HENRY JAMES

HENRY JAMES

THE LIBRARY OF AMERICA

The paper used in this publication meets the
minimum requirements of the American National Standard
for Information Sciences—Permanence of Paper for
Printed Library Materials, ANSI Z39.48–1984.

Distributed to the trade in the United States
by Penguin Group (USA) Inc.
and in Canada by Penguin Books Canada Ltd.

Library of Congress Catalog Card Number: 83–5475
For cataloging information, see end of *Notes* section.
ISBN 978-0-940450-13-4
ISBN 0-940450-13-5

Ninth Printing
The Library of America—13

Manufactured in the United States of America

Contents

WATCH AND WARD

I

R OGER LAWRENCE had come to town for the express purpose of doing a certain act, but as the hour for action
approached he felt his ardor rapidly ebbing away. Of the ardor that comes from hope, indeed, he had felt little from the
first; so little that as he whirled along in the train he wondered to find himself engaged in this fool's errand. But in
default of hope he was sustained, I may almost say, by despair. He would fail, he was sure, but he must fail again before he could rest. Meanwhile he was restless enough. In the
evening, at his hotel, having roamed aimlessly about the
streets for a couple of hours in the dark December cold, he
went up to his room and dressed, with a painful sense of
having but partly succeeded in giving himself the *tournure* of
an impassioned suitor. He was twenty-nine years old, sound
and strong, with a tender heart, and a genius, almost, for
common sense; his face told clearly of youth and kindness and
sanity, but it had little other beauty. His complexion was so
fresh as to be almost absurd in a man of his age,—an effect
rather enhanced by a precocious partial baldness. Being extremely short-sighted, he went with his head thrust forward;
but as this infirmity is considered by persons who have studied the picturesque to impart an air of distinction, he may
have the benefit of the possibility. His figure was compact and
sturdy, and, on the whole, his best point; although, owing to
an incurable personal shyness, he had a good deal of awkwardness of movement. He was fastidiously neat in his person, and extremely precise and methodical in his habits,
which were of the sort supposed to mark a man for bachelorhood. The desire to get the better of his diffidence had given
him a somewhat ponderous formalism of manner, which
many persons found extremely amusing. He was remarkable
for the spotlessness of his linen, the high polish of his boots,
and the smoothness of his hat. He carried in all weathers a
peculiarly neat umbrella. He never smoked; he drank in mod-
eration. His voice, instead of being the robust barytone which
his capacious chest led you to expect, was a mild, deferential
tenor. He was fond of going early to bed, and was suspected

3

of what is called "fussing" with his health. No one had ever
accused him of meanness, yet he passed universally for a cunning economist. In trifling matters, such as the choice of a
shoemaker or a dentist, his word carried weight; but no one
dreamed of asking his opinion in politics or literature. Here
and there, nevertheless, an observer less superficial than the
majority would have whispered you that Roger was an under-
valued man, and that in the long run he would come out even
with the best. "Have you ever studied his face?" such an
observer would say. Beneath its simple serenity, over which
his ruddy blushes seemed to pass like clouds in a summer sky,
there slumbered a fund of exquisite human expression. The
eye was excellent; small, perhaps, and somewhat dull, but
with a certain appealing depth, like the tender dumbness in
the gaze of a dog. In repose Lawrence may have looked stupid; but as he talked his face slowly brightened by gradual
fine degrees, until at the end of an hour it inspired you with
a confidence so perfect as to be in some degree a tribute to
its owner's intellect, as it certainly was to his integrity. On
this occasion Roger dressed himself with unusual care and
with a certain sober elegance. He debated for three minutes
over two cravats, and then, blushing in his mirror at his puerile vanity, he replaced the plain black tie in which he had
travelled. When he had finished dressing, it was still too early
to go forth on his errand. He went into the reading-room of
the hotel, but here there soon appeared two smokers. Wishing not to be infected by their fumes, he crossed over to the
great empty drawing-room, sat down, and beguiled his impatience with trying on a pair of lavender gloves.

While he was thus engaged there came into the room a
person who attracted his attention by the singularity of his
conduct. This was a man of less than middle age, good-looking, pale, with a rather pretentious blond mustache, and various shabby remnants of finery. His face was haggard, his
whole aspect was that of grim and hopeless misery. He
walked straight to the table in the centre of the room, and
poured out and drank without stopping three full glasses of
ice-water, as if he were striving to quench the fury of some
inner fever. He then went to the window, leaned his forehead
against the cold pane, and drummed a nervous tattoo with

his long stiff finger-nails. Finally he strode over to the fire-place, flung himself into a chair, leaned forward with his head in his hands, and groaned audibly. Lawrence, as he smoothed down his lavender gloves, watched him and reflected: "What an image of fallen prosperity, of degradation and despair! I have been fancying myself in trouble; I have been dejected, doubtful, anxious. I 'm hopeless. But what is my sentimental sorrow to this?" The unhappy gentleman rose from his chair, turned his back to the chimney-piece, and stood with folded arms gazing at Lawrence, who was seated opposite to him. The young man sustained his glance, but with sensible dis-comfort. His face was as white as ashes, his eyes were as lurid as coals. Roger had never seen anything so tragic as the two long harsh lines which descended from his nose beside his mouth, showing almost black on his chalky skin, and seeming to satirize the silly drooping ends of his fair relaxed mustache. Lawrence felt that his companion was going to address him; he began to draw off his gloves. The stranger suddenly came towards him, stopped a moment, eyed him again with inso-lent intensity, and then seated himself on the sofa beside him. His first movement was to seize the young man's arm. "He 's simply crazy!" thought Lawrence. Roger was now able to ap-preciate the pathetic disrepair of his appearance. His open waistcoat displayed a soiled and crumpled shirt-bosom, from whose empty button-holes the studs had recently been wrenched. In his normal freshness the man must have looked like a gambler with a run of luck. He spoke in a rapid, excited tone, with a hard, petulant voice.

"You 'll think me crazy, I suppose. Well, I shall be soon. Will you lend me a hundred dollars?"

"Who are you? What 's your trouble?" Roger asked.

"My name would tell you nothing. I 'm a stranger here. My trouble,—it 's a long story! But it 's grievous, I assure you. It 's pressing upon me with a fierceness that grows while I sit here talking to you. A hundred dollars would stave it off,—a few days at least. Don't refuse me!" These last words were uttered half as an entreaty, half as a threat. "Don't say you have n't got them,—a man that wears gloves like that! Come! you look like a good fellow. Look at me! I 'm a good fellow, too! I don't need to swear to my being in distress."

Lawrence was moved, disgusted, and irritated. The man's distress was real enough, but there was something flagrantly dissolute and unsavory in his expression and tone. Roger declined to entertain his request without learning more about him. From the stranger's persistent reluctance to do more than simply declare that he was from St. Louis, and repeat that he was in trouble, in hideous, overwhelming trouble, Lawrence was led to believe that he had been dabbling in crime. The more he insisted upon some definite statement of his circumstances, the more fierce and peremptory became the other's petition. Lawrence was before all things deliberate and perspicacious, the last man in the world to be hustled or bullied. It was quite out of his nature to do a thing without distinctly knowing why. He of course had no imagination, which, as we know, should always stand at the right hand of charity; but he had good store of that wholesome discretion whose place is at the left. Discretion told him that his companion was a dissolute scoundrel, who had sinned through grievous temptation, perhaps, but who had certainly sinned. His perfect misery was incontestable. Roger felt that he could not cancel his misery without in some degree sanctioning his vices. It was not in his power, at any rate, to present him, out of hand, a hundred dollars. He compromised. "I can't think of giving you the sum you ask," he said. "I have no time, moreover, to investigate your case at present. If you will meet me here to-morrow morning, I will listen to anything more you may have made up your mind to say. Meanwhile, here are ten dollars."

The man looked at the proffered note and made no movement to accept it. Then raising his eyes to Roger's face, — eyes streaming with tears of helpless rage and baffled want: "O, the devil!" he cried. "What can I do with ten dollars? Damn it, I don't know how to beg. Listen to me! If you don't give me what I ask, I shall cut my throat! Think of that! on your head be the penalty!"

Lawrence repocketed his note and rose to his feet. "No, decidedly," he said, "you don't know how to beg!" A moment after, he had left the hotel and was walking rapidly toward a well-remembered dwelling. He was shocked and discomposed by this brutal collision with want and vice; but, as he walked, the cool night air restored the healthy tone of his sensibilities. The image of his heated petitioner was speedily replaced by the calmer figure of Isabel Morton.

He had come to know her three years before, through a visit she had then made to one of his neighbors in the country. In spite of his unventurous tastes and the even tenor of his habits, Lawrence was by no means lacking, as regards life, in what the French call *les grandes curiosités*; but from an early age his curiosity had chiefly taken the form of a timid but strenuous desire to fathom the depths of matrimony. He had dreamed of this gentle bondage as other men dream of the "free unhoused condition" of celibacy. He had been born a marrying man, with a conscious desire for progeny. The world in this respect had not done him justice. It had supposed him to be wrapped up in his petty comforts; whereas, in fact, he was serving a devout apprenticeship to the profession of husband and father. Feeling at twenty-six that he had something to offer a woman, he allowed himself to become interested in Miss Morton. It was rather odd that a man of tremors and blushes should in this line have been signally bold; for Miss Morton had the reputation of being extremely fastidious, and was supposed to wear some dozen broken hearts on her girdle, as an Indian wears the scalps of his enemies.

It is said that, as a rule, men fall in love with their opposites; certainly Lawrence complied with the rule. He was the most unobtrusively natural of men; she, on the other hand, was preeminently artificial. She was pretty, but not really so pretty as she seemed; clever, but not intelligent; amiable, but not generous. She possessed in perfection the manner of society, which she lavished with indiscriminate grace on the just and the unjust, and which very effectively rounded and completed the somewhat meagre outline of her personal character. In reality, Miss Morton was keenly ambitious. A woman of simpler needs, she might very well have accepted our hero. He offered himself with urgent and obstinate warmth. She esteemed him more than any man she had known,—so she told him; but she added that the man she married must satisfy her heart. Her heart, she did not add, was bent upon a carriage and diamonds.

From the point of view of ambition, a match with Roger
Lawrence was not worth discussing. He was therefore dismissed with gracious but inexorable firmness. From this moment the young man's sentiment hardened into a passion. Six
months later he heard that Miss Morton was preparing to go
to Europe. He sought her out before her departure and urged
his suit afresh, with the same result. But his passion had cost
too much to be flung away unused. During her residence
abroad he wrote her three letters, only one of which she
briefly answered, in terms which amounted to little more than
this: "Dear Mr. Lawrence, *do* leave me alone!" At the end of
two years she returned, and was now visiting her married
brother. Lawrence had just heard of her arrival and had come
to town to make, as we have said, a supreme appeal.

Her brother and his wife were out for the evening; Roger
found her in the drawing-room, under the lamp, teaching a
stitch in crochet to her niece, a little girl of ten, who stood
leaning at her side. She seemed to him prettier than before;
although, in fact, she looked older and stouter. Her prettiness, for the most part, however, was a matter of coquetry;
and naturally, as youth departed, coquetry filled the vacancy.
She was fair and plump, and she had a very pretty trick of
suddenly turning her head and showing a charming white
throat and ear. Above her well-filled corsage these objects
produced a most agreeable effect. She always dressed in light
colors and with perfect certainty of taste. Charming as she
may have been, there was, nevertheless, about her so marked
a want of the natural, that, to admire her particularly, it was
necessary to be, like Roger, in love with her. She received him
with such flattering friendliness and so little apparent suspicion of his purpose, that he almost took heart and hope. If
she did n't fear a declaration, perhaps she desired it. For the
first half-hour it hung fire. Roger sat dumbly sensitive to the
tempered brightness of her presence. She talked to better purpose than before she went abroad, and if Roger had ever
doubted, he might have believed now with his eyes shut. For
the moment he sat tongue-tied for very modesty. Miss Morton's little niece was a very pretty child; her hair was combed
out into a golden cloud, which covered her sloping shoulders.
She kept her place beside her aunt, clasping one of the latter's

hands, and staring at Lawrence with that sweet curiosity of little girls. There glimmered mistily in the young man's brain a vision of a home-scene in the future,—a lamp-lit parlor on a winter night, a placid wife and mother, wreathed in household smiles, a golden-haired child, and, in the midst, his sentient self, drunk with possession and gratitude. As the clock struck nine, the little girl was sent to bed, having been kissed by her aunt and rekissed, or unkissed shall I say? by her aunt's lover. When she had disappeared, Roger proceeded to business. He had proposed so often to Miss Morton, that, actually, practice had begun to tell. It took but a few moments to make his meaning plain. Miss Morton addressed herself to her niece's tapestry, and as her lover went on with manly eloquence, glanced up at him from her work with womanly *finesse*. He spoke of his persistent love, of his long waiting and his passionate hope. Her acceptance of his hand was the main condition of his happiness. He should never love another woman; if she now refused him, it was the end of all things; he should continue to exist, to work and act, to eat and sleep, but he should have ceased to *live*.

"In heaven's name," he said, "don't answer me as you have answered me before."

She folded her hands, and with a serious smile; "I shall not, altogether," she said. "When I have refused you before, I have simply told you that I could n't love you. I can't love you, Mr. Lawrence! I must repeat it again to-night, but with a better reason than before. I love another man: I 'm engaged."

Roger rose to his feet like a man who has received a heavy blow and springs forward in self-defence. But he was indefensible, his assailant inattackable. He sat down again and hung his head. Miss Morton came to him and took his hand and demanded of him, as a right, that he should be resigned. "Beyond a certain point," she said, "you have no right to obtrude upon me the expression of your regret. The injury I do you in refusing you is less than that I should do you in accepting you without love."

He looked at her with his eyes full of tears. "Well! I shall never marry," he said. "There 's something you can't refuse me. Though I shall never possess you, I may at least espouse your memory and live in intimate union with your image;

spend my life on my knees before it!" She smiled at this fine talk; she had heard so much in her day! He had fancied himself prepared for the worst, but as he walked back to his hotel, it seemed intolerably bitter. Its bitterness, however, quickened his temper and prompted a violent reaction. He would now, he declared, cast his lot with pure reason. He had tried love and faith, but they would none of him. He had made a woman a goddess, and she had made him a fool. He would henceforth care neither for woman nor man, but simply for comfort, and, if need should be, for pleasure. Beneath this gathered gust of cynicism the future lay as hard and narrow as the silent street before him. He was absurdly unconscious that good-humor was lurking round the very next corner.

It was not till near morning that he was able to sleep. His sleep, however, had lasted less than an hour when it was interrupted by a loud noise from the adjoining room. He started up in bed, lending his ear to the stillness. The sound was immediately repeated; it was that of a pistol-shot. This second report was followed by a loud shrill cry. Roger jumped out of bed, thrust himself into his trousers, quitted his room, and ran to the neighboring door. It opened without difficulty, and revealed an astonishing scene. In the middle of the floor lay a man, in his trousers and shirt, his head bathed in blood, his hand grasping the pistol from which he had just sent a bullet through his brain. Beside him stood a little girl in her night-dress, her long hair on her shoulders, shrieking and wringing her hands. Stooping over the prostrate body, Roger recognized, in spite of his bedabbled visage, the person who had addressed him in the parlor of the hotel. He had kept the spirit, if not the letter, of his menace. "O father, father, father!" sobbed the little girl. Roger, overcome with horror and pity, stooped towards her and opened his arms. She, conscious of nothing but the presence of human help, rushed into his embrace and buried her head in his grasp.

The rest of the house was immediately aroused, and the room invaded by a body of lodgers and servants. Soon followed a couple of policemen, and finally the proprietor in person. The fact of suicide was so apparent that Roger's presence was easily explained. From the child nothing but sobs

could be obtained. After a vast amount of talking and pushing and staring, after a physician had affirmed that the
stranger was dead, and the ladies had passed the child from
hand to hand through a bewildering circle of caresses and
questions, the multitude dispersed, and the little girl was
borne away in triumph by the proprietor's wife, further investigation being appointed for the morrow. For Roger,
seemingly, this was to have been a night of sensations. There
came to him, as it wore away, a cruel sense of his own accidental part in his neighbor's tragedy. His refusal to help the
poor man had brought on the catastrophe. The idea haunted
him awhile; but at last, with an effort, he dismissed it. The
next man, he assured himself, would have done no more than
he, might possibly have done less. He felt, however, a certain
indefeasible fellowship in the sorrow of the little girl. He lost
no time, the next morning, in calling on the wife of the proprietor. She was a kindly woman enough, but so thoroughly
the mistress of a public house that she seemed to deal out her
very pity over a bar. She exhibited toward her *protégée* a hard
business-like charity which foreshadowed vividly to Roger's
mind the poor child's probable portion in life, and repeated
to him the little creature's story, as she had been able to learn
it. The father had come in early in the evening, in great trouble and excitement, and had made her go to bed. He had
kissed her and cried over her, and, of course, made her cry.
Late at night she was aroused by feeling him again at her
bedside, kissing her, fondling her and raving over her. He
bade her good night and passed into the adjoining room,
where she heard him fiercely knocking about. She was very
much frightened, and fancied he was out of his mind. She
knew that their troubles had lately been thickening fast, and
now the worst had come. Suddenly he called her. She asked
what he wanted, and he bade her get out of bed and come to
him. She trembled, but obeyed. On reaching the threshold of
his room she saw the gas turned low, and her father standing
in his shirt against the door at the other end. He ordered her
to stop where she was. Suddenly she heard a loud report and
felt beside her cheek the wind of a bullet. He had aimed at
her with a pistol. She retreated in terror to her own bedside and buried her head in the clothes. This, however, did

not prevent her from hearing a second report, followed by a deep groan. Venturing back again, she found her father on the floor, bleeding from the face. "He meant to kill her, of course," said the landlady, "that she might n't be left alone in the world. It 's a queer mixture of cruelty and kindness!"

It seemed to Roger an altogether pitiful tale. He related his own interview with the deceased, and the latter's menace of suicide. "It gives me," he said, "a sickening sense of connection with the calamity, though a gratuitous one, I confess. Nevertheless, I wish he had taken my ten dollars."

Of the antecedent history of the deceased they could learn little. The child had recognized Lawrence, and had broken out again into a quivering convulsion of tears. Little by little, from among her sobs, they gathered a few facts. Her father had brought her during the preceding month from St. Louis: they had stopped some time in New York. Her father had been for months in great distress and want of money. They had once had money enough; she could n't say what had become of it. Her mother had died many months before; she had no other kindred nor friends. Her father may have had friends, but she never saw them. She could indicate no source of possible assistance or sympathy. Roger put the poor little fragments of her story together. The most salient fact among them all was her absolute destitution.

"Well!" said the proprietress, "there are other people still to be attended to; I must go about my business. Perhaps you can learn something more." The little girl sat on the sofa with a pale face and swollen eyes, and with a stupefied helpless stare watched her friend depart. She was by no means a pretty child. Her clear auburn hair was thrust carelessly into a net with broken meshes, and her limbs encased in a suit of shabby, pretentious mourning. In her appearance, in spite of her childish innocence and grief, there was something undeniably vulgar. "She looks as if she belonged to a circus troupe," Roger said to himself. Her face, however, though without beauty, was not without interest. Her forehead was high and boldly rounded, and her mouth at once large and gentle. Her eyes were light in color, yet by no means colorless. A sort of arrested, concentrated brightness, a soft introversion of their rays, gave them a remarkable depth of tone. "Poor little betrayed, unfriended mortal!" thought the young man.

"What 's your name?" he asked.

"Nora Lambert," said the child.

"How old are you?"

"Twelve."

"And you live in St. Louis?"

"We used to live there. I was born there."

"Why had your father come to the East?"

"To make money, he said."

"Where was he going to live?"

"Anywhere he could find business."

"What was his business?"

"He had none. He wanted to find employment."

"To your knowledge, you say, you have no friends nor relations?"

The child gazed a few moments in silence. "He told me when he woke me up and kissed me, last night, that I had n't a friend in the world nor a person that cared for me."

Before the exquisite sadness of this statement Lawrence was silent. He leaned back in his chair and looked at the child,— the little forlorn, precocious, potential woman. His own sense of recent bereavement rose powerful in his heart and seemed to respond to hers. "Nora," he said, "come here."

She stared a moment, without moving, and then left the sofa and came slowly towards him. She was tall for her years. She laid her hand on the arm of his chair and he took it. "You have seen me before," he said. She nodded. "Do you remember my taking you last night in my arms?" It was his fancy that, for an answer, she faintly blushed. He laid his hand on her head and smoothed away her thick disordered hair. She submitted to his consoling touch with a plaintive docility. He put his arm round her waist. An irresistible sense of her childish sweetness, of her tender feminine promise, stole softly into his pulses. A dozen caressing questions rose to his lips. Had she been to school? Could she read and write? Was she musical? She murmured her answers with gathering confidence. She had never been to school; but her mother had taught her to read and write a little, and to play a little. She said, almost with a smile, that she was very backward. Lawrence felt the tears rising to his eyes; he felt in his heart the tumult of a new emotion. Was it the inexpugnable instinct of paternity? Was it the restless ghost of his buried hope? He thought of his angry vow the night before to live only for himself and turn the key on his heart. From the lips of babes and sucklings!—he softly mused. Before twenty-four hours had elapsed a child's fingers were fumbling with the key. He felt deliciously contradicted; he was after all but a lame egotist. Was he to believe, then, that he could n't live without love, and that he must take it where he found it? His promise to Miss Morton seemed still to vibrate in his heart. But there was love and love! He could be a protector, a father, a brother! What was the child before him but a tragic embodiment of the misery of isolation, a warning from his own blank future! "God forbid!" he cried. And as he did so, he drew her towards him and kissed her.

At this moment the landlord appeared with a scrap of paper, which he had found in the room of the deceased; it being the only object which gave a clew to his circumstances. He had evidently burned a mass of papers just before his death, as the grate was filled with fresh ashes. Roger read the note, which was scrawled in a hurried, vehement hand and ran as follows:—

"This is to say that I must—I must—I must! Starving, without a friend in the world, and a reputation worse than worthless,—what can I do? Life 's impossible! Try it yourself! As regards my daughter,—anything, everything is cruel; but this is the shortest way."

"She has had to take the longest, after all," said the proprietor, *sotto voce*, with a kindly wink at Roger. The landlady soon reappeared with one of the ladies who had been present overnight,—a little pushing, patronizing woman, who seemed strangely familiar with the various devices of applied charity. "I have come to arrange," she said, "about our subscription for the little one. I shall not be able to contribute myself, but I will go round among the other ladies with a paper. I 've just been seeing the reporter of the 'Universe'; he 's to insert a kind of 'appeal,' you know, in his account of the affair. Perhaps this gentleman will draw up our paper? And I think it will be a beautiful idea to take the child with me."

Lawrence was sickened. The world's tenderness had fairly begun. Nora gazed at her energetic benefactress, and then with her eyes appealed mutely to Roger. Her glance, somehow, moved him to the soul. Poor little disfathered daughter,—poor little uprooted germ of womanhood! Her innocent eyes seemed to more than beseech,—to admonish almost, and command. Should he speak and rescue her? Should he subscribe the whole sum in the name of human charity? He thought of the risk. She was an unknown quantity. Her nature, her heritage, her good and bad possibilities, were an unsolved problem. Her father had been an adventurer; what had her mother been? Conjecture was useless; she was a vague spot of light on a dark background. He was unable even to decide whether, after all, she was plain.

"If you want to take her round with you," said the landlady to her companion, "I 'd better sponge off her face."

"No indeed!" cried the other, "she 's much better as she is. If I could only have her little night-gown with the blood on it! Are you sure the bullet did n't strike your dress, deary? I'm sure we can easily get fifty names at five dollars apiece. Two hundred and fifty dollars. Perhaps this gentleman will make it three hundred. Come, sir, now!"

Thus adjured, Roger turned to the child. "Nora," he said, "you know you 're quite alone. You have no home." Her lips trembled, but her eyes were fixed and fascinated. "Do you think you could love me?" She flushed to the tender roots of her tumbled hair. "Will you come and try?" Her range of expression of course was limited; she could only answer by another burst of tears.

II

"I HAVE ADOPTED a little girl, you know," Roger said, after this, to a number of his friends; but he felt, rather, as if she had adopted him. With the downright sense of paternity he found it somewhat difficult to make his terms. It was indeed an immense satisfaction to feel, as time went on, that there was small danger of his repenting of his bargain. It seemed to him more and more that he had obeyed a divine voice; though indeed he was equally conscious that there was something grotesque in his new condition,—in the sudden assumption of paternal care by a man who had seemed to the world to rejoice so placidly in his sleek and comfortable singleness. But for all this he found himself able to look the world squarely in the face. At first it had been with an effort, a blush, and a deprecating smile that he spoke of his pious venture; but very soon he began to take a robust satisfaction in alluding to it freely, in all companies. There was but one man of whose jocular verdict he thought with some annoyance,—his cousin Hubert Lawrence, namely, who was so terribly clever and trenchant, and who had been through life a commentator formidable to his modesty, though, in the end, always absolved by his good-nature. But he made up his mind that, though Hubert might laugh, he himself was serious; and to prove it equally to himself and his friends, he determined on a great move. He annulled his personal share in business and prepared to occupy his house in the country. The latter was immediately transformed into a home for Nora,—a home admirably fitted to become the starting-point of a happy life. Roger's dwelling stood in the midst of certain paternal acres,—a little less than a "place," a little more than a farm; deep in the country, and yet at two hours' journey from town. Of recent years a dusty disorder had fallen upon the house, telling of its master's long absences and his rare and restless visits. It was but half lived in. But beneath this pulverous deposit the austerer household gods of a former generation stand erect on their pedestals. As Nora grew older, she came to love her new home with an almost passionate fondness, and to cherish all its transmitted memories as a kind compensation for her own dissevered past. There had lived with Lawrence for many years an elderly woman, of exemplary virtue, Lucinda Brown by name, who had been a personal attendant of his mother, and since her death had remained in his service as the lonely warden of his villa. Roger had an old-time regard for her, founded upon a fancy that she preserved with pious fidelity certain graceful household traditions of his mother. It seemed to him that she might communicate to little Nora, through the medium of housewifely gossip, a ray of this lady's peaceful domestic genius. Lucinda, who had been divided between hope and fear as to Roger's possibly marrying,—the fear of a diminished empire having exceeded, on the whole, the hope of company below stairs,—accepted Nora's arrival as a very comfortable compromise. The child was too young to menace her authority, and yet of sufficient importance to warrant a gradual extension of the meagre household economy. Lucinda had a vision of new carpets and curtains, of a regenerated kitchen, of a poplin dress, of her niece coming as sempstress. Nora was the narrow end of the wedge; it would broaden with her growth. Lucinda therefore was gracious.

For Roger, it seemed as if life had begun afresh and the world had put on a new face. High above the level horizon now, clearly defined against the empty sky, rose this little commanding figure, with the added magnitude that objects acquire in this position. She gave him a vast deal to think about. The child a man begets and rears weaves its existence insensibly into the tissue of his life, so that he becomes trained by fine degrees to the paternal office. But Roger had to skip experience, and spring with a bound into the paternal consciousness. In fact he missed his leap, and never tried again. Time should induct him at leisure into his proper honors, whatever they might be. He felt a strong aversion to claim in his *protégée* that prosaic right of property which belongs to the paternal name. He accepted with solemn glee his novel duties and cares, but he shrank with a tender humility of temper from all precise definition of his rights. He was too young and too sensible of his youth to wish to give this final turn to things. His heart was flattered, rather, by the idea of living at the mercy of that melting impermanence which beguiles us forever with deferred promises. It lay close to his heart, however, to drive away the dusky fears and sordid memories of Nora's anterior life. He strove to conceal the past from her childish sense by a great pictured screen, as it were, of present joys and comforts. He wished her life to date from the moment he had taken her home. He had taken her for better, for worse; but he longed to quench all baser chances in the broad daylight of prosperity. His philosophy in this as in all things was extremely simple,—to make her happy, that she might be good. Meanwhile, as he cunningly devised her happiness, his own seemed securely established. He felt twice as much a man as before, and the world seemed as much again a world. All his small stale virtues became fragrant, to his soul, with the borrowed sweetness of their unselfish use.

One of his first acts, before he left town, had been to divest her of her shabby mourning and dress her afresh in light, childish colors. He learned from the proprietor's wife at his hotel that this was considered by several ladies interested in Nora's fortunes (especially by her of the subscription) an act of awful impiety; but he held to his purpose, nevertheless. When she was freshly arrayed, he took her to a photographer and made her sit for half a dozen portraits. They were not flattering; they gave her an aged, sombre, lifeless air. He showed them to two old ladies of his acquaintance, whose judgment he valued, without saying whom they represented; the ladies pronounced her a little monster. It was directly after this that Roger hurried her away to the peaceful, uncritical country. Her manner here for a long time remained singularly docile and spiritless. She was not exactly sad, but neither was she cheerful. She smiled, as if from the fear to displease by not smiling. She had the air of a child who has been much alone, and who has learned quite to underestimate her natural right to amusement. She seemed at times hopelessly, defiantly torpid. "Good heavens!" thought Roger, as he surreptitiously watched her; "is she stupid?" He perceived at last, however, that her listless quietude covered a great deal of observation, and that she led a silent, active life of her own. His ignorance of her past distressed and vexed him, jealous as he was of admitting even to himself that she had ever lived till now. He trod on tiptoe in the region of her early memories, in the dread of reviving some dormant claim, some unclean ghost. Yet he felt that to know so little of her twelve first years was to reckon without an important factor in his problem; as if, in spite of his summons to all the fairies for this second baptism, the godmother-in-chief lurked maliciously apart, with intent to arrive at the end of years and spoil the birthday feast. Nora seemed by instinct to have perceived the fitness of her not speaking of her own affairs, and indeed displayed in the matter a precocious good taste. Among her scanty personal effects the only object referring too vividly to the past had been a small painted photograph of her mother, a languid-looking lady in a low-necked dress, with a good deal of prettiness, in spite of the rough handling of the colorist. Nora had apparently a timid reserve of vanity in the fact, which she once imparted to Roger with a kind of desperate abruptness, that her mother had been a public singer; and the heterogeneous nature of her own culture testified to some familiarity with the scenery of Bohemia. The common relations of things seemed quite reversed in her brief experience, and immaturity and precocity shared her young mind in the freest fellowship. She was ignorant of the plainest truths, and credulous of the quaintest falsities; unversed in the commonest learning, and instructed in the rarest. She barely knew that the earth is round, but she knew that Leonora is the heroine of *Il Trovatore*. She could neither write nor spell, but she could perform the most startling tricks with cards. She confessed to a passion for strong green tea, and to an interest in the romances of the Sunday newspapers which, with many other productions of the same complexion, she seemed to have perused by that subtle divining process common to illiterate children. Evidently she had sprung from a horribly vulgar soil; she was a brand snatched from the burning. She uttered various improper words with the most guileless accent and glance, and was as yet equally unsuspicious of the grammar and the Catechism. But when once Roger had straightened out her phrase, she was careful to preserve its shape; and when he had solemnly proscribed these all-too-innocent words, they seldom reappeared. For the rudiments of theological learning, also, she manifested a due respect. Considering the make-shift

process of her growth, he marvelled that it had not straggled
into even more perilous places. His impression of her father
was fatal, ineffaceable; the late Mr. Lambert had been a black-
guard. Roger had a fancy, however, that this was not all the
truth. He was free to assume that the poor fellow's wife had
been of a gentle nurture and temper; and he had even framed
on this theme an ingenious little romance, which gave him a
great deal of comfort. Mrs. Lambert had been deceived by
the lacquered plausibility of her husband, and had awaked
after marriage to a life of shifting expedients and struggling
poverty, during which she had been glad to turn to account
the voice which the friends of her happier girlhood had
praised. She had died outwearied and broken-hearted, invoking human pity on her child. Roger established in this way a
sentimental intimacy with the poor lady's spirit, and exchanged many a greeting over the little girl's head with this
vague maternal shape. But he was by no means given up to
these imaginative joys; he addressed himself vigorously to the
practical needs of the case. He determined to drive in the first
nail with his own hands, to lay the first smooth foundation-
stones of her culture, to teach her to read and write and
cipher, to associate himself largely with the growth of her
primal sense of things. Behold him thus converted into a gentle pedagogue, wooing with mild inflections the timid ven-
tures of her thought. A moted morning sunbeam used to
enter his little study and, resting on Nora's auburn hair,
seemed to make of the place a humming school-room. Roger
began also to anticipate the future needs of preceptorship. He
plunged into a course of useful reading, and devoured a
hundred volumes on education, on hygiene, on morals, on
history. He drew up a table of rules and observances for the
child's health; he weighed and measured her food, and spent
hours with Lucinda, the minister's wife, and the doctor, in
the discussion of her regimen and clothing. He bought her a
pony, and rode with her over the neighboring country,
roamed with her in the woods and fields, and made discreet
provision of society among the little damsels of the country-
side. A doting grandmother, in all this matter, could not have
shown a finer genius for detail. His zeal indeed left him very
little peace, and Lucinda often endeavored to assuage it by

the assurance that he was fretting himself away and wearing himself thin on his happiness. He passed a dozen times a week from the fear of coddling and spoiling the child to the fear of letting her run wild and grow vulgar amid too much rusticity. Sometimes he dismissed her tasks for days together, and kept her idling at his side in the winter sunshine; sometimes for a week he kept her within doors, reading to her, preaching to her, showing her prints, and telling her stories. She had an excellent musical ear, and the promise of a charming voice; Roger took counsel in a dozen quarters as to whether he ought to make her use her voice or spare it. Once he took her up to town to a *matinée* at one of the theatres, and was in anguish for a week afterwards, lest he had quickened some inherited tendency to dissipation. He used to lie awake at night, trying hard to fix in his mind the happy medium between coldness and weak fondness. With a heart full of tenderness, he used to dole out his caresses. He was in doubt for a long time as to what he should have her call him. At the outset he decided instinctively against "father." It was a question between "Mr. Lawrence" and his baptismal name. He weighed the proprieties for a week, and then he determined the child should choose for herself. She had as yet avoided addressing him by name; at last he asked what name she preferred. She stared rather blankly at the time, but a few days afterwards he heard her shouting "Roger!" from the garden under his window. She had ventured upon a small shallow pond enclosed by his land, and now coated with thin ice. The ice had cracked with a great report under her tread, and was swaying gently beneath her weight, at some yards from the edge. In her alarm her heart had chosen, and her heart's election was never subsequently gainsaid. Circumstances seemed to affect her slowly; for a long time she showed few symptoms of change. Roger in his slippers, by the fireside, in the winter evenings, used to gaze at her with an anxious soul, and wonder whether it was not only a stupid child that could sit for an hour by the chimney-corner, stroking the cat's back in absolute silence, asking no questions and telling no lies. Then, musing upon a certain positive, elderly air in her brow and eyes, he would fancy that she was wiser than he knew; that she was mocking him or judging him, and counter-plotting his pious labors with elfish gravity. Arrange it as he might, he could not call her pretty. Plain women are apt to be clever; might n't she (horror of horrors!) turn out too clever? In the evening, after she had attended Nora to bed, Lucinda would come into the little library, and she and Roger would solemnly put their heads together. In matters in which he deemed her sex gave her an advantage of judgment, he used freely to ask her opinion. She made a vast parade of motherly science, rigid spinster as she was, and hinted by many a nod and wink at the mystic depths of her penetration. As to the child's being thankless or heartless, she quite reassured him. Did n't she cry herself to sleep, under her breath, on her little pillow? Did n't she mention him every night in her prayers,—him, and him alone? However much her family may have left to be desired as a "family,"—and of its shortcomings in this respect Lucinda had an altogether awful sense,—Nora was clearly a lady in her own right. As for her plain face, they could wait awhile for a change. Plainness in a child was almost always prettiness in a woman; and at all events, if she was not to be pretty, she need never be vain.

Roger had no wish to cultivate in his young companion any expression of formal gratitude; for it was the very keystone of his plan that their relation should ripen into a perfect matter of course; but he watched patiently, like a wandering botanist for the first woodland violets for the year, for the shy field-flower of spontaneous affection. He aimed at nothing more or less than to inspire the child with a passion. Until he had detected in her glance and tone the note of passionate tenderness, his experiment must have failed. It would have succeeded on the day when she should break out into cries and tears and tell him with a clinging embrace that she loved him. So he argued with himself; but, in fact, he expected perhaps more than belongs to the lame logic of this life. As a child, she would be too irreflective to play so pretty a part; as a young girl, too self-conscious. I undertake to tell no secrets, however. Roger, thanks to a wholesome reserve of temper in the matter of sentiment, continued to possess his soul in patience. She meanwhile, seemingly, showed as little of distrust as of positive tenderness. She grew and grew in ungrudged serenity. It was in person, first, that she began gently, or rather ungently, to expand; acquiring a well-nurtured sturdiness of contour, but passing quite into the shambling and sheepish stage of girlhood. Lucinda cast about her in vain for possibilities of future beauty, and took refuge in vigorous attention to the young girl's bountiful auburn hair, which she combed and braided with a kind of fierce assiduity. The winter had passed away, the spring was well advanced. Roger, looking at his *protégée*, felt a certain sinking of the heart as he thought of his cousin Hubert's visit. As matters stood, Nora bore rather livelier testimony to his charity than to his taste.

He had debated some time as to whether he should write to Hubert and as to how he should write. Hubert Lawrence was some four years his junior; but Roger had always allowed him a large precedence in the things of the mind. Hubert had just entered the Unitarian ministry; it seemed now that grace would surely lend a generous hand to nature and complete the circle of his accomplishments. He was extremely good-looking and clever with just such a cleverness as seemed but an added personal charm. He and Roger had been much together in early life and had formed an intimacy strangely compounded of harmony and discord. Utterly unlike in temper and tone, they neither thought nor felt nor acted together on any single point. Roger was constantly differing, mutely and profoundly, and Hubert frankly and sarcastically; but each, nevertheless, seemed to find in the other a welcome counterpart and complement to his own personality. There was in their relation a large measure of healthy boyish levity which kept them from lingering long on delicate ground; but they felt at times that they belonged, by temperament, to irreconcilable camps, and that the more each of them came to lead his own life, the more their lives would diverge. Roger was of a loving turn of mind, and it cost him many a sigh that a certain glassy hardness of soul on his cousin's part was forever blunting the edge of his affection. He nevertheless had a profound regard for him; he admired his talents, he enjoyed his society, he wrapped him about with his good-will. He had told him more than once that he cared for him more than Hubert would ever believe, could in the nature of things believe,—far more than Hubert cared for him, inasmuch as Hubert's benevolence was largely spiced with contempt. "Judge what a real regard I have for you," Roger had said, "since I forgive you even that." But Hubert, who reserved his faith for heavenly mysteries, had small credence for earthly ones, and he had replied that to his perception they loved each other with a precisely equal ardor, beyond everything in life, to wit, but their own peculiar pleasure. Roger had in his mind a kind of metaphysical "idea" of a possible Hubert which the actual Hubert took a wanton satisfaction in turning upside down. Roger had drawn in his fancy a pure and ample outline, into which the wilful young minister projected a grotesquely unproportioned shadow. Roger took his cousin more *au sérieux* than the young man himself. In fact, Hubert had apparently come into the world to play. He played at life, altogether; he played at learning, he played at theology, he played at friendship; and it was to be conjectured that, on particular holidays, he would play with especial relish at love. Hubert, for some time, had been settled in New York, and of late they had exchanged but few letters. Something had been said about Hubert's coming to spend a part of his summer vacation with his cousin; now that the latter was at the head of a household and a family, Roger reminded him of their understanding. He had finally told him his little romance, with a fine bravado of indifference to his verdict; but he was, in secret, extremely anxious to obtain Hubert's judgment of the heroine. Hubert replied that he was altogether prepared for the news, and that it must be a very pretty sight to see him at dinner pinning her bib, or to hear him sermonizing her over a torn frock.

"But, pray, what relation is the young lady to me?" he added. "How far does the adoption go, and where does it stop? Your own proper daughter would be my cousin; but I take it a man is n't to have fictitious cousins grafted upon him, at this rate. I shall wait till I see her; then, if she is pleasing, I shall personally adopt her into cousinship."

He came down for a fortnight, in July, and was soon introduced to Nora. She came sidling shyly into the room, with a rent in her short-waisted frock, and the "Child's Own Book" in her hand, with her finger in the history of "The Discreet Princess." Hubert kissed her gallantly, and declared that he was happy to make her acquaintance. She retreated to a station beside Roger's knee and stood staring at the young man. *"Elle a les pieds énormes,"* said Hubert.

Roger was annoyed, partly with himself, for he made her wear big shoes. "What do you think of him?" he asked, stroking the child's hair, and hoping, half maliciously, that, with the frank perspicacity of childhood, she would utter some formidable truth about the young man. But to appreciate Hubert's failings, one must have had vital experience of them. At this time twenty-five years of age, he was a singularly handsome youth. Although of about the same height as his cousin, the pliant slimness of his figure made him look taller. He had a cool gray eye and a mass of fair curling hair. His features were cut with admirable purity; his teeth were white, his smile superb. "I think," said Nora, "that he looks like the *Prince Avenant.*"

Before Hubert went away, Roger asked him for a deliberate opinion of the child. Was she ugly or pretty? was she interesting? He found it hard, however, to induce him to consider her seriously. Hubert's observation was exercised rather less in the interest of general truth than of particular profit; and of what profit to Hubert was Nora's shambling childhood? "I can't think of her as a girl," he said; "she seems to me a boy. She climbs trees, she scales fences, she keeps rabbits, she straddles upon your old mare, bare-backed. I found her this morning wading in the pond up to her knees. She's growing up a hoyden; you ought to give her more civilized influences than she enjoys hereabouts; you ought to engage a governess, or send her to school. It's well enough now; but, my poor fellow, what will you do when she's twenty?"

You may imagine, from Hubert's sketch, that Nora's was a happy life. She had few companions, but during the long summer days, in woods and fields and orchards, Roger initiated her into all those rural mysteries which are so dear to childhood and so fondly remembered in later years. She grew more hardy and lively, more inquisitive, more active. She tasted deeply of the joy of tattered dresses and sun-burnt cheeks and arms, and long nights at the end of tired days. But Roger, pondering his cousin's words, began to believe that to keep her longer at home would be to fail of justice to the *ewig Weibliche.* The current of her growth would soon begin

to flow deeper than the plummet of a man's wit. He determined, therefore, to send her to school, and he began with
this view to investigate the merits of various establishments.
At last, after a vast amount of meditation and an extensive
correspondence with the school-keeping class, he selected one
which appeared rich in fair promises. Nora, who had never
known an hour's schooling, entered joyously upon her new
career; but she gave her friend that sweet and long-deferred
emotion of which I have spoken, when, on parting with him,
she hung upon his neck with a sort of convulsive fondness.
He took her head in his two hands and looked at her; her
eyes were streaming with tears. During the month which followed he received from her a dozen letters, sadly misspelled,
but divinely lachrymose.

It is needless to relate in detail this phase of Nora's history.
It lasted two years. Roger found that he missed her sadly; his
occupation was gone. Still, her very absence occupied him.
He wrote her long letters of advice, told her everything that
happened to him, and sent her books and useful garments and
wholesome sweets. At the end of a year he began to long
terribly to take her back again; but as his judgment forbade
this measure, he determined to beguile the following year by
travel. Before starting, he went to the little country town
which was the seat of her academy, to bid Nora farewell. He
had not seen her since she left him, as he had chosen—quite
heroically, poor fellow—to have her spend her vacation with
a school-mate, the bosom friend of this especial period. He
found her surprisingly altered. She looked three years older;
she was growing by the hour. Prettiness and symmetry had
not yet been vouchsafed to her; but Roger found in her
young imperfection a sweet assurance that her account with
nature was not yet closed. She had, moreover, a subtle grace
of her own. She had reached that charming girlish moment
when the broad freedom of childhood begins to be faintly
tempered by the sense of sex. She was coming fast, too, into
her woman's heritage of garrulity. She entertained him for a
whole morning; she took him into her confidence; she rattled
and prattled unceasingly upon all the swarming little school
interests,—her likes and aversions, her hopes and fears, her
friends and teachers, her studies and story-books. Roger sat

grinning in broad enchantment; she seemed to him to exhale the very genius of girlhood. For the first time, he became conscious of her native force; there was a vast deal of her; she overflowed. When they parted, he gave his hopes to her keeping in a long, long kiss. She kissed him too, but this time with smiles, not with tears. She neither suspected nor could she have understood the thought which, during this interview, had blossomed in her friend's mind. On leaving her, he took a long walk in the country over unknown roads. That evening he consigned his thought to a short letter, addressed to Mrs. Keith. This was the present title of the lady who had once been Miss Morton. She had married and gone abroad; where, in Rome, she had done as the Americans do, and entered the Roman Church. His letter ran as follows: —

"MY DEAR MRS. KEITH: I promised you once to be very unhappy, but I doubt whether you believed me; you did n't look as if you did. I am sure, at all events, you hoped otherwise. I am told you have become a Roman Catholic. Perhaps you have been praying for me at St. Peter's. This is the easiest way to account for my conversion to a worthier state of mind. You know that, two years ago, I adopted a homeless little girl. One of these days she will be a lovely woman. I mean to do what I can to make her one. Perhaps, six years hence, she will be grateful enough not to refuse me as you did. Pray for me more than ever. I have begun at the beginning; it will be my own fault if I have n't a perfect wife."

III

R OGER'S JOURNEY was long and various. He went to the
West Indies and to South America, whence, taking a
ship at one of the eastern ports, he sailed round the Horn and
paid a visit to Mexico. He journeyed thence to California, and
returned home across the Isthmus, stopping awhile on his upward course at various Southern cities. It was in some degree
a sentimental journey. Roger was a practical man; as he went
he gathered facts and noted manners and customs; but the
muse of observation for him was his little girl at home, the
ripening companion of his own ripe years. It was for her sake
that he used his eyes and ears and garnered information. He
had determined that she should be a lovely woman and a perfect wife; but to be worthy of such a woman as his fancy
foreshadowed, he himself had much to learn. To be a good
husband, one must first be a wise man; to educate her, he
should first educate himself. He would make it possible that
daily contact with him should be a liberal education, and that
his simple society should be a benefit. For this purpose he
should be stored with facts, tempered and tested by experience. He travelled in a spirit of solemn attention, like some
grim devotee of a former age, making a pilgrimage for the
welfare of one he loved. He kept with great labor a copious
diary, which he meant to read aloud on the winter nights of
coming years. His diary was directly addressed to Nora, she
being implied throughout as reader or auditor. He thought
at moments of his vow to Isabel Morton, and asked himself
what had become of the passion of that hour. It had betaken
itself to the common limbo of our dead passions. He rejoiced
to know that she was well and happy; he meant to write to
her again on his return and reiterate the assurance of his own
happiness. He mused ever and anon on the nature of his affection for Nora, and wondered what earthly name he could
call it by. Assuredly he was not in love with her: you could
n't fall in love with a child. But if he had not a lover's love,
he had at least a lover's jealousy; it would have made him
miserable to believe his scheme might miscarry. It would fail,
he fondly assured himself, by no fault of hers. He was sure of

her future; in that last interview at school he had guessed the answer to the riddle of her formless girlhood. If he could only be as sure of his own constancy as of her worthiness! On this point poor Roger might fairly have let his conscience rest; but to test his resolution, he deliberately courted temptation and on a dozen occasions allowed present loveliness to measure itself with absent. At the risk of a terrible increase of blushes, he bravely incurred the blandishments of various charming persons of the south. They failed signally, in every case but one, to quicken his pulses. He studied them, he noted their gifts and graces, so that he might know the range of the feminine charm. Of the utmost that women can be he wished to have personal experience. But with the sole exception I have mentioned, not a charmer of them all but shone with a radiance less magical than that dim but rounded shape which glimmered forever in the dark future, like the luminous complement of the early moon. It was at Lima that his poor little potential Nora suffered temporary eclipse. He made here the acquaintance of a young Spanish lady whose plump and full-blown innocence seemed to him divinely amiable. If ignorance is grace, what a lamentable error to be wise! He had crossed from Havana to Rio on the same vessel with her brother, a friendly young fellow, who had made him promise to come and stay with him on his arrival at Lima. Roger, in execution of this promise, passed three weeks under his roof, in the society of the lovely Señorita. She caused him to reflect, with a good deal of zeal. She moved him the more because, being wholly without coquetry, she made no attempt whatever to interest him. Her charm was the charm of absolute *naïveté* and a certain tame, unseasoned sweetness,—the sweetness of an angel who is without mundane reminiscences; to say nothing of a pair of liquid hazel eyes and a coil of crinkled blue-black hair. She could barely write her name, and from the summer twilight of her mind, which seemed to ring with amorous bird-notes, twittering in a lazy Eden, she flung a scornful shadow upon Nora's prospective condition. Roger thought of Nora, by contrast, as a creature of senseless mechanism, a thing wound up with a key, creaking and droning through the barren circle of her graces. Why travel so far round about for a wife, when here was one ready made to his heart, as illiterate as an angel and as faithful as the little page of a mediæval ballad,—and with those two perpetual love-lights beneath her silly little forehead?

Day by day, at the Señorita's side, Roger grew better pleased with the present. It was so happy, so idle, so secure! He protested against the future. He grew impatient of the stiff little figure which he had posted in the distance, to stare at him with those monstrous pale eyes: they seemed to grow and grow as he thought of them. In other words, he was in love with Teresa. She, on her side, was delighted to be loved. She caressed him with her fond dark looks and smiled perpetual assent. Late one afternoon, at the close of a long hot day, which had left with Roger the unwholesome fancy of a perpetual *siesta*, troubled by a vague confusion of dreams, they ascended together to a terrace on the top of the house. The sun had just disappeared; the lovely earth below and around was drinking in the cool of night. They stood awhile in silence; at last Roger felt that he must speak of his love. He walked away to the farther end of the terrace, casting about in his mind for the fitting words. They were hard to find. His companion spoke a little English, and he a little Spanish; but there came upon him a sudden perplexing sense of the infantine rarity of her wits. He had never done her the honor to pay her a compliment, he had never really talked with her. It was not for him to talk, but for her to perceive! She turned about, leaning back against the parapet of the terrace, looking at him and smiling. She was always smiling. She had on an old faded pink morning-dress, very much open at the throat, and a ribbon round her neck, to which was suspended a little cross of turquoise. One of the braids of her hair had fallen down, and she had drawn it forward and was plaiting the end with her plump white fingers. Her nails were not fastidiously clean. He went towards her. When he next became perfectly conscious of their relative positions, he knew that he had passionately kissed her, more than once, and that she had more than suffered him. He stood holding both her hands; he was blushing; her own complexion was undisturbed, her smile barely deepened; another of her braids had come down. He was filled with a sense of pleasure in her sweetness, tempered by a vague feeling of pain in his all-too-easy conquest. There was nothing of poor Teresita but that you could kiss her! It came upon him with a sort of horror that he had never yet distinctly told her that he loved her. "Teresa," he said, almost angrily, "I love you. Do you understand?" For all answer she raised his two hands successively to her lips. Soon after this she went off with her mother to church.

The next morning, one of his friend's clerks brought him a package of letters from his banker. One of them was a note from Nora. It ran as follows: —

> Dear Roger: I want so much to tell you that I have just got the prize for the piano. I hope you will not think it very silly to write so far only to tell you this. But I 'm so proud I want you to know it. Of the three girls who tried for it, two were seventeen. The prize is a beautiful picture called "Mozart à Vienne"; probably you have seen it. Miss Murray says I may hang it up in my bedroom. Now I have got to go and practise, for Miss Murray says I must practise more than ever. My dear Roger, I do hope you are enjoying your travels. I have learned lots of geography, following you on the map. Don't ever forget your loving
>
> Nora.

After reading this letter, Roger told his host that he would have to leave him. The young Peruvian demurred, objected, and begged for a reason.

"Well," said Roger, "I find I 'm in love with your sister." The words sounded on his ear as if some one else had spoken them. Teresa's light was quenched, and she had no more fascination than a smouldering lamp, smelling of oil.

"Why, my dear fellow," said his friend, "that seems to me a reason for staying. I shall be most happy to have you for a brother-in-law."

"It 's impossible! I 'm engaged to a young lady in my own country."

"You are in love here, you are engaged there, and you go where you are engaged! You Englishmen are strange fellows!"

"Tell Teresa that I adore her, but that I am pledged at home. I had rather not see her."

And so Roger departed from Lima, without further communion with Teresa. On his return home he received a letter from her brother, telling him of her engagement to a young merchant of Valparaiso,—an excellent match. The young lady sent him her salutations. Roger, answering his friend's letter, begged that the Doña Teresa would accept, as a wedding-present, of the accompanying trinket,—a little brooch in turquoise. It would look very well with pink!

Roger reached home in the autumn, but left Nora at school till the beginning of the Christmas holidays. He occupied the interval in refurnishing his house, and clearing the stage for the last act of the young girl's childhood. He had always possessed a modest taste for upholstery; he now began to apply it under the guidance of a delicate idea. His idea led him to prefer, in all things, the fresh and graceful to the grave and formal, and to wage war throughout his old dwelling on the lurking mustiness of the past. He had a lively regard for elegance, balanced by a horror of wanton luxury. He fancied that a woman is the better for being well dressed and well domiciled, and that vanity, too stingily treated, is sure to avenge itself. So he took her into account. Nothing annoyed him more, however, than the fear of seeing Nora a precocious fine lady; so that while he aimed at all possible purity of effect, he stayed his hand here and there before certain admonitory relics of ancestral ugliness and virtue, embodied for the most part in hair-cloth and cotton damask. Chintz and muslin, flowers and photographs and books, gave their clear light tone to the house. Nothing could be more tenderly propitious and virginal, or better chosen to chasten alike the young girl's aspirations and remind her of her protector's tenderness.

Since his return he had designedly refused himself a glimpse of her. He wished to give her a single undivided welcome to his home and his heart. Shortly before Christmas, as he had even yet not laid by his hammer and nails, Lucinda Brown was sent to fetch her from school. If Roger had expected that Nora would return with any marked accession of beauty, he would have had to say "Amen" with an effort. She had pretty well ceased to be a child; she was still his grave, imperfect Nora. She had gained her full height,—a great height, which her young strong slimness rendered the more striking. Her slender throat supported a head of massive mould, bound about with dense auburn braids. Beneath a

somewhat serious brow her large, fair eyes retained their collected light, as if uncertain where to fling it. Now and then
the lids parted widely and showered down these gathered
shafts; and if at these times a certain rare smile divided, in
harmony, her childish lips, Nora was for the moment a pass-
able beauty. But for the most part, the best charm of her face
was in a modest refinement of line, which rather evaded notice than courted it. The first impression she was likely to
produce was of a kind of awkward slender majesty. Roger
pronounced her "stately," and for a fortnight thought her too
imposing by half; but as the days went on, and the pliable
innocence of early maidenhood gave a soul to this formidable
grace, he began to feel that in essentials she was still the little
daughter of his charity. He even began to observe in her an
added consciousness of this lowly position; as if with the
growth of her mind she had come to reflect upon it, and
deem it rather less and less a matter of course. He meditated
much as to whether he should frankly talk it over with her
and allow her to feel that, for him as well, their relation could
never become commonplace. This would be in a measure un-
tender, but would it not be prudent? Ought he not, in the
interest of his final purpose, to force home to her soul in her
sensitive youth an impression of all that she owed him, so
that when his time had come, if imagination should lead her
a-wandering, gratitude would stay her steps? A dozen times
over he was on the verge of making his point, of saying,
"Nora, Nora, these are not vulgar alms; I expect a return.
One of these days you must pay your debt. Guess my riddle!
I love you less than you think,—and more! A word to the
wise." But he was silenced by a saving sense of the brutality
of such a course, and by a suspicion that, after all, it was not
needful. A passion of gratitude was silently gathering in the
young girl's heart: that heart could be trusted to keep its engagements. A deep conciliatory purpose seemed now to pervade her life, of infinite delight to Roger as little by little it
stole upon his mind, like the fragrance of a deepening spring.
He had his idea: he suspected that she had hers. They were
but opposite faces of the same deep need. Her musing silence,
her deliberate smiles, the childish keenness of her question-
ings, the growing womanly cunning of her little nameless ser-

vices and caresses, were all alike redolent of a pious sense of
suffered beneficence, which implied perfect self-devotion as a
response.

On Christmas eve they sat together alone by a blazing log-
fire in Roger's little library. He had been reading aloud a
chapter of his diary, to which Nora sat listening in dutiful
demureness, though her thoughts evidently were nearer home
than Cuba and Peru. There is no denying it was dull; he
could gossip to better purpose. He felt its dulness himself,
and closing it finally with good-humored petulance, declared
it was fit only to throw into the fire. Upon which Nora
looked up, protesting. "You must do no such thing," she
said. "You must keep your journals carefully, and one of these
days I shall have them bound in morocco and gilt, and ranged
in a row in my own bookcase."

"That 's but a polite way of burning them up," said Roger.
"They will be as little read as if they were in the fire. I don't
know how it is. They seemed to be very amusing when I
wrote them: they 're as stale as an old newspaper now. I can't
write: that 's the amount of it. I 'm a very stupid fellow,
Nora; you might as well know it first as last."

Nora's school had been of the punctilious Episcopal order,
and she had learned there the pretty custom of decorating the
house at Christmas-tide with garlands and crowns of ever-
green and holly. She had spent the day in decking out the
chimney-piece, and now, seated on a stool under the mantel-
shelf, she twisted the last little wreath, which was to complete
her design. A great still snow-storm was falling without, and
seemed to be blocking them in from the world. She bit off
the thread with which she had been binding her twigs, held
out her garland to admire its effect, and then: "I don't believe
you 're stupid, Roger," she said; "and if I did, I should n't
much care."

"Is that philosophy, or indifference?" said the young man.

"I don't know that it 's either; it 's because I know you 're
so good."

"That 's what they say about all stupid people."

Nora added another twig to her wreath and bound it up.
"I 'm sure," she said at last, "that when people are as good as

you are, they can't be stupid. I should like some one to tell me you 're stupid. I know, Roger; *I* know!"

The young man began to feel a little uneasy; it was no part of his plan that her good-will should spend itself too soon. "Dear me, Nora, if you think so well of me, I shall find it hard to live up to your expectations. I 'm afraid I shall disappoint you. I have a little gimcrack to put in your stocking to-night; but I 'm rather ashamed of it now."

"A gimcrack more or less is of small account. I 've had my stocking hanging up these three years, and everything I possess is a present from you."

Roger frowned; the conversation had taken just such a turn as he had often longed to provoke, but now it was too much for him. "O, come," he said; "I have done simply my duty to my little girl."

"But, Roger," said Nora, staring with expanded eyes, "I 'm not your little girl."

His frown darkened; his heart began to beat. "Don't talk nonsense!" he said.

"But, Roger, it 's true. I 'm no one's little girl. Do you think I 've no memory? Where is my father? Where is my mother?"

"Listen to me," said Roger, sternly. "You must n't talk of such things."

"You must n't forbid me, Roger. I can't think of them without thinking of you. This is Christmas eve! Miss Murray told us that we must never let it pass without thinking of all that it means. But without Miss Murray, I have been thinking all day of things which are hard to name,—of death and life, of my parents and you, of my incredible happiness. I feel to-night like a princess in a fairy-tale. I 'm a poor creature, without a friend, without a penny or a home; and yet, here I sit by a blazing fire, with money, with food, with clothes, with love. The snow outside is burying the stone-walls, and yet here I can sit and simply say, 'How pretty!' Suppose I were in it, wandering and begging,—I might have been! Would I think it pretty then? Roger, Roger, I 'm no one's child!" The tremor in her voice deepened, and she broke into a sudden passion of tears. Roger took her in his arms and tried to soothe away her sobs. But she disengaged

herself and went on with an almost fierce exaltation: "No, no, I
won't be comforted! I have had comfort enough, I hate it. I
want for an hour to be myself and feel how little that is, to
be my poor, wicked father's daughter, to fancy I hear my
mother's voice. I 've never spoken of them before; you must
let me to-night. You must tell me about my father; you know
something I don't. You never refused me anything, Roger;
don't refuse me this. He was n't good, like you; but now he
can do no harm. You have never mentioned his name to me,
but happy as we are here together, we should be poorly set
to work to despise him!"

Roger yielded to the vehemence of this flood of emotion.
He stood watching her with two helpless tears in his own
eyes, and then he drew her gently towards him and kissed her
on the forehead. She took up her work again, and he told
her, with every minutest detail he could recall, the story of
his sole brief interview with Mr. Lambert. Gradually he lost
the sense of effort and reluctance, and talked freely, abundantly, almost with pleasure. Nora listened with tender curiosity and with an amount of self-control which denoted the
habit of constant retrospect. She asked a hundred questions
as to Roger's impression of her father's appearance. Was n't
he wonderfully handsome? Then taking up the tale herself,
she poured out a torrent of feverish reminiscence of her childhood and unpacked her early memories with a kind of rapture
of relief. Her evident joy in this frolic of confidence gave
Roger a pitying sense of what her long silence must have cost
her. But evidently she bore him no grudge, and his present
tolerance of her rambling gossip seemed to her but another
proof of his tenderness and charity. She rose at last, and stood
before the fire, into which she had thrown the refuse of her
greenery, watching it blaze up and turn to ashes. "So much
for the past!" she said, at last. "The rest is the future. The
girls at school used to be always talking about what they
meant to do in coming years, what they hoped, what they
wished; wondering, choosing, and longing. You don't know
how girls talk, Roger; you 'd be surprised! I never used to
say much; my future is fixed. I 've nothing to choose, nothing
to hope, nothing to fear. I 'm to make you happy. That 's
simple enough. You have undertaken to bring me up, Roger;

you must do your best, because now I 'm here, it 's for long, and you 'd rather have a wise girl than a silly one." And she smiled with a kind of tentative daughterliness through the traces of her recent grief. She put her two hands on his shoulders and eyed him with arch solemnity. "You shall never repent. I shall learn everything, I shall be everything! Oh! I wish I were pretty." And she tossed back her head in impatience of her fatal plainness, with an air which forced Roger to assure her that she would do very well as she was. "If you are satisfied," she said, "I am!" For a moment Roger felt as if she were twenty years old, as if the future had flashed down on him and a proposal of marriage was at his tongue's end.

This serious Christmas eve left its traces upon many ensuing weeks. Nora's education was resumed with a certain added solemnity. Roger was no longer obliged to condescend to the level of her intelligence, and he found reason to thank his stars that he had laid up a provision of facts. He found use for all he possessed. The day of childish "lessons" was over, and Nora sought instruction in the perusal of various classical authors, in her own and other tongues, in concert with her friend. They read aloud to each other alternately, discussed their acquisitions and digested them with perhaps equal rapidity. Roger, in former years, had had but a small literary appetite; he liked a few books and knew them well, but he felt as if to settle down to an unread author were very like starting on a journey,—a case for farewells, a packing of trunks, and buying of tickets. His curiosity, now, however, imbued and quickened with a motive, led him through a hundred untrodden paths. He found it hard sometimes to keep pace with Nora's pattering step; through the flowery lanes of poetry, in especial, she would gallop without drawing breath. Was she quicker-witted than her friend, or only more superficial? Something of one, doubtless, and something of the other. Roger was forever suspecting her of a deeper penetration than his own, and hanging his head with an odd mixture of pride and humility. Her youthful brightness, at times, made him feel irretrievably dull and antiquated. His ears would tingle, his cheeks would burn, his old hope would fade into a shadow. "It 's a—" he would declare. "How can I ever have for her that charm of infallibility, that romance of omniscience, that a woman demands of her lover? She has seen me scratching my head, she has seen me counting on my fingers! Before she 's seventeen she 'll be mortally tired of me, and by the time she 's twenty I shall be fatally familiar and incurably stale. It 's very well for her to talk about life-long devotion and eternal gratitude. She does n't know the meaning of words. She must grow and outgrow, that 's her first necessity. She must come to woman's estate and pay the inevitable tribute. I can open the door and let in the lover. If her present sentiment *is* in its way a passion, I shall have had my turn. I can't hope to be the object of two passions. I must thank the Lord for small favors!" Then as he seemed to taste, in advance, the bitterness of disappointment, casting him about him angrily for some means of appeal: "I ought to go away and stay away for years and never write at all, instead of compounding ponderous diaries to make even my absence detestable. I ought to convert myself into a beneficent shadow, a vague tutelary name. Then I ought to come back in glory, fragrant with exotic perfumes and shod with shoes of mystery! Otherwise, I ought to clip the wings of her fancy and put her on half-rations. I ought to snub her and scold her and bully her and tell her she 's deplorably plain,—treat her as Rochester treats Jane Eyre. If I were only a good old Catholic, that I might shut her up in a convent and keep her childish and stupid and contented!" Roger felt that he was too doggedly conscientious; but abuse his conscience as he would, he could not make it yield an inch; so that in the constant strife between his egotistical purpose and his generous temper, the latter kept gaining ground and Nora innocently enjoyed the spoils of victory. It was his very generosity that detained him on the spot, by her side, watching her, working for her, and performing a hundred offices which in other hands would have lost their sweet precision. Roger watched intently for the signs of that inevitable hour when a young girl begins to loosen her fingers in the grasp of a guiding hand and wander softly in pursuit of that sinuous silver thread of experience which deflects, through meadows of perennial green, from the dull gray stream of the common lot. She had relapsed in the course of time into the careless gayety and the light immediate joys of girlhood. If she cherished a pious purpose in her heart, she made no indecent parade of it. But her very placidity and patience somehow afflicted her friend. She was too monotonously sweet, too easily obedient. If once in a while she would only flash out into petulance or rebellion! She kept her temper so carefully: what in the world was she keeping it for? If she would only bless him for once with an angry look and tell him that he bored her, that he worried and disgusted her!

During the second year after her return from school Roger began to fancy that she half avoided his society and resented his share in her occupations. She was fonder of lonely walks, readings and reveries. She had all of a young girl's passion for novels, and she had been in the habit of satisfying it largely. For works of fiction in general Roger had no great fondness, though he professed an especial relish for Thackeray. Nora had her favorites, but "The Newcomes," as yet, was not one of them. One evening in the early spring she sat down to a twentieth perusal of the classic tale of "The Initials." Roger, as usual, asked her to read aloud. She began and proceeded through a dozen pages. Looking up, at this point, she beheld Roger asleep. She smiled softly and privately resumed her reading. At the end of an hour, Roger, having finished his nap, rather startled her by his excessive annoyance at his lapse of consciousness. He wondered whether he had snored, but the absurd fellow was ashamed to ask her. Recovering himself finally: "The fact is, Nora," he said, "all novels seem to me stupid. They are nothing to what *I* can fancy! I have in my heart a prettier romance than any of them."

"A romance?" said Nora, simply. "Pray let me hear it. You 're quite as good a hero as this poor Mr. Hamilton. Begin!"

He stood before the fire, looking at her with almost funereal gravity. "My *dénouement* is not yet written," he said. "Wait till the story is finished; then you shall hear the whole."

As at this time Nora put on long dresses and began to arrange her hair as a young lady, it occurred to Roger that he might make some change in his own appearance and reinforce his waning attractions. He was now thirty-two; he fancied he was growing stout. Bald, corpulent, middle-aged—at this rate he would soon be shelved! He was seized with a mad desire to win back the lost graces of youth. He had a dozen interviews with his tailor, the result of which was that for a fortnight he appeared daily in a new garment. Suddenly amid this restless longing to revise and embellish himself, he determined to suppress his whiskers. This would take off five years. He appeared, therefore, one morning, in the severe simplicity of a mustache. Nora started and greeted him with a little cry of horror. "Don't you like it?" he asked.

She hung her head on one side and the other. "Well no— to be frank."

"Oh, of course to be frank! It will only take five years to grow them again. What 's the trouble?"

She gave a critical frown. "It makes you look too—too fat; too much like Mr. Vose." It is sufficient to explain that Mr. Vose was the butcher, who called every day in his cart, and who recently—Roger with horror only now remembered it—had sacrificed his whiskers to a greater singleness of effect.

"I 'm sorry!" said Roger. "It was for you I did it!"

"For me!" And Nora burst into a violent laugh.

"Why, my dear Nora," cried the young man with a certain angry vehemence, "don't I do everything in life for you?"

She relapsed into sudden gravity. And then, after much meditation: "Excuse my unfeeling levity," she said. "You might cut off your nose, Roger, and I should like your face as well." But this was but half comfort. "Too fat!" Her subtler sense had spoken, and Roger never encountered Mr. Vose for three months after this without wishing to attack him with one of his own cleavers.

He made now an heroic attempt to scale the frowning battlements of the future. He pretended to be making arrangements for a tour in Europe, and for having his house completely remodelled in his absence; noting the while attentively the effect upon Nora of his cunning machinations. But she gave no sign of suspicion that his future, to the uttermost day, could be anything but her future too. One evening, nevertheless, an incident occurred which fatally confounded his calculations,—an evening of perfect mid-spring, full of warm, vague odors, of growing day-light, of the sense of bursting sap and fresh-turned earth. Roger sat on the piazza, looking out on things with an opera-glass. Nora, who had been strolling in the garden, returned to the house and sat down on the steps of the portico. "Roger," she said, after a pause, "has it never struck you as very strange that we should be living together in this way?"

Roger's heart rose to his throat. But he was loath to concede anything to her imagination, lest he should concede too much. "It 's not especially strange," he said.

"Surely it *is* strange," she answered. "What are you? Neither my brother, nor my father, nor my uncle, nor my cousin,—nor even, by law, my guardian."

"By law! My dear child, what do you know about law?"

"I know that if I should run away and leave you now, you could n't force me to return."

"That 's fine talk! Who told you that?"

"No one; I thought of it myself. As I grow older, I ought to think of such things."

"Upon my word! Of running away and leaving me?"

"That 's but one side of the question. The other is that you can turn me out of your house this moment, and no one can force you to take me back. I ought to remember such things."

"Pray what good will it do you to remember them?"

Nora hesitated a moment. "There is always some good in not losing sight of the truth."

"The truth! you 're very young to begin to talk about it."

"Not too young. I 'm old for my age. I ought to be!" These last words were uttered with a little sigh which roused Roger to action.

"Since we 're talking about the truth," he said, "I wonder whether you know a tithe of it."

For an instant she was silent; then rising slowly to her feet: "What do you mean?" she asked. "Is there any secret in all that you 've done for me?" Suddenly she clasped her hands, and eagerly, with a smile, went on: "You said the other day you had a romance. Is it a real romance, Roger? Are you, after all, related to me,—my cousin, my brother?"

He let her stand before him, perplexed and expectant. "It 's more of a romance than that."

She slid upon her knees at his feet. "Dear Roger, do tell me," she said.

He began to stroke her hair. "You think so much," he answered; "do you never think about the future, the real future, ten years hence?"

"A great deal."

"What do you think?"

She blushed a little, and then he felt that she was drawing confidence from the steady glow of his benignant eyes. "Promise not to laugh!" she said, half laughing herself. He nodded. "I think about my husband!" she proclaimed. And then, as if she had, after all, been very absurd, and to forestall his laughter: "And about your wife!" she quickly added. "I want dreadfully to see her. Why don't you marry?"

He continued to stroke her hair in silence. At last he said sententiously: "I hope to marry one of these days."

"I wish you 'd do it now," Nora went on. "If only she 'd be nice! We should be sisters, and I should take care of the children."

"You 're too young to understand what you say, or what I mean. Little girls should n't talk about marriage. It can mean nothing to you until you come yourself to marry—as you will, of course. You 'll have to decide and choose."

"I suppose I shall. I shall refuse him."

"What do you mean?"

But without answering his question: "Were you ever in love, Roger?" she suddenly asked. "Is that your romance?"

"Almost."

"Then it 's not about me, after all?"

"It 's about you, Nora; but, after all, it 's not a romance. It 's solid, it 's real, it 's truth itself; as true as your silly novels are false. Nora, I care for no one, I shall never care for any one, but you!"

He spoke in tones so deep and solemn that she was impressed. "Do you mean, Roger, that you care so much for me that you 'll never marry?"

He rose quickly in his chair, pressing his hand over his brow. "Ah, Nora," he cried, "you 're terrible!"

Evidently she had pained him; her heart was filled with the impulse of reparation. She took his two hands in her own. "Roger," she whispered gravely, "if you don't wish it, I promise never, never, never to marry, but to be yours alone— yours alone!"

IV

THE SUMMER passed away; Nora was turned sixteen. Deeming it time she should begin to see something of the world, Roger spent the autumn in travelling. Of his tour in Europe he had ceased to talk; it was indefinitely deferred. It matters little where they went; Nora vastly enjoyed the excursion and found all spots alike delightful. For Roger, too, it was full of a certain reassuring felicity. His remoter visions were merged in the present overflow of sympathy and pride, in his happy sense of her quickened observation and in the gratified vanity of possession. Whether or no she was pretty, people certainly looked at her. He overheard them a dozen times call her "striking." *Striking!* The word seemed to him rich in meaning; if he had seen her for the first time taking the breeze on the deck of a river steamer, he certainly would have been struck. On his return home he found among his letters the following missive: —

MY DEAR SIR: I have learned, after various fruitless researches, that you have adopted my cousin. Miss Lambert, at the time she left St. Louis, was too young to know much about her family, or even to care much; and you, I suppose, have not investigated the subject. You, however, better than any one, can understand my desire to make her acquaintance. I hope you 'll not deny me the privilege. I am the second son of a half-sister of her mother, between whom and my own mother there was always the greatest affection. It was not until some time after it happened that I heard of Mr. Lambert's melancholy death. But it is useless to recur to that painful scene! I resolved to spare no trouble in ascertaining the fate of his daughter. I have only just succeeded, after having fairly given her up. I have thought it better to write to you than to her, but I beg you to give her my compliments. I anticipate no difficulty in satisfying you that I am not a humbug. I have no hope of being able to better her circumstances; but, whatever they may be, blood is blood, and cousins are cousins, especially in the West. A speedy answer will oblige

Yours truly, GEORGE FENTON.

The letter was dated in New York, from a hotel. Roger was shocked. It had been from the first a peculiar satisfaction to him that Nora began and ended so distinctly with herself. But here was a hint of indefinite continuity! Here, at last, was an echo of her past. He immediately showed the letter to Nora. As she read it, her face flushed deep with wonder and suppressed relief. She had never heard, she confessed, of her mother's half-sister. The "great affection" between the two ladies must have been anterior to Mrs. Lambert's marriage. Roger's own provisional solution of the problem was that Mrs. Lambert had married so little to the taste of her family as to forfeit all communication with them. If he had obeyed his immediate impulse, he would have written to his mysterious petitioner that Miss Lambert was sensible of the honor implied in his request, but that never having missed his society, it seemed needless that, at this time of day, she should cultivate it. But Nora had become infected by a huge curiosity; the dormant pulse of kinship had been quickened; it began to throb with delicious power. This was enough for Roger. "I don't know," he said, "whether he's an honest man or a scamp, but at a venture I suppose I must invite him down." To this Nora replied that she thought his letter was "lovely"; and Mr. Fenton received a fairly civil summons.

Whether or no he was an honest man remained to be seen; but on the face of the matter he appeared no scamp. He was, in fact, a person difficult to classify. Roger had made up his mind that he would be outrageously rough and Western; full of strange oaths and bearded, for aught he knew, like the pard. In aspect, however, Fenton was a pretty fellow enough, and his speech, if not especially conciliatory to ears polite, possessed a certain homely vigor in which ears polite might have found their account. He was as little as possible, certainly, of Roger's *monde*; but he carried about him the native fragrance of another *monde*, beside which the social perfume familiar to Roger's nostrils must have seemed a trifle stale and insipid. He was invested with a loose-fitting cosmopolitan Occidentalism, which seemed to say to Roger that, of the two, *he* was provincial. Whether or no Fenton was a good man, he was a good American; though I doubt that he would, after the saying, have sought his Mahomet's Paradise in Paris. Considering his years,—they numbered but twenty-five,—Fenton's precocity and maturity of tone were an amazing spectacle. You would have very soon confessed, however, that he had a true genius for his part, and that it became him better to play at manhood than at juvenility. He could never have been a ruddy-cheeked boy. He was tall and lean, with a keen dark eye, a smile humorous, but not exactly genial, a thin, drawling, almost feminine voice and a strange Southwestern accent. His voice, at first, might have given you certain presumptuous hopes as to a soft spot in his tough young hide; but after listening awhile to its colorless monotone, you would have felt, I think, that though it was an instrument of one string, that solitary chord had been tempered in brine. Fenton was furthermore flat-chested and high-shouldered, but without any look of debility. He wore a little dead black mustache, which, at first, you would have been likely to suspect unjustly of a borrowed tint. His straight black hair was always carefully combed, and a small diamond pin adorned the bosom of his shirt. His feet were small and slender, and his left hand was decorated with a neat specimen of tattooing. You would never have called him modest, yet you would hardly have called him impudent; for he had evidently lived with people among whom the ideas of modesty and impudence, in their finer shades, had no great circulation. He had nothing whatever of the manner of society, but it was surprising how gracefully a certain shrewd *bonhomie* and smart good-humor enabled him to dispense with it. He stood with his hands in his pockets, watching punctilio taking its course, and thinking, probably, what a d—d fool she was to go so far roundabout to a point he could reach with a single shuffle of his long legs. Roger, from the first hour of his being in the house, felt pledged to dislike him. He patronized him; he made him feel like a small boy, like an old woman; he sapped the roots of the poor fellow's comfortable consciousness of being a man of the world. Fenton was a man of twenty worlds. He had knocked about and dabbled in affairs and adventures since he was ten years old; he knew the American continent as he knew the palm of his hand; he was redolent of enterprise, of "operations," of a certain fierce friction with mankind. Roger would have liked to believe that he doubted his word, that there was a chance of his not being Nora's cousin, but a youth of an ardent swindling genius who had come into possession of a parcel of facts too provokingly pertinent to be wasted. He had evidently known the late Mr. Lambert—the poor man must have had plenty of such friends; but was he, in truth, his wife's nephew? Was not this shadowy nepotism excogitated over an unpaid hotel bill? So Roger fretfully meditated, but generally with no great gain of ground. He inclined, on the whole, to believe the young man's pretensions were valid, and to reserve his mistrust for the use he might possibly make of them. Of course Fenton had not come down to spend a stupid week in the country out of pure cousinly affection. Nora was but the means; Roger's presumptive wealth and bounty were the end. "He comes to make love to his cousin, and marry her if he can. I, who have done so much, will of course do more; settle an income directly on the bride, make my will in her favor, and die at my earliest convenience! How furious he must be," Roger continued to meditate, "to find me so young and hearty! How furious he would be if he knew a little more!" This line of argument was justified in a manner by the frank assurance which Fenton was constantly at pains to convey, that he was incapable of any other relation to a fact than a desire to turn it to pecuniary account. Roger was uneasy, yet he took a certain comfort in the belief that, thanks to his early lessons, Nora could be trusted to confine her cousin to the precinct of cousinship. In whatever he might have failed, he had certainly taught her to know a gentleman. Cousins are born, not made; but lovers may be accepted at discretion. Nora's discretion, surely, would not be wanting. I may add also that, in his desire to order all things well, Roger caught himself wondering whether, at the worst, a little precursory love-making would do any harm. The ground might be gently tickled to receive his own sowing; the petals of the young girl's nature, playfully forced apart, would leave the golden heart of the flower but the more accessible to his own vertical rays.

It was cousinship for Nora, certainly; but cousinship was much, more than Roger fancied, luckily for his peace of mind. In the utter penury of her native gifts, her tardy kinsman acquired a portentous value. She was so proud of turning out to have a cousin as well as other folks, that she lavished on the young man all the idle tenderness of her primitive instincts, the savings and sparings, such as they were, of her girlish good-will. It must be said that Fenton was not altogether unworthy of her favors. He meant no especial harm to other people, save in so far as he meant uncompromising benefit to himself. The Knight of La Mancha, on the torrid flats of Spain, never urged his gaunt steed with a grimmer pressure of the knees than that with which Fenton held himself erect on the hungry hobby of success. Shrewd as he was, he had perhaps, as well, a ray of Don Quixote's divine obliquity of vision. It is at least true that success as yet had been painfully elusive, and a part of the peril to Nora's girlish heart lay in this melancholy grace of undeserved failure. The young man's imagination was a trifle restless; he had a generous need of keeping too many irons on the fire. It had been in a kind of fanciful despair of doing better, for the time, that he had made overtures to Roger. He had learned six months before of his cousin's situation and had felt no great sentimental need of making her acquaintance; but at last, revolving many things of a certain sort, he had come to wonder whether these good people could n't be induced to play into his hands. Roger's wealth (which he largely overestimated) and Roger's obvious taste for sharing it with other people, Nora's innocence and Nora's prospects—it would surely take a great fool not to pluck the rose from so thornless a tree. He foresaw these good things melting and trickling into the shallow current of his own career. Exactly what use he meant to make of Nora he would have been at a loss to say. Plain matrimony might or might not be a prize. At any rate, it could do a clever man no harm to have a rich girl foolishly in love with him. He turned, therefore, upon his charming cousin the sunny side of his genius. He very soon began to doubt that he had ever known so delightful a person, and indeed his growing sense of her sweetness bade fair to make him bungle his naughtiness. She was altogether sweet enough to be valued for herself. She made him feel that he had never encountered a really fine girl. Nora was a young lady: how she had come to it was one of the outer mysteries; but there she was, consummate! He made no point of a man being a gentleman;

in fact, when a man was a gentleman you had rather to be
one yourself, which did n't pay; but for a woman to be a lady
was plainly pure gain. He had a fine enough sense to detect
something extremely grateful in the half-concessions, the reserve of freshness, the fugitive dignity, of gently nurtured
maidenhood. Women, to him, had seemed mostly as cut
flowers, blooming awhile in the waters of occasion, but yielding no second or rarer freshness. Nora was fast overtaking
herself in the exhilarating atmosphere of her cousin's gallantry. She had known so few young men that she had not
learned to be fastidious, and Fenton represented to her fancy
that great collective manhood of which Roger was not. He
had an irresistible air of action, alertness, and purpose. Poor
Roger, beside him, was most prosaically passive. She regarded
her cousin with something of the thrilled attention which one
bestows on the naked arrow, poised across the bow. He had,
moreover, the inestimable merit of representing her own side
of her situation. He very soon became sensible of this merit,
and you may be sure he entertained her to the top of her
bent. He gossiped by the hour about her father, and gave her
very plainly to understand that poor Mr. Lambert had been
more sinned against than sinning. His wrongs, his sufferings,
his ambitions and adventures, formed on Fenton's lips not
only a most pathetic recital, but a standing pretext for Western anecdotes, not always strictly adapted, it must be confessed, to the melting mood. Of her mother, too, he
discoursed with a wholesale fecundity of praise and reminiscence. Facts, facts, facts was Nora's demand: she got them,
and if here and there a fiction slipped into the basket, it
passed muster with the rest.

Nora was not slow to perceive that Roger had no love for
their guest, and she immediately conceded him his right of
judgment. She allowed for a certain fatal and needful antag-
onism in their common interest in herself. Fenton's presence
was a tacit infringement of Roger's prescriptive right of property. If her cousin had only never come! It might have been,
though she could not bring herself to wish it. Nora felt
vaguely that here was a chance for tact, for the woman's
peace-making art. To keep Roger in spirits, she put on a
dozen unwonted graces; she waited on him, appealed to him,

smiled at him with unwearied iteration. But the main effect of these sweet offices was to deepen her gracious radiance in her cousin's eyes. Roger's rancorous suspicion transmuted to bitterness what would otherwise have been pure delight. She was turning hypocrite; she was throwing dust in his eyes; she was plotting with that vulgar Missourian. Fenton, of course, was forced to admit that he had reckoned without his host. Roger had had the impudence not to turn out a simpleton; he was not a shepherd of the golden age; he was a dogged modern, with prosy prejudices; the wind of his favor blew as it listed. Fenton took the liberty of being extremely irritated at the other's want of ductility. "Hang the man!" he said to himself, "why can't he trust me? What is he afraid of? Why don't he take me as a friend rather than an enemy? Let him be frank, and I 'll be frank. I could put him up to things! And what does he want to do with Nora, any way?" This latter question Fenton came very soon to answer, and the answer amused him not a little. It seemed to him an extremely odd use of one's time and capital, this fashioning of a wife to order. There was in it a long-winded patience, a broad arrogance of leisure, which excited his ire. Roger might surely have found *his* fit ready made! His disappointment, a certain angry impulse to rescue his cousin from this pitiful compression of circumstance, the sense finally that what he should gain he would gain from her alone, though indeed she was too confoundedly innocent to appreciate his fierce immediate ends;—these things combined to heat the young man's humor to the fever-point and to make him strike more random blows than belonged to plain prudence.

The autumn being well advanced, the warmth of the sun had become very grateful. Nora used to spend much of the morning in strolling about the dismantled garden with her cousin. Roger would stand at the window with his honest face more nearly disfigured by a scowl than ever before. It was the old, old story, to his mind: nothing succeeds with women like just too little deference. Fenton would lounge along by Nora's side, with his hands in his pockets, a cigar in his mouth, his shoulders raised to his ears, and a pair of tattered slippers on his absurdly diminutive feet. Not only had Nora forgiven him this last breach of civility, but she had forthwith begun to work him a new pair of slippers. "What on earth," thought Roger, "do they find to talk about?" Their conversation, meanwhile, ran in some such strain as this:—

"My dear Nora," said the young man, "what on earth, week in and week out, do you and Mr. Lawrence find to talk about?"

"A great many things, George. We have lived long enough together to have a great many interests in common."

"It was a most extraordinary thing, his adopting you, if you don't mind my saying so. Imagine my adopting a little girl."

"You and Roger are very different men."

"We certainly are. What in the world did he expect to do with you?"

"Very much what he has done, I suppose. He has educated me, he has made me what I am."

"You 're a very nice little person; but, upon my word, I don't see that he 's to thank for it. A lovely girl can be neither made nor marred."

"Possibly! But I give you notice that I 'm not a lovely girl. I have it in me to be, under provocation, anything but a lovely girl. I owe everything to Roger. You must say nothing against him. I won't have it. What would have become of me—" She stopped, betrayed by her glance and voice.

"Mr. Lawrence is a model of all the virtues, I admit! But, Nora, I confess I 'm jealous of him. Does he expect to educate you forever? You seem to me to have already all the learning a pretty woman needs. What does *he* know about women? What does he expect to do with you two or three years hence? Two or three years hence, you 'll be—" And Fenton, breaking off, began to whistle with vehement gayety and executed with shuffling feet a momentary fandango. "Two or three years hence, when you look in the glass, remember I said so!"

"He means to go to Europe one of these days," said Nora, laughing.

"One of these days! One would think he expects to keep you forever. Not if I can help it. And why Europe, in the name of all that 's patriotic? Europe be hanged! You ought to come out to your own section of the country, and see your own people. I can introduce you to the best people in St.

Louis. It 's a glorious place, worth a thousand of your dismal Bostons. I 'll tell you what, my dear. You don't know it, but you 're a regular Western girl."

A certain foolish gladness in being the creature thus denominated prompted Nora to a gush of momentary laughter, of which Roger, within the window, caught the soundless ripple. "You ought to know, George," she said, "you 're Western enough yourself."

"Of course I am. I glory in it. It 's the only place for a man of ideas! In the West you can do something! Round here you 're all stuck fast in a Slough of Despond. For yourself, Nora, at bottom you 're all right; but superficially you 're just a trifle overstarched. But we 'll take it out of you! It comes of living with stiff-necked—"

Nora bent for a moment her lustrous eyes on the young man, as if to recall him to order. "I beg you to understand, once for all," she said, "that I refuse to listen to disrespectful allusions to Roger."

"I 'll say it again, just to make you look at me so. If I ever fall in love with you, it will be when you are scolding me. All I 've got to do is to attack your papa—"

"He 's not my papa. I have had one papa; that 's enough. I say it in all respect."

"If he 's not your papa, what is he? He 's a dog in the manger. He must be either one thing or the other. When you 're very little older, you'll understand that."

"He may be whatever thing you please. I shall be but one,—his best friend."

Fenton laughed with a kind of fierce hilarity. "You 're so innocent, my dear, that one does n't know where to take you. You expect, in other words, to marry him?"

Nora stopped in the path, with her eyes on her cousin. For a moment he was half confounded by their startled severity and the flush of pain in her cheek. "Marry Roger!" she said with great gravity.

"Why, he 's a man, after all!"

Nora was silent a moment; and then with a certain forced levity, walking on: "I 'd better wait till I 'm asked."

"He 'll ask you! You 'll see."

"If he does, I shall be surprised."

"You 'll pretend to be. Women always do."

"He has known me as a child," she continued, heedless of his sarcasm. "I shall always be a child, for him."

"He 'll like that," said Fenton, with heat. "He 'll like a child of twenty."

Nora, for an instant, was sunk in meditation. "As regards marriage," she said at last, with a slightly defiant emphasis, "I 'll do what Roger wishes."

Fenton lost patience. "Roger be hanged!" he cried. "You 're not his slave. You must choose for yourself and act for yourself. You must obey your own heart. You don't know what you 're talking about. One of these days your heart will say its say. Then we 'll see what becomes of Roger's wishes! If he wants to mould you to his will, he should have taken you younger—or older! Don't tell me seriously that you can ever love (don't play upon words: love, I mean, in the one sense that means anything!) such a solemn little fop as that! Don't protest, my dear girl; I must have my say. I speak in your own interest; I speak, at any rate, from my own heart. I detest the man. I came here in all deference and honesty, and he has treated me as if I were n't fit to touch with a tongs. I 'm poor, I 've my way to make, I 'm on the world; but I 'm an honest man, for all that, and as good as he, take me altogether. Why can't he show me a moment's frankness? Why can't he take me by the hand and say, 'Come, young man, I 've got capital, and you 've got brains; let 's pull together a stroke.' Does he think I want to steal his spoons or pick his pocket? Is that hospitality? If that 's the way they understand it hereabouts, I prefer the Western article!"

This passionate outbreak, prompted in about equal measure by baffled ambition and wounded sensibility, made sad havoc with Nora's strenuous loyalty to her friend. Her sense of infinite property in her cousin—the instinct of free affection alternating more gratefully than she knew with the dim consciousness of measured dependence—had become in her heart a sort of boundless and absolute rapture. She desired neither to question nor to set a term to it: she only knew that while it lasted it was potently sweet. Roger's mistrust was certainly cruel; it was crueller still that he should obtrude it on poor George's notice. She felt, however, that two angry men were muttering over her head and her main desire was to avert an explosion. She promised herself to dismiss Fenton the next day. Of course, by the very fact of this concession, Roger lost ground in her tenderness, and George acquired the grace of the persecuted. Meanwhile, Roger's jealous irritation came to a head. On the evening following the little scene I have narrated the young couple sat by the fire in the library; Fenton on a stool at his cousin's feet holding, while Nora wound them on reels, the wools which were to be applied to the manufacture of those invidious slippers. Roger, after grimly watching their mutual amenities for some time over the cover of a book, unable to master his fierce discomposure, departed with a tell-tale stride. They heard him afterwards walking up and down the piazza, where he was appealing from his troubled nerves to the ordered quietude of the stars.

"He hates me so," said Fenton, "that I believe if I were to go out there he 'd draw a knife on me."

"O George!" cried Nora, horrified.

"It 's a fact, my dear. I 'm afraid you 'll have to give me up. I wish I had never seen you!"

"At all events, we can write to each other."

"What 's writing? I don't know how to write! I will, though! I suppose he 'll open my letters. So much the worse for him!"

Nora, as she wound her spool, mused intently. "I can't believe he really grudges me our friendship. It must be something else."

Fenton, with a clinch of his fist, arrested suddenly the outflow of the skein from his hand. "It is something else," he said. "It 's our possible—more than friendship!" And he grasped her two hands in his own. "Nora, choose! Between me and him!"

She stared a moment; then her eyes filled with tears. "O George," she cried, "you make me very unhappy." She must certainly tell him to go; and yet that very movement of his which had made it doubly needful made it doubly hard. "I 'll talk to Roger," she said. "No one should be condemned unheard. We may all misunderstand each other."

Fenton, half an hour later, having, as he said, letters to

write, went up to his own room; shortly after which, Roger returned to the library. Half an hour's communion with the star-light and the long beat of the crickets had drawn the sting from his irritation. There came to him, too, a mortifying sense of his guest having outdone him in civility. This would never do. He took refuge in imperturbable good-humor, and entered the room with a *bravado* of cool indifference. But even before he had spoken, something in Nora's face caused this wholesome dose of resignation to stick in his throat. "Your cousin 's gone?" he said.

"To his own room. He has some letters to write."

"Shall I hold your wools?" Roger asked, after a pause, with a rather awkward air of overture.

"Thank you. They are all wound."

"For whom are your slippers?" He knew, of course; but the question came.

"For George. Did n't I tell you? Are n't they pretty?" And she held up her work.

"Prettier than he deserves."

Nora gave him a rapid glance and miscounted her stitch. "You don't like poor George," she said.

"Poor George" set his wound a-throbbing again. "No. Since you ask me, I don't like poor George."

Nora was silent. At last: "Well!" she said, "you 've not the same reasons as I have."

"So I 'm bound to believe!" cried Roger, with a laugh. "You must have excellent reasons."

"Excellent. He 's my own, you know."

"Your own— Oho!" And he laughed louder.

His tone forced Nora to blush. "My own cousin," she cried.

"Your own fiddlestick!" cried Roger.

She stopped her work. "What do you mean?" she asked gravely.

Roger himself began to blush a little. "I mean—I mean— that I don't half believe in your cousin. He does n't satisfy me. I don't like him. He 's a jumble of contradictions. I have nothing but his own word. I 'm not bound to take it. He tells the truth, if you like, but he tells fibs too."

"Roger, Roger," said Nora, with great softness, "do you mean that he 's an impostor?"

"The word is your own. He 's not honest."

She slowly rose from her little bench, gathering her work into the skirt of her dress. "And, doubting of his honesty, you 've let him take up his abode here, you 've let him become dear to me?"

She was making him ten times a fool! "Why, if you liked him," he said. "When did I ever refuse you anything?"

There came upon Nora a sudden unpitying sense that then and there Roger was ridiculous. "Honest or not honest," she said with vehemence, "I *do* like him. Cousin or no cousin, he 's my friend."

"Very good. But I warn you. I don't enjoy talking to you thus. But let me tell you, once for all, that your cousin, your friend,—your—whatever he is!"—He faltered an instant; Nora's eyes were fixed on him. "That he disgusts me!"

"You 're extremely unjust. You 've taken no trouble to know him. You 've treated him from the first with small civility!"

"Good heavens! Was the trouble to be all mine? Civility! he never missed it; he does n't know what it means."

"He knows more than you think. But we must talk no more about him." She rolled together her canvas and reels; and then suddenly, with passionate inconsequence, "Poor, poor George!" she cried.

Roger watched her, rankling with that unsatisfied need, familiar alike to good men and bad when vanity is at stake, of smothering feminine right in hard manly fact. "Nora," he said, cruelly, "you disappoint me."

"You must have formed great hopes of me!" she cried.

"I confess I had."

"Say good by to them then, Roger. If this is wrong, I 'm all wrong!" She spoke with a rich displeasure which transformed with admirable effect her habitual expression of docility. She had never yet come so near being beautiful. In the midst of his passionate vexation he admired her. The scene seemed for a moment a bad dream, from which, with a start, he might awake into a declaration of love.

"Your anger gives an admirable point to your remarks. Indeed, it gives a beauty to your face. Must a woman be in the wrong to be charming?" He went on, hardly knowing what

he said. But a burning blush in her cheeks recalled him to a
kind of self-abhorrence. "Would to God," he cried, "your
abominable cousin had never come between us!"

"Between us? He 's not between us. I stand as near you,
Roger, as I ever did. Of course George will leave immediately."

"Of course! I 'm not so sure. He will, I suppose, if he 's
asked."

"Of course I shall ask him."

"Nonsense. You 'll not enjoy that."

"We 're old friends by this time," said Nora, with terrible
malice. "I sha' n't in the least mind."

Roger could have choked himself. He had brought his case
to this: Fenton a martyred proscript, and Nora a brooding
victim of duty. "Do I want to turn the man out of the
house?" he cried. "Do me a favor,—I demand it. Say nothing
to him, let him stay as long as he pleases. I 'm not afraid! I
don't trust him, but I trust you. I 'm curious to see how long
he 'll have the hardihood to stay. A fortnight hence, I shall be
justified. You 'll say to me, 'Roger, you were right. George is
n't a gentleman.' There! I insist."

"A gentleman? Really, what are we talking about? Do you
mean that he wears a false diamond in his shirt? He 'll take it
off if I ask him. There 's a long way between wearing false
diamonds—"

"And stealing real ones! I don't know. I have always fancied they go together. At all events, Nora, he 's not to suspect
that he has been able to make trouble between two old
friends."

Nora stood for a moment in irresponsive meditation. "I
think he means to go," she said. "If you want him to stay,
you must ask him." And without further words she marched
out of the room. Roger followed her with his eyes. He
thought of Lady Castlewood in "Henry Esmond," who
looked "devilish handsome in a passion."

Lady Castlewood, meanwhile, ascended to her own room,
flung her work upon the floor, and, dropping into a chair,
betook herself to weeping. It was late before she slept. She
awoke with a keener consciousness of the burden of life. Her
own burden certainly was small, but her strength, as yet, was

untested. She had thought, in her many reveries, of a possible rupture of harmony with Roger, and prayed that it might never come by a fault of hers. The fault was hers now in that she had surely cared less for duty than for joy. Roger, indeed, had shown a pitiful smallness of view. This was a weakness; but who was she, to keep account of Roger's weaknesses? It was to a weakness of Roger's that she owed her food and raiment and shelter. It helped to quench her resentment that she felt, somehow, that, whether Roger smiled or frowned, George would still be George. He was not a gentleman: well and good; neither was she, for that matter, a lady. But a certain manful hardness like George's would not be amiss in the man one was to love. There was a discord now in that daily commonplace of happiness which had seemed to repeat the image of their mutual trust as a lucid pool reflects the cloudless blue. But if the discord should deepen and swell, it was sweet to think she might deafen her sense in that sturdy cousinship.

A simpler soul than Fenton's might have guessed at the trouble of this quiet household. Fenton read in it as well an omen of needful departure. He accepted the necessity with an acute sense of failure,—almost of injury. He had gained nothing but the bother of being loved. It was a bother, because it gave him a vague importunate sense of responsibility. It seemed to fling upon all things a gray shade of prohibition. Yet the matter had its brightness, too, if a man could but swallow his superstitions. He cared for Nora quite enough to tell her he loved her; he had said as much, with an easy conscience, to girls for whom he cared far less. He felt gratefully enough the cool vestment of tenderness which she had spun about him, like a web of imponderous silver; but he had other uses for his time than to go masquerading through Nora's fancy. The defeat of his hope that Roger, like an ideal *oncle de comédie*, would shower blessings and bank-notes upon his union with his cousin, involved the discomfiture of a secondary project; that, namely, of borrowing five thousand dollars. The reader will smile: but such is the *naïveté* of "smart men." He would consent, now, to be put off with five hundred. In this collapse of his visions he fell a-musing upon Nora's financial value.

"Look here," he said to her, with an air of heroic effort, "I see I'm in the way. I must be off."

"I'm sorry, George," said Nora, sadly.

"So am I. I never supposed I was proud. But I reckoned without my host!" he said with a bitter laugh. "I wish I had never come. Or rather I don't. My girl of girls!"

She began to question him soothingly about his projects and prospects; and hereupon, for once, Fenton bent his mettle to simulate a pathetic incapacity. He set forth that he was discouraged; the future was a blank. It was child's play, attempting to do anything without capital.

"And you have no capital?" said Nora, anxiously.

Fenton gave a poignant smile. "Why, my dear girl, I'm a poor man!"

"How poor?"

"Poor, poor, poor. Poor as a rat."

"You don't mean that you're penniless?"

"What's the use of my telling you? You can't help me. And it would only make you unhappy."

"If you are unhappy, I want to be!"

This golden vein of sentiment might certainly be worked. Fenton took out his pocket-book, drew from it four banknotes of five dollars each, and ranged them with a sort of mournful playfulness in a line on his knee. "That's my fortune."

"Do you mean to say that twenty dollars is all you have in the world?"

Fenton smoothed out the creases, caressingly, in the soiled and crumpled notes. "It's a great shame to bring you down to these sordid mysteries of misery," he said. "Fortune has raised you above them."

Nora's heart began to beat. "Yes, it has. I have a little money, George. Some eighty dollars."

Eighty dollars! George suppressed a groan. "He keeps you rather low."

"Why, I have little use for money, and no chance, here in the country, to spend it. Roger is extremely generous. Every few weeks he forces money upon me. I often give it away to the poor people hereabouts. Only a fortnight ago I refused to take any more on account of my having this unspent. It's agreed between us that I may give what I please in charity, and that my charities are my own affair. If I had only known of you, George, I should have appointed you my pensioner-in-chief."

George was silent. He was wondering intently how he might arrange to become the standing recipient of her overflow. Suddenly he remembered that he ought to protest. But Nora had lightly quitted the room. Fenton repocketed his twenty dollars and awaited her reappearance. Eighty dollars was not a fortune; still it was a sum. To his great annoyance, before Nora returned, Roger presented himself. The young man felt for an instant as if he had been caught in an act of sentimental burglary, and made a movement to conciliate his detector. "I 'm afraid I must bid you good by," he said.

Roger frowned and wondered whether Nora had spoken. At this moment she reappeared, flushed and out of breath with the excitement of her purpose. She had been counting over her money and held in each hand a little fluttering package of bank-notes. On seeing Roger she stopped and blushed, exchanging with her cousin a rapid glance of inquiry. He almost glared at her, whether with warning or with menace she hardly knew. Roger stood looking at her, half amazed. Suddenly, as the meaning of her errand flashed upon him, he turned a furious crimson. He made a step forward, but cautioned himself; then, folding his arms, he silently waited. Nora, after a moment's hesitation, rolling her notes together, came up to her cousin and held out the little package. Fenton kept his hands in his pockets and devoured her with his eyes. "What 's all this?" he said, brutally.

"O George!" cried Nora; and her eyes filled with tears.

Roger had divined the situation; the shabby victimization of the young girl and her kinsman's fury at the disclosure of his avidity. He was angry; but he was even more disgusted. From so vulgar a knave there was little rivalship to fear. "I 'm afraid I 'm rather a marplot," he said. "Don't insist, Nora. Wait till my back is turned."

"I have nothing to be ashamed of," said Nora.

"*You?* O, nothing whatever!" cried Roger, with a laugh.

Fenton stood leaning against the mantel-piece, desperately

sullen, with a look of vicious confusion. "It 's only I who have anything to be ashamed of," he said at last, bitterly, with an effort. "My poverty!"

Roger smiled graciously. "Honest poverty is never shameful!"

Fenton gave him an insolent stare. "Honest poverty! You know a great deal about it."

"Don't appeal to poor little Nora, man, for her savings," Roger went on. "Come to me."

"You 're unjust," said Nora. "He did n't appeal to me. I appealed to him. I guessed his poverty. He has only twenty dollars in the world."

"O, you poor little fool!" roared Fenton's eyes.

Roger was delighted. At a single stroke he might redeem his incivility and reinstate himself in Nora's affections. He took out his pocket-book. "Let me help you. It was very stupid of me not to have guessed your embarrassment." And he counted out a dozen notes.

Nora stepped to her cousin's side and passed her hand through his arm. "Don't be proud," she murmured caressingly.

Roger's notes were new and crisp. Fenton looked hard at the opposite wall, but, explain it who can, he read their successive figures,—a fifty, four twenties, six tens. He could have howled.

"Come don't be proud," repeated Roger, holding out this little bundle of wealth.

Two great passionate tears welled into the young man's eyes. The sight of Roger's sturdy sleekness, of the comfortable twinkle of patronage in his eye, was too much for him. "I sha' n't give *you* a chance to be proud," he said. "Take care! Your papers may go into the fire."

"O George!" murmured Nora; and her murmur seemed to him delicious.

He bent down his head, passed his arm around her shoulders, and kissed her on her forehead. "Good by, dearest Nora," he said.

Roger stood staring, with his proffered gift. "You decline?" he cried, almost defiantly.

" 'Decline' is n't the word. A man does n't decline an insult."

Was Fenton, then, to have the best of it, and was his own very generosity to be turned against him? Blindly, passionately, Roger crumpled the notes in his fist and tossed them into the fire. In an instant they begun to blaze.

"Roger, are you mad?" cried Nora. And she made a movement to rescue the crackling paper. Fenton burst into a laugh. He caught her by the arm, clasped her round the waist, and forced her to stand and watch the brief blaze. Pressed against his side, she felt the quick beating of his heart. As the notes disappeared her eyes sought Roger's face. He looked at her stupidly, and then turning on his heel, he walked out of the room. Her cousin, still holding her, showered upon her forehead half a dozen fierce kisses. But disengaging herself: "You must leave the house!" she cried. "Something dreadful will happen."

Fenton had soon packed his valise, and Nora, meanwhile, had ordered a vehicle to carry him to the station. She waited for him in the portico. When he came out, with his bag in his hand, she offered him again her little roll of bills. But he was a wiser man than half an hour before. He took them, turned them over and selected a one-dollar note. "I 'll keep this," he said, "in remembrance, and only spend it for my last dinner." She made him promise, however, that if trouble really overtook him, he would let her know, and in any case he would write. As the wagon went over the crest of an adjoining hill he stood up and waved his hat. His tall, gaunt young figure, as it rose dark against the cold November sunset, cast a cooling shadow across the fount of her virgin sympathies. Such was the outline, surely, of the conquering hero, not of the conquered. Her fancy followed him forth into the world with a tender impulse of comradeship.

V

ROGER'S QUARREL with his young companion, if quarrel it was, was never repaired. It had scattered its seed; they were left lying, to be absorbed in the conscious soil or dispersed by some benignant breeze of accident, as destiny might appoint. But as a manner of clearing the air of its thunder, Roger, a week after Fenton's departure, proposed she should go with him for a fortnight to town. Later, perhaps, they might arrange to remain for the winter. Nora had been longing vaguely for the relief of a change of circumstance; she assented with great good-will. They lodged at a hotel,—not the establishment at which they had made acquaintance. Here, late in the afternoon, the day after their arrival, Nora sat by the window, waiting for Roger to come and take her to dinner, and watching with the intentness of country eyes the hurrying throng in the street; thinking too at moments of a certain blue bonnet she had bought that morning, and comparing it, not uncomplacently, with the transitory bonnets on the pavement. A gentleman was introduced; Nora had not forgotten Hubert Lawrence. Hubert had occupied for more than a year past a pastoral office in the West, and had recently had little communication with his cousin. Nora he had seen but on a single occasion, that of his visit to Roger, six months after her advent. She had grown in the interval, from the little girl who slept with the "Child's Own Book" under her pillow and dreamed of the Prince Avenant, into a stately maiden who read the "Heir of Redcliffe," and mused upon the loves of the clergy. Hubert, too, had changed in his own degree. He was now thirty-one years of age and his character had lost something of a certain boyish vagueness of outline, which formerly had not been without its grace. But his elder grace was scarcely less effective. Various possible half-shadows in his personality had melted into broad, shallow lights. He was now, distinctly, one of the light-armed troops of the army of the Lord. He fought the Devil as an irresponsible skirmisher, not as a sturdy gunsman planted beside a booming sixty-pounder. The clerical cloth, as Hubert wore it, was not unmitigated sable; and in spite of his cloth, such as it was,

humanity rather than divinity got the lion's share of his attentions. He loved doubtless, in this world, the heavenward face
of things, but he loved, as regards heaven, the earthward. He
was rather an idler in the walks of theology and he was un-
committed to any very rigid convictions. He thought the old
theological positions in very bad taste, but he thought the
new theological negations in no taste at all. In fact, Hubert
believed so vaguely and languidly in the Devil that there was
but slender logic in his having undertaken the cure of souls.
He administered his spiritual medicines in homœopathic
doses. It had been maliciously said that he had turned parson
because parsons enjoy peculiar advantages in approaching the
fair sex. The presumption is in their favor. Our business,
however, is not to pick up idle reports. Hubert was, on the
whole, a decidedly light weight, and yet his want of spiritual
passion was by no means in effect a want of motive or stimulus; for the central pivot of his being continued to operate
with the most noiseless precision and regularity,—the slim,
erect, inflexible *Ego*. To the eyes of men, and especially to the
eyes of women, whatever may have been the moving cause,
the outer manifestation was supremely gracious. If Hubert
had no great firmness of faith, he had a very pretty firmness
of manner. He was gentle without timidity, frank without
arrogance, clever without pedantry. The common measure of
clerical disallowance was reduced in his hands to the tacit protest of a generous personal purity. His appearance bore various wholesome traces of the practical lessons of his Western
pastorate. This had been disagreeable; he had had to apply
himself, to devote himself, to compromise with a hundred
aversions. His talents had been worth less to him than he
expected, and he had been obliged, as the French say, to *payer
de sa personne*,—that person for which he entertained so delicate a respect,—in a peculiarly unsympathetic medium. All
this had given him a slightly jaded, overwearied look, certain
to deepen his interest in female eyes. He had actually a couple
of wrinkles in his fair seraphic forehead. He secretly rejoiced
in his wrinkles. They were his crown of glory. He had suffered, he had worked, he had been bored. Now he believed
in earthly compensations.

"Dear me!" he said, "can this be Nora Lambert?"

She had risen to meet him, and held out her hand with girlish frankness. She was dressed in a light silk dress; she seemed altogether a young woman. "I have been growing hard in all these years," she said. "I have had to overtake those *pieds énormes.*" The readers will not have forgotten that Hubert had thus qualified her lower members. Ignorant as she was, at the moment, of the French tongue, her memory had instinctively retained the words, and she had taken an early opportunity to look out *pied* in the dictionary. *Énorme*, of course, spoke for itself.

"You must have caught up with them now," Hubert said, laughing. "You 're an enormous young lady. I should never have known you." He sat down, asked various questions about Roger, and adjured her to tell him, as he said, "all about herself." The invitation was flattering, but it met only a partial compliance. Unconscious as yet of her own charm, Nora was oppressed by a secret admiration of her companion. His presence seemed to open a sudden vista in the narrow precinct of her young experience. She compared him with her cousin, and wondered that he should be at once so impressive and so different. She blushed a little, privately, for Fenton, and was not ill-pleased to think he was absent. In the light of Hubert's good manners, his admission that he was no gentleman acquired an excessive force. By this thrilling intimation of the diversity of the male sex, the mental pinafore of childhood seemed finally dismissed. Hubert was so frank and friendly, so tenderly and gallantly patronizing, that more than once she felt herself drifting toward an answering freedom of confidence; but on the verge of effusion, something absent in the tone of his assent, a vague fancy that, in the gathering dusk, he was looking at her all at his ease, rather than listening to her, converted her bravery into what she knew to be deplorable little-girlishness. On the whole, this interview may have passed for Nora's first lesson in the art, indispensable to a young lady on the threshold of society, of talking for half an hour without saying anything. The lesson was interrupted by the arrival of Roger, who greeted his cousin with almost extravagant warmth, and insisted on his staying to dinner. Roger was to take Nora after dinner to a concert, for which he felt no great enthusiasm; he proposed to Hubert, who was a musical man, to occupy his place. Hubert demurred awhile; but in the mean time Nora, having gone to prepare herself, reappeared, looking extremely well in the blue crape bonnet before mentioned, with her face bright with anticipated plea-sure. For a moment Roger was vexed at having resigned his office: Hubert immediately stepped into it. They came home late, the blue bonnet nothing the worse for wear, and the young girl's face illumined by a dozen intense impressions. She was in a fever of gayety; she treated Roger to a represen-tation of the concert, and made a great show of voice. Her departing childishness, her dawning tact, her freedom with Roger, her half-freedom with Hubert, made a charming mix-ture, and insured for her auditors the success of the entertain-ment. When she had retired, amid a mimic storm of applause from the two gentlemen, Roger solemnly addressed his cousin, "Well, what do you think of her? I hope you have no fault to find with her feet."

"I have had no observation of her feet," said Hubert; "but she will have very handsome hands. She 's a very nice crea-ture." Roger sat lounging in his chair with his hands in his pockets, his chin on his breast, and a heavy gaze fixed on Hubert. The latter was struck with his deeply preoccupied aspect. "But let us talk of you rather than of Nora," he said. "I have been waiting for a chance to tell you that you look very poorly."

"Nora or I,—it 's all one. Hubert, I live in that child!"

Hubert was startled by the sombre energy of his tone. The old polished placid Roger was in abeyance. "My dear fellow," he said, "you 're altogether wrong. Live for yourself. You may be sure she 'll do as much. You take it too hard."

"Yes, I take it too hard. It wears upon me."

"What 's the matter? Is she troublesome? Is she more than you bargained for?" Roger sat gazing at him in silence, with the same grave eye. He began to suspect Nora had turned out a losing investment. "Is she—a—vicious?" he went on. "Surely not with that sweet face!"

Roger started to his feet impatiently. "Don't misunderstand me!" he cried. "I 've been longing to see some one—to talk—to get some advice—some sympathy. I 'm fretting myself away."

"Good heavens, man, give her a thousand dollars and send her back to her family. You 've educated her."

"Her family! She has no family! She 's the loneliest as well as the sweetest, wisest, best of creatures! If she were only a tenth as good, I should be a happier man. I can't think of parting with her; not for all I possess!"

Hubert stared a moment. "Why, you 're in love!"

"Yes," said Roger, blushing. "I 'm in love."

"Come!"

"I 'm not ashamed of it," rejoined Roger, softly.

It was no business of Hubert's certainly; but he felt the least bit disappointed. "Well," he said, coolly, "why don't you marry her?"

"It 's not so simple as that!"

"She 'll not have you?"

Roger frowned impatiently. "Reflect a moment. You pretend to be a man of delicacy."

"You mean she 's too young? Nonsense. If you are sure of her, the younger the better."

"Hubert," cried Roger, "for my unutterable misery, I have a conscience. I wish to leave her free, and take the risk. I wish to be just, and let the matter work itself out. You may think me absurd, but I wish to be loved for myself, as other men are loved."

It was a specialty of Hubert's that in proportion as other people grew hot, he grew cool. To keep cool, morally, in a heated medium was, in fact, for Hubert a peculiar satisfaction. He broke into a long light laugh. "Excuse me," he said, "but there is something ludicrous in your attitude. What business has a lover with a conscience? None at all! That 's why I keep out of it. It seems to me your prerogative to be downright. If you waste any more time in hair-splitting, you 'll find your young lady has taken things in the lump!"

"Do you really think there is danger?" Roger demanded, pitifully. "Not yet awhile. She 's only a child. Tell me, rather, *is* she only a child? You 've spent the evening beside her: how does she strike a stranger?"

While Hubert's answer lingered on his lips, the door opened and Nora came in. Her errand was to demand the use of Roger's watch-key, her own having mysteriously vanished.

She had begun to take out her pins and had muffled herself for this excursion in a merino dressing-gown of sombre blue. Her hair was gathered for the night into a single massive coil, which had been loosened by the rapidity of her flight along the passage. Roger's key proved a complete misfit, so that she had recourse to Hubert's. It hung on the watch-chain which depended from his waistcoat, and some rather intimate fumbling was needed to adjust it to Nora's diminutive timepiece. It worked admirably, and she stood looking at him with a little smile of caution as it creaked on the pivot. "I would n't have troubled you," she said, "but that without my watch I should oversleep myself. You know Roger's temper, and what I should suffer if I were late for breakfast!"

Roger was ravished at this humorous sally, and when, on making her escape, she clasped one hand to her head to support her released tresses, and hurried along the corridor with the other confining the skirts of her inflated robe, he kissed his hand after her with more than jocular good-will.

"Ah! it 's as bad as that!" said Hubert, shaking his head.

"I had no idea she had such hair," cried Roger. "You 're right, it 's no case for shilly-shallying."

"Take care!" said Hubert. "She 's only a child."

Roger looked at him a moment. "My dear fellow, you 're a hypocrite."

Hubert colored the least bit, and then took up his hat and began to smooth it with his handkerchief. "Not at all. See how frank I can be. I recommend you to marry the young lady and have done with it. If you wait, it will be at your own risk. I assure you I think she's charming, and if I 'm not mistaken, this is only a hint of future possibilities. Don't sow for others to reap. If you think the harvest is n't ripe, let it ripen in milder sunbeams than these vigorous hand-kisses! Lodge her with some proper person and go to Europe; come home from Paris a year hence with her trousseau in your trunks, and I 'll perform the ceremony without another fee than the prospect of having an adorable cousin." With these words Hubert left his companion pensive.

His words reverberated in Roger's mind; I may almost say that they rankled. A couple of days later, in the hope of tenderer counsel, he called upon our friend Mrs. Keith. This lady had completely rounded the cape of matrimony, and was now buoyantly at anchor in the placid cover of well-dowered widowhood. I have heard many a young unmarried lady exclaim with a bold sweep of conception, "Ah me! I wish I were a widow!" Mrs. Keith was precisely the widow that young unmarried ladies wish to be. With her diamonds in her dressing-case and her carriage in her stable, and without a feather's weight of encumbrance, she offered a finished example of satisfied ambition. Her wants had been definite; these once gratified, she had not presumed further. She was a very much worthier woman than in those hungry virginal days when Roger had wooed her. Prosperity had agreed equally well with her beauty and her temper. The wrinkles on her brow had stood still, like Joshua's sun, and a host of good intentions and fair promises seemed to irradiate her person. Roger, as he stood before her, not only felt that his passion was incurably defunct, but allowed himself to doubt that this *veuve consolée* would have made an ideal wife. The lady, mistaking his embarrassment for the forms of smouldering ardor, determined to transmute his devotion by the subtle chemistry of friendship. This she found easy work; in ten minutes the echoes of the past were hushed in the small-talk of the present. Mrs. Keith was on the point of sailing for Europe, and had much to say of her plans and arrangements,—of the miserable rent she was to get for her house. "Why should n't one turn an honest penny?" she said. "And now," she went on, when the field had been cleared, "tell me about the young lady." This was precisely what Roger wished; but just as he was about to begin his story there came an irruption of visitors, fatal to the confidential. Mrs. Keith found means to take him aside. "Seeing is better than hearing," she said, "and I 'm dying to see her. Bring her this evening to dinner, and we shall have her to ourselves."

Mrs. Keith had long been for Nora an object of mystical veneration. Roger had been in the habit of alluding to her, not freely nor frequently, but with a certain implicit homage which more than once had set Nora wondering. She entered the lady's drawing-room that evening with an oppressive desire to please. The interest manifested by Roger in the question of what she should wear assured her that he had staked a nameless something on the impression she might make. She was not only reassured, however, but altogether captivated, by the lavish cordiality of her hostess. Mrs. Keith kissed her on both cheeks, held her at her two arms' length, gave a twist to the fall of her sash, and made her feel very plainly that she was being inspected and appraised; but all with a certain flattering light in the eye and a tender matronly smile, which rather increased than diminished the young girl's composure. Mrs. Keith was herself so elegant, so finished, so fragrant of taste and sense, that before an hour was over Nora felt that she had borrowed the hint of a dozen indispensable graces. After dinner her hostess bade her sit down to the piano. Here, feeling sure of her ground, Nora surpassed herself. Mrs. Keith beckoned to Roger to come and sit beside her on the sofa, where, as she nodded time with her head, she softly conversed under cover of the music. Prosperity, as I have intimated, had acted on her moral nature very much as a medicinal tonic—quinine or iron—acts upon the physical. She was in a comfortable glow of charity. She itched gently, she hardly knew where,—was it in heart or brain?—to render some one a service. She had on hand a small capital of sentimental patronage for which she desired a secure investment. Here was her chance. The project which Roger had imparted to her three years before seemed to her, now she had taken Nora's measure, to contain such pretty elements of success that she deemed it a sovereign pity it should not be rounded into blissful symmetry. She determined to lend an artistic hand. "Does she know it, that matter?" she asked in a whisper.

"I have never told her."

"That 's right. I approve your delicacy. Of course you 're sure of your case. She 's altogether lovely,—she 's one in a thousand. I really envy you; upon my word, Mr. Lawrence, I 'm jealous. She has a style of her own. It 's not quite beauty; it 's not quite cleverness. It belongs neither altogether to her person, nor yet to her mind. It 's a sort of 'tone.' Time will bring it out. She has pretty things, too; one of these days she may take it into her head to be a beauty of beauties. Nature never meant her to hold up her head so well for nothing. Ah, how wrinkled and becapped it makes one feel! To be sixteen

years old, with that head of hair, with health and good con-
nections, with that amount of good-will at the piano, it 's the
very best thing in the world, if they but knew it! But no! they
must leave it all behind them; they must pull their hair to
pieces, they must get rid of their complexions; they must be
twenty, they must have lovers, and go their own gait. Well,
since it must come, we must attend to the profits: they 'll take
care of the lovers. Give Nora to me for a year. She needs a
woman, a wise woman, a woman like me. Men, when they
undertake to meddle with a young girl's education, are veriest
old grandmothers. Let me take her to Europe and bring her
out in Rome. Don't be afraid; I 'll guard your interests. I 'll
bring you back the finest girl in America. I see her from
here!" And describing a great curve in the air with her fan,
Mrs. Keith inclined her head to one side in a manner suggestive of a milliner who descries in the bosom of futurity the
ideal bonnet. Looking at Roger, she saw that her point was
gained; and Nora, having just finished her piece, was accordingly summoned to the sofa and made to sit down at Mrs.
Keith's feet. Roger went and stood before the fire. "My dear
Nora," said Mrs. Keith, as if she had known her from childhood, "how would you like to go with me to Rome?"

Nora started to her feet, and stood looking open-eyed from
one to the other. "Really?" she said. "Does Roger—"

"Roger," said Mrs. Keith, "finds you so hard to manage
that he has made you over to me. I forewarn you, I 'm a
terrible woman. But if you are not afraid, I shall scold you
and pinch you no harder than I would a daughter of my
own."

"I give you up for a year," said Roger. "It 's hard, troublesome as you are."

Nora stood wavering for a moment, hesitating where to
deposit her excess of joy. Then graciously dropping on her
knees before Mrs. Keith, she bent her young head and exhaled it in an ample kiss. "I 'm not afraid of you," she said,
simply. Roger turned round and began to poke the fire.

The next day Nora went forth to buy certain articles necessary in travelling. It was raining so heavily that, at Roger's
direction, she took a carriage. Coming out of a shop, in the
course of her expedition, she encountered Hubert Lawrence,

tramping along in the wet. He helped her back to her carriage, and stood for a moment talking to her through the window. As they were going in the same direction, she invited him to get in; and on his hesitating, she added that she hoped their interview was not to end there, as she was going to Europe with Mrs. Keith. At this news Hubert jumped in and placed himself on the front seat. The knowledge that she was drifting away gave a sudden value to the present occasion. Add to this that in the light of Roger's revelation after the concert, this passive, predestined figure of hers had acquired for the young man a certain rich interest. Nora found herself strangely at ease with her companion. From time to time she strove to check the headlong course of her girlish *épanouissement*; but Hubert evidently, with his broad superior gallantry, was not the person to note to a hair's value the pitiful more or less of a school-girl's primness. Her enjoyment of his presence, her elation in the prospect of departure, made her gayety reckless. They went together to half a dozen shops and talked and laughed so distractedly over her purchases, that she made them sadly at haphazard. At last their progress was arrested by a dead-lock of vehicles in front of them, caused by the breaking down of a horse-car. The carriage drew up near the sidewalk in front of a confectioner's. On Nora's regretting the delay, and saying she was ravenous for lunch, Hubert went into the shop, and returned with a bundle of tarts. The rain came down in sheeted torrents, so that they had to close both the windows. Circled about with this watery screen, they feasted on their tarts with extraordinary relish. In a short time Hubert made another excursion, and returned with a second course. His diving to and fro in the rain excited them to extravagant mirth. Nora had bought some pocket-handkerchiefs, which were in that cohesive state common to these articles in the shop. It seemed a very pretty joke to spread the piece across their knees as a table-cloth.

"To think of picnicking in the midst of Washington Street!" cried Nora, with her lips besprinkled with flakes of pastry.

"For a young lady about to leave her native land, her home, and friends, and all that's dear to her," said Hubert, "you seem to me in very good spirits."

"Don't speak of it," said Nora. "I shall cry to-night; I know I shall."

"You 'll not be able to do this kind of thing abroad," said Hubert. "Do you know we 're monstrously improper? For a young girl it 's by no means pure gain, going to Europe. She comes into a very pretty heritage of prohibitions. You have no idea of the number of improper things a young girl can do. You 're walking on the edge of a precipice. Don't look over or you 'll lose your head and never walk straight again. Here, you 're all blindfold. Promise me not to lose this blessed bondage of American innocence. Promise me that, when you come back, we shall spend another morning together as free and delightful as this one!"

"I promise you!" said Nora; but Hubert's words had potently foreshadowed the forfeiture of sweet possibilities. For the rest of the drive she was in a graver mood. They found Roger beneath the portico of the hotel, watch in hand, staring up and down the street. Preceding events having been explained to him, he offered to drive his cousin home.

"I suppose Nora has told you," he began, as they proceeded.

"Yes! Well, I 'm sorry. She 's a charming girl."

"Ah!" Roger cried; "I knew you thought so!"

"You 're as knowing as ever! She sails, she tells me, on Wednesday next. And you, when do you sail?"

"I don't sail at all. I 'm going home."

"Are you sure of that?"

Roger gazed for a moment out of the window. "I mean for a year," he said, "to allow her perfect liberty."

"And to accept the consequences?"

"Absolutely." And Roger folded his arms.

This conversation took place on a Friday. Nora was to sail from New York on the succeeding Wednesday; for which purpose she was to leave Boston with Mrs. Keith on the Monday. The two ladies were of course to be attended to the ship by Roger. Early Sunday morning Nora received a visit from her friend. The reader will perhaps remember that Mrs. Keith was a recent convert to the Roman Catholic faith; as such, she performed her religious duties with peculiar assiduity. Her present errand was to propose that Nora should go

with her to church and join in offering a mass for their safety
at sea. "I don't want to undermine your faith, you know; but
I think it would be so nice," said Mrs. Keith. Appealing to
Roger, Nora received permission to do as she pleased; she
therefore lent herself with fervor to this pious enterprise. The
two ladies spent an hour at the foot of the altar,—an hour of
romantic delight to the younger one. On Sunday evening
Roger, who, as the day of separation approached, became
painfully anxious and reluctant, betook himself to Mrs. Keith,
with the desire to enforce upon her mind a solemn sense of
her responsibilities and of the value of the treasure he had
confided to her. Nora, left alone, sat wondering whether Hubert might not come to bid her farewell. Wandering listlessly
about the room, her eye fell on the Saturday-evening paper.
She took it up and glanced down the columns. In one of
them she perceived a list of the various church services of the
morrow. Last in the line stood this announcement: "At the
———— ———— Church, the Rev. Hubert Lawrence, at eight
o'clock." It gave her a gentle shock; it destroyed the vision of
his coming in and their having, under the lamp, by the fire,
the serious counterpart of their frolicsome *tête-à-tête* in the
carriage. She longed to show him that she was not a giggling
child, but a wise young lady. But no; in a bright, crowded
church, before a hundred eyes, he was speaking of divine
things. How did he look in the pulpit? If she could only see
him! And why not? She looked at her watch; it stood at ten
minutes to eight. She made no pause to reflect; she only felt
that she must hurry. She rang the bell and ordered a carriage,
and then, hastening to her room, put on her shawl and bonnet,—the blue crape bonnet of the concert. In a few moments she was on her way to the church. When she reached
it, her heart was beating fast; she was on the point of turning
back. But the coachman opened the carriage door with such
a flourish, that she was ashamed not to get out. She was late;
the church was full, the hymn had been sung, and the sermon
was about to begin. The sexton with great solemnity conducted her up the aisle to a pew directly beneath the pulpit.
She bent her eyes on the ground, but she knew that there was
a deep expectant silence, and that Hubert, in a white cravat,
was upright before the desk, looking at her. She sat down

beside a very grim-visaged old lady with bushy eyebrows, who stared at her so hard, that to hide her confusion she buried her head and improvised a prayer; upon which the old lady seemed to stare more intently, as if she thought her very pretentious. When she raised her head, Hubert had begun to speak; he was looking above her and beyond her, and during the sermon his level glance never met her own. Of what did he speak and what was the moral of his discourse? Nora could not have told you; yet not a soul in the audience surely, not all those listening souls together, were more devoutly attentive than she. But it was not on what he said, but on what he was, or seemed to be, that her perception was centred. Hubert Lawrence had an excellent gift of oratory. His voice was full of penetrating sweetness, and in the bright warm air of the compact little church, modulated with singular refinement, it resounded and sank with the cadence of ringing silver. His speech was silver, though I doubt that his silence was ever golden. His utterance seemed to Nora the perfection of eloquence. She thought of her brief exaltation of the morning, in the incense-thickened air of the Catholic church; but what a straighter flight to heaven was this! Hubert's weekday face was a summer cloud, with a lining of celestial brightness. Now, how the divine truth overlapped its relenting edges and seemed to transform it into a dazzling focus of light! He spoke for half an hour, but Nora took no note of time. As the service drew to a close, he gave her from the pulpit a rapid glance, which she interpreted as a request to remain. When the congregation began to disperse, a number of persons, chiefly ladies, waited for him near the pulpit, and, as he came down, met him with greetings and compliments. Nora watched him from her place, listening, smiling and passing his handkerchief over his forehead. At last they relieved him, and he came up to her. She remembered for years afterward the strange half-smile on his face. There was something in it like a pair of eyes peeping over a wall. It seemed to express so fine an acquiescence in what she had done, that, for the moment, she had a startled sense of having committed herself to something. He gave her his hand, without manifesting any surprise. "How did you get here?"

"In a carriage. I saw it in the paper at the last moment."

"Does Roger know you came?"

"No; he had gone to Mrs. Keith's."

"So you started off alone, at a moment's notice?"

She nodded, blushing. He was still holding her hand; he pressed it and dropped it. "O Hubert," cried Nora, suddenly, "*now* I know you!"

Two ladies were lingering near, apparently mother and daughter. "I must be civil to them," he said; "they have come from New York to hear me." He quickly rejoined them and conducted them toward their carriage. The younger one was extremely pretty, and looked a little like a Jewess. Nora observed that she wore a great diamond in each ear; she eyed our heroine rather severely as they passed. In a few minutes Hubert came back, and, before she knew it, she had taken his arm and he was beside her in her own carriage. They drove to the hotel in silence; he went up stairs with her. Roger had not returned. "Mrs. Keith is very agreeable," said Hubert. "But Roger knew that long ago. I suppose you have heard," he added; "but perhaps you 've not heard."

"I 've not heard," said Nora, 'but I 've suspected—"

"What?"

"No; it 's for you to say."

"Why, that Mrs. Keith might have been Mrs. Lawrence."

"Ah, I was right,—I was right," murmured Nora, with a little air of triumph. "She may be still. I wish she would!" Nora was removing her bonnet before the mirror over the chimney-piece; as she spoke, she caught Hubert's eye in the glass. He dropped it and took up his hat. "Won't you wait?" she asked.

He said he thought he had better go, but he lingered without sitting down. Nora walked about the room, she hardly knew why, smoothing the table-covers and rearranging the chairs.

"Did you cry about your departure, the other night, as you promised?" Hubert asked.

"I confess that I was so tired with our adventures, that I went straight to sleep."

"Keep your tears for a better cause. One of the greatest pleasures in life is in store for you. There are a hundred things I should like to say to you about Rome. How I only wish I were going to show it you! Let me beg you to go some day to a little place in the Via Felice, on the Pincian,—a house with a terrace adjoining the fourth floor. There is a plasterer's shop in the basement. You can reach the terrace by the common staircase. I occupied the rooms adjoining it, and it was my peculiar property. I remember I used often to share it with a poor little American sculptress who lived below. She made my bust; the Apollo Belvedere was nothing to it. I wonder what has become of her! Take a look at the view,—the view I woke up to every morning, read by, studied by, lived by. I used to alternate my periods of sight-seeing with fits of passionate study. In another winter I think I might have learned something. Your real lover of Rome oscillates with a kind of delicious pain between the city in itself and the city in literature. They keep forever referring you to each other and bandying you to and fro. If we had eyes for metaphysical things, Nora, you might see a hundred odd bits of old ambitions and day-dreams strewing that little terrace. Ah, as I sat there, how the Campagna used to take up the tale and respond to my printed page! If I know anything of the lesson of history (a man of my profession is supposed to), I learned it in that empurpled air! I should like to know who 's sitting in the same school now. Perhaps you 'll write me a word."

"I 'll piously gather up the crumbs of your feasts and make a meal of them," said Nora. "I 'll let you know how they taste."

"Pray do. And one more request. Don't let Mrs. Keith make a Catholic of you." And he put out his hand.

She shook her head slowly, as she took it. "I 'll have no Pope but you," she said.

The next moment he was gone.

VI

ROGER HAD ASSURED his cousin that he meant to return home, and indeed, after Nora's departure, he spent a fortnight in the country. But finding he had no patience left for solitude, he again came to town and established himself for the winter. A restless need of getting rid of time caused him to resume his earlier social habits. It began to be said of him that now he had disposed of that queer little girl whom he had picked up heaven knew where (whom it was certainly very good-natured of Mrs. Keith to take off his hands), he was going to look about him for a young person whom he might take to his home in earnest. Roger felt as if he were now establishing himself in society in behalf of that larger personality into which his narrow singleness was destined to expand. He was paving the way for Nora. It seemed to him that she might find it an easy way to tread. He compared her attentively with every young girl he met; many were prettier, some possessed in larger degree the air of "brightness"; but none revealed that deep-shrined natural force, lurking in the shadow of modesty like a statue in a recess, which you hardly know whether to denominate humility or pride.

One evening, at a large party, Roger found himself approached by an elderly lady who had known him from his boyhood and for whom he had a vague traditional regard, but with whom of late years he had relaxed his intercourse, from a feeling that, being a very worldly old woman, her influence on Nora might be pernicious. She had never smiled on the episode of which Nora was the heroine, and she hailed Roger's reappearance as a sign that this episode was at an end, and that he meant to begin to live as a man of taste. She was somewhat cynical in her shrewdness, and, so far as she might, she handled matters without gloves.

"I 'm glad to see you have found your wits again," she said, "and that that forlorn little orphan—Dora, Flora, what 's her name?—has n't altogether made a fool of you. You want to marry; come, don't deny it. You can no more remain unmarried than I can remain standing here. Go ask that little man for his chair. With your means and your disposition and all the rest of it, you ought by this time to be setting a good example. But it 's never too late to mend. *J'ai votre affaire.* Have you been introduced to Miss Sandys? Who *is* Miss Sandys? There you are to the life! Miss Sandys is Miss Sandys, the young lady in whose honor we are here convened. She is staying with my sister. You must have heard of her. New York, but good New York; so pretty that she might be as silly as you please, yet as clever and good as if she were as plain as I. She 's everything a man can want. If you 've not seen her it 's providential. Come; don't protest for the sake of protesting. I have thought it all out. Allow me! in this matter I have a real sixth sense. I know at a glance what will do and what won't. You 're made for each other. Come and be presented. You have just time to settle down to it before supper."

Then came into Roger's honest visage a sort of Mephistophelian glee,—the momentary intoxication of duplicity. "Well, well," he said, "let us see all that 's to be seen." And he thought of his Peruvian Teresa. Miss Sandys, however, proved no Teresa, and Roger's friend had not overstated her merits. Her beauty was remarkable; and strangely, in spite of her blooming maturity, something in her expression, her smile, reminded him forcibly of Nora. So Nora might look after ten or twelve years of evening parties. There was a hint, just a hint, of customary triumph in the poise of her head, an air of serene success in her carriage; but it was her especial charm that she seemed to melt downward and condescend from this altitude of loveliness with a benignant and considerate grace; to drop, as it were, from the zenith of her favor, with a little shake of invitation, the silken cable of a long-drawn smile. Roger felt that there was so little to be feared from her that he actually enjoyed the mere surface glow of his admiration; the sense of floating unmelted in the genial zone of her presence, like a polar ice-block in a summer sea. The more he observed her, the more she seemed to foreshadow his prospective Nora; so that at last, borrowing confidence from this phantasmal identity, he addressed her with unaffected friendliness. Miss Sandys, who was a woman of perceptions, seeing an obviously modest man swimming, as it were, in this mystical calm, became interested. She divined in

Roger's manner an unwonted force of admiration. She had feasted her fill on uttered flattery; but here was a good man whose appreciation left compliments far behind. At the end of ten minutes Roger frankly proclaimed that she reminded him singularly of a young girl he knew. "A young girl, forsooth," thought Miss Sandys. "Is he coming to his *fadaises*, like the rest of them?"

"You 're older than she," Roger added, "but I expect her to look like you some time hence."

"I gladly bequeath her my youth, as I come to give it up."

"You can never have been plain," said Roger. "My friend, just now, is no beauty. But I assure you, you encourage me."

"Tell me about this young lady," his companion rejoined. "It 's interesting to hear about people one looks like."

"I should like to tell you," said Roger, "but you would laugh at me."

"You do me injustice. Evidently this is a matter of sentiment. A bit of genuine sentiment is the best thing in the world; and when I catch myself laughing at a mortal who confesses to one, I submit to being told that I have grown old only to grow silly."

Roger smiled approval. "I can only say," he answered, "that this young friend of mine is, to me, the most interesting object in the world."

"In other words, you 're engaged to her."

"Not a bit of it."

"Why, then, she is a deaf-mute whom you have rendered vocal, or a pretty heathen whom you have brought to Sunday school."

Roger laughed exuberantly. "You 've hit it," he said; "a deaf-mute whom I have taught to speak. Add to that, that she was a little blind, and that now she recognizes me with spectacles, and you 'll admit that I have reason to be proud of my work." Then after a pause he pursued, seriously: "If anything were to happen to her—"

"If she were to lose her faculties—"

"I should be in despair; but I know what I should do. I should come to you."

"O, I should be a poor substitute!"

"I should make love to you," Roger went on.

"You would be in despair indeed. But you must bring me some supper."

Half an hour later, as the ladies were cloaking themselves, Mrs. Middleton, who had undertaken Roger's case, asked Miss Sandys for her impressions. These seemed to have been highly propitious. "He is not a shining light perhaps," the young lady said, "but he has the real moral heat that one so seldom meets. He 's in earnest; after what I have been through, that 's very pleasant. And by the way, what is this little deaf and dumb girl in whom he is interested?"

Mrs. Middleton stared. "I never heard she was deaf and dumb. Very likely. He adopted her and brought her up. He has sent her abroad—to learn the languages!"

Miss Sandys mused as they descended the stairs. "He 's a good man," she said. "I like him."

It was in consequence, doubtless, of this last remark that Roger, the next morning, received a note from his friend. "You have made a hit; I shall never forgive you, if you don't follow it up. You have only to be decently civil and then propose. Come and dine with me on Wednesday. I shall have only one guest. You know I always take a nap after dinner."

The same post that brought Mrs. Middleton's note brought him a letter from Nora. It was dated from Rome, and ran as follows:—

"I hardly know, dearest Roger, whether to begin with an apology or a scolding. We have each something to forgive, but you have certainly least. I have before me your two poor little notes, which I have been reading over for the twentieth time; trying, in this city of miracles, to work upon them the miracle of the loaves and fishes. But the miracle won't come; they remain only two very much bethumbed epistles. Dear Roger, I have been extremely vexed and uneasy. I have fancied you were ill, or, worse,—that out of sight is out of mind. It 's not with me, I assure you. I have written you *twelve* little letters. They have been short only because I have been horribly busy. To-day I declined an invitation to drive on the Campagna, on purpose to write to you. The Campagna,—do you hear? I can hardly believe that, five months ago, I was watching the ripe apples drop in the orchard at C——. We are always on our second floor on the Pincian, with plenty of sun, which you know is the great necessity here. Close at hand are the great steps of the Piazza di Spagna, where the beggars and models sit at the receipt of custom. Some of them are so handsome, sunning themselves there in their picturesqueness, that I can't help wishing I knew how to paint or draw. I wish I had been a good girl three years ago and done as you wished, and taken drawing-lessons in earnest. Dear Roger, I never neglected your advice but to my cost. Mrs. Keith is extremely kind and determined I shall have not come abroad to 'mope,' as she says. She does n't care much for sight-seeing, having done it all before; though she keeps pretty well *au courant* of the various church festivals. She very often talks of you and is very fond of you. She is full of good points, but that is her best one. My own sight-seeing habits don't at all incommode her, owing to my having made the acquaintance of a little old German lady who lives at the top of our house. She is a queer wizened oddity of a woman, but she is very clever and friendly, and she has the things of Rome on her fingers' ends. The reason of her being here is very sad and beautiful. Twelve years ago her younger sister, a beautiful girl (she has shown me her minia-ture), was deceived and abandoned by her betrothed. She fled away from her home, and after many weary wanderings found her way to Rome, and gained admission to the convent with the dreadful name,—the Sepolte Vive. Here, ever since, she has been immured. The inmates are literally buried alive; they are dead to the outer world. My poor little Mademoiselle Stamm followed her and took up her dwelling here, to be near her, though with a dead stone wall between them. For twelve years she has never seen her. Her only communication with Lisa—her conventual name she does n't even know—is once a week to deposit a bouquet of flowers, with her name attached, in the little blind wicket of the convent-wall. To do this with her own hands, she lives in Rome. She composes her bouquet with a kind of passion; I have seen her and helped her. Fortunately flowers in Rome are very cheap, for my friend is deplorably poor. I have had a little pleasure, a great pleasure rather, I confess it has been. For the past two months I have furnished the flowers, and I assure you we have had the best. I go each time with Mademoiselle Stamm to the wicket, and we put in our bouquet and see it gobbled up into the speechless maw of the cloister. It 's a dismal amusement, but I confess it interests me. I feel as if I knew this poor Lisa; though, after all, she may be dead, and we may be worshipping a shadow. But in this city of shadows and memories, what is one shadow the more? Don't think, however, that we spend all our time in this grim fashion. We go everywhere, we see everything; I could n't be in better hands. Mrs. Keith has doubts about my friend's moral influence; she accuses her of being a German philosopher in petticoats. She is a German, she wears petticoats; and having known poverty and unhappiness, she is obliged to be something of a philosopher. As for her metaphysics, they may be very wicked, but I should be too stupid to understand them, and it 's less trouble to abide by my own—and Mrs. Keith's! At all events, I have told her all about you, and she says you are the one good man she ever heard of: so it 's not for you to disapprove of her! My mornings I spend with her; after lunch I go out with Mrs. Keith. We drive to the various villas, make visits upon all kinds of people, go to studios and churches and palaces. In the evenings we hold high revel. Mrs. Keith knows every one; she receives a great many people, and we go out in proportion. It 's a most amusing world. I have seen more people in the last six weeks than I ever expected to in a lifetime. I feel so old—you would n't know me! One grows more in a month in this wonderful Rome than in a year at home. Mrs. Keith is very much liked and admired. She has lightened her mourning and looks much better; but, as she says, she will never be herself till she gets back to pink. As for me, I wear pink and blue and every color of the rainbow. It appears that everything suits me; there 's no spoiling me. You see it 's an advantage not to have a complexion. Of course, I 'm *out*,—a thousand miles out. I came out six weeks ago at the great ball of the Princess X. How the Princess X.—poor lady!—came to serve my turn, is more than I can say; but Mrs. Keith is a fairy godmother; she shod me in glass slippers and we went. I fortunately came home with my slippers on my feet. I was very much frightened when we went in. I curtesied to the Princess; and the Princess stared good-naturedly; while I heard Mrs. Keith behind me whispering, 'Lower, lower!' But I have yet to learn how to curtesy to condescending princesses. Now I can drop a little bow to a good old cardinal as smartly as you please. Mrs. Keith has presented me to half a dozen, with whom I pass, I suppose, for an interesting convert. Alas, I 'm only a convert to worldly vanities, which I confess I vastly enjoy. Dear Roger, I am hopelessly frivolous. The shrinking diffidence of childhood I have utterly cast away. I speak up at people as bold as brass. I like having them introduced to me, and having to be interested and interesting at a moment's notice. I like listening and watching; I like sitting up to the small hours; I like talking myself. But I need hardly to tell you this, at the end of my ten pages of chatter. I have talked about my own affairs, because I know they will interest you. Profit by my good example, and tell me all about yours. Do you miss me? I have read over and over your two little notes, to find some little hint that you do; but not a word! I confess I would n't have you too unhappy. I am so glad to hear you are in town, and not at that dreary, wintry C——. Is our old C—— life at an end, I wonder? Nothing can ever be the same after a winter in Rome. Sometimes I 'm half frightened at having had it in my youth. It leaves such a chance for a contrasted future! But I shall come back some day with you. And not even the Princess X. shall make me forget my winter seat by the library fire at C——, my summer seat under the great apple-tree."

This production seemed to Roger a marvel of intellectual promise and epistolary grace; it filled his eyes with grateful tears; he carried it in his pocket-book and read it to a dozen people. His tears, however, were partly those of penitence, as well as of delight. He had had a purpose in staying his own hand, though heaven knows it had ached to write. He wished to make Nora miss him and to let silence combine with absence to plead for him. Had he succeeded? Not too well, it would seem; yet well enough to make him feel that he had been cruel. His letter occupied him so intensely that it was not till within an hour of Mrs. Middleton's dinner that he remembered his engagement. In the drawing-room he found Miss Sandys, looking even more beautiful in a dark high-necked dress than in the glory of gauze and flowers. During dinner he was in excellent spirits; he uttered perhaps no epigrams, but he gave, by his laughter, an epigrammatic turn to the ladyish gossip of his companions. Mrs. Middleton entertained the best hopes. When they had left the table she betook herself to her arm-chair, and erected a little hand-screen before her face, behind which she slept or not, as you please. Roger, suddenly bethinking himself that if Miss Sandys had been made a party to the old lady's views, his alacrity of manner might compromise him, checked his vivacity, and asked his companion stiffly if she played the piano. On her confessing to this accomplishment, he of course proceeded to open the instrument, which stood in the adjoining room. Here Miss Sandys sat down and played with great resolution an exquisite composition of Schubert. As she struck the last note he uttered some superlative of praise. She was silent for a moment, and then, "That 's a thing I rarely play," she said.

"It 's very difficult, I suppose."

"It 's not only difficult, but it 's too sad."

"Sad!" cried Roger, "I should call it very joyous."

"You must be in very good spirits! I take it to have been meant for pure sadness. This is what should suit your mood!" and she attacked with great animation one of Strauss's waltzes. But she had played but a dozen chords when he interrupted her. "Spare me," he said. "I may be glad, but not with that gladness. I confess that I *am* in spirits. I have just had a letter from that young friend of whom I spoke to you."

"Your adopted daughter? Mrs. Middleton told me about her."

"Mrs. Middleton," said Roger, in downright fashion, "knows nothing about her. Mrs. Middleton," and he lowered his voice and laughed, "is not an oracle of wisdom." He glanced into the other room at their hostess and her complaisant screen. He felt with peculiar intensity that, whether she was napping or no, she was a sadly superficial—in fact a positively immoral—old woman. It seemed absurd to believe that this fair wise creature before him had lent herself to a scheme of such a one's making. He looked awhile at her deep clear eyes and the firm sweetness of her lips. It would be a satisfaction to smile with her over Mrs. Middleton's mach-

inations. "Do you know what she wants to do with us?" he
went on. "She wants to make a match between us."

He waited for her smile, but it was heralded by a blush,—
a blush portentous, formidable, tragical. Like a sudden glow
of sunset in a noonday sky, it covered her fair face and burned
on her cloudless brow. "The deuce!" thought Roger. "Can it
be,—can it be?" The smile he had invoked followed fast; but
this was not the order of nature.

"A match between *us!*" said Miss Sandys. "What a brilliant
idea!"

"Not that I can't easily imagine falling in love with you,"
Roger rejoined; "but—but—"

"But you 're in love with some one else." Her eyes, for a
moment, rested on him intently. "With your *protégée!*"

Roger hesitated. It seemed odd to be making this sacred
confidence to a stranger; but with this matter of Mrs. Middleton's little arrangement between them, she was hardly a
stranger. If he had offended her, too, the part of gallantry was
to avow everything. "Yes, I 'm in love!" he said. "And with
the young lady you so much resemble. She does n't know it.
Only one or two persons know it, save yourself. It 's the secret of my life, Miss Sandys. She is abroad. I have wished to
do what I could for her. It 's an odd sort of position, you
know. I have brought her up with the view of making her my
wife, but I 've never breathed a word of it to her. She must
choose for herself. My hope is that she 'll choose me. But
heaven knows what turn she may take, what may happen to
her over there in Rome. I hope for the best; but I think of
little else. Meanwhile I go about with a sober face, and eat
and sleep and talk, like the rest of the world; but all the while
I 'm counting the hours. Really, I don't know what has
started me up in this way. I don't suppose you 'll at all understand my situation; but you are evidently so good that I
feel as if I might count on your sympathies."

Miss Sandys listened with her eyes bent downward, and
with great gravity. When he had spoken, she gave him her
hand with a certain passionate abruptness. "You have them!"
she said. "Much good may they do you! I know nothing of
your friend, but it 's hard to fancy her disappointing you. I
perhaps don't altogether enter into your situation. It 's novel,

but it 's extremely interesting. I hope before rejecting you she
'll think twice. I don't bestow my esteem at random, but you
have it, Mr. Lawrence, absolutely." And with these words she
rose. At the same moment their hostess suspended her siesta,
and the conversation became general. It can hardly be said,
however, to have prospered. Miss Sandys talked with a certain gracious zeal which was not unallied, I imagine, to a desire to efface the trace of that superb blush I have attempted
to chronicle. Roger brooded and wondered; and Mrs. Middleton, fancying that things were not going well, expressed
her displeasure by abusing every one who was mentioned.
She took heart again for the moment when, on the young
lady's carriage being announced, the latter, turning in farewell
to Roger, asked him if he ever came to New York. "When
you are next there," she said, "you must make a point of coming to see me. You 'll have something to tell me."

After she had gone Roger demanded of Mrs. Middleton
whether she had imparted to Miss Sandys her scheme for
their common felicity. "Never mind what I said, or did n't
say," she replied. "She knows enough not to be taken un-
awares. And now tell me—" But Roger would tell her nothing. He made his escape, and as he walked home in the frosty
star-light, his face wore a broad smile of the most shameless
elation. He had gone up in the market. Nora might do worse!
There stood that beautiful woman knocking at his door.

A few evenings after this Roger called upon Hubert. Not
immediately, but on what may be called the second line of
conversation, Hubert asked him what news he had from
Nora. Roger replied by reading her letter aloud. For some
moments after he had finished Hubert was silent. " 'One
grows more in a month in this wonderful Rome,' " he said at
last, quoting, "than in a year at home."

"Grow, grow, grow, and heaven speed it!" said Roger.

"She 's growing, you may depend upon it."

"Of course she is; and yet," said Roger, discriminatingly,
"there is a kind of girlish freshness, a childish simplicity, in
her style."

"Strongly marked," said Hubert, laughing. "I have just got
a letter from her you 'd take to be written by a child of ten."

"*You* have a letter?"

"It came an hour ago. Let me read it."

"Had you written to her?"

"Not a word. But you 'll see." And Hubert in his dressing-gown, standing before the fire, with the same silver-sounding accents Nora had admired, distilled her own gentle prose into Roger's attentive ear.

" 'I have not forgotten your asking me to write to you about your beloved Pincian view. Indeed, I have been daily reminded of it by having that same view continually before my eyes. From my own window I see the same dark Rome, the same blue Campagna. I have rigorously performed my promise, however, of ascending to your little terrace. I have an old German friend here, a perfect archæologist in petticoats, in whose company I think as little of climbing to terraces and towers as of diving into catacombs and crypts. We chose the finest day of the winter, and made the pilgrimage together. The plaster-merchant is still in the basement. We saw him in his doorway, standing to dry, whitened over as if he meant personally to be cast. We reached your terrace in safety. It was flooded with light, with that tempered Roman glow which seems to be compounded of molten gold and liquid amethyst. A young painter who occupies your rooms had set up his easel under an umbrella in the open air. A young *contadina*, imported I suppose from the Piazza di Spagna, was sitting to him in the brilliant light, which deepened splendidly her brown face, her blue-black hair, and her white head-cloth. He was flattering her to his heart's content, and of course to hers. When I want my portrait painted, I shall know where to go. My friend explained to him that we had come to look at his terrace in behalf of an unhappy faraway American gentleman who had once been master of it. Hereupon he was charmingly polite. He showed us the little *salonetta*, the fragment of bas-relief inserted in the wall,—was it there in your day?—and a dozen of his own pictures. One of them was a very pretty version of the view from the terrace. Does it betray an indecent greed for applause to let you know that I bought it, and that, if you are very good and write me a delightful long letter, you shall have it when I get home? It seemed to me that you would be glad to learn that your little habitation had n't fallen away from its high tradi-

tion, and that it still is consecrated to the sunny vigils of genius and ambition. Your vigils, I suppose, were not enlivened
by dark-eyed *contadine*, though they were shared by that poor
little American sculptress. I asked the young painter if she had
left any memory behind her. Only a memory, it appears. She
died a month after his arrival. I never was so bountifully
thanked for anything as for buying our young man's picture.
As he poured out his lovely Italian gratulations, I felt like
some patronizing duchess of the Renaissance. You will have
to do your best, when I transfer it to your hands, to give as
pretty a turn to your gratitude. This is only one specimen of
a hundred delightful rambles I have had with Mlle. Stamm.
We go a great deal to the churches; I never tire of them. Not
in the least that I 'm turning Papist; though in Mrs. Keith's
society, if I chose to do so, I might treat myself to the luxury
of being a nine days' wonder, (admire my self-denial!) but
because they are so picturesque and historic; so redolent of
memories, so rich with traditions, so charged with atmosphere, so haunted with the past. I like to linger in them,—a
barbarous Western maid, doubly a heretic, an alien social and
religious,—and watch the people come and go on this eternal
business of salvation,—take their ease between the fancy
walls of the faith. To go into most of the churches is like
reading some better novel than I find most novels. They are
pitched, as it were, in various keys. On a fine day, if I have
on my best bonnet, if I have been to a party the night before,
I like to go to Sta. Maria Maggiore. Standing there, I dream,
I dream, *cugino mio*; I should be ashamed to tell you the nonsense I *do* dream! On a rainy day, when I tramp out with
Mlle. Stamm in my water-proof; when the evening before,
instead of going to a party, I have sat quietly at home reading
Rio's "Art Chrétien" (recommended by the Abbé Ledoux,
Mrs. Keith's confessor), I like to go to the Ara Cœli. There
you stand among the very *bric-à-brac* of Christian history.
Something takes you at the throat,—but you will have felt it;
I need n't try to define the indefinable. Nevertheless, in spite
of M. Rio and the Abbé Ledoux (he's a very charming old
man too, and a keeper of ladies' consciences, if there ever was
one), there is small danger of my changing my present faith
for one which will make it a sin to go and hear you preach.

Of course, we don't only haunt the churches. I know in a way the Vatican, the Capitol, and those entertaining galleries of the great palaces. You, of course, frequented them and held phantasmal revel there. I 'm stopped short on every side by my deplorable ignorance; still, as far as may be given to a silly girl, I enjoy. I wish you were here, or that I knew some benevolent man of culture. My little German duenna is a marvel of learning and communicativeness, and when she fairly harangues me, I feel as if in my single person I were a young ladies' boarding-school of fifty. But only a man can talk really to the point of this manliest of cities. Mrs. Keith sees a great many gentlemen of one sort and another; but what do they know of Brutus and Augustus, of Emperors and Popes? But I shall keep my impressions, such as they are, and we shall talk them over at our leisure. I shall bring home plenty of photographs; we shall have charming times looking at them. Roger writes that he means next winter to take a furnished house in town. You must come often and see us. We are to spend the summer in England. . . . . Do you often see Roger? I suppose so,—he wrote he was having a 'capital winter.' By the way, I 'm 'out.' I go to balls and wear Paris dresses. I toil not, neither do I spin. There is apparently no end to my banker's account, and Mrs. Keith sets me a prodigious example of buying. Is Roger meanwhile going about in patched trousers?"

At this point Hubert stopped, and on Roger's asking him if there was nothing more, declared that the rest was private. "As you please," said Roger. "By Jove! what a letter,—what a letter!"

Several months later, in September, Roger hired for the ensuing winter a small furnished house. Mrs. Keith and her companion were expected to reach home on the 10th of October. On the 6th, Roger took possession of his house. Most of the rooms had been repainted, and on preparing to establish himself in one for the night, Roger found that the fresh paint emitted such an odor as to make his position untenable. Exploring the premises he discovered in the lower regions, in a kind of sub-basement, a small vacant apartment, destined to a servant, in which he had a bed erected. It was damp, but, as he thought, not too damp, the basement being dry, as basements go. For three nights he occupied this room. On the fourth morning he woke up with a chill and a headache. By noon he had a fever. The physician, being sent for, pronounced him seriously ill, and assured him that he had been guilty of a gross imprudence. He might as well have slept in a vault. It was the first sanitary indiscretion Roger had ever committed; he had a dismal foreboding of its results. Towards evening the fever deepened and he began to lose his head. He was still distinctly conscious that Nora was to arrive on the morrrow, and sadly disgusted that she was to find him in this sorry plight. It was a bitter disappointment that he might not meet her at the steamer. Still, Hubert might. He sent for Hubert accordingly, and had him brought to his bedside. "I shall be all right in a day or two," he said, "but meanwhile some one must receive Nora. I know you 'll be glad to, you villain!"

Hubert declared that he was no villain, but that he would be happy to perform this service. As he looked at his poor fever-stricken cousin, however, he doubted strongly that Roger would be "all right" in a day or two. On the morrow he went down to the ship.

VII

ON ARRIVING at the landing-place of the European steamer Hubert found the passengers filing ashore from the tug-boat in which they had been transferred from the ship. He instructed himself, as he took his place near the gangway, to allow for change in Nora's appearance; but even with this allowance, none of the various advancing ladies seemed to be Nora. Suddenly he found himself confronted with a fair stranger, a smile, and an outstretched hand. The smile and the offered hand of course proclaimed the young lady's identity. Yet in spite of them, Hubert stood amazed. Verily, his allowance had been small. But the next moment, "Now you speak," he said, "I recognize you"; and the next he had greeted Mrs. Keith, who immediately followed her companion; after which he ushered the two ladies, with their servant and their various feminine *impedimenta*, into a carriage. Mrs. Keith was to return directly to her own house, where, hospitable even amid prospective chaos, she invited Hubert to join them at dinner. He had, of course, been obliged to inform Nora off-hand of the cause of Roger's absence, though as yet he made light of his illness. It was agreed, however, that Nora should remain with her companion until she had communicated with her guardian.

Entering Mrs. Keith's drawing-room a couple of hours later, Hubert found the young girl on her knees before the hearth. "I 'm rejoicing," she said, "in the first honest fire I 've seen since I left home." He sat down near by, and in the glow of the firelight he noted her altered aspect. A year, somehow, had made more than a year's difference. Hubert, in his intercourse with women, was accustomed to indulge in a sort of still, cool contemplation which, as a habit, found favor according to the sensibility of the ladies touching whom it was practised. It had been intimated to him more than once, in spite of his cloth, that just a certain turn of the head made this a license. But on this occasion his gaze was all respectful. He was lost in admiration. Yes, Nora was beautiful! Her beauty struck him the more that, not having witnessed the stages quick and fine by which it had come to her, he beheld now as a sudden revelation the consummate result. She had left home a simple maiden of common gifts, with no greater burden of loveliness than the slender, angular, neutral grace of youth and freshness; yet here she stood, a woman turned, perfect, mature, superb! It was as if she had bloomed into golden ripeness in the potent sunshine of a great contentment; as if, fed by the sources of æsthetic delight, her nature had risen calmly to its uttermost level and filled its measured space with a deep and lucid flood. A singular harmony and serenity seemed to pervade her person. Her beauty lay in no inordinate perfection of individual features, but in the deep sweet fellowship which reigned between smile and step and glance and tone. The total effect was an impression of the simplest and yet most stately loveliness. "Pallas Athene," said Hubert to himself, "sprang full-armed, we are told, from the brain of Jove. What a pity! What an untruth! She was born in the West, a plain, fair child; she grew through years and pinafores and all the changes of slow-coming comeliness. Then one fine day she was eighteen and she wore a black silk dress of Paris!" Meanwhile Pallas Athene had been asking about Roger. "Shall I see him to-morrow, at least?" she demanded.

"I doubt it; he 'll not get out for a number of days."

"But I can easily go to him. Dearest Roger! How things never turn out as we arrange them! I had arranged this meeting of ours to perfection! He was to dine with us here, and we were to talk, talk, talk, till midnight, and then I was to go home with him; and there we were to stand leaning on the banisters at his room door, and talk, talk, talk till morning."

"And where was I to be?" asked Hubert.

"I had n't arranged for you. But I expected to see you to-morrow. To-morrow I shall go to Roger."

"If the doctor allows," said Hubert.

Nora rose to her feet. "You don't mean to say, Hubert, that it 's as bad as *that*?" She frowned a little and bent her eyes eagerly on his face. Hubert heard Mrs. Keith's voice in the hall; in a moment their *tête-à-tête* would be at an end. Instead of answering her question—"Nora," he said, in his deepest, lowest voice, "you 're beautiful!" He caught her startled, unsatisfied glance; then he turned and greeted Mrs.

Keith. He had not pleased Nora, evidently; it was premature. So to efface the solemnity of his speech, he repeated it aloud; "I tell Nora she is beautiful!"

"Bah!" said Mrs. Keith; "you need n't tell her; she knows it."

Nora smiled unconfusedly. "O, say it all the same!"

"Was n't it the French ambassador, in Rome," Mrs. Keith demanded, "who attacked you in that fashion? He asked to be introduced. There 's an honor! '*Mademoiselle, vous êtes parfaitement belle.*'"

"Frenchwomen, as a rule, are not *parfaitement belles*," said Nora.

Hubert was a lover of the luxuries and splendors of life. He had no immediate personal need of them; he could make his terms with narrow circumstances; but his imagination was a born aristocrat. He liked to be reminded that certain things were,—ambassadors, ambassadorial compliments, old-world drawing-rooms, with duskily moulded ceilings. Nora's beauty, to his vision, took a deeper color from this homage of an old starred and gartered *diplomat*. It was sound, it had passed the ordeal. He had little need at table to play at discreet inattention. Mrs. Keith, preoccupied with her housekeeping and the "dreadful state" in which her freshly departed tenants had left her rooms, indulged in a tragic monologue and dispensed with responses. Nora, looking frankly at Hubert, consoled their hostess with gentle optimism; and Hubert returned her looks, wondering. He mused upon the mystery of beauty. What sudden gift had made her fair? She was the same tender slip of girlhood who had come trembling to hear him preach a year before; the same, yet how different! And how sufficient she had grown, withal, to her beauty! How with the added burden had come an added strength,— with the greater charm a greater force,—a force subtle, sensitive, just faintly self-suspecting. Then came the thought that all this was Roger's,—Roger's investment, Roger's property! He pitied the poor fellow, lying senseless and helpless, instead of sitting there delightedly, drawing her out and showing her off. After dinner Nora talked little, partly, as he felt, from anxiety about her friend, and partly because of that natural reserve of the altered mind when confronted with old associations. He would have been glad to believe that she was taking pensive note of his own appearance. He had made his mark in her mind a twelvemonth before. Innumerable scenes and figures had since passed over it; but his figure, Nora now discovered, had not been trampled out. Fixed there indelibly, it had grown with the growth of her imagination. She knew that she had vastly changed, and she had wondered ardently whether Hubert would have lost favor with difference. Would he suffer by contrast with people she had seen? Would he seem graceless, colorless, common? Little by little, as his presence defined itself, it became plain to her that the Hubert of the past had a lease of the future. As he rose to take his leave, she begged him to let her write a line to Roger, which he might carry.

"He 'll not be able to read it," said Hubert.

Nora mused. "I 'll write it, nevertheless. You 'll place it by his bedside, and the moment he is better he will find it at hand."

When she had left the room, Mrs. Keith demanded tribute. "Have n't I done well? Have n't I made a charming girl of her?"

"She does you vast credit," said Hubert, with a mental reservation.

"O, but wait awhile! You 've not seen her yet. She 's tired and anxious about your cousin. Wait till she comes out. My dear Mr. Lawrence, she 's perfect. She lacks nothing, she has nothing too much. You must do me justice. I saw it all in the rough, and I knew just what it wanted. I wish she were my daughter: you should see great doings! And she 's as good as gold! It 's her nature. After all, unless your nature 's right, what are you?" But before Hubert could reply to this little spasm of philosophy, Nora reappeared with her note.

The next morning Mrs. Keith went to call officially upon her mother-in-law; and Nora, left alone and thinking much of Roger's condition, conceived an intense desire to see him. He had never been so dear to her as now, and no one's right to be with him was equal to hers. She dressed hastily and repaired to the little dwelling they were to have so cosily occupied. She was admitted by her old friend Lucinda, who, between trouble and wonder, found a thousand things to say.

Nora's beauty had never received warmer tribute than the affectionate marvellings of this old woman who had known her early plainness so well. She led her into the drawing-room, opened the windows and turned her about in the light, patted her braided tresses, and rejoiced with motherly unction in her tallness and straightness and elegance. Of Roger she spoke with tearful eyes. "It would be for him to see you, my dear," she said; "he 'd not be disappointed. You 're better than his brightest dreams. O, I know all about it! He used to talk to me evenings, after you were in bed. 'Lucinda, do you think she 's pretty? Lucinda, do you think she 's plain? Lucinda, do you dress her warm? Lucinda, have you changed her shoes? And mind, Lucinda, take good care of her hair; it 's the only thing we're sure of!' Yes, my dear, you 've me to thank for these big braids. Would he feel sure of you now, poor man? You must keep yourself in cotton-wool till he recovers. You 're like a picture; you ought to be enclosed in a gilt frame and stand against the wall." Lucinda begged, however, that Nora would not insist upon seeing him; and her great reluctance betraying his evil case, Nora consented to wait. Her own slight experience could avail nothing. "He 's flighty," said Lucinda, "and I 'm afraid he would n't recognize you. If he should n't, it would do you no good; and if he should, it would do him none; it would increase his fever. He 's bad, my dear, he 's bad; but leave him to me! I nursed him as a baby; I nursed him as a boy; I 'll nurse him as a man grown. I 've seen him worse than this, with the scarlet fever at college, when his poor mother was dying at home. Baby, boy, and man, he 's always had the patience of a saint. I 'll keep him for you, Miss Nora, now I 've seen you! I should n't dare to meet him in heaven, if I were to let him miss you!"

When Lucinda had returned to her bedside duties, Nora wandered about the house with a soundless tread, taking melancholy note of the preparations Roger had made for her return. His choice, his taste, his ingenuity, were everywhere visible. The best beloved of her possessions from the old house in the country had been transferred hither and placed in such kindly half-lights as would temper justice with mercy; others had been replaced at a great cost. Nora went into the drawing-room, where the blinds were closed and the chairs and sofas shrouded in brown linen, and sat sadly revolving possibilities. How, with Roger's death, loneliness again would close about her; how he was her world, her strength, her fate! He had made her life; she needed him still to watch his work. She seemed to apprehend, as by a sudden supernatural light, the strong essence of his affection, his wisdom, his alertness, his masterly zeal. In the perfect stillness of the house she could almost hear his tread on the stairs, hear his voice utter her name with that tender adjustment of tone which conveyed a benediction in a commonplace. Her heart rose to her throat; she felt a passionate desire to scream. She buried her head in a cushion to stifle the sound; her silent tears fell upon the silk. Suddenly she heard a step in the hall; she had only time to brush them away before Hubert Lawrence came in. He greeted her with surprise. "I came to bring your note," he said; "I did n't expect to find you."

"Where can I better be?" she asked, with intensity. "I can do nothing here, but I should look ill elsewhere. Give me back my note, please. It does n't say half I feel." He returned it and stood watching her while she tore it in bits and threw it into the empty fireplace. "I have been wandering over the house," she added. "Everything tells me of poor Roger." She felt an indefinable need of protesting of her affection for him. "I never knew till now," she said, "how much I loved him. I 'm sure you don't know him, Hubert; not as I do. I don't believe any one does. People always speak of him with a little air of amusement. Even Mrs. Keith is witty at his expense. But I know him; I grew to know him in thinking of him while I was away. There 's more of him than the world knows or than the world would ever know, if it was left to his modesty and the world's stupidity!" Hubert made her a little bow, for her eloquence. "But I mean to put an end to his modesty. I mean to say, 'Come, Roger, hold up your head and speak out your mind and do yourself common justice.' I 've seen people without a quarter of his goodness who had twenty times his assurance and his success. I shall turn the tables! People shall have no favor from me, unless they recognize Roger. If they want me, they must take him too. They tell me I 'm a beauty, and I can do what I please. We shall see.

The first thing I shall do will be to tip off their hats to the best man in the world."

"I admire your spirit," said Hubert. "Dr. Johnson liked a good hater; I like a good lover. On the whole, it 's more rarely found. But are n't you the least bit Quixotic, with your terrible good-faith? No one denies that Roger is the best of the best of the best! But do what you please, Nora, you can't make pure virtue entertaining. I, as a minister, you know, have often regretted this dreadful Siamese twinship that exists between goodness and dulness. I have my own little Quixotisms. I 've tried to cut them in two; I 've dressed them in the most opposite colors; I 've called them by different names; I 've boldly denied the connection. But it 's no use; there 's a fatal family likeness! Of course you 're fond of Roger. So am I, so is every one in his heart of hearts. But what are we to do about it? The kindest thing is to leave him alone. His virtues are of the fireside. You describe him perfectly when you say that everything in the house here sings his praise—already, before he 's been here ten days! The chairs are all straight, the pictures are admirably hung, the locks are oiled, the winter fuel is stocked, the bills are paid! Look at the tidies pinned on the chairs. I 'll warrant you he pinned them with his own hands. Such is Roger! Such virtues, in a household, are priceless. He ought never to marry; his wife would die for want of occupation. What society cares for in a man is not his household virtues, but his worldly ones. It wants to see things by the large end of the telescope, not by the small. 'Be as good as you please,' says society, 'but unless you 're interesting, I 'll none of you!'"

"Interesting!" cried Nora, with a rosy flush. "I 've seen some very interesting people who have bored me to death. But if people don't care for Roger, it 's their own loss!" Pausing a moment she fixed Hubert with the searching candor of her gaze. "You 're unjust," she said.

This charge was pleasant to the young man's soul; he would not, for the world, have summarily rebutted it. "Explain, dear cousin," he said, smiling kindly. "Wherein am I unjust?"

It was the first time he had called her cousin; the word made a sweet confusion in her thoughts. But looking at him still while she collected them, "You don't care to know!" she cried. "Not when you smile so! You 're laughing at me, at Roger, at every one!" Clever men had ere this been called dreadfully satirical before by pretty women; but never, surely, with just that imperious *naïveté*. She spoke with a kind of joy in her frankness; the sense of intimacy with the young man had effaced the sense of difference.

"The scoffing fiend! That 's a pretty character to give a clergyman!" said Hubert.

"Are you, at heart, a clergyman? I 've been wondering."

"You 've heard me preach."

"Yes, a year ago, when I was a silly little girl. I want to hear you again."

"Nay, I 've gained my crown, I propose to keep it. I 'd rather not be found out. Besides, I 'm not preaching now; I 'm resting. Some people think me a clergyman, Nora," he said, lowering his voice with a hint of mock humility. "But do you know you 're formidable, with your fierce friendships and your divine suspicions? If you doubt of me, well and good. Let me walk like a Homeric god in a cloud; without my cloud, I should be sadly ungodlike. Eh! for that matter, I doubt of myself, on all but one point,—my sincere regard for Roger. I love him, I admire him, I envy him. I 'd give the world to be able to exchange my restless imagination for his silent, sturdy usefulness. I feel as if I were toiling in the sun, and he were sitting under green trees resting from an effort which he has never needed to make. Well, virtue I suppose is welcome to the shade. It 's cool, but it 's dreadfully obscure! People are free to find out the best and the worst of *me*! Here I stand, with all my imperfections on my head, tricked out with a white cravat, baptized with a *reverend*, (heaven save the mark!) equipped with platform and pulpit and text and audience,—erected into a mouthpiece of the spiritual aspirations of mankind. Well, I confess our sins; that 's good humble-minded work. And I must say, in justice, that when once I don my white cravat (I insist on the cravat, I can do nothing without it) and mount into the pulpit, a certain gift comes to me. They call it eloquence; I suppose it is. I don't know what it 's worth, but they seem to like it."

Nora sat speechless, with expanded eyes, hardly knowing

whether his humility or his audacity became him best; flattered, above all, by what she deemed the recklessness of his confidence. She had removed her hat, which she held in her hand, gently curling its great black feather. Few things in a woman could be fairer than her free uncovered brow, illumined with her gentle wonder. The moment, for Hubert, was critical. He knew that a young girl's heart stood trembling on the verge of his influence; he felt, without fatuity, that a glance might beckon her forward, a word might fix her there. Should he speak his word? This mystic precinct was haunted with the rustling ghosts of women who had ventured within and found no rest. But as the innermost meaning of Nora's beauty grew vivid before him, it seemed to him that she, at least, might purge it of its sinister memories and dedicate it to peace. He knew in his conscience that to such as Nora he was no dispenser of peace; but as he looked at her she seemed to him as an angel knocking at his gates. He could n't turn her away. Let her come, at her risk! For angels there is a special providence. "Don't think me worse than I am," he said, "but don't think me better! I shall love Roger well until I begin to fancy that you love him too well. Then—it 's absurd perhaps, but I feel it will be so—I shall be jealous."

The words were lightly uttered, but his eyes and voice gave them value. Nora colored and rose; she went to the mirror and put on her hat. Then turning round with a laugh which, to one in the secret, might have seemed to sound the coming-of-age of her maiden's fancy, "If you mean to be jealous," she said, "now 's your time! I love Roger now with all my heart. I can't do more!" She remained but a moment longer.

Her friend's illness baffled the doctors; a sceptic would have said it obeyed them. For a fortnight it went from bad to worse. Nora remained constantly at home, and played but a passive part to the little social drama enacted in Mrs. Keith's drawing-room. This lady had already cleared her stage and rung up her curtain. To the temporary indisposition of her *jeune première* she resigned herself with that serene good grace which she had always at command and which was so subtle an intermixture of kindness and shrewdness that it would have taken a wiser head than Nora's to apportion them. She valued the young girl for her social uses; but she spared her at this trying hour just as an *impressario*, with an eye to the whole season, spares a *prima donna* who is threatened with bronchitis. Between these two there was little natural sympathy, but in place of it a wondrous adjustment of caresses and civilities; little confidence, but innumerable confidences. They had quietly judged each other and each sat serenely encamped in her estimate as in a high strategical position. Nevertheless I would have trusted neither one's account of the other. Nora, for perfect fairness, had too much to learn and Mrs. Keith too much to unlearn. With her companion, however, she had unlearned much of that circumspect jealousy with which, in the interest of her remnant of youth and beauty, she taxed her commerce with most of the fashionable sisterhood. She strove to repair her one notable grievance against fate by treating Nora as a daughter. She mused with real maternal ardor upon the young girl's matrimonial possibilities, and among them upon that design of which Roger had dropped her a hint of old. He held to his purpose of course; if he had fancied Nora then, he could but fancy her now.

But were his purpose and his fancy to be viewed with undiminished complacency? What might have been great prospects for Nora as a plain, homeless child, were small prospects for a young lady gifted with beauty which, with time, would bring the world to her feet. Roger would be the best of husbands; but in Mrs. Keith's philosophy, a very good husband might stand for a very indifferent marriage. She herself had married a fool, but she had married well. Her easy, opulent widowhood was there to show it. To call things by their names, would Nora, in marrying Roger, marry money? Mrs. Keith was at loss to appraise the worldly goods of her rejected suitor. At the time of his suit she had the matter at her fingers' ends; but she suspected that since then he had been lining his pockets. He puzzled her; he had a way of seeming neither rich nor poor. When he spent largely, he had the air of one straining a point; yet when he abstained, it seemed rather from taste than necessity. She had been surprised more than once, while abroad, by his copious remittances to Nora. The point was worth looking up. The reader will agree with me that her conclusion warranted her friend either a fool or a hero; for she graciously assumed that if, financially, Roger should be found wanting, she could easily prevail upon him to give the *pas* to a possible trio of Messrs. So-and-So, millionnaires to a man. Never was better evidence that Roger passed for a good fellow. In any event, however, Mrs. Keith had no favor to spare for Hubert and his marked and increasing "attentions." She had determined to beware of a false alarm; but meanwhile she was vigilant. Hubert presented himself daily with a report of his cousin's condition,—a report most minute and exhaustive, seemingly, as a couple of hours were needed to make it. Nora, moreover, went frequently to her friend's house, wandered about aimlessly, and talked with Lucinda; and here Hubert was sure to be found, or to find her, engaged in a similar errand. Roger's malady had defined itself as virulent typhus fever; strength and reason were at the lowest ebb. Of course on these occasions Hubert walked home with the young girl; and as the autumn weather made walking delightful, they chose the longest way. They might have been seen at this period perambulating in deep discourse certain outlying regions, the connection of which with the main line of travel between Mrs. Keith's abode and Roger's was not immediately obvious. Apart from her prudent fears, Mrs. Keith had a scantier kindness for Hubert than for most comely men. She fancied of him that he meant nothing,—nothing at least but the pleasure of the hour; and the want of a certain masterly intention was of all shortcomings the one she most deprecated in a clever man. "What is he, when you come to the point?" she impatiently demanded of a friend to whom she had imparted her fears. "He 's neither fish nor flesh, neither a priest nor a layman. I like a clergyman to bring with him a little odor of sanctity,—something that rests you, after common talk. Nothing is so pleasant, near the fire, at the sober end of one's drawing-room. If he does n't fill a certain place, he 's in the way. The Reverend Hubert is sprawling everywhere at once. His manners are neither of this world nor, I hope, of the next. Last night he let me bring him a cup of tea and sat lounging in his chair while I put it in his hand. O, he knows what he 's about. He 's pretentious, with all his *nonchalance*. He finds Bible texts rather meagre fare for week-days; so he consoles himself with his pretty parishioners. To be one, you need n't go to his church. Is Nora, after all I 've done for her, going to rush into one of these random American engagements? I 'd rather she married Mr. Jenks the carpenter, outright."

But in spite of Mrs. Keith's sinister previsions, these young persons played their game in their own way, with larger moves, even, and heavier stakes, than their shrewd hostess suspected. As Nora, for the present, declined all invitations, Mrs. Keith in the evening frequently went out alone and left her perforce in the drawing-room to entertain Hubert at her ease. Roger's illness furnished a grave undercurrent to their talk and gave it a tone of hazardous melancholy. Nora's young life had known no such hours as these. She hardly knew, perhaps, just what made them what they were. She hardly wished to know; she shrank from staying the even lapse of destiny with a question. The scenes of the past year had gathered into the background like a huge distant landscape, glowing with color and swarming with life; she seemed to stand with her friend in the double shadow of a passing cloud and a rustling tree, looking off and away into tl﹒ mighty picture, caressing its fine outlines and lingering where the haze of regret lay purple in its hollows,—while he whispered the romance of hill and dale and town and stream. Never, she fondly fancied, had a young couple conversed with less of narrow exclusion; they took all history, all culture, into their confidence; the radiant light of an immense horizon seemed to shine between them. Nora had felt deliciously satisfied; she seemed to live equally in every need of her being, in soul and sense, in heart and mind. As for Hubert, he knew nothing, for the time, save that the angel was within his gates and must be treated to angelic fare. He had for the time the conscience, or the no-conscience, of a man who is feasting on the slopes of Elysium. He thought no evil, he designed no harm; the hard face of destiny was twisted into a smile. If only, for Hubert's sake, this had been an irresponsible world, without penalties to pay, without turnings to the longest lanes! If the peaches and plums in the garden of pleasure had no cheeks but ripe ones, and if, when we have eaten the fruit, we had n't to dispose of the stones! Nora's charm of charms was a cool maidenly reserve which Hubert both longed and feared to make an end of. While it soothed his conscience it irritated his ambition. He wished to know in what depth of water he stood; but no telltale ripple in this tropic calm availed to register the tide. Was he drifting in mid-ocean, or was he cruising idly among the sandy shallows? I regret to say, that as the days elapsed Hubert found his rest troubled by this folded rose-leaf of doubt; for he was not used to being baffled by feminine riddles. He determined to pluck out the heart of the mystery.

One evening, at Mrs. Keith's urgent request, Nora had pre- pared to go to the opera, as the season was to last but a week. Mrs. Keith was to dine with some friends and go thither in their company; one of the ladies was to call for Nora after dinner, and they were to join the party at the theatre. In the afternoon came a young German lady, a pianist of merit who had her way to make, a niece of Nora's regular professor, with whom Nora had an engagement to practise duets twice a week. It so happened that, owing to a violent rain, Miss Lilienthal had been unable to depart after their playing; whereupon Nora had kept her to dinner, and the two, over their sweetbread, had sworn an eternal friendship. After din- ner Nora went up to dress for the opera, and, on descending, found Hubert sitting by the fire deep in German discourse with the musical stranger. "I was afraid you 'd be going," said Hubert; "I saw *Don Giovanni* on the placards. Well, lots of pleasure! Let me stay here awhile and polish up my German with mademoiselle. It 's great fun. And when the rain 's over, Fraülein, perhaps you 'll not mind my walking home with you."

But the Fraülein was gazing in mute envy at Nora, stand- ing before her in festal array. "She can take the carriage," said Nora, "when we have used it." And then reading the burden of that wistful regard—"Have you never heard *Don Gio- vanni?*"

"Often!" said the other, with a poignant smile.

Nora reflected a moment, then drew off her gloves. "You shall go, you shall take my place. I 'll stay at home. Your dress will do; you shall wear my shawl. Let me put this flower in your hair, and here are my gloves and my fan. So! You 're charming. My gloves are large,—never mind. The others will

be delighted to have you; come to-morrow and tell me all
about it." Nora's friend, in her carriage, was already at the
door. The gentle Fraülein, half shrinking, half eager, suffered
herself to be hurried down to the carriage. On the doorstep
she turned and kissed her hostess with a fervent *"Du aller-
liebste!"* Hubert wondered whether Nora's purpose had been
to please her friend or to please herself. Was it that she preferred his society to Mozart's music? He knew that she had a
passion for Mozart. "You 've lost the opera," he said, when
she reappeared; "but let us have an opera of our own. Play
something; play Mozart." So she played Mozart for more
than an hour; and I doubt whether, among the singers who
filled the theatre with their melody, the great master found
that evening a truer interpreter than the young girl playing in
the lamplit parlor to the man she loved. She played herself
tired. "You ought to be extremely grateful," she said, as she
struck the last chord; "I have never played so well."

Later they came to speak of a novel which lay on the table,
and which Nora had been reading. "It 's very silly," she said,
"but I go on with it in spite of myself. I 'm afraid I 'm too
easily pleased; no novel is so silly I can't read it. I recommend
you this, by the way. The hero is a young clergyman endowed
with every grace, who falls in love with a fair Papist. She is
wedded to her faith, and though she loves the young man
after a fashion, she loves her religion better. To win his suit
he comes near going over to Rome; but he pulls up short and
determines the mountain shall come to Mahomet. He sets
bravely to work, converts the young lady, baptizes her with
his own hands one week, and marries her the next."

"Heaven preserve us! what a hotch-potch!" cried Hubert.
"Is that what they are doing nowadays? I very seldom read a
novel, but when I glance into one, I 'm sure to find some
such stuff as that! Nothing irritates me so as the flatness of
people's imagination. Common life—I don't say it 's a vision
of bliss, but it 's better than that! Their stories are like the
underside of a carpet,—nothing but the stringy grain of the
tissue—a muddle of figures without shape and flowers without color. When I read a novel my imagination starts off at a
gallop and leaves the narrator hidden in a cloud of dust; I
have to come jogging twenty miles back to the *dénouement*.

Your clergyman here with his Romish sweetheart must be a very pretty fellow. Why did n't he marry her first and convert her afterwards? Is n't a clergyman after all, before all, a man? I mean to write a novel about a priest who falls in love with a pretty Mahometan and swears by Allah to win her."

"Ah Hubert!" cried Nora, "would you like a clergyman to love a pretty Mahometan better than the truth?"

"The truth? A pretty Mahometan may be the truth. If you can get it in the concrete, after shivering all your days in the cold abstract, it 's worth a bit of a compromise. Nora, Nora!" he went on, stretching himself back on the sofa and flinging one arm over his head, "I stand up for passion! If a thing can take the shape of passion, that 's a fact in its favor. The greater passion is the better cause. If my love wrestles with my faith, as the angel with Jacob, and if my love stands uppermost, I 'll admit it 's a fair game. Faith is faith, under a hundred forms! Upon my word, I should like to prove it, in my own person. What a fraction of my personality is this clerical title! How little it expresses; how little it covers! On Sundays, in the pulpit, I stand up and talk to five hundred people. Does each of them, think you, appropriate his five hundredth share of my discourse? I can imagine talking to one person and saying five hundred times as much, even though she were a pretty Mahometan or a prepossessing idolatress! I can imagine being five thousand miles away from this blessed Boston,—in Turkish trousers, if you please, with a turban on my head and a chibouque in my mouth, with a great blue ball of Eastern sky staring in through the round window, high up; all in divine *insouciance* of the fact that Boston was abusing, or, worse still, forgetting me! That Eastern sky is part of the *mise en scène* of the New Testament,—it has seen greater miracles! But, my dear Nora," he added, suddenly, "don't let me muddle your convictions." And he left his sofa and came and leaned against the mantel-shelf. "This is between ourselves; I talk to you as I would to no one else. Understand me and forgive me! There are times when I must speak out and make my bow to the possible, the ideal! I must protest against the vulgar assumption of people who don't see beyond their noses; that people who do, you and I, for instance, are living up to the top of our capacity, that we are contented, satisfied,

balanced. I promise you I 'm not satisfied, not I! I 've room
for more. I only half live; I 'm like a purse filled at one end
with small coin and empty at the other. Perhaps the other will
never know the golden rattle! The Lord's will be done! I can
say that with the best of them. But I shall never pretend that
I 've known happiness, that I 've known life. On the contrary,
I shall maintain I 'm a failure! I had the wit to see, but I
lacked the courage to do—and yet I 've been called reckless,
irreverent, audacious. My dear Nora, I 'm the veriest coward
on earth; pity me if you don't despise me. There are men
born to imagine things, others born to do them. Evidently,
I 'm one of the first. But I *do* imagine them, I assure you!"

Nora listened to this flow of sweet unreason without staying her hand in the work, which, as she perceived the drift of
his talk, she had rapidly caught up, but with a beating heart
and a sense of rising tears. It was a ravishing medley of mystery and pathos and frankness. It was the agony of a restless
soul, leaping in passionate rupture from the sickening circle
of routine. Of old, she had thought of Hubert's mind as immutably placid and fixed; it gave her the notion of lucid depth
and soundless volume. But of late, with greater nearness, she
had seen the ripples on its surface and heard it beating its
banks. This was not the first time; but the waves had never
yet broken so high; she had never felt their salt spray on her
cheeks. He had rent for her sake the seamless veil of the temple and shown her its gorgeous gloom. Before her, she dis-
cerned the image of the *genius loci*, the tutelar deity, with a
dying lamp smoking at its feet and a fissure in its golden side.
The rich atmosphere confused and enchanted her. The pavement under her feet seemed to vibrate with the mournful
music of a retreating choir. She went on with her work,
mechanically taking her stitches. She felt Hubert's intense
blue eyes; the little blue flower in her tapestry grew under her
quick needle. A great door had been opened between their
hearts; she passed through it. "What is it you imagine," she
asked, with intense curiosity; "what is it you dream of
doing?"

"I dream," he said, "of breaking a law for your sake!"

The answer frightened her; it savored of the disorder of
passion. What had she to do with broken laws? She trembled

and rolled up her work. "I dream," she said, trying to smile, "of the romance of keeping laws. I expect to get a deal of pleasure out of it yet." And she left her chair. For an instant Hubert was confused. Was this the last struggle which precedes submission or the mere prudence of indifference? Nora's eyes were on the clock. It rang out eleven. "To begin with," she said, "let me keep the law of 'early to bed.' Good night!"

Hubert wondered; he hardly knew whether he was rebuked or challenged. "You 'll at least shake hands," he said, reproachfully.

A deeper consciousness had somehow been opened in her common consciousness, and she had meant in self-defence to omit this ceremony. "Good night," she repeated, letting him take her hand. Hubert gazed at her a moment and raised it to his lips. She blushed and rapidly withdrew it. "There!" cried Hubert. "I 've broken a law!"

"Much good may it do you!" she answered, and went her way. He stood for a moment, waiting, and fancying, rather fatuously, that she might come back. Then, as he took up his hat, he wondered whether she too was not a bit of a coquette.

Nora wondered on her own side whether this scene had not been the least bit a *pièce de circonstance*. For a day love and doubt fared in company. Lucinda's mournful discourse on the morrow was not of a nature to restore her calmness. "Last night," said Roger's nurse, "he was very bad. He woke out of his lethargy, but oh, on the other side of sense! He talked all night about you. If he murmurs a word, it 's always your name. He asked a dozen times if you had arrived, and forgot as often as I told him—he, dear man, who used to remember to a collar what he 'd put into the wash! He kept wondering whether anything had happened to you. Late in the evening, when the carriages began to pass, he cried out over each that it was you, and what would you think of him for not coming to meet you? 'Don't tell her how bad I am,' he says; 'I must have been in bed two or three days, have n't I, Lucinda? Say I 'll be out to-morrow; that I 've only a little cold; that she 's not to mind it, Hubert will do everything for her.' And then when, at midnight, the wind began to blow, he declared it was a storm, that your ship was on the coast.

God keep you safe! Then he asked if you were changed and grown; were you pretty, were you tall, would he know you? And he took the hand-glass and looked at himself and wondered if you would know him. He cried out that he was ugly, he was horrible, you 'd hate him. He bade me bring him his razors and let him shave; and when I would n't, he began to rage and call me names, and then he broke down and cried like a child." Hearing these things, Nora prayed almost angrily for Roger's recovery,—that he might live to see her more cunningly and lovingly his debtor. She wished to do something, she hardly knew what, not only to prove, but forever to commemorate, her devotion. Her fancy moulded with dim prevision the monumental image of some pious sacrifice. You would have marvelled to see, meanwhile, the easy breathing of her conscience. To serve Roger, to please Roger, she would give up her dream of Hubert. But best of all, if the clement skies should suffer that Hubert and she, one in all things else, should be one in his affection, one in his service!

For a couple of days she saw nothing of Hubert. On the third there came excellent news of Roger, who had taken a marked turn for the better, and was out of the woods. She had declined, for the evening, a certain most seductive invitation; but on the receipt of these tidings she revoked her refusal. Coming down to the drawing-room with Mrs. Keith, dressed and shawled, she found Hubert in waiting, with a face which uttered bad news. Roger's improvement had been momentary, a relapse had followed, and he was worse than ever. She tossed off her shawl with an energy not unnoted by her duenna. "Of course I can't go," she said. "It 's neither possible nor proper." Mrs. Keith would have given the camellia out of her *chignon* that this thing should not have happened in just this way; but she submitted with a good grace—for a duenna. Hubert went down with her to her carriage. At the foot of the stairs she stopped, and while gathering up her skirts, "Mr. Lawrence," she demanded, "are you going to remain here?"

"A little while," said Hubert, with his imperturbable smile.

"A very little while, I hope." She had been wondering whether admonition would serve as a check or a stimulus. "I need hardly to tell you that the young lady up stairs is not a person to be trifled with."

"I hardly know what you mean," said Hubert. "Am I a person to trifle?"

"Is it serious, then?"

Hubert hesitated a moment. She perceived a sudden watchful quiver in his eye, like a sword turned edge outward. She unsheathed one of her own steely beams, and for the tenth of a second there was a dainty crossing of blades. "I admire Miss Lambert," cried Hubert, "with all my heart."

"True admiration," said Mrs. Keith, "is one half respect and the other half self-denial."

Hubert laughed, ever so politely. "I 'll put that in a sermon," he said.

"O, I have a sermon to preach you," she answered. "Take your hat and go."

He made her a little bow, "I 'll go up and get my hat." Mrs. Keith, catching his eye as he closed the carriage door, wished to heaven that she had held her tongue. "I 've done him injustice." she murmured as she went. "I 've fancied him light, but I see he 's vicious." Hubert, however, kept his promise in so far as that he did take up his hat. Having held it a moment, he put it down. He had reckoned without his hostess! Nora was seated by the fire, with her bare arms folded, with a downcast brow. Dressed in pale corn-color, her white throat confined by a band of blue velvet, sewn with a dozen pearls, she was not a subject for summary farewells. Meeting her eyes, he saw they were filled with tears. "You must n't take this thing too hard," he said.

For a moment she said nothing; then she bent her face into her hands and her tears flowed. "O poor, poor Roger!" she cried.

Hubert watched her weeping in her ball-dress those primitive tears. "I 've not given him up," he said at last. "But suppose I had—" She raised her head and looked at him. "O," he cried, "I should have a hundred things to say. Both as a minister and as a man, I should preach resignation. In this crisis, let me speak my mind. Roger is part of your childhood; your childhood 's at an end. Possibly, with it, he too is to go! At all events you 're not to feel that in losing him you lose everything. I protest! As you sit here, he belongs to your past. Ask yourself what part he may play in your future. Believe me, you 'll have to settle it, you 'll have to choose. Here, in any case, *your* life begins. Your tears are for the dead past; this is the future, with its living needs. Roger's fate is only one of them."

She rose, with her tears replaced by a passionate gravity. "Ah, you don't know what you say!" she cried. "Talk of my future if you like, but not of my past! No one can speak of it, no one knows it! Such as you see me here, bedecked and bedizened, I 'm a penniless, homeless, friendless creature! But for Roger, I might be in the streets! Do you think I 've forgotten it, that I ever can? There are things that color one's life, memories that last forever. I 've my share! What am I to settle, between whom am I to choose? My love for Roger 's no choice, it 's part and parcel of my being!"

She seemed to shine, as she spoke, with a virginal faithfulness which commanded his own sincerity. Hubert was inspired. He forgot everything but that she was lovely. "I wish to heaven," he cried, "that you had never ceased to be penniless and friendless! I wish Roger had left you alone and not smothered you beneath this monstrous burden of gratitude! Give him back his gifts! Take all *I* have! In the streets? In the streets I should have found you, as lovely in your poverty as you 're now in your finery, and a thousand times more free!" He seized her hand and met her eyes with the frankness of passion. Pain and pleasure, at once, possessed Nora's heart. It was as if joy, bursting in, had trampled certain tender flowers which bloomed on the threshold. But Hubert had cried, "I love you! I love you!" and joy had taken up the words. She was unable to speak audibly; but in an instant she was spared the effort. The servant hastily came in with a note superscribed with her name. She motioned to Hubert to open it. He read it aloud. "Mr. Lawrence is sinking. You had better come. I send my carriage." Nora's voice came to her with a cry,—"He 's dying, he 's dying!"

In a minute's time she found herself wrapped in her shawl and seated with Hubert in the doctor's *coupé*. A few moments more and the doctor received them at the door of Roger's room. They passed in and Nora went straight to the bed.

Hubert stood an instant and saw her drop on her knees at the pillow. She flung back her shawl with vehemence, as if to release her hands; he was unable to see where she placed them. He went on into the adjoining chamber, of which the door stood open. The room was dark, the other lit by a night-lamp. He stood listening awhile, but heard nothing; then he began to walk slowly to and fro, past the doorway. He could see nothing but the shining train of Nora's dress lying on the carpet beyond the angle of the bed. He wanted terribly to see more, but he feared to see too much. At moments he fancied he heard whispers. This lasted some time; then the doctor came in, with what seemed to him an odd, unprofessional smile. "The young lady knows a few remedies not taught in the schools," he whispered. "He has recognized her. He 's good for to-night, at least. Half an hour ago he had no pulse at all, but this has started it. I 'll come back in an hour." After he had gone Lucinda came, self-commissioned, and shut the door in Hubert's face. He stood a moment, with an unreasoned sense of insult and defeat. Then he walked straight out of the house. But the next morning, after breakfast, a more generous sentiment moved him to return. The doctor was just coming away. "It was a Daniel come to judgment!" the doctor declared. "I verily believe she saved him. He 'll be sitting up in a fortnight!" Hubert learned that, having achieved her miracle, Nora had returned to Mrs. Keith's. What arts she had used he was left to imagine. He had still a sore feeling of having just missed a crowning joy; but there might yet be time to grasp it. He felt, too, an urgent need of catching a glimpse of the after-glow of Nora's mystical effluence. He repaired to Mrs. Keith's, hoping to find the young girl alone. But the elder lady, as luck would have it, was established in the drawing-room, and she made haste to inform him that Nora, fatigued by her "watching," had not yet left her room. But if Hubert was sombre, Mrs. Keith was radiant. Now was her chance to preach her promised sermon; she had just come into possession of facts which furnished a capital text.

"I suppose you 'll call me a meddling busybody," she said. "I confess I seem to myself a model of forbearance. Be so good as to tell me in three words whether you are in love with Nora."

Taken thus abruptly to task, Hubert, after a moment's trepidation, kept his balance. He measured the situation at a glance, and pronounced it bad. But if heroic urbanity would save it, he would be urbane. "It 's hardly a question to answer in two words," he answered, with an ingenuous smile. "I wish you could tell me!"

"Really," said Mrs. Keith, "it seems to me that by this time you might know. Tell me at least whether you are prepared to marry her?"

Hubert hesitated just an instant. "Of course not—so long as I 'm not sure I 'm in love with her!"

"And pray when will you make up your mind? And what 's to become of poor Nora meanwhile?"

"Why, Mrs. Keith, if Nora can wait, surely you can." The urbanity need not be all on his side.

"Nora can wait? That 's easily said. Is a young girl a thing to be tried like a horse, to be taken up and dropped again? O Mr. Lawrence, if I had ever doubted of the selfishness of men! What this matter has been for you, you know best yourself; but I can tell you that for Nora it has been serious!" At these words Hubert passed his hand nervously through his hair and walked to the window. "The fop!" said Mrs. Keith, *sotto voce*. "His vanity is tickled, on the very verge of exposure. If you are not consciously, passionately in love, you have no business here," she proceeded. "Retire, quietly, expeditiously, humbly. Leave Nora to me. I 'll heal her bruises. They shall have been wholesome ones."

Hubert felt that these peremptory accents implied a menace; and that the lady spoke by book. His vanity rankled, but discretion drew a long breath. For a fortnight it had been shut up in a closet. He thanked the Lord they had no witnesses; with Mrs. Keith, for once, he could afford to sing small. He remained silent for a moment, with his brow bent in meditation. Then turning suddenly, he took the bull by the horns. "Mrs. Keith," he said, "you 've done me a service. I thank you sincerely. I have gone further than I meant; I admit it. I 'm selfish, I 'm vain, I 'm anything you please. My only excuse is Nora's loveliness. It had beguiled me; I had forgotten that this is a life of hard logic." And he bravely took up his hat.

Mrs. Keith was primed for a "scene"; she was annoyed at missing it, and her easy triumph led her on. She thought, too, of the young girl up stairs, combing out her golden hair, and dreaming less of the logic than the poetry of life. She had dragged a heavy gun to the front; she determined to fire her shot. So much virtue had never inspired her with so little respect. She played a moment with the bow on her morning-dress. "Let me thank you for your great humility," she said. "Do you know I was going to be afraid of you, so that I had intrenched myself behind a great big preposterous fact? I met last evening Mrs. Chatterton of New York. You know she 's a great talker, but she talks to the point. She mentioned your engagement to a certain young lady, a dark-eyed person—need I repeat the name?" Nay, it was as well she should n't! Hubert stood before her, flushing crimson, with his blue eyes flashing cold wrath. He remained silent a moment, shaking a scornful finger at her. "For shame, madam," he cried. "That 's shocking taste! You might have been generous; it seems to me I deserve it." And with a summary bow he departed.

Mrs. Keith repented of this extra touch of zeal; the more so as she found that, practically, Nora was to be the victim of the young man's displeasure. For four days he gave no sign; Nora was left to explain his absence as she might. Even Roger's amendment failed to console her. At last, as the two ladies were sitting at lunch, his card was brought in, super-scribed *P. P. C.* Nora read it in silence, and for a moment rested her eyes on her companion with a piteous look which seemed to cry, "It 's *you* I 've to thank for this!" A torrent of remonstrances rose to Nora's lips, but they were sealed by the reflection that, though her friend might have provoked Hubert's desertion, its desperate abruptness pointed to some deeper cause. She pretended to occupy herself with her plate; but her self-control was rapidly ebbing. She silently rose and retreated to her own room, leaving Mrs. Keith moralizing over her mutton-chop, upon the miseries of young ladyhood and the immeasurable egotism of the man who had rather produce a cruel effect than none at all. The various emotions to which Nora had been recently exposed proved too much for her strength; for a week after this she was seriously ill. On the day she left her room she received a short note from Hubert.

"NEW YORK.

"DEAR FRIEND: You have, I suppose, been expecting to hear from me; but I have not written, because I am unable to write as I wish and unwilling to write as—other people would wish! I left Boston suddenly, but not unadvisedly. I shall for the present be occupied here. The last month I spent there will remain one of the best memories of my life. But it was time it should end! Remember me a little— what do I say?—forget me! Farewell. I received this morning from the doctor the best accounts of Roger."

Nora handled this letter somewhat as one may imagine a pious maiden of the antique world to have treated a messenger from the Delphic oracle. It was obscure, it was even sinister; but deep in its sacred dimness there seemed to glow a fiery particle of truth. She locked it up in her dressing-case and wondered and waited. Shortly after came a missive of a different cast. It was from her cousin, George Fenton, and also dated New York.

"DEAR NORA: You have left me to find out your return in the papers. I saw your name a month ago in the steamer's list. But I hope the fine people and things you have been seeing have n't driven me quite out of your heart, and that you have a corner left for your poor old cousin and his scrawls. I received your answer to my letter of last February; after which I immediately wrote again, but in vain! Perhaps you never got my letter; I could scarcely decipher your Italian address. Excuse my want of learning! Your photograph is a joy forever. Are you really as good looking as that? It taxes even the credulity of one who knows how pretty you used to be; how good you must be still. When I last wrote I told you of my having taken stock in an enterprise for working over refuse iron,—dreadful trade! What do you care for refuse iron? It 's awfully dirty and not fit to be talked of to a fine lady like you. Still, if you have any odd bits,—old keys, old nails,—the smallest contributions thankfully received! We think there 's money in it; if there is n't, I 'm afloat again; but again I suppose I shall drift ashore. If this fails, I think of going to Texas. I wish hugely I might see you before the bloom of my youth is sicklied o'er by an atmosphere of iron-rust. Get Mr. Lawrence to bring you to New York for a week. I suppose it would n't do for me to call on you in the light of day; but I might take service as a waiter at your hotel, and express my sentiments in strong tea and soft mutton-chops. Does he still loathe me, Mr. Lawrence? Poor man, tell him to take it easy; I sha' n't trouble him again. Are you ever lonely in the midst of your grandeur? Do you ever feel that, after all, these people are not of your blood and bone? I should like you to quarrel with them, to know a *day's* friendlessness or a day's freedom, so that you might remember that here in New York, in a dusty iron-yard, there is a poor devil who is yours without question, without condition, and till death!"

VIII

ROGER'S CONVALESCENCE went bravely on. One morning as he lay coquetting deliciously with returning sense, he became aware that a woman was sitting at his window in the sun. She seemed to be reading. He fancied vaguely that she was Lucinda; but at last it occurred to him that Lucinda was not addicted to literature, and that Lucinda's tresses, catching the light, were not of a kind to take on the likeness of a queenly crown. She was no vision; his visions had been dark and troubled; and this image was radiant and fixed. He half closed his eyes and watched her lazily through the lids. There came to him, out of his boyish past, a vague, delightful echo of the "Arabian Nights." The room was gilded by the autumn sunshine into the semblance of an enamelled harem court; he himself seemed a languid Persian, lounging on musky cushions; the fair woman at the window a Scheherazade, a Badoura. He closed his eyes completely and gave a little groan, to see if she would move. When he opened them, she had moved; she stood near his bed, looking at him. For a moment his puzzled gaze still told him nothing but that she was fictitiously fair. She smiled and smiled, and, after a little, as he only stared confusedly, she blushed, not like Badoura or Scheherazade, but like Nora. Her frequent presence after this became the great fact in his convalescence. The thought of her beauty filled the long empty hours during which he was forbidden to do anything but grow strong. Sometimes he wondered whether his impression of it was only part of the universal optimism of a man with a raging appetite. Then he would question Lucinda, who would shake her head and chuckle with elderly archness. "Wait till you 're on your feet, sir, and judge for yourself," she would say. "Go and call on her at Mrs. Keith's, and then tell me what you think." He grew well with a beating heart; he would have stayed his recovery for the very dread of facing his happiness. He muffled his pulse in a kind of brooding gravity which puzzled the young girl, who began to wonder whether his illness had left a flaw in his temper. Toward the last, Roger began to blush for his lingering aroma of medicine, and to wish to make a better appearance. He made a point, for some days, of refusing to see her,—always with a loving message, of course, conveyed through Lucinda. Meanwhile, he was shaved, anointed, and costumed. Finally, on a Sunday, he discarded his dressing-gown and sat up clothed and in his right mind. The effort, of course, gave him a huge appetite, and he dealt vigorous justice upon his luncheon. He had just finished, and his little table was still in position near his arm-chair, when Nora made her appearance. She had been to church, and on leaving church had taken a long walk. She wore one of those dark rich toilets of early winter, so becoming to fair beauties; but her face lacked freshness; she was pale and tired. On Roger's remarking it, she said the service had given her a headache; as a remedy, she had marched off briskly at haphazard, missed her way and wandered hither and thither. But here she was, safe and sound and hungry. She petitioned for a share in certain eleemosynary dainties,—that heavy crop of forbidden fruit, which blooms in convalescence,—which she had perceived wasting their sweetness in the dining-room. Hereupon she took off her bonnet and was bountifully served at Roger's table. She ate largely and hungrily, jesting at her appetite and getting back her color. Roger leaned back in his chair, watching her, carving her partridge, offering her this and that; in a word, falling in love. It happened as naturally, as he had never allowed for it. The flower of her beauty had bloomed in a night, that of his passion in a day. When at last she laid down her fork, and, sinking back in her chair, folded her hands on her arms and sat facing him with a friendly, pointless, satisfied smile, and then raising her goblet, threw back her head and showed her white throat and glanced at him over the brim, while he noted her plump ringless hand, with the little finger curled out, he felt that he was in health again. She strolled about the room, idly touching the instruments on his dressing-table and the odds and ends on his chimney-piece. Her dress, which she had released from the loops and festoons then in fashion, trailed rustling on the carpet, and lent her a sumptuous, ladyish air which seemed to give a price to this domiciliary visit. "Everywhere, everywhere, a little dust," she said. "I see it 's more than time I should be back here.

I have been waiting for you to invite me; but as you don't seem inclined, I invite myself."

Roger said nothing for a moment. Then with a blush: "I don't mean to invite you; I don't want you."

Nora stared. "Don't want me? *Par exemple!*"

"I want you as a visitor, but not as a—" And he fumbled for his word.

"As a 'regular boarder'?" she took it gayly. "You turn me out of doors?"

"No; I don't take you in—yet awhile. My dear child, I have a reason."

Nora wondered, still smiling. "I might consider this very unkind," she said, "if I had n't the patience of an angel. Could you favor me with a hint of your reason?"

"Not now," he answered. "Never fear," he cried, with a laugh. "When it comes, it will be all-sufficient!" But he imparted it, a couple of days after, to Mrs. Keith, who came late in the afternoon to present her compliments on his recovery. She displayed an almost sisterly graciousness, enhanced by a lingering spice of coquetry; but somehow, as she talked, he felt as if she were an old woman and he still a young man. It seemed a sort of hearsay that they should ever have been mistress and lover. "Nora will have told you," he said, "of my wishing you to kindly keep her awhile. I can give you no better proof of my regard, for the fact is, my dear friend, I 'm in love with her."

"Come!" she cried. "This is interesting."

"I wish her to accept me freely, as she would accept any other man. For that purpose I must cease to be, in all personal matters, her guardian."

"She must herself forget her wardship, if there is to be any sentimentalizing between you,—all but forget it, at least. Let me speak frankly," she went on. Whereupon Roger frowned a bit, for he had known her frankness to be somewhat incisive. "It 's all very well that you should be in love with her. You 're not the first. Don't be frightened; your chance is fair. The needful point is that she should be just the least bit in love with you."

He shook his head with melancholy modesty. "I don't expect that. She loves me a little, I hope; but I say nothing to her imagination. Circumstances are fatally against it. If she falls in love, it will be with a man as unlike me as possible. Nevertheless, I do hope she may, without pain, learn to think of me as a husband. I hope," he cried, with appealing eyes, "that she may see a certain rough propriety in it. After all, who can make her such a husband as I? I 'm neither handsome, nor clever, nor accomplished, nor known. She might choose from a dozen men who are. Pretty lovers doubtless they 'd make; but, my friend, it 's the *husband*, the husband, that counts!" And he beat his clenched hand on his knee. "Do they know her, have they watched her, as I have done? What are their months to my years, their vows to my acts? Mrs. Keith!"—and he grasped her hand as if to call her to witness,—"I undertake to make her happy. I know what you can say,—that a woman's happiness is worth nothing unless imagination lends a hand. Well, even as a lover, perhaps I 'm not a hopeless case! And then, I confess, other things being equal, I 'd rather Nora should n't marry a poor man."

Mrs. Keith spoke, on this hint. "You 're a rich one then?"

Roger folded up his pocket-handkerchief and patted it out on his knee, with pregnant hesitation. "Yes, I 'm rich,—I may call it so. I 'm rich!" he repeated with unction. "I can say it at last." He paused a moment, and then, with admirable *bonhomie*: "I was not altogether a pauper when you refused me. Since then, for the last six years, I have been saving and sparing and counting. My purpose has sharpened my wits, and fortune, too, has favored me. I 've speculated a little, I 've handled stock and turned this and that about, and now I can offer my wife a very pretty fortune. It 's been going on very quietly; people don't know it; but Nora, if she cares to, shall show 'em!" Mrs. Keith colored and mused; she was lost in a tardy afterthought. "It seems odd to be talking to you this way," Roger went on, exhilarated by this *résumé* of his career. "Do you remember that letter of mine from P——?"

"I did n't tear it up in a rage," she answered. "I came across it the other day."

"It was rather odd, my writing it, you know," Roger confessed. "But in my sudden desire to register a vow, I needed a friend. I turned to you as my best friend." Mrs. Keith acknowledged the honor with a little bow. Had she made a mistake of old? She very soon decided that Nora should not repeat it. Her hand-shake, as she left her friend, was generous; it seemed to assure him that he might count upon her.

When, soon after, he made his appearance in her drawing-room, she gave him many a hint as to how to play his cards. But he irritated her by his slowness; he was too circumspect by half. It was only in the evening that he took a hand in the game. During the day, he left Nora to her own affairs, and was in general neither more nor less attentive than if he had been some susceptible stranger. To spectators his present relation with the young girl was somewhat puzzling; though Mrs. Keith, "by no ambiguous giving out," had diffused a sympathetic expectancy. Roger wondered again and again whether Nora had guessed his meaning. He observed in her at times, in talk, he fancied, a forced nervous levity which seemed born of a need to conjure away the phantom of sentiment. And of this hostile need, of course, he hereupon strove to trace the lineage. He talked with her little, as yet, and never interfered in her talk with others; but he watched her devotedly from corners, and caught her words through the hum of voices, at a distance, while she exchanged soft nothings with the rank and file of her admirers. He was lost in incredulity of his good fortune; he rubbed his eyes. O heavenly favor of fate! Sometimes, as she stood before him, he caught her looking at him with heavy eyes and uncertain lips, as if she were on the verge of some passionate confidence. Adding this to that, Roger found himself rudely confronted with the suspicion that she was in love. Search as he could, however, he was unable to find his man. It was no one there present; they were all alike wasting their shot; the enemy had stolen a march and was hidden in the very heart of the citadel. He appealed distractedly to Mrs. Keith. "Love-sick,—lovesick is the word," he groaned. "I 've read of it all my days in the poets, but here it is in the flesh. Poor girl, poor girl! She plays her part well; she 's wound up tight; but the spring will snap and the watch run down. D—n the man! I 'd rather he had her than sit and see this." He saw that his friend had bad news. "Tell me everything," he said; "don't spare me."

"You 've noticed it at last," she answered. "I was afraid you would. Well! he 's not far to seek. Think it over; can't you guess? My dear Mr. Lawrence, you 're celestially simple. Your cousin Hubert is not."

"Hubert!" Roger echoed, staring. A spasm passed over his face; his eyes flashed. At last he hung his head. "Good heavens! Have I done it all for Hubert?"

"Not if I can help it!" cried Mrs. Keith, with force. "She may n't marry you; but at the worst, she sha' n't marry him!"

Roger laid his hand on her arm; first heavily, then gently. "Dear friend, she must be happy, at any cost. If she loves Hubert, she must marry him. I 'll settle an income!"

Mrs. Keith gave his knuckles a great rap with her fan. "You 'll settle a fiddlestick! You 'll keep your money and you 'll have Miss Nora. Leave it to me! If you have no regard for your rights, at least I have."

"Rights? what rights have I? I might have let her alone. I need n't have settled down on her in her helpless childhood. O, Hubert 's a happy man! Does he know it? You must write to him. I can't!"

Mrs. Keith burst into a ringing laugh. "Know it? You 're amazing! Had n't I better telegraph?"

Roger stared and frowned. "Does he suspect it then?"

Mrs. Keith rolled up her eyes. "Come," she said, "we must begin at the beginning. When you speak of your cousin, you open up a gulf. There 's not much in it, it 's true; but it 's a gulf. Your cousin is a knave,—neither more nor less. Allow me; I know what I say. He knew, of course, of your plans for Nora?" Roger nodded. "Of course he did! He took his chance, therefore, while you were well out of the way. He lost no time, and if Nora is in love with him, he can tell you why. He knew that he could n't marry her, that he should n't, that he would n't. But he made love to her, to pass the time. Happily, it passed soon. I had of course to be cautious; but as soon as I saw how things were going, I spoke, and spoke to the point. Though he 's a knave, he 's no fool; that was all he needed. He made his excuses, such as they were! I shall know in future what to think of him."

Roger shook his head mournfully. "I 'm afraid it 's not to be so easily settled. As you say, Hubert 's a gulf. I never sounded it. The fact remains, they love each other. It 's hard, but it 's fatal."

Mrs. Keith lost patience. "Don't try the heroic; you 'll break down," she cried. "You 're the best of men, but I 'll warrant you no saint. To begin with, Hubert does n't love her. He loves no one but himself! Nora must find her happiness where women as good have found it before this, in a sound, sensible marriage. She can't marry Hubert; he 's engaged to another person. Yes, I have the facts; a young girl in New York with whom he has been off and on for a couple of years, but who holds him to his bargain. I wish her joy of it! He 's not to be pitied; she 's not Nora, but she 's a nice girl, and she 's to have money. So good-by to Hubert! As for you, cut the knot! She 's a bit sentimental just now; but one sentiment, at that age, is as good as another! And, my dear man, the girl has a conscience, it 's to be hoped; give her a chance to show it. A word to the wise!"

Thus exhorted, Roger determined to act. The next day was a Sunday. While the ladies were at church he took up his position in their drawing-room. Nora came in alone; Mrs. Keith had made a pretext for ascending to her own room, where she waited, breathing stout prayers. "I 'm glad to find you," Nora said. "I have been wanting particularly to speak to you. Is n't my probation over? Can't I now come back?"

"It 's about that," he answered, "that I came to talk to you. The probation, Nora, has been mine. Has it lasted long enough! Do you love me yet? Come back to me, come back to me as my wife."

She looked at him, as he spoke, with a clear, unfrightened gaze, and, with his last words, broke frankly into a laugh. But as his own face was intensely grave, a gradual blush arrested her laugh. "Your wife, Roger?" she asked gently.

"My wife. I offer you my hand. Dear Nora, is it so incredible?"

To his uttermost meaning, somehow, her ear was still closed, as if she fancied he was half joking. "Is that the only condition on which we can live together?"

"The only one—for me!"

She looked at him, still sounding his eyes with her own. But his passion, merciful still, retreated before her frank doubt. "Ah," she said, smiling, "what a pity I have grown up!"

"Well," he said, "since you 're grown we must make the best of it. Think of it, Nora, think of it. I 'm not so old, you know. I was young when we begun. You know me so well; you 'd be safe. It would simplify matters vastly; it 's at least to think of," he went on, pleading for very tenderness, in this pitiful minor key. "I know it must seem odd; but I make you the offer!"

Nora was painfully startled. In this strange new character of a lover she seemed to see him eclipsed as a friend, now when, in the trouble of her love, she turned longingly to friendship. She was silent awhile, with her embarrassment. "Dear Roger," she answered, at last, "let me love you in the old, old way. Why need we change? Nothing is so good, so safe as that. I thank you from my heart for your offer. You 've given me too much already. Marry any woman you please, and I 'll be her serving-maid."

He had no heart to meet her eyes; he had wrought his own fate. Mechanically, he took up his hat and turned away, without speaking. She looked at him an instant, uncertain, and then, loath to part with him so abruptly, she laid her arm round his neck. "You don't think me unkind?" she said. "I 'll do anything for you on earth"—"but that," was unspoken, yet Roger heard it. The dream of years was shattered; he felt sick; he was dumb. "You forgive me?" she went on. "O Roger, Roger!" and, with a strange inconsequence of lovingness, she dropped her head on his shoulder. He held her for a moment as close as he had held his hope, and then released her as suddenly as he had parted with it. Before she knew it, he was gone.

Nora drew a long breath. It had all come and gone so fast that she was bewildered. It had been what she had heard called a "chance." Suppose she had grasped at it? She felt a kind of relief in the thought that she had been wise. That she had been cruel, she never suspected. She watched Roger, from the window, cross the street and take his way up the sunny slope. Two ladies passed him, friends as Nora saw; but he made no bow. Suddenly Nora's reflections deepened and the scene became portentous. If she had been wrong, she had been horribly wrong. She hardly dared to think of it. She ascended to her own room, to counsel with familiar privacy. In the hall, as she passed, she found Mrs. Keith at her open door. This lady put her arm round her waist, led her into the chamber toward the light. "Something has happened," she said, looking at her curiously.

"Yes, I 've had an offer. From Roger."

"Well, well?" Mrs. Keith was puzzled by her face.

"Is n't he good? To think he should have thought it necessary! It was soon settled."

"Settled, dearest? How?"

"Why—why—" And Nora began to smile the more resolutely, as her imagination had taken alarm. "I declined."

Mrs. Keith released her with a gesture almost of repulsion. "Declined? Unhappy girl!" The words were charged with a sort of righteous indignation so unusual to the speaker, that Nora's conscience took the hint.

She turned very pale. "What have I done?" she asked, appealingly.

"Done, my dear? You 've done a blind, cruel act! Look here." And Mrs. Keith having hastily ransacked a drawer, turned about with an open letter. "Read that and repent."

Nora took the letter; it was old and crumpled, the ink faded. She glanced at the date,—that of her first school-year. In a moment she had read to the closing sentence. "It will be my own fault if I have n't a perfect wife." In a moment more its heavy meaning overwhelmed her; its vital spark flashed back over the interval of years. She seemed to see Roger's bent, stunned head in the street. Mrs. Keith was frightened at her work. Nora dropped the letter and stood staring, open-mouthed, pale as death, with her poor young face blank with horror.

IX

Nora frequently wondered in after years how that Sunday afternoon had worked itself away; how, through the tumult of amazement and grief, decision, illumination, action had finally come. She had disembarrassed herself of a vague attempt of Mrs. Keith's towards some compensatory caress, and making her way half blindly to her own room, had sat down face to face with her trouble. Here, if ever, was thunder from a clear sky. Her friend's disclosure took time to swell to its full magnitude; for an hour she sat, half stunned, seeming to see it climb heaven-high and glare upon her like some monstrous blighting sun. Then at last she broke into a cry and wept. For an hour she poured out her tears; the ample flood seemed to purge and unchoke the channel of thought. Her immense pain gushed and filtered through her heart and passed out in shuddering sobs. The whole face of things was hideously altered; a sudden chasm had yawned in that backward outlook of her life which had seemed to command the very headspring of domestic security. Between the world and her, much might happen; between her and Roger, nothing! She felt horribly deluded and injured; the sense of suffered wrong absorbed for the time the thought of wrong inflicted. She was too weak for indignation, but she overflowed with a tenderness of reproach which contained the purest essence of resentment. That Roger, whom all these years she had fancied as simple as charity, should have been as double as interest, should have played a part and laid a train, that she had been living in darkness, in illusion, on lies, was a sickening, tormenting thought. The worst of the worst was, that she had been cheated of the chance to be really loyal. Why had he never told her that she wore a chain? Why, when he took her, had he not drawn up his terms and made his bargain? She would have kept it, she would have taught herself to be his wife. Duty then would have been duty; sentiment would have been sentiment; her youth would not have been so wretchedly misspent. She would have surrendered her heart gladly in its youth; doubtless it would have learned to beat to a decent and satisfied measure; but now it had throbbed to a finer music, a melody that would ring in her ears forever. But she had challenged conscience, poor girl, in retrospect; at the very whisper of its name, it stood before her as a living fact. Suddenly, with an agonizing moral convulsion, she found herself dedicating her tears to her own want of faith. She it was who had been cruel, cunning, heedless of a sacred obligation. The longer she gazed at the situation, the more without relief or issue it seemed to her; the more densely compounded of their common fatal want of wisdom. That out of it now, on her part, repentance and assent should spring, seemed as a birth of folly out of chaos. Was she to be startled back into a marriage which experience had overpassed? Yet what should she do? To be what she had been, and to be what Roger wished her to be, were now alike impossible. While she turned in her pain, longing somehow to act, Mrs. Keith knocked at the door. Nora repaired to the dressing-glass, to efface the traces of her tears; and while she stood there, she saw in her open dressing-case her last letter from her cousin. It supplied the thought she was vaguely groping for. By the time she had crossed the room and opened the door, she had welcomed and blessed this thought; and while she gravely shook her head in response to Mrs. Keith's softly urgent, "Nora, dear, won't you let me come to you?" she had passionately embraced it. "I had rather be alone," she said; "I thank you very much."

It was nearly six o'clock; Mrs. Keith was dressed for the evening. It was her gracious practice on Sundays to dine with her mother-in-law. Nora knew, therefore, that if her companion accepted this present dismissal, she would be alone for several hours.

"Can't I do something for you?" Mrs. Keith inquired, soothingly.

"Nothing at all, thank you. You 're very kind."

Mrs. Keith looked at her, wondering whether this was the irony of bitter grief; but a certain cold calmness in the young girl's face, overlying her agitation, seemed to intimate that she had taken a wise resolve. And, in fact, Nora was now soaring sublime on the wings of purpose, and viewed Mrs. Keith's offence as a diminished fact. Mrs. Keith took her hands. "Write him a line, my dear," she gently adjured.

Nora nodded. "Yes, I will write him a line."

"And when I come back, it will be all over?"

"Yes,—all over."

"God bless you, my dear." And on this theological *gracieu-seté* the two women kissed and separated. Nora returned to her dressing-case and read over her cousin's letter. Its clear friendliness seemed to ring out audibly amid this appalling hush of the harmonies of life. "I wish you might know a day's friendliness or a day's freedom, yours without question, without condition, and till death." Here was the voice of nature, of appointed protection; the sound of it aroused her early sense of native nearness to her cousin; had he been at hand she would have sought a wholesome refuge in his arms. She sat down at her writing-table, with her brow in her hands, light-headed with her passionate purpose, steadying herself to think. A day's freedom had come at last; a lifetime's freedom confronted her. For, as you will have guessed, immediate retrocession and departure had imperiously prescribed themselves. Until this had taken place, there could be nothing but deeper trouble. On the old terms there could be no clearing up; she could speak to Roger again only in perfect independence. She must throw off those suffocating bounties which had been meant to hold her to the service in which she had so miserably failed. Her failure now she felt no impulse to question, her decision no energy to revise. I shall have told my story ill if these things seem to lack logic. The fault lay deeper and dated from longer ago than her morning's words of denial. Roger and she shared it between them; it was a heavy burden for both. He had wondered, we may add, whether that lurking force which gave her the dignity that entranced him was humility or pride. Would he have wondered now?

She wrote her "line," as she had promised Mrs. Keith, rapidly, without erasure; then wrote another to Mrs. Keith, folded and directed them and laid them on her dressing-table. She remembered now, distinctly, that she had heard of a Sunday-evening train to New York. She hastened down stairs, found in a newspaper the railway advertisement, and learned that the train started at eight; satisfied herself, too, that the coast was clear of servants, and that she might depart unques-

tioned. She bade a gleeful farewell to her borrowed possessions, vain bribes, ineffective lures. She exchanged the dress
she had worn to church for an old black silk one, put a few
articles of the first necessity into a small travelling-bag, and
emptied her purse of all save a few dollars. Then bonneted,
shawled, veiled, with her bag in her hand, she went forth into
the street. She would begin as she would have to proceed;
she started for the station, savingly, on foot. Happily it was
not far off; she reached it through the wintry darkness, out
of breath, but in safety. She seemed to feel about her, as she
went, the reckless makeshift atmosphere of her childhood.
She was once more her father's daughter. She bought her
ticket and found a seat in the train without adventure; with a
sort of shame, in fact, that this great deed of hers should be
so easy to do. But as the train rattled hideously through the
long wakeful hours of the night, difficulties came thickly; in
the mere oppression of her conscious purpose, in the keener
vision at moments of Roger's distress, in a vague dread of the
great unknown into which she was rushing. But she could do
no other,—no other; with this refrain she lulled her doubts.
It was strange how, as the night elapsed and her heart-beats
seemed to keep time to the crashing swing of the train, her
pity grew for her friend. It would have been a vast relief to
be able to hate him. Her undiminished affection, forced back
on her heart, swelled and rankled there tormentingly. But unable to hate Roger, she could at least abuse herself. Every fact
of the last six years, in this new light, seemed to glow like a
portent of that morning scene, and, in contrast, her own insensibility seemed to mantle with the duskiness of sin. She
felt a passionate desire to redeem herself by work,—work of
any kind, at any cost,—the harder, the humbler the better.
Her music, she deemed, would have a marketable value; she
would write to Miss Murray, her former teacher, and beg her
to employ her or recommend her. Her lonely life would borrow something of the dignity it so sadly needed from teaching scales to little girls in pinafores. Meanwhile George,
George, was the word. She kept his letter clinched in her
hand during half the journey. But among all these things she
found time to think of one who was neither George nor
Roger. Hubert Lawrence had wished in memorable accents

that he had known her friendless and helpless. She imagined
now that her placid dependence had stirred his contempt. But
for this, *he* might have cut the knot of her destiny. As she
thought of him it seemed not misery, but happiness, to be
wandering forth alone. She wished he might see her sitting
there in poverty; she wondered whether there was a chance
of her meeting him in New York. She would tell him then
that she understood and forgave him. What had seemed cruelty was in fact magnanimity; for, of course, he had learned
Roger's plan, and on this ground had renounced. She wondered whether she might properly let him know that she was
free.

Toward morning, weariness mastered her and she fell
asleep. She was aroused by a great tumult and the stopping
of the train. It had arrived. She found with dismay that, as it
was but seven o'clock, she had two or three hours on her
hands. George would hardly be at his place of business before
ten, and the interval seemed formidable. The dusk of a winter's morning lingered still, and increased her trouble. But she
followed her companions and stood in the street. Half a
dozen hackmen attacked her; a facetious gentleman, lighting
a cigar, asked her if she would n't take a carriage with him.

She made her escape from the bustle and hurried along the
street, praying to be unnoticed. She told herself sternly that
now her difficulties had begun and must be bravely faced; but
as she stood at the street-corner, beneath an unextinguished
lamp, listening to the nascent hum of the town, she felt a
most unreasoned sinking of the heart. A Dutch grocer, behind her, was beginning to open his shop; an ash-barrel stood
beside her, and while she lingered an old woman with a filthy
bag on her back came and poked in it with a stick; a police-
man, muffled in a comforter, came lounging squarely along
the pavement and took her slender measure with his hard official eye. What a hideous sordid world! She was afraid to do
anything but walk and walk. Fortunately, in New York, in
the upper region, it is impossible to lose one's way; and she
knew that by keeping downward and to the right she would
reach her appointed refuge. The streets looked shabby and of
ill-repute; the houses seemed mean and sinister. When, to fill
her time, she stopped before the window of a small shop, the

objects within seemed, in their ugliness, to mock at the delicate needs begotten of Roger's teaching, and now come a-
begging. At last she began to feel faint and hungry, for she
had fasted since the previous morning. She ventured into an
establishment which had *Ladies' Café* inscribed in gilt letters
on a blue tablet in the window, and justified its title by an
exhibition of stale pies and fly-blown festoons of tissue-paper.
On her request, humbly preferred, for a cup of tea, she was
served staringly and condescendingly by a half-dressed young
woman, with frowzy hair and tumid eyes. The tea was bad,
yet Nora swallowed it, not to complicate the situation. The
young woman had come and sat down at her table, handled
her travelling-bag, and asked a number of plain questions;
among others, if she would n't like to go up and lie down. "I
guess it 's a dollar," said this person, to conclude her achievements, alluding to the cup of tea. Nora came afterwards to a
square, in which was an enclosure containing trees, a frozen
fountain, thawing fast, and benches. She went in and sat
down on one of the benches. Several of the others were occupied by shabby men, sullen with fasting, with their hands
thrust deep into their pockets, swinging their feet for warmth.
She felt a faint fellowship in their grim idleness; but the fact
that they were all men and she the only woman, seemed to
open out deeper depths in her loneliness. At last, when it was
nine o'clock, she made her way to Tenth Avenue and to
George's address. It was a neighborhood of storehouses and
lumber-yards, of wholesale traffic in articles she had never
heard of, and of multitudinous carts, drawn up along the
pavement. She found a large cheap-looking sign in black and
white,— *Franks and Fenton*. Beneath it was an alley, and at
the end of this alley a small office which seemed to communicate with an extension of the precinct in the rear. The office
was open; a small ragged boy was sweeping it with a broom.
From him she learned that neither Franks nor Fenton had
arrived, but that if she wanted, she might come in and wait.
She sat down in a corner, tremulous with conjecture, and
scanned the room, trying to bridge over this dull interval with
some palpable memento of her cousin. But the desk, the
stove, the iron safe, the chairs, the sordid ink-spotted walls,
were as blank and impersonal as so many columns of figures.

When at last the door opened and a man appeared, it was not
Fenton, but, presumably, Franks. Mr. Franks was a small
meagre man, with a whitish coloring, weak blue eyes and thin
yellow whiskers, laboring apparently under a chronic form of
that malady vulgarly known as the "fidgets," the opening
steps of Saint Vitus's dance. He nodded, he stumbled, he
jerked his arms and legs about with pitiful comicality. He had
a huge protuberant forehead, such a forehead as would have
done honor to a Goethe or a Newton; but poor Mr. Franks
must have been at best a man of genius *manqué*. In other
words, he was next door to a fool. He informed Nora, on
learning her errand, that his partner ("pardner" he called it)
was gone to Williamsburg on business, and would not return
till noon; meanwhile, was it anything *he* could do? Nora's
heart sank at this vision of comfort still deferred; but she
thanked Mr. Franks, and begged leave to sit in her corner and
wait. Her presence seemed to redouble his agitation; she remained for an hour gazing in painful fascination at his grotesque shrugs and spasms, as he busied himself at his desk.
The Muse of accounts, for poor Mr. Franks, was, in fact, not
habitually a young woman, thrice beautiful with trouble, sitting so sensibly at his elbow. Nora wondered how George
had come to marry his strength to such weakness; then she
guessed that it was his need of capital that had discovered a
secret affinity with Mr. Franks's need of brains. The merciless
intensity of thought begotten by her excitement suggested the
dishonorable color of this connection. From time to time Mr.
Franks wheeled about in his chair and fixed her solemnly with
his pallid glance, as if to offer her the privilege of telling him
her story; and on her failure to avail herself of it, turned back
to his ledger with a little grunt of injury and a renewal of his
vacant nods and becks. As the morning wore away, various
gentlemen of the kind designated as "parties" came in and
demanded Fenton, quite over Mr. Franks's restless head. Several of them sat awhile on tilted chairs, chewing their tooth-
picks, stroking their beards, and listening with a half-bored
grin to what appeared to be an intensely confidential exposition of Mr. Franks's wrongs. One of them, as he departed,
gave Nora a wink, as if to imply that the state of affairs between the two members of the firm was so broad a joke that

even a pretty young woman might enjoy it. At last, when they had been alone again for half an hour, Mr. Franks closed with a slap the great leathern flanks of his account-book, and sat a moment burying his head in his arms. Then he suddenly rose and stood before the young girl. "Mr. Fenton 's your cousin, Miss, you say, eh? Well, then, let me tell you that your cousin 's a rascal! I can prove it to you on them books! Where is my money, thirty thousand dollars that I put into this d—d humbug of a business? What is there to show for it? I 've been made a fool of,—as if I was n't fool enough already." The tears stood in his eyes, he stamped with the bitterness of his spite; and then thrusting his hat on his head and giving Nora's amazement no time to reply, he darted out of the door and went up the alley. Nora saw him from the window, looking up and down the street. Suddenly, while he stood and while she looked, George came up. Mr. Franks's fury seemed suddenly to evaporate; he received his companion's hand-shake and nodded toward the office, as if to tell of Nora's being there; while, to her surprise, George hereupon, without looking toward the window, turned back into the street. In a few minutes, however, he reappeared alone, and in another moment he stood before her. "Well!" he cried; "here 's a sensation!"

"George," she said, "I 've taken you at your word."

"My word? O yes!" cried George, bravely.

She instantly perceived that he was changed, and not for the better. He looked older, he was better dressed and more prosperous; but as Nora glanced at him, she felt that she had asked too much of her heart. In fact, George was the same George, only more so, as the phrase is. The lapse of a year and a half had hammered him hard. His face had acquired the settled expression of a man turning over a hard bargain with cynical suspicion. He looked at Nora from head to foot, and in a moment he had noted her simple dress and her pale face. "What on earth has happened?" he asked, closing the door with a kick.

Nora hesitated, feeling that, with words, tears might come.

"You 're sick," he said, "or you will be."

This horrible idea helped her to recall her self-control. "I 've left Mr. Lawrence," she said.

"So I see!" said George, wavering between relish and disapproval. When, a few moments before, his partner had told him that a young lady was in the office, calling herself his cousin, he had straightway placed himself on his guard. The case was delicate; so that, instead of immediately advancing, he had retreated behind a green baize door twenty yards off, had "taken something," and briskly meditated. She had taken him at his word: he knew that before she told him. But confound his word, if it came to this! It had been meant, not as an invitation to put herself under his care, but as a simple high-colored hint of his standing claims. George, however, had a native sympathy with positive measures; Nora evidently had engaged in one which, as such, might yield profit. "How do you stand?" he asked. "Have you quarrelled?"

"Don't call it a quarrel, George! He 's as kind, he 's kinder than ever!" Nora cried. "But what do you think? He has asked me to marry him."

"Eh, my dear, I told you so!"

"I did n't believe you! I ought to have believed you. But it is n't only that. It is that, years ago, he adopted me with that view. He brought me up for that purpose. He has done everything for me on that condition. I was to pay my debt and be his wife! I never dreamed of it. And now at last that I 'm a woman grown and he makes his demand, I can't, I can't!"

"You can't, eh? So you 've left him!"

"Of course I 've left him. It was the only thing to do. It was give and take. I can't give what he wants, nor can I give back all I have received. But I can refuse to take more."

Fenton sat on the edge of his desk, swinging his leg. He folded his arms and whistled a lively air, looking at Nora with a brightened eye. "I see, I see," he said.

Telling her tale had deepened her color and added to her beauty. "So here I am," she went on. "I know that I 'm dreadfully alone, that I 'm homeless and helpless. But it 's a heaven to living as I have lived. I have been content all these days, because I thought I could content him. But we never understood each other. He has given me immeasurable happiness; I know that; and he knows that I know it; don't you think he knows, George?" she cried, eager even in her reserve. "I

would have made him a sister, a friend. But I don't expect
you to understand all this. It 's enough that I 'm satisfied.
I 'm satisfied," the poor girl repeated vehemently. "I 'm not
going into the heroics; you can trust me, George. I mean to
earn my own living. I can teach; I 'm a good musician; I want
above all things to work. I shall look for some employment
without delay. All this time I might have been writing to Miss
Murray. But I was sick with impatience to see you. To come
to you was the only thing I could do; but I sha' n't trouble
you for long."

Fenton seemed to have but half caught the meaning of this
impassioned statement, for simple admiration of her radiant
purity of purpose was fast getting the better of his caution.
He gave his knee a loud slap. "Nora," he said, "you 're a great
girl!"

For a moment she was silent and thoughtful. "For heaven's
sake," she cried at last, "say nothing to make me feel that I
have done this thing too easily, too proudly and recklessly!
Really, I 'm anything but brave. I 'm full of doubts and fears."

"You 're beautiful; that 's one sure thing!" said Fenton.
"I 'd rather marry you than lose you. Poor Lawrence!" Nora
turned away in silence and walked to the window, which
grew to her eyes, for the moment, as the "glimmering square"
of the poet. "I thought you loved him so!" he added,
abruptly. Nora turned back with an effort and a blush. "If he
were to come to you now," he went on, "and go down on
his knees and beg and plead and rave and all that sort of
thing, would you still refuse him?"

She covered her face with her hands. "O George, George!"
she cried.

"He 'll follow you, of course. He 'll not let you go so
easily."

"Possibly; but I have begged him solemnly to let me take
my way. Roger is n't one to rave and rage. At all events, I
shall refuse to see him now. A year hence, perhaps. His great
desire will be, of course, that I don't suffer. I sha' n't suffer."

"By Jove, not if I can help it!" cried Fenton, with warmth.
Nora answered with a faint, grave smile, and stood looking
at him, invoking by her helpless silence some act of high protection. He colored beneath her glance with the pressure of

his thoughts. They resolved themselves chiefly into the recurring question, "What can be made of it?" While he was awaiting inspiration, he took refuge in a somewhat inexpensive piece of gallantry. "By the way, you must be hungry."

"No, I 'm not hungry," said Nora, "but I 'm tired. You must find me a lodging—in some quiet hotel."

"O, you shall be quiet enough," he answered; but he insisted that unless, meanwhile, she took some dinner, he should have her ill on his hands. They quitted the office, and he hailed a hack, which drove them over to the upper Broadway region, where they were soon established in a well-appointed restaurant. They made, however, no very hearty meal. Nora's hunger of the morning had passed away in fever, and Fenton himself was, as he would have expressed it, off his feed. Nora's head had begun to ache; she had removed her bonnet, and sat facing him at their small table, leaning wearily against the wall, her plate neglected, her arms folded, her bright eyes expanded with her trouble and consulting the uncertain future. He noted narrowly her splendid gain of beauty since their parting; but more even than by this he was struck by her brave playing of her part, and by the purity and mystery of moral temper it implied. It belonged to a line of conduct in which *he* felt no commission to dabble; but in a creature of another sort he was free to admire these luxuries of conscience. In man or woman the capacity then and there to *act* was the thing he most relished. Nora had not faltered and wavered; she had chosen, and here she sat. He felt a sort of rage that he was not the manner of man for whom such a woman might so choose, and that his own temper was pitched in so much lower a key; for as he looked askance at her beautiful absent eyes, he more than suspected that there was a positive as well as a negative side to her refusal of her friend. To refuse Roger, favored as Roger was, her heart, at least, must have accepted another. It was love, and not indifference, that had pulled the wires of her adventure. Fenton, as we have intimated, was one who, when it suited him, could ride rough-shod to his mark. "You 've told me half your story," he said, "but your eyes tell the rest. You 'll not be Roger 's wife, but you 'll not die an old maid."

She started, and her utmost effort at self-control was unable to banish a beautiful guiltiness from her blush. "To what you can learn from my eyes you are welcome," she said. "Though they may compromise me, they won't any one else."

"My dear girl," he said, "I religiously respect your secrets." But, in truth, he only half respected them. Stirred as he was by her beauty and by that sense of feminine appeal which to a man who retains aught of the generosity of manhood is the most inspiring of all motives, he was keenly mortified by the feeling that her tenderness passed him by, barely touching him with the hem of its garment. She was doing mighty fine things, but she was using him, her hard, shabby cousin, as a senseless stepping-stone. These reflections quickened his appreciation of her charm, but took the edge from his delicacy. As they rose to go, Nora, who in spite of her absent eyes had watched him well, felt that cousinship was but a name. George had been to her maturer vision a singular disappointment. His face, from the moment of their meeting, had given her warning to withdraw her trust. Was it she or he who had changed since that fervid youthful parting of sixteen months before? She, in the interval, had been refined by life; he had been vulgarized. She had seen the world. She had known better things and better men; she had known Hubert, and, more than ever, she had known Roger. But as she drew on her gloves she reflected with horror that trouble was making her fastidious. She wished to be coarse and careless; she wished that she might have eaten a heavy dinner, that she might enjoy taking George's arm. And the slower flowed the current of her confidence, the softer dropped her words. "Now, dear George," she said, with a desperate attempt at a cheerful smile, "let me know where you mean to take me."

"Upon my soul, Nora," he said, with a hard grin, "I feel as if I had a jewel I must lay in soft cotton. The thing is to find it soft enough." With George himself, perhaps, she might make terms; but she had a growing horror of his friends. Among them, probably, were the female correlatives of the men who had come to chat with Mr. Franks. She prayed he might not treat her to company. "You see I want to do the pretty thing," he went on. "I want to treat you, by Jove, as I 'd treat a queen! I can't thrust you all alone into a hotel, and I can't put up at one with you,—can I?"

"I 'm not in a position now to be fastidious," said Nora. "I sha' n't object to going alone."

"No, no!" he cried, with a flourish of his hand. "I 'll do for you what I 'd do for my own sister. I 'm not one of your pious boys, but I know the decencies. I live in the house of a lady who lets out rooms,—a very nice little woman; she and I are great cronies; I 'm sure you 'll like her. She 'll make you as snug as you ever were with our friend Roger! A female companion for a lonely girl is never amiss, you know. She 's a first-rate little woman. You 'll see!"

Nora's heart sank, but she assented. They re-entered their carriage, and a drive of moderate length brought them to a brown-stone dwelling of the third order of gentility, as one may say, stationed in a cheap and serried row. In a few moments, in a small tawdry front parlor, Nora was introduced to George's hostess, the nice little woman, Mrs. Paul by name. Nice enough she seemed, for Nora's comfort. She was youngish and fair, plump and comely, with a commendable air of remote widowhood. She was a trifle too loving on short acquaintance, perhaps; but, after all, thought Nora, who was she now, to complain of that? When the two women had gone up stairs, Fenton put on his hat,—he could never meditate without it (he had written that last letter to Nora with his beaver resting on the bridge of his nose),—and paced slowly up and down the narrow entry, chewing the end of a cigar, with his hands in his pockets and his eyes on the ground. In ten minutes Mrs. Paul reappeared. "Well, sir," she cried, "what does all this mean?"

"It means money, if you 'll not scream so loud," he answered. "Come in here." They went into the parlor and remained there for a couple of hours with closed doors. At last Fenton came forth and left the house. He walked along the street, humming gently to himself. Dusk had fallen; he stopped beneath a lighted lamp at the corner, looked up and down a moment, and then exhaled a deep, an almost melancholy sigh. Having thus purged his conscience, he proceeded to business. He consulted his watch; it was five o'clock. An empty hack rolled by; he called it and got in, breathing the motto of great spirits, "Confound the expense!" His business led him to visit successively several of the upper hotels.

Roger, he argued, starting immediately in pursuit of Nora, would have taken the first train from Boston, and would now have been more than an hour in town. Fenton could, of course, proceed only by probabilities; but according to these, Roger was to be found at one of the establishments aforesaid. Fenton knew his New York, and, from what he knew of Roger, he believed him to be at the Brevoort House. Here, in fact, he found his name freshly registered. He would give him time, however; he would take time himself. He stretched his long legs awhile on one of the divans in the hall. At last Roger appeared, strolling gloomily down the corridor, with his eyes on the ground. For a moment Fenton scarcely recognized him. He was pale and grave; distress had already made him haggard. Fenton observed that, as he passed, people stared at him. He walked slowly to the street door; whereupon Fenton, fearing he might lose him, followed him, and stood for a moment behind him. Roger turned suddenly, as if from an instinct of the other's nearness, and the two faced each other. Those dumb eyes of Roger's for once were eloquent. They glowed like living coals.

X

THE GOOD LADY who enjoyed the sinecure of being mother-in-law to Mrs. Keith passed on that especial Sunday an exceptionally dull evening. Her son's widow was oppressed and preoccupied, and took an early leave. Mrs. Keith's first question on reaching home was whether Nora had left her room. On learning that she had quitted the house alone, after dark, Mrs. Keith made her way, stirred by vague conjecture, to the empty chamber, where, of course, she speedily laid her hands on those two testamentary notes of which mention has been made. In a moment she had read the one addressed to herself. Perturbed as she was, she yet could not repress an impulse of intelligent applause. Ah, how character plays the cards! how a fine girl's very errors set her off! If Roger longed for Nora to-day, who could measure the morrow's longing? He might enjoy, however, without waiting for the morrow, this refinement of desire. In spite of the late hour, Mrs. Keith repaired to his abode, armed with the other letter, deeming this, at such a moment, a more gracious course than to send for him. The letter Roger found to be brief but pregnant. "Dear Roger," it ran, "I learned this afternoon the secret of all these years,—too late for our happiness. I have been blind; you have been too forbearing,—generous where you should have been narrowly just. I never dreamed of what this day would bring. Now, I must leave you; I can do nothing else. This is no time to thank you for these years, but I shall live to do so yet. Dear Roger, get married, and send me your children to teach. I shall live by teaching. I have a family, you know; I go to N. Y. to-night. I write this on my knees, imploring you to be happy. One of these days, when I have learned to be myself again, we shall be better friends than ever. I beg you solemnly not to follow me."

Mrs. Keith sat with her friend half the night in contemplation of this prodigious fact. For the first time in her knowledge of him she saw Roger violent,—violent with horror and self-censure, and vain imprecation of circumstance. But as the hours passed, she noted that effect of which she had had prevision: the intenser heat of his passion, the need to answer act with act. He spoke of Nora with lowered tones, with circumlocutions, as some old pagan of an unveiled goddess. Consistency is a jewel; Mrs. Keith maintained in the teeth of the event that she had given sound advice. "She 'll have you yet," she said, "if you let her alone. Take her at her word,—don't follow her. Let her knock against the world a little, and she 'll make you a better wife for this very escapade."

This philosophy seemed to Roger too stoical by half; to sit at home and let Nora knock against the world was more than he could undertake. "Wife or no wife," he said, "I must bring her back. I 'm responsible for her to Heaven. Good God! think of her afloat in that horrible city with that rascal of a half cousin—her 'family' she calls him!—for a pilot!" He took, of course, the first train to New York. How to proceed, where to look, was a hard question; but to linger and waver was agony. He was haunted, as he went, with dreadful visions of what might have befallen her; it seemed to him that he had hated her till now.

Fenton, as he recognized him, seemed a comfortable sight, in spite of his detested identity. He was better than uncertainty. "You have news for me!" Roger cried. "Where is she?"

Fenton looked about him at his leisure, feeling, agreeably, that now *he* held the cards. "Gently," he said. "Had n't we better retire?" Upon which Roger, grasping his arm with grim devotion, led him to his own bedroom. "I rather hit it," George went on. "I 'm not the fool you once tried to make me seem."

"Where is she,—tell me that!" Roger demanded.

"Allow me, dear sir," said Fenton, settling himself in spacious vantage. "If I 've come here to oblige you, you must let me take my own way. You don't suppose I 've rushed to meet you out of pure gratitude! I owe it to my cousin, in the first place, to say that I 've come without her knowledge."

"If you mean only to torture me," Roger answered, "say so outright. Is she well? is she safe?"

"Safe? the safest woman in the city, sir! A delightful home, maternal care!"

Roger wondered whether Fenton was making horrible sport of his trouble; he turned cold at the thought of maternal care of his providing. But he cautioned himself to lose nothing by arrogance. "I thank you extremely for your kindness. Nothing remains but that I should see her."

"Nothing indeed! You 're very considerate. You know that she particularly objects to seeing you."

"Possibly! But that 's for her to say. I claim the right to take the refusal from her own lips."

Fenton looked at him with an impudent parody of compassion. "Don't you think you 've had refusals enough? You must enjoy 'em!"

Roger turned away with an imprecation, but he continued to swallow his impatience. "Mr. Fenton," he said, "you have not come here, I know, to waste words, nor have I to waste temper. You see before you a desperate man. Come, make the most of me! I 'm willing, I 'm delighted, to be fleeced! You 'll help me, but not for nothing. Name your terms."

It is odd how ugly a face our passions, our projects may wear, reflected in other minds, dressed out by other hands. Fenton scowled and flinched, all but repudiated. To save the situation as far as possible, he swaggered. "Well, you see," he answered, "my assistance is worth something. Let me explain how much. You 'll not guess! I know your story; Nora has told me everything,—everything! We 've had a great talk, I can tell you! Let me give you a little hint of my story,—and excuse egotism! You proposed to her; she refused you. You offered her money, luxury, a position. She knew you, she liked you enormously, yet she refused you flat! Now reflect on this."

There was something revolting to Roger in seeing his adversary profaning these sacred mysteries; he protested. "I *have* reflected, abundantly. You can tell me nothing. Her affections," he added, stiffly, to make an end of it, "were pre-engaged."

"Exactly! You see how that complicates matters. Poor, dear little Nora!" And Fenton gave a twist to his mustache. "Imagine, if you can, how a man placed as I am feels toward a woman,—toward *the* woman! If he reciprocates, it 's love, it 's passion, it 's what you will, but it 's common enough! But when he does n't repay her in kind, when he can't, poor devil, it 's—it 's—upon my word," cried Fenton, slapping his knee, "it 's chivalry!"

For some moments Roger failed to appreciate the astounding purport of these observations; then, suddenly, it dawned upon him. "Do I understand you," he asked, in a voice gentle by force of wonder, "that *you* are the man?"

Fenton squared himself in his chair. "You 've hit it, sir. I 'm the man,—the happy, the unhappy man. Damn it, sir, it 's not my fault!"

Roger stood lost in tumultuous silence; Fenton felt his eyes penetrating him to the core. "Excuse me," said Roger, at last, "if I suggest your giving me some slight evidence of this extraordinary fact!"

"Evidence? is n't there evidence enough and to spare? When a young girl gives up home and friends and fortune and—and reputation, and rushes out into the world to throw herself into a man's arms, you may make a note of her preference, I think! But if you 'll not take my word, you may leave it! I may look at the matter once too often, let me tell you! I admire Nora with all my heart; I worship the ground she treads on; but I confess I 'm afraid of her; she 's too good for me; she was meant for a finer gentleman than I! By which I don't mean *you*, of necessity. But you have been good to her, and you have a claim. It has been cancelled, in a measure; but you wish to re-establish it. Now you see that I stand in your way; that if I had a mind to, I might stand there forever! Hang it, sir, I 'm playing the part of a saint. I have but a word to say to settle my case, and yours too! But I have my eye on a lady neither so young nor so pretty as my cousin, but whom I can marry with a better conscience, for she expects no more than I can give her. Nevertheless, I don't answer for myself. A man is n't a saint by the week! Talk about conscience when a beautiful girl sits gazing at you through a mist of tears! O, you have yourself to thank for it all! A year and a half ago, if you had n't treated me like a sharper, Nora would have been content to treat me like a cousin. But women have a fancy for an outlaw. You turned me out of doors, and Nora's heart went with me. It has followed me ever since. Here I sit with my ugly face and hold it in my hand. As I say, I don't quite know what to do with it. You propose an arrangement, I inquire your terms. A man loved is a man listened to. If I were to say to Nora to-morrow, 'My

dear girl, you 've made a mistake. You 're in a false position.
Go back to Mr. Lawrence directly, and then we 'll talk about
it!' she 'd look at me a moment with those eyes of hers, she 'd
sigh, she 'd gather herself up like a queen on trial for treason,
remanded to prison,—and she 'd march to your door. Once
she 's within it, it 's your own affair. That 's what I can do.
Now what can you do? Come, something handsome!"

Fenton spoke loud and fast, as if to deepen and outstrip
possible self-contempt. Roger listened amazedly to this prodigious tissue of falsity, impudence and greed, and at last, as
Fenton paused, and he seemed to see Nora's image blushing
piteously beneath this heavy mantle of dishonor, his disgust
broke forth. "Upon my word, sir," he cried, "you go too far;
you ask too much. Nora in love with you,—you who have
n't the grace even to lie decently! Tell me she 's ill, she 's lost,
she 's dead; but don't tell me she can fancy you for a moment
an honest man!"

Fenton rose and stood for a moment, glaring with anger at
his vain self-exposure. For an instant, Roger expected a tussle.
But Fenton deemed that he could deal harder vengeance than
by his fists. "Very good!" he cried. "You 've chosen. I don't
mind your words; you 're a fool at best, and of course you 're
twenty times a fool when you 're put out by a disagreeable
truth. But you 're not such a fool, I guess, as not to repent!"
And Fenton made a rather braver exit than you might have
expected.

Roger's recent vigil with Mrs. Keith had been hideous
enough; but he was yet to learn that a sleepless night may
contain deeper possibilities of suffering. He had flung back
Fenton's words, but they returned to the charge. When once
the gate is opened to self-torture, the whole army of fiends
files in. Before morning he had fairly out-Fentoned Fenton.
There he tossed, himself a living instance, if need were, of the
furious irresponsibility of passion; loving in the teeth of reason, of hope, of justice almost, in blind obedience to a reckless personal need. Why, if *his* passion scorned counsel, was
Nora's bound to take it? We love as we must, not as we
should; and she, poor girl, had bowed to the common law.
In the morning he slept awhile for weariness, but he awoke
to a world of agitation. If Fenton's tale was true, and if, at

Mrs. Keith's instigation, his own suspicions had done Hubert
wrong, he would go to Hubert, pour out his woes, and demand aid and comfort. He must move to find rest. Hubert's
lodging was high up town; Roger started on foot. The
weather was perfect; one of those happy days of February
which seem to snatch a mood from May,—a day when any
sorrow is twice a sorrow. All winter was a-melting; you heard
on all sides, in the still sunshine, the raising of windows; on
the edges of opposing house-tops rested a vault of vernal
blue. Where was she hidden, in the vast bright city? Hideous
seemed the streets and houses and crowds which made gross
distance of their nearness. He would have beggared himself
for the sound of her voice, though her words might damn
him. When at last he reached Hubert's dwelling a sudden
sense of all that he risked checked his steps. Hubert, after all,
and Hubert alone, was a possible rival, and it would be sad
work to put the torch in his hands! So he turned heavily back
to the Fifth Avenue and kept his way to the Park. Here, for
some time he walked about, heeding, feeling, seeing nothing
but that garish nature mocked his unsunned soul. At last he
sat down on a bench. The delicious mildness of the air almost
sickened him. It was some time before he perceived through
the mist of his thoughts that two ladies had descended from
a carriage hard by, and were approaching his bench,—the
only one near at hand. One of these ladies was of great age
and evidently infirm; she came slowly, leaning on her companion's arm; she wore a green shade over her eyes. The
younger lady, who was in the prime of youth and beauty,
supported her friend with peculiar tenderness. As Roger rose
to give them place, he dimly observed on the young lady's
face a movement of recognition, a smile,—the smile of Miss
Sandys! Blushing slightly, she frankly greeted him. He met
her with the best grace at his command, and felt her eyes, as
he spoke, scanning the trouble in his aspect. "There is no
need of my introducing you to my aunt," she said. "She has
lost her hearing, and her only pleasure is to bask in the sun."
She turned and helped this venerable invalid to settle herself
on the bench, put a shawl about her, and satisfied her feeble
needs with filial solicitude. At the end of ten minutes of commonplace talk, relieved however by certain mutual glances of

a subtler complexion, Roger felt the presence of this fine woman closing about him like some softer moral climate. At last these sympathetic eye-beams resolved themselves, on Miss Sandys's part, into speech. "You 're either very unwell, Mr. Lawrence, or very unhappy."

Roger hesitated an instant, under the empire of that stubborn aversion to complaint which, in his character, was half modesty and half philosophy. But Miss Sandys seemed to sit there eying him so like some Muse of friendship that he answered simply, "I 'm unhappy!"

"I was afraid it would come!" said Miss Sandys. "It seemed to me when we met, a year ago, that your spirits were too good for this life. You know you told me something which gives me the right—I was going to say, to be interested; let me say, at least, to be compassionate."

"I hardly remember what I told you. I only know that I admired you to a degree which may very well have loosened my tongue."

"O, it was about the charms of another you spoke! You told me about the young girl to whom you had devoted yourself."

"I was dreaming then; now I 'm awake!" Roger hung his head and poked the ground with his stick. Suddenly he looked up, and she saw that his eyes were filled with tears. "O Miss Sandys," he cried, "you 've stirred deep waters! Don't question me. I 'm ridiculous with disappointment and sorrow!"

She gently laid her hand on his arm. "Let me hear it all! I assure you I can't go away and leave you sitting here the same image of suicidal despair I found you."

Thus urged, Roger told his story. In the clear still air of her attention, it seemed to assume to his own vision a larger and more palpable outline. As he talked, he worked off the superficial disorder of his grief. He was forcibly struck, for the first time, with his own great charity; the silent respect of his companion's gaze seemed to attest it. When he came to speak of this dark contingency of Nora's love for her cousin, he threw himself frankly upon Miss Sandys's pity, upon her wisdom. "Is such a thing possible?" he asked. "Do you believe it?"

She raised her eyebrows. "You must remember that I know neither Miss Lambert nor her kinsman. I can hardly risk a judgment; I can only say this, that the general effect of your story is to diminish my esteem for women, to elevate my opinion of men."

"O, except Nora on one side, and Fenton on the other! Nora 's an angel!"

Miss Sandys gave a vexed smile. "Possibly! You 're a man, and you ought to have loved a woman. Angels have a good conscience guaranteed them; they may do what they please! If I should except any one, it would be Mr. Hubert Lawrence. I met him the other evening."

"You think it 's Hubert then?" Roger demanded mournfully.

Miss Sandys broke into a warm laugh which seemed to Roger to sound the emancipation of his puzzled spirit. "For an angel, Miss Lambert has n't lost her time on earth! But don't ask me for advice, Mr. Lawrence; at least not now and here. Come and see me to-morrow, or this evening. Don't regret having spoken; you may believe at least that the burden of your grief is shared. It was too miserable that at such a time you should be sitting here alone, feeding upon your own heart."

These seemed to Roger rich words; they lost nothing on the speaker's lips. She was indeed admirably beautiful; her face, softened by intelligent pity, was lighted by a gleam of tender irony of his patience. Was he, after all, stupidly patient, ignobly fond? There was in Miss Sandys something singularly assured and complete. Nora, in momentary contrast, seemed a flighty school-girl. He looked about him, vaguely invoking the bright empty air, longing for rest, yet dreading forfeiture. He left his place and strolled across the dull-colored turf. At the base of a tree, on its little bed of sparse raw verdure, he suddenly spied the first violet of the year. He stooped and picked it; its mild firm tint was the color of friendship. He brought it back to Miss Sandys, who now had risen with her companion and was preparing to return to the carriage. He silently offered her the violet,—a mere pin's head of bloom; a passionate throb of his heart had told him that this was all he could offer her. She took it with a sober smile; it seemed pale beneath her deep eyes. "We shall see you again?" she said.

Roger felt himself blushing to his brows. He had a vision on either hand of an offered cup,—the deep-hued wine of illusion,—the bitter draught of constancy. A certain passionate instinct answered,—an instinct deeper than his wisdom, his reason, his virtue,—deep as his love. "Not now," he said. "A year hence!"

Miss Sandys turned away and stood for a full moment as motionless as some sculptured statue of renunciation. Then, passing her arm caressingly round her companion, "Come, dear aunt," she murmured; "we must go." This little address to the stone-deaf dame was her single tribute to confusion. Roger walked with the ladies to their carriage and silently helped them to enter it. He noted the affectionate tact with which Miss Sandys adjusted her movements to those of her companion. When he lifted his hat, his friend bowed, as he fancied, with an air of redoubled compassion. She had but imagined his prior loss,—she knew his present one! "Ah, she would make a wife!" he said, as the carriage rolled away. He stood watching it for some minutes; then, as it wheeled round a turn, he was seized with a deeper, sorer sense of his impotent idleness. He would go to Hubert to accuse him, if not to appeal to him.

XI

NORA, relieved of her hostess's company, turned the key in her door and went through certain motions mechanically suggestive of her being at rest and satisfied. She unpacked her little bag and repaired her disordered toilet. She took out her writing-materials and prepared to compose a letter to Miss Murray. But she had not written many words before she lapsed into sombre thought. Now that she had seen George again and judged him, she was coming rapidly to feel that to have exchanged Roger's care for his care was, for the time, to have outraged Roger. It may have been needful, but it was none the less a revolting need. But it should pass quickly! She took refuge again in her letter and begged for an immediate reply. From time to time, as she wrote, she heard a step in the house, which she supposed to be George's; it somehow quickened her pen and the ardor of her petition. This was just finished when Mrs. Paul reappeared, bearing a salver charged with tea and toast,—a gracious attention, which Nora was unable to repudiate. The lady took advantage of it to open a conversation. Mrs. Paul's overtures, as well as her tea and toast, were the result of her close conference with Fenton; but though his instructions had made a very pretty show as he laid them down, they dwindled sensibly in the vivid glare of Nora's mistrust. Mrs. Paul, nevertheless, seated herself bravely on the bed and rubbed her plump pretty hands like the best little woman in the world. But the more Nora looked at her, the less she liked her. At the end of five minutes she had conceived a horror of her. It seemed to her that she had met just such women in reports of criminal trials. She had wondered what the heroines of these tragedies were like. Why, like Mrs. Paul, of course! They had her comely stony face, her false smile, her little tulle cap, which seemed forever to discredit coquetry. And here, in her person, sat the whole sinister sisterhood on Nora's bed, calling the young girl "my dear," wanting to take her hand and draw her out! With a defiant flourish, Nora addressed her letter with Miss Murray's honest title: "I should like to have this posted, please," she said.

"Give it to me, my dear; I 'll attend to it," said Mrs. Paul; and straightway read the address. "I suppose this is your old schoolmistress. Mr. Fenton told me all about it." Then, after turning the letter for a moment, "Keep it over a day!"

"Not an hour," said Nora, with decision. "My time is precious."

"Why, my dear," cried Mrs. Paul, "we shall be delighted to keep you a month."

"You 're very good. You know I 've my living to make."

"Don't talk about that! I make *my* living,—I know what it means! Come, let me talk to you as a friend. Don't go too far. Suppose, now, you repent? Six months hence, it may be too late. If you leave him lamenting too long, he 'll marry the first pretty girl he sees. They always do,—a man refused is just like a widower. They 're not so faithful as the widows! But let me tell you it 's not every girl that gets such a chance; if I 'd had it, I would n't have split hairs! He 'll love you the better, you see, for your having led him a little dance. But he must n't dance too long! Excuse my breaking out this way; but Mr. Fenton and I, you see, are great friends, and I feel as if his cousin was my cousin. Take back this letter and give me just one word to post,— *Come!* Poor little man! You must have a high opinion of men, my dear, to think you had n't drawn a prize!"

If Roger had wished for a proof that sentiment survived in Nora's mind, he would have found it in the disgust she felt at hearing Mrs. Paul undertake his case. She colored with her sense of the defilement of sacred things. George, surely, for an hour, at least, might have kept her story intact. "Really, madam," she answered, "I can't discuss this matter. I 'm extremely obliged to you." But Mrs. Paul was not to be so easily baffled. Poor Roger, roaming helpless and hopeless, would have been amazed to hear how warmly his cause was a-pleading. Nora, of course, made no attempt to argue the case. She waited till the lady had exhausted her eloquence, and then, "I 'm a very obstinate person," she said; "you waste your words. If you go any further I shall feel persecuted." And she rose, to signify that Mrs. Paul might do likewise. Mrs. Paul took the hint, but in an instant she had turned about the hard reverse of her fair face, in which defeated self-interest smirked

horribly. "Bah! you 're a silly girl!" she cried; and swept out
of the room. Nora, after this, determined to avoid a second
interview with George. Her bad headache furnished a sufficient pretext for escaping it. Half an hour later he knocked at
her door, quite too loudly, she thought, for good taste. When
she opened it, he stood there, excited, angry, ill-disposed.
"I 'm sorry you 're ill," he said; "but a night's rest will put
you right. I 've seen Roger."

"Roger! he 's here?"

"Yes, he 's here. But he don't know where you are. Thank
the Lord you left him! he 's a brute!" Nora would fain have
learned more,—whether he was angry, whether he was suffering, whether he had asked to see her; but at these words
she shut the door in her cousin's face. She hardly dared think
of what offered impertinence this outbreak of Fenton's was
the rebound. Her night's rest brought little comfort. Time
seemed not to cancel her disturbing thoughts, but to multiply
them. She wondered whether Roger had supposed George to
be her appointed mediator, and asked herself whether it was
not her duty to see him once again and bid him a respectfully
personal farewell. It was a long time after she rose before she
could bring herself to leave her room. She had a vague hope
that if she delayed, her companions might have gone out. But
in the dining-room, in spite of the late hour, she found
George gallantly awaiting her. He had apparently had the discretion to dismiss Mrs. Paul to the background, and apologized for her absence by saying that she had breakfasted long
since and had gone to market. He seemed to have slept off
his wrath and was full of brotherly *bonhomie*. "I suppose you
'll want to know about Roger," he said, when they were
seated at breakfast. "He had followed you directly, in spite of
your solemn request; but not out of pure affection, I think.
The little man 's mad. He expects you to back down and
come to him on your knees,—beg his pardon and promise
never to do it again. Pretty terms to marry a man on, for a
woman of spirit! But he does n't know his woman, does he,
Nora? Do you know what he intimated? indeed, he came
right out with it! That you and I want to make a match! That
you 're in love with me, Miss, and ran away to marry me.
That we expected him to forgive us and endow us with a pile

of money. But he 'll not forgive us,—not he! We may starve, we and our brats, before he looks at us. Much obliged! We shall thrive, for many a year, as brother and sister, sha' n't we, Nora? and need neither his money nor his pardon!"

In reply to this speech, Nora sat staring in pale amazement. "Roger thought," she at last found words to say, "that it was to marry *you* I refused him,—to marry *you* I came to New York?"

Fenton, with seven-and-twenty years of impudence at his back, had received in his day snubs and shocks of various shades of intensity; but he had never felt in his face so chilling a blast of reprobation as this cold disgust of Nora's. We know that the scorn of a lovely woman makes cowards brave; it may do something towards making knaves honest men. "Upon my word, my dear," he cried, "I 'm sorry I hurt your feelings. It 's rough, but it 's so!"

Nora wished in after years she had been able to laugh at this disclosure; to pretend, at least, to a mirth she so little felt. But she remained almost sternly silent, with her eyes on her plate, stirring her tea. Roger, meanwhile, was walking about under this miserable error! Let him think anything but that! "What did you reply," she asked, "to this—to this—"

"To this handsome compliment? I replied that I only wished it were true; but that I feared I had no such luck! Upon which he told me to go to the Devil—in a tone which implied that he did n't much care if you went with me."

Nora listened to this speech in sceptical silence. "Where is Roger?" she asked at last.

Fenton shot her a glance of harsh mistrust. "Where is he? What do you want to know that for?"

"Where is he, please?" she simply repeated. And then, suddenly, she wondered how and where it was the two men had happened to meet. "Where did you find him?" she went on. "How did it happen?"

Fenton drained his cup of tea at one long gulp before he answered. "My dear Nora," he said, "it 's all very well to be modest, it 's all very well to be proud; but take care you 're not ungrateful! I went purposely to look him up. I was convinced he would have followed you,—as I supposed, to beg and beg and beg again. I wanted to say to him, 'She 's safe, she 's happy, she 's in the best hands. Don't waste your time, your words, your hopes. Give her rope. Go quietly home and leave things to me. If she turns homesick, I 'll let you know.' You see I 'm frank, Nora; that 's what I meant to say. But I was received with this broadside. I found a perfect bluster of injured vanity. 'You 're her lover, she 's your mistress, and be d—d to both of you!' "

That George lied Nora did not distinctly say to herself, for she lacked practice in this range of incrimination. But she as little said to herself that this could be the truth. "I 'm not ungrateful," she answered, firmly. "But where was it?"

At this, George pushed back his chair. "Where—where? Don't you believe me? Do you want to go and ask him if it 's true? What are you, anyway? Nora, who are you, where are you? Have you put yourself into my hands or not?" A certain manly indignation was now kindled in his breast; he was equally angry with Roger, with Nora, and with himself; fate had offered him an overdose of contumely, and he felt a reckless, savage impulse to wring from the occasion that compliment to his force which had been so rudely denied to his delicacy. "Are you using me simply as a vulgar tool? Don't you care for me the least little bit? Let me suggest that for a girl in your—your ambiguous position, you are too proud, by several shades. Don't go back to Roger in a hurry! You 're not the unspotted maiden you were but two short days ago. Who am I, what am I, to the people whose opinion you care for? A very low fellow, madam; and yet with me you 've gone far to cast your lot. If you 're not prepared to do more, you should have done less. Nora, Nora," he went on, breaking into a vein none the less revolting for being more ardent, "I confess I don't understand you! But the more you puzzle me the more you fascinate me; and the less you like me the more I love you. What has there been, anyway, between you and Lawrence? Hang me if I can understand! Are you an angel of purity, or are you the most audacious of flirts?"

She had risen before he had gone far. "Spare me," she said, "the necessity of hearing your opinions or answering your questions. Be a gentleman! Tell me, I once more beg of you, where Roger is to be found?"

"Be a gentleman!" was a galling touch. He had gone too

far to be a gentleman; but in so far as a man means a bully,
he might still be a man. He placed himself before the door.
"I refuse the information," he said. "I don't mean to have
been played with, to have been buffeted hither by Roger and
thither by you! I mean to make something out of all this. I
mean to request you to remain quietly in this room. Mrs.
Paul will keep you company. You did n't treat her over-well,
yesterday; but, in her way, she 's quite as strong as you.
Meanwhile I shall go to our friend. 'She 's locked up tight,'
I 'll say; 'she 's as good as in jail. Give me five thousand dollars
and I 'll let her out.' Of course he 'll drop a hint of the law.
'O, the law! not so fast. Two can play at that game. Go to a
magistrate and present your case. I 'll go straight to the 'Her-
ald' office and demand a special reporter and the very biggest
headings. That will rather take the bloom off your meeting.'
The public don't mind details, Nora; it looks at things in the
gross; and the gross here *is* gross, for *you*! It won't hurt me!"

"Heaven forgive you!" murmured Nora, for all response to
this explosion. It made a hideous whirl about her; but she felt
that to advance in the face of it was her best safety. It sickened rather than frightened her. She went to the door. "Let
me pass!" she said.

Fenton stood motionless, leaning his head against the door,
with his eyes closed. She faced him a moment, looking at him
intently. He seemed hideous. "Coward!" she cried. He
opened his eyes at the sound; for an instant they met hers;
then a burning blush blazed out strangely on his dead complexion; he strode past her, dropped into a chair and buried
his face in his hands. "O God!" he cried. "I 'm an ass!"

Nora made it the work of a single moment to reach her
own room and fling on her bonnet and shawl, of another to
descend to the hall door. Once in the street, she never
stopped running till she had turned a corner and put the
house out of sight. She went far, hurried along by the ecstasy
of relief and escape, and it was some time before she perceived that this was but half the question, and that she was
now quite without refuge. Thrusting her hand into her
pocket to feel for her purse, she found that she had left it in
her room. Stunned and sickened as she was already, it can
hardly be said that the discovery added to her grief. She was

being precipitated toward a great decision; sooner or later made little difference. The thought of seeing Hubert Lawrence now filled her soul. That, after what had passed between them, she should so sorely need help, and yet not turn to him, seemed as great an outrage against his professions as it was an impossibility to her own heart. Reserve, prudence, mistrust, had melted away; she was conscious only of her trouble, of his ardor, and of their nearness. His address she well remembered, and she neither paused nor faltered. To say even that she reflected would be to speak amiss, for her longing and her haste were one. Between them both, you may believe, it was with a beating heart that she reached his door. The servant admitted her without visible surprise (for Nora wore, as she conceived, the air of some needy parishioner), and ushered her into the little sitting-room which, with an adjoining chamber, constituted his apartments. As she crossed the threshold, she perceived, with something of regret and relief, that he was not alone. He was sitting somewhat stiffly, with folded arms, facing the window, near which, before an easel, stood a long-haired gentleman of foreign and artistic aspect, giving the finishing touches to a portrait in crayons. Hubert was in position for a likeness of his handsome face. When Nora appeared, his handsome face remained for a moment a blank; the next it turned most eloquently pale. "Miss Lambert!" he cried.

There was such a tremor in his voice that Nora felt that, for the moment, she must have self-possession for both. "I interrupt you," she said, with excessive deference.

"We are just finishing!" Hubert answered. "It 's my portrait, you see. You must look at it." The artist made way for her before the easel, laid down his implements, and took up his hat and gloves. She looked mechanically at the picture, while Hubert accompanied him to the door, and they talked awhile about another sitting and about a frame which was to be sent home. The portrait was clever, but superficial; better looking at once, and worse looking than Hubert,—elegant, effeminate, and unreal. An impulse of wonder passed through her mind that she should happen just then to find him engaged in this odd self-reproduction. It was a different Hubert that turned and faced her as the door closed behind his com-

panion, the real Hubert, with a vengeance! He had gained
time; but surprise, admiration, conjecture, a broad hint of dismay, wrought bright confusion on his brow. Nora had
dropped into the chair vacated by the artist; and as she sat
there with clasped hands, she felt the young man reading the
riddle of her shabby dress and her excited face. For him, too,
she was the real Nora. Dismay began to prevail in his questioning eyes. He advanced, pushed towards her the chair in
which he had been posturing, and, as he seated himself, made
a half-movement to offer his hand; but before she could take
it, he had begun to play with his watch-chain. "Nora," he
asked, "what is it?"

What was it, indeed? What was her errand, and in what
words could it be told? An utter weakness had taken possession of her, a sense of having reached the goal of her journey,
the term of her strength. She dropped her eyes on her shabby
skirt, and passed her hand over it with a gesture of eloquent
simplicity. "I 've left Roger," she said.

Hubert made no answer, but his silence somehow seemed
to fill the room. He sunk back in his chair, still looking at her
with startled eyes. The fact intimidated him; he was amazed
and confused; yet he felt he must say something, and in his
confusion he uttered a gross absurdity: "Ah, with his consent?"

The sound of his voice was so grateful to her that, at first,
she hardly heeded his words. "I 'm alone," she added, "I 'm
free." It was after she had spoken, as she saw him, growing,
to his own sense, infinitely small in the large confidence of
her gaze, rise in a perfect agony of impotence and stand before her, stupidly staring, that she felt he had neither taken
her hand, nor dropped at her feet, nor divinely guessed her
trouble; that, in fact, his very silence was a summons to tell
her story and to justify herself. Her presence there was either
a rapture or a shame. Nora felt as if she had taken a jump,
and was learning in mid-air that the distance was tenfold what
she had imagined. It is strange how the hinging point of great
emotions may rest on an instant of time. These instants, however, seem as ages, viewed from within; and in such a rever-
berating moment Nora felt the spiritual substructure of a
passion melting from beneath her feet, crumbling and crash-

ing into the gulf on whose edge she stood. But her shame at
least should be brief. She rose and bridged this dizzy chasm
with some tragic counterfeit of a smile. "I 've come—I 've
come—" she began and faltered. It was a vast pity some great
actress had not been there to note upon the tablets of her art
the light, all-eloquent tremor of tone with which she trans-
posed her embarrassment into the petition, "Could you lend
me a little money?"

Hubert was simply afraid of her. At his freest and bravest,
he would have shrunk from being thus peremptorily brought
to the point; and as matters stood, he felt all the more miserably paralyzed. For him, too, this was a vital moment. All his
falsity, all his levity, all his egotism and sophism, seemed to
crowd upon him and accuse him in deafening chorus; he
seemed, under some glaring blue sky, to stand in the public
stocks for all his pleasant sins. It was with a vast sense of relief
that he heard her ask this simple favor. Money? Would
money buy his release? He took out his purse and grasped a
roll of bills; then suddenly he was overwhelmed by a sense of
his cruelty. He flung the thing on the floor and passed his
hands over his face. "Nora, Nora," he cried, "say it outright;
I disappoint you!"

He had become, in the brief space of a moment, the man
she once had loved; but if he was no longer the rose, he stood
too near it to be wantonly bruised. Men and women alike
need in some degree to respect those they have suffered to
wrong them. She stooped and picked up the porte-monnaie,
like a beggar-maid in a ballad. "A very little will do," she said.
"In a day or two I hope to be independent."

"Tell me at least what has happened!" he cried.

She hesitated a moment. "Roger has asked me to be his
wife." Hubert's head swam with the vision of all that this
simple statement embodied and implied. "I refused," Nora
added, "and, having refused, I was unwilling to live any
longer on his—on his—" Her speech at the last word melted
into silence, and she seemed to fall a-musing. But in an instant she recovered herself. "I remember your once saying
that you would have liked to see me poor and homeless. Here
I am! You ought at least," she added with a laugh, "to pay
for the exhibition!"

Hubert abruptly drew out his watch. "I expect here this moment," he said, "a young lady of whom you may have heard. She is to come and see my portrait. I 'm engaged to her. I was engaged to her five months ago. She 's rich, pretty, charming. Say but a single word, that you don't despise me, that you forgive me, and I 'll give her up, now, here, forever, and be anything you 'll take me for,—your husband, your friend, your slave!" To have been able to make this speech gave Hubert immense relief. He felt almost himself again.

Nora fixed her eyes on him, with a kind of unfathomable gentleness. "You 're engaged, you *were* engaged? How strangely you talk about giving up! Give her my compliments!" It seemed, however, that Nora was to have the chance of offering them personally. The door was thrown open and admitted two ladies whom Nora vaguely remembered to have seen. In a moment she recognized them as the persons whom, on the evening she had gone to hear Hubert preach, he had left her, after the sermon, to conduct to their carriage. The younger one was decidedly pretty, in spite of a nose a trifle too aquiline. A pair of imperious dark eyes, as bright as the diamond which glittered in each of her ears, and a nervous capricious rapidity of motion and gesture, gave her an air of girlish *brusquerie*, which was by no means without charm. Her mother's aspect, however, testified to its being as well to enjoy this charm at a distance. She was a stout, coarse-featured, good-natured woman, with a jaded, submissive expression, and seemed to proclaim by a certain bulky languor, as she followed in her daughter's wake, the subserviency of matter to mind. Both ladies were dressed to the utmost limits of the occasion, and savored potently of New York. They came into the room staring frankly at Nora, and overlooking Hubert with gracious implication of his being already one of the family. The situation was a trying one, but he faced it as he might.

"This is Miss Lambert," he said, gravely; and then with an effort to conjure away confusion with a jest, waving his hand toward his portrait, "This is the Rev. Hubert Lawrence!"

The elder lady moved toward the picture, but the other came straight to Nora. "I 've seen you before!" she cried defiantly, and with defiance in her fine eyes. "And I 've heard of

you too! Yes, you 're certainly very handsome. But pray, what
are you doing here?"

"My dear child!" said Hubert, imploringly, and with a
burning side-glance at Nora. If he had been in the pillory
before, it was not till now that the rain of missiles had begun.

"My dear Hubert," said the young lady, "what is she doing
here? I have a right to know. Have you come running after
him even here? You 're a wicked girl. You 've done me a
wrong. You 've tried to turn him away from me. You kept
him in Boston for weeks, when he ought to have been here;
when I was writing to him day after day to come. I heard all
about it! I don't know what 's the matter with you. I thought
you were so very well off! You look very poor and unhappy,
but I must say what I think!"

"My own darling, be reasonable!" murmured her mother.
"Come and look at this beautiful picture. There 's no deceit
on *that* brow!"

Nora smiled charitably. "Don't attack me," she said. "If I
ever wronged you, I was quite unconscious of it, and I beg
your pardon now."

"Nora," murmured Hubert, piteously, "spare me!"

"Ah, does he call you Nora?" cried the young lady. "The
harm 's done, madam! He 'll never be what he was. You 've
changed, Hubert!" And she turned passionately on her *fiancé*.
"You know you are! You talk to me, but you think of her.
And what is the meaning of this visit? You 're both vastly
excited; what have you been talking about?"

"Mr. Lawrence has been telling me about you," said Nora;
"how pretty, how charming, how gentle you are!"

"I 'm not gentle!" cried the other. "You 're laughing at me!
Was it to talk about my prettiness you came here? Do you go
about alone, this way? I never heard of such a thing. You 're
shameless! do you know that? But I 'm very glad of it; because once you 've done this for him, he 'll not care for you.
That 's the way with men. And I 'm not pretty either, not as
you are! You 're pale and tired; you 've got a horrid dress and
shawl, and yet you 're beautiful! Is that the way I must look
to please you?" she demanded, turning back to Hubert.

Hubert, during this spiteful *tirade*, had stood looking as

dark as thunder, and at this point he broke out fiercely, "Good God, Amy! hold your tongue. I command you."

Nora, gathering her shawl together, gave Hubert a glance. "She loves you," she said, softly.

Amy stared a moment at this vehement adjuration; then she melted into a smile and turned in ecstasy to her mother. "Good, good!" she cried. "That 's how I like him. I shall have my husband yet."

Nora left the room; and, in spite of her gesture of earnest deprecation, Hubert followed her down stairs to the street door. "Where are you going?" he asked in a whisper. "With whom are you staying?"

"I 'm alone," said Nora.

"Alone in this great city? Nora, I *will* do something for you."

"Hubert," she said, "I never in my life needed help less than at this moment. Farewell." He fancied for an instant that she was going to offer him her hand, but she only motioned him to open the door. He did so and she passed out.

She stood there on the pavement, strangely, almost absurdly, free and light of spirit. She knew neither whither she should turn nor what she should do, yet the fears which had haunted her for a whole day and night had vanished. The sky was blazing blue overhead; the opposite side of the street was all in sun; she hailed the joyous brightness of the day with a kind of answering joy. She seemed to be in the secret of the universe. A nursery-maid came along, pushing a baby in a perambulator. She stooped and greeted the child, and talked pretty nonsense to it with a fervor which left the young woman staring. Nurse and child went their way, and Nora lingered, looking up and down the empty street. Suddenly a gentleman turned into it from the cross-street above. He was walking fast; he had his hat in his hand, and with his other hand he was passing his handkerchief over his forehead. As she stood and watched him draw near, down the bright vista of the street, there came upon her a singular and altogether nameless sensation, strangely similar to one she had felt a couple of years before, when a physician had given her a dose of ether. The gentleman, she perceived, was Roger; but the

short interval of space and time which separated them seemed
to expand into a throbbing immensity and eternity. She
seemed to be watching him for an age, and, as she did so, to
be swinging through the whole circle of emotion and the full
realization of being. Yes, she was in the secret of the universe,
and the secret of the universe was, that Roger was the only
man in it who had a heart. Suddenly she felt a palpable grasp.
Roger stood before her, and had taken her hand. For a moment he said nothing; but the touch of his hand spoke loud.
They stood for an instant scanning the change in each other's
faces. "Where are you going?" said Roger, at last, imploringly.

Nora read silently in his haggard furrows the whole record
of his passion and grief. It is a strange truth that they seemed
the most beautiful things she had ever looked upon; the sight
of them was delicious. They seemed to whisper louder and
louder that secret about Roger's heart.

Nora collected herself as solemnly as one on a death-bed
making a will; but Roger was still in miserable doubt and
dread. "I 've followed you," he said, "in spite of that request
in your letter."

"Have you got my letter?" Nora asked.

"It was the only thing you had left me," he said, and drew
it, creased and crumpled, out of his pocket.

She took it from him and tore it slowly into a dozen pieces,
never taking her eyes off his own. "Don't try and forget that
I wrote it," she said. "My destroying it now means more than
that would have meant."

"What does it mean, Nora?" he asked, in hardly audible
tones.

"It means that I 'm a wiser girl to-day than *then*. I know
myself better, I know you better. O Roger!" she cried, "it
means everything!"

He passed her hand through his arm and held it there
against his heart, while he stood looking hard at the pavement, as if to steady himself amid this great convulsion of
things. Then raising his head, "Come," he said; "come!"

But she detained him, laying her other hand on his arm.
"No; you must understand first. If I 'm wiser now, I 've learnt
wisdom at my cost. I 'm not the girl you proposed to on

Sunday. I feel—I feel *dishonored*!" she said, uttering the word with a vehemence which stirred his soul to its depths.

"My own poor child!" he murmured, staring.

"There 's a young girl in that house," Nora went on, "who will tell you that I 'm shameless!"

"What house? what young girl?"

"I don't know her name. Hubert is engaged to her."

Roger gave a glance at the house behind them, as if to fling defiance and oblivion upon all that it suggested and contained. Then turning to Nora with a smile of consummate tenderness: "My dear Nora, what have *we* to do with Hubert's young girls?"

Roger, the reader will admit, was on a level with the occasion,—as with every other occasion which subsequently presented itself.

Mrs. Keith and Mrs. Lawrence are very good friends. On being complimented on possessing the confidence of so charming a woman as Mrs. Lawrence, Mrs. Keith has been known to say, opening and shutting her fan, "The fact is, Nora is under a very peculiar obligation to me." Another of Mrs. Keith's sayings may perhaps be appositely retailed,—her answer, one evening, to an inquiry as to Roger's age: "Twenty-five—*seconde jeunesse*." Hubert Lawrence, on the other hand, has already begun to pass for an elderly man. Mrs. Hubert, however, preserves the balance. She is wonderfully fresh, and, with time, has grown stout, like her mother, though she has nothing of the jaded look of that excellent lady.

RODERICK HUDSON

Contents

I

Rowland

MALLET HAD MADE his arrangements to sail for Europe
on the first of September, and having in the interval a
fortnight to spare, he determined to spend it with his cousin
Cecilia, the widow of a nephew of his father. He was urged
by the reflection that an affectionate farewell might help to
exonerate him from the charge of neglect frequently preferred
by this lady. It was not that the young man disliked her; on
the contrary, he regarded her with a tender admiration, and
he had not forgotten how, when his cousin had brought her
home on her marriage, he had seemed to feel the upward
sweep of the empty bough from which the golden fruit had
been plucked, and had then and there accepted the prospect
of bachelorhood. The truth was, that, as it will be part of the
entertainment of this narrative to exhibit, Rowland Mallet
had an uncomfortably sensitive conscience, and that, in spite
of the seeming paradox, his visits to Cecilia were rare because
she and her misfortunes were often uppermost in it. Her misfortunes were three in number: first, she had lost her husband; second, she had lost her money (or the greater part of
it); and third, she lived at Northampton, Massachusetts. Mallet's compassion was really wasted, because Cecilia was a very
clever woman, and a most skillful counter-plotter to adversity.
She had made herself a charming home, her economies were
not obtrusive, and there was always a cheerful flutter in the
folds of her crape. It was the consciousness of all this that
puzzled Mallet whenever he felt tempted to put in his oar. He
had money and he had time, but he never could decide just
how to place these gifts gracefully at Cecilia's service. He no
longer felt like marrying her: in these eight years that fancy
had died a natural death. And yet her extreme cleverness
seemed somehow to make charity difficult and patronage impossible. He would rather chop off his hand than offer her a
check, a piece of useful furniture, or a black silk dress; and
yet there was some sadness in seeing such a bright, proud
woman living in such a small, dull way. Cecilia had, more-

over, a turn for sarcasm, and her smile, which was her pretty feature, was never so pretty as when her sprightly phrase had a lurking scratch in it. Rowland remembered that, for him, she was all smiles, and suspected, awkwardly, that he ministered not a little to her sense of the irony of things. And in truth, with his means, his leisure, and his opportunities, what had he done? He had an unaffected suspicion of his uselessness. Cecilia, meanwhile, cut out her own dresses, and was personally giving her little girl the education of a princess.

This time, however, he presented himself bravely enough; for in the way of activity it was something definite, at least, to be going to Europe and to be meaning to spend the winter in Rome. Cecilia met him in the early dusk at the gate of her little garden, amid a studied combination of floral perfumes. A rosy widow of twenty-eight, half cousin, half hostess, doing the honors of an odorous cottage on a midsummer evening, was a phenomenon to which the young man's imagination was able to do ample justice. Cecilia was always gracious, but this evening she was almost joyous. She was in a happy mood, and Mallet imagined there was a private reason for it—a reason quite distinct from her pleasure in receiving her honored kinsman. The next day he flattered himself he was on the way to discover it.

For the present, after tea, as they sat on the rose-framed porch, while Rowland held his younger cousin between his knees, and she, enjoying her situation, listened timorously for the stroke of bedtime, Cecilia insisted on talking more about her visitor than about herself.

"What is it you mean to do in Europe?" she asked, lightly, giving a turn to the frill of her sleeve—just such a turn as seemed to Mallet to bring out all the latent difficulties of the question.

"Why, very much what I do here," he answered. "No great harm."

"Is it true," Cecilia asked, "that here you do no great harm? Is not a man like you doing harm when he is not doing positive good?"

"Your compliment is ambiguous," said Rowland.

"No," answered the widow, "you know what I think of you. You have a particular aptitude for beneficence. You have it in the first place in your character. You are a benevolent person. Ask Bessie if you don't hold her more gently and comfortably than any of her other admirers."

"He holds me more comfortably than Mr. Hudson," Bessie declared, roundly.

Rowland, not knowing Mr. Hudson, could but half appreciate the eulogy, and Cecilia went on to develop her idea. "Your circumstances, in the second place, suggest the idea of social usefulness. You are intelligent, you are well-informed, and your charity, if one may call it charity, would be discriminating. You are rich and unoccupied, so that it might be abundant. Therefore, I say, you are a person to do something on a large scale. Bestir yourself, dear Rowland, or we may be taught to think that virtue herself is setting a bad example."

"Heaven forbid," cried Rowland, "that I should set the examples of virtue! I am quite willing to follow them, however, and if I don't do something on the grand scale, it is that my genius is altogether imitative, and that I have not recently encountered any very striking models of grandeur. Pray, what shall I do? Found an orphan asylum, or build a dormitory for Harvard College? I am not rich enough to do either in an ideally handsome way, and I confess that, yet awhile, I feel too young to strike my *grand coup*. I am holding myself ready for inspiration. I am waiting till something takes my fancy irresistibly. If inspiration comes at forty, it will be a hundred pities to have tied up my money-bag at thirty."

"Well, I give you till forty," said Cecilia. "It 's only a word to the wise, a notification that you are expected not to run your course without having done something handsome for your fellow-men."

Nine o'clock sounded, and Bessie, with each stroke, courted a closer embrace. But a single winged word from her mother overleaped her successive intrenchments. She turned and kissed her cousin, and deposited an irrepressible tear on his moustache. Then she went and said her prayers to her mother: it was evident she was being admirably brought up. Rowland, with the permission of his hostess, lighted a cigar and puffed it awhile in silence. Cecilia's interest in his career seemed very agreeable. That Mallet was without vanity I by no means intend to affirm; but there had been times when, seeing him accept, hardly less deferentially, advice even more peremptory than the widow's, you might have asked yourself what had become of his vanity. Now, in the sweet-smelling starlight, he felt gently wooed to egotism. There was a project connected with his going abroad which it was on his tongue's end to communicate. It had no relation to hospitals or dormitories, and yet it would have sounded very generous. But it was not because it would have sounded generous that poor Mallet at last puffed it away in the fumes of his cigar. Useful though it might be, it expressed most imperfectly the young man's own personal conception of usefulness. He was extremely fond of all the arts, and he had an almost passionate enjoyment of pictures. He had seen many, and he judged them sagaciously. It had occurred to him some time before that it would be the work of a good citizen to go abroad and with all expedition and secrecy purchase certain valuable specimens of the Dutch and Italian schools as to which he had received private proposals, and then present his treasures out of hand to an American city, not unknown to æsthetic fame, in which at that time there prevailed a good deal of fruitless aspiration toward an art-museum. He had seen himself in imagination, more than once, in some mouldy old saloon of a Florentine palace, turning toward the deep embrasure of the window some scarcely-faded Ghirlandaio or Botticelli, while a host in reduced circumstances pointed out the lovely drawing of a hand. But he imparted none of these visions to Cecilia, and he suddenly swept them away with the declaration that he was of course an idle, useless creature, and that he would probably be even more so in Europe than at home. "The only thing is," he said, "that there I shall *seem* to be doing something. I shall be better entertained, and shall be therefore, I suppose, in a better humor with life. You may say that that is just the humor a useless man should keep out of. He should cultivate discontentment. I did a good many things when I was in Europe before, but I did not spend a winter in Rome. Every one assures me that this is a peculiar refinement of bliss; most people talk about Rome in the same way. It is evidently only a sort of idealized form of loafing: a passive life in Rome, thanks to the number and the quality of one's impressions, takes on a very respectable likeness to activity. It is still lotus-eating, only you sit down at table, and the lotuses are served up on rococo china. It 's all very well, but I have a distinct prevision of this—that if Roman life does n't do something substantial to make you happier, it increases tenfold your liability to moral misery. It seems to me a rash thing for a sensitive soul deliberately to cultivate its sensibilities by rambling too often among the ruins of the Palatine, or riding too often in the shadow of the aqueducts. In such recreations the chords of feeling grow tense, and after-life, to spare your intellectual nerves, must play upon them with a touch as dainty as the tread of Mignon when she danced her egg-dance."

"I should have said, my dear Rowland," said Cecilia, with a laugh, "that your nerves were tough, that your eggs were hard!"

"That being stupid, you mean, I might be happy? Upon my word I am not. I am clever enough to want more than I 've got. I am tired of myself, my own thoughts, my own affairs, my own eternal company. True happiness, we are told, consists in getting out of one's self; but the point is not only to get out—you must stay out; and to stay out you must have some absorbing errand. Unfortunately, I 've got no errand, and nobody will trust me with one. I want to care for something, or for some one. And I want to care with a certain ardor; even, if you can believe it, with a certain passion. I can't just now feel ardent and passionate about a hospital or a dormitory. Do you know I sometimes think that I 'm a man of genius, half finished? The genius has been left out, the faculty of expression is wanting; but the need for expression remains, and I spend my days groping for the latch of a closed door."

"What an immense number of words," said Cecilia after a pause, "to say you want to fall in love! I 've no doubt you have as good a genius for that as any one, if you would only trust it."

"Of course I 've thought of that, and I assure you I hold myself ready. But, evidently, I 'm not inflammable. Is there in Northampton some perfect epitome of the graces?"

"Of the graces?" said Cecilia, raising her eyebrows and suppressing too distinct a consciousness of being herself a rosy embodiment of several. "The household virtues are better represented. There are some excellent girls, and there are two or three very pretty ones. I will have them here, one by one, to tea, if you like."

"I should particularly like it; especially as I should give you a chance to see, by the profundity of my attention, that if I am not happy, it 's not for want of taking pains."

Cecilia was silent a moment; and then, "On the whole," she resumed, "I don't think there are any worth asking. There are none so very pretty, none so very pleasing."

"Are you very sure?" asked the young man, rising and throwing away his cigar-end.

"Upon my word," cried Cecilia, "one would suppose I wished to keep you for myself. Of course I am sure! But as the penalty of your insinuations, I shall invite the plainest and prosiest damsel that can be found, and leave you alone with her."

Rowland smiled. "Even against her," he said, "I should be sorry to conclude until I had given her my respectful attention."

This little profession of ideal chivalry (which closed the conversation) was not quite so fanciful on Mallet's lips as it would have been on those of many another man; as a rapid glance at his antecedents may help to make the reader perceive. His life had been a singular mixture of the rough and the smooth. He had sprung from a rigid Puritan stock, and had been brought up to think much more intently of the duties of this life than of its privileges and pleasures. His progenitors had submitted in the matter of dogmatic theology to the relaxing influences of recent years; but if Rowland's youthful consciousness was not chilled by the menace of long punishment for brief transgression, he had at least been made to feel that there ran through all things a strain of right and of wrong, as different, after all, in their complexions, as the texture, to the spiritual sense, of Sundays and week-days. His father was a chip of the primal Puritan block, a man with an icy smile and a stony frown. He had always bestowed on his son, on principle, more frowns than smiles, and if the lad had not been turned to stone himself, it was because nature had blessed him, inwardly, with a well of vivifying waters. Mrs.

Mallet had been a Miss Rowland, the daughter of a retired sea-captain, once famous on the ships that sailed from Salem and Newburyport. He had brought to port many a cargo which crowned the edifice of fortunes already almost colossal, but he had also done a little sagacious trading on his own account, and he was able to retire, prematurely for so sea-worthy a maritime organism, upon a pension of his own providing. He was to be seen for a year on the Salem wharves, smoking the best tobacco and eying the seaward horizon with an inveteracy which superficial minds interpreted as a sign of repentance. At last, one evening, he disappeared beneath it, as he had often done before; this time, however, not as a commissioned navigator, but simply as an amateur of an observing turn likely to prove oppressive to the officer in command of the vessel. Five months later his place at home knew him again, and made the acquaintance also of a handsome, blonde young woman, of redundant contours, speaking a foreign tongue. The foreign tongue proved, after much conflicting research, to be the idiom of Amsterdam, and the young woman, which was stranger still, to be Captain Rowland's wife. Why he had gone forth so suddenly across the seas to marry her, what had happened between them before, and whether—though it was of questionable propriety for a good citizen to espouse a young person of mysterious origin, who did her hair in fantastically elaborate plaits, and in whose appearance "figure" enjoyed such striking predominance—he would not have had a heavy weight on his conscience if he had remained an irresponsible bachelor; these questions and many others, bearing with varying degrees of immediacy on the subject, were much propounded but scantily answered, and this history need not be charged with resolving them. Mrs. Rowland, for so handsome a woman, proved a tranquil neighbor and an excellent housewife. Her extremely fresh complexion, however, was always suffused with an air of apathetic homesickness, and she played her part in American society chiefly by having the little squares of brick pavement in front of her dwelling scoured and polished as nearly as possible into the likeness of Dutch tiles. Rowland Mallet remembered having seen her, as a child—an immensely stout, white-faced lady, wearing a high cap of very stiff tulle, speak-

ing English with a formidable accent, and suffering from
dropsy. Captain Rowland was a little bronzed and wizened
man, with eccentric opinions. He advocated the creation of a
public promenade along the sea, with arbors and little green
tables for the consumption of beer, and a platform, surrounded by Chinese lanterns, for dancing. He especially desired the town library to be opened on Sundays, though, as
he never entered it on week-days, it was easy to turn the
proposition into ridicule. If, therefore, Mrs. Mallet was a
woman of an exquisite moral tone, it was not that she had
inherited her temper from an ancestry with a turn for casu-
istry. Jonas Mallet, at the time of his marriage, was conducting
with silent shrewdness a small, unpromising business. Both
his shrewdness and his silence increased with his years, and at
the close of his life he was an extremely well-dressed, well-
brushed gentleman, with a frigid gray eye, who said little to
anybody, but of whom everybody said that he had a very
handsome fortune. He was not a sentimental father, and the
roughness I just now spoke of in Rowland's life dated from
his early boyhood. Mr. Mallet, whenever he looked at his son,
felt extreme compunction at having made a fortune. He remembered that the fruit had not dropped ripe from the tree
into his own mouth, and determined it should be no fault of
his if the boy was corrupted by luxury. Rowland, therefore,
except for a good deal of expensive instruction in foreign
tongues and abstruse sciences, received the education of a
poor man's son. His fare was plain, his temper familiar with
the discipline of patched trousers, and his habits marked by
an exaggerated simplicity which it really cost a good deal of
money to preserve unbroken. He was kept in the country for
months together, in the midst of servants who had strict in-
junctions to see that he suffered no serious harm, but were as
strictly forbidden to wait upon him. As no school could be
found conducted on principles sufficiently rigorous, he was
attended at home by a master who set a high price on the
understanding that he was to illustrate the beauty of absti-
nence not only by precept but by example. Rowland passed
for a child of ordinary parts, and certainly, during his younger
years, was an excellent imitation of a boy who had inherited
nothing whatever that was to make life easy. He was passive,

pliable, frank, extremely slow at his books, and inordinately fond of trout-fishing. His hair, a memento of his Dutch ancestry, was of the fairest shade of yellow, his complexion absurdly rosy, and his measurement around the waist, when he was about ten years old, quite alarmingly large. This, however, was but an episode in his growth; he became afterwards a fresh-colored, yellow-bearded man, but he was never accused of anything worse than a tendency to corpulence. He emerged from childhood a simple, wholesome, round-eyed lad, with no suspicion that a less roundabout course might have been taken to make him happy, but with a vague sense that his young experience was not a fair sample of human freedom, and that he was to make a great many discoveries. When he was about fifteen, he achieved a momentous one. He ascertained that his mother was a saint. She had always been a very distinct presence in his life, but so ineffably gentle a one that his sense was fully opened to it only by the danger of losing her. She had an illness which for many months was liable at any moment to terminate fatally, and during her long-arrested convalescence she removed the mask which she had worn for years by her husband's order. Rowland spent his days at her side and felt before long as if he had made a new friend. All his impressions at this period were commented and interpreted at leisure in the future, and it was only then that he understood that his mother had been for fifteen years a perfectly unhappy woman. Her marriage had been an immitigable error which she had spent her life in trying to look straight in the face. She found nothing to oppose to her husband's will of steel but the appearance of absolute compliance; her spirit sank, and she lived for a while in a sort of helpless moral torpor. But at last, as her child emerged from babyhood, she began to feel a certain charm in patience, to discover the uses of ingenuity, and to learn that, somehow or other, one can always arrange one's life. She cultivated from this time forward a little private plot of sentiment, and it was of this secluded precinct that, before her death, she gave her son the key. Rowland's allowance at college was barely sufficient to maintain him decently, and as soon as he graduated, he was taken into his father's counting-house, to do small drudgery on a proportionate salary. For three years he earned his living as regularly as the obscure functionary in fustian who swept the office. Mr. Mallet was consistent, but the perfection of his consistency was known only on his death. He left but a third of his property to his son, and devoted the remainder to various public institutions and local charities. Rowland's third was an easy competence, and he never felt a moment's jealousy of his fellow-pensioners; but when one of the establishments which had figured most advantageously in his father's will bethought itself to affirm the existence of a later instrument, in which it had been still more handsomely treated, the young man felt a sudden passionate need to repel the claim by process of law. There was a lively tussle, but he gained his case; immediately after which he made, in another quarter, a donation of the contested sum. He cared nothing for the money, but he had felt an angry desire to protest against a destiny which seemed determined to be exclusively salutary. It seemed to him that he would bear a little spoiling. And yet he treated himself to a very modest quantity, and submitted without reserve to the great national discipline which began in 1861. When the Civil War broke out he immediately obtained a commission, and did his duty for three long years as a citizen soldier. His duty was obscure, but he never lost a certain private satisfaction in remembering that on two or three occasions it had been performed with something of an ideal precision. He had disentangled himself from business, and after the war he felt a profound disinclination to tie the knot again. He had no desire to make money, he had money enough; and although he knew, and was frequently reminded, that a young man is the better for a fixed occupation, he could discover no moral advantage in driving a lucrative trade. Yet few young men of means and leisure ever made less of a parade of idleness, and indeed idleness in any degree could hardly be laid at the door of a young man who took life in the serious, attentive, reasoning fashion of our friend. It often seemed to Mallet that he wholly lacked the prime requisite of a graceful *flâneur*— the simple, sensuous, confident relish of pleasure. He had frequent fits of extreme melancholy, in which he declared that he was neither fish nor flesh nor good red herring. He was neither an irresponsibly contemplative nature nor a sturdily practical one, and he was forever looking in vain for the uses of the things that please and the charm of the things that sustain. He was an awkward mixture of strong moral impulse and restless æsthetic curiosity, and yet he would have made a most ineffective reformer and a very indifferent artist. It seemed to him that the glow of happiness must be found either in action, of some immensely solid kind, on behalf of an idea, or in producing a masterpiece in one of the arts. Oftenest, perhaps, he wished he were a vigorous young man of genius, without a penny. As it was, he could only buy pictures, and not paint them; and in the way of action, he had to content himself with making a rule to render scrupulous moral justice to handsome examples of it in others. On the whole, he had an incorruptible modesty. With his blooming complexion and his serene gray eye, he felt the friction of existence more than was suspected; but he asked no allowance on grounds of temper, he assumed that fate had treated him inordinately well and that he had no excuse for taking an ill-natured view of life, and he undertook constantly to believe that all women were fair, all men were brave, and the world was a delightful place of sojourn, until the contrary had been distinctly proved.

*   *   *

Cecilia's blooming garden and shady porch had seemed so friendly to repose and a cigar, that she reproached him the next morning with indifference to her little parlor, not less, in its way, a monument to her ingenious taste. "And by the way," she added as he followed her in, "if I refused last night to show you a pretty girl, I can at least show you a pretty boy."

She threw open a window and pointed to a statuette which occupied the place of honor among the ornaments of the room. Rowland looked at it a moment and then turned to her with an exclamation of surprise. She gave him a rapid glance, perceived that her statuette was of altogether exceptional merit, and then smiled, knowingly, as if this had long been an agreeable certainty.

"Who did it? where did you get it?" Rowland demanded.

"Oh," said Cecilia, adjusting the light, "it 's a little thing of Mr. Hudson's."

"And who the deuce is Mr. Hudson?" asked Rowland. But he was absorbed; he lost her immediate reply. The statuette, in bronze, something less than two feet high, represented a naked youth drinking from a gourd. The attitude was perfectly simple. The lad was squarely planted on his feet, with his legs a little apart; his back was slightly hollowed, his head thrown back, and both hands raised to support the rustic cup. There was a loosened fillet of wild flowers about his head, and his eyes, under their drooped lids, looked straight into the cup. On the base was scratched the Greek word Δίψα, Thirst. The figure might have been some beautiful youth of ancient fable,—Hylas or Narcissus, Paris or Endymion. Its beauty was the beauty of natural movement; nothing had been sought to be represented but the perfection of an attitude. This had been most attentively studied, and it was exquisitely rendered. Rowland demanded more light, dropped his head on this side and that, uttered vague exclamations. He said to himself, as he had said more than once in the Louvre and the Vatican, "We ugly mortals, what beautiful creatures we are!" Nothing, in a long time, had given him so much pleasure. "Hudson—Hudson," he asked again; "who is Hudson?"

"A young man of this place," said Cecilia.

"A young man? How old?"

"I suppose he is three or four and twenty."

"Of this place, you say—of Northampton, Massachusetts?"

"He lives here, but he comes from Virginia."

"Is he a sculptor by profession?"

"He 's a law-student."

Rowland burst out laughing. "He has found something in Blackstone that I never did. He makes statues then simply for his pleasure?"

Cecilia, with a smile, gave a little toss of her head. "For mine!"

"I congratulate you," said Rowland. "I wonder whether he could be induced to do anything for me?"

"This was a matter of friendship. I saw the figure when he

had modeled it in clay, and of course greatly admired it. He said nothing at the time, but a week ago, on my birthday, he arrived in a buggy, with this. He had had it cast at the foundry at Chicopee; I believe it 's a beautiful piece of bronze. He begged me to accept."

"Upon my word," said Mallet, "he does things handsomely!" And he fell to admiring the statue again.

"So then," said Cecilia, "it 's very remarkable?"

"Why, my dear cousin," Rowland answered, "Mr. Hudson, of Virginia, is an extraordinary—" Then suddenly stopping: "Is he a great friend of yours?" he asked.

"A great friend?" and Cecilia hesitated. "I regard him as a child!"

"Well," said Rowland, "he 's a very clever child. Tell me something about him: I should like to see him."

Cecilia was obliged to go to her daughter's music-lesson, but she assured Rowland that she would arrange for him a meeting with the young sculptor. He was a frequent visitor, and as he had not called for some days it was likely he would come that evening. Rowland, left alone, examined the statuette at his leisure, and returned more than once during the day to take another look at it. He discovered its weak points, but it wore well. It had the stamp of genius. Rowland envied the happy youth who, in a New England village, without aid or encouragement, without models or resources, had found it so easy to produce a lovely work.

In the evening, as he was smoking his cigar on the veranda, a light, quick step pressed the gravel of the garden path, and in a moment a young man made his bow to Cecilia. It was rather a nod than a bow, and indicated either that he was an old friend, or that he was scantily versed in the usual social forms. Cecilia, who was sitting near the steps, pointed to a neighboring chair, but the young man seated himself abruptly on the floor at her feet, began to fan himself vigorously with his hat, and broke out into a lively objurgation upon the hot weather. "I 'm dripping wet!" he said, without ceremony.

"You walk too fast," said Cecilia. "You do everything too fast."

"I know it, I know it!" he cried, passing his hand through his abundant dark hair and making it stand out in a picturesque shock. "I can't be slow if I try. There 's something inside of me that drives me. A restless fiend!"

Cecilia gave a light laugh, and Rowland leaned forward in his hammock. He had placed himself in it at Bessie's request, and was playing that he was her baby and that she was rocking him to sleep. She sat beside him, swinging the hammock to and fro, and singing a lullaby. When he raised himself she pushed him back and said that the baby must finish its nap. "But I want to see the gentleman with the fiend inside of him," said Rowland.

"What is a fiend?" Bessie demanded. "It 's only Mr. Hudson."

"Very well, I want to see him."

"Oh, never mind him!" said Bessie, with the brevity of contempt.

"You speak as if you did n't like him."

"I don't!" Bessie affirmed, and put Rowland to bed again.

The hammock was swung at the end of the veranda, in the thickest shade of the vines, and this fragment of dialogue had passed unnoticed. Rowland submitted a while longer to be cradled, and contented himself with listening to Mr. Hudson's voice. It was a soft and not altogether masculine organ, and was pitched on this occasion in a somewhat plaintive and pettish key. The young man's mood seemed fretful; he complained of the heat, of the dust, of a shoe that hurt him, of having gone on an errand a mile to the other side of the town and found the person he was in search of had left Northampton an hour before.

"Won't you have a cup of tea?" Cecilia asked. "Perhaps that will restore your equanimity."

"Aye, by keeping me awake all night!" said Hudson. "At the best, it 's hard enough to go down to the office. With my nerves set on edge by a sleepless night, I should perforce stay at home and be brutal to my poor mother."

"Your mother is well, I hope."

"Oh, she 's as usual."

"And Miss Garland?"

"She 's as usual, too. Every one, everything, is as usual. Nothing ever happens, in this benighted town."

"I beg your pardon; things do happen, sometimes," said Cecilia. "Here is a dear cousin of mine arrived on purpose to congratulate you on your statuette." And she called to Rowland to come and be introduced to Mr. Hudson. The young man sprang up with alacrity, and Rowland, coming forward to shake hands, had a good look at him in the light projected from the parlor window. Something seemed to shine out of Hudson's face as a warning against a "compliment" of the idle, unpondered sort.

"Your statuette seems to me very good," Rowland said gravely. "It has given me extreme pleasure."

"And my cousin knows what is good," said Cecilia. "He 's a connoisseur."

Hudson smiled and stared. "A connoisseur?" he cried, laughing. "He 's the first I 've ever seen! Let me see what they look like;" and he drew Rowland nearer to the light. "Have they all such good heads as that? I should like to model yours."

"Pray do," said Cecilia. "It will keep him a while. He is running off to Europe."

"Ah, to Europe!" Hudson exclaimed with a melancholy cadence, as they sat down. "Happy man!"

But the note seemed to Rowland to be struck rather at random, for he perceived no echo of it in the boyish garrulity of his later talk. Hudson was a tall, slender young fellow, with a singularly mobile and intelligent face. Rowland was struck at first only with its responsive vivacity, but in a short time he perceived it was remarkably handsome. The features were admirably chiseled and finished, and a frank smile played over them as gracefully as a breeze among flowers. The fault of the young man's whole structure was an excessive want of breadth. The forehead, though it was high and rounded, was narrow; the jaw and the shoulders were narrow; and the result was an air of insufficient physical substance. But Mallet afterwards learned that this fair, slim youth could draw indefinitely upon a mysterious fund of nervous force, which outlasted and outwearied the endurance of many a sturdier temperament. And certainly there was life enough in his eye to furnish an immortality! It was a generous dark gray eye, in which there came and went a sort of kindling glow, which would have made a ruder visage striking, and which gave at times to Hudson's harmonious face an altogether extraordinary beauty. There was to Rowland's sympathetic sense a slightly pitiful disparity between the young sculptor's delicate countenance and the shabby gentility of his costume. He was dressed for a visit—a visit to a pretty woman. He was clad from head to foot in a white linen suit, which had never been remarkable for the felicity of its cut, and had now quite lost that crispness which garments of this complexion can as ill spare as the back-scene of a theatre the radiance of the footlights. He wore a vivid blue cravat, passed through a ring altogether too splendid to be valuable; he pulled and twisted, as he sat, a pair of yellow kid gloves; he emphasized his conversation with great dashes and flourishes of a light, silver-tipped walking-stick, and he kept constantly taking off and putting on one of those slouched sombreros which are the traditional property of the Virginian or Carolinian of romance. When this was on, he was very picturesque, in spite of his mock elegance; and when it was off, and he sat nursing it and turning it about and not knowing what to do with it, he could hardly be said to be awkward. He evidently had a natural relish for brilliant accessories, and appropriated what came to his hand. This was visible in his talk, which abounded in the florid and sonorous. He liked words with color in them.

Rowland, who was but a moderate talker, sat by in silence, while Cecilia, who had told him that she desired his opinion upon her friend, used a good deal of characteristic finesse in leading the young man to expose himself. She perfectly succeeded, and Hudson rattled away for an hour with a volubility in which boyish unconsciousness and manly shrewdness were singularly combined. He gave his opinion on twenty topics, he opened up an endless budget of local gossip, he described his repulsive routine at the office of Messrs. Striker and Spooner, counselors at law, and he gave with great felicity and gusto an account of the annual boat-race between Harvard and Yale, which he had lately witnessed at Worcester. He had looked at the straining oarsmen and the swaying crowd with the eye of the sculptor. Rowland was a good deal

amused and not a little interested. Whenever Hudson uttered
some peculiarly striking piece of youthful grandiloquence, Cecilia broke into a long, light, familiar laugh.

"What are you laughing at?" the young man then demanded. "Have I said anything so ridiculous?"

"Go on, go on," Cecilia replied. "You are too delicious!
Show Mr. Mallet how Mr. Striker read the Declaration of
Independence."

Hudson, like most men with a turn for the plastic arts, was
an excellent mimic, and he represented with a great deal of
humor the accent and attitude of a pompous country lawyer
sustaining the burden of this customary episode of our national festival. The sonorous twang, the see-saw gestures, the
odd pronunciation, were vividly depicted. But Cecilia's manner, and the young man's quick response, ruffled a little poor
Rowland's paternal conscience. He wondered whether his
cousin was not sacrificing the faculty of reverence in her clever
protégé to her need for amusement. Hudson made no serious
rejoinder to Rowland's compliment on his statuette until he
rose to go. Rowland wondered whether he had forgotten it,
and supposed that the oversight was a sign of the natural self-
sufficiency of genius. But Hudson stood a moment before he
said good night, twirled his sombrero, and hesitated for the
first time. He gave Rowland a clear, penetrating glance, and
then, with a wonderfully frank, appealing smile: "You really
meant," he asked, "what you said a while ago about that
thing of mine? It is good—essentially good?"

"I really meant it," said Rowland, laying a kindly hand on
his shoulder. "It is very good indeed. It is, as you say, essentially good. That is the beauty of it."

Hudson's eyes glowed and expanded; he looked at Rowland for some time in silence. "I have a notion you really
know," he said at last. "But if you don't, it does n't much
matter."

"My cousin asked me to-day," said Cecilia, "whether I supposed you knew yourself how good it is."

Hudson stared, blushing a little. "Perhaps not!" he cried.

"Very likely," said Mallet. "I read in a book the other day
that great talent in action—in fact the book said genius—is
a kind of somnambulism. The artist performs great feats, in a

dream. We must not wake him up, lest he should lose his balance."

"Oh, when he 's back in bed again!" Hudson answered with a laugh. "Yes, call it a dream. It was a very happy one!"

"Tell me this," said Rowland. "Did you mean anything by your young Water-drinker? Does he represent an idea? Is he a symbol?"

Hudson raised his eyebrows and gently scratched his head. "Why, he 's youth, you know; he 's innocence, he 's health, he 's strength, he 's curiosity. Yes, he 's a good many things."

"And is the cup also a symbol?"

"The cup is knowledge, pleasure, experience. Anything of that kind!"

"Well, he 's guzzling in earnest," said Rowland.

Hudson gave a vigorous nod. "Aye, poor fellow, he 's thirsty!" And on this he cried good night, and bounded down the garden path.

"Well, what do you make of him?" asked Cecilia, returning a short time afterwards from a visit of investigation as to the sufficiency of Bessie's bedclothes.

"I confess I like him," said Rowland. "He 's very immature,—but there 's stuff in him."

"He 's a strange being," said Cecilia, musingly.

"Who are his people? what has been his education?" Rowland asked.

"He has had no education, beyond what he has picked up, with little trouble, for himself. His mother is a widow, of a Massachusetts country family, a little timid, tremulous woman, who is always on pins and needles about her son. She had some property herself, and married a Virginian gentleman of good estates. He turned out, I believe, a very licentious personage, and made great havoc in their fortune. Everything, or almost everything, melted away, including Mr. Hudson himself. This is literally true, for he drank himself to death. Ten years ago his wife was left a widow, with scanty means and a couple of growing boys. She paid her husband's debts as best she could, and came to establish herself here, where by the death of a charitable relative she had inherited an old-fashioned ruinous house. Roderick, our friend, was her pride and joy, but Stephen, the elder, was her comfort and support. I remember him, later; he was an ugly, sturdy, practical lad, very different from his brother, and in his way, I imagine, a very fine fellow. When the war broke out he found that the New England blood ran thicker in his veins than the Virginian, and immediately obtained a commission. He fell in some Western battle and left his mother inconsolable. Roderick, however, has given her plenty to think about, and she has induced him, by some mysterious art, to abide, nominally at least, in a profession that he abhors, and for which he is about as fit, I should say, as I am to drive a locomotive. He grew up *à la grâce de Dieu*, and was horribly spoiled. Three or four years ago he graduated at a small college in this neighborhood, where I am afraid he had given a good deal more attention to novels and billiards than to mathematics and Greek. Since then he has been reading law, at the rate of a page a day. If he is ever admitted to practice I 'm afraid my friendship won't avail to make me give him my business. Good, bad, or indifferent, the boy is essentially an artist—an artist to his fingers' ends."

"Why, then," asked Rowland, "does n't he deliberately take up the chisel?"

"For several reasons. In the first place, I don't think he more than half suspects his talent. The flame is smouldering, but it is never fanned by the breath of criticism. He sees nothing, hears nothing, to help him to self-knowledge. He 's hopelessly discontented, but he does n't know where to look for help. Then his mother, as she one day confessed to me, has a holy horror of a profession which consists exclusively, as she supposes, in making figures of people without their clothes on. Sculpture, to her mind, is an insidious form of immorality, and for a young man of a passionate disposition she considers the law a much safer investment. Her father was a judge, she has two brothers at the bar, and her elder son had made a very promising beginning in the same line. She wishes the tradition to be perpetuated. I 'm pretty sure the law won't make Roderick's fortune, and I 'm afraid it will, in the long run, spoil his temper."

"What sort of a temper is it?"

"One to be trusted, on the whole. It is quick, but it is generous. I have known it to breathe flame and fury at ten o'clock in the evening, and soft, sweet music early on the morrow. It 's a very entertaining temper to observe. I, fortunately, can do so dispassionately, for I 'm the only person in the place he has not quarreled with."

"Has he then no society? Who is Miss Garland, whom you asked about?"

"A young girl staying with his mother, a sort of far-away cousin; a good plain girl, but not a person to delight a sculptor's eye. Roderick has a goodly share of the old Southern arrogance; he has the aristocratic temperament. He will have nothing to do with the small towns-people; he says they 're 'ignoble.' He cannot endure his mother's friends—the old ladies and the ministers and the tea-party people; they bore him to death. So he comes and lounges here and rails at everything and every one."

This graceful young scoffer reappeared a couple of evenings later, and confirmed the friendly feeling he had provoked on Rowland's part. He was in an easier mood than before, he chattered less extravagantly, and asked Rowland a number of rather naïf questions about the condition of the fine arts in New York and Boston. Cecilia, when he had gone, said that this was the wholesome effect of Rowland's praise of his statuette. Roderick was acutely sensitive, and Rowland's tranquil commendation had stilled his restless pulses. He was ruminating the full-flavored verdict of culture. Rowland felt an irresistible kindness for him, a mingled sense of his personal charm and his artistic capacity. He had an indefinable attraction—the something divine of unspotted, exuberant, confident youth. The next day was Sunday, and Rowland proposed that they should take a long walk and that Roderick should show him the country. The young man assented gleefully, and in the morning, as Rowland at the garden gate was giving his hostess Godspeed on her way to church, he came striding along the grassy margin of the road and out-whistling the music of the church bells. It was one of those lovely days of August when you feel the complete exuberance of summer just warned and checked by autumn. "Remember the day, and take care you rob no orchards," said Cecilia, as they separated.

The young men walked away at a steady pace, over hill and

dale, through woods and fields, and at last found themselves
on a grassy elevation studded with mossy rocks and red ce-
dars. Just beneath them, in a great shining curve, flowed the
goodly Connecticut. They flung themselves on the grass and
tossed stones into the river; they talked like old friends. Rowland lit a cigar, and Roderick refused one with a grimace of
extravagant disgust. He thought them vile things; he did n't
see how decent people could tolerate them. Rowland was
amused, and wondered what it was that made this ill-man-
nered speech seem perfectly inoffensive on Roderick's lips.
He belonged to the race of mortals, to be pitied or envied
according as we view the matter, who are not held to a strict
account for their aggressions. Looking at him as he lay
stretched in the shade, Rowland vaguely likened him to some
beautiful, supple, restless, bright-eyed animal, whose motions
should have no deeper warrant than the tremulous delicacy of
its structure, and be graceful even when they were most inconvenient. Rowland watched the shadows on Mount Holyoke, listened to the gurgle of the river, and sniffed the
balsam of the pines. A gentle breeze had begun to tickle their
summits, and brought the smell of the mown grass across
from the elm-dotted river meadows. He sat up beside his
companion and looked away at the far-spreading view. It
seemed to him beautiful, and suddenly a strange feeling of
prospective regret took possession of him. Something seemed
to tell him that later, in a foreign land, he would remember it
lovingly and penitently.

"It 's a wretched business," he said, "this practical quarrel
of ours with our own country, this everlasting impatience to
get out of it. Is one's only safety then in flight? This is an
American day, an American landscape, an American atmosphere. It certainly has its merits, and some day when I am
shivering with ague in classic Italy, I shall accuse myself of
having slighted them."

Roderick kindled with a sympathetic glow, and declared
that America was good enough for him, and that he had always thought it the duty of an honest citizen to stand by his
own country and help it along. He had evidently thought
nothing whatever about it, and was launching his doctrine
on the inspiration of the moment. The doctrine expanded

with the occasion, and he declared that he was above all an advocate for American art. He did n't see why we should n't produce the greatest works in the world. We were the biggest people, and we ought to have the biggest conceptions. The biggest conceptions of course would bring forth in time the biggest performances. We had only to be true to ourselves, to pitch in and not be afraid, to fling Imitation overboard and fix our eyes upon our National Individuality. "I declare," he cried, "there 's a career for a man, and I 've twenty minds to decide, on the spot, to embrace it—to be the consummate, typical, original, national American artist! It 's inspiring!"

Rowland burst out laughing and told him that he liked his practice better than his theory, and that a saner impulse than this had inspired his little Water-drinker. Roderick took no offense, and three minutes afterwards was talking volubly of some humbler theme, but half heeded by his companion, who had returned to his cogitations. At last Rowland delivered himself of the upshot of these. "How would you like," he suddenly demanded, "to go to Rome?"

Hudson stared, and, with a hungry laugh which speedily consigned our National Individuality to perdition, responded that he would like it reasonably well. "And I should like, by the same token," he added, "to go to Athens, to Constantinople, to Damascus, to the holy city of Benares, where there is a golden statue of Brahma twenty feet tall."

"Nay," said Rowland soberly, "if you were to go to Rome, you should settle down and work. Athens might help you, but for the present I should n't recommend Benares."

"It will be time to arrange details when I pack my trunk," said Hudson.

"If you mean to turn sculptor, the sooner you pack your trunk the better."

"Oh, but I 'm a practical man! What is the smallest sum per annum, on which one can keep alive the sacred fire in Rome?"

"What is the largest sum at your disposal?"

Roderick stroked his light moustache, gave it a twist, and then announced with mock pomposity: "Three hundred dollars!"

"The money question could be arranged," said Rowland. "There are ways of raising money."

"I should like to know a few! I never yet discovered one."

"One consists," said Rowland, "in having a friend with a good deal more than he wants, and not being too proud to accept a part of it."

Roderick stared a moment and his face flushed. "Do you mean—do you mean?" . . . . he stammered. He was greatly excited.

Rowland got up, blushing a little, and Roderick sprang to his feet. "In three words, if you are to be a sculptor, you ought to go to Rome and study the antique. To go to Rome you need money. I 'm fond of fine statues, but unfortunately I can't make them myself. I have to order them. I order a dozen from you, to be executed at your convenience. To help you, I pay you in advance."

Roderick pushed off his hat and wiped his forehead, still gazing at his companion. "You believe in me!" he cried at last.

"Allow me to explain," said Rowland. "I believe in you, if you are prepared to work and to wait, and to struggle, and to exercise a great many virtues. And then, I 'm afraid to say it, lest I should disturb you more than I should help you. You must decide for yourself. I simply offer you an opportunity."

Hudson stood for some time, profoundly meditative. "You have not seen my other things," he said suddenly. "Come and look at them."

"Now?"

"Yes, we 'll walk home. We 'll settle the question."

He passed his hand through Rowland's arm and they retraced their steps. They reached the town and made their way along a broad country street, dusky with the shade of magnificent elms. Rowland felt his companion's arm trembling in his own. They stopped at a large white house, flanked with melancholy hemlocks, and passed through a little front garden, paved with moss-coated bricks and ornamented with parterres bordered with high box hedges. The mansion had an air of antiquated dignity, but it had seen its best days, and evidently sheltered a shrunken household. Mrs. Hudson, Rowland was sure, might be seen in the garden of a morning, in a white apron and a pair of old gloves, engaged in frugal horticulture. Roderick's studio was behind, in the basement; a large, empty room, with the paper peeling off the walls. This represented, in the fashion of fifty years ago, a series of small fantastic landscapes of a hideous pattern, and the young sculptor had presumably torn it away in great scraps, in moments of æsthetic exasperation. On a board in a corner was a heap of clay, and on the floor, against the wall, stood some dozen medallions, busts, and figures, in various stages of completion. To exhibit them Roderick had to place them one by one on the end of a long packing-box, which served as a pedestal. He did so silently, making no explanations, and looking at them himself with a strange air of quickened curiosity. Most of the things were portraits; and the three at which he looked longest were finished busts. One was a colossal head of a negro, tossed back, defiant, with distended nostrils; one was the portrait of a young man whom Rowland immediately perceived, by the resemblance, to be his deceased brother; the last represented a gentleman with a pointed nose, a long, shaved upper lip, and a tuft on the end of his chin. This was a face peculiarly unadapted to sculpture; but as a piece of modeling it was the best, and it was admirable. It reminded Rowland in its homely veracity, its artless artfulness, of the works of the early Italian Renaissance. On the pedestal was cut the name—Barnaby Striker, Esq. Rowland remembered that this was the appellation of the legal luminary from whom his companion had undertaken to borrow a reflected ray, and although in the bust there was naught flagrantly set down in malice, it betrayed, comically to one who could relish the secret, that the features of the original had often been scanned with an irritated eye. Besides these there were several rough studies of the nude, and two or three figures of a fanciful kind. The most noticeable (and it had singular beauty) was a small modeled design for a sepulchral monument; that, evidently, of Stephen Hudson. The young soldier lay sleeping eternally, with his hand on his sword, like an old crusader in a Gothic cathedral.

Rowland made no haste to pronounce; too much depended on his judgment. "Upon my word," cried Hudson at last, "they seem to me very good."

And in truth, as Rowland looked, he saw they were good. They were youthful, awkward, and ignorant; the effort, often, was more apparent than the success. But the effort was signally powerful and intelligent; it seemed to Rowland that it needed only to let itself go to compass great things. Here and there, too, success, when grasped, had something masterly. Rowland turned to his companion, who stood with his hands in his pockets and his hair very much crumpled, looking at him askance. The light of admiration was in Rowland's eyes, and it speedily kindled a wonderful illumination on Hudson's handsome brow. Rowland said at last, gravely, "You have only to work!"

"I think I know what that means," Roderick answered. He turned away, threw himself on a rickety chair, and sat for some moments with his elbows on his knees and his head in his hands. "Work—work?" he said at last, looking up, "ah, if I could only begin!" He glanced round the room a moment and his eye encountered on the mantel-shelf the vivid physiognomy of Mr. Barnaby Striker. His smile vanished, and he stared at it with an air of concentrated enmity. "I want to begin," he cried, "and I can't make a better beginning than this! Good-by, Mr. Striker!" He strode across the room, seized a mallet that lay at hand, and before Rowland could interfere, in the interest of art if not of morals, dealt a merciless blow upon Mr. Striker's skull. The bust cracked into a dozen pieces, which toppled with a great crash upon the floor. Rowland relished neither the destruction of the image nor his companion's look in working it, but as he was about to express his displeasure the door opened and gave passage to a young girl. She came in with a rapid step and startled face, as if she had been summoned by the noise. Seeing the heap of shattered clay and the mallet in Roderick's hand, she gave a cry of horror. Her voice died away when she perceived that Rowland was a stranger, but she murmured reproachfully, "Why, Roderick, what have you done?"

Roderick gave a joyous kick to the shapeless fragments. "I 've driven the money-changers out of the temple!" he cried.

The traces retained shape enough to be recognized, and she gave a little moan of pity. She seemed not to understand the young man's allegory, but yet to feel that it pointed to some great purpose, which must be an evil one, from being expressed in such a lawless fashion, and to perceive that Rowland was in some way accountable for it. She looked at him with a sharp, frank mistrust, and turned away through the open door. Rowland looked after her with extraordinary interest.

II

Roderick

EARLY ON THE MORROW Rowland received a visit from his new friend. Roderick was in a state of extreme exhilaration, tempered, however, by a certain amount of righteous wrath. He had had a domestic struggle, but he had remained master of the situation. He had shaken the dust of Mr. Striker's office from his feet.

"I had it out last night with my mother," he said. "I dreaded the scene, for she takes things terribly hard. She does n't scold nor storm, and she does n't argue nor insist. She sits with her eyes full of tears that never fall, and looks at me, when I displease her, as if I were a perfect monster of depravity. And the trouble is that I was born to displease her. She does n't trust me; she never has and she never will. I don't know what I have done to set her against me, but ever since I can remember I have been looked at with tears. The trouble is," he went on, giving a twist to his moustache, "I 've been too absurdly docile. I 've been sprawling all my days by the maternal fireside, and my dear mother has grown used to bullying me. I 've made myself cheap! If I 'm not in my bed by eleven o'clock, the girl is sent out to explore with a lantern. When I think of it, I fairly despise my amiability. It 's rather a hard fate, to live like a saint and to pass for a sinner! I should like for six months to lead Mrs. Hudson the life some fellows lead their mothers!"

"Allow me to believe," said Rowland, "that you would like nothing of the sort. If you have been a good boy, don't spoil it by pretending you don't like it. You have been very happy, I suspect, in spite of your virtues, and there are worse fates in the world than being loved too well. I have not had the pleasure of seeing your mother, but I would lay you a wager that that is the trouble. She is passionately fond of you, and her hopes, like all intense hopes, keep trembling into fears." Rowland, as he spoke, had an instinctive vision of how such a beautiful young fellow must be loved by his female relatives.

Roderick frowned, and with an impatient gesture, "I do

her justice," he cried. "May she never do me less!" Then after
a moment's hesitation, "I 'll tell you the perfect truth," he
went on. "I have to fill a double place. I have to be my
brother as well as myself. It 's a good deal to ask of a man,
especially when he has so little talent as I for being what he
is not. When we were both young together I was the curled
darling. I had the silver mug and the biggest piece of pudding, and I stayed in-doors to be kissed by the ladies while he
made mud-pies in the garden and was never missed, of
course. Really, he was worth fifty of me! When he was
brought home from Vicksburg with a piece of shell in his
skull, my poor mother began to think she had n't loved him
enough. I remember, as she hung round my neck sobbing,
before his coffin, she told me that I must be to her everything
that he would have been. I swore in tears and in perfect good
faith that I would, but naturally I have not kept my promise.
I have been utterly different. I have been idle, restless, egotistical, discontented. I have done no harm, I believe, but I
have done no good. My brother, if he had lived, would have
made fifty thousand dollars and put gas and water into the
house. My mother, brooding night and day on her bereavement, has come to fix her ideal in offices of that sort. Judged
by that standard I 'm nowhere!"

Rowland was at loss how to receive this account of his
friend's domestic circumstances; it was plaintive, and yet the
manner seemed to him over-trenchant. "You must lose no
time in making a masterpiece," he answered; "then with the
proceeds you can give her gas from golden burners."

"So I have told her; but she only half believes either in
masterpiece or in proceeds. She can see no good in my making statues; they seem to her a snare of the enemy. She would
fain see me all my life tethered to the law, like a browsing
goat to a stake. In that way I 'm in sight. 'It 's a more regular
occupation!' that 's all I can get out of her. A more regular
damnation! Is it a fact that artists, in general, are such wicked
men? I never had the pleasure of knowing one, so I could n't
confute her with an example. She had the advantage of me,
because she formerly knew a portrait-painter at Richmond,
who did her miniature in black lace mittens (you may see it
on the parlor table), who used to drink raw brandy and beat

his wife. I promised her that, whatever I might do to my wife, I would never beat my mother, and that as for brandy, raw or diluted, I detested it. She sat silently crying for an hour, during which I expended treasures of eloquence. It 's a good thing to have to reckon up one's intentions, and I assure you, as I pleaded my cause, I was most agreeably impressed with the elevated character of my own. I kissed her solemnly at last, and told her that I had said everything and that she must make the best of it. This morning she has dried her eyes, but I warrant you it is n't a cheerful house. I long to be out of it!"

"I 'm extremely sorry," said Rowland, "to have been the prime cause of so much suffering. I owe your mother some amends; will it be possible for me to see her?"

"If you 'll see her, it will smooth matters vastly; though to tell the truth she 'll need all her courage to face you, for she considers you an agent of the foul fiend. She does n't see why you should have come here and set me by the ears: you are made to ruin ingenuous youths and desolate doting mothers. I leave it to you, personally, to answer these charges. You see, what she can't forgive—what she 'll not really ever forgive—is your taking me off to Rome. Rome is an evil word, in my mother's vocabulary, to be said in a whisper, as you 'd say 'damnation.' Northampton is in the centre of the earth and Rome far away in outlying dusk, into which it can do no Christian any good to penetrate. And there was I but yesterday a doomed *habitué* of that repository of every virtue, Mr. Striker's office!"

"And does Mr. Striker know of your decision?" asked Rowland.

"To a certainty! Mr. Striker, you must know, is not simply a good-natured attorney, who lets me dog's-ear his lawbooks. He's a particular friend and general adviser. He looks after my mother's property and kindly consents to regard me as part of it. Our opinions have always been painfully divergent, but I freely forgive him his zealous attempts to unscrew my head-piece and set it on hind part before. He never understood me, and it was useless to try to make him. We speak a different language—we 're made of a different clay. I had a fit of rage yesterday when I smashed his bust, at the thought

of all the bad blood he had stirred up in me; it did me good,
and it 's all over now. I don't hate him any more; I 'm rather
sorry for him. See how you 've improved me! I must have
seemed to him wilfully, wickedly stupid, and I 'm sure he only
tolerated me on account of his great regard for my mother.
This morning I grasped the bull by the horns. I took an armful of law-books that have been gathering the dust in my
room for the last year and a half, and presented myself at the
office. 'Allow me to put these back in their places,' I said. 'I
shall never have need for them more—never more, never
more, never more!' 'So you 've learned everything they contain?' asked Striker, leering over his spectacles. 'Better late
than never.' 'I 've learned nothing that you can teach me,' I
cried. 'But I shall tax your patience no longer. I 'm going to
be a sculptor. I 'm going to Rome. I won't bid you good-by
just yet; I shall see you again. But I bid good-by here, with
rapture, to these four detested walls—to this living tomb! I
did n't know till now how I hated it! My compliments to Mr.
Spooner, and my thanks for all you have not made of me!' "

"I 'm glad to know you are to see Mr. Striker again," Rowland answered, correcting a primary inclination to smile.
"You certainly owe him a respectful farewell, even if he has
not understood you. I confess you rather puzzle me. There is
another person," he presently added, "whose opinion as to
your new career I should like to know. What does Miss Garland think?"

Hudson looked at him keenly, with a slight blush. Then,
with a conscious smile, "What makes you suppose she thinks
anything?" he asked.

"Because, though I saw her but for a moment yesterday,
she struck me as a very intelligent person, and I am sure she
has opinions."

The smile on Roderick's mobile face passed rapidly into a
frown. "Oh, she thinks what I think!" he answered.

Before the two young men separated Rowland attempted
to give as harmonious a shape as possible to his companion's
scheme. "I have launched you, as I may say," he said, "and I
feel as if I ought to see you into port. I am older than you
and know the world better, and it seems well that we should
voyage a while together. It 's on my conscience that I ought

to take you to Rome, walk you through the Vatican, and then lock you up with a heap of clay. I sail on the fifth of September; can you make your preparations to start with me?"

Roderick assented to all this with an air of candid confidence in his friend's wisdom that outshone the virtue of pledges. "I have no preparations to make," he said with a smile, raising his arms and letting them fall, as if to indicate his unencumbered condition. "What I am to take with me I carry here!" and he tapped his forehead.

"Happy man!" murmured Rowland with a sigh, thinking of the light stowage, in his own organism, in the region indicated by Roderick, and of the heavy one in deposit at his banker's, of bags and boxes.

*   *   *

When his companion had left him he went in search of Cecilia. She was sitting at work at a shady window, and welcomed him to a low chintz-covered chair. He sat some time, thoughtfully snipping tape with her scissors; he expected criticism and he was preparing a rejoinder. At last he told her of Roderick's decision and of his own influence in it. Cecilia, besides an extreme surprise, exhibited a certain fine displeasure at his not having asked her advice.

"What would you have said, if I had?" he demanded.

"I would have said in the first place, 'Oh for pity's sake don't carry off the person in all Northampton who amuses me most!' I would have said in the second place, 'Nonsense! the boy is doing very well. Let well alone!' "

"That in the first five minutes. What would you have said later?"

"That for a man who is generally averse to meddling, you were suddenly rather officious."

Rowland's countenance fell. He frowned in silence. Cecilia looked at him askance; gradually the spark of irritation faded from her eye.

"Excuse my sharpness," she resumed at last. "But I am literally in despair at losing Roderick Hudson. His visits in the evening, for the past year, have kept me alive. They have given a silver tip to leaden days. I don't say he is of a more useful metal than other people, but he is of a different one.

Of course, however, that I shall miss him sadly is not a reason for his not going to seek his fortune. Men must work and women must weep!"

"Decidedly not!" said Rowland, with a good deal of emphasis. He had suspected from the first hour of his stay that Cecilia had treated herself to a private social luxury; he had then discovered that she found it in Hudson's lounging visits and boyish chatter, and he had felt himself wondering at last whether, judiciously viewed, her gain in the matter was not the young man's loss. It was evident that Cecilia was not judicious, and that her good sense, habitually rigid under the demands of domestic economy, indulged itself with a certain agreeable laxity on this particular point. She liked her young friend just as he was; she humored him, flattered him, laughed at him, caressed him—did everything but advise him. It was a flirtation without the benefits of a flirtation. She was too old to let him fall in love with her, which might have done him good; and her inclination was to keep him young, so that the nonsense he talked might never transgress a certain line. It was quite conceivable that poor Cecilia should relish a pastime; but if one had philanthropically embraced the idea that something considerable might be made of Roderick, it was impossible not to see that her friendship was not what might be called tonic. So Rowland reflected, in the glow of his new-born sympathy. There was a later time when he would have been grateful if Hudson's susceptibility to the relaxing influence of lovely women might have been limited to such inexpensive tribute as he rendered the excellent Cecilia.

"I only desire to remind you," she pursued, "that you are likely to have your hands full."

"I 've thought of that, and I rather like the idea; liking, as I do, the man. I told you the other day, you know, that I longed to have something on my hands. When it first occurred to me that I might start our young friend on the path of glory, I felt as if I had an unimpeachable inspiration. Then I remembered there were dangers and difficulties, and asked myself whether I had a right to step in between him and his obscurity. My sense of his really having the divine flame answered the question. He is made to do the things that humanity is the happier for! I can't do such things myself, but when I see a young man of genius standing helpless and hopeless for want of capital, I feel— and it 's no affectation of humility, I assure you—as if it would give at least a reflected usefulness to my own life to offer him his opportunity."

"In the name of humanity, I suppose, I ought to thank you. But I want, first of all, to be happy myself. You guarantee us at any rate, I hope, the masterpieces."

"A masterpiece a year," said Rowland smiling, "for the next quarter of a century."

"It seems to me that we have a right to ask more: to demand that you guarantee us not only the development of the artist, but the security of the man."

Rowland became grave again. "His security?"

"His moral, his sentimental security. Here, you see, it 's perfect. We are all under a tacit compact to preserve it. Perhaps you believe in the necessary turbulence of genius, and you intend to enjoin upon your protégé the importance of cultivating his passions."

"On the contrary, I believe that a man of genius owes as much deference to his passions as any other man, but not a particle more, and I confess I have a strong conviction that the artist is better for leading a quiet life. That is what I shall preach to my protégé, as you call him, by example as well as by precept. You evidently believe," he added in a moment, "that he will lead me a dance."

"Nay, I prophesy nothing. I only think that circumstances, with our young man, have a great influence; as is proved by the fact that although he has been fuming and fretting here for the last five years, he has nevertheless managed to make the best of it, and found it easy, on the whole, to vegetate. Transplanted to Rome, I fancy he 'll put forth a denser leafage. I should like vastly to see the change. You must write me about it, from stage to stage. I hope with all my heart that the fruit will be proportionate to the foliage. Don't think me a bird of ill omen; only remember that you will be held to a strict account."

"A man should make the most of himself, and be helped if he needs help," Rowland answered, after a long pause. "Of course when a body begins to expand, there comes in the

possibility of bursting; but I nevertheless approve of a certain
tension of one's being. It 's what a man is meant for. And then
I believe in the essential salubrity of genius—true genius."

"Very good," said Cecilia, with an air of resignation which
made Rowland, for the moment, seem to himself culpably eager. "We 'll drink then to-day at dinner to the health of our
friend."

*　　*　　*

Having it much at heart to convince Mrs. Hudson of the
purity of his intentions, Rowland waited upon her that evening. He was ushered into a large parlor, which, by the light
of a couple of candles, he perceived to be very meagrely furnished and very tenderly and sparingly used. The windows
were open to the air of the summer night, and a circle of
three persons was temporarily awed into silence by his appearance. One of these was Mrs. Hudson, who was sitting at
one of the windows, empty-handed save for the pocket-handkerchief in her lap, which was held with an air of familiarity
with its sadder uses. Near her, on the sofa, half sitting, half
lounging, in the attitude of a visitor outstaying ceremony,
with one long leg flung over the other and a large foot in a
clumsy boot swinging to and fro continually, was a lean,
sandy-haired gentleman whom Rowland recognized as the
original of the portrait of Mr. Barnaby Striker. At the table,
near the candles, busy with a substantial piece of needle-work,
sat the young girl of whom he had had a moment's quickened
glimpse in Roderick's studio, and whom he had learned to be
Miss Garland, his companion's kinswoman. This young lady's
limpid, penetrating gaze was the most effective greeting he
received. Mrs. Hudson rose with a soft, vague sound of distress, and stood looking at him shrinkingly and waveringly,
as if she were sorely tempted to retreat through the open window. Mr. Striker swung his long leg a trifle defiantly. No one,
evidently, was used to offering hollow welcomes or telling
polite fibs. Rowland introduced himself; he had come, he
might say, upon business.

"Yes," said Mrs. Hudson tremulously; "I know—my son
has told me. I suppose it is better I should see you. Perhaps
you will take a seat."

With this invitation Rowland prepared to comply, and, turning, grasped the first chair that offered itself.

"Not that one," said a full, grave voice; whereupon he perceived that a quantity of sewing-silk had been suspended and entangled over the back, preparatory to being wound on reels. He felt the least bit irritated at the curtness of the warning, coming as it did from a young woman whose countenance he had mentally pronounced interesting, and with regard to whom he was conscious of the germ of the inevitable desire to produce a responsive interest. And then he thought it would break the ice to say something playfully urbane.

"Oh, you should let me take the chair," he answered, "and have the pleasure of holding the skeins myself!"

For all reply to this sally he received a stare of undisguised amazement from Miss Garland, who then looked across at Mrs. Hudson with a glance which plainly said: "You see he's quite the insidious personage we feared." The elder lady, however, sat with her eyes fixed on the ground and her two hands tightly clasped. But touching her Rowland felt much more compassion than resentment; her attitude was not coldness, it was a kind of dread, almost a terror. She was a small, eager woman, with a pale, troubled face, which added to her apparent age. After looking at her for some minutes Rowland saw that she was still young, and that she must have been a very girlish bride. She had been a pretty one, too, though she probably had looked terribly frightened at the altar. She was very delicately made, and Roderick had come honestly by his physical slimness and elegance. She wore no cap, and her flaxen hair, which was of extraordinary fineness, was smoothed and confined with Puritanic precision. She was excessively shy, and evidently very humble-minded; it was singular to see a woman to whom the experience of life had conveyed so little reassurance as to her own resources or the chances of things turning out well. Rowland began immediately to like her, and to feel impatient to persuade her that there was no harm in him, and that, twenty to one, her son would make her a well-pleased woman yet. He foresaw that she would be easy to persuade, and that a benevolent conversational tone would probably make her pass, fluttering, from distrust into an oppressive extreme of confidence. But he had an indefinable sense that the person who was testing that strong young eyesight of hers in the dim candle-light was less readily beguiled from her mysterious feminine preconceptions. Miss Garland, according to Cecilia's judgment, as Rowland remembered, had not a countenance to inspire a sculptor; but it seemed to Rowland that her countenance might fairly inspire a man who was far from being a sculptor. She was not pretty, as the eye of habit judges prettiness, but when you made the observation you somehow failed to set it down against her, for you had already passed from measuring contours to tracing meanings. In Mary Garland's face there were many possible ones, and they gave you the more to think about that it was not—like Roderick Hudson's, for instance—a quick and mobile face, over which expression flickered like a candle in a wind. They followed each other slowly, distinctly, gravely, sincerely, and you might almost have fancied that, as they came and went, they gave her a sort of pain. She was tall and slender, and had an air of maidenly strength and decision. She had a broad forehead and dark eyebrows, a trifle thicker than those of classic beauties; her gray eye was clear but not brilliant, and her features were perfectly irregular. Her mouth was large, fortunately for the principal grace of her physiognomy was her smile, which displayed itself with magnificent amplitude. Rowland, indeed, had not yet seen her smile, but something assured him that her rigid gravity had a radiant counterpart. She wore a scanty white dress, and had a nameless rustic air which would have led one to speak of her less as a young lady than as a young woman. She was evidently a girl of a great personal force, but she lacked pliancy. She was hemming a kitchen towel with the aid of a large steel thimble. She bent her serious eyes at last on her work again, and let Rowland explain himself.

"I have become suddenly so very intimate with your son," he said at last, addressing himself to Mrs. Hudson, "that it seems just I should make your acquaintance."

"Very just," murmured the poor lady, and after a moment's hesitation was on the point of adding something more; but Mr. Striker here interposed, after a prefatory clearance of the throat.

"I should like to take the liberty," he said, "of addressing you a simple question. For how long a period of time have you been acquainted with our young friend?" He continued to kick the air, but his head was thrown back and his eyes fixed on the opposite wall, as if in aversion to the spectacle of Rowland's inevitable confusion.

"A very short time, I confess. Hardly three days."

"And yet you call yourself intimate, eh? I have been seeing Mr. Roderick daily these three years, and yet it was only this morning that I felt as if I had at last the right to say that I knew him. We had a few moments' conversation in my office which supplied the missing links in the evidence. So that now I do venture to say I 'm acquainted with Mr. Roderick! But wait three years, sir, like me!" and Mr. Striker laughed, with a closed mouth and a noiseless shake of all his long person.

Mrs. Hudson smiled confusedly, at hazard; Miss Garland kept her eyes on her stitches. But it seemed to Rowland that the latter colored a little. "Oh, in three years, of course," he said, "we shall know each other better. Before many years are over, madam," he pursued, "I expect the world to know him. I expect him to be a great man!"

Mrs. Hudson looked at first as if this could be but an insidious device for increasing her distress by the assistance of irony. Then reassured, little by little, by Rowland's benevolent visage, she gave him an appealing glance and a timorous "Really?"

But before Rowland could respond, Mr. Striker again intervened. "Do I fully apprehend your expression?" he asked. "Our young friend is to become a *great man?*"

"A great artist, I hope," said Rowland.

"This is a new and interesting view," said Mr. Striker, with an assumption of judicial calmness. "We have had hopes for Mr. Roderick, but I confess, if I have rightly understood them, they stopped short of greatness. We should n't have taken the responsibility of claiming it for him. What do you say, ladies? We all feel about him here—his mother, Miss Garland, and myself—as if his merits were rather in the line of the"—and Mr. Striker waved his hand with a series of fantastic flourishes in the air—"of the light ornamental!" Mr. Striker bore his recalcitrant pupil a grudge, but he was evi-

dently trying both to be fair and to respect the susceptibilities
of his companions. But he was unversed in the mysterious
processes of feminine emotion. Ten minutes before, there had
been a general harmony of sombre views; but on hearing
Roderick's limitations thus distinctly formulated to a
stranger, the two ladies mutely protested. Mrs. Hudson uttered a short, faint sigh, and Miss Garland raised her eyes
toward their advocate and visited him with a short, cold
glance.

"I 'm afraid, Mrs. Hudson," Rowland pursued, evading the
discussion of Roderick's possible greatness, "that you don't at
all thank me for stirring up your son's ambition on a line
which leads him so far from home. I suspect I have made you
my enemy."

Mrs. Hudson covered her mouth with her finger-tips and
looked painfully perplexed between the desire to confess the
truth and the fear of being impolite. "My cousin is no one's
enemy," Miss Garland hereupon declared, gently, but with
that same fine deliberateness with which she had made Rowland relax his grasp of the chair.

"Does she leave that to you?" Rowland ventured to ask,
with a smile.

"We are inspired with none but Christian sentiments," said
Mr. Striker; "Miss Garland perhaps most of all. Miss Garland," and Mr. Striker waved his hand again as if to perform
an introduction which had been regrettably omitted, "is
the daughter of a minister, the granddaughter of a minister, the
sister of a minister." Rowland bowed deferentially, and the
young girl went on with her sewing, with nothing, apparently, either of embarrassment or elation at the promulgation
of these facts. Mr. Striker continued: "Mrs. Hudson, I see, is
too deeply agitated to converse with you freely. She will allow
me to address you a few questions. Would you kindly inform
her, as exactly as possible, just what you propose to do with
her son?"

The poor lady fixed her eyes appealingly on Rowland's face
and seemed to say that Mr. Striker had spoken her desire,
though she herself would have expressed it less defiantly. But
Rowland saw in Mr. Striker's many-wrinkled light blue eye,
shrewd at once and good-natured, that he had no intention

of defiance, and that he was simply pompous and conceited and sarcastically compassionate of any view of things in which Roderick Hudson was regarded in a serious light.

"Do, my dear madam?" demanded Rowland. "I don't propose to do anything. He must do for himself. I simply offer him the chance. He 's to study, to work—hard, I hope."

"Not too hard, please," murmured Mrs. Hudson, pleadingly, wheeling about from recent visions of dangerous leisure. "He 's not very strong, and I 'm afraid the climate of Europe is very relaxing."

"Ah, study?" repeated Mr. Striker. "To what line of study is he to direct his attention?" Then suddenly, with an impulse of disinterested curiosity on his own account, "How do you study sculpture, anyhow?"

"By looking at models and imitating them."

"At models, eh? To what kind of models do you refer?"

"To the antique, in the first place."

"Ah, the antique," repeated Mr. Striker, with a jocose intonation. "Do you hear, madam? Roderick is going off to Europe to learn to imitate the antique."

"I suppose it 's all right," said Mrs. Hudson, twisting herself in a sort of delicate anguish.

"An antique, as I understand it," the lawyer continued, "is an image of a pagan deity, with considerable dirt sticking to it, and no arms, no nose, and no clothing. A precious model, certainly!"

"That 's a very good description of many," said Rowland, with a laugh.

"Mercy! Truly?" asked Mrs. Hudson, borrowing courage from his urbanity.

"But a sculptor's studies, you intimate, are not confined to the antique," Mr. Striker resumed. "After he has been looking three or four years at the objects I describe"—

"He studies the living model," said Rowland.

"Does it take three or four years?" asked Mrs. Hudson, imploringly.

"That depends upon the artist's aptitude. After twenty years a real artist is still studying."

"Oh, my poor boy!" moaned Mrs. Hudson, finding the prospect, under every light, still terrible.

"Now this study of the living model," Mr. Striker pursued. "Inform Mrs. Hudson about that."

"Oh dear, no!" cried Mrs. Hudson, shrinkingly.

"That too," said Rowland, "is one of the reasons for studying in Rome. It 's a handsome race, you know, and you find very well-made people."

"I suppose they 're no better made than a good tough Yankee," objected Mr. Striker, transposing his interminable legs. "The same God made us."

"Surely," sighed Mrs. Hudson, but with a questioning glance at her visitor which showed that she had already begun to concede much weight to his opinion. Rowland hastened to express his assent to Mr. Striker's proposition.

Miss Garland looked up, and, after a moment's hesitation: "Are the Roman women very beautiful?" she asked.

Rowland too, in answering, hesitated; he was looking straight at the young girl. "On the whole, I prefer ours," he said.

She had dropped her work in her lap; her hands were crossed upon it, her head thrown a little back. She had evidently expected a more impersonal answer, and she was dissatisfied. For an instant she seemed inclined to make a rejoinder, but she slowly picked up her work in silence and drew her stitches again.

Rowland had for the second time the feeling that she judged him to be a person of a disagreeably sophisticated tone. He noticed too that the kitchen towel she was hemming was terribly coarse. And yet his answer had a resonant inward echo, and he repeated to himself, "Yes, on the whole, I prefer ours."

"Well, these models," began Mr. Striker. "You put them into an attitude, I suppose."

"An attitude, exactly."

"And then you sit down and look at them."

"You must not sit too long. You must go at your clay and try to build up something that looks like them."

"Well, there you are with your model in an attitude on one side, yourself, in an attitude too, I suppose, on the other, and your pile of clay in the middle, building up, as you say. So you pass the morning. After that I hope you go out and take a walk, and rest from your exertions."

"Unquestionably. But to a sculptor who loves his work there is no time lost. Everything he looks at teaches or suggests something."

"That 's a tempting doctrine to young men with a taste for sitting by the hour with the page unturned, watching the flies buzz, or the frost melt on the window-pane. Our young friend, in this way, must have laid up stores of information which I never suspected!"

"Very likely," said Rowland, with an unresentful smile, "he will prove some day the completer artist for some of those lazy reveries."

This theory was apparently very grateful to Mrs. Hudson, who had never had the case put for her son with such ingenious hopefulness, and found herself disrelishing the singular situation of seeming to side against her own flesh and blood with a lawyer whose conversational tone betrayed the habit of cross-questioning.

"My son, then," she ventured to ask, "my son has great— what you would call great powers?"

"To my sense, very great powers."

Poor Mrs. Hudson actually smiled, broadly, gleefully, and glanced at Miss Garland, as if to invite her to do likewise. But the young girl's face remained serious, like the eastern sky when the opposite sunset is too feeble to make it glow. "Do you really know?" she asked, looking at Rowland.

"One cannot *know* in such a matter save after proof, and proof takes time. But one can believe."

"And you believe?"

"I believe."

But even then Miss Garland vouchsafed no smile. Her face became graver than ever.

"Well, well," said Mrs. Hudson, "we must hope that it is all for the best."

Mr. Striker eyed his old friend for a moment with a look of some displeasure; he saw that this was but a cunning feminine imitation of resignation, and that, through some untraceable process of transition, she was now taking more comfort in the opinions of this insinuating stranger than in his own tough dogmas. He rose to his feet, without pulling down his waistcoat, but with a wrinkled grin at the inconsistency of women. "Well, sir, Mr. Roderick's powers are nothing to me," he said, "nor no use he makes of them. Good or bad, he 's no son of mine. But, in a friendly way, I 'm glad to hear so fine an account of him. I 'm glad, madam, you 're so satisfied with the prospect. Affection, sir, you see, must have its guarantees!" He paused a moment, stroking his beard, with his head inclined and one eye half-closed, looking at Rowland. The look was grotesque, but it was significant, and it puzzled Rowland more than it amused him. "I suppose you 're a very brilliant young man," he went on, "very enlightened, very cultivated, quite up to the mark in the fine arts and all that sort of thing. I 'm a plain, practical old boy, content to follow an honorable profession in a free country. I did n't go off to the Old World to learn my business; no one took me by the hand; I had to grease my wheels myself, and, such as I am, I 'm a self-made man, every inch of me! Well, if our young friend is booked for fame and fortune, I don't suppose his going to Rome will stop him. But, mind you, it won't help him such a long way, either. If you have undertaken to put him through, there 's a thing or two you 'd better remember. The crop we gather depends upon the seed we sow. He may be the biggest genius of the age: his potatoes won't come up without his hoeing them. If he takes things so almighty easy as—well, as one or two young fellows of genius I 've had under my eye—his produce will never gain the prize. Take the word for it of a man who has made his way inch by inch, and does n't believe that we 'll wake up to find our work done because we 've lain all night a-dreaming of it; anything worth doing is devilish hard to do! If your young protajay finds things easy and has a good time and says he likes the life, it 's a sign that—as I may say—you had better step round to the office and look at the books. That 's all I desire to remark. No offense intended. I hope you 'll have a first-rate time."

Rowland could honestly reply that this seemed pregnant sense, and he offered Mr. Striker a friendly hand-shake as the latter withdrew. But Mr. Striker's rather grim view of matters cast a momentary shadow on his companions, and Mrs. Hudson seemed to feel that it necessitated between them some little friendly agreement not to be overawed.

Rowland sat for some time longer, partly because he wished to please the two women and partly because he was strangely pleased himself. There was something touching in their unworldly fears and diffident hopes, something almost terrible in the way poor little Mrs. Hudson seemed to flutter and quiver with intense maternal passion. She put forth one timid conversational venture after another, and asked Rowland a number of questions about himself, his age, his family, his occupations, his tastes, his religious opinions. Rowland had an odd feeling at last that she had begun to consider him very exemplary, and that she might make, later, some perturbing discovery. He tried, therefore, to invent something that would prepare her to find him fallible. But he could think of nothing. It only seemed to him that Miss Garland secretly mistrusted him, and that he must leave her to render him the service, after he had gone, of making him the object of a little firm derogation. Mrs. Hudson talked with low-voiced eagerness about her son.

"He 's very lovable, sir, I assure you. When you come to know him you 'll find him very lovable. He 's a little spoiled, of course; he has always done with me as he pleased; but he 's a good boy, I 'm sure he 's a good boy. And every one thinks him very attractive: I 'm sure he 'd be noticed, anywhere. Don't you think he 's very handsome, sir? He features his poor father. I had another—perhaps you 've been told. He was killed." And the poor little lady bravely smiled, for fear of doing worse. "He was a very fine boy, but very different from Roderick. Roderick is a little strange; he has never been an easy boy. Sometimes I feel like the goose—was n't it a goose, dear?" and startled by the audacity of her comparison she appealed to Miss Garland—"the goose, or the hen, who hatched a swan's egg. I have never been able to give him what he needs. I have always thought that in more—in more brilliant circumstances he might find his place and be happy. But at the same time I was afraid of the world for him; it was so large and dangerous and dreadful. No doubt I know very little about it. I never suspected, I confess, that it contained persons of such liberality as yours."

Rowland replied that, evidently, she had done the world but scanty justice. "No," objected Miss Garland, after a pause, "it is like something in a fairy tale."

"What, pray?"

"Your coming here all unknown, so rich and so polite, and carrying off my cousin in a golden cloud."

If this was badinage Miss Garland had the best of it, for Rowland almost fell a-musing silently over the question whether there was a possibility of irony in that transparent gaze. Before he withdrew, Mrs. Hudson made him tell her again that Roderick's powers were extraordinary. He had inspired her with a clinging, caressing faith in his wisdom. "He will really do great things," she asked, "the very greatest?"

"I see no reason in his talent itself why he should not."

"Well, we 'll think of that as we sit here alone," she rejoined. "Mary and I will sit here and talk about it. So I give him up," she went on, as he was going. "I 'm sure you 'll be the best of friends to him, but if you should ever forget him, or grow tired of him, or lose your interest in him, and he should come to any harm or any trouble, please, sir, remember"—And she paused, with a tremulous voice.

"Remember, my dear madam?"

"That he is all I have—that he is everything—and that it would be very terrible."

"In so far as I can help him, he shall succeed," was all Rowland could say. He turned to Miss Garland, to bid her good night, and she rose and put out her hand. She was very straightforward, but he could see that if she was too modest to be bold, she was much too simple to be shy. "Have you no charge to lay upon me?" he asked—to ask her something.

She looked at him a moment and then, although she was not shy, she blushed. "Make him do his best," she said.

Rowland noted the soft intensity with which the words were uttered. "Do you take a great interest in him?" he demanded.

"Certainly."

"Then, if he will not do his best for you, he will not do it for me." She turned away with another blush, and Rowland took his leave.

He walked homeward, thinking of many things. The great

Northampton elms interarched far above in the darkness, but
the moon had risen and through scattered apertures was
hanging the dusky vault with silver lamps. There seemed to
Rowland something intensely serious in the scene in which
he had just taken part. He had laughed and talked and
braved it out in self-defense; but when he reflected that he
was really meddling with the simple stillness of this little
New England home, and that he had ventured to disturb
so much living security in the interest of a far-away, fantastic hypothesis, he paused, amazed at his temerity. It was
true, as Cecilia had said, that for an unofficious man it was
a singular position. There stirred in his mind an odd feeling of annoyance with Roderick for having thus peremptorily enlisted his sympathies. As he looked up and down
the long vista, and saw the clear white houses glancing here
and there in the broken moonshine, he could almost have
believed that the happiest lot for any man was to make the
most of life in some such tranquil spot as that. Here were
kindness, comfort, safety, the warning voice of duty, the
perfect hush of temptation. And as Rowland looked along
the arch of silvered shadow and out into the lucid air of
the American night, which seemed so doubly vast, somehow, and strange and nocturnal, he felt like declaring that
here was beauty too—beauty sufficient for an artist not to
starve upon it. As he stood, lost in the darkness, he presently heard a rapid tread on the other side of the road, accompanied by a loud, jubilant whistle, and in a moment a
figure emerged into an open gap of moonshine. He had no
difficulty in recognizing Hudson, who was presumably returning from a visit to Cecilia. Roderick stopped suddenly
and stared up at the moon, with his face vividly illumined.
He broke out into a snatch of song:—

> "The splendor falls on castle walls
> And snowy summits old in story!"

And with a great, musical roll of his voice he went swinging
off into the darkness again, as if his thoughts had lent him
wings. He was dreaming of the inspiration of foreign
lands,—of castled crags and historic landscapes. What a pity,

after all, thought Rowland, as he went his own way, that he should n't have a taste of it!

It had been a very just remark of Cecilia's that Roderick would change with a change in his circumstances. Rowland had telegraphed to New York for another berth on his steamer, and from the hour the answer came Hudson's spirits rose to incalculable heights. He was radiant with good-humor, and his kindly jollity seemed the pledge of a brilliant future. He had forgiven his old enemies and forgotten his old grievances, and seemed every way reconciled to a world in which he was going to count as an active force. He was inexhaustibly loquacious and fantastic, and as Cecilia said, he had suddenly become so good that it was only to be feared he was going to start not for Europe but for heaven. He took long walks with Rowland, who felt more and more the fascination of what he would have called his giftedness. Rowland returned several times to Mrs. Hudson's, and found the two ladies doing their best to be happy in their companion's happiness. Miss Garland, he thought, was succeeding better than her demeanor on his first visit had promised. He tried to have some especial talk with her, but her extreme reserve forced him to content himself with such response to his rather urgent overtures as might be extracted from a keenly attentive smile. It must be confessed, however, that if the response was vague, the satisfaction was great, and that Rowland, after his second visit, kept seeing a lurking reflection of this smile in the most unexpected places. It seemed strange that she should please him so well at so slender a cost, but please him she did, prodigiously, and his pleasure had a quality altogether new to him. It made him restless, and a trifle melancholy; he walked about absently, wondering and wishing. He wondered, among other things, why fate should have condemned him to make the acquaintance of a girl whom he would make a sacrifice to know better, just as he was leaving the country for years. It seemed to him that he was turning his back on a chance of happiness—happiness of a sort of which the slenderest germ should be cultivated. He asked himself whether, feeling as he did, if he had only himself to please, he would give up his journey and—wait. He had Roderick to please now, for whom disappointment would be cruel; but he said to himself that certainly, if there were no Roderick in the case, the ship should sail without him. He asked Hudson several questions about his cousin, but Roderick, confidential on most points, seemed to have reasons of his own for being reticent on this one. His measured answers quickened Rowland's curiosity, for Miss Garland, with her own irritating half-suggestions, had only to be a subject of guarded allusion in others to become intolerably interesting. He learned from Roderick that she was the daughter of a country minister, a far-away cousin of his mother, settled in another part of the State; that she was one of a half-a-dozen daughters, that the family was very poor, and that she had come a couple of months before to pay his mother a long visit. "It is to be a very long one now," he said, "for it is settled that she is to remain while I am away."

The fermentation of contentment in Roderick's soul reached its climax a few days before the young men were to make their farewells. He had been sitting with his friends on Cecilia's veranda, but for half an hour past he had said nothing. Lounging back against a vine-wreathed column and gazing idly at the stars, he kept caroling softly to himself with that indifference to ceremony for which he always found allowance, and which in him had a sort of pleading grace. At last, springing up: "I want to strike out, hard!" he exclaimed. "I want to do something violent, to let off steam!"

"I 'll tell you what to do, this lovely weather," said Cecilia. "Give a picnic. It can be as violent as you please, and it will have the merit of leading off our emotion into a safe channel, as well as yours."

Roderick laughed uproariously at Cecilia's very practical remedy for his sentimental need, but a couple of days later, nevertheless, the picnic was given. It was to be a family party, but Roderick, in his magnanimous geniality, insisted on inviting Mr. Striker, a decision which Rowland mentally applauded. "And we 'll have Mrs. Striker, too," he said, "if she 'll come, to keep my mother in countenance; and at any rate we 'll have Miss Striker—the divine Petronilla!" The young lady thus denominated formed, with Mrs. Hudson, Miss Garland, and Cecilia, the feminine half of the company. Mr. Striker presented himself, sacrificing a morning's work, with a

magnanimity greater even than Roderick's, and foreign support was further secured in the person of Mr. Whitefoot, the
young Orthodox minister. Roderick had chosen the feasting-
place; he knew it well and had passed many a summer afternoon there, lying at his length on the grass and gazing at
the blue undulations of the horizon. It was a meadow on the
edge of a wood, with mossy rocks protruding through the
grass and a little lake on the other side. It was a cloudless
August day; Rowland always remembered it, and the scene,
and everything that was said and done, with extraordinary
distinctness. Roderick surpassed himself in friendly jollity,
and at one moment, when exhilaration was at the highest,
was seen in Mr. Striker's high white hat, drinking champagne
from a broken tea-cup to Mr. Striker's health. Miss Striker
had her father's pale blue eye; she was dressed as if she were
going to sit for her photograph, and remained for a long time
with Roderick on a little promontory overhanging the lake.
Mrs. Hudson sat all day with a little meek, apprehensive
smile. She was afraid of an "accident," though unless Miss
Striker (who indeed was a little of a romp) should push Roderick into the lake, it was hard to see what accident could
occur. Mrs. Hudson was as neat and crisp and uncrumpled at
the end of the festival as at the beginning. Mr. Whitefoot,
who but a twelvemonth later became a convert to episcopacy
and was already cultivating a certain conversational sonority,
devoted himself to Cecilia. He had a little book in his pocket,
out of which he read to her at intervals, lying stretched at her
feet, and it was a lasting joke with Cecilia, afterwards, that
she would never tell what Mr. Whitefoot's little book had
been. Rowland had placed himself near Miss Garland, while
the feasting went forward on the grass. She wore a so-called
gypsy hat—a little straw hat, tied down over her ears, so as
to cast her eyes into shadow, by a ribbon passing outside of
it. When the company dispersed, after lunch, he proposed to
her to take a stroll in the wood. She hesitated a moment and
looked toward Mrs. Hudson, as if for permission to leave her.
But Mrs. Hudson was listening to Mr. Striker, who sat gossiping to her with relaxed magniloquence, his waistcoat un-
buttoned and his hat on his nose.

"You can give your cousin your society at any time," said Rowland. "But me, perhaps, you 'll never see again."

"Why then should we wish to be friends, if nothing is to come of it?" she asked, with homely logic. But by this time she had consented, and they were treading the fallen pine-needles.

"Oh, one must take all one can get," said Rowland. "If we can be friends for half an hour, it 's so much gained."

"Do you expect never to come back to Northampton again?"

" 'Never' is a good deal to say. But I go to Europe for a long stay."

"Do you prefer it so much to your own country?"

"I will not say that. But I have the misfortune to be a rather idle man, and in Europe the burden of idleness is less heavy than here."

She was silent for a few minutes; then at last, "In that, then, we are better than Europe," she said. To a certain point Rowland agreed with her, but he demurred, to make her say more.

"Would n't it be better," she asked, "to work to get reconciled to America, than to go to Europe to get reconciled to idleness?"

"Doubtless; but you know work is hard to find."

"I come from a little place where every one has plenty," said Miss Garland. "We all work; every one I know works. And really," she added presently, "I look at you with curiosity; you are the first unoccupied man I ever saw."

"Don't look at me too hard," said Rowland, smiling. "I shall sink into the earth. What is the name of your little place?"

"West Nazareth," said Miss Garland, with her usual sobriety. "It is not so very little, though it 's smaller than Northampton."

"I wonder whether I could find any work at West Nazareth," Rowland said.

"You would not like it," Miss Garland declared reflectively. "Though there are far finer woods there than this. We have miles and miles of woods."

"I might chop down trees," said Rowland. "That is, if you allow it."

"Allow it? Why, where should we get our firewood?" Then, noticing that he had spoken jestingly, she glanced at him askance, though with no visible diminution of her gravity. "Don't you know how to do anything? Have you no profession?"

Rowland shook his head. "Absolutely none."

"What do you do all day?"

"Nothing worth relating. That 's why I am going to Europe. There, at least, if I do nothing, I shall see a great deal; and if I 'm not a producer, I shall at any rate be an observer."

"Can't we observe everywhere?"

"Certainly; and I really think that in that way I make the most of my opportunities. Though I confess," he continued, "that I often remember there are things to be seen here to which I probably have n't done justice. I should like, for instance, to see West Nazareth."

She looked round at him, open-eyed; not, apparently, that she exactly supposed he was jesting, for the expression of such a desire was not necessarily facetious; but as if he must have spoken with an ulterior motive. In fact, he had spoken from the simplest of motives. The girl beside him pleased him unspeakably, and, suspecting that her charm was essentially her own and not reflected from social circumstance, he wished to give himself the satisfaction of contrasting her with the meagre influences of her education. Miss Garland's second movement was to take him at his word. "Since you are free to do as you please, why don't you go there?"

"I am not free to do as I please now. I have offered your cousin to bear him company to Europe, he has accepted with enthusiasm, and I cannot retract."

"Are you going to Europe simply for his sake?"

Rowland hesitated a moment. "I think I may almost say so."

Miss Garland walked along in silence. "Do you mean to do a great deal for him?" she asked at last.

"What I can. But my power of helping him is very small beside his power of helping himself."

For a moment she was silent again. "You are very generous," she said, almost solemnly.

"No, I am simply very shrewd. Roderick will repay me. It 's an investment. At first, I think," he added shortly afterwards, "you would not have paid me that compliment. You distrusted me."

She made no attempt to deny it. "I did n't see why you should wish to make Roderick discontented. I thought you were rather frivolous."

"You did me injustice. I don't think I 'm that."

"It was because you are unlike other men—those, at least, whom I have seen."

"In what way?"

"Why, as you describe yourself. You have no duties, no profession, no home. You live for your pleasure."

"That 's all very true. And yet I maintain I 'm not frivolous."

"I hope not," said Miss Garland, simply. They had reached a point where the wood-path forked and put forth two divergent tracks which lost themselves in a verdurous tangle. Miss Garland seemed to think that the difficulty of choice between them was a reason for giving them up and turning back. Rowland thought otherwise, and detected agreeable grounds for preference in the left-hand path. As a compromise, they sat down on a fallen log. Looking about him, Rowland espied a curious wild shrub, with a spotted crimson leaf; he went and plucked a spray of it and brought it to Miss Garland. He had never observed it before, but she immediately called it by its name. She expressed surprise at his not knowing it; it was extremely common. He presently brought her a specimen of another delicate plant, with a little blue-streaked flower. "I suppose that 's common, too," he said, "but I have never seen it—or noticed it, at least." She answered that this one was rare, and meditated a moment before she could remember its name. At last she recalled it, and expressed surprise at his having found the plant in the woods; she supposed it grew only in open marshes. Rowland complimented her on her fund of useful information.

"It 's not especially useful," she answered; "but I like to know the names of plants as I do those of my acquaintances.

When we walk in the woods at home—which we do so much—it seems as unnatural not to know what to call the flowers as it would be to see some one in the town with whom we were not on speaking terms."

"Apropos of frivolity," Rowland said, "I 'm sure *you* have very little of it, unless at West Nazareth it is considered frivolous to walk in the woods and nod to the nodding flowers. Do kindly tell me a little about yourself." And to compel her to begin, "I know you come of a race of theologians," he went on.

"No," she replied, deliberating; "they are not theologians, though they are ministers. We don't take a very firm stand upon doctrine; we are practical, rather. We write sermons and preach them, but we do a great deal of hard work beside."

"And of this hard work what has your share been?"

"The hardest part: doing nothing."

"What do you call nothing?"

"I taught school a while: I must make the most of that. But I confess I did n't like it. Otherwise, I have only done little things at home, as they turned up."

"What kind of things?"

"Oh, every kind. If you had seen my home, you would understand."

Rowland would have liked to make her specify; but he felt a more urgent need to respect her simplicity than he had ever felt to defer to the complex circumstance of certain other women. "To be happy, I imagine," he contented himself with saying, "you need to be occupied. You need to have something to expend yourself upon."

"That is not so true as it once was; now that I am older, I am sure I am less impatient of leisure. Certainly, these two months that I have been with Mrs. Hudson, I have had a terrible amount of it. And yet I have liked it! And now that I am probably to be with her all the while that her son is away, I look forward to more with a resignation that I don't quite know what to make of."

"It is settled, then, that you are to remain with your cousin?"

"It depends upon their writing from home that I may stay. But that is probable. Only I must not forget," she said, rising, "that the ground for my doing so is that she be not left alone."

"I am glad to know," said Rowland, "that I shall probably often hear about you. I assure you I shall often think about you!" These words were half impulsive, half deliberate. They were the simple truth, and he had asked himself why he should not tell her the truth. And yet they were not all of it; her hearing the rest would depend upon the way she received this. She received it not only, as Rowland foresaw, without a shadow of coquetry, of any apparent thought of listening to it gracefully, but with a slight movement of nervous deprecation, which seemed to betray itself in the quickening of her step. Evidently, if Rowland was to take pleasure in hearing about her, it would have to be a highly disinterested pleasure. She answered nothing, and Rowland too, as he walked beside her, was silent; but as he looked along the shadow-woven wood-path, what he was really facing was a level three years of disinterestedness. He ushered them in by talking composed civility until he had brought Miss Garland back to her companions.

He saw her but once again. He was obliged to be in New York a couple of days before sailing, and it was arranged that Roderick should overtake him at the last moment. The evening before he left Northampton he went to say farewell to Mrs. Hudson. The ceremony was brief. Rowland soon perceived that the poor little lady was in the melting mood, and, as he dreaded her tears, he compressed a multitude of solemn promises into a silent hand-shake and took his leave. Miss Garland, she had told him, was in the back-garden with Roderick: he might go out to them. He did so, and as he drew near he heard Roderick's high-pitched voice ringing behind the shrubbery. In a moment, emerging, he found Miss Garland leaning against a tree, with her cousin before her talking with great emphasis. He asked pardon for interrupting them, and said he wished only to bid her good-by. She gave him her hand and he made her his bow in silence. "Don't forget," he said to Roderick, as he turned away. "And don't, in this company, repent of your bargain."

"I shall not let him," said Miss Garland, with something very like gayety. "I shall see that he is punctual. He must go!

I owe you an apology for having doubted that he ought to."
And in spite of the dusk Rowland could see that she had an
even finer smile than he had supposed.

Roderick was punctual, eagerly punctual, and they went.
Rowland for several days was occupied with material cares,
and lost sight of his sentimental perplexities. But they only
slumbered, and they were sharply awakened. The weather was
fine, and the two young men always sat together upon deck
late into the evening. One night, toward the last, they were
at the stern of the great ship, watching her grind the solid
blackness of the ocean into phosphorescent foam. They talked
on these occasions of everything conceivable, and had the air
of having no secrets from each other. But it was on Roderick's conscience that this air belied him, and he was too frank
by nature, moreover, for permanent reticence on any point.

"I must tell you something," he said at last. "I should like
you to know it, and you will be so glad to know it. Besides,
it 's only a question of time; three months hence, probably,
you would have guessed it. I am engaged to Mary Garland."

Rowland sat staring; though the sea was calm, it seemed to
him that the ship gave a great dizzying lurch. But in a moment he contrived to answer coherently: "Engaged to Miss
Garland! I never supposed—I never imagined"—

"That I was in love with her?" Roderick interrupted. "Neither did I, until this last fortnight. But you came and put me
into such ridiculous good-humor that I felt an extraordinary
desire to tell some woman that I adored her. Miss Garland is
a magnificent girl; you know her too little to do her justice. I
have been quietly learning to know her, these past three
months, and have been falling in love with her without being
conscious of it. It appeared, when I spoke to her, that she had
a kindness for me. So the thing was settled. I must of course
make some money before we can marry. It 's rather droll,
certainly, to engage one's self to a girl whom one is going to
leave the next day, for years. We shall be condemned, for
some time to come, to do a terrible deal of abstract thinking
about each other. But I wanted her blessing on my career and
I could not help asking for it. Unless a man is unnaturally
selfish he needs to work for some one else than himself, and
I am sure I shall run a smoother and swifter course for know-

ing that that fine creature is waiting, at Northampton, for news of my greatness. If ever I am a dull companion and over-addicted to moping, remember in justice to me that I am in love and that my sweetheart is five thousand miles away."

Rowland listened to all this with a sort of feeling that fortune had played him an elaborately-devised trick. It had lured him out into mid-ocean and smoothed the sea and stilled the winds and given him a singularly sympathetic comrade, and then it had turned and delivered him a thumping blow in mid-chest. "Yes," he said, after an attempt at the usual formal congratulation, "you certainly ought to do better—with Miss Garland waiting for you at Northampton."

Roderick, now that he had broken ground, was eloquent and rung a hundred changes on the assurance that he was a very happy man. Then at last, suddenly, his climax was a yawn, and he declared that he must go to bed. Rowland let him go alone, and sat there late, between sea and sky.

III

Rome

ONE WARM, STILL DAY, late in the Roman autumn, our two young men were sitting beneath one of the high-stemmed pines of the Villa Ludovisi. They had been spending an hour in the mouldy little garden-house, where the colossal mask of the famous Juno looks out with blank eyes from that dusky corner which must seem to her the last possible stage of a lapse from Olympus. Then they had wandered out into the gardens, and were lounging away the morning under the spell of their magical picturesqueness. Roderick declared that he would go nowhere else; that, after the Juno, it was a profanation to look at anything but sky and trees. There was a fresco of Guercino, to which Rowland, though he had seen it on his former visit to Rome, went dutifully to pay his respects. But Roderick, though he had never seen it, declared that it could n't be worth a fig, and that he did n't care to look at ugly things. He remained stretched on his overcoat, which he had spread on the grass, while Rowland went off envying the intellectual comfort of genius, which can arrive at serene conclusions without disagreeable processes. When the latter came back, his friend was sitting with his elbows on his knees and his head in his hands. Rowland, in the geniality of a mood attuned to the mellow charm of a Roman villa, found a good word to say for the Guercino; but he chiefly talked of the view from the little belvedere on the roof of the casino, and how it looked like the prospect from a castle turret in a fairy tale.

"Very likely," said Roderick, throwing himself back with a yawn. "But I must let it pass. I have seen enough for the present; I have reached the top of the hill. I have an indigestion of impressions; I must work them off before I go in for any more. I don't want to look at any more of other people's works, for a month—not even at Nature's own. I want to look at Roderick Hudson's. The result of it all is that I 'm not afraid. I can but try, as well as the rest of them! The fellow who did that gazing goddess yonder only made an ex-

222

periment. The other day, when I was looking at Michael Angelo's Moses, I was seized with a kind of defiance—a reaction against all this mere passive enjoyment of grandeur. It was a rousing great success, certainly, that rose there before me, but somehow it was not an inscrutable mystery, and it seemed to me, not perhaps that I should some day do as well, but that at least I *might*!"

"As you say, you can but try," said Rowland. "Success is only passionate effort."

"Well, the passion is blazing; we have been piling on fuel handsomely. It came over me just now that it is exactly three months to a day since I left Northampton. I can't believe it!"

"It certainly seems more."

"It seems like ten years. What an exquisite ass I was!"

"Do you feel so wise now?"

"Verily! Don't I look so? Surely I have n't the same face. Have n't I a different eye, a different expression, a different voice?"

"I can hardly say, because I have seen the transition. But it 's very likely. You are, in the literal sense of the word, more civilized. I dare say," added Rowland, "that Miss Garland would think so."

"That 's not what she would call it; she would say I was corrupted."

Rowland asked few questions about Miss Garland, but he always listened narrowly to his companion's voluntary observations.

"Are you very sure?" he replied.

"Why, she 's a stern moralist, and she would infer from my appearance that I had become a cynical sybarite." Roderick had, in fact, a Venetian watch-chain round his neck and a magnificent Roman intaglio on the third finger of his left hand.

"Will you think I take a liberty," asked Rowland, "if I say you judge her superficially?"

"For heaven's sake," cried Roderick, laughing, "don't tell me she 's not a moralist! It was for that I fell in love with her, and with rigid virtue in her person."

"She is a moralist, but not, as you imply, a narrow one. That 's more than a difference in degree; it 's a difference in kind. I don't know whether I ever mentioned it, but I admire her extremely. There is nothing narrow about her but her experience; everything else is large. My impression of her is of a person of great capacity, as yet wholly unmeasured and untested. Some day or other, I 'm sure, she will judge fairly and wisely of everything."

"Stay a bit!" cried Roderick; "you 're a better Catholic than the Pope. I shall be content if she judges fairly of me—of my merits, that is. The rest she must not judge at all. She 's a grimly devoted little creature; may she always remain so! Changed as I am, I adore her none the less. What becomes of all our emotions, our impressions," he went on, after a long pause, "all the material of thought that life pours into us at such a rate during such a memorable three months as these? There are twenty moments a week—a day, for that matter, some days—that seem supreme, twenty impressions that seem ultimate, that appear to form an intellectual era. But others come treading on their heels and sweeping them along, and they all melt like water into water and settle the question of precedence among themselves. The curious thing is that the more the mind takes in, the more it has space for, and that all one's ideas are like the Irish people at home who live in the different corners of a room, and take boarders."

"I fancy it is our peculiar good luck that we don't see the limits of our minds," said Rowland. "We are young, compared with what we may one day be. That belongs to youth; it is perhaps the best part of it. They say that old people do find themselves at last face to face with a solid blank wall, and stand thumping against it in vain. It resounds, it seems to have something beyond it, but it won't move! That 's only a reason for living with open doors as long as we can!"

"Open doors?" murmured Roderick. "Yes, let us close no doors that open upon Rome. For this, for the mind, is eternal summer! But though my doors may stand open to-day," he presently added, "I shall see no visitors. I want to pause and breathe; I want to dream of a statue. I have been working hard for three months; I have earned a right to a reverie."

Rowland, on his side, was not without provision for reflection, and they lingered on in broken, desultory talk. Rowland felt the need for intellectual rest, for a truce to present care

for churches, statues, and pictures, on even better grounds
than his companion, inasmuch as he had really been living
Roderick's intellectual life the past three months, as well as
his own. As he looked back on these full-flavored weeks, he
drew a long breath of satisfaction, almost of relief. Roderick,
thus far, had justified his confidence and flattered his perspicacity; he was rapidly unfolding into an ideal brilliancy. He
was changed even more than he himself suspected; he had
stepped, without faltering, into his birthright, and was spending money, intellectually, as lavishly as a young heir who has
just won an obstructive lawsuit. Roderick's glance and voice
were the same, doubtless, as when they enlivened the summer
dusk on Cecilia's veranda, but in his person, generally, there
was an indefinable expression of experience rapidly and easily
assimilated. Rowland had been struck at the outset with the
instinctive quickness of his observation and his free appropri-
ation of whatever might serve his purpose. He had not been,
for instance, half an hour on English soil before he perceived
that he was dressed like a rustic, and he had immediately re-
formed his toilet with the most unerring tact. His appetite for
novelty was insatiable, and for everything characteristically
foreign, as it presented itself, he had an extravagant greeting;
but in half an hour the novelty had faded, he had guessed the
secret, he had plucked out the heart of the mystery and was
clamoring for a keener sensation. At the end of a month, he
presented, mentally, a puzzling spectacle to his companion.
He had caught, instinctively, the key-note of the old world.
He observed and enjoyed, he criticised and rhapsodized, but
though all things interested him and many delighted him,
none surprised him; he had divined their logic and measured
their proportions, and referred them infallibly to their cate-
gories. Witnessing the rate at which he did intellectual execution on the general spectacle of European life, Rowland at
moments felt vaguely uneasy for the future; the boy was living too fast, he would have said, and giving alarming pledges
to ennui in his later years. But we must live as our pulses are
timed, and Roderick's struck the hour very often. He was, by
imagination, though he never became in manner, a natural
man of the world; he had intuitively, as an artist, what one
may call the historic consciousness. He had a relish for social

subtleties and mysteries, and, in perception, when occasion offered him an inch he never failed to take an ell. A single glimpse of a social situation of the elder type enabled him to construct the whole, with all its complex chiaroscuro, and Rowland more than once assured him that he made him believe in the metempsychosis, and that he must have lived in European society, in the last century, as a gentleman in a cocked hat and brocaded waistcoat. Hudson asked Rowland questions which poor Rowland was quite unable to answer, and of which he was equally unable to conceive where he had picked up the data. Roderick ended by answering them himself, tolerably to his satisfaction, and in a short time he had almost turned the tables and become in their walks and talks the accredited source of information. Rowland told him that when he turned sculptor a capital novelist was spoiled, and that to match his eye for social detail one would have to go to Honoré de Balzac. In all this Rowland took a generous pleasure; he felt an especial kindness for his comrade's radiant youthfulness of temperament. He was so much younger than he himself had ever been! And surely youth and genius, hand in hand, were the most beautiful sight in the world. Roderick added to this the charm of his more immediately personal qualities. The vivacity of his perceptions, the audacity of his imagination, the picturesqueness of his phrase when he was pleased,—and even more when he was displeased,—his abounding good-humor, his candor, his unclouded frankness, his unfailing impulse to share every emotion and impression with his friend; all this made comradeship a pure felicity, and interfused with a deeper amenity their long evening talks at café doors in Italian towns.

They had gone almost immediately to Paris, and had spent their days at the Louvre and their evenings at the theatre. Roderick was divided in mind as to whether Titian or Mademoiselle Delaporte was the greater artist. They had come down through France to Genoa and Milan, had spent a fortnight in Venice and another in Florence, and had now been a month in Rome. Roderick had said that he meant to spend three months in simply looking, absorbing, and reflecting, without putting pencil to paper. He looked indefatigably, and certainly saw great things—things greater, doubtless, at times, than the intentions of the artist. And yet he made few false steps and wasted little time in theories of what he ought to like and to dislike. He judged instinctively and passionately, but never vulgarly. At Venice, for a couple of days, he had half a fit of melancholy over the pretended discovery that he had missed his way, and that the only proper vestment of plastic conceptions was the coloring of Titian and Paul Veronese. Then one morning the two young men had themselves rowed out to Torcello, and Roderick lay back for a couple of hours watching a brown-breasted gondolier making superb muscular movements, in high relief, against the sky of the Adriatic, and at the end jerked himself up with a violence that nearly swamped the gondola, and declared that the only thing worth living for was to make a colossal bronze and set it aloft in the light of a public square. In Rome his first care was for the Vatican; he went there again and again. But the old imperial and papal city altogether delighted him; only there he really found what he had been looking for from the first—the complete antipodes of Northampton. And indeed Rome is the natural home of those spirits with which we just now claimed fellowship for Roderick—the spirits with a deep relish for the artificial element in life and the infinite superpositions of history. It is the immemorial city of convention. The stagnant Roman air is charged with convention; it colors the yellow light and deepens the chilly shadows. And in that still recent day the most impressive convention in all history was visible to men's eyes, in the Roman streets, erect in a gilded coach drawn by four black horses. Roderick's first fortnight was a high æsthetic revel. He declared that Rome made him feel and understand more things than he could express: he was sure that life must have there, for all one's senses, an incomparable fineness; that more interesting things must happen to one than anywhere else. And he gave Rowland to understand that he meant to live freely and largely, and be as interested as occasion demanded. Rowland saw no reason to regard this as a menace of dissipation, because, in the first place, there was in all dissipation, refine it as one might, a grossness which would disqualify it for Roderick's favor, and because, in the second, the young sculptor was a man to regard all things in the light of his art, to hand over his passions to his genius to be dealt with, and to find that he could live largely enough without exceeding the circle of wholesome curiosity. Rowland took immense satisfaction in his companion's deep impatience to *make something* of all his impressions. Some of these indeed found their way into a channel which did not lead to statues, but it was none the less a safe one. He wrote frequent long letters to Miss Garland; when Rowland went with him to post them he thought wistfully of the fortune of the great loosely-written missives, which cost Roderick unconscionable sums in postage. He received punctual answers of a more frugal form, written in a clear, minute hand, on paper vexatiously thin. If Rowland was present when they came, he turned away and thought of other things—or tried to. These were the only moments when his sympathy halted, and they were brief. For the rest he let the days go by unprotestingly, and enjoyed Roderick's serene efflorescence as he would have done a beautiful summer sunrise. Rome, for the past month, had been delicious. The annual descent of the Goths had not yet begun, and sunny leisure seemed to brood over the city.

Roderick had taken out a note-book and was roughly sketching a memento of the great Juno. Suddenly there was a noise on the gravel, and the young men, looking up, saw three persons advancing. One was a woman of middle age, with a rather grand air and a great many furbelows. She looked very hard at our friends as she passed, and glanced back over her shoulder, as if to hasten the step of a young girl who slowly followed her. She had such an expansive majesty of mien that Rowland supposed she must have some proprietary right in the villa and was not just then in a hospitable mood. Beside her walked a little elderly man, tightly buttoned in a shabby black coat, but with a flower in his lappet, and a pair of soiled light gloves. He was a grotesque-looking personage, and might have passed for a gentleman of the old school, reduced by adversity to playing cicerone to foreigners of distinction. He had a little black eye which glittered like a diamond and rolled about like a ball of quicksilver, and a white moustache, cut short and stiff, like a worn-out brush. He was smiling with extreme urbanity, and talking in a low, mellifluous voice to the lady, who evidently was not listening to him. At a considerable distance behind this couple strolled a young girl, apparently of about twenty. She was tall and slender, and dressed with extreme elegance; she led by a cord a large poodle of the most fantastic aspect. He was combed and decked like a ram for sacrifice; his trunk and haunches were of the most transparent pink, his fleecy head and shoulders as white as jeweler's cotton, and his tail and ears ornamented with long blue ribbons. He stepped along stiffly and solemnly beside his mistress, with an air of conscious elegance. There was something at first slightly ridiculous in the sight of a young lady gravely appended to an animal of these incongruous attributes, and Roderick, with his customary frankness, greeted the spectacle with a confident smile. The young girl perceived it and turned her face full upon him, with a gaze intended apparently to enforce greater deference. It was not deference, however, her face provoked, but startled, submissive admiration; Roderick's smile fell dead, and he sat eagerly staring. A pair of extraordinary dark blue eyes, a mass of dusky hair over a low forehead, a blooming oval of perfect purity, a flexible lip, just touched with disdain, the step and carriage of a tired princess—these were the general features of his vision. The young lady was walking slowly and letting her long dress rustle over the gravel; the young men had time to see her distinctly before she averted her face and went her way. She left a vague, sweet perfume behind her as she passed.

"Immortal powers!" cried Roderick, "what a vision! In the name of transcendent perfection, who is she?" He sprang up and stood looking after her until she rounded a turn in the avenue. "What a movement, what a manner, what a poise of the head! I wonder if she would sit to me."

"You had better go and ask her," said Rowland, laughing. "She is certainly most beautiful."

"Beautiful? She 's beauty itself—she 's a revelation. I don't believe she is living—she 's a phantasm, a vapor, an illusion!"

"The poodle," said Rowland, "is certainly alive."

"Nay, he too may be a grotesque phantom, like the black dog in Faust."

"I hope at least that the young lady has nothing in common with Mephistopheles. She looked dangerous."

"If beauty is immoral, as people think at Northampton," said Roderick, "she is the incarnation of evil. The mamma and the queer old gentleman, moreover, are a pledge of her reality. Who are they all?"

"The Prince and Princess Ludovisi and the *principessina*," suggested Rowland.

"There are no such people," said Roderick. "Besides, the little old man is not the papa." Rowland smiled, wondering how he had ascertained these facts, and the young sculptor went on. "The old man is a Roman, a hanger-on of. the mamma, a useful personage who now and then gets asked to dinner. The ladies are foreigners, from some Northern country; I won't say which."

"Perhaps from the State of Maine," said Rowland.

"No, she 's not an American, I 'll lay a wager on that. She 's a daughter of this elder world. We shall see her again, I pray my stars; but if we don't, I shall have done something I never expected to—I shall have had a glimpse of ideal beauty." He sat down again and went on with his sketch of the Juno, scrawled away for ten minutes, and then handed the result in silence to Rowland. Rowland uttered an exclamation of surprise and applause. The drawing represented the Juno as to the position of the head, the brow, and the broad fillet across the hair; but the eyes, the mouth, the physiognomy were a vivid portrait of the young girl with the poodle. "I have been wanting a subject," said Roderick: "there 's one made to my hand! And now for work!"

They saw no more of the young girl, though Roderick looked hopefully, for some days, into the carriages on the Pincian. She had evidently been but passing through Rome; Naples or Florence now happily possessed her, and she was guiding her fleecy companion through the Villa Reale or the Boboli Gardens with the same superb defiance of irony. Roderick went to work and spent a month shut up in his studio; he had an idea, and he was not to rest till he had embodied it. He had established himself in the basement of a huge, dusky, dilapidated old house, in that long, tortuous, and preëminently Roman street which leads from the Corso to the Bridge of St. Angelo. The black archway which admitted you might have served as the portal of the Augean stables, but

you emerged presently upon a mouldy little court, of which
the fourth side was formed by a narrow terrace, overhanging
the Tiber. Here, along the parapet, were stationed half a
dozen shapeless fragments of sculpture, with a couple of
meagre orange-trees in terra-cotta tubs, and an oleander that
never flowered. The unclean, historic river swept beneath; behind were dusky, reeking walls, spotted here and there with
hanging rags and flower-pots in windows; opposite, at a distance, were the bare brown banks of the stream, the huge
rotunda of St. Angelo, tipped with its seraphic statue, the
dome of St. Peter's, and the broad-topped pines of the Villa
Doria. The place was crumbling and shabby and melancholy,
but the river was delightful, the rent was a trifle, and everything was picturesque. Roderick was in the best humor with
his quarters from the first, and was certain that the working
mood there would be intenser in an hour than in twenty years
of Northampton. His studio was a huge, empty room with a
vaulted ceiling, covered with vague, dark traces of an old
fresco, which Rowland, when he spent an hour with his
friend, used to stare at vainly for some surviving coherence of
floating draperies and clasping arms. Roderick had lodged
himself economically in the same quarter. He occupied a fifth
floor on the Ripetta, but he was only at home to sleep, for
when he was not at work he was either lounging in Rowland's more luxurious rooms or strolling through streets and
churches and gardens.

Rowland had found a convenient corner in a stately old
palace not far from the Fountain of Trevi, and made himself
a home to which books and pictures and prints and odds and
ends of curious furniture gave an air of leisurely permanence.
He had the tastes of a collector; he spent half his afternoons
ransacking the dusty magazines of the curiosity-mongers, and
often made his way, in quest of a prize, into the heart of
impecunious Roman households, which had been prevailed
upon to listen—with closed doors and an impenetrably wary
smile—to proposals for an hereditary "antique." In the evening, often, under the lamp, amid dropped curtains and the
scattered gleam of firelight upon polished carvings and mellow paintings, the two friends sat with their heads together,
criticising intaglios and etchings, water-color drawings and il-

luminated missals. Roderick's quick appreciation of every form of artistic beauty reminded his companion of the flexible temperament of those Italian artists of the sixteenth century who were indifferently painters and sculptors, sonneteers and engravers. At times when he saw how the young sculptor's day passed in a single sustained pulsation, while his own was broken into a dozen conscious devices for disposing of the hours, and intermingled with sighs, half suppressed, some of them, for conscience' sake, over what he failed of in action and missed in possession—he felt a pang of something akin to envy. But Rowland had two substantial aids for giving patience the air of contentment: he was an inquisitive reader and a passionate rider. He plunged into bulky German octavos on Italian history, and he spent long afternoons in the saddle, ranging over the grassy desolation of the Campagna. As the season went on and the social groups began to constitute themselves, he found that he knew a great many people and that he had easy opportunity for knowing others. He enjoyed a quiet corner of a drawing-room beside an agreeable woman, and although the machinery of what calls itself society seemed to him to have many superfluous wheels, he accepted invitations and made visits punctiliously, from the conviction that the only way not to be overcome by the ridiculous side of most of such observances is to take them with exaggerated gravity. He introduced Roderick right and left, and suffered him to make his way himself—an enterprise for which Roderick very soon displayed an all-sufficient capacity. Wherever he went he made, not exactly what is called a favorable impression, but what, from a practical point of view, is better—a puzzling one. He took to evening parties as a duck to water, and before the winter was half over was the most freely and frequently discussed young man in the heterogeneous foreign colony. Rowland's theory of his own duty was to let him run his course and play his cards, only holding himself ready to point out shoals and pitfalls, and administer a friendly propulsion through tight places. Roderick's manners on the precincts of the Pincian were quite the same as his manners on Cecilia's veranda: that is, they were no manners at all. But it remained as true as before that it would have been impossible, on the whole, to violate ceremony with less of lasting offense. He interrupted, he contradicted, he spoke to people he had never seen, and left his social creditors without the smallest conversational interest on their loans; he lounged and yawned, he talked loud when he should have talked low, and low when he should have talked loud. Many people, in consequence, thought him insufferably conceited, and declared that he ought to wait till he had something to show for his powers, before he assumed the airs of a spoiled celebrity. But to Rowland and to most friendly observers this judgment was quite beside the mark, and the young man's undiluted naturalness was its own justification. He was impulsive, spontaneous, sincere; there were so many people at dinner-tables and in studios who were not, that it seemed worth while to allow this rare specimen all possible freedom of action. If Roderick took the words out of your mouth when you were just prepared to deliver them with the most effective accent, he did it with a perfect good conscience and with no pretension of a better right to being heard, but simply because he was full to overflowing of his own momentary thought and it sprang from his lips without asking leave. There were persons who waited on your periods much more deferentially, who were a hundred times more capable than Roderick of a reflective impertinence. Roderick received from various sources, chiefly feminine, enough finely-adjusted advice to have established him in life as an embodiment of the proprieties, and he received it, as he afterwards listened to criticisms on his statues, with unfaltering candor and good-humor. Here and there, doubtless, as he went, he took in a reef in his sail; but he was too adventurous a spirit to be successfully tamed, and he remained at most points the florid, rather strident young Virginian whose serene inflexibility had been the despair of Mr. Striker. All this was what friendly commentators (still chiefly feminine) alluded to when they spoke of his delightful freshness, and critics of harsher sensibilities (of the other sex) when they denounced his damned impertinence. His appearance enforced these impressions—his handsome face, his radiant, unaverted eyes, his childish, unmodulated voice. Afterwards, when those who loved him were in tears, there was something in all this unspotted comeliness that seemed to lend a mockery to the causes of their sorrow.

Certainly, among the young men of genius who, for so many ages, have gone up to Rome to test their powers, none ever made a fairer beginning than Roderick. He rode his two horses at once with extraordinary good fortune; he established the happiest *modus vivendi* betwixt work and play. He wrestled all day with a mountain of clay in his studio, and chattered half the night away in Roman drawing-rooms. It all seemed part of a kind of divine facility. He was passionately interested, he was feeling his powers; now that they had thoroughly kindled in the glowing æsthetic atmosphere of Rome, the ardent young fellow should be pardoned for believing that he never was to see the end of them. He enjoyed immeasurably, after the chronic obstruction of home, the downright act of production. He kept models in his studio till they dropped with fatigue; he drew, on other days, at the Capitol and the Vatican, till his own head swam with his eagerness, and his limbs stiffened with the cold. He had promptly set up a life-sized figure which he called an "Adam," and was pushing it rapidly toward completion. There were naturally a great many wiseheads who smiled at his precipitancy, and cited him as one more example of Yankee crudity, a capital recruit to the great army of those who wish to dance before they can walk. They were right, but Roderick was right too, for the success of his statue was not to have been foreseen; it partook, really, of the miraculous. He never surpassed it afterwards, and a good judge here and there has been known to pronounce it the finest piece of sculpture of our modern era. To Rowland it seemed to justify superbly his highest hopes of his friend, and he said to himself that if he had invested his happiness in fostering a genius, he ought now to be in possession of a boundless complacency. There was something especially confident and masterly in the artist's negligence of all such small picturesque accessories as might serve to label his figure to a vulgar apprehension. If it represented the father of the human race and the primal embodiment of human sensation, it did so in virtue of its look of balanced physical perfection, and deeply, eagerly sentient vitality. Rowland, in fraternal zeal, traveled up to Carrara and selected at the quarries the most magnificent block of marble he could find, and when it came down to Rome, the two young men had a "cel-

ebration." They drove out to Albano, breakfasted boisterously
(in their respective measure) at the inn, and lounged away the
day in the sun on the top of Monte Cavo. Roderick's head
was full of ideas for other works, which he described with
infinite spirit and eloquence, as vividly as if they were ranged
on their pedestals before him. He had an indefatigable fancy;
things he saw in the streets, in the country, things he heard
and read, effects he saw just missed or half-expressed in the
works of others, acted upon his mind as a kind of challenge,
and he was terribly restless until, in some form or other, he
had taken up the glove and set his lance in rest.

The Adam was put into marble, and all the world came to
see it. Of the criticisms passed upon it this history undertakes
to offer no record; over many of them the two young men
had a daily laugh for a month, and certain of the formulas of
the connoisseurs, restrictive or indulgent, furnished Roderick
with a permanent supply of humorous catch-words. But people enough spoke flattering good-sense to make Roderick feel
as if he were already half famous. The statue passed formally
into Rowland's possession, and was paid for as if an illus-
trious name had been chiseled on the pedestal. Poor Roderick
owed every franc of the money. It was not for this, however,
but because he was so gloriously in the mood, that, denying
himself all breathing-time, on the same day he had given the
last touch to the Adam, he began to shape the rough contour
of an Eve. This went forward with equal rapidity and success.
Roderick lost his temper, time and again, with his models,
who offered but a gross, degenerate image of his splendid
ideal; but his ideal, as he assured Rowland, became gradually
such a fixed, vivid presence, that he had only to shut his eyes
to behold a creature far more to his purpose than the poor
girl who stood posturing at forty sous an hour. The Eve was
finished in a month, and the feat was extraordinary, as well as
the statue, which represented an admirably beautiful woman.
When the spring began to muffle the rugged old city with its
clambering festoons, it seemed to him that he had done a
handsome winter's work and had fairly earned a holiday. He
took a liberal one, and lounged away the lovely Roman May,
doing nothing. He looked very contented; with himself, perhaps, at times, a trifle too obviously. But who could have said

without good reason? He was "flushed with triumph;" this classic phrase portrayed him, to Rowland's sense. He would lose himself in long reveries, and emerge from them with a quickened smile and a heightened color. Rowland grudged him none of his smiles, and took an extreme satisfaction in his two statues. He had the Adam and the Eve transported to his own apartment, and one warm evening in May he gave a little dinner in honor of the artist. It was small, but Rowland had meant it should be very agreeably composed. He thought over his friends and chose four. They were all persons with whom he lived in a certain intimacy.

One of them was an American sculptor of French extraction, or remotely, perhaps, of Italian, for he rejoiced in the somewhat fervid name of Gloriani. He was a man of forty, he had been living for years in Paris and in Rome, and he now drove a very pretty trade in sculpture of the ornamental and fantastic sort. In his youth he had had money; but he had spent it recklessly, much of it scandalously, and at twenty-six had found himself obliged to make capital of his talent. This was quite inimitable, and fifteen years of indefatigable exercise had brought it to perfection. Rowland admitted its power, though it gave him very little pleasure; what he relished in the man was the extraordinary vivacity and frankness, not to call it the impudence, of his ideas. He had a definite, practical scheme of art, and he knew at least what he meant. In this sense he was solid and complete. There were so many of the æsthetic fraternity who were floundering in unknown seas, without a notion of which way their noses were turned, that Gloriani, conscious and compact, unlimitedly intelligent and consummately clever, dogmatic only as to his own duties, and at once gracefully deferential and profoundly indifferent to those of others, had for Rowland a certain intellectual refreshment quite independent of the character of his works. These were considered by most people to belong to a very corrupt, and by many to a positively indecent school. Others thought them tremendously knowing, and paid enormous prices for them; and indeed, to be able to point to one of Gloriani's figures in a shady corner of your library was tolerable proof that you were not a fool. Corrupt things they certainly were; in the line of sculpture they were quite the latest fruit of time.

It was the artist's opinion that there is no essential difference between beauty and ugliness; that they overlap and intermingle in a quite inextricable manner; that there is no saying where one begins and the other ends; that hideousness grimaces at you suddenly from out of the very bosom of loveliness, and beauty blooms before your eyes in the lap of vileness; that it is a waste of wit to nurse metaphysical distinctions, and a sadly meagre entertainment to caress imaginary lines; that the thing to aim at is the expressive, and the way to reach it is by ingenuity; that for this purpose everything may serve, and that a consummate work is a sort of hotch-potch of the pure and the impure, the graceful and the grotesque. Its prime duty is to amuse, to puzzle, to fascinate, to savor of a complex imagination. Gloriani's statues were florid and meretricious; they looked like magnified goldsmith's work. They were extremely elegant, but they had no charm for Rowland. He never bought one, but Gloriani was such an honest fellow, and withal was so deluged with orders, that this made no difference in their friendship. The artist might have passed for a Frenchman. He was a great talker, and a very picturesque one; he was almost bald; he had a small, bright eye, a broken nose, and a moustache with waxed ends. When sometimes he received you at his lodging, he introduced you to a lady with a plain face whom he called Madame Gloriani—which she was not.

Rowland's second guest was also an artist, but of a very different type. His friends called him Sam Singleton; he was an American, and he had been in Rome a couple of years. He painted small landscapes, chiefly in water-colors: Rowland had seen one of them in a shop window, had liked it extremely, and, ascertaining his address, had gone to see him and found him established in a very humble studio near the Piazza Barberini, where, apparently, fame and fortune had not yet found him out. Rowland took a fancy to him and bought several of his pictures; Singleton made few speeches, but was grateful. Rowland heard afterwards that when he first came to Rome he painted worthless daubs and gave no promise of talent. Improvement had come, however, hand in hand with patient industry, and his talent, though of a slender and delicate order, was now incontestable. It was as yet but scant-

ily recognized, and he had hard work to live. Rowland hung
his little water-colors on the parlor wall, and found that, as
he lived with them, he grew very fond of them. Singleton was
a diminutive, dwarfish personage; he looked like a precocious
child. He had a high, protuberant forehead, a transparent
brown eye, a perpetual smile, an extraordinary expression of
modesty and patience. He listened much more willingly than
he talked, with a little fixed, grateful grin; he blushed when
he spoke, and always offered his ideas in a sidelong fashion,
as if the presumption were against them. His modesty set
them off, and they were eminently to the point. He was so
perfect an example of the little noiseless, laborious artist
whom chance, in the person of a moneyed patron, has never
taken by the hand, that Rowland would have liked to befriend him by stealth. Singleton had expressed a fervent admiration for Roderick's productions, but had not yet met the
young master. Roderick was lounging against the chimney-
piece when he came in, and Rowland presently introduced
him. The little water-colorist stood with folded hands, blushing, smiling, and looking up at him as if Roderick were himself a statue on a pedestal. Singleton began to murmur
something about his pleasure, his admiration; the desire to
make his compliment smoothly gave him a kind of grotesque
formalism. Roderick looked down at him surprised, and suddenly burst into a laugh. Singleton paused a moment and
then, with an intenser smile, went on: "Well, sir, your statues
are beautiful, all the same!"

Rowland's two other guests were ladies, and one of them,
Miss Blanchard, belonged also to the artistic fraternity. She
was an American, she was young, she was pretty, and she had
made her way to Rome alone and unaided. She lived alone,
or with no other duenna than a bushy-browed old serving-
woman, though indeed she had a friendly neighbor in the
person of a certain Madame Grandoni, who in various social
emergencies lent her a protecting wing, and had come with
her to Rowland's dinner. Miss Blanchard had a little money,
but she was not above selling her pictures. These represented
generally a bunch of dew-sprinkled roses, with the dew-drops
very highly finished, or else a wayside shrine, and a peasant
woman, with her back turned, kneeling before it. She did

backs very well, but she was a little weak in faces. Flowers, however, were her speciality, and though her touch was a little old-fashioned and finical, she painted them with remarkable skill. Her pictures were chiefly bought by the English. Rowland had made her acquaintance early in the winter, and as she kept a saddle horse and rode a great deal, he had asked permission to be her cavalier. In this way they had become almost intimate. Miss Blanchard's name was Augusta; she was slender, pale, and elegant looking; she had a very pretty head and brilliant auburn hair, which she braided with classical simplicity. She talked in a sweet, soft voice, used language at times a trifle superfine, and made literary allusions. These had often a patriotic strain, and Rowland had more than once been irritated by her quotations from Mrs. Sigourney in the cork-woods of Monte Mario, and from Mr. Willis among the ruins of Veii. Rowland was of a dozen different minds about her, and was half surprised, at times, to find himself treating it as a matter of serious moment whether he liked her or not. He admired her, and indeed there was something admirable in her combination of beauty and talent, of isolation and tranquil self-support. He used sometimes to go into the little, high-niched, ordinary room which served her as a studio, and find her working at a panel six inches square, at an open casement, profiled against the deep blue Roman sky. She received him with a meek-eyed dignity that made her seem like a painted saint on a church window, receiving the daylight in all her being. The breath of reproach passed her by with folded wings. And yet Rowland wondered why he did not like her better. If he failed, the reason was not far to seek. There was another woman whom he liked better, an image in his heart which refused to yield precedence.

On that evening to which allusion has been made, when Rowland was left alone between the starlight and the waves with the sudden knowledge that Mary Garland was to become another man's wife, he had made, after a while, the simple resolution to forget her. And every day since, like a famous philosopher who wished to abbreviate his mourning for a faithful servant, he had said to himself in substance— "Remember to forget Mary Garland." Sometimes it seemed as if he were succeeding; then, suddenly, when he was least expecting it, he would find her name, inaudibly, on his lips, and seem to see her eyes meeting his eyes. All this made him uncomfortable, and seemed to portend a possible discord. Discord was not to his taste; he shrank from imperious passions, and the idea of finding himself jealous of an unsuspecting friend was absolutely repulsive. More than ever, then, the path of duty was to forget Mary Garland, and he cultivated oblivion, as we may say, in the person of Miss Blanchard. Her fine temper, he said to himself, was a trifle cold and conscious, her purity prudish, perhaps, her culture pedantic. But since he was obliged to give up hopes of Mary Garland, Providence owed him a compensation, and he had fits of angry sadness in which it seemed to him that to attest his right to sentimental satisfaction he would be capable of falling in love with a woman he absolutely detested, if she were the best that came in his way. And what was the use, after all, of bothering about a possible which was only, perhaps, a dream? Even if Mary Garland had been free, what right had he to assume that he would have pleased her? The actual was good enough. Miss Blanchard had beautiful hair, and if she was a trifle old-maidish, there is nothing like matrimony for curing old-maidishness.

Madame Grandoni, who had formed with the companion of Rowland's rides an alliance which might have been called defensive on the part of the former and attractive on that of Miss Blanchard, was an excessively ugly old lady, highly esteemed in Roman society for her homely benevolence and her shrewd and humorous good sense. She had been the widow of a German archæologist, who had come to Rome in the early ages as an attaché of the Prussian legation on the Capitoline. Her good sense had been wanting on but a single occasion, that of her second marriage. This occasion was certainly a momentous one, but these, by common consent, are not test cases. A couple of years after her first husband's death, she had accepted the hand and the name of a Neapolitan music-master, ten years younger than herself, and with no fortune but his fiddle-bow. The marriage was most unhappy, and the Maestro Grandoni was suspected of using the fiddle-bow as an instrument of conjugal correction. He had finally run off with a *prima donna assoluta*, who, it was to be hoped, had given him a taste of the quality implied in her title. He was believed to be living still, but he had shrunk to a small black spot in Madame Grandoni's life, and for ten years she had not mentioned his name. She wore a light flaxen wig, which was never very artfully adjusted, but this mattered little, as she made no secret of it. She used to say, "I was not always so ugly as this; as a young girl I had beautiful golden hair, very much the color of my wig." She had worn from time immemorial an old blue satin dress, and a white crape shawl embroidered in colors; her appearance was ridiculous, but she had an interminable Teutonic pedigree, and her manners, in every presence, were easy and jovial, as became a lady whose ancestor had been cup-bearer to Frederick Barbarossa. Thirty years' observation of Roman society had sharpened her wits and given her an inexhaustible store of anecdotes, but she had beneath her crumpled bodice a deep-welling fund of Teutonic sentiment, which she communicated only to the objects of her particular favor. Rowland had a great regard for her, and she repaid it by wishing him to get married. She never saw him without whispering to him that Augusta Blanchard was just the girl.

It seemed to Rowland a sort of foreshadowing of matrimony to see Miss Blanchard standing gracefully on his hearth-rug and blooming behind the central bouquet at his circular dinner-table. The dinner was very prosperous and Roderick amply filled his position as hero of the feast. He had always an air of buoyant enjoyment in his work, but on this occasion he manifested a good deal of harmless pleasure in his glory. He drank freely and talked bravely; he leaned back in his chair with his hands in his pockets, and flung open the gates of his eloquence. Singleton sat gazing and listening open-mouthed, as if Apollo in person were talking. Gloriani showed a twinkle in his eye and an evident disposition to draw Roderick out. Rowland was rather regretful, for he knew that theory was not his friend's strong point, and that it was never fair to take his measure from his talk.

"As you have begun with Adam and Eve," said Gloriani, "I suppose you are going straight through the Bible." He was one of the persons who thought Roderick delightfully fresh.

"I may make a David," said Roderick, "but I shall not try

any more of the Old Testament people. I don't like the Jews;
I don't like pendulous noses. David, the boy David, is rather
an exception; you can think of him and treat him as a young
Greek. Standing forth there on the plain of battle between
the contending armies, rushing forward to let fly his stone,
he looks like a beautiful runner at the Olympic games. After
that I shall skip to the New Testament. I mean to make a
Christ."

"You 'll put nothing of the Olympic games into him, I
hope," said Gloriani.

"Oh, I shall make him very different from the Christ of
tradition; more—more"—and Roderick paused a moment to
think. This was the first that Rowland had heard of his
Christ.

"More rationalistic, I suppose," suggested Miss Blanchard.

"More idealistic!" cried Roderick. "The perfection of form,
you know, to symbolize the perfection of spirit."

"For a companion piece," said Miss Blanchard, "you ought
to make a Judas."

"Never! I mean never to make anything ugly. The Greeks
never made anything ugly, and I 'm a Hellenist; I 'm not a
Hebraist! I have been thinking lately of making a Cain, but I
should never dream of making him ugly. He should be a very
handsome fellow, and he should lift up the murderous club
with the beautiful movement of the fighters in the Greek
friezes who are chopping at their enemies."

"There 's no use trying to be a Greek," said Gloriani. "If
Phidias were to come back, he would recommend you to give
it up. I am half Italian and half French, and, as a whole, a
Yankee. What sort of a Greek should I make? I think the
Judas is a capital idea for a statue. Much obliged to you, madame, for the suggestion. What an insidious little scoundrel
one might make of him, sitting there nursing his money-bag
and his treachery! There can be a great deal of expression in
a pendulous nose, my dear sir, especially when it is cast in
green bronze."

"Very likely," said Roderick. "But it is not the sort of
expression I care for. I care only for perfect beauty. There it
is, if you want to know it! That 's as good a profession of
faith as another. In future, so far as my things are not posi-

tively beautiful, you may set them down as failures. For me, it 's either that or nothing. It 's against the taste of the day, I know; we have really lost the faculty to understand beauty in the large, ideal way. We stand like a race with shrunken muscles, staring helplessly at the weights our forefathers easily lifted. But I don't hesitate to proclaim it—I mean to lift them again! I mean to go in for big things; that 's my notion of my art. I mean to do things that will be simple and vast and infinite. You 'll see if they won't be infinite! Excuse me if I brag a little; all those Italian fellows in the Renaissance used to brag. There was a sensation once common, I am sure, in the human breast—a kind of religious awe in the presence of a marble image newly created and expressing the human type in superhuman purity. When Phidias and Praxiteles had their statues of goddesses unveiled in the temples of the Ægean, don't you suppose there was a passionate beating of hearts, a thrill of mysterious terror? I mean to bring it back; I mean to thrill the world again! I mean to produce a Juno that will make you tremble, a Venus that will make you swoon!"

"So that when we come and see you," said Madame Grandoni, "we must be sure and bring our smelling-bottles. And pray have a few soft sofas conveniently placed."

"Phidias and Praxiteles," Miss Blanchard remarked, "had the advantage of believing in their goddesses. I insist on believing, for myself, that the pagan mythology is not a fiction, and that Venus and Juno and Apollo and Mercury used to come down in a cloud into this very city of Rome where we sit talking nineteenth century English."

"Nineteenth century nonsense, my dear!" cried Madame Grandoni. "Mr. Hudson may be a new Phidias, but Venus and Juno—that 's you and I—arrived to-day in a very dirty cab; and were cheated by the driver, too."

"But, my dear fellow," objected Gloriani, "you don't mean to say you are going to make over in cold blood those poor old exploded Apollos and Hebes."

"It won't matter what you call them," said Roderick. "They shall be simply divine forms. They shall be Beauty; they shall be Wisdom; they shall be Power; they shall be Genius; they shall be Daring. That 's all the Greek divinities were."

"That 's rather abstract, you know," said Miss Blanchard.

"My dear fellow," cried Gloriani, "you 're delightfully young."

"I hope you 'll not grow any older," said Singleton, with a flush of sympathy across his large white forehead. "You can do it if you try."

"Then there are all the Forces and Mysteries and Elements of Nature," Roderick went on. "I mean to do the Morning; I mean to do the Night! I mean to do the Ocean and the Mountains; the Moon and the West Wind. I mean to make a magnificent statue of America!"

"America—the Mountains—the Moon!" said Gloriani. "You 'll find it rather hard, I 'm afraid, to compress such subjects into classic forms."

"Oh, there 's a way," cried Roderick, "and I shall think it out. My figures shall make no contortions, but they shall mean a tremendous deal."

"I 'm sure there are contortions enough in Michael Angelo," said Madame Grandoni. "Perhaps you don't approve of him."

"Oh, Michael Angelo was not me!" said Roderick, with sublimity. There was a great laugh; but after all, Roderick had done some fine things.

Rowland had bidden one of the servants bring him a small portfolio of prints, and had taken out a photograph of Roderick's little statue of the youth drinking. It pleased him to see his friend sitting there in radiant ardor, defending idealism against so knowing an apostle of corruption as Gloriani, and he wished to help the elder artist to be confuted. He silently handed him the photograph.

"Bless me!" cried Gloriani, "did he do this?"

"Ages ago," said Roderick.

Gloriani looked at the photograph a long time, with evident admiration.

"It 's deucedly pretty," he said at last. "But, my dear young friend, you can't keep this up."

"I shall do better," said Roderick.

"You will do worse! You will become weak. You will have to take to violence, to contortions, to romanticism, in self-defense. This sort of thing is like a man trying to lift himself up by the seat of his trousers. He may stand on tiptoe, but he can't do more. Here you stand on tiptoe, very gracefully, I admit; but you can't fly; there 's no use trying."

"My 'America' shall answer you!" said Roderick, shaking toward him a tall glass of champagne and drinking it down.

Singleton had taken the photograph and was poring over it with a little murmur of delight.

"Was this done in America?" he asked.

"In a square white wooden house at Northampton, Massachusetts," Roderick answered.

"Dear old white wooden houses!" said Miss Blanchard.

"If you could do as well as this there," said Singleton, blushing and smiling, "one might say that really you had only to lose by coming to Rome."

"Mallet is to blame for that," said Roderick. "But I am willing to risk the loss."

The photograph had been passed to Madame Grandoni. "It reminds me," she said, "of the things a young man used to do whom I knew years ago, when I first came to Rome. He was a German, a pupil of Overbeck and a votary of spiritual art. He used to wear a black velvet tunic and a very low shirt collar; he had a neck like a sickly crane, and let his hair grow down to his shoulders. His name was Herr Schafgans. He never painted anything so profane as a man taking a drink, but his figures were all of the simple and slender and angular pattern, and nothing if not innocent—like this one of yours. He would not have agreed with Gloriani any more than you. He used to come and see me very often, and in those days I thought his tunic and his long neck infallible symptoms of genius. His talk was all of gilded aureoles and beatific visions; he lived on weak wine and biscuits, and wore a lock of Saint Somebody's hair in a little bag round his neck. If he was not a Beato Angelico, it was not his own fault. I hope with all my heart that Mr. Hudson will do the fine things he talks about, but he must bear in mind the history of dear Mr. Schafgans as a warning against high-flown pretensions. One fine day this poor young man fell in love with a Roman model, though she had never sat to him, I believe, for she was a buxom, bold-faced, high-colored creature, and he painted

none but pale, sickly women. He offered to marry her, and
she looked at him from head to foot, gave a shrug, and consented. But he was ashamed to set up his ménage in Rome.
They went to Naples, and there, a couple of years afterwards,
I saw him. The poor fellow was ruined. His wife used to beat
him, and he had taken to drinking. He wore a ragged black
coat, and he had a blotchy, red face. Madame had turned
washerwoman and used to make him go and fetch the dirty
linen. His talent had gone heaven knows where! He was getting his living by painting views of Vesuvius in eruption on
the little boxes they sell at Sorrento."

"Moral: don't fall in love with a buxom Roman model,"
said Roderick. "I 'm much obliged to you for your story, but
I don't mean to fall in love with any one."

Gloriani had possessed himself of the photograph again,
and was looking at it curiously. "It 's a happy bit of youth,"
he said. "But you can't keep it up—you can't keep it up!"

The two sculptors pursued their discussion after dinner, in
the drawing-room. Rowland left them to have it out in a corner, where Roderick's Eve stood over them in the shaded
lamplight, in vague white beauty, like the guardian angel of
the young idealist. Singleton was listening to Madame Grandoni, and Rowland took his place on the sofa, near Miss
Blanchard. They had a good deal of familiar, desultory talk.
Every now and then Madame Grandoni looked round at
them. Miss Blanchard at last asked Rowland certain questions
about Roderick: who he was, where he came from, whether
it was true, as she had heard, that Rowland had discovered
him and brought him out at his own expense. Rowland answered her questions; to the last he gave a vague affirmative.
Finally, after a pause, looking at him, "You 're very generous," Miss Blanchard said. The declaration was made with a
certain richness of tone, but it brought to Rowland's sense
neither delight nor confusion. He had heard the words before; he suddenly remembered the grave sincerity with which
Miss Garland had uttered them as he strolled with her in the
woods the day of Roderick's picnic. They had pleased him
then; now he asked Miss Blanchard whether she would have
some tea.

When the two ladies withdrew, he attended them to their

carriage. Coming back to the drawing-room, he paused outside the open door; he was struck by the group formed by
the three men. They were standing before Roderick's statue
of Eve, and the young sculptor had lifted up the lamp and
was showing different parts of it to his companions. He was
talking ardently, and the lamplight covered his head and face.
Rowland stood looking on, for the group struck him with its
picturesque symbolism. Roderick, bearing the lamp and
glowing in its radiant circle, seemed the beautiful image of a
genius which combined sincerity with power. Gloriani, with
his head on one side, pulling his long moustache and looking
keenly from half-closed eyes at the lighted marble, represented
art with a worldly motive, skill unleavened by faith, the mere
base maximum of cleverness. Poor little Singleton, on the
other side, with his hands behind him, his head thrown back,
and his eyes following devoutly the course of Roderick's elu-
cidation, might pass for an embodiment of aspiring candor,
with feeble wings to rise on. In all this, Roderick's was certainly the *beau rôle*.

Gloriani turned to Rowland as he came up, and pointed
back with his thumb to the statue, with a smile half sardonic,
half good-natured. "A pretty thing—a devilish pretty thing,"
he said. "It 's as fresh as the foam in the milk-pail. He can do
it once, he can do it twice, he can do it at a stretch half a
dozen times. But— *but*"—

He was returning to his former refrain, but Rowland inter-
cepted him. "Oh, he will keep it up," he said, smiling, "I will
answer for him."

Gloriani was not encouraging, but Roderick had listened
smiling. He was floating unperturbed on the tide of his deep
self-confidence. Now, suddenly, however, he turned with a
flash of irritation in his eye, and demanded in a ringing voice,
"In a word, then, you prophesy that I am to fail?"

Gloriani answered imperturbably, patting him kindly on
the shoulder. "My dear fellow, passion burns out, inspiration
runs to seed. Some fine day every artist finds himself sitting
face to face with his lump of clay, with his empty canvas, with
his sheet of blank paper, waiting in vain for the revelation to
be made, for the Muse to descend. He must learn to do without the Muse! When the fickle jade forgets the way to your

studio, don't waste any time in tearing your hair and meditating on suicide. Come round and see me, and I will show you how to console yourself."

"If I break down," said Roderick, passionately, "I shall stay down. If the Muse deserts me, she shall at least have her infidelity on her conscience."

"You have no business," Rowland said to Gloriani, "to talk lightly of the Muse in this company. Mr. Singleton, too, has received pledges from her which place her constancy beyond suspicion." And he pointed out on the wall, near by, two small landscapes by the modest water-colorist.

The sculptor examined them with deference, and Singleton himself began to laugh nervously; he was trembling with hope that the great Gloriani would be pleased. "Yes, these are fresh too," Gloriani said; "extraordinarily fresh! How old are you?"

"Twenty-six, sir," said Singleton.

"For twenty-six they are famously fresh. They must have taken you a long time; you work slowly."

"Yes, unfortunately, I work very slowly. One of them took me six weeks, the other two months."

"Upon my word! The Muse pays you long visits." And Gloriani turned and looked, from head to foot, at so unlikely an object of her favors. Singleton smiled and began to wipe his forehead very hard. "Oh, you!" said the sculptor; "you 'll keep it up!"

A week after his dinner-party, Rowland went into Roderick's studio and found him sitting before an unfinished piece of work, with a hanging head and a heavy eye. He could have fancied that the fatal hour foretold by Gloriani had struck. Roderick rose with a sombre yawn and flung down his tools. "It 's no use," he said, "I give it up!"

"What is it?"

"I have struck a shallow! I have been sailing bravely, but for the last day or two my keel has been crunching the bottom."

"A difficult place?" Rowland asked, with a sympathetic inflection, looking vaguely at the roughly modeled figure.

"Oh, it 's not the poor clay!" Roderick answered. "The difficult place is *here*!" And he struck a blow on his heart. "I

don't know what 's the matter with me. Nothing comes; all
of a sudden I hate things. My old things look ugly; everything looks stupid."

Rowland was perplexed. He was in the situation of a man
who has been riding a blood horse at an even, elastic gallop,
and of a sudden feels him stumble and balk. As yet, he reflected, he had seen nothing but the sunshine of genius; he
had forgotten that it has its storms. Of course it had! And he
felt a flood of comradeship rise in his heart which would float
them both safely through the worst weather. "Why, you 're
tired!" he said. "Of course you 're tired. You have a right to
be!"

"Do you think I have a right to be?" Roderick asked, looking at him.

"Unquestionably, after all you have done."

"Well, then, right or wrong, I am tired. I certainly have
done a fair winter 's work. I want a change."

Rowland declared that it was certainly high time they
should be leaving Rome. They would go north and travel.
They would go to Switzerland, to Germany, to Holland, to
England. Roderick assented, his eye brightened, and Rowland talked of a dozen things they might do. Roderick walked
up and down; he seemed to have something to say which he
hesitated to bring out. He hesitated so rarely that Rowland
wondered, and at last asked him what was on his mind. Roderick stopped before him, frowning a little.

"I have such unbounded faith in your good-will," he said,
"that I believe nothing I can say would offend you."

"Try it," said Rowland.

"Well, then, I think my journey will do me more good if I
take it alone. I need n't say I prefer your society to that of
any man living. For the last six months it has been everything
to me. But I have a perpetual feeling that you are expecting
something of me, that you are measuring my doings by a
terrifically high standard. You are watching me; I don't want
to be watched. I want to go my own way; to work when I
choose and to loaf when I choose. It is not that I don't know
what I owe you; it is not that we are not friends. It is simply
that I want a taste of absolutely unrestricted freedom. Therefore, I say, let us separate."

Rowland shook him by the hand. "Willingly. Do as you desire, I shall miss you, and I venture to believe you 'll pass some lonely hours. But I have only one request to make: that if you get into trouble of any kind whatever, you will immediately let me know."

They began their journey, however, together, and crossed the Alps side by side, muffled in one rug, on the top of the St. Gothard coach. Rowland was going to England to pay some promised visits; his companion had no plan save to ramble through Switzerland and Germany as fancy guided him. He had money, now, that would outlast the summer; when it was spent he would come back to Rome and make another statue. At a little mountain village by the way, Roderick declared that he would stop; he would scramble about a little in the high places and doze in the shade of the pine forests. The coach was changing horses; the two young men walked along the village street, picking their way between dunghills, breathing the light, cool air, and listening to the plash of the fountain and the tinkle of cattle-bells. The coach overtook them, and then Rowland, as he prepared to mount, felt an almost overmastering reluctance.

"Say the word," he exclaimed, "and I will stop too."

Roderick frowned. "Ah, you don't trust me; you don't think I 'm able to take care of myself. That proves that I was right in feeling as if I were watched!"

"Watched, my dear fellow!" said Rowland. "I hope you may never have anything worse to complain of than being watched in the spirit in which I watch you. But I will spare you even that. Good-by!" Standing in his place, as the coach rolled away, he looked back at his friend lingering by the roadside. A great snow-mountain, behind Roderick, was beginning to turn pink in the sunset. The young man waved his hat, still looking grave. Rowland settled himself in his place, reflecting after all that this was a salubrious beginning of independence. He was among forests and glaciers, leaning on the pure bosom of nature. And then—and then—was it not in itself a guarantee against folly to be engaged to Mary Garland?

IV

Experience

ROWLAND passed the summer in England, staying with several old friends and two or three new ones. On his arrival, he felt it on his conscience to write to Mrs. Hudson and inform her that her son had relieved him of his tutelage. He felt that she considered him an incorruptible Mentor, following Roderick like a shadow, and he wished to let her know the truth. But he made the truth very comfortable, and gave a succinct statement of the young man's brilliant beginnings. He owed it to himself, he said, to remind her that he had not judged lightly, and that Roderick's present achievements were more profitable than his inglorious drudgery at Messrs. Striker & Spooner's. He was now taking a well-earned holiday and proposing to see a little of the world. He would work none the worse for this; every artist needed to knock about and look at things for himself. They had parted company for a couple of months, for Roderick was now a great man and beyond the need of going about with a keeper. But they were to meet again in Rome in the autumn, and then he should be able to send her more good news. Meanwhile, he was very happy in what Roderick had already done—especially happy in the happiness it must have brought to her. He ventured to ask to be kindly commended to Miss Garland.

His letter was promptly answered—to his surprise in Miss Garland's own hand. The same mail brought also an epistle from Cecilia. The latter was voluminous, and we must content ourselves with giving an extract.

"Your letter was filled with an echo of that brilliant Roman world, which made me almost ill with envy. For a week after I got it I thought Northampton really unpardonably tame. But I am drifting back again to my old deeps of resignation, and I rush to the window, when any one passes, with all my old gratitude for small favors. So Roderick Hudson is already a great man, and you turn out to be a great prophet? My compliments to both of you; I never heard of anything working so smoothly. And he takes it all very quietly, and does n't lose his balance nor let it turn his head? You judged him, then, in a day better than I had done in six months, for I really did not expect that he would settle down into such a jog-trot of prosperity. I believed he would do fine things, but I was sure he would intersperse them with a good many follies, and that his beautiful statues would spring up out of the midst of a straggling plantation of wild oats. But from what you tell me, Mr. Striker may now go hang himself. . . . . There is one thing, however, to say as a friend, in the way of warning. That candid soul can keep a secret, and he may have private designs on your equanimity which you don't begin to suspect. What do you think of his being engaged to Miss Garland? The two ladies had given no hint of it all winter, but a fortnight ago, when those big photographs of his statues arrived, they first pinned them up on the wall, and then trotted out into the town, made a dozen calls, and announced the news. Mrs. Hudson did, at least; Miss Garland, I suppose, sat at home writing letters. To me, I confess, the thing was a perfect surprise. I had not a suspicion that all the while he was coming so regularly to make himself agreeable on my veranda, he was quietly preferring his cousin to any one else. Not, indeed, that he was ever at particular pains to make himself agreeable! I suppose he has picked up a few graces in Rome. But he must not acquire too many: if he is too polite when he comes back, Miss Garland will count him as one of the lost. She will be a very good wife for a man of genius, and such a one as they are often shrewd enough to take. She 'll darn his stockings and keep his accounts, and sit at home and trim the lamp and keep up the fire while he studies the Beautiful in pretty neighbors at dinner-parties. The two ladies are evidently very happy, and, to do them justice, very humbly grateful to you. Mrs. Hudson never speaks of you without tears in her eyes, and I am sure she considers you a specially patented agent of Providence. Verily, it 's a good thing for a woman to be in love: Miss Garland has grown almost pretty. I met her the other night at a tea-party; she had a white rose in her hair, and sang a sentimental ballad in a fine contralto voice."

Miss Garland's letter was so much shorter that we may give it entire:—

MY DEAR SIR,—Mrs. Hudson, as I suppose you know, has been for some time unable to use her eyes. She requests me, therefore, to answer your favor of the 22d of June. She thanks you extremely for writing, and wishes me to say that she considers herself in every way under great obligations to you. Your account of her son's progress and the high estimation in which he is held has made her very happy, and she earnestly prays that all may continue well with him. He sent us, a short time ago, several large photographs of his two statues, taken from different points of view. We know little about such things, but they seem to us wonderfully beautiful. We sent them to Boston to be handsomely framed, and the man, on returning them, wrote us that he had exhibited them for a week in his store, and that they had attracted great attention. The frames are magnificent, and the pictures now hang in a row on the parlor wall. Our only quarrel with them is that they make the old papering and the engravings look dreadfully shabby. Mr. Striker stood and looked at them the other day full five minutes, and said, at last, that if Roderick's head was running on such things it was no wonder he could not learn to draw up a deed. We lead here so quiet and monotonous a life that I am afraid I can tell you nothing that will interest you. Mrs. Hudson requests me to say that the little more or less that may happen to us is of small account, as we live in our thoughts and our thoughts are fixed on her dear son. She thanks Heaven he has so good a friend. Mrs. Hudson says that this is too short a letter, but I can say nothing more.

> Yours most respectfully,
> MARY GARLAND.

It is a question whether the reader will know why, but this letter gave Rowland extraordinary pleasure. He liked its very brevity and meagreness, and there seemed to him an exquisite modesty in its saying nothing from the young girl herself. He delighted in the formal address and conclusion; they pleased him as he had been pleased by an angular gesture in some expressive girlish figure in an early painting. The letter renewed that impression of strong feeling combined with an almost rigid simplicity, which Roderick's betrothed had personally given him. And its homely stiffness seemed a vivid reflection of a life concentrated, as the young girl had borrowed warrant from her companion to say, in a single devoted idea. The monotonous days of the two women seemed to Rowland's fancy to follow each other like the tick-tick of a great time-piece, marking off the hours which separated them from the supreme felicity of clasping the far-away son and lover to lips sealed with the excess of joy. He hoped that Roderick, now that he had shaken off the oppression of his own importunate faith, was not losing a tolerant temper for the silent prayers of the two women at Northampton.

He was left to vain conjectures, however, as to Roderick's actual moods and occupations. He knew he was no letter-writer, and that, in the young sculptor's own phrase, he had at any time rather build a monument than write a note. But when a month had passed without news of him, he began to be half anxious and half angry, and wrote him three lines, in the care of a Continental banker, begging him at least to give some sign of whether he was alive or dead. A week afterwards came an answer—brief, and dated Baden-Baden. "I know I have been a great brute," Roderick wrote, "not to have sent you a word before; but really I don't know what has got into me. I have lately learned terribly well how to be idle. I am afraid to think how long it is since I wrote to my mother or to Mary. Heaven help them—poor, patient, trustful creatures! I don't know how to tell you what I am doing. It seems all amusing enough while I do it, but it would make a poor show in a narrative intended for your formidable eyes. I found Baxter in Switzerland, or rather he found me, and he grabbed me by the arm and brought me here. I was walking twenty miles a day in the Alps, drinking milk in lonely châlets, sleeping as you sleep, and thinking it was all very good fun; but Baxter told me it would never do, that the Alps were 'd——d rot,' that Baden-Baden was the place, and that if I knew what was good for me I would come along with him. It is a wonderful place, certainly, though, thank the Lord,

Baxter departed last week, blaspheming horribly at *trente et quarante*. But you know all about it and what one does—what one is liable to do. I have succumbed, in a measure, to the liabilities, and I wish I had some one here to give me a thundering good blowing up. Not you, dear friend; you would draw it too mild; you have too much of the milk of human kindness. I have fits of horrible homesickness for my studio, and I shall be devoutly grateful when the summer is over and I can go back and swing a chisel. I feel as if nothing but the chisel would satisfy me; as if I could rush in a rage at a block of unshaped marble. There are a lot of the Roman people here, English and American; I live in the midst of them and talk nonsense from morning till night. There is also some one else; and to her I don't talk sense, nor, thank heaven, mean what I say. I confess, I need a month's work to recover my self-respect."

These lines brought Rowland no small perturbation; the more, that what they seemed to point to surprised him. During the nine months of their companionship Roderick had shown so little taste for dissipation that Rowland had come to think of it as a canceled danger, and it greatly perplexed him to learn that his friend had apparently proved so pliant to opportunity. But Roderick's allusions were ambiguous, and it was possible they might simply mean that he was out of patience with a frivolous way of life and fretting wholesomely over his absent work. It was a very good thing, certainly, that idleness should prove, on experiment, to sit heavily on his conscience. Nevertheless, the letter needed, to Rowland's mind, a key: the key arrived a week later. "In common charity," Roderick wrote, "lend me a hundred pounds! I have gambled away my last franc—I have made a mountain of debts. Send me the money first; lecture me afterwards!" Rowland sent the money by return of mail; then he proceeded, not to lecture, but to think. He hung his head; he was acutely disappointed. He had no right to be, he assured himself; but so it was. Roderick was young, impulsive, unpracticed in stoicism; it was a hundred to one that he was to pay the usual vulgar tribute to folly. But his friend had regarded it as securely gained to his own belief in virtue that he was not as other foolish youths are, and that he would have been capable of looking at folly in the face and passing on his way. Rowland for a while felt a sore sense of wrath. What right had a man who was engaged to that fine girl in Northampton to behave as if his consciousness were a common blank, to be overlaid with coarse sensations? Yes, distinctly, he was disappointed. He had accompanied his missive with an urgent recommendation to leave Baden-Baden immediately, and an offer to meet Roderick at any point he would name. The answer came promptly; it ran as follows: "Send me another fifty pounds! I have been back to the tables. I will leave as soon as the money comes, and meet you at Geneva. There I will tell you everything."

There is an ancient terrace at Geneva, planted with trees and studded with benches, overlooked by gravely aristocratic old dwellings and overlooking the distant Alps. A great many generations have made it a lounging-place, a great many friends and lovers strolled there, a great many confidential talks and momentous interviews gone forward. Here, one morning, sitting on one of the battered green benches, Roderick, as he had promised, told his friend everything. He had arrived late the night before; he looked tired, and yet flushed and excited. He made no professions of penitence, but he practiced an unmitigated frankness, and his self-reprobation might be taken for granted. He implied in every phrase that he had done with it all, and that he was counting the hours till he could get back to work. We shall not rehearse his confession in detail; its main outline will be sufficient. He had fallen in with some very idle people, and had discovered that a little example and a little practice were capable of producing on his own part a considerable relish for their diversions. What could he do? He never read, and he had no studio; in one way or another he had to pass the time. He passed it in dangling about several very pretty women in wonderful Paris toilets, and reflected that it was always something gained for a sculptor to sit under a tree, looking at his leisure into a charming face and saying things that made it smile and play its muscles and part its lips and show its teeth. Attached to these ladies were certain gentlemen who walked about in clouds of perfume, rose at midday, and supped at midnight. Roderick had found himself in the mood for thinking them very amusing fellows. He was surprised at his own taste, but he let it take its course. It led him to the discovery that to live with ladies who expect you to present them with expensive bouquets, to ride with them in the Black Forest on well-looking horses, to come into their opera-boxes on nights when Patti sang and prices were consequent, to propose little light suppers at the Conversation House after the opera or drives by moonlight to the Castle, to be always arrayed and anointed, trinketed and gloved,—that to move in such society, we say, though it might be a privilege, was a privilege with a penalty attached. But the tables made such things easy; half the Baden world lived by the tables. Roderick tried them and found that at first they smoothed his path delightfully. This simplification of matters, however, was only momentary, for he soon perceived that to seem to have money, and to have it in fact, exposed a good-looking young man to peculiar liabilities. At this point of his friend's narrative, Rowland was reminded of Madame de Cruchecassée in *The Newcomes*, and though he had listened in tranquil silence to the rest of it, he found it hard not to say that all this had been, under the circumstances, a very bad business. Roderick admitted it with bitterness, and then told how much—measured simply financially—it had cost him. His luck had changed; the tables had ceased to back him, and he had found himself up to his knees in debt. Every penny had gone of the solid sum which had seemed a large equivalent of those shining statues in Rome. He had been an ass, but it was not irreparable; he could make another statue in a couple of months.

Rowland frowned. "For heaven's sake," he said, "don't play such dangerous games with your facility. If you have got facility, revere it, respect it, adore it, treasure it—don't speculate on it." And he wondered what his companion, up to his knees in debt, would have done if there had been no good-natured Rowland Mallet to lend a helping hand. But he did not formulate his curiosity audibly, and the contingency seemed not to have presented itself to Roderick's imagination. The young sculptor reverted to his late adventures again in the evening, and this time talked of them more objectively, as the phrase is; more as if they had been the adventures of another person. He related half a dozen droll things that had

happened to him, and, as if his responsibility had been disengaged by all this free discussion, he laughed extravagantly
at the memory of them. Rowland sat perfectly grave, on principle. Then Roderick began to talk of half a dozen statues that
he had in his head, and set forth his design, with his usual
vividness. Suddenly, as it was relevant, he declared that his
Baden doings had not been altogether fruitless, for that the
lady who had reminded Rowland of Madame de Cruchecassée was tremendously statuesque. Rowland at last said that it
all might pass if he felt that he was really the wiser for it. "By
the wiser," he added, "I mean the stronger in purpose, in
will."

"Oh, don't talk about will!" Roderick answered, throwing
back his head and looking at the stars. This conversation also
took place in the open air, on the little island in the shooting
Rhone where Jean-Jacques has a monument. "The will, I believe, is the mystery of mysteries. Who can answer for his
will? who can say beforehand that it 's strong? There are all
kinds of indefinable currents moving to and fro between one's
will and one's inclinations. People talk as if the two things
were essentially distinct; on different sides of one's organism,
like the heart and the liver. Mine, I know, are much nearer
together. It all depends upon circumstances. I believe there is
a certain group of circumstances possible for every man, in
which his will is destined to snap like a dry twig."

"My dear boy," said Rowland, "don't talk about the will
being 'destined.' The will is destiny itself. That 's the way to
look at it."

"Look at it, my dear Rowland," Roderick answered, "as
you find most comfortable. One conviction I have gathered
from my summer's experience," he went on—"it 's as well to
look it frankly in the face—is that I possess an almost unlimited susceptibility to the influence of a beautiful woman."

Rowland stared, then strolled away, softly whistling to
himself. He was unwilling to admit even to himself that this
speech had really the sinister meaning it seemed to have. In a
few days the two young men made their way back to Italy,
and lingered a while in Florence before going on to Rome.
In Florence Roderick seemed to have won back his old innocence and his preference for the pleasures of study over any

others. Rowland began to think of the Baden episode as a
bad dream, or at the worst as a mere sporadic piece of disorder, without roots in his companion's character. They passed
a fortnight looking at pictures and exploring for out the way
bits of fresco and carving, and Roderick recovered all his earlier fervor of appreciation and comment. In Rome he went
eagerly to work again, and finished in a month two or three
small things he had left standing on his departure. He talked
the most joyous nonsense about finding himself back in his
old quarters. On the first Sunday afternoon following their
return, on their going together to Saint Peter's, he delivered
himself of a lyrical greeting to the great church and to the city
in general, in a tone of voice so irrepressibly elevated that it
rang through the nave in rather a scandalous fashion, and almost arrested a procession of canons who were marching
across to the choir. He began to model a new statue—a female figure, of which he had said nothing to Rowland. It
represented a woman, leaning lazily back in her chair, with
her head drooping as if she were listening, a vague smile on
her lips, and a pair of remarkably beautiful arms folded in her
lap. With rather less softness of contour, it would have resembled the noble statue of Agrippina in the Capitol. Rowland
looked at it and was not sure he liked it. "Who is it? what
does it mean?" he asked.

"Anything you please!" said Roderick, with a certain petulance. "I call it A Reminiscence."

Rowland then remembered that one of the Baden ladies
had been "statuesque," and asked no more questions. This,
after all, was a way of profiting by experience. A few days
later he took his first ride of the season on the Campagna,
and as, on his homeward way, he was passing across the long
shadow of a ruined tower, he perceived a small figure at a
short distance, bent over a sketch-book. As he drew near, he
recognized his friend Singleton. The honest little painter's
face was scorched to flame-color by the light of southern
suns, and borrowed an even deeper crimson from his gleeful
greeting of his most appreciative patron. He was making a
careful and charming little sketch. On Rowland's asking him
how he had spent his summer, he gave an account of his wanderings which made poor Mallet sigh with a sense of more

contrasts than one. He had not been out of Italy, but he had been delving deep into the picturesque heart of the lovely land, and gathering a wonderful store of subjects. He had rambled about among the unvisited villages of the Apennines, pencil in hand and knapsack on back, sleeping on straw and eating black bread and beans, but feasting on local color, rioting, as it were, on chiaroscuro, and laying up a treasure of pictorial observations. He took a devout satisfaction in his hard-earned wisdom and his happy frugality. Rowland went the next day, by appointment, to look at his sketches, and spent a whole morning turning them over. Singleton talked more than he had ever done before, explained them all, and told some quaintly humorous anecdote about the production of each.

"Dear me, how I have chattered!" he said at last. "I am afraid you had rather have looked at the things in peace and quiet. I did n't know I could talk so much. But somehow, I feel very happy; I feel as if I had improved."

"That you have," said Rowland. "I doubt whether an artist ever passed a more profitable three months. You must feel much more sure of yourself."

Singleton looked for a long time with great intentness at a knot in the floor. "Yes," he said at last, in a fluttered tone, "I feel much more sure of myself. I have got more facility!" And he lowered his voice as if he were communicating a secret which it took some courage to impart. "I hardly like to say it, for fear I should after all be mistaken. But since it strikes you, perhaps it 's true. It 's a great happiness; I would not exchange it for a great deal of money."

"Yes, I suppose it 's a great happiness," said Rowland. "I shall really think of you as living here in a state of scandalous bliss. I don't believe it 's good for an artist to be in such brutally high spirits."

Singleton stared for a moment, as if he thought Rowland was in earnest; then suddenly fathoming the kindly jest, he walked about the room, scratching his head and laughing intensely to himself. "And Mr. Hudson?" he said, as Rowland was going; "I hope he is well and happy."

"He is very well," said Rowland. "He is back at work again."

"Ah, there 's a man," cried Singleton, "who has taken his start once for all, and does n't need to stop and ask himself in fear and trembling every month or two whether he is advancing or not. When he stops, it 's to rest! And where did he spend his summer?"

"The greater part of it at Baden-Baden."

"Ah, that 's in the Black Forest," cried Singleton, with profound simplicity. "They say you can make capital studies of trees there."

"No doubt," said Rowland, with a smile, laying an almost paternal hand on the little painter's yellow head. "Unfortunately trees are not Roderick's line. Nevertheless, he tells me that at Baden he made some studies. Come when you can, by the way," he added after a moment, "to his studio, and tell me what you think of something he has lately begun." Singleton declared that he would come delightedly, and Rowland left him to his work.

He met a number of his last winter's friends again, and called upon Madame Grandoni, upon Miss Blanchard, and upon Gloriani, shortly after their return. The ladies gave an excellent account of themselves. Madame Grandoni had been taking sea-baths at Rimini, and Miss Blanchard painting wild flowers in the Tyrol. Her complexion was somewhat browned, which was very becoming, and her flowers were uncommonly pretty. Gloriani had been in Paris and had come away in high good-humor, finding no one there, in the artist-world, cleverer than himself. He came in a few days to Roderick's studio, one afternoon when Rowland was present. He examined the new statue with great deference, said it was very promising, and abstained, considerately, from irritating prophecies. But Rowland fancied he observed certain signs of inward jubilation on the clever sculptor's part, and walked away with him to learn his private opinion.

"Certainly; I liked it as well as I said," Gloriani declared in answer to Rowland's anxious query; "or rather I liked it a great deal better. I did n't say how much, for fear of making your friend angry. But one can leave him alone now, for he 's coming round. I told you he could n't keep up the transcendental style, and he has already broken down. Don't you see it yourself, man?"

"I don't particularly like this new statue," said Rowland.

"That 's because you 're a purist. It 's deuced clever, it 's deuced knowing, it 's deuced pretty, but it is n't the topping high art of three months ago. He has taken his turn sooner than I supposed. What has happened to him? Has he been disappointed in love? But that 's none of my business. I congratulate him on having become a practical man."

Roderick, however, was less to be congratulated than Gloriani had taken it into his head to believe. He was discontented with his work, he applied himself to it by fits and starts, he declared that he did n't know what was coming over him; he was turning into a man of moods. "Is this of necessity what a fellow must come to"—he asked of Rowland, with a sort of peremptory flash in his eye, which seemed to imply that his companion had undertaken to insure him against perplexities and was not fulfilling his contract—"this damnable uncertainty when he goes to bed at night as to whether he is going to wake up in a working humor or in a swearing humor? Have we only a season, over before we know it, in which we can call our faculties our own? Six months ago I could stand up to my work like a man, day after day, and never dream of asking myself whether I felt like it. But now, some mornings, it 's the very devil to get going. My statue looks so bad when I come into the studio that I have twenty minds to smash it on the spot, and I lose three or four hours in sitting there, moping and getting used to it."

Rowland said that he supposed that this sort of thing was the lot of every artist and that the only remedy was plenty of courage and faith. And he reminded him of Gloriani's having forewarned him against these sterile moods the year before.

"Gloriani 's an ass!" said Roderick, almost fiercely. He hired a horse and began to ride with Rowland on the Campagna. This delicious amusement restored him in a measure to cheerfulness, but seemed to Rowland on the whole not to stimulate his industry. Their rides were always very long, and Roderick insisted on making them longer by dismounting in picturesque spots and stretching himself in the sun among a heap of overtangled stones. He let the scorching Roman luminary beat down upon him with an equanimity which Rowland found it hard to emulate. But in this situation Roderick talked so much amusing nonsense that, for the sake of his company, Rowland consented to be uncomfortable, and often forgot that, though in these diversions the days passed quickly, they brought forth neither high art nor low. And yet it was perhaps by their help, after all, that Roderick secured several mornings of ardent work on his new figure, and brought it to rapid completion. One afternoon, when it was finished, Rowland went to look at it, and Roderick asked him for his opinion.

"What do you think yourself?" Rowland demanded, not from pusillanimity, but from real uncertainty.

"I think it is curiously bad," Roderick answered. "It was bad from the first; it has fundamental vices. I have shuffled them in a measure out of sight, but I have not corrected them. I can't—I can't—I can't!" he cried passionately. "They stare me in the face—they are all I see!"

Rowland offered several criticisms of detail, and suggested certain practicable changes. But Roderick differed with him on each of these points; the thing had faults enough, but they were not those faults. Rowland, unruffled, concluded by saying that whatever its faults might be, he had an idea people in general would like it.

"I wish to heaven some person in particular would buy it, and take it off my hands and out of my sight!" Roderick cried. "What am I to do now?" he went on. "I have n't an idea. I think of subjects, but they remain mere lifeless names. They are mere words—they are not images. What am I to do?"

Rowland was a trifle annoyed. "Be a man," he was on the point of saying, "and don't, for heaven's sake, talk in that confoundedly querulous voice." But before he had uttered the words, there rang through the studio a loud, peremptory ring at the outer door.

Roderick broke into a laugh. "Talk of the devil," he said, "and you see his horns! If that 's not a customer, it ought to be."

The door of the studio was promptly flung open, and a lady advanced to the threshold—an imposing, voluminous person, who quite filled up the doorway. Rowland immediately felt that he had seen her before, but he recognized her only when she moved forward and disclosed an attendant in the person of a little bright-eyed, elderly gentleman, with a bristling white moustache. Then he remembered that just a year before he and his companion had seen in the Ludovisi gardens a wonderfully beautiful girl, strolling in the train of this conspicuous couple. He looked for her now, and in a moment she appeared, following her companions with the same nonchalant step as before, and leading her great snow-white poodle, decorated with motley ribbons. The elder lady offered the two young men a sufficiently gracious salute; the little old gentleman bowed and smiled with extreme alertness. The young girl, without casting a glance either at Roderick or at Rowland, looked about for a chair, and, on perceiving one, sank into it listlessly, pulled her poodle towards her, and began to rearrange his top-knot. Rowland saw that, even with her eyes dropped, her beauty was still dazzling.

"I trust we are at liberty to enter," said the elder lady, with majesty. "We were told that Mr. Hudson had no fixed day, and that we might come at any time. Let us not disturb you."

Roderick, as one of the lesser lights of the Roman art-world, had not hitherto been subject to incursions from inquisitive tourists, and, having no regular reception day, was not versed in the usual formulas of welcome. He said nothing, and Rowland, looking at him, saw that he was looking amazedly at the young girl and was apparently unconscious of everything else. "By Jove!" he cried precipitately, "it 's that goddess of the Villa Ludovisi!" Rowland in some confusion, did the honors as he could, but the little old gentleman begged him with the most obsequious of smiles to give himself no trouble. "I have been in many a studio!" he said, with his finger on his nose and a strong Italian accent.

"We are going about everywhere," said his companion. "I am passionately fond of art!"

Rowland smiled sympathetically, and let them turn to Roderick's statue. He glanced again at the young sculptor, to invite him to bestir himself, but Roderick was still gazing wide-eyed at the beautiful young mistress of the poodle, who by this time had looked up and was gazing straight at him. There was nothing bold in her look; it expressed a kind of languid, imperturbable indifference. Her beauty was extraordinary; it grew and grew as the young man observed her. In such a face the maidenly custom of averted eyes and ready blushes would have seemed an anomaly; nature had produced it for man's delight and meant that it should surrender itself freely and coldly to admiration. It was not immediately apparent, however, that the young lady found an answering entertainment in the physiognomy of her host; she turned her head after a moment and looked idly round the room, and at last let her eyes rest on the statue of the woman seated. It being left to Rowland to stimulate conversation, he began by complimenting her on the beauty of her dog.

"Yes, he's very handsome," she murmured. "He's a Florentine. The dogs in Florence are handsomer than the people." And on Rowland's caressing him: "His name is Stenterello," she added. "Stenterello, give your hand to the gentleman." This order was given in Italian. "Say *buon giorno a lei.*"

Stenterello thrust out his paw and gave four short, shrill barks; upon which the elder lady turned round and raised her forefinger.

"My dear, my dear, remember where you are! Excuse my foolish child," she added, turning to Roderick with an agreeable smile. "She can think of nothing but her poodle."

"I am teaching him to talk for me," the young girl went on, without heeding her mother; "to say little things in society. It will save me a great deal of trouble. Stenterello, love, give a pretty smile and say *tanti complimenti!*" The poodle wagged his white pate—it looked like one of those little pads in swan's-down, for applying powder to the face—and repeated the barking process.

"He is a wonderful beast," said Rowland.

"He is not a beast," said the young girl. "A beast is something black and dirty—something you can't touch."

"He is a very valuable dog," the elder lady explained. "He was presented to my daughter by a Florentine nobleman."

"It is not for that I care about him. It is for himself. He is better than the prince."

"My dear, my dear!" repeated the mother in deprecating accents, but with a significant glance at Rowland which seemed to bespeak his attention to the glory of possessing a daughter who could deal in that fashion with the aristocracy.

Rowland remembered that when their unknown visitors had passed before them, a year previous, in the Villa Ludovisi, Roderick and he had exchanged conjectures as to their nationality and social quality. Roderick had declared that they were old-world people; but Rowland now needed no telling to feel that he might claim the elder lady as a fellow-countrywoman. She was a person of what is called a great deal of presence, with the faded traces, artfully revived here and there, of once brilliant beauty. Her daughter had come lawfully by her loveliness, but Rowland mentally made the distinction that the mother was silly and that the daughter was not. The mother had a very silly mouth—a mouth, Rowland suspected, capable of expressing an inordinate degree of unreason. The young girl, in spite of her childish satisfaction in her poodle, was not a person of feeble understanding. Rowland received an impression that, for reasons of her own, she was playing a part. What was the part and what were her reasons? She was interesting; Rowland wondered what were her domestic secrets. If her mother was a daughter of the great Republic, it was to be supposed that the young girl was a flower of the American soil; but her beauty had a robustness and tone uncommon in the somewhat facile loveliness of our western maidenhood. She spoke with a vague foreign accent, as if she had spent her life in strange countries. The little Italian apparently divined Rowland's mute imaginings, for he presently stepped forward, with a bow like a master of ceremonies. "I have not done my duty," he said, "in not announcing these ladies. Mrs. Light, Miss Light!"

Rowland was not materially the wiser for this information, but Roderick was aroused by it to the exercise of some slight hospitality. He altered the light, pulled forward two or three figures, and made an apology for not having more to show. "I don't pretend to have anything of an exhibition—I am only a novice."

"Indeed?—a novice! For a novice this is very well," Mrs. Light declared. "Cavaliere, we have seen nothing better than this."

The Cavaliere smiled rapturously. "It is stupendous!" he murmured. "And we have been to all the studios."

"Not to all—heaven forbid!" cried Mrs. Light. "But to a

number that I have had pointed out by artistic friends. I delight in studios: they are the temples of the beautiful here below. And if you are a novice, Mr. Hudson," she went on, "you have already great admirers. Half a dozen people have told us that yours were among the things to see." This gracious speech went unanswered; Roderick had already wandered across to the other side of the studio and was revolving about Miss Light. "Ah, he 's gone to look at my beautiful daughter; he is not the first that has had his head turned," Mrs. Light resumed, lowering her voice to a confidential undertone; a favor which, considering the shortness of their acquaintance, Rowland was bound to appreciate. "The artists are all crazy about her. When she goes into a studio she is fatal to the pictures. And when she goes into a ball-room what do the other women say? Eh, Cavaliere?"

"She is very beautiful," Rowland said, gravely.

Mrs. Light, who through her long, gold-cased glass was looking a little at everything, and at nothing as if she saw it, interrupted her random murmurs and exclamations, and surveyed Rowland from head to foot. She looked at him all over; apparently he had not been mentioned to her as a feature of Roderick's establishment. It was the gaze, Rowland felt, which the vigilant and ambitious mamma of a beautiful daughter has always at her command for well-dressed young men of candid physiognomy. Her inspection in this case seemed satisfactory. "Are you also an artist?" she inquired with an almost caressing inflection. It was clear that what she meant was something of this kind: "Be so good as to assure me without delay that you are really the young man of substance and amiability that you appear."

But Rowland answered simply the formal question—not the latent one. "Dear me, no; I am only a friend of Mr. Hudson."

Mrs. Light, with a sigh, returned to the statues, and after mistaking the Adam for a gladiator, and the Eve for a Pocahontas, declared that she could not judge of such things unless she saw them in the marble. Rowland hesitated a moment, and then speaking in the interest of Roderick's renown, said that he was the happy possessor of several of his friend's works and that she was welcome to come and see them at his rooms. She bade the Cavaliere make a note of his address. "Ah, you 're a patron of the arts," she said. "That 's what I should like to be if I had a little money. I delight in beauty in every form. But all these people ask such monstrous prices. One must be a millionaire, to think of such things, eh? Twenty years ago my husband had my portrait painted, here in Rome, by Papucci, who was the great man in those days. I was in a ball dress, with all my jewels, my neck and arms, and all that. The man got six hundred francs, and thought he was very well treated. Those were the days when a family could live like princes in Italy for five thousand scudi a year. The Cavaliere once upon a time was a great dandy—don't blush, Cavaliere; any one can see that, just as any one can see that I was once a pretty woman! Get him to tell you what he made a figure upon. The railroads have brought in the vulgarians. That 's what I call it now—the invasion of the vulgarians! What are poor *we* to do?"

Rowland had begun to murmur some remedial proposition, when he was interrupted by the voice of Miss Light calling across the room, "Mamma!"

"My own love?"

"This gentleman wishes to model my bust. Please speak to him."

The Cavaliere gave a little chuckle. "Already?" he cried.

Rowland looked round, equally surprised at the promptitude of the proposal. Roderick stood planted before the young girl with his arms folded, looking at her as he would have done at the Medicean Venus. He never paid compliments, and Rowland, though he had not heard him speak, could imagine the startling distinctness with which he made his request.

"He saw me a year ago," the young girl went on, "and he has been thinking of me ever since." Her tone, in speaking, was peculiar; it had a kind of studied inexpressiveness, which was yet not the vulgar device of a drawl.

"I *must* make your daughter's bust—that 's all, madame!" cried Roderick, with warmth.

"I had rather you made the poodle's," said the young girl. "Is it very tiresome? I have spent half my life sitting for my photograph, in every conceivable attitude and with every conceivable coiffure. I think I have posed enough."

"My dear child," said Mrs. Light, "it may be one's duty to pose. But as to my daughter's sitting to you, sir—to a young sculptor whom we don't know—it is a matter that needs reflection. It is not a favor that 's to be had for the mere asking."

"If I don't make her from life," said Roderick, with energy, "I will make her from memory, and if the thing 's to be done, you had better have it done as well as possible."

"Mamma hesitates," said Miss Light, "because she does n't know whether you mean she shall pay you for the bust. I can assure you that she will not pay you a sou."

"My darling, you forget yourself," said Mrs. Light, with an attempt at majestic severity. "Of course," she added, in a moment, with a change of note, "the bust would be my own property."

"Of course!" cried Roderick, impatiently.

"Dearest mother," interposed the young girl, "how can you carry a marble bust about the world with you? Is it not enough to drag the poor original?"

"My dear, you 're nonsensical!" cried Mrs. Light, almost angrily.

"You can always sell it," said the young girl, with the same artful artlessness.

Mrs. Light turned to Rowland, who pitied her, flushed and irritated. "She is very wicked to-day!"

The Cavaliere grinned in silence and walked away on tiptoe, with his hat to his lips, as if to leave the field clear for action. Rowland, on the contrary, wished to avert the coming storm. "You had better not refuse," he said to Miss Light, "until you have seen Mr. Hudson's things in the marble. Your mother is to come and look at some that I possess."

"Thank you; I have no doubt you will see us. I dare say Mr. Hudson is very clever; but I don't care for modern sculpture. I can't look at it!"

"You shall care for my bust, I promise you!" cried Roderick, with a laugh.

"To satisfy Miss Light," said the Cavaliere, "one of the old Greeks ought to come to life."

"It would be worth his while," said Roderick, paying, to Rowland's knowledge, his first compliment.

"I might sit to Phidias, if he would promise to be very amusing and make me laugh. What do you say, Stenterello? would *you* sit to Phidias?"

"We must talk of this some other time," said Mrs. Light. "We are in Rome for the winter. Many thanks. Cavaliere, call the carriage." The Cavaliere led the way out, backing like a silver-stick, and Miss Light, following her mother, nodded, without looking at them, to each of the young men.

"Immortal powers, what a head!" cried Roderick, when they had gone. "There 's my fortune!"

"She is certainly very beautiful," said Rowland. "But I 'm sorry you have undertaken her bust."

"And why, pray?"

"I suspect it will bring trouble with it."

"What kind of trouble?"

"I hardly know. They are queer people. The mamma, I suspect, is the least bit of an adventuress. Heaven knows what the daughter is."

"She 's a goddess!" cried Roderick.

"Just so. She is all the more dangerous."

"Dangerous? What will she do to me? She does n't bite, I imagine."

"It remains to be seen. There are two kinds of women— you ought to know it by this time—the safe and the unsafe. Miss Light, if I am not mistaken, is one of the unsafe. A word to the wise!"

"Much obliged!" said Roderick, and he began to whistle a triumphant air, in honor, apparently, of the advent of his beautiful model.

In calling this young lady and her mamma "queer people," Rowland but roughly expressed his sentiment. They were so marked a variation from the monotonous troop of his fellow-country people that he felt much curiosity as to the sources of the change, especially since he doubted greatly whether, on the whole, it elevated the type. For a week he saw the two ladies driving daily in a well-appointed landau, with the Cavaliere and the poodle in the front seat. From Mrs. Light he received a gracious salute, tempered by her native majesty;

but the young girl, looking straight before her, seemed profoundly indifferent to observers. Her extraordinary beauty, however, had already made observers numerous and given the habitués of the Pincian plenty to talk about. The echoes of their commentary reached Rowland's ears; but he had little taste for random gossip, and desired a distinctly veracious informant. He had found one in the person of Madame Grandoni, for whom Mrs. Light and her beautiful daughter were a pair of old friends.

"I have known the mamma for twenty years," said this judicious critic, "and if you ask any of the people who have been living here as long as I, you will find they remember her well. I have held the beautiful Christina on my knee when she was a little wizened baby with a very red face and no promise of beauty but those magnificent eyes. Ten years ago Mrs. Light disappeared, and has not since been seen in Rome, except for a few days last winter, when she passed through on her way to Naples. Then it was you met the trio in the Ludovisi gardens. When I first knew her she was the unmarried but very marriageable daughter of an old American painter of very bad landscapes, which people used to buy from charity and use for fire-boards. His name was Savage; it used to make every one laugh, he was such a mild, melancholy, pitiful old gentleman. He had married a horrible wife, an Englishwoman who had been on the stage. It was said she used to beat poor Savage with his mahl-stick and when the domestic finances were low to lock him up in his studio and tell him he should n't come out until he had painted half a dozen of his daubs. She had a good deal of showy beauty. She would then go forth, and, her beauty helping, she would make certain people take the pictures. It helped her at last to make an English lord run away with her. At the time I speak of she had quite disappeared. Mrs. Light was then a very handsome girl, though by no means so handsome as her daughter has now become. Mr. Light was an American consul, newly appointed at one of the Adriatic ports. He was a mild, fair-whiskered young man, with some little property, and my impression is that he had got into bad company at home, and that his family procured him his place to keep him out of harm's way. He came up to Rome on a holiday, fell in love with Miss Savage, and married her on the spot. He had not been married three years when he was drowned in the Adriatic, no one ever knew how. The young widow came back to Rome, to her father, and here shortly afterwards, in the shadow of Saint Peter's, her little girl was born. It might have been supposed that Mrs. Light would marry again, and I know she had opportunities. But she overreached herself. She would take nothing less than a title and a fortune, and they were not forthcoming. She was admired and very fond of admiration; very vain, very worldly, very silly. She remained a pretty widow, with a surprising variety of bonnets and a dozen men always in her train. Giacosa dates from this period. He calls himself a Roman, but I have an impression he came up from Ancona with her. He was *l'ami de la maison.* He used to hold her bouquets, clean her gloves (I was told), run her errands, get her opera-boxes, and fight her battles with the shopkeepers. For this he needed courage, for she was smothered in debt. She at last left Rome to escape her creditors. Many of them must remember her still, but she seems now to have money to satisfy them. She left her poor old father here alone—helpless, infirm and unable to work. A subscription was shortly afterwards taken up among the foreigners, and he was sent back to America, where, as I afterwards heard, he died in some sort of asylum. From time to time, for several years, I heard vaguely of Mrs. Light as a wandering beauty at French and German watering-places. Once came a rumor that she was going to make a grand marriage in England; then we heard that the gentleman had thought better of it and left her to keep afloat as she could. She was a terribly scatter-brained creature. She pretends to be a great lady, but I consider that old Filomena, my washer-woman, is in essentials a greater one. But certainly, after all, she has been fortunate. She embarked at last on a lawsuit about some property, with her husband's family, and went to America to attend to it. She came back triumphant, with a long purse. She reappeared in Italy, and established herself for a while in Venice. Then she came to Florence, where she spent a couple of years and where I saw her. Last year she passed down to Naples, which I should have said was just the place for her, and this winter she has laid siege to Rome. She seems very prosperous. She has taken a floor in the Palazzo F——, she keeps her carriage, and Christina and she, between them, must have a pretty milliner's bill. Giacosa has turned up again, looking as if he had been kept on ice at Ancona, for her return."

"What sort of education," Rowland asked, "do you imagine the mother's adventures to have been for the daughter?"

"A strange school! But Mrs. Light told me, in Florence, that she had given her child the education of a princess. In other words, I suppose, she speaks three or four languages, and has read several hundred French novels. Christina, I suspect, is very clever. When I saw her, I was amazed at her beauty, and, certainly, if there is any truth in faces, she ought to have the soul of an angel. Perhaps she has. I don't judge her; she 's an extraordinary young person. She has been told twenty times a day by her mother, since she was five years old, that she is a beauty of beauties, that her face is her fortune, and that, if she plays her cards, she may marry a duke. If she has not been fatally corrupted, she is a very superior girl. My own impression is that she is a mixture of good and bad, of ambition and indifference. Mrs. Light, having failed to make her own fortune in matrimony, has transferred her hopes to her daughter, and nursed them till they have become a kind of monomania. She has a hobby, which she rides in secret; but some day she will let you see it. I 'm sure that if you go in some evening unannounced, you will find her scanning the tea-leaves in her cup, or telling her daughter's fortune with a greasy pack of cards, preserved for the purpose. She promises her a prince—a reigning prince. But if Mrs. Light is silly, she is shrewd, too, and, lest considerations of state should deny her prince the luxury of a love-match, she keeps on hand a few common mortals. At the worst she would take a duke, an English lord, or even a young American with a proper number of millions. The poor woman must be rather uncomfortable. She is always building castles and knocking them down again—always casting her nets and pulling them in. If her daughter were less of a beauty, her transparent ambition would be very ridiculous; but there is something in the girl, as one looks at her, that seems to make it very possible she is marked out for one of those wonderful romantic fortunes that history now and then relates. 'Who,

after all, was the Empress of the French?' Mrs. Light is forever saying. 'And beside Christina the Empress is a dowdy!' "

"And what does Christina say?"

"She makes no scruple, as you know, of saying that her
mother is a fool. What she thinks, heaven knows. I suspect
that, practically, she does not commit herself. She is excessively proud, and thinks herself good enough to occupy the
highest station in the world; but she knows that her mother
talks nonsense, and that even a beautiful girl may look awkward in making unsuccessful advances. So she remains superbly indifferent, and lets her mother take the risks. If the
prince is secured, so much the better; if he is not, she need
never confess to herself that even a prince has slighted her."

"Your report is as solid," Rowland said to Madame Grandoni, thanking her, "as if it had been prepared for the Academy of Sciences;" and he congratulated himself on having
listened to it when, a couple of days later, Mrs. Light and her
daughter, attended by the Cavaliere and the poodle, came to
his rooms to look at Roderick's statues. It was more comfortable to know just with whom he was dealing.

Mrs. Light was prodigiously gracious, and showered down
compliments not only on the statues, but on all his possessions. "Upon my word," she said, "you men know how to
make yourselves comfortable. If one of us poor women had
half as many easy-chairs and knick-knacks, we should be famously abused. It 's really selfish to be living all alone in such
a place as this. Cavaliere, how should you like this suite of
rooms and a fortune to fill them with pictures and statues?
Christina, love, look at that mosaic table. Mr. Mallet, I could
almost beg it from you. Yes, that Eve is certainly very fine.
We need n't be ashamed of such a great-grandmother as that.
If she was really such a beautiful woman, it accounts for the
good looks of some of us. Where is Mr. What 's-his-name,
the young sculptor? Why is n't he here to be complimented?"

Christina had remained but for a moment in the chair
which Rowland had placed for her, had given but a cursory
glance at the statues, and then, leaving her place, had begun
to wander round the room—looking at herself in the mirror,
touching the ornaments and curiosities, glancing at the books
and prints. Rowland's sitting-room was encumbered with

bric-à-brac, and she found plenty of occupation. Rowland presently joined her, and pointed out some of the objects he most valued.

"It 's an odd jumble," she said frankly. "Some things are very pretty—some are very ugly. But I like ugly things, when they have a certain look. Prettiness is terribly vulgar nowadays, and it is not every one that knows just the sort of ugliness that has *chic*. But chic is getting dreadfully common too. There 's a hint of it even in Madame Baldi's bonnets. I like looking at people's things," she added in a moment, turning to Rowland and resting her eyes on him. "It helps you to find out their characters."

"Am I to suppose," asked Rowland, smiling, "that you have arrived at any conclusions as to mine?"

"I am rather muddled; you have too many things; one seems to contradict another. You are very artistic and yet you are very prosaic; you have what is called a 'catholic' taste and yet you are full of obstinate little prejudices and habits of thought, which, if I knew you, I should find very tiresome. I don't think I like you."

"You make a great mistake," laughed Rowland; "I assure you I am very amiable."

"Yes, I am probably wrong, and if I knew you, I should find out I was wrong, and that would irritate me and make me dislike you more. So you see we are necessary enemies."

"No, I don't dislike you."

"Worse and worse; for you certainly will not like me."

"You are very discouraging."

"I am fond of facing the truth, though some day you will deny that. Where is that queer friend of yours?"

"You mean Mr. Hudson. He is represented by these beautiful works."

Miss Light looked for some moments at Roderick's statues. "Yes," she said, "they are not so silly as most of the things we have seen. They have no chic, and yet they are beautiful."

"You describe them perfectly," said Rowland. "They are beautiful, and yet they have no chic. That 's it!"

"If he will promise to put none into my bust, I have a mind to let him make it. A request made in those terms deserves to be granted."

"In what terms?"

"Did n't you hear him? 'Mademoiselle, you almost satisfy my conception of the beautiful. I must model your bust.' That *almost* should be rewarded. He is like me; he likes to face the truth. I think we should get on together."

The Cavaliere approached Rowland, to express the pleasure he had derived from his beautiful "collection." His smile was exquisitely bland, his accent appealing, caressing, insinuating. But he gave Rowland an odd sense of looking at a little waxen image, adjusted to perform certain gestures and emit certain sounds. It had once contained a soul, but the soul had leaked out. Nevertheless, Rowland reflected, there are more profitless things than mere sound and gesture, in a consummate Italian. And the Cavaliere, too, had soul enough left to desire to speak a few words on his own account, and call Rowland's attention to the fact that he was not, after all, a hired cicerone, but an ancient Roman gentleman. Rowland felt sorry for him; he hardly knew why. He assured him in a friendly fashion that he must come again; that his house was always at his service. The Cavaliere bowed down to the ground. "You do me too much honor," he murmured. "If you will allow me—it is not impossible!"

Mrs. Light, meanwhile, had prepared to depart. "If you are not afraid to come and see two quiet little women, we shall be most happy!" she said. "We have no statues nor pictures— we have nothing but each other. Eh, darling?"

"I beg your pardon," said Christina.

"Oh, and the Cavaliere," added her mother.

"The poodle, please!" cried the young girl.

Rowland glanced at the Cavaliere; he was smiling more blandly than ever.

A few days later Rowland presented himself, as civility demanded, at Mrs. Light's door. He found her living in one of the stately houses of the Via dell' Angelo Custode, and, rather to his surprise, was told she was at home. He passed through half a dozen rooms and was ushered into an immense saloon, at one end of which sat the mistress of the establishment, with a piece of embroidery. She received him very graciously, and then, pointing mysteriously to a large screen which was unfolded across the embrasure of one of the deep windows,

"I am keeping guard!" she said. Rowland looked interrogative; whereupon she beckoned him forward and motioned him to look behind the screen. He obeyed, and for some moments stood gazing. Roderick, with his back turned, stood before an extemporized pedestal, ardently shaping a formless mass of clay. Before him sat Christina Light, in a white dress, with her shoulders bare, her magnificent hair twisted into a classic coil, and her head admirably poised. Meeting Rowland's gaze, she smiled a little, only with her deep gray eyes, without moving. She looked divinely beautiful.

V

Christina

THE BRILLIANT Roman winter came round again, and Rowland enjoyed it, in a certain way, more deeply than before. He grew at last to feel that sense of equal possession, of intellectual nearness, which it belongs to the peculiar magic of the ancient city to infuse into minds of a cast that she never would have produced. He became passionately, unreasoningly fond of all Roman sights and sensations, and to breathe the Roman atmosphere began to seem a needful condition of being. He could not have defined and explained the nature of his great love, nor have made up the sum of it by the addition of his calculable pleasures. It was a large, vague, idle, half-profitless emotion, of which perhaps the most pertinent thing that may be said is that it enforced a sort of oppressive reconciliation to the present, the actual, the sensuous—to life on the terms that there offered themselves. It was perhaps for this very reason that, in spite of the charm which Rome flings over one's mood, there ran through Rowland's meditations an undertone of melancholy, natural enough in a mind which finds its horizon insidiously limited to the finite, even in very picturesque forms. Whether it is one that tacitly concedes to the Roman Church the monopoly of a guarantee of immortality, so that if one is indisposed to bargain with her for the precious gift, one must do without it altogether; or whether in an atmosphere so heavily weighted with echoes and memories one grows to believe that there is nothing in one's consciousness that is not foredoomed to moulder and crumble and become dust for the feet, and possible malaria for the lungs, of future generations—the fact at least remains that one parts half-willingly with one's hopes in Rome, and misses them only under some very exceptional stress of circumstance. For this reason one may perhaps say that there is no other place in which one's daily temper has such a mellow serenity, and none, at the same time, in which acute attacks of depression are more intolerable. Rowland found, in fact, a perfect response to his prevision that to live in Rome was an education to one's senses and one's imagination, but he sometimes wondered whether this was not a questionable gain in case of one's not being prepared to live wholly by one's imagination and one's senses. The tranquil profundity of his daily satisfaction seemed sometimes to turn, by a mysterious inward impulse, and face itself with questioning, admonishing, threatening eyes. "But afterwards . . . . ?" it seemed to ask, with a long reverberation; and he could give no answer but a shy affirmation that there was no such thing as afterwards, and a hope, divided against itself, that his actual way of life would last forever. He often felt heavy-hearted; he was sombre without knowing why; there were no visible clouds in his heaven, but there were cloud-shadows on his mood. Shadows projected, they often were, without his knowing it, by an undue apprehension that things after all might not go so ideally well with Roderick. When he understood his anxiety it vexed him, and he rebuked himself for taking things unmanfully hard. If Roderick chose to follow a crooked path, it was no fault of his; he had given him, he would continue to give him, all that he had offered him—friendship, sympathy, advice. He had not undertaken to provide him with unflagging strength of purpose, nor to stand bondsman for unqualified success.

If Rowland felt his roots striking and spreading in the Roman soil, Roderick also surrendered himself with renewed abandon to the local influence. More than once he declared to his companion that he meant to live and die within the shadow of Saint Peter's, and that he cared little if he never again drew breath in American air. "For a man of my temperament, Rome is the only possible place," he said; "it's better to recognize the fact early than late. So I shall never go home unless I am absolutely forced."

"What is your idea of 'force'?" asked Rowland, smiling. "It seems to me you have an excellent reason for going home some day or other."

"Ah, you mean my engagement?" Roderick answered with unaverted eyes. "Yes, I am distinctly engaged, in Northampton, and impatiently waited for!" And he gave a little sympathetic sigh. "To reconcile Northampton and Rome is rather a problem. Mary had better come out here. Even at the worst

I have no intention of giving up Rome within six or eight years, and an engagement of that duration would be rather absurd."

"Miss Garland could hardly leave your mother," Rowland observed.

"Oh, of course my mother should come. I think I will suggest it in my next letter. It will take her a year or two to make up her mind to it, but if she consents it will brighten her up. It 's too small a life, over there, even for a timid old lady. It is hard to imagine," he added, "any change in Mary being a change for the better; but I should like her to take a look at the world and have her notions stretched a little. One is never so good, I suppose, but that one can improve a little."

"If you wish your mother and Miss Garland to come," Rowland suggested, "you had better go home and bring them."

"Oh, I can't think of leaving Europe, for many a day," Roderick answered. "At present it would quite break the charm. I am just beginning to profit, to get used to things and take them naturally. I am sure the sight of Northampton Main Street would permanently upset me."

It was reassuring to hear that Roderick, in his own view, was but "just beginning" to spread his wings, and Rowland, if he had had any forebodings, might have suffered them to be modified by this declaration. This was the first time since their meeting at Geneva that Roderick had mentioned Miss Garland's name, but the ice being broken, he indulged for some time afterward in frequent allusions to his betrothed, which always had an accent of scrupulous, of almost studied, consideration. An uninitiated observer, hearing him, would have imagined her to be a person of a certain age—possibly an affectionate maiden aunt—who had once done him a kindness which he highly appreciated: perhaps presented him with a check for a thousand dollars. Rowland noted the difference between his present frankness and his reticence during the first six months of his engagement, and sometimes wondered whether it was not rather an anomaly that he should expatiate more largely as the happy event receded. He had wondered over the whole matter, first and last, in a great many different ways, and looked at it in all possible lights.

There was something terribly hard to explain in the fact of his having fallen in love with his cousin. She was not, as Rowland conceived her, the sort of girl he would have been likely to fancy, and the operation of sentiment, in all cases so mysterious, was particularly so in this one. Just why it was that Roderick should not logically have fancied Miss Garland, his companion would have been at loss to say, but I think the conviction had its roots in an unformulated comparison between himself and the accepted suitor. Roderick and he were as different as two men could be, and yet Roderick had taken it into his head to fall in love with a woman for whom he himself had been keeping in reserve, for years, a profoundly characteristic passion. That if *he* chose to conceive a great notion of the merits of Roderick's mistress, the irregularity here was hardly Roderick's, was a view of the case to which poor Rowland did scanty justice. There were women, he said to himself, whom it was every one's business to fall in love with a little—women beautiful, brilliant, artful, easily fascinating. Miss Light, for instance, was one of these; every man who spoke to her did so, if not in the language, at least with something of the agitation, the divine tremor, of a lover. There were other women—they might have great beauty, they might have small; perhaps they were generally to be classified as plain—whose triumphs in this line were rare, but immutably permanent. Such a one preëminently, was Mary Garland. Upon the doctrine of probabilities, it was unlikely that she had had an equal charm for each of them, and was it not possible, therefore, that the charm for Roderick had been simply the charm imagined, unquestioningly accepted: the general charm of youth, sympathy, kindness—of the present feminine, in short—enhanced indeed by several fine facial traits? The charm in this case for Rowland was— *the* charm!—the mysterious, individual, essential woman. There was an element in the charm, as his companion saw it, which Rowland was obliged to recognize, but which he forbore to ponder; the rather important attraction, namely, of reciprocity. As to Miss Garland being in love with Roderick and becoming charming thereby, this was a point with which his imagination ventured to take no liberties; partly because it would have been indelicate, and partly because it would have been vain. He contented himself with feeling that the young girl was still as vivid an image in his memory as she had been five days after he left her, and with drifting nearer and nearer to the impression that at just that crisis any other girl would have answered Roderick's sentimental needs as well. Any other girl indeed would do so still! Roderick had confessed as much to him at Geneva, in saying that he had been taking at Baden the measure of his susceptibility to female beauty.

His extraordinary success in modeling the bust of the beautiful Miss Light was pertinent evidence of this amiable quality. She sat to him, repeatedly, for a fortnight, and the work was rapidly finished. On one of the last days Roderick asked Rowland to come and give his opinion as to what was still wanting; for the sittings had continued to take place in Mrs. Light's apartment, the studio being pronounced too damp for the fair model. When Rowland presented himself, Christina, still in her white dress, with her shoulders bare, was standing before a mirror, readjusting her hair, the arrangement of which, on this occasion, had apparently not met the young sculptor's approval. He stood beside her, directing the operation with a peremptoriness of tone which seemed to Rowland to denote a considerable advance in intimacy. As Rowland entered, Christina was losing patience. "Do it yourself, then!" she cried, and with a rapid movement unloosed the great coil of her tresses and let them fall over her shoulders.

They were magnificent, and with her perfect face dividing their rippling flow she looked like some immaculate saint of legend being led to martyrdom. Rowland's eyes presumably betrayed his admiration, but her own manifested no consciousness of it. If Christina was a coquette, as the remarkable timeliness of this incident might have suggested, she was not a superficial one.

"Hudson 's a sculptor," said Rowland, with warmth. "But if I were only a painter!"

"Thank Heaven you are not!" said Christina. "I am having quite enough of this minute inspection of my charms."

"My dear young man, hands off!" cried Mrs. Light, coming forward and seizing her daughter's hair. "Christina, love, I am surprised."

"Is it indelicate?" Christina asked. "I beg Mr. Mallet's pardon." Mrs. Light gathered up the dusky locks and let them fall through her fingers, glancing at her visitor with a significant smile. Rowland had never been in the East, but if he had attempted to make a sketch of an old slave-merchant, calling attention to the "points" of a Circassian beauty, he would have depicted such a smile as Mrs. Light's. "Mamma 's not really shocked," added Christina in a moment, as if she had guessed her mother's by-play. "She is only afraid that Mr. Hudson might have injured my hair, and that, *per consequenza*, I should sell for less."

"You unnatural child!" cried mamma. "You deserve that I should make a fright of you!" And with half a dozen skillful passes she twisted the tresses into a single picturesque braid, placed high on the head, as a kind of coronal.

"What does your mother do when she wants to do you justice?" Rowland asked, observing the admirable line of the young girl's neck.

"I do her justice when I say she says very improper things. What is one to do with such a thorn in the flesh?" Mrs. Light demanded.

"Think of it at your leisure, Mr. Mallet," said Christina, "and when you 've discovered something, let us hear. But I must tell you that I shall not willingly believe in any remedy of yours, for you have something in your physiognomy that particularly provokes me to make the remarks that my mother so sincerely deplores. I noticed it the first time I saw you. I think it 's because your face is so broad. For some reason or other, broad faces exasperate me; they fill me with a kind of *rabbia*. Last summer, at Carlsbad, there was an Austrian count, with enormous estates and some great office at court. He was very attentive—seriously so; he was really very far gone. *Cela ne tenait qu' à moi!* But I could n't; he was impossible! He must have measured, from ear to ear, at least a yard and a half. And he was blond, too, which made it worse—as blond as Stenterello; pure fleece! So I said to him frankly, 'Many thanks, Herr Graf; your uniform is magnificent, but your face is too fat.' "

"I am afraid that mine also," said Rowland, with a smile, "seems just now to have assumed an unpardonable latitude."

"Oh, I take it you know very well that we are looking for a husband, and that none but tremendous swells need apply. Surely, before these gentlemen, mamma, I may speak freely; they are disinterested. Mr. Mallet won't do, because, though he 's rich, he 's not rich enough. Mamma made that discovery the day after we went to see you, moved to it by the promising look of your furniture. I hope she was right, eh? Unless you have millions, you know, you have no chance."

"I feel like a beggar," said Rowland.

"Oh, some better girl than I will decide some day, after mature reflection, that on the whole you have enough. Mr. Hudson, of course, is nowhere; he has nothing but his genius and his *beaux yeux*."

Roderick had stood looking at Christina intently while she delivered herself, softly and slowly, of this surprising nonsense. When she had finished, she turned and looked at him; their eyes met, and he blushed a little. "Let me model you, and he who can may marry you!" he said, abruptly.

Mrs. Light, while her daughter talked, had been adding a few touches to her coiffure. "She is not so silly as you might suppose," she said to Rowland, with dignity. "If you will give me your arm, we will go and look at the bust."

"Does that represent a silly girl?" Christina demanded, when they stood before it.

Rowland transferred his glance several times from the portrait to the original. "It represents a young lady," he said, "whom I should not pretend to judge off-hand."

"She may be a fool, but you are not sure. Many thanks! You have seen me half a dozen times. You are either very slow or I am very deep."

"I am certainly slow," said Rowland. "I don't expect to make up my mind about you within six months."

"I give you six months if you will promise then a perfectly frank opinion. Mind, I shall not forget; I shall insist upon it."

"Well, though I am slow, I am tolerably brave," said Rowland. "We shall see."

Christina looked at the bust with a sigh. "I am afraid, after all," she said, "that there 's very little wisdom in it save what the artist has put there. Mr. Hudson looked particularly wise while he was working; he scowled and growled, but he never

opened his mouth. It is very kind of him not to have represented me gaping."

"If I had talked a lot of stuff to you," said Roderick,
roundly, "the thing would not have been a tenth so good."

"Is it good, after all? Mr. Mallet is a famous connoisseur;
has he not come here to pronounce?"

The bust was in fact a very happy performance, and Roderick had risen to the level of his subject. It was thoroughly a
portrait, and not a vague fantasy executed on a graceful
theme, as the busts of pretty women, in modern sculpture,
are apt to be. The resemblance was deep and vivid; there was
extreme fidelity of detail and yet a noble simplicity. One could
say of the head that, without idealization, it was a representation of ideal beauty. Rowland, however, as we know, was
not fond of exploding into superlatives, and, after examining
the piece, contented himself with suggesting two or three alterations of detail.

"Nay, how can you be so cruel?" demanded Mrs. Light,
with soft reproachfulness. "It is surely a wonderful thing!"

"Rowland knows it 's a wonderful thing," said Roderick,
smiling. "I can tell that by his face. The other day I finished
something he thought bad, and he looked very differently
from this."

"How did Mr. Mallet look?" asked Christina.

"My dear Rowland," said Roderick, "I am speaking of my
seated woman. You looked as if you had on a pair of tight
boots."

"Ah, my child, you 'll not understand that!" cried Mrs.
Light. "You never yet had a pair that were small enough."

"It 's a pity, Mr. Hudson," said Christina, gravely, "that
you could not have introduced my feet into the bust. But we
can hang a pair of slippers round the neck!"

"I nevertheless like your statues, Roderick," Rowland rejoined, "better than your jokes. This is admirable. Miss Light,
you may be proud!"

"Thank you, Mr. Mallet, for the permission," rejoined the
young girl.

"I am dying to see it in the marble, with a red velvet screen
behind it," said Mrs. Light.

"Placed there under the Sassoferrato!" Christina went on.

"I hope you keep well in mind, Mr. Hudson, that you have not a grain of property in your work, and that if mamma chooses, she may have it photographed and the copies sold in the Piazza di Spagna, at five francs apiece, without your having a sou of the profits."

"Amen!" said Roderick. "It was so nominated in the bond. My profits are here!" and he tapped his forehead.

"It would be prettier if you said *here!*" And Christina touched her heart.

"My precious child, how you do run on!" murmured Mrs. Light.

"It is Mr. Mallet," the young girl answered. "I can't talk a word of sense so long as he is in the room. I don't say that to make you go," she added, "I say it simply to justify myself."

Rowland bowed in silence. Roderick declared that he must get at work and requested Christina to take her usual position, and Mrs. Light proposed to her visitor that they should adjourn to her boudoir. This was a small room, hardly more spacious than an alcove, opening out of the drawing-room and having no other issue. Here, as they entered, on a divan near the door, Rowland perceived the Cavaliere Giacosa, with his arms folded, his head dropped upon his breast, and his eyes closed.

"Sleeping at his post!" said Rowland with a kindly laugh.

"That 's a punishable offense," rejoined Mrs. Light, sharply. She was on the point of calling him, in the same tone, when he suddenly opened his eyes, stared a moment, and then rose with a smile and a bow.

"Excuse me, dear lady," he said, "I was overcome by the— the great heat."

"Nonsense, Cavaliere!" cried the lady, "you know we are perishing here with the cold! You had better go and cool yourself in one of the other rooms."

"I obey, dear lady," said the Cavaliere; and with another smile and bow to Rowland he departed, walking very discreetly on his toes. Rowland out-stayed him but a short time, for he was not fond of Mrs. Light, and he found nothing very inspiring in her frank intimation that if he chose, he might become a favorite. He was disgusted with himself for pleasing her; he confounded his fatal urbanity. In the court-yard of the palace he overtook the Cavaliere, who had stopped at the porter's lodge to say a word to his little girl. She was a young lady of very tender years and she wore a very dirty pinafore. He had taken her up in his arms and was singing an infantine rhyme to her, and she was staring at him with big, soft Roman eyes. On seeing Rowland he put her down with a kiss, and stepped forward with a conscious grin, an unresentful admission that he was sensitive both to chubbiness and ridicule. Rowland began to pity him again; he had taken his dismissal from the drawing-room so meekly.

"You don't keep your promise," said Rowland, "to come and see me. Don't forget it. I want you to tell me about Rome thirty years ago."

"Thirty years ago? Ah, dear sir, Rome is Rome still; a place where strange things happen! But happy things too, since I have your renewed permission to call. You do me too much honor. Is it in the morning or in the evening that I should least intrude?"

"Take your own time, Cavaliere; only come, sometime. I depend upon you," said Rowland.

The Cavaliere thanked him with an humble obeisance. To the Cavaliere, too, he felt that he was, in Roman phrase, sympathetic, but the idea of pleasing this extremely reduced gentleman was not disagreeable to him.

Miss Light's bust stood for a while on exhibition in Roderick's studio, and half the foreign colony came to see it. With the completion of his work, however, Roderick's visits at the Palazzo F—— by no means came to an end. He spent half his time in Mrs. Light's drawing-room, and began to be talked about as "attentive" to Christina. The success of the bust restored his equanimity, and in the garrulity of his good-humor he suffered Rowland to see that she was just now the object uppermost in his thoughts. Rowland, when they talked of her, was rather listener than speaker; partly because Roderick's own tone was so resonant and exultant, and partly because, when his companion laughed at him for having called her unsafe, he was too perplexed to defend himself. The impression remained that she was unsafe; that she was a complex, willful, passionate creature, who might easily engulf a

too confiding spirit in the eddies of her capricious temper.
And yet he strongly felt her charm; the eddies had a strange
fascination! Roderick, in the glow of that renewed admiration
provoked by the fixed attention of portrayal, was never weary
of descanting on the extraordinary perfection of her beauty.

"I had no idea of it," he said, "till I began to look at her
with an eye to reproducing line for line and curve for curve.
Her face is the most exquisite piece of modeling that ever
came from creative hands. Not a line without meaning, not a
hair's breadth that is not admirably finished. And then her
mouth! It 's as if a pair of lips had been shaped to utter pure
truth without doing it dishonor!" Later, after he had been
working for a week, he declared if Miss Light were inordinately plain, she would still be the most fascinating of
women. "I 've quite forgotten her beauty," he said, "or rather
I have ceased to perceive it as something distinct and defined,
something independent of the rest of her. She is all one, and
all consummately interesting!"

"What does she do—what does she say, that is so remarkable?" Rowland had asked.

"Say? Sometimes nothing—sometimes everything. She is
never the same. Sometimes she walks in and takes her place
without a word, without a smile, gravely, stiffly, as if it were
an awful bore. She hardly looks at me, and she walks away
without even glancing at my work. On other days she laughs
and chatters and asks endless questions, and pours out the
most irresistible nonsense. She is a creature of moods; you
can't count upon her; she keeps observation on the stretch.
And then, bless you, she has seen such a lot! Her talk is full
of the oddest allusions!"

"It is altogether a very singular type of young lady," said
Rowland, after the visit which I have related at length. "It
may be a charm, but it is certainly not the orthodox charm of
marriageable maidenhood, the charm of shrinking innocence
and soft docility. Our American girls are accused of being
more knowing than any others, and Miss Light is nominally
an American. But it has taken twenty years of Europe to make
her what she is. The first time we saw her, I remember you
called her a product of the old world, and certainly you were
not far wrong."

"Ah, she has an atmosphere," said Roderick, in the tone of high appreciation.

"Young unmarried women," Rowland answered, "should be careful not to have too much!"

"Ah, you don't forgive her," cried his companion, "for hitting you so hard! A man ought to be flattered at such a girl as that taking so much notice of him."

"A man is never flattered at a woman's not liking him."

"Are you sure she does n't like you? That 's to the credit of your humility. A fellow of more vanity might, on the evidence, persuade himself that he was in favor."

"He would have also," said Rowland, laughing, "to be a fellow of remarkable ingenuity!" He asked himself privately how the deuce Roderick reconciled it to his conscience to think so much more of the girl he was not engaged to than of the girl he was. But it amounted almost to arrogance, you may say, in poor Rowland to pretend to know how often Roderick thought of Miss Garland. He wondered gloomily, at any rate, whether for men of his companion's large, easy power, there was not a larger moral law than for narrow mediocrities like himself, who, yielding Nature a meagre interest on her investment (such as it was), had no reason to expect from her this affectionate laxity as to their accounts. Was it not a part of the eternal fitness of things that Roderick, while rhapsodizing about Miss Light, should have it at his command to look at you with eyes of the most guileless and unclouded blue, and to shake off your musty imputations by a toss of his picturesque brown locks? Or had he, in fact, no conscience to speak of? Happy fellow, either way!

Our friend Gloriani came, among others, to congratulate Roderick on his model and what he had made of her. "Devilish pretty, through and through!" he said as he looked at the bust. "Capital handling of the neck and throat; lovely work on the nose. You 're a detestably lucky fellow, my boy! But you ought not to have squandered such material on a simple bust; you should have made a great imaginative figure. If I could only have got hold of her, I would have put her into a statue in spite of herself. What a pity she is not a ragged Trasteverine, whom we might have for a franc an hour! I have been carrying about in my head for years a delicious design for a fantastic figure, but it has always stayed there for want of a tolerable model. I have seen intimations of the type, but Miss Light is the perfection of it. As soon as I saw her I said to myself, 'By Jove, there 's my statue in the flesh!' "

"What is your subject?" asked Roderick.

"Don't take it ill," said Gloriani. "You know I 'm the very deuce for observation. She would make a magnificent Herodias!"

If Roderick had taken it ill (which was unlikely, for we know he thought Gloriani an ass, and expected little of his wisdom), he might have been soothed by the candid incense of Sam Singleton, who came and sat for an hour in a sort of mental prostration before both bust and artist. But Roderick's attitude before his patient little devotee was one of undisguised though friendly amusement; and, indeed, judged from a strictly plastic point of view, the poor fellow's diminutive stature, his enormous mouth, his pimples and his yellow hair were sufficiently ridiculous. "Nay, don't envy our friend," Rowland said to Singleton afterwards, on his expressing, with a little groan of depreciation of his own paltry performances, his sense of the brilliancy of Roderick's talent. "You sail nearer the shore, but you sail in smoother waters. Be contented with what you are and paint me another picture."

"Oh, I don't envy Hudson anything he possesses," Singleton said, "because to take anything away would spoil his beautiful completeness. 'Complete,' that 's what he is; while we little clevernesses are like half-ripened plums, only good eating on the side that has had a glimpse of the sun. Nature has made him so, and fortune confesses to it! He is the handsomest fellow in Rome, he has the most genius, and, as a matter of course, the most beautiful girl in the world comes and offers to be his model. If that is not completeness, where shall we find it?"

One morning, going into Roderick's studio, Rowland found the young sculptor entertaining Miss Blanchard—if this is not too flattering a description of his gracefully passive tolerance of her presence. He had never liked her and never climbed into her sky-studio to observe her wonderful manipulation of petals. He had once quoted Tennyson against her:—

> "And is there any moral shut
>   Within the bosom of the rose?"

"In all Miss Blanchard's roses you may be sure there is a moral," he had said. "You can see it sticking out its head, and, if you go to smell the flower, it scratches your nose." But on this occasion she had come with a propitiatory gift—introducing her friend Mr. Leavenworth. Mr. Leavenworth was a tall, expansive, bland gentleman, with a carefully brushed whisker and a spacious, fair, well-favored face, which seemed, somehow, to have more room in it than was occupied by a smile of superior benevolence, so that (with his smooth, white forehead) it bore a certain resemblance to a large parlor with a very florid carpet, but no pictures on the walls. He held his head high, talked sonorously, and told Roderick, within five minutes, that he was a widower, traveling to distract his mind, and that he had lately retired from the proprietorship of large mines of borax in Pennsylvania. Roderick supposed at first that, in his character of depressed widower, he had come to order a tombstone; but observing then the extreme blandness of his address to Miss Blanchard, he credited him with a judicious prevision that by the time the tombstone was completed, a monument of his inconsolability might have become an anachronism. But Mr. Leavenworth was disposed to order something.

"You will find me eager to patronize our indigenous talent," he said. "I am putting up a little shanty in my native town, and I propose to make a rather nice thing of it. It has been the will of Heaven to plunge me into mourning; but art has consolations! In a tasteful home, surrounded by the memorials of my wanderings, I hope to take more cheerful views. I ordered in Paris the complete appurtenances of a dining-room. Do you think you could do something for my library? It is to be filled with well-selected authors, and I think a pure white image in this style,"—pointing to one of Roderick's statues,—"standing out against the morocco and gilt, would have a noble effect. The subject I have already fixed upon. I desire an allegorical representation of Culture. Do you think, now," asked Mr. Leavenworth, encouragingly, "you could rise to the conception?"

"A most interesting subject for a truly serious mind," remarked Miss Blanchard.

Roderick looked at her a moment, and then—"The simplest thing I could do," he said, "would be to make a full-length portrait of Miss Blanchard. I could give her a scroll in her hand, and that would do for the allegory."

Miss Blanchard colored; the compliment might be ironical; and there was ever afterwards a reflection of her uncertainty in her opinion of Roderick's genius. Mr. Leavenworth responded that with all deference to Miss Blanchard's beauty, he desired something colder, more monumental, more impersonal. "If I were to be the happy possessor of a likeness of Miss Blanchard," he added, "I should prefer to have it in no factitious disguise!"

Roderick consented to entertain the proposal, and while they were discussing it, Rowland had a little talk with the fair artist. "Who is your friend?" he asked.

"A very worthy man. The architect of his own fortune—which is magnificent. One of nature's gentlemen!"

This was a trifle sententious, and Rowland turned to the bust of Miss Light. Like every one else in Rome, by this time, Miss Blanchard had an opinion on the young girl's beauty, and, in her own fashion, she expressed it epigrammatically. "She looks half like a Madonna and half like a *ballerina*," she said.

Mr. Leavenworth and Roderick came to an understanding, and the young sculptor good-naturedly promised to do his best to rise to his patron's conception. "His conception be hanged!" Roderick exclaimed, after he had departed. "His conception is sitting on a globe with a pen in her ear and a photographic album in her hand. I shall have to conceive, myself. For the money, I ought to be able to!"

*   *   *

Mrs. Light, meanwhile, had fairly established herself in Roman society. "Heaven knows how!" Madame Grandoni said to Rowland, who had mentioned to her several evidences of the lady's prosperity. "In such a case there is nothing like audacity. A month ago she knew no one but her washerwoman, and now I am told that the cards of Roman princesses are to be seen on her table. She is evidently determined to play a great part, and she has the wit to perceive that, to make remunerative acquaintances, you must seem yourself to be worth knowing. You must have striking rooms and a confusing variety of dresses, and give good dinners, and so forth. She is spending a lot of money, and you 'll see that in two or three weeks she will take upon herself to open the season by giving a magnificent ball. Of course it is Christina's beauty that floats her. People go to see her because they are curious."

"And they go again because they are charmed," said Rowland. "Miss Christina is a very remarkable young lady."

"Oh, I know it well; I had occasion to say so to myself the other day. She came to see me, of her own free will, and for an hour she was deeply interesting. I think she 's an actress, but she believes in her part while she is playing it. She took it into her head the other day to believe that she was very unhappy, and she sat there, where you are sitting, and told me a tale of her miseries which brought tears into my eyes. She cried, herself, profusely, and as naturally as possible. She said she was weary of life and that she knew no one but me she could speak frankly to. She must speak, or she would go mad. She sobbed as if her heart would break. I assure you it 's well for you susceptible young men that you don't see her when she sobs. She said, in so many words, that her mother was an immoral woman. Heaven knows what she meant. She meant, I suppose, that she makes debts that she knows she can't pay. She said the life they led was horrible; that it was monstrous a poor girl should be dragged about the world to be sold to the highest bidder. She was meant for better things; she could be perfectly happy in poverty. It was not money she wanted. I might not believe her, but she really cared for serious things. Sometimes she thought of taking poison!"

"What did you say to that?"

"I recommended her," said Madame Grandoni, "to come and see me instead. I would help her about as much, and I was, on the whole, less unpleasant. Of course I could help her only by letting her talk herself out and kissing her and patting her beautiful hands and telling her to be patient and she would be happy yet. About once in two months I expect her to reappear, on the same errand, and meanwhile to quite forget my existence. I believe I melted down to the point of telling her that I would find some good, quiet, affectionate husband for her; but she declared, almost with fury, that she was sick unto death of husbands, and begged I would never again mention the word. And, in fact, it was a rash offer; for I am sure that there is not a man of the kind that might really make a woman happy but would be afraid to marry mademoiselle. Looked at in that way she is certainly very much to be pitied, and indeed, altogether, though I don't think she either means all she says or, by a great deal, says all that she means. I feel very sorry for her."

Rowland met the two ladies, about this time, at several entertainments, and looked at Christina with a kind of distant *attendrissement*. He imagined more than once that there had been a passionate scene between them about coming out, and wondered what arguments Mrs. Light had found effective. But Christina's face told no tales, and she moved about, beautiful and silent, looking absently over people's heads, barely heeding the men who pressed about her, and suggesting somehow that the soul of a world-wearied mortal had found its way into the blooming body of a goddess. "Where in the world has Miss Light been before she is twenty," observers asked, "to have left all her illusions behind?" And the general verdict was, that though she was incomparably beautiful, she was intolerably proud. Young ladies to whom the former distinction was not conceded were free to reflect that she was "not at all liked."

It would have been difficult to guess, however, how they reconciled this conviction with a variety of conflicting evidence, and, in especial, with the spectacle of Roderick's inveterate devotion. All Rome might behold that he, at least, "liked" Christina Light. Wherever she appeared he was either awaiting her or immediately followed her. He was perpetually at her side, trying, apparently, to preserve the thread of a disconnected talk, the fate of which was, to judge by her face, profoundly immaterial to the young lady. People in general smiled at the radiant good faith of the handsome young sculptor, and asked each other whether he really supposed that beauties of that quality were meant to wed with poor artists. But although Christina's deportment, as I have said, was one of superb inexpressiveness, Rowland had derived from Roderick no suspicion that he suffered from snubbing, and he was therefore surprised at an incident which befell one evening at a large musical party. Roderick, as usual, was in the field, and, on the ladies taking the chairs which had been arranged for them, he immediately placed himself beside Christina. As most of the gentlemen were standing, his position made him as conspicuous as Hamlet at Ophelia's feet, at the play. Rowland was leaning, somewhat apart, against the chimney-piece. There was a long, solemn pause before the music began, and in the midst of it Christina rose, left her place, came the whole length of the immense room, with every one looking at her, and stopped before him. She was neither pale nor flushed; she had a soft smile.

"Will you do me a favor?" she asked.

"A thousand!"

"Not now, but at your earliest convenience. Please remind Mr. Hudson that he is not in a New England village—that it is not the custom in Rome to address one's conversation exclusively, night after night, to the same poor girl, and that" . . . .

The music broke out with a great blare and covered her voice. She made a gesture of impatience, and Rowland offered her his arm and led her back to her seat.

The next day he repeated her words to Roderick, who burst into joyous laughter. "She 's a delightfully strange girl!" he cried. "She must do everything that comes into her head!"

"Had she never asked you before not to talk to her so much?"

"On the contrary, she has often said to me, 'Mind you now, I forbid you to leave me. Here comes that tiresome So-and-so.' She cares as little about the custom as I do. What could be a better proof than her walking up to you, with five hundred people looking at her? Is that the custom for young girls in Rome?"

"Why, then, should she take such a step?"

"Because, as she sat there, it came into her head. That 's reason enough for her. I have imagined she wishes me well, as they say here—though she has never distinguished me in such a way as that!"

*   *   *

Madame Grandoni had foretold the truth; Mrs. Light, a couple of weeks later, convoked all Roman society to a brilliant ball. Rowland went late, and found the staircase so encumbered with flower-pots and servants that he was a long time making his way into the presence of the hostess. At last he approached her, as she stood making courtesies at the door, with her daughter by her side. Some of Mrs. Light's courtesies were very low, for she had the happiness of receiving a number of the social potentates of the Roman world. She was rosy with triumph, to say nothing of a less metaphysical cause, and was evidently vastly contented with herself, with her company, and with the general promise of destiny. Her daughter was less overtly jubilant, and distributed her greetings with impartial frigidity. She had never been so beautiful. Dressed simply in vaporous white, relieved with half a dozen white roses, the perfection of her features and of her person and the mysterious depth of her expression seemed to glow with the white light of a splendid pearl. She recognized no one individually, and made her courtesy slowly, gravely, with her eyes on the ground. Rowland fancied that, as he stood before her, her obeisance was slightly exaggerated, as with an intention of irony; but he smiled philosophically to himself, and reflected, as he passed into the room, that, if she disliked him, he had nothing to reproach himself with. He walked about, had a few words with Miss Blanchard, who, with a fillet of cameos in her hair, was leaning on the arm of Mr. Leavenworth, and at last came upon the Cavaliere Giacosa, modestly stationed in a corner. The little gentleman's coat-lappet was decorated with an enormous bouquet and his neck encased in a voluminous white handkerchief of the fashion of thirty years ago. His arms were folded, and he was surveying the scene with contracted eyelids, through which you saw the glitter of his intensely dark, vivacious pupil. He immediately embarked on an elaborate apology for not having yet manifested, as he felt it, his sense of the honor Rowland had done him.

"I am always on service with these ladies, you see," he explained, "and that is a duty to which one would not willingly be faithless for an instant."

"Evidently," said Rowland, "you are a very devoted friend. Mrs. Light, in her situation, is very happy in having you."

"We are old friends," said the Cavaliere, gravely. "Old friends. I knew the signora many years ago, when she was the prettiest woman in Rome—or rather in Ancona, which is even better. The beautiful Christina, now, is perhaps the most beautiful young girl in Europe!"

"Very likely," said Rowland.

"Very well, sir, I taught her to read; I guided her little hands to touch the piano keys." And at these faded memories, the Cavaliere's eyes glittered more brightly. Rowland half expected him to proceed, with a little flash of long-repressed passion, "And now—and now, sir, they treat me as you observed the other day!" But the Cavaliere only looked out at him keenly from among his wrinkles, and seemed to say, with all the vividness of the Italian glance, "Oh, I say nothing more. I am not so shallow as to complain!"

Evidently the Cavaliere was not shallow, and Rowland repeated respectfully, "You are a devoted friend."

"That 's very true. I am a devoted friend. A man may do himself justice, after twenty years!"

Rowland, after a pause, made some remark about the beauty of the ball. It was very brilliant.

"Stupendous!" said the Cavaliere, solemnly. "It is a great day. We have four Roman princes, to say nothing of others." And he counted them over on his fingers and held up his hand triumphantly. "And there she stands, the girl to whom I—I, Giuseppe Giacosa—taught her alphabet and her piano-scales; there she stands in her incomparable beauty, and Roman princes come and bow to her. Here, in his corner, her old master permits himself to be proud."

"It is very friendly of him," said Rowland, smiling.

The Cavaliere contracted his lids a little more and gave another keen glance. "It is very natural, signore. The Christina is a good girl; she remembers my little services. But here comes," he added in a moment, "the young Prince of the Fine Arts. I am sure he has bowed lowest of all."

Rowland looked round and saw Roderick moving slowly across the room and casting about him his usual luminous, unshrinking looks. He presently joined them, nodded familiarly to the Cavaliere, and immediately demanded of Rowland, "Have you seen her?"

"I have seen Miss Light," said Rowland. "She 's magnificent."

"I 'm half crazy!" cried Roderick; so loud that several persons turned round.

Rowland saw that he was flushed, and laid his hand on his arm. Roderick was trembling. "If you will go away," Rowland said instantly, "I will go with you."

"Go away?" cried Roderick, almost angrily. "I intend to dance with her!"

The Cavaliere had been watching him attentively; he gently laid his hand on his other arm. "Softly, softly, dear young man," he said. "Let me speak to you as a friend."

"Oh, speak even as an enemy and I shall not mind it," Roderick answered, frowning.

"Be very reasonable, then, and go away."

"Why the deuce should I go away?"

"Because you are in love," said the Cavaliere.

"I might as well be in love here as in the streets."

"Carry your love as far as possible from Christina. She will not listen to you—she can't."

"She 'can't'?" demanded Roderick. "She is not a person of whom you may say that. She can if she will; she does as she chooses."

"Up to a certain point. It would take too long to explain; I only beg you to believe that if you continue to love Miss Light you will be very unhappy. Have you a princely title? have you a princely fortune? Otherwise you can never have her."

And the Cavaliere folded his arms again, like a man who has done his duty. Roderick wiped his forehead and looked askance at Rowland; he seemed to be guessing his thoughts and they made him blush a little. But he smiled blandly, and addressing the Cavaliere, "I 'm much obliged to you for the information," he said. "Now that I have obtained it, let me tell you that I am no more in love with Miss Light than you are. Mr. Mallet knows that. I admire her—yes, profoundly. But that 's no one's business but my own, and though I have, as you say, neither a princely title nor a princely fortune, I mean to suffer neither those advantages nor those who possess them to diminish my right."

"If you are not in love, my dear young man," said the Cavaliere, with his hand on his heart and an apologetic smile, "so much the better. But let me entreat you, as an affectionate friend, to keep a watch on your emotions. You are young, you are handsome, you have a brilliant genius and a generous heart, but—I may say it almost with authority—Christina is not for you!"

Whether Roderick was in love or not, he was nettled by what apparently seemed to him an obtrusive negation of an inspiring possibility. "You speak as if she had made her choice!" he cried. "Without pretending to confidential information on the subject, I am sure she has not."

"No, but she must make it soon," said the Cavaliere. And raising his forefinger, he laid it against his under lip. "She must choose a name and a fortune—and she will!"

"She will do exactly as her inclination prompts! She will marry the man who pleases her, if he has n't a dollar! I know her better than you."

The Cavaliere turned a little paler than usual, and smiled more urbanely. "No, no, my dear young man, you do not know her better than I. You have not watched her, day by day, for twenty years. I too have admired her. She is a good girl; she has never said an unkind word to me; the blessed Virgin be thanked! But she must have a brilliant destiny; it has been marked out for her, and she will submit. You had better believe me; it may save you much suffering."

"We shall see!" said Roderick, with an excited laugh.

"Certainly we shall see. But I retire from the discussion," the Cavaliere added. "I have no wish to provoke you to attempt to prove to me that I am wrong. You are already excited."

"No more than is natural to a man who in an hour or so is to dance the cotillon with Miss Light."

"The cotillon? has she promised?"

Roderick patted the air with a grand confidence. "You 'll

see!" His gesture might almost have been taken to mean that the state of his relations with Miss Light was such that they quite dispensed with vain formalities.

The Cavaliere gave an exaggerated shrug. "You make a great many mourners!"

"He has made one already!" Rowland murmured to himself. This was evidently not the first time that reference had been made between Roderick and the Cavaliere to the young man's possible passion, and Roderick had failed to consider it the simplest and most natural course to say in three words to the vigilant little gentleman that there was no cause for alarm—his affections were preoccupied. Rowland hoped, silently, with some dryness, that his motives were of a finer kind than they seemed to be. He turned away; it was irritating to look at Roderick's radiant, unscrupulous eagerness. The tide was setting toward the supper-room and he drifted with it to the door. The crowd at this point was dense, and he was obliged to wait for some minutes before he could advance. At last he felt his neighbors dividing behind him, and turning he saw Christina pressing her way forward alone. She was looking at no one, and, save for the fact of her being alone, you would not have supposed she was in her mother's house. As she recognized Rowland she beckoned to him, took his arm, and motioned him to lead her into the supper-room. She said nothing until he had forced a passage and they stood somewhat isolated.

"Take me into the most out-of-the-way corner you can find," she then said, "and then go and get me a piece of bread."

"Nothing more? There seems to be everything conceivable."

"A simple roll. Nothing more, on your peril. Only bring something for yourself."

It seemed to Rowland that the embrasure of a window (embrasures in Roman palaces are deep) was a retreat sufficiently obscure for Miss Light to execute whatever design she might have contrived against his equanimity. A roll, after he had found her a seat, was easily procured. As he presented it, he remarked that, frankly speaking, he was at loss to understand why she should have selected for the honor of a tête-à-tête an individual for whom she had so little taste.

"Ah yes, I dislike you," said Christina. "To tell the truth, I had forgotten it. There are so many people here whom I dislike more, that when I espied you just now, you seemed like an intimate friend. But I have not come into this corner to talk nonsense," she went on. "You must not think I always do, eh?"

"I have never heard you do anything else," said Rowland, deliberately, having decided that he owed her no compliments.

"Very good. I like your frankness. It 's quite true. You see, I am a strange girl. To begin with, I am frightfully egotistical. Don't flatter yourself you have said anything very clever if you ever take it into your head to tell me so. I know it much better than you. So it is, I can't help it. I am tired to death of myself; I would give all I possess to get out of myself; but somehow, at the end, I find myself so vastly more interesting than nine tenths of the people I meet. If a person wished to do me a favor I would say to him, 'I beg you, with tears in my eyes, to interest me. Be strong, be positive, be imperious, if you will; only be something,—something that, in looking at, I can forget my detestable self!' Perhaps that is nonsense too. If it is, I can't help it. I can only apologize for the nonsense I know to be such and that I talk—oh, for more reasons than I can tell you! I wonder whether, if I were to try, you would understand me."

"I am afraid I should never understand," said Rowland, "why a person should willingly talk nonsense."

"That proves how little you know about women. But I like your frankness. When I told you the other day that you displeased me, I had an idea you were more formal,—how do you say it?—more *guindé*. I am very capricious. To-night I like you better."

"Oh, I am not *guindé*," said Rowland, gravely.

"I beg your pardon, then, for thinking so. Now I have an idea that you would make a useful friend—an intimate friend—a friend to whom one could tell everything. For such a friend, what would n't I give!"

Rowland looked at her in some perplexity. Was this touching sincerity, or unfathomable coquetry? Her beautiful eyes looked divinely candid; but then, if candor was beautiful, beauty was apt to be subtle. "I hesitate to recommend myself out and out for the office," he said, "but I believe that if you were to depend upon me for anything that a friend may do, I should not be found wanting."

"Very good. One of the first things one asks of a friend is to judge one not by isolated acts, but by one's whole conduct. I care for your opinion—I don't know why."

"Nor do I, I confess," said Rowland with a laugh.

"What do you think of this affair?" she continued, without heeding his laugh.

"Of your ball? Why, it 's a very grand affair."

"It 's horrible—that 's what it is! It 's a mere rabble! There are people here whom I never saw before, people who were never asked. Mamma went about inviting every one, asking other people to invite any one they knew, doing anything to have a crowd. I hope she is satisfied! It is not my doing. I feel weary, I feel angry, I feel like crying. I have twenty minds to escape into my room and lock the door and let mamma go through with it as she can. By the way," she added in a moment, without a visible reason for the transition, "can you tell me something to read?"

Rowland stared, at the disconnectedness of the question.

"Can you recommend me some books?" she repeated. "I know you are a great reader. I have no one else to ask. We can buy no books. We can make debts for jewelry and bonnets and five-button gloves, but we can't spend a sou for ideas. And yet, though you may not believe it, I like ideas quite as well."

"I shall be most happy to lend you some books," Rowland said. "I will pick some out to-morrow and send them to you."

"No novels, please! I am tired of novels. I can imagine better stories for myself than any I read. Some good poetry, if there is such a thing nowadays, and some memoirs and histories and books of facts."

"You shall be served. Your taste agrees with my own."

She was silent a moment, looking at him. Then suddenly— "Tell me something about Mr. Hudson," she demanded. "You are great friends!"

"Oh yes," said Rowland; "we are great friends."

"Tell me about him. Come, begin!"

"Where shall I begin? You know him for yourself."

"No, I don't know him; I don't find him so easy to know. Since he has finished my bust and begun to come here disinterestedly, he has become a great talker. He says very fine things; but does he mean all he says?"

"Few of us do that."

"You do, I imagine. You ought to know, for he tells me you discovered him." Rowland was silent, and Christina continued, "Do you consider him very clever?"

"Unquestionably."

"His talent is really something out of the common way?"

"So it seems to me."

"In short, he 's a man of genius?"

"Yes, call it genius."

"And you found him vegetating in a little village and took him by the hand and set him on his feet in Rome?"

"Is that the popular legend?" asked Rowland.

"Oh, you need n't be modest. There was no great merit in it; there would have been none at least on my part in the same circumstances. Real geniuses are not so common, and if I had discovered one in the wilderness, I would have brought him out into the market-place to see how he would behave. It would be excessively amusing. You must find it so to watch Mr. Hudson, eh? Tell me this: do you think he is going to be a great man—become famous, have his life written, and all that?"

"I don't prophesy, but I have good hopes."

Christina was silent. She stretched out her bare arm and looked at it a moment absently, turning it so as to see—or almost to see—the dimple in her elbow. This was apparently a frequent gesture with her; Rowland had already observed it. It was as coolly and naturally done as if she had been in her room alone. "So he 's a man of genius," she suddenly resumed. "Don't you think I ought to be extremely flattered to have a man of genius perpetually hanging about? He is the first I ever saw, but I should have known he was not a common mortal. There is something strange about him. To begin with, he has no manners. You may say that it 's not for me to blame him, for I have none myself. That 's very true, but the difference is that I can have them when I wish to (and very charming ones too; I 'll show you some day); whereas Mr. Hudson will never have them. And yet, somehow, one sees he 's a gentleman. He seems to have something urging, driving, pushing him, making him restless and defiant. You see it in his eyes. They are the finest, by the way, I ever saw. When a person has such eyes as that you can forgive him his bad manners. I suppose that is what they call the sacred fire."

Rowland made no answer except to ask her in a moment if she would have another roll. She merely shook her head and went on: —

"Tell me how you found him. Where was he—how was he?"

"He was in a place called Northampton. Did you ever hear of it? He was studying law—but not learning it."

"It appears it was something horrible, eh?"

"Something horrible?"

"This little village. No society, no pleasures, no beauty, no life."

"You have received a false impression. Northampton is not as gay as Rome, but Roderick had some charming friends."

"Tell me about them. Who were they?"

"Well, there was my cousin, through whom I made his acquaintance: a delightful woman."

"Young—pretty?"

"Yes, a good deal of both. And very clever."

"Did he make love to her?"

"Not in the least."

"Well, who else?"

"He lived with his mother. She is the best of women."

"Ah yes, I know all that one's mother is. But she does not count as society. And who else?"

Rowland hesitated. He wondered whether Christina's insistance was the result of a general interest in Roderick's antecedents or of a particular suspicion. He looked at her; she was looking at him a little askance, waiting for his answer. As Roderick had said nothing about his engagement to the Cavaliere, it was probable that with this beautiful girl he had not been more explicit. And yet the thing was announced, it was public; that other girl was happy in it, proud of it. Rowland felt a kind of dumb anger rising in his heart. He deliberated a moment intently.

"What are you frowning at?" Christina asked.

"There was another person," he answered, "the most important of all: the young girl to whom he is engaged."

Christina stared a moment, raising her eyebrows. "Ah, Mr. Hudson is engaged?" she said, very simply. "Is she pretty?"

"She is not called a beauty," said Rowland. He meant to practice great brevity, but in a moment he added, "I have seen beauties, however, who pleased me less."

"Ah, she pleases *you*, too? Why don't they marry?"

"Roderick is waiting till he can afford to marry."

Christina slowly put out her arm again and looked at the dimple in her elbow. "Ah, he's engaged?" she repeated in the same tone. "He never told me."

Rowland perceived at this moment that the people about them were beginning to return to the dancing-room, and immediately afterwards he saw Roderick making his way toward themselves. Roderick presented himself before Miss Light.

"I don't claim that you have promised me the cotillon," he said, "but I consider that you have given me hopes which warrant the confidence that you will dance with me."

Christina looked at him a moment. "Certainly I have made no promises," she said. "It seemed to me that, as the daughter of the house, I should keep myself free and let it depend on circumstances."

"I beseech you to dance with me!" said Roderick, with vehemence.

Christina rose and began to laugh. "You say that very well, but the Italians do it better."

This assertion seemed likely to be put to the proof. Mrs. Light hastily approached, leading, rather than led by, a tall, slim young man, of an unmistakably Southern physiognomy. "My precious love," she cried, "what a place to hide in! We have been looking for you for twenty minutes; I have chosen a cavalier for you, and chosen well!"

The young man disengaged himself, made a ceremonious bow, joined his two hands, and murmured with an ecstatic smile, "May I venture to hope, dear signorina, for the honor of your hand?"

"Of course you may!" said Mrs. Light. "The honor is for us."

Christina hesitated but for a moment, then swept the young man a courtesy as profound as his own bow. "You are very kind, but you are too late. I have just accepted!"

"Ah, my own darling!" murmured—almost moaned—Mrs. Light.

Christina and Roderick exchanged a single glance—a glance brilliant on both sides. She passed her hand into his arm; he tossed his clustering locks and led her away.

A short time afterwards Rowland saw the young man whom she had rejected leaning against a doorway. He was ugly, but what is called distinguished-looking. He had a heavy black eye, a sallow complexion, a long, thin neck; his hair was cropped *en brosse*. He looked very young, yet extremely bored. He was staring at the ceiling and stroking an imperceptible moustache. Rowland espied the Cavaliere Giacosa hard by, and, having joined him, asked him the young man's name.

"Oh," said the Cavaliere, "he 's a *pezzo grosso*! A Neapolitan. Prince Casamassima."

VI

Frascati

ONE DAY, on entering Roderick's lodging (not the modest rooms on the Ripetta which he had first occupied, but a much more sumptuous apartment on the Corso), Rowland found a letter on the table addressed to himself. It was from Roderick, and consisted of but three lines: "I am gone to Frascati—for meditation. If I am not at home on Friday, you had better join me." On Friday he was still absent, and Rowland went out to Frascati. Here he found his friend living at the inn and spending his days, according to his own account, lying under the trees of the Villa Mondragone, reading Ariosto. He was in a sombre mood; "meditation" seemed not to have been fruitful. Nothing especially pertinent to our narrative had passed between the two young men since Mrs. Light's ball, save a few words bearing on an incident of that entertainment. Rowland informed Roderick, the next day, that he had told Miss Light of his engagement. "I don't know whether you 'll thank me," he had said, "but it 's my duty to let you know it. Miss Light perhaps has already done so."

Roderick looked at him a moment, intently, with his color slowly rising. "Why should n't I thank you?" he asked. "I am not ashamed of my engagement."

"As you had not spoken of it yourself, I thought you might have a reason for not having it known."

"A man does n't gossip about such a matter with strangers," Roderick rejoined, with the ring of irritation in his voice.

"With strangers—no!" said Rowland, smiling.

Roderick continued his work; but after a moment, turning round with a frown: "If you supposed I had a reason for being silent, pray why should you have spoken?"

"I did not speak idly, my dear Roderick. I weighed the matter before I spoke, and promised myself to let you know immediately afterwards. It seemed to me that Miss Light had better know that your affections are pledged."

"The Cavaliere has put it into your head, then, that I am making love to her?"

"No; in that case I would not have spoken to her first."

"Do you mean, then, that she is making love to me?"

"This is what I mean," said Rowland, after a pause. "That girl finds you interesting, and is pleased, even though she may play indifference, at your finding her so. I said to myself that it might save her some sentimental disappointment to know without delay that you are not at liberty to become indefinitely interested in other women."

"You seem to have taken the measure of my liberty with extraordinary minuteness!" cried Roderick.

"You must do me justice. I am the cause of your separation from Miss Garland, the cause of your being exposed to temptations which she hardly even suspects. How could I ever face her," Rowland demanded, with much warmth of tone, "if at the end of it all she should be unhappy?"

"I had no idea that Miss Garland had made such an impression on you. You are too zealous; I take it she did n't charge you to look after her interests."

"If anything happens to you, I am accountable. You must understand that."

"That 's a view of the situation I can't accept; in your own interest, no less than in mine. It can only make us both very uncomfortable. I know all I owe you; I feel it; you know that! But I am not a small boy nor an outer barbarian any longer, and, whatever I do, I do with my eyes open. When I do well, the merit 's mine; if I do ill, the fault 's mine! The idea that I make you nervous is detestable. Dedicate your nerves to some better cause, and believe that if Miss Garland and I have a quarrel, we shall settle it between ourselves."

Rowland had found himself wondering, shortly before, whether possibly his brilliant young friend was without a conscience; now it dimly occurred to him that he was without a heart. Rowland, as we have already intimated, was a man with a moral passion, and no small part of it had gone forth into his relations with Roderick. There had been, from the first, no protestations of friendship on either side, but Rowland had implicitly offered everything that belongs to friendship, and Roderick had, apparently, as deliberately accepted it. Rowland, indeed, had taken an exquisite satisfaction in his companion's deep, inexpressive assent to his interest in him. "Here is an uncommonly fine thing," he said to himself: "a nature unconsciously grateful, a man in whom friendship does the thing that love alone generally has the credit of— knocks the bottom out of pride!" His reflective judgment of Roderick, as time went on, had indulged in a great many irrepressible vagaries; but his affection, his sense of something in his companion's whole personality that overmastered his heart and beguiled his imagination, had never for an instant faltered. He listened to Roderick's last words, and then he smiled as he rarely smiled—with bitterness.

"I don't at all like your telling me I am too zealous," he said. "If I had not been zealous, I should never have cared a fig for you."

Roderick flushed deeply, and thrust his modeling tool up to the handle into the clay. "Say it outright! You have been a great fool to believe in me."

"I desire to say nothing of the kind, and you don't honestly believe I do!" said Rowland. "It seems to me I am really very good-natured even to reply to such nonsense."

Roderick sat down, crossed his arms, and fixed his eyes on the floor. Rowland looked at him for some moments; it seemed to him that he had never so clearly read his companion's strangely commingled character—his strength and his weakness, his picturesque personal attractiveness and his urgent egoism, his exalted ardor and his puerile petulance. It would have made him almost sick, however, to think that, on the whole, Roderick was not a generous fellow, and he was so far from having ceased to believe in him that he felt just now, more than ever, that all this was but the painful complexity of genius. Rowland, who had not a grain of genius either to make one say he was an interested reasoner, or to enable one to feel that he could afford a dangerous theory or two, adhered to his conviction of the essential salubrity of genius. Suddenly he felt an irresistible compassion for his companion; it seemed to him that his beautiful faculty of production was a double-edged instrument, susceptible of being dealt in back-handed blows at its possessor. Genius was priceless, inspired, divine; but it was also, at its hours, capricious, sinister, cruel; and men of genius, accordingly, were alternately very enviable and very helpless. It was not the first time he had had a sense of Roderick's standing helpless in the grasp of his temperament. It had shaken him, as yet, but with a half good-humored wantonness; but, henceforth, possibly, it meant to handle him more roughly. These were not times, therefore, for a friend to have a short patience.

"When you err, you say, the fault 's your own," he said at last. "It is because your faults are your own that I care about them."

Rowland's voice, when he spoke with feeling, had an extraordinary amenity. Roderick sat staring a moment longer at the floor, then he sprang up and laid his hand affectionately on his friend's shoulder. "You are the best man in the world," he said, "and I am a vile brute. Only," he added in a moment, "*you don't understand me!*" And he looked at him with eyes of such radiant lucidity that one might have said (and Rowland did almost say so, himself) that it was the fault of one's own grossness if one failed to read to the bottom of that beautiful soul.

Rowland smiled sadly. "What is it now? Explain."

"Oh, I can't explain!" cried Roderick impatiently, returning to his work. "I have only one way of expressing my deepest feelings—it 's this!" And he swung his tool. He stood looking at the half-wrought clay for a moment, and then flung the instrument down. "And even this half the time plays me false!"

Rowland felt that his irritation had not subsided, and he himself had no taste for saying disagreeable things. Nevertheless he saw no sufficient reason to forbear uttering the words he had had on his conscience from the beginning. "We must do what we can and be thankful," he said. "And let me assure you of this—that it won't help you to become entangled with Miss Light."

Roderick pressed his hand to his forehead with vehemence and then shook it in the air, despairingly; a gesture that had become frequent with him since he had been in Italy. "No, no, it 's no use; you don't understand me! But I don't blame you. You can't!"

"You think it *will* help you, then?" said Rowland, wondering.

"I think that when you expect a man to produce beautiful and wonderful works of art, you ought to allow him a certain freedom of action, you ought to give him a long rope, you ought to let him follow his fancy and look for his material wherever he thinks he may find it! A mother can't nurse her child unless she follows a certain diet; an artist can't bring his visions to maturity unless he has a certain experience. You demand of us to be imaginative, and you deny us that which feeds the imagination. In labor we must be as passionate as the inspired sibyl; in life we must be mere machines. It won't do. When you have got an artist to deal with, you must take him as he is, good and bad together. I don't say they are pleasant fellows to know or easy fellows to live with; I don't say they satisfy themselves any better than other people. I only say that if you want them to produce, you must let them conceive. If you want a bird to sing, you must not cover up its cage. Shoot them, the poor devils, drown them, exterminate them, if you will, in the interest of public morality; it may be morality would gain—I dare say it would! But if you suffer them to live, let them live on their own terms and according to their own inexorable needs!"

Rowland burst out laughing. "I have no wish whatever either to shoot you or to drown you!" he said. "Why launch such a tirade against a warning offered you altogether in the interest of your freest development? Do you really mean that you have an inexorable need of embarking on a flirtation with Miss Light?—a flirtation as to the felicity of which there may be differences of opinion, but which cannot at best, under the circumstances, be called innocent. Your last summer's adventures were more so! As for the terms on which you are to live, I had an idea you had arranged them otherwise!"

"I have arranged nothing—thank God! I don't pretend to arrange. I am young and ardent and inquisitive, and I admire Miss Light. That 's enough. I shall go as far as admiration leads me. I am not afraid. Your genuine artist may be sometimes half a madman, but he 's not a coward!"

"Suppose that in your speculation you should come to grief, not only sentimentally but artistically?"

"Come what come will! If I 'm to fizzle out, the sooner I know it the better. Sometimes I half suspect it. But let me at least go out and reconnoitre for the enemy, and not sit here waiting for him, cudgeling my brains for ideas that won't come!"

Do what he would, Rowland could not think of Roderick's theory of unlimited experimentation, especially as applied in the case under discussion, as anything but a pernicious illusion. But he saw it was vain to combat longer, for inclination was powerfully on Roderick's side. He laid his hand on Roderick's shoulder, looked at him a moment with troubled eyes, then shook his head mournfully and turned away.

"I can't work any more," said Roderick. "You have upset me! I 'll go and stroll on the Pincian." And he tossed aside his working-jacket and prepared himself for the street. As he was arranging his cravat before the glass, something occurred to him which made him thoughtful. He stopped a few moments afterward, as they were going out, with his hand on the door-knob. "You did, from your own point of view, an indiscreet thing," he said, "to tell Miss Light of my engagement."

Rowland looked at him with a glance which was partly an interrogation, but partly, also, an admission.

"If she 's the coquette you say," Roderick added, "you have given her a reason the more."

"And that 's the girl you propose to devote yourself to?" cried Rowland.

"Oh, I don't say it, mind! I only say that she 's the most interesting creature in the world! The next time you mean to render me a service, pray give me notice beforehand!"

It was perfectly characteristic of Roderick that, a fortnight later, he should have let his friend know that he depended upon him for society at Frascati, as freely as if no irritating topic had ever been discussed between them. Rowland thought him generous, and he had at any rate a liberal faculty of forgetting that he had given you any reason to be displeased with him. It was equally characteristic of Rowland that he complied with his friend's summons without a moment's hesitation. His cousin Cecilia had once told him that he was the dupe of his intense benevolence. She put the case with too little favor, or too much, as the reader chooses; it is certain, at least, that he had a constitutional tendency towards magnanimous interpretations. Nothing happened, however, to suggest to him that he was deluded in thinking that Roderick's secondary impulses were wiser than his primary ones, and that the rounded total of his nature had a harmony perfectly attuned to the most amiable of its brilliant parts. Roderick's humor, for the time, was pitched in a minor key; he was lazy, listless, and melancholy, but he had never been more friendly and kindly and appealingly submissive. Winter had begun, by the calendar, but the weather was divinely mild, and the two young men took long slow strolls on the hills and lounged away the mornings in the villas. The villas at Frascati are delicious places, and replete with romantic suggestiveness. Roderick, as he had said, was meditating, and if a masterpiece was to come of his meditations, Rowland was perfectly willing to bear him company and coax along the process. But Roderick let him know from the first that he was in a miserably sterile mood, and, cudgel his brains as he would, could think of nothing that would serve for the statue he was to make for Mr. Leavenworth.

"It is worse out here than in Rome," he said, "for here I am face to face with the dead blank of my mind! There I could n't think of anything either, but there I found things to make me forget that I needed to." This was as frank an allusion to Christina Light as could have been expected under the circumstances; it seemed, indeed, to Rowland surprisingly frank, and a pregnant example of his companion's often strangely irresponsible way of looking at harmful facts. Roderick was silent sometimes for hours, with a puzzled look on his face and a constant fold between his even eyebrows; at other times he talked unceasingly, with a slow, idle, half-nonsensical drawl. Rowland was half a dozen times on the point of asking him what was the matter with him; he was afraid he was going to be ill. Roderick had taken a great fancy to the Villa Mondragone, and used to declaim fantastic compliments to it as they strolled in the winter sunshine on the great terrace which looks toward Tivoli and the iridescent Sabine mountains. He carried his volume of Ariosto in his pocket, and took it out every now and then and spouted half a dozen

stanzas to his companion. He was, as a general thing, very
little of a reader; but at intervals he would take a fancy to one
of the classics and peruse it for a month in disjointed scraps.
He had picked up Italian without study, and had a wonderfully sympathetic accent, though in reading aloud he ruined
the sense of half the lines he rolled off so sonorously. Rowland, who pronounced badly but understood everything, once
said to him that Ariosto was not the poet for a man of his
craft; a sculptor should make a companion of Dante. So he
lent him the Inferno, which he had brought with him, and
advised him to look into it. Roderick took it with some eagerness; perhaps it would brighten his wits. He returned
it the next day with disgust; he had found it intolerably depressing.

"A sculptor should model as Dante writes—you 're right
there," he said. "But when his genius is in eclipse, Dante is a
dreadfully smoky lamp. By what perversity of fate," he went
on, "has it come about that I am a sculptor at all? A sculptor
is such a confoundedly special genius; there are so few subjects he can treat, so few things in life that bear upon his
work, so few moods in which he himself is inclined to it." (It
may be noted that Rowland had heard him a dozen times
affirm the flat reverse of all this.) "If I had only been a
painter—a little quiet, docile, matter-of-fact painter, like our
friend Singleton—I should only have to open my Ariosto
here to find a subject, to find color and attitudes, stuffs and
composition; I should only have to look up from the page at
that mouldy old fountain against the blue sky, at that cypress
alley wandering away like a procession of priests in couples,
at the crags and hollows of the Sabine hills, to find myself
grasping my brush. Best of all would be to be Ariosto himself, or one of his brotherhood. Then everything in nature
would give you a hint, and every form of beauty be part of
your stock. You would n't have to look at things only to
say,—with tears of rage half the time,—'Oh, yes, it 's wonderfully pretty, but what the deuce can I do with it?' But a
sculptor, now! That 's a pretty trade for a fellow who has got
his living to make and yet is so damnably constituted that he
can't work to order, and considers that, æsthetically, clock ornaments don't pay! You can't model the serge-coated cy-

presses, nor those mouldering old Tritons and all the sunny sadness of that dried-up fountain; you can't put the light into marble—the lovely, caressing, consenting Italian light that you get so much of for nothing. Say that a dozen times in his life a man has a complete sculpturesque vision—a vision in which the imagination recognizes a subject and the subject kindles the imagination. It is a remunerative rate of work, and the intervals are comfortable!"

One morning, as the two young men were lounging on the sun-warmed grass at the foot of one of the slanting pines of the Villa Mondragone, Roderick delivered himself of a tissue of lugubrious speculations as to the possible mischances of one's genius. "What if the watch should run down," he asked, "and you should lose the key? What if you should wake up some morning and find it stopped, inexorably, appallingly stopped? Such things have been, and the poor devils to whom they happened have had to grin and bear it. The whole matter of genius is a mystery. It bloweth where it listeth and we know nothing of its mechanism. If it gets out of order we can't mend it; if it breaks down altogether we can't set it going again. We must let it choose its own pace, and hold our breath lest it should lose its balance. It 's dealt out in different doses, in big cups and little, and when you have consumed your portion it 's as naïf to ask for more as it was for Oliver Twist to ask for more porridge. Lucky for you if you 've got one of the big cups; we drink them down in the dark, and we can't tell their size until we tip them up and hear the last gurgle. Those of some men last for life; those of others for a couple of years. Nay, what are you smiling at so damnably?" he went on. "Nothing is more common than for an artist who has set out on his journey on a high-stepping horse to find himself all of a sudden dismounted and invited to go his way on foot. You can number them by the thousand—the people of two or three successes; the poor fellows whose candle burnt out in a night. Some of them groped their way along without it, some of them gave themselves up for blind and sat down by the wayside to beg. Who shall say that I 'm not one of these? Who shall assure me that my credit is for an unlimited sum? Nothing proves it, and I never claimed it; or if I did, I did so in the mere boyish joy of shaking off the dust of Northampton. If you believed so, my dear fellow, you did so at your own risk! What am I, what are the best of us, but an experiment? Do I succeed—do I fail? It does n't depend on me. I 'm prepared for failure. It won't be a disappointment, simply because I shan't survive it. The end of my work shall be the end of my life. When I have played my last card, I shall cease to care for the game. I 'm not making vulgar threats of suicide; for destiny, I trust, won't add insult to injury by putting me to that abominable trouble. But I have a conviction that if the hour strikes *here*," and he tapped his forehead, "I shall disappear, dissolve, be carried off in a cloud! For the past ten days I have had the vision of some such fate perpetually swimming before my eyes. My mind is like a dead calm in the tropics, and my imagination as motionless as the phantom ship in the Ancient Mariner!"

Rowland listened to this outbreak, as he often had occasion to listen to Roderick's heated monologues, with a number of mental restrictions. Both in gravity and in gayety he said more than he meant, and you did him simple justice if you privately concluded that neither the glow of purpose nor the chill of despair was of so intense a character as his florid diction implied. The moods of an artist, his exaltations and depressions, Rowland had often said to himself, were like the pen-flourishes a writing-master makes in the air when he begins to set his copy. He may bespatter you with ink, he may hit you in the eye, but he writes a magnificent hand. It was nevertheless true that at present poor Roderick gave unprecedented tokens of moral stagnation, and as for genius being held by the precarious tenure he had sketched, Rowland was at a loss to see whence he could borrow the authority to contradict him. He sighed to himself, and wished that his companion had a trifle more of little Sam Singleton's evenness of impulse. But then, was Singleton a man of genius? He answered that such reflections seemed to him unprofitable, not to say morbid; that the proof of the pudding was in the eating; that he did n't know about bringing a genius that had palpably spent its last breath back to life again, but that he was satisfied that vigorous effort was a cure for a great many ills that seemed far gone. "Don't heed your mood," he said, "and don't believe there is any calm so dead that your own lungs can't ruffle it with a breeze. If you have work to do, don't wait to feel like it; set to work and you *will* feel like it."

"Set to work and produce abortions!" cried Roderick with ire. "Preach that to others. Production with me must be either pleasure or nothing. As I said just now, I must either stay in the saddle or not go at all. I won't do second-rate work; I can't if I would. I have no cleverness, apart from inspiration. I am not a Gloriani! You are right," he added after a while; "this is unprofitable talk, and it makes my head ache. I shall take a nap and see if I can dream of a bright idea or two."

He turned his face upward to the parasol of the great pine, closed his eyes, and in a short time forgot his sombre fancies. January though it was, the mild stillness seemed to vibrate with faint midsummer sounds. Rowland sat listening to them and wishing that, for the sake of his own felicity, Roderick's temper were graced with a certain absent ductility. He was brilliant, but was he, like many brilliant things, brittle? Suddenly, to his musing sense, the soft atmospheric hum was overscored with distincter sounds. He heard voices beyond a mass of shrubbery, at the turn of a neighboring path. In a moment one of them began to seem familiar, and an instant later a large white poodle emerged into view. He was slowly followed by his mistress. Miss Light paused a moment on seeing Rowland and his companion; but, though the former perceived that he was recognized, she made no bow. Presently she walked directly toward him. He rose and was on the point of waking Roderick, but she laid her finger on her lips and motioned him to forbear. She stood a moment looking at Roderick's handsome slumber.

"What delicious oblivion!" she said. "Happy man! Stenterello"—and she pointed to his face—"wake him up!"

The poodle extended a long pink tongue and began to lick Roderick's cheek.

"Why," asked Rowland, "if he is happy?"

"Oh, I want companions in misery! Besides, I want to show off my dog." Roderick roused himself, sat up, and stared. By this time Mrs. Light had approached, walking with a gentleman on each side of her. One of these was the Cavaliere Giacosa; the other was Prince Casamassima. "I should have liked to lie down on the grass and go to sleep," Christina added. "But it would have been unheard of."

"Oh, not quite," said the Prince, in English, with a tone of great precision. "There was already a Sleeping Beauty in the Wood!"

"Charming!" cried Mrs. Light. "Do you hear that, my dear?"

"When the prince says a brilliant thing, it would be a pity to lose it," said the young girl. "Your servant, sir!" And she smiled at him with a grace that might have reassured him, if he had thought her compliment ambiguous.

Roderick meanwhile had risen to his feet, and Mrs. Light began to exclaim on the oddity of their meeting and to explain that the day was so lovely that she had been charmed with the idea of spending it in the country. And who would ever have thought of finding Mr. Mallet and Mr. Hudson sleeping under a tree!

"Oh, I beg your pardon; I was not sleeping," said Rowland.

"Don't you know that Mr. Mallet is Mr. Hudson's sheep-dog?" asked Christina. "He was mounting guard to keep away the wolves."

"To indifferent purpose, madame!" said Rowland, indicating the young girl.

"Is that the way you spend your time?" Christina demanded of Roderick. "I never yet happened to learn what men were doing when they supposed women were not watching them but it was something vastly below their reputation."

"When, pray," said Roderick, smoothing his ruffled locks, "are women not watching them?"

"We shall give you something better to do, at any rate. How long have you been here? It 's an age since I have seen you. We consider you domiciled here, and expect you to play host and entertain us."

Roderick said that he could offer them nothing but to show them the great terrace, with its view; and ten minutes later the group was assembled there. Mrs. Light was extravagant in her satisfaction; Christina looked away at the Sabine mountains, in silence. The prince stood by, frowning at the rapture of the elder lady.

"This is nothing," he said at last. "My word of honor. Have you seen the terrace at San Gaetano?"

"Ah, that terrace," murmured Mrs. Light, amorously. "I suppose it is magnificent!"

"It is four hundred feet long, and paved with marble. And the view is a thousand times more beautiful than this. You see, far away, the blue, blue sea and the little smoke of Vesuvio!"

"Christina, love," cried Mrs. Light forthwith, "the prince has a terrace four hundred feet long, all paved with marble!"

The Cavaliere gave a little cough and began to wipe his eye-glass.

"Stupendous!" said Christina. "To go from one end to the other, the prince must have out his golden carriage." This was apparently an allusion to one of the other items of the young man's grandeur.

"You always laugh at me," said the prince. "I know no more what to say!"

She looked at him with a sad smile and shook her head. "No, no, dear prince, I don't laugh at you. Heaven forbid! You are much too serious an affair. I assure you I feel your importance. What did you inform us was the value of the hereditary diamonds of the Princess Casamassima?"

"Ah, you are laughing at me yet!" said the poor young man, standing rigid and pale.

"It does n't matter," Christina went on. "We have a note of it; mamma writes all those things down in a little book!"

"If you are laughed at, dear prince, at least it 's in company," said Mrs. Light, caressingly; and she took his arm, as if to resist his possible displacement under the shock of her daughter's sarcasm. But the prince looked heavy-eyed toward Rowland and Roderick, to whom the young girl was turning, as if he had much rather his lot were cast with theirs.

"Is the villa inhabited?" Christina asked, pointing to the vast melancholy structure which rises above the terrace.

"Not privately," said Roderick. "It is occupied by a Jesuits' college, for little boys."

"Can women go in?"

"I am afraid not." And Roderick began to laugh. "Fancy the poor little devils looking up from their Latin declensions and seeing Miss Light standing there!"

"I should like to see the poor little devils, with their rosy cheeks and their long black gowns, and when they were pretty, I should n't scruple to kiss them. But if I can't have that amusement I must have some other. We must not stand planted on this enchanting terrace as if we were stakes driven into the earth. We must dance, we must feast, we must do something picturesque. Mamma has arranged, I believe, that we are to go back to Frascati to lunch at the inn. I decree that we lunch here and send the Cavaliere to the inn to get the provisions! He can take the carriage, which is waiting below."

Miss Light carried out this undertaking with unfaltering ardor. The Cavaliere was summoned, and he stook to receive her commands hat in hand, with his eyes cast down, as if she had been a princess addressing her major-domo. She, however, laid her hand with friendly grace upon his button-hole, and called him a dear, good old Cavaliere, for being always so willing. Her spirits had risen with the occasion, and she talked irresistible nonsense. "Bring the best they have," she said, "no matter if it ruins us! And if the best is very bad, it will be all the more amusing. I shall enjoy seeing Mr. Mallet try to swallow it for propriety's sake! Mr. Hudson will say out like a man that it 's horrible stuff, and that he 'll be choked first! Be sure you bring a dish of maccaroni; the prince must have the diet of the Neapolitan nobility. But I leave all that to you, my poor, dear Cavaliere; you know what 's good! Only be sure, above all, you bring a guitar. Mr. Mallet will play us a tune, I 'll dance with Mr. Hudson, and mamma will pair off with the prince, of whom she is so fond!"

And as she concluded her recommendations, she patted her bland old servitor caressingly on the shoulder. He looked askance at Rowland; his little black eye glittered; it seemed to say, "Did n't I tell you she was a good girl!"

The Cavaliere returned with zealous speed, accompanied by one of the servants of the inn, laden with a basket containing the materials of a rustic luncheon. The porter of the villa was easily induced to furnish a table and half a dozen chairs, and the repast, when set forth, was pronounced a perfect success; not so good as to fail of the proper picturesqueness, nor yet so bad as to defeat the proper function of repasts. Christina continued to display the most charming animation, and compelled Rowland to reflect privately that, think what one might of her, the harmonious gayety of a beautiful girl was the most beautiful sight in nature. Her good-humor was contagious. Roderick, who an hour before had been descanting on madness and suicide, commingled his laughter with hers in ardent devotion; Prince Casamassima stroked his young moustache and found a fine, cool smile for everything; his neighbor, Mrs. Light, who had Rowland on the other side, made the friendliest confidences to each of the young men, and the Cavaliere contributed to the general hilarity by the solemnity of his attention to his plate. As for Rowland, the spirit of kindly mirth prompted him to propose the health of this useful old gentleman, as the effective author of their pleasure. A moment later he wished he had held his tongue, for although the toast was drunk with demonstrative good-will, the Cavaliere received it with various small signs of eager self-effacement which suggested to Rowland that his diminished gentility but half relished honors which had a flavor of patronage. To perform punctiliously his mysterious duties toward the two ladies, and to elude or to baffle observation on his own merits—this seemed the Cavaliere's modest programme. Rowland perceived that Mrs. Light, who was not always remarkable for tact, seemed to have divined his humor on this point. She touched her glass to her lips, but offered him no compliment and immediately gave another direction to the conversation. He had brought no guitar, so that when the feast was over there was nothing to hold the little group together. Christina wandered away with Roderick to another part of the terrace; the prince, whose smile had vanished, sat gnawing the head of his cane, near Mrs. Light, and Rowland strolled apart with the Cavaliere, to whom he wished to address a friendly word in compensation for the discomfort he had inflicted on his modesty. The Cavaliere was a mine of information upon all Roman places and people; he told Rowland a number of curious anecdotes about the old Villa Mondragone. "If history could always be taught in this fashion!" thought Rowland. "It 's the ideal—strolling up and down on the very spot commemorated, hearing sympathetic anecdotes from deeply indigenous lips." At last, as they passed, Rowland observed the mournful physiognomy of Prince Casamassima, and, glancing toward the other end of the terrace, saw that Roderick and Christina had disappeared from view. The young man was sitting upright, in an attitude, apparently habitual, of ceremonious rigidity; but his lower jaw had fallen and was propped up with his cane, and his dull dark eye was fixed upon the angle of the villa which had just eclipsed Miss Light and her companion. His features were grotesque and his expression vacuous; but there was a lurking delicacy in his face which seemed to tell you that nature had been making Casamassimas for a great many centuries, and, though she adapted her mould to circumstances, had learned to mix her material to an extraordinary fineness and to perform the whole operation with extreme smoothness. The prince was stupid, Rowland suspected, but he imagined he was amiable, and he saw that at any rate he had the great quality of regarding himself in a thoroughly serious light. Rowland touched his companion's arm and pointed to the melancholy nobleman.

"Why in the world does he not go after her and insist on being noticed!" he asked.

"Oh, he 's very proud!" said the Cavaliere.

"That 's all very well, but a gentleman who cultivates a passion for that young lady must be prepared to make sacrifices."

"He thinks he has already made a great many. He comes of a very great family—a race of princes who for six hundred years have married none but the daughters of princes. But he is seriously in love, and he would marry her to-morrow."

"And she will not have him?"

"Ah, she is very proud, too!" The Cavaliere was silent a moment, as if he were measuring the propriety of frankness. He seemed to have formed a high opinion of Rowland's discretion, for he presently continued: "It would be a great match, for she brings him neither a name nor a fortune—nothing but her beauty. But the signorina will receive no favors; I know her well! She would rather have her beauty blasted than seem to care about the marriage, and if she ever accepts the prince it will be only after he has implored her on his knees!"

"But she does care about it," said Rowland, "and to bring him to his knees she is working upon his jealousy by pretending to be interested in my friend Hudson. If you said more, you would say that, eh?"

The Cavaliere's shrewdness exchanged a glance with Rowland's. "By no means. Miss Light is a singular girl; she has many romantic ideas. She would be quite capable of interesting herself seriously in an interesting young man, like your friend, and doing her utmost to discourage a splendid suitor, like the prince. She would act sincerely and she would go very far. But it would be unfortunate for the young man," he added, after a pause, "for at the last she would retreat!"

"A singular girl, indeed!"

"She would accept the more brilliant *parti*. I can answer for it."

"And what would be her motive?"

"She would be forced. There would be circumstances . . . . I can't tell you more."

"But this implies that the rejected suitor would also come back. He might grow tired of waiting."

"Oh, this one is good! Look at him now." Rowland looked, and saw that the prince had left his place by Mrs. Light and was marching restlessly to and fro between the villa and the parapet of the terrace. Every now and then he looked at his watch. "In this country, you know," said the Cavaliere, "a young lady never goes walking alone with a handsome young man. It seems to him very strange."

"It must seem to him monstrous, and if he overlooks it he must be very much in love."

"Oh, he will overlook it. He is far gone."

"Who is this exemplary lover, then; what is he?"

"A Neapolitan; one of the oldest houses in Italy. He is a prince in your English sense of the word, for he has a princely fortune. He is very young; he is only just of age; he saw the signorina last winter in Naples. He fell in love with her from the first, but his family interfered, and an old uncle, an ecclesiastic, Monsignor B——, hurried up to Naples, seized him, and locked him up. Meantime he has passed his majority, and he can dispose of himself. His relations are moving heaven and earth to prevent his marrying Miss Light, and they have sent us word that he forfeits his property if he takes his wife out of a certain line. I have investigated the question minutely, and I find this is but a fiction to frighten us. He is perfectly free; but the estates are such that it is no wonder they wish to keep them in their own hands. For Italy, it is an extraordinary case of unincumbered property. The prince has been an orphan from his third year; he has therefore had a long minority and made no inroads upon his fortune. Besides, he is very prudent and orderly; I am only afraid that some day he will pull the purse-strings too tight. All these years his affairs have been in the hands of Monsignor B——, who has managed them to perfection—paid off mortagages, planted forests, opened up mines. It is now a magnificent fortune; such a fortune as, with his name, would justify the young man in pretending to any alliance whatsoever. And he lays it all at the feet of that young girl who is wandering in yonder *boschetto* with a penniless artist."

"He is certainly a phœnix of princes! The signora must be in a state of bliss."

The Cavaliere looked imperturbably grave. "The signora has a high esteem for his character."

"His character, by the way," rejoined Rowland, with a smile; "what sort of a character is it?"

"Eh, Prince Casamassima is a veritable prince! He is a very good young man. He is not brilliant, nor witty, but he 'll not let himself be made a fool of. He 's very grave and very devout—though he does propose to marry a Protestant. He will handle that point after marriage. He 's as you see him there: a young man without many ideas, but with a very firm grasp of a single one—the conviction that Prince Casamassima is a very great person, that he greatly honors any young lady by asking for her hand, and that things are going very strangely when the young lady turns her back upon him. The poor young man, I am sure, is profoundly perplexed. But I whisper to him every day, 'Pazienza, Signor Principe!' "

"So you firmly believe," said Rowland, in conclusion, "that Miss Light will accept him just in time not to lose him!"

"I count upon it. She would make too perfect a princess to miss her destiny."

"And you hold that nevertheless, in the mean while, in listening to, say, my friend Hudson, she will have been acting in good faith?"

The Cavaliere lifted his shoulders a trifle, and gave an inscrutable smile. "Eh, dear signore, the Christina is very romantic!"

"So much so, you intimate, that she will eventually retract, in consequence not of a change of sentiment, but of a mysterious outward pressure?"

"If everything else fails, there is that resource. But it is mysterious, as you say, and you need n't try to guess it. You will never know."

"The poor signorina, then, will suffer!"

"Not too much, I hope."

"And the poor young man! You maintain that there is nothing but disappointment in store for the infatuated youth who loses his heart to her!"

The Cavaliere hesitated. "He had better," he said in a moment, "go and pursue his studies in Florence. There are very fine antiques in the Uffizi!"

Rowland presently joined Mrs. Light, to whom her restless protégé had not yet returned. "That 's right," she said; "sit down here; I have something serious to say to you. I am going to talk to you as a friend. I want your assistance. In fact, I demand it; it 's your duty to render it. Look at that unhappy young man."

"Yes," said Rowland, "he seems unhappy."

"He is just come of age, he bears one of the greatest names in Italy and owns one of the greatest properties, and he is pining away with love for my daughter."

"So the Cavaliere tells me."

"The Cavaliere should n't gossip," said Mrs. Light dryly. "Such information should come from me. The prince is pining, as I say; he 's consumed, he 's devoured. It 's a real Italian passion; I know what that means!" And the lady gave a speaking glance, which seemed to coquet for a moment with retrospect. "Meanwhile, if you please, my daughter is hiding in the woods with your dear friend Mr. Hudson. I could cry with rage."

"If things are so bad as that," said Rowland, "it seems to me that you ought to find nothing easier than to dispatch the Cavaliere to bring the guilty couple back."

"Never in the world! My hands are tied. Do you know what Christina would do? She would tell the Cavaliere to go about his business—Heaven forgive her!—and send me word that, if she had a mind to, she would walk in the woods till midnight. Fancy the Cavaliere coming back and delivering such a message as that before the prince! Think of a girl wantonly making light of such a chance as hers! He would marry her to-morrow, at six o'clock in the morning!"

"It is certainly very sad," said Rowland.

"That costs you little to say. If you had left your precious young meddler to vegetate in his native village you would have saved me a world of distress!"

"Nay, you marched into the jaws of danger," said Rowland. "You came and disinterred poor Hudson in his own secluded studio."

"In an evil hour! I wish to Heaven you would talk with him."

"I have done my best."

"I wish, then, you would take him away. You have plenty of money. Do me a favor. Take him to travel. Go to the East—go to Timbuctoo. Then, when Christina is Princess Casamassima," Mrs. Light added in a moment, "he may come back if he chooses."

"Does she really care for him?" Rowland asked, abruptly.

"She thinks she does, possibly. She is a living riddle. She must needs follow out every idea that comes into her head. Fortunately, most of them don't last long; but this one may last long enough to give the prince a chill. If that were to happen, I don't know what I should do! I should be the most miserable of women. It would be too cruel, after all I 've suffered to make her what she is, to see the labor of years blighted by a caprice. For I can assure you, sir," Mrs. Light went on, "that if my daughter is the greatest beauty in the world, some of the credit is mine."

Rowland promptly remarked that this was obvious. He saw that the lady's irritated nerves demanded comfort from flattering reminiscence, and he assumed designedly the attitude of a zealous auditor. She began to retail her efforts, her hopes, her dreams, her presentiments, her disappointments, in the cause of her daughter's matrimonial fortunes. It was a long story, and while it was being unfolded, the prince continued to pass to and fro, stiffly and solemnly, like a pendulum marking the time allowed for the young lady to come to her senses. Mrs. Light evidently, at an early period, had gathered her maternal hopes into a sacred sheaf, which she said her prayers and burnt incense to, and treated like a sort of fetish. They had been her religion; she had none other, and she performed her devotions bravely and cheerily, in the light of day. The poor old fetish had been so caressed and manipulated, so thrust in and out of its niche, so passed from hand to hand, so dressed and undressed, so mumbled and fumbled over, that it had lost by this time much of its early freshness, and seemed a rather battered and disfeatured divinity. But it was still brought forth in moments of trouble to have its tinseled petticoat twisted about and be set up on its altar. Rowland observed that Mrs. Light had a genuine maternal conscience; she considered that she had been performing a sacred duty in bringing up Christina to set her cap for a prince, and when the future looked dark, she found consolation in thinking that destiny could never have the heart to deal a blow at so deserving a person. This conscience upside down presented to Rowland's fancy a real physical image; he was on the point, half a dozen times, of bursting out laughing.

"I don't know whether you believe in presentiments," said Mrs. Light, "and I don't care! I have had one for the last fifteen years. People have laughed at it, but they have n't laughed me out of it. It has been everything to me. I could n't have lived without it. One must believe in something! It came to me in a flash, when Christina was five years old. I remember the day and the place, as if it were yesterday. She was a very ugly baby; for the first two years I could hardly bear to look at her, and I used to spoil my own looks with crying about her. She had an Italian nurse who was very fond of her and insisted that she would grow up pretty. I could n't

believe her; I used to contradict her, and we were forever
squabbling. I was just a little silly in those days—surely I may
say it now—and I was very fond of being amused. If my
daughter was ugly, it was not that she resembled her mamma;
I had no lack of amusement. People accused me, I believe, of
neglecting my little girl; if it was so, I 've made up for it since.
One day I went to drive on the Pincio in very low spirits. A
trusted friend had greatly disappointed me. While I was there
he passed me in a carriage, driving with a horrible woman
who had made trouble between us. I got out of my carriage
to walk about, and at last sat down on a bench. I can show
you the spot at this hour. While I sat there a child came wandering along the path—a little girl of four or five, very fantastically dressed in crimson and orange. She stopped in front
of me and stared at me, and I stared at her queer little dress,
which was a cheap imitation of the costume of one of these
contadine. At last I looked up at her face, and said to myself,
'Bless me, what a beautiful child! what a splendid pair of eyes,
what a magnificent head of hair! If my poor Christina were
only like that!' The child turned away slowly, but looking
back with its eyes fixed on me. All of a sudden I gave a cry,
pounced on it, pressed it in my arms, and covered it with
kisses. It *was* Christina, my own precious child, so disguised
by the ridiculous dress which the nurse had amused herself in
making for her, that her own mother had not recognized her.
She knew me, but she said afterwards that she had not spoken
to me because I looked so angry. Of course my face was sad.
I rushed with my child to the carriage, drove home post-
haste, pulled off her rags, and, as I may say, wrapped her in
cotton. I had been blind, I had been insane; she was a creature in ten millions, she was to be a beauty of beauties, a
priceless treasure! Every day, after that, the certainty grew.
From that time I lived only for my daughter. I watched her,
I caressed her from morning till night, I worshipped her. I
went to see doctors about her, I took every sort of advice. I
was determined she should be perfection. The things that
have been done for that girl, sir—you would n't believe
them; they would make you smile! Nothing was spared; if I
had been told that she must have a bath every morning of
molten pearls, I would have found means to give it to her.

She never raised a finger for herself, she breathed nothing but perfumes, she walked upon velvet. She never was out of my sight, and from that day to this I have never said a sharp word to her. By the time she was ten years old she was beautiful as an angel, and so noticed wherever we went that I had to make her wear a veil, like a woman of twenty. Her hair reached down to her feet; her hands were the hands of a princess. Then I saw that she was as clever as she was beautiful, and that she had only to play her cards. She had masters, professors, every educational advantage. They told me she was a little prodigy. She speaks French, Italian, German, better than most natives. She has a wonderful genius for music, and might make her fortune as a pianist, if it was not made for her otherwise! I traveled all over Europe; every one told me she was a marvel. The director of the opera in Paris saw her dance at a child's party at Spa, and offered me an enormous sum if I would give her up to him and let him have her educated for the ballet. I said, 'No, I thank you, sir; she is meant to be something finer than a *princesse de théâtre*.' I had a passionate belief that she might marry absolutely whom she chose, that she might be a princess out and out. It has never left me till this hour, and I can assure you that it has sustained me in many embarrassments. Financial, some of them; I don't mind confessing it! I have raised money on that girl's face! I've taken her to the Jews and bade her put up her veil, and asked if the mother of that young lady was not safe! She, of course, was too young to understand me. And yet, as a child, you would have said she knew what was in store for her; before she could read, she had the manners, the tastes, the instincts of a little princess. She would have nothing to do with shabby things or shabby people; if she stained one of her frocks, she was seized with a kind of frenzy and tore it to pieces. At Nice, at Baden, at Brighton, wherever we stayed, she used to be sent for by all the great people to play with their children. She has played at kissing-games with people who now stand on the steps of thrones! I have gone so far as to think at times that those childish kisses were a sign—a symbol—a portent. You may laugh at me if you like, but have n't such things happened again and again without half as good a cause, and does n't history notoriously repeat itself?

There was a little Spanish girl at a second-rate English boarding-school thirty years ago! . . . . The Empress certainly is a
pretty woman; but what is my Christina, pray? I 've dreamt
of it, sometimes every night for a month. I won't tell you I
have been to consult those old women who advertise in the
newspapers; you 'll call me an old imbecile. Imbecile if you
please! I have refused magnificent offers because I believed
that somehow or other—if wars and revolutions were needed
to bring it about—we should have nothing less than *that*.
There might be another coup d'état somewhere, and another
brilliant young sovereign looking out for a wife! At last, however," Mrs. Light proceeded with incomparable gravity,
"since the overturning of the poor king of Naples and that
charming queen, and the expulsion of all those dear little old-
fashioned Italian grand-dukes, and the dreadful radical talk
that is going on all over the world, it has come to seem to
me that with Christina in such a position I should be really
very nervous. Even in such a position she would hold her
head very high, and if anything should happen to her, she
would make no concessions to the popular fury. The best
thing, if one is prudent, seems to be a nobleman of the highest possible rank, short of belonging to a reigning stock.
There you see one striding up and down, looking at his
watch, and counting the minutes till my daughter reappears!"

Rowland listened to all this with a huge compassion for the
heroine of the tale. What an education, what a history, what
a school of character and of morals! He looked at the prince
and wondered whether he too had heard Mrs. Light's story.
If he had he was a brave man. "I certainly hope you 'll keep
him," he said to Mrs. Light. "You have played a dangerous
game with your daughter; it would be a pity not to win. But
there is hope for you yet; here she comes at last!"

Christina reappeared as he spoke these words, strolling beside her companion with the same indifferent tread with
which she had departed. Rowland imagined that there was a
faint pink flush in her cheek which she had not carried away
with her, and there was certainly a light in Roderick's eyes
which he had not seen there for a week.

"Bless my soul, how they are all looking at us!" she cried,
as they advanced. "One would think we were prisoners of the

Inquisition!" And she paused and glanced from the prince to her mother, and from Rowland to the Cavaliere, and then threw back her head and burst into far-ringing laughter. "What is it, pray? Have I been very improper? Am I ruined forever? Dear prince, you are looking at me as if I had committed the unpardonable sin!"

"I myself," said the prince, "would never have ventured to ask you to walk with me alone in the country for an hour!"

"The more fool you, dear prince, as the vulgar say! Our walk has been charming. I hope you, on your side, have enjoyed each other's society."

"My dear daughter," said Mrs. Light, taking the arm of her predestined son-in-law, "I shall have something serious to say to you when we reach home. We will go back to the carriage."

"Something serious! Decidedly, it *is* the Inquisition. Mr. Hudson, stand firm, and let us agree to make no confessions without conferring previously with each other! They may put us on the rack first. Mr. Mallet, I see also," Christina added, "has something serious to say to me!"

Rowland had been looking at her with the shadow of his lately-stirred pity in his eyes. "Possibly," he said. "But it must be for some other time."

"I am at your service. I see our good-humor is gone. And I only wanted to be amiable! It is very discouraging. Cavaliere, you, only, look as if you had a little of the milk of human kindness left; from your venerable visage, at least; there is no telling what you think. Give me your arm and take me away!"

The party took its course back to the carriage, which was waiting in the grounds of the villa, and Rowland and Roderick bade their friends farewell. Christina threw herself back in her seat and closed her eyes; a manœuvre for which Rowland imagined the prince was grateful, as it enabled him to look at her without seeming to depart from his attitude of distinguished disapproval.

*   *   *

Rowland found himself aroused from sleep early the next morning, to see Roderick standing before him, dressed for departure, with his bag in his hand. "I am off," he said. "I am back to work. I have an idea. I must strike while the iron 's hot! Farewell!" And he departed by the first train. Rowland went alone by the next.

VII

Saint Cecilia's

ROWLAND WENT OFTEN to the Coliseum; he never wearied of it. One morning, about a month after his return
from Frascati, as he was strolling across the vast arena, he
observed a young woman seated on one of the fragments of
stone which are ranged along the line of the ancient parapet.
It seemed to him that he had seen her before, but he was
unable to localize her face. Passing her again, he perceived
that one of the little red-legged French soldiers at that time
on guard there had approached her and was gallantly making
himself agreeable. She smiled brilliantly, and Rowland recognized the smile (it had always pleased him) of a certain comely Assunta, who sometimes opened the door for Mrs. Light's
visitors. He wondered what she was doing alone in the Coliseum, and conjectured that Assunta had admirers as well as
her young mistress, but that, being without the same domiciliary conveniencies, she was using this massive heritage of
her Latin ancestors as a boudoir. In other words, she had an
appointment with her lover, who had better, from present
appearances, be punctual. It was a long time since Rowland
had ascended to the ruinous upper tiers of the great circus,
and, as the day was radiant and the distant views promised to
be particularly clear, he determined to give himself the pleasure. The custodian unlocked the great wooden wicket, and
he climbed through the winding shafts, where the eager Roman crowds had billowed and trampled, not pausing till he
reached the highest accessible point of the ruin. The views
were as fine as he had supposed; the lights on the Sabine
Mountains had never been more lovely. He gazed to his satisfaction and retraced his steps. In a moment he paused again
on an abutment somewhat lower, from which the glance
dropped dizzily into the interior. There are chance anfrac-
tuosities of ruin in the upper portions of the Coliseum which
offer a very fair imitation of the rugged face of an Alpine cliff.
In those days a multitude of delicate flowers and sprays of
wild herbage had found a friendly soil in the hoary crevices,

and they bloomed and nodded amid the antique masonry as freely as they would have done in the virgin rock. Rowland was turning away, when he heard a sound of voices rising up from below. He had but to step slightly forward to find himself overlooking two persons who had seated themselves on a narrow ledge, in a sunny corner. They had apparently had an eye to extreme privacy, but they had not observed that their position was commanded by Rowland's stand-point. One of these airy adventurers was a lady, thickly veiled, so that, even if he had not been standing directly above her, Rowland could not have seen her face. The other was a young man, whose face was also invisible, but who, as Rowland stood there, gave a toss of his clustering locks which was equivalent to the signature—Roderick Hudson. A moment's reflection, hereupon, satisfied him of the identity of the lady. He had been unjust to poor Assunta, sitting patient in the gloomy arena; she had not come on her own errand. Rowland's discoveries made him hesitate. Should he retire as noiselessly as possible, or should he call out a friendly good morning? While he was debating the question, he found himself distinctly hearing his friends' words. They were of such a nature as to make him unwilling to retreat, and yet to make it awkward to be discovered in a position where it would be apparent that he had heard them.

"If what you say is true," said Christina, with her usual soft deliberateness—it made her words rise with peculiar distinctness to Rowland's ear—"you are simply weak. I am sorry! I hoped—I really believed—you were not."

"No, I am not weak," answered Roderick, with vehemence; "I maintain that I am not weak! I am incomplete, perhaps; but I can't help that. Weakness is a man's own fault!"

"Incomplete, then!" said Christina, with a laugh. "It 's the same thing, so long as it keeps you from splendid achievement. Is it written, then, that I shall really never know what I have so often dreamed of?"

"What have you dreamed of?"

"A man whom I can perfectly respect!" cried the young girl, with a sudden flame. "A man, at least, whom I can unrestrictedly admire. I meet one, as I have met more than one before, whom I fondly believe to be cast in a larger mould than most of the vile human breed, to be large in character, great in talent, strong in will! In such a man as that, I say, one's weary imagination at last may rest; or it may wander if it will, yet never need to wander far from the deeps where one's heart is anchored. When I first knew you, I gave no sign, but you had struck me. I observed you, as women observe, and I fancied you had the sacred fire."

"Before heaven, I believe I have!" cried Roderick.

"Ah, but so little! It flickers and trembles and sputters; it goes out, you tell me, for whole weeks together. From your own account, it 's ten to one that in the long run you 're a failure."

"I say those things sometimes myself, but when I hear you say them they make me feel as if I could work twenty years at a sitting, on purpose to refute you!"

"Ah, the man who is strong with what I call strength," Christina replied, "would neither rise nor fall by anything I could say! I am a poor, weak woman; I have no strength myself, and I can give no strength. I am a miserable medley of vanity and folly. I am silly, I am ignorant, I am affected, I am false. I am the fruit of a horrible education, sown on a worthless soil. I am all that, and yet I believe I have one merit! I should know a great character when I saw it, and I should delight in it with a generosity which would do something toward the remission of my sins. For a man who should really give me a certain feeling—which I have never had, but which I should know when it came—I would send Prince Casamassima and his millions to perdition. I don't know what you think of me for saying all this; I suppose we have not climbed up here under the skies to play propriety. Why have you been at such pains to assure me, after all, that you are a little man and not a great one, a weak one and not a strong? I innocently imagined that your eyes declared you were strong. But your voice condemns you; I always wondered at it; it 's not the voice of a conqueror!"

"Give me something to conquer," cried Roderick, "and when I say that I thank you from my soul, my voice, whatever you think of it, shall speak the truth!"

Christina for a moment said nothing. Rowland was too interested to think of moving. "You pretend to such devotion," she went on, "and yet I am sure you have never really chosen between me and that person in America."

"Do me the favor not to speak of her," said Roderick, imploringly.

"Why not? I say no ill of her, and I think all kinds of good. I am certain she is a far better girl than I, and far more likely to make you happy."

"This is happiness, this present, palpable moment," said Roderick; "though you *have* such a genius for saying the things that torture me!"

"It 's greater happiness than you deserve, then! You have never chosen, I say; you have been afraid to choose. You have never really faced the fact that you are false, that you have broken your faith. You have never looked at it and seen that it was hideous, and yet said, 'No matter, I 'll brave the penalty, I 'll bear the shame!' You have closed your eyes; you have tried to stifle remembrance, to persuade yourself that you were not behaving as badly as you seemed to be, and there would be some way, after all, of compassing bliss and yet escaping trouble. You have faltered and drifted, you have gone on from accident to accident, and I am sure that at this present moment you can't tell what it is you really desire!"

Roderick was sitting with his knees drawn up and bent, and his hands clasped around his legs. He bent his head and rested his forehead on his knees.

Christina went on with a sort of infernal calmness: "I believe that, really, you don't greatly care for your friend in America any more than you do for me. You are one of the men who care only for themselves and for what they can make of themselves. That 's very well when they can make something great, and I could interest myself in a man of extraordinary power who should wish to turn all his passions to account. But if the power should turn out to be, after all, rather ordinary? Fancy feeling one's self ground in the mill of a third-rate talent! If you have doubts about yourself, I can't reassure you; I have too many doubts myself, about everything in this weary world. You have gone up like a rocket, in your profession, they tell me; are you going to come down like the stick? I don't pretend to know; I repeat frankly what I have said before—that all modern sculpture seems to me weak, and that the only things I care for are some of the most battered of the antiques of the Vatican. No, no, I can't reassure you; and when you tell me—with a confidence in my discretion of which, certainly, I am duly sensible—that at times you feel terribly small, why, I can only answer, 'Ah, then, my poor friend, I am afraid you are small.' The language I should like to hear, from a certain person, would be the language of absolute decision."

Roderick raised his head, but he said nothing; he seemed to be exchanging a long glance with his companion. The result of it was to make him fling himself back with an inarticulate murmur. Rowland, admonished by the silence, was on the point of turning away, but he was arrested by a gesture of the young girl. She pointed for a moment into the blue air. Roderick followed the direction of her gesture.

"Is that little flower we see outlined against that dark niche," she asked, "as intensely blue as it looks through my veil?" She spoke apparently with the amiable design of directing the conversation into a less painful channel.

Rowland, from where he stood, could see the flower she meant—a delicate plant of radiant hue, which sprouted from the top of an immense fragment of wall some twenty feet from Christina's place.

Roderick turned his head and looked at it without answering. At last, glancing round, "Put up your veil!" he said. Christina complied. "Does it look as blue now?" he asked.

"Ah, what a lovely color!" she murmured, leaning her head on one side.

"Would you like to have it?"

She stared a moment and then broke into a light laugh.

"Would you like to have it?" he repeated in a ringing voice.

"Don't look as if you would eat me up," she answered. "It 's harmless if I say yes!"

Roderick rose to his feet and stood looking at the little flower. It was separated from the ledge on which he stood by a rugged surface of vertical wall, which dropped straight into the dusky vaults behind the arena. Suddenly he took off his hat and flung it behind him. Christina then sprang to her feet.

"I will bring it you," he said.

She seized his arm. "Are you crazy? Do you mean to kill yourself?"

"I shall not kill myself. Sit down!"

"Excuse me. Not till you do!" And she grasped his arm with both hands.

Roderick shook her off and pointed with a violent gesture to her former place. "Go there!" he cried fiercely.

"You can never, never!" she murmured beseechingly, clasping her hands. "I implore you!"

Roderick turned and looked at her, and then in a voice which Rowland had never heard him use, a voice almost thunderous, a voice which awakened the echoes of the mighty ruin, he repeated, "Sit down!" She hesitated a moment and then she dropped on the ground and buried her face in her hands.

Rowland had seen all this, and he saw more. He saw Roderick clasp in his left arm the jagged corner of the vertical partition along which he proposed to pursue his crazy journey, stretch out his leg, and feel for a resting-place for his foot. Rowland had measured with a glance the possibility of his sustaining himself, and pronounced it absolutely nil. The wall was garnished with a series of narrow projections, the remains apparently of a brick cornice supporting the arch of a vault which had long since collapsed. It was by lodging his toes on these loose brackets and grasping with his hands at certain mouldering protuberances on a level with his head, that Roderick intended to proceed. The relics of the cornice were utterly worthless as a support. Rowland had observed this, and yet, for a moment, he had hesitated. If the thing *were* possible, he felt a sudden admiring glee at the thought of Roderick's doing it. It would be finely done, it would be gallant, it would have a sort of masculine eloquence as an answer to Christina's sinister persiflage. But it was not possible! Rowland left his place with a bound, and scrambled down some neighboring steps, and the next moment a stronger pair of hands than Christina's were laid upon Roderick's shoulder.

He turned, staring, pale and angry. Christina rose, pale and staring, too, but beautiful in her wonder and alarm. "My dear Roderick," said Rowland, "I am only preventing you from doing a very foolish thing. That 's an exploit for spiders, not for young sculptors of promise."

Roderick wiped his forehead, looked back at the wall, and then closed his eyes, as if with a spasm, of retarded dizziness. "I won't resist you," he said. "But I have made you obey," he added, turning to Christina. "Am I weak now?"

She had recovered her composure; she looked straight past him and addressed Rowland: "Be so good as to show me the way out of this horrible place!"

He helped her back into the corridor; Roderick followed after a short interval. Of course, as they were descending the steps, came questions for Rowland to answer, and more or less surprise. Where had he come from? how happened he to have appeared at just that moment? Rowland answered that he had been rambling overhead, and that, looking out of an aperture, he had seen a gentleman preparing to undertake a preposterous gymnastic feat, and a lady swooning away in consequence. Interference seemed justifiable, and he had made it as prompt as possible. Roderick was far from hanging his head, like a man who has been caught in the perpetration of an extravagant folly; but if he held it more erect than usual Rowland believed that this was much less because he had made a show of personal daring than because he had triumphantly proved to Christina that, like a certain person she had dreamed of, he too could speak the language of decision. Christina descended to the arena in silence, apparently occupied with her own thoughts. She betrayed no sense of the privacy of her interview with Roderick needing an explanation. Rowland had seen stranger things in New York! The only evidence of her recent agitation was that, on being joined by her maid, she declared that she was unable to walk home; she must have a carriage. A fiacre was found resting in the shadow of the Arch of Constantine, and Rowland suspected that after she had got into it she disburdened herself, under her veil, of a few natural tears.

Rowland had played eavesdropper to so good a purpose that he might justly have omitted the ceremony of denouncing himself to Roderick. He preferred, however, to let him know that he had overheard a portion of his talk with Christina.

"Of course it seems to you," Roderick said, "a proof that I am utterly infatuated."

"Miss Light seemed to me to know very well how far she could go," Rowland answered. "She was twisting you round her finger. I don't think she exactly meant to defy you; but your crazy pursuit of that flower was a proof that she could go all lengths in the way of making a fool of you."

"Yes," said Roderick, meditatively; "she is making a fool of me."

"And what do you expect to come of it?"

"Nothing good!" And Roderick put his hands into his pockets and looked as if he had announced the most colorless fact in the world.

"And in the light of your late interview, what do you make of your young lady?"

"If I could tell you that, it would be plain sailing. But she 'll not tell me again I am weak!"

"Are you very sure you are not weak?"

"I may be, but she shall never know it."

Rowland said no more until they reached the Corso, when he asked his companion whether he was going to his studio.

Roderick started out of a reverie and passed his hands over his eyes. "Oh no, I can't settle down to work after such a scene as that. I was not afraid of breaking my neck then, but I feel all in a tremor now. I will go—I will go and sit in the sun on the Pincio!"

"Promise me this, first," said Rowland, very solemnly: "that the next time you meet Miss Light, it shall be on the earth and not in the air."

Since his return from Frascati, Roderick had been working doggedly at the statue ordered by Mr. Leavenworth. To Rowland's eye he had made a very fair beginning, but he had himself insisted, from the first, that he liked neither his subject nor his patron, and that it was impossible to feel any warmth of interest in a work which was to be incorporated into the ponderous personality of Mr. Leavenworth. It was all against the grain; he wrought without love. Nevertheless after a fashion he wrought, and the figure grew beneath his hands. Miss Blanchard's friend was ordering works of art on every side, and his purveyors were in many cases persons whom Roderick declared it was infamy to be paired with. There had been grand tailors, he said, who declined to make you a coat unless you got the hat you were to wear with it from an artist of their own choosing. It seemed to him that he had an equal right to exact that his statue should not form part of the same system of ornament as the "Pearl of Perugia," a picture by an American *confrère* who had, in Mr. Leavenworth's opinion, a prodigious eye for color. As a customer, Mr. Leavenworth used to drop into Roderick's studio, to see how things were getting on, and give a friendly hint or so. He would seat himself squarely, plant his gold-topped cane between his legs, which he held very much apart, rest his large white hands on the head, and enunciate the principles of spiritual art, as he hoisted them one by one, as you might say, out of the depths of his moral consciousness. His benignant and imperturbable pomposity gave Roderick the sense of suffocating beneath a large fluffy bolster, and the worst of the matter was that the good gentleman's placid vanity had an integument whose toughness no sarcastic shaft could pierce. Roderick admitted that in thinking over the tribulations of struggling genius, the danger of dying of over-patronage had never occurred to him.

The deterring effect of the episode of the Coliseum was apparently of long continuance; if Roderick's nerves had been shaken his hand needed time to recover its steadiness. He cultivated composure upon principles of his own; by frequenting entertainments from which he returned at four o'clock in the morning, and lapsing into habits which might fairly be called irregular. He had hitherto made few friends among the artistic fraternity; chiefly because he had taken no trouble about it, and there was in his demeanor an elastic independence of the favor of his fellow-mortals which made social advances on his own part peculiarly necessary. Rowland had told him more than once that he ought to fraternize a trifle more with the other artists, and he had always answered that he had not the smallest objection to fraternizing: let them come! But they came on rare occasions, and Roderick was not punctilious about returning their visits. He declared there was not one of them whose works gave him the smallest desire to make acquaintance with the insides of their heads. For Glo-

riani he professed a superb contempt, and, having been once
to look at his wares, never crossed his threshold again. The
only one of the fraternity for whom by his own admission he
cared a straw was little Singleton; but he expressed his regard
only in a kind of sublime hilarity whenever he encountered
this humble genius, and quite forgot his existence in the intervals. He had never been to see him, but Singleton edged
his way, from time to time, timidly, into Roderick's studio,
and agreed with characteristic modesty that brilliant fellows
like the sculptor might consent to receive homage, but could
hardly be expected to render it. Roderick never exactly accepted homage, and apparently did not quite observe whether
poor Singleton spoke in admiration or in blame. Roderick's
taste as to companions was singularly capricious. There were
very good fellows, who were disposed to cultivate him, who
bored him to death; and there were others, in whom even
Rowland's good-nature was unable to discover a pretext for
tolerance, in whom he appeared to find the highest social
qualities. He used to give the most fantastic reasons for his
likes and dislikes. He would declare he could n't speak a civil
word to a man who brushed his hair in a certain fashion, and
he would explain his unaccountable fancy for an individual of
imperceptible merit by telling you that he had an ancestor
who in the thirteenth century had walled up his wife alive. "I
like to talk to a man whose ancestor has walled up his wife
alive," he would say. "You may not see the fun of it, and
think poor P—— is a very dull fellow. It 's very possible; I
don't ask you to admire him. But, for reasons of my own, I
like to have him about. The old fellow left her for three days
with her face uncovered, and placed a long mirror opposite
to her, so that she could see, as he said, if her gown was a
fit!"

His relish for an odd flavor in his friends had led him to
make the acquaintance of a number of people outside of
Rowland's well-ordered circle, and he made no secret of their
being very queer fish. He formed an intimacy, among others,
with a crazy fellow who had come to Rome as an emissary of
one of the Central American republics, to drive some ecclesiastical bargain with the papal government. The Pope had
given him the cold shoulder, but since he had not prospered

as a diplomatist, he had sought compensation as a man of the world, and his great flamboyant curricle and negro lackeys were for several weeks one of the striking ornaments of the Pincian. He spoke a queer jargon of Italian, Spanish, French, and English, humorously relieved with scraps of ecclesiastical Latin, and to those who inquired of Roderick what he found to interest him in such a fantastic jackanapes, the latter would reply, looking at his interlocutor with his lucid blue eyes, that it was worth any sacrifice to hear him talk nonsense! The two had gone together one night to a ball given by a lady of some renown in the Spanish colony, and very late, on his way home, Roderick came up to Rowland's rooms, in whose windows he had seen a light. Rowland was going to bed, but Roderick flung himself into an arm-chair and chattered for an hour. The friends of the Costa Rican envoy were as amusing as himself, and in very much the same line. The mistress of the house had worn a yellow satin dress, and gold heels to her slippers, and at the close of the entertainment had sent for a pair of castanets, tucked up her petticoats, and danced a fandango, while the gentlemen sat cross-legged on the floor. "It was awfully low," Roderick said; "all of a sudden I perceived it, and bolted. Nothing of that kind ever amuses me to the end: before it 's half over it bores me to death; it makes me sick. Hang it, why can't a poor fellow enjoy things in peace? My illusions are all broken-winded; they won't carry me twenty paces! I can't laugh and forget; my laugh dies away before it begins. Your friend Stendhal writes on his book-covers (I never got farther) that he has seen too early in life *la beauté parfaite*. I don't know how early he saw it; I saw it before I was born—in another state of being! I can't describe it positively; I can only say I don't find it anywhere now. Not at the bottom of champagne glasses; not, strange as it may seem, in that extra half-yard or so of shoulder that some women have their ball-dresses cut to expose. I don't find it at merry supper-tables, where half a dozen ugly men with pomatumed heads are rapidly growing uglier still with heat and wine; not when I come away and walk through these squalid black streets, and go out into the Forum and see a few old battered stone posts standing there like gnawed bones stuck into the earth. Everything is mean and dusky and

shabby, and the men and women who make up this so-called
brilliant society are the meanest and shabbiest of all. They
have no real spontaneity; they are all cowards and popinjays.
They have no more dignity than so many grasshoppers.
Nothing is good but one!" And he jumped up and stood
looking at one of his statues, which shone vaguely across the
room in the dim lamplight.

"Yes, do tell us," said Rowland, "what to hold on by!"

"Those things of mine were tolerably good," he answered.
"But my idea was better—and that 's what I mean!"

Rowland said nothing. He was willing to wait for Roderick
to complete the circle of his metamorphoses, but he had no
desire to officiate as chorus to the play. If Roderick chose to
fish in troubled waters, he must land his prizes himself.

"You think I 'm an impudent humbug," the latter said at
last, "coming up to moralize at this hour of the night. You
think I want to throw dust into your eyes, to put you off the
scent. That 's your eminently rational view of the case."

"Excuse me from taking any view at all," said Rowland.

"You have given me up, then?"

"No, I have merely suspended judgment. I am waiting."

"You have ceased then *positively* to believe in me?"

Rowland made an angry gesture. "Oh, cruel boy! When
you have hit your mark and made people care for you, you
should n't twist your weapon about at that rate in their vitals.
Allow me to say I am sleepy. Good night!"

Some days afterward it happened that Rowland, on a long
afternoon ramble, took his way through one of the quiet corners of the Trastevere. He was particularly fond of this part
of Rome, though he could hardly have expressed the charm
he found in it. As you pass away from the dusky, swarming
purlieus of the Ghetto, you emerge into a region of empty,
soundless, grass-grown lanes and alleys, where the shabby
houses seem mouldering away in disuse, and yet your footstep brings figures of startling Roman type to the doorways.
There are few monuments here, but no part of Rome seemed
more historic, in the sense of being weighted with a crushing
past, blighted with the melancholy of things that had had
their day. When the yellow afternoon sunshine slept on the
sallow, battered walls, and lengthened the shadows in the

grassy court-yards of small closed churches, the place acquired a strange fascination. The church of Saint Cecilia has one of these sunny, waste-looking courts; the edifice seems abandoned to silence and the charity of chance devotion. Rowland never passed it without going in, and he was generally the only visitor. He entered it now, but found that two persons had preceded him. Both were women. One was at her prayers at one of the side altars; the other was seated against a column at the upper end of the nave. Rowland walked to the altar, and paid, in a momentary glance at the clever statue of the saint in death, in the niche beneath it, the usual tribute to the charm of polished ingenuity. As he turned away he looked at the person seated and recognized Christina Light. Seeing that she perceived him, he advanced to speak to her.

She was sitting in a listless attitude, with her hands in her lap; she seemed to be tired. She was dressed simply, as if for walking and escaping observation. When he had greeted her he glanced back at her companion, and recognized the faithful Assunta.

Christina smiled. "Are you looking for Mr. Hudson? He is not here, I am happy to say."

"But you?" he asked. "This is a strange place to find you."

"Not at all! People call me a strange girl, and I might as well have the comfort of it. I came to take a walk; that, by the way, is part of my strangeness. I can't loll all the morning on a sofa, and all the afternoon in a carriage. I get horribly restless. I must move; I must do something and see something. Mamma suggests a cup of tea. Meanwhile I put on an old dress and half a dozen veils, I take Assunta under my arm, and we start on a pedestrian tour. It's a bore that I can't take the poodle, but he attracts attention. We trudge about everywhere; there is nothing I like so much. I hope you will congratulate me on the simplicity of my tastes."

"I congratulate you on your wisdom. To live in Rome and not to walk would, I think, be poor pleasure. But you are terribly far from home, and I am afraid you are tired."

"A little—enough to sit here a while."

"Might I offer you my company while you rest?"

"If you will promise to amuse me. I am in dismal spirits."

Rowland said he would do what he could, and brought a

chair and placed it near her. He was not in love with her; he disapproved of her; he mistrusted her; and yet he felt it a kind of privilege to watch her, and he found a peculiar excitement in talking to her. The background of her nature, as he would have called it, was large and mysterious, and it emitted strange, fantastic gleams and flashes. Watching for these rather quickened one's pulses. Moreover, it was not a disadvantage to talk to a girl who made one keep guard on one's composure; it diminished one's chronic liability to utter something less than revised wisdom.

Assunta had risen from her prayers, and, as he took his place, was coming back to her mistress. But Christina motioned her away. "No, no; while you are about it, say a few dozen more!" she said. "Pray for me," she added in English. "Pray, I say nothing silly. She has been at it half an hour; I envy her capacity!"

"Have you never felt in any degree," Rowland asked, "the fascination of Catholicism?"

"Yes, I have been through that, too! There was a time when I wanted immensely to be a nun; it was not a laughing matter. It was when I was about sixteen years old. I read the Imitation and the Life of Saint Catherine. I fully believed in the miracles of the saints, and I was dying to have one of my own. The least little accident that could have been twisted into a miracle would have carried me straight into the bosom of the church. I had the real religious passion. It has passed away, and, as I sat here just now, I was wondering what had become of it!"

Rowland had already been sensible of something in this young lady's tone which he would have called a want of veracity, and this epitome of her religious experience failed to strike him as an absolute statement of fact. But the trait was not disagreeable, for she herself was evidently the foremost dupe of her inventions. She had a fictitious history in which she believed much more fondly than in her real one, and an infinite capacity for extemporized reminiscence adapted to the mood of the hour. She liked to idealize herself, to take interesting and picturesque attitudes to her own imagination; and the vivacity and spontaneity of her character gave her, really, a starting-point in experience; so that the many-colored flow-

ers of fiction which blossomed in her talk were not so much
perversions, as sympathetic exaggerations, of fact. And Rowland felt that whatever she said of herself might have been,
under the imagined circumstances; impulse was there, audacity, the restless, questioning temperament. "I am afraid I
am sadly prosaic," he said, "for in these many months now
that I have been in Rome, I have never ceased for a moment to look at Catholicism simply from the outside. I
don't see an opening as big as your finger-nail where I
could creep into it!"

"What do you believe?" asked Christina, looking at him.
"Are you religious?"

"I believe in God."

Christina let her beautiful eyes wander a while, and then
gave a little sigh. "You are much to be envied!"

"You, I imagine, in that line have nothing to envy me."

"Yes, I have. Rest!"

"You are too young to say that."

"I am not young; I have never been young! My mother
took care of that. I was a little wrinkled old woman at ten."

"I am afraid," said Rowland, in a moment, "that you are
fond of painting yourself in dark colors."

She looked at him a while in silence. "Do you wish," she
demanded at last, "to win my eternal gratitude? Prove to me
that I am better than I suppose."

"I should have first to know what you really suppose."

She shook her head. "It would n't do. You would be horrified to learn even the things I imagine about myself, and
shocked at the knowledge of evil displayed in my very mistakes."

"Well, then," said Rowland, "I will ask no questions. But,
at a venture, I promise you to catch you some day in the act
of doing something very good."

"Can it be, can it be," she asked, "that you too are trying
to flatter me? I thought you and I had fallen, from the first,
into rather a truth-speaking vein."

"Oh, I have not abandoned it!" said Rowland; and he determined, since he had the credit of homely directness, to
push his advantage farther. The opportunity seemed excellent.
But while he was hesitating as to just how to begin, the

young girl said, bending forward and clasping her hands in
her lap, "Please tell me about your religion."

"Tell you about it? I can't!" said Rowland, with a good
deal of emphasis.

She flushed a little. "Is it such a mighty mystery it cannot
be put into words, nor communicated to my base ears?"

"It is simply a sentiment that makes part of my life, and I
can't detach myself from it sufficiently to talk about it."

"Religion, it seems to me, should be eloquent and aggressive. It should wish to make converts, to persuade and illumine, to sway all hearts!"

"One's religion takes the color of one's general disposition.
I am not aggressive, and certainly I am not eloquent."

"Beware, then, of finding yourself confronted with doubt
and despair! I am sure that doubt, at times, and the bitterness
that comes of it, can be terribly eloquent. To tell the truth,
my lonely musings, before you came in, were eloquent
enough, in their way. What do you know of anything but this
strange, terrible world that surrounds you? How do you
know that your faith is not a mere crazy castle in the air; one
of those castles that we are called fools for building when we
lodge them in this life?"

"I don't know it, any more than any one knows the contrary. But one's religion is extremely ingenious in doing without knowledge."

"In such a world as this it certainly needs to be!"

Rowland smiled. "What is your particular quarrel with this
world?"

"It 's a general quarrel. Nothing is true, or fixed, or permanent. We all seem to be playing with shadows more or less
grotesque. It all comes over me here so dismally! The very
atmosphere of this cold, deserted church seems to mock at
one's longing to believe in something. Who cares for it now?
who comes to it? who takes it seriously? Poor stupid Assunta
there gives in her adhesion in a jargon she does n't understand, and you and I, proper, passionless tourists, come
lounging in to rest from a walk. And yet the Catholic church
was once the proudest institution in the world, and had quite
its own way with men's souls. When such a mighty structure
as that turns out to have a flaw, what faith is one to put in

one's poor little views and philosophies? What is right and what is wrong? What is one really to care for? What is the proper rule of life? I am tired of trying to discover, and I suspect it 's not worth the trouble. Live as most amuses you!"

"Your perplexities are so terribly comprehensive," said Rowland, smiling, "that one hardly knows where to meet them first."

"I don't care much for anything you can say, because it 's sure to be half-hearted. You are not in the least contented, yourself."

"How do you know that?"

"Oh, I am an observer!"

"No one is absolutely contented, I suppose, but I assure you I complain of nothing."

"So much the worse for your honesty. To begin with, you are in love."

"You would not have me complain of that!"

"And it does n't go well. There are grievous obstacles. So much I know! You need n't protest; I ask no questions. You will tell no one—me least of all. Why does one never see you?"

"Why, if I came to see you," said Rowland, deliberating, "it would n't be, it could n't be, for a trivial reason—because I had not been in a month, because I was passing, because I admire you. It would be because I should have something very particular to say. I have not come, because I have been slow in making up my mind to say it."

"You are simply cruel. Something particular, in this ocean of inanities? In common charity, speak!"

"I doubt whether you will like it."

"Oh, I hope to heaven it 's not a compliment!"

"It may be called a compliment to your reasonableness. You perhaps remember that I gave you a hint of it the other day at Frascati."

"Has it been hanging fire all this time? Explode! I promise not to stop my ears."

"It relates to my friend Hudson." And Rowland paused. She was looking at him expectantly; her face gave no sign. "I am rather disturbed in mind about him. He seems to me at times to be in an unpromising way." He paused again, but

Christina said nothing. "The case is simply this," he went on. "It was by my advice he renounced his career at home and embraced his present one. I made him burn his ships. I brought him to Rome, I launched him in the world, and I stand surety, in a measure, to—to his mother, for his prosperity. It is not such smooth sailing as it might be, and I am inclined to put up prayers for fair winds. If he is to succeed, he must work—quietly, devotedly. It is not news to you, I imagine, that Hudson is a great admirer of yours."

Christina remained silent; she turned away her eyes with an air, not of confusion, but of deep deliberation. Surprising frankness had, as a general thing, struck Rowland as the keynote of her character, but she had more than once given him a suggestion of an unfathomable power of calculation, and her silence now had something which it is hardly extravagant to call portentous. He had of course asked himself how far it was questionable taste to inform an unprotected girl, for the needs of a cause, that another man admired her; the thing, superficially, had an uncomfortable analogy with the shrewdness that uses a cat's paw and lets it risk being singed. But he decided that even rigid discretion is not bound to take a young lady at more than her own valuation, and Christina presently reassured him as to the limits of her susceptibility. "Mr. Hudson is in love with me!" she said.

Rowland flinched a trifle. Then—"Am I," he asked, "from this point of view of mine, to be glad or sorry?"

"I don't understand you."

"Why, is Hudson to be happy, or unhappy?"

She hesitated a moment. "You wish him to be great in his profession? And for that you consider that he must be happy in his life?"

"Decidedly. I don't say it 's a general rule, but I think it is a rule for him."

"So that if he were very happy, he would become very great?"

"He would at least do himself justice."

"And by that you mean a great deal?"

"A great deal."

Christina sank back in her chair and rested her eyes on the cracked and polished slabs of the pavement. At last, looking up, "You have not forgotten, I suppose, that you told me he was engaged?"

"By no means."

"He is still engaged, then?"

"To the best of my belief."

"And yet you desire that, as you say, he should be made happy by something I can do for him?"

"What I desire is this. That your great influence with him should be exerted for his good, that it should help him and not retard him. Understand me. You probably know that your lovers have rather a restless time of it. I can answer for two of them. You don't know your own mind very well, I imagine, and you like being admired, rather at the expense of the admirer. Since we are really being frank, I wonder whether I might not say the great word."

"You need n't; I know it. I am a horrible coquette."

"No, not a horrible one, since I am making an appeal to your generosity. I am pretty sure you cannot imagine yourself marrying my friend."

"There 's nothing I cannot imagine! That is my trouble."

Rowland's brow contracted impatiently. "I cannot imagine it, then!" he affirmed.

Christina flushed faintly; then, very gently, "I am not so bad as you think," she said.

"It is not a question of badness; it is a question of whether circumstances don't make the thing an extreme improbability."

"Worse and worse. I can be bullied, then, or bribed!"

"You are not so candid," said Rowland, "as you pretend to be. My feeling is this. Hudson, as I understand him, does not need, as an artist, the stimulus of strong emotion, of passion. He 's better without it; he 's emotional and passionate enough when he 's left to himself. The sooner passion is at rest, therefore, the sooner he will settle down to work, and the fewer emotions he has that are mere emotions and nothing more, the better for him. If you cared for him enough to marry him, I should have nothing to say; I would never venture to interfere. But I strongly suspect you don't, and therefore I would suggest, most respectfully, that you should let him alone."

"And if I let him alone, as you say, all will be well with him for ever more?"

"Not immediately and not absolutely, but things will be easier. He will be better able to concentrate himself."

"What is he doing now? Wherein does he dissatisfy you?"

"I can hardly say. He 's like a watch that 's running down. He is moody, desultory, idle, irregular, fantastic."

"Heavens, what a list! And it 's all poor me?"

"No, not all. But you are a part of it, and I turn to you because you are a more tangible, sensible, responsible cause than the others."

Christina raised her hand to her eyes, and bent her head thoughtfully. Rowland was puzzled to measure the effect of his venture; she rather surprised him by her gentleness. At last, without moving, "If I were to marry him," she asked, "what would have become of his *fiancée*?"

"I am bound to suppose that she would be extremely unhappy."

Christina said nothing more, and Rowland, to let her make her reflections, left his place and strolled away. Poor Assunta, sitting patiently on a stone bench, and unprovided, on this occasion, with military consolation, gave him a bright, frank smile, which might have been construed as an expression of regret for herself, and of sympathy for her mistress. Rowland presently seated himself again near Christina.

"What do you think," she asked, looking at him, "of your friend's infidelity?"

"I don't like it."

"Was he very much in love with her?"

"He asked her to marry him. You may judge."

"Is she rich?"

"No, she is poor."

"Is she very much in love with him?"

"I know her too little to say."

She paused again, and then resumed: "You have settled in your mind, then, that I will never seriously listen to him?"

"I think it unlikely, until the contrary is proved."

"How shall it be proved? How do you know what passes between us?"

"I can judge, of course, but from appearance; but, like you,

I am an observer. Hudson has not at all the air of a prosperous suitor."

"If he is depressed, there is a reason. He has a bad conscience. One must hope so, at least. On the other hand, simply as a friend," she continued gently, "you think I can do him no good?"

The humility of her tone, combined with her beauty, as she made this remark, was inexpressibly touching, and Rowland had an uncomfortable sense of being put at a disadvantage. "There are doubtless many good things you might do, if you had proper opportunity," he said. "But you seem to be sailing with a current which leaves you little leisure for quiet benevolence. You live in the whirl and hurry of a world into which a poor artist can hardly find it to his advantage to follow you."

"In plain English, I am hopelessly frivolous. You put it very generously."

"I won't hesitate to say all my thought," said Rowland. "For better or worse, you seem to me to belong, both by character and by circumstance, to what is called the world, the great world. You are made to ornament it magnificently. You are not made to be an artist's wife."

"I see. But even from your point of view, that would depend upon the artist. Extraordinary talent might make him a member of the great world!"

Rowland smiled. "That is very true."

"If, as it is," Christina continued in a moment, "you take a low view of me—no, you need n't protest—I wonder what you would think if you knew certain things."

"What things do you mean?"

"Well, for example, how I was brought up. I have had a horrible education. There must be some good in me, since I have perceived it, since I have turned and judged my circumstances."

"My dear Miss Light!" Rowland murmured.

She gave a little, quick laugh. "You don't want to hear? you don't want to have to think about that?"

"Have I a right to? You need n't justify yourself."

She turned upon him a moment the quickened light of her beautiful eyes, then fell to musing again. "Is there not some novel or some play," she asked at last, "in which some beau-

tiful, wicked woman who has ensnared a young man sees his
father come to her and beg her to let him go?"

"Very likely," said Rowland. "I hope she consents."

"I forget. But tell me," she continued, "shall you consider—admitting your proposition—that in ceasing to flirt
with Mr. Hudson, so that he may go about his business, I do
something magnanimous, heroic, sublime—something with a
fine name like that?"

Rowland, elated with the prospect of gaining his point,
was about to reply that she would deserve the finest name in
the world; but he instantly suspected that this tone would not
please her, and, besides, it would not express his meaning.

"You do something I shall greatly respect," he contented
himself with saying.

She made no answer, and in a moment she beckoned to her
maid. "What have I to do to-day?" she asked.

Assunta meditated. "Eh, it 's a very busy day! Fortunately
I have a better memory than the signorina," she said, turning
to Rowland. She began to count on her fingers. "We have to
go to the Piè di Marmo to see about those laces that were
sent to be washed. You said also that you wished to say three
sharp words to the Buonvicini about your pink dress. You
want some moss-rosebuds for to-night, and you won't get
them for nothing! You dine at the Austrian Embassy, and
that Frenchman is to powder your hair. You 're to come
home in time to receive, for the signora gives a dance. And
so away, away till morning!"

"Ah, yes, the moss-roses!" Christina murmured, caressingly. "I must have a quantity—at least a hundred. Nothing but
buds, eh? You must sew them in a kind of immense apron,
down the front of my dress. Packed tight together, eh? It will
be delightfully barbarous. And then twenty more or so for
my hair. They go very well with powder; don't you think so?"
And she turned to Rowland. "I am going *en Pompadour*."

"Going where?"

"To the Spanish Embassy, or whatever it is."

"All down the front, signorina? *Dio buono!* You must give
me time!" Assunta cried.

"Yes, we 'll go!" And she left her place. She walked
slowly to the door of the church, looking at the pavement,

and Rowland could not guess whether she was thinking of her apron of moss-rosebuds or of her opportunity for moral sublimity. Before reaching the door she turned away and stood gazing at an old picture, indistinguishable with blackness, over an altar. At last they passed out into the court. Glancing at her in the open air, Rowland was startled; he imagined he saw the traces of hastily suppressed tears. They had lost time, she said, and they must hurry; she sent Assunta to look for a fiacre. She remained silent a while, scratching the ground with the point of her parasol, and then at last, looking up, she thanked Rowland for his confidence in her "reasonableness." "It 's really very comfortable to be asked, to be expected, to do something good, after all the horrid things one has been used to doing—instructed, commanded, forced to do! I 'll think over what you have said to me." In that deserted quarter fiacres are rare, and there was some delay in Assunta's procuring one. Christina talked of the church, of the picturesque old court, of that strange, decaying corner of Rome. Rowland was perplexed; he was ill at ease. At last the fiacre arrived, but she waited a moment longer. "So, decidedly," she suddenly asked, "I can only harm him?"

"You make me feel very brutal," said Rowland.

"And he is such a fine fellow that it would be really a great pity, eh?"

"I shall praise him no more," Rowland said.

She turned away quickly, but she lingered still. "Do you remember promising me, soon after we first met, that at the end of six months you would tell me definitely what you thought of me?"

"It was a foolish promise."

"You gave it. Bear it in mind. I will think of what you have said to me. Farewell." She stepped into the carriage, and it rolled away. Rowland stood for some minutes, looking after it, and then went his way with a sigh. If this expressed general mistrust, he ought, three days afterward, to have been reassured. He received by the post a note containing these words:—

"I have done it. Begin and respect me!

—C. L."

To be perfectly satisfactory, indeed, the note required a commentary. He called that evening upon Roderick, and found one in the information offered him at the door, by the old serving-woman—the startling information that the signorino had gone to Naples.

VIII

Provocation

ABOUT A MONTH LATER, Rowland addressed to his cousin Cecilia a letter of which the following is a portion:—
. . . . . "So much for myself; yet I tell you but a tithe of my own story unless I let you know how matters stand with poor Hudson, for he gives me more to think about just now than anything else in the world. I need a good deal of courage to begin this chapter. You warned me, you know, and I made rather light of your warning. I have had all kinds of hopes and fears, but hitherto, in writing to you, I have resolutely put the hopes foremost. Now, however, my pride has forsaken me, and I should like hugely to give expression to a little comfortable despair. I should like to say, 'My dear wise woman, you were right and I was wrong; you were a shrewd observer and I was a meddlesome donkey!' When I think of a little talk we had about the 'salubrity of genius,' I feel my ears tingle. If this is salubrity, give me raging disease! I 'm pestered to death; I go about with a chronic heartache; there are moments when I could shed salt tears. There 's a pretty portrait of the most placid of men! I wish I could make you understand; or rather, I wish you could make me! I don't understand a jot; it 's a hideous, mocking mystery; I give it up! I don't in the least give it up, you know; I 'm incapable of giving it up. I sit holding my head by the hour, racking my brain, wondering what under heaven is to be done. You told me at Northampton that I took the thing too easily; you would tell me now, perhaps, that I take it too hard. I do, altogether; but it can't be helped. Without flattering myself, I may say I 'm sympathetic. Many another man before this would have cast his perplexities to the winds and declared that Mr. Hudson must lie on his bed as he had made it. Some men, perhaps, would even say that I am making a mighty ado about nothing; that I have only to give him rope, and he will tire himself out. But he tugs at his rope altogether too hard for *me* to hold it comfortably. I certainly never pretended the thing was anything else than an experiment; I promised noth-

ing, I answered for nothing; I only said the case was hopeful, and that it would be a shame to neglect it. I have done my best, and if the machine is running down I have a right to stand aside and let it scuttle. Amen, amen! No, I can write that, but I can't feel it. I can't be just; I can only be generous. I love the poor fellow and I can't give him up. As for understanding him, that 's another matter; nowadays I don't believe even you would. One's wits are sadly pestered over here, I assure you, and I 'm in the way of seeing more than one puzzling specimen of human nature. Roderick and Miss Light, between them! . . . . Have n't I already told you about Miss Light? Last winter everything was perfection. Roderick struck out bravely, did really great things, and proved himself, as I supposed, thoroughly solid. He was strong, he was first-rate; I felt perfectly secure and sang private pæans of joy. We had passed at a bound into the open sea, and left danger behind. But in the summer I began to be puzzled, though I succeeded in not being alarmed. When we came back to Rome, however, I saw that the tide had turned and that we were close upon the rocks. It is, in fact, another case of Ulysses alongside of the Sirens; only Roderick refuses to be tied to the mast. He is the most extraordinary being, the strangest mixture of qualities. I don't understand so much force going with so much weakness— such a brilliant gift being subject to such lapses. The poor fellow is incomplete, and it is really not his own fault; Nature has given him the faculty out of hand and bidden him be hanged with it. I never knew a man harder to advise or assist, if he is not in the mood for listening. I suppose there is some key or other to his character, but I try in vain to find it; and yet I can't believe that Providence is so cruel as to have turned the lock and thrown the key away. He perplexes me, as I say, to death, and though he tires out my patience, he still fascinates me. Sometimes I think he has n't a grain of conscience, and sometimes I think that, in a way, he has an excess. He takes things at once too easily and too hard; he is both too lax and too tense, too reckless and too ambitious, too cold and too passionate. He has developed faster even than you prophesied, and for good and evil alike he takes up a formidable space. There 's too much of him for me, at any rate.

Yes, he *is* hard; there is no mistake about that. He 's inflexible, he 's brittle; and though he has plenty of spirit, plenty of soul, he has n't what I call a heart. He has something that Miss Garland took for one, and I 'm pretty sure she 's a judge. But she judged on scanty evidence. He has something that Christina Light, here, makes believe at times that she takes for one, but she is no judge at all! I think it is established that, in the long run, egotism makes a failure in conduct: is it also true that it makes a failure in the arts? . . . . Roderick's standard is immensely high; I must do him that justice. He will do nothing beneath it, and while he is waiting for inspiration, his imagination, his nerves, his senses must have something to amuse them. This is a highly philosophical way of saying that he has taken to dissipation, and that he has just been spending a month at Naples—a city where 'pleasure' is actively cultivated—in very bad company. Are they all like that, all the men of genius? There are a great many artists here who hammer away at their trade with exemplary industry; in fact I am surprised at their success in reducing the matter to a steady, daily grind: but I really don't think that one of them has his exquisite quality of talent. It is in the matter of quantity that he has broken down. The bottle won't pour; he turns it upside down; it 's no use! Sometimes he declares it 's empty—that he has done all he was made to do. This I consider great nonsense; but I would nevertheless take him on his own terms if it was only I that was concerned. But I keep thinking of those two praying, trusting neighbors of yours, and I feel wretchedly like a swindler. If his working mood came but once in five years I would willingly wait for it and maintain him in leisure, if need be, in the intervals; but that would be a sorry account to present to them. Five years of this sort of thing, moreover, would effectually settle the question. I wish he were less of a genius and more of a charlatan! He 's too confoundedly all of one piece; he won't throw overboard a grain of the cargo to save the rest. Fancy him thus with all his brilliant personal charm, his handsome head, his careless step, his look as of a nervous nineteenth-century Apollo, and you will understand that there is mighty little comfort in seeing him in a bad way. He was tolerably foolish last summer at Baden Baden, but he got on his feet, and for a while he was steady. Then he began to waver again, and at last toppled over. Now, literally, he 's lying prone. He came into my room last night, miserably tipsy. I assure you, it did n't amuse me. . . . . About Miss Light it 's a long story. She is one of the great beauties of all time, and worth coming barefoot to Rome, like the pilgrims of old, to see. Her complexion, her glance, her step, her dusky tresses, may have been seen before in a goddess, but never in a woman. And you may take this for truth, because I 'm not in love with her. On the contrary! Her education has been simply infernal. She is corrupt, perverse, as proud as the queen of Sheba, and an appalling coquette; but she is generous, and with patience and skill you may enlist her imagination in a good cause as well as in a bad one. The other day I tried to manipulate it a little. Chance offered me an interview to which it was possible to give a serious turn, and I boldly broke ground and begged her to suffer my poor friend to go in peace. After a good deal of finessing she consented, and the next day, with a single word, packed him off to Naples to drown his sorrow in debauchery. I have come to the conclusion that she is more dangerous in her virtuous moods than in her vicious ones, and that she probably has a way of turning her back which is the most provoking thing in the world. She 's an actress, she could n't forego doing the thing dramatically, and it was the dramatic touch that made it fatal. I wished her, of course, to let him down easily; but she desired to have the curtain drop on an attitude, and her attitudes deprive inflammable young artists of their reason. . . . . Roderick made an admirable bust of her at the beginning of the winter, and a dozen women came rushing to him to be done, *mutatis mutandis*, in the same style. They were all great ladies and ready to take him by the hand, but he told them all their faces did n't interest him, and sent them away vowing his destruction."

At this point of his long effusion, Rowland had paused and put by his letter. He kept it three days and then read it over. He was disposed at first to destroy it, but he decided finally to keep it, in the hope that it might strike a spark of useful suggestion from the flint of Cecilia's good sense. We know he had a talent for taking advice. And then it might be, he reflected, that his cousin's answer would throw some light on

Mary Garland's present vision of things. In his altered mood he added these few lines:—

"I unburdened myself the other day of this monstrous load of perplexity; I think it did me good, and I let it stand. I was in a melancholy muddle, and I was trying to work myself free. You know I like discussion, in a quiet way, and there is no one with whom I can have it as quietly as with you, most sagacious of cousins! There is an excellent old lady with whom I often chat, and who talks very much to the point. But Madame Grandoni has disliked Roderick from the first, and if I were to take her advice I would wash my hands of him. You will laugh at me for my long face, but you would do that in any circumstances. I am half ashamed of my letter, for I have a faith in my friend that is deeper than my doubts. He was here last evening, talking about the Naples Museum, the Aristides, the bronzes, the Pompeian frescoes, with such a beautiful intelligence that doubt of the ultimate future seemed blasphemy. I walked back to his lodging with him, and he was as mild as midsummer moonlight. He has the ineffable something that charms and convinces; my last word about him shall not be a harsh one."

Shortly after sending his letter, going one day into his friend's studio, he found Roderick suffering from the grave infliction of a visit from Mr. Leavenworth. Roderick submitted with extreme ill grace to being bored, and he was now evidently in a state of high exasperation. He had lately begun a representation of a *lazzarone* lounging in the sun; an image of serene, irresponsible, sensuous life. The real lazzarone, he had admitted, was a vile fellow; but the ideal lazzarone—and his own had been subtly idealized—was a precursor of the millennium.

Mr. Leavenworth had apparently just transferred his unhurrying gaze to the figure.

"Something in the style of the Dying Gladiator?" he sympathetically observed.

"Oh no," said Roderick seriously, "he 's not dying, he 's only drunk!"

"Ah, but intoxication, you know," Mr. Leavenworth rejoined, "is not a proper subject for sculpture. Sculpture should not deal with transitory attitudes."

"Lying dead drunk is not a transitory attitude! Nothing is more permanent, more sculpturesque, more monumental!"

"An entertaining paradox," said Mr. Leavenworth, "if we had time to exercise our wits upon it. I remember at Florence an intoxicated figure by Michael Angelo which seemed to me a deplorable aberration of a great mind. I myself touch liquor in no shape whatever. I have traveled through Europe on cold water. The most varied and attractive lists of wines are offered me, but I brush them aside. No cork has ever been drawn at my command!"

"The movement of drawing a cork calls into play a very pretty set of muscles," said Roderick. "I think I will make a figure in that position."

"A Bacchus, realistically treated! My dear young friend, never trifle with your lofty mission. Spotless marble should represent virtue, not vice!" And Mr. Leavenworth placidly waved his hand, as if to exorcise the spirit of levity, while his glance journeyed with leisurely benignity to another object— a marble replica of the bust of Miss Light. "An ideal head, I presume," he went on; "a fanciful representation of one of the pagan goddesses—a Diana, a Flora, a naiad or dryad? I often regret that our American artists should not boldly cast off that extinct nomenclature."

"She is neither a naiad nor a dryad," said Roderick, "and her name is as good as yours or mine."

"You call her"—Mr. Leavenworth blandly inquired.

"Miss Light," Rowland interposed, in charity.

"Ah, our great American beauty! Not a pagan goddess— an American, Christian lady! Yes, I have had the pleasure of conversing with Miss Light. Her conversational powers are not remarkable, but her beauty is of a high order. I observed her the other evening at a large party, where some of the proudest members of the European aristocracy were present—duchesses, princesses, countesses, and others distinguished by similar titles. But for beauty, grace, and elegance my fair countrywoman left them all nowhere. What women can compare with a truly refined American lady? The duchesses the other night had no attractions for my eyes; they looked coarse and sensual! It seemed to me that the tyranny of class distinctions must indeed be terrible when such countenances could inspire admiration. You see more beautiful girls in an hour on Broadway than in the whole tour of Europe. Miss Light, now, on Broadway, would excite no particular remark."

"She has never been there!" cried Roderick, triumphantly.

"I 'm afraid she never will be there. I suppose you have heard the news about her."

"What news?" Roderick had stood with his back turned, fiercely poking at his lazzarone; but at Mr. Leavenworth's last words he faced quickly about.

"It 's the news of the hour, I believe. Miss Light is admired by the highest people here. They tacitly recognize her superiority. She has had offers of marriage from various great lords. I was extremely happy to learn this circumstance, and to know that they all had been left sighing. She has not been dazzled by their titles and their gilded coronets. She has judged them simply as *men*, and found them wanting. One of them, however, a young Neapolitan prince, I believe, has after a long probation succeeded in making himself acceptable. Miss Light has at last said yes, and the engagement has just been announced. I am not generally a retailer of gossip of this description, but the fact was alluded to an hour ago by a lady with whom I was conversing, and here, in Europe, these conversational trifles usurp the lion's share of one's attention. I therefore retained the circumstance. Yes, I regret that Miss Light should marry one of these used-up foreigners. Americans should stand by each other. If she wanted a brilliant match we could have fixed it for her. If she wanted a fine fellow—a fine, sharp, enterprising modern man—I would have undertaken to find him for her without going out of the city of New York. And if she wanted a big fortune, I would have found her twenty that she would have had hard work to spend: money down—not tied up in fever-stricken lands and worm-eaten villas! What is the name of the young man? Prince Castaway, or some such thing!"

It was well for Mr. Leavenworth that he was a voluminous and imperturbable talker; for the current of his eloquence floated him past the short, sharp, startled cry with which Roderick greeted his "conversational trifle." The young man stood looking at him with parted lips and an excited eye.

"The position of woman," Mr. Leavenworth placidly resumed, "is certainly a very degraded one in these countries. I doubt whether a European princess can command the respect which in our country is exhibited toward the obscurest females. The civilization of a country should be measured by the deference shown to the weaker sex. Judged by that standard, where are they, over here?"

Though Mr. Leavenworth had not observed Roderick's emotion, it was not lost upon Rowland, who was making certain uncomfortable reflections upon it. He saw that it had instantly become one with the acute irritation produced by the poor gentleman's oppressive personality, and that an explosion of some sort was imminent. Mr. Leavenworth, with calm unconsciousness, proceeded to fire the mine.

"And now for our Culture!" he said in the same sonorous tones, demanding with a gesture the unveiling of the figure, which stood somewhat apart, muffled in a great sheet.

Roderick stood looking at him for a moment with concentrated rancor, and then strode to the statue and twitched off the cover. Mr. Leavenworth settled himself into his chair with an air of flattered proprietorship, and scanned the unfinished image. "I can conscientiously express myself as gratified with the general conception," he said. "The figure has considerable majesty, and the countenance wears a fine, open expression. The forehead, however, strikes me as not sufficiently intellectual. In a statue of Culture, you know, that should be the great point. The eye should instinctively seek the forehead. Could n't you heighten it up a little?"

Roderick, for all answer, tossed the sheet back over the statue. "Oblige me, sir," he said, "oblige me! Never mention that thing again."

"Never mention it? Why my dear sir"—

"Never mention it. It 's an abomination!"

"An abomination! My Culture!"

"Yours indeed!" cried Roderick. "It 's none of mine. I disown it."

"Disown it, if you please," said Mr. Leavenworth sternly, "but finish it first!"

"I 'd rather smash it!" cried Roderick.

"This is folly, sir. You must keep your engagements."

"I made no engagement. A sculptor is n't a tailor. Did you ever hear of inspiration? Mine is dead! And it 's no laughing matter. You yourself killed it."

"I—I—killed your inspiration?" cried Mr. Leavenworth, with the accent of righteous wrath. "You 're a very ungrateful boy! If ever I encouraged and cheered and sustained any one, I 'm sure I have done so to you."

"I appreciate your good intentions, and I don't wish to be uncivil. But your encouragement is—superfluous. I can't work for you!"

"I call this ill-humor, young man!" said Mr. Leavenworth, as if he had found the damning word.

"Oh, I 'm in an infernal humor!" Roderick answered.

"Pray, sir, is it my infelicitous allusion to Miss Light's marriage?"

"It 's your infelicitous everything! I don't say that to offend you; I beg your pardon if it does. I say it by way of making our rupture complete, irretrievable!"

Rowland had stood by in silence, but he now interfered. "Listen to me," he said, laying his hand on Roderick's arm. "You are standing on the edge of a gulf. If you suffer anything that has passed to interrupt your work on that figure, you take your plunge. It 's no matter that you don't like it; you will do the wisest thing you ever did if you make that effort of will necessary for finishing it. Destroy the statue then, if you like, but make the effort. I speak the truth!"

Roderick looked at him with eyes that still inexorableness made almost tender. "You too!" he simply said.

Rowland felt that he might as well attempt to squeeze water from a polished crystal as hope to move him. He turned away and walked into the adjoining room with a sense of sickening helplessness. In a few moments he came back and found that Mr. Leavenworth had departed—presumably in a manner somewhat portentous. Roderick was sitting with his elbows on his knees and his head in his hands.

Rowland made one more attempt. "You decline to think of what I urge?"

"Absolutely."

"There's one more point—that you should n't, for a month, go to Mrs. Light's."

"I go there this evening."

"That too is an utter folly."

"There are such things as necessary follies."

"You are not reflecting; you are speaking in passion."

"Why then do you make me speak?"

Rowland meditated a moment. "Is it also necessary that you should lose the best friend you have?"

Roderick looked up. "That 's for you to settle!"

His best friend clapped on his hat and strode away; in a moment the door closed behind him. Rowland walked hard for nearly a couple of hours. He passed up the Corso, out of the Porta del Popolo and into the Villa Borghese, of which he made a complete circuit. The keenness of his irritation subsided, but it left him with an intolerable weight upon his heart. When dusk had fallen, he found himself near the lodging of his friend Madame Grandoni. He frequently paid her a visit during the hour which preceded dinner, and he now ascended her unillumined staircase and rang at her relaxed bell-rope with an especial desire for diversion. He was told that, for the moment, she was occupied, but that if he would come in and wait, she would presently be with him. He had not sat musing in the firelight for ten minutes when he heard the jingle of the door-bell and then a rustling and murmuring in the hall. The door of the little saloon opened, but before the visitor appeared he had recognized her voice. Christina Light swept forward, preceded by her poodle, and almost filling the narrow parlor with the train of her dress. She was colored here and there by the flicking firelight.

"They told me you were here," she said simply, as she took a seat.

"And yet you came in? It is very brave," said Rowland.

"You are the brave one, when one thinks of it! Where is the padrona?"

"Occupied for the moment. But she is coming."

"How soon?"

"I have already waited ten minutes; I expect her from moment to moment."

"Meanwhile we are alone?" And she glanced into the dusky corners of the room.

"Unless Stenterello counts," said Rowland.

"Oh, he knows my secrets—unfortunate brute!" She sat silent awhile, looking into the firelight. Then at last, glancing at Rowland, "Come! say something pleasant!" she exclaimed.

"I have been very happy to hear of your engagement."

"No, I don't mean that. I have heard that so often, only since breakfast, that it has lost all sense. I mean some of those unexpected, charming things that you said to me a month ago at Saint Cecilia's."

"I offended you, then," said Rowland. "I was afraid I had."

"Ah, it occurred to you? Why have n't I seen you since?"

"Really, I don't know." And he began to hesitate for an explanation. "I have called, but you have never been at home."

"You were careful to choose the wrong times. You have a way with a poor girl! You sit down and inform her that she is a person with whom a respectable young man cannot associate without contamination; your friend is a very nice fellow, you are very careful of his morals, you wish him to know none but nice people, and you beg me therefore to desist. You request me to take these suggestions to heart and to act upon them as promptly as possible. They are not particularly flattering to my vanity. Vanity, however, is a sin, and I listen submissively, with an immense desire to be just. If I have many faults I know it, in a general way, and I try on the whole to do my best. '*Voyons*,' I say to myself, 'it is n't particularly charming to hear one's self made out such a low person, but it is worth thinking over; there 's probably a good deal of truth in it, and at any rate we must be as good a girl as we can. That 's the great point! And then here 's a magnificent chance for humility. If there 's doubt in the matter, let the doubt count against one's self. That is what Saint Catherine did, and Saint Theresa, and all the others, and they are said to have had in consequence the most ineffable joys. Let us go in for a little ineffable joy!' I tried it; I swallowed my rising sobs, I made you my courtesy, I determined I would not be spiteful, nor passionate, nor vengeful, nor anything that is supposed to be particularly feminine. I was a better girl than you made out—better at least than you thought; but I would let the difference go and do magnificently right, lest I should not do right enough. I thought of it a deal for six hours when I know I did n't seem to be, and then at last I did it! *Santo Dio!*"

"My dear Miss Light, my dear Miss Light!" said Rowland, pleadingly.

"Since then," the young girl went on, "I have been waiting for the ineffable joys. They have n't yet turned up!"

"Pray listen to me!" Rowland urged.

"Nothing, nothing, nothing has come of it. I have passed the dreariest month of my life!"

"My dear Miss Light, you are a very terrible young lady!" cried Rowland.

"What do you mean by that?"

"A good many things. We 'll talk them over. But first, forgive me if I have offended you!"

She looked at him a moment, hesitating, and then thrust her hands into her muff. "That means nothing. Forgiveness is between equals, and you don't regard me as your equal."

"Really, I don't understand!"

Christina rose and moved for a moment about the room. Then turning suddenly, "You don't believe in me!" she cried; "not a grain! I don't know what I would not give to *force* you to believe in me!"

Rowland sprang up, protesting, but before he had time to go far one of the scanty *portières* was raised, and Madame Grandoni came in, pulling her wig straight. "But you shall believe in me yet," murmured Christina, as she passed toward her hostess.

Madame Grandoni turned tenderly to Christina. "I must give you a very solemn kiss, my dear; you are the heroine of the hour. You have really accepted him, eh?"

"So they say!"

"But you ought to know best."

"I don't know—I don't care!" She stood with her hand in Madame Grandoni's, but looking askance at Rowland.

"That 's a pretty state of mind," said the old lady, "for a young person who is going to become a princess."

Christina shrugged her shoulders. "Every one expects me to go into ecstacies over that! Could anything be more vulgar? They may chuckle by themselves! Will you let me stay to dinner?"

"If you can dine on a *risotto*. But I imagine you are expected at home."

"You are right. Prince Casamassima dines there, en famille. But I 'm not in *his* family, yet!"

"Do you know you are very wicked? I have half a mind not to keep you."

Christina dropped her eyes, reflectively. "I beg you will let me stay," she said. "If you wish to cure me of my wickedness you must be very patient and kind with me. It will be worth the trouble. You must show confidence in me." And she gave another glance at Rowland. Then suddenly, in a different tone, "I don't know what I 'm saying!" she cried. "I am weary, I am more lonely than ever, I wish I were dead!" The tears rose to her eyes, she struggled with them an instant, and buried her face in her muff; but at last she burst into uncontrollable sobs and flung her arms upon Madame Grandoni's neck. This shrewd woman gave Rowland a significant nod, and a little shrug, over the young girl's beautiful bowed head, and then led Christina tenderly away into the adjoining room. Rowland, left alone, stood there for an instant, intolerably puzzled, face to face with Miss Light's poodle, who had set up a sharp, unearthly cry of sympathy with his mistress. Rowland vented his confusion in dealing a rap with his stick at the animal's unmelodious muzzle, and then rapidly left the house. He saw Mrs. Light's carriage waiting at the door, and heard afterwards that Christina went home to dinner.

A couple of days later he went, for a fortnight, to Florence. He had twenty minds to leave Italy altogether; and at Florence he could at least more freely decide upon his future movements. He felt profoundly, incurably disgusted. Reflective benevolence stood prudently aside, and for the time touched the source of his irritation with no softening sidelights.

It was the middle of March, and by the middle of March in Florence the spring is already warm and deep. He had an infinite relish for the place and the season, but as he strolled by the Arno and paused here and there in the great galleries, they failed to soothe his irritation. He was sore at heart, and as the days went by the soreness deepened rather than healed. He felt as if he had a complaint against fortune; good-natured

as he was, his good-nature this time quite declined to let it
pass. He had tried to be wise, he had tried to be kind, he had
embarked upon an estimable enterprise; but his wisdom, his
kindness, his energy, had been thrown back in his face. He
was disappointed, and his disappointment had an angry spark
in it. The sense of wasted time, of wasted hope and faith, kept
him constant company. There were times when the beautiful
things about him only exasperated his discontent. He went to
the Pitti Palace, and Raphael's Madonna of the Chair seemed,
in its soft serenity, to mock him with the suggestion of unattainable repose. He lingered on the bridges at sunset, and
knew that the light was enchanting and the mountains divine,
but there seemed to be something horribly invidious and unwelcome in the fact. He felt, in a word, like a man who has
been cruelly defrauded and who wishes to have his revenge.
Life owed him, he thought, a compensation, and he would
be restless and resentful until he found it. He knew—or he
seemed to know—where he should find it; but he hardly told
himself, and thought of the thing under mental protest, as a
man in want of money may think of certain funds that he
holds in trust. In his melancholy meditations the idea of
something better than all this, something that might softly,
richly interpose, something that might reconcile him to the
future, something that might make one's tenure of life deep
and zealous instead of harsh and uneven—the idea of concrete compensation, in a word—shaped itself sooner or later
into the image of Mary Garland.

Very odd, you may say, that at this time of day Rowland
should still be brooding over a plain girl of whom he had had
but the lightest of glimpses two years before; very odd that
so deep an impression should have been made by so lightly-
pressed an instrument. We must admit the oddity and offer
simply in explanation that his sentiment apparently belonged
to that species of emotion of which, by the testimony of the
poets, the very name and essence is oddity. One night he slept
but half an hour; he found his thoughts taking a turn which
excited him portentously. He walked up and down his room
half the night. It looked out on the Arno; the noise of the
river came in at the open window; he felt like dressing and
going down into the streets. Toward morning he flung him-

self into a chair; though he was wide awake he was less excited. It seemed to him that he saw his idea from the outside,
that he judged it and condemned it; yet it stood there before
him, distinct, and in a certain way imperious. During the day
he tried to banish it and forget it; but it fascinated, haunted,
at moments frightened him. He tried to amuse himself, paid
visits, resorted to several rather violent devices for diverting
his thoughts. If on the morrow he had committed a crime,
the persons whom he had seen that day would have testified
that he had talked strangely and had not seemed like himself.
He felt certainly very unlike himself; long afterwards, in retrospect, he used to reflect that during those days he had for a
while been literally *beside* himself. His idea persisted; it clung
to him like a sturdy beggar. The sense of the matter, roughly
expressed, was this: If Roderick was really going, as he himself had phrased it, to "fizzle out," one might help him on the
way—one might smooth the *descensus Averno*. For forty-eight
hours there swam before Rowland's eyes a vision of Roderick, graceful and beautiful as he passed, plunging, like a diver,
from an eminence into a misty gulf. The gulf was destruction,
annihilation, death; but if death was decreed, why should not
the agony be brief? Beyond this vision there faintly glimmered another, as in the children's game of the "magic lantern" a picture is superposed on the white wall before the last
one has quite faded. It represented Mary Garland standing
there with eyes in which the horror seemed slowly, slowly to
expire, and hanging, motionless hands which at last made no
resistance when his own offered to take them. When, of old,
a man was burnt at the stake it was cruel to have to be present; but if one was present it was kind to lend a hand to pile
up the fuel and make the flames do their work quickly and
the smoke muffle up the victim. With all deference to your
kindness, this was perhaps an obligation you would especially
feel if you had a reversionary interest in something the victim
was to leave behind him.

One morning, in the midst of all this, Rowland walked
heedlessly out of one of the city gates and found himself on
the road to Fiesole. It was a completely lovely day; the March
sun felt like May, as the English poet of Florence says; the
thick-blossomed shrubs and vines that hung over the walls of

villa and *podere* flung their odorous promise into the warm,
still air. Rowland followed the winding, climbing lanes; lingered, as he got higher, beneath the rusty cypresses, beside
the low parapets, where you look down on the charming city
and sweep the vale of the Arno; reached the little square before the cathedral, and rested awhile in the massive, dusky
church; then climbed higher, to the Franciscan convent which
is poised on the very apex of the mountain. He rang at the
little gateway; a shabby, senile, red-faced brother admitted
him with almost maudlin friendliness. There was a dreary chill
in the chapel and the corridors, and he passed rapidly through
them into the delightfully steep and tangled old garden which
runs wild over the forehead of the great hill. He had been in
it before, and he was very fond of it. The garden hangs in the
air, and you ramble from terrace to terrace and wonder how
it keeps from slipping down, in full consummation of its bereaved forlornness, into the nakedly romantic gorge beneath.
It was just noon when Rowland went in, and after roaming
about awhile he flung himself in the sun on a mossy stone
bench and pulled his hat over his eyes. The short shadows of
the brown-coated cypresses above him had grown very long,
and yet he had not passed back through the convent. One of
the monks, in his faded snuff-colored robe, came wandering
out into the garden, reading his greasy little breviary. Suddenly he came toward the bench on which Rowland had
stretched himself, and paused a moment, attentively. Rowland was lingering there still; he was sitting with his head in
his hands and his elbows on his knees. He seemed not to have
heard the sandaled tread of the good brother, but as the
monk remained watching him, he at last looked up. It was
not the ignoble old man who had admitted him, but a pale,
gaunt personage, of a graver and more ascetic, and yet of a
benignant, aspect. Rowland's face bore the traces of extreme
trouble. The *frate* kept his finger in his little book, and folded
his arms picturesquely across his breast. It can hardly be determined whether his attitude, as he bent his sympathetic Italian eye upon Rowland, was a happy accident or the result of
an exquisite spiritual discernment. To Rowland, at any rate,
under the emotion of that moment, it seemed blessedly op-

portune. He rose and approached the monk, and laid his hand on his arm.

"My brother," he said, "did you ever see the Devil?"

The frate gazed, gravely, and crossed himself. "Heaven forbid!"

"He was here," Rowland went on, "here in this lovely garden, as he was once in Paradise, half an hour ago. But have no fear; I drove him out." And Rowland stooped and picked up his hat, which had rolled away into a bed of cyclamen, in vague symbolism of an actual physical tussle.

"You have been tempted, my brother?" asked the friar, tenderly.

"Hideously!"

"And you have resisted—and conquered!"

"I believe I have conquered."

"The blessed Saint Francis be praised! It is well done. If you like, we will offer a mass for you."

"I am not a Catholic," said Rowland.

The frate smiled with dignity. "That is a reason the more."

"But it 's for you, then, to choose. Shake hands with me," Rowland added; "that will do as well; and suffer me, as I go out, to stop a moment in your chapel."

They shook hands and separated. The frate crossed himself, opened his book, and wandered away, in relief against the western sky. Rowland passed back into the convent, and paused long enough in the chapel to look for the alms-box. He had had what is vulgarly termed a great scare; he believed, very poignantly for the time, in the Devil, and he felt an irresistible need to subscribe to any institution which engaged to keep him at a distance.

The next day he returned to Rome, and the day afterwards he went in search of Roderick. He found him on the Pincian with his back turned to the crowd, looking at the sunset. "I went to Florence," Rowland said, "and I thought of going farther; but I came back on purpose to give you another piece of advice. Once more, you refuse to leave Rome?"

"Never!" said Roderick.

"The only chance that I see, then, of your reviving your sense of responsibility to—to those various sacred things you have forgotten, is in sending for your mother to join you here."

Roderick stared. "For my mother?"

"For your mother—and for Miss Garland."

Roderick still stared; and then, slowly and faintly, his face flushed. "For Mary Garland—for my mother?" he repeated. "Send for them?"

"Tell me this; I have often wondered, but till now I have forborne to ask. You are still engaged to Miss Garland?"

Roderick frowned darkly, but assented.

"It would give you pleasure, then, to see her?"

Roderick turned away and for some moments answered nothing. "Pleasure!" he said at last, huskily. "Call it pain."

"I regard you as a sick man," Rowland continued. "In such a case Miss Garland would say that her place was at your side."

Roderick looked at him some time askance, mistrustfully. "Is this a deep-laid snare?" he asked slowly.

Rowland had come back with all his patience rekindled, but these words gave it an almost fatal chill. "Heaven forgive you!" he cried bitterly. "My idea has been simply this. Try, in decency, to understand it. I have tried to befriend you, to help you, to inspire you with confidence, and I have failed. I took you from the hands of your mother and your betrothed, and it seemed to me my duty to restore you to their hands. That 's all I have to say."

He was going, but Roderick forcibly detained him. It would have been but a rough way of expressing it to say that one could never know how Roderick would take a thing. It had happened more than once that when hit hard, deservedly, he had received the blow with touching gentleness. On the other hand, he had often resented the softest taps. The secondary effect of Rowland's present admonition seemed reassuring. "I beg you to wait," he said, "to forgive that shabby speech, and to let me reflect." And he walked up and down awhile, reflecting. At last he stopped, with a look in his face that Rowland had not seen all winter. It was a strikingly beautiful look.

"How strange it is," he said, "that the simplest devices are the last that occur to one!" And he broke into a light laugh.

"To see Mary Garland is just what I want. And my mother—
my mother can't hurt me now."

"You will write, then?"

"I will telegraph. They must come, at whatever cost. Striker
can arrange it all for them."

In a couple of days he told Rowland that he had received
a telegraphic answer to his message, informing him that the
two ladies were to sail immediately for Leghorn, in one of
the small steamers which ply between that port and New
York. They would arrive, therefore, in less than a month.
Rowland passed this month of expectation in no very serene
frame of mind. His suggestion had had its source in the deepest places of his agitated conscience; but there was something
intolerable in the thought of the suffering to which the event
was probably subjecting those undefended women. They had
scraped together their scanty funds and embarked, at twenty-
four hours' notice, upon the dreadful sea, to journey tremulously to shores darkened by the shadow of deeper alarms.
He could only promise himself to be their devoted friend and
servant. Preoccupied as he was, he was able to observe that
expectation, with Roderick, took a form which seemed singular even among his characteristic singularities. If redemption—Roderick seemed to reason—was to arrive with his
mother and his affianced bride, these last moments of error
should be doubly erratic. He did nothing; but inaction, with
him, took on an unwonted air of gentle gayety. He laughed
and whistled and went often to Mrs. Light's; though Rowland knew not in what fashion present circumstances had
modified his relations with Christina. The month ebbed away
and Rowland daily expected to hear from Roderick that he
had gone to Leghorn to meet the ship. He heard nothing,
and late one evening, not having seen his friend in three or
four days, he stopped at Roderick's lodging to assure himself
that he had gone at last. A cab was standing in the street, but
as it was a couple of doors off he hardly heeded it. The hall
at the foot of the staircase was dark, like most Roman halls,
and he paused in the street-doorway on hearing the advancing footstep of a person with whom he wished to avoid coming into collision. While he did so he heard another footstep
behind him, and turning round found that Roderick in per-

son had just overtaken him. At the same moment a woman's figure advanced from within, into the light of the street-lamp, and a face, half-startled, glanced at him out of the darkness. He gave a cry—it was the face of Mary Garland. Her glance flew past him to Roderick, and in a second a startled exclamation broke from her own lips. It made Rowland turn again. Roderick stood there, pale, apparently trying to speak, but saying nothing. His lips were parted and he was wavering slightly with a strange movement—the movement of a man who has drunk too much. Then Rowland's eyes met Miss Garland's again, and her own, which had rested a moment on Roderick's, were formidable!

IX

Mary Garland

How it befell that Roderick had failed to be in Leghorn on his mother's arrival never clearly transpired; for he undertook to give no elaborate explanation of his fault. He never indulged in professions (touching personal conduct) as to the future, or in remorse as to the past, and as he would have asked no praise if he had traveled night and day to embrace his mother as she set foot on shore, he made (in Rowland's presence, at least) no apology for having left her to come in search of him. It was to be said that, thanks to an unprecedentedly fine season, the voyage of the two ladies had been surprisingly rapid, and that, according to common probabilities, if Roderick had left Rome on the morrow (as he declared that he had intended), he would have had a day or two of waiting at Leghorn. Rowland's silent inference was that Christina Light had beguiled him into letting the time slip, and it was accompanied with a silent inquiry whether she had done so unconsciously or maliciously. He had told her, presumably, that his mother and his cousin were about to arrive; and it was pertinent to remember hereupon that she was a young lady of mysterious impulses. Rowland heard in due time the story of the adventures of the two ladies from Northampton. Miss Garland's wish, at Leghorn, on finding they were left at the mercy of circumstances, had been to telegraph to Roderick and await an answer; for she knew that their arrival was a trifle premature. But Mrs. Hudson's maternal heart had taken the alarm. Roderick's sending for them was, to her imagination, a confession of illness, and his not being at Leghorn, a proof of it; an hour's delay was therefore cruel both to herself and to him. She insisted on immediate departure; and, unskilled as they were in the mysteries of foreign (or even of domestic) travel, they had hurried in trembling eagerness to Rome. They had arrived late in the evening, and, knowing nothing of inns, had got into a cab and proceeded to Roderick's lodging. At the door, poor Mrs. Hudson's frightened anxiety had overcome her, and she had sat quaking and crying in the vehicle, too weak to move. Miss Garland had bravely gone in, groped her way up the dusky staircase, reached Roderick's door, and, with the assistance of such acquaintance with the Italian tongue as she had culled from a phrase-book during the calmer hours of the voyage, had learned from the old woman who had her cousin's household economy in charge that he was in the best of health and spirits, and had gone forth a few hours before with his hat on his ear, *per divertirsi*.

These things Rowland learned during a visit he paid the two ladies the evening after their arrival. Mrs. Hudson spoke of them at great length and with an air of clinging confidence in Rowland which told him how faithfully time had served him, in her imagination. But her fright was over, though she was still catching her breath a little, like a person dragged ashore out of waters uncomfortably deep. She was excessively bewildered and confused, and seemed more than ever to demand a tender handling from her friends. Before Miss Garland, Rowland was distinctly conscious that he trembled. He wondered extremely what was going on in her mind; what was her silent commentary on the incidents of the night before. He wondered all the more, because he immediately perceived that she was greatly changed since their parting, and that the change was by no means for the worse. She was older, easier, more free, more like a young woman who went sometimes into company. She had more beauty as well, inasmuch as her beauty before had been the depth of her expression, and the sources from which this beauty was fed had in these two years evidently not wasted themselves. Rowland felt almost instantly—he could hardly have said why: it was in her voice, in her tone, in the air—that a total change had passed over her attitude towards himself. She trusted him now, absolutely; whether or no she liked him, she believed he was *solid*. He felt that during the coming weeks he would need to be solid. Mrs. Hudson was at one of the smaller hotels, and her sitting-room was frugally lighted by a couple of candles. Rowland made the most of this dim illumination to try to detect the afterglow of that frightened flash from Miss Garland's eyes the night before. It had been but a flash, for what provoked it had instantly vanished. Rowland had mur-

mured a rapturous blessing on Roderick's head, as he perceived him instantly apprehend the situation. If he had been
drinking, its gravity sobered him on the spot; in a single moment he collected his wits. The next moment, with a ringing,
jovial cry, he was folding the young girl in his arms, and the
next he was beside his mother's carriage, half smothered in
her sobs and caresses. Rowland had recommended a hotel
close at hand, and had then discreetly withdrawn. Roderick
was at this time doing his part superbly, and Miss Garland's
brow was serene. It was serene now, twenty-four hours later;
but nevertheless, her alarm had lasted an appreciable moment.
What had become of it? It had dropped down deep into her
memory, and it was lying there for the present in the shade.
But with another week, Rowland said to himself, it would
leap erect again; the lightest friction would strike a spark from
it. Rowland thought he had schooled himself to face the issue
of Mary Garland's advent, casting it even in a tragical phase;
but in her personal presence—in which he found a poignant
mixture of the familiar and the strange—he seemed to face it
and all that it might bring with it for the first time. In vulgar
parlance, he stood uneasy in his shoes. He felt like walking
on tiptoe, not to arouse the sleeping shadows. He felt, indeed, almost like saying that they might have their own way
later, if they would only allow to these first few days the clear
light of ardent contemplation. For Rowland at last was ardent, and all the bells within his soul were ringing bravely in
jubilee. Roderick, he learned, had been the whole day with
his mother, and had evidently responded to her purest trust.
He appeared to her appealing eyes still unspotted by the
world. That is what it is, thought Rowland, to be "gifted," to
escape not only the superficial, but the intrinsic penalties of
misconduct. The two ladies had spent the day within doors,
resting from the fatigues of travel. Miss Garland, Rowland
suspected, was not so fatigued as she suffered it to be assumed. She had remained with Mrs. Hudson, to attend to her
personal wants, which the latter seemed to think, now that
she was in a foreign land, with a southern climate and a Catholic religion, would forthwith become very complex and formidable, though as yet they had simply resolved themselves
into a desire for a great deal of tea and for a certain extremely

familiar old black and white shawl across her feet, as she lay on the sofa. But the sense of novelty was evidently strong upon Miss Garland, and the light of expectation was in her eye. She was restless and excited; she moved about the room and went often to the window; she was observing keenly; she watched the Italian servants intently, as they came and went; she had already had a long colloquy with the French chambermaid, who had expounded her views on the Roman question; she noted the small differences in the furniture, in the food, in the sounds that came in from the street. Rowland felt, in all this, that her intelligence, here, would have a great unfolding. He wished immensely he might have a share in it; he wished he might show her Rome. That, of course, would be Roderick's office. But he promised himself at least to take advantage of off-hours.

"It behooves you to appreciate your good fortune," he said to her. "To be young and elastic, and yet old enough and wise enough to discriminate and reflect, and to come to Italy for the first time—that is one of the greatest pleasures that life offers us. It is but right to remind you of it, so that you make the most of opportunity and do not accuse yourself, later, of having wasted the precious season."

Miss Garland looked at him, smiling intently, and went to the window again. "I expect to enjoy it," she said. "Don't be afraid; I am not wasteful."

"I am afraid we are not qualified, you know," said Mrs. Hudson. "We are told that you must know so much, that you must have read so many books. Our taste has not been cultivated. When I was a young lady at school, I remember I had a medal, with a pink ribbon, for 'proficiency in Ancient History'—the seven kings, or is it the seven hills? and Quintus Curtius and Julius Cæsar and—and that period, you know. I believe I have my medal somewhere in a drawer, now, but I have forgotten all about the kings. But after Roderick came to Italy we tried to learn something about it. Last winter Mary used to read "Corinne" to me in the evenings, and in the mornings she used to read another book, to herself. What was it, Mary, that book that was so long, you know,—in fifteen volumes?"

"It was Sismondi's Italian Republics," said Mary, simply.

Rowland could not help laughing; whereupon Mary blushed. "Did you finish it?" he asked.

"Yes, and began another—a shorter one—Roscoe's Leo the Tenth."

"Did you find them interesting?"

"Oh yes."

"Do you like history?"

"Some of it."

"That 's a woman's answer! And do you like art?"

She paused a moment. "I have never seen it!"

"You have great advantages, now, my dear, with Roderick and Mr. Mallet," said Mrs. Hudson. "I am sure no young lady ever had such advantages. You come straight to the highest authorities. Roderick, I suppose, will show you the practice of art, and Mr. Mallet, perhaps, if he will be so good, will show you the theory. As an artist's wife, you ought to know something about it."

"One learns a good deal about it, here, by simply living," said Rowland; "by going and coming about one's daily avocations."

"Dear, dear, how wonderful that we should be here in the midst of it!" murmured Mrs. Hudson. "To think of art being out there in the streets! We did n't see much of it last evening, as we drove from the depot. But the streets were so dark and we were so frightened! But we are very easy now; are n't we, Mary?"

"I am very happy," said Mary, gravely, and wandered back to the window again.

Roderick came in at this moment and kissed his mother, and then went over and joined Miss Garland. Rowland sat with Mrs. Hudson, who evidently had a word which she deemed of some value for his private ear. She followed Roderick with intensely earnest eyes.

"I wish to tell you, sir," she said, "how very grateful—how very thankful—what a happy mother I am! I feel as if I owed it all to you, sir. To find my poor boy so handsome, so prosperous, so elegant, so famous—and ever to have doubted of you! What must you think of me? You 're our guardian angel, sir. I often say so to Mary."

Rowland wore, in response to this speech, a rather haggard

brow. He could only murmur that he was glad she found
Roderick looking well. He had of course promptly asked himself whether the best discretion dictated that he should give
her a word of warning—just turn the handle of the door
through which, later, disappointment might enter. He had
determined to say nothing, but simply to wait in silence for
Roderick to find effective inspiration in those confidently expectant eyes. It was to be supposed that he was seeking for it
now; he remained sometime at the window with his cousin.
But at last he turned away and came over to the fireside with
a contraction of the eyebrows which seemed to intimate that
Miss Garland's influence was for the moment, at least, not
soothing. She presently followed him, and for an instant
Rowland observed her watching him as if she thought him
strange. "Strange enough," thought Rowland, "he may seem
to her, if he will!" Roderick directed his glance to his friend
with a certain peremptory air, which—roughly interpreted—
was equivalent to a request to share the intellectual expense
of entertaining the ladies. "Good heavens!" Rowland cried
within himself; "is he already tired of them?"

"To-morrow, of course, we must begin to put you through
the mill," Roderick said to his mother. "And be it hereby
known to Mallet that we count upon him to turn the wheel."

"I will do as you please, my son," said Mrs. Hudson. "So
long as I have you with me I don't care where I go. We must
not take up too much of Mr. Mallet's time."

"His time is inexhaustible; he has nothing under the sun to
do. Have you, Rowland? If you had seen the big hole I have
been making in it! Where will you go first? You have your
choice—from the Scala Santa to the Cloaca Maxima."

"Let us take things in order," said Rowland. "We will go
first to Saint Peter's. Miss Garland, I hope you are impatient
to see Saint Peter's."

"I would like to go first to Roderick's studio," said Miss
Garland.

"It's a very nasty place," said Roderick. "At your pleasure!"

"Yes, we must see your beautiful things before we can look
contentedly at anything else," said Mrs. Hudson.

"I have no beautiful things," said Roderick. "You may see
what there is! What makes you look so odd?"

This inquiry was abruptly addressed to his mother, who, in response, glanced appealingly at Mary and raised a startled hand to her smooth hair.

"No, it 's your face," said Roderick. "What has happened to it these two years? It has changed its expression."

"Your mother has prayed a great deal," said Miss Garland, simply.

"I did n't suppose, of course, it was from doing anything bad! It makes you a very good face—very interesting, very solemn. It has very fine lines in it; something might be done with it." And Rowland held one of the candles near the poor lady's head.

She was covered with confusion. "My son, my son," she said with dignity, "I don't understand you."

In a flash all his old alacrity had come to him. "I suppose a man may admire his own mother!" he cried. "If you please, madame, you 'll sit to me for that head. I see it, I see it! I will make something that a queen can't get done for her."

Rowland respectfully urged her to assent; he saw Roderick was in the vein and would probably do something eminently original. She gave her promise, at last, after many soft, inarticulate protests and a frightened petition that she might be allowed to keep her knitting.

Rowland returned the next day, with plenty of zeal for the part Roderick had assigned to him. It had been arranged that they should go to Saint Peter's. Roderick was in high good-humor, and, in the carriage, was watching his mother with a fine mixture of filial and professional tenderness. Mrs. Hudson looked up mistrustfully at the tall, shabby houses, and grasped the side of the barouche in her hand, as if she were in a sail-boat, in dangerous waters. Rowland sat opposite to Miss Garland. She was totally oblivious of her companions; from the moment the carriage left the hotel, she sat gazing, wide-eyed and absorbed, at the objects about them. If Rowland had felt disposed he might have made a joke of her intense seriousness. From time to time he told her the name of a place or a building, and she nodded, without looking at him. When they emerged into the great square between Bernini's colonnades, she laid her hand on Mrs. Hudson's arm and sank back in the carriage, staring up at the vast yellow façade of the church. Inside the church, Roderick gave his arm to his mother, and Rowland constituted himself the especial guide of Miss Garland. He walked with her slowly everywhere, and made the entire circuit, telling her all he knew of the history of the building. This was a great deal, but she listened attentively, keeping her eyes fixed on the dome. To Rowland himself it had never seemed so radiantly sublime as at these moments; he felt almost as if he had contrived it himself and had a right to be proud of it. He left Miss Garland a while on the steps of the choir, where she had seated herself to rest, and went to join their companions. Mrs. Hudson was watching a great circle of tattered *contadini*, who were kneeling before the image of Saint Peter. The fashion of their tatters fascinated her; she stood gazing at them in a sort of terrified pity, and could not be induced to look at anything else. Rowland went back to Miss Garland and sat down beside her.

"Well, what do you think of Europe?" he asked, smiling.

"I think it 's horrible!" she said abruptly.

"Horrible?"

"I feel so strangely—I could almost cry."

"How is it that you feel?"

"So sorry for the poor past, that seems to have died here, in my heart, in an hour!"

"But, surely, you 're pleased—you 're interested."

"I am overwhelmed. Here in a single hour, everything is changed. It is as if a wall in my mind had been knocked down at a stroke. Before me lies an immense new world, and it makes the old one, the poor little narrow, familiar one I have always known, seem pitiful."

"But you did n't come to Rome to keep your eyes fastened on that narrow little world. Forget it, turn your back on it, and enjoy all this."

"I want to enjoy it; but as I sat here just now, looking up at that golden mist in the dome, I seemed to see in it the vague shapes of certain people and things at home. To enjoy, as you say, as these things demand of one to enjoy them, is to break with one's past. And breaking is a pain!"

"Don't mind the pain, and it will cease to trouble you. Enjoy, enjoy; it is your duty. Yours especially!"

"Why mine especially?"

"Because I am very sure that you have a mind capable of doing the most liberal justice to everything interesting and beautiful. You are extremely intelligent."

"You don't know," said Miss Garland, simply.

"In that matter one *feels*. I really think that I know better than you. I don't want to seem patronizing, but I suspect that your mind is susceptible of a great development. Give it the best company, trust it, let it go!"

She looked away from him for some moments, down the gorgeous vista of the great church. "But what you say," she said at last, "means *change!*"

"Change for the better!" cried Rowland.

"How can one tell? As one stands, one knows the worst. It seems to me very frightful to develop," she added, with her complete smile.

"One is in for it in one way or another, and one might as well do it with a good grace as with a bad! Since one can't escape life, it is better to take it by the hand."

"Is *this* what you call life?" she asked.

"What do you mean by 'this'?"

"Saint Peter's—all this splendor, all Rome—pictures, ruins, statues, beggars, monks."

"It is not all of it, but it is a large part of it. All these things are impregnated with life; they are the fruits of an old and complex civilization."

"An old and complex civilization: I am afraid I don't like that."

"Don't conclude on that point just yet. Wait till you have tested it. While you wait, you will see an immense number of very beautiful things—things that you are made to understand. They won't leave you as they found you; then you can judge. Don't tell me I know nothing about your understanding. I have a right to assume it."

Miss Garland gazed awhile aloft in the dome. "I am not sure I understand that," she said.

"I hope, at least, that at a cursory glance it pleases you," said Rowland. "You need n't be afraid to tell the truth. What strikes some people is that it is so remarkably small."

"Oh, it 's large enough; it 's very wonderful. There are

things in Rome, then," she added in a moment, turning and looking at him, "that are very, *very* beautiful?"

"Lots of them."

"Some of the most beautiful things in the world?"

"Unquestionably."

"What are they? which things have most beauty?"

"That is according to taste. I should say the statues."

"How long will it take to see them all? to know, at least, something about them?"

"You can see them all, as far as mere seeing goes, in a fortnight. But to know them is a thing for one's leisure. The more time you spend among them, the more you care for them." After a moment's hesitation he went on: "Why should you grudge time? It 's all in your way, since you are to be an artist's wife."

"I have thought of that," she said. "It may be that I shall always live here, among the most beautiful things in the world!"

"Very possibly! I should like to see you ten years hence."

"I dare say I shall seem greatly altered. But I am sure of one thing."

"Of what?"

"That for the most part I shall be quite the same. I ask nothing better than to believe the fine things you say about my understanding, but even if they are true, it won't matter. I shall be what I was made, what I am now—a young woman from the country! The fruit of a civilization not old and complex, but new and simple."

"I am delighted to hear it: that 's an excellent foundation."

"Perhaps, if you show me anything more, you will not always think so kindly of it. Therefore I warn you."

"I am not frightened. I should like vastly to say something to you: Be what you are, be what you choose; but *do*, sometimes, as I tell you."

If Rowland was not frightened, neither, perhaps, was Miss Garland; but she seemed at least slightly disturbed. She proposed that they should join their companions.

Mrs. Hudson spoke under her breath; she could not be accused of the want of reverence sometimes attributed to Protestants in the great Catholic temples. "Mary, dear," she whispered, "suppose we had to kiss that dreadful brass toe. If I could only have kept our door-knocker, at Northampton, as bright as that! I think it 's so heathenish; but Roderick says he thinks it 's sublime."

Roderick had evidently grown a trifle perverse. "It 's sublimer than anything that *your* religion asks you to do!" he exclaimed.

"Surely our religion sometimes gives us very difficult duties," said Miss Garland.

"The duty of sitting in a whitewashed meeting-house and listening to a nasal Puritan! I admit that 's difficult. But it 's not sublime. I am speaking of ceremonies, of forms. It is in my line, you know, to make much of forms. I think this is a very beautiful one. Could n't you do it?" he demanded, looking at his cousin.

She looked back at him intently and then shook her head. "I think not!"

"Why not?"

"I don't know; I could n't!"

During this little discussion our four friends were standing near the venerable image of Saint Peter, and a squalid, savage-looking peasant, a tattered ruffian of the most orthodox Italian aspect, had been performing his devotions before it. He turned away, crossing himself, and Mrs. Hudson gave a little shudder of horror.

"After that," she murmured, "I suppose he thinks he is as good as any one! And here is another. Oh, what a beautiful person!"

A young lady had approached the sacred effigy, after having wandered away from a group of companions. She kissed the brazen toe, touched it with her forehead, and turned round, facing our friends. Rowland then recognized Christina Light. He was stupefied: had she suddenly embraced the Catholic faith? It was but a few weeks before that she had treated him to a passionate profession of indifference. Had she entered the church to put herself *en règle* with what was expected of a Princess Casamassima? While Rowland was mentally asking these questions she was approaching him and his friends, on her way to the great altar. At first she did not perceive them.

Mary Garland had been gazing at her. "You told me," she said gently, to Rowland, "that Rome contained some of the most beautiful things in the world. This surely is one of them!"

At this moment Christina's eye met Rowland's and before giving him any sign of recognition she glanced rapidly at his companions. She saw Roderick, but she gave him no bow; she looked at Mrs. Hudson, she looked at Mary Garland. At Mary Garland she looked fixedly, piercingly, from head to foot, as the slow pace at which she was advancing made possible. Then suddenly, as if she had perceived Roderick for the first time, she gave him a charming nod, a radiant smile. In a moment he was at her side. She stopped, and he stood talking to her; she continued to look at Miss Garland.

"Why, Roderick knows her!" cried Mrs. Hudson, in an awe-struck whisper. "I supposed she was some great princess."

"She is—almost!" said Rowland. "She is the most beautiful girl in Europe, and Roderick has made her bust."

"Her bust? Dear, dear!" murmured Mrs. Hudson, vaguely shocked. "What a strange bonnet!"

"She has very strange eyes," said Mary, and turned away.

The two ladies, with Rowland, began to descend toward the door of the church. On their way they passed Mrs. Light, the Cavaliere, and the poodle, and Rowland informed his companions of the relation in which these personages stood to Roderick's young lady.

"Think of it, Mary!" said Mrs. Hudson. "What splendid people he must know! No wonder he found Northampton dull!"

"I like the poor little old gentleman," said Mary.

"Why do you call him poor?" Rowland asked, struck with the observation.

"He seems so!" she answered simply.

As they were reaching the door they were overtaken by Roderick, whose interview with Miss Light had perceptibly brightened his eye. "So you are acquainted with princesses!" said his mother softly, as they passed into the portico.

"Miss Light is not a princess!" said Roderick, curtly.

"But Mr. Mallet says so," urged Mrs. Hudson, rather disappointed.

"I meant that she was going to be!" said Rowland.

"It 's by no means certain that she is even going to be!" Roderick answered.

"Ah," said Rowland, "I give it up!"

Roderick almost immediately demanded that his mother should sit to him, at his studio, for her portrait, and Rowland ventured to add another word of urgency. If Roderick's idea really held him, it was an immense pity that his inspiration should be wasted; inspiration, in these days, had become too precious a commodity. It was arranged therefore that, for the present, during the mornings, Mrs. Hudson should place herself at her son's service. This involved but little sacrifice, for the good lady's appetite for antiquities was diminutive and bird-like, the usual round of galleries and churches fatigued her, and she was glad to purchase immunity from sight-seeing by a regular afternoon drive. It became natural in this way that, Miss Garland having her mornings free, Rowland should propose to be the younger lady's guide in whatever explorations she might be disposed to make. She said she knew nothing about it, but she had a great curiosity, and would be glad to see anything that he would show her. Rowland could not find it in his heart to accuse Roderick of neglect of the young girl; for it was natural that the inspirations of a capricious man of genius, when they came, should be imperious; but of course he wondered how Miss Garland felt, as the young man's promised wife, on being thus expeditiously handed over to another man to be entertained. However she felt, he was certain he would know little about it. There had been, between them, none but indirect allusions to her engagement, and Rowland had no desire to discuss it more largely; for he had no quarrel with matters as they stood. They wore the same delightful aspect through the lovely month of May, and the ineffable charm of Rome at that period seemed but the radiant sympathy of nature with his happy opportunity. The weather was divine; each particular morning, as he walked from his lodging to Mrs. Hudson's modest inn, seemed to have a blessing upon it. The elder lady had usually gone off to the studio, and he found

Miss Garland sitting alone at the open window, turning the
leaves of some book of artistic or antiquarian reference that
he had given her. She always had a smile, she was always
eager, alert, responsive. She might be grave by nature, she
might be sad by circumstance, she might have secret doubts
and pangs, but she was essentially young and strong and fresh
and able to enjoy. Her enjoyment was not especially demonstrative, but it was curiously diligent. Rowland felt that it was
not amusement and sensation that she coveted, but knowledge—facts that she might noiselessly lay away, piece by
piece, in the perfumed darkness of her serious mind, so that,
under this head at least, she should not be a perfectly portion-
less bride. She never merely pretended to understand; she let
things go, in her modest fashion, at the moment, but she
watched them on their way, over the crest of the hill, and
when her fancy seemed not likely to be missed it went hurrying after them and ran breathless at their side, as it were,
and begged them for the secret. Rowland took an immense
satisfaction in observing that she never mistook the second-
best for the best, and that when she was in the presence of a
masterpiece, she recognized the occasion as a mighty one. She
said many things which he thought very profound—that is,
if they really had the fine intention he suspected. This point
he usually tried to ascertain; but he was obliged to proceed
cautiously, for in her mistrustful shyness it seemed to her that
cross-examination must necessarily be ironical. She wished to
know just where she was going—what she would gain or
lose. This was partly on account of a native intellectual purity,
a temper of mind that had not lived with its door ajar, as one
might say, upon the high-road of thought, for passing ideas
to drop in and out at their pleasure; but had made much of a
few long visits from guests cherished and honored—guests
whose presence was a solemnity. But it was even more because she was conscious of a sort of growing self-respect, a
sense of devoting her life not to her own ends, but to those
of another, whose life would be large and brilliant. She had
been brought up to think a great deal of "nature" and nature's
innocent laws; but now Rowland had spoken to her ardently
of culture; her strenuous fancy had responded, and she was
pursuing culture into retreats where the need for some intel-

lectual effort gave a noble severity to her purpose. She wished to be very sure, to take only the best, knowing it to be the best. There was something exquisite in this labor of pious self-adornment, and Rowland helped it, though its fruits were not for him. In spite of her lurking rigidity and angularity, it was very evident that a nervous, impulsive sense of beauty was constantly at play in her soul, and that her actual experience of beautiful things moved her in some very deep places. For all that she was not demonstrative, that her manner was simple, and her small-talk of no very ample flow; for all that, as she had said, she was a young woman from the country, and the country was West Nazareth, and West Nazareth was in its way a stubborn little fact, she was feeling the direct influence of the great amenities of the world, and they were shaping her with a divinely intelligent touch. "Oh exquisite virtue of circumstance!" cried Rowland to himself, "that takes us by the hand and leads us forth out of corners where, perforce, our attitudes are a trifle contracted, and beguiles us into testing mistrusted faculties!" When he said to Mary Garland that he wished he might see her ten years hence, he was paying mentally an equal compliment to circumstance and to the girl herself. Capacity was there, it could be freely trusted; observation would have but to sow its generous seed. "A superior woman"—the idea had harsh associations, but he watched it imaging itself in the vagueness of the future with a kind of hopeless confidence.

They went a great deal to Saint Peter's, for which Rowland had an exceeding affection, a large measure of which he succeeded in infusing into his companion. She confessed very speedily that to climb the long, low, yellow steps, beneath the huge florid façade, and then to push the ponderous leathern apron of the door, to find one's self confronted with that builded, luminous sublimity, was a sensation of which the keenness renewed itself with surprising generosity. In those days the hospitality of the Vatican had not been curtailed, and it was an easy and delightful matter to pass from the gorgeous church to the solemn company of the antique marbles. Here Rowland had with his companion a great deal of talk, and found himself expounding æsthetics *à perte de vue*. He discovered that she made notes of her likes and dislikes in a new-looking little memorandum book, and he wondered to what extent she reported his own discourse. These were charming hours. The galleries had been so cold all winter that Rowland had been an exile from them; but now that the sun was already scorching in the great square between the colonnades, where the twin fountains flashed almost fiercely, the marble coolness of the long, image-bordered vistas made them a delightful refuge. The great herd of tourists had almost departed, and our two friends often found themselves, for half an hour at a time, in sole and tranquil possession of the beautiful Braccio Nuovo. Here and there was an open window, where they lingered and leaned, looking out into the warm, dead air, over the towers of the city, at the soft-hued, historic hills, at the stately shabby gardens of the palace, or at some sunny, empty, grass-grown court, lost in the heart of the labyrinthine pile. They went sometimes into the chambers painted by Raphael, and of course paid their respects to the Sistine Chapel; but Mary's evident preference was to linger among the statues. Once, when they were standing before that noblest of sculptured portraits, the so-called Demosthenes, in the Braccio Nuovo, she made the only spontaneous allusion to her projected marriage, direct or indirect, that had yet fallen from her lips. "I am so glad," she said, "that Roderick is a sculptor and not a painter."

The allusion resided chiefly in the extreme earnestness with which the words were uttered. Rowland immediately asked her the reason of her gladness.

"It 's not that painting is not fine," she said, "but that sculpture is finer. It is more manly."

Rowland tried at times to make her talk about herself, but in this she had little skill. She seemed to him so much older, so much more pliant to social uses than when he had seen her at home, that he had a desire to draw from her some categorical account of her occupation and thoughts. He told her his desire and what suggested it. "It appears, then," she said, "that, after all, one *can* grow at home!"

"Unquestionably, if one has a motive. Your growth, then, was unconscious? You did not watch yourself and water your roots?"

She paid no heed to his question. "I am willing to grant," she said, "that Europe is more delightful than I supposed; and I don't think that, mentally, I had been stingy. But you must admit that America is better than you have supposed."

"I have not a fault to find with the country which produced you!" Rowland thought he might risk this, smiling.

"And yet you want me to change—to assimilate Europe, I suppose you would call it."

"I have felt that desire only on general principles. Shall I tell you what I feel now? America has made you thus far; let America finish you! I should like to ship you back without delay and see what becomes of you. That sounds unkind, and I admit there is a cold intellectual curiosity in it."

She shook her head. "The charm is broken; the thread is snapped! I prefer to remain here."

Invariably, when he was inclined to make of something they were talking of a direct application to herself, she wholly failed to assist him; she made no response. Whereupon, once, with a spark of ardent irritation, he told her she was very "secretive." At this she colored a little, and he said that in default of any larger confidence it would at least be a satisfaction to make her confess to that charge. But even this satisfaction she denied him, and his only revenge was in making, two or three times afterward, a softly ironical allusion to her slyness. He told her that she was what is called in French a *sournoise*. "Very good," she answered, almost indifferently, "and now please tell me again—I have forgotten it—what you said an 'architrave' was."

It was on the occasion of her asking him a question of this kind that he charged her, with a humorous emphasis in which, also, if she had been curious in the matter, she might have detected a spark of restless ardor, with having an insatiable avidity for facts. "You are always snatching at information," he said; "you will never consent to have any disinterested conversation."

She frowned a little, as she always did when he arrested their talk upon something personal. But this time she assented, and said that she knew she was eager for facts. "One must make hay while the sun shines," she added. "I must lay up a store of learning against dark days. Somehow, my imagination refuses to compass the idea that I may be in Rome indefinitely."

He knew he had divined her real motives; but he felt that if he might have said to her—what it seemed impossible to say—that fortune possibly had in store for her a bitter disappointment, she would have been capable of answering, immediately after the first sense of pain, "Say then that I am laying up resources for solitude!"

But all the accusations were not his. He had been watching, once, during some brief argument, to see whether she would take her forefinger out of her Murray, into which she had inserted it to keep a certain page. It would have been hard to say why this point interested him, for he had not the slightest real apprehension that she was dry or pedantic. The simple human truth was, the poor fellow was jealous of science. In preaching science to her, he had over-estimated his powers of self-effacement. Suddenly, sinking science for the moment, she looked at him very frankly and began to frown. At the same time she let the Murray slide down to the ground, and he was so charmed with this circumstance that he made no movement to pick it up.

"You are singularly inconsistent, Mr. Mallet," she said.

"How?"

"That first day that we were in Saint Peter's you said things that inspired me. You bade me plunge into all this. I was all ready; I only wanted a little push; yours was a great one; here I am in mid-ocean! And now, as a reward for my bravery, you have repeatedly snubbed me."

"Distinctly, then," said Rowland, "I strike you as inconsistent?"

"That is the word."

"Then I have played my part very ill."

"Your part? What is your part supposed to have been?"

He hesitated a moment. "That of usefulness, pure and simple."

"I don't understand you!" she said; and picking up her Murray, she fairly buried herself in it.

That evening he said something to her which necessarily increased her perplexity, though it was not uttered with such an intention. "Do you remember," he asked, "my begging

you, the other day, to do occasionally as I told you? It seemed
to me you tacitly consented."

"Very tacitly."

"I have never yet really presumed on your consent. But
now I would like you to do this: whenever you catch me in
the act of what you call inconsistency, ask me the meaning of
some architectural term. I will know what you mean; a word
to the wise!"

One morning they spent among the ruins of the Palatine,
that sunny desolation of crumbling, over-tangled fragments,
half excavated and half identified, known as the Palace of the
Cæsars. Nothing in Rome is more interesting, and no locality
has such a confusion of picturesque charms. It is a vast, rambling garden, where you stumble at every step on the disinterred bones of the past; where damp, frescoed corridors,
relics, possibly, of Nero's Golden House, serve as gigantic
bowers, and where, in the springtime, you may sit on a Latin
inscription, in the shade of a flowering almond-tree, and admire the composition of the Campagna. The day left a deep
impression on Rowland's mind, partly owing to its intrinsic
sweetness, and partly because his companion, on this occasion, let her Murray lie unopened for an hour, and asked several questions irrelevant to the Consuls and the Cæsars. She
had begun by saying that it was coming over her, after all,
that Rome was a ponderously sad place. The sirocco was
gently blowing, the air was heavy, she was tired, she looked
a little pale.

"Everything," she said, "seems to say that all things are vanity. If one is doing something, I suppose one feels a certain
strength within one to contradict it. But if one is idle, surely
it is depressing to live, year after year, among the ashes of
things that once were mighty. If I were to remain here I
should either become permanently 'low,' as they say, or I
would take refuge in some dogged daily work."

"What work?"

"I would open a school for those beautiful little beggars;
though I am sadly afraid I should never bring myself to scold
them."

"I am idle," said Rowland, "and yet I have kept up a certain
spirit."

"I don't call you idle," she answered with emphasis.

"It is very good of you. Do you remember our talking about that in Northampton?"

"During that picnic? Perfectly. Has your coming abroad succeeded, for yourself, as well as you hoped?"

"I think I may say that it has turned out as well as I expected."

"Are you happy?"

"Don't I look so?"

"So it seems to me. But"—and she hesitated a moment—"I imagine you look happy whether you are so or not."

"I'm like that ancient comic mask that we saw just now in yonder excavated fresco: I am made to grin."

"Shall you come back here next winter?"

"Very probably."

"Are you settled here forever?"

"'Forever' is a long time. I live only from year to year."

"Shall you never marry?"

Rowland gave a laugh. "'Forever'—'never!' You handle large ideas. I have not taken a vow of celibacy."

"Would n't you like to marry?"

"I should like it immensely."

To this she made no rejoinder: but presently she asked, "Why don't you write a book?"

Rowland laughed, this time more freely. "A book! What book should I write?"

"A history; something about art or antiquities."

"I have neither the learning nor the talent."

She made no attempt to contradict him; she simply said she had supposed otherwise. "You ought, at any rate," she continued in a moment, "to do something for yourself."

"For myself? I should have supposed that if ever a man seemed to live for himself"—

"I don't know how it seems," she interrupted, "to careless observers. But we know—we know that you have lived—a great deal—for *us*."

Her voice trembled slightly, and she brought out the last words with a little jerk.

"She has had that speech on her conscience," thought Rowland; "she has been thinking she owed it to me, and it seemed to her that now was her time to make it and have done with it."

She went on in a way which confirmed these reflections, speaking with due solemnity. "You ought to be made to know very well what we all feel. Mrs. Hudson tells me that she has told you what she feels. Of course Roderick has expressed himself. I have been wanting to thank you too; I do, from my heart."

Rowland made no answer; his face at this moment resembled the tragic mask much more than the comic. But Miss Garland was not looking at him; she had taken up her Murray again.

In the afternoon she usually drove with Mrs. Hudson, but Rowland frequently saw her again in the evening. He was apt to spend half an hour in the little sitting-room at the *hôtel-pension* on the slope of the Pincian, and Roderick, who dined regularly with his mother, was present on these occasions. Rowland saw him little at other times, and for three weeks no observations passed between them on the subject of Mrs. Hudson's advent. To Rowland's vision, as the weeks elapsed, the benefits to proceed from the presence of the two ladies remained shrouded in mystery. Roderick was peculiarly inscrutable. He was preoccupied with his work on his mother's portrait, which was taking a very happy turn; and often, when he sat silent, with his hands in his pockets, his legs outstretched, his head thrown back, and his eyes on vacancy, it was to be supposed that his fancy was hovering about the half-shaped image in his studio, exquisite even in its immaturity. He said little, but his silence did not of necessity imply disaffection, for he evidently found it a deep personal luxury to lounge away the hours in an atmosphere so charged with feminine tenderness. He was not alert, he suggested nothing in the way of excursions (Rowland was the prime mover in such as were attempted), but he conformed passively at least to the tranquil temper of the two women, and made no harsh comments nor sombre allusions. Rowland wondered whether he had, after all, done his friend injustice in denying him the sentiment of duty. He refused invitations, to Rowland's knowledge, in order to dine at the jejune little table-d'hôte; wherever his spirit might be, he was present in the flesh with religious constancy. Mrs. Hudson's felicity betrayed itself in a remarkable tendency to finish her sentences and wear her best black silk gown. Her tremors had trembled away; she was like a child who discovers that the shaggy monster it has so long been afraid to touch is an inanimate terror, compounded of straw and saw-dust, and that it is even a safe audacity to tickle its nose. As to whether the love-knot of which Mary Garland had the keeping still held firm, who should pronounce? The young girl, as we know, did not wear it on her sleeve. She always sat at the table, near the candles, with a piece of needle-work. This was the attitude in which Rowland had first seen her, and he thought, now that he had seen her in several others, it was not the least becoming.

X

The Cavaliere

THERE BEFELL at last a couple of days during which Rowland was unable to go to the hotel. Late in the evening of the second one Roderick came into his room. In a few moments he announced that he had finished the bust of his mother.

"And it 's magnificent!" he declared. "It 's one of the best things I have done."

"I believe it," said Rowland. "Never again talk to me about your inspiration being dead."

"Why not? This may be its last kick! I feel very tired. But it 's a masterpiece, though I do say it. They tell us we owe so much to our parents. Well, I 've paid the filial debt handsomely!" He walked up and down the room a few moments, with the purpose of his visit evidently still undischarged. "There 's one thing more I want to say," he presently resumed. "I feel as if I ought to tell you!" He stopped before Rowland with his head high and his brilliant glance unclouded. "Your invention is a failure!"

"My invention?" Rowland repeated.

"Bringing out my mother and Mary."

"A failure?"

"It 's no use! They don't help me."

Rowland had fancied that Roderick had no more surprises for him; but he was now staring at him, wide-eyed.

"They bore me!" Roderick went on.

"Oh, oh!" cried Rowland.

"Listen, listen!" said Roderick with perfect gentleness. "I am not complaining of them; I am simply stating a fact. I am very sorry for them; I am greatly disappointed."

"Have you given them a fair trial?"

"Should n't you say so? It seems to me I have behaved beautifully."

"You have done very well; I have been building great hopes on it."

"I have done too well, then. After the first forty-eight hours my own hopes collapsed. But I determined to fight it out; to stand within the temple; to let the spirit of the Lord descend! Do you want to know the result? Another week of it, and I shall begin to hate them. I shall want to poison them."

"Miserable boy!" cried Rowland. "They are the loveliest of women!"

"Very likely! But they mean no more to me than a Bible text to an atheist!"

"I utterly fail," said Rowland, in a moment, "to understand your relation to Miss Garland."

Roderick shrugged his shoulders and let his hands drop at his sides. "She adores me! That 's my relation." And he smiled strangely.

"Have you broken your engagement?"

"Broken it? You can't break a ray of moonshine."

"Have you absolutely no affection for her?"

Roderick placed his hand on his heart and held it there a moment. "Dead—dead—dead!" he said at last.

"I wonder," Rowland asked presently, "if you begin to comprehend the beauty of Miss Garland's character. She is a person of the highest merit."

"Evidently—or I would not have cared for her!"

"Has that no charm for you now?"

"Oh, don't force a fellow to say rude things!"

"Well, I can only say that you don't know what you are giving up."

Roderick gave a quickened glance. "Do *you* know, so well?"

"I admire her immeasurably."

Roderick smiled, we may almost say sympathetically. "You have not wasted time."

Rowland's thoughts were crowding upon him fast. If Roderick was resolute, why oppose him? If Mary was to be sacrificed, why, in *that* way, try to save her? There was another way; it only needed a little presumption to make it possible. Rowland tried, mentally, to summon presumption to his aid; but whether it came or not, it found conscience there before it. Conscience had only three words, but they were cogent. "For *her* sake—for *her* sake," it dumbly murmured, and Rowland resumed his argument. "I don't know what I would n't do," he said, "rather than that Miss Garland should suffer."

"There is one thing to be said," Roderick answered reflectively. "She is very strong."

"Well, then, if she 's strong, believe that with a longer chance, a better chance, she will still regain your affection."

"Do you know what you ask?" cried Roderick. "Make love to a girl I hate?"

"You *hate*?"

"As her lover, I should hate her!"

"Listen to me!" said Rowland with vehemence.

"No, listen you to me! Do you really urge my marrying a woman who would bore me to death? I would let her know it in very good season, and then where would she be?"

Rowland walked the length of the room a couple of times and then stopped suddenly. "Go your way, then! Say all this to *her*, not to me!"

"To her? I am afraid of her; I want you to help me."

"My dear Roderick," said Rowland with an eloquent smile, "I can help you no more!"

Roderick frowned, hesitated a moment, and then took his hat. "Oh, well," he said, "I am not so afraid of her as all that!" And he turned, as if to depart.

"Stop!" cried Rowland, as he laid his hand on the door.

Roderick paused and stood waiting, with his irritated brow.

"Come back; sit down there and listen to me. Of anything you were to say in your present state of mind you would live most bitterly to repent. You don't know what you really think; you don't know what you really feel. You don't know your own mind; you don't do justice to Miss Garland. All this is impossible here, under these circumstances. You 're blind, you 're deaf, you 're under a spell. To break it, you must leave Rome."

"Leave Rome! Rome was never so dear to me."

"That 's not of the smallest consequence. Leave it instantly."

"And where shall I go?"

"Go to some place where you may be alone with your mother and Miss Garland."

"Alone? You will not come?"

"Oh, if you desire it, I will come."

Roderick inclining his head a little, looked at his friend askance. "I don't understand you," he said; "I wish you liked Miss Garland either a little less, or a little more."

Rowland felt himself coloring, but he paid no heed to Roderick's speech. "You ask me to help you," he went on. "On these present conditions I can do nothing. But if you will postpone all decision as to the continuance of your engagement a couple of months longer, and meanwhile leave Rome, leave Italy, I will do what I can to 'help you,' as you say, in the event of your still wishing to break it."

"I must do without your help then! Your conditions are impossible. I will leave Rome at the time I have always intended—at the end of June. My rooms and my mother's are taken till then; all my arrangements are made accordingly. Then, I will depart; not before."

"You are not frank," said Rowland. "Your real reason for staying has nothing to do with your rooms."

Roderick's face betrayed neither embarrassment nor resentment. "If I 'm not frank, it 's for the first time in my life. Since you know so much about my real reason, let me hear it! No, stop!" he suddenly added, "I won't trouble you. You are right, I have a motive. On the twenty-fourth of June Miss Light is to be married. I take an immense interest in all that concerns her, and I wish to be present at her wedding."

"But you said the other day at Saint Peter's that it was by no means certain her marriage would take place."

"Apparently I was wrong: the invitations, I am told, are going out."

Rowland felt that it would be utterly vain to remonstrate, and that the only thing for him was to make the best terms possible. "If I offer no further opposition to your waiting for Miss Light's marriage," he said, "will you promise, meanwhile and afterwards, for a certain period, to defer to my judgment—to say nothing that may be a cause of suffering to Miss Garland?"

"For a certain period? What period?" Roderick demanded.

"Ah, don't drive so close a bargain! Don't you understand that I have taken you away from her, that I suffer in every nerve in consequence, and that I must do what I can to re-store you?"

"Do what you can, then," said Roderick gravely, putting out his hand. "Do what you can!" His tone and his hand-shake seemed to constitute a promise, and upon this they parted.

Roderick's bust of his mother, whether or no it was a dis-charge of what he called the filial debt, was at least a most admirable production. Rowland, at the time it was finished, met Gloriani one evening, and this unscrupulous genius im-mediately began to ask questions about it. "I am told our high-flying friend has come down," he said. "He has been doing a queer little old woman."

"A queer little old woman!" Rowland exclaimed. "My dear sir, she is Hudson's mother."

"All the more reason for her being queer! It is a bust for terra-cotta, eh?"

"By no means; it is for marble."

"That's a pity. It was described to me as a charming piece of quaintness: a little demure, thin-lipped old lady, with her head on one side, and the prettiest wrinkles in the world—a sort of fairy godmother."

"Go and see it, and judge for yourself," said Rowland.

"No, I see I shall be disappointed. It's quite the other thing, the sort of thing they put into the campo-santos. I wish that boy would listen to me an hour!"

But a day or two later Rowland met him again in the street, and, as they were near, proposed they should adjourn to Roderick's studio. He consented, and on entering they found the young master. Roderick's demeanor to Gloriani was never conciliatory, and on this occasion supreme indiffer-ence was apparently all he had to offer. But Gloriani, like a genuine connoisseur, cared nothing for his manners; he cared only for his skill. In the bust of Mrs. Hudson there was some-thing almost touching; it was an exquisite example of a ruling sense of beauty. The poor lady's small, neat, timorous face had certainly no great character, but Roderick had repro-duced its sweetness, its mildness, its minuteness, its still ma-ternal passion, with the most unerring art. It was perfectly unflattered, and yet admirably tender; it was the poetry of

fidelity. Gloriani stood looking at it a long time most intently.
Roderick wandered away into the neighboring room.

"I give it up!" said the sculptor at last. "I don't understand
it."

"But you like it?" said Rowland.

"Like it? It 's a pearl of pearls. Tell me this," he added: "is
he very fond of his mother; is he a very good son?" And he
gave Rowland a sharp look.

"Why, she adores him," said Rowland, smiling.

"That 's not an answer! But it 's none of my business. Only
if I, in his place, being suspected of having—what shall I call
it?—a cold heart, managed to do that piece of work, oh, oh!
I should be called a pretty lot of names. Charlatan, *poseur*,
arrangeur! But he can do as he chooses! My dear young man,
I know you don't like me," he went on, as Roderick came
back. "It 's a pity; you are strong enough not to care about
me at all. You are very strong."

"Not at all," said Roderick curtly. "I am very weak!"

"I told you last year that you would n't keep it up. I was a
great ass. You will!"

"I beg your pardon—I won't!" retorted Roderick.

"Though I 'm a great ass, all the same, eh? Well, call me
what you will, so long as you turn out this sort of thing! I
don't suppose it makes any particular difference, but I should
like to say now I believe in you."

Roderick stood looking at him for a moment with a
strange hardness in his face. It flushed slowly, and two glittering, angry tears filled his eyes. It was the first time Rowland had ever seen them there; he saw them but once again.
Poor Gloriani, he was sure, had never in his life spoken with
less of irony; but to Roderick there was evidently a sense of
mockery in his profession of faith. He turned away with a
muttered, passionate imprecation. Gloriani was accustomed
to deal with complex problems, but this time he was hopelessly puzzled. "What 's the matter with him?" he asked,
simply.

Rowland gave a sad smile, and touched his forehead. "Genius, I suppose."

Gloriani sent another parting, lingering look at the bust of
Mrs. Hudson. "Well, it 's deuced perfect, it 's deuced simple;

I *do* believe in him!" he said. "But I 'm glad I 'm not a genius. It makes," he added with a laugh, as he looked for Roderick to wave him good-by, and saw his back still turned, "it makes a more sociable studio."

Rowland had purchased, as he supposed, temporary tranquillity for Mary Garland; but his own humor in these days was not especially peaceful. He was attempting, in a certain sense, to lead the ideal life, and he found it, at the least, not easy. The days passed, but brought with them no official invitation to Miss Light's wedding. He occasionally met her, and he occasionally met Prince Casamassima; but always separately, never together. They were apparently taking their happiness in the inexpressive manner proper to people of social eminence. Rowland continued to see Madame Grandoni, for whom he felt a confirmed affection. He had always talked to her with frankness, but now he made her a confidant of all his hidden dejection. Roderick and Roderick's concerns had been a common theme with him, and it was in the natural course to talk of Mrs. Hudson's arrival and Miss Garland's fine smile. Madame Grandoni was an intelligent listener, and she lost no time in putting his case for him in a nutshell. "At one moment you tell me the girl is plain," she said; "the next you tell me she 's pretty. I will invite them, and I shall see for myself. But one thing is very clear: you are in love with her."

Rowland, for all answer, glanced round to see that no one heard her.

"More than that," she added, "you have been in love with her these two years. There was that certain something about you! . . . . I knew you were a mild, sweet fellow, but you had a touch of it more than was natural. Why did n't you tell me at once? You would have saved me a great deal of trouble. And poor Augusta Blanchard too!" And herewith Madame Grandoni communicated a pertinent fact: Augusta Blanchard and Mr. Leavenworth were going to make a match. The young lady had been staying for a month at Albano, and Mr. Leavenworth had been dancing attendance. The event was a matter of course. Rowland, who had been lately reproaching himself with a failure of attention to Miss Blanchard's doings, made some such observation.

"But you did not find it so!" cried his hostess. "It was a

matter of course, perhaps, that Mr. Leavenworth, who seems to be going about Europe with the sole view of picking up furniture for his 'home,' as he calls it, should think Miss Blanchard a very handsome piece; but it was not a matter of course—or it need n't have been—that she should be willing to become a sort of superior table-ornament. She would have accepted you if you had tried."

"You are supposing the insupposable," said Rowland. "She never gave me a particle of encouragement."

"What would you have had her do? The poor girl did her best, and I am sure that when she accepted Mr. Leavenworth she thought of you."

"She thought of the pleasure her marriage would give me."

"Ay, pleasure indeed! She is a thoroughly good girl, but she has her little grain of feminine spite, like the rest. Well, he 's richer than you, and she will have what she wants; but before I forgive you I must wait and see this new arrival— what do you call her?—Miss Garland. If I like her, I will forgive you; if I don't, I shall always bear you a grudge."

Rowland answered that he was sorry to forfeit any advantage she might offer him, but that his exculpatory passion for Miss Garland was a figment of her fancy. Miss Garland was engaged to another man, and he himself had no claims.

"Well, then," said Madame Grandoni, "if I like her, we 'll have it that you ought to be in love with her. If you fail in this, it will be a double misdemeanor. The man she 's engaged to does n't care a straw for her. Leave me alone and I 'll tell her what I think of *you*."

As to Christina Light's marriage, Madame Grandoni could make no definite statement. The young girl, of late, had made her several flying visits, in the intervals of the usual pre-matrimonial shopping and dress-fitting; she had spoken of the event with a toss of her head, as a matter which, with a wise old friend who viewed things in their essence, she need not pretend to treat as a solemnity. It was for Prince Casamassima to do that. "It is what they call a marriage of reason," she once said. "That means, you know, a marriage of madness!"

"What have you said in the way of advice?" Rowland asked.

"Very little, but that little has favored the prince. I know nothing of the mysteries of the young lady's heart. It may be a gold-mine, but at any rate it 's a mine, and it 's a long journey down into it. But the marriage in itself is an excellent marriage. It 's not only brilliant, but it 's safe. I think Christina is quite capable of making it a means of misery; but there is no position that would be sacred to her. Casamassima is an irreproachable young man; there is nothing against him but that he is a prince. It is not often, I fancy, that a prince has been put through his paces at this rate. No one knows the wedding-day; the cards of invitation have been printed half a dozen times over, with a different date; each time Christina has destroyed them. There are people in Rome who are furious at the delay; they want to get away; they are in a dreadful fright about the fever, but they are dying to see the wedding, and if the day were fixed, they would make their arrangements to wait for it. I think it very possible that after having kept them a month and produced a dozen cases of malaria, Christina will be married at midnight by an old friar, with simply the legal witnesses."

"It is true, then, that she has become a Catholic?"

"So she tells me. One day she got up in the depths of despair; at her wit's end, I suppose, in other words, for a new sensation. Suddenly it occurred to her that the Catholic church might after all hold the key, might give her what she wanted! She sent for a priest; he happened to be a clever man, and he contrived to interest her. She put on a black dress and a black lace veil, and looking handsomer than ever she rustled into the Catholic church. The prince, who is very devout, and who had her heresy sorely on his conscience, was thrown into an ecstasy. May she never have a caprice that pleases him less!"

Rowland had already asked Madame Grandoni what, to her perception, was the present state of matters between Christina and Roderick; and he now repeated his question with some earnestness of apprehension. "The girl is so deucedly dramatic," he said, "that I don't know what *coup de théâtre* she may have in store for us. Such a stroke was her turning Catholic; such a stroke would be her some day making her courtesy to a disappointed world as Princess Casamassima, married at midnight, in her bonnet. She might

do—she may do—something that would make even more
starers! I 'm prepared for anything."

"You mean that she might elope with your sculptor, eh?"

"I 'm prepared for anything!"

"Do you mean that he 's ready?"

"Do you think that *she* is?"

"They 're a precious pair! I think this. You by no means
exhaust the subject when you say that Christina is dramatic.
It 's my belief that in the course of her life she will do a
certain number of things from pure disinterested passion.
She 's immeasurably proud, and if that is often a fault in a
virtuous person, it may be a merit in a vicious one. She needs
to think well of herself; she knows a fine character, easily,
when she meets one; she hates to suffer by comparison, even
though the comparison is made by herself alone; and when
the estimate she may have made of herself grows vague, she
needs to do something to give it definite, impressive form.
What she will do in such a case will be better or worse, according to her opportunity; but I imagine it will generally be
something that will drive her mother to despair; something
of the sort usually termed 'unworldly.' "

Rowland, as he was taking his leave, after some further exchange of opinions, rendered Miss Light the tribute of a
deeply meditative sigh. "She has bothered me half to death,"
he said, "but somehow I can't manage, as I ought, to hate
her. I admire her, half the time, and a good part of the rest I
pity her."

"I think I most pity her!" said Madame Grandoni.

This enlightened woman came the next day to call upon
the two ladies from Northampton. She carried their shy affections by storm, and made them promise to drink tea with her
on the evening of the morrow. Her visit was an era in the life
of poor Mrs. Hudson, who did nothing but make sudden
desultory allusions to her, for the next thirty-six hours. "To
think of her being a foreigner!" she would exclaim, after
much intent reflection, over her knitting; "she speaks so beautifully!" Then in a little while, "She was n't so much dressed
as you might have expected. Did you notice how easy it was
in the waist? I wonder if that 's the fashion?" Or, "She 's very
old to wear a hat; I should never dare to wear a hat!" Or,

"Did you notice her hands?—very pretty hands for such a stout person. A great many rings, but nothing very handsome. I suppose they are hereditary." Or, "She 's certainly not handsome, but she 's very sweet-looking. I wonder why she does n't have something done to her teeth." Rowland also received a summons to Madame Grandoni's tea-drinking, and went betimes, as he had been requested. He was eagerly desirous to lend his mute applause to Mary Garland's début in the Roman social world. The two ladies had arrived, with Roderick, silent and careless, in attendance. Miss Blanchard was also present, escorted by Mr. Leavenworth, and the party was completed by a dozen artists of both sexes and various nationalities. It was a friendly and easy assembly, like all Madame Grandoni's parties, and in the course of the evening there was some excellent music. People played and sang for Madame Grandoni, on easy terms, who, elsewhere, were not to be heard for the asking. She was herself a superior musician, and singers found it a privilege to perform to her accompaniment. Rowland talked to various persons, but for the first time in his life his attention visibly wandered; he could not keep his eyes off Mary Garland. Madame Grandoni had said that he sometimes spoke of her as pretty and sometimes as plain; to-night, if he had had occasion to describe her appearance, he would have called her beautiful. She was dressed more than he had ever seen her; it was becoming, and gave her a deeper color and an ampler presence. Two or three persons were introduced to her who were apparently witty people, for she sat listening to them with her brilliant natural smile. Rowland, from an opposite corner, reflected that he had never varied in his appreciation of Miss Blanchard's classic contour, but that somehow, to-night, it impressed him hardly more than an effigy stamped upon a coin of low value. Roderick could not be accused of rancor, for he had approached Mr. Leavenworth with unstudied familiarity, and, lounging against the wall, with hands in pockets, was discoursing to him with candid serenity. Now that he had done him an impertinence, he evidently found him less intolerable. Mr. Leavenworth stood stirring his tea and silently opening and shutting his mouth, without looking at the young sculptor, like a large, drowsy dog snapping at flies. Rowland had

found it disagreeable to be told Miss Blanchard would have
married him for the asking, and he would have felt some embarrassment in going to speak to her if his modesty had not
found incredulity so easy. The facile side of a union with Miss
Blanchard had never been present to his mind; it had struck
him as a thing, in all ways, to be compassed with a great
effort. He had half an hour's talk with her; a farewell talk, as
it seemed to him—a farewell not to a real illusion, but to the
idea that for him, in that matter, there could ever be an acceptable *pis-aller*. He congratulated Miss Blanchard upon her
engagement, and she received his compliment with a touch of
primness. But she was always a trifle prim, even when she was
quoting Mrs. Browning and George Sand, and this harmless
defect did not prevent her responding on this occasion that
Mr. Leavenworth had a "glorious heart." Rowland wished to
manifest an extreme regard, but toward the end of the talk
his zeal relaxed, and he fell a-thinking that a certain natural
ease in a woman was the most delightful thing in the world.
There was Christina Light, who had too much, and here was
Miss Blanchard, who had too little, and there was Mary Garland (in whom the quality was wholly uncultivated), who had
just the right amount.

He went to Madame Grandoni in an adjoining room,
where she was pouring out tea.

"I will make you an excellent cup," she said, "because I
have forgiven you."

He looked at her, answering nothing; but he swallowed his
tea with great gusto, and a slight deepening of his color; by
all of which one would have known that he was gratified. In
a moment he intimated that, in so far as he had sinned, he
had forgiven himself.

"She is a lovely girl," said Madame Grandoni. "There is a
great deal there. I have taken a great fancy to her, and she
must let me make a friend of her."

"She is very plain," said Rowland, slowly, "very simple,
very ignorant."

"Which, being interpreted, means, 'She is very handsome,
very subtle, and has read hundreds of volumes on winter evenings in the country.' "

"You are a veritable sorceress," cried Rowland; "you

frighten me away!" As he was turning to leave her, there rose above the hum of voices in the drawing-room the sharp, grotesque note of a barking dog. Their eyes met in a glance of intelligence.

"There is the sorceress!" said Madame Grandoni. "The sorceress and her necromantic poodle!" And she hastened back to the post of hospitality.

Rowland followed her, and found Christina Light standing in the middle of the drawing-room, and looking about in perplexity. Her poodle, sitting on his haunches and gazing at the company, had apparently been expressing a sympathetic displeasure at the absence of a welcome. But in a moment Madame Grandoni had come to the young girl's relief, and Christina had tenderly kissed her.

"I had no idea," said Christina, surveying the assembly, "that you had such a lot of grand people, or I would not have come in. The servant said nothing; he took me for an *invitée*. I came to spend a neighborly half-hour; you know I have n't many left! It was too dismally dreary at home. I hoped I should find you alone, and I brought Stenterello to play with the cat. I don't know that if I had known about all this I would have dared to come in; but since I 've stumbled into the midst of it, I beg you 'll let me stay. I am not dressed, but am I very hideous? I will sit in a corner and no one will notice me. My dear, sweet lady, *do* let me stay. Pray, why did n't you ask me? I never have been to a little party like this. They must be very charming. No dancing—tea and conversation? No tea, thank you; but if you could spare a biscuit for Stenterello; a sweet biscuit, please. Really, why did n't you ask me? Do you have these things often? Madame Grandoni, it 's very unkind!" And the young girl, who had delivered herself of the foregoing succession of sentences in her usual low, cool, penetrating voice, uttered these last words with a certain tremor of feeling. "I see," she went on, "I do very well for balls and great banquets, but when people wish to have a cosy, friendly, comfortable evening, they leave me out, with the big flower-pots and the gilt candlesticks."

"I 'm sure you 're welcome to stay, my dear," said Madame Grandoni, "and at the risk of displeasing you I must confess that if I did n't invite you, it was because you 're too grand.

Your dress will do very well, with its fifty flounces, and there
is no need of your going into a corner. Indeed, since you 're
here, I propose to have the glory of it. You must remain
where my people can see you."

"They are evidently determined to do that by the way they
stare. Do they think I intend to dance a *tarantella*? Who are
they all; do I know them?" And lingering in the middle of
the room, with her arm passed into Madame Grandoni's, she
let her eyes wander slowly from group to group. They were
of course observing her. Standing in the little circle of lamp-
light, with the hood of an Eastern burnous, shot with silver
threads, falling back from her beautiful head, one hand gathering together its voluminous, shimmering folds, and the
other playing with the silken top-knot on the uplifted head of
her poodle, she was a figure of radiant picturesqueness. She
seemed to be a sort of extemporized *tableau vivant*. Rowland's position made it becoming for him to speak to her
without delay. As she looked at him he saw that, judging by
the light of her beautiful eyes, she was in a humor of which
she had not yet treated him to a specimen. In a simpler person he would have called it exquisite kindness; but in this
young lady's deportment the flower was one thing and the
perfume another. "Tell me about these people," she said to
him. "I had no idea there were so many people in Rome I
had not seen. What are they all talking about? It 's all beyond
me, I suppose. There is Miss Blanchard, sitting as usual in
profile against a dark object. She is like a head on a postage-
stamp. And there is that nice little old lady in black, Mrs.
Hudson. What a dear little woman for a mother! *Comme elle
est proprette!* And the other, the *fiancée*, of course she 's here.
Ah, I see!" She paused; she was looking intently at Miss Garland. Rowland measured the intentness of her glance, and
suddenly acquired a firm conviction. "I should like so much
to know her!" she said, turning to Madame Grandoni. "She
has a charming face; I am sure she 's an angel. I wish very
much you would introduce me. No, on second thoughts, I
had rather you did n't. I will speak to her bravely myself, as a
friend of her cousin." Madame Grandoni and Rowland exchanged glances of baffled conjecture, and Christina flung off
her burnous, crumpled it together, and, with uplifted finger,

tossing it into a corner, gave it in charge to her poodle. He stationed himself upon it, on his haunches, with upright vigilance. Christina crossed the room with the step and smile of a ministering angel, and introduced herself to Mary Garland. She had once told Rowland that she would show him, some day, how gracious her manners could be; she was now redeeming her promise. Rowland, watching her, saw Mary Garland rise slowly, in response to her greeting, and look at her with serious deep-gazing eyes. The almost dramatic opposition of these two keenly interesting girls touched Rowland with a nameless apprehension, and after a moment he preferred to turn away. In doing so he noticed Roderick. The young sculptor was standing planted on the train of a lady's dress, gazing across at Christina's movements with undisguised earnestness. There were several more pieces of music; Rowland sat in a corner and listened to them. When they were over, several people began to take their leave, Mrs. Hudson among the number. Rowland saw her come up to Madame Grandoni, clinging shyly to Mary Garland's arm. Miss Garland had a brilliant eye and a deep color in her cheek. The two ladies looked about for Roderick, but Roderick had his back turned. He had approached Christina, who, with an absent air, was sitting alone, where she had taken her place near Miss Garland, looking at the guests pass out of the room. Christina's eye, like Miss Garland's, was bright, but her cheek was pale. Hearing Roderick's voice, she looked up at him sharply; then silently, with a single quick gesture, motioned him away. He obeyed her, and came and joined his mother in bidding good night to Madame Grandoni. Christina, in a moment, met Rowland's glance, and immediately beckoned him to come to her. He was familiar with her spontaneity of movement, and was scarcely surprised. She made a place for him on the sofa beside her; he wondered what was coming now. He was not sure it was not a mere fancy, but it seemed to him that he had never seen her look just as she was looking then. It was a humble, touching, appealing look, and it threw into wonderful relief the nobleness of her beauty. "How many more metamorphoses," he asked himself, "am I to be treated to before we have done?"

"I want to tell you," said Christina. "I have taken an immense fancy to Miss Garland. Are n't you glad?"

"Delighted!" exclaimed poor Rowland.

"Ah, you don't believe it," she said with soft dignity.

"Is it so hard to believe?"

"Not that people in general should admire her, but that *I* should. But I want to tell you; I want to tell some one, and I can't tell Miss Garland herself. She thinks me already a horrid false creature, and if I were to express to her frankly what I think of her, I should simply disgust her. She would be quite right; she has repose, and from that point of view I and my doings must seem monstrous. Unfortunately, I have n't repose. I am trembling now; if I could ask you to feel my arm, you would see! But I want to tell you that I admire Miss Garland more than any of the people who call themselves her friends—except of course you. Oh, I know that! To begin with, she is extremely handsome, and she does n't know it."

"She is not generally thought handsome," said Rowland.

"Evidently! That 's the vulgarity of the human mind. Her head has great character, great natural style. If a woman is not to be a supreme beauty in the regular way, she will choose, if she 's wise, to look like that. She 'll not be thought pretty by people in general, and desecrated, as she passes, by the stare of every vile wretch who chooses to thrust his nose under her bonnet; but a certain number of superior people will find it one of the delightful things of life to look at her. That lot is as good as another! Then she has a beautiful character!"

"You found that out soon!" said Rowland, smiling.

"How long did it take *you*? I found it out before I ever spoke to her. I met her the other day in Saint Peter's; I knew it then. I knew it—do you want to know how long I have known it?"

"Really," said Rowland, "I did n't mean to cross-examine you."

"Do you remember mamma's ball in December? We had some talk and you then mentioned her—not by name. You said but three words, but I saw you admired her, and I knew that if you admired her she must have a beautiful character.

That 's what you require!"

"Upon my word," cried Rowland, "you make three words go very far!"

"Oh, Mr. Hudson has also spoken of her."

"Ah, that 's better!" said Rowland.

"I don't know; he does n't like her."

"Did he tell you so?" The question left Rowland's lips before he could stay it, which he would have done on a moment's reflection.

Christina looked at him intently. "No!" she said at last. "That would have been dishonorable, would n't it? But I know it from my knowledge of him. He does n't like perfection; he is not bent upon being *safe*, in his likings; he 's willing to risk something! Poor fellow, he risks too much!"

Rowland was silent; he did not care for the thrust; but he was profoundly mystified. Christina beckoned to her poodle, and the dog marched stiffly across to her. She gave a loving twist to his rose-colored top-knot, and bade him go and fetch her burnous. He obeyed, gathered it up in his teeth, and returned with great solemnity, dragging it along the floor.

"I do her justice. I do her full justice," she went on, with soft earnestness. "I like to say that, I like to be able to say it. She 's full of intelligence and courage and devotion. She does n't do me a grain of justice; but that is no harm. There is something so fine in the aversions of a good woman!"

"If you would give Miss Garland a chance," said Rowland, "I am sure she would be glad to be your friend."

"What do you mean by a chance? She has only to take it. I told her I liked her immensely, and she frowned as if I had said something disgusting. She looks very handsome when she frowns." Christina rose, with these words, and began to gather her mantle about her. "I don't often like women," she went on. "In fact I generally detest them. But I should like to know Miss Garland well. I should like to have a friendship with her; I have never had one; they must be very delightful. But I shan't have one now, either—not if she can help it! Ask her what she thinks of me; see what she will say. I don't want to know; keep it to yourself. It 's too sad. So we go through life. It 's fatality—that 's what they call it, is n't it? We please the people we don't care for, we displease those we do! But I appreciate her, I do her justice; that 's the more important thing. It 's because I have imagination. She has none. Never mind; it 's her only fault. I do her justice; I understand very well." She kept softly murmuring and looking about for Madame Grandoni. She saw the good lady near the door, and put out her hand to Rowland for good night. She held his hand an instant, fixing him with her eyes, the living splendor of which, at this moment, was something transcendent. "Yes, I do her justice," she repeated. "And you do her more; you would lay down your life for her." With this she turned away, and before he could answer, she left him. She went to Madame Grandoni, grasped her two hands, and held out her forehead to be kissed. The next moment she was gone.

"That was a happy accident!" said Madame Grandoni. "She never looked so beautiful, and she made my little party brilliant."

"Beautiful, verily!" Rowland answered. "But it was no accident."

"What was it, then?"

"It was a plan. She wished to see Miss Garland. She knew she was to be here."

"How so?"

"By Roderick, evidently."

"And why did she wish to see Miss Garland?"

"Heaven knows! I give it up!"

"Ah, the wicked girl!" murmured Madame Grandoni.

"No," said Rowland; "don't say that now. She 's too beautiful."

"Oh, you men! The best of you!"

"Well, then," cried Rowland, "she 's too good!"

The opportunity presenting itself the next day, he failed not, as you may imagine, to ask Mary Garland what she thought of Miss Light. It was a Saturday afternoon, the time at which the beautiful marbles of the Villa Borghese are thrown open to the public. Mary had told him that Roderick had promised to take her to see them, with his mother, and he joined the party in the splendid Casino. The warm weather had left so few strangers in Rome that they had the place almost to themselves. Mrs. Hudson had confessed to an invincible fear of treading, even with the help of her son's arm, the polished marble floors, and was sitting patiently on a stool, with folded hands, looking shyly, here and there, at the undraped paganism around her. Roderick had sauntered off alone, with an irritated brow, which seemed to betray the conflict between the instinct of observation and the perplexities of circumstance. Miss Garland was wandering in another direction, and though she was consulting her catalogue, Rowland fancied it was from habit; she too was preoccupied. He joined her, and she presently sat down on a divan, rather wearily, and closed her Murray. Then he asked her abruptly how Christina had pleased her.

She started the least bit at the question, and he felt that she had been thinking of Christina.

"I don't like her!" she said with decision.

"What do you think of her?"

"I think she 's false." This was said without petulance or bitterness, but with a very positive air.

"But she wished to please you; she tried," Rowland rejoined, in a moment.

"I think not. She wished to please herself!"

Rowland felt himself at liberty to say no more. No allusion to Christina had passed between them since the day they met her at Saint Peter's, but he knew that she knew, by that infallible sixth sense of a woman who loves, that this strange, beautiful girl had the power to injure her. To what extent she had the will, Mary was uncertain; but last night's interview, apparently, had not reassured her. It was, under these circumstances, equally unbecoming for Rowland either to depreciate or to defend Christina, and he had to content himself with simply having verified the girl's own assurance that she had made a bad impression. He tried to talk of indifferent matters—about the statues and the frescoes; but to-day, plainly, æsthetic curiosity, with Miss Garland, had folded its wings. Curiosity of another sort had taken its place. Mary was longing, he was sure, to question him about Christina; but she found a dozen reasons for hesitating. Her questions would imply that Roderick had not treated her with confidence, for information on this point should properly have come from him. They would imply that she was jealous, and to betray her jealousy was intolerable to her pride. For some minutes, as she sat scratching the brilliant pavement with the point of her umbrella, it was to be supposed that her pride and her anxiety held an earnest debate. At last anxiety won.

"A propos of Miss Light," she asked, "do you know her well?"

"I can hardly say that. But I have seen her repeatedly."

"Do you like her?"

"Yes and no. I think I am sorry for her."

Mary had spoken with her eyes on the pavement. At this she looked up. "Sorry for her? Why?"

"Well—she is unhappy."

"What are her misfortunes?"

"Well—she has a horrible mother, and she has had a most injurious education."

For a moment Miss Garland was silent. Then, "Is n't she very beautiful?" she asked.

"Don't you think so?"

"That 's measured by what men think! She is extremely clever, too."

"Oh, incontestably."

"She has beautiful dresses."

"Yes, any number of them."

"And beautiful manners."

"Yes—sometimes."

"And plenty of money."

"Money enough, apparently."

"And she receives great admiration."

"Very true."

"And she is to marry a prince."

"So they say."

Miss Garland rose and turned to rejoin her companions, commenting these admissions with a pregnant silence. "Poor Miss Light!" she said at last, simply. And in this it seemed to Rowland there was a touch of bitterness.

Very late on the following evening his servant brought him the card of a visitor. He was surprised at a visit at such an hour, but it may be said that when he read the inscription— Cavaliere Giuseppe Giacosa—his surprise declined. He had

had an unformulated conviction that there was to be a sequel to the apparition at Madame Grandoni's; the Cavaliere had come to usher it in.

He had come, evidently, on a portentous errand. He was as pale as ashes and prodigiously serious; his little cold black eye had grown ardent, and he had left his caressing smile at home. He saluted Rowland, however, with his usual obsequious bow.

"You have more than once done me the honor to invite me to call upon you," he said. "I am ashamed of my long delay, and I can only say to you, frankly, that my time this winter has not been my own." Rowland assented, ungrudgingly fumbled for the Italian correlative of the adage "Better late than never," begged him to be seated, and offered him a cigar. The Cavaliere sniffed imperceptibly the fragrant weed, and then declared that, if his kind host would allow him, he would reserve it for consumption at another time. He apparently desired to intimate that the solemnity of his errand left him no breath for idle smoke-puffings. Rowland stayed himself, just in time, from an enthusiastic offer of a dozen more cigars, and, as he watched the Cavaliere stow his treasure tenderly away in his pocket-book, reflected that only an Italian could go through such a performance with uncompromised dignity. "I must confess," the little old man resumed, "that even now I come on business not of my own—or my own, at least, only in a secondary sense. I have been dispatched as an ambassador, an envoy extraordinary, I may say, by my dear friend Mrs. Light."

"If I can in any way be of service to Mrs. Light, I shall be happy," Rowland said.

"Well then, dear sir, Casa Light is in commotion. The signora is in trouble—in terrible trouble." For a moment Rowland expected to hear that the signora's trouble was of a nature that a loan of five thousand francs would assuage. But the Cavaliere continued: "Miss Light has committed a great crime; she has plunged a dagger into the heart of her mother."

"A dagger!" cried Rowland.

The Cavaliere patted the air an instant with his finger-tips. "I speak figuratively. She has broken off her marriage."

"Broken it off?"

"Short! She has turned the prince from the door." And the Cavaliere, when he had made this announcement, folded his arms and bent upon Rowland his intense, inscrutable gaze. It seemed to Rowland that he detected in the polished depths of it a sort of fantastic gleam of irony or of triumph; but superficially, at least, Giacosa did nothing to discredit his character as a presumably sympathetic representative of Mrs. Light's affliction.

Rowland heard his news with a kind of fierce disgust; it seemed the sinister counterpart of Christina's preternatural mildness at Madame Grandoni's tea-party. She had been too plausible to be honest. Without being able to trace the connection, he yet instinctively associated her present rebellion with her meeting with Mary Garland. If she had not seen Mary, she would have let things stand. It was monstrous to suppose that she could have sacrificed so brilliant a fortune to a mere movement of jealousy, to a refined instinct of feminine deviltry, to a desire to frighten poor Mary from her security by again appearing in the field. Yet Rowland remembered his first impression of her; she was "dangerous," and she had measured in each direction the perturbing effect of her rupture. She was smiling her sweetest smile at it! For half an hour Rowland simply detested her, and longed to denounce her to her face. Of course all he could say to Giacosa was that he was extremely sorry. "But I am not surprised," he added.

"You are not surprised?"

"With Miss Light everything is possible. Is n't that true?"

Another ripple seemed to play for an instant in the current of the old man's irony, but he waived response. "It was a magnificent marriage," he said, solemnly. "I do not respect many people, but I respect Prince Casamassima."

"I should judge him indeed to be a very honorable young man," said Rowland.

"Eh, young as he is, he 's made of the old stuff. And now, perhaps he 's blowing his brains out. He is the last of his house; it 's a great house. But Miss Light will have put an end to it!"

"Is that the view she takes of it?" Rowland ventured to ask. This time, unmistakably, the Cavaliere smiled, but still in that very out-of-the-way place. "You have observed Miss Light with attention," he said, "and this brings me to my errand. Mrs. Light has a high opinion of your wisdom, of your kindness, and she has reason to believe you have influence with her daughter."

"I—with her daughter? Not a grain!"

"That is possibly your modesty. Mrs. Light believes that something may yet be done, and that Christina will listen to you. She begs you to come and see her before it is too late."

"But all this, my dear Cavaliere, is none of my business," Rowland objected. "I can't possibly, in such a matter, take the responsibility of advising Miss Light."

The Cavaliere fixed his eyes for a moment on the floor, in brief but intense reflection. Then looking up, "Unfortunately," he said, "she has no man near her whom she respects; she has no father!"

"And a fatally foolish mother!" Rowland gave himself the satisfaction of exclaiming.

The Cavaliere was so pale that he could not easily have turned paler; yet it seemed for a moment that his dead complexion blanched. "Eh, signore, such as she is, the mother appeals to you. A very handsome woman—disheveled, in tears, in despair, in dishabille!"

Rowland reflected a moment, not on the attractions of Mrs. Light under the circumstances thus indicated by the Cavaliere, but on the satisfaction he would take in accusing Christina to her face of having struck a cruel blow.

"I must add," said the Cavaliere, "that Mrs. Light desires also to speak to you on the subject of Mr. Hudson."

"She considers Mr. Hudson, then, connected with this step of her daughter's?"

"Intimately. He must be got out of Rome."

"Mrs. Light, then, must get an order from the Pope to remove him. It 's not in my power."

The Cavaliere assented, deferentially. "Mrs. Light is equally helpless. She would leave Rome to-morrow, but Christina will not budge. An order from the Pope would do nothing. A bull in council would do nothing."

"She 's a remarkable young lady," said Rowland, with bitterness.

But the Cavaliere rose and responded coldly, "She has a great spirit." And it seemed to Rowland that her great spirit, for mysterious reasons, gave him more pleasure than the distressing use she made of it gave him pain. He was on the point of charging him with his inconsistency, when Giacosa resumed: "But if the marriage can be saved, it must be saved. It 's a beautiful marriage. It *will* be saved."

"Notwithstanding Miss Light's great spirit to the contrary?"

"Miss Light, notwithstanding her great spirit, will call Prince Casamassima back."

"Heaven grant it!" said Rowland.

"I don't know," said the Cavaliere, solemnly, "that heaven will have much to do with it."

Rowland gave him a questioning look, but he laid his finger on his lips. And with Rowland's promise to present himself on the morrow at Casa Light, he shortly afterwards departed. He left Rowland revolving many things: Christina's magnanimity, Christina's perversity, Roderick's contingent fortune, Mary Garland's certain trouble, and the Cavaliere's own fine ambiguities.

Rowland's promise to the Cavaliere obliged him to withdraw from an excursion which he had arranged with the two ladies from Northampton. Before going to Casa Light he repaired in person to Mrs. Hudson's hotel, to make his excuses.

He found Roderick's mother sitting with tearful eyes, staring at an open note that lay in her lap. At the window sat Miss Garland, who turned her intense regard upon him as he came in. Mrs. Hudson quickly rose and came to him, holding out the note.

"In pity's name," she cried, "what is the matter with my boy? If he is ill, I entreat you to take me to him!"

"He is not ill, to my knowledge," said Rowland. "What have you there?"

"A note—a dreadful note. He tells us we are not to see him for a week. If I could only go to his room! But I am afraid, I am afraid!"

"I imagine there is no need of going to his room. What is the occasion, may I ask, of his note?"

"He was to have gone with us on this drive to—what is the place?—to Cervara. You know it was arranged yesterday morning. In the evening he was to have dined with us. But he never came, and this morning arrives this awful thing. Oh dear, I 'm so excited! Would you mind reading it?"

Rowland took the note and glanced at its half-dozen lines. "I cannot go to Cervara," they ran; "I have something else to do. This will occupy me perhaps for a week, and you 'll not see me. Don't miss me—learn not to miss me. R. H."

"Why, it means," Rowland commented, "that he has taken up a piece of work, and that it is all-absorbing. That 's very good news." This explanation was not sincere; but he had not the courage not to offer it as a stop-gap. But he found he needed all his courage to maintain it, for Miss Garland had left her place and approached him, formidably unsatisfied.

"He does not work in the evening," said Mrs. Hudson. "Can't he come for five minutes? Why does he write such a cruel, cold note to his poor mother—to poor Mary? What have we done that he acts so strangely? It 's this wicked, in-fectious, heathenish place!" And the poor lady's suppressed mistrust of the Eternal City broke out passionately. "Oh, dear Mr. Mallet," she went on, "I am sure he has the fever and he 's already delirious!"

"I am very sure it 's not that," said Miss Garland, with a certain dryness.

She was still looking at Rowland; his eyes met hers, and his own glance fell. This made him angry, and to carry off his confusion he pretended to be looking at the floor, in medita-tion. After all, what had *he* to be ashamed of? For a moment he was on the point of making a clean breast of it, of crying out, "Dearest friends, I abdicate: I can't help you!" But he checked himself; he felt so impatient to have his three words with Christina. He grasped his hat.

"I will see what it is!" he cried. And then he was glad he had not abdicated, for as he turned away he glanced again at Mary and saw that, though her eyes were full of trouble, they were not hard and accusing, but charged with appealing friendship.

He went straight to Roderick's apartment, deeming this, at an early hour, the safest place to seek him. He found him in his sitting-room, which had been closely darkened to keep out the heat. The carpets and rugs had been removed, the floor of speckled concrete was bare and lightly sprinkled with water. Here and there, over it, certain strongly perfumed flowers had been scattered. Roderick was lying on his divan in a white dressing-gown, staring up at the frescoed ceiling. The room was deliciously cool, and filled with the moist, sweet odor of the circumjacent roses and violets. All this seemed highly fantastic, and yet Rowland hardly felt surprised.

"Your mother was greatly alarmed at your note," he said, "and I came to satisfy myself that, as I believed, you are not ill." Roderick lay motionless, except that he slightly turned his head toward his friend. He was smelling a large white rose, and he continued to present it to his nose. In the darkness of the room he looked exceedingly pale, but his handsome eyes had an extraordinary brilliancy. He let them rest for some time on Rowland, lying there like a Buddhist in an intellectual swoon, whose perception should be slowly ebbing back to temporal matters. "Oh, I 'm not ill," he said at last. "I have never been better."

"Your note, nevertheless, and your absence," Rowland said, "have very naturally alarmed your mother. I advise you to go to her directly and reassure her."

"Go to her? Going to her would be worse than staying away. Staying away at present is a kindness." And he inhaled deeply his huge rose, looking up over it at Rowland. "My presence, in fact, would be indecent."

"Indecent? Pray explain."

"Why, you see, as regards Mary Garland. I am divinely happy! Does n't it strike you? You ought to agree with me. You wish me to spare her feelings; I spare them by staying away. Last night I heard something"—

"I heard it, too," said Rowland with brevity. "And it 's in honor of this piece of news that you have taken to your bed in this fashion?"

"Extremes meet! I can't get up for joy."

"May I inquire how you heard your joyous news?—from Miss Light herself?"

"By no means. It was brought me by her maid, who is in my service as well."

"Casamassima's loss, then, is to a certainty your gain?"

"I don't talk about certainties. I don't want to be arrogant, I don't want to offend the immortal gods. I 'm keeping very quiet, but I can't help being happy. I shall wait a while; I shall bide my time."

"And then?"

"And then that transcendent girl will confess to me that when she threw overboard her prince she remembered that I adored her!"

"I feel bound to tell you," was in the course of a moment Rowland's response to this speech, "that I am now on my way to Mrs. Light's."

"I congratulate you, I envy you!" Roderick murmured, imperturbably.

"Mrs. Light has sent for me to remonstrate with her daughter, with whom she has taken it into her head that I have influence. I don't know to what extent I shall remonstrate, but I give you notice I shall not speak in your interest."

Roderick looked at him a moment with a lazy radiance in his eyes. "Pray don't!" he simply answered.

"You deserve I should tell her you are a very shabby fellow."

"My dear Rowland, the comfort with you is that I can trust you. You 're incapable of doing anything disloyal."

"You mean to lie here, then, smelling your roses and nursing your visions, and leaving your mother and Miss Garland to fall ill with anxiety?"

"Can I go and flaunt my felicity in their faces? Wait till I get used to it a trifle. I have done them a palpable wrong, but I can at least forbear to add insult to injury. I may be an arrant fool, but, for the moment, I have taken it into my head to be prodigiously pleased. I should n't be able to conceal it; my pleasure would offend them; so I lock myself up as a dangerous character."

"Well, I can only say, 'May your pleasure never grow less, or your danger greater!' "

Roderick closed his eyes again, and sniffed at his rose. "God's will be done!"

On this Rowland left him and repaired directly to Mrs. Light's. This afflicted lady hurried forward to meet him.

Since the Cavaliere's report of her condition she had somewhat smoothed and trimmed the exuberance of her distress,
but she was evidently in extreme tribulation, and she clutched
Rowland by his two hands, as if, in the shipwreck of her
hopes, he were her single floating spar. Rowland greatly
pitied her, for there is something respectable in passionate
grief, even in a very bad cause; and as pity is akin to love, he
endured her rather better than he had done hitherto.

"Speak to her, plead with her, command her!" she cried,
pressing and shaking his hands. "She 'll not heed *us*, no more
than if we were a pair of clocks a-ticking. Perhaps she will
listen to you; she always liked you."

"She always disliked me," said Rowland. "But that does n't
matter now. I have come here simply because you sent
for me, not because I can help you. I cannot advise your
daughter."

"Oh, cruel, deadly man! You *must* advise her; you shan't
leave this house till you have advised her!" the poor woman
passionately retorted. "Look at me in my misery and refuse to
help me! Oh, you need n't be afraid, I know I 'm a fright, I
have n't an idea what I have on. If this goes on, we may both
as well turn scarecrows. If ever a woman was desperate, frantic, heart-broken, I am that woman. I can't begin to tell you.
To have nourished a serpent, sir, all these years! to have lavished one's self upon a viper that turns and stings her own
poor mother! To have toiled and prayed, to have pushed and
struggled, to have eaten the bread of bitterness, and all the
rest of it, sir—and at the end of all things to find myself at
this pass. It can't be, it 's too cruel, such things don't happen,
the Lord don't allow it. I 'm a religious woman, sir, and the
Lord knows all about me. With his own hand he had given
me his reward! I would have lain down in the dust and let
her walk over me; I would have given her the eyes out of my
head, if she had taken a fancy to them. No, she 's a cruel,
wicked, heartless, unnatural girl! I speak to you, Mr. Mallet,
in my dire distress, as to my *only* friend. There is n't a creature
here that I can look to—not one of them all that I have faith
in. But I always admired you. I said to Christina the first time
I saw you that there at last was a real gentleman. Come, don't
disappoint me now! I feel so terribly alone, you see; I feel

what a nasty, hard, heartless world it is that has come and devoured my dinners and danced to my fiddles, and yet that has n't a word to throw to me in my agony! Oh, the money, alone, that I have put into this thing, would melt the heart of a Turk!"

During this frenzied outbreak Rowland had had time to look round the room, and to see the Cavaliere sitting in a corner, like a major-domo on the divan of an antechamber, pale, rigid, and inscrutable.

"I have it at heart to tell you," Rowland said, "that if you consider my friend Hudson"—

Mrs. Light gave a toss of her head and hands. "Oh, it 's not that. She told me last night to bother her no longer with Hudson, Hudson! She did n't care a button for Hudson. I almost wish she did; then perhaps one might understand it. But she does n't care for anything in the wide world, except to do her own hard, wicked will, and to crush me and shame me with her cruelty."

"Ah, then," said Rowland, "I am as much at sea as you, and my presence here is an impertinence. I should like to say three words to Miss Light on my own account. But I must absolutely and inexorably decline to urge the cause of Prince Casamassima. This is simply impossible."

Mrs. Light burst into angry tears. "Because the poor boy is a prince, eh? because he 's of a great family, and has an income of millions, eh? That 's why you grudge him and hate him. I knew there were vulgar people of that way of feeling, but I did n't expect it of *you*. Make an effort, Mr. Mallet; rise to the occasion; forgive the poor fellow his splendor. Be just, be reasonable! It 's not *his* fault, and it 's not mine. He 's the best, the kindest young man in the world, and the most correct and moral and virtuous! If he were standing here in rags, I would say it all the same. The man first—the money afterwards: that was always my motto, and always will be. What do you take me for? Do you suppose I would give Christina to a *vicious* person? do you suppose I would sacrifice my precious child, little comfort as I have in her, to a man against whose character *one* word could be breathed? Casamassima is only too good, he 's a saint of saints, he 's stupidly good! There is n't such another in the length and breadth of Europe. What he has been through in this house, not a common peasant would endure. Christina has treated him as you would n't treat a dog. He has been insulted, outraged, persecuted! He has been driven hither and thither till he did n't know *where* he was. He has stood there where you stand—there, with his name and his millions and his devotion—as white as your handkerchief, with hot tears in his eyes, and me ready to go down on my knees to him and say, 'My own sweet prince, I could kiss the ground you tread on, but it is n't *decent* that I should allow you to enter my house and expose yourself to these horrors again.' And he would come back, and he would come back, and go through it all again, and take all that was given him, and only want the girl the more! I was his confidant; I know everything. He used to beg *my* forgiveness for Christina. What do you say to that? I seized him once and kissed him, I did! To find *that* and to find all the rest with it, and to believe it was a gift straight from the pitying angels of heaven, and then to see it dashed away before your eyes and to stand here helpless—oh, it 's a fate I hope *you* may ever be spared!"

"It would seem, then, that in the interest of Prince Casamassima himself I ought to refuse to interfere," said Rowland.

Mrs. Light looked at him hard, slowly drying her eyes. The intensity of her grief and anger gave her a kind of majesty, and Rowland, for the moment, felt ashamed of the ironical ring of his observation. "Very good, sir," she said. "I 'm sorry your heart is not so tender as your conscience. My compliments to your conscience! It must give you great happiness. Heaven help me! Since you fail us, we are indeed driven to the wall. But I have fought my own battles before, and I have never lost courage, and I don't see why I should break down now. Cavaliere, come here!"

Giacosa rose at her summons and advanced with his usual deferential alacrity. He shook hands with Rowland in silence.

"Mr. Mallet refuses to say a word," Mrs. Light went on. "Time presses, every moment is precious. Heaven knows what that poor boy may be doing. If at this moment a clever woman should get hold of him she might be as ugly as she pleased! It 's horrible to think of it."

The Cavaliere fixed his eyes on Rowland, and his look, which the night before had been singular, was now most extraordinary. There was a nameless force of anguish in it which seemed to grapple with the young man's reluctance, to plead, to entreat, and at the same time to be glazed over with a reflection of strange things.

Suddenly, though most vaguely, Rowland felt the presence of a new element in the drama that was going on before him. He looked from the Cavaliere to Mrs. Light, whose eyes were now quite dry, and were fixed in stony hardness on the floor.

"If you could bring yourself," the Cavaliere said, in a low, soft, caressing voice, "to address a few words of solemn remonstrance to Miss Light, you would, perhaps, do more for us than you know. You would save several persons a great pain. The dear signora, first, and then Christina herself. Christina in particular. Me too, I might take the liberty to add!"

There was, to Rowland, something acutely touching in this humble petition. He had always felt a sort of imaginative tenderness for poor little unexplained Giacosa, and these words seemed a supreme contortion of the mysterious obliquity of his life. All of a sudden, as he watched the Cavaliere, something occurred to him; it was something very odd, and it stayed his glance suddenly from again turning to Mrs. Light. His idea embarrassed him, and to carry off his embarrassment, he repeated that it was folly to suppose that *his* words would have any weight with Christina.

The Cavaliere stepped forward and laid two fingers on Rowland's breast. "Do you wish to know the truth? You are the only man whose words she remembers."

Rowland was going from surprise to surprise. "I will say what I can!" he said. By this time he had ventured to glance at Mrs. Light. She was looking at him askance, as if, upon this, she was suddenly mistrusting his motives.

"If you fail," she said sharply, "we have something else! But please to lose no time."

She had hardly spoken when the sound of a short, sharp growl caused the company to turn. Christina's fleecy poodle stood in the middle of the vast saloon, with his muzzle lowered, in pompous defiance of the three conspirators against the comfort of his mistress. This young lady's claims for him seemed justified; he was an animal of amazingly delicate instincts. He had preceded Christina as a sort of van-guard of defense, and she now slowly advanced from a neighboring room.

"You will be so good as to listen to Mr. Mallet," her mother said, in a terrible voice, "and to reflect carefully upon what he says. I suppose you will admit that *he* is disinterested. In half an hour you shall hear from me again!" And passing her hand through the Cavaliere's arm, she swept rapidly out of the room.

Christina looked hard at Rowland, but offered him no greeting. She was very pale, and, strangely enough, it at first seemed to Rowland that her beauty was in eclipse. But he very soon perceived that it had only changed its character, and that if it was a trifle less brilliant than usual, it was admirably touching and noble. The clouded light of her eyes, the magnificent gravity of her features, the conscious erectness of her head, might have belonged to a deposed sovereign or a condemned martyr. "Why have you come here at this time?" she asked.

"Your mother sent for me in pressing terms, and I was very glad to have an opportunity to speak to you."

"Have you come to help me, or to persecute me?"

"I have as little power to do one as I have desire to do the other. I came in great part to ask you a question. First, your decision is irrevocable?"

Christina's two hands had been hanging clasped in front of her; she separated them and flung them apart by an admirable gesture.

"Would you have done this if you had not seen Miss Garland?"

She looked at him with quickened attention; then suddenly, "This is interesting!" she cried. "Let us have it out." And she flung herself into a chair and pointed to another.

"You don't answer my question," Rowland said.

"You have no right, that I know of, to ask it. But it 's a very clever one; so clever that it deserves an answer. Very likely I would not."

"Last night, when I said that to myself, I was extremely angry," Rowland rejoined.

"Oh, dear, and you are not angry now?"

"I am less angry."

"How very stupid! But you can say something at least."

"If I were to say what is uppermost in my mind, I would say that, face to face with you, it is never possible to condemn you."

"*Perchè?*"

"You know, yourself! But I can at least say now what I felt last night. It seemed to me that you had consciously, cruelly dealt a blow at that poor girl. Do you understand?"

"Wait a moment!" And with her eyes fixed on him, she inclined her head on one side, meditatively. Then a cold, brilliant smile covered her face, and she made a gesture of negation. "I see your train of reasoning, but it 's quite wrong. I meant no harm to Miss Garland; I should be extremely sorry to make her suffer. Tell me you believe that."

This was said with ineffable candor. Rowland heard himself answering, "I believe it!"

"And yet, in a sense, your supposition was true," Christina continued. "I conceived, as I told you, a great admiration for Miss Garland, and I frankly confess I was jealous of her. What I envied her was simply her character! I said to myself, 'She, in my place, would n't marry Casamassima.' I could not help saying it, and I said it so often that I found a kind of inspiration in it. I hated the idea of being worse than she—of doing something that she would n't do. I might be bad by nature, but I need n't be by volition. The end of it all was that I found it impossible not to tell the prince that I was his very humble servant, but that I could not marry him."

"Are you sure it was only of Miss Garland's character that you were jealous, not of—not of"—

"Speak out, I beg you. We are talking philosophy!"

"Not of her affection for her cousin?"

"*Sure* is a good deal to ask. Still, I think I may say it! There are two reasons; one, at least, I can tell you: her affection has not a shadow's weight with Mr. Hudson! Why then should one fear it?"

"And what is the other reason?"

"Excuse me; that is my own affair."

Rowland was puzzled, baffled, charmed, inspired, almost, all at once. "I have promised your mother," he presently resumed, "to say something in favor of Prince Casamassima."

She shook her head sadly. "Prince Casamassima needs nothing that you can say for him. He is a magnificent *parti*. I know it perfectly."

"You know also of the extreme affliction of your mother?"

"Her affliction is demonstrative. She has been abusing me for the last twenty-four hours as if I were the vilest of the vile." To see Christina sit there in the purity of her beauty and say this, might have made one bow one's head with a kind of awe. "I have failed of respect to her at other times, but I have not done so now. Since we are talking philosophy," she pursued with a gentle smile, "I may say it 's a simple matter! I don't love him. Or rather, perhaps, since we are talking philosophy, I may say it 's not a simple matter. I spoke just now of inspiration. The inspiration has been great, but— I frankly confess it—the choice has been hard. Shall I tell you?" she demanded, with sudden ardor; "will you understand me? It was on the one side the world, the splendid, beautiful, powerful, interesting world. I know what that is; I have tasted of the cup, I know its sweetness. Ah, if I chose, if I let myself go, if I flung everything to the winds, the world and I would be famous friends! I know its merits, and I think, without vanity, it would see mine. You would see some fine things! I should like to be a princess, and I think I should be a very good one; I would play my part well. I am fond of luxury, I am fond of a great society, I am fond of being looked at. I am corrupt, corruptible, corruption! Ah, what a pity that could n't be, too! Mercy of Heaven!" There was a passionate tremor in her voice; she covered her face with her hands and sat motionless. Rowland saw that an intense agitation, hitherto successfully repressed, underlay her calmness, and he could easily believe that her battle had been fierce. She rose quickly and turned away, walked a few paces, and stopped. In a moment she was facing him again, with tears in her eyes and a flush in her cheeks. "But you need n't think I 'm afraid!" she said. "I have chosen, and I shall hold to it. I have something here, here, *here*!" and she patted her heart. "It 's my own. I shan't part with it. Is it what you call an ideal? I don't know; I don't care! It is brighter than the Casamassima diamonds!"

"You say that certain things are your own affair," Rowland presently rejoined; "but I must nevertheless make an attempt to learn what all this means—what it promises for my friend Hudson. Is there any hope for him?"

"This is a point I can't discuss with you minutely. I like him very much."

"Would you marry him if he were to ask you?"

"He has asked me."

"And if he asks again?"

"I shall marry no one just now."

"Roderick," said Rowland, "has great hopes."

"Does he know of my rupture with the prince?"

"He is making a great holiday of it."

Christina pulled her poodle towards her and began to smooth his silky fleece. "I like him very much," she repeated; "much more than I used to. Since you told me all that about him at Saint Cecilia's, I have felt a great friendship for him. There 's something very fine about him; he 's not afraid of anything. He is not afraid of failure; he is not afraid of ruin or death."

"Poor fellow!" said Rowland, bitterly; "he is fatally picturesque."

"Picturesque, yes; that 's what he is. I am very sorry for him."

"Your mother told me just now that you had said that you did n't care a straw for him."

"Very likely! I meant as a lover. One does n't want a lover one pities, and one does n't want—of all things in the world—a picturesque husband! I should like Mr. Hudson as something else. I wish he were my brother, so that he could never talk to me of marriage. Then I could adore him. I would nurse him, I would wait on him and save him all disagreeable rubs and shocks. I am much stronger than he, and I would stand between him and the world. Indeed, with Mr. Hudson for my brother, I should be willing to live and die an old maid!"

"Have you ever told him all this?"

"I suppose so; I 've told him five hundred things! If it would please you, I will tell him again."

"Oh, Heaven forbid!" cried poor Rowland, with a groan.

He was lingering there, weighing his sympathy against his irritation, and feeling it sink in the scale, when the curtain of a distant doorway was lifted and Mrs. Light passed across the room. She stopped half-way, and gave the young persons a flushed and menacing look. It found apparently little to reassure her, and she moved away with a passionate toss of her drapery. Rowland thought with horror of the sinister compulsion to which the young girl was to be subjected. In this ethereal flight of hers there was a certain painful effort and tension of wing; but it was none the less piteous to imagine her being rudely jerked down to the base earth she was doing her adventurous utmost to spurn. She would need all her magnanimity for her own trial, and it seemed gross to make further demands upon it on Roderick's behalf.

Rowland took up his hat. "You asked a while ago if I had come to help you," he said. "If I knew how I might help you, I should be particularly glad."

She stood silent a moment, reflecting. Then at last, looking up, "You remember," she said, "your promising me six months ago to tell me what you finally thought of me? I should like you to tell me now."

He could hardly help smiling. Madame Grandoni had insisted on the fact that Christina was an actress, though a sincere one; and this little speech seemed a glimpse of the cloven foot. She had played her great scene, she had made her point, and now she had her eye at the hole in the curtain and she was watching the house! But she blushed as she perceived his smile, and her blush, which was beautiful, made her fault venial.

"You are an excellent girl!" he said, in a particular tone, and gave her his hand in farewell.

There was a great chain of rooms in Mrs. Light's apartment, the pride and joy of the hostess on festal evenings, through which the departing visitor passed before reaching the door. In one of the first of these Rowland found himself waylaid and arrested by the distracted lady herself.

"Well, well?" she cried, seizing his arm. "Has she listened to you—have you moved her?"

"In Heaven's name, dear madame," Rowland begged, "leave the poor girl alone! She is behaving very well!"

"Behaving very well? Is that all you have to tell me? I don't believe you said a proper word to her. You are conspiring together to kill me!"

Rowland tried to soothe her, to remonstrate, to persuade her that it was equally cruel and unwise to try to force matters. But she answered him only with harsh lamentations and imprecations, and ended by telling him that her daughter was *her* property, not his, and that his interference was most insolent and most scandalous. Her disappointment seemed really to have crazed her, and his only possible rejoinder was to take a summary departure.

A moment later he came upon the Cavaliere, who was sitting with his elbows on his knees and his head in his hands, so buried in thought that Rowland had to call him before he roused himself. Giacosa looked at him a moment keenly, and then gave a shake of the head, interrogatively.

Rowland gave a shake negative, to which the Cavaliere responded by a long, melancholy sigh. "But her mother is determined to force matters," said Rowland.

"It seems that it must be!"

"Do you consider that it must be?"

"I don't differ with Mrs. Light!"

"It will be a great cruelty!"

The Cavaliere gave a tragic shrug. "Eh! it is n't an easy world."

"You should do nothing to make it harder, then."

"What will you have? It 's a magnificent marriage."

"You disappoint me, Cavaliere," said Rowland, solemnly. "I imagined you appreciated the great elevation of Miss Light's attitude. She does n't love the prince; she has let the matter stand or fall by that."

The old man grasped him by the hand and stood a moment with averted eyes. At last, looking at him, he held up two fingers.

"I have two hearts," he said, "one for myself, one for the world. This one opposes Miss Light, the other adores her! One suffers horribly at what the other does."

"I don't understand double people, Cavaliere," Rowland said, "and I don't pretend to understand you. But I have guessed that you are going to play some secret card."

"The card is Mrs. Light's, not mine," said the Cavaliere.

"It 's a menace, at any rate?"

"The sword of Damocles! It hangs by a hair. Christina is to be given ten minutes to recant, under penalty of having it fall. On the blade there is something written in strange characters. Don't scratch your head; you will not make it out."

"I think I have guessed it," Rowland said, after a pregnant silence. The Cavaliere looked at him blankly but intently, and Rowland added, "Though there are some signs, indeed, I don't understand."

"Puzzle them out at your leisure," said the Cavaliere, shaking his hand. "I hear Mrs. Light; I must go to my post. I wish you were a Catholic; I would beg you to step into the first church you come to, and pray for us the next half-hour."

"For 'us'? For whom?"

"For all of us. At any rate remember this: I worship the Christina!"

Rowland heard the rustle of Mrs. Light's dress; he turned away, and the Cavaliere went, as he said, to his post. Rowland for the next couple of days pondered his riddle.

XI

Mrs. Hudson

O F RODERICK, meanwhile, Rowland saw nothing; but he
immediately went to Mrs. Hudson and assured her that
her son was in even exceptionally good health and spirits. After this he called again on the two ladies from Northampton,
but, as Roderick's absence continued, he was able neither to
furnish nor to obtain much comfort. Miss Garland's apprehensive face seemed to him an image of his own state of
mind. He was profoundly depressed; he felt that there was a
storm in the air, and he wished it would come, without more
delay, and perform its ravages. On the afternoon of the third
day he went into Saint Peter's, his frequent resort whenever
the outer world was disagreeable. From a heart-ache to a Roman rain there were few importunate pains the great church
did not help him to forget. He had wandered there for half
an hour, when he came upon a short figure, lurking in the
shadow of one of the great piers. He saw it was that of an
artist, hastily transferring to his sketch-book a memento of
some fleeting variation in the scenery of the basilica; and in a
moment he perceived that the artist was little Sam Singleton.

Singleton pocketed his sketch-book with a guilty air, as if
it cost his modesty a pang to be detected in this greedy culture of opportunity. Rowland always enjoyed meeting him;
talking with him, in these days, was as good as a wayside
gush of clear, cold water, on a long, hot walk. There was,
perhaps, no drinking-vessel, and you had to apply your lips
to some simple natural conduit; but the result was always a
sense of extreme moral refreshment. On this occasion he mentally blessed the ingenuous little artist, and heard presently
with keen regret that he was to leave Rome on the morrow.
Singleton had come to bid farewell to Saint Peter's, and he
was gathering a few supreme memories. He had earned a
purse-full of money, and he was meaning to take a summer's
holiday; going to Switzerland, to Germany, to Paris. In the
autumn he was to return home; his family—composed, as
Rowland knew, of a father who was cashier in a bank and five

unmarried sisters, one of whom gave lyceum-lectures on
woman's rights, the whole resident at Buffalo, New York—
had been writing him peremptory letters and appealing to
him as a son, brother, and fellow-citizen. He would have been
grateful for another year in Rome, but what must be must be,
and he had laid up treasure which, in Buffalo, would seem
infinite. They talked some time; Rowland hoped they might
meet in Switzerland, and take a walk or two together. Singleton seemed to feel that Buffalo had marked him for her own;
he was afraid he should not see Rome again for many a year.

"So you expect to live at Buffalo?" Rowland asked sympathetically.

"Well, it will depend upon the views—upon the attitude—
of my family," Singleton replied. "Oh, I think I shall get on;
I think it can be done. If I find it can be done, I shall really
be quite proud of it; as an artist of course I mean, you know.
Do you know I have some nine hundred sketches? I shall live
in my portfolio. And so long as one is not in Rome, pray
what does it matter where one is? But how I shall envy all
you Romans—you and Mr. Gloriani, and Mr. Hudson, especially!"

"Don't envy Hudson; he has nothing to envy."

Singleton grinned at what he considered a harmless jest.
"Yes, he 's going to be the great man of our time! And I say,
Mr. Mallet, is n't it a mighty comfort that it 's *we* who have
turned him out?"

"Between ourselves," said Rowland, "he has disappointed
me."

Singleton stared, open-mouthed. "Dear me, what did you
expect?"

"Truly," said Rowland to himself, "what did I expect?"

"I confess," cried Singleton, "I can't judge him rationally.
He fascinates me; he 's the sort of man one makes one's hero
of."

"Strictly speaking, he is not a hero," said Rowland.

Singleton looked intensely grave, and, with almost tearful
eyes, "Is there anything amiss—anything out of the way,
about him?" he timidly asked. Then, as Rowland hesitated to
reply, he quickly added, "Please, if there is, don't tell me! I
want to know no evil of him, and I think I should hardly

believe it. In my memories of this Roman artist-life, he will be the central figure. He will stand there in radiant relief, as beautiful and unspotted as one of his own statues!"

"Amen!" said Rowland, gravely. He remembered afresh that the sea is inhabited by big fishes and little, and that the latter often find their way down the throats of the former. Singleton was going to spend the afternoon in taking last looks at certain other places, and Rowland offered to join him on his sentimental circuit. But as they were preparing to leave the church, he heard himself suddenly addressed from behind. Turning, he beheld a young woman whom he immediately recognized as Madame Grandoni's maid. Her mistress was present, she said, and begged to confer with him before he departed.

This summons obliged Rowland to separate from Singleton, to whom he bade farewell. He followed the messenger, and presently found Madame Grandoni occupying a liberal area on the steps of the tribune, behind the great altar, where, spreading a shawl on the polished red marble, she had comfortably seated herself. He expected that she had something especial to impart, and she lost no time in bringing forth her treasure.

"Don't shout very loud," she said, "remember that we are in church; there 's a limit to the noise one may make even in Saint Peter's. Christina Light was married this morning to Prince Casamassima."

Rowland did not shout at all; he gave a deep, short murmur: "Married—this morning?"

"Married this morning, at seven o'clock, *le plus tranquillement du monde*, before three or four persons. The young couple left Rome an hour afterwards."

For some moments this seemed to him really terrible; the dark little drama of which he had caught a glimpse had played itself out. He had believed that Christina would resist; that she had succumbed was a proof that the pressure had been cruel. Rowland's imagination followed her forth with an irresistible tremor into the world toward which she was rolling away, with her detested husband and her stifled ideal; but it must be confessed that if the first impulse of his compassion was for Christina, the second was for Prince Casamassima.

Madame Grandoni acknowledged an extreme curiosity as to the secret springs of these strange doings: Casamassima's sudden dismissal, his still more sudden recall, the hurried private marriage. "Listen," said Rowland, hereupon, "and I will tell you something." And he related, in detail, his last visit to Mrs. Light and his talk with this lady, with Christina, and with the Cavaliere.

"Good," she said; "it's all very curious. But it's a riddle, and I only half guess it."

"Well," said Rowland, "I desire to harm no one; but certain suppositions have taken shape in my mind which serve as a solvent to several ambiguities."

"It is very true," Madame Grandoni answered, "that the Cavaliere, as he stands, has always needed to be explained."

"He is explained by the hypothesis that, three-and-twenty years ago, at Ancona, Mrs. Light had a lover."

"I see. Ancona was dull, Mrs. Light was lively, and—three-and-twenty years ago—perhaps, the Cavaliere was fascinating. Doubtless it would be fairer to say that he was fascinated. Poor Giacosa!"

"He has had his compensation," Rowland said. "He has been passionately fond of Christina."

"Naturally. But has Christina never wondered why?"

"If she had been near guessing, her mother's shabby treatment of him would have put her off the scent. Mrs. Light's conscience has apparently told her that she could expiate an hour's too great kindness by twenty years' contempt. So she kept her secret. But what is the profit of having a secret unless you can make some use of it? The day at last came when she could turn hers to account; she could let the skeleton out of the closet and create a panic."

"I don't understand."

"Neither do I morally," said Rowland. "I only conceive that there was a horrible, fabulous scene. The poor Cavaliere stood outside, at the door, white as a corpse and as dumb. The mother and daughter had it out together. Mrs. Light burnt her ships. When she came out she had three lines of writing in her daughter's hand, which the Cavaliere was dispatched with to the prince. They overtook the young man in time, and, when he reappeared, he was delighted to dispense with further waiting. I don't know what he thought of the look in his bride's face; but that is how I roughly reconstruct history."

"Christina was forced to decide, then, that she could not afford not to be a princess?"

"She was reduced by humiliation. She was assured that it was not for her to make conditions, but to thank her stars that there were none made for her. If she persisted, she might find it coming to pass that there would be conditions, and the formal rupture—the rupture that the world would hear of and pry into—would then proceed from the prince and not from her."

"That 's all nonsense!" said Madame Grandoni, energetically.

"To us, yes; but not to the proudest girl in the world, deeply wounded in her pride, and not stopping to calculate probabilities, but muffling her shame, with an almost sensuous relief, in a splendor that stood within her grasp and asked no questions. Is it not possible that the late Mr. Light had made an outbreak before witnesses who are still living?"

"Certainly her marriage now," said Madame Grandoni, less analytically, "has the advantage that it takes her away from her—parents!"

This lady's farther comments upon the event are not immediately pertinent to our history; there were some other comments of which Rowland had a deeply oppressive foreboding. He called, on the evening of the morrow upon Mrs. Hudson, and found Roderick with the two ladies. Their companion had apparently but lately entered, and Rowland afterwards learned that it was his first appearance since the writing of the note which had so distressed his mother. He had flung himself upon a sofa, where he sat with his chin upon his breast, staring before him with a sinister spark in his eye. He fixed his gaze on Rowland, but gave him no greeting. He had evidently been saying something to startle the women; Mrs. Hudson had gone and seated herself, timidly and imploringly, on the edge of the sofa, trying to take his hand. Miss Garland was applying herself to some needlework with conscious intentness.

Mrs. Hudson gave Rowland, on his entrance, a touching

look of gratitude. "Oh, we have such blessed news!" she said. "Roderick is ready to leave Rome."

"It 's not blessed news; it 's most damnable news!" cried Roderick.

"Oh, but we are very glad, my son, and I am sure you will be when you get away. You 're looking most dreadfully thin; is n't he, Mr. Mallet? It 's plain enough you need a change. I 'm sure we will go wherever you like. Where would you like to go?"

Roderick turned his head slowly and looked at her. He had let her take his hand, which she pressed tenderly between her own. He gazed at her for some time in silence. "Poor mother!" he said at last, in a portentous tone.

"My own dear son!" murmured Mrs. Hudson in all the innocence of her trust.

"I don't care a straw where you go! I don't care a straw for anything!"

"Oh, my dear boy, you must not say that before all of us here—before Mary, before Mr. Mallet!"

"Mary—Mr. Mallet?" Roderick repeated, almost savagely. He released himself from the clasp of his mother's hand and turned away, leaning his elbows on his knees and holding his head in his hands. There was a silence; Rowland said nothing because he was watching Miss Garland. "Why should I stand on ceremony with Mary and Mr. Mallet?" Roderick presently added. "Mary pretends to believe I 'm a fine fellow, and if she believes it as she ought to, nothing I can say will alter her opinion. Mallet knows I 'm a hopeless humbug; so I need n't mince my words with him."

"Ah, my dear, don't use such dreadful language!" said Mrs. Hudson. "Are n't we all devoted to you, and proud of you, and waiting only to hear what you want, so that we may do it?"

Roderick got up, and began to walk about the room; he was evidently in a restless, reckless, profoundly demoralized condition. Rowland felt that it was literally true that he did not care a straw for anything, but he observed with anxiety that Mrs. Hudson, who did not know on what delicate ground she was treading, was disposed to chide him caressingly, as a mere expression of tenderness. He foresaw that she would bring down the hovering thunderbolt on her head.

"In God's name," Roderick cried, "don't remind me of my obligations! It 's intolerable to me, and I don't believe it 's pleasant to Mallet. I know they 're tremendous—I know I shall never repay them. I 'm bankrupt! Do you know what that means?"

The poor lady sat staring, dismayed, and Rowland angrily interfered. "Don't talk such stuff to your mother!" he cried. "Don't you see you 're frightening her?"

"Frightening her? she may as well be frightened first as last. Do I frighten you, mother?" Roderick demanded.

"Oh, Roderick, what *do* you mean?" whimpered the poor lady. "Mr. Mallet, what does he mean?"

"I mean that I 'm an angry, savage, disappointed, miserable man!" Roderick went on. "I mean that I can't do a stroke of work nor think a profitable thought! I mean that I 'm in a state of helpless rage and grief and shame! Helpless, helpless—that 's what it is. You can't help me, poor mother—not with kisses, nor tears, nor prayers! Mary can't help me—not for all the honor she does me, nor all the big books on art that she pores over. Mallet can't help me—not with all his money, nor all his good example, nor all his friendship, which I 'm so profoundly well aware of: not with it all multiplied a thousand times and repeated to all eternity! I thought you would help me, you and Mary; that 's why I sent for you. But you can't, don't think it! The sooner you give up the idea the better for you. Give up being proud of me, too; there 's nothing left of me to be proud of! A year ago I was a mighty fine fellow; but do you know what has become of me now? I have gone to the devil!"

There was something in the ring of Roderick's voice, as he uttered these words, which sent them home with convincing force. He was not talking for effect, or the mere sensuous pleasure of extravagant and paradoxical utterance, as had often enough been the case ere this; he was not even talking viciously or ill-humoredly. He was talking passionately, desperately, and from an irresistible need to throw off the oppressive burden of his mother's confidence. His cruel eloquence brought the poor lady to her feet, and she stood there with clasped hands, petrified and voiceless. Mary Garland quickly left her place, came straight to Roderick, and laid her hand on his arm, looking at him with all her tormented heart in her eyes. He made no movement to disengage himself; he simply shook his head several times, in dogged negation of her healing powers. Rowland had been living for the past month in such intolerable expectancy of disaster that now that the ice was broken, and the fatal plunge taken, his foremost feeling was almost elation; but in a moment his orderly instincts and his natural love of superficial smoothness overtook it.

"I really don't see, Roderick," he said, "the profit of your talking in just this way at just this time. Don't you see how you are making your mother suffer?"

"Do I enjoy it myself?" cried Roderick. "Is the suffering all on your side and theirs? Do I look as if I were happy, and were stirring you up with a stick for my amusement? Here we all are in the same boat; we might as well understand each other! These women must know that I 'm not to be counted on. That sounds remarkably cool, no doubt, and I certainly don't deny your right to be utterly disgusted with me."

"Will you keep what you have got to say till another time," said Mary, "and let me hear it alone?"

"Oh, I 'll let you hear it as often as you please; but what 's the use of keeping it? I 'm in the humor; it won't keep! It 's a very simple matter. I 'm a failure, that 's all; I 'm not a first-rate man. I 'm second-rate, tenth-rate, anything you please. After that, it 's all one!"

Mary Garland turned away and buried her face in her hands; but Roderick, struck, apparently, in some unwonted fashion with her gesture, drew her towards him again, and went on in a somewhat different tone. "It 's hardly worth while we should have any private talk about this, Mary," he said. "The thing would be comfortable for neither of us. It 's better, after all, that it be said once for all and dismissed. There are things I can't talk to you about. Can I, at least? You are such a queer creature!"

"I can imagine nothing you should n't talk to me about," said Mary.

"You are not afraid?" he demanded, sharply, looking at her.

She turned away abruptly, with lowered eyes, hesitating a moment. "Anything you think I should hear, I will hear," she said. And then she returned to her place at the window and took up her work.

"I have had a great blow," said Roderick. "I was a great ass, but it does n't make the blow any easier to bear."

"Mr. Mallet, tell me what Roderick means!" said Mrs. Hudson, who had found her voice, in a tone more peremptory than Rowland had ever heard her use.

"He ought to have told you before," said Roderick. "Really, Rowland, if you will allow me to say so, you ought! You could have given a much better account of all this than I myself; better, especially, in that it would have been more lenient to me. You ought to have let them down gently; it would have saved them a great deal of pain. But you always want to keep things so smooth! Allow me to say that it 's very weak of you."

"I hereby renounce such weakness!" said Rowland.

"Oh, what is it, sir; what is it?" groaned Mrs. Hudson, insistently.

"It 's what Roderick says: he 's a failure!"

Mary Garland, on hearing this declaration, gave Rowland a single glance and then rose, laid down her work, and walked rapidly out of the room. Mrs. Hudson tossed her head and timidly bristled. "This from *you*, Mr. Mallet!" she said with an injured air which Rowland found harrowing.

But Roderick, most characteristically, did not in the least resent his friend's assertion; he sent him, on the contrary, one of those large, clear looks of his, which seemed to express a stoical pleasure in Rowland's frankness, and which set his companion, then and there, wondering again, as he had so often done before, at the extraordinary contradictions of his temperament. "My dear mother," Roderick said, "if you had had eyes that were not blinded by this sad maternal vanity, you would have seen all this for yourself; you would have seen that I 'm anything but prosperous."

"Is it anything about money?" cried Mrs. Hudson. "Oh, do write to Mr. Striker!"

"Money?" said Roderick. "I have n't a cent of money; I 'm bankrupt!"

"Oh, Mr. Mallet, how could you let him?" asked Mrs. Hudson, terribly.

"Everything I have is at his service," said Rowland, feeling ill.

"Of course Mr. Mallet will help you, my son!" cried the poor lady, eagerly.

"Oh, leave Mr. Mallet alone!" said Roderick. "I have squeezed him dry; it 's not my fault, at least, if I have n't!"

"Roderick, what have you done with all your money?" his mother demanded.

"Thrown it away! It was no such great amount. I have done nothing this winter."

"You have done nothing?"

"I have done no work! Why in the world did n't you guess it and spare me all this? Could n't you see I was idle, distracted, dissipated?"

"Dissipated, my dear son?" Mrs. Hudson repeated.

"That 's over for the present! But could n't you see—could n't Mary see—that I was in a damnably bad way?"

"I have no doubt Miss Garland saw," said Rowland.

"Mary has said nothing!" cried Mrs. Hudson.

"Oh, she 's a fine girl!" Rowland said.

"Have you done anything that will hurt poor Mary?" Mrs. Hudson asked.

"I have only been thinking night and day of another woman!"

Mrs. Hudson dropped helplessly into her seat again. "Oh dear, dear, had n't we better go home?"

"Not to get out of *her* way!" Roderick said. "She has started on a career of her own, and she does n't care a straw for me. My head was filled with her; I could think of nothing else; I would have sacrificed everything to her— you, Mary, Mallet, my work, my fortune, my future, my honor! I was in a fine state, eh? I don't pretend to be giving you good news; but I 'm telling the simple, literal truth, so that you may know why I have gone to the dogs. She pretended to care greatly for all this, and to be willing to make any sacrifice in return; she had a magnificent chance, for she was being forced into a mercenary marriage with a man she detested. She led me to believe that she would give this up, and break short off, and keep herself free and sacred and pure for me. This was a great honor, and you may believe that I valued it. It turned my head, and I lived only to see my happiness come to pass. She did everything to encourage me to hope it would; everything that her infernal coquetry and falsity could suggest."

"Oh, I say, this is too much!" Rowland broke out.

"Do you defend her?" Roderick cried, with a renewal of his passion. "Do you pretend to say that she gave me no hopes?" He had been speaking with growing bitterness, quite losing sight of his mother's pain and bewilderment in the passionate joy of publishing his wrongs. Since he was hurt, he must cry out; since he was in pain, he must scatter his pain abroad. Of his never thinking of others, save as they spoke and moved from his cue, as it were, this extraordinary insensibility to the injurious effects of his eloquence was a capital example; the more so as the motive of his eloquence was never an appeal for sympathy or compassion, things to which he seemed perfectly indifferent and of which he could make no use. The great and characteristic point with him was the perfect absoluteness of his own emotions and experience. He never saw himself as part of a whole; only as the clear-cut, sharp-edged, isolated individual, rejoicing or raging, as the case might be, but needing in any case absolutely to affirm himself. All this, to Rowland, was ancient history, but his perception of it stirred within him afresh, at the sight of Roderick's sense of having been betrayed. That *he*, under the circumstances, should not in fairness be the first to lodge a complaint of betrayal was a point to which, at his leisure, Rowland was of course capable of rendering impartial justice; but Roderick's present desperation was so peremptory that it imposed itself on one's sympathies. "Do you pretend to say," he went on, "that she did n't lead me along to the very edge of fulfillment and stupefy me with all that she suffered me to believe, all that she sacredly promised? It amused her to do it, and she knew perfectly well what she really meant. She never meant to be sincere; she never dreamed she could be. She 's a ravenous flirt, and why a flirt is a flirt is more than I can tell you. I can't understand playing with those matters; for me they 're serious, whether I take them up or lay them down. I don't see what 's in your head, Rowland, to attempt to defend Miss Light; you were the first to cry out against her! You told me she was dangerous, and I pooh-poohed you. You were right; you 're always right. She 's as cold and false and heartless as she 's beautiful, and she has sold her heartless beauty to the highest bidder. I hope he knows what he gets!"

"Oh, my son," cried Mrs. Hudson, plaintively, "how could you ever care for such a dreadful creature?"

"It would take long to tell you, dear mother!"

Rowland's lately-deepened sympathy and compassion for Christina was still throbbing in his mind, and he felt that, in loyalty to it, he must say a word for her. "You believed in her too much at first," he declared, "and you believe in her too little now."

Roderick looked at him with eyes almost lurid, beneath lowering brows. "She is an angel, then, after all?—that 's what you want to prove!" he cried. "That 's consoling for me, who have lost her! You 're always right, I say; but, dear friend, in mercy, be wrong for once!"

"Oh yes, Mr. Mallet, be merciful!" said Mrs. Hudson, in a tone which, for all its gentleness, made Rowland stare. The poor fellow's stare covered a great deal of concentrated wonder and apprehension—a presentiment of what a small, sweet, feeble, elderly lady might be capable of, in the way of suddenly generated animosity. There was no space in Mrs. Hudson's tiny maternal mind for complications of feeling, and one emotion existed only by turning another over flat and perching on top of it. She was evidently not following Roderick at all in his dusky aberrations. Sitting without, in dismay, she only saw that all was darkness and trouble, and as Roderick's glory had now quite outstripped her powers of imagination and urged him beyond her jurisdiction, so that he had become a thing too precious and sacred for blame, she found it infinitely comfortable to lay the burden of their common affliction upon Rowland's broad shoulders. Had he not promised to make them all rich and happy? And this was the end of it! Rowland felt as if his trials were, in a sense, only beginning. "Had n't you better forget all this, my dear?" Mrs. Hudson said. "Had n't you better just quietly attend to your work?"

"Work, madame?" cried Roderick. "My work 's over. I can't work—I have n't worked all winter. If I were fit for anything, this sentimental collapse would have been just the thing to cure me of my apathy and break the spell of my idleness. But there 's a perfect vacuum here!" And he tapped his forehead. "It 's bigger than ever; it grows bigger every hour!"

"I 'm sure you have made a beautiful likeness of your poor little mother," said Mrs. Hudson, coaxingly.

"I had done nothing before, and I have done nothing since! I quarreled with an excellent man, the other day, from mere exasperation of my nerves, and threw away five thousand dollars!"

"Threw away—five thousand dollars!" Roderick had been wandering among formidable abstractions and allusions too dark to penetrate. But here was a concrete fact, lucidly stated, and poor Mrs. Hudson, for a moment, looked it in the face. She repeated her son's words a third time with a gasping murmur, and then, suddenly, she burst into tears. Roderick went to her, sat down beside her, put his arm round her, fixed his eyes coldly on the floor, and waited for her to weep herself out. She leaned her head on his shoulder and sobbed broken-heartedly. She said not a word, she made no attempt to scold; but the desolation of her tears was overwhelming. It lasted some time—too long for Rowland's courage. He had stood silent, wishing simply to appear very respectful; but the elation that was mentioned a while since had utterly ebbed, and he found his situation intolerable. He walked away—not, perhaps, on tiptoe, but with a total absence of bravado in his tread.

The next day, while he was at home, the servant brought him the card of a visitor. He read with surprise the name of Mrs. Hudson, and hurried forward to meet her. He found her in his sitting-room, leaning on the arm of her son and looking very pale, her eyes red with weeping, and her lips tightly compressed. Her advent puzzled him, and it was not for some time that he began to understand the motive of it. Roderick's countenance threw no light upon it; but Roderick's countenance, full of light as it was, in a way, itself, had never thrown light upon anything. He had not been in Rowland's rooms for several weeks, and he immediately began to look at those of his own works that adorned them. He lost himself in silent contemplation. Mrs. Hudson had evidently armed herself with dignity, and, so far as she might, she meant to be impressive. Her success may be measured by the fact that Rowland's whole attention centred in the fear of seeing her begin to weep. She told him that she had come to him for practical advice; she begged to remind him that she was a stranger in the land. Where were they to go, please? what were they to do? Rowland glanced at Roderick, but Roderick had his back turned and was gazing at his Adam with the intensity with which he might have examined Michael Angelo's Moses.

"Roderick says he does n't know, he does n't care," Mrs. Hudson said; "he leaves it entirely to you."

Many another man, in Rowland's place, would have greeted this information with an irate and sarcastic laugh, and told his visitors that he thanked them infinitely for their confidence, but that, really, as things stood now, they must settle these matters between themselves; many another man might have so demeaned himself, even if, like Rowland, he had been in love with Mary Garland and pressingly conscious that her destiny was also part of the question. But Rowland swallowed all hilarity and all sarcasm, and let himself seriously consider Mrs. Hudson's petition. His wits, however, were but indifferently at his command; they were dulled by his sense of the inexpressible change in Mrs. Hudson's attitude. Her visit was evidently intended as a formal reminder of the responsiblities Rowland had worn so lightly. Mrs. Hudson was doubtless too sincerely humble a person to suppose that if he had been recreant to his vows of vigilance and tenderness, her still, small presence would operate as a chastisement. But by some diminutive logical process of her own she had convinced herself that she had been weakly trustful, and that she had suffered Rowland to think too meanly, not only of her understanding, but of her social consequence. A visit in her best gown would have an admonitory effect as regards both of these attributes; it would cancel some favors received, and show him that she was no such fool! These were the reflections of a very shy woman, who, determining for once in her life to hold up her head, was perhaps carrying it a trifle extravagantly.

"You know we have very little money to spend," she said, as Rowland remained silent. "Roderick tells me that he has debts and nothing at all to pay them with. He says I must write to Mr. Striker to sell my house for what it will bring, and send me out the money. When the money comes I must give it to him. I 'm sure I don't know; I never heard of anything so dreadful! My house is all I have. But that is all Roderick will say. We must be very economical."

Before this speech was finished Mrs. Hudson's voice had begun to quaver softly, and her face, which had no capacity for the expression of superior wisdom, to look as humbly appealing as before. Rowland turned to Roderick and spoke like a school-master. "Come away from those statues, and sit down here and listen to me!"

Roderick started, but obeyed with the most graceful docility.

"What do you propose to your mother to do?" Rowland asked.

"Propose?" said Roderick, absently. "Oh, I propose nothing."

The tone, the glance, the gesture with which this was said were horribly irritating (though obviously without the slightest intention of being so), and for an instant an imprecation rose to Rowland's lips. But he checked it, and he was afterwards glad he had done so. "You must do something," he said. "Choose, select, decide!"

"My dear Rowland, how you talk!" Roderick cried. "The very point of the matter is that I can't do anything. I will do as I 'm told, but I don't call that doing. We must leave Rome, I suppose, though I don't see why. We have got no money, and you have to pay money on the railroads."

Mrs. Hudson surreptitiously wrung her hands. "Listen to him, please!" she cried. "Not leave Rome, when we have staid here later than any Christians ever did before! It 's this dreadful place that has made us so unhappy."

"That 's very true," said Roderick, serenely. "If I had not come to Rome, I would n't have risen, and if I had not risen, I should n't have fallen."

"Fallen—fallen!" murmured Mrs. Hudson. "Just hear him!"

"I will do anything you say, Rowland," Roderick added. "I will do anything you want. I have not been unkind to my mother—have I, mother? I was unkind yesterday, without meaning it; for after all, all that had to be said. Murder will out, and my low spirits can't be hidden. But we talked it over and made it up, did n't we? It seemed to me we did. Let Rowland decide it, mother; whatever he suggests will be the right thing." And Roderick, who had hardly removed his eyes from the statues, got up again and went back to look at them.

Mrs. Hudson fixed her eyes upon the floor in silence. There was not a trace in Roderick's face, or in his voice, of the bitterness of his emotion of the day before, and not a hint of his having the lightest weight upon his conscience. He looked at Rowland with his frank, luminous eye as if there had never been a difference of opinion between them; as if each had ever been for both, unalterably, and both for each.

Rowland had received a few days before a letter from a lady of his acquaintance, a worthy Scotswoman domiciled in a villa upon one of the olive-covered hills near Florence. She held her apartment in the villa upon a long lease, and she enjoyed for a sum not worth mentioning the possession of an extraordinary number of noble, stone-floored rooms, with ceilings vaulted and frescoed, and barred windows commanding the loveliest view in the world. She was a needy and thrifty spinster, who never hesitated to declare that the lovely view was all very well, but that for her own part she lived in the villa for cheapness, and that if she had a clear three hundred pounds a year she would go and really enjoy life near her sister, a baronet's lady, at Glasgow. She was now proposing to make a visit to that exhilarating city, and she desired to turn an honest penny by sub-letting for a few weeks her historic Italian chambers. The terms on which she occupied them enabled her to ask a rent almost jocosely small, and she begged Rowland to do what she called a little genteel advertising for her. Would he say a good word for her rooms to his numerous friends, as they left Rome? He said a good word for them now to Mrs. Hudson, and told her in dollars and cents how cheap a summer's lodging she might secure. He dwelt upon the fact that she would strike a truce with *tables-*

d'hôte and have a cook of her own, amenable possibly to instruction in the Northampton mysteries. He had touched a tender chord; Mrs. Hudson became almost cheerful. Her sentiments upon the table-d'hôte system and upon foreign household habits generally were remarkable, and, if we had space for it, would repay analysis; and the idea of reclaiming a lost soul to the Puritanic canons of cookery quite lightened the burden of her depression. While Rowland set forth his case Roderick was slowly walking round the magnificent Adam, with his hands in his pockets. Rowland waited for him to manifest an interest in their discussion, but the statue seemed to fascinate him and he remained calmly heedless. Rowland was a practical man; he possessed conspicuously what is called the sense of detail. He entered into Mrs. Hudson's position minutely, and told her exactly why it seemed good that she should remove immediately to the Florentine villa. She received his advice with great frigidity, looking hard at the floor and sighing, like a person well on her guard against an insidious optimism. But she had nothing better to propose, and Rowland received her permission to write to his friend that he had let the rooms.

Roderick assented to this decision without either sighs or smiles. "A Florentine villa is a good thing!" he said. "I am at your service."

"I 'm sure I hope you 'll get better there," moaned his mother, gathering her shawl together.

Roderick laid one hand on her arm and with the other pointed to Rowland's statues. "Better or worse, remember this: I did those things!" he said.

Mrs. Hudson gazed at them vaguely, and Rowland said, "Remember it yourself!"

"They are horribly good!" said Roderick.

Rowland solemnly shrugged his shoulders; it seemed to him that he had nothing more to say. But as the others were going, a last light pulsation of the sense of undischarged duty led him to address to Roderick a few words of parting advice. "You 'll find the Villa Pandolfini very delightful, very comfortable," he said. "You ought to be very contented there. Whether you work or whether you loaf, it 's a place for an artist to be happy in. I hope you will work."

"I hope I may!" said Roderick with a magnificent smile.

"When we meet again, have something to show me."

"When we meet again? Where the deuce are *you* going?" Roderick demanded.

"Oh, I hardly know; over the Alps."

"Over the Alps! You 're going to leave me?" Roderick cried.

Rowland had most distinctly meant to leave him, but his resolution immediately wavered. He glanced at Mrs. Hudson and saw that her eyebrows were lifted and her lips parted in soft irony. She seemed to accuse him of a craven shirking of trouble, to demand of him to repair his cruel havoc in her life by a solemn renewal of zeal. But Roderick's expectations were the oddest! Such as they were, Rowland asked himself why he should n't make a bargain with them. "You desire me to go with you?" he asked.

"If you don't go, I won't—that 's all! How in the world shall I get through the summer without you?"

"How will you get through it with me? That 's the question."

"I don't pretend to say; the future is a dead blank. But without you it 's not a blank—it 's certain damnation!"

"Mercy, mercy!" murmured Mrs. Hudson.

Rowland made an effort to stand firm, and for a moment succeeded. "If I go with you, will you try to work?"

Roderick, up to this moment, had been looking as unperturbed as if the deep agitation of the day before were a thing of the remote past. But at these words his face changed formidably; he flushed and scowled, and all his passion returned. "Try to work!" he cried. "Try—try! work—work! In God's name don't talk that way, or you 'll drive me mad! Do you suppose I 'm trying *not* to work? Do you suppose I stand rotting here for the fun of it? Don't you suppose I would try to work for myself before I tried for you?"

"Mr. Mallet," cried Mrs. Hudson, piteously, "will you leave me alone with *this*?"

Rowland turned to her and informed her, gently, that he would go with her to Florence. After he had so pledged himself he thought not at all of the pain of his position as mediator between the mother's resentful grief and the son's incurable weakness; he drank deep, only, of the satisfaction of not separating from Mary Garland. If the future was a blank to Roderick, it was hardly less so to himself. He had at moments a lively foreboding of impending calamity. He paid it no especial deference, but it made him feel indisposed to take the future into his account. When, on his going to take leave of Madame Grandoni, this lady asked at what time he would come back to Rome, he answered that he was coming back either never or forever. When she asked him what he meant, he said he really could n't tell her, and parted from her with much genuine emotion; the more so, doubtless, that she blessed him in a quite loving, maternal fashion, and told him she honestly believed him to be the best fellow in the world.

The Villa Pandolfini stood directly upon a small grass-grown piazza, on the top of a hill which sloped straight from one of the gates of Florence. It offered to the outer world a long, rather low façade, colored a dull, dark yellow, and pierced with windows of various sizes, no one of which, save those on the ground floor, was on the same level with any other. Within, it had a great, cool, gray cortile, with high, light arches around it, heavily-corniced doors, of majestic altitude, opening out of it, and a beautiful mediæval well on one side of it. Mrs. Hudson's rooms opened into a small garden supported on immense substructions, which were planted on the farther side of the hill, as it sloped steeply away. This garden was a charming place. Its south wall was curtained with a dense orange vine, a dozen fig-trees offered you their large-leaved shade, and over the low parapet the soft, grave Tuscan landscape kept you company. The rooms themselves were as high as chapels and as cool as royal sepulchres. Silence, peace, and security seemed to abide in the ancient house and make it an ideal refuge for aching hearts. Mrs. Hudson had a stunted, brown-faced Maddalena, who wore a crimson handkerchief passed over her coarse, black locks and tied under her sharp, pertinacious chin, and a smile which was as brilliant as a prolonged flash of lightning. She smiled at everything in life, especially the things she did n't like and which kept her talent for mendacity in healthy exercise. A glance, a word, a motion was sufficient to make her show her teeth at you like a cheerful she-wolf. This inexpugnable smile constituted her whole vocabulary in her dealings with her melancholy mistress, to whom she had been bequeathed by the late occupant of the apartment, and who, to Rowland's satisfaction, promised to be diverted from her maternal sorrows by the still deeper perplexities of Maddalena's theory of roasting, sweeping, and bed-making.

Rowland took rooms at a villa a trifle nearer Florence, whence in the summer mornings he had five minutes' walk in the sharp, black, shadow-strip projected by winding, flower-topped walls, to join his friends. The life at the Villa Pandolfini, when it had fairly defined itself, was tranquil and monotonous, but it might have borrowed from exquisite circumstance an absorbing charm. If a sensible shadow rested upon it, this was because it had an inherent vice; it was feigning a repose which it very scantily felt. Roderick had lost no time in giving the full measure of his uncompromising chagrin, and as he was the central figure of the little group, as he held its heart-strings all in his own hand, it reflected faithfully the eclipse of his own genius. No one had ventured upon the cheerful commonplace of saying that the change of air and of scene would restore his spirits; this would have had, under the circumstances, altogether too silly a sound. The change in question had done nothing of the sort, and his companions had, at least, the comfort of their perspicacity. An essential spring had dried up within him, and there was no visible spiritual law for making it flow again. He was rarely violent, he expressed little of the irritation and ennui that he must have constantly felt; it was as if he believed that a spiritual miracle for his redemption was just barely possible, and was therefore worth waiting for. The most that one could do, however, was to wait grimly and doggedly, suppressing an imprecation as, from time to time, one looked at one's watch. An attitude of positive urbanity toward life was not to be expected; it was doing one's duty to hold one's tongue and keep one's hands off one's own windpipe, and other people's. Roderick had long silences, fits of profound lethargy, almost of stupefaction. He used to sit in the garden by the hour, with his head thrown back, his legs outstretched, his hands in his pockets, and his eyes fastened upon the blinding summer sky. He would gather a dozen books about him, tumble them out on the ground, take one into his lap, and leave it with the pages unturned. These moods would alternate with hours of extreme restlessness, during which he mysteriously absented himself. He bore the heat of the Italian summer like a salamander, and used to start off at high noon for long walks over the hills. He often went down into Florence, rambled through her close, dim streets, and lounged away mornings in the churches and galleries. On many of these occasions Rowland bore him company, for they were the times when he was most like his former self. Before Michael Angelo's statues and the pictures of the early Tuscans, he quite forgot his own infelicities, and picked up the thread of his old æsthetic loquacity. He had a particular fondness for Andrea del Sarto, and affirmed that if *he* had been a painter he would have taken the author of the Madonna del Sacco for his model. He found in Florence some of his Roman friends, and went down on certain evenings to meet them. More than once he asked Mary Garland to go with him into town, and showed her the things he most cared for. He had some modeling clay brought up to the villa and deposited in a room suitable for his work; but when this had been done he turned the key in the door and the clay never was touched. His eye was heavy and his hand cold, and his mother put up a secret prayer that he might be induced to see a doctor. But on a certain occasion, when her prayer became articulate, he had a great outburst of anger and begged her to know, once for all, that his health was better than it had ever been. On the whole, and most of the time, he was a sad spectacle; he looked so hopelessly idle. If he was not querulous and bitter, it was because he had taken an extraordinary vow not to be; a vow heroic, for him, a vow which those who knew him well had the tenderness to appreciate. Talking with him was like skating on thin ice, and his companions had a constant mental vision of spots designated "dangerous."

This was a difficult time for Rowland; he said to himself that he would endure it to the end, but that it must be his last adventure of the kind. Mrs. Hudson divided her time between looking askance at her son, with her hands tightly

clasped about her pocket-handkerchief, as if she were wringing it dry of the last hour's tears, and turning her eyes much
more directly upon Rowland, in the mutest, the feeblest, the
most intolerable reproachfulness. She never phrased her accusations, but he felt that in the unillumined void of the poor
lady's mind they loomed up like vaguely-outlined monsters.
Her demeanor caused him the acutest suffering, and if, at the
outset of his enterprise, he had seen, how dimly soever, one
of those plaintive eye-beams in the opposite scale, the brilliancy of Roderick's promises would have counted for little.
They made their way to the softest spot in his conscience and
kept it chronically aching. If Mrs. Hudson had been loquacious and vulgar, he would have borne even a less valid persecution with greater fortitude. But somehow, neat and
noiseless and dismally lady-like, as she sat there, keeping her
grievance green with her soft-dropping tears, her displeasure
conveyed an overwhelming imputation of brutality. He felt
like a reckless trustee who has speculated with the widow's
mite, and is haunted with the reflection of ruin that he sees
in her tearful eyes. He did everything conceivable to be polite
to Mrs. Hudson, and to treat her with distinguished deference. Perhaps his exasperated nerves made him overshoot the
mark, and rendered his civilities a trifle peremptory. She
seemed capable of believing that he was trying to make a fool
of her; she would have thought him cruelly recreant if he had
suddenly departed in desperation, and yet she gave him no
visible credit for his constancy. Women are said by some authorities to be cruel; I don't know how true this is, but it may
at least be pertinent to remark that Mrs. Hudson was very
much of a woman. It often seemed to Rowland that he had
too decidedly forfeited his freedom, and that there was something positively grotesque in a man of his age and circumstances living in such a moral bondage.

But Mary Garland had helped him before, and she helped
him now—helped him not less than he had assured himself
she would when he found himself drifting to Florence. Yet
her help was rendered in the same unconscious, unacknowledged fashion as before; there was no explicit change in their
relations. After that distressing scene in Rome which had immediately preceded their departure, it was of course impossi-

ble that there should not be on Miss Garland's part some
frankness of allusion to Roderick's sad condition. She had
been present, the reader will remember, during only half of
his unsparing confession, and Rowland had not seen her confronted with any absolute proof of Roderick's passion for
Christina Light. But he knew that she knew far too much for
her happiness; Roderick had told him, shortly after their settlement at the Villa Pandolfini, that he had had a "tremendous talk" with his cousin. Rowland asked no questions
about it; he preferred not to know what had passed between
them. If their interview had been purely painful, he wished to
ignore it for Miss Garland's sake; and if it had sown the seeds
of reconciliation, he wished to close his eyes to it for his
own—for the sake of that unshaped idea, forever dismissed
and yet forever present, which hovered in the background of
his consciousness, with a hanging head, as it were, and yet an
unshamed glance, and whose lightest motions were an effec-
tual bribe to patience. Was the engagement broken? Rowland
wondered, yet without asking. But it hardly mattered, for if,
as was more than probable, Miss Garland had peremptorily
released her cousin, her own heart had by no means recovered
its liberty. It was very certain to Rowland's mind that if she
had given him up she had by no means ceased to care for him
passionately, and that, to exhaust her charity for his weaknesses, Roderick would have, as the phrase is, a long row to
hoe. She spoke of Roderick as she might have done of a person suffering from a serious malady which demanded much
tenderness; but if Rowland had found it possible to accuse
her of dishonesty he would have said now that she believed
appreciably less than she pretended to in her victim's being
an involuntary patient. There are women whose love is care-
taking and patronizing, and who rather prefer a weak man
because he gives them a comfortable sense of strength. It did
not in the least please Rowland to believe that Mary Garland
was one of these; for he held that such women were only
males in petticoats, and he was convinced that Miss Garland's
heart was constructed after the most perfect feminine model.
That she was a very different woman from Christina Light
did not at all prove that she was less a woman, and if the
Princess Casamassima had gone up into a high place to pub-

lish her disrelish of a man who lacked the virile will, it was
very certain that Mary Garland was not a person to put up,
at any point, with what might be called the princess's leav-
ings. It was Christina's constant practice to remind you of the
complexity of her character, of the subtlety of her mind, of
her troublous faculty of seeing everything in a dozen different
lights. Mary Garland had never pretended not to be simple;
but Rowland had a theory that she had really a more multitudinous sense of human things, a more delicate imagination,
and a finer instinct of character. She did you the honors of
her mind with a grace far less regal, but was not that faculty
of quite as remarkable an adjustment? If in poor Christina's
strangely commingled nature there was circle within circle,
and depth beneath depth, it was to be believed that Mary
Garland, though she did not amuse herself with dropping
stones into her soul, and waiting to hear them fall, laid quite
as many sources of spiritual life under contribution. She had
believed Roderick was a fine fellow when she bade him farewell beneath the Northampton elms, and this belief, to her
young, strenuous, concentrated imagination, had meant many
things. If it was to grow cold, it would be because disen-
chantment had become total and won the battle at each successive point.

Miss Garland had even in her face and carriage something
of the preoccupied and wearied look of a person who is
watching at a sick-bed; Roderick's broken fortunes, his dead
ambitions, were a cruel burden to the heart of a girl who had
believed that he possessed "genius," and supposed that genius
was to one's spiritual economy what full pockets were to
one's domestic. And yet, with her, Rowland never felt, as
with Mrs. Hudson, that undercurrent of reproach and bitterness toward himself, that impertinent implication that he had
defrauded her of happiness. Was this justice, in Miss Garland,
or was it mercy? The answer would have been difficult, for
she had almost let Rowland feel before leaving Rome that she
liked him well enough to forgive him an injury. It was partly,
Rowland fancied, that there were occasional lapses, deep and
sweet, in her sense of injury. When, on arriving at Florence,
she saw the place Rowland had brought them to in their
trouble, she had given him a look and said a few words to

him that had seemed not only a remission of guilt but a positive reward. This happened in the court of the villa—the
large gray quadrangle, overstretched, from edge to edge of
the red-tiled roof, by the soft Italian sky. Mary had felt on
the spot the sovereign charm of the place; it was reflected in
her deeply intelligent glance, and Rowland immediately accused himself of not having done the villa justice. Miss Garland took a mighty fancy to Florence, and used to look down
wistfully at the towered city from the windows and garden.
Roderick having now no pretext for not being her cicerone,
Rowland was no longer at liberty, as he had been in Rome,
to propose frequent excursions to her. Roderick's own invitations, however, were not frequent, and Rowland more than
once ventured to introduce her to a gallery or a church. These
expeditions were not so blissful, to his sense, as the rambles
they had taken together in Rome, for his companion only half
surrendered herself to her enjoyment, and seemed to have but
a divided attention at her command. Often, when she had
begun with looking intently at a picture, her silence, after an
interval, made him turn and glance at her. He usually found
that if she was looking at the picture still, she was not seeing
it. Her eyes were fixed, but her thoughts were wandering, and
an image more vivid than any that Raphael or Titian had
drawn had superposed itself upon the canvas. She asked fewer
questions than before, and seemed to have lost heart for consulting guide-books and encyclopædias. From time to time,
however, she uttered a deep, full murmur of gratification.
Florence in midsummer was perfectly void of travelers, and
the dense little city gave forth its æsthetic aroma with a larger
frankness, as the nightingale sings when the listeners have departed. The churches were deliciously cool, but the gray
streets were stifling, and the great, dove-tailed polygons of
pavement as hot to the tread as molten lava. Rowland, who
suffered from intense heat, would have found all this uncomfortable in solitude; but Florence had never charmed him so
completely as during these midsummer strolls with his preoccupied companion. One evening they had arranged to go on
the morrow to the Academy. Miss Garland kept her appointment, but as soon as she appeared, Rowland saw that something painful had befallen her. She was doing her best to look

at her ease, but her face bore the marks of tears. Rowland told her that he was afraid she was ill, and that if she preferred to give up the visit to Florence he would submit with what grace he might. She hesitated a moment, and then said she preferred to adhere to their plan. "I am not well," she presently added, "but it 's a moral malady, and in such cases I consider your company beneficial."

"But if I am to be your doctor," said Rowland, "you must tell me how your illness began."

"I can tell you very little. It began with Mrs. Hudson being unjust to me, for the first time in her life. And now I am already better!"

I mention this incident because it confirmed an impression of Rowland's from which he had derived a certain consolation. He knew that Mrs. Hudson considered her son's ill-regulated passion for Christina Light a very regrettable affair, but he suspected that her manifest compassion had been all for Roderick, and not in the least for Mary Garland. She was fond of the young girl, but she had valued her primarily, during the last two years, as a kind of assistant priestess at Roderick's shrine. Roderick had honored her by asking her to become his wife, but that poor Mary had any rights in consequence Mrs. Hudson was quite incapable of perceiving. Her sentiment on the subject was of course not very vigorously formulated, but she was unprepared to admit that Miss Garland had any ground for complaint. Roderick was very unhappy; that was enough, and Mary's duty was to join her patience and her prayers to those of his doting mother. Roderick might fall in love with whom he pleased; no doubt that women trained in the mysterious Roman arts were only too proud and too happy to make it easy for him; and it was very presuming in poor, plain Mary to feel any personal resentment. Mrs. Hudson's philosophy was of too narrow a scope to suggest that a mother may forgive where a mistress cannot, and she thought herself greatly aggrieved that Miss Garland was not so disinterested as herself. She was ready to drop dead in Roderick's service, and she was quite capable of seeing her companion falter and grow faint, without a tremor of compassion. Mary, apparently, had given some intimation of her belief that if constancy is the flower of devotion, reciprocity is the guarantee of constancy, and Mrs. Hudson had rebuked her failing faith and called it cruelty. That Miss Garland had found it hard to reason with Mrs. Hudson, that she suffered deeply from the elder lady's softly bitter imputations, and that, in short, he had companionship in misfortune—all this made Rowland find a certain luxury in his discomfort.

The party at Villa Pandolfini used to sit in the garden in the evenings, which Rowland almost always spent with them. Their entertainment was in the heavily perfumed air, in the dim, far starlight, in the crenelated tower of a neighboring villa, which loomed vaguely above them in the warm darkness, and in such conversation as depressing reflections allowed. Roderick, clad always in white, roamed about like a restless ghost, silent for the most part, but making from time to time a brief observation, characterized by the most fantastic cynicism. Roderick's contributions to the conversation were indeed always so fantastic that, though half the time they wearied him unspeakably, Rowland made an effort to treat them humorously. With Rowland alone Roderick talked a great deal more; often about things related to his own work, or about artistic and æsthetic matters in general. He talked as well as ever, or even better; but his talk always ended in a torrent of groans and curses. When this current set in, Rowland straightway turned his back or stopped his ears, and Roderick now witnessed these movements with perfect indifference. When the latter was absent from the star-lit circle in the garden, as often happened, Rowland knew nothing of his whereabouts; he supposed him to be in Florence, but he never learned what he did there. All this was not enlivening, but with an even, muffled tread the days followed each other, and brought the month of August to a close. One particular evening at this time was most enchanting; there was a perfect moon, looking so extraordinarily large that it made everything its light fell upon seem small; the heat was tempered by a soft west wind, and the wind was laden with the odors of the early harvest. The hills, the vale of the Arno, the shrunken river, the domes of Florence, were vaguely effaced by the dense moonshine; they looked as if they were melting out of sight like an exorcised vision. Rowland had found the two ladies alone at the villa, and he had sat with them for an hour. He felt absolutely hushed by the solemn splendor of the scene, but he had risked the remark that, whatever life might yet have in store for either of them, this was a night that they would never forget.

"It 's a night to remember on one's death-bed!" Miss Garland exclaimed.

"Oh, Mary, how can you!" murmured Mrs. Hudson, to whom this savored of profanity, and to whose shrinking sense, indeed, the accumulated loveliness of the night seemed to have something shameless and defiant.

They were silent after this, for some time, but at last Rowland addressed certain idle words to Miss Garland. She made no reply, and he turned to look at her. She was sitting motionless, with her head pressed to Mrs. Hudson's shoulder, and the latter lady was gazing at him through the silvered dusk with a look which gave a sort of spectral solemnity to the sad, weak meaning of her eyes. She had the air, for the moment, of a little old malevolent fairy. Miss Garland, Rowland perceived in an instant, was not absolutely motionless; a tremor passed through her figure. She was weeping, or on the point of weeping, and she could not trust herself to speak. Rowland left his place and wandered to another part of the garden, wondering at the motive of her sudden tears. Of women's sobs in general he had a sovereign dread, but these, somehow, gave him a certain pleasure. When he returned to his place Miss Garland had raised her head and banished her tears. She came away from Mrs. Hudson, and they stood for a short time leaning against the parapet.

"It seems to you very strange, I suppose," said Rowland, "that there should be any trouble in such a world as this."

"I used to think," she answered, "that if any trouble came to me I would bear it like a stoic. But that was at home, where things don't speak to us of enjoyment as they do here. Here it is such a mixture; one does n't know what to choose, what to believe. Beauty stands there—beauty such as this night and this place, and all this sad, strange summer, have been so full of—and it penetrates to one's soul and lodges there, and keeps saying that man was not made to suffer, but to enjoy. This place has undermined my stoicism, but—shall

I tell you? I feel as if I were saying something sinful—I love it!"

"If it is sinful, I absolve you," said Rowland, "in so far as I have power. We are made, I suppose, both to suffer and to enjoy. As you say, it 's a mixture. Just now and here, it seems a peculiarly strange one. But we must take things in turn."

His words had a singular aptness, for he had hardly uttered them when Roderick came out from the house, evidently in his darkest mood. He stood for a moment gazing hard at the view.

"It 's a very beautiful night, my son," said his mother, going to him timidly, and touching his arm.

He passed his hand through his hair and let it stay there, clasping his thick locks. "Beautiful?" he cried; "of course it 's beautiful! Everything is beautiful; everything is insolent, defiant, atrocious with beauty. Nothing is ugly but me—me and my poor dead brain!"

"Oh, my dearest son," pleaded poor Mrs. Hudson, "don't you feel any better?"

Roderick made no immediate answer; but at last he spoke in a different voice. "I came expressly to tell you that you need n't trouble yourselves any longer to wait for something to turn up. Nothing *will* turn up! It 's all over! I said when I came here I would give it a chance. I have given it a chance. Have n't I, eh? Have n't I, Rowland? It 's no use; the thing 's a failure! Do with me now what you please. I recommend you to set me up there at the end of the garden and shoot me."

"I feel strongly inclined," said Rowland gravely, "to go and get my revolver."

"Oh, mercy on us, what language!" cried Mrs. Hudson.

"Why not?" Roderick went on. "This would be a lovely night for it, and I should be a lucky fellow to be buried in this garden. But bury me alive, if you prefer. Take me back to Northampton."

"Roderick, will you really come?" cried his mother.

"Oh yes, I 'll go! I might as well be there as anywhere—reverting to idiocy and living upon alms. I can do nothing with all this; perhaps I should really like Northampton. If

I 'm to vegetate for the rest of my days, I can do it there better than here."

"Oh, come home, come home," Mrs. Hudson said, "and we shall all be safe and quiet and happy. My dearest son, come home with your poor mother!"

"Let us go, then, and go quickly!"

Mrs. Hudson flung herself upon his neck for gratitude. "We 'll go to-morrow!" she cried. "The Lord is very good to me!"

Mary Garland said nothing to this; but she looked at Rowland, and her eyes seemed to contain a kind of alarmed appeal. Rowland noted it with exultation, but even without it he would have broken into an eager protest.

"Are you serious, Roderick?" he demanded.

"Serious? of course not! How can a man with a crack in his brain be serious? how can a muddlehead reason? But I 'm not jesting, either; I can no more make jokes than utter oracles!"

"Are you willing to go home?"

"Willing? God forbid! I am simply amenable to force; if my mother chooses to take me, I won't resist. I can't! I have come to that!"

"Let me resist, then," said Rowland. "Go home as you are now? I can't stand by and see it."

It may have been true that Roderick had lost his sense of humor, but he scratched his head with a gesture that was almost comical in its effect. "You are a queer fellow! I should think I would disgust you horribly."

"Stay another year," Rowland simply said.

"Doing nothing?"

"You *shall* do something. I am responsible for your doing something."

"To whom are you responsible?"

Rowland, before replying, glanced at Miss Garland, and his glance made her speak quickly. "Not to me!"

"I 'm responsible to myself," Rowland declared.

"My poor, dear fellow!" said Roderick.

"Oh, Mr. Mallet, are n't you satisfied?" cried Mrs. Hudson, in the tone in which Niobe may have addressed the avenging archers, after she had seen her eldest-born fall. "It 's out of all nature keeping him here. When we 're in a poor way, surely our own dear native land is the place for us. Do leave us to ourselves, sir!"

This just failed of being a dismissal in form, and Rowland bowed his head to it. Roderick was silent for some moments; then, suddenly, he covered his face with his two hands. "Take me at least out of this terrible Italy," he cried, "where everything mocks and reproaches and torments and eludes me! Take me out of this land of impossible beauty and put me in the midst of ugliness. Set me down where nature is coarse and flat, and men and manners are vulgar. There must be something awfully ugly in Germany. Pack me off there!"

Rowland answered that if he wished to leave Italy the thing might be arranged; he would think it over and submit a proposal on the morrow. He suggested to Mrs. Hudson, in consequence, that she should spend the autumn in Switzerland, where she would find a fine tonic climate, plenty of fresh milk, and several *pensions* at three francs and a half a day. Switzerland, of course, was not ugly, but one could not have everything.

Mrs. Hudson neither thanked him nor assented; but she wept and packed her trunks. Rowland had a theory, after the scene which led to these preparations, that Mary Garland was weary of waiting for Roderick to come to his senses, that the faith which had bravely borne his manhood company hitherto, on the tortuous march he was leading it, had begun to believe it had gone far enough. This theory was not vitiated by something she said to him on the day before that on which Mrs. Hudson had arranged to leave Florence.

"Cousin Sarah, the other evening," she said, "asked you to please leave us. I think she hardly knew what she was saying, and I hope you have not taken offense."

"By no means; but I honestly believe that my leaving you would contribute greatly to Mrs. Hudson's comfort. I can be your hidden providence, you know; I can watch you at a distance, and come upon the scene at critical moments."

Miss Garland looked for a moment at the ground; and then, with sudden earnestness, "I beg you to come with us!" she said.

It need hardly be added that after this Rowland went with them.

XII

The Princess Casamassima

ROWLAND HAD a very friendly memory of a little mountain inn, accessible with moderate trouble from Lucerne, where he had once spent a blissful ten days. He had at that time been trudging, knapsack on back, over half Switzerland, and not being, on his legs, a particularly light weight, it was no shame to him to confess that he was mortally tired. The inn of which I speak presented striking analogies with a cow-stable; but in spite of this circumstance, it was crowded with hungry tourists. It stood in a high, shallow valley, with flower-strewn Alpine meadows sloping down to it from the base of certain rugged rocks whose outlines were grotesque against the evening sky. Rowland had seen grander places in Switzerland that pleased him less, and whenever afterwards he wished to think of Alpine opportunities at their best, he recalled this grassy concave among the mountain-tops, and the August days he spent there, resting deliciously, at his length, in the lee of a sun-warmed boulder, with the light cool air stirring about his temples, the wafted odors of the pines in his nostrils, the tinkle of the cattle-bells in his ears, the vast progression of the mountain shadows before his eyes, and a volume of Wordsworth in his pocket. His face, on the Swiss hill-sides, had been scorched to within a shade of the color nowadays called magenta, and his bed was a pallet in a loft, which he shared with a German botanist of colossal stature—every inch of him quaking at an open window. These had been drawbacks to felicity, but Rowland hardly cared where or how he was lodged, for he spent the livelong day under the sky, on the crest of a slope that looked at the Jungfrau. He remembered all this on leaving Florence with his friends, and he reflected that, as the midseason was over, accommodations would be more ample, and charges more modest. He communicated with his old friend the landlord, and, while September was yet young, his companions established themselves under his guidance in the grassy valley.

He had crossed the Saint Gothard Pass with them, in the

same carriage. During the journey from Florence, and especially during this portion of it, the cloud that hung over the
little party had been almost dissipated, and they had looked
at each other, in the close contiguity of the train and the post-
ing-carriage, without either accusing or consoling glances. It
was impossible not to enjoy the magnificent scenery of the
Apennines and the Italian Alps, and there was a tacit agreement among the travelers to abstain from sombre allusions.
The effect of this delicate compact seemed excellent; it en-
sured them a week's intellectual sunshine. Roderick sat and
gazed out of the window with a fascinated stare, and with a
perfect docility of attitude. He concerned himself not a particle about the itinerary, or about any of the wayside arrangements; he took no trouble, and he gave none. He assented to
everything that was proposed, talked very little, and led for a
week a perfectly contemplative life. His mother rarely removed her eyes from him; and if, a while before, this would
have extremely irritated him, he now seemed perfectly unconscious of her observation and profoundly indifferent to anything that might befall him. They spent a couple of days on
the Lake of Como, at a hotel with white porticoes smothered
in oleander and myrtle, and the terrace-steps leading down to
little boats with striped awnings. They agreed it was the
earthly paradise, and they passed the mornings strolling
through the perfumed alleys of classic villas, and the evenings
floating in the moonlight in a circle of outlined mountains, to
the music of silver-trickling oars. One day, in the afternoon,
the two young men took a long stroll together. They followed the winding footway that led toward Como, close to
the lake-side, past the gates of villas and the walls of vineyards, through little hamlets propped on a dozen arches, and
bathing their feet and their pendant tatters in the gray-green
ripple; past frescoed walls and crumbling campaniles and
grassy village piazzas, and the mouth of soft ravines that
wound upward, through belts of swinging vine and vaporous
olive and splendid chestnut, to high ledges where white chapels gleamed amid the paler boskage, and bare cliff-surfaces,
with their sun-cracked lips, drank in the azure light. It all was
confoundingly picturesque; it was the Italy that we know
from the steel engravings in old keepsakes and annuals, from

the vignettes on music-sheets and the drop-curtains at theatres; an Italy that we can never confess to ourselves—in spite
of our own changes and of Italy's—that we have ceased to
believe in. Rowland and Roderick turned aside from the little
paved footway that clambered and dipped and wound and
doubled beside the lake, and stretched themselves idly beneath a fig-tree, on a grassy promontory. Rowland had never
known anything so divinely soothing as the dreamy softness
of that early autumn afternoon. The iridescent mountains
shut him in; the little waves, beneath him, fretted the white
pebbles at the laziest intervals; the festooned vines above him
swayed just visibly in the all but motionless air.

Roderick lay observing it all with his arms thrown back and
his hands under his head. "This suits me," he said; "I could
be happy here and forget everything. Why not stay here forever?" He kept his position for a long time and seemed lost
in his thoughts. Rowland spoke to him, but he made vague
answers; at last he closed his eyes. It seemed to Rowland,
also, a place to stay in forever; a place for perfect oblivion of
the disagreeable. Suddenly Roderick turned over on his face,
and buried it in his arms. There had been something passionate in his movement; but Rowland was nevertheless surprised, when he at last jerked himself back into a sitting
posture, to perceive the trace of tears in his eyes. Roderick
turned to his friend, stretching his two hands out toward the
lake and mountains, and shaking them with an eloquent gesture, as if his heart was too full for utterance.

"Pity me, sir; pity me!" he presently cried. "Look at this
lovely world, and think what it must be to be dead to it!"

"Dead?" said Rowland.

"Dead, dead; dead and buried! Buried in an open grave,
where you lie staring up at the sailing clouds, smelling the
waving flowers, and hearing all nature live and grow above
you! That's the way I feel!"

"I am glad to hear it," said Rowland. "Death of that sort is
very near to resurrection."

"It's too horrible," Roderick went on; "it has all come over
me here tremendously! If I were not ashamed, I could shed a
bushel of tears. For one hour of what I *have* been, I would
give up anything I may be!"

"Never mind what you have been; be something better!"

"I shall never be anything again: it 's no use talking! But I don't know what secret spring has been touched since I have lain here. Something in my heart seemed suddenly to open and let in a flood of beauty and desire. I know what I have lost, and I think it horrible! Mind you, I know it, I feel it! Remember that hereafter. Don't say that he was stupefied and senseless; that his perception was dulled and his aspiration dead. Say that he trembled in every nerve with a sense of the beauty and sweetness of life; that he rebelled and protested and shrieked; that he was buried alive, with his eyes open, and his heart beating to madness; that he clung to every blade of grass and every way-side thorn as he passed; that it was the most horrible spectacle you ever witnessed; that it was an outrage, a murder, a massacre!"

"Good heavens, man, are you insane?" Rowland cried.

"I never have been saner. I don't want to be bad company, and in this beautiful spot, at this delightful hour, it seems an outrage to break the charm. But I am bidding farewell to Italy, to beauty, to honor, to life! I only want to assure you that I know what I lose. I know it in every pulse of my heart! Here, where these things are all loveliest, I take leave of them. Farewell, farewell!"

During their passage of the Saint Gothard, Roderick absented himself much of the time from the carriage, and rambled far in advance, along the huge zigzags of the road. He displayed an extraordinary activity; his light weight and slender figure made him an excellent pedestrian, and his friends frequently saw him skirting the edge of plunging chasms, loosening the stones on long, steep slopes, or lifting himself against the sky, from the top of rocky pinnacles. Mary Garland walked a great deal, but she remained near the carriage to be with Mrs. Hudson. Rowland remained near it to be with Miss Garland. He trudged by her side up that magnificent ascent from Italy, and found himself regretting that the Alps were so low, and that their trudging was not to last a week. She was exhilarated; she liked to walk; in the way of mountains, until within the last few weeks, she had seen nothing greater than Mount Holyoke, and she found that the Alps amply justified their reputation. Rowland knew that she loved nature, but he was struck afresh with the vivacity of her observation of it, and with her knowledge of plants and stones. At that season the wild flowers had mostly departed, but a few of them lingered, and Miss Garland never failed to espy them in their outlying corners. They interested her greatly; she was charmed when they were old friends, and charmed even more when they were new. She displayed a very light foot in going in quest of them, and had soon covered the front seat of the carriage with a tangle of strange vegetation. Rowland of course was alert in her service, and he gathered for her several botanical specimens which at first seemed inaccessible. One of these, indeed, had at first appeared easier of capture than his attempt attested, and he had paused a moment at the base of the little peak on which it grew, measuring the risk of farther pursuit. Suddenly, as he stood there, he remembered Roderick's defiance of danger and of Miss Light, at the Coliseum, and he was seized with a strong desire to test the courage of his companion. She had just scrambled up a grassy slope near him, and had seen that the flower was out of reach. As he prepared to approach it, she called to him eagerly to stop; the thing was impossible! Poor Rowland, whose passion had been terribly starved, enjoyed immensely the thought of having her care, for three minutes, what became of him. He was the least brutal of men, but for a moment he was perfectly indifferent to her suffering.

"I can get the flower," he called to her. "Will you trust me?"

"I don't want it; I would rather not have it!" she cried.

"Will you trust me?" he repeated, looking at her.

She looked at him and then at the flower; he wondered whether she would shriek and swoon, as Miss Light had done. "I wish it were something better!" she said simply; and then stood watching him, while he began to clamber. Rowland was not shaped for an acrobat, and his enterprise was difficult; but he kept his wits about him, made the most of narrow foot-holds and coigns of vantage, and at last secured his prize. He managed to stick it into his button-hole and then he contrived to descend. There was more than one chance for an ugly fall, but he evaded them all. It was doubtless not gracefully done, but it was done, and that was all he had proposed to himself. He was red in the face when he offered Miss Garland the flower, and she was visibly pale. She had watched him without moving. All this had passed without the knowledge of Mrs. Hudson, who was dozing beneath the hood of the carriage. Mary Garland's eyes did not perhaps display that ardent admiration which was formerly conferred by the queen of beauty at a tournament; but they expressed something in which Rowland found his reward. "Why did you do that?" she asked, gravely.

He hesitated. He felt that it was physically possible to say, "Because I love you!" but that it was not morally possible. He lowered his pitch and answered, simply, "Because I wanted to do something for you."

"Suppose you had fallen," said Miss Garland.

"I believed I would not fall. And you believed it, I think."

"I believed nothing. I simply trusted you, as you asked me."

"*Quod erat demonstrandum!*" cried Rowland. "I think you know Latin."

When our four friends were established in what I have called their grassy valley, there was a good deal of scrambling over slopes both grassy and stony, a good deal of flower-plucking on narrow ledges, a great many long walks, and, thanks to the lucid mountain air, not a little exhilaration. Mrs. Hudson was obliged to intermit her suspicions of the deleterious atmosphere of the old world, and to acknowledge the edifying purity of the breezes of Engelthal. She was certainly more placid than she had been in Italy; having always lived in the country, she had missed in Rome and Florence that social solitude mitigated by bushes and rocks which is so dear to the true New England temperament. The little unpainted inn at Engelthal, with its plank partitions, its milk-pans standing in the sun, its "help," in the form of angular young women of the country-side, reminded her of places of summer sojourn in her native land; and the beautiful historic chambers of the Villa Pandolfini passed from her memory without a regret, and without having in the least modified her ideal of domiciliary grace. Roderick had changed his sky, but he had not changed his mind; his humor was still that of which he had given Rowland a glimpse in that tragic explosion on the Lake of Como. He kept his despair to himself, and he went doggedly about the ordinary business of life; but it was easy to see that his spirit was mortally heavy, and that he lived and moved and talked simply from the force of habit. In that sad half-hour among the Italian olives there had been such a fierce sincerity in his tone, that Rowland began to abdicate the critical attitude. He began to feel that it was essentially vain to appeal to the poor fellow's will; there was no will left; its place was an impotent void. This view of the case indeed was occasionally contravened by certain indications on Roderick's part of the power of resistance to disagreeable obligations: one might still have said, if one had been disposed to be didactic at any hazard, that there was a method in his madness, that his moral energy had its sleeping and its waking hours, and that, in a cause that pleased it, it was capable of rising with the dawn. But on the other hand, pleasure, in this case, was quite at one with effort; evidently the greatest bliss in life, for Roderick, would have been to have a plastic idea. And then, it was impossible not to feel tenderly to a despair which had so ceased to be aggressive—not to forgive a great deal of apathy to a temper which had so unlearned its irritability. Roderick said frankly that Switzerland made him less miserable than Italy, and the Alps seemed less to mock at his enforced leisure than the Apennines. He indulged in long rambles, generally alone, and was very fond of climbing into dizzy places, where no sound could overtake him, and there, flinging himself on the never-trodden moss, of pulling his hat over his eyes and lounging away the hours in perfect immobility. Rowland sometimes walked with him; though Roderick never invited him, he seemed duly grateful for his society. Rowland now made it a rule to treat him like a perfectly sane man, to assume that all things were well with him, and never to allude to the prosperity he had forfeited or to the work he was not doing. He would have still said, had you questioned him, that Roderick's condition was a mood—certainly a puzzling one. It might last yet for many a weary hour; but it was a long lane that had no turning. Roderick's blues would not last forever. Rowland's interest in Miss Garland's relations with her cousin was still profoundly attentive, and perplexed as he was on all sides, he found nothing transparent here.

After their arrival at Engelthal, Roderick appeared to seek the young girl's society more than he had done hitherto, and this revival of ardor could not fail to set his friend a-wondering. They sat together and strolled together, and Miss Garland often read aloud to him. One day, on their coming to dinner, after he had been lying half the morning at her feet, in the shadow of a rock, Rowland asked him what she had been reading.

"I don't know," Roderick said, "I don't heed the sense." Miss Garland heard this, and Rowland looked at her. She looked at Roderick sharply and with a little blush. "I listen to Mary," Roderick continued, "for the sake of her voice. It 's distractingly sweet!" At this Miss Garland's blush deepened, and she looked away.

Rowland, in Florence, as we know, had suffered his imagination to wander in the direction of certain conjectures which the reader may deem unflattering to Miss Garland's constancy. He had asked himself whether her faith in Roderick had not faltered, and that demand of hers which had brought about his own departure for Switzerland had seemed almost equivalent to a confession that she needed his help to believe. Rowland was essentially a modest man, and he did not risk the supposition that Miss Garland had contrasted him with Roderick to his own advantage; but he had a certain consciousness of duty resolutely done which allowed itself to fancy, at moments, that it might be not illogically rewarded by the bestowal of such stray grains of enthusiasm as had crumbled away from her estimate of his companion. If some day she had declared, in a sudden burst of passion, that she was outwearied and sickened, and that she gave up her recreant lover, Rowland's expectation would have gone halfway to meet her. And certainly if her passion had taken this course no generous critic would utterly condemn her. She had been neglected, ignored, forsaken, treated with a contempt which no girl of a fine temper could endure. There were girls, indeed, whose fineness, like that of Burd Helen in the ballad, lay in clinging to the man of their love through thick and thin, and in bowing their head to all hard usage. This attitude had often an exquisite beauty of its own, but Rowland deemed that he had solid reason to believe it never could be Mary Garland's. She was not a passive creature; she was not soft and meek and grateful for chance bounties. With all her reserve of manner she was proud and eager; she asked much and she wanted what she asked; she believed in fine things and she never could long persuade herself that fine things missed were as beautiful as fine things achieved. Once Rowland passed an angry day. He had dreamed—it was the most insubstantial of dreams—that she had given him the right to believe that she looked to him to transmute her discontent. And yet here she was throwing herself back into Roderick's arms at his lightest overture, and playing with his own half fearful, half shameful hopes! Rowland declared to himself that his position was essentially detestable, and that all the philosophy he could bring to bear upon it would make it neither honorable nor comfortable. He would go away and make an end of it. He did not go away; he simply took a long walk, stayed away from the inn all day, and on his return found Miss Garland sitting out in the moonlight with Roderick.

Rowland, communing with himself during the restless ramble in question, had determined that he would at least cease to observe, to heed, or to care for what Miss Garland and Roderick might do or might not do together. Nevertheless, some three days afterward, the opportunity presenting itself, he deliberately broached the subject with Roderick. He knew this was inconsistent and faint-hearted; it was indulgence to the fingers that itched to handle forbidden fruit. But he said to himself that it was really more logical to be inconsistent than the reverse; for they had formerly discussed these mysteries very candidly. Was it not perfectly reasonable that he should wish to know the sequel of the situation which Roderick had then delineated? Roderick had made him promises, and it was to be expected that he should ascertain how the promises had been kept. Rowland could not say to himself that if the promises had been extorted for Mary Garland's sake, his present attention to them was equally disinterested; and so he had to admit that he was indeed faint-hearted. He may perhaps be deemed too narrow a casuist, but we have repeated more than once that he was solidly burdened with a conscience.

"I imagine," he said to Roderick, "that you are not sorry, at present, to have allowed yourself to be dissuaded from making a final rupture with Miss Garland."

Roderick eyed him with the vague and absent look which had lately become habitual to his face, and repeated "Dissuaded?"

"Don't you remember that, in Rome, you wished to break your engagement, and that I urged you to respect it, though it seemed to hang by so slender a thread? I wished you to see what would come of it? If I am not mistaken, you are reconciled to it."

"Oh yes," said Roderick, "I remember what you said; you made it a kind of personal favor to yourself that I should remain faithful. I consented, but afterwards, when I thought of it, your attitude greatly amused me. Had it ever been seen before?—a man asking another man to gratify him by *not* suspending his attentions to a pretty girl!"

"It was as selfish as anything else," said Rowland. "One man puts his selfishness into one thing, and one into another. It would have utterly marred my comfort to see Miss Garland in low spirits."

"But you liked her—you admired her, eh? So you intimated."

"I admire her profoundly."

"It was your originality then—to do you justice you have a great deal, of a certain sort—to wish her happiness secured in just that fashion. Many a man would have liked better himself to make the woman he admired happy, and would have welcomed her low spirits as an opening for sympathy. You were awfully queer about it."

"So be it!" said Rowland. "The question is, Are you not glad I was queer? Are you not finding that your affection for Miss Garland has a permanent quality which you rather underestimated?"

"I don't pretend to say. When she arrived in Rome, I found I did n't care for her, and I honestly proposed that we should have no humbug about it. If you, on the contrary, thought there was something to be gained by having a little humbug, I was willing to try it! I don't see that the situation is really changed. Mary Garland is all that she ever was—more than all. But I don't care for her! I don't care for anything, and I don't find myself inspired to make an exception in her favor. The only difference is that I don't care now, whether I care for her or not. Of course, marrying such a useless lout as I am is out of the question for any woman, and I should pay Miss Garland a poor compliment to assume that she is in a hurry to celebrate our nuptials."

"Oh, you 're in love!" said Rowland, not very logically. It must be confessed, at any cost, that this assertion was made for the sole purpose of hearing Roderick deny it.

But it quite failed of its aim. Roderick gave a liberal shrug of his shoulders and an irresponsible toss of his head. "Call it what you please! I am past caring for names."

Rowland had not only been illogical, he had also been slightly disingenuous. He did not believe that his companion was in love; he had argued the false to learn the true. The true was that Roderick was again, in some degree, under a charm, and that he found a healing virtue in Mary's presence, indisposed though he was to admit it. He had said, shortly before, that her voice was sweet to his ear; and this was a promising beginning. If her voice was sweet it was probable that her glance was not amiss, that her touch had a quiet magic, and that her whole personal presence had learned the art of not being irritating. So Rowland reasoned, and invested Mary Garland with a still finer loveliness.

It was true that she herself helped him little to definite conclusions, and that he remained in puzzled doubt as to whether these happy touches were still a matter of the heart, or had become simply a matter of the conscience. He watched for signs that she rejoiced in Roderick's renewed acceptance of her society; but it seemed to him that she was on her guard against interpreting it too largely. It was now her turn—he fancied that he sometimes gathered from certain nameless indications of glance and tone and gesture—it was now her turn to be indifferent, to care for other things. Again and again Rowland asked himself what these things were that Miss Garland might be supposed to care for, to the injury of ideal constancy; and again, having designated them, he divided them into two portions. One was that larger experience, in general, which had come to her with her arrival in Europe; the vague sense, borne in upon her imagination, that there were more things one might do with one's life than youth and ignorance and Northampton had dreamt of; the revision of old pledges in the light of new emotions. The other was the experience, in especial, of Rowland's—what? Here Rowland always paused, in perfect sincerity, to measure afresh his possible claim to the young girl's regard. What might he call it? It had been more than civility and yet it had been less than devotion. It had spoken of a desire to serve, but it had said nothing of a hope of reward. Nevertheless, Rowland's fancy hovered about the idea that it was recompensable, and his reflections ended in a reverie which perhaps did not define it, but at least, on each occasion, added a little to its volume. Since Miss Garland had asked him as a sort of favor to herself to come also to Switzerland, he thought it possible she might let him know whether he seemed to have effectively served her. The days passed without her doing so, and at last Rowland walked away to an isolated eminence some five miles from the inn and murmured to the silent rocks that she was ungrateful. Listening nature seemed not to contradict him, so that, on the morrow, he asked the young girl, with an infinitesimal touch of irony, whether it struck her that his deflection from his Florentine plan had been attended with brilliant results.

"Why, we are delighted that you are with us!" she answered.

He was anything but satisfied with this; it seemed to imply that she had forgotten that she had solemnly asked him to come. He reminded her of her request, and recalled the place and time. "That evening on the terrace, late, after Mrs. Hudson had gone to bed, and Roderick being absent."

She perfectly remembered, but the memory seemed to trouble her. "I am afraid your kindness has been a great charge upon you," she said. "You wanted very much to do something else."

"I wanted above all things to oblige you, and I made no sacrifice. But if I had made an immense one, it would be more than made up to me by any assurance that I have helped Roderick into a better mood."

She was silent a moment, and then, "Why do you ask me?" she said. "You are able to judge quite as well as I."

Rowland blushed; he desired to justify himself in the most veracious manner. "The truth is," he said, "that I am afraid I care only in the second place for Roderick's holding up his head. What I care for in the first place is *your* happiness."

"I don't know why that should be," she answered. "I have certainly done nothing to make you so much my friend. If you were to tell me you intended to leave us to-morrow, I am afraid that I should not venture to ask you to stay. But whether you go or stay, let us not talk of Roderick!"

"But that," said Rowland, "does n't answer my question. *Is* he better?"

"No!" she said, and turned away.

He was careful not to tell her that he intended to leave them. One day, shortly after this, as the two young men sat at the inn-door watching the sunset, which on that evening was very striking and lurid, Rowland made an attempt to sound his companion's present sentiment touching Christina Light. "I wonder where she is," he said, "and what sort of a life she is leading her prince."

Roderick at first made no response. He was watching a figure on the summit of some distant rocks, opposite to them. The figure was apparently descending into the valley, and in relief against the crimson screen of the western sky, it looked gigantic. "Christina Light?" Roderick at last repeated, as if arousing himself from a reverie. "Where she is? It 's extraordinary how little I care!"

"Have you, then, completely got over it?"

To this Roderick made no direct reply; he sat brooding a while. "She 's a humbug!" he presently exclaimed.

"Possibly!" said Rowland. "But I have known worse ones."

"She disappointed me!" Roderick continued in the same tone.

"Had she, then, really given you hopes?"

"Oh, don't recall it!" Roderick cried. "Why the devil should I think of it? It was only three months ago, but it seems like ten years." His friend said nothing more, and after a while he went on of his own accord. "I believed there was a future in it all! She pleased me—pleased me; and when an artist—such as I was—is pleased, you know!" And he paused again. "You never saw her as I did; you never heard her in her great moments. But there is no use talking about that! At first she would n't regard me seriously; she chaffed me and made light of me. But at last I forced her to admit I was a great man. Think of that, sir! Christina Light called me a great man. A great man was what she was looking for, and we agreed to find our happiness for life in each other. To please me she promised not to marry till I gave her leave. I was not in a marrying way myself, but it was damnation to think of another man possessing her. To spare my sensibilities, she promised to turn off her prince, and the idea of her doing so made me as happy as to see a perfect statue shaping itself in the block. You have seen how she kept her promise! When I learned it, it was as if the statue had suddenly cracked and turned hideous. She died for me, like that!" And he snapped his fingers. "Was it wounded vanity, disappointed desire, betrayed confidence? I am sure I don't know; you certainly have some name for it."

"The poor girl did the best she could," said Rowland.

"If that was her best, so much the worse for her! I have hardly thought of her these two months, but I have not forgiven her."

"Well, you may believe that you are avenged. I can't think of her as happy."

"I don't pity her!" said Roderick. Then he relapsed into silence, and the two sat watching the colossal figure as it made its way downward along the jagged silhouette of the rocks. "Who is this mighty man," cried Roderick at last, "and what is he coming down upon us for? We are small people here, and we can't undertake to keep company with giants."

"Wait till we meet him on our own level," said Rowland, "and perhaps he will not overtop us."

"For ten minutes, at least," Roderick rejoined, "he will have been a great man!" At this moment the figure sank beneath the horizon line and became invisible in the uncertain light. Suddenly Roderick said, "I would like to see her once more—simply to look at her."

"I would not advise it," said Rowland.

"It was her beauty that did it!" Roderick went on. "It was

all her beauty; in comparison, the rest was nothing. What befooled me was to think of it as *my* property! And I had made it mine—no one else had studied it as I had, no one else understood it. What does that stick of a Casamassima know about it at this hour? I should like to see it just once more; it 's the only thing in the world of which I can say so."

"I would not advise it," Rowland repeated.

"That 's right, dear Rowland," said Roderick; "don't advise! That 's no use now."

The dusk meanwhile had thickened, and they had not perceived a figure approaching them across the open space in front of the house. Suddenly it stepped into the circle of light projected from the door and windows, and they beheld little Sam Singleton stopping to stare at them. He was the giant whom they had seen descending along the rocks. When this was made apparent Roderick was seized with a fit of intense hilarity—it was the first time he had laughed in three months. Singleton, who carried a knapsack and walking-staff, received from Rowland the friendliest welcome. He was in the serenest possible humor, and if in the way of luggage his knapsack contained nothing but a comb and a second shirt, he produced from it a dozen admirable sketches. He had been trudging over half Switzerland and making everywhere the most vivid pictorial notes. They were mostly in a box at Interlaken, and in gratitude for Rowland's appreciation, he presently telegraphed for his box, which, according to the excellent Swiss method, was punctually delivered by post. The nights were cold, and our friends, with three or four other chance sojourners, sat in-doors over a fire of logs. Even with Roderick sitting moodily in the outer shadow they made a sympathetic little circle, and they turned over Singleton's drawings, while he perched in the chimney-corner, blushing and grinning, with his feet on the rounds of his chair. He had been pedestrianizing for six weeks, and he was glad to rest awhile at Engelthal. It was an economic repose, however, for he sallied forth every morning, with his sketching tools on his back, in search of material for new studies. Roderick's hilarity, after the first evening, had subsided, and he watched the little painter's serene activity with a gravity that was almost portentous. Singleton, who was not in the secret of his personal misfortunes, still treated him with timid frankness as the rising star of American art. Roderick had said to Rowland, at first, that Singleton reminded him of some curious little insect with a remarkable mechanical instinct in its *antennæ*; but as the days went by it was apparent that the modest landscapist's unflagging industry grew to have an oppressive meaning for him. It pointed a moral, and Roderick used to sit and con the moral as he saw it figured in Singleton's bent back, on the hot hill-sides, protruding from beneath his white umbrella. One day he wandered up a long slope and overtook him as he sat at work; Singleton related the incident afterwards to Rowland, who, after giving him in Rome a hint of Roderick's aberrations, had strictly kept his own counsel.

"Are you *always* like this?" said Roderick, in almost sepulchral accents.

"Like this?" repeated Singleton, blinking confusedly, with an alarmed conscience.

"You remind me of a watch that never runs down. If one listens hard one hears you always—tic-tic, tic-tic."

"Oh, I see," said Singleton, beaming ingenuously. "I am very equable."

"You are very equable, yes. And do you find it pleasant to be equable?"

Singleton turned and grinned more brightly, while he sucked the water from his camel's-hair brush. Then, with a quickened sense of his indebtedness to a Providence that had endowed him with intrinsic facilities, "Oh, delightful!" he exclaimed.

Roderick stood looking at him a moment. "Damnation!" he said at last, solemnly, and turned his back.

One morning, shortly after this, Rowland and Roderick took a long walk. They had walked before in a dozen different directions, but they had not yet crossed a charming little wooded pass, which shut in their valley on one side and descended into the vale of Engelberg. In coming from Lucerne they had approached their inn by this path, and, feeling that they knew it, had hitherto neglected it in favor of untrodden ways. But at last the list of these was exhausted, and Rowland proposed the walk to Engelberg as a novelty. The place is half bleak and half pastoral; a huge white monastery rises abruptly

from the green floor of the valley and complicates its picturesqueness with an element rare in Swiss scenery. Hard by is a
group of châlets and inns, with the usual appurtenances of a
prosperous Swiss resort—lean brown guides in baggy home-
spun, lounging under carved wooden galleries, stacks of
alpenstocks in every doorway, sun-scorched Englishmen without shirt-collars. Our two friends sat a while at the door of
an inn, discussing a pint of wine, and then Roderick, who
was indefatigable, announced his intention of climbing to a
certain rocky pinnacle which overhung the valley, and, according to the testimony of one of the guides, commanded a
view of the Lake of Lucerne. To go and come back was only
a matter of an hour, but Rowland, with the prospect of his
homeward trudge before him, confessed to a preference for
lounging on his bench, or at most strolling a trifle farther and
taking a look at the monastery. Roderick went off alone, and
his companion after a while bent his steps to the monasterial
church. It was remarkable, like most of the churches of Catholic Switzerland, for a hideous style of devotional ornament;
but it had a certain cold and musty picturesqueness, and
Rowland lingered there with some tenderness for Alpine
piety. While he was near the high-altar some people came in
at the west door; but he did not notice them, and was presently engaged in deciphering a curious old German epitaph
on one of the mural tablets. At last he turned away, wondering whether its syntax or its theology was the more uncomfortable, and, to this infinite surprise, found himself
confronted with the Prince and Princess Casamassima.

The surprise on Christina's part, for an instant, was equal,
and at first she seemed disposed to turn away without letting
it give place to a greeting. The prince, however, saluted
gravely, and then Christina, in silence, put out her hand.
Rowland immediately asked whether they were staying at Engelberg, but Christina only looked at him without speaking.
The prince answered his questions, and related that they had
been making a month's tour in Switzerland, that at Lucerne
his wife had been somewhat obstinately indisposed, and that
the physician had recommended a week's trial of the tonic air
and goat's milk of Engelberg. The scenery, said the prince,
was stupendous, but the life was terribly sad—and they had

three days more! It was a blessing, he urbanely added, to see a good Roman face.

Christina's attitude, her solemn silence and her penetrating gaze seemed to Rowland, at first, to savor of affectation; but he presently perceived that she was profoundly agitated, and that she was afraid of betraying herself. "Do let us leave this hideous edifice," she said; "there are things here that set one's teeth on edge." They moved slowly to the door, and when they stood outside, in the sunny coolness of the valley, she turned to Rowland and said, "I am extremely glad to see you." Then she glanced about her and observed, against the wall of the church, an old stone seat. She looked at Prince Casamassima a moment, and he smiled more intensely, Rowland thought, than the occasion demanded. "I wish to sit here," she said, "and speak to Mr. Mallet—alone."

"At your pleasure, dear friend," said the prince.

The tone of each was measured, to Rowland's ear; but that of Christina was dry, and that of her husband was splendidly urbane. Rowland remembered that the Cavaliere Giacosa had told him that Mrs. Light's candidate was thoroughly a prince, and our friend wondered how he relished a peremptory accent. Casamassima was an Italian of the undemonstrative type, but Rowland nevertheless divined that, like other princes before him, he had made the acquaintance of the thing called compromise. "Shall I come back?" he asked with the same smile.

"In half an hour," said Christina.

In the clear outer light, Rowland's first impression of her was that she was more beautiful than ever. And yet in three months she could hardly have changed; the change was in Rowland's own vision of her, which that last interview, on the eve of her marriage, had made unprecedentedly tender.

"How came you here?" she asked. "Are you staying in this place?"

"I am staying at Engelthal, some ten miles away; I walked over."

"Are you alone?"

"I am with Mr. Hudson."

"Is he here with you?"

"He went half an hour ago to climb a rock for a view."

"And his mother and that young girl, where are they?"

"They also are at Engelthal."

"What do you do there?"

"What do you do here?" said Rowland, smiling.

"I count the minutes till my week is up. I hate mountains; they depress me to death. I am sure Miss Garland likes them."

"She is very fond of them, I believe."

"You believe—don't you know? But I have given up trying to imitate Miss Garland," said Christina.

"You surely need imitate no one."

"Don't say that," she said gravely. "So you have walked ten miles this morning? And you are to walk back again?"

"Back again to supper."

"And Mr. Hudson too?"

"Mr. Hudson especially. He is a great walker."

"You men are happy!" Christina cried. "I believe I should enjoy the mountains if I could do such things. It is sitting still and having them scowl down at you! Prince Casamassina never rides. He only goes on a mule. He was carried up the Faulhorn on a litter."

"On a litter?" said Rowland.

"In one of those machines—a *chaise à porteurs*—like a woman."

Rowland received this information in silence; it was equally unbecoming to either to relish or deprecate its irony.

"Is Mr. Hudson to join you again? Will he come here?" Christina asked.

"I shall soon begin to expect him."

"What shall you do when you leave Switzerland?" Christina continued. "Shall you go back to Rome?"

"I rather doubt it. My plans are very uncertain."

"They depend upon Mr. Hudson, eh?"

"In a great measure."

"I want you to tell me about him. Is he still in that perverse state of mind that afflicted you so much?"

Rowland looked at her mistrustfully, without answering. He was indisposed, instinctively, to tell her that Roderick was unhappy; it was possible she might offer to help him back to happiness. She immediately perceived his hesitation.

"I see no reason why we should not be frank," she said. "I

should think we were excellently placed for that sort of thing. You remember that formerly I cared very little what I said, don't you? Well, I care absolutely not at all now. I say what I please, I do what I please! How did Mr. Hudson receive the news of my marriage?"

"Very badly," said Rowland.

"With rage and reproaches?" And as Rowland hesitated again—"With silent contempt?"

"I can tell you but little. He spoke to me on the subject, but I stopped him. I told him it was none of his business, or of mine."

"That was an excellent answer!" said Christina, softly. "Yet it was a little your business, after those sublime protestations I treated you to. I was really very fine that morning, eh?"

"You do yourself injustice," said Rowland. "I should be at liberty now to believe you were insincere."

"What does it matter now whether I was insincere or not? I can't conceive of anything mattering less. I *was* very fine— is n't it true?"

"You know what I think of you," said Rowland. And for fear of being forced to betray his suspicion of the cause of her change, he took refuge in a commonplace. "Your mother, I hope, is well."

"My mother is in the enjoyment of superb health, and may be seen every evening at the Casino, at the Baths of Lucca, confiding to every new-comer that she has married her daughter to a pearl of a prince."

Rowland was anxious for news of Mrs. Light's companion, and the natural course was frankly to inquire about him. "And the Cavaliere Giacosa is well?" he asked.

Christina hesitated, but she betrayed no other embarrassment. "The Cavaliere has retired to his native city of Ancona, upon a pension, for the rest of his natural life. He is a very good old man!"

"I have a great regard for him," said Rowland, gravely, at the same time that he privately wondered whether the Cavaliere's pension was paid by Prince Casamassima for services rendered in connection with his marriage. Had the Cavaliere received his commission? "And what do you do," Rowland continued, "on leaving this place?"

"We go to Italy—we go to Naples." She rose and stood
silent a moment, looking down the valley. The figure of
Prince Casamassima appeared in the distance, balancing his
white umbrella. As her eyes rested upon it, Rowland imagined that he saw something deeper in the strange expression
which had lurked in her face while he talked to her. At first
he had been dazzled by her blooming beauty, to which the
lapse of weeks had only added splendor; then he had seen a
heavier ray in the light of her eye—a sinister intimation of
sadness and bitterness. It was the outward mark of her sacrificed ideal. Her eyes grew cold as she looked at her husband,
and when, after a moment, she turned them upon Rowland,
they struck him as intensely tragical. He felt a singular mixture of sympathy and dread; he wished to give her a proof of
friendship, and yet it seemed to him that she had now turned
her face in a direction where friendship was impotent to interpose. She half read his feelings, apparently, and she gave a
beautiful, sad smile. "I hope we may never meet again!" she
said. And as Rowland gave her a protesting look—"You have
seen me at my best. I wish to tell you solemnly, I *was* sincere!
I know appearances are against me," she went on quickly.
"There is a great deal I can't tell you. Perhaps you have
guessed it; I care very little. You know, at any rate, I did my
best. It would n't serve; I was beaten and broken; they were
stronger than I. Now it 's another affair!"

"It seems to me you have a large chance for happiness yet,"
said Rowland, vaguely.

"Happiness? I mean to cultivate rapture; I mean to go in
for bliss ineffable! You remember I told you that I was, in
part, the world's and the devil's. Now they have taken me all.
It was their choice; may they never repent!"

"I shall hear of you," said Rowland.

"You will hear of me. And whatever you do hear, remember this: I *was* sincere!"

Prince Casamassima had approached, and Rowland looked
at him with a good deal of simple compassion as a part of
that "world" against which Christina had launched her mysterious menace. It was obvious that he was a good fellow,
and that he could not, in the nature of things, be a positively
bad husband; but his distinguished inoffensiveness only deep-

ened the infelicity of Christina's situation by depriving her
defiant attitude of the sanction of relative justice. So long as
she had been free to choose, she had esteemed him: but from
the moment she was forced to marry him she had detested
him. Rowland read in the young man's elastic Italian mask a
profound consciousness of all this; and as he found there also
a record of other curious things—of pride, of temper, of big-
otry, of an immense heritage of more or less aggressive traditions—he reflected that the matrimonial conjunction of his
two companions might be sufficiently prolific in incident.

"You are going to Naples?" Rowland said to the prince by
way of conversation.

"We are going to Paris," Christina interposed, slowly and
softly. "We are going to London. We are going to Vienna.
We are going to St. Petersburg."

Prince Casamassima dropped his eyes and fretted the earth
with the point of his umbrella. While he engaged Rowland's
attention Christina turned away. When Rowland glanced at
her again he saw a change pass over her face; she was observing something that was concealed from his own eyes by the
angle of the church-wall. In a moment Roderick stepped into
sight.

He stopped short, astonished; his face and figure were
jaded, his garments dusty. He looked at Christina from head
to foot, and then, slowly, his cheek flushed and his eye expanded. Christina returned his gaze, and for some moments
there was a singular silence. "You don't look well!" Christina
said at last.

Roderick answered nothing; he only looked and looked, as
if she had been a statue. "You are no less beautiful!" he presently cried.

She turned away with a smile, and stood a while gazing
down the valley; Roderick stared at Prince Casamassima.
Christina then put out her hand to Rowland. "Farewell," she
said. "If you are near me in future, don't try to see me!" And
then, after a pause, in a lower tone, "I *was* sincere!" She addressed herself again to Roderick and asked him some commonplace about his walk. But he said nothing; he only looked
at her. Rowland at first had expected an outbreak of reproach,
but it was evident that the danger was every moment dimin-

ishing. He was forgetting everything but her beauty, and as she stood there and let him feast upon it, Rowland was sure that she knew it. "I won't say farewell to you," she said; "we shall meet again!" And she moved gravely away. Prince Casamassima took leave courteously of Rowland; upon Roderick he bestowed a bow of exaggerated civility. Roderick appeared not to see it; he was still watching Christina, as she passed over the grass. His eyes followed her until she reached the door of her inn. Here she stopped and looked back at him.

XIII

Switzerland

ON THE HOMEWARD walk, that evening, Roderick preserved a silence which Rowland allowed to make him uneasy. Early on the morrow Roderick, saying nothing of his intentions, started off on a walk; Rowland saw him striding with light steps along the rugged path to Engelberg. He was absent all day and he gave no account of himself on his return. He said he was deadly tired, and he went to bed early. When he had left the room Miss Garland drew near to Rowland.

"I wish to ask you a question," she said. "What happened to Roderick yesterday at Engelberg?"

"You have discovered that something happened?" Rowland answered.

"I am sure of it. Was it something painful?"

"I don't know how, at the present moment, he judges it. He met the Princess Casamassima."

"Thank you!" said Miss Garland, simply, and turned away.

The conversation had been brief, but, like many small things, it furnished Rowland with food for reflection. When one is looking for symptoms one easily finds them. This was the first time Mary Garland had asked Rowland a question which it was in Roderick's power to answer, the first time she had frankly betrayed Roderick's reticence. Rowland ventured to think it marked an era.

The next morning was sultry, and the air, usually so fresh at those altitudes, was oppressively heavy. Rowland lounged on the grass a while, near Singleton, who was at work under his white umbrella, within view of the house; and then in quest of coolness he wandered away to the rocky ridge whence you looked across at the Jungfrau. To-day, however, the white summits were invisible; their heads were muffled in sullen clouds and the valleys beneath them curtained in dun-colored mist. Rowland had a book in his pocket, and he took it out and opened it. But his page remained unturned; his own thoughts were more importunate. His interview with

491

Christina Light had made a great impression upon him, and he was haunted with the memory of her almost blameless bitterness, and of all that was tragic and fatal in her latest transformation. These things were immensely appealing, and Rowland thought with infinite impatience of Roderick's having again encountered them. It required little imagination to apprehend that the young sculptor's condition had also appealed to Christina. His consummate indifference, his supreme defiance, would make him a magnificent trophy, and Christina had announced with sufficient distinctness that she had said good-by to scruples. It was her fancy at present to treat the world as a garden of pleasure, and if, hitherto, she had played with Roderick's passion on its stem, there was little doubt that now she would pluck it with an unfaltering hand and drain it of its acrid sweetness. And why the deuce need Roderick have gone marching back to destruction? Rowland's meditations, even when they began in rancor, often brought him peace; but on this occasion they ushered in a quite peculiar quality of unrest. He felt conscious of a sudden collapse in his moral energy; a current that had been flowing for two years with liquid strength seemed at last to pause and evaporate. Rowland looked away at the stagnant vapors on the mountains; their dreariness seemed a symbol of the dreariness which his own generosity had bequeathed him. At last he had arrived at the uttermost limit of the deference a sane man might pay to other people's folly; nay, rather, he had transgressed it; he had been befooled on a gigantic scale. He turned to his book and tried to woo back patience, but it gave him cold comfort and he tossed it angrily away. He pulled his hat over his eyes, and tried to wonder, dispassionately, whether atmospheric conditions had not something to do with his ill-humor. He remained for some time in this attitude, but was finally aroused from it by a singular sense that, although he had heard nothing, some one had approached him. He looked up and saw Roderick standing before him on the turf. His mood made the spectacle unwelcome, and for a moment he felt like uttering an uncivil speech. Roderick stood looking at him with an expression of countenance which had of late become rare. There was an unfamiliar spark in his eye and a certain imperious alertness in his carriage. Confirmed habit, with Rowland, came speedily to the front. "What is it now?" he asked himself, and invited Roderick to sit down. Roderick had evidently something particular to say, and if he remained silent for a time it was not because he was ashamed of it.

"I would like you to do me a favor," he said at last. "Lend me some money."

"How much do you wish?" Rowland asked.

"Say a thousand francs."

Rowland hesitated a moment. "I don't wish to be indiscreet, but may I ask what you propose to do with a thousand francs?"

"To go to Interlaken."

"And why are you going to Interlaken?"

Roderick replied without a shadow of wavering, "Because that woman is to be there."

Rowland burst out laughing, but Roderick remained serenely grave. "You have forgiven her, then?" said Rowland.

"Not a bit of it!"

"I don't understand."

"Neither do I. I only know that she is incomparably beautiful, and that she has waked me up amazingly. Besides, she asked me to come."

"She asked you?"

"Yesterday, in so many words."

"Ah, the jade!"

"Exactly. I am willing to take her for that."

"Why in the name of common sense did you go back to her?"

"Why did I find her standing there like a goddess who had just stepped out of her cloud? Why did I look at her? Before I knew where I was, the harm was done."

Rowland, who had been sitting erect, threw himself back on the grass and lay for some time staring up at the sky. At last, raising himself, "Are you perfectly serious?" he asked.

"Deadly serious."

"Your idea is to remain at Interlaken some time?"

"Indefinitely!" said Roderick; and it seemed to his companion that the tone in which he said this made it immensely well worth hearing.

"And your mother and cousin, meanwhile, are to remain here? It will soon be getting very cold, you know."

"It does n't seem much like it to-day."

"Very true; but to-day is a day by itself."

"There is nothing to prevent their going back to Lucerne. I depend upon your taking charge of them."

At this Rowland reclined upon the grass again; and again, after reflection, he faced his friend. "How would you express," he asked, "the character of the profit that you expect to derive from your excursion?"

"I see no need of expressing it. The proof of the pudding is in the eating! The case is simply this. I desire immensely to be near Christina Light, and it is such a huge refreshment to find myself again desiring something, that I propose to drift with the current. As I say, she has waked me up, and it is possible something may come of it. She makes me feel as if I were alive again. *This*," and he glanced down at the inn, "I call death!"

"That I am very grateful to hear. You really feel as if you might do something?"

"Don't ask too much. I only know that she makes my heart beat, makes me see visions."

"You feel encouraged?"

"I feel excited."

"You are really looking better."

"I am glad to hear it. Now that I have answered your questions, please to give me the money."

Rowland shook his head. "For that purpose, I can't!"

"You can't?"

"It 's impossible. Your plan is rank folly. I can't help you in it."

Roderick flushed a little, and his eye expanded. "I will borrow what money I can, then, from Mary!" This was not viciously said; it had simply the ring of passionate resolution.

Instantly it brought Rowland to terms. He took a bunch of keys from his pocket and tossed it upon the grass. "The little brass one opens my dressing-case," he said. "You will find money in it."

Roderick let the keys lie; something seemed to have struck him; he looked askance at his friend. "You are awfully gallant!"

"You certainly are not. Your proposal is an outrage."

"Very likely. It 's a proof the more of my desire."

"If you have so much steam on, then, use it for something else. You say you are awake again. I am delighted; only be so in the best sense. Is n't it very plain? If you have the energy to desire, you have also the energy to reason and to judge. If you can care to go, you can also care to stay, and staying being the more profitable course, the inspiration, on that side, for a man who has his self-confidence to win back again, should be greater."

Roderick, plainly, did not relish this simple logic, and his eye grew angry as he listened to its echo. "Oh, the devil!" he cried.

Rowland went on. "Do you believe that hanging about Christina Light will do you any good? Do you believe it won't? In either case you should keep away from her. If it won't, it 's your duty; and if it will, you can get on without it."

"Do me good?" cried Roderick. "What do I want of 'good'—what should I do with 'good'? I want what she gives me, call it by what name you will. I want to ask no questions, but to take what comes and let it fill the impossible hours! But I did n't come to discuss the matter."

"I have not the least desire to discuss it," said Rowland. "I simply protest."

Roderick meditated a moment. "I have never yet thought twice of accepting a favor of you," he said at last; "but this one sticks in my throat."

"It is not a favor; I lend you the money only under compulsion."

"Well, then, I will take it only under compulsion!" Roderick exclaimed. And he sprang up abruptly and marched away.

His words were ambiguous; Rowland lay on the grass, wondering what they meant. Half an hour had not elapsed before Roderick reappeared, heated with rapid walking, and wiping his forehead. He flung himself down and looked at his friend with an eye which expressed something purer than bravado and yet baser than conviction.

"I have done my best!" he said. "My mother is out of

money; she is expecting next week some circular notes from
London. She had only ten francs in her pocket. Mary Garland
gave me every sou she possessed in the world. It makes exactly thirty-four francs. That 's not enough."

"You asked Miss Garland?" cried Rowland.

"I asked her."

"And told her your purpose?"

"I named no names. But she knew!"

"What did she say?"

"Not a syllable. She simply emptied her purse."

Rowland turned over and buried his face in his arms. He
felt a movement of irrepressible elation, and he barely stifled
a cry of joy. Now, surely, Roderick had shattered the last link
in the chain that bound Mary to him, and after this she would
be free! . . . . When he turned about again, Roderick was
still sitting there, and he had not touched the keys which lay
on the grass.

"I don't know what is the matter with me," said Roderick,
"but I have an insurmountable aversion to taking your
money."

"The matter, I suppose, is that you have a grain of wisdom
left."

"No, it 's not that. It 's a kind of brute instinct. I find it
extremely provoking!" He sat there for some time with his
head in his hands and his eyes on the ground. His lips were
compressed, and he was evidently, in fact, in a state of profound irritation. "You have succeeded in making this thing
excessively unpleasant!" he exclaimed.

"I am sorry," said Rowland, "but I can't see it in any other
way."

"That I believe, and I resent the range of your vision pretending to be the limit of my action. You can't feel for me
nor judge for me, and there are certain things you know
nothing about. I have suffered, sir!" Roderick went on with
increasing emphasis. "I have suffered damnable torments.
Have I been such a placid, contented, comfortable man this
last six months, that when I find a chance to forget my misery, I should take such pains not to profit by it? You ask too
much, for a man who himself has no occasion to play the
hero. I don't say that invidiously; it 's your disposition, and

you can't help it. But decidedly, there are certain things you know nothing about."

Rowland listened to this outbreak with open eyes, and Roderick, if he had been less intent upon his own eloquence, would probably have perceived that he turned pale. "These things—what are they?" Rowland asked.

"They are women, principally, and what relates to women. Women for you, by what I can make out, mean nothing. You have no imagination—no sensibility!"

"That 's a serious charge," said Rowland, gravely.

"I don't make it without proof!"

"And what is your proof?"

Roderick hesitated a moment. "The way you treated Christina Light. I call that grossly obtuse."

"Obtuse?" Rowland repeated, frowning.

"Thick-skinned, beneath your good fortune."

"My good fortune?"

"There it is—it 's all news to you! You had pleased her. I don't say she was dying of love for you, but she took a fancy to you."

"We will let this pass!" said Rowland, after a silence.

"Oh, I don't insist. I have only her own word for it."

"She told you this?"

"You noticed, at least, I suppose, that she was not afraid to speak. I never repeated it, not because I was jealous, but because I was curious to see how long your ignorance would last if left to itself."

"I frankly confess it would have lasted forever. And yet I don't consider that my insensibility is proved."

"Oh, don't say that," cried Roderick, "or I shall begin to suspect—what I must do you the justice to say that I never have suspected—that you are a trifle conceited. Upon my word, when I think of all this, your protest, as you call it, against my following Christina Light seems to me thoroughly offensive. There is something monstrous in a man's pretending to lay down the law to a sort of emotion with which he is quite unacquainted—in his asking a fellow to give up a lovely woman for conscience' sake, when *he* has never had the impulse to strike a blow for one for passion's!"

"Oh, oh!" cried Rowland.

"All that 's very easy to say," Roderick went on; "but you must remember that there are such things as nerves, and senses, and imagination, and a restless demon within that may sleep sometimes for a day, or for six months, but that sooner or later wakes up and thumps at your ribs till you listen to him! If you can't understand it, take it on trust, and let a poor imaginative devil live his life as he can!"

Roderick's words seemed at first to Rowland like something heard in a dream; it was impossible they had been actually spoken—so supreme an expression were they of the insolence of egotism. Reality was never so consistent as that! But Roderick sat there balancing his beautiful head, and the echoes of his strident accent still lingered along the half-muffled mountain-side. Rowland suddenly felt that the cup of his chagrin was full to overflowing, and his long-gathered bitterness surged into the simple, wholesome passion of anger for wasted kindness. But he spoke without violence, and Roderick was probably at first far from measuring the force that lay beneath his words.

"You are incredibly ungrateful," he said. "You are talking arrogant nonsense. What do you know about my sensibilities and my imagination? How do you know whether I have loved or suffered? If I have held my tongue and not troubled you with my complaints, you find it the most natural thing in the world to put an ignoble construction on my silence. I loved quite as well as you; indeed, I think I may say rather better. I have been constant. I have been willing to give more than I received. I have not forsaken one mistress because I thought another more beautiful, nor given up the other and believed all manner of evil about her because I had not my way with her. I have been a good friend to Christina Light, and it seems to me my friendship does her quite as much honor as your love!"

"Your love—your suffering—your silence—your friendship!" cried Roderick. "I declare I don't understand!"

"I dare say not. You are not used to understanding such things—you are not used to hearing me talk of my feelings. You are altogether too much taken up with your own. Be as much so as you please; I have always respected your right. Only when I have kept myself in durance on purpose to leave you an open field, don't, by way of thanking me, come and call me an idiot."

"Oh, you claim then that you have made sacrifices?"

"Several! You have never suspected it?"

"If I had, do you suppose I would have allowed it?" cried Roderick.

"They were the sacrifices of friendship and they were easily made; only I don't enjoy having them thrown back in my teeth."

This was, under the circumstances, a sufficiently generous speech; but Roderick was not in the humor to take it generously. "Come, be more definite," he said. "Let me know where it is the shoe has pinched."

Rowland frowned; if Roderick would not take generosity, he should have full justice. "It 's a perpetual sacrifice," he said, "to live with a perfect egotist."

"I am an egotist?" cried Roderick.

"Did it never occur to you?"

"An egotist to whom you have made perpetual sacrifices?" He repeated the words in a singular tone; a tone that denoted neither exactly indignation nor incredulity, but (strange as it may seem) a sudden violent curiosity for news about himself.

"You are selfish," said Rowland; "you think only of yourself and believe only in yourself. You regard other people only as they play into your own hands. You have always been very frank about it, and the thing seemed so mixed up with the temper of your genius and the very structure of your mind, that often one was willing to take the evil with the good and to be thankful that, considering your great talent, you were no worse. But if one believed in you, as I have done, one paid a tax upon it."

Roderick leaned his elbows on his knees, clasped his hands together, and crossed them, shadewise, over his eyes. In this attitude, for a moment, he sat looking coldly at his friend. "So I have made you very uncomfortable?" he went on.

"Extremely so."

"I have been eager, grasping, obstinate, vain, ungrateful, indifferent, cruel?"

"I have accused you, mentally, of all these things, with the exception of vanity."

"You have often hated me?"

"Never. I should have parted company with you before coming to that."

"But you have wanted to part company, to bid me go my way and be hanged!"

"Repeatedly. Then I have had patience and forgiven you."

"Forgiven me, eh? Suffering all the while?"

"Yes, you may call it suffering."

"Why did you never tell me all this before?"

"Because my affection was always stronger than my resentment; because I preferred to err on the side of kindness; because I had, myself, in a measure, launched you in the world and thrown you into temptations; and because nothing short of your unwarrantable aggression just now could have made me say these painful things."

Roderick picked up a blade of long grass and began to bite it; Rowland was puzzled by his expression and manner. They seemed strangely cynical; there was something revolting in his deepening calmness. "I must have been hideous," Roderick presently resumed.

"I am not talking for your entertainment," said Rowland.

"Of course not. For my edification!" As Roderick said these words there was not a ray of warmth in his brilliant eye.

"I have spoken for my own relief," Rowland went on, "and so that you need never again go so utterly astray as you have done this morning."

"It has been a terrible mistake, then?" What his tone expressed was not willful mockery, but a kind of persistent irresponsibility which Rowland found equally exasperating. He answered nothing.

"And all this time," Roderick continued, "you have been in love? Tell me the woman."

Rowland felt an immense desire to give him a visible, palpable pang. "Her name is Mary Garland," he said.

Apparently he succeeded. The surprise was great; Roderick colored as he had never done. "Mary Garland? Heaven forgive us!"

Rowland observed the "us;" Roderick threw himself back on the turf. The latter lay for some time staring at the sky.

At last he sprang to his feet, and Rowland rose also, rejoicing keenly, it must be confessed, in his companion's confusion.

"For how long has this been?" Roderick demanded.

"Since I first knew her."

"Two years! And you have never told her?"

"Never."

"You have told no one?"

"You are the first person."

"Why have you been silent?"

"Because of your engagement."

"But you have done your best to keep that up."

"That 's another matter!"

"It 's very strange!" said Roderick, presently. "It 's like something in a novel."

"We need n't expatiate on it," said Rowland. "All I wished to do was to rebut your charge that I am an abnormal being."

But still Roderick pondered. "All these months, while I was going on! I wish you had mentioned it."

"I acted as was necessary, and that 's the end of it."

"You have a very high opinion of her?"

"The highest."

"I remember now your occasionally expressing it and my being struck with it. But I never dreamed you were in love with her. It 's a pity she does n't care for you!"

Rowland had made his point and he had no wish to prolong the conversation; but he had a desire to hear more of this, and he remained silent.

"You hope, I suppose, that some day she may?"

"I should n't have offered to say so; but since you ask me, I do."

"I don't believe it. She idolizes me, and if she never were to see me again she would idolize my memory."

This might be profound insight, and it might be profound fatuity. Rowland turned away; he could not trust himself to speak.

"My indifference, my neglect of her, must have seemed to you horrible. Altogether, I must have appeared simply hideous."

"Do you really care," Rowland asked, "what you appeared?"

"Certainly. I have been damnably stupid. Is n't an artist supposed to be a man of perceptions? I am hugely disgusted."

"Well, you understand now, and we can start afresh."

"And yet," said Roderick, "though you have suffered, in a degree, I don't believe you have suffered so much as some other men would have done."

"Very likely not. In such matters quantitative analysis is difficult."

Roderick picked up his stick and stood looking at the ground. "Nevertheless, I must have seemed hideous," he repeated—"hideous." He turned away, scowling, and Rowland offered no contradiction.

They were both silent for some time, and at last Roderick gave a heavy sigh and began to walk away. "Where are you going?" Rowland then asked.

"Oh, I don't care! To walk; you have given me something to think of." This seemed a salutary impulse, and yet Rowland felt a nameless perplexity. "To have been so stupid damns me more than anything!" Roderick went on. "Certainly, I can shut up shop now."

Rowland felt in no smiling humor, and yet, in spite of himself, he could almost have smiled at the very consistency of the fellow. It was egotism still: æsthetic disgust at the graceless contour of his conduct, but never a hint of simple sorrow for the pain he had given. Rowland let him go, and for some moments stood watching him. Suddenly Mallet became conscious of a singular and most illogical impulse—a desire to stop him, to have another word with him—not to lose sight of him. He called him and Roderick turned. "I should like to go with you," said Rowland.

"I am fit only to be alone. I am damned!"

"You had better not think of it at all," Rowland cried, "than think in that way."

"There is only one way. I have been hideous!" And he broke off and marched away with his long, elastic step, swinging his stick. Rowland watched him and at the end of a moment called to him. Roderick stopped and looked at him in silence, and then abruptly turned, and disappeared below the crest of a hill.

Rowland passed the remainder of the day uncomfortably. He was half irritated, half depressed; he had an insufferable feeling of having been placed in the wrong, in spite of his excellent cause. Roderick did not come home to dinner; but of this, with his passion for brooding away the hours on far-off mountain sides, he had almost made a habit. Mrs. Hudson appeared at the noonday repast with a face which showed that Roderick's demand for money had unsealed the fountains of her distress. Little Singleton consumed an enormous and well-earned dinner. Miss Garland, Rowland observed, had not contributed her scanty assistance to her kinsman's pursuit of the Princess Casamassima without an effort. The effort was visible in her pale face and her silence; she looked so ill that when they left the table Rowland felt almost bound to remark upon it. They had come out upon the grass in front of the inn.

"I have a headache," she said. And then suddenly, looking about at the menacing sky and motionless air, "It 's this horrible day!"

Rowland that afternoon tried to write a letter to his cousin Cecilia, but his head and his heart were alike heavy, and he traced upon the paper but a single line. "I believe there is such a thing as being too reasonable. But when once the habit is formed, what is one to do?" He had occasion to use his keys and he felt for them in his pocket; they were missing, and he remembered that he had left them lying on the hill-top where he had had his talk with Roderick. He went forth in search of them and found them where he had thrown them. He flung himself down in the same place again; he felt indisposed to walk. He was conscious that his mood had vastly changed since the morning; his extraordinary, acute sense of his rights had been replaced by the familiar, chronic sense of his duties. Only, his duties now seemed impracticable; he turned over and buried his face in his arms. He lay so a long time, thinking of many things; the sum of them all was that Roderick had beaten him. At last he was startled by an extraordinary sound; it took him a moment to perceive that it was a portentous growl of thunder. He roused himself and saw that the whole face of the sky had altered. The clouds that had hung motionless all day were moving from their stations, and getting into position, as it were, for a battle. The wind was rising; the sallow vapors were turning dark and consolidating their masses. It was a striking spectacle, but Rowland judged best to observe it briefly, as a storm was evidently imminent. He took his way down to the inn and found Singleton still at his post, profiting by the last of the rapidly-failing light to finish his study, and yet at the same time taking rapid notes of the actual condition of the clouds.

"We are going to have a most interesting storm," the little painter gleefully cried. "I should like awfully to *do* it."

Rowland adjured him to pack up his tools and decamp, and repaired to the house. The air by this time had become portentously dark, and the thunder was incessant and tremendous; in the midst of it the lightning flashed and vanished, like the treble shrilling upon the bass. The innkeeper and his servants had crowded to the doorway, and were looking at the scene with faces which seemed a proof that it was unprecedented. As Rowland approached, the group divided, to let some one pass from within, and Mrs. Hudson came forth, as white as a corpse and trembling in every limb.

"My boy, my boy, where is my boy?" she cried. "Mr. Mallet, why are you here without him? Bring him to me!"

"Has no one seen Mr. Hudson?" Rowland asked of the others. "Has he not returned?"

Each one shook his head and looked grave, and Rowland attempted to reassure Mrs. Hudson by saying that of course he had taken refuge in a châlet.

"Go and find him, go and find him!" she cried, insanely. "Don't stand there and talk, or I shall die!" It was now as dark as evening, and Rowland could just distinguish the figure of Singleton scampering homeward with his box and easel. "And where is Mary?" Mrs. Hudson went on; "what in mercy's name has become of her? Mr. Mallet, why did you ever bring us here?"

There came a prodigious flash of lightning, and the limitless tumult about them turned clearer than midsummer noonday. The brightness lasted long enough to enable Rowland to see a woman's figure on the top of an eminence near the house. It was Mary Garland, questioning the lurid darkness for Roderick. Rowland sprang out to interrupt her vigil, but in a moment he encountered her, retreating. He seized her hand and hurried her to the house, where, as soon as she stepped into the covered gallery, Mrs. Hudson fell upon her with frantic lamentations.

"Did you see nothing,—nothing?" she cried. "Tell Mr. Mallet he must go and find him, with some men, some lights, some wrappings. Go, go, go, sir! In mercy, go!"

Rowland was extremely perturbed by the poor lady's vociferous folly, for he deemed her anxiety superfluous. He had offered his suggestion with sincerity; nothing was more probable than that Roderick had found shelter in a herdsman's cabin. These were numerous on the neighboring mountains, and the storm had given fair warning of its approach. Miss Garland stood there very pale, saying nothing, but looking at him. He expected that she would check her cousin's importunity. "*Could* you find him?" she suddenly asked. "Would it be of use?"

The question seemed to him a flash intenser than the lightning that was raking the sky before them. It shattered his dream that he weighed in the scale! But before he could answer, the full fury of the storm was upon them; the rain descended in sounding torrents. Every one fell back into the house. There had been no time to light lamps, and in the little uncarpeted parlor, in the unnatural darkness, Rowland felt Mary's hand upon his arm. For a moment it had an eloquent pressure; it seemed to retract her senseless challenge, and to say that she believed, for Roderick, what he believed. But nevertheless, thought Rowland, the cry had come, her heart had spoken; her first impulse had been to sacrifice him. He had been uncertain before; here, at least, was the comfort of certainty!

It must be confessed, however, that the certainty in question did little to enliven the gloom of that formidable evening. There was a noisy crowd about him in the room— noisy even with the accompaniment of the continual thunderpeals; lodgers and servants, chattering, shuffling, and bustling, and annoying him equally by making too light of the tempest and by vociferating their alarm. In the disorder, it was some time before a lamp was lighted, and the first thing he saw, as it was swung from the ceiling, was the white face of Mrs. Hudson, who was being carried out of the room in a swoon by two stout maid-servants, with Mary Garland forcing a passage. He rendered what help he could, but when they had laid the poor woman on her bed, Miss Garland motioned him away.

"I think you make her worse," she said.

Rowland went to his own chamber. The partitions in Swiss mountain-inns are thin, and from time to time he heard Mrs. Hudson moaning, three rooms off. Considering its great fury, the storm took long to expend itself; it was upwards of three hours before the thunder ceased. But even then the rain continued to fall heavily, and the night, which had come on, was impenetrably black. This lasted till near midnight. Rowland thought of Mary Garland's challenge in the porch, but he thought even more that, although the fetid interior of a high-nestling châlet may offer a convenient refuge from an Alpine tempest, there was no possible music in the universe so sweet as the sound of Roderick's voice. At midnight, through his dripping window-pane, he saw a star, and he immediately went downstairs and out into the gallery. The rain had ceased, the cloud-masses were dissevered here and there, and several stars were visible. In a few minutes he heard a step behind him, and, turning, saw Miss Garland. He asked about Mrs. Hudson and learned that she was sleeping, exhausted by her fruitless lamentations. Miss Garland kept scanning the darkness, but she said nothing to cast doubt on Roderick's having found a refuge. Rowland noticed it. "This also have I guaranteed!" he said to himself. There was something that Mary wished to learn, and a question presently revealed it.

"What made him start on a long walk so suddenly?" she asked. "I saw him at eleven o'clock, and then he meant to go to Engelberg, and sleep."

"On his way to Interlaken?" Rowland said.

"Yes," she answered, under cover of the darkness.

"We had some talk," said Rowland, "and he seemed, for the day, to have given up Interlaken."

"Did you dissuade him?"

"Not exactly. We discussed another question, which, for the time, superseded his plan."

Miss Garland was silent. Then—"May I ask whether your discussion was violent?" she said.

"I am afraid it was agreeable to neither of us."

"And Roderick left you in—in irritation?"

"I offered him my company on his walk. He declined it."

Miss Garland paced slowly to the end of the gallery and then came back. "If he had gone to Engelberg," she said, "he would have reached the hotel before the storm began."

Rowland felt a sudden explosion of ferocity. "Oh, if you like," he cried, "he can start for Interlaken as soon as he comes back!"

But she did not even notice his wrath. "Will he come back early?" she went on.

"We may suppose so."

"He will know how anxious we are, and he will start with the first light!"

Rowland was on the point of declaring that Roderick's readiness to throw himself into the feelings of others made this extremely probable; but he checked himself and said, simply, "I expect him at sunrise."

Miss Garland bent her eyes once more upon the irresponsive darkness, and then, in silence, went into the house. Rowland, it must be averred, in spite of his resolution not to be nervous, found no sleep that night. When the early dawn began to tremble in the east, he came forth again into the open air. The storm had completely purged the atmosphere, and the day gave promise of cloudless splendor. Rowland watched the early sun-shafts slowly reaching higher, and remembered that if Roderick did not come back to breakfast, there were two things to be taken into account. One was the heaviness of the soil on the mountain-sides, saturated with the rain; this would make him walk slowly: the other was the fact that, speaking without irony, he was *not* remarkable for throwing himself into the sentiments of others. Breakfast, at the inn, was early, and by breakfast-time Roderick had not appeared. Then Rowland admitted that he was nervous. Neither Mrs. Hudson nor Miss Garland had left their apartment; Rowland had a mental vision of them sitting there praying and listening; he had no desire to see them more directly. There were a couple of men who hung about the inn as guides for the ascent of the Titlis; Rowland sent each of them forth in a different direction, to ask the news of Roderick at every châlet door within a morning's walk. Then he called Sam Singleton, whose peregrinations had made him an excellent mountaineer, and whose zeal and sympathy were now unbounded, and the two started together on a voyage of research. By the time they had lost sight of the inn, Rowland was obliged to confess that, decidedly, Roderick had had time to come back.

He wandered about for several hours, but he found only the sunny stillness of the mountain-sides. Before long he parted company with Singleton, who, to his suggestion that separation would multiply their resources, assented with a silent, frightened look which reflected too vividly his own rapidly-dawning thought. The day was magnificent; the sun was everywhere; the storm had lashed the lower slopes into a deeper flush of autumnal color, and the snow-peaks reared themselves against the near horizon in glaring blocks and dazzling spires. Rowland made his way to several châlets, but most of them were empty. He thumped at their low, foul doors with a kind of nervous, savage anger; he challenged the stupid silence to tell him something about his friend. Some of these places had evidently not been open in months. The silence everywhere was horrible; it seemed to mock at his impatience and to be a conscious symbol of calamity. In the midst of it, at the door of one of the châlets, quite alone, sat a hideous *crétin*, who grinned at Rowland over his goitre when, hardly knowing what he did, he questioned him. The creature's family was scattered on the mountain-sides; he could give Rowland no help to find them. Rowland climbed into many awkward places, and skirted, intently and peeringly, many an ugly chasm and steep-dropping ledge. But the sun, as I have said, was everywhere; it illumined the deep places over which, not knowing where to turn next, he halted and lingered, and showed him nothing but the stony Alpine void—nothing so human even as death. At noon he paused in his quest and sat down on a stone; the conviction was pressing upon him that the worst that was now possible was true. He suspended his search; he was afraid to go on. He sat there for an hour, sick to the depths of his soul. Without his knowing why, several things, chiefly trivial, that had happened during the last two years and that he had quite forgotten, became vividly present to his mind. He was aroused at last by the sound of a stone dislodged near by, which rattled down the mountain. In a moment, on a steep, rocky slope opposite to him, he beheld a figure cautiously descending—a figure which was not Roderick. It was Singleton, who had seen him and began to beckon to him.

"Come down—come down!" cried the painter, steadily making his own way down. Rowland saw that as he moved, and even as he selected his foothold and watched his steps, he was looking at something at the bottom of the cliff. This was a great rugged wall which had fallen backward from the perpendicular, and the descent, though difficult, was with care sufficiently practicable.

"What do you see?" cried Rowland.

Singleton stopped, looked across at him and seemed to hesitate; then, "Come down—come down!" he simply repeated.

Rowland's course was also a steep descent, and he attacked it so precipitately that he afterwards marveled he had not broken his neck. It was a ten minutes' headlong scramble. Halfway down he saw something that made him dizzy; he saw what Singleton had seen. In the gorge below them a vague white mass lay tumbled upon the stones. He let himself go, blindly, fiercely. Singleton had reached the rocky bottom of the ravine before him, and had bounded forward and fallen upon his knees. Rowland overtook him and his own legs collapsed. The thing that yesterday was his friend lay before him as the chance of the last breath had left it, and out of it Roderick's face stared upward, open-eyed, at the sky.

He had fallen from a great height, but he was singularly little disfigured. The rain had spent its torrents upon him, and his clothes and hair were as wet as if the billows of the ocean had flung him upon the strand. An attempt to move him would show some hideous fracture, some horrible physical dishonor; but what Rowland saw on first looking at him was only a strangely serene expression of life. The eyes were dead, but in a short time, when Rowland had closed them, the whole face seemed to awake. The rain had washed away all blood; it was as if Violence, having done her work, had stolen away in shame. Roderick's face might have shamed her; it looked admirably handsome.

"He was a beautiful man!" said Singleton.

They looked up through their horror at the cliff from which he had apparently fallen, and which lifted its blank and stony face above him, with no care now but to drink the sunshine on which his eyes were closed, and then Rowland had an immense outbreak of pity and anguish. At last they spoke of carrying him back to the inn. "There must be three or four men," Rowland said, "and they must be brought here quickly. I have not the least idea where we are."

"We are at about three hours' walk from home," said Singleton. "I will go for help; I can find my way."

"Remember," said Rowland, "whom you will have to face."

"I remember," the excellent fellow answered. "There was nothing I could ever do for him in life; I will do what I can now."

He went off, and Rowland stayed there alone. He watched for seven long hours, and his vigil was forever memorable. The most rational of men was for an hour the most passionate. He reviled himself with transcendent bitterness, he accused himself of cruelty and injustice, he would have lain down there in Roderick's place to unsay the words that had yesterday driven him forth on his lonely ramble. Roderick had been fond of saying that there are such things as necessary follies, and Rowland was now proving it. At last he grew almost used to the dumb exultation of the cliff above him. He saw that Roderick was a mass of hideous injury, and he tried to understand what had happened. Not that it helped him; before that confounding mortality one hypothesis after another faltered and swooned away. Roderick's passionate walk had carried him farther and higher than he knew; he had outstayed, supposably, the first menace of the storm, and perhaps even found a defiant entertainment in watching it. Perhaps he had simply lost himself. The tempest had overtaken him, and when he tried to return, it was too late. He had attempted to descend the cliff in the darkness, he had made the inevitable slip, and whether he had fallen fifty feet or three hundred little mattered. The condition of his body indicated the shorter fall. Now that all was over, Rowland understood how exclusively, for two years, Roderick had filled his life. His occupation was gone.

Singleton came back with four men—one of them the landlord of the inn. They had formed a sort of rude bier of the frame of a *chaise à porteurs*, and by taking a very round-about course homeward were able to follow a tolerably level path and carry their burden with a certain decency. To Rowland it seemed as if the little procession would never reach the inn; but as they drew near it he would have given his right hand for a longer delay. The people of the inn came forward to meet them, in a little silent, solemn convoy. In the doorway, clinging together, appeared the two bereaved women. Mrs. Hudson tottered forward with outstretched hands and the expression of a blind person; but before she reached her son, Mary Garland had rushed past her, and, in the face of the staring, pitying, awe-stricken crowd, had flung herself, with the magnificent movement of one whose rights were supreme, and with a loud, tremendous cry, upon the senseless vestige of her love.

That cry still lives in Rowland's ears. It interposes, persistently, against the reflection that when he sometimes—very rarely—sees her, she is unreservedly kind to him; against the memory that during the dreary journey back to America, made of course with his assistance, there was a great frankness in her gratitude, a great gratitude in her frankness. Miss Garland lives with Mrs. Hudson, at Northampton, where Rowland visits his cousin Cecilia more frequently than of old. When he calls upon Miss Garland he never sees Mrs. Hudson. Cecilia, who, having her shrewd impression that he comes to see Miss Garland as much as to see herself, does not feel obliged to seem unduly flattered, calls him, whenever he reappears, the most restless of mortals. But he always says to her in answer, "No, I assure you I am the most patient!"

THE AMERICAN

Chapter I

O N A BRILLIANT DAY in May, in the year 1868, a gentleman was reclining at his ease on the great circular divan
which at that period occupied the centre of the Salon Carré,
in the Museum of the Louvre. This commodious ottoman has
since been removed, to the extreme regret of all weak-kneed
lovers of the fine arts; but the gentleman in question had
taken serene possession of its softest spot, and, with his head
thrown back and his legs outstretched, was staring at Murillo's beautiful moon-borne Madonna in profound enjoyment
of his posture. He had removed his hat, and flung down beside him a little red guide-book and an opera-glass. The day
was warm; he was heated with walking, and he repeatedly
passed his handkerchief over his forehead, with a somewhat
wearied gesture. And yet he was evidently not a man to
whom fatigue was familiar; long, lean, and muscular, he suggested the sort of vigor that is commonly known as "toughness." But his exertions on this particular day had been of an
unwonted sort, and he had often performed great physical
feats which left him less jaded than his tranquil stroll through
the Louvre. He had looked out all the pictures to which an
asterisk was affixed in those formidable pages of fine print in
his Bädeker; his attention had been strained and his eyes dazzled, and he had sat down with an æsthetic headache. He had
looked, moreover, not only at all the pictures, but at all the
copies that were going forward around them, in the hands of
those innumerable young women in irreproachable toilets
who devote themselves, in France, to the propagation of masterpieces; and if the truth must be told, he had often admired
the copy much more than the original. His physiognomy
would have sufficiently indicated that he was a shrewd and
capable fellow, and in truth he had often sat up all night over
a bristling bundle of accounts, and heard the cock crow without a yawn. But Raphael and Titian and Rubens were a new
kind of arithmetic, and they inspired our friend, for the first
time in his life, with a vague self-mistrust.

An observer with anything of an eye for national types
would have had no difficulty in determining the local origin

of this undeveloped connoisseur, and indeed such an observer
might have felt a certain humorous relish of the almost ideal
completeness with which he filled out the national mould.
The gentleman on the divan was a powerful specimen of an
American. But he was not only a fine American; he was in
the first place, physically, a fine man. He appeared to possess
that kind of health and strength which, when found in perfection, are the most impressive—the physical capital which
the owner does nothing to "keep up." If he was a muscular
Christian, it was quite without knowing it. If it was necessary
to walk to a remote spot, he walked, but he had never known
himself to "exercise." He had no theory with regard to cold
bathing or the use of Indian clubs; he was neither an oars-
man, a rifleman, nor a fencer—he had never had time for
these amusements—and he was quite unaware that the saddle
is recommended for certain forms of indigestion. He was by
inclination a temperate man; but he had supped the night
before his visit to the Louvre at the Café Anglais—some one
had told him it was an experience not to be omitted—and he
had slept none the less the sleep of the just. His usual attitude
and carriage were of a rather relaxed and lounging kind, but
when, under a special inspiration, he straightened himself, he
looked like a grenadier on parade. He never smoked. He had
been assured—such things are said—that cigars were excellent for the health, and he was quite capable of believing it;
but he knew as little about tobacco as about homœopathy.
He had a very well-formed head, with a shapely, symmetrical
balance of the frontal and the occipital development, and a
good deal of straight, rather dry brown hair. His complexion
was brown, and his nose had a bold, well-marked arch. His
eye was of a clear, cold gray, and save for a rather abundant
mustache he was clean-shaved. He had the flat jaw and sinewy
neck which are frequent in the American type; but the traces
of national origin are a matter of expression even more than
of feature, and it was in this respect that our friend's countenance was supremely eloquent. The discriminating observer
we have been supposing might, however, perfectly have measured its expressiveness, and yet have been at a loss to describe it. It had that typical vagueness which is not vacuity,
that blankness which is not simplicity, that look of being

committed to nothing in particular, of standing in an attitude of general hospitality to the chances of life, of being very much at one's own disposal, so characteristic of many American faces. It was our friend's eye that chiefly told his story; an eye in which innocence and experience were singularly blended. It was full of contradictory suggestions, and though it was by no means the glowing orb of a hero of romance, you could find in it almost anything you looked for. Frigid and yet friendly, frank yet cautious, shrewd yet credulous, positive yet skeptical, confident yet shy, extremely intelligent and extremely good-humored, there was something vaguely defiant in its concessions, and something profoundly reassuring in its reserve. The cut of this gentleman's mustache, with the two premature wrinkles in the cheek above it, and the fashion of his garments, in which an exposed shirt-front and a cerulean cravat played perhaps an obtrusive part, completed the conditions of his identity. We have approached him, perhaps, at a not especially favorable moment; he is by no means sitting for his portrait. But listless as he lounges there, rather baffled on the æsthetic question, and guilty of the damning fault (as we have lately discovered it to be) of confounding the merit of the artist with that of his work (for he admires the squinting Madonna of the young lady with the boyish coiffure, because he thinks the young lady herself uncommonly taking), he is a sufficiently promising acquaintance. Decision, salubrity, jocosity, prosperity, seem to hover within his call; he is evidently a practical man, but the idea, in his case, has undefined and mysterious boundaries, which invite the imagination to bestir itself on his behalf.

As the little copyist proceeded with her work, she sent every now and then a responsive glance toward her admirer. The cultivation of the fine arts appeared to necessitate, to her mind, a great deal of by-play, a great standing off with folded arms and head drooping from side to side, stroking of a dimpled chin with a dimpled hand, sighing and frowning and patting of the foot, fumbling in disordered tresses for wandering hair-pins. These performances were accompanied by a restless glance, which lingered longer than elsewhere upon the gentleman we have described. At last he rose abruptly, put on his hat, and approached the young lady. He placed himself before her picture and looked at it for some moments, during which she pretended to be quite unconscious of his inspection. Then, addressing her with the single word which constituted the strength of his French vocabulary, and holding up one finger in a manner which appeared to him to illuminate his meaning, *"Combien?"* he abruptly demanded.

The artist stared a moment, gave a little pout, shrugged her shoulders, put down her palette and brushes, and stood rubbing her hands.

"How much?" said our friend, in English. "Combien?"

"Monsieur wishes to buy it?" asked the young lady in French.

"Very pretty, *splendide*. Combien?" repeated the American.

"It pleases monsieur, my little picture? It 's a very beautiful subject," said the young lady.

"The Madonna, yes; I am not a Catholic, but I want to buy it. Combien? Write it here." And he took a pencil from his pocket and showed her the fly-leaf of his guide-book. She stood looking at him and scratching her chin with the pencil. "Is it not for sale?" he asked. And as she still stood reflecting, and looking at him with an eye which, in spite of her desire to treat this avidity of patronage as a very old story, betrayed an almost touching incredulity, he was afraid he had offended her. She was simply trying to look indifferent, and wondering how far she might go. "I have n't made a mistake—*pas insulté*, no?" her interlocutor continued. "Don't you understand a little English?"

The young lady's aptitude for playing a part at short notice was remarkable. She fixed him with her conscious, perceptive eye and asked him if he spoke no French. Then, *"Donnez!"* she said briefly, and took the open guide-book. In the upper corner of the fly-leaf she traced a number, in a minute and extremely neat hand. Then she handed back the book and took up her palette again.

Our friend read the number: "2,000 francs." He said nothing for a time, but stood looking at the picture, while the copyist began actively to dabble with her paint. "For a copy, is n't that a good deal?" he asked at last. *"Pas beaucoup?"*

The young lady raised her eyes from her palette, scanned him from head to foot, and alighted with admirable sagacity upon exactly the right answer. "Yes, it 's a good deal. But my copy has remarkable qualities; it is worth nothing less."

The gentleman in whom we are interested understood no French, but I have said he was intelligent, and here is a good chance to prove it. He apprehended, by a natural instinct, the meaning of the young woman's phrase, and it gratified him to think that she was so honest. Beauty, talent, virtue; she combined everything! "But you must finish it," he said. "*Finish*, you know;" and he pointed to the unpainted hand of the figure.

"Oh, it shall be finished in perfection; in the perfection of perfections!" cried mademoiselle; and to confirm her promise, she deposited a rosy blotch in the middle of the Madonna's cheek.

But the American frowned. "Ah, too red, too red!" he rejoined. "Her complexion," pointing to the Murillo, "is more delicate."

"Delicate? Oh, it shall be delicate, monsieur; delicate as Sèvres *biscuit*. I am going to tone that down; I know all the secrets of my art. And where will you allow us to send it to you? Your address?"

"My address? Oh yes!" And the gentleman drew a card from his pocket-book and wrote something upon it. Then hesitating a moment he said, "If I don't like it when it is finished, you know, I shall not be obliged to take it."

The young lady seemed as good a guesser as himself. "Oh, I am very sure that monsieur is not capricious," she said with a roguish smile.

"Capricious?" And at this monsieur began to laugh. "Oh no, I 'm not capricious. I am very faithful. I am very constant. *Comprenez?*"

"Monsieur is constant; I understand perfectly. It 's a rare virtue. To recompense you, you shall have your picture on the first possible day; next week—as soon as it is dry. I will take the card of monsieur." And she took it and read his name: "Christopher Newman." Then she tried to repeat it aloud, and laughed at her bad accent. "Your English names are so droll!"

"Droll?" said Mr. Newman, laughing too. "Did you ever hear of Christopher Columbus?"

"*Bien sûr!* He invented America; a very great man. And is he your patron?"

"My patron?"

"Your patron-saint, in the calendar."

"Oh, exactly; my parents named me for him."

"Monsieur is American?"

"Don't you see it?" monsieur inquired.

"And you mean to carry my little picture away over there?" and she explained her phrase with a gesture.

"Oh, I mean to buy a great many pictures— *beaucoup, beaucoup,*" said Christopher Newman.

"The honor is not less for me," the young lady answered, "for I am sure monsieur has a great deal of taste."

"But you must give me your card," Newman said; "your card, you know."

The young lady looked severe for an instant, and then said, "My father will wait upon you."

But this time Mr. Newman's powers of divination were at fault. "Your card, your address," he simply repeated.

"My address?" said mademoiselle. Then, with a little shrug, "Happily for you, you are an American! It is the first time I ever gave my card to a gentleman." And, taking from her pocket a rather greasy porte-monnaie, she extracted from it a small glazed visiting card, and presented the latter to her patron. It was neatly inscribed in pencil, with a great many flourishes, "Mlle. Noémie Nioche." But Mr. Newman, unlike his companion, read the name with perfect gravity; all French names to him were equally droll.

"And precisely, here is my father, who has come to escort me home," said Mademoiselle Noémie. "He speaks English. He will arrange with you." And she turned to welcome a little old gentleman who came shuffling up, peering over his spectacles at Newman.

M. Nioche wore a glossy wig, of an unnatural color, which overhung his little meek, white, vacant face, and left it hardly more expressive than the unfeatured block upon which these articles are displayed in the barber's window. He was an exquisite image of shabby gentility. His little ill-made coat, desperately brushed, his darned gloves, his highly polished boots, his rusty, shapely hat, told the story of a person who had "had losses," and who clung to the spirit of nice habits, though the letter had been hopelessly effaced. Among other things M. Nioche had lost courage. Adversity had not only ruined him, it had frightened him, and he was evidently going through his remnant of life on tiptoe, for fear of waking up the hostile fates. If this strange gentleman was saying anything improper to his daughter, M. Nioche would entreat him huskily, as a particular favor, to forbear; but he would admit at the same time that he was very presumptuous to ask for particular favors.

"Monsieur has bought my picture," said Mademoiselle Noémie. "When it is finished you will carry it to him in a cab."

"In a cab!" cried M. Nioche; and he stared, in a bewildered way, as if he had seen the sun rising at midnight.

"Are you the young lady's father?" said Newman. "I think she said you speak English."

"Speak English—yes," said the old man, slowly rubbing his hands. "I will bring it in a cab."

"Say something, then," cried his daughter. "Thank him a little—not too much."

"A little, my daughter, a little," said M. Nioche, perplexed. "How much?"

"Two thousand!" said Mademoiselle Noémie. "Don't make a fuss, or he will take back his word."

"Two thousand!" cried the old man; and he began to fumble for his snuff-box. He looked at Newman, from head to foot, at his daughter, and then at the picture. "Take care you don't spoil it!" he cried, almost sublimely.

"We must go home," said Mademoiselle Noémie. "This is a good day's work. Take care how you carry it!" And she began to put up her utensils.

"How can I thank you?" said M. Nioche. "My English does not suffice."

"I wish I spoke French as well," said Newman, good-naturedly. "Your daughter is very clever."

"Oh, sir!" and M. Nioche looked over his spectacles with tearful eyes and nodded several times with a world of sadness. "She has had an education—*très-supérieure!* Nothing was spared. Lessons in pastel at ten francs the lesson, lessons in oil at twelve francs. I did n't look at the francs then. She 's an *artiste*, ah!"

"Do I understand you to say that you have had reverses?" asked Newman.

"Reverses? Oh, sir, misfortunes—terrible!"

"Unsuccessful in business, eh?"

"Very unsuccessful, sir."

"Oh, never fear, you 'll get on your legs again," said Newman cheerily.

The old man drooped his head on one side and looked at him with an expression of pain, as if this were an unfeeling jest.

"What does he say?" demanded Mademoiselle Noémie.

M. Nioche took a pinch of snuff. "He says I will make my fortune again."

"Perhaps he will help you. And what else?"

"He says thou art very clever."

"It is very possible. You believe it yourself, my father?"

"Believe it, my daughter? With this evidence!" And the old man turned afresh, with a staring, wondering homage, to the audacious daub on the easel.

"Ask him, then, if he would not like to learn French."

"To learn French?"

"To take lessons."

"To take lessons, my daughter? From thee?"

"From you!"

"From me, my child? How should I give lessons?"

"*Pas de raisons!* Ask him immediately!" said Mademoiselle Noémie, with soft brevity.

M. Nioche stood aghast, but under his daughter's eye he collected his wits, and, doing his best to assume an agreeable smile, he executed her commands. "Would it please you to receive instruction in our beautiful language?" he inquired, with an appealing quaver.

"To study French?" asked Newman, staring.

M. Nioche pressed his finger-tips together and slowly raised his shoulders. "A little conversation!"

"Conversation—that 's it!" murmured Mademoiselle Noémie, who had caught the word. "The conversation of the best society."

"Our French conversation is famous, you know," M. Nioche ventured to continue. "It 's a great talent."

"But is n't it awfully difficult?" asked Newman, very simply.

"Not to a man of *esprit*, like monsieur, an admirer of beauty in every form!" and M. Nioche cast a significant glance at his daughter's Madonna.

"I can't fancy myself chattering French!" said Newman with a laugh. "And yet, I suppose that the more a man knows the better."

"Monsieur expresses that very happily. *Hélas, oui!*"

"I suppose it would help me a great deal, knocking about Paris, to know the language."

"Ah, there are so many things monsieur must want to say: difficult things!"

"Everything I want to say is difficult. But you give lessons?"

Poor M. Nioche was embarrassed; he smiled more appealingly. "I am not a regular professor," he admitted. "I can't nevertheless tell him that I 'm a professor," he said to his daughter.

"Tell him it 's a very exceptional chance," answered Mademoiselle Noémie; "an *homme du monde*—one gentleman conversing with another! Remember what you are—what you have been!"

"A teacher of languages in neither case! Much more formerly and much less to day! And if he asks the price of the lessons?"

"He won't ask it," said Mademoiselle Noémie.

"What he pleases, I may say?"

"Never! That 's bad style."

"If he asks, then?"

Mademoiselle Noémie had put on her bonnet and was tying the ribbons. She smoothed them out, with her soft little chin thrust forward. "Ten francs," she said quickly.

"Oh, my daughter! I shall never dare."

"Don't dare, then! He won't ask till the end of the lessons, and then I will make out the bill."

M. Nioche turned to the confiding foreigner again, and stood rubbing his hands, with an air of seeming to plead guilty which was not intenser only because it was habitually so striking. It never occurred to Newman to ask him for a guarantee of his skill in imparting instruction; he supposed of course M. Nioche knew his own language, and his appealing forlornness was quite the perfection of what the American, for vague reasons, had always associated with all elderly foreigners of the lesson-giving class. Newman had never reflected upon philological processes. His chief impression with regard to ascertaining those mysterious correlatives of his familiar English vocables which were current in this extraordinary city of Paris was, that it was simply a matter of a good deal of unwonted and rather ridiculous muscular effort on his own part. "How did you learn English?" he asked of the old man.

"When I was young, before my miseries. Oh, I was wide awake, then. My father was a great *commerçant*; he placed me for a year in a counting-house in England. Some of it stuck to me; but I have forgotten!"

"How much French can I learn in a month?"

"What does he say?" asked Mademoiselle Noémie.

M. Nioche explained.

"He will speak like an angel!" said his daughter.

But the native integrity which had been vainly exerted to secure M. Nioche's commercial prosperity flickered up again. "*Dame*, monsieur!" he answered. "All I can teach you!" And then, recovering himself at a sign from his daughter, "I will wait upon you at your hotel."

"Oh yes, I should like to learn French," Newman went on, with democratic confidingness. "Hang me if I should ever have thought of it! I took for granted it was impossible. But if you learned my language, why should n't I learn yours?" and his frank, friendly laugh drew the sting from the jest. "Only, if we are going to converse, you know, you must think of something cheerful to converse about."

"You are very good, sir; I am overcome!" said M. Nioche, throwing out his hands. "But you have cheerfulness and happiness for two!"

"Oh no," said Newman more seriously. "You must be bright and lively; that 's part of the bargain."

M. Nioche bowed, with his hand on his heart. "Very well, sir; you have already made me lively."

"Come and bring me my picture then; I will pay you for it, and we will talk about that. That will be a cheerful subject!"

Mademoiselle Noémie had collected her accessories, and she gave the precious Madonna in charge to her father, who retreated backwards out of sight, holding it at arm's-length and reiterating his obeisances. The young lady gathered her shawl about her like a perfect Parisienne, and it was with the smile of a Parisienne that she took leave of her patron.

Chapter II

HE WANDERED back to the divan and seated himself on
the other side, in view of the great canvas on which
Paul Veronese has depicted the marriage-feast of Cana. Wearied as he was he found the picture entertaining; it had an
illusion for him; it satisfied his conception, which was ambitious, of what a splendid banquet should be. In the left-hand
corner of the picture is a young woman with yellow tresses
confined in a golden head-dress; she is bending forward and
listening, with the smile of a charming woman at a dinner-
party, to her neighbor. Newman detected her in the crowd,
admired her, and perceived that she too had her votive copyist—a young man with his hair standing on end. Suddenly
he became conscious of the germ of the mania of the "collector;" he had taken the first step; why should he not go on? It
was only twenty minutes before that he had bought the first
picture of his life, and now he was already thinking of art-
patronage as a fascinating pursuit. His reflections quickened
his good-humor, and he was on the point of approaching the
young man with another "Combien?" Two or three facts in
this relation are noticeable, although the logical chain which
connects them may seem imperfect. He knew Mademoiselle
Nioche had asked too much; he bore her no grudge for doing
so, and he was determined to pay the young man exactly the
proper sum. At this moment, however, his attention was attracted by a gentleman who had come from another part of
the room and whose manner was that of a stranger to the
gallery, although he was equipped with neither guide-book
nor opera-glass. He carried a white sun-umbrella, lined with
blue silk, and he strolled in front of the Paul Veronese,
vaguely looking at it, but much too near to see anything but
the grain of the canvas. Opposite to Christopher Newman he
paused and turned, and then our friend, who had been observing him, had a chance to verify a suspicion aroused by an
imperfect view of his face. The result of this larger scrutiny
was that he presently sprang to his feet, strode across the
room, and, with an outstretched hand, arrested the gentleman with the blue-lined umbrella. The latter stared, but put

out his hand at a venture. He was corpulent and rosy, and though his countenance, which was ornamented with a beautiful flaxen beard, carefully divided in the middle and brushed outward at the sides, was not remarkable for intensity of expression, he looked like a person who would willingly shake hands with any one. I know not what Newman thought of his face, but he found a want of response in his grasp.

"Oh, come, come," he said, laughing; "don't say, now, you don't know me—if I have *not* got a white parasol!"

The sound of his voice quickened the other's memory, his face expanded to its fullest capacity, and he also broke into a laugh. "Why, Newman—I 'll be blowed! Where in the world—I declare—who would have thought? You know you have changed."

"You have n't!" said Newman.

"Not for the better, no doubt. When did you get here?"

"Three days ago."

"Why did n't you let me know?"

"I had no idea *you* were here."

"I have been here these six years."

"It must be eight or nine since we met."

"Something of that sort. We were very young."

"It was in St. Louis, during the war. You were in the army."

"Oh no, not I! But you were."

"I believe I was."

"You came out all right?"

"I came out with my legs and arms—and with satisfaction. All that seems very far away."

"And how long have you been in Europe?"

"Seventeen days."

"First time?"

"Yes, very much so."

"Made your everlasting fortune?"

Christopher Newman was silent a moment, and then with a tranquil smile he answered, "Yes."

"And come to Paris to spend it, eh?"

"Well, we shall see. So they carry those parasols here—the men-folk?"

"Of course they do. They 're great things. They understand comfort out here."

"Where do you buy them?"

"Anywhere, everywhere."

"Well, Tristram, I 'm glad to get hold of you. You can show me the ropes. I suppose you know Paris inside out."

Mr. Tristram gave a mellow smile of self-gratulation. "Well, I guess there are not many men that can show me much. I 'll take care of you."

"It 's a pity you were not here a few minutes ago. I have just bought a picture. You might have put the thing through for me."

"Bought a picture?" said Mr. Tristram, looking vaguely round at the walls. "Why, do they sell them?"

"I mean a copy."

"Oh, I see. These," said Mr. Tristram, nodding at the Titians and Vandykes, "these, I suppose, are originals."

"I hope so," cried Newman. "I don't want a copy of a copy."

"Ah," said Mr. Tristram, mysteriously, "you can never tell. They imitate, you know, so deucedly well. It 's like the jewelers, with their false stones. Go into the Palais Royal, there; you see 'Imitation' on half the windows. The law obliges them to stick it on, you know; but you can't tell the things apart. To tell the truth," Mr. Tristram continued, with a wry face, "I don't do much in pictures. I leave that to my wife."

"Ah, you have got a wife?"

"Did n't I mention it? She 's a very nice woman; you must know her. She 's up there in the Avenue d'Iéna."

"So you are regularly fixed—house and children and all."

"Yes, a tip-top house and a couple of youngsters."

"Well," said Christopher Newman, stretching his arms a little, with a sigh, "I envy you."

"Oh no! you don't!" answered Mr. Tristram, giving him a little poke with his parasol.

"I beg your pardon; I do!"

"Well, you won't, then, when—when"—

"You don't certainly mean when I have seen your establishment?"

"When you have seen Paris, my boy. You want to be your own master here."

"Oh, I have been my own master all my life, and I 'm tired of it."

"Well, try Paris. How old are you?"

"Thirty-six."

"C'est le bel âge, as they say here."

"What does that mean?"

"It means that a man should n't send away his plate till he has eaten his fill."

"All that? I have just made arrangements to take French lessons."

"Oh, you don't want any lessons. You 'll pick it up. I never took any."

"I suppose you speak French as well as English?"

"Better!" said Mr. Tristram, roundly. "It 's a splendid language. You can say all sorts of bright things in it."

"But I suppose," said Christopher Newman, with an earnest desire for information, "that you must be bright to begin with."

"Not a bit; that 's just the beauty of it."

The two friends, as they exchanged these remarks, had remained standing where they met, and leaning against the rail which protected the pictures. Mr. Tristram at last declared that he was overcome with fatigue and should be happy to sit down. Newman recommended in the highest terms the great divan on which he had been lounging, and they prepared to seat themselves. "This is a great place; is n't it?" said Newman, with ardor.

"Great place, great place. Finest thing in the world." And then, suddenly, Mr. Tristram hesitated and looked about him. "I suppose they won't let you smoke here."

Newman stared. "Smoke? I 'm sure I don't know. You know the regulations better than I."

"I? I never was here before!"

"Never! in six years?"

"I believe my wife dragged me here once when we first came to Paris, but I never found my way back."

"But you say you know Paris so well!"

"I don't call this Paris!" cried Mr. Tristram, with assurance. "Come; let 's go over to the Palais Royal and have a smoke."

"I don't smoke," said Newman.

"A drink, then."

And Mr. Tristram led his companion away. They passed through the glorious halls of the Louvre, down the staircases, along the cool, dim galleries of sculpture, and out into the enormous court. Newman looked about him as he went, but he made no comments, and it was only when they at last emerged into the open air that he said to his friend, "It seems to me that in your place I should have come here once a week."

"Oh, no you would n't!" said Mr. Tristram. "You think so, but you would n't. You would n't have had time. You would always mean to go, but you never would go. There 's better fun than that, here in Paris. Italy 's the place to see pictures; wait till you get there. There you have to go; you can't do anything else. It 's an awful country; you can't get a decent cigar. I don't know why I went in there, to-day; I was strolling along, rather hard up for amusement. I sort of noticed the Louvre as I passed, and I thought I would go in and see what was going on. But if I had n't found you there I should have felt rather sold. Hang it, I don't care for pictures; I prefer the reality!" And Mr. Tristram tossed off this happy formula with an assurance which the numerous class of persons suffering from an overdose of 'culture' might have envied him.

The two gentlemen proceeded along the Rue de Rivoli and into the Palais Royal, where they seated themselves at one of the little tables stationed at the door of the café which projects into the great open quadrangle. The place was filled with people, the fountains were spouting, a band was playing, clusters of chairs were gathered beneath all the lime-trees, and buxom, white-capped nurses, seated along the benches, were offering to their infant charges the amplest facilities for nutrition. There was an easy, homely gayety in the whole scene, and Christopher Newman felt that it was most characteristically Parisian.

"And now," began Mr. Tristram, when they had tested the decoction which he had caused to be served to them, "now just give an account of yourself. What are your ideas, what are your plans, where have you come from and where are you going? In the first place, where are you staying?"

"At the Grand Hotel," said Newman.

Mr. Tristram puckered his plump visage. "That won't do! You must change."

"Change?" demanded Newman. "Why, it 's the finest hotel I ever was in."

"You don't want a 'fine' hotel; you want something small and quiet and elegant, where your bell is answered and your—your person is recognized."

"They keep running to see if I have rung before I have touched the bell," said Newman, "and as for my person, they are always bowing and scraping to it."

"I suppose you are always tipping them. That 's very bad style."

"Always? By no means. A man brought me something yesterday, and then stood loafing about in a beggarly manner. I offered him a chair and asked him if he would n't sit down. Was that bad style?"

"Very!"

"But he bolted, instantly. At any rate, the place amuses me. Hang your elegance, if it bores me. I sat in the court of the Grand Hotel last night until two o'clock in the morning, watching the coming and going, and the people knocking about."

"You 're easily pleased. But you can do as you choose—a man in your shoes. You have made a pile of money, eh?"

"I have made enough."

"Happy the man who can say that! Enough for what?"

"Enough to rest awhile, to forget the confounded thing, to look about me, to see the world, to have a good time, to improve my mind, and, if the fancy takes me, to marry a wife." Newman spoke slowly, with a certain dryness of accent and with frequent pauses. This was his habitual mode of utterance, but it was especially marked in the words I have just quoted.

"Jupiter! There 's a programme!" cried Mr. Tristram. "Certainly, all that takes money, especially the wife; unless indeed she gives it, as mine did. And what 's the story? How have you done it?"

Newman had pushed his hat back from his forehead, folded his arms, and stretched his legs. He listened to the music, he looked about him at the bustling crowd, at the plashing fountains, at the nurses and the babies. "I have worked!" he answered at last.

Tristram looked at him for some moments, and allowed his placid eyes to measure his friend's generous longitude and rest upon his comfortably contemplative face. "What have you worked at?" he asked.

"Oh, at several things."

"I suppose you 're a smart fellow, eh?"

Newman continued to look at the nurses and babies; they imparted to the scene a kind of primordial, pastoral simplicity. "Yes," he said at last, "I suppose I am." And then, in answer to his companion's inquiries, he related briefly his history since their last meeting. It was an intensely Western story, and it dealt with enterprises which it will be needless to introduce to the reader in detail. Newman had come out of the war with a brevet of brigadier-general, an honor which in this case—without invidious comparisons—had lighted upon shoulders amply competent to bear it. But though he could manage a fight, when need was, Newman heartily disliked the business; his four years in the army had left him with an angry, bitter sense of the waste of precious things— life and time and money and "smartness" and the early freshness of purpose; and he had addressed himself to the pursuits of peace with passionate zest and energy. He was of course as penniless when he plucked off his shoulder-straps as when he put them on, and the only capital at his disposal was his dogged resolution and his lively perception of ends and means. Exertion and action were as natural to him as respiration; a more completely healthy mortal had never trod the elastic soil of the West. His experience, moreover, was as wide as his capacity; when he was fourteen years old, necessity had taken him by his slim young shoulders and pushed him into the street, to earn that night's supper. He had not earned it, but he had earned the next night's, and afterwards, whenever he had had none, it was because he had gone without it to use the money for something else, a keener pleasure or a finer profit. He had turned his hand, with his brain in it, to many things; he had been enterprising, in an eminent sense of the term; he had been adventurous and even reckless, and he had known bitter failure as well as brilliant success; but he was a born experimentalist, and he had always found something to enjoy in the pressure of necessity, even when it was as irritating as the haircloth shirt of the mediæval monk. At one time failure seemed inexorably his portion; ill-luck became his bed-fellow, and whatever he touched he turned, not to gold, but to ashes. His most vivid conception of a supernatural element in the world's affairs had come to him once when this pertinacity of misfortune was at its climax; there seemed to him something stronger in life than his own will. But the mysterious something could only be the devil, and he was accordingly seized with an intense personal enmity to this impertinent force. He had known what it was to have utterly exhausted his credit, to be unable to raise a dollar, and to find himself at nightfall in a strange city, without a penny to mitigate its strangeness. It was under these circumstances that he made his entrance into San Francisco, the scene, subsequently, of his happiest strokes of fortune. If he did not, like Dr. Franklin in Philadelphia, march along the street munching a penny-loaf, it was only because he had not the penny-loaf necessary to the performance. In his darkest days he had had but one simple, practical impulse—the desire, as he would have phrased it, to see the thing through. He did so at last, buffeted his way into smooth waters, and made money largely. It must be admitted, rather nakedly, that Christopher Newman's sole aim in life had been to make money; what he had been placed in the world for was, to his own perception, simply to wrest a fortune, the bigger the better, from defiant opportunity. This idea completely filled his horizon and satisfied his imagination. Upon the uses of money, upon what one might do with a life into which one had succeeded in injecting the golden stream, he had up to his thirty-fifth year very scantily reflected. Life had been for him an open game, and he had played for high stakes. He had won at last and carried off his winnings; and now what was he to do with them? He was a man to whom, sooner or later, the question was sure to present itself, and the answer to it belongs to our story. A vague sense that more answers were possible than his philosophy had hitherto dreamt of had already taken possession of him, and it seemed softly and agreeably to deepen as he lounged in this brilliant corner of Paris with his friend.

"I must confess," he presently went on, "that here I don't feel at all smart. My remarkable talents seem of no use. I feel as simple as a little child, and a little child might take me by the hand and lead me about."

"Oh, I 'll be your little child," said Tristram, jovially; "I 'll take you by the hand. Trust yourself to me."

"I am a good worker," Newman continued, "but I rather think I am a poor loafer. I have come abroad to amuse myself, but I doubt whether I know how."

"Oh, that 's easily learned."

"Well, I may perhaps learn it, but I am afraid I shall never do it by rote. I have the best will in the world about it, but my genius does n't lie in that direction. As a loafer I shall never be original, as I take it that you are."

"Yes," said Tristram, "I suppose I am original; like all those immoral pictures in the Louvre."

"Besides," Newman continued, "I don't want to work at pleasure, any more than I played at work. I want to take it easily. I feel deliciously lazy, and I should like to spend six months as I am now, sitting under a tree and listening to a band. There 's only one thing; I want to hear some good music."

"Music and pictures! Lord, what refined tastes! You are what my wife calls intellectual. I an't, a bit. But we can find something better for you to do than to sit under a tree. To begin with, you must come to the club."

"What club?"

"The Occidental. You will see all the Americans there; all the best of them, at least. Of course you play poker?"

"Oh, I say," cried Newman, with energy, "you are not going to lock me up in a club and stick me down at a card-table! I have n't come all this way for that."

"What the deuce *have* you come for! You were glad enough to play poker in St. Louis, I recollect, when you cleaned me out."

"I have come to see Europe, to get the best out of it I can. I want to see all the great things, and do what the clever people do."

"The clever people? Much obliged. You set me down as a blockhead, then?"

Newman was sitting sidewise in his chair, with his elbow on the back and his head leaning on his hand. Without moving he looked a while at his companion, with his dry, guarded, half-inscrutable, and yet altogether good-natured smile. "Introduce me to your wife!" he said at last.

Tristram bounced about in his chair. "Upon my word, I won't. She does n't want any help to turn up her nose at me, nor do you, either!"

"I don't turn up my nose at you, my dear fellow; nor at any one, or anything. I 'm not proud, I assure you I 'm not proud. That 's why I am willing to take example by the clever people."

"Well, if I 'm not the rose, as they say here, I have lived near it. I can show you some clever people, too. Do you know General Packard? Do you know C. P. Hatch? Do you know Miss Kitty Upjohn?"

"I shall be happy to make their acquaintance; I want to cultivate society."

Tristram seemed restless and suspicious; he eyed his friend askance, and then, "What are you up to, any way?" he demanded. "Are you going to write a book?"

Christopher Newman twisted one end of his mustache a while, in silence, and at last he made answer. "One day, a couple of months ago, something very curious happened to me. I had come on to New York on some important business; it was rather a long story—a question of getting ahead of another party, in a certain particular way, in the stock-market. This other party had once played me a very mean trick. I owed him a grudge, I felt awfully savage at the time, and I vowed that, when I got a chance, I would, figuratively speaking, put his nose out of joint. There was a matter of some sixty thousand dollars at stake. If I put it out of his way, it was a blow the fellow would feel, and he really deserved no quarter. I jumped into a hack and went about my business, and it was in this hack—this immortal, historical hack—that the curious thing I speak of occurred. It was a hack like any other, only a trifle dirtier, with a greasy line along the top of the drab cushions, as if it had been used for a great many Irish funerals. It is possible I took a nap; I had been traveling all night, and though I was excited with my errand, I felt the want of sleep. At all events I woke up suddenly, from a sleep or from a kind of a reverie, with the most extraordinary feeling in the world—a mortal disgust for the thing I was going to do. It came upon me like *that!*"—and he snapped his fingers—"as abruptly as an old wound that begins to ache. I could n't tell the meaning of it; I only felt that I loathed the whole business and wanted to wash my hands of it. The idea of losing that sixty thousand dollars, of letting it utterly slide and scuttle and never hearing of it again, seemed the sweetest thing in the world. And all this took place quite independently of my will, and I sat watching it as if it were a play at the theatre. I could feel it going on inside of me. You may depend upon it that there are things going on inside of us that we understand mighty little about."

"Jupiter! you make my flesh creep!" cried Tristram. "And while you sat in your hack, watching the play, as you call it, the other man marched in and bagged your sixty thousand dollars?"

"I have not the least idea. I hope so, poor devil! but I never found out. We pulled up in front of the place I was going to in Wall Street, but I sat still in the carriage, and at last the driver scrambled down off his seat to see whether his carriage had not turned into a hearse. I could n't have got out, any more than if I had been a corpse. What was the matter with me? Momentary idiocy, you 'll say. What I wanted to get out of was Wall Street. I told the man to drive down to the Brooklyn ferry and to cross over. When we were over, I told him to drive me out into the country. As I had told him originally to drive for dear life down town, I suppose he thought me insane. Perhaps I was, but in that case I am insane still. I spent the morning looking at the first green leaves on Long Island. I was sick of business; I wanted to throw it all up and break off short; I had money enough, or if I had n't I ought to have. I seemed to feel a new man inside my old skin, and I longed for a new world. When you want a thing so very badly you had better treat yourself to it. I did n't understand the matter, not in the least; but I gave the old horse the bridle and let him find his way. As soon as I could get out of the game I sailed for Europe. That is how I come to be sitting here."

"You ought to have bought up that hack," said Tristram; "it is n't a safe vehicle to have about. And you have really sold out, then; you have retired from business?"

"I have made over my hand to a friend; when I feel disposed, I can take up the cards again. I dare say that a twelve-month hence the operation will be reversed. The pendulum will swing back again. I shall be sitting in a gondola or on a dromedary, and all of a sudden I shall want to clear out. But for the present I am perfectly free. I have even bargained that I am to receive no business letters."

"Oh, it 's a real *caprice de prince*," said Tristram. "I back out; a poor devil like me can't help you to spend such very magnificent leisure as that. You should get introduced to the crowned heads."

Newman looked at him a moment, and then, with his easy smile, "How does one do it?" he asked.

"Come, I like that!" cried Tristram. "It shows you are in earnest."

"Of course I am in earnest. Did n't I say I wanted the best? I know the best can't be had for mere money, but I rather think money will do a good deal. In addition, I am willing to take a good deal of trouble."

"You are not bashful, eh?"

"I have n't the least idea. I want the biggest kind of entertainment a man can get. People, places, art, nature, everything! I want to see the tallest mountains, and the bluest lakes, and the finest pictures, and the handsomest churches, and the most celebrated men, and the most beautiful women."

"Settle down in Paris, then. There are no mountains that I know of, and the only lake is in the Bois du Boulogne, and not particularly blue. But there is everything else: plenty of pictures and churches, no end of celebrated men, and several beautiful women."

"But I can't settle down in Paris at this season, just as summer is coming on."

"Oh, for the summer go up to Trouville."

"What is Trouville?"

"The French Newport. Half the Americans go."

"Is it anywhere near the Alps?"

"About as near as Newport is to the Rocky Mountains."

"Oh, I want to see Mont Blanc," said Newman, "and Amsterdam, and the Rhine, and a lot of places. Venice in particular. I have great ideas about Venice."

"Ah," said Mr. Tristram, rising, "I see I shall have to introduce you to my wife!"

Chapter III

H E PERFORMED this ceremony on the following day, when, by appointment, Christopher Newman went to dine with him. Mr. and Mrs. Tristram lived behind one of those chalk-colored façades which decorate with their pompous sameness the broad avenues manufactured by Baron Haussmann in the neighborhood of the Arc de Triomphe. Their apartment was rich in the modern conveniences, and Tristram lost no time in calling his visitor's attention to their principal household treasures, the gas-lamps and the furnace-holes. "Whenever you feel homesick," he said, "you must come up here. We 'll stick you down before a register, under a good big burner, and"—

"And you will soon get over your homesickness," said Mrs. Tristram.

Her husband stared; his wife often had a tone which he found inscrutable; he could not tell for his life whether she was in jest or in earnest. The truth is that circumstances had done much to cultivate in Mrs. Tristram a marked tendency to irony. Her taste on many points differed from that of her husband, and though she made frequent concessions it must be confessed that her concessions were not always graceful. They were founded upon a vague project she had of some day doing something very positive, something a trifle passionate. What she meant to do she could by no means have told you; but meanwhile, nevertheless, she was buying a good conscience, by installments.

It should be added, without delay, to anticipate misconception, that her little scheme of independence did not definitely involve the assistance of another person, of the opposite sex; she was not saving up virtue to cover the expenses of a flirtation. For this there were various reasons. To begin with, she had a very plain face and she was entirely without illusions as to her appearance. She had taken its measure to a hair's breadth, she knew the worst and the best, she had accepted herself. It had not been, indeed, without a struggle. As a young girl she had spent hours with her back to her mirror, crying her eyes out; and later she had from despera-

tion and bravado adopted the habit of proclaiming herself the
most ill-favored of women, in order that she might—as in
common politeness was inevitable—be contradicted and reassured. It was since she had come to live in Europe that she
had begun to take the matter philosophically. Her observation, acutely exercised here, had suggested to her that a woman's first duty is not to be beautiful, but to be pleasing, and
she encountered so many women who pleased without beauty
that she began to feel that she had discovered her mission.
She had once heard an enthusiastic musician, out of patience
with a gifted bungler, declare that a fine voice is really an
obstacle to singing properly; and it occurred to her that it
might perhaps be equally true that a beautiful face is an obstacle to the acquisition of charming manners. Mrs. Tristram,
then, undertook to be exquisitely agreeable, and she brought
to the task a really touching devotion. How well she would
have succeeded I am unable to say; unfortunately she broke
off in the middle. Her own excuse was the want of encouragement in her immediate circle. But I am inclined to think
that she had not a real genius for the matter, or she would
have pursued the charming art for itself. The poor lady was
very incomplete. She fell back upon the harmonies of the toilet, which she thoroughly understood, and contented herself
with dressing in perfection. She lived in Paris, which she pretended to detest, because it was only in Paris that one could
find things to exactly suit one's complexion. Besides out of
Paris it was always more or less of a trouble to get ten-button
gloves. When she railed at this serviceable city and you asked
her where she would prefer to reside, she returned some very
unexpected answer. She would say in Copenhagen, or in Bar-
celona; having, while making the tour of Europe, spent a couple of days at each of these places. On the whole, with her
poetic furbelows and her misshapen, intelligent little face, she
was, when you knew her, a decidedly interesting woman. She
was naturally shy, and if she had been born a beauty, she
would (having no vanity) probably have remained shy. Now,
she was both diffident and importunate; extremely reserved
sometimes with her friends, and strangely expansive with
strangers. She despised her husband; despised him too much,
for she had been perfectly at liberty not to marry him. She

had been in love with a clever man who had slighted her, and she had married a fool in the hope that this thankless wit, reflecting on it, would conclude that she had no appreciation of merit, and that he had flattered himself in supposing that she cared for his own. Restless, discontented, visionary, without personal ambitions, but with a certain avidity of imagination, she was, as I have said before, eminently incomplete. She was full—both for good and for ill—of beginnings that came to nothing; but she had nevertheless, morally, a spark of the sacred fire.

Newman was fond, under all circumstances, of the society of women, and now that he was out of his native element and deprived of his habitual interests, he turned to it for compensation. He took a great fancy to Mrs. Tristram; she frankly repaid it, and after their first meeting he passed a great many hours in her drawing-room. After two or three talks they were fast friends. Newman's manner with women was peculiar, and it required some ingenuity on a lady's part to discover that he admired her. He had no gallantry, in the usual sense of the term; no compliments, no graces, no speeches. Very fond of what is called chaffing, in his dealings with men, he never found himself on a sofa beside a member of the softer sex without feeling extremely serious. He was not shy, and so far as awkwardness proceeds from a struggle with shyness, he was not awkward; grave, attentive, submissive, often silent, he was simply swimming in a sort of rapture of respect. This emotion was not at all theoretic, it was not even in a high degree sentimental; he had thought very little about the "position" of women, and he was not familiar either sympathetically or otherwise, with the image of a President in petticoats. His attitude was simply the flower of his general good-nature, and a part of his instinctive and genuinely democratic assumption of every one's right to lead an easy life. If a shaggy pauper had a right to bed and board and wages and a vote, women, of course, who were weaker than paupers, and whose physical tissue was in itself an appeal, should be maintained, sentimentally, at the public expense. Newman was willing to be taxed for this purpose, largely, in proportion to his means. Moreover, many of the common traditions with regard to women were with him fresh personal impres-

sions; he had never read a novel! He had been struck with
their acuteness, their subtlety, their tact, their felicity of judgment. They seemed to him exquisitely organized. If it is true
that one must always have in one's work here below a religion, or at least an ideal, of some sort, Newman found his
metaphysical inspiration in a vague acceptance of final responsibility to some illumined feminine brow.

He spent a great deal of time in listening to advice from
Mrs. Tristram; advice, it must be added, for which he had
never asked. He would have been incapable of asking for it,
for he had no perception of difficulties, and consequently no
curiosity about remedies. The complex Parisian world about
him seemed a very simple affair; it was an immense, amazing
spectacle, but it neither inflamed his imagination nor irritated
his curiosity. He kept his hands in his pockets, looked on
good-humoredly, desired to miss nothing important, observed a great many things narrowly, and never reverted to
himself. Mrs. Tristram's "advice" was a part of the show, and
a more entertaining element, in her abundant gossip, than the
others. He enjoyed her talking about himself; it seemed a part
of her beautiful ingenuity; but he never made an application
of anything she said, or remembered it when he was away
from her. For herself, she appropriated him; he was the most
interesting thing she had had to think about in many a
month. She wished to do something with him—she hardly
knew what. There was so much of him; he was so rich and
robust, so easy, friendly, well-disposed, that he kept her fancy
constantly on the alert. For the present, the only thing she
could do was to like him. She told him that he was "horribly
Western," but in this compliment the adverb was tinged with
insincerity. She led him about with her, introduced him to
fifty people, and took extreme satisfaction in her conquest.
Newman accepted every proposal, shook hands universally
and promiscuously, and seemed equally unfamiliar with trepidation or with elation. Tom Tristram complained of his
wife's avidity, and declared that he could never have a clear
five minutes with his friend. If he had known how things
were going to turn out, he never would have brought him to
the Avenue d'Iéna. The two men, formerly, had not been intimate, but Newman remembered his earlier impression of his

host, and did Mrs. Tristram, who had by no means taken him into her confidence, but whose secret he presently discovered, the justice to admit that her husband was a rather degenerate mortal. At twenty-five he had been a good fellow, and in this respect he was unchanged; but of a man of his age one expected something more. People said he was sociable, but this was as much a matter of course as for a dipped sponge to expand; and it was not a high order of sociability. He was a great gossip and tattler, and to produce a laugh would hardly have spared the reputation of his aged mother. Newman had a kindness for old memories, but he found it impossible not to perceive that Tristram was nowadays a very light weight. His only aspirations were to hold out at poker, at his club, to know the names of all the *cocottes*, to shake hands all round, to ply his rosy gullet with truffles and champagne, and to create uncomfortable eddies and obstructions among the constituent atoms of the American colony. He was shamefully idle, spiritless, sensual, snobbish. He irritated our friend by the tone of his allusions to their native country, and Newman was at a loss to understand why the United States were not good enough for Mr. Tristram. He had never been a very conscious patriot, but it vexed him to see them treated as little better than a vulgar smell in his friend's nostrils, and he finally broke out and swore that they were the greatest country in the world, that they could put all Europe into their breeches' pockets, and that an American who spoke ill of them ought to be carried home in irons and compelled to live in Boston. (This, for Newman, was putting it very vindictively.) Tristram was a comfortable man to snub; he bore no malice, and he continued to insist on Newman's finishing his evenings at the Occidental Club.

Christopher Newman dined several times in the Avenue d'Iéna, and his host always proposed an early adjournment to this institution. Mrs. Tristram protested, and declared that her husband exhausted his ingenuity in trying to displease her.

"Oh no, I never try, my love," he answered. "I know you loathe me quite enough when I take my chance."

Newman hated to see a husband and wife on these terms, and he was sure one or other of them must be very unhappy.

He knew it was not Tristram. Mrs. Tristram had a balcony before her windows, upon which, during the June evenings, she was fond of sitting, and Newman used frankly to say that he preferred the balcony to the club. It had a fringe of perfumed plants in tubs, and enabled you to look up the broad street and see the Arch of Triumph vaguely massing its heroic sculptures in the summer starlight. Sometimes Newman kept his promise of following Mr. Tristram, in half an hour, to the Occidental, and sometimes he forgot it. His hostess asked him a great many questions about himself, but on this subject he was an indifferent talker. He was not what is called subjective, though when he felt that her interest was sincere, he made an almost heroic attempt to be. He told her a great many things he had done, and regaled her with anecdotes of Western life; she was from Philadelphia, and with her eight years in Paris, talked of herself as a languid Oriental. But some other person was always the hero of the tale, by no means always to his advantage; and Newman's own emotions were but scantily chronicled. She had an especial wish to know whether he had ever been in love—seriously, passionately—and, failing to gather any satisfaction from his allusions, she at last directly inquired. He hesitated a while, and at last he said, "No!" She declared that she was delighted to hear it, as it confirmed her private conviction that he was a man of no feeling.

"Really?" he asked, very gravely. "Do you think so? How do you recognize a man of feeling?"

"I can't make out," said Mrs. Tristram, "whether you are very simple or very deep."

"I 'm very deep. That 's a fact."

"I believe that if I were to tell you with a certain air that you have no feeling, you would implicitly believe me."

"A certain air?" said Newman. "Try it and see."

"You would believe me, but you would not care," said Mrs. Tristram.

"You have got it all wrong. I should care immensely, but I should n't believe you. The fact is I have never had time to feel things. I have had to *do* them, to make myself felt."

"I can imagine that you may have done that tremendously, sometimes."

"Yes, there 's no mistake about that."

"When you are in a fury it can't be pleasant."

"I am never in a fury."

"Angry, then, or displeased."

"I am never angry, and it is so long since I have been displeased that I have quite forgotten it."

"I don't believe," said Mrs. Tristram, "that you are never angry. A man ought to be angry sometimes, and you are neither good enough nor bad enough always to keep your temper."

"I lose it perhaps once in five years."

"The time is coming round, then," said his hostess. "Before I have known you six months I shall see you in a fine fury."

"Do you mean to put me into one?"

"I should not be sorry. You take things too coolly. It exasperates me. And then you are too happy. You have what must be the most agreeable thing in the world, the consciousness of having bought your pleasure beforehand and paid for it. You have not a day of reckoning staring you in the face. Your reckonings are over."

"Well, I suppose I am happy," said Newman, meditatively.

"You have been odiously successful."

"Successful in copper," said Newman, "only so-so in railroads, and a hopeless fizzle in oil."

"It is very disagreeable to know how Americans have made their money. Now you have the world before you. You have only to enjoy."

"Oh, I suppose I am very well off," said Newman. "Only I am tired of having it thrown up at me. Besides, there are several drawbacks. I am not intellectual."

"One does n't expect it of you," Mrs. Tristram answered. Then in a moment, "Besides, you are!"

"Well, I mean to have a good time, whether or no," said Newman. "I am not cultivated, I am not even educated; I know nothing about history, or art, or foreign tongues, or any other learned matters. But I am not a fool, either, and I shall undertake to know something about Europe by the time I have done with it. I feel something under my ribs here," he added in a moment, "that I can't explain—a sort of a mighty hankering, a desire to stretch out and haul in."

"Bravo!" said Mrs. Tristram, "that is very fine. You are the great Western Barbarian, stepping forth in his innocence and might, gazing a while at this poor effete Old World, and then swooping down on it."

"Oh, come," said Newman. "I am not a barbarian, by a good deal. I am very much the reverse. I have seen barbarians; I know what they are."

"I don't mean that you are a Comanche chief, or that you wear a blanket and feathers. There are different shades."

"I am a highly civilized man," said Newman. "I stick to that. If you don't believe it, I should like to prove it to you."

Mrs. Tristram was silent a while. "I should like to make you prove it," she said, at last. "I should like to put you in a difficult place."

"Pray do," said Newman.

"That has a little conceited sound!" his companion rejoined.

"Oh," said Newman, "I have a very good opinion of myself."

"I wish I could put it to the test. Give me time, and I will." And Mrs. Tristram remained silent for some time afterwards, as if she was trying to keep her pledge. It did not appear that evening that she succeeded; but as he was rising to take his leave she passed suddenly, as she was very apt to do, from the tone of unsparing persiflage to that of almost tremulous sympathy. "Speaking seriously," she said, "I believe in you, Mr. Newman. You flatter my patriotism."

"Your patriotism?" Christopher demanded.

"Even so. It would take too long to explain, and you probably would not understand. Besides, you might take it—really, you might take it for a declaration. But it has nothing to do with you personally; it 's what you represent. Fortunately you don't know all that, or your conceit would increase insufferably."

Newman stood staring and wondering what under the sun he "represented."

"Forgive all my meddlesome chatter and forget my advice. It is very silly in me to undertake to tell you what to do. When you are embarrassed, do as you think best, and you will do very well. When you are in a difficulty, judge for yourself."

"I shall remember everything you have told me," said Newman. "There are so many forms and ceremonies over here"—

"Forms and ceremonies are what I mean, of course."

"Ah, but I want to observe them," said Newman. "Have n't I as good a right as another? They don't scare me, and you need n't give me leave to violate them. I won't take it."

"That is not what I mean. I mean, observe them in your own way. Settle nice questions for yourself. Cut the knot or untie it, as you choose."

"Oh, I am sure I shall never fumble over it!" said Newman.

The next time that he dined in the Avenue d'Iéna was a Sunday, a day on which Mr. Tristram left the cards unshuffled, so that there was a trio in the evening on the balcony. The talk was of many things, and at last Mrs. Tristram suddenly observed to Christopher Newman that it was high time he should take a wife.

"Listen to her; she has the audacity!" said Tristram, who on Sunday evenings was always rather acrimonious.

"I don't suppose you have made up your mind not to marry?" Mrs. Tristram continued.

"Heaven forbid!" cried Newman. "I am sternly resolved on it."

"It 's very easy," said Tristram; "fatally easy!"

"Well, then, I suppose you do not mean to wait till you are fifty."

"On the contrary, I am in a great hurry."

"One would never suppose it. Do you expect a lady to come and propose to you?"

"No; I am willing to propose. I think a great deal about it."

"Tell me some of your thoughts."

"Well," said Newman, slowly, "I want to marry very well."

"Marry a woman of sixty, then," said Tristram.

" 'Well' in what sense?"

"In every sense. I shall be hard to please."

"You must remember that, as the French proverb says, the most beautiful girl in the world can give but what she has."

"Since you ask me," said Newman, "I will say frankly that I want extremely to marry. It is time, to begin with; before I know it I shall be forty. And then I'm lonely and helpless and dull. But if I marry now, so long as I did n't do it in hot haste when I was twenty, I must do it with my eyes open. I want to do the thing in handsome style. I not only want to make no mistakes, but I want to make a great hit. I want to take my pick. My wife must be a magnificent woman."

"Voilà ce qui s'appelle parler!" cried Mrs. Tristram.

"Oh, I have thought an immense deal about it."

"Perhaps you think too much. The best thing is simply to fall in love."

"When I find the woman who pleases me, I shall love her enough. My wife shall be very comfortable."

"You are superb! There 's a chance for the magnificent woman."

"You are not fair," Newman rejoined. "You draw a fellow out and put him off his guard, and then you laugh at him."

"I assure you," said Mrs. Tristram, "that I am very serious. To prove it, I will make you a proposal. Should you like me, as they say here, to marry you?"

"To hunt up a wife for me?"

"She is already found. I will bring you together."

"Oh, come," said Tristram, "we don't keep a matrimonial bureau. He will think you want your commission."

"Present me to a woman who comes up to my notions," said Newman, "and I will marry her to-morrow."

"You have a strange tone about it, and I don't quite understand you. I did n't suppose you would be so cold-blooded and calculating."

Newman was silent a while. "Well," he said, at last, "I want a great woman. I stick to that. That's one thing I *can* treat myself to, and if it is to be had I mean to have it. What else have I toiled and struggled for, all these years? I have succeeded, and now what am I to do with my success? To make it perfect, as I see it, there must be a beautiful woman perched on the pile, like a statue on a monument. She must be as good as she is beautiful, and as clever as she is good. I can give my wife a good deal, so I am not afraid to ask a good deal myself. She shall have everything a woman can desire; I shall not even object to her being too good for me; she may be cleverer and wiser than I can understand, and I shall only be the better pleased. I want to possess, in a word, the best article in the market."

"Why did n't you tell a fellow all this at the outset?" Tristram demanded. "I have been trying so to make you fond of *me!*"

"This is very interesting," said Mrs. Tristram. "I like to see a man know his own mind."

"I have known mine for a long time," Newman went on. "I made up my mind tolerably early in life that a beautiful wife was the thing best worth having, here below. It is the greatest victory over circumstances. When I say beautiful, I mean beautiful in mind and in manners, as well as in person. It is a thing every man has an equal right to; he may get it if he can. He does n't have to be born with certain faculties, on purpose; he needs only to be a man. Then he needs only to use his will, and such wits as he has, and to try."

"It strikes me that your marriage is to be rather a matter of vanity."

"Well, it is certain," said Newman, "that if people notice my wife and admire her, I shall be mightily tickled."

"After this," cried Mrs. Tristram, "call any man modest!"

"But none of them will admire her so much as I."

"I see you have a taste for splendor."

Newman hesitated a little; and then, "I honestly believe I have!" he said.

"And I suppose you have already looked about you a good deal."

"A good deal, according to opportunity."

"And you have seen nothing that satisfied you?"

"No," said Newman, half reluctantly, "I am bound to say in honesty that I have seen nothing that really satisfied me."

"You remind me of the heroes of the French romantic poets, Rolla and Fortunio and all those other insatiable gentlemen for whom nothing in this world was handsome enough. But I see you are in earnest, and I should like to help you."

"Who the deuce is it, darling, that you are going to put upon him?" Tristram cried. "We know a good many pretty girls, thank Heaven, but magnificent women are not so common."

"Have you any objections to a foreigner?" his wife continued, addressing Newman, who had tilted back his chair, and, with his feet on a bar of the balcony railing and his hands in his pockets, was looking at the stars.

"No Irish need apply," said Tristram.

Newman meditated a while. "As a foreigner, no," he said at last; "I have no prejudices."

"My dear fellow, you have no suspicions!" cried Tristram. "You don't know what terrible customers these foreign women are; especially the 'magnificent' ones. How should you like a fair Circassian, with a dagger in her belt?"

Newman administered a vigorous slap to his knee. "I would marry a Japanese, if she pleased me," he affirmed.

"We had better confine ourselves to Europe," said Mrs. Tristram. "The only thing is, then, that the person be in herself to your taste?"

"She is going to offer you an unappreciated governess!" Tristram groaned.

"Assuredly. I won't deny that, other things being equal, I should prefer one of my own country-women. We should speak the same language, and that would be a comfort. But I am not afraid of a foreigner. Besides, I rather like the idea of taking in Europe, too. It enlarges the field of selection. When you choose from a greater number, you can bring your choice to a finer point."

"You talk like Sardanapalus!" exclaimed Tristram.

"You say all this to the right person," said Newman's hostess. "I happen to number among my friends the loveliest woman in the world. Neither more nor less. I don't say a very charming person or a very estimable woman or a very great beauty; I say simply the loveliest woman in the world."

"The deuce!" cried Tristram, "you have kept very quiet about her. Were you afraid of me?"

"You have seen her," said his wife, "but you have no perception of such merit as Claire's."

"Ah, her name is Claire? I give it up."

"Does your friend wish to marry?" asked Newman.

"Not in the least. It is for you to make her change her

mind. It will not be easy; she has had one husband, and he gave her a low opinion of the species."

"Oh, she is a widow, then?" said Newman.

"Are you already afraid? She was married at eighteen, by her parents, in the French fashion, to a disagreeable old man. But he had the good taste to die a couple of years afterward, and she is now twenty-five."

"So she is French?"

"French by her father, English by her mother. She is really more English than French, and she speaks English as well as you or I—or rather much better. She belongs to the very top of the basket, as they say here. Her family, on each side, is of fabulous antiquity; her mother is the daughter of an English Catholic earl. Her father is dead, and since her widowhood she has lived with her mother and a married brother. There is another brother, younger, who I believe is wild. They have an old hotel in the Rue de l'Université, but their fortune is small, and they make a common household, for economy's sake. When I was a girl I was put into a convent here for my education, while my father made the tour of Europe. It was a silly thing to do with me, but it had the advantage that it made me acquainted with Claire de Bellegarde. She was younger than I, but we became fast friends. I took a tremendous fancy to her, and she returned my passion as far as she could. They kept such a tight rein on her that she could do very little, and when I left the convent she had to give me up. I was not of her *monde*; I am not now, either, but we sometimes meet. They are terrible people—her monde; all mounted upon stilts a mile high, and with pedigrees long in proportion. It is the skim of the milk of the old noblesse. Do you know what a Legitimist is, or an Ultramontane? Go into Madame de Cintré's drawing-room some afternoon, at five o'clock, and you will see the best-preserved specimens. I say go, but no one is admitted who can't show his fifty quarterings."

"And this is the lady you propose to me to marry?" asked Newman. "A lady I can't even approach?"

"But you said just now that you recognized no obstacles."

Newman looked at Mrs. Tristram a while, stroking his mustache. "Is she a beauty?" he demanded.

"No."

"Oh, then it 's no use"—

"She is not a beauty, but she is beautiful, two very different things. A beauty has no faults in her face; the face of a beautiful woman may have faults that only deepen its charm."

"I remember Madame de Cintré, now," said Tristram. "She is as plain as a pike-staff. A man would n't look at her twice."

"In saying that *he* would not look at her twice, my husband sufficiently describes her," Mrs. Tristram rejoined.

"Is she good; is she clever?" Newman asked.

"She is perfect! I won't say more than that. When you are praising a person to another who is to know her, it is bad policy to go into details. I won't exaggerate. I simply recommend her. Among all women I have known she stands alone; she is of a different clay."

"I should like to see her," said Newman, simply.

"I will try to manage it. The only way will be to invite her to dinner. I have never invited her before, and I don't know that she will come. Her old feudal countess of a mother rules the family with an iron hand, and allows her to have no friends but of her own choosing, and to visit only in a certain sacred circle. But I can at least ask her."

At this moment Mrs. Tristram was interrupted; a servant stepped out upon the balcony and announced that there were visitors in the drawing-room. When Newman's hostess had gone in to receive her friends, Tom Tristram approached his guest.

"Don't put your foot into *this*, my boy," he said, puffing the last whiffs of his cigar. "There 's nothing in it!"

Newman looked askance at him, inquisitive. "You tell another story, eh?"

"I say simply that Madame de Cintré is a great white doll of a woman, who cultivates quiet haughtiness."

"Ah, she 's haughty, eh?"

"She looks at you as if you were so much thin air, and cares for you about as much."

"She is very proud, eh?"

"Proud? As proud as I 'm humble."

"And not good-looking?"

Tristram shrugged his shoulders: "It 's a kind of beauty you must be *intellectual* to understand. But I must go in and amuse the company."

Some time elapsed before Newman followed his friends into the drawing-room. When he at last made his appearance there he remained but a short time, and during this period sat perfectly silent, listening to a lady to whom Mrs. Tristram had straightway introduced him and who chattered, without a pause, with the full force of an extraordinarily high-pitched voice. Newman gazed and attended. Presently he came to bid good-night to Mrs. Tristram.

"Who is that lady?" he asked.

"Miss Dora Finch. How do you like her?"

"She 's too noisy."

"She is thought so bright! Certainly, you are fastidious," said Mrs. Tristram.

Newman stood a moment, hesitating. Then at last, "Don't forget about your friend," he said; "Madame What's-her-name? the proud beauty. Ask her to dinner, and give me good notice." And with this he departed.

Some days later he came back; it was in the afternoon. He found Mrs. Tristram in her drawing-room; with her was a visitor, a woman young and pretty, dressed in white. The two ladies had risen and the visitor was apparently taking her leave. As Newman approached, he received from Mrs. Tristram a glance of the most vivid significance, which he was not immediately able to interpret.

"This is a good friend of ours," she said, turning to her companion, "Mr. Christopher Newman. I have spoken of you to him and he has an extreme desire to make your acquaintance. If you had consented to come and dine, I should have offered him an opportunity."

The stranger turned her face toward Newman, with a smile. He was not embarrassed, for his unconscious *sang-froid* was boundless; but as he became aware that this was the proud and beautiful Madame de Cintré, the loveliest woman in the world, the promised perfection, the proposed ideal, he made an instinctive movement to gather his wits together. Through the slight preoccupation that it produced he had a sense of a long, fair face, and of two eyes that were both brilliant and mild.

"I should have been most happy," said Madame de Cintré. "Unfortunately, as I have been telling Mrs. Tristram, I go on Monday to the country."

Newman had made a solemn bow. "I am very sorry," he said.

"Paris is getting too warm," Madame de Cintré added, taking her friend's hand again in farewell.

Mrs. Tristram seemed to have formed a sudden and somewhat venturesome resolution, and she smiled more intensely, as women do when they take such resolutions. "I want Mr. Newman to know you," she said, dropping her head on one side and looking at Madame de Cintré's bonnet ribbons.

Christopher Newman stood gravely silent, while his native penetration admonished him. Mrs. Tristram was determined to force her friend to address him a word of encouragement which should be more than one of the common formulas of politeness; and if she was prompted by charity, it was by the charity that begins at home. Madame de Cintré was her dearest Claire, and her especial admiration, but Madame de Cintré had found it impossible to dine with her, and Madame de Cintré should for once be forced gently to render tribute to Mrs. Tristram.

"It would give me great pleasure," she said, looking at Mrs. Tristram.

"That 's a great deal," cried the latter, "for Madame de Cintré to say!"

"I am very much obliged to you," said Newman. "Mrs. Tristram can speak better for me than I can speak for myself."

Madame de Cintré looked at him again, with the same soft brightness. "Are you to be long in Paris?" she asked.

"We shall keep him," said Mrs. Tristram.

"But you are keeping *me!*" and Madame de Cintré shook her friend's hand.

"A moment longer," said Mrs. Tristram.

Madame de Cintré looked at Newman again; this time without her smile. Her eyes lingered a moment. "Will you come and see me?" she asked.

Mrs. Tristram kissed her. Newman expressed his thanks, and she took her leave. Her hostess went with her to the door, and left Newman alone a moment. Presently she returned, rubbing her hands. "It was a fortunate chance," she said. "She had come to decline my invitation. You triumphed on the spot, making her ask you, at the end of three minutes, to her house."

"It was you who triumphed," said Newman. "You must not be too hard upon her."

Mrs. Tristram stared. "What do you mean?"

"She did not strike me as so proud. I should say she was shy."

"You are very discriminating. And what do you think of her face?"

"It 's handsome!" said Newman.

"I should think it was! Of course you will go and see her."

"To-morrow!" cried Newman.

"No, not to-morrow; the next day. That will be Sunday; she leaves Paris on Monday. If you don't see her, it will at least be a beginning." And she gave him Madame de Cintré's address.

He walked across the Seine, late in the summer afternoon, and made his way through those gray and silent streets of the Faubourg St. Germain whose houses present to the outer world a face as impassive and as suggestive of the concentration of privacy within as the blank walls of Eastern seraglios. Newman thought it a queer way for rich people to live; his ideal of grandeur was a splendid façade, diffusing its brilliancy outward too, irradiating hospitality. The house to which he had been directed had a dark, dusty, painted portal, which swung open in answer to his ring. It admitted him into a wide, graveled court, surrounded on three sides with closed windows, and with a doorway facing the street, approached by three steps and surmounted by a tin canopy. The place was all in the shade; it answered to Newman's conception of a convent. The portress could not tell him whether Madame de Cintré was visible; he would please to apply at the farther door. He crossed the court; a gentleman was sitting, bare-headed, on the steps of the portico, playing with a beautiful pointer. He rose as Newman approached, and, as he laid his hand upon the bell, said with a smile, in English, that he was afraid Newman would be kept waiting; the servants were scattered, he himself had been ringing, he did n't know what the deuce was in them. He was a young man, his English was excellent, and his smile very frank. Newman pronounced the name of Madame de Cintré.

"I think," said the young man, "that my sister is visible. Come in, and if you will give me your card I will carry it to her myself."

Newman had been accompanied on his present errand by a slight sentiment, I will not say of defiance—a readiness for aggression or defense, as they might prove needful—but of reflective, good-humored suspicion. He took from his pocket, while he stood on the portico, a card upon which, under his name, he had written the words "San Francisco," and while he presented it he looked warily at his interlocutor. His glance was singularly reassuring; he liked the young man's face; it strongly resembled that of Madame de Cintré. He was evidently her brother. The young man, on his side, had made a rapid inspection of Newman's person. He had taken the card and was about to enter the house with it when another figure appeared on the threshold—an older man, of a fine presence, wearing evening dress. He looked hard at Newman, and Newman looked at him. "Madame de Cintré," the younger man repeated, as an introduction of the visitor. The other took the card from his hand, read it in a rapid glance, looked again at Newman from head to foot, hesitated a moment, and then said, gravely but urbanely, "Madame de Cintré is not at home."

The younger man made a gesture, and then, turning to Newman, "I am very sorry, sir," he said.

Newman gave him a friendly nod, to show that he bore him no malice, and retraced his steps. At the porter's lodge he stopped; the two men were still standing on the portico.

"Who is the gentleman with the dog?" he asked of the old woman who reappeared. He had begun to learn French.

"That is Monsieur le Comte."

"And the other?"

"That is Monsieur le Marquis."

"A marquis?" said Christopher in English, which the old woman fortunately did not understand. "Oh, then he's not the butler!"

Chapter IV

E ARLY ONE MORNING, before Christopher Newman was
dressed, a little old man was ushered into his apartment,
followed by a youth in a blouse, bearing a picture in a brilliant frame. Newman, among the distractions of Paris, had
forgotten M. Nioche and his accomplished daughter; but this
was an effective reminder.

"I am afraid you had given me up, sir," said the old man,
after many apologies and salutations. "We have made you
wait so many days. You accused us, perhaps, of inconstancy,
of bad faith. But behold me at last! And behold also the
pretty Madonna. Place it on a chair, my friend, in a good
light, so that monsieur may admire it." And M. Nioche, addressing his companion, helped him to dispose the work of
art.

It had been endued with a layer of varnish an inch thick,
and its frame, of an elaborate pattern, was at least a foot wide.
It glittered and twinkled in the morning light, and looked, to
Newman's eyes, wonderfully splendid and precious. It seemed
to him a very happy purchase, and he felt rich in the possession of it. He stood looking at it complacently, while he proceeded with his toilet, and M. Nioche, who had dismissed his
own attendant, hovered near, smiling and rubbing his hands.

"It has wonderful *finesse*," he murmured, caressingly. "And
here and there are marvelous touches; you probably perceive
them, sir. It attracted great attention on the Boulevard, as we
came along. And then a gradation of tones! That 's what it is
to know how to paint. I don't say it because I am her father,
sir; but as one man of taste addressing another I cannot help
observing that you have there an exquisite work. It is hard to
produce such things and to have to part with them. If our
means only allowed us the luxury of keeping it! I really may
say, sir"—and M. Nioche gave a little feebly insinuating
laugh—"I really may say that I envy you! You see," he added
in a moment, "we have taken the liberty of offering you a
frame. It increases by a trifle the value of the work, and it will
save you the annoyance—so great for a person of your delicacy—of going about to bargain at the shops."

The language spoken by M. Nioche was a singular compound, which I shrink from the attempt to reproduce in its integrity. He had apparently once possessed a certain knowledge of English, and his accent was oddly tinged with the cockneyism of the British metropolis. But his learning had grown rusty with disuse, and his vocabulary was defective and capricious. He had repaired it with large patches of French, with words anglicized by a process of his own, and with native idioms literally translated. The result, in the form in which he in all humility presented it, would be scarcely comprehensible to the reader, so that I have ventured to trim and sift it. Newman only half understood it, but it amused him, and the old man's decent forlornness appealed to his democratic instincts. The assumption of a fatality in misery always irritated his strong good nature—it was almost the only thing that did so; and he felt the impulse to wipe it out, as it were, with the sponge of his own prosperity. The papa of Mademoiselle Noémie, however, had apparently on this occasion been vigorously indoctrinated, and he showed a certain tremulous eagerness to cultivate unexpected opportunities.

"How much do I owe you, then, with the frame?" asked Newman.

"It will make in all three thousand francs," said the old man, smiling agreeably, but folding his hands in instinctive suppliance.

"Can you give me a receipt?"

"I have brought one," said M. Nioche. "I took the liberty of drawing it up, in case monsieur should happen to desire to discharge his debt." And he drew a paper from his pocket-book and presented it to his patron. The document was written in a minute, fantastic hand, and couched in the choicest language.

Newman laid down the money, and M. Nioche dropped the napoleons one by one, solemnly and lovingly, into an old leathern purse.

"And how is your young lady?" asked Newman. "She made a great impression on me."

"An impression? Monsieur is very good. Monsieur admires her appearance?"

"She is very pretty, certainly."

"Alas, yes, she is very pretty!"

"And what is the harm in her being pretty?"

M. Nioche fixed his eyes upon a spot on the carpet and shook his head. Then looking up at Newman with a gaze that seemed to brighten and expand, "Monsieur knows what Paris is. She is dangerous to beauty, when beauty has n't the sou."

"Ah, but that is not the case with your daughter. She is rich, now."

"Very true; we are rich for six months. But if my daughter were a plain girl I should sleep better, all the same."

"You are afraid of the young men?"

"The young and the old!"

"She ought to get a husband."

"Ah, monsieur, one does n't get a husband for nothing. Her husband must take her as she is: I can't give her a sou. But the young men don't see with that eye."

"Oh," said Newman, "her talent is in itself a dowry."

"Ah, sir, it needs first to be converted into specie!" and M. Nioche slapped his purse tenderly before he stowed it away. "The operation does n't take place every day."

"Well, your young men are very shabby," said Newman; "that 's all I can say. They ought to pay for your daughter, and not ask money themselves."

"Those are very noble ideas, monsieur; but what will you have? They are not the ideas of this country. We want to know what we are about when we marry."

"How big a portion does your daughter want?"

M. Nioche stared, as if he wondered what was coming next; but he promptly recovered himself, at a venture, and replied that he knew a very nice young man, employed by an insurance company, who would content himself with fifteen thousand francs.

"Let your daughter paint half a dozen pictures for me, and she shall have her dowry."

"Half a dozen pictures—her dowry! Monsieur is not speaking inconsiderately?"

"If she will make me six or eight copies in the Louvre as pretty as that Madonna, I will pay her the same price," said Newman.

Poor M. Nioche was speechless a moment, with amazement and gratitude, and then he seized Newman's hand, pressed it between his own ten fingers, and gazed at him with watery eyes. "As pretty as that? They shall be a thousand times prettier—they shall be magnificent, sublime. Ah, if I only knew how to paint, myself, sir, so that I might lend a hand! What can I do to thank you? *Voyons!*" And he pressed his forehead while he tried to think of something.

"Oh, you have thanked me enough," said Newman.

"Ah, here it is, sir!" cried M. Nioche. "To express my gratitude, I will charge you nothing for the lessons in French conversation."

"The lessons? I had quite forgotten them. Listening to your English," added Newman, laughing, "is almost a lesson in French."

"Ah, I don't profess to teach English, certainly," said M. Nioche. "But for my own admirable tongue I am still at your service."

"Since you are here, then," said Newman, "we will begin. This is a very good hour. I am going to have my coffee; come every morning at half-past nine and have yours with me."

"Monsieur offers me my coffee, also?" cried M. Nioche. "Truly, my *beaux jours* are coming back."

"Come," said Newman, "let us begin. The coffee is almighty hot. How do you say that in French?"

Every day, then, for the following three weeks, the minutely respectable figure of M. Nioche made its appearance, with a series of little inquiring and apologetic obeisances, among the aromatic fumes of Newman's morning beverage. I don't know how much French our friend learned, but, as he himself said, if the attempt did him no good, it could at any rate do him no harm. And it amused him; it gratified that irregularly sociable side of his nature which had always expressed itself in a relish for ungrammatical conversation, and which often, even in his busy and preoccupied days, had made him sit on rail fences in young Western towns, in the twilight, in gossip hardly less than fraternal with humorous loafers and obscure fortune-seekers. He had notions, wherever he went, about talking with the natives; he had been assured, and his judgment approved the advice, that in traveling abroad it was an excellent thing to look into the life of the country. M. Nioche was very much of a native and, though his life might not be particularly worth looking into, he was a palpable and smoothly-rounded unit in that picturesque Parisian civilization which offered our hero so much easy entertainment and propounded so many curious problems to his inquiring and practical mind. Newman was fond of statistics; he liked to know how things were done; it gratified him to learn what taxes were paid, what profits were gathered, what commercial habits prevailed, how the battle of life was fought. M. Nioche, as a reduced capitalist, was familiar with these considerations, and he formulated his information, which he was proud to be able to impart, in the neatest possible terms and with a pinch of snuff between finger and thumb. As a Frenchman—quite apart from Newman's napoleons—M. Nioche loved conversation, and even in his decay his urbanity had not grown rusty. As a Frenchman, too, he could give a clear account of things, and—still as a Frenchman—when his knowledge was at fault he could supply its lapses with the most convenient and ingenious hypotheses. The little shrunken financier was intensely delighted to have questions asked him, and he scraped together information, by frugal processes, and took notes, in his little greasy pocketbook, of incidents which might interest his munificent friend. He read old almanacs at the book-stalls on the quays, and he began to frequent another café, where more newspapers were taken and his post-prandial *demitasse* cost him a penny extra, and where he used to con the tattered sheets for curious anecdotes, freaks of nature, and strange coincidences. He would relate with solemnity the next morning that a child of five years of age had lately died at Bordeaux, whose brain had been found to weigh sixty ounces—the brain of a Napoleon or a Washington! or that Madame P——, *charcutière* in the Rue de Clichy, had found in the wadding of an old petticoat the sum of three hundred and sixty francs, which she had lost five years before. He pronounced his words with great distinctness and sonority, and Newman assured him that his way of dealing with the French tongue was very superior to the bewildering chatter that he heard in other mouths. Upon this M. Nioche's accent became more finely trenchant than ever; he offered to read extracts from Lamartine, and he protested that, although he did endeavor according to his feeble lights to cultivate refinement of diction, monsieur, if he wanted the real thing, should go to the Théâtre Français.

Newman took an interest in French thriftiness and conceived a lively admiration for Parisian economies. His own economic genius was so entirely for operations on a larger scale, and, to move at his ease, he needed so imperatively the sense of great risks and great prizes, that he found an ungrudging entertainment in the spectacle of fortunes made by the aggregation of copper coins, and in the minute subdivision of labor and profit. He questioned M. Nioche about his own manner of life, and felt a friendly mixture of compassion and respect over the recital of his delicate frugalities. The worthy man told him how, at one period, he and his daughter had supported existence, comfortably, upon the sum of fifteen sous *per diem*; recently, having succeeded in hauling ashore the last floating fragments of the wreck of his fortune, his budget had been a trifle more ample. But they still had to count their sous very narrowly, and M. Nioche intimated with a sigh that Mademoiselle Noémie did not bring to this task that zealous coöperation which might have been desired.

"But what will you have?" he asked, philosophically. "One is young, one is pretty, one needs new dresses and fresh gloves; one can't wear shabby gowns among the splendors of the Louvre."

"But your daughter earns enough to pay for her own clothes," said Newman.

M. Nioche looked at him with weak, uncertain eyes. He would have liked to be able to say that his daughter's talents were appreciated, and that her crooked little daubs commanded a market; but it seemed a scandal to abuse the credulity of this free-handed stranger, who, without a suspicion or a question, had admitted him to equal social rights. He compromised, and declared that while it was obvious that Mademoiselle Noémie's reproductions of the old masters had only to be seen to be coveted, the prices which, in consideration of their altogether peculiar degree of finish, she felt obliged to ask for them had kept purchasers at a respectful distance. "Poor little one!" said M. Nioche, with a sigh; "it is almost a pity that her work is so perfect! It would be in her interest to paint less well."

"But if Mademoiselle Noémie has this devotion to her art," Newman once observed, "why should you have those fears for her that you spoke of the other day?"

M. Nioche meditated: there was an inconsistency in his position; it made him chronically uncomfortable. Though he had no desire to destroy the goose with the golden eggs—Newman's benevolent confidence—he felt a tremulous impulse to speak out all his trouble. "Ah, she is an artist, my dear sir, most assuredly," he declared. "But, to tell you the truth, she is also a *franche coquette*. I am sorry to say," he added in a moment, shaking his head with a world of harmless bitterness, "that she comes honestly by it. Her mother was one before her!"

"You were not happy with your wife?" Newman asked.

M. Nioche gave half a dozen little backward jerks of his head. "She was my purgatory, monsieur!"

"She deceived you?"

"Under my nose, year after year. I was too stupid, and the temptation was too great. But I found her out at last. I have only been once in my life a man to be afraid of; I know it very well: it was in that hour! Nevertheless I don't like to think of it. I loved her—I can't tell you how much. She was a bad woman."

"She is not living?"

"She has gone to her account."

"Her influence on your daughter, then," said Newman encouragingly, "is not to be feared."

"She cared no more for her daughter than for the sole of her shoe! But Noémie has no need of influence. She is sufficient to herself. She is stronger than I."

"She does n't obey you, eh?"

"She can't obey, monsieur, since I don't command. What would be the use? It would only irritate her and drive her to some *coup de tête*. She is very clever, like her mother; she would waste no time about it. As a child—when I was happy, or supposed I was—she studied drawing and painting with first-class professors, and they assured me she had a talent. I was delighted to believe it, and when I went into society I used to carry her pictures with me in a portfolio and hand them round to the company. I remember, once, a lady thought I was offering them for sale, and I took it very ill. We don't know what we may come to! Then came my dark days, and my explosion with Madame Nioche. Noémie had no more twenty-franc lessons; but in the course of time, when she grew older, and it became highly expedient that she should do something that would help to keep us alive, she bethought herself of her palette and brushes. Some of our friends in the *quartier* pronounced the idea fantastic: they recommended her to try bonnet making, to get a situation in a shop, or—if she was more ambitious—to advertise for a place of *dame de compagnie*. She did advertise, and an old lady wrote her a letter and bade her come and see her. The old lady liked her, and offered her her living and six hundred francs a year; but Noémie discovered that she passed her life in her arm-chair and had only two visitors, her confessor and her nephew: the confessor very strict, and the nephew a man of fifty, with a broken nose and a government clerkship of two thousand francs. She threw her old lady over, bought a paint-box, a canvas, and a new dress, and went and set up her easel in the Louvre. There, in one place and another, she has passed the last two years; I can't say it has made us millionaires. But Noémie tells me that Rome was not built in a day, that she is making great progress, that I must leave her to her own devices. The fact is, without prejudice to her genius, that she has no idea of burying herself alive. She likes to see the world, and to be seen. She says, herself, that she can't work in the dark. With her appearance it is very natural. Only, I can't help worrying and trembling and wondering what may happen to her there all alone, day after day, amid all that coming and going of strangers. I can't be always at her side. I go with her in the morning, and I come to fetch her away, but she won't have me near her in the interval; she says I make her nervous. As if it did n't make me nervous to wander about all day without her! Ah, if anything were to happen to her!" cried M. Nioche, clenching his two fists and jerking back his head again, portentously.

"Oh, I guess nothing will happen," said Newman.

"I believe I should shoot her!" said the old man, solemnly.

"Oh, we 'll marry her," said Newman, "since that 's how you manage it; and I will go and see her to-morrow at the Louvre and pick out the pictures she is to copy for me."

M. Nioche had brought Newman a message from his daughter, in acceptance of his magnificent commission, the young lady declaring herself his most devoted servant, promising her most zealous endeavor, and regretting that the proprieties forbade her coming to thank him in person. The morning after the conversation just narrated, Newman reverted to his intention of meeting Mademoiselle Noémie at the Louvre. M. Nioche appeared preoccupied, and left his budget of anecdotes unopened; he took a great deal of snuff, and sent certain oblique, appealing glances toward his stalwart pupil. At last, when he was taking his leave, he stood a moment, after he had polished his hat with his calico pocket-handkerchief, with his small, pale eyes fixed strangely upon Newman.

"What 's the matter?" our hero demanded.

"Excuse the solicitude of a father's heart!" said M. Nioche. "You inspire me with boundless confidence, but I can't help giving you a warning. After all, you are a man, you are young and at liberty. Let me beseech you, then, to respect the innocence of Mademoiselle Nioche!"

Newman had wondered what was coming, and at this he broke into a laugh. He was on the point of declaring that his own innocence struck him as the more exposed, but he contented himself with promising to treat the young girl with nothing less than veneration. He found her waiting for him, seated upon the great divan in the Salon Carré. She was not in her working-day costume, but wore her bonnet and gloves and carried her parasol, in honor of the occasion. These articles had been selected with unerring taste, and a fresher, prettier image of youthful alertness and blooming discretion was not to be conceived. She made Newman a most respectful curtsey and expressed her gratitude for his liberality in a wonderfully graceful little speech. It annoyed him to have a charming young girl stand there thanking him, and it made him feel uncomfortable to think that this perfect young lady, with her excellent manners and her finished intonation, was literally in his pay. He assured her, in such French as he could muster, that the thing was not worth mentioning, and that he considered her services a great favor.

"Whenever you please, then," said Mademoiselle Noémie, "we will pass the review."

They walked slowly round the room, then passed into the others and strolled about for half an hour. Mademoiselle Noémie evidently relished her situation, and had no desire to bring her public interview with her striking-looking patron to a close. Newman perceived that prosperity agreed with her. The little thin-lipped, peremptory air with which she had addressed her father on the occasion of their former meeting had given place to the most lingering and caressing tones.

"What sort of pictures do you desire?" she asked. "Sacred, or profane?"

"Oh, a few of each," said Newman. "But I want something bright and gay."

"Something gay? There is nothing very gay in this solemn old Louvre. But we will see what we can find. You speak French to-day like a charm. My father has done wonders."

"Oh, I am a bad subject," said Newman. "I am too old to learn a language."

"Too old? *Quelle folie!*" cried Mademoiselle Noémie, with a clear, shrill laugh. "You are a very young man. And how do you like my father?"

"He is a very nice old gentleman. He never laughs at my blunders."

"He is very comme il faut, my papa," said Mademoiselle Noémie, "and as honest as the day. Oh, an exceptional probity! You could trust him with millions."

"Do you always obey him?" asked Newman.

"Obey him?"

"Do you do what he bids you?"

The young girl stopped and looked at him; she had a spot of color in either cheek, and in her expressive French eye, which projected too much for perfect beauty, there was a slight gleam of audacity. "Why do you ask me that?" she demanded.

"Because I want to know."

"You think me a bad girl?" And she gave a strange smile.

Newman looked at her a moment; he saw that she was

pretty, but he was not in the least dazzled. He remembered poor M. Nioche's solicitude for her "innocence," and he laughed out again as his eyes met hers. Her face was the oddest mixture of youth and maturity, and beneath her candid brow her searching little smile seemed to contain a world of ambiguous intentions. She was pretty enough, certainly, to make her father nervous; but, as regards her innocence, Newman felt ready on the spot to affirm that she had never parted with it. She had simply never had any; she had been looking at the world since she was ten years old, and he would have been a wise man who could tell her any secrets. In her long mornings at the Louvre she had not only studied Madonnas and St. Johns; she had kept an eye upon all the variously embodied human nature around her, and she had formed her conclusions. In a certain sense, it seemed to Newman, M. Nioche might be at rest; his daughter might do something very audacious, but she would never do anything foolish. Newman, with his long-drawn, leisurely smile, and his even, unhurried utterance, was always, mentally, taking his time; and he asked himself, now, what she was looking at him in that way for. He had an idea that she would like him to confess that he did think her a bad girl.

"Oh, no," he said at last; "it would be very bad manners in me to judge you that way. I don't know you."

"But my father has complained to you," said Mademoiselle Noémie.

"He says you are a coquette."

"He shouldn't go about saying such things to gentlemen! But you don't believe it."

"No," said Newman gravely, "I don't believe it."

She looked at him again, gave a shrug and a smile, and then pointed to a small Italian picture, a Marriage of St. Catherine. "How should you like that?" she asked.

"It doesn't please me," said Newman. "The young lady in the yellow dress is not pretty."

"Ah, you are a great connoisseur," murmured Mademoiselle Noémie.

"In pictures? Oh, no; I know very little about them."

"In pretty women, then."

"In that I am hardly better."

"What do you say to that, then?" the young girl asked, indicating a superb Italian portrait of a lady. "I will do it for you on a smaller scale."

"On a smaller scale? Why not as large as the original?"

Mademoiselle Noémie glanced at the glowing splendor of the Venetian masterpiece and gave a little toss of her head. "I don't like that woman. She looks stupid."

"I do like her," said Newman. "Decidedly, I must have her, as large as life. And just as stupid as she is there."

The young girl fixed her eyes on him again, and with her mocking smile, "It certainly ought to be easy for me to make her look stupid!" she said.

"What do you mean?" asked Newman, puzzled.

She gave another little shrug. "Seriously, then, you want that portrait—the golden hair, the purple satin, the pearl necklace, the two magnificent arms?"

"Everything—just as it is."

"Would nothing else do, instead?"

"Oh, I want some other things, but I want that too."

Mademoiselle Noémie turned away a moment, walked to the other side of the hall, and stood there, looking vaguely about her. At last she came back. "It must be charming to be able to order pictures at such a rate. Venetian portraits, as large as life! You go at it *en prince*. And you are going to travel about Europe that way?"

"Yes, I intend to travel," said Newman.

"Ordering, buying, spending money?"

"Of course I shall spend some money."

"You are very happy to have it. And you are perfectly free?"

"How do you mean, free?"

"You have nothing to bother you—no family, no wife, no *fiancée*?"

"Yes, I am tolerably free."

"You are very happy," said Mademoiselle Noémie, gravely.

"Je le veux bien!" said Newman, proving that he had learned more French than he admitted.

"And how long shall you stay in Paris?" the young girl went on.

"Only a few days more."

"Why do you go away?"

"It is getting hot, and I must go to Switzerland."

"To Switzerland? That 's a fine country. I would give my new parasol to see it! Lakes and mountains, romantic valleys and icy peaks! Oh, I congratulate you. Meanwhile, I shall sit here through all the hot summer, daubing at your pictures."

"Oh, take your time about it," said Newman. "Do them at your convenience."

They walked farther and looked at a dozen other things. Newman pointed out what pleased him, and Mademoiselle Noémie generally criticised it, and proposed something else. Then suddenly she diverged and began to talk about some personal matter.

"What made you speak to me the other day in the Salon Carré?" she abruptly asked.

"I admired your picture."

"But you hesitated a long time."

"Oh, I do nothing rashly," said Newman.

"Yes, I saw you watching me. But I never supposed you were going to speak to me. I never dreamed I should be walking about here with you to-day. It 's very curious."

"It is very natural," observed Newman.

"Oh, I beg your pardon; not to me. Coquette as you think me, I have never walked about in public with a gentleman before. What was my father thinking of, when he consented to our interview?"

"He was repenting of his unjust accusations," replied Newman.

Mademoiselle Noémie remained silent; at last she dropped into a seat. "Well then, for those five it is fixed," she said. "Five copies as brilliant and beautiful as I can make them. We have one more to choose. Should n't you like one of those great Rubenses—the marriage of Marie de Médicis? Just look at it and see how handsome it is."

"Oh, yes; I should like that," said Newman. "Finish off with that."

"Finish off with that—good!" And she laughed. She sat a moment, looking at him, and then she suddenly rose and stood before him, with her hands hanging and clasped in front of her. "I don't understand you," she said with a smile. "I don't understand how a man can be so ignorant."

"Oh, I am ignorant, certainly," said Newman, putting his hands into his pockets.

"It 's ridiculous! I don't know how to paint."

"You don't know how?"

"I paint like a cat; I can't draw a straight line. I never sold a picture until you bought that thing the other day." And as she offered this surprising information she continued to smile.

Newman burst into a laugh. "Why do you tell me this?" he asked.

"Because it irritates me to see a clever man blunder so. My pictures are grotesque."

"And the one I possess"—

"That one is rather worse than usual."

"Well," said Newman, "I like it all the same!"

She looked at him askance. "That is a very pretty thing to say," she answered; "but it is my duty to warn you before you go farther. This order of yours is impossible, you know. What do you take me for? It is work for ten men. You pick out the six most difficult pictures in the Louvre, and you expect me to go to work as if I were sitting down to hem a dozen pocket handkerchiefs. I wanted to see how far you would go."

Newman looked at the young girl in some perplexity. In spite of the ridiculous blunder of which he stood convicted, he was very far from being a simpleton, and he had a lively suspicion that Mademoiselle Noémie's sudden frankness was not essentially more honest than her leaving him in error would have been. She was playing a game; she was not simply taking pity on his æsthetic verdancy. What was it she expected to win? The stakes were high and the risk was great; the prize therefore must have been commensurate. But even granting that the prize might be great, Newman could not resist a movement of admiration for his companion's intrepidity. She was throwing away with one hand, whatever she might intend to do with the other, a very handsome sum of money.

"Are you joking," he said, "or are you serious?"

"Oh, serious!" cried Mademoiselle Noémie, but with her extraordinary smile.

"I know very little about pictures or how they are painted.

If you can't do all that, of course you can't. Do what you can, then."

"It will be very bad," said Mademoiselle Noémie.

"Oh," said Newman, laughing, "if you are determined it shall be bad, of course it will. But why do you go on painting badly?"

"I can do nothing else; I have no real talent."

"You are deceiving your father, then."

The young girl hesitated a moment. "He knows very well!"

"No," Newman declared; "I am sure he believes in you."

"He is afraid of me. I go on painting badly, as you say, because I want to learn. I like it, at any rate. And I like being here; it is a place to come to, every day; it is better than sitting in a little dark, damp room, on a court, or selling buttons and whalebones over a counter."

"Of course it is much more amusing," said Newman. "But for a poor girl is n't it rather an expensive amusement?"

"Oh, I am very wrong, there is no doubt about that," said Mademoiselle Noémie. "But rather than earn my living as some girls do — toiling with a needle, in little black holes, out of the world — I would throw myself into the Seine."

"There is no need of that," Newman answered; "your father told you my offer?"

"Your offer?"

"He wants you to marry, and I told him I would give you a chance to earn your *dot*."

"He told me all about it, and you see the account I make of it! Why should you take such an interest in my marriage?"

"My interest was in your father. I hold to my offer; do what you can, and I will buy what you paint."

She stood for some time, meditating, with her eyes on the ground. At last, looking up, "What sort of a husband can you get for twelve thousand francs?" she asked.

"Your father tells me he knows some very good young men."

"Grocers and butchers and little *maîtres de cafés*! I will not marry at all if I can't marry well."

"I would advise you not to be too fastidious," said Newman. "That 's all the advice I can give you."

"I am very much vexed at what I have said!" cried the young girl. "It has done me no good. But I could n't help it."

"What good did you expect it to do you?"

"I could n't help it, simply."

Newman looked at her a moment. "Well, your pictures may be bad," he said, "but you are too clever for me, nevertheless. I don't understand you. Good-by!" And he put out his hand.

She made no response, and offered him no farewell. She turned away and seated herself sidewise on a bench, leaning her head on the back of her hand, which clasped the rail in front of the pictures. Newman stood a moment and then turned on his heel and retreated. He had understood her better than he confessed; this singular scene was a practical commentary upon her father's statement that she was a frank coquette.

Chapter V

WHEN NEWMAN related to Mrs. Tristram his fruitless visit to Madame de Cintré, she urged him not to be discouraged, but to carry out his plan of "seeing Europe" during the summer, and return to Paris in the autumn and settle down comfortably for the winter. "Madame de Cintré will keep," she said; "she is not a woman who will marry from one day to another." Newman made no distinct affirmation that he would come back to Paris; he even talked about Rome and the Nile, and abstained from professing any especial interest in Madame de Cintré's continued widowhood. This circumstance was at variance with his habitual frankness, and may perhaps be regarded as characteristic of the incipient stage of that passion which is more particularly known as the mysterious one. The truth is that the expression of a pair of eyes that were at once brilliant and mild had become very familiar to his memory, and he would not easily have resigned himself to the prospect of never looking into them again. He communicated to Mrs. Tristram a number of other facts, of greater or less importance, as you choose; but on this particular point he kept his own counsel. He took a kindly leave of M. Nioche, having assured him that, so far as he was concerned, the blue-cloaked Madonna herself might have been present at his interview with Mademoiselle Noémie; and left the old man nursing his breast-pocket, in an ecstasy which the acutest misfortune might have been defied to dissipate. Newman then started on his travels, with all his usual appearance of slow-strolling leisure, and all his essential directness and intensity of aim. No man seemed less in a hurry, and yet no man achieved more in brief periods. He had certain practical instincts which served him excellently in his trade of tourist. He found his way in foreign cities by divination, his memory was excellent when once his attention had been at all cordially given, and he emerged from dialogues in foreign tongues, of which he had, formally, not understood a word, in full possession of the particular fact he had desired to ascertain. His appetite for facts was capacious, and although many of those which he noted would have seemed wofully dry and colorless

to the ordinary sentimental traveler, a careful inspection of
the list would have shown that he had a soft spot in his imagination. In the charming city of Brussels—his first stopping-
place after leaving Paris—he asked a great many questions
about the street-cars, and took extreme satisfaction in the
reappearance of this familiar symbol of American civilization;
but he was also greatly struck with the beautiful Gothic tower
of the Hôtel de Ville, and wondered whether it would not be
possible to "get up" something like it in San Francisco. He
stood for half an hour in the crowded square before this edifice, in imminent danger from carriage-wheels, listening to a
toothless old cicerone mumble in broken English the touching history of Counts Egmont and Horn; and he wrote the
names of these gentlemen—for reasons best known to himself—on the back of an old letter.

At the outset, on his leaving Paris, his curiosity had not
been intense; passive entertainment, in the Champs Élysées
and at the theatres, seemed about as much as he need expect
of himself, and although, as he had said to Tristram, he
wanted to see the mysterious, satisfying *best*, he had not the
Grand Tour in the least on his conscience, and was not given
to cross-questioning the amusement of the hour. He believed
that Europe was made for him, and not he for Europe. He
had said that he wanted to improve his mind, but he would
have felt a certain embarrassment, a certain shame, even—a
false shame, possibly—if he had caught himself looking intellectually into the mirror. Neither in this nor in any other respect had Newman a high sense of responsibility; it was his
prime conviction that a man's life should be easy, and that he
should be able to resolve privilege into a matter of course.
The world, to his sense, was a great bazar, where one might
stroll about and purchase handsome things; but he was no
more conscious, individually, of social pressure than he admitted the existence of such a thing as an obligatory purchase.
He had not only a dislike, but a sort of moral mistrust, of
uncomfortable thoughts, and it was both uncomfortable and
slightly contemptible to feel obliged to square one's self with
a standard. One's standard was the ideal of one's own good-
humored prosperity, the prosperity which enabled one to give
as well as take. To expand, without bothering about it—

without shiftless timidity on one side, or loquacious eagerness on the other—to the full compass of what he would have called a "pleasant" experience, was Newman's most definite programme of life. He had always hated to hurry to catch railroad trains, and yet he had always caught them; and just so an undue solicitude for "culture" seemed a sort of silly dawdling at the station, a proceeding properly confined to women, foreigners, and other unpractical persons. All this admitted, Newman enjoyed his journey, when once he had fairly entered the current, as profoundly as the most zealous *dilettante*. One's theories, after all, matter little; it is one's humor that is the great thing. Our friend was intelligent, and he could not help that. He lounged through Belgium and Holland and the Rhineland, through Switzerland and Northern Italy, planning about nothing, but seeing everything. The guides and *valets de place* found him an excellent subject. He was always approachable, for he was much addicted to standing about in the vestibules and porticoes of inns, and he availed himself little of the opportunities for impressive seclusion which are so liberally offered in Europe to gentlemen who travel with long purses. When an excursion, a church, a gallery, a ruin, was proposed to him, the first thing Newman usually did, after surveying his postulant in silence, from head to foot, was to sit down at a little table and order something to drink. The cicerone, during this process, usually retreated to a respectful distance; otherwise I am not sure that Newman would not have bidden him sit down and have a glass also, and tell him as an honest fellow whether his church or his gallery was really worth a man's trouble. At last he rose and stretched his long legs, beckoned to the man of monuments, looked at his watch, and fixed his eye on his adversary. "What is it?" he asked. "How far?" And whatever the answer was, although he sometimes seemed to hesitate, he never declined. He stepped into an open cab, made his conductor sit beside him to answer questions, bade the driver go fast (he had a particular aversion to slow driving) and rolled, in all probability through a dusty suburb, to the goal of his pilgrimage. If the goal was a disappointment, if the church was meagre, or the ruin a heap of rubbish, Newman never protested or berated his cicerone; he looked with an impartial eye upon great monuments and small, made the guide recite his lesson, listened to it religiously, asked if there was nothing else to be seen in the neighborhood, and drove back again at a rattling pace. It is to be feared that his perception of the difference between good architecture and bad was not acute, and that he might sometimes have been seen gazing with culpable serenity at inferior productions. Ugly churches were a part of his pastime in Europe, as well as beautiful ones, and his tour was altogether a pastime. But there is sometimes nothing like the imagination of those people who have none, and Newman, now and then, in an unguided stroll in a foreign city, before some lonely, sad-towered church, or some angular image of one who had rendered civic service in an unknown past, had felt a singular inward tremor. It was not an excitement or a perplexity; it was a placid, fathomless sense of diversion.

He encountered by chance in Holland a young American, with whom, for a time, he formed a sort of traveler's partnership. They were men of a very different cast, but each, in his way, was so good a fellow that, for a few weeks at least, it seemed something of a pleasure to share the chances of the road. Newman's comrade, whose name was Babcock, was a young Unitarian minister; a small, spare, neatly-attired man, with a strikingly candid physiognomy. He was a native of Dorchester, Massachusetts, and had spiritual charge of a small congregation in another suburb of the New England metropolis. His digestion was weak, and he lived chiefly on Graham bread and hominy—a regimen to which he was so much attached that his tour seemed to him destined to be blighted when, on landing on the Continent, he found that these delicacies did not flourish under the *table d'hôte* system. In Paris he had purchased a bag of hominy at an establishment which called itself an American Agency, and at which the New York illustrated papers were also to be procured, and he had carried it about with him, and shown extreme serenity and fortitude in the somewhat delicate position of having his hominy prepared for him and served at anomalous hours, at the hotels he successively visited. Newman had once spent a morning, in the course of business, at Mr. Babcock's birthplace, and, for reasons too recondite to unfold, his visit there always as-

sumed in his mind a jocular cast. To carry out his joke, which
certainly seems poor so long as it is not explained, he used
often to address his companion as "Dorchester." Fellow-travelers very soon grow intimate; but it is highly improbable
that at home these extremely dissimilar characters would have
found any very convenient points of contact. They were, indeed, as different as possible. Newman, who never reflected
on such matters, accepted the situation with great equanimity, but Babcock used to meditate over it privately; used often, indeed, to retire to his room early in the evening for the
express purpose of considering it conscientiously and impar-
tially. He was not sure that it was a good thing for him to
associate with our hero, whose way of taking life was so little
his own. Newman was an excellent, generous fellow; Mr.
Babcock sometimes said to himself that he was a *noble* fellow,
and, certainly, it was impossible not to like him. But would it
not be desirable to try to exert an influence upon him, to try
to quicken his moral life and sharpen his sense of duty? He
liked everything, he accepted everything, he found amusement in everything; he was not discriminating, he had not a
high tone. The young man from Dorchester accused Newman
of a fault which he considered very grave, and which he did
his best to avoid: what he would have called a want of "moral
reaction." Poor Mr. Babcock was extremely fond of pictures
and churches, and carried Mrs. Jameson's works about in his
trunk; he delighted in æsthetic analysis, and received peculiar
impressions from everything he saw. But nevertheless in his
secret soul he detested Europe, and he felt an irritating need
to protest against Newman's gross intellectual hospitality. Mr.
Babcock's moral *malaise*, I am afraid, lay deeper than where
any definition of mine can reach it. He mistrusted the European temperament, he suffered from the European climate, he
hated the European dinner-hour; European life seemed to
him unscrupulous and impure. And yet he had an exquisite
sense of beauty; and as beauty was often inextricably associated with the above displeasing conditions, as he wished,
above all, to be just and dispassionate, and as he was, furthermore, extremely devoted to "culture," he could not bring
himself to decide that Europe was utterly bad. But he
thought it was very bad indeed, and his quarrel with Newman

was that this unregulated epicure had a sadly insufficient perception of the bad. Babcock himself really knew as little about the bad, in any quarter of the world, as a nursing infant; his most vivid realization of evil had been the discovery that one of his college classmates, who was studying architecture in Paris, had a love affair with a young woman who did not expect him to marry her. Babcock had related this incident to Newman, and our hero had applied an epithet of an unflattering sort to the young girl. The next day his companion asked him whether he was very sure he had used exactly the right word to characterize the young architect's mistress. Newman stared and laughed. "There are a great many words to express that idea," he said; "you can take your choice!"

"Oh, I mean," said Babcock, "was she possibly not to be considered in a different light? Don't you think she *really* expected him to marry her?"

"I am sure I don't know," said Newman. "Very likely she did; I have no doubt she is a grand woman." And he began to laugh again.

"I did n't mean that either," said Babcock; "I was only afraid that I might have seemed yesterday not to remember—not to consider; well, I think I will write to Percival about it."

And he had written to Percival (who answered him in a really impudent fashion), and he had reflected that it was, somehow, raw and reckless in Newman to assume in that offhand manner that the young woman in Paris might be "grand." The brevity of Newman's judgments very often shocked and discomposed him. He had a way of damning people without farther appeal, or of pronouncing them capital company in the face of uncomfortable symptoms, which seemed unworthy of a man whose conscience had been properly cultivated. And yet poor Babcock liked him, and remembered that even if he was sometimes perplexing and painful, this was not a reason for giving him up. Goethe recommended seeing human nature in the most various forms, and Mr. Babcock thought Goethe perfectly splendid. He often tried, in odd half-hours of conversation, to infuse into Newman a little of his own spiritual starch, but Newman's personal texture was too loose to admit of stiffening. His mind could no more hold principles than a sieve can hold water. He admired principles extremely, and thought Babcock a mighty fine little fellow for having so many. He accepted all that his high-strung companion offered him, and put them away in what he supposed to be a very safe place; but poor Babcock never afterwards recognized his gifts among the articles that Newman had in daily use.

They traveled together through Germany and into Switzerland, where for three or four weeks they trudged over passes and lounged upon blue lakes. At last they crossed the Simplon and made their way to Venice. Mr. Babcock had become gloomy and even a trifle irritable; he seemed moody, absent, preoccupied; he got his plans into a tangle, and talked one moment of doing one thing and the next of doing another. Newman led his usual life, made acquaintances, took his ease in the galleries and churches, spent an unconscionable amount of time in strolling in the Piazza San Marco, bought a great many bad pictures, and for a fortnight enjoyed Venice grossly. One evening, coming back to his inn, he found Babcock waiting for him in the little garden beside it. The young man walked up to him, looking very dismal, thrust out his hand, and said with solemnity that he was afraid they must part. Newman expressed his surprise and regret, and asked why a parting had become necessary. "Don't be afraid I 'm tired of you," he said.

"You are not tired of me?" demanded Babcock, fixing him with his clear gray eye.

"Why the deuce should I be? You are a very plucky fellow. Besides, I don't grow tired of things."

"We don't understand each other," said the young minister.

"Don't I understand you?" cried Newman. "Why, I hoped I did. But what if I don't; where 's the harm?"

"I don't understand *you*," said Babcock. And he sat down and rested his head on his hand, and looked up mournfully at his immeasurable friend.

"Oh Lord, I don't mind that!" cried Newman, with a laugh.

"But it 's very distressing to me. It keeps me in a state of unrest. It irritates me; I can't settle anything. I don't think it 's good for me."

"You worry too much; that 's what 's the matter with you," said Newman.

"Of course it must seem so to you. You think I take things too hard, and I think you take things too easily. We can never agree."

"But we have agreed very well all along."

"No, I have n't agreed," said Babcock, shaking his head. "I am very uncomfortable. I ought to have separated from you a month ago."

"Oh, horrors! I 'll agree to anything!" cried Newman.

Mr. Babcock buried his head in both hands. At last, looking up, "I don't think you appreciate my position," he said. "I try to arrive at the truth about everything. And then you go too fast. For me, you are too passionate, too extravagant. I feel as if I ought to go over all this ground we have traversed again, by myself, alone. I am afraid I have made a great many mistakes."

"Oh, you need n't give so many reasons," said Newman. "You are simply tired of my company. You have a good right to be."

"No, no, I am not tired!" cried the pestered young divine. "It is very wrong to be tired."

"I give it up!" laughed Newman. "But of course it will never do to go on making mistakes. Go your way, by all means. I shall miss you; but you have seen I make friends very easily. You will be lonely, yourself; but drop me a line, when you feel like it, and I will wait for you anywhere."

"I think I will go back to Milan. I am afraid I did n't do justice to Luini."

"Poor Luini!" said Newman.

"I mean that I am afraid I overestimated him. I don't think that he is a painter of the first rank."

"Luini?" Newman exclaimed; "why, he 's enchanting— he 's magnificent! There is something in his genius that is like a beautiful woman. It gives one the same feeling."

Mr. Babcock frowned and winced. And it must be added that this was, for Newman, an unusually metaphysical flight; but in passing through Milan he had taken a great fancy to the painter. "There you are again!" said Mr. Babcock. "Yes, we had better separate." And on the morrow he retraced his steps and proceeded to tone down his impressions of the great Lombard artist.

A few days afterwards Newman received a note from his late companion which ran as follows:—

MY DEAR MR. NEWMAN,—I am afraid that my conduct at Venice, a week ago, seemed to you strange and ungrateful, and I wish to explain my position, which, as I said at the time, I do not think you appreciate. I had long had it on my mind to propose that we should part company, and this step was not really so abrupt as it seemed. In the first place, you know, I am traveling in Europe on funds supplied by my congregation, who kindly offered me a vacation and an opportunity to enrich my mind with the treasures of nature and art in the Old World. I feel, therefore, as if I ought to use my time to the very best advantage. I have a high sense of responsibility. You appear to care only for the pleasure of the hour, and you give yourself up to it with a violence which I confess I am not able to emulate. I feel as if I must arrive at some conclusion and fix my belief on certain points. Art and life seem to me intensely serious things, and in our travels in Europe we should especially remember the immense seriousness of Art. You seem to hold that if a thing amuses you for the moment, that is all you need ask for it; and your relish for mere amusement is also much higher than mine. You put, moreover, a kind of reckless confidence into your pleasure which at times, I confess, has seemed to me—shall I say it?—almost cynical. Your way at any rate is not my way, and it is unwise that we should attempt any longer to pull together. And yet, let me add that I know there is a great deal to be said for your way; I have felt its attraction, in your society, very strongly. But for this I should have left you long ago. But I was so perplexed. I hope I have not done wrong. I feel as if I had a great deal of lost time to make up. I beg you take all this as I mean it, which, Heaven knows, is not invidiously. I have a great personal esteem for you, and hope that some day, when I have recovered my balance, we shall meet again. I hope you will continue to enjoy your travels; only *do* remember that Life and Art *are* extremely serious. Believe me your sincere friend and well-wisher,

BENJAMIN BABCOCK.

P.S. I am greatly perplexed by Luini.

This letter produced in Newman's mind a singular mixture of exhilaration and awe. At first, Mr. Babcock's tender conscience seemed to him a capital farce, and his traveling back to Milan only to get into a deeper muddle appeared, as the reward of his pedantry, exquisitely and ludicrously just. Then Newman reflected that these are mighty mysteries; that possibly he himself was indeed that baleful and barely mentionable thing, a cynic, and that his manner of considering the treasures of art and the privileges of life was probably very base and immoral. Newman had a great contempt for immorality, and that evening, for a good half hour, as he sat watching the star-sheen on the warm Adriatic, he felt rebuked and depressed. He was at a loss how to answer Babcock's letter. His good nature checked his resenting the young minister's lofty admonitions, and his tough, inelastic sense of humor forbade his taking them seriously. He wrote no answer at all, but a day or two afterward he found in a curiosity shop a grotesque little statuette in ivory, of the sixteenth century, which he sent off to Babcock without a commentary. It represented a gaunt, ascetic-looking monk, in a tattered gown and cowl, kneeling with clasped hands and pulling a portentously long face. It was a wonderfully delicate piece of carving, and in a moment, through one of the rents of his gown, you espied a fat capon hung round the monk's waist. In Newman's intention what did the figure symbolize? Did it mean that he was going to try to be as "high-toned" as the monk looked at first, but that he feared he should succeed no better than the friar, on a closer inspection, proved to have done? It is not supposable that he intended a satire upon Babcock's own asceticism, for this would have been a truly cynical stroke. He made his late companion, at any rate, a very valuable little present.

Newman, on leaving Venice, went through the Tyrol to Vienna, and then returned westward, through Southern Germany. The autumn found him at Baden-Baden, where he spent several weeks. The place was charming, and he was in no hurry to depart; besides, he was looking about him and deciding what to do for the winter. His summer had been very full, and as he sat under the great trees beside the miniature river that trickles past the Baden flower-beds, he slowly rummaged it over. He had seen and done a great deal, enjoyed and observed a great deal; he felt older, and yet he felt younger too. He remembered Mr. Babcock and his desire to form conclusions, and he remembered also that he had profited very little by his friend's exhortation to cultivate the same respectable habit. Could he not scrape together a few conclusions? Baden-Baden was the prettiest place he had seen yet, and orchestral music in the evening, under the stars, was decidedly a great institution. This was one of his conclusions! But he went on to reflect that he had done very wisely to pull up stakes and come abroad; this seeing of the world was a very interesting thing. He had learned a great deal; he could n't say just what, but he had it there under his hat-band. He had done what he wanted; he had seen the great things, and he had given his mind a chance to "improve," if it would. He cheerfully believed that it had improved. Yes, this seeing of the world was very pleasant, and he would willingly do a little more of it. Thirty-six years old as he was, he had a handsome stretch of life before him yet, and he need not begin to count his weeks. Where should he take the world next? I have said he remembered the eyes of the lady whom he had found standing in Mrs. Tristram's drawing-room; four months had elapsed, and he had not forgotten them yet. He had looked— he had made a point of looking—into a great many other eyes in the interval, but the only ones he thought of now were Madame de Cintré's. If he wanted to see more of the world, should he find it in Madame de Cintré's eyes? He would certainly find something there, call it this world or the next. Throughout these rather formless meditations he sometimes thought of his past life and the long array of years (they had begun so early) during which he had had nothing in his head but "enterprise." They seemed far away now, for his present attitude was more than a holiday, it was almost a rupture. He had told Tristram that the pendulum was swinging back, and it appeared that the backward swing had not yet ended. Still "enterprise," which was over in the other quarter, wore to his mind a different aspect at different hours. In its train a thousand forgotten episodes came trooping back into his memory. Some of them he looked complacently enough in the face; from some he averted his head. They were old efforts, old exploits, antiquated examples of "smartness" and sharpness. Some of them, as he looked at them, he felt decidedly proud of; he admired himself as if he had been looking at another man. And, in fact, many of the qualities that make a great deed were there: the decision, the resolution, the courage, the celerity, the clear eye, and the strong hand. Of certain other achievements it would be going too far to say that he was ashamed of them, for Newman had never had a stomach for dirty work. He was blessed with a natural impulse to disfigure with a direct, unreasoning blow the comely visage of temptation. And certainly, in no man could a want of integrity have been less excusable. Newman knew the crooked from the straight at a glance, and the former had cost him, first and last, a great many moments of lively disgust. But none the less some of his memories seemed to wear at present a rather graceless and sordid mien, and it struck him that if he had never done anything very ugly, he had never, on the other hand, done anything particularly beautiful. He had spent his years in the unremitting effort to add thousands to thousands, and, now that he stood well outside of it, the business of money-getting appeared tolerably dry and sterile. It is very well to sneer at money-getting after you have filled your pockets, and Newman, it may be said, should have begun somewhat earlier to moralize thus delicately. To this it may be answered that he might have made another fortune, if he chose; and we ought to add that he was not exactly moralizing. It had come back to him simply that what he had been looking at all summer was a very rich and beautiful world, and that it had not all been made by sharp railroad men and stock-brokers.

During his stay at Baden-Baden he received a letter from Mrs. Tristram, scolding him for the scanty tidings he had sent to his friends of the Avenue d'Iéna, and begging to be definitely informed that he had not concocted any horrid scheme for wintering in outlying regions, but was coming back sanely and promptly to the most comfortable city in the world. Newman's answer ran as follows:—

"I supposed you knew I was a miserable letter-writer, and did n't expect anything of me. I don't think I have written twenty letters of pure friendship in my whole life; in America I conducted my correspondence altogether by telegrams. This is a letter of pure friendship; you have got hold of a curiosity, and I hope you will value it. You want to know everything that has happened to me these three months. The best way to tell you, I think, would be to send you my half dozen guide-books, with my pencil-marks in the margin. Wherever you find a scratch, or a cross, or a 'Beautiful!' or a 'So true!' or a 'Too thin!' you may know that I have had a sensation of some sort or other. That has been about my history, ever since I left you. Belgium, Holland, Switzerland, Germany, Italy, I have been through the whole list, and I don't think I am any the worse for it. I know more about Madonnas and church-steeples than I supposed any man could. I have seen some very pretty things, and shall perhaps talk them over this win-ter, by your fireside. You see, my face is not altogether set against Paris. I have had all kinds of plans and visions, but your letter has blown most of them away. 'L'appétit vient en mangeant,' says the French proverb, and I find that the more I see of the world the more I want to see. Now that I am in the shafts, why should n't I trot to the end of the course? Sometimes I think of the far East, and keep rolling the names of Eastern cities under my tongue: Damascus and Bagdad, Medina and Mecca. I spent a week last month in the company of a returned missionary, who told me I ought to be ashamed to be loafing about Europe when there are such big things to be seen out there. I do want to explore, but I think I would rather explore over in the Rue de l'Université. Do you ever hear from that pretty lady? If you can get her to promise she will be at home the next time I call, I will go back to Paris straight. I am more than ever in the state of mind I told you about that evening; I want a first-class wife. I have kept an eye on all the pretty girls I have come across this summer, but none of them came up to my notion, or anywhere near it. I should have enjoyed all this a thousand times more if I had had the lady just mentioned by my side. The nearest approach to her was a Unitarian minister from Boston, who very soon demanded a separation, for incompatibility of temper. He told me I was low-minded, immoral, a devotee of 'art for art'—whatever that is: all of which greatly afflicted me, for he was really a sweet little fellow. But shortly afterwards I met an Englishman, with whom I struck up an acquaintance which at first seemed to promise well—a very bright man, who writes in the London papers and knows Paris nearly as well as Tristram. We knocked about for a week together, but he very soon gave me up in disgust. I was too virtuous by half; I was too stern a moralist. He told me, in a friendly way, that I was cursed with a conscience; that I judged things like a Methodist and talked about them like an old lady. This was rather bewildering. Which of my two critics was I to believe? I did n't worry about it and very soon made up my mind they were both idiots. But there is one thing in which no one will ever have the impudence to pretend I am wrong; that is, in being your faithful friend,

C.N."

Chapter VI

N EWMAN gave up Damascus and Bagdad and returned to
Paris before the autumn was over. He established himself in some rooms selected for him by Tom Tristram, in accordance with the latter's estimate of what he called his social
position. When Newman learned that his social position was
to be taken into account, he professed himself utterly incom-
petent, and begged Tristram to relieve him of the care. "I did
n't know I had a social position," he said, "and if I have, I
have n't the smallest idea of what it is. Is n't a social position
knowing some two or three thousand people and inviting
them to dinner? I know you and your wife and little old Mr.
Nioche, who gave me French lessons last spring. Can I invite
you to dinner to meet each other? If I can, you must come
to-morrow."

"That is not very grateful to me," said Mrs. Tristram, "who
introduced you last year to every creature I know."

"So you did; I had quite forgotten. But I thought you
wanted me to forget," said Newman, with that tone of simple
deliberateness which frequently marked his utterance, and
which an observer would not have known whether to pronounce a somewhat mysteriously humorous affectation of ignorance or a modest aspiration to knowledge; "you told me
you disliked them all."

"Ah, the way you remember what I say is at least very flattering! But in future," added Mrs. Tristram, "pray forget all
the wicked things and remember only the good ones. It will
be easily done, and it will not fatigue your memory. But I
forewarn you that if you trust my husband to pick out your
rooms, you are in for something hideous."

"Hideous, darling?" cried Tristram.

"To-day I must say nothing wicked; otherwise I should use
stronger language."

"What do you think she would say, Newman?" asked Tristram. "If she really tried, now? She can express displeasure,
volubly, in two or three languages; that 's what it is to be
intellectual. It gives her the start of me completely, for I can't
swear, for the life of me, except in English. When I get mad

587

I have to fall back on our dear old mother tongue. There 's nothing like it, after all."

Newman declared that he knew nothing about tables and chairs, and that he would accept, in the way of a lodging, with his eyes shut, anything that Tristram should offer him. This was partly pure veracity on our hero's part, but it was also partly charity. He knew that to pry about and look at rooms, and make people open windows, and poke into sofas with his cane, and gossip with landladies, and ask who lived above and who below—he knew that this was of all pastimes the dearest to Tristram's heart, and he felt the more disposed to put it in his way as he was conscious that, as regards his obliging friend, he had suffered the warmth of ancient good-fellowship somewhat to abate. Besides, he had no taste for upholstery; he had even no very exquisite sense of comfort or convenience. He had a relish for luxury and splendor, but it was satisfied by rather gross contrivances. He scarcely knew a hard chair from a soft one, and he possessed a talent for stretching his legs which quite dispensed with adventitious facilities. His idea of comfort was to inhabit very large rooms, have a great many of them, and be conscious of their possessing a number of patented mechanical devices—half of which he should never have occasion to use. The apartments should be light and brilliant and lofty; he had once said that he liked rooms in which you wanted to keep your hat on. For the rest, he was satisfied with the assurance of any respectable person that everything was "handsome." Tristram accordingly secured for him an apartment to which this epithet might be lavishly applied. It was situated on the Boulevard Haussmann, on a first floor, and consisted of a series of rooms, gilded from floor to ceiling a foot thick, draped in various light shades of satin, and chiefly furnished with mirrors and clocks. Newman thought them magnificent, thanked Tristram heartily, immediately took possession, and had one of his trunks standing for three months in his drawing-room.

One day Mrs. Tristram told him that her beautiful friend, Madame de Cintré, had returned from the country; that she had met her three days before, coming out of the Church of St. Sulpice; she herself having journeyed to that distant quarter in quest of an obscure lace-mender, of whose skill she had heard high praise.

"And how were those eyes?" Newman asked.

"Those eyes were red with weeping, if you please!" said Mrs. Tristram. "She had been to confession."

"It does n't tally with your account of her," said Newman, "that she should have sins to confess."

"They were not sins; they were sufferings."

"How do you know that?"

"She asked me to come and see her; I went this morning."

"And what does she suffer from?"

"I did n't ask her. With her, somehow, one is very discreet. But I guessed, easily enough. She suffers from her wicked old mother and her Grand Turk of a brother. They persecute her. But I can almost forgive them, because, as I told you, she is a saint, and a persecution is all that she needs to bring out her saintliness and make her perfect."

"That 's a comfortable theory for her. I hope you will never impart it to the old folks. Why does she let them bully her? Is she not her own mistress?"

"Legally, yes, I suppose; but morally, no. In France you must never say nay to your mother, whatever she requires of you. She may be the most abominable old woman in the world, and make your life a purgatory; but, after all, she is *ma mère*, and you have no right to judge her. You have simply to obey. The thing has a fine side to it. Madame de Cintré bows her head and folds her wings."

"Can't she at least make her brother leave off?"

"Her brother is the *chef de la famille*, as they say; he is the head of the clan. With those people the family is everything; you must act, not for your own pleasure, but for the advantage of the family."

"I wonder what *my* family would like me to do!" exclaimed Tristram.

"I wish you had one!" said his wife.

"But what do they want to get out of that poor lady?" Newman asked.

"Another marriage. They are not rich, and they want to bring more money into the family."

"There 's your chance, my boy!" said Tristram.

"And Madame de Cintré objects," Newman continued.

"She has been sold once; she naturally objects to being sold again. It appears that the first time they made rather a poor bargain; M. de Cintré left a scanty property."

"And to whom do they want to marry her now?"

"I thought it best not to ask; but you may be sure it is to some horrid old nabob, or to some dissipated little duke."

"There 's Mrs. Tristram, as large as life!" cried her husband. "Observe the richness of her imagination. She has not asked a single question—it 's vulgar to ask questions—and yet she knows everything. She has the history of Madame de Cintré's marriage at her fingers' ends. She has seen the lovely Claire on her knees, with loosened tresses and streaming eyes, and the rest of them standing over her with spikes and goads and red-hot irons, ready to come down on her if she refuses the tipsy duke. The simple truth is that they have made a fuss about her milliner's bill or refused her an opera-box."

Newman looked from Tristram to his wife with a certain mistrust in each direction. "Do you really mean," he asked of Mrs. Tristram, "that your friend is being forced into an unhappy marriage?"

"I think it extremely probable. Those people are very capable of that sort of thing."

"It is like something in a play," said Newman; "that dark old house over there looks as if wicked things had been done in it, and might be done again."

"They have a still darker old house in the country, Madame de Cintré tells me, and there, during the summer, this scheme must have been hatched."

"*Must* have been; mind that!" said Tristram.

"After all," suggested Newman, after a silence, "she may be in trouble about something else."

"If it is something else, then it is something worse," said Mrs. Tristram, with rich decision.

Newman was silent a while, and seemed lost in meditation. "Is it possible," he asked at last, "that they do that sort of thing over here? that helpless women are bullied into marrying men they hate?"

"Helpless women, all over the world, have a hard time of

it," said Mrs. Tristram. "There is plenty of bullying every-where."

"A great deal of that kind of thing goes on in New York," said Tristram. "Girls are bullied or coaxed or bribed, or all three together, into marrying nasty fellows. There is no end of that always going on in the Fifth Avenue, and other bad things besides. The Mysteries of the Fifth Avenue! Some one ought to show them up."

"I don't believe it!" said Newman, very gravely. "I don't believe that, in America, girls are ever subjected to compulsion. I don't believe there have been a dozen cases of it since the country began."

"Listen to the voice of the spread eagle!" cried Tristram.

"The spread eagle ought to use his wings," said Mrs. Tristram. "Fly to the rescue of Madame de Cintré!"

"To her rescue?"

"Pounce down, seize her in your talons, and carry her off. Marry her yourself."

Newman, for some moments, answered nothing; but presently, "I should suppose she had heard enough of marrying," he said. "The kindest way to treat her would be to admire her, and yet never to speak of it. But that sort of thing is infamous," he added; "it makes me feel savage to hear of it."

He heard of it, however, more than once afterward. Mrs. Tristram again saw Madame de Cintré, and again found her looking very sad. But on these occasions there had been no tears; her beautiful eyes were clear and still. "She is cold, calm, and hopeless," Mrs. Tristram declared, and she added that on her mentioning that her friend Mr. Newman was again in Paris and was faithful in his desire to make Madame de Cintré's acquaintance, this lovely woman had found a smile in her despair, and declared that she was sorry to have missed his visit in the spring and that she hoped he had not lost courage. "I told her something about you," said Mrs. Tristram.

"That 's a comfort," said Newman, placidly. "I like people to know about me."

A few days after this, one dusky autumn afternoon, he went again to the Rue de l'Université. The early evening had closed in as he applied for admittance at the stoutly guarded Hôtel de Bellegarde. He was told that Madame de Cintré was at home; he crossed the court, entered the farther door, and was conducted through a vestibule, vast, dim, and cold, up a broad stone staircase with an ancient iron balustrade, to an apartment on the second floor. Announced and ushered in, he found himself in a sort of paneled boudoir, at one end of which a lady and gentleman were seated before the fire. The gentleman was smoking a cigarette; there was no light in the room save that of a couple of candles and the glow from the hearth. Both persons rose to welcome Newman, who, in the firelight, recognized Madame de Cintré. She gave him her hand with a smile which seemed in itself an illumination, and, pointing to her companion, said softly, "My brother." The gentleman offered Newman a frank, friendly greeting, and our hero then perceived him to be the young man who had spoken to him in the court of the hotel on his former visit and who had struck him as a good fellow.

"Mrs. Tristram has spoken to me a great deal of you," said Madame de Cintré gently, as she resumed her former place.

Newman, after he had seated himself, began to consider what, in truth, was his errand. He had an unusual, unexpected sense of having wandered into a strange corner of the world. He was not given, as a general thing, to anticipating danger, or forecasting disaster, and he had had no social tremors on this particular occasion. He was not timid and he was not impudent. He felt too kindly toward himself to be the one, and too good-naturedly toward the rest of the world to be the other. But his native shrewdness sometimes placed his ease of temper at its mercy; with every disposition to take things simply, it was obliged to perceive that some things were not so simple as others. He felt as one does in missing a step, in an ascent, where one expected to find it. This strange, pretty woman, sitting in fire-side talk with her brother, in the gray depths of her inhospitable-looking house—what had he to say to her? She seemed enveloped in a sort of fantastic privacy; on what grounds had he pulled away the curtain? For a moment he felt as if he had plunged into some medium as deep as the ocean, and as if he must exert himself to keep from sinking. Meanwhile he was looking at Madame de Cintré, and she was settling herself in her chair and drawing in her long dress and turning her face towards him. Their eyes met; a moment afterwards she looked away and motioned to her brother to put a log on the fire. But the moment, and the glance which traversed it, had been sufficient to relieve Newman of the first and the last fit of personal embarrassment he was ever to know. He performed the movement which was so frequent with him, and which was always a sort of symbol of his taking mental possession of a scene—he extended his legs. The impression Madame de Cintré had made upon him on their first meeting came back in an instant; it had been deeper than he knew. She was pleasing, she was interesting; he had opened a book and the first lines held his attention.

She asked him several questions: how lately he had seen Mrs. Tristram, how long he had been in Paris, how long he expected to remain there, how he liked it. She spoke English without an accent, or rather with that distinctively British accent which, on his arrival in Europe, had struck Newman as an altogether foreign tongue, but which, in women, he had come to like extremely. Here and there Madame de Cintré's utterance had a faint shade of strangeness, but at the end of ten minutes Newman found himself waiting for these soft roughnesses. He enjoyed them, and he marveled to see that gross thing, error, brought down to so fine a point.

"You have a beautiful country," said Madame de Cintré, presently.

"Oh, magnificent!" said Newman. "You ought to see it."

"I shall never see it," said Madame de Cintré with a smile.

"Why not?" asked Newman.

"I don't travel; especially so far."

"But you go away sometimes; you are not always here?"

"I go away in summer, a little way, to the country."

Newman wanted to ask her something more, something personal, he hardly knew what. "Don't you find it rather—rather quiet here?" he said; "so far from the street?" Rather "gloomy," he was going to say, but he reflected that that would be impolite.

"Yes, it is very quiet," said Madame de Cintré; "but we like that."

"Ah, you like that," repeated Newman, slowly.

"Besides, I have lived here all my life."

"Lived here all your life," said Newman, in the same way.

"I was born here, and my father was born here before me, and my grandfather, and my great-grandfathers. Were they not, Valentin?" and she appealed to her brother.

"Yes, it 's a family habit to be born here!" the young man said with a laugh, and rose and threw the remnant of his cigarette into the fire, and then remained leaning against the chimney-piece. An observer would have perceived that he wished to take a better look at Newman, whom he covertly examined, while he stood stroking his mustache.

"Your house is tremendously old, then," said Newman.

"How old is it, brother?" asked Madame de Cintré.

The young man took the two candles from the mantel-shelf, lifted one high in each hand, and looked up toward the cornice of the room, above the chimney-piece. This latter feature of the apartment was of white marble, and in the familiar rococo style of the last century; but above it was a paneling of an earlier date, quaintly carved, painted white, and gilded here and there. The white had turned to yellow, and the gilding was tarnished. On the top, the figures ranged themselves into a sort of shield, on which an armorial device was cut. Above it, in relief, was a date—1627. "There you have it," said the young man. "That is old or new, according to your point of view."

"Well, over here," said Newman, "one's point of view gets shifted round considerably." And he threw back his head and looked about the room. "Your house is of a very curious style of architecture," he said.

"Are you interested in architecture?" asked the young man at the chimney-piece.

"Well, I took the trouble, this summer," said Newman, "to examine—as well as I can calculate—some four hundred and seventy churches. Do you call that interested?"

"Perhaps you are interested in theology," said the young man.

"Not particularly. Are you a Roman Catholic, madam?" And he turned to Madame de Cintré.

"Yes, sir," she answered, gravely.

Newman was struck with the gravity of her tone; he threw

back his head and began to look round the room again. "Had you never noticed that number up there?" he presently asked.

She hesitated a moment, and then, "In former years," she said.

Her brother had been watching Newman's movement. "Perhaps you would like to examine the house," he said.

Newman slowly brought down his eyes and looked at him; he had a vague impression that the young man at the chimney-piece was inclined to irony. He was a handsome fellow, his face wore a smile, his mustaches were curled up at the ends, and there was a little dancing gleam in his eye. "Damn his French impudence!" Newman was on the point of saying to himself. "What the deuce is he grinning at?" He glanced at Madame de Cintré; she was sitting with her eyes fixed on the floor. She raised them, they met his, and she looked at her brother. Newman turned again to this young man and observed that he strikingly resembled his sister. This was in his favor, and our hero's first impression of the Count Valentin, moreover, had been agreeable. His mistrust expired, and he said he would be very glad to see the house.

The young man gave a frank laugh, and laid his hand on one of the candlesticks. "Good, good!" he exclaimed. "Come, then."

But Madame de Cintré rose quickly and grasped his arm. "Ah, Valentin!" she said. "What do you mean to do?"

"To show Mr. Newman the house. It will be very amusing."

She kept her hand on his arm, and turned to Newman with a smile. "Don't let him take you," she said; "you will not find it amusing. It is a musty old house, like any other."

"It is full of curious things," said the count, resisting. "Besides, I want to do it; it is a rare chance."

"You are very wicked, brother," Madame de Cintré answered.

"Nothing venture, nothing have!" cried the young man. "Will you come?"

Madame de Cintré stepped toward Newman, gently clasping her hands and smiling softly. "Would you not prefer my society, here, by my fire, to stumbling about dark passages after my brother?"

"A hundred times!" said Newman. "We will see the house some other day."

The young man put down his candlestick with mock solemnity, and, shaking his head, "Ah, you have defeated a great scheme, sir!" he said.

"A scheme? I don't understand," said Newman.

"You would have played your part in it all the better. Perhaps some day I shall have a chance to explain it."

"Be quiet, and ring for the tea," said Madame de Cintré.

The young man obeyed, and presently a servant brought in the tea, placed the tray on a small table, and departed. Madame de Cintré, from her place, busied herself with making it. She had but just begun when the door was thrown open and a lady rushed in, making a loud rustling sound. She stared at Newman, gave a little nod and a "Monsieur!" and then quickly approached Madame de Cintré and presented her forehead to be kissed. Madame de Cintré saluted her, and continued to make tea. The new-comer was young and pretty, it seemed to Newman; she wore her bonnet and cloak, and a train of royal proportions. She began to talk rapidly in French. "Oh, give me some tea, my beautiful one, for the love of God! I'm exhausted, mangled, massacred." Newman found himself quite unable to follow her; she spoke much less distinctly than M. Nioche.

"That is my sister-in-law," said the Count Valentin, leaning towards him.

"She is very pretty," said Newman.

"Exquisite," answered the young man, and this time, again, Newman suspected him of irony.

His sister-in-law came round to the other side of the fire with her cup of tea in her hand, holding it out at arm's-length, so that she might not spill it on her dress, and uttering little cries of alarm. She placed the cup on the mantel-shelf and began to unpin her veil and pull off her gloves, looking meanwhile at Newman.

"Is there any thing I can do for you, my dear lady?" the Count Valentin asked, in a sort of mock-caressing tone.

"Present monsieur," said his sister-in-law.

The young man answered, "Mr. Newman!"

"I can't courtesy to you, monsieur, or I shall spill my tea," said the lady. "So Claire receives strangers, like that?" she added, in a low voice, in French, to her brother-in-law.

"Apparently!" he answered with a smile. Newman stood a moment, and then he approached Madame de Cintré. She looked up at him as if she were thinking of something to say. But she seemed to think of nothing; so she simply smiled. He sat down near her and she handed him a cup of tea. For a few moments they talked about that, and meanwhile he looked at her. He remembered what Mrs. Tristram had told him of her "perfection," and of her having, in combination, all the brilliant things that he dreamed of finding. This made him observe her not only without mistrust, but without uneasy conjectures; the presumption, from the first moment he looked at her, had been in her favor. And yet, if she was beautiful, it was not a dazzling beauty. She was tall and moulded in long lines; she had thick, fair hair, a wide forehead, and features with a sort of harmonious irregularity. Her clear gray eyes were strikingly expressive; they were both gentle and intelligent, and Newman liked them immensely; but they had not those depths of splendor—those many-colored rays—which illumine the brow of famous beauties. Madame de Cintré was rather thin, and she looked younger than probably she was. In her whole person there was something both youthful and subdued, slender and yet ample, tranquil yet shy; a mixture of immaturity and repose, of innocence and dignity. What had Tristram meant, Newman wondered, by calling her proud? She was certainly not proud now, to him; or if she was, it was of no use, it was lost upon him; she must pile it up higher if she expected him to mind it. She was a beautiful woman, and it was very easy to get on with her. Was she a countess, a *marquise*, a kind of historical formation? Newman, who had rarely heard these words used, had never been at pains to attach any particular image to them; but they occurred to him now and seemed charged with a sort of melodious meaning. They signified something fair and softly bright, that had easy motions and spoke very agreeably.

"Have you many friends in Paris; do you go out?" asked Madame de Cintré, who had at last thought of something to say.

"Do you mean do I dance, and all that?"

"Do you go *dans le monde*, as we say?"

"I have seen a good many people. Mrs. Tristram has taken me about. I do whatever she tells me."

"By yourself, you are not fond of amusements?"

"Oh yes, of some sorts. I am not fond of dancing, and that sort of thing; I am too old and sober. But I want to be amused; I came to Europe for that."

"But you can be amused in America, too."

"I could n't; I was always at work. But after all, that was my amusement."

At this moment Madame de Bellegarde came back for another cup of tea, accompanied by the Count Valentin. Madame de Cintré, when she had served her, began to talk again with Newman, and recalling what he had last said, "In your own country you were very much occupied?" she asked.

"I was in business. I have been in business since I was fifteen years old."

"And what was your business?" asked Madame de Bellegarde, who was decidedly not so pretty as Madame de Cintré.

"I have been in everything," said Newman. "At one time I sold leather; at one time I manufactured wash-tubs."

Madame de Bellegarde made a little grimace. "Leather? I don't like that. Wash-tubs are better. I prefer the smell of soap. I hope at least they made your fortune." She rattled this off with the air of a woman who had the reputation of saying everything that came into her head, and with a strong French accent.

Newman had spoken with cheerful seriousness, but Madame de Bellegarde's tone made him go on, after a meditative pause, with a certain light grimness of jocularity. "No, I lost money on wash-tubs, but I came out pretty square on leather."

"I have made up my mind, after all," said Madame de Bellegarde, "that the great point is—how do you call it?—to come out square. I am on my knees to money; I don't deny it. If you have it, I ask no questions. For that I am a real democrat—like you, monsieur. Madame de Cintré is very proud; but I find that one gets much more pleasure in this sad life if one does n't look too close."

"Just Heaven, dear madam, how you go at it," said the Count Valentin, lowering his voice.

"He 's a man one can speak to, I suppose, since my sister receives him," the lady answered. "Besides, it 's very true; those are my ideas."

"Ah, you call them ideas," murmured the young man.

"But Mrs. Tristram told me you had been in the army—in your war," said Madame de Cintré.

"Yes, but that is not business!" said Newman.

"Very true!" said M. de Bellegarde. "Otherwise perhaps I should not be penniless."

"Is it true," asked Newman in a moment, "that you are so proud? I had already heard it."

Madame de Cintré smiled. "Do you find me so?"

"Oh," said Newman, "I am no judge. If you are proud with me, you will have to tell me. Otherwise I shall not know it."

Madame de Cintré began to laugh. "That would be pride in a sad position!" she said.

"It would be partly," Newman went on, "because I should n't want to know it. I want you to treat me well."

Madame de Cintré, whose laugh had ceased, looked at him with her head half averted, as if she feared what he was going to say.

"Mrs. Tristram told you the literal truth," he went on; "I want very much to know you. I did n't come here simply to call to-day; I came in the hope that you might ask me to come again."

"Oh, pray come often," said Madame de Cintré.

"But will you be at home?" Newman insisted. Even to himself he seemed a trifle "pushing," but he was, in truth, a trifle excited.

"I hope so!" said Madame de Cintré.

Newman got up. "Well, we shall see," he said, smoothing his hat with his coat-cuff.

"Brother," said Madame de Cintré, "invite Mr. Newman to come again."

The Count Valentin looked at our hero from head to foot with his peculiar smile, in which impudence and urbanity seemed perplexingly commingled. "Are you a brave man?" he asked, eying him askance.

"Well, I hope so," said Newman.

"I rather suspect so. In that case, come again."

"Ah, what an invitation!" murmured Madame de Cintré, with something painful in her smile.

"Oh, I want Mr. Newman to come—particularly," said the young man. "It will give me great pleasure. I shall be desolate if I miss one of his visits. But I maintain he must be brave. A stout heart, sir!" And he offered Newman his hand.

"I shall not come to see you; I shall come to see Madame de Cintré," said Newman.

"You will need all the more courage."

"Ah, Valentin!" said Madame de Cintré, appealingly.

"Decidedly," cried Madame de Bellegarde, "I am the only person here capable of saying something polite! Come to see me; you will need no courage," she said.

Newman gave a laugh which was not altogether an assent, and took his leave. Madame de Cintré did not take up her sister's challenge to be gracious, but she looked with a certain troubled air at the retreating guest.

Chapter VII

O NE EVENING, very late, about a week after his visit to Madame de Cintré, Newman's servant brought him a card. It was that of young M. de Bellegarde. When, a few moments later, he went to receive his visitor, he found him standing in the middle of his great gilded parlor and eying it from cornice to carpet. M. de Bellegarde's face, it seemed to Newman, expressed a sense of lively entertainment. "What the devil is he laughing at now?" our hero asked himself. But he put the question without acrimony, for he felt that Madame de Cintré's brother was a good fellow, and he had a presentiment that on this basis of good fellowship they were destined to understand each other. Only, if there was anything to laugh at, he wished to have a glimpse of it too.

"To begin with," said the young man, as he extended his hand, "have I come too late?"

"Too late for what?" asked Newman.

"To smoke a cigar with you."

"You would have to come early to do that," said Newman. "I don't smoke."

"Ah, you are a strong man!"

"But I keep cigars," Newman added. "Sit down."

"Surely, I may not smoke here," said M. de Bellegarde.

"What is the matter? Is the room too small?"

"It is too large. It is like smoking in a ball-room, or a church."

"That is what you were laughing at just now?" Newman asked; "the size of my room?"

"It is not size only," replied M. de Bellegarde, "but splendor, and harmony, and beauty of detail. It was the smile of admiration."

Newman looked at him a moment, and then, "So it *is* very ugly?" he inquired.

"Ugly, my dear sir? It is magnificent."

"That is the same thing, I suppose," said Newman. "Make yourself comfortable. Your coming to see me, I take it, is an act of friendship. You were not obliged to. Therefore, if anything around here amuses you, it will be all in a pleasant way.

Laugh as loud as you please; I like to see my visitors cheerful. Only, I must make this request: that you explain the joke to me as soon as you can speak. I don't want to lose anything, myself."

M. de Bellegarde stared, with a look of unresentful perplexity. He laid his hand on Newman's sleeve and seemed on the point of saying something, but he suddenly checked himself, leaned back in his chair, and puffed at his cigar. At last, however, breaking silence,—"Certainly," he said, "my coming to see you is an act of friendship. Nevertheless I was in a measure obliged to do so. My sister asked me to come, and a request from my sister is, for me, a law. I was near you, and I observed lights in what I supposed were your rooms. It was not a ceremonious hour for making a call, but I was not sorry to do something that would show I was not performing a mere ceremony."

"Well, here I am as large as life," said Newman, extending his legs.

"I don't know what you mean," the young man went on, "by giving me unlimited leave to laugh. Certainly I am a great laugher, and it is better to laugh too much than too little. But it is not in order that we may laugh together— or separately—that I have, I may say, sought your acquaintance. To speak with almost impudent frankness, you interest me!" All this was uttered by M. de Bellegarde with the modulated smoothness of the man of the world, and, in spite of his excellent English, of the Frenchman; but Newman, at the same time that he sat noting its harmonious flow, perceived that it was not mere mechanical urbanity. Decidedly, there was something in his visitor that he liked. M. de Bellegarde was a foreigner to his finger-tips, and if Newman had met him on a Western prairie he would have felt it proper to address him with a "How-d'ye-do, Mosseer?" But there was something in his physiognomy which seemed to cast a sort of aerial bridge over the impassable gulf produced by difference of race. He was below the middle height, and robust and agile in figure. Valentin de Bellegarde, Newman afterwards learned, had a mortal dread of the robustness overtaking the agility; he was afraid of growing stout; he was too short, as he said, to afford a belly. He rode and fenced and practiced gymnastics with unremitting zeal, and if you greeted him with a "How well you are looking!" he started and turned pale. In your *well* he read a grosser monosyllable. He had a round head, high above the ears, a crop of hair at once dense and silky, a broad, low forehead, a short nose, of the ironical and inquiring rather than of the dogmatic or sensitive cast, and a mustache as delicate as that of a page in a romance. He resembled his sister not in feature, but in the expression of his clear, bright eye, completely void of introspection, and in the way he smiled. The great point in his face was that it was intensely alive—frankly, ardently, gallantly alive. The look of it was like a bell, of which the handle might have been in the young man's soul: at a touch of the handle it rang with a loud, silver sound. There was something in his quick, light brown eye which assured you that he was not economizing his consciousness. He was not living in a corner of it to spare the furniture of the rest. He was squarely encamped in the centre and he was keeping open house. When he smiled, it was like the movement of a person who in emptying a cup turns it upside down: he gave you the last drop of his jollity. He inspired Newman with something of the same kindness that our hero used to feel in his earlier years for those of his companions who could perform strange and clever tricks—make their joints crack in queer places or whistle at the back of their mouths.

"My sister told me," M. de Bellegarde continued, "that I ought to come and remove the impression that I had taken such great pains to produce upon you; the impression that I am a lunatic. Did it strike you that I behaved very oddly the other day?"

"Rather so," said Newman.

"So my sister tells me." And M. de Bellegarde watched his host for a moment through his smoke-wreaths. "If that is the case, I think we had better let it stand. I did n't try to make you think I was a lunatic, at all; on the contrary, I wanted to produce a favorable impression. But if, after all, I made a fool of myself, it was the intention of Providence. I should injure myself by protesting too much, for I should seem to set up a claim for wisdom which, in the sequel of our acquaintance, I could by no means justify. Set me down as a lunatic with intervals of sanity."

"Oh, I guess you know what you are about," said Newman.

"When I am sane, I am very sane; that I admit," M. de Bellegarde answered. "But I did n't come here to talk about myself. I should like to ask you a few questions. You allow me?"

"Give me a specimen," said Newman.

"You live here all alone?"

"Absolutely. With whom should I live?"

"For the moment," said M. de Bellegarde with a smile, "I am asking questions, not answering them. You have come to Paris for your pleasure?"

Newman was silent a while. Then, at last, "Every one asks me that!" he said with his mild slowness. "It sounds so awfully foolish."

"But at any rate you had a reason."

"Oh, I came for my pleasure!" said Newman. "Though it is foolish, it is true."

"And you are enjoying it?"

Like any other good American, Newman thought it as well not to truckle to the foreigner. "Oh, so-so," he answered.

M. de Bellegarde puffed his cigar again in silence. "For myself," he said at last, "I am entirely at your service. Anything I can do for you I shall be very happy to do. Call upon me at your convenience. Is there any one you desire to know—anything you wish to see? It is a pity you should not enjoy Paris."

"Oh, I do enjoy it!" said Newman, good-naturedly. "I 'm much obliged to you."

"Honestly speaking," M. de Bellegarde went on, "there is something absurd to me in hearing myself make you these offers. They represent a great deal of good-will, but they represent little else. You are a successful man and I am a failure, and it 's a turning of the tables to talk as if I could lend you a hand."

"In what way are you a failure?" asked Newman.

"Oh, I 'm not a tragical failure!" cried the young man with a laugh. "I have not fallen from a height, and my fiasco has made no noise. You, evidently, are a success. You have made a fortune, you have built up an edifice, you are a financial, commercial power, you can travel about the world until you have found a soft spot, and lie down in it with the consciousness of having earned your rest. Is not that true? Well, imagine the exact reverse of all that, and you have me. I have done nothing—I can do nothing!"

"Why not?"

"It 's a long story. Some day I will tell you. Meanwhile, I 'm right, eh? You are a success? You have made a fortune? It 's none of my business, but, in short, you are rich?"

"That 's another thing that it sounds foolish to say," said Newman. "Hang it, no man is rich!"

"I have heard philosophers affirm," laughed M. de Bellegarde, "that no man was poor; but your formula strikes me as an improvement. As a general thing, I confess, I don't like successful people, and I find clever men who have made great fortunes very offensive. They tread on my toes; they make me uncomfortable. But as soon as I saw you, I said to myself, 'Ah, there is a man with whom I shall get on. He has the good-nature of success and none of the *morgue*; he has not our confoundedly irritable French vanity.' In short, I took a fancy to you. We are very different, I 'm sure, I don't believe there is a subject on which we think or feel alike. But I rather think we shall get on, for there is such a thing, you know, as being too different to quarrel."

"Oh, I never quarrel," said Newman.

"Never? Sometimes it 's a duty—or at least it 's a pleasure. Oh, I have had two or three delicious quarrels in my day!" and M. de Bellegarde's handsome smile assumed, at the memory of these incidents, an almost voluptuous intensity.

With the preamble embodied in his share of the foregoing fragment of dialogue, he paid our hero a long visit; as the two men sat with their heels on Newman's glowing hearth, they heard the small hours of the morning striking larger from a far-off belfry. Valentin de Bellegarde was, by his own confession, at all times a great chatterer, and on this occasion he was evidently in a particularly loquacious mood. It was a tradition of his race that people of its blood always conferred a favor by their smiles, and as his enthusiasms were as rare as his civility was constant, he had a double reason for not suspecting that his friendship could ever be importunate. Moreover, the flower of an ancient stem as he was, tradition (since I have used the word) had in his temperament nothing of disagreeable rigidity. It was muffled in sociability and urbanity, as an old dowager in her laces and strings of pearls. Valentin was what is called in France a *gentilhomme*, of the purest source, and his rule of life, so far as it was definite, was to play the part of a gentilhomme. This, it seemed to him, was enough to occupy comfortably a young man of ordinary good parts. But all that he was he was by instinct and not by theory, and the amiability of his character was so great that certain of the aristocratic virtues, which in some aspects seem rather brittle and trenchant, acquired in his application of them an extreme geniality. In his younger years he had been suspected of low tastes, and his mother had greatly feared he would make a slip in the mud of the highway and bespatter the family shield. He had been treated, therefore, to more than his share of schooling and drilling, but his instructors had not succeeded in mounting him upon stilts. They could not spoil his safe spontaneity, and he remained the least cautious and the most lucky of young nobles. He had been tied with so short a rope in his youth that he had now a mortal grudge against family discipline. He had been known to say, within the limits of the family, that, light-headed as he was, the honor of the name was safer in his hands than in those of some of its other members, and that if a day ever came to try it, they should see. His talk was an odd mixture of almost boyish garrulity and of the reserve and discretion of the man of the world, and he seemed to Newman, as afterwards young members of the Latin races often seemed to him, now amusingly juvenile and now appallingly mature. In America, Newman reflected, lads of twenty-five and thirty have old heads and young hearts, or at least young morals; here they have young heads and very aged hearts, morals the most grizzled and wrinkled.

"What I envy you is your liberty," observed M. de Bellegarde, "your wide range, your freedom to come and go, your not having a lot of people, who take themselves awfully seriously, expecting something of you. I live," he added with a sigh, "beneath the eyes of my admirable mother."

"It is your own fault; what is to hinder your ranging?" said Newman.

"There is a delightful simplicity in that remark! Everything is to hinder me. To begin with, I have not a penny."

"I had not a penny when I began to range."

"Ah, but your poverty was your capital. Being an American, it was impossible you should remain what you were born, and being born poor—do I understand it?—it was therefore inevitable that you should become rich. You were in a position that makes one's mouth water; you looked round you and saw a world full of things you had only to step up to and take hold of. When I was twenty, I looked around me and saw a world with everything ticketed 'Hands off!' and the deuce of it was that the ticket seemed meant only for me. I could n't go into business, I could n't make money, because I was a Bellegarde. I could n't go into politics, because I was a Bellegarde—the Bellegardes don't recognize the Bonapartes. I could n't go into literature, because I was a dunce. I could n't marry a rich girl, because no Bellegarde had ever married a *roturière*, and it was not proper that I should begin. We shall have to come to it, yet. Marriageable heiresses, *de notre bord*, are not to be had for nothing; it must be name for name, and fortune for fortune. The only thing I could do was to go and fight for the Pope. That I did, punctiliously, and received an apostolic flesh-wound at Castelfidardo. It did neither the Holy Father nor me any good, that I could see. Rome was doubtless a very amusing place in the days of Caligula, but it has sadly fallen off since. I passed three years in the Castle of St. Angelo, and then came back to secular life."

"So you have no profession—you do nothing," said Newman.

"I do nothing! I am supposed to amuse myself, and, to tell the truth, I have amused myself. One can, if one knows how. But you can't keep it up forever. I am good for another five years, perhaps, but I foresee that after that I shall lose my appetite. Then what shall I do? I think I shall turn monk. Seriously, I think I shall tie a rope round my waist and go into a monastery. It was an old custom, and the old customs were very good. People understood life quite as well as we do. They kept the pot boiling till it cracked, and then they put it on the shelf altogether.

"Are you very religious?" asked Newman, in a tone which gave the inquiry a grotesque effect.

M. de Bellegarde evidently appreciated the comical element in the question, but he looked at Newman a moment with extreme soberness. "I am a very good Catholic. I respect the Church. I adore the blessed Virgin. I fear the Devil."

"Well, then," said Newman, "you are very well fixed. You have got pleasure in the present and religion in the future; what do you complain of?"

"It 's a part of one's pleasure to complain. There is something in your own circumstances that irritates me. You are the first man I have ever envied. It 's singular, but so it is. I have known many men who, besides any factitious advantages that I may possess, had money and brains into the bargain; but somehow they have never disturbed my good-humor. But you have got something that I should have liked to have. It is not money, it is not even brains—though no doubt yours are excellent. It is not your six feet of height, though I should have rather liked to be a couple of inches taller. It 's a sort of air you have of being thoroughly at home in the world. When I was a boy, my father told me that it was by such an air as that that people recognized a Bellegarde. He called my attention to it. He did n't advise me to cultivate it; he said that as we grew up it always came of itself. I supposed it had come to me, because I think I have always had the feeling. My place in life was made for me, and it seemed easy to occupy it. But you who, as I understand it, have made your own place, you who, as you told us the other day, have manufactured wash-tubs—you strike me, somehow, as a man who stands at his ease, who looks at things from a height. I fancy you going about the world like a man traveling on a railroad in which he owns a large amount of stock. You make me feel as if I had missed something. What is it?"

"It is the proud consciousness of honest toil—of having manufactured a few wash-tubs," said Newman, at once jocose and serious.

"Oh no; I have seen men who had done even more, men who had made not only wash-tubs, but soap—strong-smelling yellow soap, in great bars; and they never made me the least uncomfortable."

"Then it 's the privilege of being an American citizen," said Newman. "That sets a man up."

"Possibly," rejoined M. de Bellegarde. "But I am forced to say that I have seen a great many American citizens who did n't seem at all set up or in the least like large stockholders. I never envied them. I rather think the thing is an accomplishment of your own."

"Oh, come," said Newman, "you will make me proud!"

"No, I shall not. You have nothing to do with pride, or with humility—that is a part of this easy manner of yours. People are proud only when they have something to lose, and humble when they have something to gain."

"I don't know what I have to lose," said Newman, "but I certainly have something to gain."

"What is it?" asked his visitor.

Newman hesitated a while. "I will tell you when I know you better."

"I hope that will be soon! Then, if I can help you to gain it, I shall be happy."

"Perhaps you may," said Newman.

"Don't forget, then, that I am your servant," M. de Bellegarde answered; and shortly afterwards he took his departure.

During the next three weeks Newman saw Bellegarde several times, and without formally swearing an eternal friendship the two men established a sort of comradeship. To Newman, Bellegarde was the ideal Frenchman, the Frenchman of tradition and romance, so far as our hero was acquainted with these mystical influences. Gallant, expansive, amusing, more pleased himself with the effect he produced than those (even when they were well pleased) for whom he produced it; a master of all the distinctively social virtues and a votary of all agreeable sensations; a devotee of something mysterious and sacred to which he occasionally alluded in terms more ecstatic even than those in which he spoke of the last pretty woman, and which was simply the beautiful though somewhat superannuated image of *honor*; he was irresistibly entertaining and enlivening, and he formed a character to which Newman was as capable of doing justice when he had once been placed in contact with it, as he was unlikely, in musing upon the possible mixtures of our human ingredients, mentally to have foreshadowed it. Bellegarde did not in the least cause him to modify his needful premise that all Frenchmen are of a frothy and imponderable substance; he simply reminded him that light materials may be beaten up into a most agreeable compound. No two companions could be more different, but their differences made a capital basis for a friendship of which the distinctive characteristic was that it was extremely amusing to each.

Valentin de Bellegarde lived in the basement of an old house in the Rue d'Anjou St. Honoré, and his small apartments lay between the court of the house and an old garden which spread itself behind it—one of those large, sunless, humid gardens into which you look unexpectingly in Paris from back windows, wondering how among the grudging habitations they find their space. When Newman returned Bellegarde's visit, he hinted that *his* lodging was at least as much a laughing matter as his own. But its oddities were of a different cast from those of our hero's gilded saloons on the Boulevard Haussmann: the place was low, dusky, contracted, and crowded with curious bric-à-brac. Bellegarde, penniless patrician as he was, was an insatiable collector, and his walls were covered with rusty arms and ancient panels and platters, his doorways draped in faded tapestries, his floors muffled in the skins of beasts. Here and there was one of those uncomfortable tributes to elegance in which the upholsterer's art, in France, is so prolific; a curtained recess with a sheet of looking-glass in which, among the shadows, you could see nothing; a divan on which, for its festoons and furbelows, you could not sit: a fire-place draped, flounced, and frilled to the complete exclusion of fire. The young man's possessions were in picturesque disorder, and his apartment was pervaded by the odor of cigars, mingled with perfumes more inscrutable. Newman thought it a damp, gloomy place to live in, and was puzzled by the obstructive and fragmentary character of the furniture.

Bellegarde, according to the custom of his country, talked

very generously about himself, and unveiled the mysteries of
his private history with an unsparing hand. Inevitably, he had
a vast deal to say about women, and he used frequently to
indulge in sentimental and ironical apostrophes to these authors of his joys and woes. "Oh, the women, the women, and
the things they have made me do!" he would exclaim with a
lustrous eye. "*C'est égal*, of all the follies and stupidities I have
committed for them I would not have missed one!" On this
subject Newman maintained an habitual reserve; to expatiate
largely upon it had always seemed to him a proceeding
vaguely analogous to the cooing of pigeons and the chattering of monkeys, and even inconsistent with a fully developed
human character. But Bellegarde's confidences greatly amused
him, and rarely displeased him, for the generous young
Frenchman was not a cynic. "I really think," he had once said,
"that I am not more depraved than most of my contemporaries. They are tolerably depraved, my contemporaries!" He
said wonderfully pretty things about his female friends, and,
numerous and various as they had been, declared that on the
whole there was more good in them than harm. "But you are
not to take that as advice," he added. "As an authority I am
very untrustworthy. I 'm prejudiced in their favor; I 'm an
idealist!" Newman listened to him with his impartial smile,
and was glad, for his own sake, that he had fine feelings; but
he mentally repudiated the idea of a Frenchman having discovered any merit in the amiable sex which he himself did not
suspect. M. de Bellegarde, however, did not confine his conversation to the autobiographical channel; he questioned our
hero largely as to the events of his own life, and Newman
told him some better stories than any that Bellegarde carried
in his budget. He narrated his career, in fact, from the beginning, through all its variations, and whenever his companion's
credulity, or his habits of gentility, appeared to protest, it
amused him to heighten the color of the episode. Newman
had sat with Western humorists in knots, round cast-iron
stoves, and seen "tall" stories grow taller without toppling
over, and his own imagination had learned the trick of piling
up consistent wonders. Bellegarde's regular attitude at last became that of laughing self-defense; to maintain his reputation
as an all-knowing Frenchman, he doubted of everything,

wholesale. The result of this was that Newman found it impossible to convince him of certain time-honored verities.

"But the details don't matter," said M. de Bellegarde. "You have evidently had some surprising adventures; you have seen some strange sides of life, you have revolved to and fro over a whole continent as I walk up and down the Boulevard. You are a man of the world with a vengeance! You have spent some deadly dull hours, and you have done some extremely disagreeable things: you have shoveled sand, as a boy, for supper, and you have eaten roast dog in a gold-diggers' camp. You have stood casting up figures for ten hours at a time, and you have sat through Methodist sermons for the sake of looking at a pretty girl in another pew. All that is rather stiff, as we say. But at any rate you have done something and you are something; you have used your will and you have made your fortune. You have not stupefied yourself with debauchery and you have not mortgaged your fortune to social conveniences. You take things easily, and you have fewer prejudices even than I, who pretend to have none, but who in reality have three or four. Happy man, you are strong and you are free. But what the deuce," demanded the young man in conclusion, "do you propose to do with such advantages? Really to use them you need a better world than this. There is nothing worth your while here."

"Oh, I think there is something," said Newman.

"What is it?"

"Well," murmured Newman, "I will tell you some other time!"

In this way our hero delayed from day to day broaching a subject which he had very much at heart. Meanwhile, however, he was growing practically familiar with it; in other words, he had called again, three times, on Madame de Cintré. On only two of these occasions had he found her at home, and on each of them she had other visitors. Her visitors were numerous and extremely loquacious, and they exacted much of their hostess's attention. She found time, however, to bestow a little of it on Newman, in an occasional vague smile, the very vagueness of which pleased him, allowing him as it did to fill it out mentally, both at the time and afterwards, with such meanings as most pleased him. He sat by without speaking, looking at the entrances and exits, the greetings and chatterings, of Madame de Cintré's visitors. He felt as if he were at the play, and as if his own speaking would be an interruption; sometimes he wished he had a book, to follow the dialogue; he half expected to see a woman in a white cap and pink ribbons come and offer him one for two francs. Some of the ladies looked at him very hard—or very soft, as you please; others seemed profoundly unconscious of his presence. The men looked only at Madame de Cintré. This was inevitable; for whether one called her beautiful or not she entirely occupied and filled one's vision, just as an agreeable sound fills one's ear. Newman had but twenty distinct words with her, but he carried away an impression to which solemn promises could not have given a higher value. She was part of the play that he was seeing acted, quite as much as her companions; but how she filled the stage and how much better she did it! Whether she rose or seated herself; whether she went with her departing friends to the door and lifted up the heavy curtain as they passed out, and stood an instant looking after them and giving them the last nod; or whether she leaned back in her chair with her arms crossed and her eyes resting, listening and smiling; she gave Newman the feeling that he should like to have her always before him, moving slowly to and fro along the whole scale of expressive hospitality. If it might be *to* him, it would be well; if it might be *for* him, it would be still better! She was so tall and yet so light, so active and yet so still, so elegant and yet so simple, so frank and yet so mysterious! It was the mystery—it was what she was off the stage, as it were—that interested Newman most of all. He could not have told you what warrant he had for talking about mysteries; if it had been his habit to express himself in poetic figures he might have said that in observing Madame de Cintré he seemed to see the vague circle which sometimes accompanies the partly-filled disk of the moon. It was not that she was reserved; on the contrary, she was as frank as flowing water. But he was sure she had qualities which she herself did not suspect.

He had abstained for several reasons from saying some of these things to Bellegarde. One reason was that before proceeding to any act he was always circumspect, conjectural, contemplative; he had little eagerness, as became a man who felt that whenever he really began to move he walked with long steps. And then, it simply pleased him not to speak—it occupied him, it excited him. But one day Bellegarde had been dining with him, at a restaurant, and they had sat long over their dinner. On rising from it, Bellegarde proposed that, to help them through the rest of the evening, they should go and see Madame Dandelard. Madame Dandelard was a little Italian lady who had married a Frenchman who proved to be a rake and a brute and the torment of her life. Her husband had spent all her money, and then, lacking the means of obtaining more expensive pleasures, had taken, in his duller hours, to beating her. She had a blue spot somewhere, which she showed to several persons, including Bellegarde. She had obtained a separation from her husband, collected the scraps of her fortune (they were very meagre) and come to live in Paris, where she was staying at a *hôtel garni*. She was always looking for an apartment, and visiting, inquiringly, those of other people. She was very pretty, very child-like, and she made very extraordinary remarks. Bellegarde had made her acquaintance, and the source of his interest in her was, according to his own declaration, a curiosity as to what would become of her. "She is poor, she is pretty, and she is silly," he said; "it seems to me she can go only one way. It 's a pity, but it can't be helped. I will give her six months. She has nothing to fear from me, but I am watching the process. I am curious to see just how things will go. Yes, I know what you are going to say: this horrible Paris hardens one's heart. But it quickens one's wits, and it ends by teaching one a refinement of observation! To see this little woman's little drama play itself out, now, is, for me, an intellectual pleasure."

"If she is going to throw herself away," Newman had said, "you ought to stop her."

"Stop her? How stop her?"

"Talk to her; give her some good advice."

Bellegarde laughed. "Heaven deliver us both! Imagine the situation! Go and advise her yourself."

It was after this that Newman had gone with Bellegarde to see Madame Dandelard. When they came away, Bellegarde reproached his companion. "Where was your famous advice?" he asked. "I did n't hear a word of it."

"Oh, I give it up," said Newman, simply.

"Then you are as bad as I!" said Bellegarde.

"No, because I don't take an 'intellectual pleasure' in her prospective adventures. I don't in the least want to see her going down hill. I had rather look the other way. But why," he asked, in a moment, "don't you get your sister to go and see her?"

Bellegarde stared. "Go and see Madame Dandelard—my sister?"

"She might talk to her to very good purpose."

Bellegarde shook his head with sudden gravity. "My sister can't see that sort of person. Madame Dandelard is nothing at all; they would never meet."

"I should think," said Newman, "that your sister might see whom she pleased." And he privately resolved that after he knew her a little better he would ask Madame de Cintré to go and talk to the foolish little Italian lady.

After his dinner with Bellegarde, on the occasion I have mentioned, he demurred to his companion's proposal that they should go again and listen to Madame Dandelard describe her sorrows and her bruises. "I have something better in mind," he said; "come home with me and finish the evening before my fire."

Bellegarde always welcomed the prospect of a long stretch of conversation, and before long the two men sat watching the great blaze which scattered its scintillations over the high adornments of Newman's ballroom.

Chapter VIII

"TELL ME SOMETHING about your sister," Newman began abruptly.

Bellegarde turned and gave him a quick look. "Now that I think of it, you have never yet asked me a question about her."

"I know that very well."

"If it is because you don't trust me, you are very right," said Bellegarde. "I can't talk of her rationally. I admire her too much."

"Talk of her as you can," rejoined Newman. "Let yourself go."

"Well, we are very good friends; we are such a brother and sister as have not been seen since Orestes and Electra. You have seen her; you know what she is: tall, thin, light, imposing, and gentle, half a *grande dame* and half an angel; a mixture of pride and humility, of the eagle and the dove. She looks like a statue which had failed as stone, resigned itself to its grave defects, and come to life as flesh and blood, to wear white capes and long trains. All I can say is that she really possesses every merit that her face, her glance, her smile, the tone of her voice, lead you to expect; it is saying a great deal. As a general thing, when a woman seems very charming, I should say 'Beware!' But in proportion as Claire seems charming you may fold your arms and let yourself float with the current; you are safe. She is so good! I have never seen a woman half so perfect or so complete. She has everything; that is all I can say about her. There!" Bellegarde concluded; "I told you I should rhapsodize."

Newman was silent a while, as if he were turning over his companion's words. "She is very good, eh?" he repeated at last.

"Divinely good!"

"Kind, charitable, gentle, generous?"

"Generosity itself; kindness double-distilled!"

"Is she clever?"

"She is the most intelligent woman I know. Try her, some day, with something difficult, and you will see."

"Is she fond of admiration?"

"Parbleu!" cried Bellegarde; "what woman is not?"

"Ah, when they are too fond of admiration they commit all kinds of follies to get it."

"I did not say she was too fond!" Bellegarde exclaimed. "Heaven forbid I should say anything so idiotic. She is not *too* anything! If I were to say she was ugly, I should not mean she was too ugly. She is fond of pleasing, and if you are pleased she is grateful. If you are not pleased, she lets it pass and thinks the worse neither of you nor of herself. I imagine, though, she hopes the saints in heaven are, for I am sure she is incapable of trying to please by any means of which they would disapprove."

"Is she grave or gay?" asked Newman.

"She is both; not alternately, for she is always the same. There is gravity in her gayety, and gayety in her gravity. But there is no reason why she should be particularly gay."

"Is she unhappy?"

"I won't say that, for unhappiness is according as one takes things, and Claire takes them according to some receipt communicated to her by the Blessed Virgin in a vision. To be unhappy is to be disagreeable, which, for her, is out of the question. So she has arranged her circumstances so as to be happy in them."

"She is a philosopher," said Newman.

"No, she is simply a very nice woman."

"Her circumstances, at any rate, have been disagreeable?"

Bellegarde hesitated a moment—a thing he very rarely did. "Oh, my dear fellow, if I go into the history of my family I shall give you more than you bargain for."

"No, on the contrary, I bargain for that," said Newman.

"We shall have to appoint a special séance, then, beginning early. Suffice it for the present that Claire has not slept on roses. She made at eighteen a marriage that was expected to be brilliant, but that turned out like a lamp that goes out; all smoke and bad smell. M. de Cintré was sixty years old, and an odious old gentleman. He lived, however, but a short time, and after his death his family pounced upon his money, brought a lawsuit against his widow, and pushed things very hard. Their case was a good one, for M. de Cintré, who had been trustee for some of his relatives, appeared to have been guilty of some very irregular practices. In the course of the suit some revelations were made as to his private history which my sister found so displeasing that she ceased to defend herself and washed her hands of the property. This required some pluck, for she was between two fires, her husband's family opposing her and her own family forcing her. My mother and my brother wished her to cleave to what they regarded as her rights. But she resisted firmly, and at last bought her freedom—obtained my mother's assent to dropping the suit at the price of a promise."

"What was the promise?"

"To do anything else, for the next ten years, that was asked of her—anything, that is, but marry."

"She had disliked her husband very much?"

"No one knows how much!"

"The marriage had been made in your horrible French way," Newman continued, "made by the two families, without her having any voice?"

"It was a chapter for a novel. She saw M. de Cintré for the first time a month before the wedding, after everything, to the minutest detail, had been arranged. She turned white when she looked at him, and white she remained till her wedding-day. The evening before the ceremony she swooned away, and she spent the whole night in sobs. My mother sat holding her two hands, and my brother walked up and down the room. I declared it was revolting and told my sister publicly that if she would refuse, downright, I would stand by her. I was told to go about my business, and she became Comtesse de Cintré."

"Your brother," said Newman, reflectively, "must be a very nice young man."

"He is very nice, though he is not young. He is upward of fifty; fifteen years my senior. He has been a father to my sister and me. He is a very remarkable man; he has the best manners in France. He is extremely clever; indeed he is very learned. He is writing a history of The Princesses of France Who Never Married." This was said by Bellegarde with extreme gravity, looking straight at Newman, and with an eye that betokened no mental reservation; or that, at least, almost betokened none.

Newman perhaps discovered there what little there was, for he presently said, "You don't love your brother."

"I beg your pardon," said Bellegarde, ceremoniously; "well-bred people always love their brothers."

"Well, I don't love him, then!" Newman answered.

"Wait till you know him!" rejoined Bellegarde, and this time he smiled.

"Is your mother also very remarkable?" Newman asked, after a pause.

"For my mother," said Bellegarde, now with intense gravity, "I have the highest admiration. She is a very extraordinary woman. You cannot approach her without perceiving it."

"She is the daughter, I believe, of an English nobleman."

"Of the Earl of St. Dunstan's."

"Is the Earl of St. Dunstan's a very old family?"

"So-so; the sixteenth century. It is on my father's side that we go back—back, back, back. The family antiquaries themselves lose breath. At last they stop, panting and fanning themselves, somewhere in the ninth century, under Charlemagne. That is where we begin."

"There is no mistake about it?" said Newman.

"I'm sure I hope not. We have been mistaken at least for several centuries."

"And you have always married into old families?"

"As a rule; though in so long a stretch of time there have been some exceptions. Three or four Bellegardes, in the seventeenth and eighteenth centuries, took wives out of the bourgeoisie—married lawyers' daughters."

"A lawyer's daughter; that's very bad, is it?" asked Newman.

"Horrible! one of us, in the middle ages, did better: he married a beggar-maid, like King Cophetua. That was really better; it was like marrying a bird or a monkey; one did n't have to think about her family at all. Our women have always done well; they have never even gone into the *petite noblesse*. There is, I believe, not a case on record of a misalliance among the women."

Newman turned this over a while, and then at last he said,

"You offered, the first time you came to see me, to render me any service you could. I told you that some time I would mention something you might do. Do you remember?"

"Remember? I have been counting the hours."

"Very well; here 's your chance. Do what you can to make your sister think well of me."

Bellegarde stared, with a smile. "Why, I 'm sure she thinks as well of you as possible, already."

"An opinion founded on seeing me three or four times? That is putting me off with very little. I want something more. I have been thinking of it a good deal, and at last I have decided to tell you. I should like very much to marry Madame de Cintré."

Bellegarde had been looking at him with quickened expectancy, and with the smile with which he had greeted Newman's allusion to his promised request. At this last announcement he continued to gaze; but his smile went through two or three curious phases. It felt, apparently, a momentary impulse to broaden; but this it immediately checked. Then it remained for some instants taking counsel with itself, at the end of which it decreed a retreat. It slowly effaced itself and left a look of seriousness modified by the desire not to be rude. Extreme surprise had come into the Count Valentin's face; but he had reflected that it would be uncivil to leave it there. And yet, what the deuce was he to do with it? He got up, in his agitation, and stood before the chimney-piece, still looking at Newman. He was a longer time thinking what to say than one would have expected.

"If you can't render me the service I ask," said Newman, "say it out!"

"Let me hear it again, distinctly," said Bellegarde. "It 's very important, you know. I shall plead your cause with my sister, because you want—you want to marry her? That 's it, eh?"

"Oh, I don't say plead my cause, exactly; I shall try and do that myself. But say a good word for me, now and then—let her know that you think well of me."

At this, Bellegarde gave a little light laugh.

"What I want chiefly, after all," Newman went on, "is just to let you know what I have in mind. I suppose that is what you expect, is n't it? I want to do what is customary over here. If there is any thing particular to be done, let me know and I will do it. I would n't for the world approach Madame de Cintré without all the proper forms. If I ought to go and tell your mother, why I will go and tell her. I will go and tell your brother, even. I will go and tell any one you please. As I don't know any one else, I begin by telling you. But that, if it is a social obligation, is a pleasure as well."

"Yes, I see—I see," said Bellegarde, lightly stroking his chin. "You have a very right feeling about it, but I 'm glad you have begun with me." He paused, hesitated, and then turned away and walked slowly the length of the room. Newman got up and stood leaning against the mantel-shelf, with his hands in his pockets, watching Bellegarde's promenade. The young Frenchman came back and stopped in front of him. "I give it up," he said; "I will not pretend I am not surprised. I am—hugely! *Ouf!* It 's a relief."

"That sort of news is always a surprise," said Newman. "No matter what you have done, people are never prepared. But if you are so surprised, I hope at least you are pleased."

"Come!" said Bellegarde. "I am going to be tremendously frank. I don't know whether I am pleased or horrified."

"If you are pleased, I shall be glad," said Newman, "and I shall be—encouraged. If you are horrified, I shall be sorry, but I shall not be discouraged. You must make the best of it."

"That is quite right—that is your only possible attitude. You are perfectly serious?"

"Am I a Frenchman, that I should not be?" asked Newman. "But why is it, by the bye, that you should be horrified?"

Bellegarde raised his hand to the back of his head and rubbed his hair quickly up and down, thrusting out the tip of his tongue as he did so. "Why, you are not noble, for instance," he said.

"The devil I am not!" exclaimed Newman.

"Oh," said Bellegarde a little more seriously, "I did not know you had a title."

"A title? What do you mean by a title?" asked Newman. "A count, a duke, a marquis? I don't know anything about that, I don't know who is and who is not. But I say I am noble. I don't exactly know what you mean by it, but it 's a fine word and a fine idea; I put in a claim to it."

"But what have you to show, my dear fellow; what proofs?"

"Anything you please! But you don't suppose I am going to undertake to prove that I am noble. It is for you to prove the contrary."

"That 's easily done. You have manufactured wash-tubs."

Newman stared a moment. "Therefore I am not noble? I don't see it. Tell me something I have *not* done—something I cannot do."

"You cannot marry a woman like Madame de Cintré for the asking."

"I believe you mean," said Newman slowly, "that I am not good enough."

"Brutally speaking—yes!"

Bellegarde had hesitated a moment, and while he hesitated Newman's attentive glance had grown somewhat eager. In answer to these last words he for a moment said nothing. He simply blushed a little. Then he raised his eyes to the ceiling and stood looking at one of the rosy cherubs that was painted upon it. "Of course I don't expect to marry any woman for the asking," he said at last; "I expect first to make myself acceptable to her. She must like me, to begin with. But that I am not good enough to make a trial is rather a surprise."

Bellegarde wore a look of mingled perplexity, sympathy, and amusement. "You should not hesitate, then, to go up to-morrow and ask a duchess to marry you?"

"Not if I thought she would suit me. But I am very fastidious; she might not at all."

Bellegarde's amusement began to prevail. "And you should be surprised if she refused you?"

Newman hesitated a moment. "It sounds conceited to say yes, but nevertheless I think I should. For I should make a very handsome offer."

"What would it be?"

"Everything she wishes. If I get hold of a woman that comes up to my standard, I shall think nothing too good for her. I have been a long time looking, and I find such women are rare. To combine the qualities I require seems to be difficult, but when the difficulty is vanquished it deserves a reward. My wife shall have a good position, and I am not afraid to say that I shall be a good husband."

"And these qualities that you require—what are they?"

"Goodness, beauty, intelligence, a fine education, personal elegance—everything, in a word, that makes a splendid woman."

"And noble birth, evidently," said Bellegarde.

"Oh, throw that in, by all means, if it 's there. The more the better!"

"And my sister seems to you to have all these things?"

"She is exactly what I have been looking for. She is my dream realized."

"And you would make her a very good husband?"

"That is what I wanted you to tell her."

Bellegarde laid his hand on his companion's arm a moment, looked at him with his head on one side, from head to foot, and then, with a loud laugh, and shaking the other hand in the air, turned away. He walked again the length of the room, and again he came back and stationed himself in front of Newman. "All this is very interesting—it is very curious. In what I said just now I was speaking, not for myself, but for my traditions, my superstitions. For myself, really, your proposal tickles me. It startled me at first, but the more I think of it the more I see in it. It 's no use attempting to explain anything; you won't understand me. After all, I don't see why you need; it 's no great loss."

"Oh, if there is anything more to explain, try it! I want to proceed with my eyes open. I will do my best to understand."

"No," said Bellegarde, "it 's disagreeable to me; I give it up. I liked you the first time I saw you, and I will abide by that. It would be quite odious for me to come talking to you as if I could patronize you. I have told you before that I envy you; *vous m'imposez*, as we say. I did n't know you much until within five minutes. So we will let things go, and I will say nothing to you that, if our positions were reversed, you would not say to me."

I do not know whether, in renouncing the mysterious opportunity to which he alluded, Bellegarde felt that he was doing something very generous. If so, he was not rewarded;

his generosity was not appreciated. Newman quite failed to recognize the young Frenchman's power to wound his feelings, and he had now no sense of escaping or coming off easily. He did not thank his companion even with a glance. "My eyes are open, though," he said, "so far as that you have practically told me that your family and your friends will turn up their noses at me. I have never thought much about the reasons that make it proper for people to turn up their noses, and so I can only decide the question off-hand. Looking at it in that way I can't see anything in it. I simply think, if you want to know, that I'm as good as the best. Who the best are, I don't pretend to say. I have never thought much about that either. To tell the truth, I have always had rather a good opinion of myself; a man who is successful can't help it. But I will admit that I was conceited. What I don't say yes to is that I don't stand high—as high as any one else. This is a line of speculation I should not have chosen, but you must remember you began it yourself. I should never have dreamed that I was on the defensive, or that I had to justify myself; but if your people will have it so, I will do my best."

"But you offered, a while ago, to make your court, as we say, to my mother and my brother."

"Damn it!" cried Newman, "I want to be polite."

"Good!" rejoined Bellegarde; "this will go far, it will be very entertaining. Excuse my speaking of it in that cold-blooded fashion, but the matter must, of necessity, be for me something of a spectacle. It's positively exciting. But apart from that I sympathize with you, and I shall be actor, so far as I can, as well as spectator. You are a capital fellow; I believe in you and I back you. The simple fact that you appreciate my sister will serve as the proof I was asking for. All men are equal—especially men of taste!"

"Do you think," asked Newman presently, "that Madame de Cintré is determined not to marry?"

"That is my impression. But that is not against you; it's for you to make her change her mind."

"I am afraid it will be hard," said Newman, gravely.

"I don't think it will be easy. In a general way I don't see why a widow should ever marry again. She has gained the benefits of matrimony—freedom and consideration—and she has got rid of the drawbacks. Why should she put her head into the noose again? Her usual motive is ambition: if a man can offer her a great position, make her a princess or an ambassadress, she may think the compensation sufficient."

"And—in that way—is Madame de Cintré ambitious?"

"Who knows?" said Bellegarde, with a profound shrug. "I don't pretend to say all that she is or all that she is not. I think she might be touched by the prospect of becoming the wife of a great man. But in a certain way, I believe, whatever she does will be the *improbable*. Don't be too confident, but don't absolutely doubt. Your best chance for success will be precisely in being, to her mind, unusual, unexpected, original. Don't try to be any one else; be simply yourself, out and out. Something or other can't fail to come of it; I am very curious to see what."

"I am much obliged to you for your advice," said Newman. "And," he added with a smile, "I am glad, for your sake, I am going to be so amusing."

"It will be more than amusing," said Bellegarde; "it will be inspiring. I look at it from my point of view, and you from yours. After all, anything for a change! And only yesterday I was yawning so as to dislocate my jaw, and declaring that there was nothing new under the sun! If it is n't new to see you come into the family as a suitor, I am very much mistaken. Let me say that, my dear fellow; I won't call it anything else, bad or good; I will simply call it *new*." And overcome with a sense of the novelty thus foreshadowed, Valentin de Bellegarde threw himself into a deep arm-chair before the fire, and, with a fixed, intense smile, seemed to read a vision of it in the flame of the logs. After a while he looked up. "Go ahead, my boy; you have my good wishes," he said. "But it is really a pity you don't understand me, that you don't know just what I am doing."

"Oh," said Newman, laughing, "don't do anything wrong. Leave me to myself, rather, or defy me, out and out. I would n't lay any load on your conscience."

Bellegarde sprang up again; he was evidently excited; there was a warmer spark even than usual in his eye. "You never will understand—you never will know," he said; "and if you succeed, and I turn out to have helped you, you will never be grateful, not as I shall deserve you should be. You will be an excellent fellow always, but you will not be grateful. But it does n't matter, for I shall get my own fun out of it." And he broke into an extravagant laugh. "You look puzzled," he added; "you look almost frightened."

"It *is* a pity," said Newman, "that I don't understand you. I shall lose some very good jokes."

"I told you, you remember, that we were very strange people," Bellegarde went on. "I give you warning again. We are! My mother is strange, my brother is strange, and I verily believe that I am stranger than either. You will even find my sister a little strange. Old trees have crooked branches, old houses have queer cracks, old races have odd secrets. Remember that we are eight hundred years old!"

"Very good," said Newman; "that 's the sort of thing I came to Europe for. You come into my programme."

"*Touchez-là*, then," said Bellegarde, putting out his hand. "It 's a bargain: I accept you; I espouse your cause. It 's because I like you, in a great measure; but that is not the only reason!" And he stood holding Newman's hand and looking at him askance.

"What is the other one?"

"I am in the Opposition. I dislike some one else."

"Your brother?" asked Newman, in his unmodulated voice.

Bellegarde laid his finger upon his lips with a whispered *hush!* "Old races have strange secrets!" he said. "Put yourself into motion, come and see my sister, and be assured of my sympathy!" And on this he took his leave.

Newman dropped into a chair before his fire, and sat a long time staring into the blaze.

Chapter IX

H E WENT TO SEE Madame de Cintré the next day, and
was informed by the servant that she was at home. He
passed as usual up the large, cold staircase and through a spacious vestibule above, where the walls seemed all composed
of small door panels, touched with long-faded gilding;
whence he was ushered into the sitting-room in which he had
already been received. It was empty, and the servant told him
that Madame la Comtesse would presently appear. He had
time, while he waited, to wonder whether Bellegarde had
seen his sister since the evening before, and whether in this
case he had spoken to her of their talk. In this case Madame
de Cintré's receiving him was an encouragement. He felt a
certain trepidation as he reflected that she might come in with
the knowledge of his supreme admiration and of the project
he had built upon it in her eyes; but the feeling was not disagreeable. Her face could wear no look that would make it
less beautiful, and he was sure beforehand that however she
might take the proposal he had in reserve, she would not take
it in scorn or in irony. He had a feeling that if she could only
read the bottom of his heart and measure the extent of his
good will toward her, she would be entirely kind.

She came in at last, after so long an interval that he wondered whether she had been hesitating. She smiled with her
usual frankness, and held out her hand; she looked at him
straight with her soft and luminous eyes, and said, without a
tremor in her voice, that she was glad to see him and that she
hoped he was well. He found in her what he had found before—that faint perfume of a personal shyness worn away by
contact with the world, but the more perceptible the more
closely you approached her. This lingering diffidence seemed
to give a peculiar value to what was definite and assured in
her manner; it made it seem like an accomplishment, a beautiful talent, something that one might compare to an exquisite
touch in a pianist. It was, in fact, Madame de Cintré's "authority," as they say of artists, that especially impressed and
fascinated Newman; he always came back to the feeling that
when he should complete himself by taking a wife, that was

the way he should like his wife to interpret him to the world. The only trouble, indeed, was that when the instrument was so perfect it seemed to interpose too much between you and the genius that used it. Madame de Cintré gave Newman the sense of an elaborate education, of her having passed through mysterious ceremonies and processes of culture in her youth, of her having been fashioned and made flexible to certain exalted social needs. All this, as I have affirmed, made her seem rare and precious—a very expensive article, as he would have said, and one which a man with an ambition to have everything about him of the best would find it highly agreeable to possess. But looking at the matter with an eye to private felicity, Newman wondered where, in so exquisite a compound, nature and art showed their dividing line. Where did the special intention separate from the habit of good manners? Where did urbanity end and sincerity begin? Newman asked himself these questions even while he stood ready to accept the admired object in all its complexity; he felt that he could do so in profound security, and examine its mechanism afterwards, at leisure.

"I am very glad to find you alone," he said. "You know I have never had such good luck before."

"But you have seemed before very well contented with your luck," said Madame de Cintré. "You have sat and watched my visitors with an air of quiet amusement. What have you thought of them?"

"Oh, I have thought the ladies were very elegant and very graceful, and wonderfully quick at repartee. But what I have chiefly thought has been that they only helped me to admire you." This was not gallantry on Newman's part—an art in which he was quite unversed. It was simply the instinct of the practical man, who had quite made up his mind what he wanted, and was now beginning to take active steps to obtain it.

Madame de Cintré started slightly, and raised her eyebrows; she had evidently not expected so fervid a compliment. "Oh, in that case," she said with a laugh, "your finding me alone is not good luck for me. I hope some one will come in quickly."

"I hope not," said Newman. "I have something particular to say to you. Have you seen your brother?"

"Yes; I saw him an hour ago."

"Did he tell you that he had seen me last night?"

"He said so."

"And did he tell you what we had talked about?"

Madame de Cintré hesitated a moment. As Newman asked these questions she had grown a little pale, as if she regarded what was coming as necessary, but not as agreeable. "Did you give him a message to me?" she asked.

"It was not exactly a message—I asked him to render me a service."

"The service was to sing your praises, was it not?" And she accompanied this question with a little smile, as if to make it easier to herself.

"Yes, that is what it really amounts to," said Newman. "Did he sing my praises?"

"He spoke very well of you. But when I know that it was by your special request, of course I must take his eulogy with a grain of salt."

"Oh, that makes no difference," said Newman. "Your brother would not have spoken well of me unless he believed what he was saying. He is too honest for that."

"Are you very deep?" said Madame de Cintré. "Are you trying to please me by praising my brother. I confess it is a good way."

"For me, any way that succeeds will be good. I will praise your brother all day, if that will help me. He is a noble little fellow. He has made me feel, in promising to do what he can to help me, that I can depend upon him."

"Don't make too much of that," said Madame de Cintré. "He can help you very little."

"Of course I must work my way myself. I know that very well; I only want a chance to. In consenting to see me, after what he told you, you almost seem to be giving me a chance."

"I am seeing you," said Madame de Cintré, slowly and gravely, "because I promised my brother I would."

"Blessings on your brother's head!" cried Newman. "What I told him last evening was this: that I admired you more than any woman I had ever seen, and that I should like immensely to make you my wife." He uttered these words with great directness and firmness, and without any sense of confusion. He was full of his idea, he had completely mastered it, and he seemed to look down on Madame de Cintré, with all her gathered elegance, from the height of his bracing good conscience. It is probable that this particular tone and manner were the very best he could have hit upon. Yet the light, just visibly forced smile with which his companion had listened to him died away, and she sat looking at him with her lips parted and her face as solemn as a tragic mask. There was evidently something very painful to her in the scene to which he was subjecting her, and yet her impatience of it found no angry voice. Newman wondered whether he was hurting her; he could not imagine why the liberal devotion he meant to express should be disagreeable. He got up and stood before her, leaning one hand on the chimney-piece. "I know I have seen you very little to say this," he said, "so little that it may make what I say seem disrespectful. That is my misfortune! I could have said it the first time I saw you. Really, I had seen you before; I had seen you in imagination; you seemed almost an old friend. So what I say is not mere gallantry and compliments and nonsense—I can't talk that way, I don't know how, and I would n't, to you, if I could. It 's as serious as such words can be. I feel as if I knew you and knew what a beautiful, admirable woman you are. I shall know better, perhaps, some day, but I have a general notion now. You are just the woman I have been looking for, except that you are far more perfect. I won't make any protestations and vows, but you can trust me. It is very soon, I know, to say all this; it is almost offensive. But why not gain time if one can? And if you want time to reflect—of course you do—the sooner you begin, the better for me. I don't know what you think of me; but there is no great mystery about me; you see what I am. Your brother told me that my antecedents and occupations were against me; that your family stands, somehow, on a higher level than I do. That is an idea which of course I don't understand and don't accept. But you don't care anything about that. I can assure you that I am a very solid fellow, and that if I give my mind to it I can arrange things so that in a very few years I shall not need to waste time in explaining who I am and what I am. You will decide for yourself whether you like me or not. What there is you see before you. I honestly believe I have no hidden vices or nasty tricks. I am kind, kind, kind! Everything that a man can give a woman I will give you. I have a large fortune, a very large fortune; some day, if you will allow me, I will go into details. If you want brilliancy, everything in the way of brilliancy that money can give you, you shall have. And as regards anything you may give up, don't take for granted too much that its place cannot be filled. Leave that to me; I 'll take care of you; I shall know what you need. Energy and ingenuity can arrange everything. I 'm a strong man! There, I have said what I had on my heart! It was better to get it off. I am very sorry if it 's disagreeable to you; but think how much better it is that things should be clear. Don't answer me now, if you don't wish it. Think about it; think about it as slowly as you please. Of course I have n't said, I can't say, half I mean, especially about my admiration for you. But take a favorable view of me; it will only be just."

During this speech, the longest that Newman had ever made, Madame de Cintré kept her gaze fixed upon him, and it expanded at the last into a sort of fascinated stare. When he ceased speaking she lowered her eyes and sat for some moments looking down and straight before her. Then she slowly rose to her feet, and a pair of exceptionally keen eyes would have perceived that she was trembling a little in the movement. She still looked extremely serious. "I am very much obliged to you for your offer," she said. "It seems very strange, but I am glad you spoke without waiting any longer. It is better the subject should be dismissed. I appreciate all you say; you do me great honor. But I have decided not to marry."

"Oh, don't say that!" cried Newman, in a tone absolutely *naïf* from its pleading and caressing cadence. She had turned away, and it made her stop a moment with her back to him. "Think better of that. You are too young, too beautiful, too much made to be happy and to make others happy. If you are afraid of losing your freedom, I can assure you that this freedom here, this life you now lead, is a dreary bondage to what I will offer you. You shall do things that I don't think you have ever thought of. I will take you to live anywhere in the wide world that you propose. Are you unhappy? You give me a feeling that you *are* unhappy. You have no right to be, or to be made so. Let me come in and put an end to it."

Madame de Cintré stood there a moment longer, looking away from him. If she was touched by the way he spoke, the thing was conceivable. His voice, always very mild and interrogative, gradually became as soft and as tenderly argumentative as if he had been talking to a much-loved child. He stood watching her, and she presently turned round again, but this time she did not look at him, and she spoke in a quietness in which there was a visible trace of effort.

"There are a great many reasons why I should not marry," she said, "more than I can explain to you. As for my happiness, I am very happy. Your offer seems strange to me, for more reasons also than I can say. Of course you have a perfect right to make it. But I cannot accept it—it is impossible. Please never speak of this matter again. If you cannot promise me this, I must ask you not to come back."

"Why is it impossible?" Newman demanded. "You may think it is, at first, without its really being so. I did n't expect you to be pleased at first, but I do believe that if you will think of it a good while, you may be satisfied."

"I don't know you," said Madame de Cintré. "Think how little I know you."

"Very little, of course, and therefore I don't ask for your ultimatum on the spot. I only ask you not to say no, and to let me hope. I will wait as long as you desire. Meanwhile you can see more of me and know me better, look at me as a possible husband—as a candidate—and make up your mind."

Something was going on, rapidly, in Madame de Cintré's thoughts; she was weighing a question there, beneath Newman's eyes, weighing it and deciding it. "From the moment I don't very respectfully beg you to leave the house and never return," she said, "I listen to you, I seem to give you hope. I *have* listened to you—against my judgment. It is because you are eloquent. If I had been told this morning that I should consent to consider you as a possible husband, I should have thought my informant a little crazy. I *am* listening to you, you see!" And she threw her hands out for a moment and let them drop with a gesture in which there was just the slightest expression of appealing weakness.

"Well, as far as saying goes, I have said everything," said Newman. "I believe in you, without restriction, and I think all the good of you that it is possible to think of a human creature. I firmly believe that in marrying me you will be *safe*. As I said just now," he went on with a smile, "I have no bad ways. I can *do* so much for you. And if you are afraid that I am not what you have been accustomed to, not refined and delicate and punctilious, you may easily carry that too far. I *am* delicate! You shall see!"

Madame de Cintré walked some distance away, and paused before a great plant, an azalea, which was flourishing in a porcelain tub before her window. She plucked off one of the flowers and, twisting it in her fingers, retraced her steps. Then she sat down in silence, and her attitude seemed to be a consent that Newman should say more.

"Why should you say it is impossible you should marry?" he continued. "The only thing that could make it really impossible would be your being already married. Is it because you have been unhappy in marriage? That is all the more reason! Is it because your family exert a pressure upon you, interfere with you, annoy you? That is still another reason; you ought to be perfectly free, and marriage will make you so. I don't say anything against your family—understand that!" added Newman, with an eagerness which might have made a perspicacious observer smile. "Whatever way you feel toward them is the right way, and anything that you should wish me to do to make myself agreeable to them I will do as well as I know how. Depend upon that!"

Madame de Cintré rose again and came toward the fireplace, near which Newman was standing. The expression of pain and embarrassment had passed out of her face, and it was illuminated with something which, this time at least, Newman need not have been perplexed whether to attribute to habit or to intention, to art or to nature. She had the air of a woman who has stepped across the frontier of friendship and, looking around her, finds the region vast. A certain checked and controlled exaltation seemed mingled with the usual level radiance of her glance. "I will not refuse to see you again," she said, "because much of what you have said has given me pleasure. But I will see you only on this condition: that you say nothing more in the same way for a long time."

"For how long?"

"For six months. It must be a solemn promise."

"Very well; I promise."

"Good-by, then," she said, and extended her hand.

He held it a moment, as if he were going to say something more. But he only looked at her; then he took his departure.

That evening, on the Boulevard, he met Valentin de Bellegarde. After they had exchanged greetings, Newman told him that he had seen Madame de Cintré a few hours before.

"I know it," said Bellegarde. "I dined in the Rue de l'Université." And then, for some moments, both men were silent. Newman wished to ask Bellegarde what visible impression his visit had made, and the Count Valentin had a question of his own. Bellegarde spoke first.

"It 's none of my business, but what the deuce did you say to my sister?"

"I am willing to tell you," said Newman, "that I made her an offer of marriage."

"Already!" And the young man gave a whistle. " 'Time is money!' Is that what you say in America? And Madame de Cintré?" he added, with an interrogative inflection.

"She did not accept my offer."

"She could n't, you know, in that way."

"But I 'm to see her again," said Newman.

"Oh, the strangeness of woman!" exclaimed Bellegarde. Then he stopped, and held Newman off at arms'-length. "I look at you with respect!" he exclaimed. "You have achieved what we call a personal success! Immediately, now, I must present you to my brother."

"Whenever you please!" said Newman.

Chapter X

NEWMAN continued to see his friends the Tristrams with
a good deal of frequency, though if you had listened to
Mrs. Tristram's account of the matter you would have supposed that they had been cynically repudiated for the sake of
grander acquaintance. "We were all very well so long as we
had no rivals—we were better than nothing. But now that
you have become the fashion, and have your pick every day
of three invitations to dinner, we are tossed into the corner.
I am sure it is very good of you to come and see us once a
month; I wonder you don't send us your cards in an enve-
lope. When you do, pray have them with black edges; it will
be for the death of my last illusion." It was in this incisive
strain that Mrs. Tristram moralized over Newman's so-called
neglect, which was in reality a most exemplary constancy. Of
course she was joking, but there was always something ironical in her jokes, as there was always something jocular in her
gravity.

"I know no better proof that I have treated you very well,"
Newman had said, "than the fact that you make so free with
my character. Familiarity breeds contempt; I have made myself too cheap. If I had a little proper pride I would stay away
a while, and when you asked me to dinner say I was going to
the Princess Borealska's. But I have not any pride where my
pleasure is concerned, and to keep you in the humor to see
me—if you must see me only to call me bad names—I will
agree to anything you choose; I will admit that I am the biggest snob in Paris." Newman, in fact, had declined an invitation personally given by the Princess Borealska, an inquiring
Polish lady to whom he had been presented, on the ground
that on that particular day he always dined at Mrs. Tristram's;
and it was only a tenderly perverse theory of his hostess of
the Avenue d'Iéna that he was faithless to his early friendships. She needed the theory to explain a certain moral irritation by which she was often visited; though, if this
explanation was unsound, a deeper analyst than I must give
the right one. Having launched our hero upon the current
which was bearing him so rapidly along, she appeared but

half-pleased at its swiftness. She had succeeded too well; she had played her game too cleverly and she wished to mix up the cards. Newman had told her, in due season, that her friend was "satisfactory." The epithet was not romantic, but Mrs. Tristram had no difficulty in perceiving that, in essentials, the feeling which lay beneath it was. Indeed, the mild, expansive brevity with which it was uttered, and a certain look, at once appealing and inscrutable, that issued from Newman's half-closed eyes as he leaned his head against the back of his chair, seemed to her the most eloquent attestation of a mature sentiment that she had ever encountered. Newman was, according to the French phrase, only abounding in her own sense, but his temperate raptures exerted a singular effect upon that ardor which she herself had so freely manifested a few months before. She now seemed inclined to take a purely critical view of Madame de Cintré, and wished to have it understood that she did not in the least answer for her being a compendium of all the virtues. "No woman was ever so good as that woman seems," she said. "Remember what Shakespeare calls Desdemona; 'a supersubtle Venetian.' Madame de Cintré is a supersubtle Parisian. She is a charming woman, and she has five hundred merits; but you had better keep that in mind." Was Mrs. Tristram simply finding out that she was jealous of her dear friend on the other side of the Seine, and that in undertaking to provide Newman with an ideal wife she had counted too much on her own disinterestedness? We may be permitted to doubt it. The inconsistent little lady of the Avenue d'Iéna had an insuperable need of changing her place, intellectually. She had a lively imagination, and she was capable, at certain times, of imagining the direct reverse of her most cherished beliefs, with a vividness more intense than that of conviction. She got tired of thinking aright; but there was no serious harm in it, as she got equally tired of thinking wrong. In the midst of her mysterious perversities she had admirable flashes of justice. One of these occurred when Newman related to her that he had made a formal proposal to Madame de Cintré. He repeated in a few words what he had said, and in a great many what she had answered. Mrs. Tristram listened with extreme interest.

"But after all," said Newman, "there is nothing to congratulate me upon. It is not a triumph."

"I beg your pardon," said Mrs. Tristram; "it is a great triumph. It is a great triumph that she did not silence you at the first word, and request you never to speak to her again."

"I don't see that," observed Newman.

"Of course you don't; Heaven forbid you should! When I told you to go your own way and do what came into your head, I had no idea you would go over the ground so fast. I never dreamed you would offer yourself after five or six morning-calls. As yet, what had you done to make her like you? You had simply sat—not very straight—and stared at her. But she does like you."

"That remains to be seen."

"No, that is proved. What will come of it remains to be seen. That you should propose to marry her, without more ado, could never have come into her head. You can form very little idea of what passed through her mind as you spoke; if she ever really marries you, the affair will be characterized by the usual justice of all human things towards women. You will think you take generous views of her; but you will never begin to know through what a strange sea of feeling she passed before she accepted you. As she stood there in front of you the other day, she plunged into it. She said 'Why not?' to something which, a few hours earlier, had been inconceivable. She turned about on a thousand gathered prejudices and traditions as on a pivot, and looked where she had never looked hitherto. When I think of it—when I think of Claire de Cintré and all that she represents, there seems to me something very fine in it. When I recommended you to try your fortune with her I of course thought well of you, and in spite of your sins I think so still. But I confess I don't see quite what you are and what you have done, to make such a woman do this sort of thing for you."

"Oh, there is something very fine in it!" said Newman with a laugh, repeating her words. He took an extreme satisfaction in hearing that there was something fine in it. He had not the least doubt of it himself, but he had already begun to value the world's admiration of Madame de Cintré, as adding to the prospective glory of possession.

It was immediately after this conversation that Valentin de Bellegarde came to conduct his friend to the Rue de l'Université to present him to the other members of his family. "You are already introduced," he said, "and you have begun to be talked about. My sister has mentioned your successive visits to my mother, and it was an accident that my mother was present at none of them. I have spoken of you as an American of immense wealth, and the best fellow in the world, who is looking for something very superior in the way of a wife."

"Do you suppose," asked Newman, "that Madame de Cintré has related to your mother the last conversation I had with her?"

"I am very certain that she has not; she will keep her own counsel. Meanwhile you must make your way with the rest of the family. Thus much is known about you: you have made a great fortune in trade, you are a little eccentric, and you frankly admire our dear Claire. My sister-in-law, whom you remember seeing in Madame de Cintré's sitting-room, took, it appears, a fancy to you; she has described you as having *beaucoup de cachet*. My mother, therefore, is curious to see you."

"She expects to laugh at me, eh?" said Newman.

"She never laughs. If she does not like you, don't hope to purchase favor by being amusing. Take warning by me!"

This conversation took place in the evening, and half an hour later Valentin ushered his companion into an apartment of the house of the Rue de l'Université into which he had not yet penetrated, the salon of the dowager Marquise de Bellegarde. It was a vast, high room, with elaborate and ponderous mouldings, painted a whitish gray, along the upper portion of the walls and the ceiling; with a great deal of faded and carefully repaired tapestry in the doorways and chair-backs; a Turkey carpet in light colors, still soft and deep, in spite of great antiquity, on the floor; and portraits of each of Madame de Bellegarde's children, at the age of ten, suspended against an old screen of red silk. The room was illumined, exactly enough for conversation, by half a dozen candles, placed in odd corners, at a great distance apart. In a deep arm-chair, near the fire, sat an old lady in black; at the other

end of the room another person was seated at the piano, playing a very expressive waltz. In this latter person Newman recognized the young Marquise de Bellegarde.

Valentin presented his friend, and Newman walked up to
the old lady by the fire and shook hands with her. He received a rapid impression of a white, delicate, aged face, with
a high forehead, a small mouth, and a pair of cold blue eyes
which had kept much of the freshness of youth. Madame de
Bellegarde looked hard at him, and returned his hand-shake
with a sort of British positiveness which reminded him that
she was the daughter of the Earl of St. Dunstan's. Her daughter-in-law stopped playing and gave him an agreeable smile.
Newman sat down and looked about him, while Valentin
went and kissed the hand of the young marquise.

"I ought to have seen you before," said Madame de Bellegarde. "You have paid several visits to my daughter."

"Oh, yes," said Newman, smiling; "Madame de Cintré and
I are old friends by this time."

"You have gone fast," said Madame de Bellegarde.

"Not so fast as I should like," said Newman, bravely.

"Oh, you are very ambitious," answered the old lady.

"Yes, I confess I am," said Newman, smiling.

Madame de Bellegarde looked at him with her cold fine
eyes, and he returned her gaze, reflecting that she was a possible adversary and trying to take her measure. Their eyes remained in contact for some moments. Then Madame de
Bellegarde looked away, and without smiling, "I am very ambitious, too," she said.

Newman felt that taking her measure was not easy; she was
a formidable, inscrutable little woman. She resembled her
daughter, and yet she was utterly unlike her. The coloring in
Madame de Cintré was the same, and the high delicacy of her
brow and nose was hereditary. But her face was a larger and
freer copy, and her mouth in especial a happy divergence
from that conservative orifice, a little pair of lips at once
plump and pinched, that looked, when closed, as if they could
not open wider than to swallow a gooseberry or to emit an
"Oh, dear, no!" which probably had been thought to give the
finishing touch to the aristocratic prettiness of the Lady
Emmeline Atheling as represented, forty years before, in sev-

eral Books of Beauty. Madame de Cintré's face had, to Newman's eye, a range of expression as delightfully vast as the
wind-streaked, cloud-flecked distance on a Western prairie.
But her mother's white, intense, respectable countenance,
with its formal gaze, and its circumscribed smile, suggested a
document signed and sealed; a thing of parchment, ink, and
ruled lines. "She is a woman of conventions and proprieties,"
he said to himself as he looked at her; "her world is the world
of things immutably decreed. But how she is at home in it,
and what a paradise she finds it! She walks about in it as if it
were a blooming park, a Garden of Eden; and when she sees
'This is genteel,' or 'This is improper,' written on a mile-stone
she stops ecstatically, as if she were listening to a nightingale
or smelling a rose." Madame de Bellegarde wore a little black
velvet hood tied under her chin, and she was wrapped in an
old black cashmere shawl.

"You are an American?" she said presently. "I have seen
several Americans."

"There are several in Paris," said Newman jocosely.

"Oh, really?" said Madame de Bellegarde. "It was in England I saw these, or somewhere else; not in Paris. I think it
must have been in the Pyrenees, many years ago. I am told
your ladies are very pretty. One of these ladies was very
pretty! such a wonderful complexion! She presented me a
note of introduction from some one—I forget whom—and
she sent with it a note of her own. I kept her letter a long
time afterwards, it was so strangely expressed. I used to know
some of the phrases by heart. But I have forgotten them now,
it is so many years ago. Since then I have seen no more Americans. I think my daughter-in-law has; she is a great gad-
about; she sees every one."

At this the younger lady came rustling forward, pinching
in a very slender waist, and casting idly preoccupied glances
over the front of her dress, which was apparently designed
for a ball. She was, in a singular way, at once ugly and pretty;
she had protuberant eyes, and lips that were strangely red.
She reminded Newman of his friend, Mademoiselle Nioche;
this was what that much-obstructed young lady would have
liked to be. Valentin de Bellegarde walked behind her at a

distance, hopping about to keep off the far-spreading train of her dress.

"You ought to show more of your shoulders behind," he said very gravely. "You might as well wear a standing ruff as such a dress as that."

The young woman turned her back to the mirror over the chimney-piece, and glanced behind her, to verify Valentin's assertion. The mirror descended low, and yet it reflected nothing but a large unclad flesh surface. The young marquise put her hands behind her and gave a downward pull to the waist of her dress. "Like that, you mean?" she asked.

"That is a little better," said Bellegarde in the same tone, "but it leaves a good deal to be desired."

"Oh, I never go to extremes," said his sister-in-law. And then, turning to Madame de Bellegarde, "What were you calling me just now, madame?"

"I called you a gad-about," said the old lady. "But I might call you something else, too."

"A gad-about? What an ugly word! What does it mean?"

"A very beautiful person," Newman ventured to say, seeing that it was in French.

"That is a pretty compliment but a bad translation," said the young marquise. And then, looking at him a moment, "Do you dance?"

"Not a step."

"You are very wrong," she said, simply. And with another look at her back in the mirror she turned away.

"Do you like Paris?" asked the old lady, who was apparently wondering what was the proper way to talk to an American.

"Yes, rather," said Newman. And then he added, with a friendly intonation, "Don't you?"

"I can't say I know it. I know my house—I know my friends—I don't know Paris."

"Oh, you lose a great deal," said Newman, sympathetically.

Madame de Bellegarde stared; it was presumably the first time she had been condoled with on her losses.

"I am content with what I have," she said with dignity.

Newman's eyes, at this moment, were wandering round the

room, which struck him as rather sad and shabby; passing from the high casements, with their small, thickly-framed panes, to the sallow tints of two or three portraits in pastel, of the last century, which hung between them. He ought, obviously, to have answered that the contentment of his hostess was quite natural—she had a great deal; but the idea did not occur to him during the pause of some moments which followed.

"Well, my dear mother," said Valentin, coming and leaning against the chimney-piece, "what do you think of my dear friend Newman? Is he not the excellent fellow I told you?"

"My acquaintance with Mr. Newman has not gone very far," said Madame de Bellegarde. "I can as yet only appreciate his great politeness."

"My mother is a great judge of these matters," said Valentin to Newman. "If you have satisfied her, it is a triumph."

"I hope I shall satisfy you, some day," said Newman, looking at the old lady. "I have done nothing yet."

"You must not listen to my son; he will bring you into trouble. He is a sad scatterbrain."

"Oh, I like him—I like him," said Newman, genially.

"He amuses you, eh?"

"Yes, perfectly."

"Do you hear that, Valentin?" said Madame de Bellegarde. "You amuse Mr. Newman."

"Perhaps we shall all come to that!" Valentin exclaimed.

"You must see my other son," said Madame de Bellegarde. "He is much better than this one. But he will not amuse you."

"I don't know—I don't know!" murmured Valentin, reflectively. "But we shall very soon see. Here comes *Monsieur mon frère*."

The door had just opened to give ingress to a gentleman who stepped forward and whose face Newman remembered. He had been the author of our hero's discomfiture the first time he tried to present himself to Madame de Cintré. Valentin de Bellegarde went to meet his brother, looked at him a moment, and then, taking him by the arm, led him up to Newman.

"This is my excellent friend Mr. Newman," he said very blandly. "You must know him."

"I am delighted to know Mr. Newman," said the marquis with a low bow, but without offering his hand.

"He is the old woman at second-hand," Newman said to himself, as he returned M. de Bellegarde's greeting. And this was the starting-point of a speculative theory, in his mind, that the late marquis had been a very amiable foreigner, with an inclination to take life easily and a sense that it was difficult for the husband of the stilted little lady by the fire to do so. But if he had taken little comfort in his wife he had taken much in his two younger children, who were after his own heart, while Madame de Bellegarde had paired with her eldest-born.

"My brother has spoken to me of you," said M. de Bellegarde; "and as you are also acquainted with my sister, it was time we should meet." He turned to his mother and gallantly bent over her hand, touching it with his lips, and then he assumed an attitude before the chimney-piece. With his long, lean face, his high-bridged nose and his small, opaque eye he looked much like an Englishman. His whiskers were fair and glossy, and he had a large dimple, of unmistakably British origin, in the middle of his handsome chin. He was "distinguished" to the tips of his polished nails, and there was not a movement of his fine, perpendicular person that was not noble and majestic. Newman had never yet been confronted with such an incarnation of the art of taking one's self seriously; he felt a sort of impulse to step backward, as you do to get a view of a great façade.

"Urbain," said young Madame de Bellegarde, who had apparently been waiting for her husband to take her to her ball, "I call your attention to the fact that I am dressed."

"That is a good idea," murmured Valentin.

"I am at your orders, my dear friend," said M. de Bellegarde. "Only, you must allow me first the pleasure of a little conversation with Mr. Newman."

"Oh, if you are going to a party, don't let me keep you," objected Newman. "I am very sure we shall meet again. Indeed, if you would like to converse with me I will gladly name an hour." He was eager to make it known that he would readily answer all questions and satisfy all exactions.

M. de Bellegarde stood in a well-balanced position before

the fire, caressing one of his fair whiskers with one of his white hands, and looking at Newman, half askance, with eyes from which a particular ray of observation made its way through a general meaningless smile. "It is very kind of you to make such an offer," he said. "If I am not mistaken, your occupations are such as to make your time precious. You are in—a—as we say, *dans les affaires*."

"In business, you mean? Oh no, I have thrown business overboard for the present. I am 'loafing,' as *we* say. My time is quite my own."

"Ah, you are taking a holiday," rejoined M. de Bellegarde. " 'Loafing.' Yes, I have heard that expression."

"Mr. Newman is American," said Madame de Bellegarde.

"My brother is a great ethnologist," said Valentin.

"An ethnologist?" said Newman. "Ah, you collect negroes' skulls, and that sort of thing."

The marquis looked hard at his brother, and began to caress his other whisker. Then, turning to Newman, with sustained urbanity, "You are traveling for your pleasure?" he asked.

"Oh, I am knocking about to pick up one thing and another. Of course I get a good deal of pleasure out of it."

"What especially interests you?" inquired the marquis.

"Well, everything interests me," said Newman. "I am not particular. Manufactures are what I care most about."

"That has been your specialty?"

"I can't say I have had any specialty. My specialty has been to make the largest possible fortune in the shortest possible time." Newman made this last remark very deliberately; he wished to open the way, if it were necessary, to an authoritative statement of his means.

M. de Bellegarde laughed agreeably. "I hope you have succeeded," he said.

"Yes, I have made a fortune in a reasonable time. I am not so old, you see."

"Paris is a very good place to spend a fortune. I wish you great enjoyment of yours." And M. de Bellegarde drew forth his gloves and began to put them on.

Newman for a few moments watched him sliding his white hands into the white kid, and as he did so his feelings took a singular turn. M. de Bellegarde's good wishes seemed to descend out of the white expanse of his sublime serenity with the soft, scattered movement of a shower of snow-flakes. Yet Newman was not irritated; he did not feel that he was being patronized; he was conscious of no especial impulse to introduce a discord into so noble a harmony. Only he felt himself suddenly in personal contact with the forces with which his friend Valentin had told him that he would have to contend, and he became sensible of their intensity. He wished to make some answering manifestation, to stretch himself out at his own length, to sound a note at the uttermost end of *his* scale. It must be added that if this impulse was not vicious or malicious, it was by no means void of humorous expectancy. Newman was quite as ready to give play to that loosely-adjusted smile of his, if his hosts should happen to be shocked, as he was far from deliberately planning to shock them.

"Paris is a very good place for idle people," he said, "or it is a very good place if your family has been settled here for a long time, and you have made acquaintances and got your relations round you; or if you have got a good big house like this, and a wife and children and mother and sister, and everything comfortable. I don't like that way of living all in rooms next door to each other. But I am not an idler. I try to be, but I can't manage it; it goes against the grain. My business habits are too deep-seated. Then, I have n't any house to call my own, or anything in the way of a family. My sisters are five thousand miles away, my mother died when I was a youngster, and I have n't any wife; I wish I had! So, you see, I don't exactly know what to do with myself. I am not fond of books, as you are, sir, and I get tired of dining out and going to the opera. I miss my business activity. You see, I began to earn my living when I was almost a baby, and until a few months ago I have never had my hand off the plow. Elegant leisure comes hard."

This speech was followed by a profound silence of some moments, on the part of Newman's entertainers. Valentin stood looking at him fixedly, with his hands in his pockets, and then he slowly, with a half-sidling motion, went out of the room. The marquis continued to draw on his gloves and to smile benignantly.

"You began to earn your living when you were a mere baby?" said the marquise.

"Hardly more—a small boy."

"You say you are not fond of books," said M. de Bellegarde; "but you must do yourself the justice to remember that your studies were interrupted early."

"That is very true; on my tenth birthday I stopped going to school. I thought it was a grand way to keep it. But I picked up some information afterwards," said Newman, reassuringly.

"You have some sisters?" asked old Madame de Bellegarde.

"Yes, two sisters. Splendid women!"

"I hope that for them the hardships of life commenced less early."

"They married very early, if you call that a hardship, as girls do in our Western country. One of them is married to the owner of the largest india-rubber house in the West."

"Ah, you make houses also of india-rubber?" inquired the marquise.

"You can stretch them as your family increases," said young Madame de Bellegarde, who was muffling herself in a long white shawl.

Newman indulged in a burst of hilarity, and explained that the house in which his brother-in-law lived was a large wooden structure, but that he manufactured and sold india-rubber on a colossal scale.

"My children have some little india-rubber shoes which they put on when they go to play in the Tuileries in damp weather," said the young marquise. "I wonder whether your brother-in-law made them."

"Very likely," said Newman; "if he did, you may be very sure they are well made."

"Well, you must not be discouraged," said M. de Bellegarde, with vague urbanity.

"Oh, I don't mean to be. I have a project which gives me plenty to think about, and that is an occupation." And then Newman was silent a moment, hesitating, yet thinking rapidly; he wished to make his point, and yet to do so forced him to speak out in a way that was disagreeable to him. Nevertheless he continued, addressing himself to old Madame de Bellegarde, "I will tell you my project; perhaps you can help me. I want to take a wife."

"It is a very good project, but I am no matchmaker," said the old lady.

Newman looked at her an instant, and then, with perfect sincerity, "I should have thought you were," he declared.

Madame de Bellegarde appeared to think him too sincere. She murmured something sharply in French, and fixed her eyes on her son. At this moment the door of the room was thrown open, and with a rapid step Valentin reappeared.

"I have a message for you," he said to his sister-in-law. "Claire bids me to request you not to start for your ball. She will go with you."

"Claire will go with us!" cried the young marquise. "En voilà, du nouveau!"

"She has changed her mind; she decided half an hour ago, and she is sticking the last diamond into her hair," said Valentin.

"What has taken possession of my daughter?" demanded Madame de Bellegarde, sternly. "She has not been into the world these three years. Does she take such a step at half an hour's notice, and without consulting me?"

"She consulted me, dear mother, five minutes since," said Valentin, "and I told her that such a beautiful woman—she is beautiful, you will see—had no right to bury herself alive."

"You should have referred Claire to her mother, my brother," said M. de Bellegarde, in French. "This is very strange."

"I refer her to the whole company!" said Valentin. "Here she comes!" And he went to the open door, met Madame de Cintré on the threshold, took her by the hand, and led her into the room. She was dressed in white; but a long blue cloak, which hung almost to her feet, was fastened across her shoulders by a silver clasp. She had tossed it back, however, and her long white arms were uncovered. In her dense, fair hair there glittered a dozen diamonds. She looked serious and, Newman thought, rather pale; but she glanced round her, and, when she saw him, smiled and put out her hand. He thought her tremendously handsome. He had a chance to look at her full in the face, for she stood a moment in the centre of the room, hesitating, apparently, what she should do, without meeting his eyes. Then she went up to her mother, who sat in her deep chair by the fire, looking at Madame de Cintré almost fiercely. With her back turned to the others, Madame de Cintré held her cloak apart to show her dress.

"What do you think of me?" she asked.

"I think you are audacious," said the marquise. "It was but three days ago, when I asked you, as a particular favor to myself, to go to the Duchess de Lusignan's, that you told me you were going nowhere and that one must be consistent. Is this your consistency? Why should you distinguish Madame Robineau? Who is it you wish to please to-night?"

"I wish to please myself, dear mother," said Madame de Cintré. And she bent over and kissed the old lady.

"I don't like surprises, my sister," said Urbain de Bellegarde; "especially when one is on the point of entering a drawing-room."

Newman at this juncture felt inspired to speak. "Oh, if you are going into a room with Madame de Cintré, you need n't be afraid of being noticed yourself!"

M. de Bellegarde turned to his sister with a smile too intense to be easy. "I hope you appreciate a compliment that is paid you at your brother's expense," he said. "Come, come, madam." And offering Madame de Cintré his arm he led her rapidly out of the room. Valentin rendered the same service to young Madame de Bellegarde, who had apparently been reflecting on the fact that the ball dress of her sister-in-law was much less brilliant than her own, and yet had failed to derive absolute comfort from the reflection. With a farewell smile she sought the complement of her consolation in the eyes of the American visitor, and perceiving in them a certain mysterious brilliancy, it is not improbable that she may have flattered herself she had found it.

Newman, left alone with old Madame de Bellegarde, stood before her a few moments in silence. "Your daughter is very beautiful," he said at last.

"She is very strange," said Madame de Bellegarde.

"I am glad to hear it," Newman rejoined, smiling. "It makes me hope."

"Hope what?"

"That she will consent, some day, to marry me."

The old lady slowly rose to her feet. "That really is your project, then?"

"Yes; will you favor it?"

"Favor it?" Madame de Bellegarde looked at him a moment and then shook her head. "No!" she said, softly.

"Will you suffer it, then? Will you let it pass?"

"You don't know what you ask. I am a very proud and meddlesome old woman."

"Well, I am very rich," said Newman.

Madame de Bellegarde fixed her eyes on the floor, and Newman thought it probable she was weighing the reasons in favor of resenting the brutality of this remark. But at last, looking up, she said simply, "How rich?"

Newman expressed his income in a round number which had the magnificent sound that large aggregations of dollars put on when they are translated into francs. He added a few remarks of a financial character, which completed a sufficiently striking presentment of his resources.

Madame de Bellegarde listened in silence. "You are very frank," she said finally. "I will be the same. I would rather favor you, on the whole, than suffer you. It will be easier."

"I am thankful for any terms," said Newman. "But, for the present, you have suffered me long enough. Good night!" And he took his leave.

Chapter XI

NEWMAN, on his return to Paris, had not resumed the study of French conversation with M. Nioche; he found that he had too many other uses for his time. M. Nioche, however, came to see him very promptly, having learned his whereabouts by a mysterious process to which his patron never obtained the key. The shrunken little capitalist repeated his visit more than once. He seemed oppressed by a humiliating sense of having been overpaid, and wished apparently to redeem his debt by the offer of grammatical and statistical information in small installments. He wore the same decently melancholy aspect as a few months before; a few months more or less of brushing could make little difference in the antique lustre of his coat and hat. But the poor old man's spirit was a trifle more threadbare; it seemed to have received some hard rubs during the summer. Newman inquired with interest about Mademoiselle Noémie; and M. Nioche, at first, for answer, simply looked at him in lachrymose silence.

"Don't ask me, sir," he said at last. "I sit and watch her, but I can do nothing."

"Do you mean that she misconducts herself?"

"I don't know, I am sure. I can't follow her. I don't understand her. She has something in her head; I don't know what she is trying to do. She is too deep for me."

"Does she continue to go to the Louvre? Has she made any of those copies for me?"

"She goes to the Louvre, but I see nothing of the copies. She has something on her easel; I suppose it is one of the pictures you ordered. Such a magnificent order ought to give her fairy-fingers. But she is not in earnest. I can't say anything to her; I am afraid of her. One evening, last summer, when I took her to walk in the Champs Élysées, she said some things to me that frightened me."

"What were they?"

"Excuse an unhappy father from telling you," said M. Nioche, unfolding his calico pocket-handkerchief.

Newman promised himself to pay Mademoiselle Noémie another visit at the Louvre. He was curious about the progress of his copies, but it must be added that he was still more curious about the progress of the young lady herself. He went one afternoon to the great museum, and wandered through several of the rooms in fruitless quest of her. He was bending his steps to the long hall of the Italian masters, when suddenly he found himself face to face with Valentin de Bellegarde. The young Frenchman greeted him with ardor, and assured him that he was a godsend. He himself was in the worst of humors and he wanted some one to contradict.

"In a bad humor among all these beautiful things?" said Newman. "I thought you were so fond of pictures, especially the old black ones. There are two or three here that ought to keep you in spirits."

"Oh, to-day," answered Valentin, "I am not in a mood for pictures, and the more beautiful they are the less I like them. Their great staring eyes and fixed positions irritate me. I feel as if I were at some big, dull party, in a room full of people I should n't wish to speak to. What should I care for their beauty? It 's a bore, and, worse still, it 's a reproach. I have a great many *ennuis*; I feel vicious."

"If the Louvre has so little comfort for you, why in the world did you come here?" Newman asked.

"That is one of my ennuis. I came to meet my cousin—a dreadful English cousin, a member of my mother's family— who is in Paris for a week for her husband, and who wishes me to point out the 'principal beauties.' Imagine a woman who wears a green crape bonnet in December and has straps sticking out of the ankles of her interminable boots! My mother begged I would do something to oblige them. I have undertaken to play *valet de place* this afternoon. They were to have met me here at two o'clock, and I have been waiting for them twenty minutes. Why does n't she arrive? She has at least a pair of feet to carry her. I don't know whether to be furious at their playing me false, or delighted to have escaped them."

"I think in your place I would be furious," said Newman, "because they may arrive yet, and then your fury will still be of use to you. Whereas if you were delighted and they were afterwards to turn up, you might not know what to do with your delight."

"You give me excellent advice, and I already feel better. I will be furious; I will let them go to the deuce and I myself will go with you—unless by chance you too have a rendezvous."

"It is not exactly a rendezvous," said Newman. "But I have in fact come to see a person, not a picture."

"A woman, presumably?"

"A young lady."

"Well," said Valentin, "I hope for you with all my heart that she is not clothed in green tulle and that her feet are not too much out of focus."

"I don't know much about her feet, but she has very pretty hands."

Valentin gave a sigh. "And on that assurance I must part with you?"

"I am not certain of finding my young lady," said Newman, "and I am not quite prepared to lose your company on the chance. It does not strike me as particularly desirable to introduce you to her, and yet I should rather like to have your opinion of her."

"Is she pretty?"

"I guess you will think so."

Bellegarde passed his arm into that of his companion. "Conduct me to her on the instant! I should be ashamed to make a pretty woman wait for my verdict."

Newman suffered himself to be gently propelled in the direction in which he had been walking, but his step was not rapid. He was turning something over in his mind. The two men passed into the long gallery of the Italian masters, and Newman, after having scanned for a moment its brilliant vista, turned aside into the smaller apartment devoted to the same school, on the left. It contained very few persons, but at the farther end of it sat Mademoiselle Nioche, before her easel. She was not at work; her palette and brushes had been laid down beside her, her hands were folded in her lap, and she was leaning back in her chair and looking intently at two ladies on the other side of the hall, who, with their backs turned to her, had stopped before one of the pictures. These ladies were apparently persons of high fashion; they were dressed with great splendor, and their long silken trains and furbelows were spread over the polished floor. It was at their dresses Mademoiselle Noémie was looking, though what she was thinking of I am unable to say. I hazard the supposition that she was saying to herself that to be able to drag such a train over a polished floor was a felicity worth any price. Her reflections, at any rate, were disturbed by the advent of Newman and his companion. She glanced at them quickly, and then, coloring a little, rose and stood before her easel.

"I came here on purpose to see you," said Newman in his bad French, offering to shake hands. And then, like a good American, he introduced Valentin formally: "Allow me to make you acquainted with the Comte Valentin de Bellegarde."

Valentin made a bow which must have seemed to Mademoiselle Noémie quite in harmony with the impressiveness of his title, but the graceful brevity of her own response made no concession to underbred surprise. She turned to Newman, putting up her hands to her hair and smoothing its delicately-felt roughness. Then, rapidly, she turned the canvas that was on her easel over upon its face. "You have not forgotten me?" she asked.

"I shall never forget you," said Newman. "You may be sure of that."

"Oh," said the young girl, "there are a great many different ways of remembering a person." And she looked straight at Valentin de Bellegarde, who was looking at her as a gentleman may when a "verdict" is expected of him.

"Have you painted anything for me?" said Newman. "Have you been industrious?"

"No, I have done nothing." And taking up her palette, she began to mix her colors at hazard.

"But your father tells me you have come here constantly."

"I have nowhere else to go! Here, all summer, it was cool, at least."

"Being here, then," said Newman, "you might have tried something."

"I told you before," she answered, softly, "that I don't know how to paint."

"But you have something charming on your easel, now," said Valentin, "if you would only let me see it."

She spread out her two hands, with the fingers expanded, over the back of the canvas—those hands which Newman had called pretty, and which, in spite of several paint-stains, Valentin could now admire. "My painting is not charming," she said.

"It is the only thing about you that is not, then, mademoiselle," quoth Valentin, gallantly.

She took up her little canvas and silently passed it to him. He looked at it, and in a moment she said, "I am sure you are a judge."

"Yes," he answered, "I am."

"You know, then, that that is very bad."

"Mon Dieu," said Valentin, shrugging his shoulders, "let us distinguish."

"You know that I ought not to attempt to paint," the young girl continued.

"Frankly, then, mademoiselle, I think you ought not."

She began to look at the dresses of the two splendid ladies again—a point on which, having risked one conjecture, I think I may risk another. While she was looking at the ladies she was seeing Valentin de Bellegarde. He, at all events, was seeing her. He put down the roughly-besmeared canvas and addressed a little click with his tongue, accompanied by an elevation of the eyebrows, to Newman.

"Where have you been all these months?" asked Mademoiselle Noémie of our hero. "You took those great journeys, you amused yourself well?"

"Oh, yes," said Newman, "I amused myself well enough."

"I am very glad," said Mademoiselle Noémie with extreme gentleness; and she began to dabble in her colors again. She was singularly pretty, with the look of serious sympathy that she threw into her face.

Valentin took advantage of her downcast eyes to telegraph again to his companion. He renewed his mysterious physiognomical play, making at the same time a rapid tremulous movement in the air with his fingers. He was evidently finding Mademoiselle Noémie extremely interesting; the blue devils had departed, leaving the field clear.

"Tell me something about your travels," murmured the young girl.

"Oh, I went to Switzerland,—to Geneva and Zermatt and Zürich and all those places you know; and down to Venice, and all through Germany, and down the Rhine, and into Holland and Belgium—the regular round. How do you say that, in French—the regular round?" Newman asked of Valentin.

Mademoiselle Nioche fixed her eyes an instant on Bellegarde, and then with a little smile, "I don't understand monsieur," she said, "when he says so much at once. Would you be so good as to translate?"

"I would rather talk to you out of my own head," Valentin declared.

"No," said Newman, gravely, still in his bad French, "you must not talk to Mademoiselle Nioche, because you say discouraging things. You ought to tell her to work, to persevere."

"And we French, mademoiselle," said Valentin, "are accused of being false flatterers!"

"I don't want any flattery, I want only the truth. But I know the truth."

"All I say is that I suspect there are some things that you can do better than paint," said Valentin.

"I know the truth—I know the truth," Mademoiselle Noémie repeated. And, dipping a brush into a clot of red paint, she drew a great horizontal daub across her unfinished picture.

"What is that?" asked Newman.

Without answering, she drew another long crimson daub, in a vertical direction, down the middle of her canvas, and so, in a moment, completed the rough indication of a cross. "It is the sign of the truth," she said at last.

The two men looked at each other, and Valentin indulged in another flash of physiognomical eloquence. "You have spoiled your picture," said Newman.

"I know that very well. It was the only thing to do with it. I had sat looking at it all day without touching it. I had begun to hate it. It seemed to me something was going to happen."

"I like it better that way than as it was before," said Valentin. "Now it is more interesting. It tells a story. Is it for sale, mademoiselle?"

"Everything I have is for sale," said Mademoiselle Noémie. "How much is this thing?"

"Ten thousand francs," said the young girl, without a smile.

"Everything that Mademoiselle Nioche may do at present is mine in advance," said Newman. "It makes part of an order I gave her some months ago. So you can't have this."

"Monsieur will lose nothing by it," said the young girl, looking at Valentin. And she began to put up her utensils.

"I shall have gained a charming memory," said Valentin. "You are going away? your day is over?"

"My father is coming to fetch me," said Mademoiselle Noémie.

She had hardly spoken when, through the door behind her, which opens on one of the great white stone staircases of the Louvre, M. Nioche made his appearance. He came in with his usual even, patient shuffle, and he made a low salute to the two gentlemen who were standing before his daughter's easel. Newman shook his hand with muscular friendliness, and Valentin returned his greeting with extreme deference. While the old man stood waiting for Noémie to make a parcel of her implements, he let his mild, oblique gaze hover toward Bellegarde, who was watching Mademoiselle Noémie put on her bonnet and mantle. Valentin was at no pains to disguise his scrutiny. He looked at a pretty girl as he would have listened to a piece of music. Attention, in each case, was simple good manners. M. Nioche at last took his daughter's paint-box in one hand and the bedaubed canvas, after giving it a solemn, puzzled stare, in the other, and led the way to the door. Mademoiselle Noémie made the young men the salute of a duchess, and followed her father.

"Well," said Newman, "what do you think of her?"

"She is very remarkable. *Diable, diable, diable!*" repeated M. de Bellegarde, reflectively; "she is very remarkable."

"I am afraid she is a sad little adventuress," said Newman.

"Not a little one—a great one. She has the material." And Valentin began to walk away slowly, looking vaguely at the pictures on the walls, with a thoughtful illumination in his eye. Nothing could have appealed to his imagination more than the possible adventures of a young lady endowed with the "material" of Mademoiselle Nioche. "She is very interesting," he went on. "She is a beautiful type."

"A beautiful type? What the deuce do you mean?" asked Newman.

"I mean from the artistic point of view. She is an artist,—outside of her painting, which obviously is execrable."

"But she is not beautiful. I don't even think her very pretty."

"She is quite pretty enough for her purposes, and it is a face and figure on which everything tells. If she were prettier she would be less intelligent, and her intelligence is half of her charm."

"In what way," asked Newman, who was much amused at his companion's immediate philosophization of Mademoiselle Nioche, "does her intelligence strike you as so remarkable?"

"She has taken the measure of life, and she has determined to *be* something—to succeed at any cost. Her painting, of course, is a mere trick to gain time. She is waiting for her chance; she wishes to launch herself, and to do it well. She knows her Paris. She is one of fifty thousand, so far as the mere ambition goes; but I am very sure that in the way of resolution and capacity she is a rarity. And in one gift—perfect heartlessness—I will warrant she is unsurpassed. She has not as much heart as will go on the point of a needle. That is an immense virtue. Yes, she is one of the celebrities of the future."

"Heaven help us!" said Newman, "how far the artistic point of view may take a man! But in this case I must request that you don't let it take you too far. You have learned a wonderful deal about Mademoiselle Noémie in a quarter of an hour. Let that suffice; don't follow up your researches."

"My dear fellow," cried Bellegarde with warmth, "I hope I have too good manners to intrude."

"You are not intruding. The girl is nothing to me. In fact, I rather dislike her. But I like her poor old father, and for his sake I beg you to abstain from any attempt to verify your theories."

"For the sake of that seedy old gentleman who came to fetch her?" demanded Valentin, stopping short. And on Newman's assenting, "Ah no, ah no," he went on with a smile.

"You are quite wrong, my dear fellow; you need n't mind him."

"I verily believe that you are accusing the poor gentleman of being capable of rejoicing in his daughter's dishonor."

"Voyons," said Valentin; "who is he? what is he?"

"He is what he looks like: as poor as a rat, but very high-toned."

"Exactly. I noticed him perfectly; be sure I do him justice. He has had losses, *des malheurs*, as we say. He is very low-spirited, and his daughter is too much for him. He is the pink of respectability, and he has sixty years of honesty on his back. All this I perfectly appreciate. But I know my fellow-men and my fellow-Parisians, and I will make a bargain with you." Newman gave ear to his bargain and he went on. "He would rather his daughter were a good girl than a bad one, but if the worst comes to the worst, the old man will not do what Virginius did. Success justifies everything. If Mademoiselle Noémie makes a figure, her papa will feel—well, we will call it relieved. And she will make a figure. The old gentleman's future is assured."

"I don't know what Virginius did, but M. Nioche will shoot Miss Noémie," said Newman. "After that, I suppose his future will be assured in some snug prison."

"I am not a cynic; I am simply an observer," Valentin rejoined. "Mademoiselle Noémie interests me; she is extremely remarkable. If there is a good reason, in honor or decency, for dismissing her from my thoughts forever, I am perfectly willing to do it. Your estimate of the papa's sensibilities is a good reason until it is invalidated. I promise you not to look at the young girl again until you tell me that you have changed your mind about the papa. When he has given distinct proof of being a philosopher, you will raise your interdict. Do you agree to that?"

"Do you mean to bribe him?"

"Oh, you admit, then, that he is bribable? No, he would ask too much, and it would not be exactly fair. I mean simply to wait. You will continue, I suppose, to see this interesting couple, and you will give me the news yourself."

"Well," said Newman, "if the old man turns out a humbug, you may do what you please. I wash my hands of the matter."

"For the girl herself, you may be at rest. I don't know what harm she may do to me, but I certainly can't hurt her."

"It seems to me," said Newman, "that you are very well matched. You are both hard cases, and M. Nioche and I, I believe, are the only virtuous men to be found in Paris."

Soon after this M. de Bellegarde, in punishment for his levity, received a stern poke in the back from a pointed instrument. Turning quickly round he found the weapon to be a parasol wielded by a lady in a green gauze bonnet. Valentin's English cousins had been drifting about unpiloted, and evidently deemed that they had a grievance. Newman left him to their mercies, but with a boundless faith in his power to plead his cause.

Chapter XII

THREE DAYS after his introduction to the family of Madame de Cintré, Newman, coming in toward evening, found upon his table the card of the Marquis de Bellegarde. On the following day he received a note informing him that the Marquise de Bellegarde would be grateful for the honor of his company at dinner.

He went, of course, though he had to break another engagement to do it. He was ushered into the room in which Madame de Bellegarde had received him before, and here he found his venerable hostess, surrounded by her entire family. The room was lighted only by the crackling fire, which illumined the very small pink slippers of a lady who, seated in a low chair, was stretching out her toes before it. This lady was the younger Madame de Bellegarde. Madame de Cintré was seated at the other end of the room, holding a little girl against her knee, the child of her brother Urbain, to whom she was apparently relating a wonderful story. Valentin was sitting on a puff, close to his sister-in-law, into whose ear he was certainly distilling the finest nonsense. The marquis was stationed before the fire, with his head erect and his hands behind him, in an attitude of formal expectancy.

Old Madame de Bellegarde stood up to give Newman her greeting, and there was that in the way she did so which seemed to measure narrowly the extent of her condescension. "We are all alone, you see; we have asked no one else," she said, austerely.

"I am very glad you did n't; this is much more sociable," said Newman. "Good evening, sir," and he offered his hand to the marquis.

M. de Bellegarde was affable, but in spite of his dignity he was restless. He began to pace up and down the room, he looked out of the long windows, he took up books and laid them down again. Young Madame de Bellegarde gave Newman her hand without moving and without looking at him.

"You may think that is coldness," explained Valentin; "but it is not, it is warmth. It shows she is treating you as an intimate. Now she detests me, and yet she is always looking at me."

660

"No wonder I detest you if I am always looking at you!" cried the lady. "If Mr. Newman does not like my way of shaking hands, I will do it again."

But this charming privilege was lost upon our hero, who was already making his way across the room to Madame de Cintré. She looked at him as she shook hands, but she went on with the story she was telling her little niece. She had only two or three phrases to add, but they were apparently of great moment. She deepened her voice, smiling as she did so, and the little girl gazed at her with round eyes.

"But in the end the young prince married the beautiful Florabella," said Madame de Cintré, "and carried her off to live with him in the Land of the Pink Sky. There she was so happy that she forgot all her troubles, and went out to drive every day of her life in an ivory coach drawn by five hundred white mice. Poor Florabella," she explained to Newman, "had suffered terribly."

"She had had nothing to eat for six months," said little Blanche.

"Yes, but when the six months were over, she had a plum-cake as big as that ottoman," said Madame de Cintré. "That quite set her up again."

"What a checkered career!" said Newman. "Are you very fond of children?" He was certain that she was, but he wished to make her say it.

"I like to talk with them," she answered; "we can talk with them so much more seriously than with grown persons. That is great nonsense that I have been telling Blanche, but it is a great deal more serious than most of what we say in society."

"I wish you would talk to me, then, as if I were Blanche's age," said Newman, laughing. "Were you happy at your ball, the other night?"

"Ecstatically!"

"Now you are talking the nonsense that we talk in society," said Newman. "I don't believe that."

"It was my own fault if I was not happy. The ball was very pretty, and every one very amiable."

"It was on your conscience," said Newman, "that you had annoyed your mother and your brother."

Madame de Cintré looked at him a moment without answering. "That is true," she replied at last. "I had undertaken more than I could carry out. I have very little courage; I am not a heroine." She said this with a certain soft emphasis; but then, changing her tone, "I could never have gone through the sufferings of the beautiful Florabella," she added, "not even for her prospective rewards."

Dinner was announced, and Newman betook himself to the side of old Madame de Bellegarde. The dining-room, at the end of a cold corridor, was vast and sombre; the dinner was simple and delicately excellent. Newman wondered whether Madame de Cintré had had something to do with ordering the repast, and greatly hoped she had. Once seated at table, with the various members of the ancient house of Bellegarde around him, he asked himself the meaning of his position. Was the old lady responding to his advances? Did the fact that he was a solitary guest augment his credit or diminish it? Were they ashamed to show him to other people, or did they wish to give him a sign of sudden adoption into their last reserve of favor? Newman was on his guard; he was watchful and conjectural; and yet at the same time he was vaguely indifferent. Whether they gave him a long rope or a short one he was there now, and Madame de Cintré was opposite to him. She had a tall candlestick on each side of her; she would sit there for the next hour, and that was enough. The dinner was extremely solemn and measured; he wondered whether this was always the state of things in "old families." Madame de Bellegarde held her head very high, and fixed her eyes, which looked peculiarly sharp in her little, finely-wrinkled white face, very intently upon the table-service. The marquis appeared to have decided that the fine arts offered a safe subject of conversation, as not leading to startling personal revelations. Every now and then, having learned from Newman that he had been through the museums of Europe, he uttered some polished aphorism upon the flesh-tints of Rubens and the good taste of Sansovino. His manners seemed to indicate a fine, nervous dread that something disagreeable might happen if the atmosphere were not purified by allusions of a thoroughly superior cast. "What under the sun is the man afraid of?" Newman asked himself. "Does he think I am going to offer to swap jack-knives with him?" It was useless to shut his eyes to the fact that the marquis was profoundly disagreeable to him. He had never been a man of strong personal aversions; his nerves had not been at the mercy of the mystical qualities of his neighbors. But here was a man towards whom he was irresistibly in opposition; a man of forms and phrases and postures; a man full of possible impertinences and treacheries. M. de Bellegarde made him feel as if he were standing bare-footed on a marble floor; and yet, to gain his desire, Newman felt perfectly able to stand. He wondered what Madame de Cintré thought of his being accepted, if accepted it was. There was no judging from her face, which expressed simply the desire to be gracious in a manner which should require as little explicit recognition as possible. Young Madame de Bellegarde had always the same manners; she was always preoccupied, distracted, listening to everything and hearing nothing, looking at her dress, her rings, her finger-nails, seeming rather bored, and yet puzzling you to decide what was her ideal of social diversion. Newman was enlightened on this point later. Even Valentin did not quite seem master of his wits; his vivacity was fitful and forced, yet Newman observed that in the lapses of his talk he appeared excited. His eyes had an intenser spark than usual. The effect of all this was that Newman, for the first time in his life, was not himself; that he measured his movements, and counted his words, and resolved that if the occasion demanded that he should appear to have swallowed a ramrod, he would meet the emergency.

After dinner M. de Bellegarde proposed to his guest that they should go into the smoking-room, and he led the way toward a small, somewhat musty apartment, the walls of which were ornamented with old hangings of stamped leather and trophies of rusty arms. Newman refused a cigar, but he established himself upon one of the divans, while the marquis puffed his own weed before the fire-place, and Valentin sat looking through the light fumes of a cigarette from one to the other.

"I can't keep quiet any longer," said Valentin, at last. "I must tell you the news and congratulate you. My brother seems unable to come to the point; he revolves around his announcement like the priest around the altar. You are accepted as a candidate for the hand of our sister."

"Valentin, be a little proper!" murmured the marquis, with a look of the most delicate irritation contracting the bridge of his high nose.

"There has been a family council," the young man continued; "my mother and Urbain have put their heads together, and even my testimony has not been altogether excluded. My mother and the marquis sat at a table covered with green cloth; my sister-in-law and I were on a bench against the wall. It was like a committee at the Corps Législatif. We were called up, one after the other, to testify. We spoke of you very handsomely. Madame de Bellegarde said that if she had not been told who you were, she would have taken you for a duke—an American duke, the Duke of California. I said that I could warrant you grateful for the smallest favors—modest, humble, unassuming. I was sure that you would know your own place, always, and never give us occasion to remind you of certain differences. After all, you could n't help it if you were not a duke. There were none in your country; but if there had been, it was certain that, smart and active as you are, you would have got the pick of the titles. At this point I was ordered to sit down, but I think I made an impression in your favor."

M. de Bellegarde looked at his brother with dangerous coldness, and gave a smile as thin as the edge of a knife. Then he removed a spark of cigar-ash from the sleeve of his coat; he fixed his eyes for a while on the cornice of the room, and at last he inserted one of his white hands into the breast of his waistcoat. "I must apologize to you for the deplorable levity of my brother," he said, "and I must notify you that this is probably not the last time that his want of tact will cause you serious embarrassment."

"No, I confess I have no tact," said Valentin. "Is your embarrassment really painful, Newman? The marquis will put you right again; his own touch is deliciously delicate."

"Valentin, I am sorry to say," the marquis continued, "has never possessed the tone, the manner, that belong to a young man in his position. It has been a great affliction to his mother, who is very fond of the old traditions. But you must remember that he speaks for no one but himself."

"Oh, I don't mind him, sir," said Newman, good-humoredly. "I know what he amounts to."

"In the good old times," said Valentin, "marquises and counts used to have their appointed fools and jesters, to crack jokes for them. Nowadays we see a great strapping democrat keeping a count about him to play the fool. It's a good situation, but I certainly am very degenerate."

M. de Bellegarde fixed his eyes for some time on the floor. "My mother informed me," he said presently, "of the announcement that you made to her the other evening."

"That I desired to marry your sister?" said Newman.

"That you wished to arrange a marriage," said the marquis, slowly, "with my sister, the Comtesse de Cintré. The proposal was serious, and required, on my mother's part, a great deal of reflection. She naturally took me into her counsels, and I gave my most zealous attention to the subject. There was a great deal to be considered; more than you appear to imagine. We have viewed the question on all its faces, we have weighed one thing against another. Our conclusion has been that we favor your suit. My mother has desired me to inform you of our decision. She will have the honor of saying a few words to you on the subject, herself. Meanwhile, by us, the heads of the family, you are accepted."

Newman got up and came nearer to the marquis. "You will do nothing to hinder me, and all you can to help me, eh?"

"I will recommend my sister to accept you."

Newman passed his hand over his face, and pressed it for a moment upon his eyes. This promise had a great sound, and yet the pleasure he took in it was embittered by his having to stand there so and receive his passport from M. de Bellegarde. The idea of having this gentleman mixed up with his wooing and wedding was more and more disagreeable to him. But Newman had resolved to go through the mill, as he imaged it, and he would not cry out at the first turn of the wheel. He was silent a while, and then he said, with a certain dryness which Valentin told him afterwards had a very grand air, "I am much obliged to you."

"I take note of the promise," said Valentin, "I register the vow."

M. de Bellegarde began to gaze at the cornice again; he apparently had something more to say. "I must do my mother the justice," he resumed, "I must do myself the justice, to say that our decision was not easy. Such an arrangement was not what we had expected. The idea that my sister should marry a gentleman—ah—in business, was something of a novelty."

"So I told you, you know," said Valentin raising his finger at Newman.

"The novelty has not quite worn away, I confess," the marquis went on; "perhaps it never will, entirely. But possibly that is not altogether to be regretted," and he gave his thin smile again. "It may be that the time has come when we should make some concession to novelty. There had been no novelties in our house for a great many years. I made the observation to my mother, and she did me the honor to admit that it was worthy of attention."

"My dear brother," interrupted Valentin, "is not your memory just here leading you the least bit astray? Our mother is, I may say, distinguished for her small respect for abstract reasoning. Are you very sure that she replied to your striking proposition in the gracious manner you describe? You know how terribly incisive she is sometimes. Did n't she, rather, do you the honor to say, 'A fiddlestick for your phrases! There are better reasons than that'?"

"Other reasons were discussed," said the marquis, without looking at Valentin, but with an audible tremor in his voice; "some of them possibly were better. We are conservative, Mr. Newman, but we are not also bigots. We judged the matter liberally. We have no doubt that everything will be comfortable."

Newman had stood listening to these remarks with his arms folded and his eyes fastened upon M. de Bellegarde. "Comfortable?" he said, with a sort of grim flatness of intonation. "Why should n't we be comfortable? If you are not, it will be your own fault; I have everything to make *me* so."

"My brother means that with the lapse of time you may get used to the change"—and Valentin paused, to light another cigarette.

"What change?" asked Newman in the same tone.

"Urbain," said Valentin, very gravely, "I am afraid that Mr. Newman does not quite realize the change. We ought to insist upon that."

"My brother goes too far," said M. de Bellegarde. "It is his fatal want of tact again. It is my mother's wish, and mine, that no such allusions should be made. Pray never make them yourself. We prefer to assume that the person accepted as the possible husband of my sister is one of ourselves, and that he should have no explanations to make. With a little discretion on both sides, everything, I think, will be easy. That is exactly what I wished to say—that we quite understand what we have undertaken, and that you may depend upon our adhering to our resolution."

Valentin shook his hands in the air and then buried his face in them. "I have less tact than I might have, no doubt; but oh, my brother, if you knew what you yourself were saying!" And he went off into a long laugh.

M. de Bellegarde's face flushed a little, but he held his head higher, as if to repudiate this concession to vulgar perturbability. "I am sure you understand me," he said to Newman.

"Oh no, I don't understand you at all," said Newman. "But you need n't mind that. I don't care. In fact, I think I had better not understand you. I might not like it. That would n't suit me at all, you know. I want to marry your sister, that 's all; to do it as quickly as possible, and to find fault with nothing. I don't care how I do it. I am not marrying you, you know, sir. I have got my leave, and that is all I want."

"You had better receive the last word from my mother," said the marquis.

"Very good; I will go and get it," said Newman; and he prepared to return to the drawing-room.

M. de Bellegarde made a motion for him to pass first, and when Newman had gone out he shut himself into the room with Valentin. Newman had been a trifle bewildered by the audacious irony of the younger brother, and he had not needed its aid to point the moral of M. de Bellegarde's transcendent patronage. He had wit enough to appreciate the force of that civility which consists in calling your attention to the impertinences it spares you. But he had felt warmly the delicate sympathy with himself that underlay Valentin's fraternal irreverence, and he was most unwilling that his friend should pay a tax upon it. He paused a moment in the corridor, after he had gone a few steps, expecting to hear the resonance of M. de Bellegarde's displeasure; but he detected only a perfect stillness. The stillness itself seemed a trifle portentous; he reflected however that he had no right to stand listening, and he made his way back to the salon. In his absence several persons had come in. They were scattered about the room in groups, two or three of them having passed into a small boudoir, next to the drawing-room, which had now been lighted and opened. Old Madame de Bellegarde was in her place by the fire, talking to a very old gentleman in a wig and a profuse white neckcloth of the fashion of 1820. Madame de Cintré was bending a listening head to the historic confidences of an old lady who was presumably the wife of the old gentleman in the neckcloth, an old lady in a red satin dress and an ermine cape, who wore across her forehead a band with a topaz set in it. Young Madame de Bellegarde, when Newman came in, left some people among whom she was sitting, and took the place that she had occupied before dinner. Then she gave a little push to the puff that stood near her, and by a glance at Newman seemed to indicate that she had placed it in position for him. He went and took possession of it; the marquis's wife amused and puzzled him.

"I know your secret," she said, in her bad but charming English; "you need make no mystery of it. You wish to marry my sister-in-law. *C'est un beau choix*. A man like you ought to marry a tall, thin woman. You must know that I have spoken in your favor; you owe me a famous taper!"

"You have spoken to Madame de Cintré?" said Newman.

"Oh no, not that. You may think it strange, but my sister-in-law and I are not so intimate as that. No; I spoke to my husband and my mother-in-law; I said I was sure we could do what we chose with you."

"I am much obliged to you," said Newman, laughing; "but you can't."

"I know that very well; I did n't believe a word of it. But I wanted you to come into the house; I thought we should be friends."

"I am very sure of it," said Newman.

"Don't be too sure. If you like Madame de Cintré so much, perhaps you will not like me. We are as different as blue and pink. But you and I have something in common. I have come into this family by marriage; you want to come into it in the same way."

"Oh no, I don't!" interrupted Newman. "I only want to take Madame de Cintré out of it."

"Well, to cast your nets you have to go into the water. Our positions are alike; we shall be able to compare notes. What do you think of my husband? It 's a strange question, is n't it? But I shall ask you some stranger ones yet."

"Perhaps a stranger one will be easier to answer," said Newman. "You might try me."

"Oh, you get off very well; the old Comte de la Rochefidèle, yonder, could n't do it better. I told them that if we only gave you a chance you would be a perfect *talon rouge*. I know something about men. Besides, you and I belong to the same camp. I am a ferocious democrat. By birth I am vieille roche; a good little bit of the history of France is the history of my family. Oh, you never heard of us, of course! *Ce que c'est que la gloire!* We are much better than the Bellegardes, at any rate. But I don't care a pin for my pedigree; I want to belong to my time. I 'm a revolutionist, a radical, a child of the age! I am sure I go beyond you. I like clever people, wherever they come from, and I take my amusement wherever I find it. I don't pout at the Empire; here all the world pouts at the Empire. Of course I have to mind what I say; but I expect to take my revenge with you." Madame de Bellegarde discoursed for some time longer in this sympathetic strain, with an eager abundance which seemed to indicate that her opportunities for revealing her esoteric philosophy were indeed rare. She hoped that Newman would never be afraid of her, however he might be with the others, for, really, she went very far indeed. "Strong people"—*les gens forts*—were in her opinion equal, all the world over. Newman listened to her with an attention at once beguiled and irritated. He wondered what the deuce she, too, was driving at, with her hope that he would not be afraid of her and her protestations of equality. In so far as he could understand her, she was wrong;

a silly, rattling woman was certainly not the equal of a sensible man, preoccupied with an ambitious passion. Madame de Bellegarde stopped suddenly, and looked at him sharply, shaking her fan. "I see you don't believe me," she said, "you are too much on your guard. You will not form an alliance, offensive or defensive? You are very wrong; I could help you."

Newman answered that he was very grateful and that he would certainly ask for help; she should see. "But first of all," he said, "I must help myself." And he went to join Madame de Cintré.

"I have been telling Madame de la Rochefidèle that you are an American," she said, as he came up. "It interests her greatly. Her father went over with the French troops to help you in your battles in the last century, and she has always, in consequence, wanted greatly to see an American. But she has never succeeded till to-night. You are the first—to her knowledge—that she has ever looked at."

Madame de la Rochefidèle had an aged, cadaverous face, with a falling of the lower jaw which prevented her from bringing her lips together, and reduced her conversation to a series of impressive but inarticulate gutturals. She raised an antique eye-glass, elaborately mounted in chased silver, and looked at Newman from head to foot. Then she said something to which he listened deferentially, but which he completely failed to understand.

"Madame de la Rochefidèle says that she is convinced that she must have seen Americans without knowing it," Madame de Cintré explained. Newman thought it probable she had seen a great many things without knowing it; and the old lady, again addressing herself to utterance, declared—as interpreted by Madame de Cintré—that she wished she had known it.

At this moment the old gentleman who had been talking to the elder Madame de Bellegarde drew near, leading the marquise on his arm. His wife pointed out Newman to him, apparently explaining his remarkable origin. M. de la Rochefidèle, whose old age was rosy and rotund, spoke very neatly and clearly; almost as prettily, Newman thought, as M.

Nioche. When he had been enlightened, he turned to Newman with an inimitable elderly grace.

"Monsieur is by no means the first American that I have seen," he said. "Almost the first person I ever saw—to notice him—was an American."

"Ah?" said Newman, sympathetically.

"The great Dr. Franklin," said M. de la Rochefidèle. "Of course I was very young. He was received very well in our *monde*."

"Not better than Mr. Newman," said Madame de Bellegarde. "I beg he will offer me his arm into the other room. I could have offered no higher privilege to Dr. Franklin."

Newman, complying with Madame de Bellegarde's request, perceived that her two sons had returned to the drawing-room. He scanned their faces an instant for traces of the scene that had followed his separation from them, but the marquis seemed neither more nor less frigidly grand than usual, and Valentin was kissing ladies' hands with at least his habitual air of self-abandonment to the act. Madame de Bellegarde gave a glance at her eldest son, and by the time she had crossed the threshold of her boudoir he was at her side. The room was now empty and offered a sufficient degree of privacy. The old lady disengaged herself from Newman's arm and rested her hand on the arm of the marquis; and in this position she stood a moment, holding her head high and biting her small under-lip. I am afraid the picture was lost upon Newman, but Madame de Bellegarde was, in fact, at this moment a striking image of the dignity which—even in the case of a little time-shrunken old lady—may reside in the habit of unquestioned authority and the absoluteness of a social theory favorable to yourself.

"My son has spoken to you as I desired," she said, "and you understand that we shall not interfere. The rest will lie with yourself."

"M. de Bellegarde told me several things I did n't understand," said Newman, "but I made out that. You will leave me an open field. I am much obliged."

"I wish to add a word that my son probably did not feel at liberty to say," the marquise rejoined. "I must say it for my own peace of mind. We are stretching a point; we are doing you a great favor."

"Oh, your son said it very well; did n't you?" said Newman.

"Not so well as my mother," declared the marquis.

"I can only repeat—I am much obliged."

"It is proper I should tell you," Madame de Bellegarde went on, "that I am very proud, and that I hold my head very high. I may be wrong, but I am too old to change. At least I know it, and I don't pretend to anything else. Don't flatter yourself that my daughter is not proud. She is proud in her own way—a somewhat different way from mine. You will have to make your terms with that. Even Valentin is proud, if you touch the right spot—or the wrong one. Urbain is proud; that you see for yourself. Sometimes I think he is a little too proud; but I would n't change him. He is the best of my children; he cleaves to his old mother. But I have said enough to show you that we are all proud together. It is well that you should know the sort of people you have come among."

"Well," said Newman, "I can only say, in return, that I am *not* proud; I shan't mind you! But you speak as if you intended to be very disagreeable."

"I shall not enjoy having my daughter marry you, and I shall not pretend to enjoy it. If you don't mind that, so much the better."

"If you stick to your own side of the contract we shall not quarrel; that is all I ask of you," said Newman. "Keep your hands off, and give me an open field. I am very much in earnest, and there is not the slightest danger of my getting discouraged or backing out. You will have me constantly before your eyes; if you don't like it, I am sorry for you. I will do for your daughter, if she will accept me, everything that a man can do for a woman. I am happy to tell you that, as a promise—a pledge. I consider that on your side you make me an equal pledge. You will not back out, eh?"

"I don't know what you mean by 'backing out,' " said the marquise. "It suggests a movement of which I think no Bellegarde has ever been guilty."

"Our word is our word," said Urbain. "We have given it."

"Well, now," said Newman, "I am very glad you are so proud. It makes me believe that you will keep it."

The marquise was silent a moment, and then, suddenly, "I shall always be polite to you, Mr. Newman," she declared, "but, decidedly, I shall never like you."

"Don't be too sure," said Newman, laughing.

"I am so sure that I will ask you to take me back to my arm-chair without the least fear of having my sentiments modified by the service you render me." And Madame de Bellegarde took his arm, and returned to the salon and to her customary place.

M. de la Rochefidèle and his wife were preparing to take their leave, and Madame de Cintré's interview with the mumbling old lady was at an end. She stood looking about her, asking herself, apparently, to whom she should next speak, when Newman came up to her.

"Your mother has given me leave—very solemnly—to come here often," he said. "I mean to come often."

"I shall be glad to see you," she answered, simply. And then, in a moment, "You probably think it very strange that there should be such a solemnity—as you say—about your coming."

"Well, yes; I do, rather."

"Do you remember what my brother Valentin said, the first time you came to see me—that we were a strange, strange family?"

"It was not the first time I came, but the second," said Newman.

"Very true. Valentin annoyed me at the time; but now I know you better, I may tell you he was right. If you come often, you will see!" and Madame de Cintré turned away.

Newman watched her a while, talking with other people, and then he took his leave. He shook hands last with Valentin de Bellegarde, who came out with him to the top of the staircase. "Well, you have got your permit," said Valentin. "I hope you liked the process."

"I like your sister, more than ever. But don't worry your brother any more for my sake," Newman added. "I don't mind him. I am afraid he came down on you in the smoking-room, after I went out."

"When my brother comes down on me," said Valentin, "he falls hard. I have a peculiar way of receiving him. I must say," he continued, "that they came up to the mark much sooner than I expected. I don't understand it; they must have had to turn the screw pretty tight. It 's a tribute to your millions."

"Well, it 's the most precious one they have ever received," said Newman.

He was turning away when Valentin stopped him, looking at him with a brilliant, softly-cynical glance. "I should like to know whether, within a few days, you have seen your venerable friend M. Nioche."

"He was yesterday at my rooms," Newman answered.

"What did he tell you?"

"Nothing particular."

"You did n't see the muzzle of a pistol sticking out of his pocket?"

"What are you driving at?" Newman demanded. "I thought he seemed rather cheerful, for him."

Valentin broke into a laugh. "I am delighted to hear it! I win my bet. Mademoiselle Noémie has thrown her cap over the mill, as we say. She has left the paternal domicile. She is launched! And M. Nioche is rather cheerful—*for him!* Don't brandish your tomahawk at that rate; I have not seen her nor communicated with her since that day at the Louvre. Andromeda has found another Perseus than I. My information is exact; on such matters it always is. I suppose that now you will raise your protest."

"My protest be hanged!" murmured Newman, disgustedly.

But his tone found no echo in that in which Valentin, with his hand on the door, to return to his mother's apartment, exclaimed, "But I shall see her now! She is very remarkable—she is very remarkable!"

Chapter XIII

NEWMAN kept his promise, or his menace, of going often to the Rue de l'Université, and during the next six weeks he saw Madame de Cintré more times than he could have numbered. He flattered himself that he was not in love, but his biographer may be supposed to know better. He claimed, at least, none of the exemptions and emoluments of the romantic passion. Love, he believed, made a fool of a man, and his present emotion was not folly but wisdom; wisdom sound, serene, well-directed. What he felt was an intense, all-consuming tenderness, which had for its object an extraordinarily graceful and delicate, and at the same time impressive, woman who lived in a large gray house on the left bank of the Seine. This tenderness turned very often into a positive heart-ache; a sign in which, certainly, Newman ought to have read the appellation which science has conferred upon his sentiment. When the heart has a heavy weight upon it, it hardly matters whether the weight be of gold or of lead; when, at any rate, happiness passes into that place in which it becomes identical with pain, a man may admit that the reign of wisdom is temporarily suspended. Newman wished Madame de Cintré so well that nothing he could think of doing for her in the future rose to the high standard which his present mood had set itself. She seemed to him so felicitous a product of nature and circumstance that his invention, musing on future combinations, was constantly catching its breath with the fear of stumbling into some brutal compression or mutilation of her beautiful personal harmony. This is what I mean by Newman's tenderness: Madame de Cintré pleased him so, exactly as she was, that his desire to interpose between her and the troubles of life had the quality of a young mother's eagerness to protect the sleep of her first-born child. Newman was simply charmed, and he handled his charm as if it were a music-box which would stop if one shook it. There can be no better proof of the hankering epicure that is hidden in every man's temperament, waiting for a signal from some divine confederate that he may safely peep out. Newman at last was enjoying, purely, freely, deeply. Certain of Madame de Cintré's personal qualities—the luminous sweetness of her eyes, the delicate mobility of her face, the deep liquidity of her voice—filled all his consciousness. A rose-crowned Greek of old, gazing at a marble goddess with his whole bright intellect resting satisfied in the act, could not have been a more complete embodiment of the wisdom that loses itself in the enjoyment of quiet harmonies.

He made no violent love to her—no sentimental speeches. He never trespassed on what she had made him understand was for the present forbidden ground. But he had, nevertheless, a comfortable sense that she knew better from day to day how much he admired her. Though in general he was no great talker, he talked much, and he succeeded perfectly in making her say many things. He was not afraid of boring her, either by his discourse or by his silence; and whether or no he did occasionally bore her, it is probable that on the whole she liked him only the better for his absence of embarrassed scruples. Her visitors, coming in often while Newman sat there, found a tall, lean, silent man in a half-lounging attitude, who laughed out sometimes when no one had meant to be droll, and remained grave in the presence of calculated witticisms, for the appreciation of which he had apparently not the proper culture.

It must be confessed that the number of subjects upon which Newman had no ideas was extremely large, and it must be added that as regards those subjects upon which he was without ideas he was also perfectly without words. He had little of the small change of conversation, and his stock of ready-made formulas and phrases was the scantiest. On the other hand he had plenty of attention to bestow, and his estimate of the importance of a topic did not depend upon the number of clever things he could say about it. He himself was almost never bored, and there was no man with whom it would have been a greater mistake to suppose that silence meant displeasure. What it was that entertained him during some of his speechless sessions I must, however, confess myself unable to determine. We know in a general way that a great many things which were old stories to a great many people had the charm of novelty to him, but a complete list of his new impressions would probably contain a number of surprises for us. He told Madame de Cintré a hundred long stories; he explained to her, in talking of the United States, the working of various local institutions and mercantile customs. Judging by the sequel she was interested, but one would not have been sure of it beforehand. As regards her own talk, Newman was very sure himself that she herself enjoyed it: this was as a sort of amendment to the portrait that Mrs. Tristram had drawn of her. He discovered that she had naturally an abundance of gayety. He had been right at first in saying she was shy; her shyness, in a woman whose circumstances and tranquil beauty afforded every facility for well-mannered hardihood, was only a charm the more. For Newman it had lasted some time, and even when it went it left something behind it which for a while performed the same office. Was this the tearful secret of which Mrs. Tristram had had a glimpse, and of which, as of her friend's reserve, her high-breeding, and her profundity, she had given a sketch of which the outlines were, perhaps, rather too heavy? Newman supposed so, but he found himself wondering less every day what Madame de Cintré's secrets might be, and more convinced that secrets were, in themselves, hateful things to her. She was a woman for the light, not for the shade; and her natural line was not picturesque reserve and mysterious melancholy, but frank, joyous, brilliant action, with just so much meditation as was necessary, and not a grain more. To this, apparently, he had succeeded in bringing her back. He felt, himself, that he was an antidote to oppressive secrets; what he offered her was, in fact, above all things a vast, sunny immunity from the need of having any.

He often passed his evenings, when Madame de Cintré had so appointed it, at the chilly fireside of Madame de Bellegarde, contenting himself with looking across the room, through narrowed eyelids, at his mistress, who always made a point, before her family, of talking to some one else. Madame de Bellegarde sat by the fire conversing neatly and coldly with whomsoever approached her, and glancing round the room with her slowly-restless eye, the effect of which, when it lighted upon him, was to Newman's sense identical with that of a sudden spurt of damp air. When he shook hands with her he always asked her with a laugh whether she could "stand him" another evening, and she replied, without a laugh, that thank God she had always been able to do her duty. Newman, talking once of the marquise to Mrs. Tristram, said that after all it was very easy to get on with her; it always was easy to get on with out-and-out rascals.

"And is it by that elegant term," said Mrs. Tristram, "that you designate the Marquise de Bellegarde?"

"Well," said Newman, "she is wicked, she is an old sinner."

"What is her crime?" asked Mrs. Tristram.

"I should n't wonder if she had murdered some one—all from a sense of duty, of course."

"How can you be so dreadful?" sighed Mrs. Tristram.

"I am not dreadful. I am speaking of her favorably."

"Pray what will you say when you want to be severe?"

"I shall keep my severity for some one else—for the marquis. There 's a man I can't swallow, mix the drink as I will."

"And what has *he* done?"

"I can't quite make out; it is something dreadfully bad, something mean and underhand, and not redeemed by audacity, as his mother's misdemeanors may have been. If he has never committed murder, he has at least turned his back and looked the other way while some one else was committing it."

In spite of this invidious hypothesis, which must be taken for nothing more than an example of the capricious play of "American humor," Newman did his best to maintain an easy and friendly style of communication with M. de Bellegarde. So long as he was in personal contact with people he disliked extremely to have anything to forgive them, and he was capable of a good deal of unsuspected imaginative effort (for the sake of his own personal comfort) to assume for the time that they were good fellows. He did his best to treat the marquis as one; he believed honestly, moreover, that he could not, in reason, be such a confounded fool as he seemed. Newman's familiarity was never importunate; his sense of human equality was not an aggressive taste or an æsthetic theory, but something as natural and organic as a physical appetite which had never been put on a scanty allowance and consequently was innocent of ungraceful eagerness. His tranquil unsuspectingness of the relativity of his own place in the social scale was probably irritating to M. de Bellegarde, who saw himself reflected in the mind of his potential brother-in-law in a crude and colorless form, unpleasantly dissimilar to the impressive image projected upon his own intellectual mirror. He never forgot himself for an instant, and replied to what he must have considered Newman's "advances" with mechanical politeness. Newman, who was constantly forgetting himself, and indulging in an unlimited amount of irresponsible inquiry and conjecture, now and then found himself confronted by the conscious, ironical smile of his host. What the deuce M. de Bellegarde was smiling at he was at a loss to divine. M. de Bellegarde's smile may be supposed to have been, for himself, a compromise between a great many emotions. So long as he smiled he was polite, and it was proper he should be polite. A smile, moreover, committed him to nothing more than politeness, and left the degree of politeness agreeably vague. A smile, too, was neither dissent—which was too serious—nor agreement, which might have brought on terrible complications. And then a smile covered his own personal dignity, which in this critical situation he was resolved to keep immaculate; it was quite enough that the glory of his house should pass into eclipse. Between him and Newman, his whole manner seemed to declare, there could be no interchange of opinion; he was holding his breath so as not to inhale the odor of democracy. Newman was far from being versed in European politics, but he liked to have a general idea of what was going on about him, and he accordingly asked M. de Bellegarde several times what he thought of public affairs. M. de Bellegarde answered with suave concision that he thought as ill of them as possible, that they were going from bad to worse, and that the age was rotten to its core. This gave Newman, for the moment, an almost kindly feeling for the marquis; he pitied a man for whom the world was so cheerless a place, and the next time he saw M. de Bellegarde he attempted to call his attention to some of the brilliant features of the time. The marquis presently replied that he had but a single political conviction, which was enough for him: he believed in the divine right of Henry of Bourbon, Fifth of his name, to the throne of France. Newman stared, and after this he ceased to talk politics with M.

de Bellegarde. He was not horrified nor scandalized, he was not even amused; he felt as he should have felt if he had discovered in M. de Bellegarde a taste for certain oddities of diet; an appetite, for instance, for fishbones or nutshells. Under these circumstances, of course, he would never have broached dietary questions with him.

One afternoon, on his calling on Madame de Cintré, Newman was requested by the servant to wait a few moments, as his hostess was not at liberty. He walked about the room a while, taking up her books, smelling her flowers, and looking at her prints and photographs (which he thought prodigiously pretty), and at last he heard the opening of a door to which his back was turned. On the threshold stood an old woman whom he remembered to have met several times in entering and leaving the house. She was tall and straight and dressed in black, and she wore a cap which, if Newman had been initiated into such mysteries, would have been a sufficient assurance that she was not a Frenchwoman; a cap of pure British composition. She had a pale, decent, depressed-looking face, and a clear, dull, English eye. She looked at Newman a moment, both intently and timidly, and then she dropped a short, straight English curtsey.

"Madame de Cintré begs you will kindly wait," she said. "She has just come in; she will soon have finished dressing."

"Oh, I will wait as long as she wants," said Newman. "Pray tell her not to hurry."

"Thank you, sir," said the woman, softly; and then, instead of retiring with her message, she advanced into the room. She looked about her for a moment, and presently went to a table and began to arrange certain books and knicknacks. Newman was struck with the high respectability of her appearance; he was afraid to address her as a servant. She busied herself for some moments with putting the table in order and pulling the curtains straight, while Newman walked slowly to and fro. He perceived at last, from her reflection in the mirror, as he was passing, that her hands were idle and that she was looking at him intently. She evidently wished to say something, and Newman, perceiving it, helped her to begin.

"You are English?" he asked.

"Yes, sir, please," she answered, quickly and softly; "I was born in Wiltshire."

"And what do you think of Paris?"

"Oh, I don't think of Paris, sir," she said in the same tone. "It is so long since I have been here."

"Ah, you have been here very long?"

"It is more than forty years, sir. I came over with Lady Emmeline."

"You mean with old Madame de Bellegarde?"

"Yes, sir. I came with her when she was married. I was my lady's own woman."

"And you have been with her ever since?"

"I have been in the house ever since. My lady has taken a younger person. You see I am very old. I do nothing regular now. But I keep about."

"You look very strong and well," said Newman, observing the erectness of her figure, and a certain venerable rosiness in her cheek.

"Thank God I am not ill, sir; I hope I know my duty too well to go panting and coughing about the house. But I am an old woman, sir, and it is as an old woman that I venture to speak to you."

"Oh, speak out," said Newman, curiously. "You need n't be afraid of me."

"Yes, sir. I think you are kind. I have seen you before."

"On the stairs, you mean?"

"Yes, sir. When you have been coming to see the countess. I have taken the liberty of noticing that you come often."

"Oh yes; I come very often," said Newman, laughing. "You need not have been very wide-awake to notice that."

"I have noticed it with pleasure, sir," said the ancient tire-woman, gravely. And she stood looking at Newman with a strange expression of face. The old instinct of deference and humility was there; the habit of decent self-effacement and knowledge of her "own place." But there mingled with it a certain mild audacity, born of the occasion and of a sense, probably, of Newman's unprecedented approachableness, and, beyond this, a vague indifference to the old proprieties; as if my lady's own woman had at last begun to reflect that, since my lady had taken another person, she had a slight reversionary property in herself.

"You take a great interest in the family?" said Newman.

"A deep interest, sir. Especially in the countess."

"I am glad of that," said Newman. And in a moment he added, smiling, "So do I!"

"So I supposed, sir. We can't help noticing these things and having our ideas; can we, sir?"

"You mean as a servant?" said Newman.

"Ah, there it is, sir. I am afraid that when I let my thoughts meddle with such matters I am no longer a servant. But I am so devoted to the countess; if she were my own child I could n't love her more. That is how I come to be so bold, sir. They say you want to marry her."

Newman eyed his interlocutress and satisfied himself that she was not a gossip, but a zealot; she looked anxious, appealing, discreet. "It is quite true," he said. "I want to marry Madame de Cintré."

"And to take her away to America?"

"I will take her wherever she wants to go."

"The farther away the better, sir!" exclaimed the old woman, with sudden intensity. But she checked herself, and, taking up a paper-weight in mosaic, began to polish it with her black apron. "I don't mean anything against the house or the family, sir. But I think a great change would do the poor countess good. It is very sad here."

"Yes, it 's not very lively," said Newman. "But Madame de Cintré is gay herself."

"She is everything that is good. You will not be vexed to hear that she has been gayer for a couple of months past than she had been in many a day before."

Newman was delighted to gather this testimony to the prosperity of his suit, but he repressed all violent marks of elation. "Has Madame de Cintré been in bad spirits before this?" he asked.

"Poor lady, she had good reason. M. de Cintré was no husband for a sweet young lady like that. And then, as I say, it has been a sad house. It is better, in my humble opinion, that she were out of it. So, if you will excuse me for saying so, I hope she will marry you."

"I hope she will!" said Newman.

"But you must not lose courage, sir, if she does n't make up her mind at once. That is what I wanted to beg of you, sir. Don't give it up, sir. You will not take it ill if I say it 's a great risk for any lady at any time; all the more when she has got rid of one bad bargain. But if she can marry a good, kind, respectable gentleman, I think she had better make up her mind to it. They speak very well of you, sir, in the house, and, if you will allow me to say so, I like your face. You have a very different appearance from the late count: he was n't five feet high. And they say your fortune is beyond everything. There 's no harm in that. So I beseech you to be patient, sir, and bide your time. If I don't say this to you, sir, perhaps no one will. Of course it is not for me to make any promises. I can answer for nothing. But I think your chance is not so bad, sir. I am nothing but a weary old woman in my quiet corner, but one woman understands another, and I think I make out the countess. I received her in my arms when she came into the world, and her first wedding day was the saddest of my life. She owes it to me to show me another and a brighter one. If you will hold firm, sir—and you look as if you would—I think we may see it."

"I am much obliged to you for your encouragement," said Newman, heartily. "One can't have too much. I mean to hold firm. And if Madame de Cintré marries me, you must come and live with her."

The old woman looked at him strangely, with her soft, lifeless eyes. "It may seem a heartless thing to say, sir, when one has been forty years in a house, but I may tell you that I should like to leave this place."

"Why, it 's just the time to say it," said Newman, fervently. "After forty years one wants a change."

"You are very kind, sir;" and this faithful servant dropped another curtsey and seemed disposed to retire. But she lingered a moment and gave a timid, joyless smile. Newman was disappointed, and his fingers stole half shyly, half irritably into his waistcoat-pocket. His informant noticed the movement. "Thank God I am not a Frenchwoman," she said. "If I were, I would tell you with a brazen simper, old as I am, that if you please, monsieur, my information is worth something.

Let me tell you so in my own decent English way. It *is* worth something."

"How much, please?" said Newman.

"Simply this: a promise not to hint to the countess that I have said these things."

"If that is all, you have it," said Newman.

"That is all, sir. Thank you, sir. Good day, sir." And having once more slid down telescope-wise into her scanty petticoats, the old woman departed. At the same moment Madame de Cintré came in by an opposite door. She noticed the movement of the other *portière* and asked Newman who had been entertaining him.

"The British female!" said Newman. "An old lady in a black dress and a cap, who curtsies up and down, and expresses herself ever so well."

"An old lady who curtsies and expresses herself? . . . . Ah, you mean poor Mrs. Bread. I happen to know that you have made a conquest of her."

"Mrs. Cake, she ought to be called," said Newman. "She is very sweet. She is a delicious old woman."

Madame de Cintré looked at him a moment. "What can she have said to you? She is an excellent creature, but we think her rather dismal."

"I suppose," Newman answered presently, "that I like her because she has lived near you so long. Since your birth, she told me."

"Yes," said Madame de Cintré, simply; "she is very faithful; I can trust her."

Newman had never made any reflections to this lady upon her mother and her brother Urbain; had given no hint of the impression they made upon him. But, as if she had guessed his thoughts, she seemed careful to avoid all occasion for making him speak of them. She never alluded to her mother's domestic decrees; she never quoted the opinions of the marquis. They had talked, however, of Valentin, and she had made no secret of her extreme affection for her younger brother. Newman listened sometimes with a certain harmless jealousy; he would have liked to divert some of her tender allusions to his own credit. Once Madame de Cintré told him with a little air of triumph about something that Valentin had done which she thought very much to his honor. It was a service he had rendered to an old friend of the family; something more "serious" than Valentin was usually supposed capable of being. Newman said he was glad to hear of it, and then began to talk about something which lay upon his own heart. Madame de Cintré listened, but after a while she said, "I don't like the way you speak of my brother Valentin." Hereupon Newman, surprised, said that he had never spoken of him but kindly.

"It is too kindly," said Madame de Cintré. "It is a kindness that costs nothing; it is the kindness you show to a child. It is as if you did n't respect him."

"Respect him? Why I think I do."

"You think? If you are not sure, it is no respect."

"Do you respect him?" said Newman. "If you do, I do."

"If one loves a person, that is a question one is not bound to answer," said Madame de Cintré.

"You should not have asked it of me, then. I am very fond of your brother."

"He amuses you. But you would not like to resemble him."

"I should n't like to resemble any one. It is hard enough work resembling one's self."

"What do you mean," asked Madame de Cintré, "by resembling one's self?"

"Why, doing what is expected of one. Doing one's duty."

"But that is only when one is very good."

"Well, a great many people are good," said Newman. "Valentin is quite good enough for me."

Madame de Cintré was silent for a short time. "He is not good enough for me," she said at last. "I wish he would do something."

"What can he do?" asked Newman.

"Nothing. Yet he is very clever."

"It is a proof of cleverness," said Newman, "to be happy without doing anything."

"I don't think Valentin is happy, in reality. He is clever, generous, brave; but what is there to show for it? To me there is something sad in his life, and sometimes I have a sort of foreboding about him. I don't know why, but I fancy he will have some great trouble—perhaps an unhappy end."

"Oh, leave him to me," said Newman, jovially. "I will watch over him and keep harm away."

One evening, in Madame de Bellegarde's salon, the conversation had flagged most sensibly. The marquis walked up and down in silence, like a sentinel at the door of some smooth-fronted citadel of the proprieties; his mother sat staring at the fire; young Madame de Bellegarde worked at an enormous band of tapestry. Usually there were three or four visitors, but on this occasion a violent storm sufficiently accounted for the absence of even the most devoted habitués. In the long silences the howling of the wind and the beating of the rain were distinctly audible. Newman sat perfectly still, watching the clock, determined to stay till the stroke of eleven, but not a moment longer. Madame de Cintré had turned her back to the circle, and had been standing for some time within the uplifted curtain of a window, with her forehead against the pane, gazing out into the deluged darkness. Suddenly she turned round toward her sister-in-law.

"For Heaven's sake," she said, with peculiar eagerness, "go to the piano and play something."

Madame de Bellegarde held up her tapestry and pointed to a little white flower. "Don't ask me to leave this. I am in the midst of a masterpiece. My flower is going to smell very sweet; I am putting in the smell with this gold-colored silk. I am holding my breath; I can't leave off. Play something yourself."

"It is absurd for me to play when you are present," said Madame de Cintré. But the next moment she went to the piano and began to strike the keys with vehemence. She played for some time, rapidly and brilliantly; when she stopped, Newman went to the piano and asked her to begin again. She shook her head, and, on his insisting, she said, "I have not been playing for you; I have been playing for myself." She went back to the window again and looked out, and shortly afterwards left the room. When Newman took leave, Urbain de Bellegarde accompanied him, as he always did, just three steps down the staircase. At the bottom stood a servant with his overcoat. He had just put it on when he saw Madame de Cintré coming towards him across the vestibule.

"Shall you be at home on Friday?" Newman asked.

She looked at him a moment before answering his question. "You don't like my mother and my brother," she said.

He hesitated a moment, and then he said softly, "No."

She laid her hand on the balustrade and prepared to ascend the stairs, fixing her eyes on the first step.

"Yes, I shall be at home on Friday," and she passed up the wide dusky staircase.

On the Friday, as soon as he came in, she asked him to please to tell her why he disliked her family.

"Dislike your family?" he exclaimed. "That has a horrid sound. I did n't say so, did I? I did n't mean it, if I did."

"I wish you would tell me what you think of them," said Madame de Cintré.

"I don't think of any of them but you."

"That is because you dislike them. Speak the truth; you can't offend me."

"Well, I don't exactly love your brother," said Newman. "I remember now. But what is the use of my saying so? I had forgotten it."

"You are too good-natured," said Madame de Cintré gravely. Then, as if to avoid the appearance of inviting him to speak ill of the marquis, she turned away, motioning him to sit down.

But he remained standing before her and said presently, "What is of much more importance is that they don't like me."

"No—they don't," she said.

"And don't you think they are wrong?" Newman asked. "I don't believe I am a man to dislike."

"I suppose that a man who may be liked may also be disliked. And my brother—my mother," she added, "have not made you angry?"

"Yes, sometimes."

"You have never shown it."

"So much the better."

"Yes, so much the better. They think they have treated you very well."

"I have no doubt they might have handled me much more roughly," said Newman. "I am much obliged to them. Honestly."

"You are generous," said Madame de Cintré. "It 's a disagreeable position."

"For them, you mean. Not for me."

"For me," said Madame de Cintré.

"Not when their sins are forgiven!" said Newman. "They don't think I am as good as they are. I do. But we shan't quarrel about it."

"I can't even agree with you without saying something that has a disagreeable sound. The presumption was against you. That you probably don't understand."

Newman sat down and looked at her for some time. "I don't think I really understand it. But when you say it, I believe it."

"That 's a poor reason," said Madame de Cintré, smiling.

"No, it 's a very good one. You have a high spirit, a high standard; but with you it 's all natural and unaffected; you don't seem to have stuck your head into a vise, as if you were sitting for the photograph of propriety. You think of me as a fellow who has had no idea in life but to make money and drive sharp bargains. That 's a fair description of me, but it is not the whole story. A man ought to care for something else, though I don't know exactly what. I cared for money-making, but I never cared particularly for the money. There was nothing else to do, and it was impossible to be idle. I have been very easy to others, and to myself. I have done most of the things that people asked me—I don't mean rascals. As regards your mother and your brother," Newman added, "there is only one point upon which I feel that I might quarrel with them. I don't ask them to sing my praises to you, but I ask them to let you alone. If I thought they talked ill of me to you, I should come down upon them."

"They have let me alone, as you say. They have not talked ill of you."

"In that case," cried Newman, "I declare they are only too good for this world!"

Madame de Cintré appeared to find something startling in his exclamation. She would, perhaps, have replied, but at this moment the door was thrown open and Urbain de Bellegarde stepped across the threshold. He appeared surprised at finding Newman, but his surprise was but a momentary shadow across the surface of an unwonted joviality. Newman had never seen the marquis so exhilarated; his pale, unlighted countenance had a sort of thin transfiguration. He held open the door for some one else to enter, and presently appeared old Madame de Bellegarde, leaning on the arm of a gentleman whom Newman had not seen before. He had already risen, and Madame de Cintré rose, as she always did before her mother. The marquis, who had greeted Newman almost genially, stood apart, slowly rubbing his hands. His mother came forward with her companion. She gave a majestic little nod at Newman, and then she released the strange gentleman, that he might make his bow to her daughter.

"My daughter," she said, "I have brought you an unknown relative, Lord Deepmere. Lord Deepmere is our cousin, but he has done only to-day what he ought to have done long ago—come to make our acquaintance."

Madame de Cintré smiled, and offered Lord Deepmere her hand. "It is very extraordinary," said this noble laggard, "but this is the first time that I have ever been in Paris for more than three or four weeks."

"And how long have you been here now?" asked Madame de Cintré.

"Oh, for the last two months," said Lord Deepmere.

These two remarks might have constituted an impertinence; but a glance at Lord Deepmere's face would have satisfied you, as it apparently satisfied Madame de Cintré, that they constituted only a naïveté. When his companions were seated, Newman, who was out of the conversation, occupied himself with observing the new-comer. Observation, however, as regards Lord Deepmere's person, had no great range. He was a small, meagre man, of some three and thirty years of age, with a bald head, a short nose, and no front teeth in the upper jaw; he had round, candid, blue eyes, and several pimples on his chin. He was evidently very shy, and he laughed a great deal, catching his breath with an odd, startling sound, as the most convenient imitation of repose. His physiognomy denoted great simplicity, a certain amount of brutality, and a probable failure in the past to profit by rare educational advantages. He remarked that Paris was awfully jolly, but that for real, thorough-paced entertainment it was nothing to Dublin. He even preferred Dublin to London. Had Madame de Cintré ever been to Dublin? They must all come over there some day, and he would show them some Irish sport. He always went to Ireland for the fishing, and he came to Paris for the new Offenbach things. They always brought them out in Dublin, but he could n't wait. He had been nine times to hear La Pomme de Paris. Madame de Cintré, leaning back, with her arms folded, looked at Lord Deepmere with a more visibly puzzled face than she usually showed to society. Madame de Bellegarde, on the other hand, wore a fixed smile. The marquis said that among light operas his favorite was the Gazza Ladra. The marquise then began a series of inquiries about the duke and the cardinal, the old countess and Lady Barbara, after listening to which, and to Lord Deepmere's somewhat irreverent responses, for a quarter of an hour, Newman rose to take his leave. The marquis went with him three steps into the hall.

"Is he Irish?" asked Newman, nodding in the direction of the visitor.

"His mother was the daughter of Lord Finucane," said the marquis; "he has great Irish estates. Lady Bridget, in the complete absence of male heirs, either direct or collateral—a most extraordinary circumstance—came in for everything. But Lord Deepmere's title is English and his English property is immense. He is a charming young man."

Newman answered nothing, but he detained the marquis as the latter was beginning gracefully to recede. "It is a good time for me to thank you," he said, "for sticking so punctiliously to our bargain, for doing so much to help me on with your sister."

The marquis stared. "Really, I have done nothing that I can boast of," he said.

"Oh, don't be modest," Newman answered, laughing. "I can't flatter myself that I am doing so well simply by my own merit. And thank your mother for me, too!" And he turned away, leaving M. de Bellegarde looking after him.

Chapter XIV

T HE NEXT TIME Newman came to the Rue de l'Université
he had the good fortune to find Madame de Cintré
alone. He had come with a definite intention, and he lost no
time in executing it. She wore, moreover, a look which he
eagerly interpreted as expectancy.

"I have been coming to see you for six months, now," he
said, "and I have never spoken to you a second time of marriage. That was what you asked me; I obeyed. Could any man
have done better?"

"You have acted with great delicacy," said Madame de
Cintré.

"Well, I 'm going to change, now," said Newman. "I don't
mean that I am going to be indelicate; but I 'm going to go
back to where I began. I *am* back there. I have been all round
the circle. Or rather, I have never been away from there. I
have never ceased to want what I wanted then. Only now I
am more sure of it, if possible; I am more sure of myself, and
more sure of you. I know you better, though I don't know
anything I did n't believe three months ago. You are everything—you are beyond everything—I can imagine or desire.
You know me now; you *must* know me. I won't say that you
have seen the best—but you have seen the worst. I hope you
have been thinking all this while. You must have seen that I
was only waiting; you can't suppose that I was changing.
What will you say to me, now? Say that everything is clear
and reasonable, and that I have been very patient and considerate, and deserve my reward. And then give me your hand.
Madame de Cintré, do that. Do it."

"I knew you were only waiting," she said; "and I was very
sure this day would come. I have thought about it a great
deal. At first I was half afraid of it. But I am not afraid of it
now." She paused a moment, and then she added, "It 's a
relief."

She was sitting on a low chair, and Newman was on an
ottoman, near her. He leaned a little and took her hand,
which for an instant she let him keep. "That means that I
have not waited for nothing," he said. She looked at him for

a moment, and he saw her eyes fill with tears. "With me," he went on, "you will be as safe—as safe"—and even in his ardor he hesitated a moment for a comparison—"as safe," he said, with a kind of simple solemnity, "as in your father's arms."

Still she looked at him and her tears increased. Then, abruptly, she buried her face on the cushioned arm of the sofa beside her chair, and broke into noiseless sobs. "I am weak— I am weak," he heard her say.

"All the more reason why you should give yourself up to me," he answered. "Why are you troubled? There is nothing here that should trouble you. I offer you nothing but happiness. Is that so hard to believe?"

"To you everything seems so simple," she said, raising her head. "But things are not so. I like you extremely. I liked you six months ago, and now I am sure of it, as you say you are sure. But it is not easy, simply for that, to decide to marry you. There are a great many things to think about."

"There ought to be only one thing to think about—that we love each other," said Newman. And as she remained silent he quickly added, "Very good; if you can't accept that, don't tell me so."

"I should be very glad to think of nothing," she said at last; "not to think at all; only to shut both my eyes and give myself up. But I can't. I'm cold, I'm old, I'm a coward; I never supposed I should marry again, and it seems to me very strange I should ever have listened to you. When I used to think, as a girl, of what I should do if I were to marry freely, by my own choice, I thought of a very different man from you."

"That's nothing against me," said Newman with an immense smile; "your taste was not formed."

His smile made Madame de Cintré smile. "Have you formed it?" she asked. And then she said, in a different tone, "Where do you wish to live?"

"Anywhere in the wide world you like. We can easily settle that."

"I don't know why I ask you," she presently continued. "I care very little. I think if I were to marry you I could live almost anywhere. You have some false ideas about me; you think that I need a great many things—that I must have a brilliant, worldly life. I am sure you are prepared to take a great deal of trouble to give me such things. But that is very arbitrary; I have done nothing to prove that." She paused again, looking at him, and her mingled sound and silence were so sweet to him that he had no wish to hurry her, any more than he would have had a wish to hurry a golden sunrise. "Your being so different, which at first seemed a difficulty, a trouble, began one day to seem to me a pleasure, a great pleasure. I was glad you were different. And yet if I had said so, no one would have understood me; I don't mean simply to my family."

"They would have said I was a queer monster, eh?" said Newman.

"They would have said I could never be happy with you— you were too different; and I would have said it was just *because* you were so different that I might be happy. But they would have given better reasons than I. My only reason"— and she paused again.

But this time, in the midst of his golden sunrise, Newman felt the impulse to grasp at a rosy cloud. "Your only reason is that you love me!" he murmured with an eloquent gesture, and for want of a better reason Madame de Cintré reconciled herself to this one.

*   *   *

Newman came back the next day, and in the vestibule, as he entered the house, he encountered his friend Mrs. Bread. She was wandering about in honorable idleness, and when his eyes fell upon her she delivered him one of her curtsies. Then turning to the servant who had admitted him, she said, with the combined majesty of her native superiority and of a rugged English accent, "You may retire; I will have the honor of conducting monsieur." In spite of this combination, however, it appeared to Newman that her voice had a slight quaver, as if the tone of command were not habitual to it. The man gave her an impertinent stare, but he walked slowly away, and she led Newman up-stairs. At half its course the staircase gave a bend, forming a little platform. In the angle of the wall stood an indifferent statue of an eighteenth-century nymph, simpering, sallow, and cracked. Here Mrs. Bread stopped and looked with shy kindness at her companion.

"I know the good news, sir," she murmured.

"You have a good right to be first to know it," said Newman. "You have taken such a friendly interest."

Mrs. Bread turned away and began to blow the dust off the statue, as if this might be mockery.

"I suppose you want to congratulate me," said Newman. "I am greatly obliged." And then he added, "You gave me much pleasure the other day."

She turned round, apparently reassured. "You are not to think that I have been told anything," she said; "I have only guessed. But when I looked at you, as you came in, I was sure I had guessed aright."

"You are very sharp," said Newman. "I am sure that in your quiet way you see everything."

"I am not a fool, sir, thank God. I have guessed something else beside," said Mrs. Bread.

"What's that?"

"I need n't tell you that, sir; I don't think you would believe it. At any rate it would n't please you."

"Oh, tell me nothing but what will please me," laughed Newman. "That is the way you began."

"Well, sir, I suppose you won't be vexed to hear that the sooner everything is over the better."

"The sooner we are married, you mean? The better for me, certainly."

"The better for every one."

"The better for you, perhaps. You know you are coming to live with us," said Newman.

"I 'm extremely obliged to you, sir, but it is not of myself I was thinking. I only wanted, if I might take the liberty, to recommend you to lose no time."

"Whom are you afraid of?"

Mrs. Bread looked up the staircase and then down, and then she looked at the undusted nymph, as if she possibly had sentient ears. "I am afraid of every one," she said.

"What an uncomfortable state of mind!" said Newman. "Does 'every one' wish to prevent my marriage?"

"I am afraid of already having said too much," Mrs. Bread

replied. "I won't take it back, but I won't say any more." And she took her way up the staircase again and led him into Madame de Cintré's salon.

Newman indulged in a brief and silent imprecation when he found that Madame de Cintré was not alone. With her sat her mother, and in the middle of the room stood young Madame de Bellegarde, in her bonnet and mantle. The old marquise, who was leaning back in her chair with a hand clasping the knob of each arm, looked at him fixedly, without moving. She seemed barely conscious of his greeting; she appeared to be musing intently. Newman said to himself that her daughter had been announcing her engagement and that the old lady found the morsel hard to swallow. But Madame de Cintré, as she gave him her hand, gave him also a look by which she appeared to mean that he should understand something. Was it a warning or a request? Did she wish to enjoin speech or silence? He was puzzled, and young Madame de Bellegarde's pretty grin gave him no information.

"I have not told my mother," said Madame de Cintré, abruptly, looking at him.

"Told me what?" demanded the marquise. "You tell me too little; you should tell me everything."

"That is what I do," said Madame Urbain, with a little laugh.

"Let *me* tell your mother," said Newman.

The old lady stared at him again, and then turned to her daughter. "You are going to marry him?" she cried, softly.

"Oui ma mère," said Madame de Cintré.

"Your daughter has consented, to my great happiness," said Newman.

"And when was this arrangement made?" asked Madame de Bellegarde. "I seem to be picking up the news by chance!"

"My suspense came to an end yesterday," said Newman.

"And how long was mine to have lasted?" said the marquise to her daughter. She spoke without irritation; with a sort of cold, noble displeasure.

Madame de Cintré stood silent, with her eyes on the ground. "It is over now," she said.

"Where is my son—where is Urbain?" asked the marquise. "Send for your brother and inform him."

Young Madame de Bellegarde laid her hand on the bell-rope. "He was to make some visits with me, and I was to go and knock—very softly, very softly—at the door of his study. But he can come to me!" She pulled the bell, and in a few moments Mrs. Bread appeared, with a face of calm inquiry.

"Send for your brother," said the old lady.

But Newman felt an irresistible impulse to speak, and to speak in a certain way. "Tell the marquis we want him," he said to Mrs. Bread, who quietly retired.

Young Madame de Bellegarde went to her sister-in-law and embraced her. Then she turned to Newman, with an intense smile. "She is charming. I congratulate you."

"I congratulate you, sir," said Madame de Bellegarde, with extreme solemnity. "My daughter is an extraordinarily good woman. She may have faults, but I don't know them."

"My mother does not often make jokes," said Madame de Cintré; "but when she does they are terrible."

"She is ravishing," the Marquise Urbain resumed, looking at her sister-in-law, with her head on one side. "Yes, I congratulate you."

Madame de Cintré turned away, and, taking up a piece of tapestry, began to ply the needle. Some minutes of silence elapsed, which were interrupted by the arrival of M. de Bellegarde. He came in with his hat in his hand, gloved, and was followed by his brother Valentin, who appeared to have just entered the house. M. de Bellegarde looked around the circle and greeted Newman with his usual finely-measured courtesy. Valentin saluted his mother and his sisters, and, as he shook hands with Newman, gave him a glance of acute interrogation.

"Arrivez donc, messieurs!" cried young Madame de Bellegarde. "We have great news for you."

"Speak to your brother, my daughter," said the old lady.

Madame de Cintré had been looking at her tapestry. She raised her eyes to her brother. "I have accepted Mr. Newman."

"Your sister has consented," said Newman. "You see, after all, I knew what I was about."

"I am charmed!" said M. de Bellegarde, with superior benignity.

"So am I," said Valentin to Newman. "The marquis and I are charmed. I can't marry, myself, but I can understand it. I can't stand on my head, but I can applaud a clever acrobat. My dear sister, I bless your union."

The marquis stood looking for a while into the crown of his hat. "We have been prepared," he said at last, "but it is inevitable that in face of the event one should experience a certain emotion." And he gave a most unhilarious smile.

"I feel no emotion that I was not perfectly prepared for," said his mother.

"I can't say that for myself," said Newman, smiling, but differently from the marquis. "I am happier than I expected to be. I suppose it 's the sight of your happiness!"

"Don't exaggerate that," said Madame de Bellegarde, getting up and laying her hand upon her daughter's arm. "You can't expect an honest old woman to thank you for taking away her beautiful, only daughter."

"You forgot me, dear madame," said the young marquise, demurely.

"Yes, she is very beautiful," said Newman.

"And when is the wedding, pray?" asked young Madame de Bellegarde; "I must have a month to think over a dress."

"That must be discussed," said the marquise.

"Oh, we will discuss it, and let you know!" Newman exclaimed.

"I have no doubt we shall agree," said Urbain.

"If you don't agree with Madame de Cintré, you will be very unreasonable."

"Come, come, Urbain," said young Madame de Bellegarde. "I must go straight to my tailor's."

The old lady had been standing with her hand on her daughter's arm, looking at her fixedly. She gave a little sigh, and murmured, "No, I did *not* expect it! You are a fortunate man," she added, turning to Newman, with an expressive nod.

"Oh, I know that!" he answered. "I feel tremendously proud. I feel like crying it on the house-tops,—like stopping people in the street to tell them."

Madame de Bellegarde narrowed her lips. "Pray don't," she said.

"The more people that know it, the better," Newman declared. "I have n't yet announced it here, but I telegraphed it this morning to America."

"Telegraphed it to America?" the old lady murmured.

"To New York, to St. Louis, and to San Francisco; those are the principal cities, you know. To-morrow I shall tell my friends here."

"Have you many?" asked Madame de Bellegarde, in a tone of which I am afraid that Newman but partly measured the impertinence.

"Enough to bring me a great many hand-shakes and congratulations. To say nothing," he added, in a moment, "of those I shall receive from your friends."

"They will not use the telegraph," said the marquise, taking her departure.

M. de Bellegarde, whose wife, her imagination having apparently taken flight to the tailor's, was fluttering her silken wings in emulation, shook hands with Newman, and said with a more persuasive accent than the latter had ever heard him use, "You may count upon me." Then his wife led him away.

Valentin stood looking from his sister to our hero. "I hope you have both reflected seriously," he said.

Madame de Cintré smiled. "We have neither your powers of reflection nor your depth of seriousness; but we have done our best."

"Well, I have a great regard for each of you," Valentin continued. "You are charming young people. But I am not satisfied, on the whole, that you belong to that small and superior class—that exquisite group—composed of persons who are worthy to remain unmarried. These are rare souls; they are the salt of the earth. But I don't mean to be invidious; the marrying people are often very nice."

"Valentin holds that women should marry, and that men should not," said Madame de Cintré. "I don't know how he arranges it."

"I arrange it by adoring you, my sister," said Valentin, ardently. "Good-by."

"Adore some one whom you can marry," said Newman. "I will arrange that for you some day. I foresee that I am going to turn apostle."

Valentin was on the threshold; he looked back a moment, with a face that had turned grave. "I adore some one I can't marry!" he said. And he dropped the portière and departed.

"They don't like it," said Newman, standing alone before Madame de Cintré.

"No," she said, after a moment; "they don't like it."

"Well, now, do you mind that?" asked Newman.

"Yes!" she said, after another interval.

"That 's a mistake."

"I can't help it. I should prefer that my mother were pleased."

"Why the deuce," demanded Newman, "is she not pleased? She gave you leave to marry me."

"Very true; I don't understand it. And yet I do 'mind it,' as you say. You will call it superstitious."

"That will depend upon how much you let it bother you. Then I shall call it an awful bore."

"I will keep it to myself," said Madame de Cintré. "It shall not bother you." And then they talked of their marriage-day, and Madame de Cintré assented unreservedly to Newman's desire to have it fixed for an early date.

Newman's telegrams were answered with interest. Having dispatched but three electric missives, he received no less than eight gratulatory bulletins in return. He put them into his pocket-book, and the next time he encountered old Madame de Bellegarde drew them forth and displayed them to her. This, it must be confessed, was a slightly malicious stroke; the reader must judge in what degree the offense was venial. Newman knew that the marquise disliked his telegrams, though he could see no sufficient reason for it. Madame de Cintré, on the other hand, liked them, and, most of them being of a humorous cast, laughed at them immoderately, and inquired into the character of their authors. Newman, now that his prize was gained, felt a peculiar desire that his triumph should be manifest. He more than suspected that the Bellegardes were keeping quiet about it, and allowing it, in their select circle, but a limited resonance; and it pleased him to think that if he were to take the trouble he might, as he phrased it, break all the windows. No man likes being repudiated, and yet Newman, if he was not flattered, was not exactly offended. He had not this good excuse for his somewhat aggressive impulse to promulgate his felicity; his sentiment was of another quality. He wanted for once to make the heads of the house of Bellegarde *feel* him; he knew not when he should have another chance. He had had for the past six months a sense of the old lady and her son looking straight over his head, and he was now resolved that they should toe a mark which he would give himself the satisfaction of drawing.

"It is like seeing a bottle emptied when the wine is poured too slowly," he said to Mrs. Tristram. "They make me want to joggle their elbows and force them to spill their wine."

To this Mrs. Tristram answered that he had better leave them alone and let them do things in their own way. "You must make allowances for them," she said. "It is natural enough that they should hang fire a little. They thought they accepted you when you made your application; but they are not people of imagination, they could not project themselves into the future, and now they will have to begin again. But they *are* people of honor, and they will do whatever is necessary."

Newman spent a few moments in narrow-eyed meditation. "I am not hard on them," he presently said, "and to prove it I will invite them all to a festival."

"To a festival?"

"You have been laughing at my great gilded rooms all winter; I will show you that they are good for something. I will give a party. What is the grandest thing one can do here? I will hire all the great singers from the opera, and all the first people from the Théâtre Français, and I will give an entertainment."

"And whom will you invite?"

"You, first of all. And then the old lady and her son. And then every one among her friends whom I have met at her house or elsewhere, every one who has shown me the minimum of politeness, every duke of them and his wife. And then all my friends, without exception: Miss Kitty Upjohn, Miss Dora Finch, General Packard, C. P. Hatch, and all the rest. And every one shall know what it is about: that is, to celebrate my engagement to the Countess de Cintré. What do you think of the idea?"

"I think it is odious!" said Mrs. Tristram. And then in a moment: "I think it is delicious!"

The very next evening Newman repaired to Madame de Bellegarde's salon, where he found her surrounded by her children, and invited her to honor his poor dwelling by her presence on a certain evening a fortnight distant.

The marquise stared a moment. "My dear sir," she cried, "what do you want to do to me?"

"To make you acquainted with a few people, and then to place you in a very easy chair and ask you to listen to Madame Frezzolini's singing."

"You mean to give a concert?"

"Something of that sort."

"And to have a crowd of people?"

"All my friends, and I hope some of yours and your daughter's. I want to celebrate my engagement."

It seemed to Newman that Madame de Bellegarde turned pale. She opened her fan, a fine old painted fan of the last century, and looked at the picture, which represented a *fête champêtre*—a lady with a guitar, singing, and a group of dancers round a garlanded Hermes.

"We go out so little," murmured the marquis, "since my poor father's death."

"But *my* dear father is still alive, my friend," said his wife. "I am only waiting for my invitation to accept it," and she glanced with amiable confidence at Newman. "It will be magnificent; I am very sure of that."

I am sorry to say, to the discredit of Newman's gallantry, that this lady's invitation was not then and there bestowed; he was giving all his attention to the old marquise. She looked up at last, smiling. "I can't think of letting you offer me a fête," she said, "until I have offered you one. We want to present you to our friends; we will invite them all. We have it very much at heart. We must do things in order. Come to me about the 25th; I will let you know the exact day immediately. We shall not have any one so fine as Madame Frezzolini, but we shall have some very good people. After that you may talk of your own fête." The old lady spoke with a certain quick eagerness, smiling more agreeably as she went on.

It seemed to Newman a handsome proposal, and such proposals always touched the sources of his good-nature. He said to Madame de Bellegarde that he should be glad to come on the 25th or any other day, and that it mattered very little whether he met his friends at her house or at his own. I have said that Newman was observant, but it must be admitted that on this occasion he failed to notice a certain delicate glance which passed between Madame de Bellegarde and the marquis, and which we may presume to have been a commentary upon the innocence displayed in that latter clause of his speech.

Valentin de Bellegarde walked away with Newman that evening, and when they had left the Rue de l'Université some distance behind them he said reflectively, "My mother is very strong—very strong." Then in answer to an interrogative movement of Newman's he continued, "She was driven to the wall, but you would never have thought it. Her fête of the 25th was an invention of the moment. She had no idea whatever of giving a fête, but finding it the only issue from your proposal, she looked straight at the dose—excuse the expression—and bolted it, as you saw, without winking. She is very strong."

"Dear me!" said Newman, divided between relish and compassion. "I don't care a straw for her fête; I am willing to take the will for the deed."

"No, no," said Valentin, with a little inconsequent touch of family pride. "The thing will be done now, and done handsomely."

Chapter XV

VALENTIN DE BELLEGARDE's announcement of the secession of Mademoiselle Nioche from her father's domicile, and his irreverent reflections upon the attitude of this anxious parent in so grave a catastrophe, received a practical commentary in the fact that M. Nioche was slow to seek another interview with his late pupil. It had cost Newman some disgust to be forced to assent to Valentin's somewhat cynical interpretation of the old man's philosophy, and, though circumstances seemed to indicate that he had not given himself up to a noble despair, Newman thought it very possible he might be suffering more keenly than was apparent. M. Nioche had been in the habit of paying him a respectful little visit every two or three weeks, and his absence might be a proof quite as much of extreme depression as of a desire to conceal the success with which he had patched up his sorrow. Newman presently learned from Valentin several details touching this new phase of Mademoiselle Noémie's career.

"I told you she was remarkable," this unshrinking observer declared, "and the way she has managed this performance proves it. She has had other chances, but she was resolved to take none but the best. She did you the honor to think for a while that you might be such a chance. You were not; so she gathered up her patience and waited a while longer. At last her occasion came along, and she made her move with her eyes wide open. I am very sure she had no innocence to lose, but she had all her respectability. Dubious little damsel as you thought her, she had kept a firm hold of that; nothing could be proved against her, and she was determined not to let her reputation go till she had got her equivalent. About her equivalent she had high ideas. Apparently her ideal has been satisfied. It is fifty years old, bald-headed, and deaf, but it is very easy about money."

"And where in the world," asked Newman, "did you pick up this valuable information?"

"In conversation. Remember my frivolous habits. In conversation with a young woman engaged in the humble trade of glove-cleaner, who keeps a small shop in the Rue St. Roch.

M. Nioche lives in the same house, up six pair of stairs, across the court, in and out of whose ill-swept doorway Miss Noémie has been flitting for the last five years. The little glove-cleaner was an old acquaintance; she used to be the friend of a friend of mine, who has married and dropped such friends. I often saw her in his society. As soon as I espied her behind her clear little window-pane, I recollected her. I had on a spotlessly fresh pair of gloves, but I went in and held up my hands, and said to her, 'Dear mademoiselle, what will you ask me for cleaning these?' 'Dear count,' she answered immediately, 'I will clean them for you for nothing.' She had instantly recognized me, and I had to hear her history for the last six years. But after that, I put her upon that of her neighbors. She knows and admires Noémie, and she told me what I have just repeated."

A month elapsed without M. Nioche reappearing, and Newman, who every morning read two or three suicides in the "Figaro," began to suspect that, mortification proving stubborn, he had sought a balm for his wounded pride in the waters of the Seine. He had a note of M. Nioche's address in his pocket-book, and finding himself one day in the *quartier*, he determined in so far as he might to clear up his doubts. He repaired to the house in the Rue St. Roch which bore the recorded number, and observed in a neighboring basement, behind a dangling row of neatly inflated gloves, the attentive physiognomy of Bellegarde's informant—a sallow person in a dressing-gown—peering into the street as if she were expecting that amiable nobleman to pass again. But it was not to her that Newman applied; he simply asked of the portress if M. Nioche were at home. The portress replied, as the portress invariably replies, that her lodger had gone out barely three minutes before; but then, through the little square hole of her lodge-window taking the measure of Newman's fortunes, and seeing them, by an unspecified process, refresh the dry places of servitude to occupants of fifth floors on courts, she added that M. Nioche would have had just time to reach the Café de la Patrie, round the second corner to the left, at which establishment he regularly spent his afternoons. Newman thanked her for the information, took the second turning to the left, and arrived at the Café de la Patrie. He felt a momentary hesitation to go in; was it not rather mean to "follow up" poor old Nioche at that rate? But there passed across his vision an image of a haggard little septuagenarian taking measured sips of a glass of sugar and water and finding them quite impotent to sweeten his desolation. He opened the door and entered, perceiving nothing at first but a dense cloud of tobacco smoke. Across this, however, in a corner, he presently descried the figure of M. Nioche, stirring the contents of a deep glass, with a lady seated in front of him. The lady's back was turned to Newman, but M. Nioche very soon perceived and recognized his visitor. Newman had gone toward him, and the old man rose slowly, gazing at him with a more blighted expression even than usual.

"If you are drinking hot punch," said Newman, "I suppose you are not dead. That 's all right. Don't move."

M. Nioche stood staring, with a fallen jaw, not daring to put out his hand. The lady, who sat facing him, turned round in her place and glanced upward with a spirited toss of her head, displaying the agreeable features of his daughter. She looked at Newman sharply, to see how he was looking at her; then—I don't know what she discovered—she said graciously, "How d' ye do, monsieur? won't you come into our little corner?"

"Did you come—did you come after *me?*" asked M. Nioche, very softly.

"I went to your house to see what had become of you. I thought you might be sick," said Newman.

"It is very good of you, as always," said the old man. "No, I am not well. Yes, I am *seek.*"

"Ask monsieur to sit down," said Mademoiselle Nioche. "Garçon, bring a chair."

"Will you do us the honor to *seat?*" said M. Nioche, timorously, and with a double foreignness of accent.

Newman said to himself that he had better see the thing out, and he took a chair at the end of the table, with Mademoiselle Nioche on his left and her father on the other side. "You will take something, of course," said Miss Noémie, who was sipping a glass of madeira. Newman said that he believed not, and then she turned to her papa with a smile. "What an honor, eh? he has come only for us." M. Nioche drained his pungent glass at a long draught, and looked out from eyes more lachrymose in consequence. "But you did n't come for me, eh?" Mademoiselle Noémie went on. "You did n't expect to find me here?"

Newman observed the change in her appearance. She was very elegant and prettier than before; she looked a year or two older, and it was noticeable that, to the eye, she had only gained in respectability. She looked "lady-like." She was dressed in quiet colors, and she wore her expensively unobtrusive toilet with a grace that might have come from years of practice. Her present self-possession and *aplomb* struck Newman as really infernal, and he inclined to agree with Valentin de Bellegarde that the young lady was very remarkable. "No, to tell the truth, I did n't come for you," he said, "and I did n't expect to find you. I was told," he added in a moment, "that you had left your father."

"*Quelle horreur!*" cried Mademoiselle Nioche with a smile. "Does one leave one's father? You have the proof of the contrary."

"Yes, convincing proof," said Newman glancing at M. Nioche. The old man caught his glance obliquely, with his faded, deprecating eye, and then, lifting his empty glass, pretended to drink again.

"Who told you that?" Noémie demanded. "I know very well. It was M. de Bellegarde. Why don't you say yes? You are not polite."

"I am embarrassed," said Newman.

"I set you a better example. I know M. de Bellegarde told you. He knows a great deal about me—or he thinks he does. He has taken a great deal of trouble to find out, but half of it is n't true. In the first place, I have n't left my father; I am much too fond of him. Is n't it so, little father? M. de Bellegarde is a charming young man; it is impossible to be cleverer. I know a good deal about him too; you can tell him that when you next see him."

"No," said Newman, with a sturdy grin; "I won't carry any messages for you."

"Just as you please," said Mademoiselle Nioche. "I don't depend upon you, nor does M. de Bellegarde either. He is very much interested in me; he can be left to his own devices. He is a contrast to you."

"Oh, he is a great contrast to me, I have no doubt," said Newman. "But I don't exactly know how you mean it."

"I mean it in this way. First of all, he never offered to help me to a *dot* and a husband." And Mademoiselle Nioche paused, smiling. "I won't say that is in his favor, for I do you justice. What led you, by the way, to make me such a queer offer? You did n't care for me."

"Oh yes, I did," said Newman.

"How so?"

"It would have given me real pleasure to see you married to a respectable young fellow."

"With six thousand francs of income!" cried Mademoiselle Nioche. "Do you call that caring for me? I 'm afraid you know little about women. You were not *galant*; you were not what you might have been."

Newman flushed, a trifle fiercely. "Come!" he exclaimed, "that 's rather strong. I had no idea I had been so shabby."

Mademoiselle Nioche smiled as she took up her muff. "It is something, at any rate, to have made you angry."

Her father had leaned both his elbows on the table, and his head, bent forward, was supported in his hands, the thin white fingers of which were pressed over his ears. In this position he was staring fixedly at the bottom of his empty glass, and Newman supposed he was not hearing. Mademoiselle Noémie buttoned her furred jacket and pushed back her chair, casting a glance charged with the consciousness of an expensive appearance first down over her flounces and then up at Newman.

"You had better have remained an honest girl," Newman said, quietly.

M. Nioche continued to stare at the bottom of his glass, and his daughter got up, still bravely smiling. "You mean that I look so much like one? That 's more than most women do nowadays. Don't judge me yet a while," she added. "I mean to succeed; that 's what I mean to do. I leave you; I don't mean to be seen in cafés, for one thing. I can't think what you want of my poor father; he 's very comfortable now. It is n't his fault, either. Au revoir, little father." And she tapped the old man on the head with her muff. Then she stopped a minute, looking at Newman. "Tell M. de Bellegarde, when he wants news of me, to come and get it from *me*!" And she turned and departed, the white-aproned waiter, with a bow, holding the door wide open for her.

M. Nioche sat motionless, and Newman hardly knew what to say to him. The old man looked dismally foolish. "So you determined not to shoot her, after all," Newman said, presently.

M. Nioche, without moving, raised his eyes and gave him a long, peculiar look. It seemed to confess everything, and yet not to ask for pity, nor to pretend, on the other hand, to a rugged ability to do without it. It might have expressed the state of mind of an innocuous insect, flat in shape and conscious of the impending pressure of a boot-sole, and reflecting that he was perhaps too flat to be crushed. M. Nioche's gaze was a profession of moral flatness. "You despise me terribly," he said, in the weakest possible voice.

"Oh no," said Newman, "it is none of my business. It 's a good plan to take things easily."

"I made you too many fine speeches," M. Nioche added. "I meant them at the time."

"I am sure I am very glad you did n't shoot her," said Newman. "I was afraid you might have shot yourself. That is why I came to look you up." And he began to button his coat.

"Neither," said M. Nioche. "You despise me, and I can't explain to you. I hoped I should n't see you again."

"Why, that 's rather shabby," said Newman. "You should n't drop your friends that way. Besides, the last time you came to see me I thought you particularly jolly."

"Yes, I remember," said M. Nioche, musingly; "I was in a fever. I did n't know what I said, what I did. It was delirium."

"Ah, well, you are quieter now."

M. Nioche was silent a moment. "As quiet as the grave," he whispered softly.

"Are you very unhappy?" asked Newman.

M. Nioche rubbed his forehead slowly, and even pushed back his wig a little, looking askance at his empty glass. "Yes—yes. But that 's an old story. I have always been unhappy. My daughter does what she will with me. I take what she gives me, good or bad. I have no spirit, and when you have no spirit you must keep quiet. I shan't trouble you any more."

"Well," said Newman, rather disgusted at the smooth operation of the old man's philosophy, "that 's as you please."

M. Nioche seemed to have been prepared to be despised, but nevertheless he made a feeble movement of appeal from Newman's faint praise. "After all," he said, "she is my daughter, and I can still look after her. If she will do wrong, why she will. But there are many different paths, there are degrees. I can give her the benefit—give her the benefit"—and M. Nioche paused, staring vaguely at Newman, who began to suspect that his brain had softened—"the benefit of my experience," M. Nioche added.

"Your experience?" inquired Newman, both amused and amazed.

"My experience of business," said M. Nioche, gravely.

"Ah, yes," said Newman, laughing, "that will be a great advantage to her!" And then he said good-by, and offered the poor, foolish old man his hand.

M. Nioche took it and leaned back against the wall, holding it a moment and looking up at him. "I suppose you think my wits are going," he said. "Very likely; I have always a pain in my head. That 's why I can't explain, I can't tell you. And she 's so strong, she makes me walk as she will, anywhere! But there 's this—there 's this." And he stopped, still staring up at Newman. His little white eyes expanded and glittered for a moment like those of a cat in the dark. "It 's not as it seems. I have n't forgiven her. Oh, no!"

"That 's right; don't," said Newman. "She 's a bad case."

"It 's horrible, it 's terrible," said M. Nioche; "but do you want to know the truth? I hate her! I take what she gives me, and I hate her more. To-day she brought me three hundred francs; they are here in my waistcoat pocket. Now I hate her almost cruelly. No, I have n't forgiven her."

"Why did you accept the money?" Newman asked.

"If I had n't," said M. Nioche, "I should have hated her still more. That 's what misery is. No, I have n't forgiven her."

"Take care you don't hurt her!" said Newman, laughing again. And with this he took his leave. As he passed along the glazed side of the café, on reaching the street, he saw the old man motioning the waiter, with a melancholy gesture, to replenish his glass.

One day, a week after his visit to the Café de la Patrie, he called upon Valentin de Bellegarde, and by good fortune found him at home. Newman spoke of his interview with M. Nioche and his daughter, and said he was afraid Valentin had judged the old man correctly. He had found the couple hobnobbing together in all amity; the old gentleman's rigor was purely theoretic. Newman confessed that he was disappointed; he should have expected to see M. Nioche take high ground.

"High ground, my dear fellow," said Valentin, laughing; "there is no high ground for him to take. The only perceptible eminence in M. Nioche's horizon is Montmartre, which is not an edifying quarter. You can't go mountaineering in a flat country."

"He remarked, indeed," said Newman, "that he had not forgiven her. But she 'll never find it out."

"We must do him the justice to suppose he does n't like the thing," Valentin rejoined. "Mademoiselle Nioche is like the great artists whose biographies we read, who at the beginning of their career have suffered opposition in the domestic circle. Their vocation has not been recognized by their families, but the world has done it justice. Mademoiselle Nioche has a vocation."

"Oh, come," said Newman, impatiently, "you take the little baggage too seriously."

"I know I do; but when one has nothing to think about, one must think of little baggages. I suppose it is better to be serious about light things than not to be serious at all. This little baggage entertains me."

"Oh, she has discovered that. She knows you have been hunting her up and asking questions about her. She is very much tickled by it. That 's rather annoying."

"Annoying, my dear fellow," laughed Valentin; "not the least!"

"Hanged if I should want to have a greedy little adventuress like that know I was giving myself such pains about her!" said Newman.

"A pretty woman is always worth one's pains," objected Valentin. "Mademoiselle Nioche is welcome to be tickled by my curiosity, and to know that I am tickled that she is tickled. She is not so much tickled, by the way."

"You had better go and tell her," Newman rejoined. "She gave me a message for you of some such drift."

"Bless your quiet imagination," said Valentin, "I have been to see her—three times in five days. She is a charming hostess; we talk of Shakespeare and the musical glasses. She is extremely clever and a very curious type; not at all coarse or wanting to be coarse; determined not to be. She means to take very good care of herself. She is extremely perfect; she is as hard and clear-cut as some little figure of a sea-nymph in an antique intaglio, and I will warrant that she has not a grain more of sentiment or heart than if she were scooped out of a big amethyst. You can't scratch her even with a diamond. Extremely pretty,—really, when you know her, she is wonderfully pretty,—intelligent, determined, ambitious, unscrupulous, capable of looking at a man strangled without changing color, she is, upon my honor, extremely entertaining."

"It's a fine list of attractions," said Newman; "they would serve as a police-detective's description of a favorite criminal. I should sum them up by another word than 'entertaining.'"

"Why, that is just the word to use. I don't say she is laudable or lovable. I don't want her as my wife or my sister. But she is a very curious and ingenious piece of machinery; I like to see it in operation."

"Well, I have seen some very curious machines, too," said Newman; "and once, in a needle factory, I saw a gentleman from the city, who had stepped too near one of them, picked up as neatly as if he had been prodded by a fork, swallowed down straight, and ground into small pieces."

Reëntering his domicile, late in the evening, three days after Madame de Bellegarde had made her bargain with him—the expression is sufficiently correct—touching the entertainment at which she was to present him to the world, he found on his table a card of goodly dimensions bearing an announcement that this lady would be at home on the 27th of the month, at ten o'clock in the evening. He stuck it into the frame of his mirror and eyed it with some complacency; it seemed an agreeable emblem of triumph, documentary evidence that his prize was gained. Stretched out in a chair, he was looking at it lovingly, when Valentin de Bellegarde was shown into the room. Valentin's glance presently followed the direction of Newman's, and he perceived his mother's invitation.

"And what have they put into the corner?" he asked. "Not the customary 'music,' 'dancing,' or 'tableaux vivants'? They ought at least to put 'An American.'"

"Oh, there are to be several of us," said Newman. "Mrs. Tristram told me to-day that she had received a card and sent an acceptance."

"Ah, then, with Mrs. Tristram and her husband you will have support. My mother might have put on her card 'Three Americans.' But I suspect you will not lack amusement. You will see a great many of the best people in France. I mean the long pedigrees and the high noses, and all that. Some of them are awful idiots; I advise you to take them up cautiously."

"Oh, I guess I shall like them," said Newman. "I am prepared to like every one and everything in these days; I am in high good-humor."

Valentin looked at him a moment in silence and then dropped himself into a chair with an unwonted air of weariness. "Happy man!" he said with a sigh. "Take care you don't become offensive."

"If any one chooses to take offense, he may. I have a good conscience," said Newman.

"So you are really in love with my sister."

"Yes, sir!" said Newman, after a pause.

"And she also?"

"I guess she likes me," said Newman.

"What is the witchcraft you have used?" Valentin asked. "How do *you* make love?"

"Oh, I have n't any general rules," said Newman. "In any way that seems acceptable."

"I suspect that, if one knew it," said Valentin, laughing,

"you are a terrible customer. You walk in seven-league boots."

"There is something the matter with you to-night," Newman said in response to this. "You are vicious. Spare me all discordant sounds until after my marriage. Then, when I have settled down for life, I shall be better able to take things as they come."

"And when does your marriage take place?"

"About six weeks hence."

Valentin was silent a while, and then he said, "And you feel very confident about the future?"

"Confident. I knew what I wanted, exactly, and I know what I have got."

"You are sure you are going to be happy?"

"Sure?" said Newman. "So foolish a question deserves a foolish answer. Yes!"

"You are not afraid of anything?"

"What should I be afraid of? You can't hurt me unless you kill me by some violent means. That I should indeed consider a tremendous sell. I want to live and I mean to live. I can't die of illness, I am too ridiculously tough; and the time for dying of old age won't come round yet a while. I can't lose my wife, I shall take too good care of her. I may lose my money, or a large part of it; but that won't matter, for I shall make twice as much again. So what have I to be afraid of?"

"You are not afraid it may be rather a mistake for an American man of business to marry a French countess?"

"For the countess, possibly; but not for the man of business, if you mean me! But my countess shall not be disappointed; I answer for her happiness!" And as if he felt the impulse to celebrate his happy certitude by a bonfire, he got up to throw a couple of logs upon the already blazing hearth. Valentin watched for a few moments the quickened flame, and then, with his head leaning on his hand, gave a melancholy sigh. "Got a headache?" Newman asked.

"*Je suis triste,*" said Valentin, with Gallic simplicity.

"You are sad, eh? Is it about the lady you said the other night that you adored and that you could n't marry?"

"Did I really say that? It seemed to me afterwards that the

words had escaped me. Before Claire it was bad taste. But I felt gloomy as I spoke, and I feel gloomy still. Why did you ever introduce me to that girl?"

"Oh, it 's Noémie, is it? Lord deliver us! You don't mean to say you are lovesick about her?"

"Lovesick, no; it 's not a grand passion. But the cold-blooded little demon sticks in my thoughts; she has bitten me with those even little teeth of hers; I feel as if I might turn rabid and do something crazy in consequence. It 's very low; it 's disgustingly low. She 's the most mercenary little jade in Europe. Yet she really affects my peace of mind; she is always running in my head. It 's a striking contrast to your noble and virtuous attachment—a vile contrast! It is rather pitiful that it should be the best I am able to do for myself at my present respectable age. I am a nice young man, eh, *en somme*? You can't warrant my future, as you do your own."

"Drop that girl, short," said Newman; "don't go near her again, and your future will do. Come over to America and I will get you a place in a bank."

"It is easy to say drop her," said Valentin, with a light laugh. "You can't drop a pretty woman like that. One must be polite, even with Noémie. Besides, I 'll not have her suppose I am afraid of her."

"So, between politeness and vanity, you will get deeper into the mud? Keep them both for something better. Remember, too, that I did n't want to introduce you to her; you insisted. I had a sort of uneasy feeling about it."

"Oh, I don't reproach you," said Valentin. "Heaven forbid! I would n't for the world have missed knowing her. She is really extraordinary. The way she has already spread her wings is amazing. I don't know when a woman has amused me more. But excuse me," he added in an instant; "she does n't amuse you, at second hand, and the subject is an impure one. Let us talk of something else." Valentin introduced another topic, but within five minutes Newman observed that, by a bold transition, he had reverted to Mademoiselle Nioche, and was giving pictures of her manners and quoting specimens of her *mots*. These were very witty, and, for a young woman who six months before had been painting the most artless madonnas, startlingly cynical. But at last, abruptly, he stopped, became thoughtful, and for some time afterwards said nothing. When he rose to go it was evident that his thoughts were still running upon Mademoiselle Nioche. "Yes, she 's a frightful little monster!" he said.

Chapter XVI

THE NEXT TEN DAYS were the happiest that Newman had ever known. He saw Madame de Cintré every day, and never saw either old Madame de Bellegarde or the elder of his prospective brothers-in-law. Madame de Cintré at last seemed to think it becoming to apologize for their never being present. "They are much taken up," she said, "with doing the honors of Paris to Lord Deepmere." There was a smile in her gravity as she made this declaration, and it deepened as she added, "He is our seventh cousin, you know, and blood is thicker than water. And then, he is so interesting!" And with this she laughed.

Newman met young Madame de Bellegarde two or three times, always roaming about with graceful vagueness, as if in search of an unattainable ideal of amusement. She always reminded him of a painted perfume-bottle with a crack in it; but he had grown to have a kindly feeling for her, based on the fact of her owing conjugal allegiance to Urbain de Bellegarde. He pitied M. de Bellegarde's wife, especially since she was a silly, thirstily-smiling little brunette, with a suggestion of an unregulated heart. The small marquise sometimes looked at him with an intensity too marked not to be innocent, for coquetry is more finely shaded. She apparently wanted to ask him something or tell him something; he wondered what it was. But he was shy of giving her an opportunity, because, if her communication bore upon the aridity of her matrimonial lot, he was at a loss to see how he could help her. He had a fancy, however, of her coming up to him some day and saying (after looking round behind her) with a little passionate hiss, "I know you detest my husband; let me have the pleasure of assuring you for once that you are right. Pity a poor woman who is married to a clock-image in *papier-mâché*!" Possessing, however, in default of a competent knowledge of the principles of etiquette, a very downright sense of the "meanness" of certain actions, it seemed to him to belong to his position to keep on his guard; he was not going to put it into the power of these people to say that in their house he had done anything unpleasant. As it was, Madame de Bellegarde used to give him news of the dress she meant to wear at his wedding, and which had not yet, in her creative imagination, in spite of many interviews with the tailor, resolved itself into its composite totality. "I told you pale blue bows on the sleeves, at the elbows," she said. "But to-day I don't see my blue bows at all. I don't know what has become of them. To-day I see pink—a tender pink. And then I pass through strange, dull phases in which neither blue nor pink says anything to me. And yet I must have the bows."

"Have them green or yellow," said Newman.

"*Malheureux!*" the little marquise would cry. "Green bows would break your marriage—your children would be illegitimate!"

Madame de Cintré was calmly happy before the world, and Newman had the felicity of fancying that before him, when the world was absent, she was almost agitatedly happy. She said very tender things. "I take no pleasure in you. You never give me a chance to scold you, to correct you. I bargained for that, I expected to enjoy it. But you won't do anything dreadful; you are dismally inoffensive. It is very stupid; there is no excitement for me; I might as well be marrying some one else."

"I am afraid it 's the worst I can do," Newman would say in answer to this. "Kindly overlook the deficiency." He assured her that he, at least, would never scold her; she was perfectly satisfactory. "If you only knew," he said, "how exactly you are what I coveted! And I am beginning to understand why I coveted it; the having it makes all the difference that I expected. Never was a man so pleased with his good fortune. You have been holding your head for a week past just as I wanted my wife to hold hers. You say just the things I want her to say. You walk about the room just as I want her to walk. You have just the taste in dress that I want her to have. In short, you come up to the mark, and, I can tell you, my mark was high."

These observations seemed to make Madame de Cintré rather grave. At last she said, "Depend upon it, I don't come up to the mark; your mark is too high. I am not all that you suppose; I am a much smaller affair. She is a magnificent

woman, your ideal. Pray, how did she come to such perfection?"

"She was never anything else," Newman said.

"I really believe," Madame de Cintré went on, "that she is
better than my own ideal. Do you know that is a very handsome compliment? Well, sir, I will make her my own!"

Mrs. Tristram came to see her dear Claire after Newman
had announced his engagement, and she told our hero the
next day that his good fortune was simply absurd. "For the
ridiculous part of it is," she said, "that you are evidently going
to be as happy as if you were marrying Miss Smith or Miss
Thompson. I call it a brilliant match for you, but you get
brilliancy without paying any tax upon it. Those things are
usually a compromise, but here you have everything, and
nothing crowds anything else out. You will be brilliantly
happy as well." Newman thanked her for her pleasant, encouraging way of saying things; no woman could encourage
or discourage better. Tristram's way of saying things was different; he had been taken by his wife to call upon Madame
de Cintré, and he gave an account of the expedition.

"You don't catch me giving an opinion on your countess
this time," he said; "I put my foot in it once. That 's a d—d
underhand thing to do, by the way—coming round to sound
a fellow upon the woman you are going to marry. You deserve anything you get. Then of course you rush and tell her,
and she takes care to make it pleasant for the poor spiteful
wretch the first time he calls. I will do you the justice to say,
however, that you don't seem to have told Madame de
Cintré; or if you have she 's uncommonly magnanimous. She
was very nice; she was tremendously polite. She and Lizzie
sat on the sofa, pressing each other's hands and calling each
other *chère belle*, and Madame de Cintré sent me with every
third word a magnificent smile, as if to give me to understand
that I too was a handsome dear. She quite made up for past
neglect, I assure you; she was very pleasant and sociable. Only
in an evil hour it came into her head to say that she must
present us to her mother—her mother wished to know your
friends. I did n't want to know her mother, and I was on the
point of telling Lizzie to go in alone and let me wait for her
outside. But Lizzie, with her usual infernal ingenuity, guessed

my purpose and reduced me by a glance of her eye. So they marched off arm in arm, and I followed as I could. We found the old lady in her arm-chair, twiddling her aristocratic thumbs. She looked at Lizzie from head to foot; but at that game Lizzie, to do her justice, was a match for her. My wife told her we were great friends of Mr. Newman. The marquise stared a moment, and then said, 'Oh, Mr. Newman! My daughter has made up her mind to marry a Mr. Newman.' Then Madame de Cintré began to fondle Lizzie again, and said it was this dear lady that had planned the match and brought them together. 'Oh, 't is you I have to thank for my American son-in-law,' the old lady said to Mrs. Tristram. 'It was a very clever thought of yours. Be sure of my gratitude.' And then she began to look at me and presently said, 'Pray, are you engaged in some species of manufacture?' I wanted to say that I manufactured broomsticks for old witches to ride on, but Lizzie got in ahead of me. 'My husband, Madame la Marquise,' she said, 'belongs to that unfortunate class of persons who have no profession and no business, and do very little good in the world.' To get her poke at the old woman she did n't care where she shoved me. 'Dear me,' said the marquise, 'we all have our duties.' 'I am sorry mine compel me to take leave of you,' said Lizzie. And we bundled out again. But you have a mother-in-law, in all the force of the term."

"Oh," said Newman, "my mother-in-law desires nothing better than to let me alone."

Betimes, on the evening of the 27th, he went to Madame de Bellegarde's ball. The old house in the Rue de l'Université looked strangely brilliant. In the circle of light projected from the outer gate a detachment of the populace stood watching the carriages roll in; the court was illumined with flaring torches and the portico carpeted with crimson. When Newman arrived there were but a few people present. The marquise and her two daughters were at the top of the staircase, where the sallow old nymph in the angle peeped out from a bower of plants. Madame de Bellegarde, in purple and fine laces, looked like an old lady painted by Vandyke; Madame de Cintré was dressed in white. The old lady greeted Newman with majestic formality, and, looking round her, called several of the persons who were standing near. They were elderly gentlemen, of what Valentin de Bellegarde had designated as the high-nosed category; two or three of them wore cordons and stars. They approached with measured alertness, and the marquise said that she wished to present them to Mr. Newman, who was going to marry her daughter. Then she introduced successively three dukes, three counts, and a baron. These gentlemen bowed and smiled most agreeably, and Newman indulged in a series of impartial hand-shakes, accompanied by a "Happy to make your acquaintance, sir." He looked at Madame de Cintré, but she was not looking at him. If his personal self-consciousness had been of a nature to make him constantly refer to her, as the critic before whom, in company, he played his part, he might have found it a flattering proof of her confidence that he never caught her eyes resting upon him. It is a reflection Newman did not make, but we may nevertheless risk it, that in spite of this circumstance she probably saw every movement of his little finger. Young Madame de Bellegarde was dressed in an audacious toilet of crimson crape, bestrewn with huge silver moons—thin crescents and full disks.

"You don't say anything about my dress," she said to Newman.

"I feel," he answered, "as if I were looking at you through a telescope. It is very strange."

"If it is strange it matches the occasion. But I am not a heavenly body."

"I never saw the sky at midnight that particular shade of crimson," said Newman.

"That is my originality; any one could have chosen blue. My sister-in-law would have chosen a lovely shade of blue, with a dozen little delicate moons. But I think crimson is much more amusing. And I give my idea, which is moonshine."

"Moonshine and bloodshed," said Newman.

"A murder by moonlight," laughed Madame de Bellegarde. "What a delicious idea for a toilet! To make it complete, there is the silver dagger, you see, stuck into my hair. But here comes Lord Deepmere," she added in a moment. "I must find out what he thinks of it." Lord Deepmere came up, looking very red in the face, and laughing. "Lord Deepmere can't decide which he prefers, my sister-in-law or me," said Madame de Bellegarde. "He likes Claire because she is his cousin, and me because I am not. But he has no right to make love to Claire, whereas I am perfectly *disponible*. It is very wrong to make love to a woman who is engaged, but it is very wrong not to make love to a woman who is married."

"Oh, it 's very jolly making love to married women," said Lord Deepmere, "because they can't ask you to marry them."

"Is that what the others do, the spinsters?" Newman inquired.

"Oh dear, yes," said Lord Deepmere; "in England all the girls ask a fellow to marry them."

"And a fellow brutally refuses," said Madame de Bellegarde.

"Why, really, you know, a fellow can't marry any girl that asks him," said his lordship.

"Your cousin won't ask you. She is going to marry Mr. Newman."

"Oh, that 's a very different thing!" laughed Lord Deepmere.

"You would have accepted *her*, I suppose. That makes me hope that after all you prefer me."

"Oh, when things are nice I never prefer one to the other," said the young Englishman. "I take them all."

"Ah, what a horror! I won't be taken in that way; I must be kept apart," cried Madame de Bellegarde. "Mr. Newman is much better; he knows how to choose. Oh, he chooses as if he were threading a needle. He prefers Madame de Cintré to any conceivable creature or thing."

"Well, you can't help my being her cousin," said Lord Deepmere to Newman, with candid hilarity.

"Oh no, I can't help that," said Newman, laughing back; "neither can she!"

"And you can't help my dancing with her," said Lord Deepmere, with sturdy simplicity.

"I could prevent that only by dancing with her myself," said Newman. "But unfortunately I don't know how to dance."

"Oh, you may dance without knowing how; may you not,

milord?" said Madame de Bellegarde. But to this Lord Deepmere replied that a fellow ought to know how to dance if he
did n't want to make an ass of himself; and at this same moment Urbain de Bellegarde joined the group, slow-stepping
and with his hands behind him.

"This is a very splendid entertainment," said Newman,
cheerfully. "The old house looks very bright."

"If *you* are pleased, we are content," said the marquis, lifting his shoulders and bending them forward.

"Oh, I suspect every one is pleased," said Newman. "How
can they help being pleased when the first thing they see as
they come in is your sister, standing there as beautiful as an
angel?"

"Yes, she is very beautiful," rejoined the marquis, solemnly.
"But that is not so great a source of satisfaction to other people, naturally, as to you."

"Yes, I am satisfied, marquis, I am satisfied," said Newman,
with his protracted enunciation. "And now tell me," he
added, looking round, "who some of your friends are."

M. de Bellegarde looked about him in silence, with his
head bent and his hand raised to his lower lip, which he
slowly rubbed. A stream of people had been pouring into the
salon in which Newman stood with his host, the rooms were
filling up and the spectacle had become brilliant. It borrowed
its splendor chiefly from the shining shoulders and profuse
jewels of the women, and from the voluminous elegance of
their dresses. There were no uniforms, as Madame de Bellegarde's door was inexorably closed against the myrmidons of
the upstart power which then ruled the fortunes of France,
and the great company of smiling and chattering faces was
not graced by any very frequent suggestions of harmonious
beauty. It is a pity, nevertheless, that Newman had not been
a physiognomist, for a great many of the faces were irregularly agreeable, expressive, and suggestive. If the occasion had
been different they would hardly have pleased him; he would
have thought the women not pretty enough and the men too
smirking; but he was now in a humor to receive none but
agreeable impressions, and he looked no more narrowly than
to perceive that every one was brilliant, and to feel that the
sum of their brilliancy was a part of his credit. "I will present

you to some people," said M. de Bellegarde after a while. "I will make a point of it, in fact. You will allow me?"

"Oh, I will shake hands with any one you want," said Newman. "Your mother just introduced me to half a dozen old gentlemen. Take care you don't pick up the same parties again."

"Who are the gentlemen to whom my mother presented you?"

"Upon my word, I forget them," said Newman, laughing. "The people here look very much alike."

"I suspect they have not forgotten you," said the marquis. And he began to walk through the rooms. Newman, to keep near him in the crowd, took his arm; after which, for some time, the marquis walked straight along, in silence. At last, reaching the farther end of the suite of reception-rooms, Newman found himself in the presence of a lady of monstrous proportions, seated in a very capacious arm-chair, with several persons standing in a semicircle round her. This little group had divided as the marquis came up, and M. de Bellegarde stepped forward and stood for an instant silent and obsequious, with his hat raised to his lips, as Newman had seen some gentlemen stand in churches as soon as they entered their pews. The lady, indeed, bore a very fair likeness to a reverend effigy in some idolatrous shrine. She was monumentally stout and imperturbably serene. Her aspect was to Newman almost formidable; he had a troubled consciousness of a triple chin, a small piercing eye, a vast expanse of uncovered bosom, a nodding and twinkling tiara of plumes and gems, and an immense circumference of satin petticoat. With her little circle of beholders this remarkable woman reminded him of the Fat Lady at a fair. She fixed her small, unwinking eyes at the new-comers.

"Dear duchess," said the marquis, "let me present you our good friend Mr. Newman, of whom you have heard us speak. Wishing to make Mr. Newman known to those who are dear to us, I could not possibly fail to begin with you."

"Charmed, dear friend; charmed, monsieur," said the duchess in a voice which, though small and shrill, was not disagreeable, while Newman executed his obeisance. "I came on purpose to see monsieur. I hope he appreciates the compliment. You have only to look at me to do so, sir," she continued, sweeping her person with a much-encompassing glance. Newman hardly knew what to say, though it seemed that to a duchess who joked about her corpulence one might say almost anything. On hearing that the duchess had come on purpose to see Newman, the gentlemen who surrounded her turned a little and looked at him with sympathetic curiosity. The marquis with supernatural gravity mentioned to him the name of each, while the gentleman who bore it bowed; they were all what are called in France *beaux noms*. "I wanted extremely to see you," the duchess went on. "*C'est positif.* In the first place, I am very fond of the person you are going to marry; she is the most charming creature in France. Mind you treat her well, or you shall hear some news of me. But you look as if you were good. I am told you are very remarkable. I have heard all sorts of extraordinary things about you. Voyons, are they true?"

"I don't know what you can have heard," said Newman.

"Oh, you have your *légende*. We have heard that you have had a career the most checkered, the most bizarre. What is that about your having founded a city some ten years ago in the great West, a city which contains to-day half a million of inhabitants? Is n't it half a million, messieurs? You are exclusive proprietor of this flourishing settlement, and are consequently fabulously rich, and you would be richer still if you did n't grant lands and houses free of rent to all new-comers who will pledge themselves never to smoke cigars. At this game, in three years, we are told, you are going to be made president of America."

The duchess recited this amazing "legend" with a smooth self-possession which gave the speech, to Newman's mind, the air of being a bit of amusing dialogue in a play, delivered by a veteran comic actress. Before she had ceased speaking he had burst into loud, irrepressible laughter. "Dear duchess, dear duchess," the marquis began to murmur, soothingly. Two or three persons came to the door of the room to see who was laughing at the duchess. But the lady continued with the soft, serene assurance of a person who, as a duchess, was certain of being listened to, and, as a garrulous woman, was independent of the pulse of her auditors. "But I know

you are very remarkable. You must be, to have endeared
yourself to this good marquis and to his admirable mother.
They don't bestow their esteem on all the world. They are
very exacting. I myself am not very sure at this hour of really
possessing it. Eh, Bellegarde? To please you, I see, one must
be an American millionaire. But your real triumph, my dear
sir, is pleasing the countess; she is as difficult as a princess in
a fairy tale. Your success is a miracle. What is your secret? I
don't ask you to reveal it before all these gentlemen, but come
and see me some day and give me a specimen of your talents."

"The secret is with Madame de Cintré," said Newman.
"You must ask her for it. It consists in her having a great deal
of charity."

"Very pretty!" said the duchess. "That 's a very nice specimen, to begin with. What, Bellegarde, are you already taking
monsieur away?"

"I have a duty to perform, dear friend," said the marquis,
pointing to the other groups.

"Ah, for you I know what that means. Well, I have seen
monsieur; that is what I wanted. He can't persuade me that
he is n't very clever. Farewell."

As Newman passed on with his host, he asked who the
duchess was. "The greatest lady in France," said the marquis.
M. de Bellegarde then presented his prospective brother-in-
law to some twenty other persons of both sexes, selected apparently for their typically august character. In some cases this
character was written in a good round hand upon the countenance of the wearer; in others Newman was thankful for
such help as his companion's impressively brief intimation
contributed to the discovery of it. There were large, majestic
men, and small, demonstrative men; there were ugly ladies in
yellow lace and quaint jewels, and pretty ladies with white
shoulders from which jewels and everything else were absent.
Every one gave Newman extreme attention, every one smiled,
every one was charmed to make his acquaintance, every one
looked at him with that soft hardness of good society which
puts out its hand but keeps its fingers closed over the coin. If
the marquis was going about as a bear-leader, if the fiction of
Beauty and the Beast was supposed to have found its com-
panion-piece, the general impression appeared to be that the

bear was a very fair imitation of humanity. Newman found
his reception among the marquis's friends very "pleasant;" he
could not have said more for it. It was pleasant to be treated
with so much explicit politeness; it was pleasant to hear neatly
turned civilities, with a flavor of wit, uttered from beneath
carefully-shaped mustaches; it was pleasant to see clever
Frenchwomen—they all seemed clever—turn their backs to
their partners to get a good look at the strange American
whom Claire de Cintré was to marry, and reward the object
of the exhibition with a charming smile. At last, as he turned
away from a battery of smiles and other amenities, Newman
caught the eye of the marquis looking at him heavily; and
thereupon, for a single instant, he checked himself. "Am I
behaving like a d—d fool?" he asked himself. "Am I stepping
about like a terrier on his hind legs?" At this moment he perceived Mrs. Tristram at the other side of the room, and he
waived his hand in farewell to M. de Bellegarde and made his
way toward her.

"Am I holding my head too high?" he asked. "Do I look as
if I had the lower end of a pulley fastened to my chin?"

"You look like all happy men, very ridiculous," said Mrs.
Tristram. "It 's the usual thing, neither better nor worse. I
have been watching you for the last ten minutes, and I have
been watching M. de Bellegarde. He does n't like it."

"The more credit to him for putting it through," replied
Newman. "But I shall be generous. I shan't trouble him any
more. But I am very happy. I can't stand still here. Please to
take my arm and we will go for a walk."

He led Mrs. Tristram through all the rooms. There were a
great many of them, and, decorated for the occasion and filled
with a stately crowd, their somewhat tarnished nobleness recovered its lustre. Mrs. Tristram, looking about her, dropped
a series of softly-incisive comments upon her fellow-guests.
But Newman made vague answers; he hardly heard her; his
thoughts were elsewhere. They were lost in a cheerful sense
of success, of attainment and victory. His momentary care as
to whether he looked like a fool passed away, leaving him
simply with a rich contentment. He had got what he wanted.
The savor of success had always been highly agreeable to him,
and it had been his fortune to know it often. But it had never

before been so sweet, been associated with so much that was brilliant and suggestive and entertaining. The lights, the flowers, the music, the crowd, the splendid women, the jewels, the strangeness even of the universal murmur of a clever foreign tongue, were all a vivid symbol and assurance of his having grasped his purpose and forced along his groove. If Newman's smile was larger than usual, it was not tickled vanity that pulled the strings; he had no wish to be shown with the finger or to achieve a personal success. If he could have looked down at the scene, invisible, from a hole in the roof, he would have enjoyed it quite as much. It would have spoken to him about his own prosperity and deepened that easy feeling about life to which, sooner or later, he made all experience contribute. Just now the cup seemed full.

"It is a very pretty party," said Mrs. Tristram, after they had walked a while. "I have seen nothing objectionable except my husband leaning against the wall and talking to an individual whom I suppose he takes for a duke, but whom I more than suspect to be the functionary who attends to the lamps. Do you think you could separate them? Knock over a lamp!"

I doubt whether Newman, who saw no harm in Tristram's conversing with an ingenious mechanic, would have complied with this request; but at this moment Valentin de Bellegarde drew near. Newman, some weeks previously, had presented Madame de Cintré's youngest brother to Mrs. Tristram, for whose merits Valentin professed a discriminating relish and to whom he had paid several visits.

"Did you ever read Keats's Belle Dame sans Merci?" asked Mrs. Tristram. "You remind me of the hero of the ballad:—

'Oh, what can ail thee, knight-at-arms,
    Alone and palely loitering?' "

"If I am alone, it is because I have been deprived of your society," said Valentin. "Besides it is good manners for no man except Newman to look happy. This is all to his address. It is not for you and me to go before the curtain."

"You promised me last spring," said Newman to Mrs. Tristram, "that six months from that time I should get into a monstrous rage. It seems to me the time's up, and yet the nearest I can come to doing anything rough now is to offer you a café glacé."

"I told you we should do things grandly," said Valentin. "I don't allude to the cafés glacés. But every one is here, and my sister told me just now that Urbain had been adorable."

"He 's a good fellow, he 's a good fellow," said Newman. "I love him as a brother. That reminds me that I ought to go and say something polite to your mother."

"Let it be something very polite indeed," said Valentin. "It may be the last time you will feel so much like it!"

Newman walked away, almost disposed to clasp old Madame de Bellegarde round the waist. He passed through several rooms and at last found the old marquise in the first saloon, seated on a sofa, with her young kinsman, Lord Deepmere, beside her. The young man looked somewhat bored; his hands were thrust into his pockets and his eyes were fixed upon the toes of his shoes, his feet being thrust out in front of him. Madame de Bellegarde appeared to have been talking to him with some intensity and to be waiting for an answer to what she had said, or for some sign of the effect of her words. Her hands were folded in her lap, and she was looking at his lordship's simple physiognomy with an air of politely suppressed irritation.

Lord Deepmere looked up as Newman approached, met his eyes, and changed color.

"I am afraid I disturb an interesting interview," said Newman.

Madame de Bellegarde rose, and her companion rising at the same time, she put her hand into his arm. She answered nothing for an instant, and then, as he remained silent, she said with a smile, "It would be polite for Lord Deepmere to say it was very interesting."

"Oh, I 'm not polite!" cried his lordship. "But it *was* interesting."

"Madame de Bellegarde was giving you some good advice, eh?" said Newman; "toning you down a little?"

"I was giving him some excellent advice," said the marquise, fixing her fresh, cold eyes upon our hero. "It 's for him to take it."

"Take it, sir—take it," Newman exclaimed. "Any advice

the marquise gives you to-night must be good. For to-night, marquise, you must speak from a cheerful, comfortable spirit, and that makes good advice. You see everything going on so brightly and successfully round you. Your party is magnificent; it was a very happy thought. It is much better than that thing of mine would have been."

"If you are pleased I am satisfied," said Madame de Bellegarde. "My desire was to please you."

"Do you want to please me a little more?" said Newman. "Just drop our lordly friend; I am sure he wants to be off and shake his heels a little. Then take my arm and walk through the rooms."

"My desire was to please you," the old lady repeated. And she liberated Lord Deepmere, Newman rather wondering at her docility. "If this young man is wise," she added, "he will go and find my daughter and ask her to dance."

"I have been indorsing your advice," said Newman, bending over her and laughing, "I suppose I must swallow that!"

Lord Deepmere wiped his forehead and departed, and Madame de Bellegarde took Newman's arm. "Yes, it 's a very pleasant, sociable entertainment," the latter declared, as they proceeded on their circuit. "Every one seems to know every one and to be glad to see every one. The marquis has made me acquainted with ever so many people, and I feel quite like one of the family. It 's an occasion," Newman continued, wanting to say something thoroughly kind and comfortable, "that I shall always remember, and remember very pleasantly."

"I think it is an occasion that we shall none of us forget," said the marquise, with her pure, neat enunciation.

People made way for her as she passed, others turned round and looked at her, and she received a great many greetings and pressings of the hand, all of which she accepted with the most delicate dignity. But though she smiled upon every one, she said nothing until she reached the last of the rooms, where she found her elder son. Then, "This is enough, sir," she declared with measured softness to Newman, and turned to the marquis. He put out both his hands and took both hers, drawing her to a seat with an air of the tenderest veneration. It was a most harmonious family group, and Newman discreetly retired. He moved through the rooms for some time longer, circulating freely, overtopping most people by his great height, renewing acquaintance with some of the groups to which Urbain de Bellegarde had presented him, and expending generally the surplus of his equanimity. He continued to find it all extremely agreeable; but the most agreeable things have an end, and the revelry on this occasion began to deepen to a close. The music was sounding its ultimate strains and people were looking for the marquise, to make their farewells. There seemed to be some difficulty in finding her, and Newman heard a report that she had left the ball, feeling faint. "She has succumbed to the emotions of the evening," he heard a lady say. "Poor, dear marquise; I can imagine all that they may have been for her!" But he learned immediately afterwards that she had recovered herself and was seated in an arm-chair near the doorway, receiving parting compliments from great ladies who insisted upon her not rising. He himself set out in quest of Madame de Cintré. He had seen her move past him many times in the rapid circles of a waltz, but in accordance with her explicit instructions he had exchanged no words with her since the beginning of the evening. The whole house having been thrown open, the apartments of the *rez-de-chaussée* were also accessible, though a smaller number of persons had gathered there. Newman wandered through them, observing a few scattered couples to whom this comparative seclusion appeared grateful, and reached a small conservatory which opened into the garden. The end of the conservatory was formed by a clear sheet of glass, unmasked by plants, and admitting the winter starlight so directly that a person standing there would seem to have passed into the open air. Two persons stood there now, a lady and a gentleman; the lady Newman, from within the room and although she had turned her back to it, immediately recognized as Madame de Cintré. He hesitated as to whether he would advance, but as he did so she looked round, feeling apparently that he was there. She rested her eyes on him a moment and then turned again to her companion.

"It is almost a pity not to tell Mr. Newman," she said softly, but in a tone that Newman could hear.

"Tell him if you like!" the gentleman answered, in the voice of Lord Deepmere.

"Oh, tell me by all means!" said Newman advancing.

Lord Deepmere, he observed, was very red in the face, and he had twisted his gloves into a tight cord, as if he had been squeezing them dry. These, presumably, were tokens of violent emotion, and it seemed to Newman that the traces of a corresponding agitation were visible in Madame de Cintré's face. The two had been talking with much vivacity. "What I should tell you is only to my lord's credit," said Madame de Cintré, smiling frankly enough.

"He would n't like it any better for that!" said my lord, with his awkward laugh.

"Come; what 's the mystery?" Newman demanded. "Clear it up. I don't like mysteries."

"We must have some things we don't like, and go without some we do," said the ruddy young nobleman, laughing still.

"It 's to Lord Deepmere's credit, but it is not to every one's," said Madame de Cintré. "So I shall say nothing about it. You may be sure," she added; and she put out her hand to the Englishman, who took it half shyly, half impetuously. "And now go and dance!" she said.

"Oh yes, I feel awfully like dancing!" he answered. "I shall go and get tipsy." And he walked away with a gloomy guffaw.

"What has happened between you?" Newman asked.

"I can't tell you—now," said Madame de Cintré. "Nothing that need make you unhappy."

"Has the little Englishman been trying to make love to you?"

She hesitated, and then she uttered a grave "No! he 's a very honest little fellow."

"But you are agitated. Something is the matter."

"Nothing, I repeat, that need make you unhappy. My agitation is over. Some day I will tell you what it was; not now. I can't now!"

"Well, I confess," remarked Newman, "I don't want to hear anything unpleasant. I am satisfied with everything—most of all with you. I have seen all the ladies and talked with a great many of them; but I am satisfied with you." Madame de

Cintré covered him for a moment with her large, soft glance, and then turned her eyes away into the starry night. So they stood silent a moment, side by side. "Say you are satisfied with me," said Newman.

He had to wait a moment for the answer; but it came at last, low yet distinct: "I am very happy."

It was presently followed by a few words from another source, which made them both turn round. "I am sadly afraid Madame de Cintré will take a chill. I have ventured to bring a shawl." Mrs. Bread stood there softly solicitous, holding a white drapery in her hand.

"Thank you," said Madame de Cintré, "the sight of those cold stars gives one a sense of frost. I won't take your shawl, but we will go back into the house."

She passed back and Newman followed her, Mrs. Bread standing respectfully aside to make way for them. Newman paused an instant before the old woman, and she glanced up at him with a silent greeting. "Oh, yes," he said, "you must come and live with us."

"Well then, sir, if you will," she answered, "you have not seen the last of me!"

Chapter XVII

NEWMAN was fond of music and went often to the opera. A couple of evenings after Madame de Bellegarde's ball he sat listening to "Don Giovanni," having in honor of this work, which he had never yet seen represented, come to occupy his orchestra-chair before the rising of the curtain. Frequently he took a large box and invited a party of his compatriots; this was a mode of recreation to which he was much addicted. He liked making up parties of his friends and conducting them to the theatre, and taking them to drive on high drags or to dine at remote restaurants. He liked doing things which involved his paying for people; the vulgar truth is that he enjoyed "treating" them. This was not because he was what is called purse-proud; handling money in public was on the contrary positively disagreeable to him; he had a sort of personal modesty about it, akin to what he would have felt about making a toilet before spectators. But just as it was a gratification to him to be handsomely dressed, just so it was a private satisfaction to him (he enjoyed it very clandestinely) to have interposed, pecuniarily, in a scheme of pleasure. To set a large group of people in motion and transport them to a distance, to have special conveyances, to charter railway-carriages and steamboats, harmonized with his relish for bold processes, and made hospitality seem more active and more to the purpose. A few evenings before the occasion of which I speak he had invited several ladies and gentlemen to the opera to listen to Madame Alboni—a party which included Miss Dora Finch. It befell, however, that Miss Dora Finch, sitting near Newman in the box, discoursed brilliantly, not only during the entr'actes, but during many of the finest portions of the performance, so that Newman had really come away with an irritated sense that Madame Alboni had a thin, shrill voice, and that her musical phrase was much garnished with a laugh of the giggling order. After this he promised himself to go for a while to the opera alone.

When the curtain had fallen upon the first act of "Don Giovanni" he turned round in his place to observe the house. Presently, in one of the boxes, he perceived Urbain de Belle-

garde and his wife. The little marquise was sweeping the
house very busily with a glass, and Newman, supposing that
she saw him, determined to go and bid her good evening. M.
de Bellegarde was leaning against a column, motionless, looking straight in front of him, with one hand in the breast of
his white waistcoat and the other resting his hat on his thigh.
Newman was about to leave his place when he noticed in that
obscure region devoted to the small boxes which in France
are called, not inaptly, "bathing-tubs," a face which even the
dim light and the distance could not make wholly indistinct.
It was the face of a young and pretty woman, and it was
surmounted with a coiffure of pink roses and diamonds. This
person was looking round the house, and her fan was moving
to and fro with the most practiced grace; when she lowered
it, Newman perceived a pair of plump white shoulders and
the edge of a rose-colored dress. Beside her, very close to the
shoulders, and talking, apparently with an earnestness which
it pleased her scantily to heed, sat a young man with a red
face and a very low shirt-collar. A moment's gazing left Newman with no doubts; the pretty young woman was Noémie
Nioche. He looked hard into the depths of the box, thinking
her father might perhaps be in attendance, but from what he
could see the young man's eloquence had no other auditor.
Newman at last made his way out, and in doing so he passed
beneath the *baignoire* of Mademoiselle Noémie. She saw him
as he approached and gave him a nod and smile which
seemed meant as an assurance that she was still a good-natured girl, in spite of her enviable rise in the world. Newman
passed into the foyer and walked through it. Suddenly he
paused in front of a gentleman seated on one of the divans.
The gentleman's elbows were on his knees; he was leaning
forward and staring at the pavement, lost apparently in meditations of a somewhat gloomy cast. But in spite of his bent
head Newman recognized him, and in a moment sat down
beside him. Then the gentleman looked up and displayed the
expressive countenance of Valentin de Bellegarde.

"What in the world are you thinking of so hard?" asked
Newman.

"A subject that requires hard thinking to do it justice," said
Valentin. "My immeasurable idiocy."

"What is the matter now?"

"The matter now is that I am a man again, and no more a fool than usual. But I came within an inch of taking that girl *au sérieux.*"

"You mean the young lady below stairs, in a baignoire, in a pink dress?" said Newman.

"Did you notice what a brilliant kind of pink it was?" Valentin inquired, by way of answer. "It makes her look as white as new milk."

"White or black, as you please. But you have stopped going to see her?"

"Oh, bless you, no. Why should I stop? I have changed, but she has n't," said Valentin. "I see she is a vulgar little wretch, after all. But she is as amusing as ever, and one *must* be amused."

"Well, I am glad she strikes you so unpleasantly," Newman rejoined. "I suppose you have swallowed all those fine words you used about her the other night. You compared her to a sapphire, or a topaz, or an amethyst—some precious stone; what was it?"

"I don't remember," said Valentin, "it may have been to a carbuncle! But she won't make a fool of me now. She has no real charm. It 's an awfully low thing to make a mistake about a person of that sort."

"I congratulate you," Newman declared, "upon the scales having fallen from your eyes. It 's a great triumph; it ought to make you feel better."

"Yes, it makes me feel better!" said Valentin, gayly. Then, checking himself, he looked askance at Newman. "I rather think you are laughing at me. If you were not one of the family I would take it up."

"Oh, no, I 'm not laughing, any more than I am one of the family. You make me feel badly. You are too clever a fellow, you are made of too good stuff, to spend your time in ups and downs over that class of goods. The idea of splitting hairs about Miss Nioche! It seems to me awfully foolish. You say you have given up taking her seriously; but you take her seriously so long as you take her at all."

Valentin turned round in his place and looked a while at Newman, wrinkling his forehead and rubbing his knees.

"Vous parlez d'or. But she has wonderfully pretty arms. Would you believe I did n't know it till this evening?"

"But she is a vulgar little wretch, remember, all the same," said Newman.

"Yes; the other day she had the bad taste to begin to abuse her father, to his face, in my presence. I should n't have expected it of her; it was a disappointment; heigho!"

"Why, she cares no more for her father than for her doormat," said Newman. "I discovered that the first time I saw her."

"Oh, that 's another affair; she may think of the poor old beggar what she pleases. But it was low in her to call him bad names; it quite threw me off. It was about a frilled petticoat that he was to have fetched from the washer-woman's; he appeared to have neglected this graceful duty. She almost boxed his ears. He stood there staring at her with his little blank eyes and smoothing his old hat with his coat-tail. At last he turned round and went out without a word. Then I told her it was in very bad taste to speak so to one's papa. She said she should be so thankful to me if I would mention it to her whenever her taste was at fault; she had immense confidence in mine. I told her I could n't have the bother of forming her manners; I had had an idea they were already formed, after the best models. She had disappointed me. But I shall get over it," said Valentin, gayly.

"Oh, time 's a great consoler!" Newman answered with humorous sobriety. He was silent a moment, and then he added, in another tone, "I wish you would think of what I said to you the other day. Come over to America with us, and I will put you in the way of doing some business. You have got a very good head, if you will only use it."

Valentin made a genial grimace. "My head is much obliged to you. Do you mean the place in a bank?"

"There are several places, but I suppose you would consider the bank the most aristocratic."

Valentin burst into a laugh. "My dear fellow, at night all cats are gray! When one derogates there are no degrees."

Newman answered nothing for a minute. Then, "I think you will find there are degrees in success," he said with a certain dryness.

Valentin had leaned forward again, with his elbows on his knees, and he was scratching the pavement with his stick. At last he said, looking up, "Do you really think I ought to do something?"

Newman laid his hand on his companion's arm and looked at him a moment through sagaciously-narrowed eyelids. "Try it and see. You are not good enough for it, but we will stretch a point."

"Do you really think I can make some money? I should like to see how it feels to have a little."

"Do what I tell you, and you shall be rich," said Newman. "Think of it." And he looked at his watch and prepared to resume his way to Madame de Bellegarde's box.

"Upon my word I will think of it," said Valentin. "I will go and listen to Mozart another half hour—I can always think better to music—and profoundly meditate upon it."

The marquis was with his wife when Newman entered their box; he was bland, remote, and correct as usual; or, as it seemed to Newman, even more than usual.

"What do you think of the opera?" asked our hero. "What do you think of the Don?"

"We all know what Mozart is," said the marquis; "our impressions don't date from this evening. Mozart is youth, freshness, brilliancy, facility—a little too great facility, perhaps. But the execution is here and there deplorably rough."

"I am very curious to see how it ends," said Newman.

"You speak as if it were a feuilleton in the 'Figaro,'" observed the marquis. "You have surely seen the opera before?"

"Never," said Newman. "I am sure I should have remembered it. Donna Elvira reminds me of Madame de Cintré; I don't mean in her circumstances, but in the music she sings."

"It is a very nice distinction," laughed the marquis lightly. "There is no great possibility, I imagine, of Madame de Cintré being forsaken."

"Not much!" said Newman. "But what becomes of the Don?"

"The devil comes down—or comes up," said Madame de Bellegarde, "and carries him off. I suppose Zerlina reminds you of me."

"I will go to the foyer for a few moments," said the marquis, "and give you a chance to say that the commander—the man of stone—resembles me." And he passed out of the box.

The little marquise stared an instant at the velvet ledge of the balcony, and then murmured, "Not a man of stone, a man of wood." Newman had taken her husband's empty chair. She made no protest, and then she turned suddenly and laid her closed fan upon his arm. "I am very glad you came in," she said. "I want to ask you a favor. I wanted to do so on Thursday, at my mother-in-law's ball, but you would give me no chance. You were in such very good spirits that I thought you might grant my little favor then; not that you look particularly doleful now. It is something you must promise me; now is the time to take you; after you are married you will be good for nothing. Come, promise!"

"I never sign a paper without reading it first," said Newman. "Show me your document."

"No, you must sign with your eyes shut; I will hold your hand. Come, before you put your head into the noose. You ought to be thankful to me for giving you a chance to do something amusing."

"If it is so amusing," said Newman, "it will be in even better season after I am married."

"In other words," cried Madame de Bellegarde, "you will not do it at all. You will be afraid of your wife."

"Oh, if the thing is intrinsically improper," said Newman, "I won't go into it. If it is not, I will do it after my marriage."

"You talk like a treatise on logic, and English logic into the bargain!" exclaimed Madame de Bellegarde. "Promise, then, after you are married. After all, I shall enjoy keeping you to it."

"Well, then, after I am married," said Newman serenely.

The little marquise hesitated a moment, looking at him, and he wondered what was coming. "I suppose you know what my life is," she presently said. "I have no pleasure, I see nothing, I do nothing. I live in Paris as I might live at Poitiers. My mother-in-law calls me—what is the pretty word?— a gad-about? accuses me of going to unheard-of places, and thinks it ought to be joy enough for me to sit at home and count over my ancestors on my fingers. But why should I bother about my ancestors? I am sure they never bothered about me. I don't propose to live with a green shade on my eyes; I hold that things were made to look at. My husband, you know, has principles, and the first on the list is that the Tuileries are dreadfully vulgar. If the Tuileries are vulgar, his principles are tiresome. If I chose I might have principles quite as well as he. If they grew on one's family tree I should only have to give mine a shake to bring down a shower of the finest. At any rate, I prefer clever Bonapartes to stupid Bourbons."

"Oh, I see; you want to go to court," said Newman, vaguely conjecturing that she might wish him to appeal to the United States legation to smooth her way to the imperial halls.

The marquise gave a little sharp laugh. "You are a thousand miles away. I will take care of the Tuileries myself; the day I decide to go they will be very glad to have me. Sooner or later I shall dance in an imperial quadrille. I know what you are going to say: 'How will you dare?' But I *shall* dare. I am afraid of my husband; he is soft, smooth, irreproachable, everything that you know; but I am afraid of him—horribly afraid of him. And yet I shall arrive at the Tuileries. But that will not be this winter, nor perhaps next, and meantime I must live. For the moment, I want to go somewhere else; it 's my dream. I want to go to the Bal Bullier."

"To the Bal Bullier?" repeated Newman, for whom the words at first meant nothing.

"The ball in the Latin Quarter, where the students dance with their mistresses. Don't tell me you have not heard of it."

"Oh yes," said Newman; "I have heard of it; I remember now. I have even been there. And you want to go there?"

"It is silly, it is low, it is anything you please. But I want to go. Some of my friends have been, and they say it is aw-fully *drôle*. My friends go everywhere; it is only I who sit moping at home."

"It seems to me you are not at home now," said Newman, "and I should n't exactly say you were moping."

"I am bored to death. I have been to the opera twice a week for the last eight years. Whenever I ask for anything my mouth is stopped with that: Pray, madam, have n't you an opera box? Could a woman of taste want more? In the first place, my opera box was down in my *contrat*; they have to give it to me. To-night, for instance, I should have preferred a thousand times to go to the Palais Royal. But my husband won't go to the Palais Royal because the ladies of the court go there so much. You may imagine, then, whether he would take me to Bullier's; he says it is a mere imitation—and a bad one—of what they do at the Princess Kleinfuss's. But as I don't go to the Princess Kleinfuss's, the next best thing is to go to Bullier's. It is my dream, at any rate; it 's a fixed idea. All I ask of you is to give me your arm; you are less compromising than any one else. I don't know why, but you are. I can arrange it. I shall risk something, but that is my own affair. Besides, fortune favors the bold. Don't refuse me; it is my dream!"

Newman gave a loud laugh. It seemed to him hardly worth while to be the wife of the Marquis de Bellegarde, a daughter of the crusaders, heiress of six centuries of glories and traditions, to have centred one's aspirations upon the sight of a couple of hundred young ladies kicking off young men's hats. It struck him as a theme for the moralist; but he had no time to moralize upon it. The curtain rose again; M. de Bellegarde returned, and Newman went back to his seat.

He observed that Valentin de Bellegarde had taken his place in the baignoire of Mademoiselle Nioche, behind this young lady and her companion, where he was visible only if one carefully looked for him. In the next act Newman met him in the lobby and asked him if he had reflected upon possible emigration. "If you really meant to meditate," he said, "you might have chosen a better place for it."

"Oh, the place was not bad," said Valentin. "I was not thinking of that girl. I listened to the music, and, without thinking of the play or looking at the stage, I turned over your proposal. At first it seemed quite fantastic. And then a certain fiddle in the orchestra—I could distinguish it—began to say as it scraped away, 'Why not, why not?' And then, in that rapid movement, all the fiddles took it up and the conductor's stick seemed to beat it in the air: 'Why not, why not?' I 'm sure I can't say! I don't see why not. I don't see why I should n't do something. It appears to me really a very bright idea. This sort of thing is certainly very stale. And then

I could come back with a trunk full of dollars. Besides, I might possibly find it amusing. They call me a *raffiné*; who knows but that I might discover an unsuspected charm in shop-keeping? It would really have a certain romantic, picturesque side; it would look well in my biography. It would look as if I were a strong man, a first-rate man, a man who dominated circumstances."

"Never mind how it would look," said Newman. "It always looks well to have half a million of dollars. There is no reason why you should n't have them if you will mind what I tell you—I alone—and not talk to other parties." He passed his arm into that of his companion, and the two walked for some time up and down one of the less frequented corridors. Newman's imagination began to glow with the idea of converting his bright, impracticable friend into a first-class man of business. He felt for the moment a sort of spiritual zeal, the zeal of the propagandist. Its ardor was in part the result of that general discomfort which the sight of all uninvested capital produced in him; so fine an intelligence as Bellegarde's ought to be dedicated to high uses. The highest uses known to Newman's experience were certain transcendent sagacities in the handling of railway stock. And then his zeal was quickened by his personal kindness for Valentin; he had a sort of pity for him which he was well aware he never could have made the Comte de Bellegarde understand. He never lost a sense of its being pitiable that Valentin should think it a large life to revolve in varnished boots between the Rue d'Anjou and the Rue de l'Université, taking the Boulevard des Italiens on the way, when over there in America one's promenade was a continent, and one's Boulevard stretched from New York to San Francisco. It mortified him, moreover, to think that Valentin lacked money; there was a painful grotesqueness in it. It affected him as the ignorance of a companion, otherwise without reproach, touching some rudimentary branch of learning would have done. There were things that one knew about as a matter of course, he would have said in such a case. Just so, if one pretended to be easy in the world, one had money as a matter of course; one had made it! There was something almost ridiculously anomalous to Newman in the sight of lively pretensions unaccompanied by large investments in railroads; though I may add that he would not have maintained that such investments were in themselves a proper ground for pretensions. "I will make you do something," he said to Valentin; "I will put you through. I know half a dozen things in which we can make a place for you. You will see some lively work. It will take you a little while to get used to the life, but you will work in before long, and at the end of six months—after you have done a thing or two on your own account—you will like it. And then it will be very pleasant for you, having your sister over there. It will be pleasant for her to have you, too. Yes, Valentin," continued Newman, pressing his friend's arm genially, "I think I see just the opening for you. Keep quiet and I 'll push you right in."

Newman pursued this favoring strain for some time longer. The two men strolled about for a quarter of an hour. Valentin listened and questioned, many of his questions making Newman laugh loud at the naïveté of his ignorance of the vulgar processes of money-getting; smiling himself, too, half ironical and half curious. And yet he was serious; he was fascinated by Newman's plain prose version of the legend of El Dorado. It is true, however, that though to accept an "opening" in an American mercantile house might be a bold, original, and in its consequences extremely agreeable thing to do, he did not quite see himself objectively doing it. So that when the bell rang to indicate the close of the entr'acte, there was a certain mock-heroism in his saying, with his brilliant smile, "Well, then, put me through; push me in! I make myself over to you. Dip me into the pot and turn me into gold."

They had passed into the corridor which encircled the row of baignoires, and Valentin stopped in front of the dusky little box in which Mademoiselle Nioche had bestowed herself, laying his hand on the door-knob. "Oh, come, are you going back there?" asked Newman.

"Mon Dieu, oui," said Valentin.

"Have n't you another place?"

"Yes, I have my usual place, in the stalls."

"You had better go and occupy it, then."

"I see her very well from there, too," added Valentin, serenely; "and to-night she is worth seeing. But," he added in a moment, "I have a particular reason for going back just now."

"Oh, I give you up," said Newman. "You are infatuated!"

"No, it is only this. There is a young man in the box whom I shall annoy by going in, and I want to annoy him."

"I am sorry to hear it," said Newman. "Can't you leave the poor fellow alone?"

"No, he has given me cause. The box is not his; Noémie came in alone and installed herself. I went and spoke to her, and in a few moments she asked me to go and get her fan from the pocket of her cloak, which the *ouvreuse* had carried off. In my absence this gentleman came in and took the chair beside Noémie in which I had been sitting. My reappearance disgusted him, and he had the grossness to show it. He came within an ace of being impertinent. I don't know who he is; he is some vulgar wretch. I can't think where she picks up such acquaintances. He has been drinking, too, but he knows what he is about. Just now, in the second act, he was unmannerly again. I shall put in another appearance for ten minutes—time enough to give him an opportunity to commit himself, if he feels inclined. I really can't let the brute suppose that he is keeping me out of the box."

"My dear fellow," said Newman, remonstrantly, "what child's play! You are not going to pick a quarrel about that girl, I hope."

"That girl has nothing to do with it, and I have no intention of picking a quarrel. I am not a bully nor a fire-eater. I simply wish to make a point that a gentleman must."

"Oh, damn your point!" said Newman. "That is the trouble with you Frenchmen; you must be always making points. Well," he added, "be short. But if you are going in for this kind of thing, we must ship you off to America in advance."

"Very good," Valentin answered, "whenever you please. But if I go to America, I must not let this gentleman suppose that it is to run away from him."

And they separated. At the end of the act Newman observed that Valentin was still in the baignoire. He strolled into the corridor again, expecting to meet him, and when he was within a few yards of Mademoiselle Nioche's box saw his friend pass out, accompanied by the young man who had been seated beside its fair occupant. The two gentlemen walked with some quickness of step to a distant part of the lobby, where Newman perceived them stop and stand talking. The manner of each was perfectly quiet, but the stranger, who looked flushed, had begun to wipe his face very emphatically with his pocket-handkerchief. By this time Newman was abreast of the baignoire; the door had been left ajar, and he could see a pink dress inside. He immediately went in. Mademoiselle Nioche turned and greeted him with a brilliant smile.

"Ah, you have at last decided to come and see me?" she exclaimed. "You just save your politeness. You find me in a fine moment. Sit down." There was a very becoming little flush in her cheek, and her eye had a noticeable spark. You would have said that she had received some very good news.

"Something has happened here!" said Newman, without sitting down.

"You find me in a very fine moment," she repeated. "Two gentlemen—one of them is M. de Bellegarde, the pleasure of whose acquaintance I owe to you—have just had words about your humble servant. Very big words too. They can't come off without crossing swords. A duel—that will give me a push!" cried Mademoiselle Noémie, clapping her little hands. "C'est ça qui pose une femme!"

"You don't mean to say that Bellegarde is going to fight about *you*!" exclaimed Newman, disgustedly.

"Nothing less!" and she looked at him with a hard little smile. "No, no, you are not *galant*! And if you prevent this affair I shall owe you a grudge—and pay my debt!"

Newman uttered an imprecation which, though brief—it consisted simply of the interjection "Oh!" followed by a geographical, or more correctly, perhaps, a theological noun in four letters—had better not be transferred to these pages. He turned his back without more ceremony upon the pink dress and went out of the box. In the corridor he found Valentin and his companion walking towards him. The latter was thrusting a card into his waistcoat pocket. Mademoiselle Noémie's jealous votary was a tall, robust young man with a thick nose, a prominent blue eye, a Germanic physiognomy, and a massive watch-chain. When they reached the box, Valentin with an emphasized bow made way for him to pass in first. Newman touched Valentin's arm as a sign that he wished to speak with him, and Bellegarde answered that he would be with him in an instant. Valentin entered the box after the robust young man, but a couple of minutes afterwards he reappeared, largely smiling.

"She is immensely tickled," he said. "She says we will make her fortune. I don't want to be fatuous, but I think it is very possible."

"So you are going to fight?" said Newman.

"My dear fellow, don't look so mortally disgusted. It was not my own choice. The thing is all arranged."

"I told you so!" groaned Newman.

"I told *him* so," said Valentin, smiling.

"What did he do to you?"

"My good friend, it does n't matter what. He used an expression—I took it up."

"But I insist upon knowing; I can't, as your elder brother, have you rushing into this sort of nonsense."

"I am very much obliged to you," said Valentin. "I have nothing to conceal, but I can't go into particulars now and here."

"We will leave this place, then. You can tell me outside."

"Oh no, I can't leave this place; why should I hurry away? I will go to my orchestra-stall and sit out the opera."

"You will not enjoy it; you will be preoccupied."

Valentin looked at him a moment, colored a little, smiled, and patted him on the arm. "You are delightfully simple! Before an affair a man is quiet. The quietest thing I can do is to go straight to my place."

"Ah," said Newman, "you want her to see you there—you and your quietness. I am not so simple! It is a poor business."

Valentin remained, and the two men, in their respective places, sat out the rest of the performance, which was also enjoyed by Mademoiselle Nioche and her truculent admirer. At the end Newman joined Valentin again, and they went into the street together. Valentin shook his head at his friend's proposal that he should get into Newman's own vehicle, and stopped on the edge of the pavement. "I must go off alone," he said; "I must look up a couple of friends who will take charge of this matter."

"I will take charge of it," Newman declared. "Put it into my hands."

"You are very kind, but that is hardly possible. In the first place, you are, as you said just now, almost my brother; you are about to marry my sister. That alone disqualifies you; it casts doubts on your impartiality. And if it did n't, it would be enough for me that I strongly suspect you of disapproving of the affair. You would try to prevent a meeting."

"Of course I should," said Newman. "Whoever your friends are, I hope they will do that."

"Unquestionably they will. They will urge that excuses be made, proper excuses. But you would be too good-natured. You won't do."

Newman was silent a moment. He was keenly annoyed, but he saw it was useless to attempt interference. "When is this precious performance to come off?" he asked.

"The sooner the better," said Valentin. "The day after to-morrow, I hope."

"Well," said Newman, "I have certainly a claim to know the facts. I can't consent to shut my eyes to the matter."

"I shall be most happy to tell you the facts," said Valentin. "They are very simple, and it will be quickly done. But now everything depends on my putting my hands on my friends without delay. I will jump into a cab; you had better drive to my room and wait for me there. I will turn up at the end of an hour."

Newman assented protestingly, let his friend go, and then betook himself to the picturesque little apartment in the Rue d'Anjou. It was more than an hour before Valentin returned, but when he did so he was able to announce that he had found one of his desired friends, and that this gentleman had taken upon himself the care of securing an associate. Newman had been sitting without lights by Valentin's faded fire, upon which he had thrown a log; the blaze played over the richly-encumbered little sitting-room and produced fantastic gleams and shadows. He listened in silence to Valentin's account of what had passed between him and the gentleman whose card he had in his pocket—M. Stanislas Kapp, of Strasbourg—after his return to Mademoiselle Nioche's box. This hospitable young lady had espied an acquaintance on the other side of the house, and had expressed her displeasure at his not having the civility to come and pay her a visit. "Oh, let him alone!" M. Stanislas Kapp had hereupon exclaimed. "There are too many people in the box already." And he had fixed his eyes with a demonstrative stare upon M. de Bellegarde. Valentin had promptly retorted that if there were too many people in the box it was easy for M. Kapp to diminish the number. "I shall be most happy to open the door for *you*!" M. Kapp exclaimed. "I shall be delighted to fling you into the pit!" Valentin had answered. "Oh, do make a rumpus and get into the papers!" Miss Noémie had gleefully ejaculated. "M. Kapp, turn him out; or, M. de Bellegarde, pitch him into the pit, into the orchestra—anywhere! I don't care who does which, so long as you make a scene." Valentin answered that they would make no scene, but that the gentleman would be so good as to step into the corridor with him. In the corridor, after a brief further exchange of words, there had been an exchange of cards. M. Stanislas Kapp was very stiff. He evidently meant to force his offence home.

"The man, no doubt, was insolent," Newman said; "but if you had n't gone back into the box the thing would n't have happened."

"Why, don't you see," Valentin replied, "that the event proves the extreme propriety of my going back into the box? M. Kapp wished to provoke me; he was awaiting his chance. In such a case—that is, when he has been, so to speak, notified—a man must be on hand to receive the provocation. My not returning would simply have been tantamount to my saying to M. Stanislas Kapp, 'Oh, if you are going to be disagreeable'"—

"'You must manage it by yourself; damned if I'll help you!' That would have been a thoroughly sensible thing to say. The only attraction for you seems to have been the prospect of M. Kapp's impertinence," Newman went on. "You told me you were not going back for that girl."

"Oh, don't mention that girl any more," murmured Valentin. "She's a bore."

"With all my heart. But if that is the way you feel about her, why could n't you let her alone?"

Valentin shook his head with a fine smile. "I don't think you quite understand, and I don't believe I can make you. She understood the situation; she knew what was in the air; she was watching us."

"A cat may look at a king! What difference does that make?"

"Why, a man can't back down before a woman."

"I don't call her a woman. You said yourself she was a stone," cried Newman.

"Well," Valentin rejoined, "there is no disputing about tastes. It 's a matter of feeling; it 's measured by one's sense of honor."

"Oh, confound your sense of honor!" cried Newman.

"It is vain talking," said Valentin; "words have passed, and the thing is settled."

Newman turned away, taking his hat. Then pausing with his hand on the door, "What are you going to use?" he asked.

"That is for M. Stanislas Kapp, as the challenged party, to decide. My own choice would be a short, light sword. I handle it well. I 'm an indifferent shot."

Newman had put on his hat; he pushed it back, gently scratching his forehead, high up. "I wish it were pistols," he said. "I could show you how to lodge a bullet!"

Valentin broke into a laugh. "What is it some English poet says about consistency? It 's a flower, or a star, or a jewel. Yours has the beauty of all three!" But he agreed to see Newman again on the morrow, after the details of his meeting with M. Stanislas Kapp should have been arranged.

In the course of the day Newman received three lines from him, saying that it had been decided that he should cross the frontier, with his adversary, and that he was to take the night express to Geneva. He should have time, however, to dine with Newman. In the afternoon Newman called upon Madame de Cintré, but his visit was brief. She was as gracious and sympathetic as he had ever found her, but she was sad, and she confessed, on Newman's charging her with her red eyes, that she had been crying. Valentin had been with her a couple of hours before, and his visit had left her with a painful impression. He had laughed and gossiped, he had brought her no bad news, he had only been, in his manner, rather more affectionate than usual. His fraternal tenderness had touched her, and on his departure she had burst into tears. She had felt as if something strange and sad were going to happen; she had tried to reason away the fancy, and the effort had only given her a headache. Newman, of course, was perforce tongue-tied about Valentin's projected duel, and his dramatic talent was not equal to satirizing Madame de Cintré's presentiment as pointedly as perfect security demanded. Before he went away he asked Madame de Cintré whether Valentin had seen his mother.

"Yes," she said, "but he did n't make her cry."

It was in Newman's own apartment that Valentin dined, having brought his portmanteau, so that he might adjourn directly to the railway. M. Stanislas Kapp had positively declined to make excuses, and he, on his side, obviously, had none to offer. Valentin had found out with whom he was dealing. M. Stanislas Kapp was the son and heir of a rich brewer of Strasbourg, a youth of a sanguineous—and sanguinary—temperament. He was making ducks and drakes of the paternal brewery, and although he passed in a general way for a good fellow, he had already been observed to be quarrelsome after dinner. "Que voulez-vous?" said Valentin. "Brought up on beer, he can't stand champagne." He had chosen pistols. Valentin, at dinner, had an excellent appetite; he made a point, in view of his long journey, of eating more than usual. He took the liberty of suggesting to Newman a slight modification in the composition of a certain fish-sauce; he thought it would be worth mentioning to the cook. But Newman had no thoughts for fish-sauce; he felt thoroughly discontented. As he sat and watched his amiable and clever companion going through his excellent repast with the delicate deliberation of hereditary epicurism, the folly of so charming a fellow traveling off to expose his agreeable young life for the sake of M. Stanislas and Mademoiselle Noémie struck him with intolerable force. He had grown fond of Valentin, he felt now how fond; and his sense of helplessness only increased his irritation.

"Well, this sort of thing may be all very well," he cried at last, "but I declare I don't see it. I can't stop you, perhaps, but at least I can protest. I do protest, violently."

"My dear fellow, don't make a scene," said Valentin. "Scenes in these cases are in very bad taste."

"Your duel itself is a scene," said Newman; "that 's all it is! It 's a wretched theatrical affair. Why don't you take a band of music with you outright? It 's d—d barbarous and it 's d—d corrupt, both."

"Oh, I can't begin, at this time of day, to defend the theory of dueling," said Valentin. "It is our custom, and I think it is a good thing. Quite apart from the goodness of the cause in which a duel may be fought, it has a kind of picturesque charm which in this age of vile prose seems to me greatly to recommend it. It 's a remnant of a higher-tempered time; one ought to cling to it. Depend upon it, a duel is never amiss."

"I don't know what you mean by a higher-tempered time," said Newman. "Because your great-grandfather was an ass, is that any reason why you should be? For my part I think we had better let our temper take care of itself; it generally seems to me quite high enough; I am not afraid of being too meek. If your great-grandfather were to make himself unpleasant to me, I think I could manage him, yet."

"My dear friend," said Valentin, smiling, "you can't invent anything that will take the place of satisfaction for an insult. To demand it and to give it are equally excellent arrangements."

"Do you call this sort of thing satisfaction?" Newman asked. "Does it satisfy you to receive a present of the carcass of that coarse fop? does it gratify you to make him a present of yours? If a man hits you, hit him back; if a man libels you, haul him up."

"Haul him up, into court? Oh, that is very nasty!" said Valentin.

"The nastiness is his—not yours. And for that matter, what you are doing is not particularly nice. You are too good for it. I don't say you are the most useful man in the world, or the cleverest, or the most amiable. But you are too good to go and get your throat cut for a prostitute."

Valentin flushed a little, but he laughed. "I shan't get my throat cut if I can help it. Moreover, one's honor has n't two different measures. It only knows that it is hurt; it does n't ask when, or how, or where."

"The more fool it is!" said Newman.

Valentin ceased to laugh; he looked grave. "I beg you not to say any more," he said. "If you do I shall almost fancy you don't care about—about"—and he paused.

"About what?"

"About that matter—about one's honor."

"Fancy what you please," said Newman. "Fancy while you are at it that I care about *you*—though you are not worth it. But come back without damage," he added in a moment, "and I will forgive you. And then," he continued, as Valentin was going, "I will ship you straight off to America."

"Well," answered Valentin, "if I am to turn over a new page, this may figure as a tail-piece to the old." And then he lit another cigar and departed.

"Blast that girl!" said Newman as the door closed upon Valentin.

Chapter XVIII

NEWMAN went the next morning to see Madame de Cintré, timing his visit so as to arrive after the noonday breakfast. In the court of the *hôtel*, before the portico, stood Madame de Bellegarde's old square carriage. The servant who opened the door answered Newman's inquiry with a slightly embarrassed and hesitating murmur, and at the same moment Mrs. Bread appeared in the background, dim-visaged as usual, and wearing a large black bonnet and shawl.

"What is the matter?" asked Newman. "Is Madame la Comtesse at home, or not?"

Mrs. Bread advanced, fixing her eyes upon him; he observed that she held a sealed letter, very delicately, in her fingers. "The countess has left a message for you, sir; she has left this," said Mrs. Bread, holding out the letter, which Newman took.

"Left it? Is she out? Is she gone away?"

"She is going away, sir; she is leaving town," said Mrs. Bread.

"Leaving town!" exclaimed Newman. "What has happened?"

"It is not for me to say, sir," said Mrs. Bread, with her eyes on the ground. "But I thought it would come."

"What would come, pray?" Newman demanded. He had broken the seal of the letter, but he still questioned. "She is in the house? She is visible?"

"I don't think she expected you this morning," the old waiting-woman replied. "She was to leave immediately."

"Where is she going?"

"To Fleurières."

"To Fleurières? But surely I can see her?"

Mrs. Bread hesitated a moment, and then clasping together her two hands, "I will take you!" she said. And she led the way up-stairs. At the top of the staircase she paused and fixed her dry, sad eyes upon Newman. "Be very easy with her," she said; "she is most unhappy!" Then she went on to Madame de Cintré's apartment; Newman, perplexed and alarmed, followed her rapidly. Mrs. Bread threw open the door, and

Newman pushed back the curtain at the farther side of its deep embrasure. In the middle of the room stood Madame de Cintré; her face was pale and she was dressed for traveling. Behind her, before the fire-place, stood Urbain de Bellegarde, looking at his finger-nails; near the marquis sat his mother, buried in an arm-chair, and with her eyes immediately fixing themselves upon Newman. He felt, as soon as he entered the room, that he was in the presence of something evil; he was startled and pained, as he would have been by a threatening cry in the stillness of the night. He walked straight to Madame de Cintré and seized her by the hand.

"What is the matter?" he asked, commandingly; "what is happening?"

Urbain de Bellegarde stared, then left his place and came and leaned upon his mother's chair, behind. Newman's sudden irruption had evidently discomposed both mother and son. Madame de Cintré stood silent, with her eyes resting upon Newman's. She had often looked at him with all her soul, as it seemed to him; but in this present gaze there was a sort of bottomless depth. She was in distress; it was the most touching thing he had ever seen. His heart rose into his throat, and he was on the point of turning to her companions, with an angry challenge; but she checked him, pressing the hand that held her own.

"Something very grave has happened," she said. "I cannot marry you."

Newman dropped her hand and stood staring, first at her and then at the others. "Why not?" he asked, as quietly as possible.

Madame de Cintré almost smiled, but the attempt was strange. "You must ask my mother, you must ask my brother."

"Why can't she marry me?" said Newman, looking at them.

Madame de Bellegarde did not move in her place, but she was as pale as her daughter. The marquis looked down at her. She said nothing for some moments, but she kept her keen, clear eyes upon Newman, bravely. The marquis drew himself up and looked at the ceiling. "It 's impossible!" he said softly.

"It 's improper," said Madame de Bellegarde.

Newman began to laugh. "Oh, you are fooling!" he exclaimed.

"My sister, you have no time; you are losing your train," said the marquis.

"Come, is he mad?" asked Newman.

"No; don't think that," said Madame de Cintré. "But I am going away."

"Where are you going?"

"To the country, to Fleurières; to be alone."

"To leave me?" said Newman, slowly.

"I can't see you, now," said Madame de Cintré.

"*Now*—why not?"

"I am ashamed," said Madame de Cintré, simply.

Newman turned toward the marquis. "What have you done to her—what does it mean?" he asked with the same effort at calmness, the fruit of his constant practice in taking things easily. He was excited, but excitement with him was only an intenser deliberateness; it was the swimmer stripped.

"It means that I have given you up," said Madame de Cintré. "It means that."

Her face was too charged with tragic expression not fully to confirm her words. Newman was profoundly shocked, but he felt as yet no resentment against her. He was amazed, bewildered, and the presence of the old marquise and her son seemed to smite his eyes like the glare of a watchman's lantern. "Can't I see you alone?" he asked.

"It would be only more painful. I hoped I should not see you—I should escape. I wrote to you. Good-by." And she put out her hand again.

Newman put both his own into his pockets. "I will go with you," he said.

She laid her two hands on his arm. "Will you grant me a last request?" and as she looked at him, urging this, her eyes filled with tears. "Let me go alone—let me go in peace. I can't call it peace—it 's death. But let me bury myself. So—good-by."

Newman passed his hand into his hair and stood slowly rubbing his head and looking through his keenly-narrowed eyes from one to the other of the three persons before him. His lips were compressed, and the two lines which had formed themselves beside his mouth might have made it appear at a first glance that he was smiling. I have said that his excitement was an intenser deliberateness, and now he looked grimly deliberate. "It seems very much as if you had interfered, marquis," he said slowly. "I thought you said you would n't interfere. I know you don't like me; but that does n't make any difference. I thought you promised me you would n't interfere. I thought you swore on your honor that you would n't interfere. Don't you remember, marquis?"

The marquis lifted his eyebrows; but he was apparently determined to be even more urbane than usual. He rested his two hands upon the back of his mother's chair and bent forward, as if he were leaning over the edge of a pulpit or a lecture-desk. He did not smile, but he looked softly grave. "Excuse me, sir," he said, "I assured you that I would not influence my sister's decision. I adhered, to the letter, to my engagement. Did I not, sister?"

"Don't appeal, my son," said the marquise, "your word is sufficient."

"Yes—she accepted me," said Newman. "That is very true; I can't deny that. At least," he added, in a different tone, turning to Madame de Cintré, "you *did* accept me?"

Something in the tone seemed to move her strongly. She turned away, burying her face in her hands.

"But you have interfered now, have n't you?" inquired Newman of the marquis.

"Neither then nor now have I attempted to influence my sister. I used no persuasion then, I have used no persuasion to-day."

"And what have you used?"

"We have used authority," said Madame de Bellegarde in a rich, bell-like voice.

"Ah, you have used authority," Newman exclaimed. "They have used authority," he went on, turning to Madame de Cintré. "What is it? how did they use it?"

"My mother commanded," said Madame de Cintré.

"Commanded you to give me up—I see. And you obey—I see. But why do you obey?" asked Newman.

Madame de Cintré looked across at the old marquise; her

eyes slowly measured her from head to foot. "I am afraid of my mother," she said.

Madame de Bellegarde rose with a certain quickness, crying, "This is a most indecent scene!"

"I have no wish to prolong it," said Madame de Cintré; and turning to the door she put out her hand again. "If you can pity me a little, let me go alone."

Newman shook her hand quietly and firmly. "I 'll come down there," he said. The portière dropped behind her, and Newman sank with a long breath into the nearest chair. He leaned back in it, resting his hands on the knobs of the arms and looking at Madame de Bellegarde and Urbain. There was a long silence. They stood side by side, with their heads high and their handsome eyebrows arched.

"So you make a distinction?" Newman said at last. "You make a distinction between persuading and commanding? It 's very neat. But the distinction is in favor of commanding. That rather spoils it."

"We have not the least objection to defining our position," said M. de Bellegarde. "We understand that it should not at first appear to you quite clear. We rather expect, indeed, that you should not do us justice."

"Oh, I 'll do you justice," said Newman. "Don't be afraid. Please proceed."

The marquise laid her hand on her son's arm, as if to deprecate the attempt to define their position. "It is quite useless," she said, "to try and arrange this matter so as to make it agreeable to you. It can never be agreeable to you. It is a disappointment, and disappointments are unpleasant. I thought it over carefully and tried to arrange it better; but I only gave myself a headache and lost my sleep. Say what we will, you will think yourself ill-treated, and you will publish your wrongs among your friends. But we are not afraid of that. Besides, your friends are not our friends, and it will not matter. Think of us as you please. I only beg you not to be violent. I have never in my life been present at a violent scene of any kind, and at my age I can't be expected to begin."

"Is *that* all you have got to say?" asked Newman, slowly rising out of his chair. "That 's a poor show for a clever lady like you, marquise. Come, try again."

"My mother goes to the point, with her usual honesty and intrepidity," said the marquis, toying with his watch-guard. "But it is perhaps well to say a little more. We of course quite repudiate the charge of having broken faith with you. We left you entirely at liberty to make yourself agreeable to my sister. We left her quite at liberty to entertain your proposal. When she accepted you we said nothing. We therefore quite observed our promise. It was only at a later stage of the affair, and on quite a different basis, as it were, that we determined to speak. It would have been better, perhaps, if we had spoken before. But really, you see, nothing has yet been done."

"Nothing has yet been done?" Newman repeated the words, unconscious of their comical effect. He had lost the sense of what the marquis was saying; M. de Bellegarde's superior style was a mere humming in his ears. All that he understood, in his deep and simple indignation, was that the matter was not a violent joke, and that the people before him were perfectly serious. "Do you suppose I can take this?" he asked. "Do you suppose it can matter to me what you say? Do you suppose I can seriously listen to you? You are simply crazy!"

Madame de Bellegarde gave a rap with her fan in the palm of her hand. "If you don't take it you can leave it, sir. It matters very little what you do. My daughter has given you up."

"She does n't mean it," Newman declared after a moment.

"I think I can assure you that she does," said the marquis.

"Poor woman, what damnable thing have you done to her?" cried Newman.

"Gently, gently!" murmured M. de Bellegarde.

"She told you," said the old lady. "I commanded her."

Newman shook his head, heavily. "This sort of thing can't be, you know," he said. "A man can't be used in this fashion. You have got no right; you have got no power."

"My power," said Madame de Bellegarde, "is in my children's obedience."

"In their fear, your daughter said. There is something very strange in it. Why should your daughter be afraid of you?" added Newman, after looking a moment at the old lady. "There is some foul play."

The marquise met his gaze without flinching, and as if she did not hear or heed what he said. "I did my best," she said, quietly. "I could endure it no longer."

"It was a bold experiment!" said the marquis.

Newman felt disposed to walk to him, clutch his neck with his fingers and press his windpipe with his thumb. "I need n't tell you how you strike me," he said; "of course you know that. But I should think you would be afraid of your friends—all those people you introduced me to the other night. There were some very nice people among them; you may depend upon it there were some honest men and women."

"Our friends approve us," said M. de Bellegarde; "there is not a family among them that would have acted otherwise. And however that may be, we take the cue from no one. The Bellegardes have been used to set the example, not to wait for it."

"You would have waited long before any one would have set you such an example as this," exclaimed Newman. "Have I done anything wrong?" he demanded. "Have I given you reason to change your opinion? Have you found out anything against me? I can't imagine."

"Our opinion," said Madame de Bellegarde, "is quite the same as at first—exactly. We have no ill-will towards yourself; we are very far from accusing you of misconduct. Since your relations with us began you have been, I frankly confess, less—less peculiar than I expected. It is not your disposition that we object to, it is your antecedents. We really cannot reconcile ourselves to a commercial person. We fancied in an evil hour that we could; it was a great misfortune. We determined to persevere to the end, and to give you every advantage. I was resolved that you should have no reason to accuse me of a want of loyalty. We let the thing certainly go very far; we introduced you to our friends. To tell the truth, it was that, I think, that broke me down. I succumbed to the scene that took place on Thursday night in these rooms. You must excuse me if what I say is disagreeable to you, but we cannot release ourselves without an explanation."

"There can be no better proof of our good faith," said the marquis, "than our committing ourselves to you in the eyes

of the world the other evening. We endeavored to bind ourselves—to tie our hands, as it were."

"But it was that," added his mother, "that opened our eyes
and broke our bonds. We should have been most uncomfortable! You know," she added in a moment, "that you were
forewarned. I told you we were very proud."

Newman took up his hat and began mechanically to
smooth it; the very fierceness of his scorn kept him from
speaking. "You are not proud enough," he observed at last.

"In all this matter," said the marquis, smiling, "I really see
nothing but our humility."

"Let us have no more discussion than is necessary," resumed Madame de Bellegarde. "My daughter told you everything when she said she gave you up."

"I am not satisfied about your daughter," said Newman; "I
want to know what you did to her. It is all very easy talking
about authority and saying you commanded her. She did n't
accept me blindly, and she would n't have given me up
blindly. Not that I believe yet she has really given me up; she
will talk it over with me. But you have frightened her, you
have bullied her, you have *hurt* her. What was it you did to
her?"

"I did very little!" said Madame de Bellegarde, in a tone
which gave Newman a chill when he afterwards remembered
it.

"Let me remind you that we offered you these explanations," the marquis observed, "with the express understanding that you should abstain from violence of language."

"I am not violent," Newman answered, "it is you who are
violent! But I don't know that I have much more to say to
you. What you expect of me, apparently, is to go my way,
thanking you for favors received, and promising never to
trouble you again."

"We expect of you to act like a clever man," said Madame
de Bellegarde. "You have shown yourself that already, and
what we have done is altogether based upon your being so.
When one must submit, one must. Since my daughter absolutely withdraws, what will be the use of your making a
noise?"

"It remains to be seen whether your daughter absolutely

withdraws. Your daughter and I are still very good friends; nothing is changed in that. As I say, I will talk it over with her."

"That will be of no use," said the old lady. "I know my daughter well enough to know that words spoken as she just now spoke to you are final. Besides, she has promised me."

"I have no doubt her promise is worth a great deal more than your own," said Newman; "nevertheless I don't give her up."

"Just as you please! But if she won't even see you,—and she won't,—your constancy must remain purely Platonic."

Poor Newman was feigning a greater confidence than he felt. Madame de Cintré's strange intensity had in fact struck a chill to his heart; her face, still impressed upon his vision, had been a terribly vivid image of renunciation. He felt sick, and suddenly helpless. He turned away and stood for a moment with his hand on the door; then he faced about and after the briefest hesitation broke out with a different accent. "Come, think of what this must be to me, and let her alone! Why should you object to me so—what 's the matter with me? I can't hurt you, I would n't if I could. I 'm the most unobjectionable fellow in the world. What if I am a commercial person? What under the sun do you mean? A commercial person? I will be any sort of a person you want. I never talked to you about business. Let her go, and I will ask no questions. I will take her away, and you shall never see me or hear of me again. I will stay in America if you like. I 'll sign a paper promising never to come back to Europe! All I want is not to lose her!"

Madame de Bellegarde and her son exchanged a glance of lucid irony, and Urbain said, "My dear sir, what you propose is hardly an improvement. We have not the slightest objection to seeing you, as an amiable foreigner, and we have every reason for not wishing to be eternally separated from my sister. We object to the marriage; and in that way," and M. de Bellegarde gave a small, thin laugh, "she would be more married than ever."

"Well, then," said Newman, "where is this place of yours—Fleurières? I know it is near some old city on a hill."

"Precisely. Poitiers is on a hill," said Madame de Bellegarde. "I don't know how old it is. We are not afraid to tell you."

"It is Poitiers, is it? Very good," said Newman. "I shall immediately follow Madame de Cintré."

"The trains after this hour won't serve you," said Urbain.

"I shall hire a special train!"

"That will be a very silly waste of money," said Madame de Bellegarde.

"It will be time enough to talk about waste three days hence," Newman answered; and clapping his hat on his head, he departed.

He did not immediately start for Fleurières; he was too stunned and wounded for consecutive action. He simply walked; he walked straight before him, following the river, till he got out of the *enceinte* of Paris. He had a burning, tingling sense of personal outrage. He had never in his life received so absolute a check; he had never been pulled up, or, as he would have said, "let down," so short; and he found the sensation intolerable; he strode along, tapping the trees and lamp-posts fiercely with his stick and inwardly raging. To lose Madame de Cintré after he had taken such jubilant and triumphant possession of her was as great an affront to his pride as it was an injury to his happiness. And to lose her by the interference and the dictation of others, by an impudent old woman and a pretentious fop stepping in with their "authority"! It was too preposterous, it was too pitiful. Upon what he deemed the unblushing treachery of the Bellegardes Newman wasted little thought; he consigned it, once for all, to eternal perdition. But the treachery of Madame de Cintré herself amazed and confounded him; there was a key to the mystery, of course, but he groped for it in vain. Only three days had elapsed since she stood beside him in the starlight, beautiful and tranquil as the trust with which he had inspired her, and told him that she was happy in the prospect of their marriage. What was the meaning of the change? of what infernal potion had she tasted? Poor Newman had a terrible apprehension that she had really changed. His very admiration for her attached the idea of force and weight to her rupture. But he did not rail at her as false, for he was sure she was unhappy. In his walk he had crossed one of the bridges of the Seine, and he still followed, unheedingly, the long, un-broken quay. He had left Paris behind him, and he was al-most in the country; he was in the pleasant suburb of Auteuil. He stopped at last, looked around him without seeing or car-ing for its pleasantness, and then slowly turned and at a slower pace retraced his steps. When he came abreast of the fantastic embankment known as the Trocadero, he reflected, through his throbbing pain, that he was near Mrs. Tristram's dwelling, and that Mrs. Tristram, on particular occasions, had much of a woman's kindness in her utterance. He felt that he needed to pour out his ire, and he took the road to her house. Mrs. Tristram was at home and alone, and as soon as she had looked at him, on his entering the room, she told him that she knew what he had come for. Newman sat down heavily, in silence, looking at her.

"They have backed out!" she said. "Well, you may think it strange, but I felt something the other night in the air." Pres-ently he told her his story; she listened, with her eyes fixed on him. When he had finished she said quietly, "They want her to marry Lord Deepmere." Newman stared. He did not know that she knew anything about Lord Deepmere. "But I don't think she will," Mrs. Tristram added.

"*She* marry that poor little cub!" cried Newman. "Oh, Lord! And yet, why did she refuse me?"

"But that is n't the only thing," said Mrs. Tristram. "They really could n't endure you any longer. They had overrated their courage. I must say, to give the devil his due, that there is something rather fine in that. It was your commercial qual-ity in the abstract they could n't swallow. That is really aris-tocratic. They wanted your money, but they have given you up for an idea."

Newman frowned most ruefully, and took up his hat again. "I thought you would encourage me!" he said, with almost childlike sadness.

"Excuse me," she answered very gently. "I feel none the less sorry for you, especially as I am at the bottom of your trou-bles. I have not forgotten that I suggested the marriage to you. I don't believe that Madame de Cintré has any intention of marrying Lord Deepmere. It is true he is not younger than she, as he looks. He is thirty-three years old; I looked in the Peerage. But no—I can't believe her so horribly, cruelly false."

"Please say nothing against her," said Newman.

"Poor woman, she *is* cruel. But of course you will go after her and you will plead powerfully. Do you know that as you are now," Mrs. Tristram pursued, with characteristic audacity of comment, "you are extremely eloquent, even without speaking? To resist you a woman must have a very fixed idea in her head. I wish I had done you a wrong, that you might come to me in that fine fashion! But go to Madame de Cintré at any rate, and tell her that she is a puzzle even to me. I am very curious to see how far family discipline will go."

Newman sat a while longer, leaning his elbows on his knees and his head in his hands, and Mrs. Tristram continued to temper charity with philosophy and compassion with criticism. At last she inquired, "And what does the Count Valentin say to it?" Newman started; he had not thought of Valentin and his errand on the Swiss frontier since the morning. The reflection made him restless again, and he took his leave. He went straight to his apartment, where, upon the table of the vestibule, he found a telegram. It ran (with the date and place) as follows: "I am seriously ill; please to come to me as soon as possible. V. B." Newman groaned at this miserable news, and at the necessity of deferring his journey to the Château de Fleurières. But he wrote to Madame de Cintré these few lines; they were all he had time for:—

"I don't give you up, and I don't really believe you give me up. I don't understand it, but we shall clear it up together. I can't follow you to-day, as I am called to see a friend at a distance who is very ill, perhaps dying. But I shall come to you as soon as I can leave my friend. Why should n't I say that he is your brother? C. N."

After this he had only time to catch the night express to Geneva.

Chapter XIX

NEWMAN possessed a remarkable talent for sitting still when it was necessary, and he had an opportunity to use it on his journey to Switzerland. The successive hours of the night brought him no sleep; but he sat motionless in his corner of the railway-carriage, with his eyes closed, and the most observant of his fellow-travelers might have envied him his apparent slumber. Toward morning slumber really came, as an effect of mental rather than of physical fatigue. He slept for a couple of hours, and at last, waking, found his eyes resting upon one of the snow-powdered peaks of the Jura, behind which the sky was just reddening with the dawn. But he saw neither the cold mountain nor the warm sky; his consciousness began to throb again, on the very instant, with a sense of his wrong. He got out of the train half an hour before it reached Geneva, in the cold morning twilight, at the station indicated in Valentin's telegram. A drowsy stationmaster was on the platform with a lantern, and the hood of his overcoat over his head, and near him stood a gentleman who advanced to meet Newman. This personage was a man of forty, with a tall, lean figure, a sallow face, a dark eye, a neat mustache, and a pair of fresh gloves. He took off his hat, looking very grave, and pronounced Newman's name. Our hero assented and said, "You are M. de Bellegarde's friend?"

"I unite with you in claiming that sad honor," said the gentleman. "I had placed myself at M. de Bellegarde's service in this melancholy affair, together with M. de Grosjoyaux, who is now at his bedside. M. de Grosjoyaux, I believe, has had the honor of meeting you in Paris, but as he is a better nurse than I he remained with our poor friend. Bellegarde has been eagerly expecting you."

"And how is Bellegarde?" said Newman. "He was badly hit?"

"The doctor has condemned him; we brought a surgeon with us. But he will die in the best sentiments. I sent last evening for the curé of the nearest French village, who spent an hour with him. The curé was quite satisfied."

"Heaven forgive us!" groaned Newman. "I would rather

the doctor were satisfied! And can he see me—shall he know me?"

"When I left him, half an hour ago, he had fallen asleep, after a feverish, wakeful night. But we shall see." And Newman's companion proceeded to lead the way out of the station to the village, explaining as he went that the little party was lodged in the humblest of Swiss inns, where, however, they had succeeded in making M. de Bellegarde much more comfortable than could at first have been expected. "We are old companions in arms," said Valentin's second; "it is not the first time that one of us has helped the other to lie easily. It is a very nasty wound, and the nastiest thing about it is that Bellegarde's adversary was no shot. He put his bullet where he could. It took it into its head to walk straight into Bellegarde's left side, just below the heart."

As they picked their way in the gray, deceptive dawn, between the manure-heaps of the village street, Newman's new acquaintance narrated the particulars of the duel. The conditions of the meeting had been that if the first exchange of shots should fail to satisfy one of the two gentlemen, a second should take place. Valentin's first bullet had done exactly what Newman's companion was convinced he had intended it to do; it had grazed the arm of M. Stanislas Kapp, just scratching the flesh. M. Kapp's own projectile, meanwhile, had passed at ten good inches from the person of Valentin. The representatives of M. Stanislas had demanded another shot, which was granted. Valentin had then fired aside and the young Alsatian had done effective execution. "I saw, when we met him on the ground," said Newman's informant, "that he was not going to be *commode*. It is a kind of bovine temperament." Valentin had immediately been installed at the inn, and M. Stanislas and his friends had withdrawn to regions unknown. The police authorities of the canton had waited upon the party at the inn, had been extremely majestic, and had drawn up a long *procès-verbal*; but it was probable that they would wink at so very gentlemanly a bit of bloodshed. Newman asked whether a message had not been sent to Valentin's family, and learned that up to a late hour on the preceding evening Valentin had opposed it. He had refused to believe his wound was dangerous. But after his interview with the curé he had consented, and a telegram had been dispatched to his mother. "But the marquise had better hurry!" said Newman's conductor.

"Well, it 's an abominable affair!" said Newman. "That 's all I have got to say!" To say this, at least, in a tone of infinite disgust, was an irresistible need.

"Ah, you don't approve?" questioned his conductor, with curious urbanity.

"Approve?" cried Newman. "I wish that when I had him there, night before last, I had locked him up in my *cabinet de toilette!*"

Valentin's late second opened his eyes, and shook his head up and down two or three times, gravely, with a little flute-like whistle. But they had reached the inn, and a stout maid-servant in a night-cap was at the door with a lantern, to take Newman's traveling-bag from the porter who trudged behind him. Valentin was lodged on the ground-floor at the back of the house, and Newman's companion went along a stone-faced passage and softly opened a door. Then he beckoned to Newman, who advanced and looked into the room, which was lighted by a single shaded candle. Beside the fire sat M. de Grosjoyaux asleep in his dressing-gown—a little plump, fair man whom Newman had seen several times in Valentin's company. On the bed lay Valentin, pale and still, with his eyes closed—a figure very shocking to Newman, who had seen it hitherto awake to its finger tips. M. de Grosjoyaux's colleague pointed to an open door beyond, and whispered that the doctor was within, keeping guard. So long as Valentin slept, or seemed to sleep, of course Newman could not approach him; so our hero withdrew for the present, committing himself to the care of the half-waked *bonne*. She took him to a room above-stairs, and introduced him to a bed on which a magnified bolster, in yellow calico, figured as a counterpane. Newman lay down, and, in spite of his counterpane, slept for three or four hours. When he awoke, the morning was advanced and the sun was filling his window, and he heard, outside of it, the clucking of hens. While he was dressing there came to his door a messenger from M. de Grosjoyaux and his companion proposing that he should breakfast with them. Presently he went down-stairs to the little stone-

paved dining-room, where the maid-servant, who had taken
off her night-cap, was serving the repast. M. de Grosjoyaux
was there, surprisingly fresh for a gentleman who had been
playing sick-nurse half the night, rubbing his hands and
watching the breakfast table attentively. Newman renewed acquaintance with him, and learned that Valentin was still sleeping; the surgeon, who had had a fairly tranquil night, was at
present sitting with him. Before M. de Grosjoyaux's associate
reappeared, Newman learned that his name was M. Ledoux,
and that Bellegarde's acquaintance with him dated from the
days when they served together in the Pontifical Zouaves. M.
Ledoux was the nephew of a distinguished Ultramontane
bishop. At last the bishop's nephew came in with a toilet in
which an ingenious attempt at harmony with the peculiar situation was visible, and with a gravity tempered by a decent
deference to the best breakfast that the Croix Helvétique had
ever set forth. Valentin's servant, who was allowed only in
scanty measure the honor of watching with his master, had
been lending a light Parisian hand in the kitchen. The two
Frenchmen did their best to prove that if circumstances might
overshadow, they could not really obscure, the national talent
for conversation, and M. Ledoux delivered a neat little eulogy
on poor Bellegarde, whom he pronounced the most charming
Englishman he had ever known.

"Do you call him an Englishman?" Newman asked.

M. Ledoux smiled a moment and then made an epigram.
"C'est plus qu'un Anglais—c'est un Anglomane!" Newman
said soberly that he had never noticed it; and M. de Grosjoyaux remarked that it was really too soon to deliver a funeral
oration upon poor Bellegarde. "Evidently," said M. Ledoux.
"But I could n't help observing this morning to Mr. Newman
that when a man has taken such excellent measures for his
salvation as our dear friend did last evening, it seems almost
a pity he should put it in peril again by returning to the
world." M. Ledoux was a great Catholic, and Newman
thought him a queer mixture. His countenance, by daylight,
had a sort of amiably saturnine cast; he had a very large thin
nose, and looked like a Spanish picture. He appeared to think
dueling a very perfect arrangement, provided, if one should
get hit, one could promptly see the priest. He seemed to take

a great satisfaction in Valentin's interview with the curé, and
yet his conversation did not at all indicate a sanctimonious
habit of mind. M. Ledoux had evidently a high sense of the
becoming, and was prepared to be urbane and tasteful on all
points. He was always furnished with a smile (which pushed
his mustache up under his nose) and an explanation. *Savoir-
vivre*—knowing how to live—was his specialty, in which he
included knowing how to die; but, as Newman reflected,
with a good deal of dumb irritation, he seemed disposed to
delegate to others the application of his learning on this latter
point. M. de Grosjoyaux was of quite another complexion,
and appeared to regard his friend's theological unction as the
sign of an inaccessibly superior mind. He was evidently doing
his utmost, with a kind of jovial tenderness, to make life
agreeable to Valentin to the last, and help him as little as
possible to miss the Boulevard des Italiens; but what chiefly
occupied his mind was the mystery of a bungling brewer's
son making so neat a shot. He himself could snuff a candle,
etc., and yet he confessed that he could not have done better
than this. He hastened to add that on the present occasion he
would have made a point of not doing so well. It was not an
occasion for that sort of murderous work, *que diable!* He
would have picked out some quiet fleshy spot and just tapped
it with a harmless ball. M. Stanislas Kapp had been deplorably heavy-handed; but really, when the world had come to
that pass that one granted a meeting to a brewer's son! . . . .
This was M. de Grosjoyaux's nearest approach to a general-
ization. He kept looking through the window, over the
shoulder of M. Ledoux, at a slender tree which stood at the
end of a lane, opposite to the inn, and seemed to be measuring its distance from his extended arm and secretly wishing
that, since the subject had been introduced, propriety did not
forbid a little speculative pistol-practice.

Newman was in no humor to enjoy good company. He
could neither eat nor talk; his soul was sore with grief and
anger, and the weight of his double sorrow was intolerable.
He sat with his eyes fixed upon his plate, counting the minutes, wishing at one moment that Valentin would see him
and leave him free to go in quest of Madame de Cintré and
his lost happiness, and mentally calling himself a vile brute

the next, for the impatient egotism of the wish. He was very poor company, himself, and even his acute preoccupation and his general lack of the habit of pondering the impression he produced did not prevent him from reflecting that his companions must be puzzled to see how poor Bellegarde came to take such a fancy to this taciturn Yankee that he must needs have him at his death-bed. After breakfast he strolled forth alone into the village and looked at the fountain, the geese, the open barn doors, the brown, bent old women, showing their hugely darned stocking-heels at the ends of their slowly-clicking sabots, and the beautiful view of snowy Alp and purple Jura at either end of the little street. The day was brilliant; early spring was in the air and in the sunshine, and the winter's damp was trickling out of the cottage eaves. It was birth and brightness for all nature, even for chirping chickens and waddling goslings, and it was to be death and burial for poor, foolish, generous, delightful Bellegarde. Newman walked as far as the village church, and went into the small grave-yard beside it, where he sat down and looked at the awkward tablets which were planted around. They were all sordid and hideous, and Newman could feel nothing but the hardness and coldness of death. He got up and came back to the inn, where he found M. Ledoux having coffee and a cigarette at a little green table which he had caused to be carried into the small garden. Newman, learning that the doctor was still sitting with Valentin, asked M. Ledoux if he might not be allowed to relieve him; he had a great desire to be useful to his poor friend. This was easily arranged; the doctor was very glad to go to bed. He was a youthful and rather jaunty practitioner, but he had a clever face, and the ribbon of the Legion of Honor in his button-hole; Newman listened attentively to the instructions he gave him before retiring, and took mechanically from his hand a small volume which the surgeon recommended as a help to wakefulness, and which turned out to be an old copy of "Faublas." Valentin was still lying with his eyes closed, and there was no visible change in his condition. Newman sat down near him, and for a long time narrowly watched him. Then his eyes wandered away with his thoughts upon his own situation, and rested upon the chain of the Alps, disclosed by the drawing of the scant white cotton curtain of the window, through which the sunshine passed and lay in squares upon the red-tiled floor. He tried to interweave his reflections with hope, but he only half succeeded. What had happened to him seemed to have, in its violence and audacity, the force of a real calamity—the strength and insolence of Destiny herself. It was unnatural and monstrous, and he had no arms against it. At last a sound struck upon the stillness, and he heard Valentin's voice.

"It can't be about *me* you are pulling that long face!" He found, when he turned, that Valentin was lying in the same position; but his eyes were open, and he was even trying to smile. It was with a very slender strength that he returned the pressure of Newman's hand. "I have been watching you for a quarter of an hour," Valentin went on; "you have been looking as black as thunder. You are greatly disgusted with me, I see. Well, of course! So am I!"

"Oh, I shall not scold you," said Newman. "I feel too badly. And how are you getting on?"

"Oh, I 'm getting off! They have quite settled that; have n't they?"

"That 's for you to settle; you can get well if you try," said Newman, with resolute cheerfulness.

"My dear fellow, how can I try? Trying is violent exercise, and that sort of thing is n't in order for a man with a hole in his side as big as your hat, that begins to bleed if he moves a hair's-breadth. I knew you would come," he continued; "I knew I should wake up and find you here; so I 'm not surprised. But last night I was very impatient. I did n't see how I could keep still until you came. It was a matter of keeping still, just like this; as still as a mummy in his case. You talk about trying; I tried that! Well, here I am yet—these twenty hours. It seems like twenty days." Bellegarde talked slowly and feebly, but distinctly enough. It was visible, however, that he was in extreme pain, and at last he closed his eyes. Newman begged him to remain silent and spare himself; the doctor had left urgent orders. "Oh," said Valentin, "let us eat and drink, for to-morrow—to-morrow"—and he paused again. "No, not to-morrow, perhaps, but to-day. I can't eat and drink, but I can talk. What 's to be gained, at this pass, by renun—renunciation? I must n't use such big words. I was always a chatterer; Lord, how I have talked in my day!"

"That 's a reason for keeping quiet now," said Newman. "We know how well you talk, you know."

But Valentin, without heeding him, went on in the same weak, dying drawl. "I wanted to see you because you have seen my sister. Does she know—will she come?"

Newman was embarrassed. "Yes, by this time she must know."

"Did n't you tell her?" Valentin asked. And then, in a moment, "Did n't you bring me any message from her?" His eyes rested upon Newman's with a certain soft keenness.

"I did n't see her after I got your telegram," said Newman. "I wrote to her."

"And she sent you no answer?"

Newman was obliged to reply that Madame de Cintré had left Paris. "She went yesterday to Fleurières."

"Yesterday—to Fleurières? Why did she go to Fleurières? What day is this? What day was yesterday? Ah, then I shan't see her," said Valentin, sadly. "Fleurières is too far!" And then he closed his eyes again. Newman sat silent, summoning pious invention to his aid, but he was relieved at finding that Valentin was apparently too weak to reason or to be curious. Bellegarde, however, presently went on. "And my mother—and my brother—will they come? Are they at Fleurières?"

"They were in Paris, but I did n't see them, either," Newman answered. "If they received your telegram in time, they will have started this morning. Otherwise they will be obliged to wait for the night-express, and they will arrive at the same hour as I did."

"They won't thank me—they won't thank me," Valentin murmured. "They will pass an atrocious night, and Urbain does n't like the early morning air. I don't remember ever in my life to have seen him before noon—before breakfast. No one ever saw him. We don't know how he is then. Perhaps he 's different. Who knows? Posterity, perhaps, will know. That 's the time he works, in his *cabinet*, at the history of the Princesses. But I had to send for them—had n't I? And then I want to see my mother sit there where you sit, and say good-by to her. Perhaps, after all, I don't know her, and she will have some surprise for me. Don't think you know her yet, yourself; perhaps she may surprise *you*. But if I can't see Claire, I don't care for anything. I have been thinking of it—and in my dreams, too. Why did she go to Fleurières to-day? She never told me. What has happened? Ah, she ought to have guessed I was here—this way. It is the first time in her life she ever disappointed me. Poor Claire!"

"You know we are not man and wife quite yet,—your sister and I," said Newman. "She does n't yet account to me for all her actions." And, after a fashion, he smiled.

Valentin looked at him a moment. "Have you quarreled?"

"Never, never, never!" Newman exclaimed.

"How happily you say that!" said Valentin. "You are going to be happy—*va!*" In answer to this stroke of irony, none the less powerful for being so unconscious, all poor Newman could do was to give a helpless and transparent stare. Valentin continued to fix him with his own rather over-bright gaze, and presently he said, "But something *is* the matter with you. I watched you just now; you have n't a bridegroom's face."

"My dear fellow," said Newman, "how can I show *you* a bridegroom's face? If you think I enjoy seeing you lie there and not being able to help you"—

"Why, you are just the man to be cheerful; don't forfeit your rights! I 'm a proof of your wisdom. When was a man ever gloomy when he could say, 'I told you so?' You told me so, you know. You did what you could about it. You said some very good things; I have thought them over. But, my dear friend, I was right, all the same. This is the regular way."

"I did n't do what I ought," said Newman. "I ought to have done something else."

"For instance?"

"Oh, something or other. I ought to have treated you as a small boy."

"Well, I 'm a very small boy, now," said Valentin. "I 'm rather less than an infant. An infant is helpless, but it 's generally voted promising. I 'm not promising, eh? Society can't lose a less valuable member."

Newman was strongly moved. He got up and turned his back upon his friend and walked away to the window, where he stood looking out, but only vaguely seeing. "No, I don't like the look of your back," Valentin continued. "I have always been an observer of backs; yours is quite out of sorts."

Newman returned to his bedside and begged him to be quiet. "Be quiet and get well," he said. "That 's what you must do. Get well and help me."

"I told you you were in trouble! How can I help you?" Valentin asked.

"I 'll let you know when you are better. You were always curious; there is something to get well for!" Newman answered, with resolute animation.

Valentin closed his eyes and lay a long time without speaking. He seemed even to have fallen asleep. But at the end of half an hour he began to talk again. "I am rather sorry about that place in the bank. Who knows but that I might have become another Rothschild? But I was n't meant for a banker; bankers are not so easy to kill. Don't you think I have been very easy to kill? It 's not like a serious man. It 's really very mortifying. It 's like telling your hostess you must go, when you count upon her begging you to stay, and then finding she does no such thing. 'Really—so soon? You 've only just come!' Life does n't make me any such polite little speech."

Newman for some time said nothing, but at last he broke out. "It 's a bad case—it 's a bad case—it 's the worst case I ever met. I don't want to say anything unpleasant, but I can't help it. I 've seen men dying before—and I 've seen men shot. But it always seemed more natural; they were not so clever as you. Damnation—damnation! You might have done something better than this. It 's about the meanest winding-up of a man's affairs that I can imagine!"

Valentin feebly waved his hand to and fro. "Don't insist—don't insist! It is mean—decidedly mean. For you see at the bottom—down at the bottom, in a little place as small as the end of a wine-funnel—I agree with you!"

A few moments after this the doctor put his head through the half-opened door and, perceiving that Valentin was awake, came in and felt his pulse. He shook his head and declared that he had talked too much—ten times too much. "Nonsense!" said Valentin; "a man sentenced to death can never talk too much. Have you never read an account of an execution in a newspaper? Don't they always set a lot of people at the prisoner—lawyers, reporters, priests—to make him talk? But it 's not Mr. Newman's fault; he sits there as mum as a death's-head."

The doctor observed that it was time his patient's wound should be dressed again; MM. de Grosjoyaux and Ledoux, who had already witnessed this delicate operation, taking Newman's place as assistants. Newman withdrew and learned from his fellow-watchers that they had received a telegram from Urbain de Bellegarde to the effect that their message had been delivered in the Rue de l'Université too late to allow him to take the morning train, but that he would start with his mother in the evening. Newman wandered away into the village again, and walked about restlessly for two or three hours. The day seemed terribly long. At dusk he came back and dined with the doctor and M. Ledoux. The dressing of Valentin's wound had been a very critical operation; the doctor did n't really see how he was to endure a repetition of it. He then declared that he must beg of Mr. Newman to deny himself for the present the satisfaction of sitting with M. de Bellegarde; more than any one else, apparently, he had the flattering but inconvenient privilege of exciting him. M. Ledoux, at this, swallowed a glass of wine in silence; he must have been wondering what the deuce Bellegarde found so exciting in the American.

Newman, after dinner, went up to his room, where he sat for a long time staring at his lighted candle, and thinking that Valentin was dying down-stairs. Late, when the candle had burnt low, there came a soft tap at his door. The doctor stood there with a candlestick and a shrug.

"He must amuse himself, still!" said Valentin's medical adviser. "He insists upon seeing you, and I am afraid you must come. I think, at this rate, that he will hardly outlast the night."

Newman went back to Valentin's room, which he found lighted by a taper on the hearth. Valentin begged him to light a candle. "I want to see your face," he said. "They say you excite me," he went on, as Newman complied with this request, "and I confess I do feel excited. But it is n't you—it 's my own thoughts. I have been thinking—thinking. Sit down there, and let me look at you again." Newman seated himself, folded his arms, and bent a heavy gaze upon his friend. He seemed to be playing a part, mechanically, in a lugubrious comedy. Valentin looked at him for some time. "Yes, this morning I was right; you have something on your mind heavier than Valentin de Bellegarde. Come, I 'm a dying man and it 's indecent to deceive me. Something happened after I left Paris. It was not for nothing that my sister started off at this season of the year for Fleurières. Why was it? It sticks in my crop. I have been thinking it over, and if you don't tell me I shall guess."

"I had better not tell you," said Newman. "It won't do you any good."

"If you think it will do me any good not to tell me, you are very much mistaken. There is trouble about your marriage."

"Yes," said Newman. "There is trouble about my marriage."

"Good!" And Valentin was silent again. "They have stopped it."

"They have stopped it," said Newman. Now that he had spoken out, he found a satisfaction in it which deepened as he went on. "Your mother and brother have broken faith. They have decided that it can't take place. They have decided that I am not good enough, after all. They have taken back their word. Since you insist, there it is!"

Valentin gave a sort of groan, lifted his hands a moment, and then let them drop.

"I am sorry not to have anything better to tell you about them," Newman pursued. "But it 's not my fault. I was, indeed, very unhappy when your telegram reached me; I was quite upside down. You may imagine whether I feel any better now."

Valentin moaned gaspingly, as if his wound were throbbing. "Broken faith, broken faith!" he murmured. "And my sister—my sister?"

"Your sister is very unhappy; she has consented to give me up. I don't know why. I don't know what they have done to her; it must be something pretty bad. In justice to her you ought to know it. They have made her suffer. I have n't seen her alone, but only before them! We had an interview yesterday morning. They came out, flat, in so many words. They told me to go about my business. It seems to me a very bad case. I 'm angry, I 'm sore, I 'm sick."

Valentin lay there staring, with his eyes more brilliantly lighted, his lips soundlessly parted, and a flush of color in his pale face. Newman had never before uttered so many words in the plaintive key, but now, in speaking to Valentin in the poor fellow's extremity, he had a feeling that he was making his complaint somewhere within the presence of the power that men pray to in trouble; he felt his outgush of resentment as a sort of spiritual privilege.

"And Claire,"—said Bellegarde,—"Claire? She has given you up?"

"I don't really believe it," said Newman.

"No, don't believe it, don't believe it. She is gaining time; excuse her."

"I pity her!" said Newman.

"Poor Claire!" murmured Valentin. "But they—but they" —and he paused again. "You saw them; they dismissed you, face to face?"

"Face to face. They were very explicit."

"What did they say?"

"They said they could n't stand a commercial person."

Valentin put out his hand and laid it upon Newman's arm. "And about their promise—their engagement with you?"

"They made a distinction. They said it was to hold good only until Madame de Cintré accepted me."

Valentin lay staring a while, and his flush died away. "Don't tell me any more," he said at last; "I 'm ashamed."

"You? You are the soul of honor," said Newman, simply.

Valentin groaned and turned away his head. For some time nothing more was said. Then Valentin turned back again and found a certain force to press Newman's arm. "It 's very bad—very bad. When my people—when my race—come to that, it is time for me to withdraw. I believe in my sister; she will explain. Excuse her. If she can't—if she can't, forgive her. She has suffered. But for the others it is very bad—very bad. You take it very hard? No, it 's a shame to make you say so." He closed his eyes and again there was a silence. Newman felt almost awed; he had evoked a more solemn spirit than he expected. Presently Valentin looked at him again, removing his hand from his arm. "I apologize," he said. "Do you understand? Here on my death-bed. I apologize for my family. For my mother. For my brother. For the ancient house of Bellegarde. *Voilà!*" he added, softly.

Newman for all answer took his hand and pressed it with a world of kindness. Valentin remained quiet, and at the end of half an hour the doctor softly came in. Behind him, through the half-open door, Newman saw the two questioning faces of MM. de Grosjoyaux and Ledoux. The doctor laid his hand on Valentin's wrist and sat looking at him. He gave no sign and the two gentlemen came in, M. Ledoux having first beckoned to some one outside. This was M. le curé, who carried in his hand an object unknown to Newman, and covered with a white napkin. M. le curé was short, round, and red: he advanced, pulling off his little black cap to Newman, and deposited his burden on the table; and then he sat down in the best arm-chair, with his hands folded across his person. The other gentlemen had exchanged glances which expressed unanimity as to the timeliness of their presence. But for a long time Valentin neither spoke nor moved. It was Newman's belief, afterwards, that M. le curé went to sleep. At last, abruptly, Valentin pronounced Newman's name. His friend went to him, and he said in French, "You are not alone. I want to speak to you alone." Newman looked at the doctor, and the doctor looked at the curé, who looked back at him; and then the doctor and the curé, together, gave a shrug. "Alone—for five minutes," Valentin repeated. "Please leave us."

The curé took up his burden again and led the way out, followed by his companions. Newman closed the door behind them and came back to Valentin's bedside. Bellegarde had watched all this intently.

"It 's very bad, it 's very bad," he said, after Newman had seated himself close to him. "The more I think of it the worse it is."

"Oh, don't think of it," said Newman.

But Valentin went on, without heeding him. "Even if they should come round again, the shame—the baseness—is there."

"Oh, they won't come round!" said Newman.

"Well, you can make them."

"Make them?"

"I can tell you something—a great secret—an immense secret. You can use it against them—frighten them, force them."

"A secret!" Newman repeated. The idea of letting Valentin, on his death-bed, confide him an "immense secret" shocked him, for the moment, and made him draw back. It seemed an illicit way of arriving at information, and even had a vague analogy with listening at a key-hole. Then, suddenly, the thought of "forcing" Madame de Bellegarde and her son became attractive, and Newman bent his head closer to Valentin's lips. For some time, however, the dying man said nothing more. He only lay and looked at his friend with his kindled, expanded, troubled eye, and Newman began to believe that he had spoken in delirium. But at last he said,—

"There was something done—something done at Fleurières. It was foul play. My father—something happened to him. I don't know; I have been ashamed—afraid to know. But I know there is something. My mother knows—Urbain knows."

"Something happened to your father?" said Newman, urgently.

Valentin looked at him, still more wide-eyed. "He did n't get well."

"Get well of what?"

But the immense effort which Valentin had made, first to decide to utter these words and then to bring them out, appeared to have taken his last strength. He lapsed again into silence, and Newman sat watching him. "Do you understand?" he began again, presently. "At Fleurières. You can find out. Mrs. Bread knows. Tell her I begged you to ask her. Then tell them that, and see. It may help you. If not, tell every one. It will—it will"—here Valentin's voice sank to the feeblest murmur—"it will avenge you!"

The words died away in a long, soft groan. Newman stood up, deeply impressed, not knowing what to say; his heart was beating violently. "Thank you," he said at last. "I am much obliged." But Valentin seemed not to hear him; he remained silent, and his silence continued. At last Newman went and opened the door. M. le curé reëntered, bearing his sacred vessel and followed by the three gentlemen and by Valentin's servant. It was almost processional.

Chapter XX

VALENTIN DE BELLEGARDE died, tranquilly, just as the cold, faint March dawn began to illumine the faces of the little knot of friends gathered about his bedside. An hour afterwards Newman left the inn and drove to Geneva; he was naturally unwilling to be present at the arrival of Madame de Bellegarde and her first-born. At Geneva, for the moment, he remained. He was like a man who has had a fall and wants to sit still and count his bruises. He instantly wrote to Madame de Cintré, relating to her the circumstances of her brother's death—with certain exceptions—and asking her what was the earliest moment at which he might hope that she would consent to see him. M. Ledoux had told him that he had reason to know that Valentin's will—Bellegarde had a great deal of elegant personal property to dispose of—contained a request that he should be buried near his father in the church-yard of Fleurières, and Newman intended that the state of his own relations with the family should not deprive him of the satisfaction of helping to pay the last earthly honors to the best fellow in the world. He reflected that Valentin's friend-ship was older than Urbain's enmity, and that at a funeral it was easy to escape notice. Madame de Cintré's answer to his letter enabled him to time his arrival at Fleurières. This answer was very brief; it ran as follows:—

"I thank you for your letter, and for your being with Valentin. It is a most inexpressible sorrow to me that I was not. To see you will be nothing but a distress to me; there is no need, therefore, to wait for what you call brighter days. It is all one now, and I shall have no brighter days. Come when you please; only notify me first. My brother is to be buried here on Friday, and my family is to remain here. C. de C."

As soon as he received this letter Newman went straight to Paris and to Poitiers. The journey took him far southward, through green Touraine and across the far-shining Loire, into a country where the early spring deepened about him as he went. But he had never made a journey during which he heeded less what he would have called the lay of the land. He obtained lodging at the inn at Poitiers, and the next morning drove in a couple of hours to the village of Fleurières. But here, preoccupied though he was, he could not fail to notice the picturesqueness of the place. It was what the French call a *petit bourg*; it lay at the base of a sort of huge mound on the summit of which stood the crumbling ruins of a feudal castle, much of whose sturdy material, as well as that of the wall which dropped along the hill to inclose the clustered houses defensively, had been absorbed into the very substance of the village. The church was simply the former chapel of the castle, fronting upon its grass-grown court, which, however, was of generous enough width to have given up its quaintest corner to a little graveyard. Here the very head-stones themselves seemed to sleep, as they slanted into the grass; the patient elbow of the rampart held them together on one side, and in front, far beneath their mossy lids, the green plains and blue distances stretched away. The way to church, up the hill, was impracticable to vehicles. It was lined with peasants, two or three rows deep, who stood watching old Madame de Bellegarde slowly ascend it, on the arm of her elder son, behind the pall-bearers of the other. Newman chose to lurk among the common mourners who murmured "Madame la Comtesse" as a tall figure veiled in black passed before them. He stood in the dusky little church while the service was going forward, but at the dismal tomb-side he turned away and walked down the hill. He went back to Poitiers, and spent two days in which patience and impatience were singularly commingled. On the third day he sent Madame de Cintré a note, saying that he would call upon her in the afternoon, and in accordance with this he again took his way to Fleurières. He left his vehicle at the tavern in the village street, and obeyed the simple instructions which were given him for finding the château.

"It is just beyond there," said the landlord, and pointed to the tree-tops of the park, above the opposite houses. Newman followed the first cross-road to the right—it was bordered with mouldy cottages—and in a few moments saw before him the peaked roofs of the towers. Advancing farther, he found himself before a vast iron gate, rusty and closed; here

he paused a moment, looking through the bars. The château
was near the road; this was at once its merit and its defect;
but its aspect was extremely impressive. Newman learned afterwards, from a guide-book of the province, that it dated
from the time of Henry IV. It presented to the wide, paved
area which preceded it and which was edged with shabby
farm-buildings an immense façade of dark, time-stained brick,
flanked by two low wings, each of which terminated in a little
Dutch-looking pavilion capped with a fantastic roof. Two
towers rose behind, and behind the towers was a mass of elms
and beeches, now just faintly green. But the great feature was
a wide, green river which washed the foundations of the château. The building rose from an island in the circling stream,
so that this formed a perfect moat spanned by a two-arched
bridge without a parapet. The dull brick walls, which here
and there made a grand, straight sweep; the ugly little cupolas
of the wings, the deep-set windows, the long, steep pinnacles
of mossy slate, all mirrored themselves in the tranquil river.
Newman rang at the gate, and was almost frightened at the
tone with which a big rusty bell above his head replied to
him. An old woman came out from the gate-house and
opened the creaking portal just wide enough for him to pass,
and he went in, across the dry, bare court and the little
cracked white slabs of the causeway on the moat. At the door
of the château he waited for some moments, and this gave
him a chance to observe that Fleurières was not "kept up,"
and to reflect that it was a melancholy place of residence. "It
looks," said Newman to himself—and I give the comparison
for what it is worth—"like a Chinese penitentiary." At last
the door was opened by a servant whom he remembered to
have seen in the Rue de l'Université. The man's dull face
brightened as he perceived our hero, for Newman, for indefinable reasons, enjoyed the confidence of the liveried gentry.
The footman led the way across a great central vestibule, with
a pyramid of plants in tubs in the middle and glass doors all
around, to what appeared to be the principal drawing-room
of the château. Newman crossed the threshold of a room of
superb proportions, which made him feel at first like a tourist
with a guide-book and a cicerone awaiting a fee. But when
his guide had left him alone, with the observation that he

would call Madame la Comtesse, Newman perceived that the salon contained little that was remarkable save a dark ceiling with curiously carved rafters, some curtains of elaborate, antiquated tapestry, and a dark oaken floor, polished like a mirror. He waited some minutes, walking up and down; but at length, as he turned at the end of the room, he saw that Madame de Cintré had come in by a distant door. She wore a black dress, and she stood looking at him. As the length of the immense room lay between them he had time to look at her before they met in the middle of it.

He was dismayed at the change in her appearance. Pale, heavy-browed, almost haggard, with a sort of monastic rigidity in her dress, she had little but her pure features in common with the woman whose radiant good grace he had hitherto admired. She let her eyes rest on his own, and she let him take her hand; but her eyes looked like two rainy autumn moons, and her touch was portentously lifeless.

"I was at your brother's funeral," Newman said. "Then I waited three days. But I could wait no longer."

"Nothing can be lost or gained by waiting," said Madame de Cintré. "But it was very considerate of you to wait, wronged as you have been."

"I 'm glad you think I have been wronged," said Newman, with that oddly humorous accent with which he often uttered words of the gravest meaning.

"Do I need to say so?" she asked. "I don't think I have wronged, seriously, many persons; certainly not consciously. To you, to whom I have done this hard and cruel thing, the only reparation I can make is to say, 'I know it, I feel it!' The reparation is pitifully small!"

"Oh, it 's a great step forward!" said Newman, with a gracious smile of encouragement. He pushed a chair towards her and held it, looking at her urgently. She sat down, mechanically, and he seated himself near her; but in a moment he got up, restlessly, and stood before her. She remained seated, like a troubled creature who had passed through the stage of restlessness.

"I say nothing is to be gained by my seeing you," she went on, "and yet I am very glad you came. Now I can tell you what I feel. It is a selfish pleasure, but it is one of the last I shall have." And she paused, with her great misty eyes fixed upon him. "I know how I have deceived and injured you; I know how cruel and cowardly I have been. I see it as vividly as you do—I feel it to the ends of my fingers." And she unclasped her hands, which were locked together in her lap, lifted them, and dropped them at her side. "Anything that you may have said of me in your angriest passion is nothing to what I have said to myself."

"In my angriest passion," said Newman, "I have said nothing hard of you. The very worst thing I have said of you yet is that you are the loveliest of women." And he seated himself before her again, abruptly.

She flushed a little, but even her flush was pale. "That is because you think I will come back. But I will not come back. It is in that hope you have come here, I know; I am very sorry for you. I would do almost anything for you. To say that, after what I have done, seems simply impudent; but what can I say that will not seem impudent? To wrong you and apologize—that is easy enough. I should not have wronged you." She stopped a moment, looking at him, and motioned him to let her go on. "I ought never to have listened to you at first; that was the wrong. No good could come of it. I felt it, and yet I listened; that was your fault. I liked you too much; I believed in you."

"And don't you believe in me now?"

"More than ever. But now it does n't matter. I have given you up."

Newman gave a powerful thump with his clenched fist upon his knee. "Why, why, why?" he cried. "Give me a reason—a decent reason. You are not a child—you are not a minor, nor an idiot. You are not obliged to drop me because your mother told you to. Such a reason is n't worthy of you."

"I know that; it 's not worthy of me. But it 's the only one I have to give. After all," said Madame de Cintré, throwing out her hands, "think me an idiot and forget me! That will be the simplest way."

Newman got up and walked away with a crushing sense that his cause was lost, and yet with an equal inability to give up fighting. He went to one of the great windows, and looked out at the stiffly embanked river and the formal gardens which lay beyond it. When he turned round, Madame de Cintré had risen; she stood there silent and passive. "You are not frank," said Newman; "you are not honest. Instead of saying that you are imbecile, you should say that other people are wicked. Your mother and your brother have been false and cruel; they have been so to me, and I am sure they have been so to you. Why do you try to shield them? Why do you sacrifice me to them? I'm not false; I'm not cruel. You don't know what you give up; I can tell you that—you don't. They bully you and plot about you; and I—I"— And he paused, holding out his hands. She turned away and began to leave him. "You told me the other day that you were afraid of your mother," he said, following her. "What did you mean?"

Madame de Cintré shook her head. "I remember; I was sorry afterwards."

"You were sorry when she came down and put on the thumb-screws. In God's name what *is* it she does to you?"

"Nothing. Nothing that you can understand. And now that I have given you up, I must not complain of her to you."

"That's no reasoning!" cried Newman. "Complain of her, on the contrary. Tell me all about it, frankly and trustfully, as you ought, and we will talk it over so satisfactorily that you won't give me up."

Madame de Cintré looked down some moments, fixedly; and then, raising her eyes, she said, "One good at least has come of this: I have made you judge me more fairly. You thought of me in a way that did me great honor; I don't know why you had taken it into your head. But it left me no loop-hole for escape—no chance to be the common, weak creature I am. It was not my fault; I warned you from the first. But I ought to have warned you more. I ought to have convinced you that I was doomed to disappoint you. But I *was*, in a way, too proud. You see what my superiority amounts to, I hope!" she went on, raising her voice with a tremor which even then and there Newman thought beautiful. "I am too proud to be honest, I am not too proud to be faithless. I am timid and cold and selfish. I am afraid of being uncomfortable."

"And you call marrying me uncomfortable!" said Newman, staring.

Madame de Cintré blushed a little and seemed to say that if begging his pardon in words was impudent, she might at least thus mutely express her perfect comprehension of his finding her conduct odious. "It is not marrying you; it is doing all that would go with it. It 's the rupture, the defiance, the insisting upon being happy in my own way. What right have I to be happy when—when"—And she paused.

"When what?" said Newman.

"When others have been most unhappy!"

"What others?" Newman asked. "What have you to do with any others but me? Besides you said just now that you wanted happiness, and that you should find it by obeying your mother. You contradict yourself."

"Yes, I contradict myself; that shows you that I am not even intelligent."

"You are laughing at me!" cried Newman. "You are mocking me!"

She looked at him intently, and an observer might have said that she was asking herself whether she might not most quickly end their common pain by confessing that she was mocking him. "No; I am not," she presently said.

"Granting that you are not intelligent," he went on, "that you are weak, that you are common, that you are nothing that I have believed you were—what I ask of you is not a heroic effort, it is a very common effort. There is a great deal on my side to make it easy. The simple truth is that you don't care enough about me to make it."

"I am cold," said Madame de Cintré. "I am as cold as that flowing river."

Newman gave a great rap on the floor with his stick, and a long, grim laugh. "Good, good!" he cried. "You go altogether too far—you overshoot the mark. There is n't a woman in the world as bad as you would make yourself out. I see your game; it 's what I said. You are blackening yourself to whiten others. You don't want to give me up, at all; you like me—you like me. I know you do; you have shown it, and I have felt it. After that, you may be as cold as you please! They have bullied you, I say; they have tortured you. It 's an outrage, and I insist upon saving you from the extravagance of your own generosity. Would you chop off your hand if your mother requested it?"

Madame de Cintré looked a little frightened. "I spoke of my mother too blindly, the other day. I am my own mistress, by law and by her approval. She can do nothing to me; she has done nothing. She has never alluded to those hard words I used about her."

"She has made you feel them, I 'll promise you!" said Newman.

"It 's my conscience that makes me feel them."

"Your conscience seems to me to be rather mixed!" exclaimed Newman, passionately.

"It has been in great trouble, but now it is very clear," said Madame de Cintré. "I don't give you up for any worldly advantage or for any worldly happiness."

"Oh, you don't give me up for Lord Deepmere, I know," said Newman. "I won't pretend, even to provoke you, that I think that. But that 's what your mother and your brother wanted, and your mother, at that villainous ball of hers—I liked it at the time, but the very thought of it now makes me rabid—tried to push him on to make up to you."

"Who told you this?" said Madame de Cintré, softly.

"Not Valentin. I observed it. I guessed it. I did n't know at the time that I was observing it, but it stuck in my memory. And afterwards, you recollect, I saw Lord Deepmere with you in the conservatory. You said then that you would tell me at another time what he had said to you."

"That was before—before *this*," said Madame de Cintré.

"It does n't matter," said Newman; "and, besides, I think I know. He 's an honest little Englishman. He came and told you what your mother was up to—that she wanted him to supplant me; not being a commercial person. If he would make you an offer she would undertake to bring you over and give me the slip. Lord Deepmere is n't very intellectual, so she had to spell it out to him. He said he admired you 'no end,' and that he wanted you to know it; but he did n't like being mixed up with that sort of underhand work, and he came to you and told tales. That was about the amount of it, was n't it? And then you said you were perfectly happy."

"I don't see why we should talk of Lord Deepmere," said

Madame de Cintré. "It was not for that you came here. And about my mother, it does n't matter what you suspect and what you know. When once my mind has been made up, as it is now, I should not discuss these things. Discussing anything, now, is very idle. We must try and live each as we can. I believe you will be happy again; even, sometimes, when you think of me. When you do so, think this—that it was not easy, and that I did the best I could. I have things to reckon with that you don't know. I mean I have feelings. I must do as they force me—I must, I must. They would haunt me otherwise," she cried, with vehemence; "they would kill me!"

"I know what your feelings are: they are superstitions! They are the feeling that, after all, though I *am* a good fellow, I have been in business; the feeling that your mother's looks are law and your brother's words are gospel; that you all hang together, and that it's a part of the everlasting proprieties that they should have a hand in everything you do. It makes my blood boil. That *is* cold; you are right. And what I feel here," and Newman struck his heart and became more poetical than he knew, "is a glowing fire!"

A spectator less preoccupied than Madame de Cintré's distracted wooer would have felt sure from the first that her appealing calm of manner was the result of violent effort, in spite of which the tide of agitation was rapidly rising. On these last words of Newman's it overflowed, though at first she spoke low, for fear of her voice betraying her. "No, I was not right—I am not cold! I believe that if I am doing what seems so bad, it is not mere weakness and falseness. Mr. Newman, it's like a religion. I can't tell you—I can't! It's cruel of you to insist. I don't see why I should n't ask you to believe me—and pity me. It's like a religion. There's a curse upon the house; I don't know what—I don't know why—don't ask me. We must all bear it. I have been too selfish; I wanted to escape from it. You offered me a great chance—besides my liking you. It seemed good to change completely, to break, to go away. And then I admired you. But I can't—it has overtaken and come back to me." Her self-control had now completely abandoned her, and her words were broken with long sobs. "Why do such dreadful things happen to us—why is my brother Valentin killed, like a beast, in the midst of his youth and his gayety and his brightness and all that we loved him for? Why are there things I can't ask about—that I am afraid to know? Why are there places I can't look at, sounds I can't hear? Why is it given to me to choose, to decide, in a case so hard and so terrible as this? I am not meant for that—I am not made for boldness and defiance. I was made to be happy in a quiet, natural way." At this Newman gave a most expressive groan, but Madame de Cintré went on. "I was made to do gladly and gratefully what is expected of me. My mother has always been very good to me; that's all I can say. I must not judge her; I must not criticise her. If I did, it would come back to me. I can't change!"

"No," said Newman, bitterly; "*I* must change—if I break in two in the effort!"

"You are different. You are a man; you will get over it. You have all kinds of consolation. You were born—you were trained, to changes. Besides—besides, I shall always think of you."

"I don't care for that!" cried Newman. "You are cruel—you are terribly cruel. God forgive you! You may have the best reasons and the finest feelings in the world; that makes no difference. You are a mystery to me; I don't see how such hardness can go with such loveliness."

Madame de Cintré fixed him a moment with her swimming eyes. "You believe I am hard, then?"

Newman answered her look, and then broke out, "You are a perfect, faultless creature! Stay by me!"

"Of course I am hard," she went on. "Whenever we give pain we are hard. And we *must* give pain; that's the world,—the hateful, miserable world! Ah!" and she gave a long, deep sigh, "I can't even say I am glad to have known you—though I am. That too is to wrong you. I can say nothing that is not cruel. Therefore let us part, without more of this. Good-by!" And she put out her hand.

Newman stood and looked at it without taking it, and then raised his eyes to her face. He felt, himself, like shedding tears of rage. "What are you going to do?" he asked. "Where are you going?"

"Where I shall give no more pain and suspect no more evil. I am going out of the world."

"Out of the world?"

"I am going into a convent."

"Into a convent!" Newman repeated the words with the deepest dismay; it was as if she had said she was going into an hospital. "Into a convent—*you!*"

"I told you that it was not for my worldly advantage or pleasure I was leaving you."

But still Newman hardly understood. "You are going to be a nun," he went on, "in a cell—for life—with a gown and white veil?"

"A nun—a Carmelite nun," said Madame de Cintré. "For life, with God's leave."

The idea struck Newman as too dark and horrible for belief, and made him feel as he would have done if she had told him that she was going to mutilate her beautiful face, or drink some potion that would make her mad. He clasped his hands and began to tremble, visibly.

"Madame de Cintré, don't, don't!" he said. "I beseech you! On my knees, if you like, I 'll beseech you."

She laid her hand upon his arm, with a tender, pitying, almost reassuring gesture. "You don't understand," she said. "You have wrong ideas. It 's nothing horrible. It is only peace and safety. It is to be out of the world, where such troubles as this come to the innocent, to the best. And for life— that 's the blessing of it! They can't begin again."

Newman dropped into a chair and sat looking at her with a long, inarticulate murmur. That this superb woman, in whom he had seen all human grace and household force, should turn from him and all the brightness that he offered her—him and his future and his fortune and his fidelity—to muffle herself in ascetic rags and entomb herself in a cell, was a confounding combination of the inexorable and the grotesque. As the image deepened before him the grotesque seemed to expand and overspread it; it was a reduction to the absurd of the trial to which he was subjected. "You—you a nun!" he exclaimed; "you with your beauty defaced—you behind locks and bars! Never, never, if I can prevent it!" And he sprang to his feet with a violent laugh.

"You can't prevent it," said Madame de Cintré; "and it ought—a little—to satisfy you. Do you suppose I will go on living in the world, still beside you, and yet not with you? It is all arranged. Good-by, good-by."

This time he took her hand, took it in both his own. "Forever?" he said. Her lips made an inaudible movement and his own uttered a deep imprecation. She closed her eyes, as if with the pain of hearing it; then he drew her towards him and clasped her to his breast. He kissed her white face; for an instant she resisted and for a moment she submitted; then, with force, she disengaged herself and hurried away over the long shining floor. The next moment the door closed behind her.

Newman made his way out as he could.

Chapter XXI

THERE IS a pretty public walk at Poitiers, laid out upon the crest of the high hill around which the little city clusters, planted with thick trees and looking down upon the fertile fields in which the old English princes fought for their right and held it. Newman paced up and down this quiet promenade for the greater part of the next day and let his eyes wander over the historic prospect; but he would have been sadly at a loss to tell you afterwards whether the latter was made up of coal-fields or of vineyards. He was wholly given up to his grievance, of which reflection by no means diminished the weight. He feared that Madame de Cintré was irretrievably lost; and yet, as he would have said himself, he didn't see his way clear to giving her up. He found it impossible to turn his back upon Fleurières and its inhabitants; it seemed to him that some germ of hope or reparation must lurk there somewhere, if he could only stretch his arm out far enough to pluck it. It was as if he had his hand on a door-knob and were closing his clenched fist upon it: he had thumped, he had called, he had pressed the door with his powerful knee and shaken it with all his strength, and dead, damning silence had answered him. And yet something held him there— something hardened the grasp of his fingers. Newman's satisfaction had been too intense, his whole plan too deliberate and mature, his prospect of happiness too rich and comprehensive, for this fine moral fabric to crumble at a stroke. The very foundation seemed fatally injured, and yet he felt a stubborn desire still to try to save the edifice. He was filled with a sorer sense of wrong than he had ever known, or than he had supposed it possible he should know. To accept his injury and walk away without looking behind him was a stretch of good-nature of which he found himself incapable. He looked behind him intently and continually, and what he saw there did not assuage his resentment. He saw himself trustful, generous, liberal, patient, easy, pocketing frequent irritation and furnishing unlimited modesty. To have eaten humble pie, to have been snubbed and patronized and satirized and have consented to take it as one of the conditions of the bargain—

to have done this, and done it all for nothing, surely gave one a right to protest. And to be turned off because one was a commercial person! As if he had ever talked or dreamt of the commercial since his connection with the Bellegardes began—as if he had made the least circumstance of the commercial—as if he would not have consented to confound the commercial fifty times a day, if it might have increased by a hair's breadth the chance of the Bellegardes' not playing him a trick! Granted that being commercial was fair ground for having a trick played upon one, how little they knew about the class so designated and its enterprising way of not standing upon trifles! It was in the light of his injury that the weight of Newman's past endurance seemed so heavy; his actual irritation had not been so great, merged as it was in his vision of the cloudless blue that over-arched his immediate wooing. But now his sense of outrage was deep, rancorous, and ever present; he felt that he was a good fellow wronged. As for Madame de Cintré's conduct, it struck him with a kind of awe, and the fact that he was powerless to understand it or feel the reality of its motives only deepened the force with which he had attached himself to her. He had never let the fact of her Catholicism trouble him; Catholicism to him was nothing but a name, and to express a mistrust of the form in which her religious feelings had moulded themselves would have seemed to him on his own part a rather pretentious affectation of Protestant zeal. If such superb white flowers as that could bloom in Catholic soil, the soil was not insalubrious. But it was one thing to be a Catholic, and another to turn nun—on your hands! There was something lugubriously comical in the way Newman's thoroughly contemporaneous optimism was confronted with this dusky old-world expedient. To see a woman made for him and for motherhood to his children juggled away in this tragic travesty—it was a thing to rub one's eyes over, a nightmare, an illusion, a hoax. But the hours passed away without disproving the thing, and leaving him only the after-sense of the vehemence with which he had embraced Madame de Cintré. He remembered her words and her looks; he turned them over and tried to shake the mystery out of them and to infuse them with an endurable meaning. What had she meant by her feeling being a kind of religion? It was the religion simply of the family laws, the religion of which her implacable little mother was the high priestess. Twist the thing about as her generosity would, the one certain fact was that they had used force against her. Her generosity had tried to screen them, but Newman's heart rose into his throat at the thought that they should go scot-free.

The twenty-four hours wore themselves away, and the next morning Newman sprang to his feet with the resolution to return to Fleurières and demand another interview with Madame de Bellegarde and her son. He lost no time in putting it into practice. As he rolled swiftly over the excellent road in the little calèche furnished him at the inn at Poitiers, he drew forth, as it were, from the very safe place in his mind to which he had consigned it, the last information given him by poor Valentin. Valentin had told him he could do something with it, and Newman thought it would be well to have it at hand. This was of course not the first time, lately, that Newman had given it his attention. It was information in the rough,—it was dark and puzzling; but Newman was neither helpless nor afraid. Valentin had evidently meant to put him in possession of a powerful instrument, though he could not be said to have placed the handle very securely within his grasp. But if he had not really told him the secret, he had at least given him the clew to it—a clew of which that queer old Mrs. Bread held the other end. Mrs. Bread had always looked to Newman as if she knew secrets; and as he apparently enjoyed her esteem, he suspected she might be induced to share her knowledge with him. So long as there was only Mrs. Bread to deal with, he felt easy. As to what there was to find out, he had only one fear—that it might not be bad enough. Then, when the image of the marquise and her son rose before him again, standing side by side, the old woman's hand in Urbain's arm, and the same cold, unsociable fixedness in the eyes of each, he cried out to himself that the fear was groundless. There was blood in the secret at the very least! He arrived at Fleurières almost in a state of elation; he had satisfied himself, logically, that in the presence of his threat of exposure they would, as he mentally phrased it, rattle down like unwound buckets. He remembered indeed that he must first catch his hare—first ascertain what there was to expose;

but after that, why should n't his happiness be as good as new again? Mother and son would drop their lovely victim in terror and take to hiding, and Madame de Cintré, left to herself, would surely come back to him. Give her a chance and she would rise to the surface, return to the light. How could she fail to perceive that his house would be much the most comfortable sort of convent?

Newman, as he had done before, left his conveyance at the inn and walked the short remaining distance to the château. When he reached the gate, however, a singular feeling took possession of him—a feeling which, strange as it may seem, had its source in its unfathomable good nature. He stood there a while, looking through the bars at the large, time-stained face of the edifice, and wondering to what crime it was that the dark old house, with its flowery name, had given convenient occasion. It had given occasion, first and last, to tyrannies and sufferings enough, Newman said to himself; it was an evil-looking place to live in. Then, suddenly, came the reflection—What a horrible rubbish-heap of iniquity to fumble in! The attitude of inquisitor turned its ignobler face, and with the same movement Newman declared that the Bellegardes should have another chance. He would appeal once more directly to their sense of fairness, and not to their fear; and if they should be accessible to reason, he need know nothing worse about them than what he already knew. That was bad enough.

The gate-keeper let him in through the same stiff crevice as before, and he passed through the court and over the little rustic bridge on the moat. The door was opened before he had reached it, and, as if to put his clemency to rout with the suggestion of a richer opportunity, Mrs. Bread stood there awaiting him. Her face, as usual, looked as hopelessly blank as the tide-smoothed sea-sand, and her black garments seemed of an intenser sable. Newman had already learned that her strange inexpressiveness could be a vehicle for emotion, and he was not surprised at the muffled vivacity with which she whispered, "I thought you would try again, sir. I was looking out for you."

"I am glad to see you," said Newman; "I think you are my friend."

Mrs. Bread looked at him opaquely. "I wish you well, sir; but it 's vain wishing now."

"You know, then, how they have treated me?"

"Oh, sir," said Mrs. Bread, dryly, "I know everything."

Newman hesitated a moment. "Everything?"

Mrs. Bread gave him a glance somewhat more lucent. "I know at least too much, sir."

"One can never know too much. I congratulate you. I have come to see Madame de Bellegarde and her son," Newman added. "Are they at home? If they are not, I will wait."

"My lady is always at home," Mrs. Bread replied, "and the marquis is mostly with her."

"Please then tell them—one or the other, or both—that I am here and that I desire to see them."

Mrs. Bread hesitated. "May I take a great liberty, sir?"

"You have never taken a liberty but you have justified it," said Newman, with diplomatic urbanity.

Mrs. Bread dropped her wrinkled eyelids as if she were curtseying; but the curtsey stopped there; the occasion was too grave. "You have come to plead with them again, sir? Perhaps you don't know this—that Madame de Cintré returned this morning to Paris."

"Ah, she 's gone!" And Newman, groaning, smote the pavement with his stick.

"She has gone straight to the convent—the Carmelites they call it. I see you know, sir. My lady and the marquis take it very ill. It was only last night she told them."

"Ah, she had kept it back, then?" cried Newman. "Good, good! And they are very fierce?"

"They are not pleased," said Mrs. Bread. "But they may well dislike it. They tell me it 's most dreadful, sir; of all the nuns in Christendom the Carmelites are the worst. You may say they are really not human, sir; they make you give up everything—forever. And to think of *her* there! If I was one that cried, sir, I could cry."

Newman looked at her an instant. "We must n't cry, Mrs. Bread; we must act. Go and call them!" And he made a movement to enter farther.

But Mrs. Bread gently checked him. "May I take another liberty? I am told you were with my dearest Mr. Valentin, in his last hours. If you would tell me a word about him! The poor count was my own boy, sir; for the first year of his life he was hardly out of my arms; I taught him to speak. And the count spoke so well, sir! He always spoke well to his poor old Bread. When he grew up and took his pleasure he always had a kind word for me. And to die in that wild way! They have a story that he fought with a wine-merchant. I can't believe that, sir! And was he in great pain?"

"You are a wise, kind old woman, Mrs. Bread," said Newman. "I hoped I might see you with my own children in your arms. Perhaps I shall, yet." And he put out his hand. Mrs. Bread looked for a moment at his open palm, and then, as if fascinated by the novelty of the gesture, extended her own lady-like fingers. Newman held her hand firmly and deliberately, fixing his eyes upon her. "You want to know all about Mr. Valentin?" he said.

"It would be a sad pleasure, sir."

"I can tell you everything. Can you sometimes leave this place?"

"The château, sir? I really don't know. I never tried."

"Try, then; try hard. Try this evening, at dusk. Come to me in the old ruin there on the hill, in the court before the church. I will wait for you there; I have something very important to tell you. An old woman like you can do as she pleases."

Mrs. Bread stared, wondering, with parted lips. "Is it from the count, sir?" she asked.

"From the count—from his death-bed," said Newman.

"I will come, then. I will be bold, for once, for *him*."

She led Newman into the great drawing-room with which he had already made acquaintance, and retired to execute his commands. Newman waited a long time; at last he was on the point of ringing and repeating his request. He was looking round him for a bell when the marquis came in with his mother on his arm. It will be seen that Newman had a logical mind when I say that he declared to himself, in perfect good faith, as a result of Valentin's dark hints, that his adversaries looked grossly wicked. "There is no mistake about it now," he said to himself as they advanced. "They 're a bad lot; they have pulled off the mask." Madame de Bellegarde and her son certainly bore in their faces the signs of extreme perturbation; they looked like people who had passed a sleepless night. Confronted, moreover, with an annoyance which they hoped they had disposed of, it was not natural that they should have any very tender glances to bestow upon Newman. He stood before them, and such eye-beams as they found available they leveled at him; Newman feeling as if the door of a sepulchre had suddenly been opened, and the damp darkness were being exhaled.

"You see I have come back," he said. "I have come to try again."

"It would be ridiculous," said M. de Bellegarde, "to pretend that we are glad to see you or that we don't question the taste of your visit."

"Oh, don't talk about taste," said Newman, with a laugh, "or that will bring us round to yours! If I consulted my taste I certainly should n't come to see you. Besides, I will make as short work as you please. Promise me to raise the blockade— to set Madame de Cintré at liberty—and I will retire instantly."

"We hesitated as to whether we would see you," said Madame de Bellegarde; "and we were on the point of declining the honor. But it seemed to me that we should act with civility, as we have always done, and I wished to have the satisfaction of informing you that there are certain weaknesses that people of our way of feeling can be guilty of but once."

"You may be weak but once, but you will be audacious many times, madam," Newman answered. "I did n't come, however, for conversational purposes. I came to say this, simply: that if you will write immediately to your daughter that you withdraw your opposition to her marriage, I will take care of the rest. You don't want her to turn nun—you know more about the horrors of it than I do. Marrying a commercial person is better than that. Give me a letter to her, signed and sealed, saying you retract and that she may marry me with your blessing, and I will take it to her at the convent and bring her out. There 's your chance—I call those easy terms."

"We look at the matter otherwise, you know. We call them very hard terms," said Urbain de Bellegarde. They had all remained standing rigidly in the middle of the room. "I think my mother will tell you that she would rather her daughter should become Sœur Catherine than Mrs. Newman."

But the old lady, with the serenity of supreme power, let her son make her epigrams for her. She only smiled, almost sweetly, shaking her head and repeating, "But once, Mr. Newman; but once!"

Nothing that Newman had ever seen or heard gave him such a sense of marble hardness as this movement and the tone that accompanied it. "Could anything compel you?" he asked. "Do you know of anything that would force you?"

"This language, sir," said the marquis, "addressed to people in bereavement and grief is beyond all qualification."

"In most cases," Newman answered, "your objection would have some weight, even admitting that Madame de Cintré's present intentions make time precious. But I have thought of what you speak of, and I have come here to-day without scruple simply because I consider your brother and you two very different parties. I see no connection between you. Your brother was ashamed of you. Lying there wounded and dying, the poor fellow apologized to me for your conduct. He apologized to me for that of his mother."

For a moment the effect of these words was as if Newman had struck a physical blow. A quick flush leaped into the faces of Madame de Bellegarde and her son, and they exchanged a glance like a twinkle of steel. Urbain uttered two words which Newman but half heard, but of which the sense came to him as it were in the reverberation of the sound, "Le misérable!"

"You show little respect for the living," said Madame de Bellegarde, "but at least respect the dead. Don't profane— don't insult—the memory of my innocent son."

"I speak the simple truth," Newman declared, "and I speak it for a purpose. I repeat it—distinctly. Your son was utterly disgusted—your son apologized."

Urbain de Bellegarde was frowning portentously, and Newman supposed he was frowning at poor Valentin's invidious image. Taken by surprise, his scant affection for his brother had made a momentary concession to dishonor. But not for an appreciable instant did his mother lower her flag.

"You are immensely mistaken, sir," she said. "My son was sometimes light, but he was never indecent. He died faithful to his name."

"You simply misunderstood him," said the marquis, beginning to rally. "You affirm the impossible!"

"Oh, I don't care for poor Valentin's apology," said Newman. "It was far more painful than pleasant to me. This atrocious thing was not his fault; he never hurt me, or any one else; he was the soul of honor. But it shows how he took it."

"If you wish to prove that my poor brother, in his last moments, was out of his head, we can only say that under the melancholy circumstances nothing was more possible. But confine yourself to that."

"He was quite in his right mind," said Newman, with gentle but dangerous doggedness; "I have never seen him so bright and clever. It was terrible to see that witty, capable fellow dying such a death. You know I was very fond of your brother. And I have further proof of his sanity," Newman concluded.

The marquise gathered herself together majestically. "This is too gross!" she cried. "We decline to accept your story, sir—we repudiate it. Urbain, open the door." She turned away, with an imperious motion to her son, and passed rapidly down the length of the room. The marquis went with her and held the door open. Newman was left standing.

He lifted his finger, as a sign to M. de Bellegarde, who closed the door behind his mother and stood waiting. Newman slowly advanced, more silent, for the moment, than life. The two men stood face to face. Then Newman had a singular sensation; he felt his sense of injury almost brimming over into jocularity. "Come," he said, "you don't treat me well; at least admit that."

M. de Bellegarde looked at him from head to foot, and then, in the most delicate, best-bred voice, "I detest you, personally," he said.

"That's the way I feel to you, but for politeness' sake I don't say it," said Newman. "It's singular I should want so much to be your brother-in-law, but I can't give it up. Let me try once more." And he paused a moment. "You have a secret—you have a skeleton in the closet." M. de Bellegarde continued to look at him hard, but Newman could not see whether his eyes betrayed anything; the look of his eyes was always so strange. Newman paused again, and then went on. "You and your mother have committed a crime." At this M. de Bellegarde's eyes certainly did change; they seemed to flicker, like blown candles. Newman could see that he was profoundly startled; but there was something admirable in his self-control.

"Continue," said M. de Bellegarde.

Newman lifted a finger and made it waver a little in the air. "Need I continue? You are trembling."

"Pray where did you obtain this interesting information?" M. de Bellegarde asked, very softly.

"I shall be strictly accurate," said Newman. "I won't pretend to know more than I do. At present that is all I know. You have done something that you must hide, something that would damn you if it were known, something that would disgrace the name you are so proud of. I don't know what it is, but I can find out. Persist in your present course and I *will* find out. Change it, let your sister go in peace, and I will leave you alone. It 's a bargain?"

The marquis almost succeeded in looking untroubled; the breaking up of the ice in his handsome countenance was an operation that was necessarily gradual. But Newman's mildly-syllabled argumentation seemed to press, and press, and presently he averted his eyes. He stood some moments, reflecting.

"My brother told you this," he said, looking up.

Newman hesitated a moment. "Yes, your brother told me."

The marquis smiled, handsomely. "Did n't I say that he was out of his mind?"

"He was out of his mind if I don't find out. He was very much in it if I do."

M. de Bellegarde gave a shrug. "Eh, sir, find out or not, as you please."

"I don't frighten you?" demanded Newman.

"That 's for you to judge."

"No, it 's for you to judge, at your leisure. Think it over, feel yourself all round. I will give you an hour or two. I can't give you more, for how do we know how fast they may be making Madame de Cintré a nun? Talk it over with your

mother; let her judge whether she is frightened. I don't believe she is as easily frightened, in general, as you; but you
will see. I will go and wait in the village, at the inn, and I beg
you to let me know as soon as possible. Say by three o'clock.
A simple *yes* or *no* on paper will do. Only, you know, in case
of a *yes* I shall expect you, this time, to stick to your bargain."
And with this Newman opened the door and let himself out.
The marquis did not move, and Newman, retiring, gave him
another look. "At the inn, in the village," he repeated. Then
he turned away altogether and passed out of the house.

He was extremely excited by what he had been doing, for
it was inevitable that there should be a certain emotion in
calling up the spectre of dishonor before a family a thousand
years old. But he went back to the inn and contrived to wait
there, deliberately, for the next two hours. He thought it
more than probable that Urbain de Bellegarde would give no
sign; for an answer to his challenge, in either sense, would be
a confession of guilt. What he most expected was silence—in
other words defiance. But he prayed that, as he imaged it, his
shot might bring them down. It did bring, by three o'clock,
a note, delivered by a footman; a note addressed in Urbain
de Bellegarde's handsome English hand. It ran as follows:—

> "I cannot deny myself the satisfaction of letting you
> know that I return to Paris, to-morrow, with my mother,
> in order that we may see my sister and confirm her in the
> resolution which is the most effectual reply to your auda-
> cious pertinacity.
>
> "HENRI-URBAIN DE BELLEGARDE."

Newman put the letter into his pocket, and continued his
walk up and down the inn-parlor. He had spent most of his
time, for the past week, in walking up and down. He continued to measure the length of the little *salle* of the Armes de
France until the day began to wane, when he went out to
keep his rendezvous with Mrs. Bread. The path which led up
the hill to the ruin was easy to find, and Newman in a short
time had followed it to the top. He passed beneath the rugged arch of the castle wall, and looked about him in the early
dusk for an old woman in black. The castle yard was empty,
but the door of the church was open. Newman went into the

little nave and of course found a deeper dusk than without. A couple of tapers, however, twinkled on the altar and just enabled him to perceive a figure seated by one of the pillars. Closer inspection helped him to recognize Mrs. Bread, in spite of the fact that she was dressed with unwonted splendor. She wore a large black silk bonnet, with imposing bows of crape, and an old black satin dress disposed itself in vaguely lustrous folds about her person. She had judged it proper to the occasion to appear in her stateliest apparel. She had been sitting with her eyes fixed upon the ground, but when Newman passed before her she looked up at him, and then she rose.

"Are you a Catholic, Mrs. Bread?" he asked.

"No, sir; I 'm a good Church-of-England woman, very Low," she answered. "But I thought I should be safer in here than outside. I was never out in the evening before, sir."

"We shall be safer," said Newman, "where no one can hear us." And he led the way back into the castle court and then followed a path beside the church, which he was sure must lead into another part of the ruin. He was not deceived. It wandered along the crest of the hill and terminated before a fragment of wall pierced by a rough aperture which had once been a door. Through this aperture Newman passed and found himself in a nook peculiarly favorable to quiet conversation, as probably many an earnest couple, otherwise assorted than our friends, had assured themselves. The hill sloped abruptly away, and on the remnant of its crest were scattered two or three fragments of stone. Beneath, over the plain, lay the gathered twilight, through which, in the near distance, gleamed two or three lights from the château. Mrs. Bread rustled slowly after her guide, and Newman, satisfying himself that one of the fallen stones was steady, proposed to her to sit upon it. She cautiously complied, and he placed himself upon another, near her.

Chapter XXII

"I AM very much obliged to you for coming," Newman said. "I hope it won't get you into trouble."

"I don't think I shall be missed. My lady, in these days, is not fond of having me about her." This was said with a certain fluttered eagerness which increased Newman's sense of having inspired the old woman with confidence.

"From the first, you know," he answered, "you took an interest in my prospects. You were on my side. That gratified me, I assure you. And now that you know what they have done to me, I am sure you are with me all the more."

"They have not done well—I must say it," said Mrs. Bread. "But you must n't blame the poor countess; they pressed her hard."

"I would give a million of dollars to know what they did to her!" cried Newman.

Mrs. Bread sat with a dull, oblique gaze fixed upon the lights of the château. "They worked on her feelings; they knew that was the way. She is a delicate creature. They made her feel wicked. She is only too good."

"Ah, they made her feel wicked," said Newman, slowly; and then he repeated it. "They made her feel wicked,—they made her feel wicked." The words seemed to him for the moment a vivid description of infernal ingenuity.

"It was because she was so good that she gave up—poor sweet lady!" added Mrs. Bread.

"But she was better to them than to me," said Newman.

"She was afraid," said Mrs. Bread, very confidently; "she has always been afraid, or at least for a long time. That was the real trouble, sir. She was like a fair peach, I may say, with just one little speck. She had one little sad spot. You pushed her into the sunshine, sir, and it almost disappeared. Then they pulled her back into the shade and in a moment it began to spread. Before we knew it she was gone. She was a delicate creature."

This singular attestation of Madame de Cintré's delicacy, for all its singularity, set Newman's wound aching afresh. "I see," he presently said; "she knew something bad about her mother."

"No, sir, she knew nothing," said Mrs. Bread, holding her head very stiff and keeping her eyes fixed upon the glimmering windows of the château.

"She guessed something, then, or suspected it."

"She was afraid to know," said Mrs. Bread.

"But *you* know, at any rate," said Newman.

She slowly turned her vague eyes upon Newman, squeezing her hands together in her lap. "You are not quite faithful, sir. I thought it was to tell me about Mr. Valentin you asked me to come here."

"Oh, the more we talk of Mr. Valentin the better," said Newman. "That 's exactly what I want. I was with him, as I told you, in his last hour. He was in a great deal of pain, but he was quite himself. You know what that means; he was bright and lively and clever."

"Oh, he would always be clever, sir," said Mrs. Bread. "And did he know of your trouble?"

"Yes, he guessed it of himself."

"And what did he say to it?"

"He said it was a disgrace to his name—but it was not the first."

"Lord, Lord!" murmured Mrs. Bread.

"He said that his mother and his brother had once put their heads together and invented something even worse."

"You should n't have listened to that, sir."

"Perhaps not. But I *did* listen, and I don't forget it. Now I want to know what it is they did."

Mrs. Bread gave a soft moan. "And you have enticed me up into this strange place to tell you?"

"Don't be alarmed," said Newman. "I won't say a word that shall be disagreeable to you. Tell me as it suits you, and when it suits you. Only remember that it was Mr. Valentin's last wish that you should."

"Did he say that?"

"He said it with his last breath—'Tell Mrs. Bread I told you to ask her.' "

"Why did n't he tell you himself?"

"It was too long a story for a dying man; he had no breath

left in his body. He could only say that he wanted me to know—that, wronged as I was, it was my right to know."

"But how will it help you, sir?" said Mrs. Bread.

"That's for me to decide. Mr. Valentin believed it would, and that's why he told me. Your name was almost the last word he spoke."

Mrs. Bread was evidently awe-struck by this statement; she shook her clasped hands slowly up and down. "Excuse me, sir," she said, "if I take a great liberty. Is it the solemn truth you are speaking? I *must* ask you that; must I not, sir?"

"There's no offense. It *is* the solemn truth; I solemnly swear it. Mr. Valentin himself would certainly have told me more if he had been able."

"Oh, sir, if he knew more!"

"Don't you suppose he did?"

"There's no saying what he knew about anything," said Mrs. Bread, with a mild head-shake. "He was so mightily clever. He could make you believe he knew things that he did n't, and that he did n't know others that he had better not have known."

"I suspect he knew something about his brother that kept the marquis civil to him," Newman propounded; "he made the marquis feel him. What he wanted now was to put me in his place; he wanted to give me a chance to make the marquis feel *me*."

"Mercy on us!" cried the old waiting-woman, "how wicked we all are!"

"I don't know," said Newman; "some of us are wicked, certainly. I am very angry, I am very sore, and I am very bitter, but I don't know that I am wicked. I have been cruelly injured. They have hurt me, and I want to hurt them. I don't deny that; on the contrary, I tell you plainly that that is the use I want to make of your secret."

Mrs. Bread seemed to hold her breath. "You want to publish them—you want to shame them?"

"I want to bring them down,—down, down, down! I want to turn the tables upon them—I want to mortify them as they mortified me. They took me up into a high place and made me stand there for all the world to see me, and then they stole behind me and pushed me into this bottomless pit, where I lie howling and gnashing my teeth! I made a fool of myself before all their friends; but I shall make something worse of them."

This passionate sally, which Newman uttered with the greater fervor that it was the first time he had had a chance to say all this aloud, kindled two small sparks in Mrs. Bread's fixed eyes. "I suppose you have a right to your anger, sir; but think of the dishonor you will draw down on Madame de Cintré."

"Madame de Cintré is buried alive," cried Newman. "What are honor or dishonor to her? The door of the tomb is at this moment closing behind her."

"Yes, it 's most awful," moaned Mrs. Bread.

"She has moved off, like her brother Valentin, to give me room to work. It 's as if it were done on purpose."

"Surely," said Mrs. Bread, apparently impressed by the ingenuity of this reflection. She was silent for some moments; then she added, "And would you bring my lady before the courts?"

"The courts care nothing for my lady," Newman replied. "If she has committed a crime, she will be nothing for the courts but a wicked old woman."

"And will they hang her, sir?"

"That depends upon what she has done." And Newman eyed Mrs. Bread intently.

"It would break up the family most terribly, sir!"

"It 's time such a family should be broken up!" said Newman, with a laugh.

"And me at my age out of place, sir!" sighed Mrs. Bread.

"Oh, I will take care of you! You shall come and live with me. You shall be my housekeeper, or anything you like. I will pension you for life."

"Dear, dear, sir, you think of everything." And she seemed to fall a-brooding.

Newman watched her a while, and then he said suddenly, "Ah, Mrs. Bread, you are too fond of my lady!"

She looked at him as quickly. "I would n't have you say that, sir. I don't think it any part of my duty to be fond of my lady. I have served her faithfully this many a year; but if she were to die to-morrow, I believe, before Heaven, I should n't shed a tear for her." Then, after a pause, "I have no reason to love her!" Mrs. Bread added. "The most she has done for me has been not to turn me out of the house." Newman felt that decidedly his companion was more and more confidential—that if luxury is corrupting, Mrs. Bread's conservative habits were already relaxed by the spiritual comfort of this preconcerted interview, in a remarkable locality, with a free-spoken millionaire. All his native shrewdness admonished him that his part was simply to let her take her time—let the charm of the occasion work. So he said nothing; he only looked at her kindly. Mrs. Bread sat nursing her lean elbows. "My lady once did me a great wrong," she went on at last. "She has a terrible tongue when she is vexed. It was many a year ago, but I have never forgotten it. I have never mentioned it to a human creature; I have kept my grudge to myself. I dare say I have been wicked, but my grudge has grown old with me. It has grown good for nothing, too, I dare say; but it has lived along, as I have lived. It will die when I die,—not before!"

"And what *is* your grudge?" Newman asked.

Mrs. Bread dropped her eyes and hesitated. "If I were a foreigner, sir, I should make less of telling you; it comes harder to a decent Englishwoman. But I sometimes think I have picked up too many foreign ways. What I was telling you belongs to a time when I was much younger and very different looking to what I am now. I had a very high color, sir, if you can believe it; indeed I was a very smart lass. My lady was younger, too, and the late marquis was youngest of all—I mean in the way he went on, sir; he had a very high spirit; he was a magnificent man. He was fond of his pleasure, like most foreigners, and it must be owned that he sometimes went rather below him to take it. My lady was often jealous, and, if you 'll believe it, sir, she did me the honor to be jealous of me. One day I had a red ribbon in my cap, and my lady flew out at me and ordered me to take it off. She accused me of putting it on to make the marquis look at me. I don't know that I was impertinent, but I spoke up like an honest girl and did n't count my words. A red ribbon indeed! As if it was my ribbons the marquis looked at! My lady knew afterwards that I was perfectly respectable, but she never said a word to show that she believed it. But the marquis did!" Mrs. Bread presently added, "I took off my red ribbon and put it away in a drawer, where I have kept it to this day. It 's faded now, it 's a very pale pink; but there it lies. My grudge has faded, too; the red has all gone out of it; but it lies here yet." And Mrs. Bread stroked her black satin bodice.

Newman listened with interest to this decent narrative, which seemed to have opened up the deeps of memory to his companion. Then, as she remained silent, and seemed to be losing herself in retrospective meditation upon her perfect respectability, he ventured upon a short cut to his goal. "So Madame de Bellegarde was jealous; I see. And M. de Bellegarde admired pretty women, without distinction of class. I suppose one must n't be hard upon him, for they probably did n't all behave so properly as you. But years afterwards it could hardly have been jealousy that turned Madame de Bellegarde into a criminal."

Mrs. Bread gave a weary sigh. "We are using dreadful words, sir, but I don't care now. I see you have your idea, and I have no will of my own. My will was the will of my children, as I called them; but I have lost my children now. They are dead—I may say it of both of them; and what should I care for the living? What is any one in the house to me now—what am I to them? My lady objects to me—she has objected to me these thirty years. I should have been glad to be something to young Madame de Bellegarde, though I never was nurse to the present marquis. When he was a baby I was too young; they would n't trust me with him. But his wife told her own maid, Mamselle Clarisse, the opinion she had of me. Perhaps you would like to hear it, sir."

"Oh, immensely," said Newman.

"She said that if I would sit in her children's school-room I should do very well for a penwiper! When things have come to that I don't think I need stand upon ceremony."

"Decidedly not," said Newman. "Go on, Mrs. Bread."

Mrs. Bread, however, relapsed again into troubled dumbness, and all Newman could do was to fold his arms and wait. But at last she appeared to have set her memories in order. "It was when the late marquis was an old man and his eldest son had been two years married. It was when the time came on for marrying Mademoiselle Claire; that 's the way they talk of it here, you know, sir. The marquis's health was bad; he was very much broken down. My lady had picked out M. de Cintré, for no good reason that I could see. But there are reasons, I very well know, that are beyond me, and you must be high in the world to understand them. Old M. de Cintré was very high, and my lady thought him almost as good as herself; that 's saying a good deal. Mr. Urbain took sides with his mother, as he always did. The trouble, I believe, was that my lady would give very little money, and all the other gentlemen asked more. It was only M. de Cintré that was satisfied. The Lord willed it he should have that one soft spot; it was the only one he had. He may have been very grand in his birth, and he certainly was very grand in his bows and speeches; but that was all the grandeur he had. I think he was like what I have heard of comedians; not that I have ever seen one. But I know he painted his face. He might paint it all he would; he could never make me like it! The marquis could n't abide him, and declared that sooner than take such a husband as that Mademoiselle Claire should take none at all. He and my lady had a great scene; it came even to our ears in the servants' hall. It was not their first quarrel, if the truth must be told. They were not a loving couple, but they did n't often come to words, because, I think, neither of them thought the other's doings worth the trouble. My lady had long ago got over her jealousy, and she had taken to indifference. In this, I must say, they were well matched. The marquis was very easygoing; he had a most gentlemanly temper. He got angry only once a year, but then it was very bad. He always took to bed directly afterwards. This time I speak of he took to bed as usual, but he never got up again. I 'm afraid the poor gentleman was paying for his dissipation; is n't it true they mostly do, sir, when they get old? My lady and Mr. Urbain kept quiet, but I know my lady wrote letters to M. de Cintré. The marquis got worse and the doctors gave him up. My lady, she gave him up too, and if the truth must be told, she gave him up gladly. When once he was out of the way she could do what she pleased with her daughter, and it was all arranged that my poor innocent child should be handed over to M. de Cintré. You don't know what Mademoiselle was in those days, sir; she was the sweetest young creature in France, and knew as little of what was going on around her as the lamb does of the butcher. I used to nurse the marquis, and I was always in his room. It was here at Fleurières, in the autumn. We had a doctor from Paris, who came and stayed two or three weeks in the house. Then there came two others, and there was a consultation, and these two others, as I said, declared that the marquis could n't be saved. After this they went off, pocketing their fees, but the other one stayed and did what he could. The marquis himself kept crying out that he would n't die, that he did n't want to die, that he would live and look after his daughter. Mademoiselle Claire and the viscount—that was Mr. Valentin, you know—were both in the house. The doctor was a clever man,—that I could see myself,—and I think he believed that the marquis might get well. We took good care of him, he and I, between us, and one day, when my lady had almost ordered her mourning, my patient suddenly began to mend. He got better and better, till the doctor said he was out of danger. What was killing him was the dreadful fits of pain in his stomach. But little by little they stopped, and the poor marquis began to make his jokes again. The doctor found something that gave him great comfort—some white stuff that we kept in a great bottle on the chimney-piece. I used to give it to the marquis through a glass tube; it always made him easier. Then the doctor went away, after telling me to keep on giving him the mixture whenever he was bad. After that there was a little doctor from Poitiers, who came every day. So we were alone in the house—my lady and her poor husband and their three children. Young Madame de Bellegarde had gone away, with her little girl, to her mother's. You know she is very lively, and her maid told me that she did n't like to be where people were dying." Mrs. Bread paused a moment, and then she went on with the same quiet consistency. "I think you have guessed, sir, that when the marquis began to turn my lady was disappointed." And she paused again, bending upon Newman a face which seemed to grow whiter as the darkness settled down upon them.

Newman had listened eagerly—with an eagerness greater even than that with which he had bent his ear to Valentin de

Bellegarde's last words. Every now and then, as his companion looked up at him, she reminded him of an ancient tabby
cat, protracting the enjoyment of a dish of milk. Even her
triumph was measured and decorous; the faculty of exultation
had been chilled by disuse. She presently continued. "Late
one night I was sitting by the marquis in his room, the great
red room in the west tower. He had been complaining a little,
and I gave him a spoonful of the doctor's dose. My lady had
been there in the early part of the evening; she sat for more
than an hour by his bed. Then she went away and left me
alone. After midnight she came back, and her eldest son was
with her. They went to the bed and looked at the marquis,
and my lady took hold of his hand. Then she turned to me
and said he was not so well; I remember how the marquis,
without saying anything, lay staring at her. I can see his white
face, at this moment, in the great black square between the
bed-curtains. I said I did n't think he was very bad; and she
told me to go to bed—she would sit a while with him. When
the marquis saw me going he gave a sort of groan, and called
out to me not to leave him; but Mr. Urbain opened the door
for me and pointed the way out. The present marquis—perhaps you have noticed, sir—has a very proud way of giving
orders, and I was there to take orders. I went to my room,
but I was n't easy; I could n't tell you why. I did n't undress;
I sat there waiting and listening. For what, would you have
said, sir? I could n't have told you; for surely a poor gentleman might be comfortable with his wife and his son. It was
as if I expected to hear the marquis moaning after me again.
I listened, but I heard nothing. It was a very still night; I
never knew a night so still. At last the very stillness itself
seemed to frighten me, and I came out of my room and went
very softly down-stairs. In the anteroom, outside of the marquis's chamber, I found Mr. Urbain walking up and down.
He asked me what I wanted, and I said I came back to relieve
my lady. He said *he* would relieve my lady, and ordered me
back to bed; but as I stood there, unwilling to turn away, the
door of the room opened and my lady came out. I noticed
she was very pale; she was very strange. She looked a moment
at the count and at me, and then she held out her arms to the
count. He went to her, and she fell upon him and hid her

face. I went quickly past her into the room and to the marquis's bed. He was lying there, very white, with his eyes shut, like a corpse. I took hold of his hand and spoke to him, and he felt to me like a dead man. Then I turned round; my lady and Mr. Urbain were there. 'My poor Bread,' said my lady, 'M. le Marquis is gone.' Mr. Urbain knelt down by the bed and said softly, 'Mon père, mon père.' I thought it wonderful strange, and asked my lady what in the world had happened, and why she had n't called me. She said nothing had happened; that she had only been sitting there with the marquis, very quiet. She had closed her eyes, thinking she might sleep, and she had slept, she did n't know how long. When she woke up he was dead. 'It 's death, my son, it 's death,' she said to the count. Mr. Urbain said they must have the doctor, immediately, from Poitiers, and that he would ride off and fetch him. He kissed his father's face, and then he kissed his mother and went away. My lady and I stood there at the bedside. As I looked at the poor marquis it came into my head that he was not dead, that he was in a kind of swoon. And then my lady repeated, 'My poor Bread, it 's death, it 's death;' and I said, 'Yes, my lady, it 's certainly death.' I said just the opposite to what I believed; it was my notion. Then my lady said we must wait for the doctor, and we sat there and waited. It was a long time; the poor marquis neither stirred nor changed. 'I have seen death before,' said my lady, 'and it 's terribly like this.' 'Yes please, my lady,' said I; and I kept thinking. The night wore away without the count's coming back, and my lady began to be frightened. She was afraid he had had an accident in the dark, or met with some wild people. At last she got so restless that she went below to watch in the court for her son's return. I sat there alone and the marquis never stirred."

Here Mrs. Bread paused again, and the most artistic of romancers could not have been more effective. Newman made a movement as if he were turning over the page of a novel. "So he *was* dead!" he exclaimed.

"Three days afterwards he was in his grave," said Mrs. Bread, sententiously. "In a little while I went away to the front of the house and looked out into the court, and there, before long, I saw Mr. Urbain ride in alone. I waited a bit, to hear him come up-stairs with his mother, but they stayed below, and I went back to the marquis's room. I went to the bed and held up the light to him, but I don't know why I did n't let the candlestick fall. The marquis's eyes were open— open wide! they were staring at me. I knelt down beside him and took his hands, and begged him to tell me, in the name of wonder, whether he was alive or dead. Still he looked at me a long time, and then he made me a sign to put my ear close to him: 'I am dead,' he said, 'I am dead. The marquise has killed me.' I was all in a tremble; I did n't understand him. I did n't know what had become of him. He seemed both a man and a corpse, if you can fancy, sir. 'But you 'll get well now, sir,' I said. And then he whispered again, ever so weak: 'I would n't get well for a kingdom. I would n't be that woman's husband again.' And then he said more; he said she had murdered him. I asked him what she had done to him, but he only replied, 'Murder, murder. And she 'll kill my daughter,' he said; 'my poor unhappy child.' And he begged me to prevent that, and then he said that he was dying, that he was dead. I was afraid to move or to leave him; I was almost dead myself. All of a sudden he asked me to get a pencil and write for him; and then I had to tell him that I could n't manage a pencil. He asked me to hold him up in bed while he wrote himself, and I said he could never, never do such a thing. But he seemed to have a kind of terror that gave him strength. I found a pencil in the room and a piece of paper and a book, and I put the paper on the book and the pencil into his hand, and moved the candle near him. You will think all this very strange, sir; and very strange it was. The strangest part of it was that I believed he was dying, and that I was eager to help him to write. I sat on the bed and put my arm round him, and held him up. I felt very strong; I believe I could have lifted him and carried him. It was a wonder how he wrote, but he did write, in a big scratching hand; he almost covered one side of the paper. It seemed a long time; I suppose it was three or four minutes. He was groaning, terribly, all the while. Then he said it was ended, and I let him down upon his pillows, and he gave me the paper and told me to fold it, and hide it, and to give it to those who would act upon it. 'Whom do you mean?' I said.

'Who are those who will act upon it?' But he only groaned, for an answer; he could n't speak, for weakness. In a few minutes he told me to go and look at the bottle on the chimney-piece. I knew the bottle he meant; the white stuff that was good for his stomach. I went and looked at it, but it was empty. When I came back his eyes were open and he was staring at me; but soon he closed them and he said no more. I hid the paper in my dress; I did n't look at what was written upon it, though I can read very well, sir, if I have n't any handwriting. I sat down near the bed, but it was nearly half an hour before my lady and the count came in. The marquis looked as he did when they left him, and I never said a word about his having been otherwise. Mr. Urbain said that the doctor had been called to a person in childbirth, but that he promised to set out for Fleurières immediately. In another half hour he arrived, and as soon as he had examined the marquis he said that we had had a false alarm. The poor gentleman was very low, but he was still living. I watched my lady and her son when he said this, to see if they looked at each other, and I am obliged to admit that they did n't. The doctor said there was no reason he should die; he had been going on so well. And then he wanted to know how he had suddenly fallen off; he had left him so very hearty. My lady told her little story again—what she had told Mr. Urbain and me—and the doctor looked at her and said nothing. He stayed all the next day at the château, and hardly left the marquis. I was always there. Mademoiselle and Mr. Valentin came and looked at their father, but he never stirred. It was a strange, deathly stupor. My lady was always about; her face was as white as her husband's, and she looked very proud, as I had seen her look when her orders or her wishes had been disobeyed. It was as if the poor marquis had defied her; and the way she took it made me afraid of her. The apothecary from Poitiers kept the marquis along through the day, and we waited for the other doctor from Paris, who, as I told you, had been staying at Fleurières. They had telegraphed for him early in the morning, and in the evening he arrived. He talked a bit outside with the doctor from Poitiers, and then they came in to see the marquis together. I was with him, and so was Mr. Urbain. My lady had been to receive the doctor from

Paris, and she did n't come back with him into the room. He
sat down by the marquis; I can see him there now, with his
hand on the marquis's wrist, and Mr. Urbain watching him
with a little looking-glass in his hand. 'I 'm sure he 's better,'
said the little doctor from Poitiers; 'I 'm sure he 'll come
back.' A few moments after he had said this the marquis
opened his eyes, as if he were waking up, and looked at us,
from one to the other. I saw him look at me, very softly, as
you 'd say. At the same moment my lady came in on tiptoe;
she came up to the bed and put in her head between me and
the count. The marquis saw her and gave a long, most wonderful moan. He said something we could n't understand, and
he seemed to have a kind of spasm. He shook all over and
then closed his eyes, and the doctor jumped up and took hold
of my lady. He held her for a moment a bit roughly. The
marquis was stone dead! This time there were those there that
knew."

Newman felt as if he had been reading by starlight the report of highly important evidence in a great murder case.
"And the paper—the paper!" he said, excitedly. "What was
written upon it?"

"I can't tell you, sir," answered Mrs. Bread. "I could n't
read it; it was in French."

"But could no one else read it?"

"I never asked a human creature."

"No one has ever seen it?"

"If you see it you 'll be the first."

Newman seized the old woman's hand in both his own
and pressed it vigorously. "I thank you ever so much for
that," he cried. "I want to be the first; I want it to be my
property and no one else's! You 're the wisest old woman
in Europe. And what did you do with the paper?" This information had made him feel extraordinarily strong. "Give it
to me quick!"

Mrs. Bread got up with a certain majesty. "It is not so easy
as that, sir. If you want the paper, you must wait."

"But waiting is horrible, you know," urged Newman.

"I am sure *I* have waited; I have waited these many years,"
said Mrs. Bread.

"That is very true. You have waited for me. I won't forget

it. And yet, how comes it you did n't do as M. de Bellegarde said, show the paper to some one?"

"To whom should I show it?" answered Mrs. Bread, mournfully. "It was not easy to know, and many 's the night I have lain awake thinking of it. Six months afterwards, when they married Mademoiselle to her vicious old husband, I was very near bringing it out. I thought it was my duty to do something with it, and yet I was mightily afraid. I did n't know what was written on the paper or how bad it might be, and there was no one I could trust enough to ask. And it seemed to me a cruel kindness to do that sweet young creature, letting her know that her father had written her mother down so shamefully; for that 's what he did, I suppose. I thought she would rather be unhappy with her husband than be unhappy that way. It was for her and for my dear Mr. Valentin I kept quiet. Quiet I call it, but for me it was a weary quietness. It worried me terribly, and it changed me altogether. But for others I held my tongue, and no one, to this hour, knows what passed between the poor marquis and me."

"But evidently there were suspicions," said Newman. "Where did Mr. Valentin get his ideas?"

"It was the little doctor from Poitiers. He was very ill-satisfied, and he made a great talk. He was a sharp Frenchman, and coming to the house, as he did, day after day, I suppose he saw more than he seemed to see. And indeed the way the poor marquis went off as soon as his eyes fell on my lady was a most shocking sight for any one. The medical gentleman from Paris was much more accommodating, and he hushed up the other. But for all he could do Mr. Valentin and Mademoiselle heard something; they knew their father's death was somehow against nature. Of course they could n't accuse their mother, and, as I tell you, I was as dumb as that stone. Mr. Valentin used to look at me sometimes, and his eyes seemed to shine, as if he were thinking of asking me something. I was dreadfully afraid he would speak, and I always looked away and went about my business. If I were to tell him, I was sure he would hate me afterwards, and that I could never have borne. Once I went up to him and took a great liberty; I kissed him, as I had kissed him when he was a child.

'You ought n't to look so sad, sir,' I said; 'believe your poor old Bread. Such a gallant, handsome young man can have nothing to be sad about.' And I think he understood me; he understood that I was begging off, and he made up his mind in his own way. He went about with his unasked question in his mind, as I did with my untold tale; we were both afraid of bringing dishonor on a great house. And it was the same with Mademoiselle. She did n't know what had happened; she would n't know. My lady and Mr. Urbain asked me no questions because they had no reason. I was as still as a mouse. When I was younger my lady thought me a hussy, and now she thought me a fool. How should I have any ideas?"

"But you say the little doctor from Poitiers made a talk," said Newman. "Did no one take it up?"

"I heard nothing of it, sir. They are always talking scandal in these foreign countries—you may have noticed—and I suppose they shook their heads over Madame de Bellegarde. But after all, what could they say? The marquis had been ill, and the marquis had died; he had as good a right to die as any one. The doctor could n't say he had not come honestly by his cramps. The next year the little doctor left the place and bought a practice in Bordeaux, and if there has been any gossip it died out. And I don't think there could have been much gossip about my lady that any one would listen to. My lady is so very respectable."

Newman, at this last affirmation, broke into an immense, resounding laugh. Mrs. Bread had begun to move away from the spot where they were sitting, and he helped her through the aperture in the wall and along the homeward path. "Yes," he said, "my lady's respectability is delicious; it will be a great crash!" They reached the empty space in front of the church, where they stopped a moment, looking at each other with something of an air of closer fellow-ship—like two sociable conspirators. "But what was it," said Newman, "what was it she did to her husband? She did n't stab him or poison him."

"I don't know, sir; no one saw it."

"Unless it was Mr. Urbain. You say he was walking up and

down, outside the room. Perhaps he looked through the key-hole. But no; I think that with his mother he would take it on trust."

"You may be sure I have often thought of it," said Mrs. Bread. "I am sure she did n't touch him with her hands. I saw nothing on him, anywhere. I believe it was in this way. He had a fit of his great pain, and he asked her for his medicine. Instead of giving it to him she went and poured it away, before his eyes. Then he saw what she meant, and, weak and helpless as he was, he was frightened, he was terrified. 'You want to kill me,' he said. 'Yes, M. le Marquis, I want to kill you,' says my lady, and sits down and fixes her eyes upon him. You know my lady's eyes, I think, sir; it was with them she killed him; it was with the terrible strong will she put into them. It was like a frost on flowers."

"Well, you are a very intelligent woman; you have shown great discretion," said Newman. "I shall value your services as housekeeper extremely."

They had begun to descend the hill, and Mrs. Bread said nothing until they reached the foot. Newman strolled lightly beside her; his head was thrown back and he was gazing at all the stars; he seemed to himself to be riding his vengeance along the Milky Way. "So you are serious, sir, about that?" said Mrs. Bread, softly.

"About your living with me? Why of course I take care of you to the end of your days. You can't live with those people any longer. And you ought n't to, you know, after this. You give me the paper, and you move away."

"It seems very flighty in me to be taking a new place at this time of life," observed Mrs. Bread, lugubriously. "But if you are going to turn the house upside down, I would rather be out of it."

"Oh," said Newman, in the cheerful tone of a man who feels rich in alternatives, "I don't think I shall bring in the constables, if that 's what you mean. Whatever Madame de Bellegarde did, I am afraid the law can't take hold of it. But I am glad of that; it leaves it altogether to me!"

"You are a mighty bold gentleman, sir," murmured Mrs. Bread, looking at him round the edge of her great bonnet.

He walked with her back to the château; the curfew had
tolled for the laborious villagers of Fleurières, and the street
was unlighted and empty. She promised him that he should
have the marquis's manuscript in half an hour. Mrs. Bread
choosing not to go in by the great gate, they passed round
by a winding lane to a door in the wall of the park, of which
she had the key, and which would enable her to enter the
château from behind. Newman arranged with her that he
should await outside the wall her return with the coveted
document.

She went in, and his half hour in the dusky lane seemed
very long. But he had plenty to think about. At last the door
in the wall opened and Mrs. Bread stood there, with one
hand on the latch and the other holding out a scrap of white
paper, folded small. In a moment he was master of it, and it
had passed into his waistcoat pocket. "Come and see me in
Paris," he said; "we are to settle your future, you know; and
I will translate poor M. de Bellegarde's French to you." Never
had he felt so grateful as at this moment for M. Nioche's
instructions.

Mrs. Bread's dull eyes had followed the disappearance of
the paper, and she gave a heavy sigh. "Well, you have done
what you would with me, sir, and I suppose you will do it
again. You *must* take care of me now. You are a terribly positive gentleman."

"Just now," said Newman, "I 'm a terribly impatient gentleman!" And he bade her good-night and walked rapidly
back to the inn. He ordered his vehicle to be prepared for his
return to Poitiers, and then he shut the door of the common
salle and strode toward the solitary lamp on the chimney-
piece. He pulled out the paper and quickly unfolded it. It was
covered with pencil-marks, which at first, in the feeble light,
seemed indistinct. But Newman's fierce curiosity forced a
meaning from the tremulous signs. The English of them was
as follows: —

"My wife has tried to kill me, and she has done it; I am
dying, dying horribly. It is to marry my dear daughter to
M. de Cintré. With all my soul I protest, — I forbid it. I am
not insane, — ask the doctors, ask Mrs. B——. It was alone

with me here, to-night; she attacked me and put me to death. It is murder, if murder ever was. Ask the doctors.

"HENRI-URBAIN DE BELLEGARDE."

Chapter XXIII

NEWMAN returned to Paris the second day after his interview with Mrs. Bread. The morrow he had spent at Poitiers, reading over and over again the little document which he had lodged in his pocket-book, and thinking what he would do in the circumstances and how he would do it. He would not have said that Poitiers was an amusing place; yet the day seemed very short. Domiciled once more in the Boulevard Haussmann, he walked over to the Rue de l'Université and inquired of Madame de Bellegarde's portress whether the marquise had come back. The portress told him that she had arrived, with M. le Marquis, on the preceding day, and further informed him that if he desired to enter, Madame de Bellegarde and her son were both at home. As she said these words the little white-faced old woman who peered out of the dusky gate-house of the Hotel de Bellegarde gave a small wicked smile—a smile which seemed to Newman to mean, "Go in if you dare!" She was evidently versed in the current domestic history; she was placed where she could feel the pulse of the house. Newman stood a moment, twisting his mustache and looking at her; then he abruptly turned away. But this was not because he was afraid to go in—though he doubted whether, if he did so, he should be able to make his way, unchallenged, into the presence of Madame de Cintré's relatives. Confidence—excessive confidence, perhaps—quite as much as timidity prompted his retreat. He was nursing his thunder-bolt; he loved it; he was unwilling to part with it. He seemed to be holding it aloft in the rumbling, vaguely-flashing air, directly over the heads of his victims, and he fancied he could see their pale, upturned faces. Few specimens of the human countenance had ever given him such pleasure as these, lighted in the lurid fashion I have hinted at, and he was disposed to sip the cup of contemplative revenge in a leisurely fashion. It must be added, too, that he was at a loss to see exactly how he could arrange to witness the operation of his thunder. To send in his card to Madame de Bellegarde would be a waste of ceremony; she would certainly decline to receive him. On the other hand he could not force his way into her presence. It annoyed him keenly to think that he might be reduced to the blind satisfaction of writing her a letter; but he consoled himself in a measure with the reflection that a letter might lead to an interview. He went home, and feeling rather tired—nursing a vengeance was, it must be confessed, a rather fatiguing process; it took a good deal out of one—flung himself into one of his brocaded fauteuils, stretched his legs, thrust his hands into his pockets, and, while he watched the reflected sunset fading from the ornate house-tops on the opposite side of the Boulevard, began mentally to compose a cool epistle to Madame de Bellegarde. While he was so occupied his servant threw open the door and announced ceremoniously, "Madame Brett!"

Newman roused himself, expectantly, and in a few moments perceived upon his threshold the worthy woman with whom he had conversed to such good purpose on the starlit hill-top of Fleurières. Mrs. Bread had made for this visit the same toilet as for her former expedition. Newman was struck with her distinguished appearance. His lamp was not lit, and as her large, grave face gazed at him through the light dusk from under the shadow of her ample bonnet, he felt the incongruity of such a person presenting herself as a servant. He greeted her with high geniality and bade her come in and sit down and make herself comfortable. There was something which might have touched the springs both of mirth and of melancholy in the ancient maidenliness with which Mrs. Bread endeavored to comply with these directions. She was not playing at being fluttered, which would have been simply ridiculous; she was doing her best to carry herself as a person so humble that, for her, even embarrassment would have been pretentious; but evidently she had never dreamed of its being in her horoscope to pay a visit, at night-fall, to a friendly single gentleman who lived in theatrical-looking rooms on one of the new Boulevards.

"I truly hope I am not forgetting my place, sir," she murmured.

"Forgetting your place?" cried Newman. "Why, you are remembering it. This is your place, you know. You are already in my service; your wages, as housekeeper, began a fortnight ago. I can tell you my house wants keeping! Why don't you take off your bonnet and stay?"

"Take off my bonnet?" said Mrs. Bread, with timid literalness. "Oh, sir, I have n't my cap. And with your leave, sir, I could n't keep house in my best gown."

"Never mind your gown," said Newman, cheerfully. "You shall have a better gown than that."

Mrs. Bread stared solemnly and then stretched her hands over her lustreless satin skirt, as if the perilous side of her situation were defining itself. "Oh, sir, I am fond of my own clothes," she murmured.

"I hope you have left those wicked people, at any rate," said Newman.

"Well, sir, here I am!" said Mrs. Bread. "That 's all I can tell you. Here I sit, poor Catherine Bread. It 's a strange place for me to be. I don't know myself; I never supposed I was so bold. But indeed, sir, I have gone as far as my own strength will bear me."

"Oh, come, Mrs. Bread," said Newman, almost caressingly, "don't make yourself uncomfortable. Now 's the time to feel lively, you know."

She began to speak again with a trembling voice. "I think it would be more respectable if I could—if I could"—and her voice trembled to a pause.

"If you could give up this sort of thing altogether?" said Newman, kindly, trying to anticipate her meaning, which he supposed might be a wish to retire from service.

"If I could give up everything, sir! All I should ask is a decent Protestant burial."

"Burial!" cried Newman, with a burst of laughter. "Why, to bury you now would be a sad piece of extravagance. It 's only rascals who have to be buried to get respectable. Honest folks like you and me can live our time out—and live together. Come! did you bring your baggage?"

"My box is locked and corded; but I have n't yet spoken to my lady."

"Speak to her, then, and have done with it. I should like to have your chance!" cried Newman.

"I would gladly give it you, sir. I have passed some weary hours in my lady's dressing-room; but this will be one of the longest. She will tax me with ingratitude."

"Well," said Newman, "so long as you can tax her with murder"—

"Oh, sir, I can't; not I," sighed Mrs. Bread.

"You don't mean to say anything about it? So much the better. Leave that to me."

"If she calls me a thankless old woman," said Mrs. Bread, "I shall have nothing to say. But it is better so," she softly added. "She shall be my lady to the last. That will be more respectable."

"And then you will come to me and I shall be your gentleman," said Newman; "that will be more respectable still!"

Mrs. Bread rose, with lowered eyes, and stood a moment; then, looking up, she rested her eyes upon Newman's face. The disordered proprieties were somehow settling to rest. She looked at Newman so long and so fixedly, with such a dull, intense devotedness, that he himself might have had a pretext for embarrassment. At last she said gently, "You are not looking well, sir."

"That 's natural enough," said Newman. "I have nothing to feel well about. To be very indifferent and very fierce, very dull and very jovial, very sick and very lively, all at once,— why, it rather mixes one up."

Mrs. Bread gave a noiseless sigh. "I can tell you something that will make you feel duller still, if you want to feel all one way. About Madame de Cintré."

"What can you tell me?" Newman demanded. "Not that you have seen her?"

She shook her head. "No, indeed, sir, nor ever shall. That 's the dullness of it. Nor my lady. Nor M. de Bellegarde."

"You mean that she is kept so close."

"Close, close," said Mrs. Bread, very softly.

These words, for an instant, seemed to check the beating of Newman's heart. He leaned back in his chair, staring up at the old woman. "They have tried to see her, and she would n't—she could n't?"

"She refused—forever! I had it from my lady's own maid," said Mrs. Bread, "who had it from my lady. To speak of it to such a person my lady must have felt the shock. Madame de Cintré won't see them now, and now is her only chance. A while hence she will have no chance."

"You mean the other women—the mothers, the daughters, the sisters; what is it they call them?—won't let her?"

"It is what they call the rule of the house,—or of the order, I believe," said Mrs. Bread. "There is no rule so strict as that of the Carmelites. The bad women in the reformatories are fine ladies to them. They wear old brown cloaks—so the *femme de chambre* told me—that you would n't use for a horse blanket. And the poor countess was so fond of soft-feeling dresses; she would never have anything stiff! They sleep on the ground," Mrs. Bread went on; "they are no better, no better,"—and she hesitated for a comparison,—"they are no better than tinkers' wives. They give up everything, down to the very name their poor old nurses called them by. They give up father and mother, brother and sister,—to say nothing of other persons," Mrs. Bread delicately added. "They wear a shroud under their brown cloaks and a rope round their waists, and they get up on winter nights and go off into cold places to pray to the Virgin Mary. The Virgin Mary is a hard mistress!"

Mrs. Bread, dwelling on these terrible facts, sat dry-eyed and pale, with her hands clasped in her satin lap. Newman gave a melancholy groan and fell forward, leaning his head in his hands. There was a long silence, broken only by the ticking of the great gilded clock on the chimney-piece.

"Where is this place—where is the convent?" Newman asked at last, looking up.

"There are two houses," said Mrs. Bread. "I found out; I thought you would like to know—though it 's poor comfort, I think. One is in the Avenue de Messine; they have learned that Madame de Cintré is there. The other is in the Rue d'Enfer. That 's a terrible name; I suppose you know what it means."

Newman got up and walked away to the end of his long room. When he came back Mrs. Bread had got up, and stood by the fire with folded hands. "Tell me this," he said. "Can I get near her—even if I don't see her? Can I look through a grating, or some such thing, at the place where she is?"

It is said that all women love a lover, and Mrs. Bread's sense of the preëstablished harmony which kept servants in their "place," even as planets in their orbits (not that Mrs. Bread had ever consciously likened herself to a planet), barely availed to temper the maternal melancholy with which she leaned her head on one side and gazed at her new employer. She probably felt for the moment as if, forty years before, she had held him also in her arms. "That would n't help you, sir. It would only make her seem farther away."

"I want to go there, at all events," said Newman. "Avenue de Messine, you say? And what is it they call themselves?"

"Carmelites," said Mrs. Bread.

"I shall remember that."

Mrs. Bread hesitated a moment, and then, "It 's my duty to tell you this, sir," she went on. "The convent has a chapel, and some people are admitted on Sunday to the Mass. You don't see the poor creatures that are shut up there, but I am told you can hear them sing. It 's a wonder they have any heart for singing! Some Sunday I shall make bold to go. It seems to me I should know *her* voice in fifty."

Newman looked at his visitor very gratefully; then he held out his hand and shook hers. "Thank you," he said. "If any one can get in, I will." A moment later Mrs. Bread proposed, deferentially, to retire, but he checked her and put a lighted candle into her hand. "There are half a dozen rooms there I don't use," he said, pointing through an open door. "Go and look at them and take your choice. You can live in the one you like best." From this bewildering opportunity Mrs. Bread at first recoiled; but finally, yielding to Newman's gentle, re-assuring push, she wandered off into the dusk with her tremulous taper. She remained absent a quarter of an hour, during which Newman paced up and down, stopped occasionally to look out of the window at the lights on the Boulevard, and then resumed his walk. Mrs. Bread's relish for her investigations apparently increased as she proceeded; but at last she reappeared and deposited her candlestick on the chimney-piece.

"Well, have you picked one out?" asked Newman.

"A room, sir? They are all too fine for a dingy old body like me. There is n't one that has n't a bit of gilding."

"It 's only tinsel, Mrs. Bread," said Newman. "If you stay there a while it will all peel off of itself." And he gave a dismal smile.

"Oh, sir, there are things enough peeling off already!" re-joined Mrs. Bread, with a head-shake. "Since I was there I thought I would look about me. I don't believe you know, sir. The corners are most dreadful. You do want a house-keeper, that you do; you want a tidy Englishwoman that is n't above taking hold of a broom."

Newman assured her that he suspected, if he had not mea-sured, his domestic abuses, and that to reform them was a mission worthy of her powers. She held her candlestick aloft again and looked round the salon with compassionate glances; then she intimated that she accepted the mission, and that its sacred character would sustain her in her rupture with Madame de Bellegarde. With this she curtsied herself away.

She came back the next day with her worldly goods, and Newman, going into his drawing-room, found her upon her aged knees before a divan, sewing up some detached fringe. He questioned her as to her leave-taking with her late mis-tress, and she said it had proved easier than she feared. "I was perfectly civil, sir, but the Lord helped me to remember that a good woman has no call to tremble before a bad one."

"I should think so!" cried Newman. "And does she know you have come to me?"

"She asked me where I was going, and I mentioned your name," said Mrs. Bread.

"What did she say to that?"

"She looked at me very hard, and she turned very red. Then she bade me leave her. I was all ready to go, and I had got the coachman, who is an Englishman, to bring down my poor box and to fetch me a cab. But when I went down my-self to the gate I found it closed. My lady had sent orders to the porter not to let me pass, and by the same orders the porter's wife—she is a dreadful sly old body—had gone out in a cab to fetch home M. de Bellegarde from his club."

Newman slapped his knee. "She *is* scared! she *is* scared!" he cried, exultantly.

"I was frightened too, sir," said Mrs. Bread, "but I was also mightily vexed. I took it very high with the porter and asked him by what right he used violence to an honorable English-woman who had lived in the house for thirty years before he was heard of. Oh, sir, I was very grand, and I brought the man down. He drew his bolts and let me out, and I promised the cabman something handsome if he would drive fast. But he was terribly slow; it seemed as if we should never reach your blessed door. I am all of a tremble still; it took me five minutes, just now, to thread my needle."

Newman told her, with a gleeful laugh, that if she chose she might have a little maid on purpose to thread her needles; and he went away murmuring to himself again that the old woman *was* scared—she *was* scared!

He had not shown Mrs. Tristram the little paper that he carried in his pocket-book, but since his return to Paris he had seen her several times, and she had told him that he seemed to her to be in a strange way—an even stranger way than his sad situation made natural. Had his disappointment gone to his head? He looked like a man who was going to be ill, and yet she had never seen him more restless and active. One day he would sit hanging his head and looking as if he were firmly resolved never to smile again; another he would indulge in laughter that was almost unseemly and make jokes that were bad even for him. If he was trying to carry off his sorrow, he at such times really went too far. She begged him of all things not to be "strange." Feeling in a measure responsible as she did for the affair which had turned out so ill for him, she could endure anything but his strangeness. He might be melancholy if he would, or he might be stoical; he might be cross and cantankerous with her and ask her why she had ever dared to meddle with his destiny: to this she would submit; for this she would make allowances. Only, for Heaven's sake, let him not be incoherent. That would be extremely unpleasant. It was like people talking in their sleep; they always frightened her. And Mrs. Tristram intimated that, taking very high ground as regards the moral obligation which events had laid upon her, she proposed not to rest quiet until she should have confronted him with the least inadequate substitute for Madame de Cintré that the two hemispheres contained.

"Oh," said Newman, "we are even now, and we had better not open a new account! You may bury me some day, but you shall never marry me. It 's too rough. I hope, at any rate," he added, "that there is nothing incoherent in this— that I want to go next Sunday to the Carmelite chapel in the Avenue de Messine. You know one of the Catholic ministers—an abbé, is that it?—I have seen him here, you know; that motherly old gentleman with the big waist-band. Please ask him if I need a special leave to go in, and if I do, beg him to obtain it for me."

Mrs. Tristram gave expression to the liveliest joy. "I am so glad you have asked me to do something!" she cried. "You shall get into the chapel if the abbé is disfrocked for his share in it." And two days afterwards she told him that it was all arranged; the abbé was enchanted to serve him, and if he would present himself civilly at the convent gate there would be no difficulty.

Chapter XXIV

S UNDAY was as yet two days off; but meanwhile, to beguile his impatience, Newman took his way to the Avenue de Messine and got what comfort he could in staring at the blank outer wall of Madame de Cintré's present residence. The street in question, as some travelers will remember, adjoins the Parc Monceau, which is one of the prettiest corners of Paris. The quarter has an air of modern opulence and convenience which seems at variance with the ascetic institution, and the impression made upon Newman's gloomily-irritated gaze by the fresh-looking, windowless expanse behind which the woman he loved was perhaps even then pledging herself to pass the rest of her days was less exasperating than he had feared. The place suggested a convent with the modern improvements—an asylum in which privacy, though unbroken, might be not quite identical with privation, and meditation, though monotonous, might be of a cheerful cast. And yet he knew the case was otherwise; only at present it was not a reality to him. It was too strange and too mocking to be real; it was like a page torn out of a romance, with no context in his own experience.

On Sunday morning, at the hour which Mrs. Tristram had indicated, he rang at the gate in the blank wall. It instantly opened and admitted him into a clean, cold-looking court, from beyond which a dull, plain edifice looked down upon him. A robust lay sister with a cheerful complexion emerged from a porter's lodge, and, on his stating his errand, pointed to the open door of the chapel, an edifice which occupied the right side of the court and was preceded by a high flight of steps. Newman ascended the steps and immediately entered the open door. Service had not yet begun; the place was dimly lighted, and it was some moments before he could distinguish its features. Then he saw it was divided by a large close iron screen into two unequal portions. The altar was on the hither side of the screen, and between it and the entrance were disposed several benches and chairs. Three or four of these were occupied by vague, motionless figures—figures that he presently perceived to be women, deeply absorbed in

their devotion. The place seemed to Newman very cold; the
smell of the incense itself was cold. Besides this there was a
twinkle of tapers and here and there a glow of colored glass.
Newman seated himself; the praying women kept still, with
their backs turned. He saw they were visitors like himself and
he would have liked to see their faces; for he believed that
they were the mourning mothers and sisters of other women
who had had the same pitiless courage as Madame de Cintré.
But they were better off than he, for they at least shared the
faith to which the others had sacrificed themselves. Three or
four persons came in; two of them were elderly gentlemen.
Every one was very quiet. Newman fastened his eyes upon
the screen behind the altar. That was the convent, the real
convent, the place where she was. But he could see nothing;
no light came through the crevices. He got up and approached the partition very gently, trying to look through.
But behind it there was darkness, with nothing stirring. He
went back to his place, and after that a priest and two altar
boys came in and began to say mass. Newman watched their
genuflections and gyrations with a grim, still enmity; they
seemed aids and abettors of Madame de Cintré's desertion;
they were mouthing and droning out their triumph. The
priest's long, dismal intonings acted upon his nerves and
deepened his wrath; there was something defiant in his unin-
telligible drawl; it seemed meant for Newman himself. Suddenly there arose from the depths of the chapel, from behind
the inexorable grating, a sound which drew his attention from
the altar—the sound of a strange, lugubrious chant, uttered
by women's voices. It began softly, but it presently grew
louder, and as it increased it became more of a wail and a
dirge. It was the chant of the Carmelite nuns, their only human utterance. It was their dirge over their buried affections
and over the vanity of earthly desires. At first Newman was
bewildered—almost stunned—by the strangeness of the
sound; then, as he comprehended its meaning, he listened intently and his heart began to throb. He listened for Madame
de Cintré's voice, and in the very heart of the tuneless harmony he imagined he made it out. (We are obliged to believe
that he was wrong, inasmuch as she had obviously not yet
had time to become a member of the invisible sisterhood.)

The chant kept on, mechanical and monotonous, with dismal repetitions and despairing cadences. It was hideous, it was horrible; as it continued, Newman felt that he needed all his self-control. He was growing more agitated; he felt tears in his eyes. At last, as in its full force the thought came over him that this confused, impersonal wail was all that either he or the world she had deserted should ever hear of the voice he had found so sweet, he felt that he could bear it no longer. He rose abruptly and made his way out. On the threshold he paused, listened again to the dreary strain, and then hastily descended into the court. As he did so he saw that the good sister with the high-colored cheeks and the fan-like frill to her coiffure, who had admitted him, was in conference at the gate with two persons who had just come in. A second glance informed him that these persons were Madame de Bellegarde and her son, and that they were about to avail themselves of that method of approach to Madame de Cintré which Newman had found but a mockery of consolation. As he crossed the court M. de Bellegarde recognized him; the marquis was coming to the steps, leading his mother. The old lady also gave Newman a look, and it resembled that of her son. Both faces expressed a franker perturbation, something more akin to the humbleness of dismay, than Newman had yet seen in them. Evidently he startled the Bellegardes, and they had not their grand behavior immediately in hand. Newman hurried past them, guided only by the desire to get out of the convent walls and into the street. The gate opened itself at his approach; he strode over the threshold and it closed behind him. A carriage, which appeared to have been standing there, was just turning away from the sidewalk. Newman looked at it for a moment, blankly; then he became conscious, through the dusky mist that swam before his eyes, that a lady seated in it was bowing to him. The vehicle had turned away before he recognized her; it was an ancient landau with one half the cover lowered. The lady's bow was very positive and accompanied with a smile; a little girl was seated beside her. He raised his hat, and then the lady bade the coachman stop. The carriage halted again beside the pavement, and she sat there and beckoned to Newman—beckoned with the demonstrative grace of Madame Urbain de Bellegarde. Newman hesi-

tated a moment before he obeyed her summons; during this
moment he had time to curse his stupidity for letting the others escape him. He had been wondering how he could get at
them; fool that he was for not stopping them then and there!
What better place than beneath the very prison walls to which
they had consigned the promise of his joy? He had been too
bewildered to stop them, but now he felt ready to wait for
them at the gate. Madame Urbain, with a certain attractive
petulance, beckoned to him again, and this time he went over
to the carriage. She leaned out and gave him her hand, looking at him kindly, and smiling.

"Ah monsieur," she said, "you don't include me in your
wrath? I had nothing to do with it."

"Oh, I don't suppose *you* could have prevented it!" Newman answered in a tone which was not that of studied gallantry.

"What you say is too true for me to resent the small account it makes of my influence. I forgive you, at any rate,
because you look as if you had seen a ghost."

"I have!" said Newman.

"I am glad, then, I did n't go in with Madame de Bellegarde and my husband. You must have seen them, eh? Was
the meeting affectionate? Did you hear the chanting? They
say it 's like the lamentations of the damned. I would n't go
in: one is certain to hear that soon enough. Poor Claire—in
a white shroud and a big brown cloak! That 's the *toilette* of
the Carmelites, you know. Well, she was always fond of long,
loose things. But I must not speak of her to you; only I must
say that I am very sorry for you, that if I could have helped
you I would, and that I think every one has been very shabby.
I was afraid of it, you know; I felt it in the air for a fortnight
before it came. When I saw you at my mother-in-law's ball,
taking it all so easily, I felt as if you were dancing on your
grave. But what could I do? I wish you all the good I can
think of. You will say that is n't much! Yes; they have been
very shabby; I am not a bit afraid to say it; I assure you every
one thinks so. We are not all like that. I am sorry I am not
going to see you again; you know I think you very good
company. I would prove it by asking you to get into the carriage and drive with me for a quarter of an hour, while I wait

for my mother-in-law. Only if we were seen—considering what has passed, and every one knows you have been turned away—it might be thought I was going a little too far, even for me. But I shall see you sometimes—somewhere, eh? You know"—this was said in English—"we have a plan for a little amusement."

Newman stood there with his hand on the carriage-door, listening to this consolatory murmur with an unlighted eye. He hardly knew what Madame de Bellegarde was saying; he was only conscious that she was chattering ineffectively. But suddenly it occurred to him that, with her pretty professions, there was a way of making her effective; she might help him to get at the old woman and the marquis. "They are coming back soon—your companions?" he said. "You are waiting for them?"

"They will hear the mass out; there is nothing to keep them longer. Claire has refused to see them."

"I want to speak to them," said Newman; "and you can help me, you can do me a favor. Delay your return for five minutes and give me a chance at them. I will wait for them here."

Madame de Bellegarde clasped her hands with a tender grimace. "My poor friend, what do you want to do to them? To beg them to come back to you? It will be wasted words. They will never come back!"

"I want to speak to them, all the same. Pray do what I ask you. Stay away and leave them to me for five minutes; you need n't be afraid; I shall not be violent; I am very quiet."

"Yes, you look very quiet! If they had *le cœur tendre* you would move them. But they have n't! However, I will do better for you than what you propose. The understanding is not that I shall come back for them. I am going into the Parc Monceau with my little girl to give her a walk, and my mother-in-law, who comes so rarely into this quarter, is to profit by the same opportunity to take the air. We are to wait for her in the park, where my husband is to bring her to us. Follow me now; just within the gates I shall get out of my carriage. Sit down on a chair in some quiet corner and I will bring them near you. There 's devotion for you! *Le reste vous regarde.*"

This proposal seemed to Newman extremely felicitous; it revived his drooping spirit, and he reflected that Madame Urbain was not such a goose as she seemed. He promised immediately to overtake her, and the carriage drove away.

The Parc Monceau is a very pretty piece of landscape-gardening, but Newman, passing into it, bestowed little attention upon its elegant vegetation, which was full of the freshness of spring. He found Madame de Bellegarde promptly, seated in one of the quiet corners of which she had spoken, while before her, in the alley, her little girl, attended by the footman and the lap-dog, walked up and down as if she were taking a lesson in deportment. Newman sat down beside the mamma, and she talked a great deal, apparently with the design of convincing him that—if he would only see it—poor dear Claire did not belong to the most fascinating type of woman. She was too tall and thin, too stiff and cold; her mouth was too wide and her nose too narrow. She had no dimples anywhere. And then she was eccentric, eccentric in cold blood; she was an Anglaise, after all. Newman was very impatient; he was counting the minutes until his victims should reappear. He sat silent, leaning upon his cane, looking absently and insensibly at the little marquise. At length Madame de Bellegarde said she would walk toward the gate of the park and meet her companions; but before she went she dropped her eyes, and, after playing a moment with the lace of her sleeve, looked up again at Newman.

"Do you remember," she asked, "the promise you made me three weeks ago?" And then, as Newman, vainly consulting his memory, was obliged to confess that the promise had escaped it, she declared that he had made her, at the time, a very queer answer—an answer at which, viewing it in the light of the sequel, she had fair ground for taking offense. "You promised to take me to Bullier's after your marriage. After your marriage—you made a great point of that. Three days after that your marriage was broken off. Do you know, when I heard the news, the first thing I said to myself? 'Oh heaven, now he won't go with me to Bullier's!' And I really began to wonder if you had not been expecting the rupture."

"Oh, my dear lady," murmured Newman, looking down the path to see if the others were not coming.

"I shall be good-natured," said Madame de Bellegarde. "One must not ask too much of a gentleman who is in love with a cloistered nun. Besides, I can't go to Bullier's while we are in mourning. But I have n't given it up for that. The *partie* is arranged; I have my cavalier. Lord Deepmere, if you please! He has gone back to his dear Dublin; but a few months hence I am to name any evening and he will come over from Ireland, on purpose. That 's what I call gallantry!"

Shortly after this Madame de Bellegarde walked away with her little girl. Newman sat in his place; the time seemed terribly long. He felt how fiercely his quarter of an hour in the convent chapel had raked over the glowing coals of his resentment. Madame de Bellegarde kept him waiting, but she proved as good as her word. At last she reappeared at the end of the path, with her little girl and her footman; beside her slowly walked her husband, with his mother on his arm. They were a long time advancing, during which Newman sat unmoved. Tingling as he was with passion, it was extremely characteristic of him that he was able to moderate his expression of it, as he would have turned down a flaring gas-burner. His native coolness, shrewdness, and deliberateness, his lifelong submissiveness to the sentiment that words were acts and acts were steps in life, and that in this matter of taking steps curveting and prancing were exclusively reserved for quadrupeds and foreigners—all this admonished him that rightful wrath had no connection with being a fool and indulging in spectacular violence. So as he rose, when old Madame de Bellegarde and her son were close to him, he only felt very tall and light. He had been sitting beside some shrubbery, in such a way as not to be noticeable at a distance; but M. de Bellegarde had evidently already perceived him. His mother and he were holding their course, but Newman stepped in front of them, and they were obliged to pause. He lifted his hat slightly, and looked at them for a moment; they were pale with amazement and disgust.

"Excuse me for stopping you," he said in a low tone, "but I must profit by the occasion. I have ten words to say to you. Will you listen to them?"

The marquis glared at him and then turned to his mother.

"Can Mr. Newman possibly have anything to say that is worth our listening to?"

"I assure you I have something," said Newman; "besides, it is my duty to say it. It 's a notification—a warning."

"Your duty?" said old Madame de Bellegarde, her thin lips curving like scorched paper. "That is your affair, not ours."

Madame Urbain meanwhile had seized her little girl by the hand, with a gesture of surprise and impatience which struck Newman, intent as he was upon his own words, with its dramatic effectiveness. "If Mr. Newman is going to make a scene in public," she exclaimed, "I will take my poor child out of the *mêlée*. She is too young to see such naughtiness!" and she instantly resumed her walk.

"You had much better listen to me," Newman went on. "Whether you do or not, things will be disagreeable for you; but at any rate you will be prepared."

"We have already heard something of your threats," said the marquis, "and you know what we think of them."

"You think a good deal more than you admit. A moment," Newman added in reply to an exclamation of the old lady. "I remember perfectly that we are in a public place, and you see I am very quiet. I am not going to tell your secret to the passers-by; I shall keep it, to begin with, for certain picked listeners. Any one who observes us will think that we are having a friendly chat, and that I am complimenting you, madam, on your venerable virtues."

The marquis gave three short sharp raps on the ground with his stick. "I demand of you to step out of our path!" he hissed.

Newman instantly complied, and M. de Bellegarde stepped forward with his mother. Then Newman said, "Half an hour hence Madame de Bellegarde will regret that she did n't learn exactly what I mean."

The marquise had taken a few steps, but at these words she paused, looking at Newman with eyes like two scintillating globules of ice. "You are like a peddler with something to sell," she said, with a little cold laugh which only partially concealed the tremor in her voice.

"Oh, no, not to sell," Newman rejoined; "I give it to you for nothing." And he approached nearer to her, looking her straight in the eyes. "You killed your husband," he said, almost in a whisper. "That is, you tried once and failed, and then, without trying, you succeeded."

Madame de Bellegarde closed her eyes and gave a little cough, which, as a piece of dissimulation, struck Newman as really heroic. "Dear mother," said the marquis, "does this stuff amuse you so much?"

"The rest is more amusing," said Newman. "You had better not lose it."

Madame de Bellegarde opened her eyes; the scintillations had gone out of them; they were fixed and dead. But she smiled superbly with her narrow little lips, and repeated Newman's word. "Amusing? Have I killed some one else?"

"I don't count your daughter," said Newman, "though I might! Your husband knew what you were doing. I have a proof of it whose existence you have never suspected." And he turned to the marquis, who was terribly white—whiter than Newman had ever seen any one out of a picture. "A paper written by the hand, and signed with the name, of Henri-Urbain de Bellegarde. Written after you, madam, had left him for dead, and while you, sir, had gone—not very fast—for the doctor."

The marquis looked at his mother; she turned away, looking vaguely round her. "I must sit down," she said in a low tone, going toward the bench on which Newman had been sitting.

"Could n't you have spoken to me alone?" said the marquis to Newman, with a strange look.

"Well, yes, if I could have been sure of speaking to your mother alone, too," Newman answered. "But I have had to take you as I could get you."

Madame de Bellegarde, with a movement very eloquent of what he would have called her "grit," her steel-cold pluck and her instinctive appeal to her own personal resources, drew her hand out of her son's arm and went and seated herself upon the bench. There she remained, with her hands folded in her lap, looking straight at Newman. The expression of her face was such that he fancied at first that she was smiling; but he went and stood in front of her, and saw that her elegant features were distorted by agitation. He saw, however, equally, that she was resisting her agitation with all the rigor of her inflexible will, and there was nothing like either fear or submission in her stony stare. She had been startled, but she was not terrified. Newman had an exasperating feeling that she would get the better of him still; he would not have believed it possible that he could so utterly fail to be touched by the sight of a woman (criminal or other) in so tight a place. Madame de Bellegarde gave a glance at her son which seemed tantamount to an injunction to be silent and leave her to her own devices. The marquis stood beside her, with his hands behind him, looking at Newman.

"What paper is this you speak of?" asked the old lady, with an imitation of tranquillity which would have been applauded in a veteran actress.

"Exactly what I have told you," said Newman. "A paper written by your husband after you had left him for dead, and during the couple of hours before you returned. You see he had the time; you should n't have stayed away so long. It declares distinctly his wife's murderous intent."

"I should like to see it," Madame de Bellegarde observed.

"I thought you might," said Newman, "and I have taken a copy." And he drew from his waistcoat pocket a small, folded sheet.

"Give it to my son," said Madame de Bellegarde. Newman handed it to the marquis, whose mother, glancing at him, said simply, "Look at it." M. de Bellegarde's eyes had a pale eagerness which it was useless for him to try to dissimulate; he took the paper in his light-gloved fingers and opened it. There was a silence, during which he read it. He had more than time to read it, but still he said nothing; he stood staring at it. "Where is the original?" asked Madame de Bellegarde, in a voice which was really a consummate negation of impatience.

"In a very safe place. Of course I can't show you that," said Newman. "You might want to take hold of it," he added with conscious quaintness. "But that 's a very correct copy—except, of course, the handwriting. I am keeping the original to show some one else."

M. de Bellegarde at last looked up, and his eyes were still very eager. "To whom do you mean to show it?"

"Well, I 'm thinking of beginning with the duchess," said Newman; "that stout lady I saw at your ball. She asked me to come and see her, you know. I thought at the moment I should n't have much to say to her; but my little document will give us something to talk about."

"You had better keep it, my son," said Madame de Bellegarde.

"By all means," said Newman; "keep it and show it to your mother when you get home."

"And after showing it to the duchess?"—asked the marquis, folding the paper and putting it away.

"Well, I 'll take up the dukes," said Newman. "Then the counts and the barons—all the people you had the cruelty to introduce me to in a character of which you meant immediately to deprive me. I have made out a list."

For a moment neither Madame de Bellegarde nor her son said a word; the old lady sat with her eyes upon the ground; M. de Bellegarde's blanched pupils were fixed upon her face. Then, looking at Newman, "Is that all you have to say?" she asked.

"No, I want to say a few words more. I want to say that I hope you quite understand what I 'm about. This is my revenge, you know. You have treated me before the world—convened for the express purpose—as if I were not good enough for you. I mean to show the world that, however bad I may be, you are not quite the people to say it."

Madame de Bellegarde was silent again, and then she broke her silence. Her self-possession continued to be extraordinary. "I need n't ask you who has been your accomplice. Mrs. Bread told me that you had purchased her services."

"Don't accuse Mrs. Bread of venality," said Newman. "She has kept your secret all these years. She has given you a long respite. It was beneath her eyes your husband wrote that paper; he put it into her hands with a solemn injunction that she was to make it public. She was too good-hearted to make use of it."

The old lady appeared for an instant to hesitate, and then, "She was my husband's mistress," she said, softly. This was the only concession to self-defense that she condescended to make.

"I doubt that," said Newman.

Madame de Bellegarde got up from her bench. "It was not to your opinions I undertook to listen, and if you have nothing left but them to tell me I think this remarkable interview may terminate." And turning to the marquis she took his arm again. "My son," she said, "say something!"

M. de Bellegarde looked down at his mother, passing his hand over his forehead, and then, tenderly, caressingly, "What shall I say?" he asked.

"There is only one thing to say," said the marquise. "That it was really not worth while to have interrupted our walk."

But the marquis thought he could improve this. "Your paper 's a forgery," he said to Newman.

Newman shook his head a little, with a tranquil smile. "M. de Bellegarde," he said, "your mother does better. She has done better all along, from the first of my knowing you. You 're a mighty plucky woman, madam," he continued. "It 's a great pity you have made me your enemy. I should have been one of your greatest admirers."

"Mon pauvre ami," said Madame de Bellegarde to her son in French, and as if she had not heard these words, "you must take me immediately to my carriage."

Newman stepped back and let them leave him; he watched them a moment and saw Madame Urbain, with her little girl, come out of a by-path to meet them. The old lady stooped and kissed her grandchild. "Damn it, she *is* plucky!" said Newman, and he walked home with a slight sense of being balked. She was so inexpressively defiant! But on reflection he decided that what he had witnessed was no real sense of security, still less a real innocence. It was only a very superior style of brazen assurance. "Wait till she reads the paper!" he said to himself; and he concluded that he should hear from her soon.

He heard sooner than he expected. The next morning, before midday, when he was about to give orders for his breakfast to be served, M. de Bellegarde's card was brought to him. "She has read the paper and she has passed a bad night," said Newman. He instantly admitted his visitor, who came in with the air of the ambassador of a great power meeting the delegate of a barbarous tribe whom an absurd accident had enabled for the moment to be abominably annoying. The ambassador, at all events, had passed a bad night, and his faultlessly careful toilet only threw into relief the frigid rancor in his eyes and the mottled tones of his refined complexion. He stood before Newman a moment, breathing quickly and softly, and shaking his forefinger curtly as his host pointed to a chair.

"What I have come to say is soon said," he declared, "and can only be said without ceremony."

"I am good for as much or for as little as you desire," said Newman.

The marquis looked round the room a moment, and then, "On what terms will you part with your scrap of paper?"

"On none!" And while Newman, with his head on one side and his hands behind him sounded the marquis's turbid gaze with his own, he added, "Certainly, that is not worth sitting down about."

M. de Bellegarde meditated a moment, as if he had not heard Newman's refusal. "My mother and I, last evening," he said, "talked over your story. You will be surprised to learn that we think your little document is—a"—and he held back his word a moment—"is genuine."

"You forget that with you I am used to surprises!" exclaimed Newman, with a laugh.

"The very smallest amount of respect that we owe to my father's memory," the marquis continued, "makes us desire that he should not be held up to the world as the author of so—so infernal an attack upon the reputation of a wife whose only fault was that she had been submissive to accumulated injury."

"Oh, I see," said Newman. "It 's for your father's sake." And he laughed the laugh in which he indulged when he was most amused—a noiseless laugh, with his lips closed.

But M. de Bellegarde's gravity held good. "There are a few of my father's particular friends for whom the knowledge of so—so unfortunate an—inspiration—would be a real grief. Even say we firmly established by medical evidence the presumption of a mind disordered by fever, *il en resterait quelque chose*. At the best it would look ill in him. Very ill!"

"Don't try medical evidence," said Newman. "Don't touch

the doctors and they won't touch you. I don't mind your knowing that I have not written to them."

Newman fancied that he saw signs in M. de Bellegarde's discolored mask that this information was extremely pertinent. But it may have been merely fancy; for the marquis remained majestically argumentative. "For instance, Madame d'Outreville," he said, "of whom you spoke yesterday. I can imagine nothing that would shock her more."

"Oh, I am quite prepared to shock Madame d'Outreville, you know. That 's on the cards. I expect to shock a great many people."

M. de Bellegarde examined for a moment the stitching on the back of one of his gloves. Then, without looking up, "We don't offer you money," he said. "That we suppose to be useless."

Newman, turning away, took a few turns about the room, and then came back. "What *do* you offer me? By what I can make out, the generosity is all to be on my side."

The marquis dropped his arms at his side and held his head a little higher. "What we offer you is a chance—a chance that a gentleman should appreciate. A chance to abstain from inflicting a terrible blot upon the memory of a man who certainly had his faults, but who, personally, had done you no wrong."

"There are two things to say to that," said Newman. "The first is, as regards appreciating your 'chance,' that you don't consider me a gentleman. That 's your great point, you know. It 's a poor rule that won't work both ways. The second is that—well, in a word, you are talking great nonsense!"

Newman, who in the midst of his bitterness had, as I have said, kept well before his eyes a certain ideal of saying nothing rude, was immediately somewhat regretfully conscious of the sharpness of these words. But he speedily observed that the marquis took them more quietly than might have been expected. M. de Bellegarde, like the stately ambassador that he was, continued the policy of ignoring what was disagreeable in his adversary's replies. He gazed at the gilded arabesques on the opposite wall, and then presently transferred his glance to Newman, as if he too were a large grotesque in a rather vulgar system of chamber-decoration. "I suppose you know that as regards yourself, it won't do at all."

"How do you mean it won't do?"

"Why, of course you damn yourself. But I suppose that 's in your programme. You propose to throw mud at us; you believe, you hope, that some of it may stick. We know, of course, it can't," explained the marquis in a tone of conscious lucidity; "but you take the chance, and are willing at any rate to show that you yourself have dirty hands."

"That 's a good comparison; at least half of it is," said Newman. "I take the chance of something sticking. But as regards my hands, they are clean. I have taken the matter up with my finger-tips."

M. de Bellegarde looked a moment into his hat. "All our friends are quite with us," he said. "They would have done exactly as we have done."

"I shall believe that when I hear them say it. Meanwhile I shall think better of human nature."

The marquis looked into his hat again. "Madame de Cintré was extremely fond of her father. If she knew of the existence of the few written words of which you propose to make this scandalous use, she would demand of you proudly for his sake to give it up to her, and she would destroy it without reading it."

"Very possibly," Newman rejoined. "But she will not know. I was in that convent yesterday and I know what *she* is doing. Lord deliver us! You can guess whether it made me feel forgiving!"

M. de Bellegarde appeared to have nothing more to suggest; but he continued to stand there, rigid and elegant, as a man who believed that his mere personal presence had an argumentative value. Newman watched him, and, without yielding an inch on the main issue, felt an incongruously good-natured impulse to help him to retreat in good order.

"Your visit 's a failure, you see," he said. "You offer too little."

"Propose something yourself," said the marquis.

"Give me back Madame de Cintré in the same state in which you took her from me."

M. de Bellegarde threw back his head and his pale face flushed. "Never!" he said.

"You can't!"

"We would n't if we could! In the sentiment which led us to deprecate her marriage nothing is changed."

" 'Deprecate' is good!" cried Newman. "It was hardly worth while to come here only to tell me that you are not ashamed of yourselves. I could have guessed that!"

The marquis slowly walked toward the door, and Newman, following, opened it for him. "What you propose to do will be very disagreeable," M. de Bellegarde said. "That is very evident. But it will be nothing more."

"As I understand it," Newman answered, "that will be quite enough!"

M. de Bellegarde stood a moment looking on the ground, as if he were ransacking his ingenuity to see what else he could do to save his father's reputation. Then, with a little cold sigh, he seemed to signify that he regretfully surrendered the late marquis to the penalty of his turpitude. He gave a hardly perceptible shrug, took his neat umbrella from the servant in the vestibule, and, with his gentlemanly walk, passed out. Newman stood listening till he heard the door close; then he slowly exclaimed, "Well, I ought to begin to be satisfied now!"

Chapter XXV

NEWMAN called upon the comical duchess and found her at home. An old gentleman with a high nose and a gold-headed cane was just taking leave of her; he made Newman a protracted obeisance as he retired, and our hero supposed that he was one of the mysterious grandees with whom he had shaken hands at Madame de Bellegarde's ball. The duchess, in her arm-chair, from which she did not move, with a great flower-pot on one side of her, a pile of pink-covered novels on the other, and a large piece of tapestry depending from her lap, presented an expansive and imposing front; but her aspect was in the highest degree gracious, and there was nothing in her manner to check the effusion of his confidence. She talked to him about flowers and books, getting launched with marvelous promptitude; about the theatres, about the peculiar institutions of his native country, about the humidity of Paris, about the pretty complexions of the American ladies, about his impressions of France and his opinion of its female inhabitants. All this was a brilliant monologue on the part of the duchess, who, like many of her country-women, was a person of an affirmative rather than an interrogative cast of mind, who made *mots* and put them herself into circulation, and who was apt to offer you a present of a convenient little opinion, neatly enveloped in the gilt paper of a happy Gallicism. Newman had come to her with a grievance, but he found himself in an atmosphere in which apparently no cognizance was taken of grievances; an atmosphere into which the chill of discomfort had never penetrated, and which seemed exclusively made up of mild, sweet, stale intellectual perfumes. The feeling with which he had watched Madame d'Outreville at the treacherous festival of the Bellegardes came back to him; she struck him as a wonderful old lady in a comedy, particularly well up in her part. He observed before long that she asked him no questions about their common friends; she made no allusion to the circumstances under which he had been presented to her. She neither feigned ignorance of a change in these circumstances nor pretended to condole with him upon it; but she smiled and discoursed and compared the tender-tinted wools of her tapestry, as if the Bellegardes and their wickedness were not of this world. "She is fighting shy!" said Newman to himself; and, having made the observation, he was prompted to observe, farther, how the duchess would carry off her indifference. She did so in a masterly manner. There was not a gleam of disguised consciousness in those small, clear, demonstrative eyes which constituted her nearest claim to personal loveliness; there was not a symptom of apprehension that Newman would trench upon the ground she proposed to avoid. "Upon my word, she does it very well," he tacitly commented. "They all hold together bravely, and, whether any one else can trust them or not, they can certainly trust each other."

Newman, at this juncture, fell to admiring the duchess for her fine manners. He felt, most accurately, that she was not a grain less urbane than she would have been if his marriage were still in prospect; but he felt also that she was not a particle more urbane. He had come, so reasoned the duchess— Heaven knew why he had come, after what had happened; and for the half hour, therefore, she would be *charmante*. But she would never see him again. Finding no ready-made opportunity to tell his story, Newman pondered these things more dispassionately than might have been expected; he stretched his legs, as usual, and even chuckled a little, appreciatively and noiselessly. And then as the duchess went on relating a *mot* with which her mother had snubbed the great Napoleon, it occurred to Newman that her evasion of a chapter of French history more interesting to himself might possibly be the result of an extreme consideration for his feelings. Perhaps it was delicacy on the duchess's part—not policy. He was on the point of saying something himself, to make the chance which he had determined to give her still better, when the servant announced another visitor. The duchess, on hearing the name—it was that of an Italian prince—gave a little imperceptible pout, and said to Newman, rapidly: "I beg you to remain; I desire this visit to be short." Newman said to himself, at this, that Madame d'Outreville intended, after all, that they should discuss the Bellegardes together.

The prince was a short, stout man, with a head disproportionately large. He had a dusky complexion and a bushy eyebrow, beneath which his eye wore a fixed and somewhat defiant expression; he seemed to be challenging you to insinuate that he was top-heavy. The duchess, judging from her charge to Newman, regarded him as a bore; but this was not apparent from the unchecked flow of her conversation. She made a fresh series of *mots*, characterized with great felicity the Italian intellect and the taste of the figs at Sorrento, predicted the ultimate future of the Italian kingdom (disgust with the brutal Sardinian rule and complete reversion, throughout the peninsula, to the sacred sway of the Holy Father), and, finally, gave a history of the love affairs of the Princess X——. This narrative provoked some rectifications on the part of the prince, who, as he said, pretended to know something about that matter; and having satisfied himself that Newman was in no laughing mood, either with regard to the size of his head or anything else, he entered into the controversy with an animation for which the duchess, when she set him down as a bore, could not have been prepared. The sentimental vicissitudes of the Princess X—— led to a discussion of the heart history of Florentine nobility in general; the duchess had spent five weeks in Florence and had gathered much information on the subject. This was merged, in turn, in an examination of the Italian heart *per se*. The duchess took a brilliantly heterodox view—thought it the least susceptible organ of its kind that she had ever encountered, related examples of its want of susceptibility, and at last declared that for her the Italians were a people of ice. The prince became flame to refute her, and his visit really proved charming. Newman was naturally out of the conversation; he sat with his head a little on one side, watching the interlocutors. The duchess, as she talked, frequently looked at him with a smile, as if to intimate, in the charming manner of her nation, that it lay only with him to say something very much to the point. But he said nothing at all, and at last his thoughts began to wander. A singular feeling came over him—a sudden sense of the folly of his errand. What under the sun had he to say to the duchess, after all? Wherein would it profit him to tell her that the Bellegardes were traitors and that the old lady, into the bargain, was a murderess? He seemed morally to have turned a sort of somersault, and to find things looking differently in consequence. He felt a sudden stiffening of his will and quickening of his reserve. What in the world had he been thinking of when he fancied the duchess could help him, and that it would conduce to his comfort to make her think ill of the Bellegardes? What did her opinion of the Bellegardes matter to him? It was only a shade more important than the opinion the Bellegardes entertained of her. The duchess help him—that cold, stout, soft, artificial woman help him?—she who in the last twenty minutes had built up between them a wall of polite conversation in which she evidently flattered herself that he would never find a gate. Had it come to that— that he was asking favors of conceited people, and appealing for sympathy where he had no sympathy to give? He rested his arms on his knees, and sat for some minutes staring into his hat. As he did so his ears tingled—he had come very near being an ass. Whether or no the duchess would hear his story, he would n't tell it. Was he to sit there another half hour for the sake of exposing the Bellegardes? The Bellegardes be hanged! He got up abruptly, and advanced to shake hands with his hostess.

"You can't stay longer?" she asked, very graciously.

"I am afraid not," he said.

She hesitated a moment, and then, "I had an idea you had something particular to say to me," she declared.

Newman looked at her; he felt a little dizzy; for the moment he seemed to be turning his somersault again. The little Italian prince came to his help: "Ah, madam, who has not that?" he softly sighed.

"Don't teach Mr. Newman to say *fadaises*," said the duchess. "It is his merit that he does n't know how."

"Yes, I don't know how to say fadaises," said Newman, "and I don't want to say anything unpleasant."

"I am sure you are very considerate," said the duchess with a smile; and she gave him a little nod for good-by, with which he took his departure.

Once in the street, he stood for some time on the pavement, wondering whether, after all, he was not an ass not to have discharged his pistol. And then again he decided that to talk to any one whomsoever about the Bellegardes would be extremely disagreeable to him. The least disagreeable thing, under the circumstances, was to banish them from his mind, and never think of them again. Indecision had not hitherto been one of Newman's weaknesses, and in this case it was not of long duration. For three days after this he did not, or at least he tried not to, think of the Bellegardes. He dined with Mrs. Tristram, and on her mentioning their name, he begged her almost severely to desist. This gave Tom Tristram a much-coveted opportunity to offer his condolences.

He leaned forward, laying his hand on Newman's arm, compressing his lips and shaking his head. "The fact is, my dear fellow, you see, that you ought never to have gone into it. It was not your doing, I know—it was all my wife. If you want to come down on her, I'll stand off; I give you leave to hit her as hard as you like. You know she has never had a word of reproach from me in her life, and I think she is in need of something of the kind. Why did n't you listen to *me*? You know I did n't believe in the thing. I thought it at the best an amiable delusion. I don't profess to be a Don Juan or a gay Lothario,—that class of man, you know; but I do pretend to know something about the harder sex. I have never disliked a woman in my life that she has not turned out badly. I was not at all deceived in Lizzie, for instance; I always had my doubts about her. Whatever you may think of my present situation, I must at least admit that I got into it with my eyes open. Now suppose you had got into something like this box with Madame de Cintré. You may depend upon it she would have turned out a stiff one. And upon my word I don't see where you could have found your comfort. Not from the marquis, my dear Newman; he was n't a man you could go and talk things over with in a sociable, common-sense way. Did he ever seem to want to have you on the premises—did he ever try to see you alone? Did he ever ask you to come and smoke a cigar with him of an evening, or step in, when you had been calling on the ladies, and take something? I don't think you would have got much encouragement out of *him*. And as for the old lady, she struck one as an uncommonly strong dose. They have a great expression here, you know; they call it 'sympathetic.' Everything is sympathetic—or ought to be. Now Madame de Bellegarde is about as sympathetic as that mustard-pot. They 're a d—d

cold-blooded lot, any way; I felt it awfully at that ball of
theirs. I felt as if I were walking up and down in the Armory,
in the Tower of London! My dear boy, don't think me a
vulgar brute for hinting at it, but you may depend upon it,
all they wanted was your money. I know something about
that; I can tell when people want one's money! Why they
stopped wanting yours I don't know; I suppose because they
could get some one else's without working so hard for it. It
is n't worth finding out. It may be that it was not Madame
de Cintré that backed out first; very likely the old woman put
her up to it. I suspect she and her mother are really as thick
as thieves, eh? You are well out of it, my boy; make up your
mind to that. If I express myself strongly it is all because I
love you so much; and from that point of view I may say I
should as soon have thought of making up to that piece of
pale high-mightiness as I should have thought of making up
to the Obelisk in the Place de la Concorde."

Newman sat gazing at Tristram during this harangue with
a lack-lustre eye; never yet had he seemed to himself to have
outgrown so completely the phase of equal comradeship with
Tom Tristram. Mrs. Tristram's glance at her husband had
more of a spark; she turned to Newman with a slightly lurid
smile. "You must at least do justice," she said, "to the felicity
with which Mr. Tristram repairs the indiscretions of a too
zealous wife."

But even without the aid of Tom Tristram's conversational
felicities, Newman would have begun to think of the Bellegardes again. He could cease to think of them only when he
ceased to think of his loss and privation, and the days had as
yet but scantily lightened the weight of this incommodity. In
vain Mrs. Tristram begged him to cheer up; she assured him
that the sight of his countenance made her miserable.

"How can I help it?" he demanded with a trembling voice.
"I feel like a widower—and a widower who has not even the
consolation of going to stand beside the grave of his wife—
who has not the right to wear so much mourning as a weed
on his hat. I feel," he added in a moment, "as if my wife had
been murdered and her assassins were still at large."

Mrs. Tristram made no immediate rejoinder, but at last she
said, with a smile which, in so far as it was a forced one, was

less successfully simulated than such smiles, on her lips, usually were: "Are you very sure that you would have been happy?"

Newman stared a moment, and then shook his head. "That 's weak," he said; "that won't do."

"Well," said Mrs. Tristram with a more triumphant bravery, "I don't believe you would have been happy."

Newman gave a little laugh. "Say I should have been miserable, then; it 's a misery I should have preferred to any happiness."

Mrs. Tristram began to muse. "I should have been curious to see; it would have been very strange."

"Was it from curiosity that you urged me to try and marry her?"

"A little," said Mrs. Tristram, growing still more audacious. Newman gave her the one angry look he had been destined ever to give her, turned away and took up his hat. She watched him a moment, and then she said, "That sounds very cruel, but it is less so than it sounds. Curiosity has a share in almost everything I do. I wanted very much to see, first, whether such a marriage could actually take place; second, what would happen if it should take place."

"So you did n't believe," said Newman, resentfully.

"Yes, I believed—I believed that it would take place, and that you would be happy. Otherwise I should have been, among my speculations, a very heartless creature. *But*," she continued, laying her hand upon Newman's arm and hazarding a grave smile, "it was the highest flight ever taken by a tolerably bold imagination!"

Shortly after this she recommended him to leave Paris and travel for three months. Change of scene would do him good, and he would forget his misfortune sooner in absence from the objects which had witnessed it. "I really feel," Newman rejoined, "as if to leave *you*, at least, would do me good— and cost me very little effort. You are growing cynical; you shock me and pain me."

"Very good," said Mrs. Tristram, good-naturedly or cynically, as may be thought most probable. "I shall certainly see you again."

Newman was very willing to get away from Paris; the brilliant streets he had walked through in his happier hours, and which then seemed to wear a higher brilliancy in honor of his happiness, appeared now to be in the secret of his defeat and to look down upon it in shining mockery. He would go somewhere; he cared little where; and he made his preparations. Then, one morning, at hap-hazard, he drove to the train that would transport him to Boulogne and dispatch him thence to the shores of Britain. As he rolled along in the train he asked himself what had become of his revenge, and he was able to say that it was provisionally pigeon-holed in a very safe place; it would keep till called for.

He arrived in London in the midst of what is called "the season," and it seemed to him at first that he might here put himself in the way of being diverted from his heavy-heartedness. He knew no one in all England, but the spectacle of the mighty metropolis roused him somewhat from his apathy. Anything that was enormous usually found favor with Newman, and the multitudinous energies and industries of England stirred within him a dull vivacity of contemplation. It is on record that the weather, at that moment, was of the finest English quality; he took long walks and explored London in every direction; he sat by the hour in Kensington Gardens and beside the adjoining Drive, watching the people and the horses and the carriages; the rosy English beauties, the wonderful English dandies, and the splendid flunkies. He went to the opera and found it better than in Paris; he went to the theatre and found a surprising charm in listening to dialogue the finest points of which came within the range of his comprehension. He made several excursions into the country, recommended by the waiter at his hotel, with whom, on this and similar points, he had established confidential relations. He watched the deer in Windsor Forest and admired the Thames from Richmond Hill; he ate white-bait and brown-bread and butter at Greenwich, and strolled in the grassy shadow of the cathedral of Canterbury. He also visited the Tower of London and Madame Tussaud's exhibition. One day he thought he would go to Sheffield, and then, thinking again, he gave it up. Why should he go to Sheffield? He had a feeling that the link which bound him to a possible interest in the manufacture of cutlery was broken. He had no

desire for an "inside view" of any successful enterprise whatever, and he would not have given the smallest sum for the
privilege of talking over the details of the most "splendid"
business with the shrewdest of overseers.

One afternoon he had walked into Hyde Park, and was
slowly threading his way through the human maze which
edges the Drive. The stream of carriages was no less dense,
and Newman, as usual, marveled at the strange, dingy figures
which he saw taking the air in some of the stateliest vehicles.
They reminded him of what he had read of eastern and southern countries, in which grotesque idols and fetiches were
sometimes taken out of their temples and carried abroad in
golden chariots to be displayed to the multitude. He saw a
great many pretty cheeks beneath high-plumed hats as he
squeezed his way through serried waves of crumpled muslin;
and sitting on little chairs at the base of the great serious
English trees, he observed a number of quiet-eyed maidens
who seemed only to remind him afresh that the magic of
beauty had gone out of the world with Madame de Cintré:
to say nothing of other damsels, whose eyes were not quiet,
and who struck him still more as a satire on possible consolation. He had been walking for some time, when, directly in
front of him, borne back by the summer breeze, he heard a
few words uttered in that bright Parisian idiom from which
his ears had begun to alienate themselves. The voice in which
the words were spoken made them seem even more like a
thing with which he had once been familiar, and as he bent
his eyes it lent an identity to the commonplace elegance of
the back hair and shoulders of a young lady walking in the
same direction as himself. Mademoiselle Nioche, apparently,
had come to seek a more rapid advancement in London, and
another glance led Newman to suppose that she had found it.
A gentleman was strolling beside her, lending a most attentive
ear to her conversation and too entranced to open his lips.
Newman did not hear his voice, but perceived that he presented the dorsal expression of a well-dressed Englishman.
Mademoiselle Nioche was attracting attention: the ladies who
passed her turned round to survey the Parisian perfection of
her toilet. A great cataract of flounces rolled down from the
young lady's waist to Newman's feet; he had to step aside to

avoid treading upon them. He stepped aside, indeed, with a decision of movement which the occasion scarcely demanded; for even this imperfect glimpse of Miss Noémie had excited his displeasure. She seemed an odious blot upon the face of nature; he wanted to put her out of his sight. He thought of Valentin de Bellegarde, still green in the earth of his burial—his young life clipped by this flourishing impudence. The perfume of the young lady's finery sickened him; he turned his head and tried to deflect his course; but the pressure of the crowd kept him near her a few minutes longer, so that he heard what she was saying.

"Ah, I am sure he will miss me," she murmured. "It was very cruel in me to leave him; I am afraid you will think me a very heartless creature. He might perfectly well have come with us. I don't think he is very well," she added; "it seemed to me to-day that he was not very gay."

Newman wondered whom she was talking about, but just then an opening among his neighbors enabled him to turn away, and he said to himself that she was probably paying a tribute to British propriety and playing at tender solicitude about her papa. Was that miserable old man still treading the path of vice in her train? Was he still giving her the benefit of his experience of affairs, and had he crossed the sea to serve as her interpreter? Newman walked some distance farther, and then began to retrace his steps, taking care not to traverse again the orbit of Mademoiselle Nioche. At last he looked for a chair under the trees, but he had some difficulty in finding an empty one. He was about to give up the search when he saw a gentleman rise from the seat he had been occupying, leaving Newman to take it without looking at his neighbors. He sat there for some time without heeding them; his attention was lost in the irritation and bitterness produced by his recent glimpse of Miss Noémie's iniquitous vitality. But at the end of a quarter of an hour, dropping his eyes, he perceived a small pug-dog squatted upon the path near his feet—a diminutive but very perfect specimen of its interesting species. The pug was sniffing at the fashionable world, as it passed him, with his little black muzzle, and was kept from extending his investigation by a large blue ribbon attached to his collar with an enormous rosette and held in the hand of a person seated next to Newman. To this person Newman transferred his attention, and immediately perceived that he was the object of all that of his neighbor, who was staring up at him from a pair of little fixed white eyes. These eyes Newman instantly recognized; he had been sitting for the last quarter of an hour beside M. Nioche. He had vaguely felt that some one was staring at him. M. Nioche continued to stare; he appeared afraid to move, even to the extent of evading Newman's glance.

"Dear me," said Newman; "are you here, too?" And he looked at his neighbor's helplessness more grimly than he knew. M. Nioche had a new hat and a pair of kid gloves; his clothes, too, seemed to belong to a more recent antiquity than of yore. Over his arm was suspended a lady's mantilla— a light and brilliant tissue, fringed with white lace—which had apparently been committed to his keeping; and the little dog's blue ribbon was wound tightly round his hand. There was no expression of recognition in his face—or of anything indeed save a sort of feeble, fascinated dread; Newman looked at the pug and the lace mantilla, and then he met the old man's eyes again. "You know me, I see," he pursued. "You might have spoken to me before." M. Nioche still said nothing, but it seemed to Newman that his eyes began faintly to water. "I did n't expect," our hero went on, "to meet you so far from—from the Café de la Patrie." The old man remained silent, but decidedly Newman had touched the source of tears. His neighbor sat staring and Newman added, "What 's the matter, M. Nioche? You used to talk—to talk very prettily. Don't you remember you even gave lessons in conversation?"

At this M. Nioche decided to change his attitude. He stooped and picked up the pug, lifted it to his face and wiped his eyes on its little soft back. "I am afraid to speak to you," he presently said, looking over the puppy's shoulder. "I hoped you would n't notice me. I should have moved away, but I was afraid that if I moved you would notice me. So I sat very still."

"I suspect you have a bad conscience, sir," said Newman.

The old man put down the little dog and held it carefully in his lap. Then he shook his head, with his eyes still fixed upon his interlocutor. "No, Mr. Newman, I have a good conscience," he murmured.

"Then why should you want to slink away from me?"

"Because—because you don't understand my position."

"Oh, I think you once explained it to me," said Newman. "But it seems improved."

"Improved!" exclaimed M. Nioche, under his breath. "Do you call this improvement?" And he glanced at the treasures in his arms.

"Why, you are on your travels," Newman rejoined. "A visit to London in the season is certainly a sign of prosperity."

M. Nioche, in answer to this cruel piece of irony, lifted the puppy up to his face again, peering at Newman with his small blank eye-holes. There was something almost imbecile in the movement, and Newman hardly knew whether he was taking refuge in a convenient affectation of unreason, or whether he had in fact paid for his dishonor by the loss of his wits. In the latter case, just now, he felt little more tenderly to the foolish old man than in the former. Responsible or not, he was equally an accomplice of his detestably mischievous daughter. Newman was going to leave him abruptly, when a ray of entreaty appeared to disengage itself from the old man's misty gaze. "Are you going away?" he asked.

"Do you want me to stay?" said Newman.

"I should have left you—from consideration. But my dignity suffers at your leaving me—that way."

"Have you got anything particular to say to me?"

M. Nioche looked round him to see that no one was listening, and then he said, very softly but distinctly, "I have *not* forgiven her!"

Newman gave a short laugh, but the old man seemed for the moment not to perceive it; he was gazing away, absently, at some metaphysical image of his implacability. "It does n't much matter whether you forgive her or not," said Newman. "There are other people who won't, I assure you."

"What has she done?" M. Nioche softly questioned, turning round again. "I don't know what she does, you know."

"She has done a devilish mischief; it does n't matter what," said Newman. "She 's a nuisance; she ought to be stopped."

M. Nioche stealthily put out his hand and laid it very

gently upon Newman's arm. "Stopped, yes," he whispered. "That's it. Stopped short. She is running away—she must be stopped." Then he paused a moment and looked round him. "I mean to stop her," he went on. "I am only waiting for my chance."

"I see," said Newman, laughing briefly again. "She is running away and you are running after her. You have run a long distance!"

But M. Nioche stared insistently: "I shall stop her!" he softly repeated.

He had hardly spoken when the crowd in front of them separated, as if by the impulse to make way for an important personage. Presently, through the opening, advanced Mademoiselle Nioche, attended by the gentleman whom Newman had lately observed. His face being now presented to our hero, the latter recognized the irregular features, the hardly more regular complexion, and the amiable expression of Lord Deepmere. Noémie, on finding herself suddenly confronted with Newman, who, like M. Nioche, had risen from his seat, faltered for a barely perceptible instant. She gave him a little nod, as if she had seen him yesterday, and then, with a good-natured smile, "*Tiens*, how we keep meeting!" she said. She looked consummately pretty, and the front of her dress was a wonderful work of art. She went up to her father, stretching out her hands for the little dog, which he submissively placed in them, and she began to kiss it and murmur over it: "To think of leaving him all alone,—what a wicked, abominable creature he must believe me! He has been very unwell," she added, turning and affecting to explain to Newman, with a spark of infernal impudence, fine as a needle-point, in her eye. "I don't think the English climate agrees with him."

"It seems to agree wonderfully well with his mistress," said Newman.

"Do you mean me? I have never been better, thank you," Miss Noémie declared. "But with *milord*"—and she gave a brilliant glance at her late companion—"how can one help being well?" She seated herself in the chair from which her father had risen, and began to arrange the little dog's rosette.

Lord Deepmere carried off such embarrassment as might be incidental to this unexpected encounter with the inferior grace of a male and a Briton. He blushed a good deal, and greeted the object of his late momentary aspiration to rivalry in the favor of a person other than the mistress of the invalid pug with an awkward nod and a rapid ejaculation—an ejaculation to which Newman, who often found it hard to understand the speech of English people, was able to attach no meaning. Then the young man stood there, with his hand on his hip, and with a conscious grin, staring askance at Miss Noémie. Suddenly an idea seemed to strike him, and he said, turning to Newman, "Oh, you know her?"

"Yes," said Newman, "I know her. I don't believe you do."

"Oh dear, yes, I do!" said Lord Deepmere, with another grin. "I knew her in Paris—by my poor cousin Bellegarde, you know. He knew her, poor fellow, did n't he? It was she, you know, who was at the bottom of his affair. Awfully sad, was n't it?" continued the young man, talking off his embarrassment as his simple nature permitted. "They got up some story about its being for the Pope; about the other man having said something against the Pope's morals. They always do that, you know. They put it on the Pope because Bellegarde was once in the Zouaves. But it was about *her* morals—*she* was the Pope!" Lord Deepmere pursued, directing an eye illumined by this pleasantry toward Mademoiselle Nioche, who was bending gracefully over her lap-dog, apparently absorbed in conversation with it. "I dare say you think it rather odd that I should—a—keep up the acquaintance," the young man resumed. "But she could n't help it, you know, and Bellegarde was only my twentieth cousin. I dare say you think it 's rather cheeky, my showing with her in Hyde Park. But you see she is n't known yet, and she 's in such very good form"—And Lord Deepmere's conclusion was lost in the attesting glance which he again directed toward the young lady.

Newman turned away; he was having more of her than he relished. M. Nioche had stepped aside on his daughter's approach, and he stood there, within a very small compass, looking down hard at the ground. It had never yet, as between him and Newman, been so apposite to place on record the fact that he had not forgiven his daughter. As Newman was moving away he looked up and drew near to him, and

Newman, seeing the old man had something particular to say, bent his head for an instant.

"You will see it some day in the papers," murmured M. Nioche.

Our hero departed to hide his smile, and to this day, though the newspapers form his principal reading, his eyes have not been arrested by any paragraph forming a sequel to this announcement.

Chapter XXVI

IN THAT UNINITIATED observation of the great spectacle of English life upon which I have touched, it might be supposed that Newman passed a great many dull days. But the dullness of his days pleased him; his melancholy, which was settling into a secondary stage, like a healing wound, had in it a certain acrid, palatable sweetness. He had company in his thoughts, and for the present he wanted no other. He had no desire to make acquaintances, and he left untouched a couple of notes of introduction which had been sent him by Tom Tristram. He thought, a great deal of Madame de Cintré— sometimes with a dogged tranquillity which might have seemed, for a quarter of an hour at a time, a near neighbor to forgetfulness. He lived over again the happiest hours he had known—that silver chain of numbered days in which his afternoon visits, tending sensibly to the ideal result, had subtilized his good humor to a sort of spiritual intoxication. He came back to reality, after such reveries, with a somewhat muffled shock; he had begun to feel the need of accepting the unchangeable. At other times the reality became an infamy again and the unchangeable an imposture, and he gave himself up to his angry restlessness till he was weary. But on the whole he fell into a rather reflective mood. Without in the least intending it or knowing it, he attempted to read the moral of his strange misadventure. He asked himself, in his quieter hours, whether perhaps, after all, he *was* more commercial than was pleasant. We know that it was in obedience to a strong reaction against questions exclusively commercial that he had come out to pick up æsthetic entertainment in Europe; it may therefore be understood that he was able to conceive that a man might be too commercial. He was very willing to grant it, but the concession, as to his own case, was not made with any very oppressive sense of shame. If he had been too commercial, he was ready to forget it, for in being so he had done no man any wrong that might not be as easily forgotten. He reflected with sober placidity that at least there were no monuments of his "meanness" scattered about the world. If there was any reason in the nature of things why his connection with business should have cast a shadow upon a connection—even a connection broken—with a woman justly proud, he was willing to sponge it out of his life forever. The thing seemed a possibility; he could not feel it, doubtless, as keenly as some people, and it hardly seemed worth while to flap his wings very hard to rise to the idea; but he could feel it enough to make any sacrifice that still remained to be made. As to what such sacrifice was now to be made to, here Newman stopped short before a blank wall over which there sometimes played a shadowy imagery. He had a fancy of carrying out his life as he would have directed it if Madame de Cintré had been left to him—of making it a religion to do nothing that she would have disliked. In this, certainly, there was no sacrifice; but there was a pale, oblique ray of inspiration. It would be lonely entertainment—a good deal like a man talking to himself in the mirror for want of better company. Yet the idea yielded Newman several half hours' dumb exaltation as he sat, with his hands in his pockets and his legs stretched, over the relics of an expensively poor dinner, in the undying English twilight. If, however, his commercial imagination was dead, he felt no contempt for the surviving actualities begotten by it. He was glad he had been prosperous and had been a great man of business rather than a small one; he was extremely glad he was rich. He felt no impulse to sell all he had and give to the poor, or to retire into meditative economy and asceticism. He was glad he was rich and tolerably young; if it was possible to think too much about buying and selling, it was a gain to have a good slice of life left in which not to think about them. Come, what should he think about now? Again and again Newman could think only of one thing; his thoughts always came back to it, and as they did so, with an emotional rush which seemed physically to express itself in a sudden upward choking, he leaned forward—the waiter having left the room—and, resting his arms on the table, buried his troubled face.

He remained in England till midsummer, and spent a month in the country, wandering about among cathedrals, castles, and ruins. Several times, taking a walk from his inn into meadows and parks, he stopped by a well-worn stile, looked across through the early evening at a gray church tower, with its dusky nimbus of thick-circling swallows, and remembered that this might have been part of the entertainment of his honeymoon. He had never been so much alone or indulged so little in accidental dialogue. The period of recreation appointed by Mrs. Tristram had at last expired, and he asked himself what he should do now. Mrs. Tristram had written to him, proposing to him that he should join her in the Pyrenees; but he was not in the humor to return to France. The simplest thing was to repair to Liverpool and embark on the first American steamer. Newman made his way to the great seaport and secured his berth; and the night before sailing he sat in his room at the hotel, staring down, vacantly and wearily, at an open portmanteau. A number of papers were lying upon it, which he had been meaning to look over; some of them might conveniently be destroyed. But at last he shuffled them roughly together, and pushed them into a corner of the valise; they were business papers, and he was in no humor for sifting them. Then he drew forth his pocket-book and took out a paper of smaller size than those he had dismissed. He did not unfold it; he simply sat looking at the back of it. If he had momentarily entertained the idea of destroying it, the idea quickly expired. What the paper suggested was the feeling that lay in his innermost heart and that no reviving cheerfulness could long quench—the feeling that after all and above all he was a good fellow wronged. With it came a hearty hope that the Bellegardes were enjoying their suspense as to what he would do yet. The more it was prolonged the more they would enjoy it! He had hung fire once, yes; perhaps, in his present queer state of mind, he might hang fire again. But he restored the little paper to his pocket-book very tenderly, and felt better for thinking of the suspense of the Bellegardes. He felt better every time he thought of it after that, as he sailed the summer seas. He landed in New York and journeyed across the continent to San Francisco, and nothing that he observed by the way contributed to mitigate his sense of being a good fellow wronged.

He saw a great many other good fellows—his old friends—but he told none of them of the trick that had been played him. He said simply that the lady he was to have married had changed her mind, and when he was asked if he had changed his own, he said, "Suppose we change the subject." He told his friends that he had brought home no "new ideas" from Europe, and his conduct probably struck them as an eloquent proof of failing invention. He took no interest in chatting about his affairs and manifested no desire to look over his accounts. He asked half a dozen questions which, like those of an eminent physician inquiring for particular symptoms, showed that he still knew what he was talking about; but he made no comments and gave no directions. He not only puzzled the gentlemen on the stock exchange, but he was himself surprised at the extent of his indifference. As it seemed only to increase, he made an effort to combat it; he tried to interest himself and to take up his old occupations. But they appeared unreal to him; do what he would he somehow could not believe in them. Sometimes he began to fear that there was something the matter with his head; that his brain, perhaps, had softened, and that the end of his strong activities had come. This idea came back to him with an exasperating force. A hopeless, helpless loafer, useful to no one and detestable to himself—this was what the treachery of the Bellegardes had made of him. In his restless idleness he came back from San Francisco to New York, and sat for three days in the lobby of his hotel, looking out through a huge wall of plate-glass at the unceasing stream of pretty girls in Parisian-looking dresses, undulating past with little parcels nursed against their neat figures. At the end of three days he returned to San Francisco, and having arrived there he wished he had stayed away. He had nothing to do, his occupation was gone, and it seemed to him that he should never find it again. He had nothing to do *here*, he sometimes said to himself; but there was something beyond the ocean that he was still to do; something that he had left undone experimentally and speculatively, to see if it could content itself to remain undone. But it was not content: it kept pulling at his heart-strings and thumping at his reason; it murmured in his ears and hovered perpetually before his eyes. It interposed between all new resolutions and their fulfillment; it seemed like a stubborn ghost, dumbly entreating to be laid. Till that was done he should never be able to do anything else.

One day, toward the end of the winter, after a long interval, he received a letter from Mrs. Tristram, who apparently was animated by a charitable desire to amuse and distract her correspondent. She gave him much Paris gossip, talked of General Packard and Miss Kitty Upjohn, enumerated the new plays at the theatre, and inclosed a note from her husband, who had gone down to spend a month at Nice. Then came her signature, and after this her postscript. The latter consisted of these few lines: "I heard three days since from my friend, the Abbé Aubert, that Madame de Cintré last week took the veil at the Carmelites. It was on her twenty-seventh birthday, and she took the name of her patroness, St. Veronica. Sister Veronica has a life-time before her!"

This letter came to Newman in the morning; in the evening he started for Paris. His wound began to ache with its first fierceness, and during his long bleak journey the thought of Madame de Cintré's "life-time," passed within prison walls on whose outer side he might stand, kept him perpetual company. Now he would fix himself in Paris forever; he would extort a sort of happiness from the knowledge that if she was not there, at least the stony sepulchre that held her was. He descended, unannounced, upon Mrs. Bread, whom he found keeping lonely watch in his great empty saloons on the Boulevard Haussmann. They were as neat as a Dutch village; Mrs. Bread's only occupation had been removing individual dust-particles. She made no complaint, however, of her loneliness, for in her philosophy a servant was but a mysteriously projected machine, and it would be as fantastic for a housekeeper to comment upon a gentleman's absences as for a clock to remark upon not being wound up. No particular clock, Mrs. Bread supposed, kept all the time, and no particular servant could enjoy all the sunshine diffused by the career of an exacting master. She ventured, nevertheless, to express a modest hope that Newman meant to remain a while in Paris. Newman laid his hand on hers and shook it gently. "I mean to remain forever," he said.

He went after this to see Mrs. Tristram, to whom he had telegraphed, and who expected him. She looked at him a moment and shook her head. "This won't do," she said; "you have come back too soon." He sat down and asked about her husband and her children, tried even to inquire about Miss Dora Finch. In the midst of this—"Do you know where she is?" he asked, abruptly.

Mrs. Tristram hesitated a moment; of course he could n't mean Miss Dora Finch. Then she answered, properly: "She has gone to the other house—in the Rue d'Enfer." After Newman had sat a while longer, looking very sombre, she went on: "You are not so good a man as I thought. You are more—you are more"—

"More what?" Newman asked.

"More unforgiving."

"Good God!" cried Newman; "do you expect me to forgive?"

"No, not that. I have not forgiven, so of course you can't. But you might forget! You have a worse temper about it than I should have expected. You look wicked—you look dangerous."

"I may be dangerous," he said; "but I am not wicked. No, I am not wicked." And he got up to go. Mrs. Tristram asked him to come back to dinner; but he answered that he did not feel like pledging himself to be present at an entertainment, even as a solitary guest. Later in the evening, if he should be able, he would come.

He walked away through the city, beside the Seine and over it, and took the direction of the Rue d'Enfer. The day had the softness of early spring; but the weather was gray and humid. Newman found himself in a part of Paris which he little knew—a region of convents and prisons, of streets bordered by long dead walls and traversed by few wayfarers. At the intersection of two of these streets stood the house of the Carmelites—a dull, plain edifice, with a high-shouldered blank wall all round it. From without Newman could see its upper windows, its steep roof and its chimneys. But these things revealed no symptoms of human life; the place looked dumb, deaf, inanimate. The pale, dead, discolored wall stretched beneath it, far down the empty side street—a vista without a human figure. Newman stood there a long time; there were no passers; he was free to gaze his fill. This seemed the goal of his journey; it was what he had come for. It was a strange satisfaction, and yet it was a satisfaction; the barren stillness of the place seemed to be his own release from ineffectual longing. It told him that the woman within was lost beyond recall, and that the days and years of the future would pile themselves above her like the huge immovable slab of a tomb. These days and years, in this place, would always be just so gray and silent. Suddenly, from the thought of their seeing him stand there, again the charm utterly departed. He would never stand there again; it was gratuitous dreariness. He turned away with a heavy heart, but with a heart lighter than the one he had brought. Everything was over, and he too at last could rest. He walked down through narrow, winding streets to the edge of the Seine again, and there he saw, close above him, the soft, vast towers of Notre Dame. He crossed one of the bridges and stood a moment in the empty place before the great cathedral; then he went in beneath the grossly-imaged portals. He wandered some distance up the nave and sat down in the splendid dimness. He sat a long time; he heard far-away bells chiming off, at long intervals, to the rest of the world. He was very tired; this was the best place he could be in. He said no prayers; he had no prayers to say. He had nothing to be thankful for, and he had nothing to ask; nothing to ask, because now he must take care of himself. But a great cathedral offers a very various hospitality, and Newman sat in his place, because while he was there he was out of the world. The most unpleasant thing that had ever happened to him had reached its formal conclusion, as it were; he could close the book and put it away. He leaned his head for a long time on the chair in front of him; when he took it up he felt that he was himself again. Somewhere in his mind, a tight knot seemed to have loosened. He thought of the Bellegardes; he had almost forgotten them. He remembered them as people he had meant to do something to. He gave a groan as he remembered what he had meant to do; he was annoyed at having meant to do it; the bottom, suddenly, had fallen out of his revenge. Whether it was Christian charity or unregenerate good nature—what it was, in the background of his soul—I don't pretend to say; but Newman's last thought was that of course he would let the Bellegardes go. If he had spoken it aloud he would have said that he did n't want to hurt them. He was ashamed of having wanted to hurt them. They had hurt him, but such things were really not his game. At last he got up and came out of the darkening church; not with the elastic step of a man who has won a victory or taken a resolve, but strolling soberly, like a good-natured man who is still a little ashamed.

Going home, he said to Mrs. Bread that he must trouble her to put back his things into the portmanteau she had had unpacked the evening before. His gentle stewardess looked at him through eyes a trifle bedimmed. "Dear me, sir," she exclaimed, "I thought you said that you were going to stay forever."

"I meant that I was going to stay away forever," said Newman kindly. And since his departure from Paris on the following day he has certainly not returned. The gilded apartments I have so often spoken of stand ready to receive him; but they serve only as a spacious residence for Mrs. Bread, who wanders eternally from room to room, adjusting the tassels of the curtains, and keeps her wages, which are regularly brought her by a banker's clerk, in a great pink Sèvres vase on the drawing-room mantel-shelf.

Late in the evening Newman went to Mrs. Tristram's and found Tom Tristram by the domestic fire-side. "I 'm glad to see you back in Paris," this gentleman declared. "You know it 's really the only place for a white man to live." Mr. Tristram made his friend welcome, according to his own rosy light, and offered him a convenient résumé of the Franco-American gossip of the last six months. Then at last he got up and said he would go for half an hour to the club. "I suppose a man who has been for six months in California wants a little intellectual conversation. I 'll let my wife have a go at you."

Newman shook hands heartily with his host, but did not ask him to remain; and then he relapsed into his place on the sofa, opposite to Mrs. Tristram. She presently asked him what he had done after leaving her. "Nothing particular," said Newman.

"You struck me," she rejoined, "as a man with a plot in his head. You looked as if you were bent on some sinister errand, and after you had left me I wondered whether I ought to have let you go."

"I only went over to the other side of the river—to the Carmelites," said Newman.

Mrs. Tristram looked at him a moment and smiled. "What did you do there? Try to scale the wall?"

"I did nothing. I looked at the place for a few minutes and then came away."

Mrs. Tristram gave him a sympathetic glance. "You did n't happen to meet M. de Bellegarde," she asked, "staring hopelessly at the convent wall as well? I am told he takes his sister's conduct very hard."

"No, I did n't meet him, I am happy to say," Newman answered, after a pause.

"They are in the country," Mrs. Tristram went on; "at—what is the name of the place?—Fleurières. They returned there at the time you left Paris and have been spending the year in extreme seclusion. The little marquise must enjoy it; I expect to hear that she has eloped with her daughter's music-master!"

Newman was looking at the light wood-fire; but he listened to this with extreme interest. At last he spoke: "I mean never to mention the name of those people again, and I don't want to hear anything more about them." And then he took out his pocket-book and drew forth a scrap of paper. He looked at it an instant, then got up and stood by the fire. "I am going to burn them up," he said. "I am glad to have you as a witness. There they go!" And he tossed the paper into the flame.

Mrs. Tristram sat with her embroidery needle suspended. "What is that paper?" she asked.

Newman leaning against the fire-place, stretched his arms and drew a longer breath than usual. Then after a moment, "I can tell you now," he said. "It was a paper containing a secret of the Bellegardes—something which would damn them if it were known."

Mrs. Tristram dropped her embroidery with a reproachful moan. "Ah, why did n't you show it to me?"

"I thought of showing it to you—I thought of showing it to every one. I thought of paying my debt to the Bellegardes that way. So I told them, and I frightened them. They have been staying in the country, as you tell me, to keep out of the explosion. But I have given it up."

Mrs. Tristram began to take slow stitches again. "Have you quite given it up?"

"Oh yes."

"Is it very bad, this secret?"

"Yes, very bad."

"For myself," said Mrs. Tristram, "I am sorry you have given it up. I should have liked immensely to see your paper. They have wronged me too, you know, as your sponsor and guarantee, and it would have served for my revenge as well. How did you come into possession of your secret?"

"It 's a long story. But honestly, at any rate."

"And they knew you were master of it?"

"Oh, I told them."

"Dear me, how interesting!" cried Mrs. Tristram. "And you humbled them at your feet?"

Newman was silent a moment. "No, not at all. They pretended not to care—not to be afraid. But I know they did care—they were afraid."

"Are you very sure?"

Newman stared a moment. "Yes, I 'm sure."

Mrs. Tristram resumed her slow stitches. "They defied you, eh?"

"Yes," said Newman, "it was about that."

"You tried by the threat of exposure to make them retract?" Mrs. Tristram pursued.

"Yes, but they would n't. I gave them their choice, and they chose to take their chance of bluffing off the charge and convicting me of fraud. But they *were* frightened," Newman added, "and I have had all the vengeance I want."

"It is most provoking," said Mrs. Tristram, "to hear your talk of the 'charge' when the charge is burnt up. Is it quite consumed?" she asked, glancing at the fire.

Newman assured her that there was nothing left of it.

"Well then," she said, "I suppose there is no harm in saying that you probably did not make them so very uncomfortable. My impression would be that since, as you say, they defied you, it was because they believed that, after all, you would never really come to the point. Their confidence, after counsel taken of each other, was not in their innocence, nor in their talent for bluffing things off; it was in your remarkable good nature! You see they were right."

Newman instinctively turned to see if the little paper was in fact consumed; but there was nothing left of it.

THE END

THE EUROPEANS

I

A NARROW GRAVE-YARD in the heart of a bustling, indifferent city, seen from the windows of a gloomy-looking inn, is at no time an object of enlivening suggestion; and the spectacle is not at its best when the mouldy tombstones and funereal umbrage have received the ineffectual refreshment of a dull, moist snow-fall. If, while the air is thickened by this frosty drizzle, the calendar should happen to indicate that the blessed vernal season is already six weeks old, it will be admitted that no depressing influence is absent from the scene. This fact was keenly felt on a certain 12th of May, upwards of thirty years since, by a lady who stood looking out of one of the windows of the best hotel in the ancient city of Boston. She had stood there for half an hour—stood there, that is, at intervals; for from time to time she turned back into the room and measured its length with a restless step. In the chimney-place was a red-hot fire which emitted a small blue flame; and in front of the fire, at a table, sat a young man who was busily plying a pencil. He had a number of sheets of paper cut into small equal squares, and he was apparently covering them with pictorial designs—strange-looking figures. He worked rapidly and attentively, sometimes threw back his head and held out his drawing at arm's-length, and kept up a soft, gay-sounding humming and whistling. The lady brushed past him in her walk; her much-trimmed skirts were voluminous. She never dropped her eyes upon his work; she only turned them, occasionally, as she passed, to a mirror suspended above the toilet-table on the other side of the room. Here she paused a moment, gave a pinch to her waist with her two hands, or raised these members—they were very plump and pretty—to the multifold braids of her hair, with a movement half caressing, half corrective. An attentive observer might have fancied that during these periods of desultory self-inspection her face forgot its melancholy; but as soon as she neared the window again it began to proclaim that she was a very ill-pleased woman. And indeed, in what met her eyes there was little to be pleased with. The window-panes were battered by the sleet; the head-stones in the grave-yard beneath seemed to be holding themselves askance to keep it out of their faces. A tall iron railing protected them from the street, and on the other side of the railing an assemblage of Bostonians were trampling about in the liquid snow. Many of them were looking up and down; they appeared to be waiting for something. From time to time a strange vehicle drew near to the place where they stood,—such a vehicle as the lady at the window, in spite of a considerable acquaintance with human inventions, had never seen before: a huge, low omnibus, painted in brilliant colors, and decorated apparently with jangling bells, attached to a species of groove in the pavement, through which it was dragged, with a great deal of rumbling, bouncing and scratching, by a couple of remarkably small horses. When it reached a certain point the people in front of the grave-yard, of whom much the greater number were women, carrying satchels and parcels, projected themselves upon it in a compact body—a movement suggesting the scramble for places in a life-boat at sea—and were engulfed in its large interior. Then the life-boat—or the life-car, as the lady at the window of the hotel vaguely designated it—went bumping and jingling away upon its invisible wheels, with the helmsman (the man at the wheel) guiding its course incongruously from the prow. This phenomenon was repeated every three minutes, and the supply of eagerly-moving women in cloaks, bearing reticules and bundles, renewed itself in the most liberal manner. On the other side of the grave-yard was a row of small red brick houses, showing a series of homely, domestic-looking backs; at the end opposite the hotel a tall wooden church-spire, painted white, rose high into the vagueness of the snow-flakes. The lady at the window looked at it for some time; for reasons of her own she thought it the ugliest thing she had ever seen. She hated it, she despised it; it threw her into a state of irritation that was quite out of proportion to any sensible motive. She had never known herself to care so much about church-spires.

She was not pretty; but even when it expressed perplexed irritation her face was most interesting and agreeable. Neither was she in her first youth; yet, though slender, with a great deal of extremely well-fashioned roundness of contour—a suggestion both of maturity and flexibility—she carried her three and thirty years as a light-wristed Hebe might have carried a brimming wine-cup. Her complexion was fatigued, as the French say; her mouth was large, her lips too full, her teeth uneven, her chin rather commonly modeled; she had a thick nose, and when she smiled—she was constantly smiling—the lines beside it rose too high, toward her eyes. But these eyes were charming: gray in color, brilliant, quickly glancing, gently resting, full of intelligence. Her forehead was very low—it was her only handsome feature; and she had a great abundance of crisp dark hair, finely frizzled, which was always braided in a manner that suggested some Southern or Eastern, some remotely foreign, woman. She had a large collection of ear-rings, and wore them in alternation; and they seemed to give a point to her Oriental or exotic aspect. A compliment had once been paid her, which, being repeated to her, gave her greater pleasure than anything she had ever heard. "A pretty woman?" some one had said. "Why, her features are very bad." "I don't know about her features," a very discerning observer had answered; "but she carries her head like a pretty woman." You may imagine whether, after this, she carried her head less becomingly.

She turned away from the window at last, pressing her hands to her eyes. "It 's too horrible!" she exclaimed. "I shall go back—I shall go back!" And she flung herself into a chair before the fire.

"Wait a little, dear child," said the young man softly, sketching away at his little scraps of paper.

The lady put out her foot; it was very small, and there was an immense rosette on her slipper. She fixed her eyes for a while on this ornament, and then she looked at the glowing bed of anthracite coal in the grate. "Did you ever see anything so hideous as that fire?" she demanded. "Did you ever see anything so—so *affreux* as—as everything?" She spoke English with perfect purity; but she brought out this French epithet in a manner that indicated that she was accustomed to using French epithets.

"I think the fire is very pretty," said the young man, glancing at it a moment. "Those little blue tongues, dancing on top of the crimson embers, are extremely picturesque. They are like a fire in an alchemist's laboratory."

"You are too good-natured, my dear," his companion declared.

The young man held out one of his drawings, with his head on one side. His tongue was gently moving along his under-lip. "Good-natured—yes. Too good-natured—no."

"You are irritating," said the lady, looking at her slipper.

He began to retouch his sketch. "I think you mean simply that you are irritated."

"Ah, for that, yes!" said his companion, with a little bitter laugh. "It 's the darkest day of my life—and you know what that means."

"Wait till to-morrow," rejoined the young man.

"Yes, we have made a great mistake. If there is any doubt about it to-day, there certainly will be none to-morrow. Ce sera clair, au moins!"

The young man was silent a few moments, driving his pencil. Then at last, "There are no such things as mistakes," he affirmed.

"Very true—for those who are not clever enough to perceive them. Not to recognize one's mistakes—that would be happiness in life," the lady went on, still looking at her pretty foot.

"My dearest sister," said the young man, always intent upon his drawing, "it 's the first time you have told me I am not clever."

"Well, by your own theory I can't call it a mistake," answered his sister, pertinently enough.

The young man gave a clear, fresh laugh. "You, at least, are clever enough, dearest sister," he said.

"I was not so when I proposed this."

"Was it you who proposed it?" asked her brother.

She turned her head and gave him a little stare. "Do you desire the credit of it?"

"If you like, I will take the blame," he said, looking up with a smile.

"Yes," she rejoined in a moment, "you make no difference in these things. You have no sense of property."

The young man gave his joyous laugh again. "If that means I have no property, you are right!"

"Don't joke about your poverty," said his sister. "That is quite as vulgar as to boast about it."

"My poverty! I have just finished a drawing that will bring me fifty francs!"

"Voyons," said the lady, putting out her hand.

He added a touch or two, and then gave her his sketch. She looked at it, but she went on with her idea of a moment before. "If a woman were to ask you to marry her you would say, 'Certainly, my dear, with pleasure!' And you would marry her and be ridiculously happy. Then at the end of three months you would say to her, 'You know that blissful day when I begged you to be mine!'"

The young man had risen from the table, stretching his arms a little; he walked to the window. "That is a description of a charming nature," he said.

"Oh, yes, you have a charming nature; I regard that as our capital. If I had not been convinced of that I should never have taken the risk of bringing you to this dreadful country."

"This comical country, this delightful country!" exclaimed the young man, and he broke into the most animated laughter.

"Is it those women scrambling into the omnibus?" asked his companion. "What do you suppose is the attraction?"

"I suppose there is a very good-looking man inside," said the young man.

"In each of them? They come along in hundreds, and the men in this country don't seem at all handsome. As for the women—I have never seen so many at once since I left the convent."

"The women are very pretty," her brother declared, "and the whole affair is very amusing. I must make a sketch of it." And he came back to the table quickly, and picked up his utensils—a small sketching-board, a sheet of paper, and three or four crayons. He took his place at the window with these things, and stood there glancing out, plying his pencil with an air of easy skill. While he worked he wore a brilliant smile. Brilliant is indeed the word at this moment for his strongly-lighted face. He was eight and twenty years old; he had a short, slight, well-made figure. Though he bore a noticeable resemblance to his sister, he was a better favored person: fair-haired, clear-faced, witty-looking, with a delicate finish of feature and an expression at once urbane and not at all serious, a warm blue eye, an eyebrow finely drawn and excessively arched—an eyebrow which, if ladies wrote sonnets to those of their lovers, might have been made the subject of such a piece of verse—and a light moustache that flourished upwards as if blown that way by the breath of a constant smile. There was something in his physiognomy at once benevolent and picturesque. But, as I have hinted, it was not at all serious. The young man's face was, in this respect, singular; it was not at all serious, and yet it inspired the liveliest confidence.

"Be sure you put in plenty of snow," said his sister. "Bonté divine, what a climate!"

"I shall leave the sketch all white, and I shall put in the little figures in black," the young man answered, laughing. "And I shall call it—what is that line in Keats?—Mid-May's Eldest Child!"

"I don't remember," said the lady, "that mamma ever told me it was like this."

"Mamma never told you anything disagreeable. And it 's not like this—every day. You will see that to-morrow we shall have a splendid day."

"Qu'en savez-vous? To-morrow I shall go away."

"Where shall you go?"

"Anywhere away from here. Back to Silberstadt. I shall write to the Reigning Prince."

The young man turned a little and looked at her, with his crayon poised. "My dear Eugenia," he murmured, "were you so happy at sea?"

Eugenia got up; she still held in her hand the drawing her brother had given her. It was a bold, expressive sketch of a group of miserable people on the deck of a steamer, clinging together and clutching at each other, while the vessel lurched downward, at a terrific angle, into the hollow of a wave. It was extremely clever, and full of a sort of tragi-comical power. Eugenia dropped her eyes upon it and made a sad grimace. "How can you draw such odious scenes?" she asked. "I should like to throw it into the fire!" And she tossed the paper away. Her brother watched, quietly, to see where it went. It fluttered down to the floor, where he let it lie. She came toward the window, pinching in her waist. "Why don't you reproach me—abuse me?" she asked. "I think I should feel better then. Why don't you tell me that you hate me for bringing you here?"

"Because you would not believe it. I adore you, dear sister! I am delighted to be here, and I am charmed with the prospect."

"I don't know what had taken possession of me. I had lost my head," Eugenia went on.

The young man, on his side, went on plying his pencil. "It is evidently a most curious and interesting country. Here we are, and I mean to enjoy it."

His companion turned away with an impatient step, but presently came back. "High spirits are doubtless an excellent thing," she said; "but you give one too much of them, and I can't see that they have done you any good."

The young man stared, with lifted eyebrows, smiling; he tapped his handsome nose with his pencil. "They have made me happy!"

"That was the least they could do; they have made you nothing else. You have gone through life thanking fortune for such very small favors that she has never put herself to any trouble for you."

"She must have put herself to a little, I think, to present me with so admirable a sister."

"Be serious, Felix. You forget that I am your elder."

"With a sister, then, so elderly!" rejoined Felix, laughing. "I hoped we had left seriousness in Europe."

"I fancy you will find it here. Remember that you are nearly thirty years old, and that you are nothing but an obscure Bohemian—a penniless correspondent of an illustrated newspaper."

"Obscure as much as you please, but not so much of a Bohemian as you think. And not at all penniless! I have a hundred pounds in my pocket. I have an engagement to make fifty sketches, and I mean to paint the portraits of all our cousins, and of all *their* cousins, at a hundred dollars a head."

"You are not ambitious," said Eugenia.

"You are, dear Baroness," the young man replied.

The Baroness was silent a moment, looking out at the sleet-darkened grave-yard and the bumping horse-cars. "Yes, I am ambitious," she said at last. "And my ambition has brought me to this dreadful place!" She glanced about her—the room had a certain vulgar nudity; the bed and the window were curtainless—and she gave a little passionate sigh. "Poor old ambition!" she exclaimed. Then she flung herself down upon a sofa which stood near against the wall, and covered her face with her hands.

Her brother went on with his drawing, rapidly and skillfully; after some moments he sat down beside her and showed her his sketch. "Now, don't you think that's pretty good for an obscure Bohemian?" he asked. "I have knocked off another fifty francs."

Eugenia glanced at the little picture as he laid it on her lap. "Yes, it is very clever," she said. And in a moment she added, "Do you suppose our cousins do that?"

"Do what?"

"Get into those things, and look like that."

Felix meditated awhile. "I really can't say. It will be interesting to discover."

"Oh, the rich people can't!" said the Baroness.

"Are you very sure they are rich?" asked Felix, lightly.

His sister slowly turned in her place, looking at him. "Heavenly powers!" she murmured. "You have a way of bringing out things!"

"It will certainly be much pleasanter if they are rich," Felix declared.

"Do you suppose if I had not known they were rich I would ever have come?"

The young man met his sister's somewhat peremptory eye with his bright, contented glance. "Yes, it certainly will be pleasanter," he repeated.

"That is all I expect of them," said the Baroness. "I don't count upon their being clever or friendly—at first—or elegant or interesting. But I assure you I insist upon their being rich."

Felix leaned his head upon the back of the sofa and looked awhile at the oblong patch of sky to which the window served as frame. The snow was ceasing; it seemed to him that the sky had begun to brighten. "I count upon their being rich," he said at last, "and powerful, and clever, and friendly, and elegant, and interesting, and generally delightful! Tu vas voir." And he bent forward and kissed his sister. "Look there!" he went on. "As a portent, even while I speak, the sky is turning the color of gold; the day is going to be splendid."

And indeed, within five minutes the weather had changed. The sun broke out through the snow-clouds and jumped into the Baroness's room. "Bonté divine," exclaimed this lady, "what a climate!"

"We will go out and see the world," said Felix.

And after a while they went out. The air had grown warm as well as brilliant; the sunshine had dried the pavements. They walked about the streets at hazard, looking at the people and the houses, the shops and the vehicles, the blazing blue sky and the muddy crossings, the hurrying men and the slow-strolling maidens, the fresh red bricks and the bright green trees, the extraordinary mixture of smartness and shabbiness. From one hour to another the day had grown vernal; even in the bustling streets there was an odor of earth and blossom. Felix was immensely entertained. He had called it a comical country, and he went about laughing at everything he saw. You would have said that American civilization expressed itself to his sense in a tissue of capital jokes. The jokes were certainly excellent, and the young man's merriment was joyous and genial. He possessed what is called the pictorial sense; and this first glimpse of democratic manners stirred the same sort of attention that he would have given to the movements of a lively young person with a bright complexion. Such attention would have been demonstrative and complimentary; and in the present case Felix might have passed for an undispirited young exile revisiting the haunts of his childhood. He kept looking at the violent blue of the sky, at the scintillating air, at the scattered and multiplied patches of color.

"Comme c'est bariolé, eh?" he said to his sister in that foreign tongue which they both appeared to feel a mysterious prompting occasionally to use.

"Yes, it is bariolé indeed," the Baroness answered. "I don't like the coloring; it hurts my eyes."

"It shows how extremes meet," the young man rejoined. "Instead of coming to the West we seem to have gone to the

East. The way the sky touches the house-tops is just like
Cairo; and the red and blue sign-boards patched over the face
of everything remind one of Mahometan decorations."

"The young women are not Mahometan," said his companion. "They can't be said to hide their faces. I never saw anything so bold."

"Thank Heaven they don't hide their faces!" cried Felix.
"Their faces are uncommonly pretty."

"Yes, their faces are often very pretty," said the Baroness,
who was a very clever woman. She was too clever a woman
not to be capable of a great deal of just and fine observation.
She clung more closely than usual to her brother's arm; she
was not exhilarated, as he was; she said very little, but she
noted a great many things and made her reflections. She was
a little excited; she felt that she had indeed come to a strange
country, to make her fortune. Superficially, she was conscious
of a good deal of irritation and displeasure; the Baroness was
a very delicate and fastidious person. Of old, more than once,
she had gone, for entertainment's sake and in brilliant company, to a fair in a provincial town. It seemed to her now that
she was at an enormous fair—that the entertainment and the
désagréments were very much the same. She found herself alternately smiling and shrinking; the show was very curious,
but it was probable, from moment to moment, that one
would be jostled. The Baroness had never seen so many people walking about before; she had never been so mixed up
with people she did not know. But little by little she felt that
this fair was a more serious undertaking. She went with her
brother into a large public garden, which seemed very pretty,
but where she was surprised at seeing no carriages. The afternoon was drawing to a close; the coarse, vivid grass and the
slender tree-boles were gilded by the level sunbeams—gilded
as with gold that was fresh from the mine. It was the hour at
which ladies should come out for an airing and roll past a
hedge of pedestrians, holding their parasols askance. Here,
however, Eugenia observed no indications of this custom, the
absence of which was more anomalous as there was a charming avenue of remarkably graceful, arching elms in the most
convenient contiguity to a large, cheerful street, in which, evidently, among the more prosperous members of the *bour-*

geoisie, a great deal of pedestrianism went forward. Our friends passed out into this well lighted promenade, and Felix noticed a great many more pretty girls and called his sister's attention to them. This latter measure, however, was superfluous; for the Baroness had inspected, narrowly, these charming young ladies.

"I feel an intimate conviction that our cousins are like that," said Felix.

The Baroness hoped so, but this is not what she said. "They are very pretty," she said, "but they are mere little girls. Where are the women—the women of thirty?"

"Of thirty-three, do you mean?" her brother was going to ask; for he understood often both what she said and what she did not say. But he only exclaimed upon the beauty of the sunset, while the Baroness, who had come to seek her fortune, reflected that it would certainly be well for her if the persons against whom she might need to measure herself should all be mere little girls. The sunset was superb; they stopped to look at it; Felix declared that he had never seen such a gorgeous mixture of colors. The Baroness also thought it splendid; and she was perhaps the more easily pleased from the fact that while she stood there she was conscious of much admiring observation on the part of various nice-looking people who passed that way, and to whom a distinguished, strikingly-dressed woman with a foreign air, exclaiming upon the beauties of nature on a Boston street corner in the French tongue, could not be an object of indifference. Eugenia's spirits rose. She surrendered herself to a certain tranquil gayety. If she had come to seek her fortune, it seemed to her that her fortune would be easy to find. There was a promise of it in the gorgeous purity of the western sky; there was an intimation in the mild, unimpertinent gaze of the passers of a certain natural facility in things.

"You will not go back to Silberstadt, eh?" asked Felix.

"Not to-morrow," said the Baroness.

"Nor write to the Reigning Prince?"

"I shall write to him that they evidently know nothing about him over here."

"He will not believe you," said the young man. "I advise you to let him alone."

Felix himself continued to be in high good humor. Brought up among ancient customs and in picturesque cities, he yet found plenty of local color in the little Puritan metropolis. That evening, after dinner, he told his sister that he should go forth early on the morrow to look up their cousins.

"You are very impatient," said Eugenia.

"What can be more natural," he asked, "after seeing all those pretty girls to-day? If one's cousins are of that pattern, the sooner one knows them the better."

"Perhaps they are not," said Eugenia. "We ought to have brought some letters—to some other people."

"The other people would not be our kinsfolk."

"Possibly they would be none the worse for that," the Baroness replied.

Her brother looked at her with his eyebrows lifted. "That was not what you said when you first proposed to me that we should come out here and fraternize with our relatives. You said that it was the prompting of natural affection; and when I suggested some reasons against it you declared that the *voix du sang* should go before everything."

"You remember all that?" asked the Baroness.

"Vividly! I was greatly moved by it."

She was walking up and down the room, as she had done in the morning; she stopped in her walk and looked at her brother. She apparently was going to say something, but she checked herself and resumed her walk. Then, in a few moments, she said something different, which had the effect of an explanation of the suppression of her earlier thought. "You will never be anything but a child, dear brother."

"One would suppose that you, madam," answered Felix, laughing, "were a thousand years old."

"I am—sometimes," said the Baroness.

"I will go, then, and announce to our cousins the arrival of a personage so extraordinary. They will immediately come and pay you their respects."

Eugenia paced the length of the room again, and then she stopped before her brother, laying her hand upon his arm. "They are not to come and see me," she said. "You are not to allow that. That is not the way I shall meet them first." And in answer to his interrogative glance she went on. "You will go and examine, and report. You will come back and tell me who they are and what they are; their number, gender, their respective ages—all about them. Be sure you observe everything; be ready to describe to me the locality, the accessories—how shall I say it?—the mise en scène. Then, at my own time, at my own hour, under circumstances of my own choosing, I will go to them. I will present myself—I will appear before them!" said the Baroness, this time phrasing her idea with a certain frankness.

"And what message am I to take to them?" asked Felix, who had a lively faith in the justness of his sister's arrangements.

She looked at him a moment—at his expression of agreeable veracity; and, with that justness that he admired, she replied, "Say what you please. Tell my story in the way that seems to you most—natural." And she bent her forehead for him to kiss.

II

THE NEXT DAY was splendid, as Felix had prophesied; if the winter had suddenly leaped into spring, the spring had for the moment as quickly leaped into summer. This was an observation made by a young girl who came out of a large square house in the country, and strolled about in the spacious garden which separated it from a muddy road. The flowering shrubs and the neatly-disposed plants were basking in the abundant light and warmth; the transparent shade of the great elms—they were magnificent trees—seemed to thicken by the hour; and the intensely habitual stillness offered a submissive medium to the sound of a distant church-bell. The young girl listened to the church-bell; but she was not dressed for church. She was bare-headed; she wore a white muslin waist, with an embroidered border, and the skirt of her dress was of colored muslin. She was a young lady of some two or three and twenty years of age, and though a young person of her sex walking bare-headed in a garden, of a Sunday morning in spring-time, can, in the nature of things, never be a displeasing object, you would not have pronounced this innocent Sabbath-breaker especially pretty. She was tall and pale, thin and a little awkward; her hair was fair and perfectly straight; her eyes were dark, and they had the singularity of seeming at once dull and restless—differing herein, as you see, fatally from the ideal "fine eyes," which we always imagine to be both brilliant and tranquil. The doors and windows of the large square house were all wide open, to admit the purifying sunshine, which lay in generous patches upon the floor of a wide, high, covered piazza adjusted to two sides of the mansion—a piazza on which several straw-bottomed rocking-chairs and half a dozen of those small cylindrical stools in green and blue porcelain, which suggest an affiliation between the residents and the Eastern trade, were symmetrically disposed. It was an ancient house—ancient in the sense of being eighty years old; it was built of wood, painted a clean, clear, faded gray, and adorned along the front, at intervals, with flat wooden pilasters, painted white. These pilasters appeared to support a kind of classic pediment, which was decorated in the middle by a large triple window in a boldly carved frame, and in each of its smaller angles by a glazed circular aperture. A large white door, furnished with a highly-polished brass knocker, presented itself to the rural-looking road, with which it was connected by a spacious pathway, paved with worn and cracked, but very clean, bricks. Behind it there were meadows and orchards, a barn and a pond; and facing it, a short distance along the road, on the opposite side, stood a smaller house, painted white, with external shutters painted green, a little garden on one hand and an orchard on the other. All this was shining in the morning air, through which the simple details of the picture addressed themselves to the eye as distinctly as the items of a "sum" in addition.

A second young lady presently came out of the house, across the piazza, descended into the garden and approached the young girl of whom I have spoken. This second young lady was also thin and pale; but she was older than the other; she was shorter; she had dark, smooth hair. Her eyes, unlike the other's, were quick and bright; but they were not at all restless. She wore a straw bonnet with white ribbons, and a long, red, India scarf, which, on the front of her dress, reached to her feet. In her hand she carried a little key.

"Gertrude," she said, "are you very sure you had better not go to church?"

Gertrude looked at her a moment, plucked a small sprig from a lilac-bush, smelled it and threw it away. "I am not very sure of anything!" she answered.

The other young lady looked straight past her, at the distant pond, which lay shining between the long banks of fir-trees. Then she said in a very soft voice, "This is the key of the dining-room closet. I think you had better have it, if any one should want anything."

"Who is there to want anything?" Gertrude demanded. "I shall be all alone in the house."

"Some one may come," said her companion.

"Do you mean Mr. Brand?"

"Yes, Gertrude. He may like a piece of cake."

"I don't like men that are always eating cake!" Gertrude declared, giving a pull at the lilac-bush.

Her companion glanced at her, and then looked down on the ground. "I think father expected you would come to church," she said. "What shall I say to him?"

"Say I have a bad headache."

"Would that be true?" asked the elder lady, looking straight at the pond again.

"No, Charlotte," said the younger one simply.

Charlotte transferred her quiet eyes to her companion's face. "I am afraid you are feeling restless."

"I am feeling as I always feel," Gertrude replied, in the same tone.

Charlotte turned away; but she stood there a moment. Presently she looked down at the front of her dress. "Does n't it seem to you, somehow, as if my scarf were too long?" she asked.

Gertrude walked half round her, looking at the scarf. "I don't think you wear it right," she said.

"How should I wear it, dear?"

"I don't know; differently from that. You should draw it differently over your shoulders, round your elbows; you should look differently behind."

"How should I look?" Charlotte inquired.

"I don't think I can tell you," said Gertrude, plucking out the scarf a little behind. "I could do it myself, but I don't think I can explain it."

Charlotte, by a movement of her elbows, corrected the laxity that had come from her companion's touch. "Well, some day you must do it for me. It does n't matter now. Indeed, I don't think it matters," she added, "how one looks behind."

"I should say it mattered more," said Gertrude. "Then you don't know who may be observing you. You are not on your guard. You can't try to look pretty."

Charlotte received this declaration with extreme gravity. "I don't think one should ever try to look pretty," she rejoined, earnestly.

Her companion was silent. Then she said, "Well, perhaps it 's not of much use."

Charlotte looked at her a little, and then kissed her. "I hope you will be better when we come back."

"My dear sister, I am very well!" said Gertrude.

Charlotte went down the large brick walk to the garden gate; her companion strolled slowly toward the house. At the gate Charlotte met a young man, who was coming in—a tall, fair young man, wearing a high hat and a pair of thread gloves. He was handsome, but rather too stout. He had a pleasant smile. "Oh, Mr. Brand!" exclaimed the young lady.

"I came to see whether your sister was not going to church," said the young man.

"She says she is not going; but I am very glad you have come. I think if you were to talk to her a little" . . . . And Charlotte lowered her voice. "It seems as if she were restless."

Mr. Brand smiled down on the young lady from his great height. "I shall be very glad to talk to her. For that I should be willing to absent myself from almost any occasion of worship, however attractive."

"Well, I suppose you know," said Charlotte, softly, as if positive acceptance of this proposition might be dangerous. "But I am afraid I shall be late."

"I hope you will have a pleasant sermon," said the young man.

"Oh, Mr. Gilman is always pleasant," Charlotte answered. And she went on her way.

Mr. Brand went into the garden, where Gertrude, hearing the gate close behind him, turned and looked at him. For a moment she watched him coming; then she turned away. But almost immediately she corrected this movement, and stood still, facing him. He took off his hat and wiped his forehead as he approached. Then he put on his hat again and held out his hand. His hat being removed, you would have perceived that his forehead was very large and smooth, and his hair abundant but rather colorless. His nose was too large, and his mouth and eyes were too small; but for all this he was, as I have said, a young man of striking appearance. The expression of his little clean-colored blue eyes was irresistibly gentle and serious; he looked, as the phrase is, as good as gold. The young girl, standing in the garden path, glanced, as he came up, at his thread gloves.

"I hoped you were going to church," he said. "I wanted to walk with you."

"I am very much obliged to you," Gertrude answered. "I am not going to church."

She had shaken hands with him; he held her hand a moment. "Have you any special reason for not going?"

"Yes, Mr. Brand," said the young girl.

"May I ask what it is?"

She looked at him smiling; and in her smile, as I have intimated, there was a certain dullness. But mingled with this dullness was something sweet and suggestive. "Because the sky is so blue!" she said.

He looked at the sky, which was magnificent, and then said, smiling too, "I have heard of young ladies staying at home for bad weather, but never for good. Your sister, whom I met at the gate, tells me you are depressed," he added.

"Depressed? I am never depressed."

"Oh, surely, sometimes," replied Mr. Brand, as if he thought this a regrettable account of one's self.

"I am never depressed," Gertrude repeated. "But I am sometimes wicked. When I am wicked I am in high spirits. I was wicked just now to my sister."

"What did you do to her?"

"I said things that puzzled her—on purpose."

"Why did you do that, Miss Gertrude?" asked the young man.

She began to smile again. "Because the sky is so blue!"

"You say things that puzzle *me*," Mr. Brand declared.

"I always know when I do it," proceeded Gertrude. "But people puzzle me more, I think. And they don't seem to know!"

"This is very interesting," Mr. Brand observed, smiling.

"You told me to tell you about my—my struggles," the young girl went on.

"Let us talk about them. I have so many things to say."

Gertrude turned away a moment; and then, turning back, "You had better go to church," she said.

"You know," the young man urged, "that I have always one thing to say."

Gertrude looked at him a moment. "Please don't say it now!"

"We are all alone," he continued, taking off his hat; "all alone in this beautiful Sunday stillness."

Gertrude looked around her, at the breaking buds, the shining distance, the blue sky to which she had referred as a pretext for her irregularities. "That 's the reason," she said, "why I don't want you to speak. Do me a favor; go to church."

"May I speak when I come back?" asked Mr. Brand.

"If you are still disposed," she answered.

"I don't know whether you are wicked," he said, "but you are certainly puzzling."

She had turned away; she raised her hands to her ears. He looked at her a moment, and then he slowly walked to church.

She wandered for a while about the garden, vaguely and without purpose. The church-bell had stopped ringing; the stillness was complete. This young lady relished highly, on occasions, the sense of being alone—the absence of the whole family and the emptiness of the house. To-day, apparently, the servants had also gone to church; there was never a figure at the open windows; behind the house there was no stout negress in a red turban, lowering the bucket into the great shingle-hooded well. And the front door of the big, un-guarded home stood open, with the trustfulness of the golden age; or what is more to the purpose, with that of New England's silvery prime. Gertrude slowly passed through it, and went from one of the empty rooms to the other—large, clear-colored rooms, with white wainscots, ornamented with thin-legged mahogany furniture, and, on the walls, with old-fashioned engravings, chiefly of scriptural subjects, hung very high. This agreeable sense of solitude, of having the house to herself, of which I have spoken, always excited Gertrude's imagination; she could not have told you why, and neither can her humble historian. It always seemed to her that she must do something particular—that she must honor the occasion; and while she roamed about, wondering what she could do, the occasion usually came to an end. To-day she wondered more than ever. At last she took down a book; there was no library in the house, but there were books in all the rooms. None of them were forbidden books, and Gertrude had not stopped at home for the sake of a chance to climb to the inaccessible shelves. She possessed herself of a very obvious volume—one of the series of the Arabian Nights—and she brought it out into the portico and sat down with it in her lap. There, for a quarter of an hour, she read the history of the loves of the Prince Camaralzaman and the Princess Badoura. At last, looking up, she beheld, as it seemed to her, the Prince Camaralzaman standing before her. A beautiful young man was making her a very low bow—a magnificent bow, such as she had never seen before. He appeared to have dropped from the clouds; he was wonderfully handsome; he smiled—smiled as if he were smiling on purpose. Extreme surprise, for a moment, kept Gertrude sitting still; then she rose, without even keeping her finger in her book. The young man, with his hat in his hand, still looked at her, smiling and smiling. It was very strange.

"Will you kindly tell me," said the mysterious visitor, at last, "whether I have the honor of speaking to Miss Wentworth?"

"My name is Gertrude Wentworth," murmured the young woman.

"Then—then—I have the honor—the pleasure—of being your cousin."

The young man had so much the character of an apparition that this announcement seemed to complete his unreality. "What cousin? Who are you?" said Gertrude.

He stepped back a few paces and looked up at the house; then glanced round him at the garden and the distant view. After this he burst out laughing. "I see it must seem to you very strange," he said. There was, after all, something substantial in his laughter. Gertrude looked at him from head to foot. Yes, he was remarkably handsome; but his smile was almost a grimace. "It is very still," he went on, coming nearer again. And as she only looked at him, for reply, he added, "Are you all alone?"

"Every one has gone to church," said Gertrude.

"I was afraid of that!" the young man exclaimed. "But I hope you are not afraid of me."

"You ought to tell me who you are," Gertrude answered.

"I am afraid of you!" said the young man. "I had a different plan. I expected the servant would take in my card, and that you would put your heads together, before admitting me, and make out my identity."

Gertrude had been wondering with a quick intensity which brought its result; and the result seemed an answer—a wondrous, delightful answer—to her vague wish that something would befall her. "I know—I know," she said. "You come from Europe."

"We came two days ago. You have heard of us, then—you believe in us?"

"We have known, vaguely," said Gertrude, "that we had relations in France."

"And have you ever wanted to see us?" asked the young man.

Gertrude was silent a moment. "I have wanted to see you."

"I am glad, then, it is you I have found. We wanted to see you, so we came."

"On purpose?" asked Gertrude.

The young man looked round him, smiling still. "Well, yes; on purpose. Does that sound as if we should bore you?" he added. "I don't think we shall—I really don't think we shall. We are rather fond of wandering, too; and we were glad of a pretext."

"And you have just arrived?"

"In Boston, two days ago. At the inn I asked for Mr. Wentworth. He must be your father. They found out for me where he lived; they seemed often to have heard of him. I determined to come, without ceremony. So, this lovely morning, they set my face in the right direction, and told me to walk straight before me, out of town. I came on foot because I wanted to see the country. I walked and walked, and here I am! It 's a good many miles."

"It is seven miles and a half," said Gertrude, softly. Now that this handsome young man was proving himself a reality she found herself vaguely trembling; she was deeply excited. She had never in her life spoken to a foreigner, and she had often thought it would be delightful to do so. Here was one who had suddenly been engendered by the Sabbath stillness for her private use; and such a brilliant, polite, smiling one! She found time and means to compose herself, however: to

remind herself that she must exercise a sort of official hospitality. "We are very—very glad to see you," she said. "Won't
you come into the house?" And she moved toward the open
door.

"You are not afraid of me, then?" asked the young man
again, with his light laugh.

She wondered a moment, and then, "We are not afraid—
here," she said.

"Ah, comme vous devez avoir raison!" cried the young
man, looking all round him, appreciatively. It was the first
time that Gertrude had heard so many words of French spoken. They gave her something of a sensation. Her companion
followed her, watching, with a certain excitement of his own,
this tall, interesting-looking girl, dressed in her clear, crisp
muslin. He paused in the hall, where there was a broad white
staircase with a white balustrade. "What a pleasant house!" he
said. "It 's lighter inside than it is out."

"It 's pleasanter here," said Gertrude, and she led the way
into the parlor,—a high, clean, rather empty-looking room.
Here they stood looking at each other,—the young man
smiling more than ever; Gertrude, very serious, trying to
smile.

"I don't believe you know my name," he said. "I am called
Felix Young. Your father is my uncle. My mother was his half
sister, and older than he."

"Yes," said Gertrude, "and she turned Roman Catholic and
married in Europe."

"I see you know," said the young man. "She married and
she died. Your father's family did n't like her husband. They
called him a foreigner; but he was not. My poor father was
born in Sicily, but his parents were American."

"In Sicily?" Gertrude murmured.

"It is true," said Felix Young, "that they had spent their
lives in Europe. But they were very patriotic. And so are we."

"And you are Sicilian," said Gertrude.

"Sicilian, no! Let 's see. I was born at a little place—a dear
little place—in France. My sister was born at Vienna."

"So you are French," said Gertrude.

"Heaven forbid!" cried the young man. Gertrude's eyes
were fixed upon him almost insistently. He began to laugh

again. "I can easily be French, if that will please you."

"You are a foreigner of some sort," said Gertrude.

"Of some sort—yes; I suppose so. But who can say of what sort? I don't think we have ever had occasion to settle the question. You know there are people like that. About their country, their religion, their profession, they can't tell."

Gertrude stood there gazing; she had not asked him to sit down. She had never heard of people like that; she wanted to hear. "Where do you live?" she asked.

"They can't tell that, either!" said Felix. "I am afraid you will think they are little better than vagabonds. I have lived anywhere—everywhere. I really think I have lived in every city in Europe." Gertrude gave a little long soft exhalation. It made the young man smile at her again; and his smile made her blush a little. To take refuge from blushing she asked him if, after his long walk, he was not hungry or thirsty. Her hand was in her pocket; she was fumbling with the little key that her sister had given her. "Ah, my dear young lady," he said, clasping his hands a little, "if you could give me, in charity, a glass of wine!"

Gertrude gave a smile and a little nod, and went quickly out of the room. Presently she came back with a very large decanter in one hand and a plate in the other, on which was placed a big, round cake with a frosted top. Gertrude, in taking the cake from the closet, had had a moment of acute consciousness that it composed the refection of which her sister had thought that Mr. Brand would like to partake. Her kinsman from across the seas was looking at the pale, high-hung engravings. When she came in he turned and smiled at her, as if they had been old friends meeting after a separation. "You wait upon me yourself?" he asked. "I am served like the gods!" She had waited upon a great many people, but none of them had ever told her that. The observation added a certain lightness to the step with which she went to a little table where there were some curious red glasses—glasses covered with little gold sprigs, which Charlotte used to dust every morning with her own hands. Gertrude thought the glasses very handsome, and it was a pleasure to her to know that the wine was good; it was her father's famous madeira. Felix

Young thought it excellent; he wondered why he had been told that there was no wine in America. She cut him an immense triangle out of the cake, and again she thought of Mr. Brand. Felix sat there, with his glass in one hand and his huge morsel of cake in the other—eating, drinking, smiling, talking. "I am very hungry," he said. "I am not at all tired; I am never tired. But I am very hungry."

"You must stay to dinner," said Gertrude. "At two o'clock. They will all have come back from church; you will see the others."

"Who are the others?" asked the young man. "Describe them all."

"You will see for yourself. It is you that must tell me; now, about your sister."

"My sister is the Baroness Münster," said Felix.

On hearing that his sister was a Baroness, Gertrude got up and walked about slowly, in front of him. She was silent a moment. She was thinking of it. "Why did n't she come, too?" she asked.

"She did come; she is in Boston, at the hotel."

"We will go and see her," said Gertrude, looking at him.

"She begs you will not!" the young man replied. "She sends you her love; she sent me to announce her. She will come and pay her respects to your father."

Gertrude felt herself trembling again. A Baroness Münster, who sent a brilliant young man to "announce" her; who was coming, as the Queen of Sheba came to Solomon, to pay her "respects" to quiet Mr. Wentworth—such a personage presented herself to Gertrude's vision with a most effective unexpectedness. For a moment she hardly knew what to say. "When will she come?" she asked at last.

"As soon as you will allow her—to-morrow. She is very impatient," answered Felix, who wished to be agreeable.

"To-morrow, yes," said Gertrude. She wished to ask more about her; but she hardly knew what could be predicated of a Baroness Münster. "Is she—is she—married?"

Felix had finished his cake and wine; he got up, fixing upon the young girl his bright, expressive eyes. "She is married to a German prince—Prince Adolf, of Silberstadt-Schreckenstein. He is not the reigning prince; he is a younger brother."

Gertrude gazed at her informant; her lips were slightly parted. "Is she a—a *Princess*?" she asked at last.

"Oh, no," said the young man; "her position is rather a singular one. It 's a morganatic marriage."

"Morganatic?" These were new names and new words to poor Gertrude.

"That 's what they call a marriage, you know, contracted between a scion of a ruling house and—and a common mortal. They made Eugenia a Baroness, poor woman; but that was all they could do. Now they want to dissolve the marriage. Prince Adolf, between ourselves, is a ninny; but his brother, who is a clever man, has plans for him. Eugenia, naturally enough, makes difficulties; not, however, that I think she cares much—she 's a very clever woman; I 'm sure you 'll like her—but she wants to bother them. Just now everything is *en l'air*."

The cheerful, off-hand tone in which her visitor related this darkly romantic tale seemed to Gertrude very strange; but it seemed also to convey a certain flattery to herself, a recognition of her wisdom and dignity. She felt a dozen impressions stirring within her, and presently the one that was uppermost found words. "They want to dissolve her marriage?" she asked.

"So it appears."

"And against her will?"

"Against her right."

"She must be very unhappy!" said Gertrude.

Her visitor looked at her, smiling; he raised his hand to the back of his head and held it there a moment. "So she says," he answered. "That 's her story. She told me to tell it you."

"Tell me more," said Gertrude.

"No, I will leave that to her; she does it better."

Gertrude gave her little excited sigh again. "Well, if she is unhappy," she said, "I am glad she has come to us."

She had been so interested that she failed to notice the sound of a footstep in the portico; and yet it was a footstep that she always recognized. She heard it in the hall, and then she looked out of the window. They were all coming back from church—her father, her sister and brother, and their cousins, who always came to dinner on Sunday. Mr. Brand had come in first; he was in advance of the others, because, apparently, he was still disposed to say what she had not wished him to say an hour before. He came into the parlor, looking for Gertrude. He had two little books in his hand. On seeing Gertrude's companion he slowly stopped, looking at him.

"Is this a cousin?" asked Felix.

Then Gertrude saw that she must introduce him; but her ears, and, by sympathy, her lips, were full of all that he had been telling her. "This is the Prince," she said, "the Prince of Silberstadt-Schreckenstein!"

Felix burst out laughing, and Mr. Brand stood staring, while the others, who had passed into the house, appeared behind him in the open door-way.

III

THAT EVENING at dinner Felix Young gave his sister, the
Baroness Münster, an account of his impressions. She
saw that he had come back in the highest possible spirits; but
this fact, to her own mind, was not a reason for rejoicing.
She had but a limited confidence in her brother's judgment;
his capacity for taking rose-colored views was such as to vul-
garize one of the prettiest of tints. Still, she supposed he
could be trusted to give her the mere facts; and she invited
him with some eagerness to communicate them. "I suppose,
at least, they did n't turn you out from the door;" she said.
"You have been away some ten hours."

"Turn me from the door!" Felix exclaimed. "They took me
to their hearts; they killed the fatted calf."

"I know what you want to say: they are a collection of
angels."

"Exactly," said Felix. "They are a collection of angels—
simply."

"C'est bien vague," remarked the Baroness. "What are they
like?"

"Like nothing you ever saw."

"I am sure I am much obliged; but that is hardly more
definite. Seriously, they were glad to see you?"

"Enchanted. It has been the proudest day of my life. Never,
never have I been so lionized! I assure you, I was cock of the
walk. My dear sister," said the young man, "nous n'avons qu'à
nous tenir; we shall be great swells!"

Madame Münster looked at him, and her eye exhibited a
slight responsive spark. She touched her lips to a glass of
wine, and then she said, "Describe them. Give me a picture."

Felix drained his own glass. "Well, it 's in the country,
among the meadows and woods; a wild sort of place, and yet
not far from here. Only, such a road, my dear! Imagine one
of the Alpine glaciers reproduced in mud. But you will not
spend much time on it, for they want you to come and stay,
once for all."

"Ah," said the Baroness, "they want me to come and stay,
once for all? Bon."

"It 's intensely rural, tremendously natural; and all over-hung with this strange white light, this far-away blue sky. There 's a big wooden house—a kind of three-story bunga-low; it looks like a magnified Nüremberg toy. There was a gentleman there that made a speech to me about it and called it a 'venerable mansion;' but it looks as if it had been built last night."

"Is it handsome—is it elegant?" asked the Baroness.

Felix looked at her a moment, smiling. "It 's very clean! No splendors, no gilding, no troops of servants; rather straight-backed chairs. But you might eat off the floors, and you can sit down on the stairs."

"That must be a privilege. And the inhabitants are straight-backed too, of course."

"My dear sister," said Felix, "the inhabitants are charming."

"In what style?"

"In a style of their own. How shall I describe it? It 's prim-itive; it 's patriarchal; it 's the *ton* of the golden age."

"And have they nothing golden but their ton? Are there no symptoms of wealth?"

"I should say there was wealth without symptoms. A plain, homely way of life: nothing for show, and very little for—what shall I call it?—for the senses: but a great *aisance*, and a lot of money, out of sight, that comes forward very quietly for subscriptions to institutions, for repairing tenements, for paying doctor 's bills; perhaps even for portioning daughters."

"And the daughters?" Madame Münster demanded. "How many are there?"

"There are two, Charlotte and Gertrude."

"Are they pretty?"

"One of them," said Felix.

"Which is that?"

The young man was silent, looking at his sister. "Char-lotte," he said at last.

She looked at him in return. "I see. You are in love with Gertrude. They must be Puritans to their finger-tips; anything but gay!"

"No, they are not gay," Felix admitted. "They are sober; they are even severe. They are of a pensive cast; they take things hard. I think there is something the matter with

them; they have some melancholy memory or some depressing expectation. It 's not the epicurean temperament.
My uncle, Mr. Wentworth, is a tremendously high-toned
old fellow; he looks as if he were undergoing martyrdom,
not by fire, but by freezing. But we shall cheer them up;
we shall do them good. They will take a good deal of stirring up; but they are wonderfully kind and gentle. And
they are appreciative. They think one clever; they think one
remarkable!"

"That is very fine, so far as it goes," said the Baroness. "But
are we to be shut up to these three people, Mr. Wentworth
and the two young women—what did you say their names
were—Deborah and Hephzibah?"

"Oh, no; there is another little girl, a cousin of theirs, a
very pretty creature; a thorough little American. And then
there is the son of the house."

"Good!" said the Baroness. "We are coming to the gentlemen. What of the son of the house?"

"I am afraid he gets tipsy."

"He, then, has the epicurean temperament! How old is
he?"

"He is a boy of twenty; a pretty young fellow, but I am
afraid he has vulgar tastes. And then there is Mr. Brand—a
very tall young man, a sort of lay-priest. They seem to think
a good deal of him, but I don't exactly make him out."

"And is there nothing," asked the Baroness, "between these
extremes—this mysterious ecclesiastic and that intemperate
youth?"

"Oh, yes, there is Mr. Acton. I think," said the young man,
with a nod at his sister, "that you will like Mr. Acton."

"Remember that I am very fastidious," said the Baroness.
"Has he very good manners?"

"He will have them with you. He is a man of the world;
he has been to China."

Madame Münster gave a little laugh. "A man of the
Chinese world! He must be very interesting."

"I have an idea that he brought home a fortune," said Felix.

"That is always interesting. Is he young, good-looking,
clever?"

"He is less than forty; he has a baldish head; he says witty things. I rather think," added the young man, "that he will admire the Baroness Münster."

"It is very possible," said this lady. Her brother never knew how she would take things; but shortly afterwards she declared that he had made a very pretty description and that on the morrow she would go and see for herself.

They mounted, accordingly, into a great barouche—a vehicle as to which the Baroness found nothing to criticise but the price that was asked for it and the fact that the coachman wore a straw hat. (At Silberstadt Madame Münster had had liveries of yellow and crimson.) They drove into the country, and the Baroness, leaning far back and swaying her lace-fringed parasol, looked to right and to left and surveyed the way-side objects. After a while she pronounced them "affreux." Her brother remarked that it was apparently a country in which the foreground was inferior to the *plans reculés*: and the Baroness rejoined that the landscape seemed to be all foreground. Felix had fixed with his new friends the hour at which he should bring his sister; it was four o'clock in the afternoon. The large, clean-faced house wore, to his eyes, as the barouche drove up to it, a very friendly aspect; the high, slender elms made lengthening shadows in front of it. The Baroness descended; her American kinsfolk were stationed in the portico. Felix waved his hat to them, and a tall, lean gentleman, with a high forehead and a clean shaven face, came forward toward the garden gate. Charlotte Wentworth walked at his side. Gertrude came behind, more slowly. Both of these young ladies wore rustling silk dresses. Felix ushered his sister into the gate. "Be very gracious," he said to her. But he saw the admonition was superfluous. Eugenia was prepared to be gracious as only Eugenia could be. Felix knew no keener pleasure than to be able to admire his sister unrestrictedly; for if the opportunity was frequent, it was not inveterate. When she desired to please she was to him, as to every one else, the most charming woman in the world. Then he forgot that she was ever anything else; that she was sometimes hard and perverse; that he was occasionally afraid of her. Now, as she took his arm to pass into the garden, he felt that she desired, that she proposed, to please, and this situation made him very happy. Eugenia would please.

The tall gentleman came to meet her, looking very rigid and grave. But it was a rigidity that had no illiberal meaning. Mr. Wentworth's manner was pregnant, on the contrary, with a sense of grand responsibility, of the solemnity of the occasion, of its being difficult to show sufficient deference to a lady at once so distinguished and so unhappy. Felix had observed on the day before his characteristic pallor; and now he perceived that there was something almost cadaverous in his uncle's high-featured white face. But so clever were this young man's quick sympathies and perceptions that he already learned that in these semi-mortuary manifestations there was no cause for alarm. His light imagination had gained a glimpse of Mr. Wentworth's spiritual mechanism, and taught him that, the old man being infinitely conscientious, the special operation of conscience within him announced itself by several of the indications of physical faintness.

The Baroness took her uncle's hand, and stood looking at him with her ugly face and her beautiful smile. "Have I done right to come?" she asked.

"Very right, very right," said Mr. Wentworth, solemnly. He had arranged in his mind a little speech; but now it quite faded away. He felt almost frightened. He had never been looked at in just that way—with just that fixed, intense smile—by any woman; and it perplexed and weighed upon him, now, that the woman who was smiling so and who had instantly given him a vivid sense of her possessing other unprecedented attributes, was his own niece, the child of his own father's daughter. The idea that his niece should be a German Baroness, married "morganatically" to a Prince, had already given him much to think about. Was it right, was it just, was it acceptable? He always slept badly, and the night before he had lain awake much more even than usual, asking himself these questions. The strange word "morganatic" was constantly in his ears; it reminded him of a certain Mrs. Morgan whom he had once known and who had been a bold, unpleasant woman. He had a feeling that it was his duty, so long as the Baroness looked at him, smiling in that way, to meet her glance with his own scrupulously adjusted, consciously frigid organs of vision; but on this occasion he failed to perform his duty to the last. He looked away toward his daughters. "We are very glad to see you," he had said. "Allow me to introduce my daughters—Miss Charlotte Wentworth, Miss Gertrude Wentworth."

The Baroness thought she had never seen people less demonstrative. But Charlotte kissed her and took her hand, looking at her sweetly and solemnly. Gertrude seemed to her almost funereal, though Gertrude might have found a source of gayety in the fact that Felix, with his magnificent smile, had been talking to her; he had greeted her as a very old friend. When she kissed the Baroness she had tears in her eyes. Madame Münster took each of these young women by the hand, and looked at them all over. Charlotte thought her very strange-looking and singularly dressed; she could not have said whether it was well or ill. She was glad, at any rate, that they had put on their silk gowns—especially Gertrude. "My cousins are very pretty," said the Baroness, turning her eyes from one to the other. "Your daughters are very handsome, sir."

Charlotte blushed quickly; she had never yet heard her personal appearance alluded to in a loud, expressive voice. Gertrude looked away—not at Felix; she was extremely pleased. It was not the compliment that pleased her; she did not believe it; she thought herself very plain. She could hardly have told you the source of her satisfaction; it came from something in the way the Baroness spoke, and it was not diminished—it was rather deepened, oddly enough—by the young girl's disbelief. Mr. Wentworth was silent; and then he asked, formally, "Won't you come into the house?"

"These are not all; you have some other children," said the Baroness.

"I have a son," Mr. Wentworth answered.

"And why does n't he come to meet me?" Eugenia cried. "I am afraid he is not so charming as his sisters."

"I don't know; I will see about it," the old man declared.

"He is rather afraid of ladies," Charlotte said, softly.

"He is very handsome," said Gertrude, as loud as she could.

"We will go in and find him. We will draw him out of his *cachette*." And the Baroness took Mr. Wentworth's arm, who was not aware that he had offered it to her, and who, as they walked toward the house, wondered whether he ought to have offered it and whether it was proper for her to take it if it had not been offered. "I want to know you well," said the Baroness, interrupting these meditations, "and I want you to know me."

"It seems natural that we should know each other," Mr. Wentworth rejoined. "We are near relatives."

"Ah, there comes a moment in life when one reverts, irresistibly, to one's natural ties—to one's natural affections. You must have found that!" said Eugenia.

Mr. Wentworth had been told the day before by Felix that Eugenia was very clever, very brilliant, and the information had held him in some suspense. This was the cleverness, he supposed; the brilliancy was beginning. "Yes, the natural affections are very strong," he murmured.

"In some people," the Baroness declared. "Not in all." Charlotte was walking beside her; she took hold of her hand again, smiling always. "And you, *cousine*, where did you get that enchanting complexion?" she went on; "such lilies and roses?" The roses in poor Charlotte's countenance began speedily to predominate over the lilies, and she quickened her step and reached the portico. "This is the country of complexions," the Baroness continued, addressing herself to Mr. Wentworth. "I am convinced they are more delicate. There are very good ones in England—in Holland; but they are very apt to be coarse. There is too much red."

"I think you will find," said Mr. Wentworth, "that this country is superior in many respects to those you mention. I have been to England and Holland."

"Ah, you have been to Europe?" cried the Baroness. "Why did n't you come and see me? But it 's better, after all, this way," she said. They were entering the house; she paused and looked round her. "I see you have arranged your house—your beautiful house—in the—in the Dutch taste!"

"The house is very old," remarked Mr. Wentworth. "General Washington once spent a week here."

"Oh, I have heard of Washington," cried the Baroness. "My father used to tell me of him."

Mr. Wentworth was silent a moment, and then, "I found he was very well known in Europe," he said.

Felix had lingered in the garden with Gertrude; he was standing before her and smiling, as he had done the day before. What had happened the day before seemed to her a kind of dream. He had been there and he had changed everything; the others had seen him, they had talked with him; but that he should come again, that he should be part of the future, part of her small, familiar, much-meditating life—this needed, afresh, the evidence of her senses. The evidence had come to her senses now; and her senses seemed to rejoice in it. "What do you think of Eugenia?" Felix asked. "Is n't she charming?"

"She is very brilliant," said Gertrude. "But I can't tell yet. She seems to me like a singer singing an air. You can't tell till the song is done."

"Ah, the song will never be done!" exclaimed the young man, laughing. "Don't you think her handsome?"

Gertrude had been disappointed in the beauty of the Baroness Münster; she had expected her, for mysterious reasons, to resemble a very pretty portrait of the Empress Josephine, of which there hung an engraving in one of the parlors, and which the younger Miss Wentworth had always greatly admired. But the Baroness was not at all like that—not at all. Though different, however, she was very wonderful, and Gertrude felt herself most suggestively corrected. It was strange, nevertheless, that Felix should speak in that positive way about his sister's beauty. "I think I *shall* think her handsome," Gertrude said. "It must be very interesting to know her. I don't feel as if I ever could."

"Ah, you will know her well; you will become great friends," Felix declared, as if this were the easiest thing in the world.

"She is very graceful," said Gertrude, looking after the Baroness, suspended to her father's arm. It was a pleasure to her to say that any one was graceful.

Felix had been looking about him. "And your little cousin, of yesterday," he said, "who was so wonderfully pretty—what has become of her?"

"She is in the parlor," Gertrude answered. "Yes, she is very pretty." She felt as if it were her duty to take him straight into the house, to where he might be near her cousin. But after hesitating a moment she lingered still. "I did n't believe you would come back," she said.

"Not come back!" cried Felix, laughing. "You did n't know, then, the impression made upon this susceptible heart of mine."

She wondered whether he meant the impression her cousin Lizzie had made. "Well," she said, "I did n't think we should ever see you again."

"And pray what did you think would become of me?"

"I don't know. I thought you would melt away."

"That 's a compliment to my solidity! I melt very often," said Felix, "but there is always something left of me."

"I came and waited for you by the door, because the others did," Gertrude went on. "But if you had never appeared I should not have been surprised."

"I hope," declared Felix, looking at her, "that you would have been disappointed."

She looked at him a little, and shook her head. "No—no!"

"Ah, *par exemple!*" cried the young man. "You deserve that I should never leave you."

Going into the parlor they found Mr. Wentworth performing introductions. A young man was standing before the Baroness, blushing a good deal, laughing a little, and shifting his weight from one foot to the other—a slim, mild-faced young man, with neatly-arranged features, like those of Mr. Wentworth. Two other gentlemen, behind him, had risen from their seats, and a little apart, near one of the windows, stood a remarkably pretty young girl. The young girl was knitting a stocking; but, while her fingers quickly moved, she looked with wide, brilliant eyes at the Baroness.

"And what is your son's name?" said Eugenia, smiling at the young man.

"My name is Clifford Wentworth, ma'am," he said in a tremulous voice.

"Why did n't you come out to meet me, Mr. Clifford Wentworth?" the Baroness demanded, with her beautiful smile.

"I did n't think you would want me," said the young man, slowly sidling about.

"One always wants a *beau cousin*,—if one has one! But if you are very nice to me in future I won't remember it against you." And Madame Münster transferred her smile to the other persons present. It rested first upon the candid countenance and long-skirted figure of Mr. Brand, whose eyes were intently fixed upon Mr. Wentworth, as if to beg him not to prolong an anomalous situation. Mr. Wentworth pronounced his name. Eugenia gave him a very charming glance, and then looked at the other gentleman.

This latter personage was a man of rather less than the usual stature and the usual weight, with a quick, observant, agreeable dark eye, a small quantity of thin dark hair, and a small mustache. He had been standing with his hands in his pockets; and when Eugenia looked at him he took them out. But he did not, like Mr. Brand, look evasively and urgently at their host. He met Eugenia's eyes; he appeared to appreciate the privilege of meeting them. Madame Münster instantly felt that he was, intrinsically, the most important person present. She was not unconscious that this impression was in some degree manifested in the little sympathetic nod with which she acknowledged Mr. Wentworth's announcement, "My cousin, Mr. Acton!"

"Your cousin—not mine?" said the Baroness.

"It only depends upon you," Mr. Acton declared, laughing.

The Baroness looked at him a moment, and noticed that he had very white teeth. "Let it depend upon your behavior," she said. "I think I had better wait. I have cousins enough. Unless I can also claim relationship," she added, "with that charming young lady," and she pointed to the young girl at the window.

"That 's my sister," said Mr. Acton. And Gertrude Wentworth put her arm round the young girl and led her forward. It was not, apparently, that she needed much leading. She came toward the Baroness with a light, quick step, and with perfect self-possession, rolling her stocking round its needles. She had dark blue eyes and dark brown hair; she was wonderfully pretty.

Eugenia kissed her, as she had kissed the other young women, and then held her off a little, looking at her. "Now this is quite another *type*," she said; she pronounced the word in the French manner. "This is a different outline, my uncle, a different character, from that of your own daughters. This,

Felix," she went on, "is very much more what we have always thought of as the American type."

The young girl, during this exposition, was smiling askance at every one in turn, and at Felix out of turn. "I find only one type here!" cried Felix, laughing. "The type adorable!"

This sally was received in perfect silence, but Felix, who learned all things quickly, had already learned that the silences frequently observed among his new acquaintances were not necessarily restrictive or resentful. It was, as one might say, the silence of expectation, of modesty. They were all standing round his sister, as if they were expecting her to acquit herself of the exhibition of some peculiar faculty, some brilliant talent. Their attitude seemed to imply that she was a kind of conversational mountebank, attired, intellectually, in gauze and spangles. This attitude gave a certain ironical force to Madame Münster's next words. "Now this is your circle," she said to her uncle. "This is your *salon*. These are your regular habitués, eh? I am so glad to see you all together."

"Oh," said Mr. Wentworth, "they are always dropping in and out. You must do the same."

"Father," interposed Charlotte Wentworth, "they must do something more." And she turned her sweet, serious face, that seemed at once timid and placid, upon their interesting visitor. "What is your name?" she asked.

"Eugenia-Camilla-Dolores," said the Baroness, smiling. "But you need n't say all that."

"I will say Eugenia, if you will let me. You must come and stay with us."

The Baroness laid her hand upon Charlotte's arm very tenderly; but she reserved herself. She was wondering whether it would be possible to "stay" with these people. "It would be very charming—very charming," she said; and her eyes wandered over the company, over the room. She wished to gain time before committing herself. Her glance fell upon young Mr. Brand, who stood there, with his arms folded and his hand on his chin, looking at her. "The gentleman, I suppose, is a sort of ecclesiastic," she said to Mr. Wentworth, lowering her voice a little.

"He is a minister," answered Mr. Wentworth.

"A Protestant?" asked Eugenia.

"I am a Unitarian, madam," replied Mr. Brand, impressively.

"Ah, I see," said Eugenia. "Something new." She had never heard of this form of worship.

Mr. Acton began to laugh, and Gertrude looked anxiously at Mr. Brand.

"You have come very far," said Mr. Wentworth.

"Very far—very far," the Baroness replied, with a graceful shake of her head—a shake that might have meant many different things.

"That 's a reason why you ought to settle down with us," said Mr. Wentworth, with that dryness of utterance which, as Eugenia was too intelligent not to feel, took nothing from the delicacy of his meaning.

She looked at him, and for an instant, in his cold, still face, she seemed to see a far-away likeness to the vaguely remembered image of her mother. Eugenia was a woman of sudden emotions, and now, unexpectedly, she felt one rising in her heart. She kept looking round the circle; she knew that there was admiration in all the eyes that were fixed upon her. She smiled at them all.

"I came to look—to try—to ask," she said. "It seems to me I have done well. I am very tired; I want to rest." There were tears in her eyes. The luminous interior, the gentle, tranquil people, the simple, serious life—the sense of these things pressed upon her with an overmastering force, and she felt herself yielding to one of the most genuine emotions she had ever known. "I should like to stay here," she said. "Pray take me in."

Though she was smiling, there were tears in her voice as well as in her eyes. "My dear niece," said Mr. Wentworth, softly. And Charlotte put out her arms and drew the Baroness toward her; while Robert Acton turned away, with his hands stealing into his pockets.

IV

A FEW DAYS after the Baroness Münster had presented herself to her American kinsfolk she came, with her brother, and took up her abode in that small white house adjacent to Mr. Wentworth's own dwelling of which mention has already been made. It was on going with his daughters to return her visit that Mr. Wentworth placed this comfortable cottage at her service; the offer being the result of a domestic colloquy, diffused through the ensuing twenty-four hours, in the course of which the two foreign visitors were discussed and analyzed with a great deal of earnestness and subtlety. The discussion went forward, as I say, in the family circle; but that circle on the evening following Madame Münster's return to town, as on many other occasions, included Robert Acton and his pretty sister. If you had been present, it would probably not have seemed to you that the advent of these brilliant strangers was treated as an exhilarating occurrence, a pleasure the more in this tranquil household, a prospective source of entertainment. This was not Mr. Wentworth's way of treating any human occurrence. The sudden irruption into the well-ordered consciousness of the Wentworths of an element not allowed for in its scheme of usual obligations required a readjustment of that sense of responsibility which constituted its principal furniture. To consider an event, crudely and baldly, in the light of the pleasure it might bring them was an intellectual exercise with which Felix Young's American cousins were almost wholly unacquainted, and which they scarcely supposed to be largely pursued in any section of human society. The arrival of Felix and his sister was a satisfaction, but it was a singularly joyless and inelastic satisfaction. It was an extension of duty, of the exercise of the more recondite virtues; but neither Mr. Wentworth, nor Charlotte, nor Mr. Brand, who, among these excellent people, was a great promoter of reflection and aspiration, frankly adverted to it as an extension of enjoyment. This function was ultimately assumed by Gertrude Wentworth, who was a peculiar girl, but the full compass of whose peculiarities had not been exhibited before they very ingeniously found their pretext in the presence of these possibly too agreeable foreigners. Gertrude, however, had to struggle with a great accumulation of obstructions, both of the subjective, as the metaphysicians say, and of the objective, order; and indeed it is no small part of the purpose of this little history to set forth her struggle. What seemed paramount in this abrupt enlargement of Mr. Wentworth's sympathies and those of his daughters was an extension of the field of possible mistakes; and the doctrine, as it may almost be called, of the oppressive gravity of mistakes was one of the most cherished traditions of the Wentworth family.

"I don't believe she wants to come and stay in this house," said Gertrude; Madame Münster, from this time forward, receiving no other designation than the personal pronoun. Charlotte and Gertrude acquired considerable facility in addressing her, directly, as "Eugenia;" but in speaking of her to each other they rarely called her anything but "she."

"Does n't she think it good enough for her?" cried little Lizzie Acton, who was always asking unpractical questions that required, in strictness, no answer, and to which indeed she expected no other answer than such as she herself invariably furnished in a small, innocently-satirical laugh.

"She certainly expressed a willingness to come," said Mr. Wentworth.

"That was only politeness," Gertrude rejoined.

"Yes, she is very polite—very polite," said Mr. Wentworth.

"She is too polite," his son declared, in a softly growling tone which was habitual to him, but which was an indication of nothing worse than a vaguely humorous intention. "It is very embarrassing."

"That is more than can be said of you, sir," said Lizzie Acton, with her little laugh.

"Well, I don't mean to encourage her," Clifford went on.

"I 'm sure I don't care if you do!" cried Lizzie.

"She will not think of you, Clifford," said Gertrude, gravely.

"I hope not!" Clifford exclaimed.

"She will think of Robert," Gertrude continued, in the same tone.

Robert Acton began to blush; but there was no occasion

for it, for every one was looking at Gertrude—every one, at least, save Lizzie, who, with her pretty head on one side, contemplated her brother.

"Why do you attribute motives, Gertrude?" asked Mr. Wentworth.

"I don't attribute motives, father," said Gertrude. "I only say she will think of Robert; and she will!"

"Gertrude judges by herself!" Acton exclaimed, laughing. "Don't you, Gertrude? Of course the Baroness will think of me. She will think of me from morning till night."

"She will be very comfortable here," said Charlotte, with something of a housewife's pride. "She can have the large northeast room. And the French bedstead," Charlotte added, with a constant sense of the lady's foreignness.

"She will not like it," said Gertrude; "not even if you pin little tidies all over the chairs."

"Why not, dear?" asked Charlotte, perceiving a touch of irony here, but not resenting it.

Gertrude had left her chair; she was walking about the room; her stiff silk dress, which she had put on in honor of the Baroness, made a sound upon the carpet. "I don't know," she replied. "She will want something more—more private."

"If she wants to be private she can stay in her room," Lizzie Acton remarked.

Gertrude paused in her walk, looking at her. "That would not be pleasant," she answered. "She wants privacy and pleasure together."

Robert Acton began to laugh again. "My dear cousin, what a picture!"

Charlotte had fixed her serious eyes upon her sister; she wondered whence she had suddenly derived these strange notions. Mr. Wentworth also observed his younger daughter.

"I don't know what her manner of life may have been," he said; "but she certainly never can have enjoyed a more refined and salubrious home."

Gertrude stood there looking at them all. "She is the wife of a Prince," she said.

"We are all princes here," said Mr. Wentworth; "and I don't know of any palace in this neighborhood that is to let."

"Cousin William," Robert Acton interposed, "do you want

to do something handsome? Make them a present, for three months, of the little house over the way."

"You are very generous with other people's things!" cried his sister.

"Robert is very generous with his own things," Mr. Wentworth observed dispassionately, and looking, in cold meditation, at his kinsman.

"Gertrude," Lizzie went on, "I had an idea you were so fond of your new cousin."

"Which new cousin?" asked Gertrude.

"I don't mean the Baroness!" the young girl rejoined, with her laugh. "I thought you expected to see so much of him."

"Of Felix? I hope to see a great deal of him," said Gertrude, simply.

"Then why do you want to keep him out of the house?"

Gertrude looked at Lizzie Acton, and then looked away.

"Should you want me to live in the house with you, Lizzie?" asked Clifford.

"I hope you never will. I hate you!" Such was this young lady's reply.

"Father," said Gertrude, stopping before Mr. Wentworth and smiling, with a smile the sweeter, as her smile always was, for its rarity; "do let them live in the little house over the way. It will be lovely!"

Robert Acton had been watching her. "Gertrude is right," he said. "Gertrude is the cleverest girl in the world. If I might take the liberty, I should strongly recommend their living there."

"There is nothing there so pretty as the northeast room," Charlotte urged.

"She will make it pretty. Leave her alone!" Acton exclaimed.

Gertrude, at his compliment, had blushed and looked at him: it was as if some one less familiar had complimented her. "I am sure she will make it pretty. It will be very interesting. It will be a place to go to. It will be a foreign house."

"Are we very sure that we need a foreign house?" Mr. Wentworth inquired. "Do you think it desirable to establish a foreign house—in this quiet place?"

"You speak," said Acton, laughing, "as if it were a question of the poor Baroness opening a wine-shop or a gaming-table."

"It would be too lovely!" Gertrude declared again, laying her hand on the back of her father's chair.

"That she should open a gaming-table?" Charlotte asked, with great gravity.

Gertrude looked at her a moment, and then, "Yes, Charlotte," she said, simply.

"Gertrude is growing pert," Clifford Wentworth observed, with his humorous young growl. "That comes of associating with foreigners."

Mr. Wentworth looked up at his daughter, who was standing beside him; he drew her gently forward. "You must be careful," he said. "You must keep watch. Indeed, we must all be careful. This is a great change; we are to be exposed to peculiar influences. I don't say they are bad. I don't judge them in advance. But they may perhaps make it necessary that we should exercise a great deal of wisdom and self-control. It will be a different tone."

Gertrude was silent a moment, in deference to her father's speech; then she spoke in a manner that was not in the least an answer to it. "I want to see how they will live. I am sure they will have different hours. She will do all kinds of little things differently. When we go over there it will be like going to Europe. She will have a boudoir. She will invite us to dinner—very late. She will breakfast in her room."

Charlotte gazed at her sister again. Gertrude's imagination seemed to her to be fairly running riot. She had always known that Gertrude had a great deal of imagination—she had been very proud of it. But at the same time she had always felt that it was a dangerous and irresponsible faculty; and now, to her sense, for the moment, it seemed to threaten to make her sister a strange person who should come in suddenly, as from a journey, talking of the peculiar and possibly unpleasant things she had observed. Charlotte's imagination took no journeys whatever; she kept it, as it were, in her pocket, with the other furniture of this receptacle—a thimble, a little box of peppermint, and a morsel of court-plaster. "I don't believe she would have any dinner—or any breakfast," said Miss Wentworth. "I don't believe she knows how to do anything herself. I should have to get her ever so many servants, and she would n't like them."

"She has a maid," said Gertrude; "a French maid. She mentioned her."

"I wonder if the maid has a little fluted cap and red slippers," said Lizzie Acton. "There was a French maid in that play that Robert took me to see. She had pink stockings; she was very wicked."

"She was a *soubrette*," Gertrude announced, who had never seen a play in her life. "They call that a soubrette. It will be a great chance to learn French." Charlotte gave a little soft, helpless groan. She had a vision of a wicked, theatrical person, clad in pink stockings and red shoes, and speaking, with confounding volubility, an incomprehensible tongue, flitting through the sacred penetralia of that large, clean house. "That is one reason in favor of their coming here," Gertrude went on. "But we can make Eugenia speak French to us, and Felix. I mean to begin—the next time."

Mr. Wentworth had kept her standing near him, and he gave her his earnest, thin, unresponsive glance again. "I want you to make me a promise, Gertrude," he said.

"What is it?" she asked, smiling.

"Not to get excited. Not to allow these—these occurrences to be an occasion for excitement."

She looked down at him a moment, and then she shook her head. "I don't think I can promise that, father. I am excited already."

Mr. Wentworth was silent a while; they all were silent, as if in recognition of something audacious and portentous.

"I think they had better go to the other house," said Charlotte, quietly.

"I shall keep them in the other house," Mr. Wentworth subjoined, more pregnantly.

Gertrude turned away; then she looked across at Robert Acton. Her cousin Robert was a great friend of hers; she often looked at him this way instead of saying things. Her glance on this occasion, however, struck him as a substitute for a larger volume of diffident utterance than usual, inviting him to observe, among other things, the inefficiency of her father's design—if design it was—for diminishing, in the interest of quiet nerves, their occasions of contact with their foreign relatives. But Acton immediately complimented Mr. Wentworth upon his liberality. "That 's a very nice thing to do," he said, "giving them the little house. You will have treated them handsomely, and, whatever happens, you will be glad of it." Mr. Wentworth was liberal, and he knew he was liberal. It gave him pleasure to know it, to feel it, to see it recorded; and this pleasure is the only palpable form of self-indulgence with which the narrator of these incidents will be able to charge him.

"A three days' visit at most, over there, is all I should have found possible," Madame Münster remarked to her brother, after they had taken possession of the little white house. "It would have been too *intime*—decidedly too intime. Break-fast, dinner, and tea *en famille*—it would have been the end of the world if I could have reached the third day." And she made the same observation to her maid Augustine, an intelligent person, who enjoyed a liberal share of her confidence. Felix declared that he would willingly spend his life in the bosom of the Wentworth family; that they were the kindest, simplest, most amiable people in the world, and that he had taken a prodigious fancy to them all. The Baroness quite agreed with him that they were simple and kind; they were thoroughly nice people, and she liked them extremely. The girls were perfect ladies; it was impossible to be more of a lady than Charlotte Wentworth, in spite of her little village air. "But as for thinking them the best company in the world," said the Baroness, "that is another thing; and as for wishing to live *porte à porte* with them, I should as soon think of wishing myself back in the convent again, to wear a bom-bazine apron and sleep in a dormitory." And yet the Baroness was in high good humor; she had been very much pleased. With her lively perception and her refined imagination, she was capable of enjoying anything that was characteristic, anything that was good of its kind. The Wentworth household seemed to her very perfect in its kind—wonderfully peaceful and unspotted; pervaded by a sort of dove-colored freshness that had all the quietude and benevolence of what she deemed to be Quakerism, and yet seemed to be founded upon a degree of material abundance for which, in certain matters of detail, one might have looked in vain at the frugal little court of Silberstadt-Schreckenstein. She perceived immediately that her American relatives thought and talked very little about money; and this of itself made an impression upon Eugenia's imagination. She perceived at the same time that if Charlotte or Gertrude should ask their father for a very considerable sum he would at once place it in their hands; and this made a still greater impression. The greatest impression of all, perhaps, was made by another rapid induction. The Baroness had an immediate conviction that Robert Acton would put his hand into his pocket every day in the week if that rattle-pated little sister of his should bid him. The men in this country, said the Baroness, are evidently very obliging. Her declaration that she was looking for rest and retirement had been by no means wholly untrue; nothing that the Baroness said was wholly untrue. It is but fair to add, perhaps, that nothing that she said was wholly true. She wrote to a friend in Germany that it was a return to nature; it was like drinking new milk, and she was very fond of new milk. She said to herself, of course, that it would be a little dull; but there can be no better proof of her good spirits than the fact that she thought she should not mind its being a little dull. It seemed to her, when from the piazza of her eleemosynary cottage she looked out over the soundless fields, the stony pastures, the clear-faced ponds, the rugged little orchards, that she had never been in the midst of so peculiarly intense a stillness; it was almost a delicate sensual pleasure. It was all very good, very innocent and safe, and out of it something good must come. Augustine, indeed, who had an unbounded faith in her mistress's wisdom and far-sightedness, was a great deal perplexed and depressed. She was always ready to take her cue when she understood it; but she liked to understand it, and on this occasion comprehension failed. What, indeed, was the Baroness doing *dans cette galère*? what fish did she expect to land out of these very stagnant waters? The game was evidently a deep one. Augustine could trust her; but the sense of walking in the dark betrayed itself in the physiognomy of this spare, sober, sallow, middle-aged person, who had nothing in common with Gertrude Wentworth's conception of a soubrette, by the most ironical scowl that had ever rested upon the unpretending tokens of the peace and plenty of the Wentworths. Fortunately, Augustine could quench skepticism in action. She quite agreed with her mistress—or rather she quite out-stripped her mistress—in thinking that the little white house was pitifully bare. "Il faudra," said Augustine, "lui faire un peu de toilette." And she began to hang up *portières* in the doorways; to place wax candles, procured after some research, in unexpected situations; to dispose anomalous draperies over the arms of sofas and the backs of chairs. The Baroness had brought with her to the New World a copious provision of the element of costume; and the two Miss Wentworths, when they came over to see her, were somewhat bewildered by the obtrusive distribution of her wardrobe. There were India shawls suspended, curtain-wise, in the parlor door, and curi-ous fabrics, corresponding to Gertrude's metaphysical vision of an opera-cloak, tumbled about in the sitting-places. There were pink silk blinds in the windows, by which the room was strangely bedimmed; and along the chimney-piece was dis-posed a remarkable band of velvet, covered with coarse, dirty-looking lace. "I have been making myself a little comfortable," said the Baroness, much to the confusion of Charlotte, who had been on the point of proposing to come and help her put her superfluous draperies away. But what Charlotte mistook for an almost culpably delayed subsidence Gertrude very pres-ently perceived to be the most ingenious, the most interest-ing, the most romantic intention. "What is life, indeed, without curtains?" she secretly asked herself; and she ap-peared to herself to have been leading hitherto an existence singularly garish and totally devoid of festoons.

Felix was not a young man who troubled himself greatly about anything—least of all about the conditions of enjoy-ment. His faculty of enjoyment was so large, so unconsciously eager, that it may be said of it that it had a permanent ad-vance upon embarrassment and sorrow. His sentient faculty was intrinsically joyous, and novelty and change were in themselves a delight to him. As they had come to him with a great deal of frequency, his life had been more agreeable than appeared. Never was a nature more perfectly fortunate. It was not a restless, apprehensive, ambitious spirit, running a race with the tyranny of fate, but a temper so unsuspicious as to put Adversity off her guard, dodging and evading her with the easy, natural motion of a wind-shifted flower. Felix extracted entertainment from all things, and all his faculties—his imagination, his intelligence, his affections, his senses—had a hand in the game. It seemed to him that Eugenia and he had been very well treated; there was something absolutely touching in that combination of paternal liberality and social considerateness which marked Mr. Wentworth's deportment. It was most uncommonly kind of him, for instance, to have given them a house. Felix was positively amused at having a house of his own; for the little white cottage among the apple-trees—the chalet, as Madame Münster always called it—was much more sensibly his own than any domiciliary *quatrième*, looking upon a court, with the rent overdue. Felix had spent a good deal of his life in looking into courts, with a perhaps slightly tattered pair of elbows resting upon the ledge of a high-perched window, and the thin smoke of a cigarette rising into an atmosphere in which street-cries died away and the vibration of chimes from ancient belfries became sensible. He had never known anything so infinitely rural as these New England fields; and he took a great fancy to all their pastoral roughnesses. He had never had a greater sense of luxurious security; and at the risk of making him seem a rather sordid adventurer I must declare that he found an irresistible charm in the fact that he might dine every day at his uncle's. The charm was irresistible, however, because his fancy flung a rosy light over this homely privilege. He appreciated highly the fare that was set before him. There was a kind of fresh-looking abundance about it which made him think that people must have lived so in the mythological era, when they spread their tables upon the grass, replenished them from cornucopias, and had no particular need of kitchen stoves. But the great thing that Felix enjoyed was having found a family—sitting in the midst of gentle, generous people whom he might call by their first names. He had never known anything more charming than the attention they paid to what he said. It was like a large sheet of clean, fine-grained drawing-paper, all ready to be washed over with effective splashes of water-color. He had never had any cousins, and he had never before found himself in contact so unrestricted with young unmarried ladies. He was extremely fond of the society of ladies, and it was new to him that it might be enjoyed in just this manner. At first he hardly knew what to make of his state of mind. It seemed to him that he was in love, indiscriminately, with three girls at once. He saw that Lizzie Acton was more brilliantly pretty than Charlotte and Gertrude; but this was scarcely a superiority. His pleasure came from something they had in common—a part of which was, indeed, that physical delicacy which seemed to make it proper that they should always dress in thin materials and clear colors. But they were delicate in other ways, and it was most agreeable to him to feel that these latter delicacies were appreciable by contact, as it were. He had known, fortunately, many virtuous gentlewomen, but it now appeared to him that in his relations with them (especially when they were unmarried) he had been looking at pictures under glass. He perceived at present what a nuisance the glass had been—how it perverted and interfered, how it caught the reflection of other objects and kept you walking from side to side. He had no need to ask himself whether Charlotte and Gertrude, and Lizzie Acton, were in the right light; they were always in the right light. He liked everything about them: he was, for instance, not at all above liking the fact that they had very slender feet and high insteps. He liked their pretty noses; he liked their surprised eyes and their hesitating, not at all positive way of speaking; he liked so much knowing that he was perfectly at liberty to be alone for hours, anywhere, with either of them; that preference for one to the other, as a companion of solitude, remained a minor affair. Charlotte Wentworth's sweetly severe features were as agreeable as Lizzie Acton's wonderfully expressive blue eyes; and Gertrude's air of being always ready to walk about and listen was as charming as anything else, especially as she walked very gracefully. After a while Felix began to distinguish; but even then he would often wish, suddenly, that they were not all so sad. Even Lizzie Acton, in spite of her fine little chatter and laughter, appeared sad. Even Clifford Wentworth, who had extreme youth in his favor, and kept a buggy with enormous wheels and a little sorrel mare with the prettiest legs in the world—even this fortunate lad was apt to have an averted, uncomfortable glance, and to edge away from you at times, in the manner of a person with a bad conscience. The only person in the circle with no sense of oppression of any kind was, to Felix's perception, Robert Acton.

It might perhaps have been feared that after the completion of those graceful domiciliary embellishments which have been mentioned Madame Münster would have found herself confronted with alarming possibilities of *ennui*. But as yet she had not taken the alarm. The Baroness was a restless soul, and she projected her restlessness, as it may be said, into any situation that lay before her. Up to a certain point her restlessness might be counted upon to entertain her. She was always expecting something to happen, and, until it was disappointed, expectancy itself was a delicate pleasure. What the Baroness expected just now it would take some ingenuity to set forth; it is enough that while she looked about her she found something to occupy her imagination. She assured herself that she was enchanted with her new relatives; she professed to herself that, like her brother, she felt it a sacred satisfaction to have found a family. It is certain that she enjoyed to the utmost the gentleness of her kinsfolk's deference. She had, first and last, received a great deal of admiration, and her experience of well-turned compliments was very considerable; but she knew that she had never been so real a power, never counted for so much, as now when, for the first time, the standard of comparison of her little circle was a prey to vagueness. The sense, indeed, that the good people about her had, as regards her remarkable self, no standard of comparison at all gave her a feeling of almost illimitable power. It was true, as she said to herself, that if for this reason they would be able to discover nothing against her, so they would perhaps neglect to perceive some of her superior points; but she always wound up her reflections by declaring that she would take care of that.

Charlotte and Gertrude were in some perplexity between their desire to show all proper attention to Madame Münster and their fear of being importunate. The little house in the orchard had hitherto been occupied during the summer months by intimate friends of the family, or by poor relations who found in Mr. Wentworth a landlord attentive to repairs and oblivious of quarter-day. Under these circumstances the open door of the small house and that of the large one, facing each other across their homely gardens, levied no tax upon hourly visits. But the Misses Wentworth received an impression that Eugenia was no friend to the primitive custom of "dropping in;" she evidently had no idea of living without a door-keeper. "One goes into your house as into an inn—except that there are no servants rushing forward," she said to Charlotte. And she added that that was very charming. Gertrude explained to her sister that she meant just the reverse; she did n't like it at all. Charlotte inquired why she should tell an untruth, and Gertrude answered that there was probably some very good reason for it which they should discover when they knew her better. "There can surely be no good reason for telling an untruth," said Charlotte. "I hope she does not think so."

They had of course desired, from the first, to do everything in the way of helping her to arrange herself. It had seemed to Charlotte that there would be a great many things to talk about; but the Baroness was apparently inclined to talk about nothing.

"Write her a note, asking her leave to come and see her. I think that is what she will like," said Gertrude.

"Why should I give her the trouble of answering me?" Charlotte asked. "She will have to write a note and send it over."

"I don't think she will take any trouble," said Gertrude, profoundly.

"What then will she do?"

"That is what I am curious to see," said Gertrude, leaving her sister with an impression that her curiosity was morbid.

They went to see the Baroness without preliminary correspondence; and in the little salon which she had already created, with its becoming light and its festoons, they found Robert Acton.

Eugenia was intensely gracious, but she accused them of neglecting her cruelly. "You see Mr. Acton has had to take pity upon me," she said. "My brother goes off sketching, for hours; I can never depend upon him. So I was to send Mr. Acton to beg you to come and give me the benefit of your wisdom."

Gertrude looked at her sister. She wanted to say, "*That* is what she would have done." Charlotte said that they hoped the Baroness would always come and dine with them; it would give them so much pleasure; and, in that case, she would spare herself the trouble of having a cook.

"Ah, but I must have a cook!" cried the Baroness. "An old negress in a yellow turban. I have set my heart upon that. I want to look out of my window and see her sitting there on the grass, against the background of those crooked, dusky little apple-trees, pulling the husks off a lapful of Indian corn. That will be local color, you know. There is n't much of it here—you don't mind my saying that, do you?—so one must make the most of what one can get. I shall be most happy to dine with you whenever you will let me; but I want to be able to ask you sometimes. And I want to be able to ask Mr. Acton," added the Baroness.

"You must come and ask me at home," said Acton. "You must come and see me; you must dine with me first. I want to show you my place; I want to introduce you to my mother." He called again upon Madame Münster, two days later. He was constantly at the other house; he used to walk across the fields from his own place, and he appeared to have fewer scruples than his cousins with regard to dropping in. On this occasion he found that Mr. Brand had come to pay his respects to the charming stranger; but after Acton's arrival the young theologian said nothing. He sat in his chair with his two hands clasped, fixing upon his hostess a grave, fascinated stare. The Baroness talked to Robert Acton, but, as she talked, she turned and smiled at Mr. Brand, who never took his eyes off her. The two men walked away together; they were going to Mr. Wentworth's. Mr. Brand still said nothing; but after they had passed into Mr. Wentworth's garden he stopped and looked back for some time at the little white house. Then, looking at his companion, with his head bent a little to one side and his eyes somewhat contracted, "Now I suppose that 's what is called conversation," he said; "real conversation."

"It 's what I call a very clever woman," said Acton, laughing.

"It is most interesting," Mr. Brand continued. "I only wish she would speak French; it would seem more in keeping. It must be quite the style that we have heard about, that we have read about—the style of conversation of Madame de Staël, of Madame Récamier."

Acton also looked at Madame Münster's residence among its hollyhocks and apple-trees. "What I should like to know," he said, smiling, "is just what has brought Madame Récamier to live in that place!"

V

Mr. WENTWORTH, with his cane and his gloves in his hand, went every afternoon to call upon his niece. A couple of hours later she came over to the great house to tea. She had let the proposal that she should regularly dine there fall to the ground; she was in the enjoyment of whatever satisfaction was to be derived from the spectacle of an old negress in a crimson turban shelling peas under the apple-trees. Charlotte, who had provided the ancient negress, thought it must be a strange household, Eugenia having told her that Augustine managed everything, the ancient negress included—Augustine who was naturally devoid of all acquaintance with the expurgatory English tongue. By far the most immoral sentiment which I shall have occasion to attribute to Charlotte Wentworth was a certain emotion of disappointment at finding that, in spite of these irregular conditions, the domestic arrangements at the small house were apparently not—from Eugenia's peculiar point of view—strikingly offensive. The Baroness found it amusing to go to tea; she dressed as if for dinner. The tea-table offered an anomalous and picturesque repast; and on leaving it they all sat and talked in the large piazza, or wandered about the garden in the starlight, with their ears full of those sounds of strange insects which, though they are supposed to be, all over the world, a part of the magic of summer nights, seemed to the Baroness to have beneath these western skies an incomparable resonance.

Mr. Wentworth, though, as I say, he went punctiliously to call upon her, was not able to feel that he was getting used to his niece. It taxed his imagination to believe that she was really his half-sister's child. His sister was a figure of his early years; she had been only twenty when she went abroad, never to return, making in foreign parts a willful and undesirable marriage. His aunt, Mrs. Whiteside, who had taken her to Europe for the benefit of the tour, gave, on her return, so lamentable an account of Mr. Adolphus Young, to whom the headstrong girl had united her destiny, that it operated as a chill upon family feeling—especially in the case of the half-brothers. Catherine had done nothing subsequently to propitiate her family; she had not even written to them in a way that indicated a lucid appreciation of their suspended sympathy; so that it had become a tradition in Boston circles that the highest charity, as regards this young lady, was to think it well to forget her, and to abstain from conjecture as to the extent to which her aberrations were reproduced in her descendants. Over these young people—a vague report of their existence had come to his ears—Mr. Wentworth had not, in the course of years, allowed his imagination to hover. It had plenty of occupation nearer home, and though he had many cares upon his conscience the idea that he had been an unnatural uncle was, very properly, never among the number. Now that his nephew and niece had come before him, he perceived that they were the fruit of influences and circumstances very different from those under which his own familiar progeny had reached a vaguely-qualified maturity. He felt no provocation to say that these influences had been exerted for evil; but he was sometimes afraid that he should not be able to like his distinguished, delicate, lady-like niece. He was paralyzed and bewildered by her foreignness. She spoke, somehow, a different language. There was something strange in her words. He had a feeling that another man, in his place, would accommodate himself to her tone; would ask her questions and joke with her, reply to those pleasantries of her own which sometimes seemed startling as addressed to an uncle. But Mr. Wentworth could not do these things. He could not even bring himself to attempt to measure her position in the world. She was the wife of a foreign nobleman who desired to repudiate her. This had a singular sound, but the old man felt himself destitute of the materials for a judgment. It seemed to him that he ought to find them in his own experience, as a man of the world and an almost public character; but they were not there, and he was ashamed to confess to himself—much more to reveal to Eugenia by interrogations possibly too innocent—the unfurnished condition of this repository.

It appeared to him that he could get much nearer, as he would have said, to his nephew; though he was not sure that Felix was altogether safe. He was so bright and handsome and talkative that it was impossible not to think well of him; and yet it seemed as if there were something almost impudent, almost vicious—or as if there ought to be—in a young man being at once so joyous and so positive. It was to be observed that while Felix was not at all a serious young man there was somehow more of him—he had more weight and volume and resonance—than a number of young men who were distinctly serious. While Mr. Wentworth meditated upon this anomaly his nephew was admiring him unrestrictedly. He thought him a most delicate, generous, high-toned old gentleman, with a very handsome head, of the ascetic type, which he promised himself the profit of sketching. Felix was far from having made a secret of the fact that he wielded the paint-brush, and it was not his own fault if it failed to be generally understood that he was prepared to execute the most striking likenesses on the most reasonable terms. "He is an artist—my cousin is an artist," said Gertrude; and she offered this information to every one who would receive it. She offered it to herself, as it were, by way of admonition and reminder; she repeated to herself at odd moments, in lonely places, that Felix was invested with this sacred character. Gertrude had never seen an artist before; she had only read about such people. They seemed to her a romantic and mysterious class, whose life was made up of those agreeable accidents that never happened to other persons. And it merely quickened her meditations on this point that Felix should declare, as he repeatedly did, that he was really not an artist. "I have never gone into the thing seriously," he said. "I have never studied; I have had no training. I do a little of everything, and nothing well. I am only an amateur."

It pleased Gertrude even more to think that he was an amateur than to think that he was an artist; the former word, to her fancy, had an even subtler connotation. She knew, however, that it was a word to use more soberly. Mr. Wentworth used it freely; for though he had not been exactly familiar with it, he found it convenient as a help toward classifying Felix, who, as a young man extremely clever and active and apparently respectable and yet not engaged in any recognized business, was an importunate anomaly. Of course the Baroness and her brother—she was always spoken of first—were a welcome topic of conversation between Mr. Wentworth and his daughters and their occasional visitors.

"And the young man, your nephew, what is his profession?" asked an old gentleman—Mr. Broderip, of Salem—who had been Mr. Wentworth's classmate at Harvard College in the year 1809, and who came into his office in Devonshire Street. (Mr. Wentworth, in his later years, used to go but three times a week to his office, where he had a large amount of highly confidential trust-business to transact.)

"Well, he 's an amateur," said Felix's uncle, with folded hands, and with a certain satisfaction in being able to say it. And Mr. Broderip had gone back to Salem with a feeling that this was probably a "European" expression for a broker or a grain exporter.

"I should like to do your head, sir," said Felix to his uncle one evening, before them all—Mr. Brand and Robert Acton being also present. "I think I should make a very fine thing of it. It 's an interesting head; it 's very mediæval."

Mr. Wentworth looked grave; he felt awkwardly, as if all the company had come in and found him standing before the looking-glass. "The Lord made it," he said. "I don't think it is for man to make it over again."

"Certainly the Lord made it," replied Felix, laughing, "and he made it very well. But life has been touching up the work. It is a very interesting type of head. It 's delightfully wasted and emaciated. The complexion is wonderfully bleached." And Felix looked round at the circle, as if to call their attention to these interesting points. Mr. Wentworth grew visibly paler. "I should like to do you as an old prelate, an old cardinal, or the prior of an order."

"A prelate, a cardinal?" murmured Mr. Wentworth. "Do you refer to the Roman Catholic priesthood?"

"I mean an old ecclesiastic who should have led a very pure, abstinent life. Now I take it that has been the case with you, sir; one sees it in your face," Felix proceeded. "You have been very—a—very moderate. Don't you think one always sees that in a man's face?"

"You see more in a man's face than I should think of looking for," said Mr. Wentworth coldly.

The Baroness rattled her fan, and gave her brilliant laugh. "It is a risk to look so close!" she exclaimed. "My uncle has some peccadilloes on his conscience." Mr. Wentworth looked at her, painfully at a loss; and in so far as the signs of a pure and abstinent life were visible in his face they were then probably peculiarly manifest. "You are a *beau vieillard*, dear uncle," said Madame Münster, smiling with her foreign eyes.

"I think you are paying me a compliment," said the old man.

"Surely, I am not the first woman that ever did so!" cried the Baroness.

"I think you are," said Mr. Wentworth gravely. And turning to Felix he added, in the same tone, "Please don't take my likeness. My children have my daguerreotype. That is quite satisfactory."

"I won't promise," said Felix, "not to work your head into something!"

Mr. Wentworth looked at him and then at all the others; then he got up and slowly walked away.

"Felix," said Gertrude, in the silence that followed, "I wish you would paint my portrait."

Charlotte wondered whether Gertrude was right in wishing this; and she looked at Mr. Brand as the most legitimate way of ascertaining. Whatever Gertrude did or said, Charlotte always looked at Mr. Brand. It was a standing pretext for looking at Mr. Brand—always, as Charlotte thought, in the interest of Gertrude's welfare. It is true that she felt a tremulous interest in Gertrude being right; for Charlotte, in her small, still way, was an heroic sister.

"We should be glad to have your portrait, Miss Gertrude," said Mr. Brand.

"I should be delighted to paint so charming a model," Felix declared.

"Do you think you are so lovely, my dear?" asked Lizzie Acton, with her little inoffensive pertness, biting off a knot in her knitting.

"It is not because I think I am beautiful," said Gertrude, looking all round. "I don't think I am beautiful, at all." She spoke with a sort of conscious deliberateness; and it seemed very strange to Charlotte to hear her discussing this question so publicly. "It is because I think it would be amusing to sit and be painted. I have always thought that."

"I am sorry you have not had better things to think about, my daughter," said Mr. Wentworth.

"You are very beautiful, cousin Gertrude," Felix declared.

"That 's a compliment," said Gertrude. "I put all the compliments I receive into a little money-jug that has a slit in the side. I shake them up and down, and they rattle. There are not many yet—only two or three."

"No, it 's not a compliment," Felix rejoined. "See; I am careful not to give it the form of a compliment. I did n't think you were beautiful at first. But you have come to seem so little by little."

"Take care, now, your jug does n't burst!" exclaimed Lizzie.

"I think sitting for one's portrait is only one of the various forms of idleness," said Mr. Wentworth. "Their name is legion."

"My dear sir," cried Felix, "you can't be said to be idle when you are making a man work so!"

"One might be painted while one is asleep," suggested Mr. Brand, as a contribution to the discussion.

"Ah, do paint me while I am asleep," said Gertrude to Felix, smiling. And she closed her eyes a little. It had by this time become a matter of almost exciting anxiety to Charlotte what Gertrude would say or would do next.

She began to sit for her portrait on the following day—in the open air, on the north side of the piazza. "I wish you would tell me what you think of us—how we seem to you," she said to Felix, as he sat before his easel.

"You seem to me the best people in the world," said Felix.

"You say that," Gertrude resumed, "because it saves you the trouble of saying anything else."

The young man glanced at her over the top of his canvas. "What else should I say? It would certainly be a great deal of trouble to say anything different."

"Well," said Gertrude, "you have seen people before that you have liked, have you not?"

"Indeed I have, thank Heaven!"

"And they have been very different from us," Gertrude went on.

"That only proves," said Felix, "that there are a thousand different ways of being good company."

"Do you think us good company?" asked Gertrude.

"Company for a king!"

Gertrude was silent a moment; and then, "There must be a thousand different ways of being dreary," she said; "and sometimes I think we make use of them all."

Felix stood up quickly, holding up his hand. "If you could only keep that look on your face for half an hour—while I catch it!" he said. "It is uncommonly handsome."

"To look handsome for half an hour—that is a great deal to ask of me," she answered.

"It would be the portrait of a young woman who has taken some vow, some pledge, that she repents of," said Felix, "and who is thinking it over at leisure."

"I have taken no vow, no pledge," said Gertrude, very gravely; "I have nothing to repent of."

"My dear cousin, that was only a figure of speech. I am very sure that no one in your excellent family has anything to repent of."

"And yet we are always repenting!" Gertrude exclaimed. "That is what I mean by our being dreary. You know it perfectly well; you only pretend that you don't."

Felix gave a quick laugh. "The half hour is going on, and yet you are handsomer than ever. One must be careful what one says, you see."

"To me," said Gertrude, "you can say anything."

Felix looked at her, as an artist might, and painted for some time in silence.

"Yes, you seem to me different from your father and sister—from most of the people you have lived with," he observed.

"To say that one's self," Gertrude went on, "is like saying—by implication, at least—that one is better. I am not better; I am much worse. But they say themselves that I am different. It makes them unhappy."

"Since you accuse me of concealing my real impressions, I

may admit that I think the tendency—among you generally—is to be made unhappy too easily."

"I wish you would tell that to my father," said Gertrude.

"It might make him more unhappy!" Felix exclaimed,
laughing.

"It certainly would. I don't believe you have seen people
like that."

"Ah, my dear cousin, how do you know what I have seen?"
Felix demanded. "How can I tell you?"

"You might tell me a great many things, if you only would.
You have seen people like yourself—people who are bright
and gay and fond of amusement. We are not fond of amusement."

"Yes," said Felix, "I confess that rather strikes me. You
don't seem to me to get all the pleasure out of life that you
might. You don't seem to me to enjoy. . . . . Do you mind
my saying this?" he asked, pausing.

"Please go on," said the girl, earnestly.

"You seem to me very well placed for enjoying. You have
money and liberty and what is called in Europe a 'position.'
But you take a painful view of life, as one may say."

"One ought to think it bright and charming and delightful,
eh?" asked Gertrude.

"I should say so—if one can. It is true it all depends upon
that," Felix added.

"You know there is a great deal of misery in the world,"
said his model.

"I have seen a little of it," the young man rejoined. "But it
was all over there—beyond the sea. I don't see any here. This
is a paradise."

Gertrude said nothing; she sat looking at the dahlias and
the currant-bushes in the garden, while Felix went on with
his work. "To 'enjoy,' " she began at last, "to take life—not
painfully, must one do something wrong?"

Felix gave his long, light laugh again. "Seriously, I think
not. And for this reason, among others: you strike me as very
capable of enjoying, if the chance were given you, and yet at
the same time as incapable of wrong-doing."

"I am sure," said Gertrude, "that you are very wrong in

telling a person that she is incapable of that. We are never nearer to evil than when we believe that."

"You are handsomer than ever," observed Felix, irrelevantly.

Gertrude had got used to hearing him say this. There was not so much excitement in it as at first. "What ought one to do?" she continued. "To give parties, to go to the theatre, to read novels, to keep late hours?"

"I don't think it 's what one does or one does n't do that promotes enjoyment," her companion answered. "It is the general way of looking at life."

"They look at it as a discipline—that 's what they do here. I have often been told that."

"Well, that 's very good. But there is another way," added Felix, smiling: "to look at it as an opportunity."

"An opportunity—yes," said Gertrude. "One would get more pleasure that way."

"I don't attempt to say anything better for it than that it has been my own way—and that is not saying much!" Felix had laid down his palette and brushes; he was leaning back, with his arms folded, to judge the effect of his work. "And you know," he said, "I am a very petty personage."

"You have a great deal of talent," said Gertrude.

"No—no," the young man rejoined, in a tone of cheerful impartiality, "I have not a great deal of talent. It is nothing at all remarkable. I assure you I should know if it were. I shall always be obscure. The world will never hear of me." Gertrude looked at him with a strange feeling. She was thinking of the great world which he knew and which she did not, and how full of brilliant talents it must be, since it could afford to make light of his abilities. "You need n't in general attach much importance to anything I tell you," he pursued; "but you may believe me when I say this,—that I am little better than a good-natured feather-head."

"A feather-head?" she repeated.

"I am a species of Bohemian."

"A Bohemian?" Gertrude had never heard this term before, save as a geographical denomination; and she quite failed to understand the figurative meaning which her companion appeared to attach to it. But it gave her pleasure.

Felix had pushed back his chair and risen to his feet; he slowly came toward her, smiling. "I am a sort of adventurer," he said, looking down at her.

She got up, meeting his smile. "An adventurer?" she repeated. "I should like to hear your adventures."

For an instant she believed that he was going to take her hand; but he dropped his own hands suddenly into the pockets of his painting-jacket. "There is no reason why you should n't," he said. "I have been an adventurer, but my adventures have been very innocent. They have all been happy ones; I don't think there are any I should n't tell. They were very pleasant and very pretty; I should like to go over them in memory. Sit down again, and I will begin," he added in a moment, with his naturally persuasive smile.

Gertrude sat down again on that day, and she sat down on several other days. Felix, while he plied his brush, told her a great many stories, and she listened with charmed avidity. Her eyes rested upon his lips; she was very serious; sometimes, from her air of wondering gravity, he thought she was displeased. But Felix never believed for more than a single moment in any displeasure of his own producing. This would have been fatuity if the optimism it expressed had not been much more a hope than a prejudice. It is beside the matter to say that he had a good conscience; for the best conscience is a sort of self-reproach, and this young man's brilliantly healthy nature spent itself in objective good intentions which were ignorant of any test save exactness in hitting their mark. He told Gertrude how he had walked over France and Italy with a painter's knapsack on his back, paying his way often by knocking off a flattering portrait of his host or hostess. He told her how he had played the violin in a little band of musicians—not of high celebrity—who traveled through foreign lands giving provincial concerts. He told her also how he had been a momentary ornament of a troupe of strolling actors, engaged in the arduous task of interpreting Shakespeare to French and German, Polish and Hungarian audiences.

While this periodical recital was going on, Gertrude lived in a fantastic world; she seemed to herself to be reading a romance that came out in daily numbers. She had known nothing so delightful since the perusal of "Nicholas Nickleby." One afternoon she went to see her cousin, Mrs. Acton, Robert's mother, who was a great invalid, never leaving the house. She came back alone, on foot, across the fields—this being a short way which they often used. Felix had gone to Boston with her father, who desired to take the young man to call upon some of his friends, old gentlemen who remembered his mother—remembered her, but said nothing about her—and several of whom, with the gentle ladies their wives, had driven out from town to pay their respects at the little house among the apple-trees, in vehicles which reminded the Baroness, who received her visitors with discriminating civility, of the large, light, rattling barouche in which she herself had made her journey to this neighborhood. The afternoon was waning; in the western sky the great picture of a New England sunset, painted in crimson and silver, was suspended from the zenith; and the stony pastures, as Gertrude traversed them, thinking intently to herself, were covered with a light, clear glow. At the open gate of one of the fields she saw from the distance a man's figure; he stood there as if he were waiting for her, and as she came nearer she recognized Mr. Brand. She had a feeling as of not having seen him for some time; she could not have said for how long, for it yet seemed to her that he had been very lately at the house.

"May I walk back with you?" he asked. And when she had said that he might if he wanted, he observed that he had seen her and recognized her half a mile away.

"You must have very good eyes," said Gertrude.

"Yes, I have very good eyes, Miss Gertrude," said Mr. Brand. She perceived that he meant something; but for a long time past Mr. Brand had constantly meant something, and she had almost got used to it. She felt, however, that what he meant had now a renewed power to disturb her, to perplex and agitate her. He walked beside her in silence for a moment, and then he added, "I have had no trouble in seeing that you are beginning to avoid me. But perhaps," he went on, "one need n't have had very good eyes to see that."

"I have not avoided you," said Gertrude, without looking at him.

"I think you have been unconscious that you were avoiding

me," Mr. Brand replied. "You have not even known that I was there."

"Well, you are here now, Mr. Brand!" said Gertrude, with a little laugh. "I know that very well."

He made no rejoinder. He simply walked beside her slowly, as they were obliged to walk over the soft grass. Presently they came to another gate, which was closed. Mr. Brand laid his hand upon it, but he made no movement to open it; he stood and looked at his companion. "You are very much interested—very much absorbed," he said.

Gertrude glanced at him; she saw that he was pale and that he looked excited. She had never seen Mr. Brand excited before, and she felt that the spectacle, if fully carried out, would be impressive, almost painful. "Absorbed in what?" she asked. Then she looked away at the illuminated sky. She felt guilty and uncomfortable, and yet she was vexed with herself for feeling so. But Mr. Brand, as he stood there looking at her with his small, kind, persistent eyes, represented an immense body of half-obliterated obligations, that were rising again into a certain distinctness.

"You have new interests, new occupations," he went on. "I don't know that I can say that you have new duties. We have always old ones, Gertrude," he added.

"Please open the gate, Mr. Brand," she said; and she felt as if, in saying so, she were cowardly and petulant. But he opened the gate, and allowed her to pass; then he closed it behind himself. Before she had time to turn away he put out his hand and held her an instant by the wrist.

"I want to say something to you," he said.

"I know what you want to say," she answered. And she was on the point of adding, "And I know just how you will say it;" but these words she kept back.

"I love you, Gertrude," he said. "I love you very much; I love you more than ever."

He said the words just as she had known he would; she had heard them before. They had no charm for her; she had said to herself before that it was very strange. It was supposed to be delightful for a woman to listen to such words; but these seemed to her flat and mechanical. "I wish you would forget that," she declared.

"How can I—why should I?" he asked.

"I have made you no promise—given you no pledge," she said, looking at him, with her voice trembling a little.

"You have let me feel that I have an influence over you. You have opened your mind to me."

"I never opened my mind to you, Mr. Brand!" Gertrude cried, with some vehemence.

"Then you were not so frank as I thought—as we all thought."

"I don't see what any one else had to do with it!" cried the girl.

"I mean your father and your sister. You know it makes them happy to think you will listen to me."

She gave a little laugh. "It does n't make them happy," she said. "Nothing makes them happy. No one is happy here."

"I think your cousin is very happy—Mr. Young," rejoined Mr. Brand, in a soft, almost timid tone.

"So much the better for him!" And Gertrude gave her little laugh again.

The young man looked at her a moment. "You are very much changed," he said.

"I am glad to hear it," Gertrude declared.

"I am not. I have known you a long time, and I have loved you as you were."

"I am much obliged to you," said Gertrude. "I must be going home."

He on his side, gave a little laugh.

"You certainly do avoid me—you see!"

"Avoid me, then," said the girl.

He looked at her again; and then, very gently, "No I will not avoid you," he replied; "but I will leave you, for the present, to yourself. I think you will remember—after a while—some of the things you have forgotten. I think you will come back to me; I have great faith in that."

This time his voice was very touching; there was a strong, reproachful force in what he said, and Gertrude could answer nothing. He turned away and stood there, leaning his elbows on the gate and looking at the beautiful sunset. Gertrude left him and took her way home again; but when she reached the middle of the next field she suddenly burst into tears. Her tears seemed to her to have been a long time gathering, and for some moments it was a kind of glee to shed them. But they presently passed away. There was something a little hard about Gertrude; and she never wept again.

VI

GOING of an afternoon to call upon his niece, Mr. Wentworth more than once found Robert Acton sitting in her little drawing-room. This was in no degree, to Mr. Wentworth, a perturbing fact, for he had no sense of competing with his young kinsman for Eugenia's good graces. Madame Münster's uncle had the highest opinion of Robert Acton, who, indeed, in the family at large, was the object of a great deal of undemonstrative appreciation. They were all proud of him, in so far as the charge of being proud may be brought against people who were, habitually, distinctly guiltless of the misdemeanor known as "taking credit." They never boasted of Robert Acton, nor indulged in vainglorious reference to him; they never quoted the clever things he had said, nor mentioned the generous things he had done. But a sort of frigidly-tender faith in his unlimited goodness was a part of their personal sense of right; and there can, perhaps, be no better proof of the high esteem in which he was held than the fact that no explicit judgment was ever passed upon his actions. He was no more praised than he was blamed; but he was tacitly felt to be an ornament to his circle. He was the man of the world of the family. He had been to China and brought home a collection of curiosities; he had made a fortune—or rather he had quintupled a fortune already considerable; he was distinguished by that combination of celibacy, "property," and good humor which appeals to even the most subdued imaginations; and it was taken for granted that he would presently place these advantages at the disposal of some well-regulated young woman of his own "set." Mr. Wentworth was not a man to admit to himself that—his paternal duties apart—he liked any individual much better than all other individuals; but he thought Robert Acton extremely judicious; and this was perhaps as near an approach as he was capable of to the eagerness of preference, which his temperament repudiated as it would have disengaged itself from something slightly unchaste. Acton was, in fact, very judicious—and something more beside; and indeed it must be claimed for Mr. Wentworth that in the more illicit parts of his preference there hovered the vague adumbration of a belief that his cousin's final merit was a certain enviable capacity for whistling, rather gallantly, at the sanctions of mere judgment—for showing a larger courage, a finer quality of pluck, than common occasion demanded. Mr. Wentworth would never have risked the intimation that Acton was made, in the smallest degree, of the stuff of a hero; but this is small blame to him, for Robert would certainly never have risked it himself. Acton certainly exercised great discretion in all things—beginning with his estimate of himself. He knew that he was by no means so much of a man of the world as he was supposed to be in local circles; but it must be added that he knew also that his natural shrewdness had a reach of which he had never quite given local circles the measure. He was addicted to taking the humorous view of things, and he had discovered that even in the narrowest circles such a disposition may find frequent opportunities. Such opportunities had formed for some time—that is, since his return from China, a year and a half before—the most active element in this gentleman's life, which had just now a rather indolent air. He was perfectly willing to get married. He was very fond of books, and he had a handsome library; that is, his books were much more numerous than Mr. Wentworth's. He was also very fond of pictures; but it must be confessed, in the fierce light of contemporary criticism, that his walls were adorned with several rather abortive masterpieces. He had got his learning—and there was more of it than commonly appeared—at Harvard College; and he took a pleasure in old associations, which made it a part of his daily contentment to live so near this institution that he often passed it in driving to Boston. He was extremely interested in the Baroness Münster.

She was very frank with him; or at least she intended to be. "I am sure you find it very strange that I should have settled down in this out-of-the-way part of the world!" she said to him three or four weeks after she had installed herself. "I am certain you are wondering about my motives. They are very pure." The Baroness by this time was an old inhabitant; the best society in Boston had called upon her, and Clifford Wentworth had taken her several times to drive in his buggy.

Robert Acton was seated near her, playing with a fan; there

were always several fans lying about her drawing-room, with long ribbons of different colors attached to them, and Acton was always playing with one. "No, I don't find it at all strange," he said slowly, smiling. "That a clever woman should turn up in Boston, or its suburbs—that does not require so much explanation. Boston is a very nice place."

"If you wish to make me contradict you," said the Baroness, "*vous vous y prenez mal*. In certain moods there is nothing I am not capable of agreeing to. Boston is a paradise, and we are in the suburbs of Paradise."

"Just now I am not at all in the suburbs; I am in the place itself," rejoined Acton, who was lounging a little in his chair. He was, however, not always lounging; and when he was he was not quite so relaxed as he pretended. To a certain extent, he sought refuge from shyness in this appearance of relaxation; and like many persons in the same circumstances he somewhat exaggerated the appearance. Beyond this, the air of being much at his ease was a cover for vigilant observation. He was more than interested in this clever woman, who, whatever he might say, was clever not at all after the Boston fashion; she plunged him into a kind of excitement, held him in vague suspense. He was obliged to admit to himself that he had never yet seen a woman just like this—not even in China. He was ashamed, for inscrutable reasons, of the vivacity of his emotion, and he carried it off, superficially, by taking, still superficially, the humorous view of Madame Münster. It was not at all true that he thought it very natural of her to have made this pious pilgrimage. It might have been said of him in advance that he was too good a Bostonian to regard in the light of an eccentricity the desire of even the remotest alien to visit the New England metropolis. This was an impulse for which, surely, no apology was needed; and Madame Münster was the fortunate possessor of several New England cousins. In fact, however, Madame Münster struck him as out of keeping with her little circle; she was at the best a very agreeable, a gracefully mystifying anomaly. He knew very well that it would not do to address these reflections too crudely to Mr. Wentworth; he would never have remarked to the old gentleman that he wondered what the Baroness was up to. And indeed he had no great desire to share his vague mistrust with any one. There was a personal pleasure in it; the greatest pleasure he had known at least since he had come from China. He would keep the Baroness, for better or worse, to himself; he had a feeling that he deserved to enjoy a monopoly of her, for he was certainly the person who had most adequately gauged her capacity for social intercourse. Before long it became apparent to him that the Baroness was disposed to lay no tax upon such a monopoly.

One day (he was sitting there again and playing with a fan) she asked him to apologize, should the occasion present itself, to certain people in Boston for her not having returned their calls. "There are half a dozen places," she said; "a formidable list. Charlotte Wentworth has written it out for me, in a terrifically distinct hand. There is no ambiguity on the subject; I know perfectly where I must go. Mr. Wentworth informs me that the carriage is always at my disposal, and Charlotte offers to go with me, in a pair of tight gloves and a very stiff petticoat. And yet for three days I have been putting it off. They must think me horribly vicious."

"You ask me to apologize," said Acton, "but you don't tell me what excuse I can offer."

"That is more," the Baroness declared, "than I am held to. It would be like my asking you to buy me a bouquet and giving you the money. I have no reason except that—somehow—it 's too violent an effort. It is not inspiring. Would n't that serve as an excuse, in Boston? I am told they are very sincere; they don't tell fibs. And then Felix ought to go with me, and he is never in readiness. I don't see him. He is always roaming about the fields and sketching old barns, or taking ten-mile walks, or painting some one's portrait, or rowing on the pond, or flirting with Gertrude Wentworth."

"I should think it would amuse you to go and see a few people," said Acton. "You are having a very quiet time of it here. It 's a dull life for you."

"Ah, the quiet,—the quiet!" the Baroness exclaimed. "That 's what I like. It 's rest. That 's what I came here for. Amusement? I have had amusement. And as for seeing people—I have already seen a great many in my life. If it did n't sound ungracious I should say that I wish very humbly your people here would leave me alone!"

Acton looked at her a moment, and she looked at him. She was a woman who took being looked at remarkably well. "So you have come here for rest?" he asked.

"So I may say. I came for many of those reasons that are no reasons—don't you know?—and yet that are really the best: to come away, to change, to break with everything. When once one comes away one must arrive somewhere, and I asked myself why I should n't arrive here."

"You certainly had time on the way!" said Acton, laughing.

Madame Münster looked at him again; and then, smiling: "And I have certainly had time, since I got here, to ask myself why I came. However, I never ask myself idle questions. Here I am, and it seems to me you ought only to thank me."

"When you go away you will see the difficulties I shall put in your path."

"You mean to put difficulties in my path?" she asked, re-arranging the rosebud in her corsage.

"The greatest of all—that of having been so agreeable"—

"That I shall be unable to depart? Don't be too sure. I have left some very agreeable people over there."

"Ah," said Acton, "but it was to come here, where I am!"

"I did n't know of your existence. Excuse me for saying anything so rude; but, honestly speaking, I did not. No," the Baroness pursued, "it was precisely not to see you—such people as you—that I came."

"Such people as me?" cried Acton.

"I had a sort of longing to come into those natural relations which I knew I should find here. Over there I had only, as I may say, artificial relations. Don't you see the difference?"

"The difference tells against me," said Acton. "I suppose I am an artificial relation."

"Conventional," declared the Baroness; "very conventional."

"Well, there is one way in which the relation of a lady and a gentleman may always become natural," said Acton.

"You mean by their becoming lovers? That may be natural or not. And at any rate," rejoined Eugenia, "*nous n'en sommes pas là!*"

They were not, as yet; but a little later, when she began to go with him to drive, it might almost have seemed that they were. He came for her several times, alone, in his high "wagon," drawn by a pair of charming light-limbed horses. It was different, her having gone with Clifford Wentworth, who was her cousin, and so much younger. It was not to be imagined that she should have a flirtation with Clifford, who was a mere shame-faced boy, and whom a large section of Boston society supposed to be "engaged" to Lizzie Acton. Not, indeed, that it was to be conceived that the Baroness was a possible party to any flirtation whatever; for she was undoubtedly a married lady. It was generally known that her matrimonial condition was of the "morganatic" order; but in its natural aversion to suppose that this meant anything less than absolute wedlock, the conscience of the community took refuge in the belief that it implied something even more.

Acton wished her to think highly of American scenery, and he drove her to great distances, picking out the prettiest roads and the largest points of view. If we are good when we are contented, Eugenia's virtues should now certainly have been uppermost; for she found a charm in the rapid movement through a wild country, and in a companion who from time to time made the vehicle dip, with a motion like a swallow's flight, over roads of primitive construction, and who, as she felt, would do a great many things that she might ask him. Sometimes, for a couple of hours together, there were almost no houses; there were nothing but woods and rivers and lakes and horizons adorned with bright-looking mountains. It seemed to the Baroness very wild, as I have said, and lovely; but the impression added something to that sense of the enlargement of opportunity which had been born of her arrival in the New World.

One day—it was late in the afternoon—Acton pulled up his horses on the crest of a hill which commanded a beautiful prospect. He let them stand a long time to rest, while he sat there and talked with Madame Münster. The prospect was beautiful in spite of there being nothing human within sight. There was a wilderness of woods, and the gleam of a distant river, and a glimpse of half the hill-tops in Massachusetts. The road had a wide, grassy margin, on the further side of which there flowed a deep, clear brook; there were wild flowers in the grass, and beside the brook lay the trunk of a fallen tree.

Acton waited a while; at last a rustic wayfarer came trudging along the road. Acton asked him to hold the horses—a service he consented to render, as a friendly turn to a fellow-citizen. Then he invited the Baroness to descend, and the two wandered away, across the grass, and sat down on the log beside the brook.

"I imagine it does n't remind you of Silberstadt," said Acton. It was the first time that he had mentioned Silberstadt to her, for particular reasons. He knew she had a husband there, and this was disagreeable to him; and, furthermore, it had been repeated to him that this husband wished to put her away—a state of affairs to which even indirect reference was to be deprecated. It was true, nevertheless, that the Baroness herself had often alluded to Silberstadt; and Acton had often wondered why her husband wished to get rid of her. It was a curious position for a lady—this being known as a repudiated wife; and it is worthy of observation that the Baroness carried it off with exceeding grace and dignity. She had made it felt, from the first, that there were two sides to the question, and that her own side, when she should choose to present it, would be replete with touching interest.

"It does not remind me of the town, of course," she said, "of the sculptured gables and the Gothic churches, of the wonderful Schloss, with its moat and its clustering towers. But it has a little look of some other parts of the principality. One might fancy one's self among those grand old German forests, those legendary mountains; the sort of country one sees from the windows at Shreckenstein."

"What is Shreckenstein?" asked Acton.

"It is a great castle,—the summer residence of the Reigning Prince."

"Have you ever lived there?"

"I have stayed there," said the Baroness. Acton was silent; he looked a while at the uncastled landscape before him. "It is the first time you have ever asked me about Silberstadt," she said. "I should think you would want to know about my marriage; it must seem to you very strange."

Acton looked at her a moment. "Now you would n't like me to say that!"

"You Americans have such odd ways!" the Baroness declared. "You never ask anything outright; there seem to be so many things you can't talk about."

"We Americans are very polite," said Acton, whose national consciousness had been complicated by a residence in foreign lands, and who yet disliked to hear Americans abused. "We don't like to tread upon people's toes," he said. "But I should like very much to hear about your marriage. Now tell me how it came about."

"The Prince fell in love with me," replied the Baroness simply. "He pressed his suit very hard. At first he did n't wish me to marry him; on the contrary. But on that basis I refused to listen to him. So he offered me marriage—in so far as he might. I was young, and I confess I was rather flattered. But if it were to be done again now, I certainly should not accept him."

"How long ago was this?" asked Acton.

"Oh—several years," said Eugenia. "You should never ask a woman for dates."

"Why, I should think that when a woman was relating history" . . . . Acton answered. "And now he wants to break it off?"

"They want him to make a political marriage. It is his brother's idea. His brother is very clever."

"They must be a precious pair!" cried Robert Acton.

The Baroness gave a little philosophic shrug. "Que voulez-vous? They are princes. They think they are treating me very well. Silberstadt is a perfectly despotic little state, and the Reigning Prince may annul the marriage by a stroke of his pen. But he has promised me, nevertheless, not to do so without my formal consent."

"And this you have refused?"

"Hitherto. It is an indignity, and I have wished at least to make it difficult for them. But I have a little document in my writing-desk which I have only to sign and send back to the Prince."

"Then it will be all over?"

The Baroness lifted her hand, and dropped it again. "Of course I shall keep my title; at least, I shall be at liberty to keep it if I choose. And I suppose I shall keep it. One must have a name. And I shall keep my pension. It is very small— it is wretchedly small; but it is what I live on."

"And you have only to sign that paper?" Acton asked.

The Baroness looked at him a moment. "Do you urge it?"

He got up slowly, and stood with his hands in his pockets. "What do you gain by not doing it?"

"I am supposed to gain this advantage—that if I delay, or temporize, the Prince may come back to me, may make a stand against his brother. He is very fond of me, and his brother has pushed him only little by little."

"If he were to come back to you," said Acton, "would you—would you take him back?"

The Baroness met his eyes; she colored just a little. Then she rose. "I should have the satisfaction of saying, 'Now it is my turn. I break with your serene highness!' "

They began to walk toward the carriage. "Well," said Robert Acton, "it 's a curious story! How did you make his acquaintance?"

"I was staying with an old lady—an old Countess—in Dresden. She had been a friend of my father's. My father was dead; I was very much alone. My brother was wandering about the world in a theatrical troupe."

"Your brother ought to have stayed with you," Acton observed, "and kept you from putting your trust in princes."

The Baroness was silent a moment, and then, "He did what he could," she said. "He sent me money. The old Countess encouraged the Prince; she was even pressing. It seems to me," Madame Münster added, gently, "that—under the circumstances—I behaved very well."

Acton glanced at her, and made the observation—he had made it before—that a woman looks the prettier for having unfolded her wrongs or her sufferings. "Well," he reflected, audibly, "I should like to see you send his serene highness—somewhere!"

Madame Münster stooped and plucked a daisy from the grass. "And not sign my renunciation?"

"Well, I don't know—I don't know," said Acton.

"In one case I should have my revenge; in another case I should have my liberty."

Acton gave a little laugh as he helped her into the carriage. "At any rate," he said, "take good care of that paper."

A couple of days afterward he asked her to come and see his house. The visit had already been proposed, but it had been put off in consequence of his mother's illness. She was a constant invalid, and she had passed these recent years, very patiently, in a great flowered arm-chair at her bedroom window. Lately, for some days, she had been unable to see any one; but now she was better, and she sent the Baroness a very civil message. Acton had wished their visitor to come to dinner; but Madame Münster preferred to begin with a simple call. She had reflected that if she should go to dinner Mr. Wentworth and his daughters would also be asked, and it had seemed to her that the peculiar character of the occasion would be best preserved in a *tête-à-tête* with her host. Why the occasion should have a peculiar character she explained to no one. As far as any one could see, it was simply very pleasant. Acton came for her and drove her to his door, an operation which was rapidly performed. His house the Baroness mentally pronounced a very good one; more articulately, she declared that it was enchanting. It was large and square and painted brown; it stood in a well-kept shrubbery, and was approached, from the gate, by a short drive. It was, moreover, a much more modern dwelling than Mr. Wentworth's, and was more redundantly upholstered and expensively ornamented. The Baroness perceived that her entertainer had analyzed material comfort to a sufficiently fine point. And then he possessed the most delightful *chinoiseries*—trophies of his sojourn in the Celestial Empire: pagodas of ebony and cabinets of ivory; sculptured monsters, grinning and leering on chimney-pieces, in front of beautifully figured hand-screens; porcelain dinner-sets, gleaming behind the glass doors of mahogany buffets; large screens, in corners, covered with tense silk and embroidered with mandarins and dragons. These things were scattered all over the house, and they gave Eugenia a pretext for a complete domiciliary visit. She liked it, she enjoyed it; she thought it a very nice place. It had a mixture of the homely and the liberal, and though it was almost a museum, the large, little-used rooms were as fresh and clean as a well-kept dairy. Lizzie Acton told her that she dusted all the pagodas and other curiosities every day with her own hands; and the Baroness answered that she was evidently a household fairy. Lizzie had not at all the look of a young lady who dusted things; she wore such pretty dresses and had such delicate fingers that it was difficult to imagine her immersed in sordid cares. She came to meet Madame Münster on her arrival, but she said nothing, or almost nothing, and the Baroness again reflected—she had had occasion to do so before—that American girls had no manners. She disliked this little American girl, and she was quite prepared to learn that she had failed to commend herself to Miss Acton. Lizzie struck her as positive and explicit almost to pertness; and the idea of her combining the apparent incongruities of a taste for housework and the wearing of fresh, Parisian-looking dresses suggested the possession of a dangerous energy. It was a source of irritation to the Baroness that in this country it should seem to matter whether a little girl were a trifle less or a trifle more of a nonentity; for Eugenia had hitherto been conscious of no moral pressure as regards the appreciation of diminutive virgins. It was perhaps an indication of Lizzie's pertness that she very soon retired and left the Baroness on her brother's hands. Acton talked a great deal about his chinoiseries; he knew a good deal about porcelain and bric-a-brac. The Baroness, in her progress through the house, made, as it were, a great many stations. She sat down everywhere, confessed to being a little tired, and asked about the various objects with a curious mixture of alertness and inattention. If there had been any one to say it to she would have declared that she was positively in love with her host; but she could hardly make this declaration—even in the strictest confidence—to Acton himself. It gave her, nevertheless, a pleasure that had some of the charm of unwontedness to feel, with that admirable keenness with which she was capable of feeling things, that he had a disposition without any edges; that even his humorous irony always expanded toward the point. One's impression of his honesty was almost like carrying a bunch of flowers; the perfume was most agreeable, but they were occasionally an inconvenience. One could trust him, at any rate, round all the corners of the world; and, withal, he was not absolutely simple, which would have been excess; he was only relatively simple, which was quite enough for the Baroness.

Lizzie reappeared to say that her mother would now be

happy to receive Madame Münster; and the Baroness followed her to Mrs. Acton's apartment. Eugenia reflected, as she went, that it was not the affectation of impertinence that made her dislike this young lady, for on that ground she could easily have beaten her. It was not an aspiration on the girl's part to rivalry, but a kind of laughing, childishly-mocking indifference to the results of comparison. Mrs. Acton was an emaciated, sweet-faced woman of five and fifty, sitting with pillows behind her, and looking out on a clump of hemlocks. She was very modest, very timid, and very ill; she made Eugenia feel grateful that she herself was not like that—neither so ill, nor, possibly, so modest. On a chair, beside her, lay a volume of Emerson's Essays. It was a great occasion for poor Mrs. Acton, in her helpless condition, to be confronted with a clever foreign lady, who had more manner than any lady—any dozen ladies—that she had ever seen.

"I have heard a great deal about you," she said, softly, to the Baroness.

"From your son, eh?" Eugenia asked. "He has talked to me immensely of you. Oh, he talks of you as you would like," the Baroness declared; "as such a son *must* talk of such a mother!"

Mrs. Acton sat gazing; this was part of Madame Münster's "manner." But Robert Acton was gazing too, in vivid consciousness that he had barely mentioned his mother to their brilliant guest. He never talked of this still maternal presence,—a presence refined to such delicacy that it had almost resolved itself, with him, simply into the subjective emotion of gratitude. And Acton rarely talked of his emotions. The Baroness turned her smile toward him, and she instantly felt that she had been observed to be fibbing. She had struck a false note. But who were these people to whom such fibbing was not pleasing? If they were annoyed, the Baroness was equally so; and after the exchange of a few civil inquiries and low-voiced responses she took leave of Mrs. Acton. She begged Robert not to come home with her; she would get into the carriage alone; she preferred that. This was imperious, and she thought he looked disappointed. While she stood before the door with him—the carriage was turning in the gravel-walk—this thought restored her serenity.

When she had given him her hand in farewell she looked at him a moment. "I have almost decided to dispatch that paper," she said.

He knew that she alluded to the document that she had called her renunciation; and he assisted her into the carriage without saying anything. But just before the vehicle began to move he said, "Well, when you have in fact dispatched it, I hope you will let me know!"

VII

FELIX YOUNG finished Gertrude's portrait, and he afterwards transferred to canvas the features of many members of that circle of which it may be said that he had become for the time the pivot and the centre. I am afraid it must be confessed that he was a decidedly flattering painter, and that he imparted to his models a romantic grace which seemed easily and cheaply acquired by the payment of a hundred dollars to a young man who made "sitting" so entertaining. For Felix was paid for his pictures, making, as he did, no secret of the fact that in guiding his steps to the Western world affectionate curiosity had gone hand in hand with a desire to better his condition. He took his uncle's portrait quite as if Mr. Wentworth had never averted himself from the experiment; and as he compassed his end only by the exercise of gentle violence, it is but fair to add that he allowed the old man to give him nothing but his time. He passed his arm into Mr. Wentworth's one summer morning—very few arms indeed had ever passed into Mr. Wentworth's—and led him across the garden and along the road into the studio which he had extemporized in the little house among the apple-trees. The grave gentleman felt himself more and more fascinated by his clever nephew, whose fresh, demonstrative youth seemed a compendium of experiences so strangely numerous. It appeared to him that Felix must know a great deal; he would like to learn what he thought about some of those things as regards which his own conversation had always been formal, but his knowledge vague. Felix had a confident, gayly trenchant way of judging human actions which Mr. Wentworth grew little by little to envy; it seemed like criticism made easy. Forming an opinion—say on a person's conduct—was, with Mr. Wentworth, a good deal like fumbling in a lock with a key chosen at hazard. He seemed to himself to go about the world with a big bunch of these ineffectual instruments at his girdle. His nephew, on the other hand, with a single turn of the wrist, opened any door as adroitly as a horse-thief. He felt obliged to keep up the convention that an uncle is always wiser than a nephew, even if he could keep it up no otherwise than by listening in serious silence to Felix's quick, light, constant discourse. But there came a day when he lapsed from consistency and almost asked his nephew's advice.

"Have you ever entertained the idea of settling in the United States?" he asked one morning, while Felix brilliantly plied his brush.

"My dear uncle," said Felix, "excuse me if your question makes me smile a little. To begin with, I have never entertained an idea. Ideas often entertain *me*; but I am afraid I have never seriously made a plan. I know what you are going to say; or rather, I know what you think, for I don't think you will say it—that this is very frivolous and loose-minded on my part. So it is; but I am made like that; I take things as they come, and somehow there is always some new thing to follow the last. In the second place, I should never propose to *settle*. I can't settle, my dear uncle; I 'm not a settler. I know that is what strangers are supposed to do here; they always settle. But I have n't—to answer your question—entertained that idea."

"You intend to return to Europe and resume your irregular manner of life?" Mr. Wentworth inquired.

"I can't say I intend. But it 's very likely I shall go back to Europe. After all, I am a European. I feel that, you know. It will depend a good deal upon my sister. She 's even more of a European than I; here, you know, she 's a picture out of her setting. And as for 'resuming,' dear uncle, I really have never given up my irregular manner of life. What, for me, could be more irregular than this?"

"Than what?" asked Mr. Wentworth, with his pale gravity.

"Well, than everything! Living in the midst of you, this way; this charming, quiet, serious family life; fraternizing with Charlotte and Gertrude; calling upon twenty young ladies and going out to walk with them; sitting with you in the evening on the piazza and listening to the crickets, and going to bed at ten o'clock."

"Your description is very animated," said Mr. Wentworth; "but I see nothing improper in what you describe."

"Neither do I, dear uncle. It is extremely delightful; I should n't like it if it were improper. I assure you I don't like improper things; though I dare say you think I do," Felix went on, painting away.

"I have never accused you of that."

"Pray don't," said Felix, "because, you see, at bottom I am a terrible Philistine."

"A Philistine?" repeated Mr. Wentworth.

"I mean, as one may say, a plain, God-fearing man." Mr. Wentworth looked at him reservedly, like a mystified sage, and Felix continued, "I trust I shall enjoy a venerable and venerated old age. I mean to live long. I can hardly call that a plan, perhaps; but it 's a keen desire—a rosy vision. I shall be a lively, perhaps even a frivolous old man!"

"It is natural," said his uncle, sententiously, "that one should desire to prolong an agreeable life. We have perhaps a selfish indisposition to bring our pleasure to a close. But I presume," he added, "that you expect to marry."

"That too, dear uncle, is a hope, a desire, a vision," said Felix. It occurred to him for an instant that this was possibly a preface to the offer of the hand of one of Mr. Wentworth's admirable daughters. But in the name of decent modesty and a proper sense of the hard realities of this world, Felix banished the thought. His uncle was the incarnation of benevolence, certainly; but from that to accepting—much more postulating—the idea of a union between a young lady with a dowry presumptively brilliant and a penniless artist with no prospect of fame, there was a very long way. Felix had lately become conscious of a luxurious preference for the society— if possible unshared with others—of Gertrude Wentworth; but he had relegated this young lady, for the moment, to the coldly brilliant category of unattainable possessions. She was not the first woman for whom he had entertained an unpractical admiration. He had been in love with duchesses and countesses, and he had made, once or twice, a perilously near approach to cynicism in declaring that the disinterestedness of women had been overrated. On the whole, he had tempered audacity with modesty; and it is but fair to him now to say explicitly that he would have been incapable of taking advantage of his present large allowance of familiarity to make love to the younger of his handsome cousins. Felix had

grown up among traditions in the light of which such a proceeding looked like a grievous breach of hospitality. I have
said that he was always happy, and it may be counted among
the present sources of his happiness that he had as regards
this matter of his relations with Gertrude a deliciously good
conscience. His own deportment seemed to him suffused
with the beauty of virtue—a form of beauty that he admired
with the same vivacity with which he admired all other forms.

"I think that if you marry," said Mr. Wentworth presently,
"it will conduce to your happiness."

"*Sicurissimo!*" Felix exclaimed; and then, arresting his
brush, he looked at his uncle with a smile. "There is something I feel tempted to say to you. May I risk it?"

Mr. Wentworth drew himself up a little. "I am very safe; I don't
repeat things." But he hoped Felix would not risk too much.

Felix was laughing at his answer.

"It 's odd to hear you telling me how to be happy. I don't
think you know yourself, dear uncle. Now, does that sound
brutal?"

The old man was silent a moment, and then, with a dry
dignity that suddenly touched his nephew: "We may sometimes point out a road we are unable to follow."

"Ah, don't tell me you have had any sorrows," Felix rejoined. "I did n't suppose it, and I did n't mean to allude to
them. I simply meant that you all don't amuse yourselves."

"Amuse ourselves? We are not children."

"Precisely not! You have reached the proper age. I was saying that the other day to Gertrude," Felix added. "I hope it
was not indiscreet."

"If it was," said Mr. Wentworth, with a keener irony than
Felix would have thought him capable of, "it was but your
way of amusing yourself. I am afraid you have never had a
trouble."

"Oh, yes, I have!" Felix declared, with some spirit; "before
I knew better. But you don't catch me at it again."

Mr. Wentworth maintained for a while a silence more expressive than a deep-drawn sigh. "You have no children," he
said at last.

"Don't tell me," Felix exclaimed, "that your charming
young people are a source of grief to you!"

"I don't speak of Charlotte." And then, after a pause, Mr. Wentworth continued, "I don't speak of Gertrude. But I feel considerable anxiety about Clifford. I will tell you another time."

The next time he gave Felix a sitting his nephew reminded him that he had taken him into his confidence. "How is Clifford to-day?" Felix asked. "He has always seemed to me a young man of remarkable discretion. Indeed, he is only too discreet; he seems on his guard against me—as if he thought me rather light company. The other day he told his sister— Gertrude repeated it to me—that I was always laughing at him. If I laugh it is simply from the impulse to try and inspire him with confidence. That is the only way I have."

"Clifford's situation is no laughing matter," said Mr. Wentworth. "It is very peculiar, as I suppose you have guessed."

"Ah, you mean his love affair with his cousin?"

Mr. Wentworth stared, blushing a little. "I mean his absence from college. He has been suspended. We have decided not to speak of it unless we are asked."

"Suspended?" Felix repeated.

"He has been requested by the Harvard authorities to absent himself for six months. Meanwhile he is studying with Mr. Brand. We think Mr. Brand will help him; at least we hope so."

"What befell him at college?" Felix asked. "He was too fond of pleasure? Mr. Brand certainly will not teach him any of those secrets!"

"He was too fond of something of which he should not have been fond. I suppose it is considered a pleasure."

Felix gave his light laugh. "My dear uncle, is there any doubt about its being a pleasure? *C'est de son âge*, as they say in France."

"I should have said rather it was a vice of later life—of disappointed old age."

Felix glanced at his uncle, with his lifted eyebrows, and then, "Of what are you speaking?" he demanded, smiling.

"Of the situation in which Clifford was found."

"Ah, he was found—he was caught?"

"Necessarily, he was caught. He could n't walk; he staggered."

"Oh," said Felix, "he drinks! I rather suspected that, from something I observed the first day I came here. I quite agree with you that it is a low taste. It 's not a vice for a gentleman. He ought to give it up."

"We hope for a good deal from Mr. Brand's influence," Mr. Wentworth went on. "He has talked to him from the first. And he never touches anything himself."

"I will talk to him—I will talk to him!" Felix declared, gayly.

"What will you say to him?" asked his uncle, with some apprehension.

Felix for some moments answered nothing. "Do you mean to marry him to his cousin?" he asked at last.

"Marry him?" echoed Mr. Wentworth. "I should n't think his cousin would want to marry him."

"You have no understanding, then, with Mrs. Acton?"

Mr. Wentworth stared, almost blankly. "I have never discussed such subjects with her."

"I should think it might be time," said Felix. "Lizzie Acton is admirably pretty, and if Clifford is dangerous . . . ."

"They are not engaged," said Mr. Wentworth. "I have no reason to suppose they are engaged."

"Par exemple!" cried Felix. "A clandestine engagement? Trust me, Clifford, as I say, is a charming boy. He is incapable of that. Lizzie Acton, then, would not be jealous of another woman."

"I certainly hope not," said the old man, with a vague sense of jealousy being an even lower vice than a love of liquor.

"The best thing for Clifford, then," Felix propounded, "is to become interested in some clever, charming woman." And he paused in his painting, and, with his elbows on his knees, looked with bright communicativeness at his uncle. "You see, I believe greatly in the influence of women. Living with women helps to make a man a gentleman. It is very true Clifford has his sisters, who are so charming. But there should be a different sentiment in play from the fraternal, you know. He has Lizzie Acton; but she, perhaps, is rather immature."

"I suspect Lizzie has talked to him, reasoned with him," said Mr. Wentworth.

"On the impropriety of getting tipsy—on the beauty of

temperance? That is dreary work for a pretty young girl. No," Felix continued; "Clifford ought to frequent some agreeable woman, who, without ever mentioning such unsavory subjects, would give him a sense of its being very ridiculous to be fuddled. If he could fall in love with her a little, so much the better. The thing would operate as a cure."

"Well, now, what lady should you suggest?" asked Mr. Wentworth.

"There is a clever woman under your hand. My sister."

"Your sister—under my hand?" Mr. Wentworth repeated.

"Say a word to Clifford. Tell him to be bold. He is well disposed already; he has invited her two or three times to drive. But I don't think he comes to see her. Give him a hint to come—to come often. He will sit there of an afternoon, and they will talk. It will do him good."

Mr. Wentworth meditated. "You think she will exercise a helpful influence?"

"She will exercise a civilizing—I may call it a sobering—influence. A charming, clever, witty woman always does—especially if she is a little of a coquette. My dear uncle, the society of such women has been half my education. If Clifford is suspended, as you say, from college, let Eugenia be his preceptress."

Mr. Wentworth continued thoughtful. "You think Eugenia is a coquette?" he asked.

"What pretty woman is not?" Felix demanded in turn. But this, for Mr. Wentworth, could at the best have been no answer, for he did not think his niece pretty. "With Clifford," the young man pursued, "Eugenia will simply be enough of a coquette to be a little ironical. That 's what he needs. So you recommend him to be nice with her, you know. The suggestion will come best from you."

"Do I understand," asked the old man, "that I am to suggest to my son to make a—a profession of—of affection to Madame Münster?"

"Yes, yes—a profession!" cried Felix sympathetically.

"But, as I understand it, Madame Münster is a married woman."

"Ah," said Felix, smiling, "of course she can't marry him. But she will do what she can."

Mr. Wentworth sat for some time with his eyes on the floor; at last he got up. "I don't think," he said, "that I can undertake to recommend my son any such course." And without meeting Felix's surprised glance he broke off his sitting, which was not resumed for a fortnight.

Felix was very fond of the little lake which occupied so many of Mr. Wentworth's numerous acres, and of a remarkable pine grove which lay upon the further side of it, planted upon a steep embankment and haunted by the summer breeze. The murmur of the air in the far off tree-tops had a strange distinctness; it was almost articulate. One afternoon the young man came out of his painting-room and passed the open door of Eugenia's little salon. Within, in the cool dimness, he saw his sister, dressed in white, buried in her armchair, and holding to her face an immense bouquet. Opposite to her sat Clifford Wentworth, twirling his hat. He had evidently just presented the bouquet to the Baroness, whose fine eyes, as she glanced at him over the big roses and geraniums, wore a conversational smile. Felix, standing on the threshold of the cottage, hesitated for a moment as to whether he should retrace his steps and enter the parlor. Then he went his way and passed into Mr. Wentworth's garden. That civilizing process to which he had suggested that Clifford should be subjected appeared to have come on of itself. Felix was very sure, at least, that Mr. Wentworth had not adopted his ingenious device for stimulating the young man's æsthetic consciousness. "Doubtless he supposes," he said to himself, after the conversation that has been narrated, "that I desire, out of fraternal benevolence, to procure for Eugenia the amusement of a flirtation—or, as he probably calls it, an intrigue—with the too susceptible Clifford. It must be admitted—and I have noticed it before—that nothing exceeds the license occasionally taken by the imagination of very rigid people." Felix, on his own side, had of course said nothing to Clifford; but he had observed to Eugenia that Mr. Wentworth was much mortified at his son's low tastes. "We ought to do something to help them, after all their kindness to us," he had added. "Encourage Clifford to come and see you, and inspire him with a taste for conversation. That will supplant the other, which only comes from his puerility, from his not taking his position in the world—that of a rich young man of ancient stock—seriously enough. Make him a little more serious. Even if he makes love to you it is no great matter."

"I am to offer myself as a superior form of intoxication—a substitute for a brandy bottle, eh?" asked the Baroness. "Truly, in this country one comes to strange uses."

But she had not positively declined to undertake Clifford's higher education, and Felix, who had not thought of the matter again, being haunted with visions of more personal profit, now reflected that the work of redemption had fairly begun. The idea in prospect had seemed of the happiest, but in operation it made him a trifle uneasy. "What if Eugenia—what if Eugenia"—he asked himself softly; the question dying away in his sense of Eugenia's undetermined capacity. But before Felix had time either to accept or to reject its admonition, even in this vague form, he saw Robert Acton turn out of Mr. Wentworth's inclosure, by a distant gate, and come toward the cottage in the orchard. Acton had evidently walked from his own house along a shady by-way and was intending to pay a visit to Madame Münster. Felix watched him a moment; then he turned away. Acton could be left to play the part of Providence and interrupt—if interruption were needed—Clifford's entanglement with Eugenia.

Felix passed through the garden toward the house and toward a postern gate which opened upon a path leading across the fields, beside a little wood, to the lake. He stopped and looked up at the house; his eyes rested more particularly upon a certain open window, on the shady side. Presently Gertrude appeared there, looking out into the summer light. He took off his hat to her and bade her good-day; he remarked that he was going to row across the pond, and begged that she would do him the honor to accompany him. She looked at him a moment; then, without saying anything, she turned away. But she soon reappeared below in one of those quaint and charming Leghorn hats, tied with white satin bows, that were worn at that period; she also carried a green parasol. She went with him to the edge of the lake, where a couple of boats were always moored; they got into one of them, and Felix, with gentle strokes, propelled it to the opposite shore. The day was the perfection of summer weather; the little lake was the color of sunshine; the plash of the oars was the only sound, and they found themselves listening to it. They disembarked, and, by a winding path, ascended the pine-crested mound which overlooked the water, whose white expanse glittered between the trees. The place was delightfully cool, and had the added charm that—in the softly sounding pine boughs—you seemed to hear the coolness as well as feel it. Felix and Gertrude sat down on the rust-colored carpet of pine-needles and talked of many things. Felix spoke at last, in the course of talk, of his going away; it was the first time he had alluded to it.

"You are going away?" said Gertrude, looking at him.

"Some day—when the leaves begin to fall. You know I can't stay forever."

Gertrude transferred her eyes to the outer prospect, and then, after a pause, she said, "I shall never see you again."

"Why not?" asked Felix. "We shall probably both survive my departure."

But Gertrude only repeated, "I shall never see you again. I shall never hear of you," she went on. "I shall know nothing about you. I knew nothing about you before, and it will be the same again."

"I knew nothing about you then, unfortunately," said Felix. "But now I shall write to you."

"Don't write to me. I shall not answer you," Gertrude declared.

"I should of course burn your letters," said Felix.

Gertrude looked at him again. "Burn my letters? You sometimes say strange things."

"They are not strange in themselves," the young man answered. "They are only strange as said to you. You will come to Europe."

"With whom shall I come?" She asked this question simply; she was very much in earnest. Felix was interested in her earnestness; for some moments he hesitated. "You can't tell me that," she pursued. "You can't say that I shall go with my father and my sister; you don't believe that."

"I shall keep your letters," said Felix, presently, for all answer.

"I never write. I don't know how to write." Gertrude, for

some time, said nothing more; and her companion, as he looked at her, wished it had not been "disloyal" to make love to the daughter of an old gentleman who had offered one hospitality. The afternoon waned; the shadows stretched themselves; and the light grew deeper in the western sky. Two persons appeared on the opposite side of the lake, coming from the house and crossing the meadow. "It is Charlotte and Mr. Brand," said Gertrude. "They are coming over here." But Charlotte and Mr. Brand only came down to the edge of the water, and stood there, looking across; they made no motion to enter the boat that Felix had left at the mooring-place. Felix waved his hat to them; it was too far to call. They made no visible response, and they presently turned away and walked along the shore.

"Mr. Brand is not demonstrative," said Felix. "He is never demonstrative to me. He sits silent, with his chin in his hand, looking at me. Sometimes he looks away. Your father tells me he is so eloquent; and I should like to hear him talk. He looks like such a noble young man. But with me he will never talk. And yet I am so fond of listening to brilliant imagery!"

"He is very eloquent," said Gertrude; "but he has no brilliant imagery. I have heard him talk a great deal. I knew that when they saw us they would not come over here."

"Ah, he is making *la cour*, as they say, to your sister? They desire to be alone?"

"No," said Gertrude, gravely, "they have no such reason as that for being alone."

"But why does n't he make la cour to Charlotte?" Felix inquired. "She is so pretty, so gentle, so good."

Gertrude glanced at him, and then she looked at the distantly-seen couple they were discussing. Mr. Brand and Charlotte were walking side by side. They might have been a pair of lovers, and yet they might not. "They think I should not be here," said Gertrude.

"With me? I thought you did n't have those ideas."

"You don't understand. There are a great many things you don't understand."

"I understand my stupidity. But why, then, do not Charlotte and Mr. Brand, who, as an elder sister and a clergyman, are free to walk about together, come over and make me wiser by breaking up the unlawful interview into which I have lured you?"

"That is the last thing they would do," said Gertrude.

Felix stared at her a moment, with his lifted eyebrows. "Je n'y comprends rien!" he exclaimed; then his eyes followed for a while the retreating figures of this critical pair. "You may say what you please," he declared; "it is evident to me that your sister is not indifferent to her clever companion. It is agreeable to her to be walking there with him. I can see that from here." And in the excitement of observation Felix rose to his feet.

Gertrude rose also, but she made no attempt to emulate her companion's discovery; she looked rather in another direction. Felix's words had struck her; but a certain delicacy checked her. "She is certainly not indifferent to Mr. Brand; she has the highest opinion of him."

"One can see it—one can see it," said Felix, in a tone of amused contemplation, with his head on one side. Gertrude turned her back to the opposite shore; it was disagreeable to her to look, but she hoped Felix would say something more. "Ah, they have wandered away into the wood," he added.

Gertrude turned round again. "She is *not* in love with him," she said; it seemed her duty to say that.

"Then he is in love with her; or if he is not, he ought to be. She is such a perfect little woman of her kind. She reminds me of a pair of old-fashioned silver sugar-tongs; you know I am very fond of sugar. And she is very nice with Mr. Brand; I have noticed that; very gentle and gracious."

Gertrude reflected a moment. Then she took a great resolution. "She wants him to marry me," she said. "So of course she is nice."

Felix's eyebrows rose higher than ever. "To marry you! Ah, ah, this is interesting. And you think one must be very nice with a man to induce him to do that?"

Gertrude had turned a little pale, but she went on, "Mr. Brand wants it himself."

Felix folded his arms and stood looking at her. "I see—I see," he said quickly. "Why did you never tell me this before?"

"It is disagreeable to me to speak of it even now. I wished simply to explain to you about Charlotte."

"You don't wish to marry Mr. Brand, then?"

"No," said Gertrude, gravely.

"And does your father wish it?"

"Very much."

"And you don't like him—you have refused him?"

"I don't wish to marry him."

"Your father and sister think you ought to, eh?"

"It is a long story," said Gertrude. "They think there are good reasons. I can't explain it. They think I have obligations, and that I have encouraged him."

Felix smiled at her, as if she had been telling him an amusing story about some one else. "I can't tell you how this interests me," he said. "Now you don't recognize these reasons—these obligations?"

"I am not sure; it is not easy." And she picked up her parasol and turned away, as if to descend the slope.

"Tell me this," Felix went on, going with her: "are you likely to give in—to let them persuade you?"

Gertrude looked at him with the serious face that she had constantly worn, in opposition to his almost eager smile. "I shall never marry Mr. Brand," she said.

"I see!" Felix rejoined. And they slowly descended the hill together, saying nothing till they reached the margin of the pond. "It is your own affair," he then resumed; "but do you know, I am not altogether glad? If it were settled that you were to marry Mr. Brand I should take a certain comfort in the arrangement. I should feel more free. I have no right to make love to you myself, eh?" And he paused, lightly pressing his argument upon her.

"None whatever," replied Gertrude quickly—too quickly.

"Your father would never hear of it; I have n't a penny. Mr. Brand, of course, has property of his own, eh?"

"I believe he has some property; but that has nothing to do with it."

"With you, of course not; but with your father and sister it must have. So, as I say, if this were settled, I should feel more at liberty."

"More at liberty?" Gertrude repeated. "Please unfasten the boat."

Felix untwisted the rope and stood holding it. "I should be able to say things to you that I can't give myself the pleasure of saying now," he went on. "I could tell you how much I admire you, without seeming to pretend to that which I have no right to pretend to. I should make violent love to you," he added, laughing, "if I thought you were so placed as not to be offended by it."

"You mean if I were engaged to another man? That is strange reasoning!" Gertrude exclaimed.

"In that case you would not take me seriously."

"I take every one seriously," said Gertrude. And without his help she stepped lightly into the boat.

Felix took up the oars and sent it forward. "Ah, this is what you have been thinking about? It seemed to me you had something on your mind. I wish very much," he added, "that you would tell me some of these so-called reasons—these obligations."

"They are not real reasons—good reasons," said Gertrude, looking at the pink and yellow gleams in the water.

"I can understand that! Because a handsome girl has had a spark of coquetry, that is no reason."

"If you mean me, it 's not that. I have not done that."

"It is something that troubles you, at any rate," said Felix.

"Not so much as it used to," Gertrude rejoined.

He looked at her, smiling always. "That is not saying much, eh?" But she only rested her eyes, very gravely, on the lighted water. She seemed to him to be trying to hide the signs of the trouble of which she had just told him. Felix felt, at all times, much the same impulse to dissipate visible melancholy that a good housewife feels to brush away dust. There was something he wished to brush away now; suddenly he stopped rowing and poised his oars. "Why should Mr. Brand have addressed himself to you, and not to your sister?" he asked. "I am sure she would listen to him."

Gertrude, in her family, was thought capable of a good deal of levity; but her levity had never gone so far as this. It moved her greatly, however, to hear Felix say that he was sure of something; so that, raising her eyes toward him, she tried intently, for some moments, to conjure up this wonderful image of a love-affair between her own sister and her own suitor. We know that Gertrude had an imaginative mind; so that it is not impossible that this effort should have been partially successful. But she only murmured, "Ah, Felix! ah, Felix!"

"Why should n't they marry? Try and make them marry!" cried Felix.

"Try and make them?"

"Turn the tables on them. Then they will leave you alone. I will help you as far as I can."

Gertrude's heart began to beat; she was greatly excited; she had never had anything so interesting proposed to her before. Felix had begun to row again, and he now sent the boat home with long strokes. "I believe she does care for him!" said Gertrude, after they had disembarked.

"Of course she does, and we will marry them off. It will make them happy; it will make every one happy. We shall have a wedding and I will write an epithalamium."

"It seems as if it would make me happy," said Gertrude.

"To get rid of Mr. Brand, eh? To recover your liberty?"

Gertrude walked on. "To see my sister married to so good a man."

Felix gave his light laugh. "You always put things on those grounds; you will never say anything for yourself. You are all so afraid, here, of being selfish. I don't think you know how," he went on. "Let me show you! It will make me happy for myself, and for just the reverse of what I told you a while ago. After that, when I make love to you, you will have to think I mean it."

"I shall never think you mean anything," said Gertrude. "You are too fantastic."

"Ah," cried Felix, "that 's a license to say everything! Gertrude, I adore you!"

VIII

CHARLOTTE and Mr. Brand had not returned when they reached the house; but the Baroness had come to tea, and Robert Acton also, who now regularly asked for a place at this generous repast or made his appearance later in the evening. Clifford Wentworth, with his juvenile growl, remarked upon it.

"You are always coming to tea nowadays, Robert," he said. "I should think you had drunk enough tea in China."

"Since when is Mr. Acton more frequent?" asked the Baroness.

"Since you came," said Clifford. "It seems as if you were a kind of attraction."

"I suppose I am a curiosity," said the Baroness. "Give me time and I will make you a salon."

"It would fall to pieces after you go!" exclaimed Acton.

"Don't talk about her going, in that familiar way," Clifford said. "It makes me feel gloomy."

Mr. Wentworth glanced at his son, and taking note of these words, wondered if Felix had been teaching him, according to the programme he had sketched out, to make love to the wife of a German prince.

Charlotte came in late with Mr. Brand; but Gertrude, to whom, at least, Felix had taught something, looked in vain, in her face, for the traces of a guilty passion. Mr. Brand sat down by Gertrude, and she presently asked him why they had not crossed the pond to join Felix and herself.

"It is cruel of you to ask me that," he answered, very softly. He had a large morsel of cake before him; but he fingered it without eating it. "I sometimes think you are growing cruel," he added.

Gertrude said nothing; she was afraid to speak. There was a kind of rage in her heart; she felt as if she could easily persuade herself that she was persecuted. She said to herself that it was quite right that she should not allow him to make her believe she was wrong. She thought of what Felix had said to her; she wished indeed Mr. Brand would marry Charlotte. She looked away from him and spoke no more. Mr. Brand ended by eating his cake, while Felix sat opposite, describing to Mr. Wentworth the students' duels at Heidelberg. After tea they all dispersed themselves, as usual, upon the piazza and in the garden; and Mr. Brand drew near to Gertrude again.

"I did n't come to you this afternoon because you were not alone," he began; "because you were with a newer friend."

"Felix? He is an old friend by this time."

Mr. Brand looked at the ground for some moments. "I thought I was prepared to hear you speak in that way," he resumed. "But I find it very painful."

"I don't see what else I can say," said Gertrude.

Mr. Brand walked beside her for a while in silence; Gertrude wished he would go away. "He is certainly very accomplished. But I think I ought to advise you."

"To advise me?"

"I think I know your nature."

"I think you don't," said Gertrude, with a soft laugh.

"You make yourself out worse than you are—to please him," Mr. Brand said, gently.

"Worse—to please him? What do you mean?" asked Gertrude, stopping.

Mr. Brand stopped also, and with the same soft straightforwardness, "He does n't care for the things you care for—the great questions of life."

Gertrude, with her eyes on his, shook her head. "I don't care for the great questions of life. They are much beyond me."

"There was a time when you did n't say that," said Mr. Brand.

"Oh," rejoined Gertrude, "I think you made me talk a great deal of nonsense. And it depends," she added, "upon what you call the great questions of life. There are some things I care for."

"Are they the things you talk about with your cousin?"

"You should not say things to me against my cousin, Mr. Brand," said Gertrude. "That is dishonorable."

He listened to this respectfully; then he answered, with a little vibration of the voice, "I should be very sorry to do anything dishonorable. But I don't see why it is dishonorable to say that your cousin is frivolous."

"Go and say it to himself!"

"I think he would admit it," said Mr. Brand. "That is the tone he would take. He would not be ashamed of it."

"Then I am not ashamed of it!" Gertrude declared. "That is probably what I like him for. I am frivolous myself."

"You are trying, as I said just now, to lower yourself."

"I am trying for once to be natural!" cried Gertrude passionately. "I have been pretending, all my life; I have been dishonest; it is you that have made me so!" Mr. Brand stood gazing at her, and she went on, "Why should n't I be frivolous, if I want? One has a right to be frivolous, if it 's one's nature. No, I don't care for the great questions. I care for pleasure—for amusement. Perhaps I am fond of wicked things; it is very possible!"

Mr. Brand remained staring; he was even a little pale, as if he had been frightened. "I don't think you know what you are saying!" he exclaimed.

"Perhaps not. Perhaps I am talking nonsense. But it is only with you that I talk nonsense. I never do so with my cousin."

"I will speak to you again, when you are less excited," said Mr. Brand.

"I am always excited when you speak to me. I must tell you that—even if it prevents you altogether, in future. Your speaking to me irritates me. With my cousin it is very different. That seems quiet and natural."

He looked at her, and then he looked away, with a kind of helpless distress, at the dusky garden and the faint summer stars. After which, suddenly turning back, "Gertrude, Gertrude!" he softly groaned. "Am I really losing you?"

She was touched—she was pained; but it had already occurred to her that she might do something better than say so. It would not have alleviated her companion's distress to perceive, just then, whence she had sympathetically borrowed this ingenuity. "I am not sorry for you," Gertrude said; "for in paying so much attention to me you are following a shadow—you are wasting something precious. There is something else you might have that you don't look at—something better than I am. That is a reality!" And then, with intention, she looked at him and tried to smile a little. He thought this smile of hers very strange; but she turned away and left him.

She wandered about alone in the garden wondering what Mr. Brand would make of her words, which it had been a singular pleasure for her to utter. Shortly after, passing in front of the house, she saw at a distance two persons standing near the garden gate. It was Mr. Brand going away and bidding good-night to Charlotte, who had walked down with him from the house. Gertrude saw that the parting was prolonged. Then she turned her back upon it. She had not gone very far, however, when she heard her sister slowly following her. She neither turned round nor waited for her; she knew what Charlotte was going to say. Charlotte, who at last overtook her, in fact presently began; she had passed her arm into Gertrude's.

"Will you listen to me, dear, if I say something very particular?"

"I know what you are going to say," said Gertrude. "Mr. Brand feels very badly."

"Oh, Gertrude, how can you treat him so?" Charlotte demanded. And as her sister made no answer she added, "After all he has done for you!"

"What has he done for me?"

"I wonder you can ask, Gertrude. He has helped you so. You told me so yourself, a great many times. You told me that he helped you to struggle with your—your peculiarities. You told me that he had taught you how to govern your temper."

For a moment Gertrude said nothing. Then, "Was my temper very bad?" she asked.

"I am not accusing you, Gertrude," said Charlotte.

"What are you doing, then?" her sister demanded, with a short laugh.

"I am pleading for Mr. Brand—reminding you of all you owe him."

"I have given it all back," said Gertrude, still with her little laugh. "He can take back the virtue he imparted! I want to be wicked again."

Her sister made her stop in the path, and fixed upon her, in the darkness, a sweet, reproachful gaze. "If you talk this way I shall almost believe it. Think of all we owe Mr. Brand. Think of how he has always expected something of you. Think how much he has been to us. Think of his beautiful influence upon Clifford."

"He is very good," said Gertrude, looking at her sister. "I know he is very good. But he should n't speak against Felix."

"Felix is good," Charlotte answered, softly but promptly. "Felix is very wonderful. Only he is so different. Mr. Brand is much nearer to us. I should never think of going to Felix with a trouble—with a question. Mr. Brand is much more to us, Gertrude."

"He is very—very good," Gertrude repeated. "He is more to you; yes, much more. Charlotte," she added suddenly, "you are in love with him!"

"Oh, Gertrude!" cried poor Charlotte; and her sister saw her blushing in the darkness.

Gertrude put her arm round her. "I wish he would marry you!" she went on.

Charlotte shook herself free. "You must not say such things!" she exclaimed, beneath her breath.

"You like him more than you say, and he likes you more than he knows."

"This is very cruel of you!" Charlotte Wentworth murmured.

But if it was cruel Gertrude continued pitiless. "Not if it 's true," she answered. "I wish he would marry you."

"Please don't say that."

"I mean to tell him so!" said Gertrude.

"Oh, Gertrude, Gertrude!" her sister almost moaned.

"Yes, if he speaks to me again about myself. I will say, 'Why don't you marry Charlotte? She 's a thousand times better than I.' "

"You *are* wicked; you *are* changed!" cried her sister.

"If you don't like it you can prevent it," said Gertrude. "You can prevent it by keeping him from speaking to me!" And with this she walked away, very conscious of what she had done; measuring it and finding a certain joy and a quickened sense of freedom in it.

Mr. Wentworth was rather wide of the mark in suspecting that Clifford had begun to pay unscrupulous compliments to his brilliant cousin; for the young man had really more scruples than he received credit for in his family. He had a certain transparent shamefacedness which was in itself a proof that he was not at his ease in dissipation. His collegiate peccadilloes had aroused a domestic murmur as disagreeable to the young man as the creaking of his boots would have been to a house-breaker. Only, as the house-breaker would have simplified matters by removing his *chaussures*, it had seemed to Clifford that the shortest cut to comfortable relations with people— relations which should make him cease to think that when they spoke to him they meant something improving—was to renounce all ambition toward a nefarious development. And, in fact, Clifford's ambition took the most commendable form. He thought of himself in the future as the well-known and much-liked Mr. Wentworth, of Boston, who should, in the natural course of prosperity, have married his pretty cousin, Lizzie Acton; should live in a wide-fronted house, in view of the Common; and should drive, behind a light wagon, over the damp autumn roads, a pair of beautifully matched sorrel horses. Clifford's vision of the coming years was very simple; its most definite features were this element of familiar matrimony and the duplication of his resources for trotting. He had not yet asked his cousin to marry him; but he meant to do so as soon as he had taken his degree. Lizzie was serenely conscious of his intention, and she had made up her mind that he would improve. Her brother, who was very fond of this light, quick, competent little Lizzie, saw on his side no reason to interpose. It seemed to him a graceful social law that Clifford and his sister should become engaged; he himself was not engaged, but every one else, fortunately, was not such a fool as he. He was fond of Clifford, as well, and had his own way—of which it must be confessed he was a little ashamed—of looking at those aberrations which had led to the young man's compulsory retirement from the neighboring seat of learning. Acton had seen the world, as he said to himself; he had been to China and had knocked about among men. He had learned the essential difference between a nice young fellow and a mean young fellow, and was satisfied that there was no harm in Clifford. He believed—although it must be added that he had not quite the courage to declare it—in the doctrine of wild oats, and thought it a useful preventive of superfluous fears. If Mr. Wentworth and Charlotte and Mr. Brand would only apply it in Clifford's case, they would be happier; and Acton thought it a pity they should not be happier. They took the boy's misdemeanors too much to heart; they talked to him too solemnly; they frightened and bewildered him. Of course there was the great standard of morality, which forbade that a man should get tipsy, play at billiards for money, or cultivate his sensual consciousness; but what fear was there that poor Clifford was going to run a tilt at any great standard? It had, however, never occurred to Acton to dedicate the Baroness Münster to the redemption of a refractory collegian. The instrument, here, would have seemed to him quite too complex for the operation. Felix, on the other hand, had spoken in obedience to the belief that the more charming a woman is the more numerous, literally, are her definite social uses.

Eugenia herself, as we know, had plenty of leisure to enumerate her uses. As I have had the honor of intimating, she had come four thousand miles to seek her fortune; and it is not to be supposed that after this great effort she could neglect any apparent aid to advancement. It is my misfortune that in attempting to describe in a short compass the deportment of this remarkable woman I am obliged to express things rather brutally. I feel this to be the case, for instance, when I say that she had primarily detected such an aid to advancement in the person of Robert Acton, but that she had afterwards remembered that a prudent archer has always a second bowstring. Eugenia was a woman of finely-mingled motive, and her intentions were never sensibly gross. She had a sort of æsthetic ideal for Clifford which seemed to her a disinterested reason for taking him in hand. It was very well for a fresh-colored young gentleman to be ingenuous; but Clifford, really, was crude. With such a pretty face he ought to have prettier manners. She would teach him that, with a beautiful name, the expectation of a large property, and, as they said in Europe, a social position, an only son should know how to carry himself.

Once Clifford had begun to come and see her by himself and for himself, he came very often. He hardly knew why he should come; he saw her almost every evening at his father's house; he had nothing particular to say to her. She was not a young girl, and fellows of his age called only upon young girls. He exaggerated her age; she seemed to him an old woman; it was happy that the Baroness, with all her intelligence, was incapable of guessing this. But gradually it struck Clifford that visiting old women might be, if not a natural, at least, as they say of some articles of diet, an acquired taste. The Baroness was certainly a very amusing old woman; she talked to him as no lady—and indeed no gentleman—had ever talked to him before.

"You should go to Europe and make the tour," she said to him one afternoon. "Of course, on leaving college you will go."

"I don't want to go," Clifford declared. "I know some fellows who have been to Europe. They say you can have better fun here."

"That depends. It depends upon your idea of fun. Your friends probably were not introduced."

"Introduced?" Clifford demanded.

"They had no opportunity of going into society; they formed no *relations*." This was one of a certain number of words that the Baroness often pronounced in the French manner.

"They went to a ball, in Paris; I know that," said Clifford.

"Ah, there are balls and balls; especially in Paris. No, you must go, you know; it is not a thing from which you can dispense yourself. You need it."

"Oh, I 'm very well," said Clifford. "I 'm not sick."

"I don't mean for your health, my poor child. I mean for your manners."

"I have n't got any manners!" growled Clifford.

"Precisely. You don't mind my assenting to that, eh?" asked the Baroness with a smile. "You must go to Europe and get a few. You can get them better there. It is a pity you might not have come while I was living in—in Germany. I would have introduced you; I had a charming little circle. You would perhaps have been rather young; but the younger one begins, I think, the better. Now, at any rate, you have no time to lose, and when I return you must immediately come to me."

All this, to Clifford's apprehension, was a great mixture—his beginning young, Eugenia's return to Europe, his being introduced to her charming little circle. What was he to begin, and what was her little circle? His ideas about her marriage had a good deal of vagueness; but they were in so far definite as that he felt it to be a matter not to be freely mentioned. He sat and looked all round the room; he supposed she was alluding in some way to her marriage.

"Oh, I don't want to go to Germany," he said; it seemed to him the most convenient thing to say.

She looked at him a while, smiling with her lips, but not with her eyes.

"You have scruples?" she asked.

"Scruples?" said Clifford.

"You young people, here, are very singular; one does n't know where to expect you. When you are not extremely improper you are so terribly proper. I dare say you think that, owing to my irregular marriage, I live with loose people. You were never more mistaken. I have been all the more particular."

"Oh, no," said Clifford, honestly distressed. "I never thought such a thing as that."

"Are you very sure? I am convinced that your father does, and your sisters. They say to each other that here I am on my good behavior, but that over there—married by the left hand—I associate with light women."

"Oh, no," cried Clifford, energetically, "they don't say such things as that to each other!"

"If they think them they had better say them," the Baroness rejoined. "Then they can be contradicted. Please contradict that whenever you hear it, and don't be afraid of coming to see me on account of the company I keep. I have the honor of knowing more distinguished men, my poor child, than you are likely to see in a life-time. I see very few women; but those are women of rank. So, my dear young Puritan, you need n't be afraid. I am not in the least one of those who think that the society of women who have lost their place in the *vrai monde* is necessary to form a young man. I have never taken that tone. I have kept my place myself, and I think we are a much better school than the others. Trust me, Clifford, and I will prove that to you," the Baroness continued, while she made the agreeable reflection that she could not, at least, be accused of perverting her young kinsman. "So if you ever fall among thieves don't go about saying I sent you to them."

Clifford thought it so comical that he should know—in spite of her figurative language—what she meant, and that she should mean what he knew, that he could hardly help laughing a little, although he tried hard. "Oh, no! oh, no!" he murmured.

"Laugh out, laugh out, if I amuse you!" cried the Baroness. "I am here for that!" And Clifford thought her a very amusing person indeed. "But remember," she said on this occasion, "that you are coming—next year—to pay me a visit over there."

About a week afterwards she said to him, point-blank, "Are you seriously making love to your little cousin?"

"Seriously making love"—these words, on Madame Münster's lips, had to Clifford's sense a portentous and embarrassing sound; he hesitated about assenting, lest he should commit himself to more than he understood. "Well, I should n't say it if I was!" he exclaimed.

"Why would n't you say it?" the Baroness demanded. "Those things ought to be known."

"I don't care whether it is known or not," Clifford rejoined. "But I don't want people looking at me."

"A young man of your importance ought to learn to bear observation—to carry himself as if he were quite indifferent to it. I won't say, exactly, unconscious," the Baroness explained. "No, he must seem to know he is observed, and to think it natural he should be; but he must appear perfectly used to it. Now you have n't that, Clifford; you have n't that at all. You must have that, you know. Don't tell me you are not a young man of importance," Eugenia added. "Don't say anything so flat as that."

"Oh, no, you don't catch me saying that!" cried Clifford.

"Yes, you must come to Germany," Madame Münster continued. "I will show you how people can be talked about, and yet not seem to know it. You will be talked about, of course, with me; it will be said you are my lover. I will show you how little one may mind that—how little I shall mind it."

Clifford sat staring, blushing and laughing. "I shall mind it a good deal!" he declared.

"Ah, not too much, you know; that would be uncivil. But I give you leave to mind it a little; especially if you have a passion for Miss Acton. *Voyons*; as regards that, you either have or you have not. It is very simple to say it."

"I don't see why you want to know," said Clifford.

"You ought to want me to know. If one is arranging a marriage, one tells one's friends."

"Oh, I 'm not arranging anything," said Clifford.

"You don't intend to marry your cousin?"

"Well, I expect I shall do as I choose!"

The Baroness leaned her head upon the back of her chair and closed her eyes, as if she were tired. Then opening them again, "Your cousin is very charming!" she said.

"She is the prettiest girl in this place," Clifford rejoined.

" 'In this place' is saying little; she would be charming anywhere. I am afraid you are entangled."

"Oh, no, I 'm not entangled."

"Are you engaged? At your age that is the same thing."

Clifford looked at the Baroness with some audacity. "Will you tell no one?"

"If it 's as sacred as that—no."

"Well, then—we are not!" said Clifford.

"That 's the great secret—that you are not, eh?" asked the Baroness, with a quick laugh. "I am very glad to hear it. You are altogether too young. A young man in your position must choose and compare; he must see the world first. Depend upon it," she added, "you should not settle that matter before you have come abroad and paid me that visit. There are several things I should like to call your attention to first."

"Well, I am rather afraid of that visit," said Clifford. "It seems to me it will be rather like going to school again."

The Baroness looked at him a moment.

"My dear child," she said, "there is no agreeable man who has not, at some moment, been to school to a clever woman—probably a little older than himself. And you must be thankful when you get your instructions gratis. With me you would get it gratis."

The next day Clifford told Lizzie Acton that the Baroness thought her the most charming girl she had ever seen.

Lizzie shook her head. "No, she does n't!" she said.

"Do you think everything she says," asked Clifford, "is to be taken the opposite way?"

"I think that is!" said Lizzie.

Clifford was going to remark that in this case the Baroness must desire greatly to bring about a marriage between Mr. Clifford Wentworth and Miss Elizabeth Acton; but he resolved, on the whole, to suppress this observation.

IX

IT SEEMED to Robert Acton, after Eugenia had come to his house, that something had passed between them which made them a good deal more intimate. It was hard to say exactly what, except her telling him that she had taken her resolution with regard to the Prince Adolf; for Madame Münster's visit had made no difference in their relations. He came to see her very often; but he had come to see her very often before. It was agreeable to him to find himself in her little drawing-room; but this was not a new discovery. There was a change, however, in this sense: that if the Baroness had been a great deal in Acton's thoughts before, she was now never out of them. From the first she had been personally fascinating; but the fascination now had become intellectual as well. He was constantly pondering her words and motions; they were as interesting as the factors in an algebraic problem. This is saying a good deal; for Acton was extremely fond of mathematics. He asked himself whether it could be that he was in love with her, and then hoped he was not; hoped it not so much for his own sake as for that of the amatory passion itself. If this was love, love had been overrated. Love was a poetic impulse, and his own state of feeling with regard to the Baroness was largely characterized by that eminently prosaic sentiment—curiosity. It was true, as Acton with his quietly cogitative habit observed to himself, that curiosity, pushed to a given point, might become a romantic passion; and he certainly thought enough about this charming woman to make him restless and even a little melancholy. It puzzled and vexed him at times to feel that he was not more ardent. He was not in the least bent upon remaining a bachelor. In his younger years he had been—or he had tried to be—of the opinion that it would be a good deal "jollier" not to marry, and he had flattered himself that his single condition was something of a citadel. It was a citadel, at all events, of which he had long since leveled the outworks. He had removed the guns from the ramparts; he had lowered the draw-bridge across the moat. The draw-bridge had swayed lightly under Madame Münster's step; why should he not cause it to be raised again, so that she might be kept prisoner? He had an idea that she would become—in time at least, and on learning the conveniences of the place for making a lady comfortable—a tolerably patient captive. But the draw-bridge was never raised, and Acton's brilliant visitor was as free to depart as she had been to come. It was part of his curiosity to know why the deuce so susceptible a man was *not* in love with so charming a woman. If her various graces were, as I have said, the factors in an algebraic problem, the answer to this question was the indispensable unknown quantity. The pursuit of the unknown quantity was extremely absorbing; for the present it taxed all Acton's faculties.

Toward the middle of August he was obliged to leave home for some days; an old friend, with whom he had been associated in China, had begged him to come to Newport, where he lay extremely ill. His friend got better, and at the end of a week Acton was released. I use the word "released" advisedly; for in spite of his attachment to his Chinese comrade he had been but a half-hearted visitor. He felt as if he had been called away from the theatre during the progress of a remarkably interesting drama. The curtain was up all this time, and he was losing the fourth act; that fourth act which would have been so essential to a just appreciation of the fifth. In other words, he was thinking about the Baroness, who, seen at this distance, seemed a truly brilliant figure. He saw at Newport a great many pretty women, who certainly were figures as brilliant as beautiful light dresses could make them; but though they talked a great deal—and the Baroness's strong point was perhaps also her conversation—Madame Münster appeared to lose nothing by the comparison. He wished she had come to Newport too. Would it not be possible to make up, as they said, a party for visiting the famous watering-place and invite Eugenia to join it? It was true that the complete satisfaction would be to spend a fortnight at Newport with Eugenia alone. It would be a great pleasure to see her, in society, carry everything before her, as he was sure she would do. When Acton caught himself thinking these thoughts he began to walk up and down, with his hands in his pockets, frowning a little and looking at the floor. What did it prove—for it certainly proved something—this lively disposition to be "off" somewhere with Madame Münster, away from all the rest of them? Such a vision, certainly, seemed a refined implication of matrimony, after the Baroness should have formally got rid of her informal husband. At any rate, Acton, with his characteristic discretion, forbore to give expression to whatever else it might imply, and the narrator of these incidents is not obliged to be more definite.

He returned home rapidly, and, arriving in the afternoon, lost as little time as possible in joining the familiar circle at Mr. Wentworth's. On reaching the house, however, he found the piazzas empty. The doors and windows were open, and their emptiness was made clear by the shafts of lamp-light from the parlors. Entering the house, he found Mr. Wentworth sitting alone in one of these apartments, engaged in the perusal of the "North American Review." After they had exchanged greetings and his cousin had made discreet inquiry about his journey, Acton asked what had become of Mr. Wentworth's companions.

"They are scattered about, amusing themselves as usual," said the old man. "I saw Charlotte, a short time since, seated, with Mr. Brand, upon the piazza. They were conversing with their customary animation. I suppose they have joined her sister, who, for the hundredth time, was doing the honors of the garden to her foreign cousin."

"I suppose you mean Felix," said Acton. And on Mr. Wentworth's assenting, he said, "And the others?"

"Your sister has not come this evening. You must have seen her at home," said Mr. Wentworth.

"Yes. I proposed to her to come. She declined."

"Lizzie, I suppose, was expecting a visitor," said the old man, with a kind of solemn slyness.

"If she was expecting Clifford, he had not turned up."

Mr. Wentworth, at this intelligence, closed the "North American Review" and remarked that he had understood Clifford to say that he was going to see his cousin. Privately, he reflected that if Lizzie Acton had had no news of his son, Clifford must have gone to Boston for the evening: an unnatural course of a summer night, especially when accompanied with disingenuous representations.

"You must remember that he has two cousins," said Acton,

laughing. And then, coming to the point, "If Lizzie is not here," he added, "neither apparently is the Baroness."

Mr. Wentworth stared a moment, and remembered that queer proposition of Felix's. For a moment he did not know whether it was not to be wished that Clifford, after all, might have gone to Boston. "The Baroness has not honored us to-night," he said. "She has not come over for three days."

"Is she ill?" Acton asked.

"No; I have been to see her."

"What is the matter with her?"

"Well," said Mr. Wentworth, "I infer she has tired of us."

Acton pretended to sit down, but he was restless; he found it impossible to talk with Mr. Wentworth. At the end of ten minutes he took up his hat and said that he thought he would "go off." It was very late; it was ten o'clock.

His quiet-faced kinsman looked at him a moment. "Are you going home?" he asked.

Acton hesitated, and then answered that he had proposed to go over and take a look at the Baroness.

"Well, *you* are honest, at least," said Mr. Wentworth, sadly.

"So are you, if you come to that!" cried Acton, laughing. "Why should n't I be honest?"

The old man opened the "North American" again, and read a few lines. "If we have ever had any virtue among us, we had better keep hold of it now," he said. He was not quoting.

"We have a Baroness among us," said Acton. "That 's what we must keep hold of!" He was too impatient to see Madame Münster again to wonder what Mr. Wentworth was talking about. Nevertheless, after he had passed out of the house and traversed the garden and the little piece of road that separated him from Eugenia's provisional residence, he stopped a moment outside. He stood in her little garden; the long window of her parlor was open, and he could see the white curtains, with the lamp-light shining through them, swaying softly to and fro in the warm night wind. There was a sort of excitement in the idea of seeing Madame Münster again; he became aware that his heart was beating rather faster than usual. It was this that made him stop, with a half-amused surprise. But in a moment he went along the piazza, and, approaching the open window, tapped upon its lintel with his stick. He could see the Baroness within; she was standing in the middle of the room. She came to the window and pulled aside the curtain; then she stood looking at him a moment. She was not smiling; she seemed serious.

"Mais entrez donc!" she said at last. Acton passed in across the window-sill; he wondered, for an instant, what was the matter with her. But the next moment she had begun to smile and had put out her hand. "Better late than never," she said. "It is very kind of you to come at this hour."

"I have just returned from my journey," said Acton.

"Ah, very kind, very kind," she repeated, looking about her where to sit.

"I went first to the other house," Acton continued. "I expected to find you there."

She had sunk into her usual chair; but she got up again, and began to move about the room. Acton had laid down his hat and stick; he was looking at her, conscious that there was in fact a great charm in seeing her again. "I don't know whether I ought to tell you to sit down," she said. "It is too late to begin a visit."

"It 's too early to end one," Acton declared; "and we need n't mind the beginning."

She looked at him again, and, after a moment, dropped once more into her low chair, while he took a place near her. "We are in the middle, then?" she asked. "Was that where we were when you went away? No, I have n't been to the other house."

"Not yesterday, nor the day before, eh?"

"I don't know how many days it is."

"You are tired of it," said Acton.

She leaned back in her chair; her arms were folded. "That is a terrible accusation, but I have not the courage to defend myself."

"I am not attacking you," said Acton. "I expected something of this kind."

"It 's a proof of extreme intelligence. I hope you enjoyed your journey."

"Not at all," Acton declared. "I would much rather have been here with you."

"Now you *are* attacking me," said the Baroness. "You are contrasting my inconstancy with your own fidelity."

"I confess I never get tired of people I like."

"Ah, you are not a poor wicked foreign woman, with irritable nerves and a sophisticated mind!"

"Something has happened to you since I went away," said Acton, changing his place.

"Your going away—that is what has happened to me."

"Do you mean to say that you have missed me?" he asked.

"If I had meant to say it, it would not be worth your making a note of. I am very dishonest and my compliments are worthless."

Acton was silent for some moments. "You have broken down," he said at last.

Madame Münster left her chair, and began to move about.

"Only for a moment. I shall pull myself together again."

"You had better not take it too hard. If you are bored, you need n't be afraid to say so—to me at least."

"You should n't say such things as that," the Baroness answered. "You should encourage me."

"I admire your patience; that is encouraging."

"You should n't even say that. When you talk of my patience you are disloyal to your own people. Patience implies suffering; and what have I had to suffer?"

"Oh, not hunger, not unkindness, certainly," said Acton, laughing. "Nevertheless, we all admire your patience."

"You all detest me!" cried the Baroness, with a sudden vehemence, turning her back toward him.

"You make it hard," said Acton, getting up, "for a man to say something tender to you." This evening there was something particularly striking and touching about her; an unwonted softness and a look of suppressed emotion. He felt himself suddenly appreciating the fact that she had behaved very well. She had come to this quiet corner of the world under the weight of a cruel indignity, and she had been so gracefully, modestly thankful for the rest she found there. She had joined that simple circle over the way; she had mingled in its plain, provincial talk; she had shared its meagre and savorless pleasures. She had set herself a task, and she had rigidly performed it. She had conformed to the angular conditions of New England life, and she had had the tact and pluck to carry it off as if she liked them. Acton felt a more downright need than he had ever felt before to tell her that he admired her and that she struck him as a very superior woman. All along, hitherto, he had been on his guard with her; he had been cautious, observant, suspicious. But now a certain light tumult in his blood seemed to tell him that a finer degree of confidence in this charming woman would be its own reward. "We don't detest you," he went on. "I don't know what you mean. At any rate, I speak for myself; I don't know anything about the others. Very likely, you detest them for the dull life they make you lead. Really, it would give me a sort of pleasure to hear you say so."

Eugenia had been looking at the door on the other side of the room; now she slowly turned her eyes toward Robert Acton. "What can be the motive," she asked, "of a man like you—an honest man, a *galant homme*—in saying so base a thing as that?"

"Does it sound very base?" asked Acton, candidly. "I suppose it does, and I thank you for telling me so. Of course, I don't mean it literally."

The Baroness stood looking at him. "How do you mean it?" she asked.

This question was difficult to answer, and Acton, feeling the least bit foolish, walked to the open window and looked out. He stood there, thinking a moment, and then he turned back. "You know that document that you were to send to Germany," he said. "You called it your 'renunciation.' Did you ever send it?"

Madame Münster's eyes expanded; she looked very grave. "What a singular answer to my question!"

"Oh, it is n't an answer," said Acton. "I have wished to ask you, many times. I thought it probable you would tell me yourself. The question, on my part, seems abrupt now; but it would be abrupt at any time."

The Baroness was silent a moment; and then, "I think I have told you too much!" she said.

This declaration appeared to Acton to have a certain force; he had indeed a sense of asking more of her than he offered her. He returned to the window, and watched, for a moment, a little star that twinkled through the lattice of the piazza. There were at any rate offers enough he could make; perhaps he had hitherto not been sufficiently explicit in doing so. "I wish you would ask something of me," he presently said. "Is there nothing I can do for you? If you can't stand this dull life any more, let me amuse you!"

The Baroness had sunk once more into a chair, and she had taken up a fan which she held, with both hands, to her mouth. Over the top of the fan her eyes were fixed on him. "You are very strange to-night," she said, with a little laugh.

"I will do anything in the world," he rejoined, standing in front of her. "Should n't you like to travel about and see something of the country? Won't you go to Niagara? You ought to see Niagara, you know."

"With you, do you mean?"

"I should be delighted to take you."

"You alone?"

Acton looked at her, smiling, and yet with a serious air. "Well, yes; we might go alone," he said.

"If you were not what you are," she answered, "I should feel insulted."

"How do you mean—what I am?"

"If you were one of the gentlemen I have been used to all my life. If you were not a queer Bostonian."

"If the gentlemen you have been used to have taught you to expect insults," said Acton, "I am glad I am what I am. You had much better come to Niagara."

"If you wish to 'amuse' me," the Baroness declared, "you need go to no further expense. You amuse me very effectually."

He sat down opposite to her; she still held her fan up to her face, with her eyes only showing above it. There was a moment's silence, and then he said, returning to his former question, "Have you sent that document to Germany?"

Again there was a moment's silence. The expressive eyes of Madame Münster seemed, however, half to break it.

"I will tell you—at Niagara!" she said.

She had hardly spoken when the door at the further end of the room opened—the door upon which, some minutes previous, Eugenia had fixed her gaze. Clifford Wentworth stood there, blushing and looking rather awkward. The Baroness rose, quickly, and Acton, more slowly, did the same. Clifford gave him no greeting; he was looking at Eugenia.

"Ah, you were here?" exclaimed Acton.

"He was in Felix's studio," said Madame Münster. "He wanted to see his sketches."

Clifford looked at Robert Acton, but said nothing; he only fanned himself with his hat. "You chose a bad moment," said Acton; "you had n't much light."

"I had n't any!" said Clifford, laughing.

"Your candle went out?" Eugenia asked. "You should have come back here and lighted it again."

Clifford looked at her a moment. "So I have—come back. But I have left the candle!"

Eugenia turned away. "You are very stupid, my poor boy. You had better go home."

"Well," said Clifford, "good night!"

"Have n't you a word to throw to a man when he has safely returned from a dangerous journey?" Acton asked.

"How do you do?" said Clifford. "I thought—I thought you were"—and he paused, looking at the Baroness again.

"You thought I was at Newport, eh? So I was—this morning."

"Good night, clever child!" said Madame Münster, over her shoulder.

Clifford stared at her—not at all like a clever child; and then, with one of his little facetious growls, took his departure.

"What is the matter with him?" asked Acton, when he was gone. "He seemed rather in a muddle."

Eugenia, who was near the window, glanced out, listening a moment. "The matter—the matter"—she answered. "But you don't say such things here."

"If you mean that he had been drinking a little, you can say that."

"He does n't drink any more. I have cured him. And in return—he 's in love with me."

It was Acton's turn to stare. He instantly thought of his sister; but he said nothing about her. He began to laugh. "I don't wonder at his passion! But I wonder at his forsaking your society for that of your brother's paint-brushes."

Eugenia was silent a little. "He had not been in the studio. I invented that at the moment."

"Invented it? For what purpose?"

"He has an idea of being romantic. He has adopted the habit of coming to see me at midnight—passing only through the orchard and through Felix's painting-room, which has a door opening that way. It seems to amuse him," added Eugenia, with a little laugh.

Acton felt more surprise than he confessed to, for this was a new view of Clifford, whose irregularities had hitherto been quite without the romantic element. He tried to laugh again, but he felt rather too serious, and after a moment's hesitation his seriousness explained itself. "I hope you don't encourage him," he said. "He must not be inconstant to poor Lizzie."

"To your sister?"

"You know they are decidedly intimate," said Acton.

"Ah," cried Eugenia, smiling, "has she—has she"—

"I don't know," Acton interrupted, "what she has. But I always supposed that Clifford had a desire to make himself agreeable to her."

"Ah, par exemple!" the Baroness went on. "The little monster! The next time he becomes sentimental I will him tell that he ought to be ashamed of himself."

Acton was silent a moment. "You had better say nothing about it."

"I had told him as much already, on general grounds," said the Baroness. "But in this country, you know, the relations of young people are so extraordinary that one is quite at sea. They are not engaged when you would quite say they ought to be. Take Charlotte Wentworth, for instance, and that young ecclesiastic. If I were her father I should insist upon his marrying her; but it appears to be thought there is no urgency. On the other hand, you suddenly learn that a boy of twenty and a little girl who is still with her governess—your sister has no governess? Well, then, who is never away from her mamma—a young couple, in short, between whom you have noticed nothing beyond an exchange of the childish pleasantries characteristic of their age, are on the point of setting up as man and wife." The Baroness spoke with a certain exaggerated volubility which was in contrast with the languid grace that had characterized her manner before Clifford made his appearance. It seemed to Acton that there was a spark of irritation in her eye—a note of irony (as when she spoke of Lizzie being never away from her mother) in her voice. If Madame Münster was irritated, Robert Acton was vaguely mystified; she began to move about the room again, and he looked at her without saying anything. Presently she took out her watch, and, glancing at it, declared that it was three o'clock in the morning and that he must go.

"I have not been here an hour," he said, "and they are still sitting up at the other house. You can see the lights. Your brother has not come in."

"Oh, at the other house," cried Eugenia, "they are terrible people! I don't know what they may do over there. I am a quiet little humdrum woman; I have rigid rules and I keep them. One of them is not to have visitors in the small hours—especially clever men like you. So good night!"

Decidedly, the Baroness was incisive; and though Acton bade her good night and departed, he was still a good deal mystified.

The next day Clifford Wentworth came to see Lizzie, and Acton, who was at home and saw him pass through the garden, took note of the circumstance. He had a natural desire to make it tally with Madame Münster's account of Clifford's disaffection; but his ingenuity, finding itself unequal to the task, resolved at last to ask help of the young man's candor. He waited till he saw him going away, and then he went out and overtook him in the grounds.

"I wish very much you would answer me a question," Acton said. "What were you doing, last night, at Madame Münster's?"

Clifford began to laugh and to blush, by no means like a young man with a romantic secret. "What did she tell you?" he asked.

"That is exactly what I don't want to say."

"Well, I want to tell you the same," said Clifford; "and unless I know it perhaps I can't."

They had stopped in a garden path; Acton looked hard at

his rosy young kinsman. "She said she could n't fancy what had got into you; you appeared to have taken a violent dislike to her."

Clifford stared, looking a little alarmed. "Oh, come," he growled, "you don't mean that!"

"And that when—for common civility's sake—you came occasionally to the house you left her alone and spent your time in Felix's studio, under pretext of looking at his sketches."

"Oh, come!" growled Clifford, again.

"Did you ever know me to tell an untruth?"

"Yes, lots of them!" said Clifford, seeing an opening, out of the discussion, for his sarcastic powers. "Well," he presently added, "I thought you were my father."

"You knew some one was there?"

"We heard you coming in."

Acton meditated. "You had been with the Baroness, then?"

"I was in the parlor. We heard your step outside. I thought it was my father."

"And on that," asked Acton, "you ran away?"

"She told me to go—to go out by the studio."

Acton meditated more intensely; if there had been a chair at hand he would have sat down. "Why should she wish you not to meet your father?"

"Well," said Clifford, "father does n't like to see me there."

Acton looked askance at his companion and forbore to make any comment upon this assertion. "Has he said so," he asked, "to the Baroness?"

"Well, I hope not," said Clifford. "He has n't said so—in so many words—to me. But I know it worries him; and I want to stop worrying him. The Baroness knows it, and she wants me to stop, too."

"To stop coming to see her?"

"I don't know about that; but to stop worrying father. Eugenia knows everything," Clifford added, with an air of knowingness of his own.

"Ah," said Acton, interrogatively, "Eugenia knows everything?"

"She knew it was not father coming in."

"Then why did you go?"

Clifford blushed and laughed afresh. "Well, I was afraid it was. And besides, she told me to go, at any rate."

"Did she think it was I?" Acton asked.

"She did n't say so."

Again Robert Acton reflected. "But you did n't go," he presently said; "you came back."

"I could n't get out of the studio," Clifford rejoined. "The door was locked, and Felix has nailed some planks across the lower half of the confounded windows to make the light come in from above. So they were no use. I waited there a good while, and then, suddenly, I felt ashamed. I did n't want to be hiding away from my own father. I could n't stand it any longer. I bolted out, and when I found it was you I was a little flurried. But Eugenia carried it off, did n't she?" Clifford added, in the tone of a young humorist whose perception had not been permanently clouded by the sense of his own discomfort.

"Beautifully!" said Acton. "Especially," he continued, "when one remembers that you were very imprudent and that she must have been a good deal annoyed."

"Oh," cried Clifford, with the indifference of a young man who feels that however he may have failed of felicity in behavior he is extremely just in his impressions, "Eugenia does n't care for anything!"

Acton hesitated a moment. "Thank you for telling me this," he said at last. And then, laying his hand on Clifford's shoulder, he added, "Tell me one thing more: are you by chance a little in love with the Baroness?"

"No, sir!" said Clifford, almost shaking off his hand.

X

THE FIRST SUNDAY that followed Robert Acton's return from Newport witnessed a change in the brilliant weather that had long prevailed. The rain began to fall and the day was cold and dreary. Mr. Wentworth and his daughters put on overshoes and went to church, and Felix Young, without overshoes, went also, holding an umbrella over Gertrude. It is to be feared that, in the whole observance, this was the privilege he most highly valued. The Baroness remained at home; she was in neither a cheerful nor a devotional mood. She had, however, never been, during her residence in the United States, what is called a regular attendant at divine service; and on this particular Sunday morning of which I began with speaking she stood at the window of her little drawing-room, watching the long arm of a rose-tree that was attached to her piazza, but a portion of which had disengaged itself, sway to and fro, shake and gesticulate, against the dusky drizzle of the sky. Every now and then, in a gust of wind, the rose-tree scattered a shower of water-drops against the window-pane; it appeared to have a kind of human movement—a menacing, warning intention. The room was very cold; Madame Münster put on a shawl and walked about. Then she determined to have some fire; and summoning her ancient negress, the contrast of whose polished ebony and whose crimson turban had been at first a source of satisfaction to her, she made arrangements for the production of a crackling flame. This old woman's name was Azarina. The Baroness had begun by thinking that there would be a savory wildness in her talk, and, for amusement, she had encouraged her to chatter. But Azarina was dry and prim; her conversation was anything but African; she reminded Eugenia of the tiresome old ladies she met in society. She knew, however, how to make a fire; so that after she had laid the logs, Eugenia, who was terribly bored, found a quarter of an hour's entertainment in sitting and watching them blaze and sputter. She had thought it very likely Robert Acton would come and see her; she had not met him since that infelicitous evening. But the morning waned without his coming; several times she thought she heard his step on the piazza; but it was only a window-shutter shaking in a rain-gust. The Baroness, since the beginning of that episode in her career of which a slight sketch has been attempted in these pages, had had many moments of irritation. But to-day her irritation had a peculiar keenness; it appeared to feed upon itself. It urged her to do something; but it suggested no par-ticularly profitable line of action. If she could have done something at the moment, on the spot, she would have stepped upon a European steamer and turned her back, with a kind of rapture, upon that profoundly mortifying failure, her visit to her American relations. It is not exactly apparent why she should have termed this enterprise a failure, inas-much as she had been treated with the highest distinction for which allowance had been made in American institutions. Her irritation came, at bottom, from the sense, which, always present, had suddenly grown acute, that the social soil on this big, vague continent was somehow not adapted for growing those plants whose fragrance she especially inclined to inhale and by which she liked to see herself surrounded—a species of vegetation for which she carried a collection of seedlings, as we may say, in her pocket. She found her chief happiness in the sense of exerting a certain power and making a certain impression; and now she felt the annoyance of a rather wea-ried swimmer who, on nearing shore, to land, finds a smooth straight wall of rock when he had counted upon a clean firm beach. Her power, in the American air, seemed to have lost its prehensile attributes; the smooth wall of rock was insur-mountable. "Surely je n'en suis pas là," she said to herself, "that I let it make me uncomfortable that a Mr. Robert Acton should n't honor me with a visit!" Yet she was vexed that he had not come; and she was vexed at her vexation.

Her brother, at least, came in, stamping in the hall and shaking the wet from his coat. In a moment he entered the room, with a glow in his cheek and half-a-dozen rain-drops glistening on his mustache. "Ah, you have a fire," he said.

"Les beaux jours sont passés," replied the Baroness.

"Never, never! They have only begun," Felix declared, planting himself before the hearth. He turned his back to the fire, placed his hands behind him, extended his legs and looked away through the window with an expression of face which seemed to denote the perception of rose-color even in the tints of a wet Sunday.

His sister, from her chair, looked up at him, watching him; and what she saw in his face was not grateful to her present mood. She was puzzled by many things, but her brother's disposition was a frequent source of wonder to her. I say frequent and not constant, for there were long periods during which she gave her attention to other problems. Sometimes she had said to herself that his happy temper, his eternal gayety, was an affectation, a *pose*; but she was vaguely conscious that during the present summer he had been a highly successful comedian. They had never yet had an explanation; she had not known the need of one. Felix was presumably following the bent of his disinterested genius, and she felt that she had no advice to give him that he would understand. With this, there was always a certain element of comfort about Felix— the assurance that he would not interfere. He was very delicate, this pure-minded Felix; in effect, he was her brother, and Madame Münster felt that there was a great propriety, every way, in that. It is true that Felix was delicate; he was not fond of explanations with his sister; this was one of the very few things in the world about which he was uncomfortable. But now he was not thinking of anything uncomfortable.

"Dear brother," said Eugenia at last, "do stop making *les yeux doux* at the rain."

"With pleasure. I will make them at you!" answered Felix.

"How much longer," asked Eugenia, in a moment, "do you propose to remain in this lovely spot?"

Felix stared. "Do you want to go away—already?"

" 'Already' is delicious. I am not so happy as you."

Felix dropped into a chair, looking at the fire. "The fact is I *am* happy," he said in his light, clear tone.

"And do you propose to spend your life in making love to Gertrude Wentworth?"

"Yes!" said Felix, smiling sidewise at his sister.

The Baroness returned his glance, much more gravely; and then, "Do you like her?" she asked.

"Don't you?" Felix demanded.

The Baroness was silent a moment. "I will answer you in the words of the gentleman who was asked if he liked music: 'Je ne la crains pas!' "

"She admires you immensely," said Felix.

"I don't care for that. Other women should not admire one."

"They should dislike you?"

Again Madame Münster hesitated. "They should hate me! It's a measure of the time I have been losing here that they don't."

"No time is lost in which one has been happy!" said Felix, with a bright sententiousness which may well have been a little irritating.

"And in which," rejoined his sister, with a harsher laugh, "one has secured the affections of a young lady with a fortune!"

Felix explained, very candidly and seriously. "I have secured Gertrude's affection, but I am by no means sure that I have secured her fortune. That may come—or it may not."

"Ah, well, it *may*! That's the great point."

"It depends upon her father. He does n't smile upon our union. You know he wants her to marry Mr. Brand."

"I know nothing about it!" cried the Baroness. "Please to put on a log." Felix complied with her request and sat watching the quickening of the flame. Presently his sister added, "And you propose to elope with mademoiselle?"

"By no means. I don't wish to do anything that's disagreeable to Mr. Wentworth. He has been far too kind to us."

"But you must choose between pleasing yourself and pleasing him."

"I want to please every one!" exclaimed Felix, joyously. "I have a good conscience. I made up my mind at the outset that it was not my place to make love to Gertrude."

"So, to simplify matters, she made love to you!"

Felix looked at his sister with sudden gravity. "You say you are not afraid of her," he said. "But perhaps you ought to be—a little. She's a very clever person."

"I begin to see it!" cried the Baroness. Her brother, making no rejoinder, leaned back in his chair, and there was a long silence. At last, with an altered accent, Madame Münster put another question. "You expect, at any rate, to marry?"

"I shall be greatly disappointed if we don't."

"A disappointment or two will do you good!" the Baroness declared. "And, afterwards, do you mean to turn American?"

"It seems to me I am a very good American already. But we shall go to Europe. Gertrude wants extremely to see the world."

"Ah, like me, when I came here!" said the Baroness, with a little laugh.

"No, not like you," Felix rejoined, looking at his sister with a certain gentle seriousness. While he looked at her she rose from her chair, and he also got up. "Gertrude is not at all like you," he went on; "but in her own way she is almost as clever." He paused a moment; his soul was full of an agreeable feeling and of a lively disposition to express it. His sister, to his spiritual vision, was always like the lunar disk when only a part of it is lighted. The shadow on this bright surface seemed to him to expand and to contract; but whatever its proportions, he always appreciated the moonlight. He looked at the Baroness, and then he kissed her. "I am very much in love with Gertrude," he said. Eugenia turned away and walked about the room, and Felix continued. "She is very interesting, and very different from what she seems. She has never had a chance. She is very brilliant. We will go to Europe and amuse ourselves."

The Baroness had gone to the window, where she stood looking out. The day was drearier than ever; the rain was doggedly falling. "Yes, to amuse yourselves," she said at last, "you had decidedly better go to Europe!" Then she turned round, looking at her brother. A chair stood near her; she leaned her hands upon the back of it. "Don't you think it is very good of me," she asked, "to come all this way with you simply to see you properly married—if properly it is?"

"Oh, it will be properly!" cried Felix, with light eagerness.

The Baroness gave a little laugh. "You are thinking only of yourself, and you don't answer my question. While you are amusing yourself—with the brilliant Gertrude—what shall I be doing?"

"Vous serez de la partie!" cried Felix.

"Thank you: I should spoil it." The Baroness dropped her eyes for some moments. "Do you propose, however, to leave me here?" she inquired.

Felix smiled at her. "My dearest sister, where you are concerned I never propose. I execute your commands."

"I believe," said Eugenia, slowly, "that you are the most heartless person living. Don't you see that I am in trouble?"

"I saw that you were not cheerful, and I gave you some good news."

"Well, let me give you some news," said the Baroness. "You probably will not have discovered it for yourself. Robert Acton wants to marry me."

"No, I had not discovered that. But I quite understand it. Why does it make you unhappy?"

"Because I can't decide."

"Accept him, accept him!" cried Felix, joyously. "He is the best fellow in the world."

"He is immensely in love with me," said the Baroness.

"And he has a large fortune. Permit me in turn to remind you of that."

"Oh, I am perfectly aware of it," said Eugenia. "That 's a great item in his favor. I am terribly candid." And she left her place and came nearer her brother, looking at him hard. He was turning over several things; she was wondering in what manner he really understood her.

There were several ways of understanding her: there was what she said, and there was what she meant, and there was something, between the two, that was neither. It is probable that, in the last analysis, what she meant was that Felix should spare her the necessity of stating the case more exactly and should hold himself commissioned to assist her by all honorable means to marry the best fellow in the world. But in all this it was never discovered what Felix understood.

"Once you have your liberty, what are your objections?" he asked.

"Well, I don't particularly like him."

"Oh, try a little."

"I am trying now," said Eugenia. "I should succeed better if he did n't live here. I could never live here."

"Make him go to Europe," Felix suggested.

"Ah, there you speak of happiness based upon violent effort," the Baroness rejoined. "That is not what I am looking for. He would never live in Europe."

"He would live anywhere, with you!" said Felix, gallantly.

His sister looked at him still, with a ray of penetration in her charming eyes; then she turned away again. "You see, at all events," she presently went on, "that if it had been said of me that I had come over here to seek my fortune it would have to be added that I have found it!"

"Don't leave it lying!" urged Felix, with smiling solemnity.

"I am much obliged to you for your interest," his sister declared, after a moment. "But promise me one thing: *pas de zèle!* If Mr. Acton should ask you to plead his cause, excuse yourself."

"I shall certainly have the excuse," said Felix, "that I have a cause of my own to plead."

"If he should talk of me—favorably," Eugenia continued, "warn him against dangerous illusions. I detest importunities; I want to decide at my leisure, with my eyes open."

"I shall be discreet," said Felix, "except to you. To you I will say, Accept him outright."

She had advanced to the open door-way, and she stood looking at him. "I will go and dress and think of it," she said; and he heard her moving slowly to her apartments.

Late in the afternoon the rain stopped, and just afterwards there was a great flaming, flickering, trickling sunset. Felix sat in his painting-room and did some work; but at last, as the light, which had not been brilliant, began to fade, he laid down his brushes and came out to the little piazza of the cottage. Here he walked up and down for some time, looking at the splendid blaze of the western sky and saying, as he had often said before, that this was certainly the country of sunsets. There was something in these glorious deeps of fire that quickened his imagination; he always found images and promises in the western sky. He thought of a good many things—of roaming about the world with Gertrude Wentworth; he seemed to see their possible adventures, in a glowing frieze, between the cloud-bars; then of what Eugenia had just been telling him. He wished very much that Madame

Münster would make a comfortable and honorable marriage. Presently, as the sunset expanded and deepened, the fancy took him of making a note of so magnificent a piece of coloring. He returned to his studio and fetched out a small panel, with his palette and brushes, and, placing the panel against a window-sill, he began to daub with great gusto. While he was so occupied he saw Mr. Brand, in the distance, slowly come down from Mr. Wentworth's house, nursing a large folded umbrella. He walked with a joyless, meditative tread, and his eyes were bent upon the ground. Felix poised his brush for a moment, watching him; then, by a sudden impulse, as he drew nearer, advanced to the garden-gate and signaled to him—the palette and bunch of brushes contributing to this effect.

Mr. Brand stopped and started; then he appeared to decide to accept Felix's invitation. He came out of Mr. Wentworth's gate and passed along the road; after which he entered the little garden of the cottage. Felix had gone back to his sunset; but he made his visitor welcome while he rapidly brushed it in.

"I wanted so much to speak to you that I thought I would call you," he said, in the friendliest tone. "All the more that you have been to see me so little. You have come to see my sister; I know that. But you have n't come to see me—the celebrated artist. Artists are very sensitive, you know; they notice those things." And Felix turned round, smiling, with a brush in his mouth.

Mr. Brand stood there with a certain blank, candid majesty, pulling together the large flaps of his umbrella. "Why should I come to see you?" he asked. "I know nothing of Art."

"It would sound very conceited, I suppose," said Felix, "if I were to say that it would be a good little chance for you to learn something. You would ask me why you should learn; and I should have no answer to that. I suppose a minister has no need for Art, eh?"

"He has need for good temper, sir," said Mr. Brand, with decision.

Felix jumped up, with his palette on his thumb and a movement of the liveliest deprecation. "That 's because I keep you standing there while I splash my red paint! I beg a thousand pardons! You see what bad manners Art gives a man; and how right you are to let it alone. I did n't mean you should stand, either. The piazza, as you see, is ornamented with rustic chairs; though indeed I ought to warn you that they have nails in the wrong places. I was just making a note of that sunset. I never saw such a blaze of different reds. It looks as if the Celestial City were in flames, eh? If that were really the case I suppose it would be the business of you theologians to put out the fire. Fancy me—an ungodly artist—quietly sitting down to paint it!"

Mr. Brand had always credited Felix Young with a certain impudence, but it appeared to him that on this occasion his impudence was so great as to make a special explanation—or even an apology—necessary. And the impression, it must be added, was sufficiently natural. Felix had at all times a brilliant assurance of manner which was simply the vehicle of his good spirits and his good will; but at present he had a special design, and as he would have admitted that the design was audacious, so he was conscious of having summoned all the arts of conversation to his aid. But he was so far from desiring to offend his visitor that he was rapidly asking himself what personal compliment he could pay the young clergyman that would gratify him most. If he could think of it, he was prepared to pay it down. "Have you been preaching one of your beautiful sermons to-day?" he suddenly asked, laying down his palette. This was not what Felix had been trying to think of, but it was a tolerable stop-gap.

Mr. Brand frowned—as much as a man can frown who has very fair, soft eyebrows, and, beneath them, very gentle, tranquil eyes. "No, I have not preached any sermon to-day. Did you bring me over here for the purpose of making that inquiry?"

Felix saw that he was irritated, and he regretted it immensely; but he had no fear of not being, in the end, agreeable to Mr. Brand. He looked at him, smiling and laying his hand on his arm. "No, no, not for that—not for that. I wanted to ask you something; I wanted to tell you something. I am sure it will interest you very much. Only—as it is something rather private—we had better come into my little studio. I have a western window; we can still see the sunset. *Andiamo!*" And he gave a little pat to his companion's arm.

He led the way in; Mr. Brand stiffly and softly followed. The twilight had thickened in the little studio; but the wall opposite the western window was covered with a deep pink flush. There were a great many sketches and half-finished canvasses suspended in this rosy glow, and the corners of the room were vague and dusky. Felix begged Mr. Brand to sit down; then glancing round him, "By Jove, how pretty it looks!" he cried. But Mr. Brand would not sit down; he went and leaned against the window; he wondered what Felix wanted of him. In the shadow, on the darker parts of the wall, he saw the gleam of three or four pictures that looked fantastic and surprising. They seemed to represent naked figures. Felix stood there, with his head a little bent and his eyes fixed upon his visitor, smiling intensely, pulling his mustache. Mr. Brand felt vaguely uneasy. "It is very delicate—what I want to say," Felix began. "But I have been thinking of it for some time."

"Please to say it as quickly as possible," said Mr. Brand.

"It 's because you are a clergyman, you know," Felix went on. "I don't think I should venture to say it to a common man."

Mr. Brand was silent a moment. "If it is a question of yielding to a weakness, of resenting an injury, I am afraid I am a very common man."

"My dearest friend," cried Felix, "this is not an injury; it 's a benefit—a great service! You will like it extremely. Only it 's so delicate!" And, in the dim light, he continued to smile intensely. "You know I take a great interest in my cousins—in Charlotte and Gertrude Wentworth. That 's very evident from my having traveled some five thousand miles to see them." Mr. Brand said nothing and Felix proceeded. "Coming into their society as a perfect stranger I received of course a great many new impressions, and my impressions had a great freshness, a great keenness. Do you know what I mean?"

"I am not sure that I do; but I should like you to continue."

"I think my impressions have always a good deal of fresh-

ness," said Mr. Brand's entertainer; "but on this occasion it
was perhaps particularly natural that—coming in, as I say,
from outside—I should be struck with things that passed unnoticed among yourselves. And then I had my sister to help
me; and she is simply the most observant woman in the
world."

"I am not surprised," said Mr. Brand, "that in our little
circle two intelligent persons should have found food for observation. I am sure that, of late, I have found it myself!"

"Ah, but I shall surprise you yet!" cried Felix, laughing.
"Both my sister and I took a great fancy to my cousin Charlotte."

"Your cousin Charlotte?" repeated Mr. Brand.

"We fell in love with her from the first!"

"You fell in love with Charlotte?" Mr. Brand murmured.

"*Dame!*" exclaimed Felix, "she 's a very charming person;
and Eugenia was especially smitten." Mr. Brand stood staring, and he pursued, "Affection, you know, opens one's eyes,
and we noticed something. Charlotte is not happy! Charlotte
is in love." And Felix, drawing nearer, laid his hand again
upon his companion's arm.

There was something akin to an acknowledgment of fascination in the way Mr. Brand looked at him; but the young
clergyman retained as yet quite enough self-possession to be
able to say, with a good deal of solemnity, "She is not in love
with you."

Felix gave a light laugh, and rejoined with the alacrity of a
maritime adventurer who feels a puff of wind in his sail. "Ah,
no; if she were in love with me I should know it! I am not
so blind as you."

"As I?"

"My dear sir, you are stone blind. Poor Charlotte is dead
in love with *you*!"

Mr. Brand said nothing for a moment; he breathed a little
heavily. "Is that what you wanted to say to me?" he asked.

"I have wanted to say it these three weeks. Because of late
she has been worse. I told you," added Felix, "it was very
delicate."

"Well, sir"—Mr. Brand began; "well, sir"—

"I was sure you did n't know it," Felix continued. "But

don't you see—as soon as I mention it—how everything is explained?" Mr. Brand answered nothing; he looked for a chair and softly sat down. Felix could see that he was blushing; he had looked straight at his host hitherto, but now he looked away. The foremost effect of what he had heard had been a sort of irritation of his modesty. "Of course," said Felix, "I suggest nothing; it would be very presumptuous in me to advise you. But I think there is no doubt about the fact."

Mr. Brand looked hard at the floor for some moments; he was oppressed with a mixture of sensations. Felix, standing there, was very sure that one of them was profound surprise. The innocent young man had been completely unsuspicious of poor Charlotte's hidden flame. This gave Felix great hope; he was sure that Mr. Brand would be flattered. Felix thought him very transparent, and indeed he was so; he could neither simulate nor dissimulate. "I scarcely know what to make of this," he said at last, without looking up; and Felix was struck with the fact that he offered no protest or contradiction. Evidently Felix had kindled a train of memories—a retrospective illumination. It was making, to Mr. Brand's astonished eyes, a very pretty blaze; his second emotion had been a gratification of vanity.

"Thank me for telling you," Felix rejoined. "It 's a good thing to know."

"I am not sure of that," said Mr. Brand.

"Ah, don't let her languish!" Felix murmured, lightly and softly.

"You *do* advise me, then?" And Mr. Brand looked up.

"I congratulate you!" said Felix, smiling. He had thought at first his visitor was simply appealing; but he saw he was a little ironical.

"It is in your interest; you have interfered with me," the young clergyman went on.

Felix still stood and smiled. The little room had grown darker, and the crimson glow had faded; but Mr. Brand could see the brilliant expression of his face. "I won't pretend not to know what you mean," said Felix at last. "But I have not really interfered with you. Of what you had to lose—with another person—you have lost nothing. And think what you have gained!"

"It seems to me I am the proper judge, on each side," Mr. Brand declared. He got up, holding the brim of his hat against his mouth and staring at Felix through the dusk.

"You have lost an illusion!" said Felix.

"What do you call an illusion?"

"The belief that you really know—that you have ever really known—Gertrude Wentworth. Depend upon that," pursued Felix. "I don't know her yet; but I have no illusions; I don't pretend to."

Mr. Brand kept gazing, over his hat. "She has always been a lucid, limpid nature," he said, solemnly.

"She has always been a dormant nature. She was waiting for a touchstone. But now she is beginning to awaken."

"Don't praise her to me!" said Mr. Brand, with a little quaver in his voice. "If you have the advantage of me that is not generous."

"My dear sir, I am melting with generosity!" exclaimed Felix. "And I am not praising my cousin. I am simply attempting a scientific definition of her. She does n't care for abstractions. Now I think the contrary is what you have always fancied—is the basis on which you have been building. She is extremely preoccupied with the concrete. I care for the concrete, too. But Gertrude is stronger than I; she whirls me along!"

Mr. Brand looked for a moment into the crown of his hat. "It 's a most interesting nature."

"So it is," said Felix. "But it pulls—it pulls—like a runaway horse. Now I like the feeling of a runaway horse; and if I am thrown out of the vehicle it is no great matter. But if *you* should be thrown, Mr. Brand"—and Felix paused a moment—"another person also would suffer from the accident."

"What other person?"

"Charlotte Wentworth!"

Mr. Brand looked at Felix for a moment sidewise, mistrustfully; then his eyes slowly wandered over the ceiling. Felix was sure he was secretly struck with the romance of the situation. "I think this is none of our business," the young minister murmured.

"None of mine, perhaps; but surely yours!"

Mr. Brand lingered still, looking at the ceiling; there was

evidently something he wanted to say. "What do you mean by Miss Gertrude being strong?" he asked abruptly.

"Well," said Felix meditatively, "I mean that she has had a great deal of self-possession. She was waiting—for years; even when she seemed, perhaps, to be living in the present. She knew how to wait; she had a purpose. That 's what I mean by her being strong."

"But what do you mean by her purpose?"

"Well—the purpose to see the world!"

Mr. Brand eyed his strange informant askance again; but he said nothing. At last he turned away, as if to take leave. He seemed bewildered, however; for instead of going to the door he moved toward the opposite corner of the room. Felix stood and watched him for a moment—almost groping about in the dusk; then he led him to the door, with a tender, almost fraternal movement. "Is that all you have to say?" asked Mr. Brand.

"Yes, it 's all—but it will bear a good deal of thinking of."

Felix went with him to the garden-gate, and watched him slowly walk away into the thickening twilight with a relaxed rigidity that tried to rectify itself. "He is offended, excited, bewildered, perplexed—and enchanted!" Felix said to himself. "That 's a capital mixture."

XI

SINCE THAT VISIT paid by the Baroness Münster to Mrs.
Acton, of which some account was given at an earlier
stage of this narrative, the intercourse between these two ladies had been neither frequent nor intimate. It was not that
Mrs. Acton had failed to appreciate Madame Münster's
charms; on the contrary, her perception of the graces of manner and conversation of her brilliant visitor had been only too
acute. Mrs. Acton was, as they said in Boston, very "intense,"
and her impressions were apt to be too many for her. The
state of her health required the restriction of emotion; and
this is why, receiving, as she sat in her eternal arm-chair, very
few visitors, even of the soberest local type, she had been
obliged to limit the number of her interviews with a lady
whose costume and manner recalled to her imagination—
Mrs. Acton's imagination was a marvel—all that she had ever
read of the most stirring historical periods. But she had sent
the Baroness a great many quaintly-worded messages and a
great many nosegays from her garden and baskets of beautiful
fruit. Felix had eaten the fruit, and the Baroness had arranged
the flowers and returned the baskets and the messages. On
the day that followed that rainy Sunday of which mention has
been made, Eugenia determined to go and pay the beneficent
invalid a "*visite d'adieux*;" so it was that, to herself, she qualified her enterprise. It may be noted that neither on the Sunday evening nor on the Monday morning had she received
that expected visit from Robert Acton. To his own consciousness, evidently he was "keeping away;" and as the Baroness,
on her side, was keeping away from her uncle's, whither, for
several days, Felix had been the unembarrassed bearer of apologies and regrets for absence, chance had not taken the cards
from the hands of design. Mr. Wentworth and his daughters
had respected Eugenia's seclusion; certain intervals of mysterious retirement appeared to them, vaguely, a natural part of
the graceful, rhythmic movement of so remarkable a life. Gertrude especially held these periods in honor; she wondered
what Madame Münster did at such times, but she would not
have permitted herself to inquire too curiously.

The long rain had freshened the air, and twelve hours' brilliant sunshine had dried the roads; so that the Baroness, in the late afternoon, proposing to walk to Mrs. Acton's, exposed herself to no great discomfort. As with her charming undulating step she moved along the clean, grassy margin of the road, beneath the thickly-hanging boughs of the orchards, through the quiet of the hour and place and the rich maturity of the summer, she was even conscious of a sort of luxurious melancholy. The Baroness had the amiable weakness of attaching herself to places—even when she had begun with a little aversion; and now, with the prospect of departure, she felt tenderly toward this well-wooded corner of the Western world, where the sunsets were so beautiful and one's ambitions were so pure. Mrs. Acton was able to receive her; but on entering this lady's large, freshly-scented room the Baroness saw that she was looking very ill. She was wonderfully white and transparent, and, in her flowered arm-chair, she made no attempt to move. But she flushed a little—like a young girl, the Baroness thought—and she rested her clear, smiling eyes upon those of her visitor. Her voice was low and monotonous, like a voice that had never expressed any human passions.

"I have come to bid you good-by," said Eugenia. "I shall soon be going away."

"When are you going away?"

"Very soon—any day."

"I am very sorry," said Mrs. Acton. "I hoped you would stay—always."

"Always?" Eugenia demanded.

"Well, I mean a long time," said Mrs. Acton, in her sweet, feeble tone. "They tell me you are so comfortable—that you have got such a beautiful little house."

Eugenia stared—that is, she smiled; she thought of her poor little *chalet* and she wondered whether her hostess were jesting. "Yes, my house is exquisite," she said; "though not to be compared to yours."

"And my son is so fond of going to see you," Mrs. Acton added. "I am afraid my son will miss you."

"Ah, dear madame," said Eugenia, with a little laugh, "I can't stay in America for your son!"

"Don't you like America?"

The Baroness looked at the front of her dress. "If I liked it—that would not be staying for your son!"

Mrs. Acton gazed at her with her grave, tender eyes, as if she had not quite understood. The Baroness at last found something irritating in the sweet, soft stare of her hostess; and if one were not bound to be merciful to great invalids she would almost have taken the liberty of pronouncing her, mentally, a fool. "I am afraid, then, I shall never see you again," said Mrs. Acton. "You know I am dying."

"Ah, dear madame," murmured Eugenia.

"I want to leave my children cheerful and happy. My daughter will probably marry her cousin."

"Two such interesting young people," said the Baroness, vaguely. She was not thinking of Clifford Wentworth.

"I feel so tranquil about my end," Mrs. Acton went on. "It is coming so easily, so surely." And she paused, with her mild gaze always on Eugenia's.

The Baroness hated to be reminded of death; but even in its imminence, so far as Mrs. Acton was concerned, she preserved her good manners. "Ah, madame, you are too charming an invalid," she rejoined.

But the delicacy of this rejoinder was apparently lost upon her hostess, who went on in her low, reasonable voice. "I want to leave my children bright and comfortable. You seem to me all so happy here—just as you are. So I wish you could stay. It would be so pleasant for Robert."

Eugenia wondered what she meant by its being pleasant for Robert; but she felt that she would never know what such a woman as that meant. She got up; she was afraid Mrs. Acton would tell her again that she was dying. "Good-by, dear madame," she said. "I must remember that your strength is precious."

Mrs. Acton took her hand and held it a moment. "Well, you *have* been happy here, have n't you? And you like us all, don't you? I wish you would stay," she added, "in your beautiful little house."

She had told Eugenia that her waiting-woman would be in the hall, to show her down-stairs; but the large landing outside her door was empty, and Eugenia stood there looking about. She felt irritated; the dying lady had not "*la main heu-reuse*." She passed slowly down-stairs, still looking about. The broad staircase made a great bend, and in the angle was a high window, looking westward, with a deep bench, covered with a row of flowering plants in curious old pots of blue china-ware. The yellow afternoon light came in through the flowers and flickered a little on the white wainscots. Eugenia paused a moment; the house was perfectly still, save for the ticking, somewhere, of a great clock. The lower hall stretched away at the foot of the stairs, half covered over with a large Oriental rug. Eugenia lingered a little, noticing a great many things. "Comme c'est bien!" she said to herself; such a large, solid, irreproachable basis of existence the place seemed to her to indicate. And then she reflected that Mrs. Acton was soon to withdraw from it. The reflection accompanied her the rest of the way down-stairs, where she paused again, making more observations. The hall was extremely broad, and on either side of the front door was a wide, deeply-set window, which threw the shadows of everything back into the house. There were high-backed chairs along the wall and big Eastern vases upon tables, and, on either side, a large cabinet with a glass front and little curiosities within, dimly gleaming. The doors were open—into the darkened parlor, the library, the dining-room. All these rooms seemed empty. Eugenia passed along, and stopped a moment on the threshold of each. "Comme c'est bien!" she murmured again; she had thought of just such a house as this when she decided to come to America. She opened the front door for herself—her light tread had sum-moned none of the servants—and on the threshold she gave a last look. Outside, she was still in the humor for curious contemplation; so instead of going directly down the little drive, to the gate, she wandered away towards the garden, which lay to the right of the house. She had not gone many yards over the grass before she paused quickly; she perceived a gentleman stretched upon the level verdure, beneath a tree. He had not heard her coming, and he lay motionless, flat on his back, with his hands clasped under his head, staring up at the sky; so that the Baroness was able to reflect, at her leisure, upon the question of his identity. It was that of a person who had lately been much in her thoughts; but her first impulse, nevertheless, was to turn away; the last thing she desired was to have the air of coming in quest of Robert Acton. The gentleman on the grass, however, gave her no time to decide; he could not long remain unconscious of so agreeable a presence. He rolled back his eyes, stared, gave an exclamation, and then jumped up. He stood an instant, looking at her.

"Excuse my ridiculous position," he said.

"I have just now no sense of the ridiculous. But, in case you have, don't imagine I came to see you."

"Take care," rejoined Acton, "how you put it into my head! I was thinking of you."

"The occupation of extreme leisure!" said the Baroness. "To think of a woman when you are in that position is no compliment."

"I did n't say I was thinking well!" Acton affirmed, smiling.

She looked at him, and then she turned away.

"Though I did n't come to see you," she said, "remember at least that I am within your gates."

"I am delighted—I am honored! Won't you come into the house?"

"I have just come out of it. I have been calling upon your mother. I have been bidding her farewell."

"Farewell?" Acton demanded.

"I am going away," said the Baroness. And she turned away again, as if to illustrate her meaning.

"When are you going?" asked Acton, standing a moment in his place. But the Baroness made no answer, and he followed her.

"I came this way to look at your garden," she said, walking back to the gate, over the grass. "But I must go."

"Let me at least go with you." He went with her, and they said nothing till they reached the gate. It was open, and they looked down the road which was darkened over with long bosky shadows. "Must you go straight home?" Acton asked.

But she made no answer. She said, after a moment, "Why have you not been to see me?" He said nothing, and then she went on, "Why don't you answer me?"

"I am trying to invent an answer," Acton confessed.

"Have you none ready?"

"None that I can tell you," he said. "But let me walk with you now."

"You may do as you like."

She moved slowly along the road, and Acton went with her. Presently he said, "If I had done as I liked I would have come to see you several times."

"Is that invented?" asked Eugenia.

"No, that is natural. I stayed away because"—

"Ah, here comes the reason, then!"

"Because I wanted to think about you."

"Because you wanted to lie down!" said the Baroness. "I have seen you lie down—almost—in my drawing-room."

Acton stopped in the road, with a movement which seemed to beg her to linger a little. She paused, and he looked at her awhile; he thought her very charming. "You are jesting," he said; "but if you are really going away it is very serious."

"If I stay," and she gave a little laugh, "it is more serious still!"

"When shall you go?"

"As soon as possible."

"And why?"

"Why should I stay?"

"Because we all admire you so."

"That is not a reason. I am admired also in Europe." And she began to walk homeward again.

"What could I say to keep you?" asked Acton. He wanted to keep her, and it was a fact that he had been thinking of her for a week. He was in love with her now; he was conscious of that, or he thought he was; and the only question with him was whether he could trust her.

"What you can say to keep me?" she repeated. "As I want very much to go it is not in my interest to tell you. Besides, I can't imagine."

He went on with her in silence; he was much more affected by what she had told him than appeared. Ever since that evening of his return from Newport her image had had a terrible power to trouble him. What Clifford Wentworth had told him—that had affected him, too, in an adverse sense; but it had not liberated him from the discomfort of a charm of which his intelligence was impatient. "She is not honest, she is not honest," he kept murmuring to himself. That is what he had been saying to the summer sky, ten minutes before. Unfortunately, he was unable to say it finally, definitively; and now that he was near her it seemed to matter wonderfully little. "She is a woman who will lie," he had said to himself. Now, as he went along, he reminded himself of this observation; but it failed to frighten him as it had done before. He almost wished he could make her lie and then convict her of it, so that he might see how he should like that. He kept thinking of this as he walked by her side, while she moved forward with her light, graceful dignity. He had sat with her before; he had driven with her; but he had never walked with her.

"By Jove, how *comme il faut* she is!" he said, as he observed her sidewise. When they reached the cottage in the orchard she passed into the gate without asking him to follow; but she turned round, as he stood there, to bid him good-night.

"I asked you a question the other night which you never answered," he said. "Have you sent off that document—liberating yourself?"

She hesitated for a single moment—very naturally. Then, "Yes," she said, simply.

He turned away; he wondered whether that would do for his lie. But he saw her again that evening, for the Baroness reappeared at her uncle's. He had little talk with her, however; two gentlemen had driven out from Boston, in a buggy, to call upon Mr. Wentworth and his daughters, and Madame Münster was an object of absorbing interest to both of the visitors. One of them, indeed, said nothing to her; he only sat and watched with intense gravity, and leaned forward solemnly, presenting his ear (a very large one), as if he were deaf, whenever she dropped an observation. He had evidently been impressed with the idea of her misfortunes and reverses: he never smiled. His companion adopted a lighter, easier style; sat as near as possible to Madame Münster; attempted to draw her out, and proposed every few moments a new topic of conversation. Eugenia was less vividly responsive than usual and had less to say than, from her brilliant reputation, her interlocutor expected, upon the relative merits of European and American institutions; but she was inaccessible to Robert Acton, who roamed about the piazza with his hands in his pockets, listening for the grating sound of the buggy from Boston, as it should be brought round to the side-door. But he listened in vain, and at last he lost patience. His sister came to him and begged him to take her home, and he presently went off with her. Eugenia observed him leaving the house with Lizzie; in her present mood the fact seemed a contribution to her irritated conviction that he had several precious qualities. "Even that *mal-élevée* little girl," she reflected, "makes him do what she wishes."

She had been sitting just within one of the long windows that opened upon the piazza; but very soon after Acton had gone away she got up abruptly, just when the talkative gentleman from Boston was asking her what she thought of the "moral tone" of that city. On the piazza she encountered Clifford Wentworth, coming round from the other side of the house. She stopped him; she told him she wished to speak to him.

"Why did n't you go home with your cousin?" she asked.

Clifford stared. "Why, Robert has taken her," he said.

"Exactly so. But you don't usually leave that to him."

"Oh," said Clifford, "I want to see those fellows start off. They don't know how to drive."

"It is not, then, that you have quarreled with your cousin?"

Clifford reflected a moment, and then with a simplicity which had, for the Baroness, a singularly baffling quality, "Oh, no; we have made up!" he said.

She looked at him for some moments; but Clifford had begun to be afraid of the Baroness's looks, and he endeavored, now, to shift himself out of their range. "Why do you never come to see me any more?" she asked. "Have I displeased you?"

"Displeased me? Well, I guess not!" said Clifford, with a laugh.

"Why have n't you come, then?"

"Well, because I am afraid of getting shut up in that back room."

Eugenia kept looking at him. "I should think you would like that."

"Like it!" cried Clifford.

"I should, if I were a young man calling upon a charming woman."

"A charming woman is n't much use to me when I am shut up in that back room!"

"I am afraid I am not of much use to you anywhere!" said Madame Münster. "And yet you know how I have offered to be."

"Well," observed Clifford, by way of response, "there comes the buggy."

"Never mind the buggy. Do you know I am going away?"

"Do you mean now?"

"I mean in a few days. I leave this place."

"You are going back to Europe?"

"To Europe, where you are to come and see me."

"Oh, yes, I 'll come out there," said Clifford.

"But before that," Eugenia declared, "you must come and see me here."

"Well, I shall keep clear of that back room!" rejoined her simple young kinsman.

The Baroness was silent a moment. "Yes, you must come frankly—boldly. That will be very much better. I see that now."

"I see it!" said Clifford. And then, in an instant, "What 's the matter with that buggy?" His practiced ear had apparently detected an unnatural creak in the wheels of the light vehicle which had been brought to the portico, and he hurried away to investigate so grave an anomaly.

The Baroness walked homeward, alone, in the starlight, asking herself a question. Was she to have gained nothing—was she to have gained nothing?

Gertrude Wentworth had held a silent place in the little circle gathered about the two gentlemen from Boston. She was not interested in the visitors; she was watching Madame Münster, as she constantly watched her. She knew that Eugenia also was not interested—that she was bored; and Gertrude was absorbed in study of the problem how, in spite of her indifference and her absent attention, she managed to have such a charming manner. That was the manner Gertrude would have liked to have; she determined to cultivate it, and she wished that—to give her the charm—she might in future

very often be bored. While she was engaged in these researches, Felix Young was looking for Charlotte, to whom he
had something to say. For some time, now, he had had something to say to Charlotte, and this evening his sense of the
propriety of holding some special conversation with her had
reached the motive-point—resolved itself into acute and delightful desire. He wandered through the empty rooms on the
large ground-floor of the house, and found her at last in a
small apartment denominated, for reasons not immediately
apparent, Mr. Wentworth's "office:" an extremely neat and
well-dusted room, with an array of law-books, in time-dark-
ened sheep-skin, on one of the walls; a large map of the
United States on the other, flanked on either side by an old
steel engraving of one of Raphael's Madonnas; and on the
third several glass cases containing specimens of butterflies
and beetles. Charlotte was sitting by a lamp, embroidering a
slipper. Felix did not ask for whom the slipper was destined;
he saw it was very large.

He moved a chair toward her and sat down, smiling as
usual, but, at first, not speaking. She watched him, with her
needle poised, and with a certain shy, fluttered look which
she always wore when he approached her. There was something in Felix's manner that quickened her modesty, her self-
consciousness; if absolute choice had been given her she
would have preferred never to find herself alone with him;
and in fact, though she thought him a most brilliant, distinguished, and well-meaning person, she had exercised a
much larger amount of tremulous tact than he had ever
suspected, to circumvent the accident of *tête-à-tête*. Poor
Charlotte could have given no account of the matter that
would not have seemed unjust both to herself and to her
foreign kinsman; she could only have said—or rather, she
would never have said it—that she did not like so much
gentleman's society at once. She was not reassured, accordingly, when he began, emphasizing his words with a kind
of admiring radiance, "My dear cousin, I am enchanted at
finding you alone."

"I am very often alone," Charlotte observed. Then she
quickly added, "I don't mean I am lonely!"

"So clever a woman as you is never lonely," said Felix.

"You have company in your beautiful work." And he glanced at the big slipper.

"I like to work," declared Charlotte, simply.

"So do I!" said her companion. "And I like to idle too. But it is not to idle that I have come in search of you. I want to tell you something very particular."

"Well," murmured Charlotte; "of course, if you must"—

"My dear cousin," said Felix, "it 's nothing that a young lady may not listen to. At least I suppose it is n't. But *voyons*; you shall judge. I am terribly in love."

"Well, Felix," began Miss Wentworth, gravely. But her very gravity appeared to check the development of her phrase.

"I am in love with your sister; but in love, Charlotte—in love!" the young man pursued. Charlotte had laid her work in her lap; her hands were tightly folded on top of it; she was staring at the carpet. "In short, I 'm in love, dear lady," said Felix. "Now I want you to help me."

"To help you?" asked Charlotte, with a tremor.

"I don't mean with Gertrude; she and I have a perfect understanding; and oh, how well she understands one! I mean with your father and with the world in general, including Mr. Brand."

"Poor Mr. Brand!" said Charlotte, slowly, but with a simplicity which made it evident to Felix that the young minister had not repeated to Miss Wentworth the talk that had lately occurred between them.

"Ah, now, don't say 'poor' Mr. Brand! I don't pity Mr. Brand at all. But I pity your father a little, and I don't want to displease him. Therefore, you see, I want you to plead for me. You don't think me very shabby, eh?"

"Shabby?" exclaimed Charlotte softly, for whom Felix represented the most polished and iridescent qualities of mankind.

"I don't mean in my appearance," rejoined Felix, laughing; for Charlotte was looking at his boots. "I mean in my conduct. You don't think it 's an abuse of hospitality?"

"To—to care for Gertrude?" asked Charlotte.

"To have really expressed one's self. Because I *have* expressed myself, Charlotte; I must tell you the whole truth—I have! Of course I want to marry her—and here is the difficulty. I held off as long as I could; but she is such a terribly fascinating person! She 's a strange creature, Charlotte; I don't believe you really know her." Charlotte took up her tapestry again, and again she laid it down. "I know your father has had higher views," Felix continued; "and I think you have shared them. You have wanted to marry her to Mr. Brand."

"Oh, no," said Charlotte, very earnestly. "Mr. Brand has always admired her. But we did not want anything of that kind."

Felix stared. "Surely, marriage was what you proposed."

"Yes; but we did n't wish to force her."

"A la bonne heure! That 's very unsafe you know. With these arranged marriages there is often the deuce to pay."

"Oh, Felix," said Charlotte, "we did n't want to 'arrange.' "

"I am delighted to hear that. Because in such cases—even when the woman is a thoroughly good creature—she can't help looking for a compensation. A charming fellow comes along—and *voilà!*" Charlotte sat mutely staring at the floor, and Felix presently added, "Do go on with your slipper, I like to see you work."

Charlotte took up her variegated canvas, and began to draw vague blue stitches in a big round rose. "If Gertrude is so—so strange," she said, "why do you want to marry her?"

"Ah, that 's it, dear Charlotte! I like strange women; I always have liked them. Ask Eugenia! And Gertrude is wonderful; she says the most beautiful things!"

Charlotte looked at him, almost for the first time, as if her meaning required to be severely pointed. "You have a great influence over her."

"Yes—and no!" said Felix. "I had at first, I think; but now it is six of one and half-a-dozen of the other; it is reciprocal. She affects me strongly—for she is so strong. I don't believe you know her; it 's a beautiful nature."

"Oh, yes, Felix; I have always thought Gertrude's nature beautiful."

"Well, if you think so now," cried the young man, "wait and see! She 's a folded flower. Let me pluck her from the parent tree and you will see her expand. I 'm sure you will enjoy it."

"I don't understand you," murmured Charlotte. "I *can't*, Felix."

"Well, you can understand this—that I beg you to say a good word for me to your father. He regards me, I naturally believe, as a very light fellow, a Bohemian, an irregular character. Tell him I am not all this; if I ever was, I have forgotten it. I am fond of pleasure—yes; but of innocent pleasure. Pain is all one; but in pleasure, you know, there are tremendous distinctions. Say to him that Gertrude is a folded flower and that I am a serious man!"

Charlotte got up from her chair slowly rolling up her work. "We know you are very kind to every one, Felix," she said. "But we are extremely sorry for Mr. Brand."

"Of course you are—you especially! Because," added Felix hastily, "you are a woman. But I don't pity him. It ought to be enough for any man that you take an interest in him."

"It is not enough for Mr. Brand," said Charlotte, simply. And she stood there a moment, as if waiting conscientiously for anything more that Felix might have to say.

"Mr. Brand is not so keen about his marriage as he was," he presently said. "He is afraid of your sister. He begins to think she is wicked."

Charlotte looked at him now with beautiful, appealing eyes—eyes into which he saw the tears rising. "Oh, Felix, Felix," she cried, "what have you done to her?"

"I think she was asleep; I have waked her up!"

But Charlotte, apparently, was really crying, she walked straight out of the room. And Felix, standing there and meditating, had the apparent brutality to take satisfaction in her tears.

Late that night Gertrude, silent and serious, came to him in the garden; it was a kind of appointment. Gertrude seemed to like appointments. She plucked a handful of heliotrope and stuck it into the front of her dress, but she said nothing. They walked together along one of the paths, and Felix looked at the great, square, hospitable house, massing itself vaguely in the starlight, with all its windows darkened.

"I have a little of a bad conscience," he said. "I ought n't to meet you this way till I have got your father's consent."

Gertrude looked at him for some time. "I don't understand you."

"You very often say that," he said. "Considering how little we understand each other, it is a wonder how well we get on!"

"We have done nothing but meet since you came here—but meet alone. The first time I ever saw you we were alone," Gertrude went on. "What is the difference now? Is it because it is at night?"

"The difference, Gertrude," said Felix, stopping in the path, "the difference is that I love you more—more than before!" And then they stood there, talking, in the warm stillness and in front of the closed dark house. "I have been talking to Charlotte—been trying to bespeak her interest with your father. She has a kind of sublime perversity; was ever a woman so bent upon cutting off her own head?"

"You are too careful," said Gertrude; "you are too diplomatic."

"Well," cried the young man, "I did n't come here to make any one unhappy!"

Gertrude looked round her awhile in the odorous darkness. "I will do anything you please," she said.

"For instance?" asked Felix, smiling.

"I will go away. I will do anything you please."

Felix looked at her in solemn admiration. "Yes, we will go away," he said. "But we will make peace first."

Gertrude looked about her again, and then she broke out, passionately, "Why do they try to make one feel guilty? Why do they make it so difficult? Why can't they understand?"

"I will make them understand!" said Felix. He drew her hand into his arm, and they wandered about in the garden, talking, for an hour.

XII

FELIX ALLOWED Charlotte time to plead his cause; and then, on the third day, he sought an interview with his uncle. It was in the morning; Mr. Wentworth was in his office; and, on going in, Felix found that Charlotte was at that moment in conference with her father. She had, in fact, been constantly near him since her interview with Felix; she had made up her mind that it was her duty to repeat very literally her cousin's passionate plea. She had accordingly followed Mr. Wentworth about like a shadow, in order to find him at hand when she should have mustered sufficient composure to speak. For poor Charlotte, in this matter, naturally lacked composure; especially when she meditated upon some of Felix's intimations. It was not cheerful work, at the best, to keep giving small hammer-taps to the coffin in which one had laid away, for burial, the poor little unacknowledged offspring of one's own misbehaving heart; and the occupation was not rendered more agreeable by the fact that the ghost of one's stifled dream had been summoned from the shades by the strange, bold words of a talkative young foreigner. What had Felix meant by saying that Mr. Brand was not so keen? To herself her sister's justly depressed suitor had shown no sign of faltering. Charlotte trembled all over when she allowed herself to believe for an instant now and then that, privately, Mr. Brand might have faltered; and as it seemed to give more force to Felix's words to repeat them to her father, she was waiting until she should have taught herself to be very calm. But she had now begun to tell Mr. Wentworth that she was extremely anxious. She was proceeding to develop this idea, to enumerate the objects of her anxiety, when Felix came in.

Mr. Wentworth sat there, with his legs crossed, lifting his dry, pure countenance from the Boston "Advertiser." Felix entered smiling, as if he had something particular to say, and his uncle looked at him as if he both expected and deprecated this event. Felix vividly expressing himself had come to be a formidable figure to his uncle, who had not yet arrived at definite views as to a proper tone. For the first time in his life, as I have said, Mr. Wentworth shirked a responsibility; he earnestly desired that it might not be laid upon him to determine how his nephew's lighter propositions should be treated. He lived under an apprehension that Felix might yet beguile him into assent to doubtful inductions, and his conscience instructed him that the best form of vigilance was the avoidance of discussion. He hoped that the pleasant episode of his nephew's visit would pass away without a further lapse of consistency.

Felix looked at Charlotte with an air of understanding, and then at Mr. Wentworth, and then at Charlotte again. Mr. Wentworth bent his refined eyebrows upon his nephew and stroked down the first page of the "Advertiser." "I ought to have brought a bouquet," said Felix, laughing. "In France they always do."

"We are not in France," observed Mr. Wentworth, gravely, while Charlotte earnestly gazed at him.

"No, luckily, we are not in France, where I am afraid I should have a harder time of it. My dear Charlotte, have you rendered me that delightful service?" And Felix bent toward her as if some one had been presenting him.

Charlotte looked at him with almost frightened eyes; and Mr. Wentworth thought this might be the beginning of a discussion. "What is the bouquet for?" he inquired, by way of turning it off.

Felix gazed at him, smiling. "Pour la demande!" And then, drawing up a chair, he seated himself, hat in hand, with a kind of conscious solemnity.

Presently he turned to Charlotte again. "My good Charlotte, my admirable Charlotte," he murmured, "you have not played me false—you have not sided against me?"

Charlotte got up, trembling extremely, though imperceptibly. "You must speak to my father yourself," she said. "I think you are clever enough."

But Felix, rising too, begged her to remain. "I can speak better to an audience!" he declared.

"I hope it is nothing disagreeable," said Mr. Wentworth.

"It 's something delightful, for me!" And Felix, laying down his hat, clasped his hands a little between his knees. "My dear uncle," he said, "I desire, very earnestly, to marry your daughter Gertrude." Charlotte sank slowly into her chair again, and Mr. Wentworth sat staring, with a light in his face that might have been flashed back from an iceberg. He stared and stared; he said nothing. Felix fell back, with his hands still clasped. "Ah—you don't like it. I was afraid!" He blushed deeply, and Charlotte noticed it—remarking to herself that it was the first time she had ever seen him blush. She began to blush herself and to reflect that he might be much in love.

"This is very abrupt," said Mr. Wentworth, at last.

"Have you never suspected it, dear uncle?" Felix inquired. "Well, that proves how discreet I have been. Yes, I thought you would n't like it."

"It is very serious, Felix," said Mr. Wentworth.

"You think it 's an abuse of hospitality!" exclaimed Felix, smiling again.

"Of hospitality?—an abuse?" his uncle repeated very slowly.

"That is what Felix said to me," said Charlotte, conscientiously.

"Of course you think so; don't defend yourself!" Felix pursued. "It *is* an abuse, obviously; the most I can claim is that it is perhaps a pardonable one. I simply fell head over heels in love; one can hardly help that. Though you are Gertrude's progenitor I don't believe you know how attractive she is. Dear uncle, she contains the elements of a singularly—I may say a strangely—charming woman!"

"She has always been to me an object of extreme concern," said Mr. Wentworth. "We have always desired her happiness."

"Well, here it is!" Felix declared. "I will make her happy. She believes it, too. Now had n't you noticed that?"

"I had noticed that she was much changed," Mr. Wentworth declared, in a tone whose unexpressive, unimpassioned quality appeared to Felix to reveal a profundity of opposition. "It may be that she is only becoming what you call a charming woman."

"Gertrude, at heart, is so earnest, so true," said Charlotte, very softly, fastening her eyes upon her father.

"I delight to hear you praise her!" cried Felix.

"She has a very peculiar temperament," said Mr. Wentworth.

"Eh, even that is praise!" Felix rejoined. "I know I am not the man you might have looked for. I have no position and no fortune; I can give Gertrude no place in the world. A place in the world—that 's what she ought to have; that would bring her out."

"A place to do her duty!" remarked Mr. Wentworth.

"Ah, how charmingly she does it—her duty!" Felix exclaimed, with a radiant face. "What an exquisite conception she has of it! But she comes honestly by that, dear uncle." Mr. Wentworth and Charlotte both looked at him as if they were watching a greyhound doubling. "Of course with me she will hide her light under a bushel," he continued; "I being the bushel! Now I know you like me—you have certainly proved it. But you think I am frivolous and penniless and shabby! Granted—granted—a thousand times granted. I have been a loose fish—a fiddler, a painter, an actor. But there is this to be said: In the first place, I fancy you exaggerate; you lend me qualities I have n't had. I have been a Bohemian—yes; but in Bohemia I always passed for a gentleman. I wish you could see some of my old *camarades*—they would tell you! It was the liberty I liked, but not the opportunities! My sins were all peccadilloes; I always respected my neighbor's property—my neighbor's wife. Do you see, dear uncle?" Mr. Wentworth ought to have seen; his cold blue eyes were intently fixed. "And then, *c'est fini!* It 's all over. Je me range. I have settled down to a jog-trot. I find I can earn my living—a very fair one—by going about the world and painting bad portraits. It 's not a glorious profession, but it is a perfectly respectable one. You won't deny that, eh? Going about the world, I say? I must not deny that, for that I am afraid I shall always do—in quest of agreeable sitters. When I say agreeable, I mean susceptible of delicate flattery and prompt of payment. Gertrude declares she is willing to share my wanderings and help to pose my models. She even thinks it will be charming; and that brings me to my third point. Gertrude likes me. Encourage her a little and she will tell you so."

Felix's tongue obviously moved much faster than the imagination of his auditors; his eloquence, like the rocking of a boat in a deep, smooth lake, made long eddies of silence. And he seemed to be pleading and chattering still, with his brightly eager smile, his uplifted eyebrows, his expressive mouth, after he had ceased speaking, and while, with his glance quickly turning from the father to the daughter, he sat waiting for the effect of his appeal. "It is not your want of means," said Mr. Wentworth, after a period of severe reticence.

"Now it 's delightful of you to say that! Only don't say it 's my want of character. Because I have a character—I assure you I have; a small one, a little slip of a thing, but still something tangible."

"Ought you not to tell Felix that it is Mr. Brand, father?" Charlotte asked, with infinite mildness.

"It is not only Mr. Brand," Mr. Wentworth solemnly declared. And he looked at his knee for a long time. "It is difficult to explain," he said. He wished, evidently, to be very just. "It rests on moral grounds, as Mr. Brand says. It is the question whether it is the best thing for Gertrude."

"What is better—what is better, dear uncle?" Felix rejoined urgently, rising in his urgency and standing before Mr. Wentworth. His uncle had been looking at his knee; but when Felix moved he transferred his gaze to the handle of the door which faced him. "It is usually a fairly good thing for a girl to marry the man she loves!" cried Felix.

While he spoke, Mr. Wentworth saw the handle of the door begin to turn; the door opened and remained slightly ajar, until Felix had delivered himself of the cheerful axiom just quoted. Then it opened altogether and Gertrude stood there. She looked excited; there was a spark in her sweet, dull eyes. She came in slowly, but with an air of resolution, and, closing the door softly, looked round at the three persons present. Felix went to her with tender gallantry, holding out his hand, and Charlotte made a place for her on the sofa. But Gertrude put her hands behind her and made no motion to sit down.

"We are talking of you!" said Felix.

"I know it," she answered. "That 's why I came." And she fastened her eyes on her father, who returned her gaze very fixedly. In his own cold blue eyes there was a kind of pleading, reasoning light.

"It is better you should be present," said Mr. Wentworth. "We are discussing your future."

"Why discuss it?" asked Gertrude. "Leave it to me."

"That is, to me!" cried Felix.

"I leave it, in the last resort, to a greater wisdom than ours," said the old man.

Felix rubbed his forehead gently. "But *en attendant* the last resort, your father lacks confidence," he said to Gertrude.

"Have n't you confidence in Felix?" Gertrude was frowning; there was something about her that her father and Charlotte had never seen. Charlotte got up and came to her, as if to put her arm round her; but suddenly, she seemed afraid to touch her.

Mr. Wentworth, however, was not afraid. "I have had more confidence in Felix than in you," he said.

"Yes, you have never had confidence in me—never, never! I don't know why."

"Oh sister, sister!" murmured Charlotte.

"You have always needed advice," Mr. Wentworth declared. "You have had a difficult temperament."

"Why do you call it difficult? It might have been easy, if you had allowed it. You would n't let me be natural. I don't know what you wanted to make of me. Mr. Brand was the worst."

Charlotte at last took hold of her sister. She laid her two hands upon Gertrude's arm. "He cares so much for you," she almost whispered.

Gertrude looked at her intently an instant; then kissed her. "No, he does not," she said.

"I have never seen you so passionate," observed Mr. Wentworth, with an air of indignation mitigated by high principles.

"I am sorry if I offend you," said Gertrude.

"You offend me, but I don't think you are sorry."

"Yes, father, she is sorry," said Charlotte.

"I would even go further, dear uncle," Felix interposed. "I would question whether she really offends you. How can she offend you?"

To this Mr. Wentworth made no immediate answer. Then, in a moment, "She has not profited as we hoped."

"Profited? Ah *voilà!*" Felix exclaimed.

Gertrude was very pale; she stood looking down. "I have told Felix I would go away with him," she presently said.

"Ah, you have said some admirable things!" cried the young man.

"Go away, sister?" asked Charlotte.

"Away—away; to some strange country."

"That is to frighten you," said Felix, smiling at Charlotte.

"To—what do you call it?" asked Gertrude, turning an instant to Felix. "To Bohemia."

"Do you propose to dispense with preliminaries?" asked Mr. Wentworth, getting up.

"Dear uncle, *vous plaisantez!*" cried Felix. "It seems to me that these are preliminaries."

Gertrude turned to her father. "I *have* profited," she said. "You wanted to form my character. Well, my character is formed—for my age. I know what I want; I have chosen. I am determined to marry this gentleman."

"You had better consent, sir," said Felix very gently.

"Yes, sir, you had better consent," added a very different voice.

Charlotte gave a little jump, and the others turned to the direction from which it had come. It was the voice of Mr. Brand, who had stepped through the long window which stood open to the piazza. He stood patting his forehead with his pocket-handkerchief; he was very much flushed; his face wore a singular expression.

"Yes, sir, you had better consent," Mr. Brand repeated, coming forward. "I know what Miss Gertrude means."

"My dear friend!" murmured Felix, laying his hand caressingly on the young minister's arm.

Mr. Brand looked at him; then at Mr. Wentworth; lastly at Gertrude. He did not look at Charlotte. But Charlotte's earnest eyes were fastened to his own countenance; they were asking an immense question of it. The answer to this question could not come all at once; but some of the elements of it were there. It was one of the elements of it that Mr. Brand was very red, that he held his head very high, that he had a bright, excited eye and an air of embarrassed boldness—the air of a man who has taken a resolve, in the execution of which he apprehends the failure, not of his moral, but of his personal, resources. Charlotte thought he looked very grand; and it is incontestable that Mr. Brand felt very grand. This, in fact, was the grandest moment of his life; and it was natural that such a moment should contain opportunities of awkwardness for a large, stout, modest young man.

"Come in, sir," said Mr. Wentworth, with an angular wave of his hand. "It is very proper that you should be present."

"I know what you are talking about," Mr. Brand rejoined. "I heard what your nephew said."

"And he heard what you said!" exclaimed Felix, patting him again on the arm.

"I am not sure that I understood," said Mr. Wentworth, who had angularity in his voice as well as in his gestures.

Gertrude had been looking hard at her former suitor. She had been puzzled, like her sister; but her imagination moved more quickly than Charlotte's. "Mr. Brand asked you to let Felix take me away," she said to her father.

The young minister gave her a strange look. "It is not because I don't want to see you any more," he declared, in a tone intended as it were for publicity.

"I should n't think you would want to see me any more," Gertrude answered, gently.

Mr. Wentworth stood staring. "Is n't this rather a change, sir?" he inquired.

"Yes, sir." And Mr. Brand looked anywhere; only still not at Charlotte. "Yes, sir," he repeated. And he held his handkerchief a few moments to his lips.

"Where are our moral grounds?" demanded Mr. Wentworth, who had always thought Mr. Brand would be just the thing for a younger daughter with a peculiar temperament.

"It is sometimes very moral to change, you know," suggested Felix.

Charlotte had softly left her sister's side. She had edged gently toward her father, and now her hand found its way into his arm. Mr. Wentworth had folded up the "Advertiser" into a surprisingly small compass, and, holding the roll with one hand, he earnestly clasped it with the other.

Mr. Brand was looking at him; and yet, though Charlotte was so near, his eyes failed to meet her own. Gertrude watched her sister.

"It is better not to speak of change," said Mr. Brand. "In one sense there is no change. There was something I desired—something I asked of you; I desire something still—I ask it of you." And he paused a moment; Mr. Wentworth looked bewildered. "I should like, in my ministerial capacity, to unite this young couple."

Gertrude, watching her sister, saw Charlotte flushing intensely, and Mr. Wentworth felt her pressing upon his arm. "Heavenly Powers!" murmured Mr. Wentworth. And it was the nearest approach to profanity he had ever made.

"That is very nice; that is very handsome!" Felix exclaimed.

"I don't understand," said Mr. Wentworth; though it was plain that every one else did.

"That is very beautiful, Mr. Brand," said Gertrude, emulating Felix.

"I should like to marry you. It will give me great pleasure."

"As Gertrude says, it 's a beautiful idea," said Felix.

Felix was smiling, but Mr. Brand was not even trying to. He himself treated his proposition very seriously. "I have thought of it, and I should like to do it," he affirmed.

Charlotte, meanwhile, was staring with expanded eyes. Her imagination, as I have said, was not so rapid as her sister's, but now it had taken several little jumps. "Father," she murmured, "consent!"

Mr. Brand heard her; he looked away. Mr. Wentworth, evidently, had no imagination at all. "I have always thought," he began, slowly, "that Gertrude's character required a special line of development."

"Father," repeated Charlotte, "*consent*."

Then, at last, Mr. Brand looked at her. Her father felt her leaning more heavily upon his folded arm than she had ever done before; and this, with a certain sweet faintness in her voice, made him wonder what was the matter. He looked down at her and saw the encounter of her gaze with the young theologian's; but even this told him nothing, and he continued to be bewildered. Nevertheless, "I consent," he said at last, "since Mr. Brand recommends it."

"I should like to perform the ceremony very soon," observed Mr. Brand, with a sort of solemn simplicity.

"Come, come, that 's charming!" cried Felix, profanely.

Mr. Wentworth sank into his chair. "Doubtless, when you understand it," he said, with a certain judicial asperity.

Gertrude went to her sister and led her away, and Felix having passed his arm into Mr. Brand's and stepped out of the long window with him, the old man was left sitting there in unillumined perplexity.

Felix did no work that day. In the afternoon, with Gertrude, he got into one of the boats and floated about with idly-dipping oars. They talked a good deal of Mr. Brand—though not exclusively.

"That was a fine stroke," said Felix. "It was really heroic."

Gertrude sat musing, with her eyes upon the ripples. "That was what he wanted to be; he wanted to do something fine."

"He won't be comfortable till he has married us," said Felix. "So much the better."

"He wanted to be magnanimous; he wanted to have a fine moral pleasure. I know him so well," Gertrude went on. Felix looked at her; she spoke slowly, gazing at the clear water. "He thought of it a great deal, night and day. He thought it would be beautiful. At last he made up his mind that it was his duty, his duty to do just that—nothing less than that. He felt exalted; he felt sublime. That 's how he likes to feel. It is better for him than if I had listened to him."

"It 's better for me," smiled Felix. "But do you know, as regards the sacrifice, that I don't believe he admired you when this decision was taken quite so much as he had done a fortnight before?"

"He never admired me. He admires Charlotte; he pitied me. I know him so well."

"Well, then, he did n't pity you so much."

Gertrude looked at Felix a little, smiling. "You should n't permit yourself," she said, "to diminish the splendor of his action. He admires Charlotte," she repeated.

"That 's capital!" said Felix laughingly, and dipping his oars. I cannot say exactly to which member of Gertrude's phrase he alluded; but he dipped his oars again, and they kept floating about.

Neither Felix nor his sister, on that day, was present at Mr. Wentworth's at the evening repast. The two occupants of the chalet dined together, and the young man informed his companion that his marriage was now an assured fact. Eugenia congratulated him, and replied that if he were as reasonable a husband as he had been, on the whole, a brother, his wife would have nothing to complain of.

Felix looked at her a moment, smiling. "I hope," he said, "not to be thrown back on my reason."

"It is very true," Eugenia rejoined, "that one's reason is dismally flat. It 's a bed with the mattress removed."

But the brother and sister, later in the evening, crossed over to the larger house, the Baroness desiring to compliment her prospective sister-in-law. They found the usual circle upon the piazza, with the exception of Clifford Wentworth and Lizzie Acton; and as every one stood up as usual to welcome the Baroness, Eugenia had an admiring audience for her compliment to Gertrude.

Robert Acton stood on the edge of the piazza, leaning against one of the white columns, so that he found himself next to Eugenia while she acquitted herself of a neat little discourse of congratulation.

"I shall be so glad to know you better," she said; "I have seen so much less of you than I should have liked. Naturally; now I see the reason why! You will love me a little, won't you? I think I may say I gain on being known." And terminating these observations with the softest cadence of her voice, the Baroness imprinted a sort of grand official kiss upon Gertrude's forehead.

Increased familiarity had not, to Gertrude's imagination, diminished the mysterious impressiveness of Eugenia's personality, and she felt flattered and transported by this little ceremony. Robert Acton also seemed to admire it, as he admired so many of the gracious manifestations of Madame Münster's wit.

They had the privilege of making him restless, and on this occasion he walked away, suddenly, with his hands in his pockets, and then came back and leaned against his column. Eugenia was now complimenting her uncle upon his daughter's engagement, and Mr. Wentworth was listening with his usual plain yet refined politeness. It is to be supposed that by this time his perception of the mutual relations of the young people who surrounded him had become more acute; but he still took the matter very seriously, and he was not at all exhilarated.

"Felix will make her a good husband," said Eugenia. "He will be a charming companion; he has a great quality—indestructible gayety."

"You think that 's a great quality?" asked the old man.

Eugenia meditated, with her eyes upon his. "You think one gets tired of it, eh?"

"I don't know that I am prepared to say that," said Mr. Wentworth.

"Well, we will say, then, that it is tiresome for others but delightful for one's self. A woman's husband, you know, is supposed to be her second self; so that, for Felix and Gertrude, gayety will be a common property."

"Gertrude was always very gay," said Mr. Wentworth. He was trying to follow this argument.

Robert Acton took his hands out of his pockets and came a little nearer to the Baroness. "You say you gain by being known," he said. "One certainly gains by knowing you."

"What have *you* gained?" asked Eugenia.

"An immense amount of wisdom."

"That 's a questionable advantage for a man who was already so wise!"

Acton shook his head. "No, I was a great fool before I knew you!"

"And being a fool you made my acquaintance? You are very complimentary."

"Let me keep it up," said Acton, laughing. "I hope, for our pleasure, that your brother's marriage will detain you."

"Why should I stop for my brother's marriage when I would not stop for my own?" asked the Baroness.

"Why should n't you stop in either case, now that, as you say, you have dissolved that mechanical tie that bound you to Europe?"

The Baroness looked at him a moment. "As I say? You look as if you doubted it."

"Ah," said Acton, returning her glance, "that is a remnant

of my old folly! We have other attractions," he added. "We are to have another marriage."

But she seemed not to hear him; she was looking at him still. "My word was never doubted before," she said.

"We are to have another marriage," Acton repeated, smiling.

Then she appeared to understand. "Another marriage?" And she looked at the others. Felix was chattering to Gertrude; Charlotte, at a distance, was watching them; and Mr. Brand, in quite another quarter, was turning his back to them, and, with his hands under his coat-tails and his large head on one side, was looking at the small, tender crescent of a young moon. "It ought to be Mr. Brand and Charlotte," said Eugenia, "but it does n't look like it."

"There," Acton answered, "you must judge just now by contraries. There is more than there looks to be. I expect that combination one of these days; but that is not what I meant."

"Well," said the Baroness, "I never guess my own lovers; so I can't guess other people's."

Acton gave a loud laugh, and he was about to add a rejoinder when Mr. Wentworth approached his niece. "You will be interested to hear," the old man said, with a momentary aspiration toward jocosity, "of another matrimonial venture in our little circle."

"I was just telling the Baroness," Acton observed.

"Mr. Acton was apparently about to announce his own engagement," said Eugenia.

Mr. Wentworth's jocosity increased. "It is not exactly that; but it is in the family. Clifford, hearing this morning that Mr. Brand had expressed a desire to tie the nuptial knot for his sister, took it into his head to arrange that, while his hand was in, our good friend should perform a like ceremony for himself and Lizzie Acton."

The Baroness threw back her head and smiled at her uncle; then turning, with an intenser radiance, to Robert Acton, "I am certainly very stupid not to have thought of that," she said. Acton looked down at his boots, as if he thought he had perhaps reached the limits of legitimate experimentation, and for a moment Eugenia said nothing more. It had been, in fact, a sharp knock, and she needed to recover herself. This was done, however, promptly enough. "Where are the young people?" she asked.

"They are spending the evening with my mother."

"Is not the thing very sudden?"

Acton looked up. "Extremely sudden. There had been a tacit understanding; but within a day or two Clifford appears to have received some mysterious impulse to precipitate the affair."

"The impulse," said the Baroness, "was the charms of your very pretty sister."

"But my sister's charms were an old story; he had always known her." Acton had begun to experiment again.

Here, however, it was evident the Baroness would not help him. "Ah, one can't say! Clifford is very young; but he is a nice boy."

"He's a likeable sort of boy, and he will be a rich man." This was Acton's last experiment. Madame Münster turned away.

She made but a short visit and Felix took her home. In her little drawing-room she went almost straight to the mirror over the chimney-piece, and, with a candle uplifted, stood looking into it. "I shall not wait for your marriage," she said to her brother. "To-morrow my maid shall pack up."

"My dear sister," Felix exclaimed, "we are to be married immediately! Mr. Brand is too uncomfortable."

But Eugenia, turning and still holding her candle aloft, only looked about the little sitting-room at her gimcracks and curtains and cushions. "My maid shall pack up," she repeated. "*Bonté divine*, what rubbish! I feel like a strolling actress; these are my 'properties.' "

"Is the play over, Eugenia?" asked Felix.

She gave him a sharp glance. "I have spoken my part."

"With great applause!" said her brother.

"Oh, applause—applause!" she murmured. And she gathered up two or three of her dispersed draperies. She glanced at the beautiful brocade, and then, "I don't see how I can have endured it!" she said.

"Endure it a little longer. Come to my wedding."

"Thank you; that's your affair. My affairs are elsewhere."

"Where are you going?"

"To Germany—by the first ship."

"You have decided not to marry Mr. Acton?"

"I have refused him," said Eugenia.

Her brother looked at her in silence. "I am sorry," he rejoined at last. "But I was very discreet, as you asked me to be. I said nothing."

"Please continue, then, not to allude to the matter," said Eugenia.

Felix inclined himself gravely. "You shall be obeyed. But your position in Germany?" he pursued.

"Please to make no observations upon it."

"I was only going to say that I supposed it was altered."

"You are mistaken."

"But I thought you had signed"—

"I have not signed!" said the Baroness.

Felix urged her no further, and it was arranged that he should immediately assist her to embark.

Mr. Brand was indeed, it appeared, very impatient to consummate his sacrifice and deliver the nuptial benediction which would set it off so handsomely; but Eugenia's impatience to withdraw from a country in which she had not found the fortune she had come to seek was even less to be mistaken. It is true she had not made any very various exertion; but she appeared to feel justified in generalizing—in deciding that the conditions of action on this provincial continent were not favorable to really superior women. The elder world was, after all, their natural field. The unembarrassed directness with which she proceeded to apply these intelligent conclusions appeared to the little circle of spectators who have figured in our narrative but the supreme exhibition of a character to which the experience of life had imparted an inimitable pliancy. It had a distinct effect upon Robert Acton, who, for the two days preceding her departure, was a very restless and irritated mortal. She passed her last evening at her uncle's, where she had never been more charming; and in parting with Clifford Wentworth's affianced bride she drew from her own finger a curious old ring and presented it to her with the prettiest speech and kiss. Gertrude, who as an affianced bride was also indebted to her gracious bounty, admired this little incident extremely, and Robert Acton almost wondered whether it did not give him the right, as Lizzie's brother and guardian, to offer in return a handsome present to the Baroness. It would have made him extremely happy to be able to offer a handsome present to the Baroness; but he abstained from this expression of his sentiments, and they were in consequence, at the very last, by so much the less comfortable. It was almost at the very last that he saw her— late the night before she went to Boston to embark.

"For myself, I wish you might have stayed," he said. "But not for your own sake."

"I don't make so many differences," said the Baroness. "I am simply sorry to be going."

"That 's a much deeper difference than mine," Acton declared; "for you mean you are simply glad!"

Felix parted with her on the deck of the ship. "We shall often meet over there," he said.

"I don't know," she answered. "Europe seems to me much larger than America."

Mr. Brand, of course, in the days that immediately followed, was not the only impatient spirit; but it may be said that of all the young spirits interested in the event none rose more eagerly to the level of the occasion. Gertrude left her father's house with Felix Young; they were imperturbably happy and they went far away. Clifford and his young wife sought their felicity in a narrower circle, and the latter's influence upon her husband was such as to justify, strikingly, that theory of the elevating effect of easy intercourse with clever women which Felix had propounded to Mr. Wentworth. Gertrude was for a good while a distant figure, but she came back when Charlotte married Mr. Brand. She was present at the wedding feast, where Felix's gayety confessed to no change. Then she disappeared, and the echo of a gayety of her own, mingled with that of her husband, often came back to the home of her earlier years. Mr. Wentworth at last found himself listening for it; and Robert Acton, after his mother's death, married a particularly nice young girl.

THE END

CONFIDENCE

I

IT WAS in the early days of April; Bernard Longueville had been spending the winter in Rome. He had travelled northward with the consciousness of several social duties that appealed to him from the further side of the Alps, but he was under the charm of the Italian spring, and he made a pretext for lingering. He had spent five days at Siena, where he had intended to spend but two, and still it was impossible to continue his journey. He was a young man of a contemplative and speculative turn, and this was his first visit to Italy, so that if he dallied by the way he should not be harshly judged. He had a fancy for sketching, and it was on his conscience to take a few pictorial notes. There were two old inns at Siena, both of them very shabby and very dirty. The one at which Longueville had taken up his abode was entered by a dark, pestiferous arch-way, surmounted by a sign which at a distance might have been read by the travellers as the Dantean injunction to renounce all hope. The other was not far off, and the day after his arrival, as he passed it, he saw two ladies going in who evidently belonged to the large fraternity of Anglo-Saxon tourists, and one of whom was young and carried herself very well. Longueville had his share—or more than his share—of gallantry, and this incident awakened a regret. If he had gone to the other inn he might have had charming company: at his own establishment there was no one but an æsthetic German who smoked bad tobacco in the dining-room. He remarked to himself that this was always his luck, and the remark was characteristic of the man; it was charged with the feeling of the moment, but it was not absolutely just; it was the result of an acute impression made by the particular occasion; but it failed in appreciation of a providence which had sprinkled Longueville's career with happy accidents—accidents, especially, in which his characteristic gallantry was not allowed to rust for want of exercise. He lounged, however, contentedly enough through these bright, still days of a Tuscan April, drawing much entertainment from the high picturesqueness of the things about him. Siena, a few years since, was a flawless gift of the Middle Ages to the modern imagination. No other Italian city could have been more interesting to an observer fond of reconstructing obsolete manners. This was a taste of Bernard Longueville's, who had a relish for serious literature, and at one time had made several lively excursions into mediæval history. His friends thought him very clever, and at the same time had an easy feeling about him which was a tribute to his freedom from pedantry. He was clever indeed, and an excellent companion; but the real measure of his brilliancy was in the success with which he entertained himself. He was much addicted to conversing with his own wit, and he greatly enjoyed his own society. Clever as he often was in talking with his friends, I am not sure that his best things, as the phrase is, were not for his own ears. And this was not on account of any cynical contempt for the understanding of his fellow-creatures: it was simply because what I have called his own society was more of a stimulus than that of most other people. And yet he was not for this reason fond of solitude; he was, on the contrary, a very sociable animal. It must be admitted at the outset that he had a nature which seemed at several points to contradict itself, as will probably be perceived in the course of this narration.

He entertained himself greatly with his reflections and meditations upon Sienese architecture and early Tuscan art, upon Italian street-life and the geological idiosyncrasies of the Apennines. If he had only gone to the other inn, that nice-looking girl whom he had seen passing under the dusky portal with her face turned away from him might have broken bread with him at this intellectual banquet. Then came a day, however, when it seemed for a moment that if she were disposed she might gather up the crumbs of the feast. Longueville, every morning after breakfast, took a turn in the great square of Siena—the vast *piazza*, shaped like a horse-shoe, where the market is held beneath the windows of that crenellated palace from whose overhanging cornice a tall, straight tower springs up with a movement as light as that of a single plume in the bonnet of a captain. Here he strolled about, watching a brown *contadino* disembarrass his donkey, noting the progress of half an hour's chaffer over a bundle of carrots, wishing a young girl with eyes like animated agates would let him sketch her, and gazing up at intervals at the beautiful, slim tower, as it played at contrasts with the large blue air. After he had spent the greater part of a week in these grave considerations, he made up his mind to leave Siena. But he was not content with what he had done for his portfolio. Siena was eminently sketchable, but he had not been industrious. On the last morning of his visit, as he stood staring about him in the crowded piazza, and feeling that, in spite of its picturesqueness, this was an awkward place for setting up an easel, he bethought himself, by contrast, of a quiet corner in another part of the town, which he had chanced upon in one of his first walks—an angle of a lonely terrace that abutted upon the city-wall, where three or four superannuated objects seemed to slumber in the sunshine—the open door of an empty church, with a faded fresco exposed to the air in the arch above it, and an ancient beggar-woman sitting beside it on a three-legged stool. The little terrace had an old polished parapet, about as high as a man's breast, above which was a view of strange, sad-colored hills. Outside, to the left, the wall of the town made an outward bend, and exposed its rugged and rusty complexion. There was a smooth stone bench set into the wall of the church, on which Longueville had rested for an hour, observing the composition of the little picture of which I have indicated the elements, and of which the parapet of the terrace would form the foreground. The thing was what painters call a subject, and he had promised himself to come back with his utensils. This morning he returned to the inn and took possession of them, and then he made his way through a labyrinth of empty streets, lying on the edge of the town, within the wall, like the superfluous folds of a garment whose wearer has shrunken with old age. He reached his little grass-grown terrace, and found it as sunny and as private as before. The old mendicant was mumbling petitions, sacred and profane, at the church door; but save for this the stillness was unbroken. The yellow sunshine warmed the brown surface of the city-wall, and lighted the hollows of the Etruscan hills. Longueville settled himself on the empty bench, and, arranging his little portable apparatus, began to ply his brushes. He worked for some time smoothly and rapidly, with an agreeable sense of the absence of obstacles. It seemed almost an interruption when, in the silent air, he heard a distant bell in the town strike noon. Shortly after this, there was another interruption. The sound of a soft footstep caused him to look up; whereupon he saw a young woman standing there and bending her eyes upon the graceful artist. A second glance assured him that she was that nice girl whom he had seen going into the other inn with her mother, and suggested that she had just emerged from the little church. He suspected, however—I hardly know why—that she had been looking at him for some moments before he perceived her. It would perhaps be impertinent to inquire what she thought of him; but Longueville, in the space of an instant, made two or three reflections upon the young lady. One of them was to the effect that she was a handsome creature, but that she looked rather bold; the burden of the other was that—yes, decidedly—she was a compatriot. She turned away almost as soon as she met his eyes; he had hardly time to raise his hat, as, after a moment's hesitation, he proceeded to do. She herself appeared to feel a certain hesitation; she glanced back at the church door, as if under the impulse to retrace her steps. She stood there a moment longer—long enough to let him see that she was a person of easy attitudes—and then she walked away slowly to the parapet of the terrace. Here she stationed herself, leaning her arms upon the high stone ledge, presenting her back to Longueville, and gazing at rural Italy. Longueville went on with his sketch, but less attentively than before. He wondered what this young lady was doing there alone, and then it occurred to him that her companion—her mother, presumably—was in the church. The two ladies had been in the church when he arrived; women liked to sit in churches; they had been there more than half an hour, and the mother had not enough of it even yet. The young lady, however, at present preferred the view that Longueville was painting; he became aware that she had placed herself in the very centre of his foreground. His first feeling was that she would spoil it; his second was that she would improve it. Little by little she turned more into profile, leaning only one arm upon the parapet, while the other hand, holding her folded parasol, hung down at her side. She was motionless; it was almost as if she were standing there on purpose to be drawn. Yes, certainly she improved the picture. Her profile, delicate and thin, defined itself against the sky, in the clear shadow of a coquettish hat; her figure was light; she bent and leaned easily; she wore a gray dress, fastened up as was then the fashion, and displaying the broad edge of a crimson petticoat. She kept her position; she seemed absorbed in the view. "Is she *posing*—is she attitudinizing for my benefit?" Longueville asked of himself. And then it seemed to him that this was a needless assumption, for the prospect was quite beautiful enough to be looked at for itself, and there was nothing impossible in a pretty girl having a love of fine landscape. "But posing or not," he went on, "I will put her into my sketch. She has simply put herself in. It will give it a human interest. There is nothing like having a human interest." So, with the ready skill that he possessed, he introduced the young girl's figure into his foreground, and at the end of ten minutes he had almost made something that had the form of a likeness. "If she will only be quiet for another ten minutes," he said, "the thing will really be a picture." Unfortunately, the young lady was not quiet; she had apparently had enough of her attitude and her view. She turned away, facing Longueville again, and slowly came back, as if to re-enter the church. To do so she had to pass near him, and as she approached he instinctively got up, holding his drawing in one hand. She looked at him again, with that expression that he had mentally characterized as "bold," a few minutes before—with dark, intelligent eyes. Her hair was dark and dense; she was a strikingly handsome girl.

"I am so sorry you moved," he said, confidently, in English. "You were so—so beautiful."

She stopped, looking at him more directly than ever; and she looked at his sketch, which he held out toward her. At the sketch, however, she only glanced, whereas there was observation in the eye that she bent upon Longueville. He never knew whether she had blushed; he afterward thought she might have been frightened. Nevertheless, it was not exactly terror that appeared to dictate her answer to Longueville's speech.

"I am much obliged to you. Don't you think you have looked at me enough?"

"By no means. I should like so much to finish my drawing."

"I am not a professional model," said the young lady.

"No. That 's my difficulty," Longueville answered, laughing. "I can't propose to remunerate you."

The young lady seemed to think this joke in indifferent taste. She turned away in silence; but something in her expression, in his feeling at the time, in the situation, incited Longueville to higher play. He felt a lively need of carrying his point.

"You see it will be pure kindness," he went on,—"a simple act of charity. Five minutes will be enough. Treat me as an Italian beggar."

She had laid down his sketch and had stepped forward. He stood there, obsequious, clasping his hands and smiling.

His interruptress stopped and looked at him again, as if she thought him a very odd person; but she seemed amused. Now, at any rate, she was not frightened. She seemed even disposed to provoke him a little.

"I wish to go to my mother," she said.

"Where is your mother?" the young man asked.

"In the church, of course. I did n't come here alone!"

"Of course not; but you may be sure that your mother is very contented. I have been in that little church. It is charming. She is just resting there; she is probably tired. If you will kindly give me five minutes more, she will come out to you."

"Five minutes?" the young girl asked.

"Five minutes will do. I shall be eternally grateful." Longueville was amused at himself as he said this. He cared infinitely less for his sketch than the words appeared to imply; but, somehow, he cared greatly that this graceful stranger should do what he had proposed.

The graceful stranger dropped an eye on the sketch again.

"Is your picture so good as that?" she asked.

"I have a great deal of talent," he answered, laughing. "You shall see for yourself, when it is finished."

She turned slowly toward the terrace again.

"You certainly have a great deal of talent, to induce me to do what you ask." And she walked to where she had stood before. Longueville made a movement to go with her, as if to show her the attitude he meant; but, pointing with decision to his easel, she said—

"You have only five minutes." He immediately went back to his work, and she made a vague attempt to take up her position. "You must tell me if this will do," she added, in a moment.

"It will do beautifully," Longueville answered, in a happy tone, looking at her and plying his brush. "It is immensely good of you to take so much trouble."

For a moment she made no rejoinder, but presently she said—

"Of course if I pose at all I wish to pose well."

"You pose admirably," said Longueville.

After this she said nothing, and for several minutes he painted rapidly and in silence. He felt a certain excitement, and the movement of his thoughts kept pace with that of his brush. It was very true that she posed admirably; she was a fine creature to paint. Her prettiness inspired him, and also her audacity, as he was content to regard it for the moment. He wondered about her—who she was, and what she was—perceiving that the so-called audacity was not vulgar boldness, but the play of an original and probably interesting character. It was obvious that she was a perfect lady, but it was equally obvious that she was irregularly clever. Longueville's little figure was a success—a charming success, he thought, as he put on the last touches. While he was doing this, his model's companion came into view. She came out of the church, pausing a moment as she looked from her daughter to the young man in the corner of the terrace; then she walked straight over to the young girl. She was a delicate little gentlewoman, with a light, quick step.

Longueville's five minutes were up; so, leaving his place, he approached the two ladies, sketch in hand. The elder one, who had passed her hand into her daughter's arm, looked up at him with clear, surprised eyes; she was a charming old woman. Her eyes were very pretty, and on either side of them, above a pair of fine dark brows, was a band of silvery hair, rather coquettishly arranged.

"It is my portrait," said her daughter, as Longueville drew near. "This gentleman has been sketching me."

"Sketching you, dearest?" murmured her mother. "Was n't it rather sudden?"

"Very sudden—very abrupt!" exclaimed the young girl with a laugh.

"Considering all that, it 's very good," said Longueville, offering his picture to the elder lady, who took it and began to examine it. "I can't tell you how much I thank you," he said to his model.

"It 's very well for you to thank me now," she replied. "You really had no right to begin."

"The temptation was so great."

"We should resist temptation. And you should have asked my leave."

"I was afraid you would refuse it; and you stood there, just in my line of vision."

"You should have asked me to get out of it."

"I should have been very sorry. Besides, it would have been extremely rude."

The young girl looked at him a moment.

"Yes, I think it would. But what you have done is ruder."

"It is a hard case!" said Longueville. "What could I have done, then, decently?"

"It 's a beautiful drawing," murmured the elder lady, handing the thing back to Longueville. Her daughter, meanwhile, had not even glanced at it.

"You might have waited till I should go away," this argumentative young person continued.

Longueville shook his head.

"I never lose opportunities!"

"You might have sketched me afterwards, from memory."

Longueville looked at her, smiling.

"Judge how much better my memory will be now!"

She also smiled a little, but instantly became serious.

"For myself, it 's an episode I shall try to forget. I don't like the part I have played in it."

"May you never play a less becoming one!" cried Longueville. "I hope that your mother, at least, will accept a memento of the occasion." And he turned again with his sketch to her companion, who had been listening to the girl's conversation with this enterprising stranger, and looking from one to the other with an air of earnest confusion. "Won't you do me the honor of keeping my sketch?" he said. "I think it really looks like your daughter."

"Oh, thank you, thank you; I hardly dare," murmured the lady, with a deprecating gesture.

"It will serve as a kind of amends for the liberty I have taken," Longueville added; and he began to remove the drawing from its paper block.

"It makes it worse for you to give it to us," said the young girl.

"Oh, my dear, I am sure it 's lovely!" exclaimed her mother. "It 's wonderfully like you."

"I think that also makes it worse!"

Longueville was at last nettled. The young lady's perversity was perhaps not exactly malignant; but it was certainly ungracious. She seemed to desire to present herself as a beautiful tormentress.

"How does it make it worse?" he asked, with a frown.

He believed she was clever, and she was certainly ready. Now, however, she reflected a moment before answering.

"That you should give us your sketch," she said at last.

"It was to your mother I offered it," Longueville observed.

But this observation, the fruit of his irritation, appeared to have no effect upon the young girl.

"Is n't it what painters call a study?" she went on. "A study is of use to the painter himself. Your justification would be that you should keep your sketch, and that it might be of use to you."

"My daughter is a study, sir, you will say," said the elder lady in a little, light, conciliating voice, and graciously accepting the drawing again.

"I will admit," said Longueville, "that I am very inconsistent. Set it down to my esteem, madam," he added, looking at the mother.

"That 's for you, mamma," said his model, disengaging her arm from her mother's hand and turning away.

The mamma stood looking at the sketch with a smile which seemed to express a tender desire to reconcile all accidents.

"It 's extremely beautiful," she murmured, "and if you insist on my taking it—"

"I shall regard it as a great honor."

"Very well, then; with many thanks, I will keep it." She looked at the young man a moment, while her daughter walked away. Longueville thought her a delightful little person; she struck him as a sort of transfigured Quakeress—a mystic with a practical side. "I am sure you think she 's a strange girl," she said.

"She is extremely pretty."

"She is very clever," said the mother.

"She is wonderfully graceful."

"Ah, but she 's good!" cried the old lady.

"I am sure she comes honestly by that," said Longueville, expressively, while his companion, returning his salutation with a certain scrupulous grace of her own, hurried after her daughter.

Longueville remained there staring at the view but not especially seeing it. He felt as if he had at once enjoyed and lost an opportunity. After a while he tried to make a sketch of the old beggar-woman who sat there in a sort of palsied immobility, like a rickety statue at a church-door. But his attempt to reproduce her features was not gratifying, and he suddenly laid down his brush. She was not pretty enough—she had a bad profile.

II

Two months later Bernard Longueville was at Venice, still under the impression that he was leaving Italy. He was not a man who made plans and held to them. He made them, indeed—few men made more—but he made them as a basis for variation. He had gone to Venice to spend a fortnight, and his fortnight had taken the form of eight enchanting weeks. He had still a sort of conviction that he was carrying out his plans; for it must be confessed that where his pleasure was concerned he had considerable skill in accommodating his theory to his practice. His enjoyment of Venice was extreme, but he was roused from it by a summons he was indisposed to resist. This consisted of a letter from an intimate friend who was living in Germany—a friend whose name was Gordon Wright. He had been spending the winter in Dresden, but his letter bore the date of Baden-Baden. As it was not long, I may give it entire.

"I wish very much that you would come to this place. I think you have been here before, so that you know how pretty it is, and how amusing. I shall probably be here the rest of the summer. There are some people I know and whom I want you to know. Be so good as to arrive. Then I will thank you properly for your various Italian rhapsodies. I can't reply on the same scale—I have n't the time. Do you know what I am doing? I am making love. I find it a most absorbing occupation. That is literally why I have not written to you before. I have been making love ever since the last of May. It takes an immense amount of time, and everything else has got terribly behindhand. I don't mean to say that the experiment itself has gone on very fast; but I am trying to push it forward. I have n't yet had time to test its success; but in this I want your help. You know we great physicists never make an experiment without an 'assistant'—a humble individual who burns his fingers and stains his clothes in the cause of science, but whose interest in the problem is only indirect. I want you to be my assistant, and I will guarantee that your burns and stains shall not be dangerous. She is an extremely interesting girl, and I really want you to see her—I want to know what you think of her. She wants to know you, too, for I have talked a good deal about you. There you have it, if gratified vanity will help you on the way. Seriously, this is a real request. I want your opinion, your impression. I want to see how she will affect you. I don't say I ask for your advice; that, of course, you will not undertake to give. But I desire a definition, a characterization; you know you toss off those things. I don't see why I should n't tell you all this—I have always told you everything. I have never pretended to know anything about women, but I have always supposed that you knew everything. You certainly have always had the tone of that sort of omniscience. So come here as soon as possible and let me see that you are not a humbug. She 's a very handsome girl."

Longueville was so much amused with this appeal that he very soon started for Germany. In the reader, Gordon Wright's letter will, perhaps, excite surprise rather than hilarity; but Longueville thought it highly characteristic of his friend. What it especially pointed to was Gordon's want of imagination—a deficiency which was a matter of common jocular allusion between the two young men, each of whom kept a collection of acknowledged oddities as a playground for the other's wit. Bernard had often spoken of his comrade's want of imagination as a bottomless pit, into which Gordon was perpetually inviting him to lower himself. "My dear fellow," Bernard said, "you must really excuse me; I cannot take these subterranean excursions. I should lose my breath down there; I should never come up alive. You know I have dropped things down—little jokes and metaphors, little fantasies and paradoxes—and I have never heard them touch bottom!" This was an epigram on the part of a young man who had a lively play of fancy; but it was none the less true that Gordon Wright had a firmly-treading, rather than a winged, intellect. Every phrase in his letter seemed, to Bernard, to march in stout-soled walking-boots, and nothing could better express his attachment to the process of reasoning things out than this proposal that his friend should come and make a chemical analysis—a geometrical survey—of the lady of his love. "That I shall have any difficulty in forming an opinion, and any difficulty in expressing it when formed—

of this he has as little idea as that he shall have any difficulty in accepting it when expressed." So Bernard reflected, as he rolled in the train to Munich. "Gordon's mind," he went on, "has no atmosphere; his intellectual process goes on in the void. There are no currents and eddies to affect it, no high winds nor hot suns, no changes of season and temperature. His premises are neatly arranged, and his conclusions are perfectly calculable."

Yet for the man on whose character he so freely exercised his wit Bernard Longueville had a strong affection. It is nothing against the validity of a friendship that the parties to it have not a mutual resemblance. There must be a basis of agreement, but the structure reared upon it may contain a thousand disparities. These two young men had formed an alliance of old, in college days, and the bond between them had been strengthened by the simple fact of its having survived the sentimental revolutions of early life. Its strongest link was a sort of mutual respect. Their tastes, their pursuits were different; but each of them had a high esteem for the other's character. It may be said that they were easily pleased; for it is certain that neither of them had performed any very conspicuous action. They were highly civilized young Americans, born to an easy fortune and a tranquil destiny, and unfamiliar with the glitter of golden opportunities. If I did not shrink from disparaging the constitution of their native land for their own credit, I should say that it had never been very definitely proposed to these young gentlemen to distinguish themselves. On reaching manhood, they had each come into property sufficient to make violent exertion superfluous. Gordon Wright, indeed, had inherited a large estate. Their wants being tolerably modest, they had not been tempted to strive for the glory of building up commercial fortunes—the most obvious career open to young Americans. They had, indeed, embraced no career at all, and if summoned to give an account of themselves would, perhaps, have found it hard to tell any very impressive story. Gordon Wright was much interested in physical science, and had ideas of his own on what is called the endowment of research. His ideas had taken a practical shape, and he had distributed money very freely among the investigating classes, after which he had gone to spend a couple of years in Germany, supposing it to be the land of laboratories. Here we find him at present, cultivating relations with several learned bodies and promoting the study of various tough branches of human knowledge, by paying the expenses of difficult experiments. The experiments, it must be added, were often of his own making, and he must have the honor of whatever brilliancy attaches, in the estimation of the world, to such pursuits. It was not, indeed, a brilliancy that dazzled Bernard Longueville, who, however, was not easily dazzled by anything. It was because he regarded him in so plain and direct a fashion, that Bernard had an affection for his friend—an affection to which it would perhaps be difficult to assign a definite cause. Personal sympathies are doubtless caused by something; but the causes are remote, mysterious to our daily vision, like those of the particular state of the weather. We content ourselves with remarking that it is fine or that it rains, and the enjoyment of our likes and dislikes is by no means apt to borrow its edge from the keenness of our analysis. Longueville had a relish for fine quality—superior savour; and he was sensible of this merit in the simple, candid, manly, affectionate nature of his comrade, which seemed to him an excellent thing of its kind. Gordon Wright had a tender heart and a strong will—a combination which, when the understanding is not too limited, is often the motive of admirable actions. There might sometimes be a question whether Gordon's understanding were sufficiently unlimited, but the impulses of a generous temper often play a useful part in filling up the gaps of an incomplete imagination, and the general impression that Wright produced was certainly that of intelligent good-nature. The reasons for appreciating Bernard Longueville were much more manifest. He pleased superficially, as well as fundamentally. Nature had sent him into the world with an armful of good gifts. He was very good-looking—tall, dark, agile, perfectly finished, so good-looking that he might have been a fool and yet be forgiven. As has already been intimated, however, he was far from being a fool. He had a number of talents, which, during three or four years that followed his leaving college, had received the discipline of the study of the law. He had not made much of the law; but he had made something of his talents. He was almost always spoken of as "accomplished;" people asked why he did n't do something. This question was never satisfactorily answered, the feeling being that Longueville did more than many people in causing it to be asked. Moreover, there was one thing he did constantly— he enjoyed himself. This is manifestly not a career, and it has been said at the outset that he was not attached to any of the recognized professions. But without going into details, he was a charming fellow—clever, urbane, free-handed, and with that fortunate quality in his appearance which is known as distinction.

III

H E HAD NOT SPECIFIED, in writing to Gordon Wright, the day on which he should arrive at Baden-Baden; it must be confessed that he was not addicted to specifying days. He came to his journey's end in the evening, and, on presenting himself at the hotel from which his friend had dated his letter, he learned that Gordon Wright had betaken himself after dinner, according to the custom of Baden-Baden, to the grounds of the Conversation-house. It was eight o'clock, and Longueville, after removing the stains of travel, sat down to dine. His first impulse had been to send for Gordon to come and keep him company at his repast; but on second thought he determined to make it as brief as possible. Having brought it to a close, he took his way to the Kursaal. The great German watering-place is one of the prettiest nooks in Europe, and of a summer evening in the gaming days, five-and-twenty years ago, it was one of the most brilliant scenes. The lighted windows of the great temple of hazard (of as chaste an architecture as if it had been devoted to a much purer divinity) opened wide upon the gardens and groves; the little river that issues from the bosky mountains of the Black Forest flowed, with an air of brook-like innocence, past the expensive hotels and lodging-houses; the orchestra, in a high pavilion on the terrace of the Kursaal, played a discreet accompaniment to the conversation of the ladies and gentlemen who, scattered over the large expanse on a thousand little chairs, preferred for the time the beauties of nature to the shuffle of coin and the calculation of chance; while the faint summer stars, twinkling above the vague black hills and woods, looked down at the indifferent groups without venturing to drop their light upon them.

Longueville, noting all this, went straight into the gaming-rooms; he was curious to see whether his friend, being fond of experiments, was trying combinations at roulette. But he was not to be found in any of the gilded chambers, among the crowd that pressed in silence about the tables; so that Bernard presently came and began to wander about the lamp-lit terrace, where innumerable groups, seated and strolling, made the place a gigantic *conversazione*. It seemed to him very agreeable and amusing, and he remarked to himself that, for a man who was supposed not to take especially the Epicurean view of life, Gordon Wright, in coming to Baden, had certainly made himself comfortable. Longueville went his way, glancing from one cluster of talkers to another; and at last he saw a face which brought him to a stop. He stood a moment looking at it; he knew he had seen it before. He had an excellent memory for faces; but it was some time before he was able to attach an identity to this one. Where had he seen a little elderly lady with an expression of timorous vigilance, and a band of hair as softly white as a dove's wing? The answer to the question presently came— Where but in a grass-grown corner of an old Italian town? The lady was the mother of his inconsequent model, so that this mysterious personage was probably herself not far off. Before Longueville had time to verify this induction, he found his eyes resting upon the broad back of a gentleman seated close to the old lady, and who, turning away from her, was talking to a young girl. It was nothing but the back of this gentleman that he saw, but nevertheless, with the instinct of true friendship, he recognized in this featureless expanse the robust personality of Gordon Wright. In a moment he had stepped forward and laid his hand upon Wright's shoulder.

His friend looked round, and then sprang up with a joyous exclamation and grasp of the hand.

"My dear fellow—my dear Bernard! What on earth— when did you arrive?"

While Bernard answered and explained a little, he glanced from his friend's good, gratified face at the young girl with whom Wright had been talking, and then at the lady on the other side, who was giving him a bright little stare. He raised his hat to her and to the young girl, and he became conscious, as regards the latter, of a certain disappointment. She was very pretty; she was looking at him; but she was not the heroine of the little incident of the terrace at Siena.

"It 's just like Longueville, you know," Gordon Wright went on; "he always comes at you from behind; he 's so awfully fond of surprises." He was laughing; he was greatly pleased; he introduced Bernard to the two ladies. "You must know Mrs. Vivian; you must know Miss Blanche Evers."

Bernard took his place in the little circle; he wondered whether he ought to venture upon a special recognition of Mrs. Vivian. Then it seemed to him that he should leave the option of this step with the lady, especially as he had detected recognition in her eye. But Mrs. Vivian ventured upon nothing special; she contented herself with soft generalities—with remarking that she always liked to know when people would arrive; that, for herself, she never enjoyed surprises.

"And yet I imagine you have had your share," said Longueville, with a smile. He thought this might remind her of the moment when she came out of the little church at Siena and found her daughter posturing to an unknown painter.

But Mrs. Vivian, turning her benignant head about, gave but a superficial reply.

"Oh, I have had my share of everything, good and bad. I don't complain of anything." And she gave a little deprecating laugh.

Gordon Wright shook hands with Bernard again; he seemed really very glad to see him. Longueville, remembering that Gordon had written to him that he had been "making love," began to seek in his countenance for the ravages of passion. For the moment, however, they were not apparent; the excellent, honest fellow looked placid and contented. Gordon Wright had a clear gray eye, short, straight, flaxen hair, and a healthy diffusion of color. His features were thick and rather irregular; but his countenance—in addition to the merit of its expression—derived a certain grace from a powerful yellow moustache, to which its wearer occasionally gave a martial twist. Gordon Wright was not tall, but he was strong, and in his whole person there was something well-planted and sturdy. He almost always dressed in light-colored garments, and he wore round his neck an eternal blue cravat. When he was agitated he grew very red. While he questioned Longueville about his journey and his health, his whereabouts and his intentions, the latter, among his own replies, endeavored to read in Wright's eyes some account of his present situation. Was that pretty girl at his side the ambiguous object of his adoration, and, in that case, what was the function of the elder lady, and what had become of her argumentative daughter? Perhaps this was another, a younger daughter, though, indeed, she bore no resemblance to either of Longueville's friends. Gordon Wright, in spite of Bernard's interrogative glances, indulged in no optical confidences. He had too much to tell. He would keep his story till they should be alone together. It was impossible that they should adjourn just yet to social solitude; the two ladies were under Gordon's protection. Mrs. Vivian—Bernard felt a satisfaction in learning her name; it was as if a curtain, half pulled up and stopped by a hitch, had suddenly been raised altogether— Mrs. Vivian sat looking up and down the terrace at the crowd of loungers and talkers with an air of tender expectation. She was probably looking for her elder daughter, and Longueville could not help wishing also that this young lady would arrive. Meanwhile, he saw that the young girl to whom Gordon had been devoting himself was extremely pretty, and appeared eminently approachable. Longueville had some talk with her, reflecting that if she were the person concerning whom Gordon had written him, it behooved him to appear to take an interest in her. This view of the case was confirmed by Gordon Wright's presently turning away to talk with Mrs. Vivian, so that his friend might be at liberty to make acquaintance with their companion.

Though she had not been with the others at Siena, it seemed to Longueville, with regard to her, too, that this was not the first time he had seen her. She was simply the American pretty girl, whom he had seen a thousand times. It was a numerous sisterhood, pervaded by a strong family likeness. This young lady had charming eyes (of the color of Gordon's cravats), which looked everywhere at once and yet found time to linger in some places, where Longueville's own eyes frequently met them. She had soft brown hair, with a silky-golden thread in it, beautifully arranged and crowned by a smart little hat that savoured of Paris. She had also a slender little figure, neatly rounded, and delicate, narrow hands, prettily gloved. She moved about a great deal in her place, twisted her little flexible body and tossed her head, fingered her hair and examined the ornaments of her dress. She had a great deal of conversation, Longueville speedily learned, and she expressed herself with extreme frankness and decision. He asked her, to begin with, if she had been long at Baden, but the impetus of this question was all she required. Turning her charming, conscious, coquettish little face upon him, she instantly began to chatter.

"I have been here about four weeks. I don't know whether you call that long. It does n't seem long to me; I have had such a lovely time. I have met ever so many people here I know—every day some one turns up. Now you have turned up to-day."

"Ah, but you don't know me," said Longueville, laughing.

"Well, I have heard a great deal about you!" cried the young girl, with a pretty little stare of contradiction. "I think you know a great friend of mine, Miss Ella Maclane, of Baltimore. She 's travelling in Europe now." Longueville's memory did not instantly respond to this signal, but he expressed that rapturous assent which the occasion demanded, and even risked the observation that the young lady from Baltimore was very pretty. "She 's far too lovely," his companion went on. "I have often heard her speak of you. I think you know her sister rather better than you know her. She has not been out very long. She is just as interesting as she can be. Her hair comes down to her feet. She 's travelling in Norway. She has been everywhere you can think of, and she 's going to finish off with Finland. You can't go any further than that, can you? That 's one comfort; she will have to turn round and come back. I want her dreadfully to come to Baden-Baden."

"I wish she would," said Longueville. "Is she travelling alone?"

"Oh, no. They 've got some Englishman. They say he 's devoted to Ella. Every one seems to have an Englishman, now. We 've got one here, Captain Lovelock, the Honourable Augustus Lovelock. Well, they 're awfully handsome. Ella Maclane is dying to come to Baden-Baden. I wish you 'd write to her. Her father and mother have got some idea in their heads; they think it 's improper—what do you call it?— immoral. I wish you would write to her and tell her it is n't. I wonder if they think that Mrs. Vivian would come to a place that 's immoral. Mrs. Vivian says she would take her in a moment; she does n't seem to care how many she has. I declare, she 's only too kind. You know I 'm in Mrs. Vivian's care. My mother 's gone to Marienbad. She would let me go with Mrs. Vivian anywhere, on account of the influence—she thinks so much of Mrs. Vivian's influence. I have always heard a great deal about it, have n't you? I must say it 's lovely; it 's had a wonderful effect upon me. I don't want to praise myself, but it has. You ask Mrs. Vivian if I have n't been good. I have been just as good as I can be. I have been so peaceful, I have just sat here this way. Do you call this immoral? You 're not obliged to gamble if you don't want to. Ella Maclane's father seems to think you get drawn in. I 'm sure I have n't been drawn in. I know what you 're going to say—you 're going to say I have been drawn out. Well, I have, to-night. We just sit here so quietly—there 's nothing to do but to talk. We make a little party by ourselves—are you going to belong to our party? Two of us are missing— Miss Vivian and Captain Lovelock. Captain Lovelock has gone with her into the rooms to explain the gambling—Miss Vivian always wants everything explained. I am sure I understood it the first time I looked at the tables. Have you ever seen Miss Vivian? She 's very much admired, she 's so very unusual. Black hair 's so uncommon—I see you have got it too—but I mean for young ladies. I am sure one sees everything here. There 's a woman that comes to the tables—a Portuguese countess—who has hair that is positively blue. I can't say I admire it when it comes to that shade. Blue 's my favorite color, but I prefer it in the eyes," continued Longueville's companion, resting upon him her own two brilliant little specimens of the tint.

He listened with that expression of clear amusement which is not always an indication of high esteem, but which even pretty chatterers, who are not the reverse of estimable, often prefer to masculine inattention; and while he listened Bernard, according to his wont, made his reflections. He said to himself that there were two kinds of pretty girls—the acutely conscious and the finely unconscious. Mrs. Vivian's *protégée* was a member of the former category; she belonged to the genus coquette. We all have our conception of the indispensable, and the indispensable, to this young lady, was a spectator; almost any male biped would serve the purpose. To her spectator she addressed, for the moment, the whole volume of her being—addressed it in her glances, her attitudes, her exclamations, in a hundred little experiments of tone and gesture and position. And these rustling artifices were so innocent and obvious that the directness of her desire to be well with her observer became in itself a grace; it led Bernard afterward to say to himself that the natural vocation and *métier* of little girls for whom existence was but a shimmering surface, was to prattle and ruffle their plumage; their view of life and its duties was as simple and superficial as that of an Oriental *bayadere*. It surely could not be with regard to this transparent little flirt that Gordon Wright desired advice; you could literally see the daylight—or rather the Baden gaslight—on the other side of her. She sat there for a minute, turning her little empty head to and fro, and catching Bernard's eye every time she moved; she had for the instant the air of having exhausted all topics. Just then a young lady, with a gentleman at her side, drew near to the little group, and Longueville, perceiving her, instantly got up from his chair.

"There 's a beauty of the unconscious class!" he said to himself. He knew her face very well; he had spent half an hour in copying it.

"Here comes Miss Vivian!" said Gordon Wright, also getting up, as if to make room for the daughter near the mother.

She stopped in front of them, smiling slightly, and then she rested her eyes upon Longueville. Their gaze at first was full and direct, but it expressed nothing more than civil curiosity. This was immediately followed, however, by the light of recognition—recognition embarrassed, and signalling itself by a blush.

Miss Vivian's companion was a powerful, handsome fellow, with a remarkable auburn beard, who struck the observer immediately as being uncommonly well dressed. He carried his hands in the pockets of a little jacket, the button-hole of which was adorned with a blooming rose. He approached Blanche Evers, smiling and dandling his body a little, and making her two or three jocular bows.

"Well, I hope you have lost every penny you put on the

table!" said the young girl, by way of response to his obeisances.

He began to laugh and repeat them.

"I don't care what I lose, so long—so long—"

"So long as what, pray?"

"So long as you let me sit down by you!" And he dropped, very gallantly, into a chair on the other side of her.

"I wish you would lose all your property!" she replied, glancing at Bernard.

"It would be a very small stake," said Captain Lovelock. "Would you really like to see me reduced to misery?"

While this graceful dialogue rapidly established itself, Miss Vivian removed her eyes from Longueville's face and turned toward her mother. But Gordon Wright checked this movement by laying his hand on Longueville's shoulder and proceeding to introduce his friend.

"This is the accomplished creature, Mr. Bernard Longueville, of whom you have heard me speak. One of his accomplishments, as you see, is to drop down from the moon."

"No, I don't drop from the moon," said Bernard, laughing. "I drop from—Siena!" He offered his hand to Miss Vivian, who for an appreciable instant hesitated to extend her own. Then she returned his salutation, without any response to his allusion to Siena.

She declined to take a seat, and said she was tired and preferred to go home. With this suggestion her mother immediately complied, and the two ladies appealed to the indulgence of little Miss Evers, who was obliged to renounce the society of Captain Lovelock. She enjoyed this luxury, however, on the way to Mrs. Vivian's lodgings, toward which they all slowly strolled, in the sociable Baden fashion. Longueville might naturally have found himself next Miss Vivian, but he received an impression that she avoided him. She walked in front, and Gordon Wright strolled beside her, though Longueville noticed that they appeared to exchange but few words. He himself offered his arm to Mrs. Vivian, who paced along with a little lightly-wavering step, making observations upon the beauties of Baden and the respective merits of the hotels.

IV

"WHICH OF THEM is it?" asked Longueville of his friend, after they had bidden good-night to the three ladies and to Captain Lovelock, who went off to begin, as he said, the evening. They stood, when they had turned away from the door of Mrs. Vivian's lodgings, in the little, rough-paved German street.

"Which of them is what?" Gordon asked, staring at his companion.

"Oh, come," said Longueville, "you are not going to begin to play at modesty at this hour! Did n't you write to me that you had been making violent love?"

"Violent? No."

"The more shame to you! Has your love-making been feeble?"

His friend looked at him a moment rather soberly.

"I suppose you thought it a queer document—that letter I wrote you."

"I thought it characteristic," said Longueville smiling.

"Is n't that the same thing?"

"Not in the least. I have never thought you a man of oddities." Gordon stood there looking at him with a serious eye, half appealing, half questioning; but at these last words he glanced away. Even a very modest man may wince a little at hearing himself denied the distinction of a few variations from the common type. Longueville made this reflection, and it struck him, also, that his companion was in a graver mood than he had expected; though why, after all, should he have been in a state of exhilaration? "Your letter was a very natural, interesting one," Bernard added.

"Well, you see," said Gordon, facing his companion again, "I have been a good deal preoccupied."

"Obviously, my dear fellow!"

"I want very much to marry."

"It 's a capital idea," said Longueville.

"I think almost as well of it," his friend declared, "as if I had invented it. It has struck me for the first time."

These words were uttered with a mild simplicity which provoked Longueville to violent laughter.

"My dear fellow," he exclaimed, "you have, after all, your little oddities."

Singularly enough, however, Gordon Wright failed to appear flattered by this concession.

"I did n't send for you to laugh at me," he said.

"Ah, but I have n't travelled three hundred miles to cry! Seriously, solemnly, then, it is one of these young ladies that has put marriage into your head?"

"Not at all. I had it in my head."

"Having a desire to marry, you proceeded to fall in love."

"I am not in love!" said Gordon Wright, with some energy.

"Ah, then, my dear fellow, why did you send for me?"

Wright looked at him an instant in silence.

"Because I thought you were a good fellow, as well as a clever one."

"A good fellow!" repeated Longueville. "I don't understand your confounded scientific nomenclature. But excuse me; I won't laugh. I am not a clever fellow; but I *am* a good one." He paused a moment, and then laid his hand on his companion's shoulder. "My dear Gordon, it 's no use; you *are* in love."

"Well, I don't want to be," said Wright.

"Heavens, what a horrible sentiment!"

"I want to marry with my eyes open. I want to *know* my wife. You don't know people when you are in love with them. Your impressions are colored."

"They are supposed to be, slightly. And you object to color?"

"Well, as I say, I want to know the woman I marry, as I should know any one else. I want to see her as clearly."

"Depend upon it, you have too great an appetite for knowledge; you set too high an esteem upon the dry light of science."

"Ah!" said Gordon promptly; "of course I want to be fond of her."

Bernard, in spite of his protest, began to laugh again.

"My dear Gordon, you are better than your theories. Your passionate heart contradicts your frigid intellect. I repeat it— you *are* in love."

"Please don't repeat it again," said Wright.

Bernard took his arm, and they walked along.

"What shall I call it, then? You are engaged in making studies for matrimony."

"I don't in the least object to your calling it that. My studies are of extreme interest."

"And one of those young ladies is the fair volume that contains the precious lesson," said Longueville. "Or perhaps your text-book is in two volumes?"

"No; there is one of them I am not studying at all. I never could do two things at once."

"That proves you are in love. One can't be in love with two women at once, but one may perfectly have two of them—or as many as you please—up for a competitive examination. However, as I asked you before, which of these young ladies is it that you have selected?"

Gordon Wright stopped abruptly, eying his friend.

"Which should you say?"

"Ah, that's not a fair question," Bernard urged. "It would be invidious for me to name one rather than the other, and if I were to mention the wrong one, I should feel as if I had been guilty of a rudeness towards the other. Don't you see?"

Gordon saw, perhaps, but he held to his idea of making his companion commit himself.

"Never mind the rudeness. I will do the same by you some day, to make it up. Which of them should you think me likely to have taken a fancy to? On general grounds, now, from what you know of me?" He proposed this problem with an animated eye.

"You forget," his friend said, "that though I know, thank heaven, a good deal of you, I know very little of either of those girls. I have had too little evidence."

"Yes, but you are a man who notices. That's why I wanted you to come."

"I spoke only to Miss Evers."

"Yes, I know you have never spoken to Miss Vivian." Gordon Wright stood looking at Bernard and urging his point as he pronounced these words. Bernard felt peculiarly conscious of his gaze. The words represented an illusion, and Longueville asked himself quickly whether it were not his duty to dispel it. The answer came more slowly than the question, but still it came, in the shape of a negative. The illusion was but a trifling one, and it was not for him, after all, to let his friend know that he had already met Miss Vivian. It was for the young girl herself, and since she had not done so—although she had the opportunity—Longueville said to himself that he was bound in honor not to speak. These reflections were very soon made, but in the midst of them our young man, thanks to a great agility of mind, found time to observe, tacitly, that it was odd, just there, to see his "honor" thrusting in its nose. Miss Vivian, in her own good time, would doubtless mention to Gordon the little incident of Siena. It was Bernard's fancy, for a moment, that he already knew it, and that the remark he had just uttered had an ironical accent; but this impression was completely dissipated by the tone in which he added— "All the same, you noticed her."

"Oh, yes; she is very noticeable."

"Well, then," said Gordon, "you will see. I should like you to make it out. Of course, if I am really giving my attention to one to the exclusion of the other, it will be easy to discover."

Longueville was half amused, half irritated by his friend's own relish of his little puzzle. " 'The exclusion of the other' has an awkward sound," he answered, as they walked on. "Am I to notice that you are very rude to one of the young ladies?"

"Oh dear, no. Do you think there is a danger of that?"

"Well," said Longueville, "I have already guessed."

Gordon Wright remonstrated. "Don't guess yet—wait a few days. I won't tell you now."

"Let us see if he does n't tell me," said Bernard, privately. And he meditated a moment. "When I presented myself, you were sitting very close to Miss Evers and talking very earnestly. Your head was bent toward her—it was very lover-like. Decidedly, Miss Evers is the object!"

For a single instant Gordon Wright hesitated, and then— "I hope I have n't seemed rude to Miss Vivian!" he exclaimed.

Bernard broke into a light laugh. "My dear Gordon, you are very much in love!" he remarked, as they arrived at their hotel.

V

LIFE AT BADEN-BADEN proved a very sociable affair, and Bernard Longueville perceived that he should not lack opportunity for the exercise of those gifts of intelligence to which Gordon Wright had appealed. The two friends took long walks through the woods and over the mountains, and they mingled with human life in the crowded precincts of the Conversation-house. They engaged in a ramble on the morning after Bernard's arrival, and wandered far away, over hill and dale. The Baden forests are superb, and the composition of the landscape is most effective. There is always a bosky dell in the foreground, and a purple crag embellished with a ruined tower at a proper angle. A little timber-and-plaster village peeps out from a tangle of plum-trees, and a way-side tavern, in comfortable recurrence, solicits concessions to the national custom of frequent refreshment. Gordon Wright, who was a dogged pedestrian, always enjoyed doing his ten miles, and Longueville, who was an incorrigible stroller, felt a keen relish for the picturesqueness of the country. But it was not, on this occasion, of the charms of the landscape or the pleasures of locomotion that they chiefly discoursed. Their talk took a more closely personal turn. It was a year since they had met, and there were many questions to ask and answer, many arrears of gossip to make up. As they stretched themselves on the grass on a sun-warmed hill-side, beneath a great German oak whose arms were quiet in the blue summer air, there was a lively exchange of impressions, opinions, speculations, anecdotes. Gordon Wright was surely an excellent friend. He took an interest in you. He asked no idle questions and made no vague professions; but he entered into your situation, he examined it in detail, and what he learned he never forgot. Months afterwards, he asked you about things which you yourself had forgotten. He was not a man of whom it would be generally said that he had the gift of sympathy; but he gave his attention to a friend's circumstances with a conscientious fixedness which was at least very far removed from indifference. Bernard had the gift of sympathy—or at least he was supposed to have it; but even he, familiar as he must therefore have been with the practice of this charming virtue, was at times so struck with his friend's fine faculty of taking other people's affairs seriously that he constantly exclaimed to himself, "The excellent fellow—the admirable nature!"

Bernard had two or three questions to ask about the three persons who appeared to have formed for some time his companion's principal society, but he was indisposed to press them. He felt that he should see for himself, and at a prospect of entertainment of this kind, his fancy always kindled. Gordon was, moreover, at first rather shy of confidences, though after they had lain on the grass ten minutes there was a good deal said.

"Now what do you think of her face?" Gordon asked, after staring a while at the sky through the oak-boughs.

"Of course, in future," said Longueville, "whenever you make use of the personal pronoun feminine, I am to understand that Miss Vivian is indicated."

"Her name is Angela," said Gordon; "but of course I can scarcely call her that."

"It's a beautiful name," Longueville rejoined; "but I may say, in answer to your question, that I am not struck with the fact that her face corresponds to it."

"You don't think her face beautiful, then?"

"I don't think it angelic. But how can I tell? I have only had a glimpse of her."

"Wait till she looks at you and speaks—wait till she smiles," said Gordon.

"I don't think I saw her smile—at least, not at me, directly. I hope she will!" Longueville went on. "But who is she—this beautiful girl with the beautiful name?"

"She is her mother's daughter," said Gordon Wright. "I don't really know a great deal more about her than that."

"And who is her mother?"

"A delightful little woman, devoted to Miss Vivian. She is a widow, and Angela is her only child. They have lived a great deal in Europe; they have but a modest income. Over here, Mrs. Vivian says, they can get a lot of things for their money that they can't get at home. So they stay, you see. When they are at home they live in New York. They know some of my people there. When they are in Europe they live about in different places. They are fond of Italy. They are extremely nice; it 's impossible to be nicer. They are very fond of books, fond of music, and art, and all that. They always read in the morning. They only come out rather late in the day."

"I see they are very superior people," said Bernard. "And little Miss Evers—what does she do in the morning? I know what she does in the evening!"

"I don't know what her regular habits are. I have n't paid much attention to her. She is very pretty."

"*Wunderschön!*" said Bernard. "But you were certainly talking to her last evening."

"Of course I talk to her sometimes. She is totally different from Angela Vivian—not nearly so cultivated; but she seems very charming."

"A little silly, eh?" Bernard suggested.

"She certainly is not so wise as Miss Vivian."

"That would be too much to ask, eh? But the Vivians, as kind as they are wise, have taken her under their protection."

"Yes," said Gordon, "they are to keep her another month or two. Her mother has gone to Marienbad, which I believe is thought a dull place for a young girl; so that, as they were coming here, they offered to bring her with them. Mrs. Evers is an old friend of Mrs. Vivian, who, on leaving Italy, had come up to Dresden to be with her. They spent a month there together; Mrs. Evers had been there since the winter. I think Mrs. Vivian really came to Baden-Baden—she would have preferred a less expensive place—to bring Blanche Evers. Her mother wanted her so much to come."

"And was it for her sake that Captain Lovelock came, too?" Bernard asked.

Gordon Wright stared a moment.

"I 'm sure I don't know!"

"Of course you can't be interested in that," said Bernard smiling. "Who is Captain Lovelock?"

"He is an Englishman. I believe he is what 's called aristocratically connected—the younger brother of a lord, or something of that sort."

"Is he a clever man?"

"I have n't talked with him much, but I doubt it. He is rather rakish; he plays a great deal."

"But is that considered here a proof of rakishness?" asked Bernard. "Have n't you played a little yourself?"

Gordon hesitated a moment.

"Yes, I have played a little. I wanted to try some experiments. I had made some arithmetical calculations of probabilities, which I wished to test."

Bernard gave a long laugh.

"I am delighted with the reasons you give for amusing yourself! Arithmetical calculations!"

"I assure you they are the real reasons!" said Gordon, blushing a little.

"That 's just the beauty of it. You were not afraid of being 'drawn in,' as little Miss Evers says?"

"I am never drawn in, whatever the thing may be. I go in, or I stay out; but I am not drawn," said Gordon Wright.

"You were not drawn into coming with Mrs. Vivian and her daughter from Dresden to this place?"

"I did n't come with them; I came a week later."

"My dear fellow," said Bernard, "that distinction is unworthy of your habitual candor."

"Well, I was not fascinated; I was not overmastered. I wanted to come to Baden."

"I have no doubt you did. Had you become very intimate with your friends in Dresden?"

"I had only seen them three times."

"After which you followed them to this place? Ah, don't say you were not fascinated!" cried Bernard, laughing and springing to his feet.

VI

THAT EVENING, in the gardens of the Kursaal, he renewed acquaintance with Angela Vivian. Her mother came, as usual, to sit and listen to the music, accompanied by Blanche Evers, who was in turn attended by Captain Lovelock. This little party found privacy in the crowd; they seated themselves in a quiet corner in an angle of one of the barriers of the terrace, while the movement of the brilliant Baden world went on around them. Gordon Wright engaged in conversation with Mrs. Vivian, while Bernard enjoyed an interview with her daughter. This young lady continued to ignore the fact of their previous meeting, and our hero said to himself that all he wished was to know what she preferred—he would rigidly conform to it. He conformed to her present programme; he had ventured to pronounce the word Siena the evening before, but he was careful not to pronounce it again. She had her reasons for her own reserve; he wondered what they were, and it gave him a certain pleasure to wonder. He enjoyed the consciousness of their having a secret together, and it became a kind of entertaining suspense to see how long she would continue to keep it. For himself, he was in no hurry to let the daylight in; the little incident at Siena had been, in itself, a charming affair; but Miss Vivian's present attitude gave it a sort of mystic consecration. He thought she carried it off very well—the theory that she had not seen him before; last evening she had been slightly confused, but now she was as self-possessed as if the line she had taken were a matter of conscience. Why should it be a matter of conscience? Was she in love with Gordon Wright, and did she wish, in consequence, to forget—and wish him not to suspect—that she had ever received an expression of admiration from another man? This was not likely; it was not likely, at least, that Miss Vivian wished to pass for a prodigy of innocence; for if to be admired is to pay a tribute to corruption, it was perfectly obvious that so handsome a girl must have tasted of the tree of knowledge. As for her being in love with Gordon Wright, that of course was another affair, and Bernard did not pretend, as yet, to have an opinion on this point, beyond hoping very much that she might be.

He was not wrong in the impression of her good looks that he had carried away from the short interview at Siena. She had a charmingly chiselled face, with a free, pure outline, a clear, fair complexion, and the eyes and hair of a dusky beauty. Her features had a firmness which suggested tranquillity, and yet her expression was light and quick, a combination—or a contradiction—which gave an original stamp to her beauty. Bernard remembered that he had thought it a trifle "bold"; but he now perceived that this had been but a vulgar misreading of her dark, direct, observant eye. The eye was a charming one; Bernard discovered in it, little by little, all sorts of things; and Miss Vivian was, for the present, simply a handsome, intelligent, smiling girl. He gave her an opportunity to make an allusion to Siena; he said to her that his friend told him that she and her mother had been spending the winter in Italy.

"Oh yes," said Angela Vivian; "we were in the far south; we were five months at Sorrento."

"And nowhere else?"

"We spent a few days in Rome. We usually prefer the quiet places; that is my mother's taste."

"It was not your mother's taste, then," said Bernard, "that brought you to Baden?"

She looked at him a moment.

"You mean that Baden is not quiet?"

Longueville glanced about at the moving, murmuring crowd, at the lighted windows of the Conversation-house, at the great orchestra perched up in its pagoda.

"This is not my idea of absolute tranquillity."

"Nor mine, either," said Miss Vivian. "I am not fond of absolute tranquillity."

"How do you arrange it, then, with your mother?"

Again she looked at him a moment, with her clever, slightly mocking smile.

"As you see. By making her come where I wish."

"You have a strong will," said Bernard. "I see that."

"No. I have simply a weak mother. But I make sacrifices too, sometimes."

"What do you call sacrifices?"

"Well, spending the winter at Sorrento."

Bernard began to laugh, and then he told her she must have had a very happy life—"to call a winter at Sorrento a sacrifice."

"It depends upon what one gives up," said Miss Vivian.

"What did you give up?"

She touched him with her mocking smile again.

"That is not a very civil question, asked in that way."

"You mean that I seem to doubt your abnegation?"

"You seem to insinuate that I had nothing to renounce. I gave up—I gave up—" and she looked about her, considering a little—"I gave up society."

"I am glad you remember what it was," said Bernard. "If I have seemed uncivil, let me make it up. When a woman speaks of giving up society, what she means is giving up admiration. You can never have given up that—you can never have escaped from it. You must have found it even at Sorrento."

"It may have been there, but I never found it. It was very respectful—it never expressed itself."

"That is the deepest kind," said Bernard.

"I prefer the shallower varieties," the young girl answered.

"Well," said Bernard, "you must remember that although shallow admiration expresses itself, all the admiration that expresses itself is not shallow."

Miss Vivian hesitated a moment.

"Some of it is impertinent," she said, looking straight at him, rather gravely.

Bernard hesitated about as long.

"When it is impertinent it is shallow. That comes to the same thing."

The young girl frowned a little.

"I am not sure that I understand—I am rather stupid. But you see how right I am in my taste for such places as this. I have to come here to hear such ingenious remarks."

"You should add that my coming, as well, has something to do with it."

"Everything!" said Miss Vivian.

"Everything? Does no one else make ingenious remarks? Does n't my friend Wright?"

"Mr. Wright says excellent things, but I should not exactly call them ingenious remarks."

"It is not what Wright says; it 's what he does. That 's the charm!" said Bernard.

His companion was silent for a moment. "That 's not usually a charm; good conduct is not thought pleasing."

"It surely is not thought the reverse!" Bernard exclaimed.

"It does n't rank—in the opinion of most people—among the things that make men agreeable."

"It depends upon what you call agreeable."

"Exactly so," said Miss Vivian. "It all depends on that."

"But the agreeable," Bernard went on—"it is n't after all, fortunately, such a subtle idea! The world certainly is agreed to think that virtue is a beautiful thing."

Miss Vivian dropped her eyes a moment, and then, looking up,

"Is it a charm?" she asked.

"For me there is no charm without it," Bernard declared.

"I am afraid that for me there is," said the young girl.

Bernard was puzzled—he who was not often puzzled. His companion struck him as altogether too clever to be likely to indulge in a silly affectation of cynicism. And yet, without this, how could one account for her sneering at virtue?

"You talk as if you had sounded the depths of vice!" he said, laughing. "What do you know about other than virtuous charms?"

"I know, of course, nothing about vice; but I have known virtue when it was very tiresome."

"Ah, then it was a poor affair. It was poor virtue. The best virtue is never tiresome."

Miss Vivian looked at him a little, with her fine discriminating eye.

"What a dreadful thing to have to think any virtue poor!"

This was a touching reflection, and it might have gone further had not the conversation been interrupted by Mrs. Vivian's appealing to her daughter to aid a defective recollection of a story about a Spanish family they had met at Biarritz, with which she had undertaken to entertain Gordon Wright. After this, the little circle was joined by a party of American friends who were spending a week at Baden, and the conversation became general.

VII

B UT ON THE FOLLOWING EVENING, Bernard again found himself seated in friendly colloquy with this interesting girl, while Gordon Wright discoursed with her mother on one side, and little Blanche Evers chattered to the admiring eyes of Captain Lovelock on the other.

"You and your mother are very kind to that little girl," our hero said; "you must be a great advantage to her."

Angela Vivian directed her eyes to her neighbors, and let them rest a while on the young girl's little fidgeting figure and her fresh, coquettish face. For some moments she said nothing, and to Longueville, turning over several things in his mind, and watching her, it seemed that her glance was one of disfavor. He divined, he scarcely knew how, that her esteem for her pretty companion was small.

"I don't know that I am very kind," said Miss Vivian. "I have done nothing in particular for her."

"Mr. Wright tells me you came to this place mainly on her account."

"I came for myself," said Miss Vivian. "The consideration you speak of perhaps had weight with my mother."

"You are not an easy person to say appreciative things to," Bernard rejoined. "One is tempted to say them; but you don't take them."

The young girl colored as she listened to this observation.

"I don't think you know," she murmured, looking away. Then, "Set it down to modesty," she added.

"That, of course, is what I have done. To what else could one possibly attribute an indifference to compliments?"

"There is something else. One might be proud."

"There you are again!" Bernard exclaimed. "You won't even let me praise your modesty."

"I would rather you should rebuke my pride."

"That is so humble a speech that it leaves no room for rebuke."

For a moment Miss Vivian said nothing.

"Men are singularly base," she declared presently, with a little smile. "They don't care in the least to say things that might help a person. They only care to say things that may seem effective and agreeable."

"I see: you think that to say agreeable things is a great misdemeanor."

"It comes from their vanity," Miss Vivian went on, as if she had not heard him. "They wish to appear agreeable and get credit for cleverness and *tendresse*, no matter how silly it would be for another person to believe them."

Bernard was a good deal amused, and a little nettled.

"Women, then," he said, "have rather a fondness for producing a bad impression—they like to appear disagreeable?"

His companion bent her eyes upon her fan for a moment as she opened and closed it.

"They are capable of resigning themselves to it—for a purpose."

Bernard was moved to extreme merriment.

"For what purpose?"

"I don't know that I mean for a purpose," said Miss Vivian; "but for a necessity."

"Ah, what an odious necessity!"

"Necessities usually are odious. But women meet them. Men evade them and shirk them."

"I contest your proposition. Women are themselves necessities; but they are not odious ones!" And Bernard added, in a moment, "One could n't evade them, if they were!"

"I object to being called a necessity," said Angela Vivian. "It diminishes one's merit."

"Ah, but it enhances the charm of life!"

"For men, doubtless!"

"The charm of life is very great," Bernard went on, looking up at the dusky hills and the summer stars, seen through a sort of mist of music and talk, and of powdery light projected from the softly lurid windows of the gaming-rooms. "The charm of life is extreme. I am unacquainted with odious necessities. I object to nothing!"

Angela Vivian looked about her as he had done—looked perhaps a moment longer at the summer stars; and if she had not already proved herself a young lady of a contradictory turn, it might have been supposed she was just then tacitly admitting the charm of life to be considerable.

"Do you suppose Miss Evers often resigns herself to being disagreeable—for a purpose?" asked Longueville, who had glanced at Captain Lovelock's companion again.

"She can't be disagreeable; she is too gentle, too soft."

"Do you mean too silly?"

"I don't know that I call her silly. She is not very wise; but she has no pretensions—absolutely none—so that one is not struck with anything incongruous."

"What a terrible description! I suppose one ought to have a few pretensions."

"You see one comes off more easily without them," said Miss Vivian.

"Do you call that coming off easily?"

She looked at him a moment gravely.

"I am very fond of Blanche," she said.

"Captain Lovelock is rather fond of her," Bernard went on.

The girl assented.

"He is completely fascinated—he is very much in love with her."

"And do they mean to make an international match?"

"I hope not; my mother and I are greatly troubled."

"Is n't he a good fellow?"

"He is a good fellow; but he is a mere trifler. He has n't a penny, I believe, and he has very expensive habits. He gambles a great deal. We don't know what to do."

"You should send for the young lady's mother."

"We have written to her pressingly. She answers that Blanche can take care of herself, and that she must stay at Marienbad to finish her cure. She has just begun a new one."

"Ah well," said Bernard, "doubtless Blanche can take care of herself."

For a moment his companion said nothing; then she exclaimed—

"It 's what a girl ought to be able to do!"

"I am sure you are!" said Bernard.

She met his eyes, and she was going to make some rejoinder; but before she had time to speak, her mother's little, clear, conciliatory voice interposed. Mrs. Vivian appealed to her daughter, as she had done the night before.

"Dear Angela, what was the name of the gentleman who

delivered that delightful course of lectures that we heard in Geneva, on—what was the title?—'The Redeeming Features of the Pagan Morality.'"

Angela flushed a little.

"I have quite forgotten his name, mamma," she said, without looking round.

"Come and sit by me, my dear, and we will talk them over. I wish Mr. Wright to hear about them," Mrs. Vivian went on.

"Do you wish to convert him to paganism?" Bernard asked.

"The lectures were very dull; they had no redeeming features," said Angela, getting up, but turning away from her mother. She stood looking at Bernard Longueville; he saw she was annoyed at her mother's interference. "Every now and then," she said, "I take a turn through the gaming-rooms. The last time, Captain Lovelock went with me. Will you come to-night?"

Bernard assented with expressive alacrity; he was charmed with her not wishing to break off her conversation with him.

"Ah, we 'll all go!" said Mrs. Vivian, who had been listening, and she invited the others to accompany her to the Kursaal.

They left their places, but Angela went first, with Bernard Longueville by her side; and the idea of her having publicly braved her mother, as it were, for the sake of his society, lent for the moment an almost ecstatic energy to his tread. If he had been tempted to presume upon his triumph, however, he would have found a check in the fact that the young girl herself tasted very soberly of the sweets of defiance. She was silent and grave; she had a manner which took the edge from the wantonness of filial independence. Yet, for all this, Bernard was pleased with his position; and, as he walked with her through the lighted and crowded rooms, where they soon detached themselves from their companions, he felt that peculiar satisfaction which best expresses itself in silence. Angela looked a while at the rows of still, attentive faces, fixed upon the luminous green circle, across which little heaps of louis d'or were being pushed to and fro, and she continued to say nothing. Then at last she exclaimed simply, "Come away!" They turned away and passed into another chamber, in which there was no gambling. It was an immense apartment, apparently a ball-room; but at present it was quite unoccupied. There were green velvet benches all around it, and a great polished floor stretched away, shining in the light of chandeliers adorned with innumerable glass drops. Miss Vivian stood a moment on the threshold; then she passed in, and they stopped in the middle of the place, facing each other, and with their figures reflected as if they had been standing on a sheet of ice. There was no one in the room; they were entirely alone.

"Why don't you recognize me?" Bernard murmured quickly.

"Recognize you?"

"Why do you seem to forget our meeting at Siena?"

She might have answered if she had answered immediately; but she hesitated, and while she did so something happened at the other end of the room which caused her to shift her glance. A green velvet *portière* suspended in one of the doorways—not that through which our friends had passed—was lifted, and Gordon Wright stood there, holding it up, and looking at them. His companions were behind him.

"Ah, here they are!" cried Gordon, in his loud, clear voice.

This appeared to strike Angela Vivian as an interruption, and Bernard saw it very much in the same light.

VIII

H E FORBORE to ask her his question again—she might
tell him at her convenience. But the days passed by,
and she never told him—she had her own reasons. Bernard
talked with her very often; conversation formed indeed the
chief entertainment of the quiet little circle of which he was a
member. They sat on the terrace and talked in the mingled
starlight and lamplight, and they strolled in the deep green
forests and wound along the side of the gentle Baden hills,
under the influence of colloquial tendencies. The Black Forest
is a country of almost unbroken shade, and in the still days of
midsummer the whole place was covered with a motionless
canopy of verdure. Our friends were not extravagant or audacious people, and they looked at Baden life very much from
the outside—they sat aloof from the brightly lighted drama
of professional revelry. Among themselves as well, however,
a little drama went forward in which each member of the
company had a part to play. Bernard Longueville had been
surprised at first at what he would have called Miss Vivian's
approachableness—at the frequency with which he encountered opportunities for sitting near her and entering into conversation. He had expected that Gordon Wright would deem
himself to have established an anticipatory claim upon the
young lady's attention, and that, in pursuance of this claim,
he would occupy a recognized place at her side. Gordon was,
after all, wooing her; it was very natural he should seek her
society. In fact, he was never very far off; but Bernard, for
three or four days, had the anomalous consciousness of being
still nearer. Presently, however, he perceived that he owed
this privilege simply to his friend's desire that he should become acquainted with Miss Vivian—should receive a vivid
impression of a person in whom Gordon was so deeply interested. After this result might have been supposed to be at-
tained, Gordon Wright stepped back into his usual place and
showed her those small civilities which were the only homage
that the quiet conditions of their life rendered possible—
walked with her, talked with her, brought her a book to read,
a chair to sit upon, a couple of flowers to place in the bosom

of her gown, treated her, in a word, with a sober but by no means inexpressive gallantry. He had not been making violent love, as he told Longueville, and these demonstrations were certainly not violent. Bernard said to himself that if he were not in the secret, a spectator would scarcely make the discovery that Gordon cherished an even very safely tended flame. Angela Vivian, on her side, was not strikingly responsive. There was nothing in her deportment to indicate that she was in love with her systematic suitor. She was perfectly gracious and civil. She smiled in his face when he shook hands with her; she looked at him and listened when he talked; she let him stroll beside her in the Lichtenthal Alley; she read, or appeared to read, the books he lent her, and she decorated herself with the flowers he offered. She seemed neither bored nor embarrassed, neither irritated nor oppressed. But it was Bernard's belief that she took no more pleasure in his attentions than a pretty girl must always take in any recognition of her charms. "If she 's not indifferent," he said to himself, "she is, at any rate, impartial—profoundly impartial."

It was not till the end of a week that Gordon Wright told him exactly how his business stood with Miss Vivian and what he had reason to expect and hope—a week during which their relations had been of the happiest and most comfortable cast, and during which Bernard, rejoicing in their long walks and talks, in the charming weather, in the beauty and entertainment of the place, and in other things besides, had not ceased to congratulate himself on coming to Baden. Bernard, after the first day, had asked his friend no questions. He had a great respect for opportunity, coming either to others or to himself, and he left Gordon to turn his lantern as fitfully as might be upon the subject which was tacitly open between them, but of which as yet only the mere edges had emerged into light. Gordon, on his side, seemed content for the moment with having his clever friend under his hand; he reserved him for final appeal or for some other mysterious use.

"You can't tell me you don't know her now," he said, one evening as the two young men strolled along the Lichtenthal Alley—"now that you have had a whole week's observation of her."

"What is a week's observation of a singularly clever and complicated woman?" Bernard asked.

"Ah, your week has been of some use. You have found out she is complicated!" Gordon rejoined.

"My dear Gordon," Longueville exclaimed, "I don't see what it signifies to you that I should find Miss Vivian out! When a man 's in love, what need he care what other people think of the loved object?"

"It would certainly be a pity to care too much. But there is some excuse for him in the loved object being, as you say, complicated."

"Nonsense! That 's no excuse. The loved object is always complicated."

Gordon walked on in silence a moment.

"Well, then, I don't care a button what you think!"

"Bravo! That 's the way a man should talk," cried Longueville.

Gordon indulged in another fit of meditation, and then he said—

"Now that leaves you at liberty to say what you please."

"Ah, my dear fellow, you are ridiculous!" said Bernard.

"That 's precisely what I want you to say. You always think me too reasonable."

"Well, I go back to my first assertion. I don't know Miss Vivian—I mean I don't know her to have opinions about her. I don't suppose you wish me to string you off a dozen mere *banalités*—'She 's a charming girl—evidently a superior person—has a great deal of style.'"

"Oh no," said Gordon; "I know all that. But, at any rate," he added, "you like her, eh?"

"I do more," said Longueville. "I admire her."

"Is that doing more?" asked Gordon, reflectively.

"Well, the greater, whichever it is, includes the less."

"You won't commit yourself," said Gordon. "My dear Bernard," he added, "I thought you knew such an immense deal about women!"

Gordon Wright was of so kindly and candid a nature that it is hardly conceivable that this remark should have been framed to make Bernard commit himself by putting him on his mettle. Such a view would imply indeed on Gordon's part a greater familiarity with the uses of irony than he had ever possessed, as well as a livelier conviction of the irritable nature of his friend's vanity. In fact, however, it may be confided to the reader that Bernard was pricked in a tender place, though the resentment of vanity was not visible in his answer.

"You were quite wrong," he simply said. "I am as ignorant of women as a monk in his cloister."

"You try to prove too much. You don't think her sympathetic!" And as regards this last remark, Gordon Wright must be credited with a certain ironical impulse.

Bernard stopped impatiently.

"I ask you again, what does it matter to you what I think of her?"

"It matters in this sense—that she has refused me."

"Refused you? Then it is all over, and nothing matters."

"No, it is n't over," said Gordon, with a positive head-shake. "Don't you see it is n't over?"

Bernard smiled, laid his hand on his friend's shoulder and patted it a little.

"Your attitude might almost pass for that of resignation."

"I 'm not resigned!" said Gordon Wright.

"Of course not. But when were you refused?"

Gordon stood a minute with his eyes fixed on the ground. Then, at last looking up,

"Three weeks ago—a fortnight before you came. But let us walk along," he said, "and I will tell you all about it."

"I proposed to her three weeks ago," said Gordon, as they walked along. "My heart was very much set upon it. I was very hard hit—I was deeply smitten. She had been very kind to me—she had been charming—I thought she liked me. Then I thought her mother was pleased, and would have liked it. Mrs. Vivian, in fact, told me as much; for of course I spoke to her first. Well, Angela does like me—or at least she did—and I see no reason to suppose she has changed. Only she did n't like me enough. She said the friendliest and pleasantest things to me, but she thought that she knew me too little, and that I knew her even less. She made a great point of that—that I had no right, as yet, to trust her. I told her that if she would trust me, I was perfectly willing to trust her; but she answered that this was poor reasoning. She said that I was trustworthy and that she was not, and—in short, all sorts of nonsense. She abused herself roundly—accused herself of no end of defects."

"What defects, for instance?"

"Oh, I have n't remembered them. She said she had a bad temper—that she led her mother a dreadful life. Now, poor Mrs. Vivian says she is an angel."

"Ah yes," Bernard observed; "Mrs. Vivian says that, very freely."

"Angela declared that she was jealous, ungenerous, unforgiving—all sorts of things. I remember she said 'I am very false,' and I think she remarked that she was cruel."

"But this did n't put you off," said Bernard.

"Not at all. She was making up."

"She makes up very well!" Bernard exclaimed, laughing.

"Do you call that well?"

"I mean it was very clever."

"It was not clever from the point of view of wishing to discourage me."

"Possibly. But I am sure," said Bernard, "that if I had been present at your interview—excuse the impudence of the hypothesis—I should have been struck with the young lady's—" and he paused a moment.

"With her what?"

"With her ability."

"Well, her ability was not sufficient to induce me to give up my idea. She told me that after I had known her six months I should detest her."

"I have no doubt she could make you do it if she should try. That 's what I mean by her ability."

"She calls herself cruel," said Gordon, "but she has not had the cruelty to try. She has been very reasonable—she has been perfect. I agreed with her that I would drop the subject for a while, and that meanwhile we should be good friends. We should take time to know each other better and act in accordance with further knowledge. There was no hurry, since we trusted each other—wrong as my trust might be. She had no wish that I should go away. I was not in the least disagreeable to her; she liked me extremely, and I was perfectly free to try and please her. Only I should drop my proposal, and be free to take it up again or leave it alone, later, as I should choose. If she felt differently then, I should have the benefit of it, and if I myself felt differently, I should also have the benefit of it."

"That 's a very comfortable arrangement. And that 's your present situation?" asked Bernard.

Gordon hesitated a moment.

"More or less, but not exactly."

"Miss Vivian feels differently?" said Bernard.

"Not that I know of."

Gordon's companion, with a laugh, clapped him on the shoulder again.

"Admirable youth, you are a capital match!"

"Are you alluding to my money?"

"To your money and to your modesty. There is as much of one as of the other—which is saying a great deal."

"Well," said Gordon, "in spite of that enviable combination, I am not happy."

"I thought you seemed pensive!" Bernard exclaimed. "It 's you, then, who feel differently."

Gordon gave a sigh.

"To say that is to say too much."

"What shall we say, then?" his companion asked, kindly.

Gordon stopped again; he stood there looking up at a certain particularly lustrous star which twinkled—the night was cloudy—in an open patch of sky, and the vague brightness shone down on his honest and serious visage.

"I don't understand her," he said.

"Oh, I 'll say that with you any day!" cried Bernard. "I can't help you there."

"You *must* help me;" and Gordon Wright deserted his star. "You must keep me in good humor."

"Please to walk on, then. I don't in the least pity you; she is very charming with you."

"True enough; but insisting on that is not the way to keep me in good humor—when I feel as I do."

"How is it you feel?"

"Puzzled to death—bewildered—depressed!"

This was but the beginning of Gordon Wright's list; he went on to say that though he "thought as highly" of Miss

Vivian as he had ever done, he felt less at his ease with her than in the first weeks of their acquaintance, and this condition made him uncomfortable and unhappy.

"I don't know what 's the matter," said poor Gordon. "I don't know what has come between us. It is n't her fault—I don't make her responsible for it. I began to notice it about a fortnight ago—before you came; shortly after that talk I had with her that I have just described to you. Her manner has n't changed and I have no reason to suppose that she likes me any the less; but she makes a strange impression on me—she makes me uneasy. It 's only her nature coming out, I suppose—what you might call her originality. She 's thoroughly original—she 's a kind of mysterious creature. I suppose that what I feel is a sort of fascination; but that is just what I don't like. Hang it, I don't want to be fascinated—I object to being fascinated!"

This little story had taken some time in the telling, so that the two young men had now reached their hotel.

"Ah, my dear Gordon," said Bernard, "we speak a different language. If you don't want to be fascinated, what is one to say to you? 'Object to being fascinated!' There 's a man easy to satisfy! *Raffiné, va!*"

"Well, see here now," said Gordon, stopping in the doorway of the inn; "when it comes to the point, do you like it yourself?"

"When it comes to the point?" Bernard exclaimed. "I assure you I don't wait till then. I like the beginning—I delight in the approach of it—I revel in the prospect."

"That 's just what I did. But now that the thing has come—I don't revel. To be fascinated is to be mystified. Damn it, I like my liberty—I like my judgment!"

"So do I—like yours," said Bernard, laughing, as they took their bedroom candles.

IX

BERNARD talked of this matter rather theoretically, inasmuch as to his own sense, he was in a state neither of incipient nor of absorbed fascination. He got on very easily, however, with Angela Vivian, and felt none of the mysterious discomfort alluded to by his friend. The element of mystery attached itself rather to the young lady's mother, who gave him the impression that for undiscoverable reasons she avoided his society. He regretted her evasive deportment, for he found something agreeable in this shy and scrupulous little woman, who struck him as a curious specimen of a society of which he had once been very fond. He learned that she was of old New England stock, but he had not needed this information to perceive that Mrs. Vivian was animated by the genius of Boston. "She has the Boston temperament," he said, using a phrase with which he had become familiar and which evoked a train of associations. But then he immediately added that if Mrs. Vivian was a daughter of the Puritans, the Puritan strain in her disposition had been mingled with another element. "It is the Boston temperament sophisticated," he said; "perverted a little—perhaps even corrupted. It is the local east-wind with an infusion from climates less tonic." It seemed to him that Mrs. Vivian was a Puritan grown worldly—a Bostonian relaxed; and this impression, oddly enough, contributed to his wish to know more of her. He felt like going up to her very politely and saying, "Dear lady and most honored compatriot, what in the world have I done to displease you? You don't approve of me, and I am dying to know the reason why. I should be so happy to exert myself to be agreeable to you. It's no use; you give me the cold shoulder. When I speak to you, you look the other way; it is only when I speak to your daughter that you look at me. It is true that at those times you look at me very hard, and if I am not greatly mistaken, you are not gratified by what you see. You count the words I address to your beautiful Angela—you time our harmless little interviews. You interrupt them indeed whenever you can; you call her away—you appeal to her; you cut across the conversation. You are always laying plots to keep us apart. Why can't you leave me alone? I assure you I am the most innocent of men. Your beautiful Angela can't possibly be injured by my conversation, and I have no designs whatever upon her peace of mind. What on earth have I done to offend you?"

These observations Bernard Longueville was disposed to make, and one afternoon, the opportunity offering, they rose to his lips and came very near passing them. In fact, however, at the last moment, his eloquence took another turn. It was the custom of the orchestra at the Kursaal to play in the afternoon, and as the music was often good, a great many people assembled under the trees, at three o'clock, to listen to it. This was not, as a regular thing, an hour of re-union for the little group in which we are especially interested; Miss Vivian, in particular, unless an excursion of some sort had been agreed upon the day before, was usually not to be seen in the precincts of the Conversation-house until the evening. Bernard, one afternoon, at three o'clock, directed his steps to this small world-centre of Baden, and, passing along the terrace, soon encountered little Blanche Evers strolling there under a pink parasol and accompanied by Captain Lovelock. This young lady was always extremely sociable; it was quite in accordance with her habitual geniality that she should stop and say how d' ye do to our hero.

"Mr. Longueville is growing very frivolous," she said, "coming to the Kursaal at all sorts of hours."

"There is nothing frivolous in coming here with the hope of finding you," the young man answered. "That is very serious."

"It would be more serious to lose Miss Evers than to find her," remarked Captain Lovelock, with gallant jocosity.

"I wish you would lose me!" cried the young girl. "I think I should like to be lost. I might have all kinds of adventures."

"I 'guess' so!" said Captain Lovelock, hilariously.

"Oh, I should find my way. I can take care of myself!" Blanche went on.

"Mrs. Vivian does n't think so," said Bernard, who had just perceived this lady, seated under a tree with a book, over the top of which she was observing her pretty *protégée*. Blanche looked toward her and gave her a little nod and a smile. Then chattering on to the young men—

"She 's awfully careful. I never saw any one so careful. But I suppose she is right. She promised my mother she would be tremendously particular; but I don't know what she thinks I would do."

"That is n't flattering to me," said Captain Lovelock. "Mrs. Vivian does n't approve of me—she wishes me in Jamaica. What does she think me capable of?"

"And me, now?" Bernard asked. "She likes me least of all, and I, on my side, think she 's so nice."

"Can't say I 'm very sweet on her," said the Captain. "She strikes me as feline."

Blanche Evers gave a little cry of horror.

"Stop, sir, this instant! I won't have you talk that way about a lady who has been so kind to me."

"She is n't so kind to you. She would like to lock you up where I can never see you."

"I 'm sure I should n't mind that!" cried the young girl, with a little laugh and a toss of her head. "Mrs. Vivian has the most perfect character—that 's why my mother wanted me to come with her. And if she promised my mother she would be careful, is n't she right to keep her promise? She 's a great deal more careful than mamma ever was, and that 's just what mamma wanted. She would never take the trouble herself. And then she was always scolding me. Mrs. Vivian never scolds me. She only watches me, but I don't mind that."

"I wish she would watch you a little less and scold you a little more," said Captain Lovelock.

"I have no doubt you wish a great many horrid things," his companion rejoined, with delightful asperity.

"Ah, unfortunately I never have anything I wish!" sighed Lovelock.

"Your wishes must be comprehensive," said Bernard. "It seems to me you have a good deal."

The Englishman gave a shrug.

"It 's less than you might think. She is watching us more furiously than ever," he added, in a moment, looking at Mrs. Vivian. "Mr. Gordon Wright is the only man she likes. She is awfully fond of Mr. Gordon Wright."

"Ah, Mrs. Vivian shows her wisdom!" said Bernard.

"He is certainly very handsome," murmured Blanche Evers, glancing several times, with a very pretty aggressiveness, at Captain Lovelock. "I must say I like Mr. Gordon Wright. Why in the world did you come here without him?" she went on, addressing herself to Bernard. "You two are so awfully inseparable. I don't think I ever saw you alone before."

"Oh, I have often seen Mr. Gordon Wright alone," said Captain Lovelock—"that is, alone with Miss Vivian. That 's what the old lady likes; she can't have too much of that."

The young girl, poised for an instant in one of her pretty attitudes, looked at him from head to foot.

"Well, I call that scandalous! Do you mean that she wants to make a match?"

"I mean that the young man has six thousand a year."

"It 's no matter what he has—six thousand a year is n't much! And we don't do things in that way in our country. We have n't those horrid match-making arrangements that you have in your dreadful country. American mothers are not like English mothers."

"Oh, any one can see, of course," said Captain Lovelock, "that Mr. Gordon Wright is dying of love for Miss Vivian."

"I can't see it!" cried Blanche.

"He dies easier than I, eh?"

"I wish you would die!" said Blanche. "At any rate, Angela is not dying of love for Mr. Wright."

"Well, she will marry him all the same," Lovelock declared.

Blanche Evers glanced at Bernard.

"Why don't you contradict that?" she asked. "Why don't you speak up for your friend?"

"I am quite ready to speak for my friend," said Bernard, "but I am not ready to speak for Miss Vivian."

"Well, I am," Blanche declared. "She won't marry him."

"If she does n't, I 'll eat my hat!" said Captain Lovelock. "What do you mean," he went on, "by saying that in America a pretty girl's mother does n't care for a young fellow's property?"

"Well, they don't—we consider that dreadful. Why don't you say so, Mr. Longueville?" Blanche demanded. "I never saw any one take things so quietly. Have n't you got any patriotism?"

"My patriotism is modified by an indisposition to generalize," said Bernard, laughing. "On this point permit me not to generalize. I am interested in the particular case—in ascertaining whether Mrs. Vivian thinks very often of Gordon Wright's income."

Miss Evers gave a little toss of disgust.

"If you are so awfully impartial, you had better go and ask her."

"That 's a good idea—I think I will go and ask her," said Bernard.

Captain Lovelock returned to his argument.

"Do you mean to say that your mother would be indifferent to the fact that I have n't a shilling in the world?"

"Indifferent?" Blanche demanded. "Oh no, she would be sorry for you. She is very charitable—she would give you a shilling!"

"She would n't let you marry me," said Lovelock.

"She would n't have much trouble to prevent it!" cried the young girl.

Bernard had had enough of this intellectual fencing.

"Yes, I will go and ask Mrs. Vivian," he repeated. And he left his companions to resume their walk.

X

IT HAD SEEMED to him a good idea to interrogate Mrs. Vivian; but there are a great many good ideas that are never put into execution. As he approached her with a smile and a salutation, and, with the air of asking leave to take a liberty, seated himself in the empty chair beside her, he felt a humorous relish of her own probable dismay which relaxed the investigating impulse. His impulse was now simply to prove to her that he was the most unobjectionable fellow in the world—a proposition which resolved itself into several ingenious observations upon the weather, the music, the charms and the drawbacks of Baden, the merits of the volume that she held in her lap. If Mrs. Vivian should be annoyed, should be fluttered, Bernard would feel very sorry for her; there was nothing in the world that he respected more than the moral consciousness of a little Boston woman whose view of life was serious and whose imagination was subject to alarms. He held it to be a temple of delicacy, where one should walk on tiptoe, and he wished to exhibit to Mrs. Vivian the possible lightness of his own step. She herself was incapable of being rude or ungracious, and now that she was fairly confronted with the plausible object of her mistrust, she composed herself to her usual attitude of refined liberality. Her book was a volume of Victor Cousin.

"You must have an extraordinary power of abstracting your mind," Bernard said to her, observing it. "Studying philosophy at the Baden Kursaal strikes me as a real intellectual feat."

"Don't you think we need a little philosophy here?"

"By all means—what we bring with us. But I should n't attempt the use of the text-book on the spot."

"You should n't speak of yourself as if you were not clever," said Mrs. Vivian. "Every one says you are so very clever."

Longueville stared; there was an unexpectedness in the speech and an incongruity in Mrs. Vivian's beginning to flatter him. He needed to remind himself that if she was a Bostonian, she was a Bostonian perverted.

"Ah, my dear madam, every one is no one," he said, laughing.

1094

"It was Mr. Wright, in particular," she rejoined. "He has always told us that."

"He is blinded by friendship."

"Ah yes, we know about your friendship," said Mrs. Vivian. "He has told us about that."

"You are making him out a terrible talker!"

"We think he talks so well—we are so very fond of his conversation."

"It 's usually excellent," said Bernard. "But it depends a good deal on the subject."

"Oh," rejoined Mrs. Vivian, "we always let him choose his subjects." And dropping her eyes as if in sudden reflection, she began to smooth down the crumpled corner of her volume.

It occurred to Bernard that—by some mysterious impulse—she was suddenly presenting him with a chance to ask her the question that Blanche Evers had just suggested. Two or three other things as well occurred to him. Captain Lovelock had been struck with the fact that she favored Gordon Wright's addresses to her daughter, and Captain Lovelock had a grotesque theory that she had set her heart upon seeing this young lady come into six thousand a year. Miss Evers's devoted swain had never struck Bernard as a brilliant reasoner, but our friend suddenly found himself regarding him as one of the inspired. The form of depravity into which the New England conscience had lapsed on Mrs. Vivian's part was an undue appreciation of a possible son-in-law's income! In this illuminating discovery everything else became clear. Mrs. Vivian disliked her humble servant because he had not thirty thousand dollars a year, and because at a moment when it was Angela's prime duty to concentrate her thoughts upon Gordon Wright's great advantages, a clever young man of paltry fortune was a superfluous diversion.

"When you say clever, everything is relative," he presently observed. "Now, there is Captain Lovelock; he has a certain kind of cleverness; he is very observant."

Mrs. Vivian glanced up with a preoccupied air.

"We don't like Captain Lovelock," she said.

"I have heard him say capital things," Bernard answered.

"We think him brutal," said Mrs. Vivian. "Please don't praise Captain Lovelock."

"Oh, I only want to be just."

Mrs. Vivian for a moment said nothing.

"Do you want very much to be just?" she presently asked.

"It 's my most ardent desire."

"I 'm glad to hear that—and I can easily believe it," said Mrs. Vivian.

Bernard gave her a grateful smile, but while he smiled, he asked himself a serious question. "Why the deuce does she go on flattering me?—You have always been very kind to me," he said aloud.

"It 's on Mr. Wright's account," she answered demurely.

In speaking the words I have just quoted, Bernard Longueville had felt himself, with a certain compunction, to be skirting the edge of clever impudence; but Mrs. Vivian's quiet little reply suggested to him that her cleverness, if not her impudence, was almost equal to his own. He remarked to himself that he had not yet done her justice.

"You bring everything back to Gordon Wright," he said, continuing to smile.

Mrs. Vivian blushed a little.

"It is because he is really at the foundation of everything that is pleasant for us here. When we first came we had some very disagreeable rooms, and as soon as he arrived he found us some excellent ones—that were less expensive. And then, Mr. Longueville," she added, with a soft, sweet emphasis which should properly have contradicted the idea of audacity, but which, to Bernard's awakened sense, seemed really to impart a vivid color to it, "he was also the cause of your joining our little party."

"Oh, among his services that should never be forgotten. You should set up a tablet to commemorate it, in the wall of the Kursaal!—The wicked little woman!" Bernard mentally subjoined.

Mrs. Vivian appeared quite unruffled by his sportive sarcasm, and she continued to enumerate her obligations to Gordon Wright.

"There are so many ways in which a gentleman can be of assistance to three poor lonely women, especially when he is at the same time so friendly and so delicate as Mr. Wright. I don't know what we should have done without him, and I feel as if every one ought to know it. He seems like a very old friend. My daughter and I quite worship him. I will not conceal from you that when I saw you coming through the grounds a short time ago without him I was very much disappointed. I hope he is not ill."

Bernard sat listening, with his eyes on the ground.

"Oh no, he is simply at home writing letters."

Mrs. Vivian was silent a moment.

"I suppose he has a very large correspondence."

"I really don't know. Just now that I am with him he has a smaller one than usual."

"Ah yes. When you are separated I suppose you write volumes to each other. But he must have a great many business letters."

"It is very likely," said Bernard. "And if he has, you may be sure he writes them."

"Order and method!" Mrs. Vivian exclaimed. "With his immense property those virtues are necessary."

Bernard glanced at her a moment.

"My dear Lovelock," he said to himself, "you are not such a fool as you seem. — Gordon's virtues are always necessary, doubtless," he went on. "But should you say his property was immense?"

Mrs. Vivian made a delicate little movement of deprecation. "Oh, don't ask me to say! I know nothing about it; I only supposed he was rich."

"He is rich; but he is not a Crœsus."

"Oh, you fashionable young men have a standard of luxury!" said Mrs. Vivian, with a little laugh. "To a poverty-stricken widow such a fortune as Mr. Wright's seems magnificent."

"Don't call me such horrible names!" exclaimed Bernard. "Our friend has certainly money enough and to spare."

"That was all I meant. He once had occasion to allude to his property, but he was so modest, so reserved in the tone he took about it, that one hardly knew what to think."

"He is ashamed of being rich," said Bernard. "He would be sure to represent everything unfavorably."

"That 's just what I thought!" This ejaculation was more eager than Mrs. Vivian might have intended, but even had it been less so, Bernard was in a mood to appreciate it. "I felt that we should make allowances for his modesty. But it was in very good taste," Mrs. Vivian added.

"He 's a fortunate man," said Bernard. "He gets credit for his good taste—and he gets credit for the full figure of his income as well!"

"Ah," murmured Mrs. Vivian, rising lightly, as if to make her words appear more casual, "I don't know the full figure of his income."

She was turning away, and Bernard, as he raised his hat and separated from her, felt that it was rather cruel that he should let her go without enlightening her ignorance. But he said to himself that she knew quite enough. Indeed, he took a walk along the Lichtenthal Alley and carried out this line of reflection. Whether or no Miss Vivian were in love with Gordon Wright, her mother was enamored of Gordon's fortune, and it had suddenly occurred to her that instead of treating the friend of her daughter's suitor with civil mistrust, she would help her case better by giving him a hint of her state of mind and appealing to his sense of propriety. Nothing could be more natural than that Mrs. Vivian should suppose that Bernard desired his friend's success; for, as our thoughtful hero said to himself, what she had hitherto taken it into her head to fear was not that Bernard should fall in love with her daughter, but that her daughter should fall in love with him. Watering-place life is notoriously conducive to idleness of mind, and Bernard strolled for half an hour along the overarched avenue, glancing alternately at these two insupposable cases.

A few days afterward, late in the evening, Gordon Wright came to his room at the hotel.

"I have just received a letter from my sister," he said. "I am afraid I shall have to go away."

"Ah, I 'm sorry for that," said Bernard, who was so well pleased with the actual that he desired no mutation.

"I mean only for a short time," Gordon explained. "My poor sister writes from England, telling me that my brother-in-law is suddenly obliged to go home. She has decided not to remain behind, and they are to sail a fortnight hence. She wants very much to see me before she goes, and as I don't know when I shall see her again, I feel as if I ought to join her immediately and spend the interval with her. That will take about a fortnight."

"I appreciate the sanctity of family ties and I project myself into your situation," said Bernard. "On the other hand, I don't envy you a breathless journey from Baden to Folkestone."

"It 's the coming back that will be breathless," exclaimed Gordon, smiling.

"You will certainly come back, then?"

"Most certainly. Mrs. Vivian is to be here another month."

"I understand. Well, we shall miss you very much."

Gordon Wright looked for a moment at his companion.

"You will stay here, then? I am so glad of that."

"I was taking it for granted; but on reflection—what do you recommend?"

"I recommend you to stay."

"My dear fellow, your word is law," said Bernard.

"I want you to take care of those ladies," his friend went on. "I don't like to leave them alone."

"You are joking!" cried Bernard. "When did you ever hear of my 'taking care' of any one? It 's as much as I can do to take care of myself."

"This is very easy," said Gordon. "I simply want to feel that they have a man about them."

"They will have a man at any rate—they have the devoted Lovelock."

"That 's just why I want them to have another. He has only an eye to Miss Evers, who, by the way, is extremely bored with him. You look after the others. You have made yourself very agreeable to them, and they like you extremely."

"Ah," said Bernard, laughing, "if you are going to be coarse and flattering, I collapse. If you are going to titillate my vanity, I succumb."

"It won't be so disagreeable," Gordon observed, with an intention vaguely humorous.

"Oh no, it won't be disagreeable. I will go to Mrs. Vivian every morning, hat in hand, for my orders."

Gordon Wright, with his hands in his pockets and a meditative expression, took several turns about the room.

"It will be a capital chance," he said, at last, stopping in front of his companion.

"A chance for what?"

"A chance to arrive at a conclusion about my young friend."

Bernard gave a gentle groan.

"Are you coming back to that? Did n't I arrive at a conclusion long ago? Did n't I tell you she was a delightful girl?"

"Do you call that a conclusion? The first comer could tell me that at the end of an hour."

"Do you want me to invent something different?" Bernard asked. "I can't invent anything better."

"I don't want you to invent anything. I only want you to observe her—to study her in complete independence. You will have her to yourself—my absence will leave you at liberty. Hang it, sir," Gordon declared, "I should think you would like it!"

"Damn it, sir, you 're delicious!" Bernard answered; and he broke into an irrepressible laugh. "I don't suppose it 's for my pleasure that you suggest the arrangement."

Gordon took a turn about the room again.

"No, it 's for mine. At least, it 's for my benefit."

"For your benefit?"

"I have got all sorts of ideas—I told you the other day. They are all mixed up together and I want a fresh impression."

"My impressions are never fresh," Bernard replied.

"They would be if you had a little good-will—if you entered a little into my dilemma." The note of reproach was so distinct in these words that Bernard stood staring. "You never take anything seriously," his companion went on.

Bernard tried to answer as seriously as possible.

"Your dilemma seems to me of all dilemmas the strangest."

"That may be; but different people take things differently. Don't you see," Gordon went on with a sudden outbreak of passion—"don't you see that I am horribly divided in mind? I care immensely for Angela Vivian—and yet—and yet—I am afraid of her."

"Afraid of her?"

"I am afraid she 's cleverer than I—that she would be a difficult wife; that she might do strange things."

"What sort of things?"

"Well, that she might flirt, for instance."

"That 's not a thing for a man to fear."

"Not when he supposes his wife to be fond of him—no. But I don't suppose that—I have given that up. If I should induce Angela Vivian to accept me she would do it on grounds purely reasonable. She would think it best, simply. That would give her a chance to repent."

Bernard sat for some time looking at his friend.

"You say she is cleverer than you. It 's impossible to be cleverer than you."

"Oh, come, Longueville!" said Gordon, angrily.

"I am speaking very seriously. You have done a remarkably clever thing. You have impressed me with the reality, and with—what shall I term it?—the estimable character of what you call your dilemma. Now this fresh impression of mine— what do you propose to do with it when you get it?"

"Such things are always useful. It will be a good thing to have."

"I am much obliged to you; but do you propose to let anything depend upon it? Do you propose to take or to leave Miss Vivian—that is, to return to the charge or to give up trying—in consequence of my fresh impression?"

Gordon seemed perfectly unembarrassed by this question, in spite of the ironical light which it projected upon his sentimental perplexity.

"I propose to do what I choose!" he said.

"That 's a relief to me," Bernard rejoined. "This idea of yours is, after all, only the play of the scientific mind."

"I shall contradict you flat if I choose," Gordon went on.

"Ah, it 's well to warn me of that," said Bernard, laughing. "Even the most sincere judgment in the world likes to be notified a little of the danger of being contradicted."

"Is yours the most sincere judgment in the world?" Gordon demanded.

"That 's a very pertinent question. Does n't it occur to you that you may have reason to be jealous—leaving me alone, with an open field, with the woman of your choice?"

"I wish to heaven I could be jealous!" Gordon exclaimed. "That would simplify the thing—that would give me a lift."

And the next day, after some more talk, it seemed really with a hope of this contingency—though, indeed, he laughed about it—that he started for England.

XI

FOR THE THREE OR FOUR DAYS that followed Gordon Wright's departure, Bernard saw nothing of the ladies who had been committed to his charge. They chose to remain in seclusion, and he was at liberty to interpret this fact as an expression of regret at the loss of Gordon's good offices. He knew other people at Baden, and he went to see them and endeavored, by cultivating their society, to await in patience the re-appearance of Mrs. Vivian and her companions. But on the fourth day he became conscious that other people were much less interesting than the trio of American ladies who had lodgings above the confectioner's, and he made bold to go and knock at their door. He had been asked to take care of them, and this function presupposed contact. He had met Captain Lovelock the day before, wandering about with a rather crest-fallen aspect, and the young Englishman had questioned him eagerly as to the whereabouts of Mrs. Vivian.

"Gad, I believe they 've left the place—left the place without giving a fellow warning!" cried Lovelock.

"Oh no, I think they are here still," said Bernard. "My friend Wright has gone away for a week or two, but I suspect the ladies are simply staying at home."

"Gad, I was afraid your friend Wright had taken them away with him; he seems to keep them all in his pocket. I was afraid he had given them marching orders; they 'd have been sure to go—they 're so awfully fond of his pocket! I went to look them up yesterday—upon my word I did. They live at a baker's in a little back-street; people do live in rum places when they come abroad! But I assure you, when I got there, I 'm damned if I could make out whether they were there or not. I don't speak a word of German, and there was no one there but the baker's wife. She was a low brute of a woman— she could n't understand a word I said, though she gave me plenty of her own tongue. I had to give it up. They were not at home, but whether they had left Baden or not—that was beyond my finding out. If they are here, why the deuce don't they show? Fancy coming to Baden-Baden to sit moping at a pastry-cook's!"

Captain Lovelock was evidently irritated, and it was Bernard's impression that the turn of luck over yonder where the gold-pieces were chinking had something to do with the state of his temper. But more fortunate himself, he ascertained from the baker's wife that though Mrs. Vivian and her daughter had gone out, their companion, "the youngest lady—the little young lady"—was above in the sitting-room.

Blanche Evers was sitting at the window with a book, but she relinquished the volume with an alacrity that showed it had not been absorbing, and began to chatter with her customary frankness.

"Well, I must say I am glad to see *some one*!" cried the young girl, passing before the mirror and giving a touch to her charming tresses.

"Even if it's only me," Bernard exclaimed, laughing.

"I did n't mean that. I am sure I am very glad to see you—I should think you would have found out that by this time. I mean I'm glad to see any one—especially a man. I suppose it's improper for me to say that—especially to you! There—you see I do think more of you than of some gentlemen. Why especially to you? Well, because you always seem to me to want to take advantage. I did n't say a base advantage; I did n't accuse you of anything dreadful. I'm sure I want to take advantage, too—I take it whenever I can. You see I take advantage of your being here—I've got so many things to say. I have n't spoken a word in three days, and I'm sure it is a pleasant change—a gentleman's visit. All of a sudden we have gone into mourning; I'm sure I don't know who's dead. Is it Mr. Gordon Wright? It's some idea of Mrs. Vivian's—I'm sure it is n't mine. She thinks we have been often enough to the Kursaal. I don't know whether she thinks it's wicked, or what. If it's wicked the harm's already done; I can't be any worse than I am now. I have seen all the improper people and I have learnt all their names; Captain Lovelock has told me their names, plenty of times. I don't see what good it does me to be shut up here with all those names running in my ears. I must say I do prefer society. We have n't been to the Kursaal for four days—we have only gone out for a drive. We have taken the most interminable drives. I do believe we have seen every old ruin in the whole country. Mrs. Vivian and Angela are so awfully fond of scenery—they talk about it by the half-hour. They talk about the mountains and trees as if they were people they knew—as if they were gentlemen! I mean as if the mountains and trees were gentlemen. Of course scenery 's lovely, but you can't walk about with a tree. At any rate, that has been all our society—foliage! Foliage and women; but I suppose women are a sort of foliage. They are always rustling about and dropping off. That 's why I could n't make up my mind to go out with them this afternoon. They 've gone to see the Waterworths—the Waterworths arrived yesterday and are staying at some hotel. Five daughters—all unmarried! I don't know what kind of foliage they are; some peculiar kind—they don't drop off. I thought I had had about enough ladies' society—three women all sticking together! I don't think it 's good for a young girl to have nothing but ladies' society—it 's so awfully limited. I suppose I ought to stand up for my own sex and tell you that when we are alone together we want for nothing. But we want for everything, as it happens! Women's talk *is* limited— every one knows that. That 's just what mamma did n't want when she asked Mrs. Vivian to take charge of me. Now, Mr. Longueville, what are you laughing at?—you are always laughing at me. She wanted me to be unlimited—is that what you say? Well, she did n't want me to be narrowed down; she wanted me to have plenty of conversation. She wanted me to be fitted for society—that 's what mamma wanted. She wanted me to have ease of manner; she thinks that if you don't acquire it when you are young you never have it at all. She was so happy to think I should come to Baden; but she would n't approve of the life I 've been leading the last four days. That 's no way to acquire ease of manner—sitting all day in a small parlor with two persons of one's own sex! Of course Mrs. Vivian's influence—that 's the great thing. Mamma said it was like the odor of a flower. But you don't want to keep smelling a flower all day, even the sweetest; that 's the shortest way to get a headache. Apropos of flowers, do you happen to have heard whether Captain Lovelock is alive or dead? Do I call him a flower? No; I call him a flower-pot.

He always has some fine young plant in his button-hole. He has n't been near me these ten years—I never heard of anything so rude!"

Captain Lovelock came on the morrow, Bernard finding him in Mrs. Vivian's little sitting-room on paying a second visit. On this occasion the two other ladies were at home and Bernard was not exclusively indebted to Miss Evers for entertainment. It was to this source of hospitality, however, that Lovelock mainly appealed, following the young girl out upon the little balcony that was suspended above the confectioner's window. Mrs. Vivian sat writing at one of the windows of the sitting-room, and Bernard addressed his conversation to Angela.

"Wright requested me to keep an eye on you," he said; "but you seem very much inclined to keep out of my jurisdiction."

"I supposed you had gone away," she answered—"now that your friend is gone."

"By no means. Gordon is a charming fellow, but he is by no means the only attraction of Baden. Besides, I have promised him to look after you—to take care of you."

The girl looked at him a moment in silence—a little askance.

"I thought you had probably undertaken something of that sort," she presently said.

"It was of course a very natural request for Gordon to make."

Angela got up and turned away; she wandered about the room and went and stood at one of the windows. Bernard found the movement abrupt and not particularly gracious; but the young man was not easy to snub. He followed her, and they stood at the second window—the long window that opened upon the balcony. Miss Evers and Captain Lovelock were leaning on the railing, looking into the street and apparently amusing themselves highly with what they saw.

"I am not sure it was a natural request for him to make," said Angela.

"What could have been more so—devoted as he is to you?"

She hesitated a moment; then with a little laugh—

"He ought to have locked us up and said nothing about it."

"It 's not so easy to lock you up," said Bernard. "I know Wright has great influence with you, but you are after all independent beings."

"I am not an independent being. If my mother and Mr. Wright were to agree together to put me out of harm's way they could easily manage it."

"You seem to have been trying something of that sort," said Bernard. "You have been so terribly invisible."

"It was because I thought you had designs upon us; that you were watching for us—to take care of us."

"You contradict yourself! You said just now that you believed I had left Baden."

"That was an artificial—a conventional speech. Is n't a lady always supposed to say something of that sort to a visitor by way of pretending to have noticed that she has not seen him?"

"You know I would never have left Baden without coming to bid you good-bye," said Bernard.

The girl made no rejoinder; she stood looking out at the little sunny, slanting, rough-paved German street.

"Are you taking care of us now?" she asked in a moment. "Has the operation begun? Have you heard the news, mamma?" she went on. "Do you know that Mr. Wright has made us over to Mr. Longueville, to be kept till called for? Suppose Mr. Wright should never call for us!"

Mrs. Vivian left her writing-table and came toward Bernard, smiling at him and pressing her hands together.

"There is no fear of that, I think," she said. "I am sure I am very glad we have a gentleman near us. I think you will be a very good care-taker, Mr. Longueville, and I recommend my daughter to put great faith in your judgment." And Mrs. Vivian gave him an intense—a pleading, almost affecting—little smile.

"I am greatly touched by your confidence and I shall do everything I can think of to merit it," said the young man.

"Ah, mamma's confidence is wonderful!" Angela exclaimed. "There was never anything like mamma's confidence. I am very different; I have no confidence. And then I don't like being deposited, like a parcel, or being watched, like a curious animal. I am too fond of my liberty."

"That is the second time you have contradicted yourself,"

said Bernard. "You said just now that you were not an independent being."

Angela turned toward him quickly, smiling and frowning at once.

"You *do* watch one, certainly! I see it has already begun." Mrs. Vivian laid her hand upon her daughter's with a little murmur of tender deprecation, and the girl bent over and kissed her. "Mamma will tell you it 's the effect of agitation," she said—"that I am nervous, and don't know what I say. I am supposed to be agitated by Mr. Wright's departure; is n't that it, mamma?"

Mrs. Vivian turned away, with a certain soft severity.

"I don't know, my daughter. I don't understand you."

A charming pink flush had come into Angela's cheek and a noticeable light into her eye. She looked admirably handsome, and Bernard frankly gazed at her. She met his gaze an instant, and then she went on.

"Mr. Longueville does n't understand me either. You must know that I *am* agitated," she continued. "Every now and then I have moments of talking nonsense. It 's the air of Baden, I think; it 's too exciting. It 's only lately I have been so. When you go away I shall be horribly ashamed."

"If the air of Baden has such an effect upon you," said Bernard, "it is only a proof the more that you need the solicitous attention of your friends."

"That may be; but, as I told you just now, I have no confidence—none whatever, in any one or anything. Therefore, for the present, I shall withdraw from the world—I shall seclude myself. Let us go on being quiet, mamma. Three or four days of it have been so charming. Let the parcel lie till it 's called for. It is much safer it should n't be touched at all. I shall assume that, metaphorically speaking, Mr. Wright, who, as you have intimated, is our earthly providence, has turned the key upon us. I am locked up. I shall not go out, except upon the balcony!" And with this, Angela stepped out of the long window and went and stood beside Miss Evers.

Bernard was extremely amused, but he was also a good deal puzzled, and it came over him that it was not a wonder that poor Wright should not have found this young lady's disposition a perfectly decipherable page. He remained in the room with Mrs. Vivian—he stood there looking at her with his agreeably mystified smile. She had turned away, but on perceiving that her daughter had gone outside she came toward Bernard again, with her habitual little air of eagerness mitigated by discretion. There instantly rose before his mind the vision of that moment when he had stood face to face with this same apologetic mamma, after Angela had turned her back, on the grass-grown terrace at Siena. To make the vision complete, Mrs. Vivian took it into her head to utter the same words.

"I am sure you think she is a strange girl."

Bernard recognized them, and he gave a light laugh.

"You told me that the first time you ever saw me—in that quiet little corner of an Italian town."

Mrs. Vivian gave a little faded, elderly blush.

"Don't speak of that," she murmured, glancing at the open window. "It was a little accident of travel."

"I am dying to speak of it," said Bernard. "It was such a charming accident for me! Tell me this, at least—have you kept my sketch?"

Mrs. Vivian colored more deeply and glanced at the window again.

"No," she just whispered.

Bernard looked out of the window too. Angela was leaning against the railing of the balcony, in profile, just as she had stood while he painted her, against the polished parapet at Siena. The young man's eyes rested on her a moment, then, as he glanced back at her mother:

"Has *she* kept it?" he asked.

"I don't know," said Mrs. Vivian, with decision.

The decision was excessive—it expressed the poor lady's distress at having her veracity tested. "Dear little daughter of the Puritans—she can't tell a fib!" Bernard exclaimed to himself. And with this flattering conclusion he took leave of her.

XII

IT WAS AFFIRMED at an early stage of this narrative that he was a young man of a contemplative and speculative turn, and he had perhaps never been more true to his character than during an hour or two that evening as he sat by himself on the terrace of the Conversation-house, surrounded by the crowd of its frequenters, but lost in his meditations. The place was full of movement and sound, but he had tilted back his chair against the great green box of an orange-tree, and in this easy attitude, vaguely and agreeably conscious of the music, he directed his gaze to the star-sprinkled vault of the night. There were people coming and going whom he knew, but he said nothing to any one—he preferred to be alone; he found his own company quite absorbing. He felt very happy, very much amused, very curiously preoccupied. The feeling was a singular one. It partook of the nature of intellectual excitement. He had a sense of having received *carte blanche* for the expenditure of his wits. Bernard liked to feel his intelligence at play; this is, perhaps, the highest luxury of a clever man. It played at present over the whole field of Angela Vivian's oddities of conduct—for, since his visit in the afternoon, Bernard had felt that the spectacle was considerably enlarged. He had come to feel, also, that poor Gordon's predicament was by no means an unnatural one. Longueville had begun to take his friend's dilemma very seriously indeed. The girl was certainly a curious study.

The evening drew to a close and the crowd of Bernard's fellow-loungers dispersed. The lighted windows of the Kursaal still glittered in the bosky darkness, and the lamps along the terrace had not been extinguished; but the great promenade was almost deserted; here and there only a lingering couple—the red tip of a cigar and the vague radiance of a light dress—gave animation to the place. But Bernard sat there still in his tilted chair, beneath his orange-tree; his imagination had wandered very far and he was awaiting its return to the fold. He was on the point of rising, however, when he saw three figures come down the empty vista of the terrace—figures which even at a distance had a familiar air. He immediately left his seat and, taking a dozen steps, recognized Angela Vivian, Blanche Evers and Captain Lovelock. In a moment he met them in the middle of the terrace.

Blanche immediately announced that they had come for a midnight walk.

"And if you think it 's improper," she exclaimed, "it 's not my invention—it 's Miss Vivian's."

"I beg pardon—it 's mine," said Captain Lovelock. "I desire the credit of it. I started the idea; you never would have come without me."

"I think it would have been more proper to come without you than with you," Blanche declared. "You know you 're a dreadful character."

"I 'm much worse when I 'm away from you than when I 'm with you," said Lovelock. "You keep me in order."

The young girl gave a little cry.

"I don't know what you call order! You can't be worse than you have been to-night."

Angela was not listening to this; she turned away a little, looking about at the empty garden.

"This is the third time to-day that you have contradicted yourself," he said. Though he spoke softly he went nearer to her; but she appeared not to hear him—she looked away.

"You ought to have been there, Mr. Longueville," Blanche went on. "We have had a most lovely night; we sat all the evening on Mrs. Vivian's balcony, eating ices. To sit on a balcony, eating ices—that 's my idea of heaven."

"With an angel by your side," said Captain Lovelock.

"You are not my idea of an angel," retorted Blanche.

"I 'm afraid you 'll never learn what the angels are really like," said the Captain. "That 's why Miss Evers got Mrs. Vivian to take rooms over the baker's—so that she could have ices sent up several times a day. Well, I 'm bound to say the baker's ices are not bad."

"Considering that they have been baked! But they affect the mind," Blanche went on. "They would have affected Captain Lovelock's—only he has n't any. They certainly affected Angela's—putting it into her head, at eleven o'clock, to come out to walk."

Angela did nothing whatever to defend herself against

this ingenious sally; she simply stood there in graceful abstraction. Bernard was vaguely vexed at her neither looking at him nor speaking to him; her indifference seemed a contravention of that right of criticism which Gordon had bequeathed to him.

"I supposed people went to bed at eleven o'clock," he said.

Angela glanced about her, without meeting his eye.

"They seem to have gone."

Miss Evers strolled on, and her Captain of course kept pace with her; so that Bernard and Miss Vivian were left standing together. He looked at her a moment in silence, but her eye still avoided his own.

"You are remarkably inconsistent," Bernard presently said. "You take a solemn vow of seclusion this afternoon, and no sooner have you taken it than you proceed to break it in this outrageous manner."

She looked at him now—a long time—longer than she had ever done before.

"This is part of the examination, I suppose," she said.

Bernard hesitated an instant.

"What examination?"

"The one you have undertaken—on Mr. Wright's behalf."

"What do you know about that?"

"Ah, you admit it then?" the girl exclaimed, with an eager laugh.

"I don't in the least admit it," said Bernard, conscious only for the moment of the duty of loyalty to his friend and feeling that negation here was simply a point of honor.

"I trust more to my own conviction than to your denial. You have engaged to bring your superior wisdom and your immense experience to bear upon me! That 's the understanding."

"You must think us a pretty pair of wiseacres," said Bernard.

"There it is—you already begin to answer for what I think. When Mr. Wright comes back you will be able to tell him that I am 'outrageous'!" And she turned away and walked on, slowly following her companions.

"What do you care what I tell him?" Bernard asked. "You don't care a straw."

She said nothing for a moment, then, suddenly, she stopped again, dropping her eyes.

"I beg your pardon," she said, very gently; "I care a great deal. It 's as well that you should know that."

Bernard stood looking at her; her eyes were still lowered.

"Do you know what I shall tell him? I shall tell him that about eleven o'clock at night you become peculiarly attractive."

She went on again a few steps; Miss Evers and Captain Lovelock had turned round and were coming toward her.

"It is very true that I am outrageous," she said; "it was extremely silly and in very bad taste to come out at this hour. Mamma was not at all pleased, and I was very unkind to her. I only wanted to take a turn, and now we will go back." On the others coming up she announced this resolution, and though Captain Lovelock and his companion made a great outcry, she carried her point. Bernard offered no opposition. He contented himself with walking back to her mother's lodging with her almost in silence. The little winding streets were still and empty; there was no sound but the chatter and laughter of Blanche and her attendant swain. Angela said nothing.

This incident presented itself at first to Bernard's mind as a sort of declaration of war. The girl had guessed that she was to be made a subject of speculative scrutiny. The idea was not agreeable to her independent spirit, and she placed herself boldly on the defensive. She took her stand upon her right to defeat his purpose by every possible means—to perplex, elude, deceive him—in plain English, to make a fool of him. This was the construction which for several days Bernard put upon her deportment, at the same time that he thought it immensely clever of her to have guessed what had been going on in his mind. She made him feel very much ashamed of his critical attitude, and he did everything he could think of to put her off her guard and persuade her that for the moment he had ceased to be an observer. His position at moments seemed to him an odious one, for he was firmly resolved that between him and the woman to whom his friend had proposed there should be nothing in the way of a vulgar flirtation. Under the circumstances, it savoured both of flirtation and of vulgarity that they should even fall out with each other—a consummation which appeared to be more or less definitely impending. Bernard remarked to himself that his own only reasonable line of conduct would be instantly to leave Baden, but I am almost ashamed to mention the fact which led him to modify this decision. It was simply that he was induced to make the reflection that he had really succeeded in putting Miss Vivian off her guard. How he had done so he would have found it difficult to explain, inasmuch as in one way or another, for a week, he had spent several hours in talk with her. The most effective way of putting her off her guard would have been to leave her alone, to forswear the privilege of conversation with her, to pass the days in other society. This course would have had the drawback of not enabling him to measure the operation of so ingenious a policy, and Bernard liked, of all the things in the world, to know when he was successful. He believed, at all events, that he was successful now, and that the virtue of his conversation itself had persuaded this keen and brilliant girl that he was thinking of anything in the world but herself. He flattered himself that the civil indifference of his manner, the abstract character of the topics he selected, the irrelevancy of his allusions and the laxity of his attention, all contributed to this result.

Such a result was certainly a remarkable one, for it is almost superfluous to intimate that Miss Vivian was, in fact, perpetually in his thoughts. He made it a point of conscience not to think of her, but he was thinking of her most when his conscience was most lively. Bernard had a conscience—a conscience which, though a little irregular in its motions, gave itself in the long run a great deal of exercise; but nothing could have been more natural than that, curious, imaginative, audacious as he was, and delighting, as I have said, in the play of his singularly nimble intelligence, he should have given himself up to a sort of unconscious experimentation. "I will leave her alone—I will be hanged if I attempt to draw her out!" he said to himself; and meanwhile he was roaming afield and plucking personal impressions in great fragrant handfuls. All this, as I say, was natural, given the man and the situation; the only oddity is that he should have fancied himself able to persuade the person most interested that he had renounced his advantage.

He remembered her telling him that she cared very much what he should say of her on Gordon Wright's return, and he felt that this declaration had a particular significance. After this, of her own movement, she never spoke of Gordon, and Bernard made up his mind that she had promised her mother to accept him if he should repeat his proposal, and that as her heart was not in the matter she preferred to drop a veil over the prospect. "She is going to marry him for his money," he said, "because her mother has brought out the advantages of the thing. Mrs. Vivian's persuasive powers have carried the day, and the girl has made herself believe that it does n't matter that she does n't love him. Perhaps it does n't—to her; it 's hard, in such a case, to put one's self in the woman's point of view. But I should think it would matter, some day or other, to poor Gordon. She herself can't help suspecting it may make a difference in his happiness, and she therefore does n't wish to seem any worse to him than is necessary. She wants me to speak well of her; if she intends to deceive him she expects me to back her up. The wish is doubtless natural, but for a proud girl it is rather an odd favor to ask. Oh yes, she 's a proud girl, even though she has been able to arrange it with her conscience to make a mercenary marriage. To expect me to help her is perhaps to treat me as a friend; but she ought to remember—or at least I ought to remember—that Gordon is an older friend than she. Inviting me to help her as against my oldest friend—is n't there a grain of impudence in that?"

It will be gathered that Bernard's meditations were not on the whole favorable to this young lady, and it must be affirmed that he was forcibly struck with an element of cynicism in her conduct. On the evening of her so-called midnight visit to the Kursaal she had suddenly sounded a note of sweet submissiveness which re-appeared again at frequent intervals. She was gentle, accessible, tenderly gracious, expressive, demonstrative, almost flattering. From his own personal point of view Bernard had no complaint to make of this maidenly urbanity, but he kept reminding himself that *he* was not in question and that everything must be looked at in the light

of Gordon's requirements. There was all this time an absurd
logical twist in his view of things. In the first place he was
not to judge at all; and in the second he was to judge strictly
on Gordon's behalf. This latter clause always served as a justification when the former had failed to serve as a deterrent.
When Bernard reproached himself for thinking too much of
the girl, he drew comfort from the reflection that he was not
thinking well. To let it gradually filter into one's mind,
through a superficial complexity of more reverent preconceptions, that she was an extremely clever coquette— *this*, surely,
was not to think well! Bernard had luminous glimpses of another situation, in which Angela Vivian's coquetry should
meet with a different appreciation; but just now it was not an
item to be entered on the credit side of Wright's account.
Bernard wiped his pen, mentally speaking, as he made this
reflection, and felt like a grizzled old book-keeper, of incorruptible probity. He saw her, as I have said, very often; she
continued to break her vow of shutting herself up, and at the
end of a fortnight she had reduced it to imperceptible parti-
cles. On four different occasions, presenting himself at Mrs.
Vivian's lodgings, Bernard found Angela there alone. She
made him welcome, receiving him as an American girl, in
such circumstances, is free to receive the most gallant of visitors. She smiled and talked and gave herself up to charming
gayety, so that there was nothing for Bernard to say but that
now at least she was off her guard with a vengeance. Happily
he was on his own! He flattered himself that he remained so
on occasions that were even more insidiously relaxing—
when, in the evening, she strolled away with him to parts of
the grounds of the Conversation-house, where the music sank
to sweeter softness and the murmur of the tree-tops of the
Black Forest, stirred by the warm night-air, became almost
audible; or when, in the long afternoons, they wandered in
the woods apart from the others—from Mrs. Vivian and the
amiable object of her more avowed solicitude, the object of
the sportive adoration of the irrepressible, the ever-present
Lovelock. They were constantly having parties in the woods
at this time—driving over the hills to points of interest which
Bernard had looked out in the guide-book. Bernard, in such
matters, was extremely alert and considerate; he developed an

unexpected talent for arranging excursions, and he had taken regularly into his service the red-waistcoated proprietor of a big Teutonic landau, which had a courier's seat behind and was always at the service of the ladies. The functionary in the red waistcoat was a capital charioteer; he was constantly proposing new drives, and he introduced our little party to treasures of romantic scenery.

XIII

MORE THAN A FORTNIGHT had elapsed, but Gordon Wright had not re-appeared, and Bernard suddenly decided that he would leave Baden. He found Mrs. Vivian and her daughter, very opportunely, in the garden of the pleasant, homely Schloss which forms the residence of the Grand Dukes of Baden during their visits to the scene of our narrative, and which, perched upon the hill-side directly above the little town, is surrounded with charming old shrubberies and terraces. To this garden a portion of the public is admitted, and Bernard, who liked the place, had been there more than once. One of the terraces had a high parapet, against which Angela was leaning, looking across the valley. Mrs. Vivian was not at first in sight, but Bernard presently perceived her seated under a tree with Victor Cousin in her hand. As Bernard approached the young girl, Angela, who had not seen him, turned round.

"Don't move," he said. "You were just in the position in which I painted your portrait at Siena."

"Don't speak of that," she answered.

"I have never understood," said Bernard, "why you insist upon ignoring that charming incident."

She resumed for a moment her former position, and stood looking at the opposite hills.

"That 's just how you were—in profile—with your head a little thrown back."

"It was an odious incident!" Angela exclaimed, rapidly changing her attitude.

Bernard was on the point of making a rejoinder, but he thought of Gordon Wright and held his tongue. He presently told her that he intended to leave Baden on the morrow.

They were walking toward her mother. She looked round at him quickly.

"Where are you going?"

"To Paris," he said, quite at hazard; for he had not in the least determined where to go.

"To Paris—in the month of August?" And she gave a little laugh. "What a happy inspiration!"

She gave a little laugh, but she said nothing more, and Bernard gave no further account of his plan. They went and sat down near Mrs. Vivian for ten minutes, and then they got up again and strolled to another part of the garden. They had it all to themselves, and it was filled with things that Bernard liked—inequalities of level, with mossy steps connecting them, rose-trees trained upon old brick walls, horizontal trellises arranged like Italian pergolas, and here and there a towering poplar, looking as if it had survived from some more primitive stage of culture, with its stiff boughs motionless and its leaves forever trembling. They made almost the whole circuit of the garden, and then Angela mentioned very quietly that she had heard that morning from Mr. Wright, and that he would not return for another week.

"You had better stay," she presently added, as if Gordon's continued absence were an added reason.

"I don't know," said Bernard. "It is sometimes difficult to say what one had better do."

I hesitate to bring against him that most inglorious of all charges, an accusation of sentimental fatuity, of the disposition to invent obstacles to enjoyment so that he might have the pleasure of seeing a pretty girl attempt to remove them. But it must be admitted that if Bernard really thought at present that he had better leave Baden, the observation I have just quoted was not so much a sign of this conviction as of the hope that his companion would proceed to gainsay it. The hope was not disappointed, though I must add that no sooner had it been gratified than Bernard began to feel ashamed of it.

"This certainly is not one of those cases," said Angela. "The thing is surely very simple now."

"What makes it so simple?"

She hesitated a moment.

"The fact that I ask you to stay."

"You ask me?" he repeated, softly.

"Ah," she exclaimed, "one does n't say those things twice!"

She turned away, and they went back to her mother, who gave Bernard a wonderful little look of half urgent, half remonstrant inquiry. As they left the garden he walked beside Mrs. Vivian, Angela going in front of them at a distance. The elder lady began immediately to talk to him of Gordon Wright.

"He 's not coming back for another week, you know," she said. "I am sorry he stays away so long."

"Ah yes," Bernard answered, "it seems very long indeed."

And it had, in fact, seemed to him very long.

"I suppose he is always likely to have business," said Mrs. Vivian.

"You may be very sure it is not for his pleasure that he stays away."

"I know he is faithful to old friends," said Mrs. Vivian. "I am sure he has not forgotten us."

"I certainly count upon that," Bernard exclaimed—"remembering him as we do!"

Mrs. Vivian glanced at him gratefully.

"Oh yes, we remember him—we remember him daily, hourly. At least, I can speak for my daughter and myself. He has been so very kind to us." Bernard said nothing, and she went on. "And you have been so very kind to us, too, Mr. Longueville. I want so much to thank you."

"Oh no, don't!" said Bernard, frowning. "I would rather you should n't."

"Of course," Mrs. Vivian added, "I know it 's all on his account; but that makes me wish to thank you all the more. Let me express my gratitude, in advance, for the rest of the time, till he comes back. That 's more responsibility than you bargained for," she said, with a little nervous laugh.

"Yes, it 's more than I bargained for. I am thinking of going away."

Mrs. Vivian almost gave a little jump, and then she paused on the Baden cobble-stones, looking up at him.

"If you *must* go, Mr. Longueville—don't sacrifice yourself!"

The exclamation fell upon Bernard's ear with a certain softly mocking cadence which was sufficient, however, to make this organ tingle.

"Oh, after all, you know," he said, as they walked on— "after all, you know, I am not like Wright—I have no business."

He walked with the ladies to the door of their lodging.

Angela kept always in front. She stood there, however, at the little confectioner's window until the others came up. She let her mother pass in, and then she said to Bernard, looking at him—

"Shall I see you again?"

"Some time, I hope."

"I mean—are you going away?"

Bernard looked for a moment at a little pink sugar cherub—a species of Cupid, with a gilded bow—which figured among the pastry-cook's enticements. Then he said—

"I will come and tell you this evening."

And in the evening he went to tell her; she had mentioned during the walk in the garden of the Schloss that they should not go out. As he approached Mrs. Vivian's door he saw a figure in a light dress standing in the little balcony. He stopped and looked up, and then the person in the light dress, leaning her hands on the railing, with her shoulders a little raised, bent over and looked down at him. It was very dark, but even through the thick dusk he thought he perceived the finest brilliancy of Angela Vivian's smile.

"I shall not go away," he said, lifting his voice a little.

She made no answer; she only stood looking down at him through the warm dusk and smiling. He went into the house, and he remained at Baden-Baden till Gordon came back.

XIV

G ORDON asked him no questions for twenty-four hours after his return, then suddenly he began:

"Well, have n't you something to say to me?"

It was at the hotel, in Gordon's apartment, late in the afternoon. A heavy thunder-storm had broken over the place an hour before, and Bernard had been standing at one of his friend's windows, rather idly, with his hands in his pockets, watching the rain-torrents dance upon the empty pavements. At last the deluge abated, the clouds began to break—there was a promise of a fine evening. Gordon Wright, while the storm was at its climax, sat down to write letters, and wrote half a dozen. It was after he had sealed, directed and affixed a postage-stamp to the last of the series that he addressed to his companion the question I have just quoted.

"Do you mean about Miss Vivian?" Bernard asked, without turning round from the window.

"About Miss Vivian, of course." Bernard said nothing and his companion went on. "Have you nothing to tell me about Miss Vivian?"

Bernard presently turned round looking at Gordon and smiling a little.

"She 's a delightful creature!"

"That won't do—you have tried that before," said Gordon. "No," he added in a moment, "that won't do." Bernard turned back to the window, and Gordon continued, as he remained silent. "I shall have a right to consider your saying nothing a proof of an unfavorable judgment. You don't like her!"

Bernard faced quickly about again, and for an instant the two men looked at each other.

"Ah, my dear Gordon," Longueville murmured.

"*Do* you like her then?" asked Wright, getting up.

"No!" said Longueville.

"That 's just what I wanted to know, and I am much obliged to you for telling me."

"I am not obliged to you for asking me. I was in hopes you would n't."

"You dislike her very much then?" Gordon exclaimed, gravely.

"Won't disliking her, simply, do?" said Bernard.

"It will do very well. But it will do a little better if you will tell me why. Give me a reason or two."

"Well," said Bernard, "I tried to make love to her and she boxed my ears."

"The devil!" cried Gordon.

"I mean morally, you know."

Gordon stared; he seemed a little puzzled.

"You tried to make love to her morally?"

"She boxed my ears morally," said Bernard, laughing out.

"Why did you try to make love to her?"

This inquiry was made in a tone so expressive of an un-biassed truth-seeking habit that Bernard's mirth was not immediately quenched. Nevertheless, he replied with sufficient gravity—

"To test her fidelity to you. Could you have expected anything else? You told me you were afraid she was a latent coquette. You gave me a chance, and I tried to ascertain."

"And you found she was not. Is that what you mean?"

"She 's as firm as a rock. My dear Gordon, Miss Vivian is as firm as the firmest of your geological formations."

Gordon shook his head with a strange positive persistence.

"You are talking nonsense. You are not serious. You are not telling me the truth. I don't believe that you attempted to make love to her. You would n't have played such a game as that. It would n't have been honorable."

Bernard flushed a little; he was irritated.

"Oh come, don't make too much of a point of that! Did n't you tell me before that it was a great opportunity?"

"An opportunity to be wise—not to be foolish!"

"Ah, there is only one sort of opportunity," cried Bernard. "You exaggerate the reach of human wisdom."

"Suppose she had let you make love to her," said Gordon. "That would have been a beautiful result of your experiment."

"I should have seemed to you a rascal, perhaps, but I should have saved you from a latent coquette. You would owe some thanks for that."

"And now you have n't saved me," said Gordon, with a simple air of noting a fact.

"You assume—in spite of what I say—that she *is* a coquette!"

"I assume something because you evidently conceal something. I want the whole truth."

Bernard turned back to the window with increasing irritation.

"If he wants the whole truth he shall have it," he said to himself.

He stood a moment in thought and then he looked at his companion again.

"I think she would marry you—but I don't think she cares for you."

Gordon turned a little pale, but he clapped his hands together.

"Very good," he exclaimed. "That 's exactly how I want you to speak."

"Her mother has taken a great fancy to your fortune and it has rubbed off on the girl, who has made up her mind that it would be a pleasant thing to have thirty thousand a year, and that her not caring for you is an unimportant detail."

"I see—I see," said Gordon, looking at his friend with an air of admiration for his frank and lucid way of putting things.

Now that he had begun to be frank and lucid, Bernard found a charm in it, and the impulse under which he had spoken urged him almost violently forward.

"The mother and daughter have agreed together to bag you, and Angela, I am sure, has made a vow to be as nice to you after marriage as possible. Mrs. Vivian has insisted upon the importance of that; Mrs. Vivian is a great moralist."

Gordon kept gazing at his friend; he seemed positively fascinated.

"Yes, I have noticed that in Mrs. Vivian," he said.

"Ah, she 's a very nice woman!"

"It 's not true, then," said Gordon, "that you tried to make love to Angela?"

Bernard hesitated a single instant.

"No, it is n't true. I calumniated myself, to save her reputation. You insisted on my giving you a reason for my not liking her—I gave you that one."

"And your real reason—"

"My real reason is that I believe she would do you what I can't help regarding as an injury."

"Of course!" and Gordon, dropping his interested eyes, stared for some moments at the carpet. "But it is n't true, then, that you discovered her to be a coquette?"

"Ah, that 's another matter."

"You did discover it all the same?"

"Since you want the whole truth—I did!"

"How did you discover it?" Gordon asked, clinging to his right of interrogation.

Bernard hesitated.

"You must remember that I saw a great deal of her."

"You mean that she encouraged you?"

"If I had not been a very faithful friend I might have thought so."

Gordon laid his hand appreciatively, gratefully, on Bernard's shoulder.

"And even that did n't make you like her?"

"Confound it, you make me blush!" cried Bernard, blushing a little in fact. "I have said quite enough; excuse me from drawing the portrait of too insensible a man. It was my point of view; I kept thinking of you."

Gordon, with his hand still on his friend's arm, patted it an instant in response to this declaration; then he turned away.

"I am much obliged to you. That 's my notion of friendship. You have spoken out like a man."

"Like a man, yes. Remember that. Not in the least like an oracle."

"I prefer an honest man to all the oracles," said Gordon.

"An honest man has his impressions! I have given you mine—they pretend to be nothing more. I hope they have n't offended you."

"Not in the least."

"Nor distressed, nor depressed, nor in any way discomposed you?"

"For what do you take me? I asked you a favor—a service; I imposed it on you. You have done the thing, and my part is simple gratitude."

"Thank you for nothing," said Bernard, smiling. "You have asked me a great many questions; there is one that in turn I have a right to ask you. What do you propose to do in consequence of what I have told you?"

"I propose to do nothing."

This declaration closed the colloquy, and the young men separated. Bernard saw Gordon no more that evening; he took for granted he had gone to Mrs. Vivian's. The burden of Longueville's confidences was a heavy load to carry there, but Bernard ventured to hope that he would deposit it at the door. He had given Gordon his impressions, and the latter might do with them what he chose—toss them out of the window, or let them grow stale with heedless keeping. So Bernard meditated, as he wandered about alone for the rest of the evening. It was useless to look for Mrs. Vivian's little circle, on the terrace of the Conversation-house, for the storm in the afternoon had made the place so damp that it was almost forsaken of its frequenters. Bernard spent the evening in the gaming-rooms, in the thick of the crowd that pressed about the tables, and by way of a change—he had hitherto been almost nothing of a gambler—he laid down a couple of pieces at roulette. He had played but two or three times, without winning a penny; but now he had the agreeable sensation of drawing in a small handful of gold. He continued to play, and he continued to win. His luck surprised and excited him—so much so that after it had repeated itself half a dozen times he left the place and walked about for half an hour in the outer darkness. He felt amused and exhilarated, but the feeling amounted almost to agitation. He, nevertheless, returned to the tables, where he again found success awaiting him. Again and again he put his money on a happy number, and so steady a run of luck began at last to attract attention. The rumor of it spread through the rooms, and the crowd about the roulette received a large contingent of spectators. Bernard felt that they were looking more or less eagerly for a turn of the tide; but he was in the humor for disappointing them, and he left the place, while his luck was still running high, with ten thousand francs in his pocket. It was very late when he returned to the inn—so late that he forbore to knock at Gordon's door. But though he betook himself to his own quarters, he was far from finding, or even seeking, immediate rest. He knocked about, as he would have said, for half the night—not because he was delighted at having won ten thousand francs, but rather because all of a sudden he found himself disgusted at the manner in which he had spent the evening. It was extremely characteristic of Bernard Longueville that his pleasure should suddenly transform itself into flatness. What he felt was not regret or repentance. He had it not in the least on his conscience that he had given countenance to the reprehensible practice of gaming. It was annoyance that he had passed out of his own control—that he had obeyed a force which he was unable to measure at the time. He had been drunk and he was turning sober. In spite of a great momentary appearance of frankness and a lively relish of any conjunction of agreeable circumstances exerting a pressure to which one could respond, Bernard had really little taste for giving himself up, and he never did so without very soon wishing to take himself back. He had now given himself to something that was not himself, and the fact that he had gained ten thousand francs by it was an insufficient salve to an aching sense of having ceased to be his own master. He had not been playing—he had been played with. He had been the sport of a blind, brutal chance, and he felt humiliated by having been favored by so rudely-operating a divinity. Good luck and bad luck? Bernard felt very scornful of the distinction, save that good luck seemed to him rather the more vulgar. As the night went on his disgust deepened, and at last the weariness it brought with it sent him to sleep. He slept very late, and woke up to a disagreeable consciousness. At first, before collecting his thoughts, he could not imagine what he had on his mind—was it that he had spoken ill of Angela Vivian? It brought him extraordinary relief to remember that he had gone to bed in extreme ill-humor with his exploits at roulette. After he had dressed himself and just as he was leaving his room, a servant brought him a note superscribed in Gordon's hand—a note of which the following proved to be the contents.

"Seven o'clock, A.M.

"My dear Bernard: Circumstances have determined me to leave Baden immediately, and I shall take the train that starts an hour hence. I am told that you came in very late last night, so I won't disturb you for a painful parting at this unnatural hour. I came to this decision last evening, and I put up my things; so I have nothing to do but to take myself off. I shall go to Basel, but after that I don't know where, and in so comfortless an uncertainty I don't ask you to follow me. Perhaps I shall go to America; but in any case I shall see you sooner or later. Meanwhile, my dear Bernard, be as happy as your brilliant talents should properly make you, and believe me yours ever,   G.W.

"P.S. It is perhaps as well that I should say that I am leaving in consequence of something that happened last evening, but not—by any traceable process—in consequence of the talk we had together. I may also add that I am in very good health and spirits."

Bernard lost no time in learning that his friend had in fact departed by the eight o'clock train—the morning was now well advanced; and then, over his breakfast, he gave himself up to meditative surprise. What had happened during the evening—what had happened after their conversation in Gordon's room? He had gone to Mrs. Vivian's—what had happened there? Bernard found it difficult to believe that he had gone there simply to notify her that, having talked it over with an intimate friend, he gave up her daughter, or to mention to the young lady herself that he had ceased to desire the honor of her hand. Gordon alluded to some definite occurrence, yet it was inconceivable that he should have allowed himself to be determined by Bernard's words—his diffident and irresponsible impression. Bernard resented this idea as an injury to himself, yet it was difficult to imagine what else could have happened. There was Gordon's word for it, however, that there was no "traceable" connection between the circumstances which led to his sudden departure and the information he had succeeded in extracting from his friend.

What did he mean by a "traceable" connection? Gordon never used words idly, and he meant to make of this point an intelligible distinction. It was this sense of his usual accuracy of expression that assisted Bernard in fitting a meaning to his late companion's letter. He intended to intimate that he had come back to Baden with his mind made up to relinquish his suit, and that he had questioned Bernard simply from moral curiosity—for the sake of intellectual satisfaction. Nothing was altered by the fact that Bernard had told him a sorry tale; it had not modified his behavior—that effect would have been traceable. It had simply affected his imagination, which was a consequence of the imponderable sort. This view of the case was supported by Gordon's mention of his good spirits. A man always had good spirits when he had acted in harmony with a conviction. Of course, after renouncing the attempt to make himself acceptable to Miss Vivian, the only possible thing for Gordon had been to leave Baden. Bernard, continuing to meditate, at last convinced himself that there had been no explicit rupture, that Gordon's last visit had simply been a visit of farewell, that its character had sufficiently signified his withdrawal, and that he had now gone away because, after giving the girl up, he wished very naturally not to meet her again. This was, on Bernard's part, a sufficiently coherent view of the case; but nevertheless, an hour afterward, as he strolled along the Lichtenthal Alley, he found himself stopping suddenly and exclaiming under his breath—"Have I done her an injury? Have I affected her prospects?" Later in the day he said to himself half a dozen times that he had simply warned Gordon against an incongruous union.

XV

Now that Gordon was gone, at any rate, gone for good, and not to return, he felt a sudden and singular sense of freedom. It was a feeling of unbounded expansion, quite out of proportion, as he said to himself, to any assignable cause. Everything suddenly appeared to have become very optional; but he was quite at a loss what to do with his liberty. It seemed a harmless use to make of it, in the afternoon, to go and pay another visit to the ladies who lived at the confectioner's. Here, however, he met a reception which introduced a fresh element of perplexity into the situation that Gordon had left behind him. The door was opened to him by Mrs. Vivian's maid-servant, a sturdy daughter of the Schwartzwald, who informed him that the ladies—with much regret—were unable to receive any one.

"They are very busy—and they are ill," said the young woman, by way of explanation.

Bernard was disappointed, and he felt like arguing the case.

"Surely," he said, "they are not both ill and busy! When you make excuses, you should make them agree with each other."

The Teutonic soubrette fixed her round blue eyes a minute upon the patch of blue sky revealed to her by her open door.

"I say what I can, *lieber Herr*. It 's not my fault if I 'm not so clever as a French mamsell. One of the ladies is busy, the other is ill. There you have it."

"Not quite," said Bernard. "You must remember that there are three of them."

"Oh, the little one—the little one weeps."

"Miss Evers weeps!" exclaimed Bernard, to whom the vision of this young lady in tears had never presented itself.

"That happens to young ladies when they are unhappy," said the girl; and with an artless yet significant smile she carried a big red hand to the left side of a broad bosom.

"I am sorry she is unhappy; but which of the other ladies is ill?"

"The mother is very busy."

"And the daughter is ill?"

The young woman looked at him an instant, smiling again, and the light in her little blue eyes indicated confusion, but not perversity.

"No, the mamma is ill," she exclaimed, "and the daughter is very busy. They are preparing to leave Baden."

"To leave Baden? When do they go?"

"I don't quite know, *lieber Herr*; but very soon."

With this information Bernard turned away. He was rather surprised, but he reflected that Mrs. Vivian had not proposed to spend her life on the banks of the Oos, and that people were leaving Baden every day in the year. In the evening, at the Kursaal, he met Captain Lovelock, who was wandering about with an air of explosive sadness.

"Damn it, they 're going—yes, they 're going," said the Captain, after the two young men had exchanged a few allusions to current events. "Fancy their leaving us in that heartless manner! It 's not the time to run away—it 's the time to keep your rooms, if you 're so lucky as to have any. The races begin next week and there 'll be a tremendous crowd. All the grand-ducal people are coming. Miss Evers wanted awfully to see the Grand Duke, and I promised her an introduction. I can't make out what Mrs. Vivian is up to. I bet you a ten-pound note she 's giving chase. Our friend Wright has come back and gone off again, and Mrs. Vivian means to strike camp and follow. She 'll pot him yet; you see if she does n't!"

"She is running away from you, dangerous man!" said Bernard.

"Do you mean on account of Miss Evers? Well, I admire Miss Evers—I don't mind admitting that; but I ain't dangerous," said Captain Lovelock, with a lustreless eye. "How can a fellow be dangerous when he has n't ten shillings in his pocket? Desperation, do you call it? But Miss Evers has n't money, so far as I have heard. I don't ask you," Lovelock continued—"I don't care a damn whether she has or not. She 's a devilish charming girl, and I don't mind telling you I 'm hit. I stand no chance—I know I stand no chance. Mrs. Vivian 's down on me, and, by Jove, Mrs. Vivian 's right. I 'm not the husband to pick out for a young woman of expensive habits and no expectations. Gordon Wright 's the sort of young man that 's wanted, and, hang me, if Mrs. Vivian did n't want him so much for her own daughter, I believe she 'd try and bag him for the little one. Gad, I believe that to keep me off she would like to cut him in two and give half to each of them! I 'm afraid of that little woman. She has got a little voice like a screw-driver. But for all that, if I could get away from this cursed place, I would keep the girl in sight—hang me if I would n't! I 'd cut the races—dash me if I would n't! But I 'm in pawn, if you know what that means. I owe a beastly lot of money at the inn, and that impudent little beggar of a landlord won't let me out of his sight. The luck 's dead against me at those filthy tables; I have n't won a farthing in three weeks. I wrote to my brother the other day, and this morning I got an answer from him—a cursed, canting letter of good advice, remarking that he had already paid my debts seven times. It does n't happen to be seven; it 's only six, or six and a half! Does he expect me to spend the rest of my life at the Hôtel de Hollande? Perhaps he would like me to engage as a waiter there and pay it off by serving at the table d'hôte. It would be convenient for him the next time he comes abroad with his seven daughters and two governesses. I hate the smell of their beastly table d'hôte! You 're sorry I 'm hard up? I 'm sure I 'm much obliged to you. Can you be of any service? My dear fellow, if you are bent on throwing your money about the place I 'm not the man to stop you." Bernard's winnings of the previous night were burning a hole, as the phrase is, in his pocket. Ten thousand francs had never before seemed to him so heavy a load to carry, and to lighten the weight of his good luck by lending fifty pounds to a less fortunate fellow-player was an operation that not only gratified his good-nature but strongly commended itself to his conscience. His conscience, however, made its conditions. "My dear Longueville," Lovelock went on, "I have always gone in for family feeling, early associations, and all that sort of thing. That 's what made me confide my difficulties to Dovedale. But, upon my honor, you remind me of the good Samaritan, or that sort of person; you are fonder of me than my own brother! I 'll take fifty pounds with pleasure, thank you, and you shall have them again—at the earliest opportunity. My earliest convenience—will that do? Damn it, it *is* a convenience, is n't it? You make your conditions. My dear fellow, I accept them in advance. That I 'm not to follow up Miss Evers—is that what you mean? Have you been commissioned by the family to buy me off? It 's devilish cruel to take advantage of my poverty! Though I 'm poor, I 'm honest. But I *am* honest, my dear Longueville; that 's the point. I 'll give you my word, and I 'll keep it. I won't go near that girl again—I won't think of her till I 've got rid of your fifty pounds. It 's a dreadful encouragement to extravagance, but that 's your lookout. I 'll stop for their beastly races and the young lady shall be sacred."

Longueville called the next morning at Mrs. Vivian's, and learned that the three ladies had left Baden by the early train, a couple of hours before. This fact produced in his mind a variety of emotions—surprise, annoyance, embarrassment. In spite of his effort to think it natural they should go, he found something precipitate and inexplicable in the manner of their going, and he declared to himself that one of the party, at least, had been unkind and ungracious in not giving him a chance to say good-bye. He took refuge by anticipation, as it were, in this reflection, whenever, for the next three or four days, he foresaw himself stopping short, as he had done before, and asking himself whether he had done an injury to Angela Vivian. This was an idle and unpractical question, inasmuch as the answer was not forthcoming; whereas it was quite simple and conclusive to say, without the note of interrogation, that she was, in spite of many attractive points, an abrupt and capricious young woman. During the three or four days in question, Bernard lingered on at Baden, uncertain what to do or where to go, feeling as if he had received a sudden check—a sort of spiritual snub—which arrested the accumulation of motive. Lovelock, also, whom Bernard saw every day, appeared to think that destiny had given him a slap in the face, for he had not enjoyed the satisfaction of a last interview with Miss Evers.

"I thought she might have written me a note," said the Captain; "but it appears she does n't write. Some girls don't write, you know."

Bernard remarked that it was possible Lovelock would still have news of Miss Blanche; and before he left Baden he learned that she had addressed her forsaken swain a charming little note from Lausanne, where the three ladies had paused in their flight from Baden, and where Mrs. Vivian had decreed that for the present they should remain.

"I 'm devilish glad she writes," said Captain Lovelock; "some girls do write, you know."

Blanche found Lausanne most horrid after Baden, for whose delights she languished. The delights of Baden, however, were not obvious just now to her correspondent, who had taken Bernard's fifty pounds into the Kursaal and left them there. Bernard, on learning his misfortune, lent him another fifty, with which he performed a second series of unsuccessful experiments; and our hero was not at his ease until he had passed over to his luckless friend the whole amount of his own winnings, every penny of which found its way through Captain Lovelock's fingers back into the bank. When this operation was completed, Bernard left Baden, the Captain gloomily accompanying him to the station.

I have said that there had come over Bernard a singular sense of freedom. One of the uses he made of his freedom was to undertake a long journey. He went to the East and remained absent from Europe for upward of two years—a period of his life of which it is not proposed to offer a complete history. The East is a wonderful region, and Bernard, investigating the mysteries of Asia, saw a great many curious and beautiful things. He had moments of keen enjoyment; he laid up a great store of impressions and even a considerable sum of knowledge. But, nevertheless, he was not destined to look back upon this episode with any particular complacency. It was less delightful than it was supposed to be; it was less successful than it might have been. By what unnatural element the cup of pleasure was adulterated, he would have been very much at a loss to say; but it was an incontestable fact that at times he sipped it as a medicine, rather than quaffed it as a nectar. When people congratulated him on his opportunity of seeing the world, and said they envied him the privilege of seeing it so well, he felt even more than the usual degree of irritation produced by an insinuation that fortune thinks so poorly of us as to give us easy terms. Misplaced sympathy is the least available of superfluities, and Bernard at this time found himself thinking that there was a good deal of impertinence in the world. He would, however, readily have confessed that, in so far as he failed to enjoy his Oriental wanderings, the fault was his own; though he would have made mentally the gratifying reflection that never was a fault less deliberate. If, during the period of which I speak, his natural gayety had sunk to a minor key, a partial explanation may be found in the fact that he was deprived of the society of his late companion. It was an odd circumstance that the two young men had not met since Gordon's abrupt departure from Baden. Gordon went to Berlin, and shortly afterward to America, so that they were on opposite sides of the globe. Before he returned to his own country, Bernard made by letter two or three offers to join him in Europe, anywhere that was agreeable to him. Gordon answered that his movements were very uncertain, and that he should be sorry to trouble Bernard to follow him about. He had put him to this inconvenience in making him travel from Venice to Baden, and one such favor at a time was enough to ask, even of the most obliging of men. Bernard was, of course, afraid that what he had told Gordon about Angela Vivian was really the cause of a state of things which, as between two such good friends, wore a perceptible resemblance to alienation. Gordon had given her up; but he bore Bernard a grudge for speaking ill of her, and so long as this disagreeable impression should last, he preferred not to see him. Bernard was frank enough to charge the poor fellow with a lingering rancor, of which he made, indeed, no great crime. But Gordon denied the allegation, and assured him that, to his own perception, there was no decline in their intimacy. He only requested, as a favor and as a tribute to "just susceptibilities," that Bernard would allude no more either to Miss Vivian or to what had happened at Baden. This request was easy to comply with, and Bernard, in writing, strictly conformed to it; but it seemed to him that the act of doing so was in itself a cooling-off. What would be a better proof of what is called a "tension" than an agreement to avoid a natural topic? Bernard moralized a little over Gordon's "just susceptibilities," and felt that the existence of a perverse resentment in so honest a nature was a fact gained to his acquaintance with psychological science. It cannot be said, however, that he suffered this fact to occupy at all times the foreground of his consciousness. Bernard was like some great painters; his foregrounds were very happily arranged. He heard nothing of Mrs. Vivian and her daughter, beyond a rumor that they had gone to Italy; and he learned, on apparently good authority, that Blanche Evers had returned to New York with her mother. He wondered whether Captain Lovelock was still in pawn at the Hôtel de Hollande. If he did not allow himself to wonder too curiously whether he had done a harm to Gordon, it may be affirmed that he was haunted by the recurrence of that other question, of which mention has already been made. Had he done a harm to Angela Vivian, and did she know that he had done it? This inquiry by no means made him miserable, and it was far from awaiting him regularly on his pillow. But it visited him at intervals, and sometimes in the strangest places—suddenly, abruptly, in the stillness of an Indian temple, or amid the shrillness of an Oriental crowd. He became familiar with it at last; he called it his Jack-in-the-box. Some invisible touch of circumstance would press the spring, and the little image would pop up, staring him in the face and grinning an interrogation. Bernard always clapped down the lid, for he regarded this phenomenon as strikingly inane. But if it was more frequent than any pang of conscience connected with the remembrance of Gordon himself, this last sentiment was certainly lively enough to make it a great relief to hear at last a rumor that the excellent fellow was about to be married. The rumor reached him at Athens; it was vague and indirect, and it omitted the name of his betrothed. But Bernard made the most of it, and took comfort in the thought that his friend had recovered his spirits and his appetite for matrimony.

XVI

IT WAS NOT till our hero reached Paris, on his return from
the distant East, that the rumor I have just mentioned acquired an appreciable consistency. Here, indeed, it took the
shape of authentic information. Among a number of delayed
letters which had been awaiting him at his banker's he found
a communication from Gordon Wright. During the previous
year or two his correspondence with this trusted—and trusting—friend had not been frequent, and Bernard had received
little direct news of him. Three or four short letters had overtaken him in his wanderings—letters as cordial, to all appearance, if not as voluminous, as the punctual missives of an
earlier time. Bernard made a point of satisfying himself that
they were as cordial; he weighed them in the scales of impartial suspicion. It seemed to him on the whole that there was
no relaxation of Gordon's epistolary tone. If he wrote less
often than he used to do, that was a thing that very commonly happened as men grew older. The closest intimacies,
moreover, had phases and seasons, intermissions and revivals,
and even if his friend had, in fact, averted his countenance
from him, this was simply the accomplishment of a periodical
revolution which would bring them in due order face to face
again. Bernard made a point, himself, of writing tolerably often and writing always in the friendliest tone. He made it a
matter of conscience—he liked to feel that he was treating
Gordon generously, and not demanding an eye for an eye.
The letter he found in Paris was so short that I may give it
entire.

"My dear Bernard (it ran), I must write to you before I
write to any one else, though unfortunately you are so far
away that you can't be the first to congratulate me. Try and
not be the last, however. I am going to be married—as soon
as possible. You know the young lady, so you can appreciate
the situation. Do you remember little Blanche Evers, whom
we used to see three years ago at Baden-Baden? Of course
you remember her, for I know you used often to talk with
her. You will be rather surprised, perhaps, at my having selected her as the partner of a life-time; but we manage these

matters according to our lights. I am very much in love with her, and I hold that an excellent reason. I have been ready any time this year or two to fall in love with some simple, trusting, child-like nature. I find this in perfection in this charming young girl. I find her so natural and fresh. I remember telling you once that I did n't wish to be fascinated—that I wanted to estimate scientifically the woman I should marry. I have altogether got over that, and I don't know how I ever came to talk such nonsense. I am fascinated now, and I assure you I like it! The best of it is that I find it does n't in the least prevent my estimating Blanche. I judge her very fairly—I see just what she is. She 's simple—that 's what I want; she 's tender—that 's what I long for. You will remember how pretty she is; I need n't remind you of that. She was much younger then, and she has greatly developed and improved in these two or three years. But she will always be young and innocent—I don't want her to improve too much. She came back to America with her mother the winter after we met her at Baden, but I never saw her again till three months ago. Then I saw her with new eyes, and I wondered I could have been so blind. But I was n't ready for her till then, and what makes me so happy now is to know that I have come to my present way of feeling by experience. That gives me confidence—you see I am a reasoner still. But I am under the charm, for all my reason. We are to be married in a month—try and come back to the wedding. Blanche sends you a message, which I will give you verbatim. 'Tell him I am not such a silly little chatterbox as I used to be at Baden. I am a great deal wiser; I am almost as clever as Angela Vivian.' She has an idea you thought Miss Vivian very clever—but it is not true that she is equally so. I am very happy; come home and see."

Bernard went home, but he was not able to reach the United States in time for Gordon's wedding, which took place at midsummer. Bernard, arriving late in the autumn, found his friend a married man of some months' standing, and was able to judge, according to his invitation, whether he appeared happy. The first effect of the letter I have just quoted had been an immense surprise; the second had been a series of reflections which were quite the negative of surprise;

and these operations of Bernard's mind had finally merged themselves in a simple sentiment of jollity. He was delighted that Gordon should be married; he felt jovial about it; he was almost indifferent to the question of whom he had chosen. Certainly, at first, the choice of Blanche Evers seemed highly incongruous; it was difficult to imagine a young woman less shaped to minister to Gordon's strenuous needs than the light-hearted and empty-headed little flirt whose inconsequent prattle had remained for Bernard one of the least importunate memories of a charming time. Blanche Evers was a pretty little goose—the prettiest of little geese, perhaps, and doubtless the most amiable; but she was not a companion for a peculiarly serious man, who would like his wife to share his view of human responsibilities. What a singular selection— what a queer infatuation! Bernard had no sooner committed himself to this line of criticism than he stopped short, with the sudden consciousness of error carried almost to the point of *naïveté*. He exclaimed that Blanche Evers was exactly the sort of girl that men of Gordon Wright's stamp always ended by falling in love with, and that poor Gordon knew very much better what he was about in this case than he had done in trying to solve the deep problem of a comfortable life with Angela Vivian. This was what your strong, solid, sensible fellows always came to; they paid, in this particular, a larger tribute to pure fancy than the people who were supposed habitually to cultivate that muse. Blanche Evers was what the French call an article of fantasy, and Gordon had taken a pleasure in finding her deliciously useless. He cultivated utility in other ways, and it pleased and flattered him to feel that he could afford, morally speaking, to have a kittenish wife. He had within himself a fund of common sense to draw upon, so that to espouse a paragon of wisdom would be but to carry water to the fountain. He could easily make up for the deficiencies of a wife who was a little silly, and if she charmed and amused him, he could treat himself to the luxury of these sensations for themselves. He was not in the least afraid of being ruined by it, and if Blanche's birdlike chatter and turns of the head had made a fool of him, he knew it perfectly well, and simply took his stand upon his rights. Every man has a right to a little flower-bed, and life is not all mere kitchen-gardening. Bernard rapidly extemporized this rough explanation of the surprise his friend had offered him, and he found it all-sufficient for his immediate needs. He wrote Blanche a charming note, to which she replied with a great deal of spirit and grace. Her little letter was very prettily turned, and Bernard, reading it over two or three times, said to himself that, to do her justice, she might very well have polished her intellect a trifle during these two or three years. As she was older, she could hardly help being wiser. It even occurred to Bernard that she might have profited by the sort of experience that is known as the discipline of suffering. What had become of Captain Lovelock and that tender passion which was apparently none the less genuine for having been expressed in the slang of a humorous period? Had they been permanently separated by judicious guardians, and had she been obliged to obliterate his image from her lightly-beating little heart? Bernard had felt sure at Baden that, beneath her contemptuous airs and that impertinent consciousness of the difficulties of conquest by which a pretty American girl attests her allegiance to a civilization in which young women occupy the highest place—he had felt sure that Blanche had a high appreciation of her handsome Englishman, and that if Lovelock should continue to relish her charms, he might count upon the advantages of reciprocity. But it occurred to Bernard that Captain Lovelock had perhaps been faithless; that, at least, the discourtesy of chance and the inhumanity of an elder brother might have kept him an eternal prisoner at the Hôtel de Hollande (where, for all Bernard knew to the contrary, he had been obliged to work out his destiny in the arduous character of a polyglot waiter); so that the poor young girl, casting backward glances along the path of Mrs. Vivian's retreat, and failing to detect the onward rush of a rescuing cavalier, had perforce believed herself forsaken, and had been obliged to summon philosophy to her aid. It was very possible that her philosophic studies had taught her the art of reflection; and that, as she would have said herself, she was tremendously toned down. Once, at Baden, when Gordon Wright happened to take upon himself to remark that little Miss Evers was bored by her English gallant, Bernard had ventured to observe, *in petto*, that Gordon knew nothing about it. But all this was of no consequence now, and Bernard steered further and further away from the liability to detect fallacies in his friend. Gordon had engaged himself to marry, and our critical hero had not a grain of fault to find with this resolution. It was a capital thing; it was just what he wanted; it would do him a world of good. Bernard rejoiced with him sincerely, and regretted extremely that a series of solemn engagements to pay visits in England should prevent his being present at the nuptials.

They were well over, as I have said, when he reached New York. The honeymoon had waned, and the business of married life had begun. Bernard, at the end, had sailed from England rather abruptly. A friend who had a remarkably good cabin on one of the steamers was obliged by a sudden detention to give it up, and on his offering it to Longueville, the latter availed himself gratefully of this opportunity of being a little less discomposed than usual by the Atlantic billows. He therefore embarked at two days' notice, a fortnight earlier than he had intended and than he had written to Gordon to expect him. Gordon, of course, had written that he was to seek no hospitality but that which Blanche was now prepared—they had a charming house—so graciously to dispense; but Bernard, nevertheless, leaving the ship early in the morning, had betaken himself to an hotel. He wished not to anticipate his welcome, and he determined to report himself to Gordon first and to come back with his luggage later in the day. After purifying himself of his sea-stains, he left his hotel and walked up the Fifth Avenue with all a newly-landed voyager's enjoyment of terrestrial locomotion. It was a charming autumn day; there was a golden haze in the air; he supposed it was the Indian summer. The broad sidewalk of the Fifth Avenue was scattered over with dry leaves—crimson and orange and amber. He tossed them with his stick as he passed; they rustled and murmured with the motion, and it reminded him of the way he used to kick them in front of him over these same pavements in his riotous infancy. It was a pleasure, after many wanderings, to find himself in his native land again, and Bernard Longueville, as he went, paid his compliments to his mother-city. The brightness and gayety of the place seemed a greeting to a returning son, and he felt a throb of affection for the freshest, the youngest, the easiest and most good-natured of great capitals. On presenting himself at Gordon's door, Bernard was told that the master of the house was not at home; he went in, however, to see the mistress. She was in her drawing-room, alone; she had on her bonnet, as if she had been going out. She gave him a joyous, demonstrative little welcome; she was evidently very glad to see him. Bernard had thought it possible she had "improved," and she was certainly prettier than ever. He instantly perceived that she was still a chatterbox; it remained to be seen whether the quality of her discourse were finer.

"Well, Mr. Longueville," she exclaimed, "where in the world did you drop from, and how long did it take you to cross the Atlantic? Three days, eh? It could n't have taken you many more, for it was only the other day that Gordon told me you were not to sail till the 20th. You changed your mind, eh? I did n't know you ever changed your mind. Gordon never changes his. That 's not a reason, eh, because you are not a bit like Gordon. Well, I never thought you were, except that you are a man. Now what are you laughing at? What should you like me call you? You *are* a man, I suppose; you are not a god. That 's what you would like me to call you, I have no doubt. I must keep that for Gordon? I shall certainly keep it a good while. I know a good deal more about gentlemen than I did when I last saw you, and I assure you I don't think they are a bit god-like. I suppose that 's why you always drop down from the sky—you think it 's more divine. I remember that 's the way you arrived at Baden when we were there together; the first thing we knew, you were standing in the midst of us. Do you remember that evening when you presented yourself? You came up and touched Gordon on the shoulder, and he gave a little jump. He will give another little jump when he sees you to-day. He gives a great many little jumps; I keep him skipping about! I remember perfectly the way we were sitting that evening at Baden, and the way you looked at me when you came up. I saw you before Gordon— I see a good many things before Gordon. What did you look at me that way for? I always meant to ask you. I was dying to know."

"For the simplest reason in the world," said Bernard. "Because you were so pretty."

"Ah no, it was n't that! I know all about that look. It was something else—as if you knew something about me. I don't know what you can have known. There was very little to know about me, except that I was intensely silly. Really, I was awfully silly that summer at Baden—you would n't believe how silly I was. But I don't see how you could have known that—before you had spoken to me. It came out in my conversation—it came out awfully. My mother was a good deal disappointed in Mrs. Vivian's influence; she had expected so much from it. But it was not poor Mrs. Vivian's fault, it was some one's else. Have you ever seen the Vivians again? They are always in Europe; they have gone to live in Paris. That evening when you came up and spoke to Gordon, I never thought that three years afterward I should be married to him, and I don't suppose you did either. Is that what you meant by looking at me? Perhaps you can tell the future. I wish you would tell *my* future!"

"Oh, I can tell that easily," said Bernard.

"What will happen to me?"

"Nothing particular; it will be a little dull—the perfect happiness of a charming woman married to the best fellow in the world."

"Ah, what a horrid future!" cried Blanche, with a little petulant cry. "I want to be happy, but I certainly don't want to be dull. If you say that again you will make me repent of having married the best fellow in the world. I mean to be happy, but I certainly shall not be dull if I can help it."

"I was wrong to say that," said Bernard, "because, after all, my dear young lady, there must be an excitement in having so kind a husband as you have got. Gordon's devotion is quite capable of taking a new form—of inventing a new kindness—every day in the year."

Blanche looked at him an instant, with less than her usual consciousness of her momentary pose.

"My husband *is* very kind," she said gently.

She had hardly spoken the words when Gordon came in. He stopped a moment on seeing Bernard, glanced at his wife, blushed, flushed, and with a loud, frank exclamation of pleasure, grasped his friend by both hands. It was so long since he had seen Bernard that he seemed a good deal moved; he stood there smiling, clasping his hands, looking him in the eyes, unable for some moments to speak. Bernard, on his side, was greatly pleased; it was delightful to him to look into Gordon's honest face again and to return his manly grasp. And he looked well—he looked happy; to see that was more delightful yet. During these few instants, while they exchanged a silent pledge of renewed friendship, Bernard's elastic perception embraced several things besides the consciousness of his own pleasure. He saw that Gordon looked well and happy, but that he looked older, too, and more serious, more marked by life. He looked as if something had happened to him—as, in fact, something had. Bernard saw a latent spark in his friend's eye that seemed to question his own for an impression of Blanche—to question it eagerly, and yet to deprecate judgment. He saw, too—with the fact made more vivid by Gordon's standing there beside her in his manly sincerity and throwing it into contrast—that Blanche was the same little posturing coquette of a Blanche whom, at Baden, he would have treated it as a broad joke that Gordon Wright should dream of marrying. He saw, in a word, that it was what it had first struck him as being—an incongruous union. All this was a good deal for Bernard to see in the course of half a minute, especially through the rather opaque medium of a feeling of irreflective joy; and his impressions at this moment have a value only in so far as they were destined to be confirmed by larger opportunity.

"You have come a little sooner than we expected," said Gordon; "but you are all the more welcome."

"It was rather a risk," Blanche observed. "One should be notified, when one wishes to make a good impression."

"Ah, my dear lady," said Bernard, "you made your impression—as far as I am concerned—a long time ago, and I doubt whether it would have gained anything to-day by your having prepared an effect."

They were standing before the fire-place, on the great hearth-rug, and Blanche, while she listened to this speech, was feeling, with uplifted arm, for a curl that had strayed from her chignon.

"She prepares her effects very quickly," said Gordon, laughing gently. "They follow each other very fast!"

Blanche kept her hand behind her head, which was bent slightly forward; her bare arm emerged from her hanging sleeve, and, with her eyes glancing upward from under her lowered brows, she smiled at her two spectators. Her husband laid his hand on Bernard's arm.

"Is n't she pretty?" he cried; and he spoke with a sort of tender delight in being sure at least of this point.

"Tremendously pretty!" said Bernard. "I told her so half an hour before you came in."

"Ah, it was time I should arrive!" Gordon exclaimed.

Blanche was manifestly not in the least discomposed by this frank discussion of her charms, for the air of distinguished esteem adopted by both of her companions diminished the crudity of their remarks. But she gave a little pout of irritated modesty—it was more becoming than anything she had done yet—and declared that if they wished to talk her over, they were very welcome; but she should prefer their waiting till she got out of the room. So she left them, reminding Bernard that he was to send for his luggage and remain, and promising to give immediate orders for the preparation of his apartment. Bernard opened the door for her to pass out; she gave him a charming nod as he stood there, and he turned back to Gordon with the reflection of her smile in his face. Gordon was watching him; Gordon was dying to know what he thought of her. It was a curious mania of Gordon's, this wanting to know what one thought of the women he loved; but Bernard just now felt abundantly able to humor it. He was so pleased at seeing him tightly married.

"She 's a delightful creature," Bernard said, with cordial vagueness, shaking hands with his friend again.

Gordon glanced at him a moment, and then, coloring a little, looked straight out of the window; whereupon Bernard remembered that these were just the terms in which, at Baden, after his companion's absence, he had attempted to qualify Angela Vivian. Gordon was conscious—he was conscious of the oddity of his situation.

"Of course it surprised you," he said, in a moment, still looking out of the window.

"What, my dear fellow?"

"My marriage."

"Well, you know," said Bernard, "everything surprises me. I am of a very conjectural habit of mind. All sorts of ideas come into my head, and yet when the simplest things happen I am always rather startled. I live in a reverie, and I am perpetually waked up by people doing things."

Gordon transferred his eyes from the window to Bernard's face—to his whole person.

"You are waked up? But you fall asleep again!"

"I fall asleep very easily," said Bernard.

Gordon looked at him from head to foot, smiling and shaking his head.

"You are not changed," he said. "You have travelled in unknown lands; you have had, I suppose, all sorts of adventures; but you are the same man I used to know."

"I am sorry for that!"

"You have the same way of representing—of misrepresenting, yourself."

"Well, if I am not changed," said Bernard, "I can ill afford to lose so valuable an art."

"Taking you altogether, I am glad you are the same," Gordon answered, simply; "but you must come into my part of the house."

XVII

Yes, he was conscious—he was very conscious; so Bernard reflected during the two or three first days of his visit to his friend. Gordon knew it must seem strange to so irreverent a critic that a man who had once aspired to the hand of so intelligent a girl—putting other things aside—as Angela Vivian should, as the Ghost in "Hamlet" says, have "declined upon" a young lady who, in force of understanding, was so very much Miss Vivian's inferior; and this knowledge kept him ill at his ease and gave him a certain pitiable awkwardness. Bernard's sense of the anomaly grew rapidly less acute; he made various observations which helped it to seem natural. Blanche was wonderfully pretty; she was very graceful, innocent, amusing. Since Gordon had determined to marry a little goose, he had chosen the animal with extreme discernment. It had quite the plumage of a swan, and it sailed along the stream of life with an extraordinary lightness of motion. He asked himself indeed at times whether Blanche were really so silly as she seemed; he doubted whether any woman could be so silly as Blanche seemed. He had a suspicion at times that, for ends of her own, she was playing a part—the suspicion arising from the fact that, as usually happens in such cases, she over-played it. Her empty chatter, her futility, her childish coquetry and frivolity—such light wares could hardly be the whole substance of any woman's being; there was something beneath them which Blanche was keeping out of sight. She had a scrap of a mind somewhere, and even a little particle of a heart. If one looked long enough one might catch a glimpse of these possessions. But why should she keep them out of sight, and what were the ends that she proposed to serve by this uncomfortable perversity? Bernard wondered whether she were fond of her husband, and he heard it intimated by several good people in New York who had had some observation of the courtship, that she had married him for his money. He was very sorry to find that this was taken for granted, and he determined, on the whole, not to believe it. He was disgusted with the idea of such a want of gratitude; for, if Gordon Wright had loved Miss Evers for herself, the young lady might certainly have discovered the intrinsic value of so disinterested a suitor. Her mother had the credit of having made the match. Gordon was known to be looking for a wife; Mrs. Evers had put her little feather-head of a daughter very much forward, and Gordon was as easily captivated as a child by the sound of a rattle. Blanche had an affection for him now, however; Bernard saw no reason to doubt that, and certainly she would have been a very flimsy creature indeed if she had not been touched by his inexhaustible kindness. She had every conceivable indulgence, and if she married him for his money, at least she had got what she wanted. She led the most agreeable life conceivable, and she ought to be in high good-humor. It was impossible to have a prettier house, a prettier carriage, more jewels and laces for the adornment of a plump little person. It was impossible to go to more parties, to give better dinners, to have fewer privations or annoyances. Bernard was so much struck with all this that, advancing rapidly in the intimacy of his gracious hostess, he ventured to call her attention to her blessings. She answered that she was perfectly aware of them, and there was no pretty speech she was not prepared to make about Gordon.

"I know what you want to say," she went on; "you want to say that he spoils me, and I don't see why you should hesitate. You generally say everything you want, and you need n't be afraid of me. He does n't spoil me, simply because I am so bad I can't be spoiled; but that 's of no consequence. I was spoiled ages ago; every one spoiled me—every one except Mrs. Vivian. I was always fond of having everything I want, and I generally managed to get it. I always had lovely clothes; mamma thought that was a kind of a duty. If it was a duty, I don't suppose it counts as a part of the spoiling. But I was very much indulged, and I know I have everything now. Gordon is a perfect husband; I believe if I were to ask him for a present of his nose, he would cut it off and give it to me. I think I will ask him for a small piece of it some day; it will rather improve him to have an inch or two less. I don't say he 's handsome; but he 's just as good as he can be. Some people say that if you are very fond of a person you always think them handsome; but I don't agree with that at all. I am very fond of Gordon, and yet I am not blinded by affection, as regards his personal appearance. He 's too light for my taste, and too red. And because you think people handsome, it does n't follow that you are fond of them. I used to have a friend who was awfully handsome—the handsomest man I ever saw—and I was perfectly conscious of his defects. But I 'm not conscious of Gordon's, and I don't believe he has got any. He 's so intensely kind; it 's quite pathetic. One would think he had done me an injury in marrying me, and that he wanted to make up for it. If he has done me an injury I have n't discovered it yet, and I don't believe I ever shall. I certainly shall not as long as he lets me order all the clothes I want. I have ordered five dresses this week, and I mean to order two more. When I told Gordon, what do you think he did? He simply kissed me. Well, if that 's not expressive, I don't know what he could have done. He kisses me about seventeen times a day. I suppose it 's very improper for a woman to tell any one how often her husband kisses her; but, as you happen to have seen him do it, I don't suppose you will be scandalized. I know you are not easily scandalized; I am not afraid of you. You are scandalized at my getting so many dresses? Well, I told you I was spoiled—I freely acknowledge it. That 's why I was afraid to tell Gordon—because when I was married I had such a lot of things; I was supposed to have dresses enough to last for a year. But Gordon had n't to pay for them, so there was no harm in my letting him feel that he has a wife. If he thinks I am extravagant, he can easily stop kissing me. You don't think it would be easy to stop? It 's very well, then, for those that have never begun!"

Bernard had a good deal of conversation with Blanche, of which, so far as she was concerned, the foregoing remarks may serve as a specimen. Gordon was away from home during much of the day; he had a chemical laboratory in which he was greatly interested, and which he took Bernard to see; it was fitted up with the latest contrivances for the pursuit of experimental science, and was the resort of needy young students, who enjoyed, at Gordon's expense, the opportunity for pushing their researches. The place did great honor to Gordon's liberality and to his ingenuity; but Blanche, who had also paid it a visit, could never speak of it without a pretty little shudder.

"Nothing would induce me to go there again," she declared, "and I consider myself very fortunate to have escaped from it with my life. It 's filled with all sorts of horrible things, that fizzle up and go off, or that make you turn some dreadful color if you look at them. I expect to hear a great clap some day, and half an hour afterward to see Gordon brought home in several hundred small pieces, put up in a dozen little bottles. I got a horrid little stain in the middle of my dress that one of the young men—the young *savants*—was so good as to drop there. Did you see the young *savants* who work under Gordon's orders? I thought they were too forlorn; there is n't one of them you would look at. If you can believe it, there was n't one of them that looked at me; they took no more notice of me than if I had been the charwoman. They might have shown me some attention, at least, as the wife of the proprietor. What is it that Gordon 's called—is n't there some other name? If you say 'proprietor,' it sounds as if he kept an hotel. I certainly don't want to pass for the wife of an hotel-keeper. What does he call himself? He must have some name. I hate telling people he 's a chemist; it sounds just as if he kept a shop. That 's what they call the druggists in England, and I formed the habit while I was there. It makes me feel as if he were some dreadful little man, with big green bottles in the window and 'night-bell' painted outside. He does n't call himself anything? Well, that 's exactly like Gordon! I wonder he consents to have a name at all. When I was telling some one about the young men who work under his orders—the young *savants*—he said I must not say that—I must not speak of their working 'under his orders.' I don't know what he would like me to say! Under his inspiration!"

During the hours of Gordon's absence, Bernard had frequent colloquies with his friend's wife, whose irresponsible prattle amused him, and in whom he tried to discover some faculty, some quality, which might be a positive guarantee of Gordon's future felicity. But often, of course, Gordon was an auditor as well; I say an auditor, because it seemed to Bernard that he had grown to be less of a talker than of yore. Doubtless, when a man finds himself united to a garrulous wife, he naturally learns to hold his tongue; but sometimes, at the close of one of Blanche's discursive monologues, on glancing at her husband just to see how he took it, and seeing him sit perfectly silent, with a fixed, inexpressive smile, Bernard said to himself that Gordon found the lesson of listening attended with some embarrassments. Gordon, as the years went by, was growing a little inscrutable; but this, too, in certain circumstances, was a usual tendency. The operations of the mind, with deepening experience, became more complex, and people were less apt to emit immature reflections at forty than they had been in their earlier days. Bernard felt a great kindness in these days for his old friend; he never yet had seemed to him such a good fellow, nor appealed so strongly to the benevolence of his disposition. Sometimes, of old, Gordon used to irritate him; but this danger appeared completely to have passed away. Bernard prolonged his visit; it gave him pleasure to be able to testify in this manner to his good will. Gordon was the kindest of hosts, and if in conversation, when his wife was present, he gave precedence to her superior powers, he had at other times a good deal of pleasant bachelor-talk with his guest. He seemed very happy; he had plenty of occupation and plenty of practical intentions. The season went on, and Bernard enjoyed his life. He enjoyed the keen and brilliant American winter, and he found it very pleasant to be treated as a distinguished stranger in his own land—a situation to which his long and repeated absences had relegated him. The hospitality of New York was profuse; the charm of its daughters extreme; the radiance of its skies superb. Bernard was the restless and professionless mortal that we know, wandering in life from one vague experiment to another, constantly gratified and never satisfied, to whom no imperious finality had as yet presented itself; and, nevertheless, for a time he contrived to limit his horizon to the passing hour, and to make a good many hours pass in the drawing-room of a demonstrative flirt.

For Mrs. Gordon was a flirt; that had become tolerably obvious. Bernard had known of old that Blanche Evers was one, and two or three months' observation of his friend's wife assured him that she did not judge a certain ethereal coquetry to be inconsistent with the conjugal character. Blanche flirted, in fact, more or less with all men, but her opportunity for playing her harmless batteries upon Bernard were of course exceptionally large. The poor fellow was perpetually under fire, and it was inevitable that he should reply with some precision of aim. It seemed to him all child's play, and it is certain that when his back was turned to his pretty hostess he never found himself thinking of her. He had not the least reason to suppose that she thought of him—excessive concentration of mind was the last vice of which he accused her. But before the winter was over, he discovered that Mrs. Gordon Wright was being talked about, and that his own name was, as the newspapers say, mentioned in connection with that of his friend's wife. The discovery greatly disgusted him; Bernard Longueville's chronicler must do him the justice to say that it failed to yield him an even transient thrill of pleasure. He thought it very improbable that this vulgar rumor had reached Gordon's ears; but he nevertheless—very naturally—instantly made up his mind to leave the house. He lost no time in saying to Gordon that he had suddenly determined to go to California, and that he was sure he must be glad to get rid of him. Gordon expressed no surprise and no regret. He simply laid his hand on his shoulder and said, very quietly, looking at him in the eyes—

"Very well; the pleasantest things must come to an end."

It was not till an hour afterwards that Bernard said to himself that his friend's manner of receiving the announcement of his departure had been rather odd. He had neither said a word about his staying longer nor urged him to come back again, and there had been (it now seemed to Bernard) an audible undertone of relief in the single sentence with which he assented to his visitor's withdrawal. Could it be possible that poor Gordon was jealous of him, that he had heard this loathsome gossip, or that his own observation had given him an alarm? He had certainly never betrayed the smallest sense of injury; but it was to be remembered that even if he were uneasy, Gordon was quite capable, with his characteristic habit of weighing everything, his own honor included, in scrupulously adjusted scales, of denying himself the luxury of active suspicion. He would never have let a half suspicion

make a difference in his conduct, and he would not have dis-
simulated; he would simply have resisted belief. His hospitality had been without a flaw, and if he had really been wishing
Bernard out of his house, he had behaved with admirable self-
control. Bernard, however, followed this train of thought a
very short distance. It was odious to him to believe that he
could have appeared to Gordon, however guiltlessly, to have
invaded even in imagination the mystic line of the marital
monopoly; not to say that, moreover, if one came to that, he
really cared about as much for poor little Blanche as for the
weather-cock on the nearest steeple. He simply hurried his
preparations for departure, and he told Blanche that he
should have to bid her farewell on the following day. He had
found her in the drawing-room, waiting for dinner. She was
expecting company to dine, and Gordon had not yet come
down.

She was sitting in the vague glow of the fire-light, in a
wonderful blue dress, with two little blue feet crossed on the
rug and pointed at the hearth. She received Bernard's announcement with small satisfaction, and expended a great
deal of familiar ridicule on his project of a journey to California. Then, suddenly getting up and looking at him a moment—

"I know why you are going," she said.

"I am glad to hear my explanations have not been lost."

"Your explanations are all nonsense. You are going for another reason."

"Well," said Bernard, "if you insist upon it, it 's because
you are too sharp with me."

"It 's because of me. So much as that is true." Bernard
wondered what she was going to say—if she were going to
be silly enough to allude to the most impudent of fictions;
then, as she stood opening and closing her blue fan and smiling at him in the fire-light, he felt that she was silly enough
for anything. "It 's because of all the talk—it 's because of
Gordon. You need n't be afraid of Gordon."

"Afraid of him? I don't know what you mean," said Bernard, gravely.

Blanche gave a little laugh.

"You have discovered that people are talking about us—

about you and me. I must say I wonder you care. I don't care, and if it 's because of Gordon, you might as well know that he does n't care. If he does n't care, I don't see why I should; and if I don't, I don't see why you should!"

"You pay too much attention to such insipid drivel in even mentioning it."

"Well, if I have the credit of saying what I should n't—to you or to any one else—I don't see why I should n't have the advantage too. Gordon does n't care—he does n't care what I do or say. He does n't care a pin for me!"

She spoke in her usual rattling, rambling voice, and brought out this declaration with a curious absence of resentment.

"You talk about advantage," said Bernard. "I don't see what advantage it is to you to say that."

"I want to—I must—I will! That 's the advantage!" This came out with a sudden sharpness of tone; she spoke more excitedly. "He does n't care a button for me, and he never did! I don't know what he married me for. He cares for something else—he thinks of something else. I don't know what it is—I suppose it 's chemistry!"

These words gave Bernard a certain shock, but he had his intelligence sufficiently in hand to contradict them with energy.

"You labor under a monstrous delusion," he exclaimed. "Your husband thinks you fascinating."

This epithet, pronounced with a fine distinctness, was ringing in the air when the door opened and Gordon came in. He looked for a moment from Bernard to his wife, and then, approaching the latter, he said, softly—

"Do you know that he leaves us to-morrow?"

XVIII

BERNARD left then and went to California; but when he arrived there he asked himself why he had come, and was unable to mention any other reason than that he had announced it. He began to feel restless again, and to drift back to that chronic chagrin which had accompanied him through his long journey in the East. He succeeded, however, in keeping these unreasonable feelings at bay for some time, and he strove to occupy himself, to take an interest in Californian problems. Bernard, however, was neither an economist nor a cattle-fancier, and he found that, as the phrase is, there was not a great deal to take hold of. He wandered about, admired the climate and the big peaches, thought a while of going to Japan, and ended by going to Mexico. In this way he passed several months, and justified, in the eyes of other people at least, his long journey across the Continent. At last he made it again, in the opposite sense. He went back to New York, where the summer had already begun, and here he invented a solution for the difficulty presented by life to a culpably unoccupied and ill-regulated man. The solution was not in the least original, and I am almost ashamed to mention so stale and conventional a device. Bernard simply hit upon the plan of returning to Europe. Such as it was, however, he carried it out with an audacity worthy of a better cause, and was sensibly happier since he had made up his mind to it. Gordon Wright and his wife were out of town, but Bernard went into the country, as boldly as you please, to inform them of his little project and take a long leave of them. He had made his arrangements to sail immediately, and, as at such short notice it was impossible to find good quarters on one of the English vessels, he had engaged a berth on a French steamer, which would convey him to Havre. On going down to Gordon's house in the country, he was conscious of a good deal of eagerness to know what had become of that latent irritation of which Blanche had given him a specimen. Apparently it had quite subsided; Blanche was wreathed in smiles; she was living in a bower of roses. Bernard, indeed, had no opportunity for investigating her state of mind, for he found several people in the house, and Blanche, who had an exalted standard of the duties of a hostess, was occupied in making life agreeable to her guests, most of whom were gentlemen. She had in this way that great remedy for dissatisfaction which Bernard lacked—something interesting to do. Bernard felt a good deal of genuine sadness in taking leave of Gordon, to whom he contrived to feel even more kindly than in earlier days. He had quite forgotten that Gordon was jealous of him—which he was not, as Bernard said. Certainly, Gordon showed nothing of it now, and nothing could have been more friendly than their parting. Gordon, also, for a man who was never boisterous, seemed very contented. He was fond of exercising hospitality, and he confessed to Bernard that he was just now in the humor for having his house full of people. Fortune continued to gratify this generous taste; for just as Bernard was coming away another guest made his appearance. The new-comer was none other than the Honourable Augustus Lovelock, who had just arrived in New York, and who, as he added, had long desired to visit the United States. Bernard merely witnessed his arrival, and was struck with the fact that as he presented himself—it seemed quite a surprise—Blanche really stopped chattering.

XIX

I HAVE CALLED IT a stale expedient on Bernard Longueville's part to "go to Europe" again, like the most commonplace American; and it is certain that, as our young man
stood and looked out of the window of his inn at Havre, an
hour after his arrival at that sea-port, his adventure did not
strike him as having any great freshness. He had no plans nor
intentions; he had not even any very definite desires. He had
felt the impulse to come back to Europe, and he had obeyed
it; but now that he had arrived, his impulse seemed to have
little more to say to him. He perceived it, indeed—mentally—in the attitude of a small street-boy playing upon his
nose with that vulgar gesture which is supposed to represent
the elation of successful fraud. There was a large blank wall
before his window, painted a dirty yellow and much discolored by the weather; a broad patch of summer sunlight rested
upon it and brought out the full vulgarity of its complexion.
Bernard stared a while at this blank wall, which struck him in
some degree as a symbol of his own present moral prospect.
Then suddenly he turned away, with the declaration that,
whatever truth there might be in symbolism, he, at any rate,
had not come to Europe to spend the precious remnant of
his youth in a malodorous Norman sea-port. The weather was
very hot, and neither the hotel nor the town at large appeared
to form an attractive *séjour* for persons of an irritable nostril.
To go to Paris, however, was hardly more attractive than to
remain at Havre, for Bernard had a lively vision of the heated
bitumen and the glaring frontages of the French capital. But
if a Norman town was close and dull, the Norman country
was notoriously fresh and entertaining, and the next morning
Bernard got into a calèche, with his luggage, and bade its
proprietor drive him along the coast. Once he had begun to
rumble through this charming landscape, he was in much better humor with his situation; the air was freshened by a
breeze from the sea; the blooming country, without walls or
fences, lay open to the traveller's eye; the grain-fields and
copses were shimmering in the summer wind; the pink-faced
cottages peeped through the ripening orchard-boughs, and

the gray towers of the old churches were silvered by the morning-light of France.

At the end of some three hours, Bernard arrived at a little watering-place which lay close upon the shore, in the embrace of a pair of white-armed cliffs. It had a quaint and primitive aspect and a natural picturesqueness which commended it to Bernard's taste. There was evidently a great deal of nature about it, and at this moment, nature, embodied in the clear, gay sunshine, in the blue and quiet sea, in the daisied grass of the high-shouldered downs, had an air of inviting the intelligent observer to postpone his difficulties. Blanquais-les-Galets, as Bernard learned the name of this unfashionable resort to be, was twenty miles from a railway, and the place wore an expression of unaffected rusticity. Bernard stopped at an inn for his noonday breakfast, and then, with his appreciation quickened by the homely felicity of this repast, determined to go no further. He engaged a room at the inn, dismissed his vehicle, and gave himself up to the contemplation of French sea-side manners. These were chiefly to be observed upon a pebbly strand which lay along the front of the village and served as the gathering-point of its idler inhabitants. Bathing in the sea was the chief occupation of these good people, including, as it did, prolonged spectatorship of the process and infinite conversation upon its mysteries. The little world of Blanquais appeared to form a large family party, of highly developed amphibious habits, which sat gossiping all day upon the warm pebbles, occasionally dipping into the sea and drying itself in the sun, without any relaxation of personal intimacy. All this was very amusing to Bernard, who in the course of the day took a bath with the rest. The ocean was, after all, very large, and when one took one's plunge one seemed to have it quite to one's self. When he had dressed himself again, Bernard stretched himself on the beach, feeling happier than he had done in a long time, and pulled his hat over his eyes. The feeling of happiness was an odd one; it had come over him suddenly, without visible cause; but, such as it was, our hero made the most of it. As he lay there it seemed to deepen; his immersion and his exercise in the salt water had given him an agreeable languor. This presently became a drowsiness which was not less agreeable, and Bernard felt himself going to sleep. There were sounds in the air above his head—sounds of the crunching and rattling of the loose, smooth stones as his neighbors moved about on them; of high-pitched French voices exchanging colloquial cries; of the plash of the bathers in the distant water, and the short, soft breaking of the waves. But these things came to his ears more vaguely and remotely, and at last they faded away. Bernard enjoyed half an hour of that light and easy slumber which is apt to overtake idle people in recumbent attitudes in the open air on August afternoons. It brought with it an exquisite sense of rest, and the rest was not spoiled by the fact that it was animated by a charming dream. Dreams are vague things, and this one had the defects of its species; but it was somehow concerned with the image of a young lady whom Bernard had formerly known, and who had beautiful eyes, into which—in the dream—he found himself looking. He waked up to find himself looking into the crown of his hat, which had been resting on the bridge of his nose. He removed it, and half raised himself, resting on his elbow and preparing to taste, in another position, of a little more of that exquisite rest of which mention has just been made. The world about him was still amusing and charming; the chatter of his companions, losing itself in the large sea-presence, the plash of the divers and swimmers, the deep blue of the ocean and the silvery white of the cliff, had that striking air of indifference to the fact that his mind had been absent from them which we are apt to find in mundane things on emerging from a nap. The same people were sitting near him on the beach—the same, and yet not quite the same. He found himself noticing a person whom he had not noticed before—a young lady, who was seated in a low portable chair, some dozen yards off, with her eyes bent upon a book. Her head was in shade; her large parasol made, indeed, an awning for her whole person, which in this way, in the quiet attitude of perusal, seemed to abstract itself from the glare and murmur of the beach. The clear shadow of her umbrella—it was lined with blue—was deep upon her face; but it was not deep enough to prevent Bernard from recognizing a profile that he knew. He suddenly sat upright, with an intensely quickened vision. Was he dreaming still, or had he waked? In a moment he felt that he was acutely awake; he heard her, across the interval, turn the page of her book. For a single instant, as she did so, she looked with level brows at the glittering ocean; then, lowering her eyes, she went on with her reading. In this barely perceptible movement he saw Angela Vivian; it was wonderful how well he remembered her. She was evidently reading very seriously; she was much interested in her book. She was alone; Bernard looked about for her mother, but Mrs. Vivian was not in sight. By this time Bernard had become aware that he was agitated; the exquisite rest of a few moments before had passed away. His agitation struck him as unreasonable; in a few minutes he made up his mind that it was absurd. He had done her an injury—yes; but as she sat there losing herself in a French novel—Bernard could see it was a French novel—he could not make out that she was the worse for it. It had not affected her appearance; Miss Vivian was still a handsome girl. Bernard hoped she would not look toward him or recognize him; he wished to look at her at his ease; to think it over; to make up his mind. The idea of meeting Angela Vivian again had often come into his thoughts; I may, indeed, say that it was a tolerably famil-iar presence there; but the fact, nevertheless, now presented itself with all the violence of an accident for which he was totally unprepared. He had often asked himself what he should say to her, how he should carry himself, and how he should probably find the young lady; but, with whatever in-genuity he might at the moment have answered these ques-tions, his intelligence at present felt decidedly overtaxed. She was a very pretty girl to whom he had done a wrong; this was the final attitude into which, with a good deal of prelim-inary shifting and wavering, she had settled in his recollec-tion. The wrong was a right, doubtless, from certain points of view; but from the girl's own it could only seem an injury to which its having been inflicted by a clever young man with whom she had been on agreeable terms, necessarily added a touch of baseness.

In every disadvantage that a woman suffers at the hands of a man, there is inevitably, in what concerns the man, an ele-ment of cowardice. When I say "inevitably," I mean that this is what the woman sees in it. This is what Bernard believed that Angela Vivian saw in the fact that by giving his friend a bad account of her he had prevented her making an opulent marriage. At first he had said to himself that, whether he had held his tongue or spoken, she had already lost her chance; but with time, somehow, this reflection had lost its weight in the scale. It conveyed little re-assurance to his irritated conscience—it had become imponderable and impertinent. At the moment of which I speak it entirely failed to present itself, even for form's sake; and as he sat looking at this superior creature who came back to him out of an episode of his past, he thought of her simply as an unprotected woman toward whom he had been indelicate. It is not an agreeable thing for a delicate man like Bernard Longueville to have to accommodate himself to such an accident, but this is nevertheless what it seemed needful that he should do. If she bore him a grudge he must think it natural; if she had vowed him a hatred he must allow her the comfort of it. He had done the only thing possible, but that made it no better for her. He had wronged her. The circumstances mattered nothing, and as he could not make it up to her, the only reasonable thing was to keep out of her way. He had stepped into her path now, and the proper thing was to step out of it. If it could give her no pleasure to see him again, it could certainly do him no good to see her. He had seen her by this time pretty well—as far as mere seeing went, and as yet, apparently, he was none the worse for that; but his hope that he should himself escape unperceived had now become acute. It is singular that this hope should not have led him instantly to turn his back and move away; but the explanation of his imprudent delay is simply that he wished to see a little more of Miss Vivian. He was unable to bring himself to the point. Those clever things that he might have said to her quite faded away. The only good taste was to take himself off, and spare her the trouble of inventing civilities that she could not feel. And yet he continued to sit there from moment to moment, arrested, detained, fascinated, by the accident of her not looking round—of her having let him watch her so long. She turned another page, and another, and her reading absorbed her still. He was so near her that he could have touched her dress with the point of his umbrella. At last she raised her eyes and rested them a while on the blue horizon, straight in front of her, but as yet without turning them aside. This, however, augmented the danger of her doing so, and Bernard, with a good deal of an effort, rose to his feet. The effort, doubtless, kept the movement from being either as light or as swift as it might have been, and it vaguely attracted his neighbor's attention. She turned her head and glanced at him, with a glance that evidently expected but to touch him and pass. It touched him, and it was on the point of passing; then it suddenly checked itself; she had recognized him. She looked at him, straight and open-eyed, out of the shadow of her parasol, and Bernard stood there—motionless now—receiving her gaze. How long it lasted need not be narrated. It was probably a matter of a few seconds, but to Bernard it seemed a little eternity. He met her eyes, he looked straight into her face; now that she had seen him he could do nothing else. Bernard's little eternity, however, came to an end; Miss Vivian dropped her eyes upon her book again. She let them rest upon it only a moment; then she closed it and slowly rose from her chair, turning away from Bernard. He still stood looking at her—stupidly, foolishly, helplessly enough, as it seemed to him; no sign of recognition had been exchanged. Angela Vivian hesitated a minute; she now had her back turned to him, and he fancied her light, flexible figure was agitated by her indecision. She looked along the sunny beach which stretched its shallow curve to where the little bay ended and the white wall of the cliffs began. She looked down toward the sea, and up toward the little Casino which was perched on a low embankment, communicating with the beach at two or three points by a short flight of steps. Bernard saw—or supposed he saw—that she was asking herself whither she had best turn to avoid him. He had not blushed when she looked at him—he had rather turned a little pale; but he blushed now, for it really seemed odious to have literally driven the poor girl to bay. Miss Vivian decided to take refuge in the Casino, and she passed along one of the little pathways of planks that were laid here and there across the beach, and directed herself to the nearest flight of steps. Before she had gone two paces a complete change came over Bernard's feeling; his only wish now was to speak to her—to explain—to tell her he would go away. There was another row of steps at a short distance behind him; he rapidly ascended them and reached the little terrace of the Casino. Miss Vivian stood there; she was apparently hesitating again which way to turn. Bernard came straight up to her, with a gallant smile and a greeting. The comparison is a coarse one, but he felt that he was taking the bull by the horns. Angela Vivian stood watching him arrive.

"You did n't recognize me," he said, "and your not recognizing me made me—made me hesitate."

For a moment she said nothing, and then—

"You are more timid than you used to be!" she answered.

He could hardly have said what expression he had expected to find in her face; his apprehension had, perhaps, not painted her obtrusively pale and haughty, aggressively cold and stern; but it had figured something different from the look he encountered. Miss Vivian was simply blushing—that was what Bernard mainly perceived; he saw that her surprise had been extreme—complete. Her blush was re-assuring; it contradicted the idea of impatient resentment, and Bernard took some satisfaction in noting that it was prolonged.

"Yes, I am more timid than I used to be," he said.

In spite of her blush, she continued to look at him very directly; but she had always done that—she always met one's eye; and Bernard now instantly found all the beauty that he had ever found before in her pure, unevasive glance.

"I don't know whether I am more brave," she said; "but I must tell the truth—I instantly recognized you."

"You gave no sign!"

"I supposed I gave a striking one—in getting up and going away."

"Ah!" said Bernard, "as I say, I am more timid than I was, and I did n't venture to interpret that as a sign of recognition."

"It was a sign of surprise."

"Not of pleasure!" said Bernard. He felt this to be a venturesome, and from the point of view of taste perhaps a reprehensible, remark; but he made it because he was now feeling his ground, and it seemed better to make it gravely than with assumed jocosity.

"Great surprises are to me never pleasures," Angela answered; "I am not fond of shocks of any kind. The pleasure is another matter. I have not yet got over my surprise."

"If I had known you were here, I would have written to you beforehand," said Bernard, laughing.

Miss Vivian, beneath her expanded parasol, gave a little shrug of her shoulders.

"Even that would have been a surprise."

"You mean a shock, eh? Did you suppose I was dead?"

Now, at last, she lowered her eyes, and her blush slowly died away.

"I knew nothing about it."

"Of course you could n't know, and we are all mortal. It was natural that you should n't expect—simply on turning your head—to find me lying on the pebbles at Blanquais-les-Galets. You were a great surprise to me, as well; but I differ from you—I like surprises."

"It is rather refreshing to hear that one is a surprise," said the girl.

"Especially when in that capacity one is liked!" Bernard exclaimed.

"I don't say that—because such sensations pass away. I am now beginning to get over mine."

The light mockery of her tone struck him as the echo of an unforgotten air. He looked at her a moment, and then he said—

"You are not changed; I find you quite the same."

"I am sorry for that!" And she turned away.

"What are you doing?" he asked. "Where are you going?"

She looked about her, without answering, up and down the little terrace. The Casino at Blanquais was a much more modest place of reunion than the Conversation-house at Baden-Baden. It was a small, low structure of brightly painted wood, containing but three or four rooms, and furnished all along its front with a narrow covered gallery, which offered a delusive shelter from the rougher moods of the fine, fresh weather. It was somewhat rude and shabby—the subscription for the season was low—but it had a simple picturesqueness. Its little terrace was a very convenient place for a stroll, and the great view of the ocean and of the marble-white crags that

formed the broad gate-way of the shallow bay, was a sufficient compensation for the absence of luxuries. There were a
few people sitting in the gallery, and a few others scattered
upon the terrace; but the pleasure-seekers of Blanquais were,
for the most part, immersed in the salt water or disseminated
on the grassy downs.

"I am looking for my mother," said Angela Vivian.

"I hope your mother is well."

"Very well, thank you."

"May I help you to look for her?" Bernard asked.

Her eyes paused in their quest, and rested a moment upon
her companion.

"She is not here," she said presently. "She has gone home."

"What do you call home?" Bernard demanded.

"The sort of place that we always call home; a bad little
house that we have taken for a month."

"Will you let me come and see it?"

"It 's nothing to see."

Bernard hesitated a moment.

"Is that a refusal?"

"I should never think of giving it so fine a name."

"There would be nothing fine in forbidding me your door.
Don't think that!" said Bernard, with rather a forced laugh.

It was difficult to know what the girl thought; but she said,
in a moment—

"We shall be very happy to see you. I am going home."

"May I walk with you so far?" asked Bernard.

"It is not far; it 's only three minutes." And Angela moved
slowly to the gate of the Casino.

XX

BERNARD walked beside her, and for some moments nothing was said between them. As the silence continued, he became aware of it, and it vexed him that she should leave certain things unsaid. She had asked him no question—neither whence he had come, nor how long he would stay, nor what had happened to him since they parted. He wished to see whether this was intention or accident. He was already complaining to himself that she expressed no interest in him, and he was perfectly aware that this was a ridiculous feeling. He had come to speak to her in order to tell her that he was going away, and yet, at the end of five minutes, he had asked leave to come and see her. This sudden gyration of mind was grotesque, and Bernard knew it; but, nevertheless, he had an immense expectation that, if he should give her time, she would manifest some curiosity as to his own situation. He tried to give her time; he held his tongue; but she continued to say nothing. They passed along a sort of winding lane, where two or three fishermen's cottages, with old brown nets suspended on the walls and drying in the sun, stood open to the road, on the other side of which was a patch of salt-looking grass, browsed by a donkey that was not fastidious.

"It 's so long since we parted, and we have so much to say to each other!" Bernard exclaimed at last, and he accompanied this declaration with a laugh much more spontaneous than the one he had given a few moments before.

It might have gratified him, however, to observe that his companion appeared to see no ground for joking in the idea that they should have a good deal to say to each other.

"Yes, it 's a long time since we spent those pleasant weeks at Baden," she rejoined. "Have you been there again?"

This was a question, and though it was a very simple one, Bernard was charmed with it.

"I would n't go back for the world!" he said. "And you?"

"Would I go back? Oh yes; I thought it so agreeable."

With this he was less pleased; he had expected the traces of resentment, and he was actually disappointed at not finding them. But here was the little house of which his companion had spoken, and it seemed, indeed, a rather bad one. That is, it was one of those diminutive structures which are known at French watering-places as "chalets," and, with an exiguity of furniture, are let for the season to families that pride themselves upon their powers of contraction. This one was a very humble specimen of its class, though it was doubtless a not inadequate abode for two quiet and frugal women. It had a few inches of garden, and there were flowers in pots in the open windows, where some extremely fresh white curtains were gently fluttering in the breath of the neighboring ocean. The little door stood wide open.

"This is where we live," said Angela; and she stopped and laid her hand upon the little garden-gate.

"It 's very fair," said Bernard. "I think it 's better than the pastry-cook's at Baden."

They stood there, and she looked over the gate at the geraniums. She did not ask him to come in; but, on the other hand, keeping the gate closed, she made no movement to leave him. The Casino was now quite out of sight, and the whole place was perfectly still. Suddenly, turning her eyes upon Bernard with a certain strange inconsequence—

"I have not seen you here before," she observed.

He gave a little laugh.

"I suppose it 's because I only arrived this morning. I think that if I had been here you would have noticed me."

"You arrived this morning?"

"Three or four hours ago. So, if the remark were not in questionable taste, I should say we had not lost time."

"You may say what you please," said Angela, simply. "Where did you come from?"

Interrogation, now it had come, was most satisfactory, and Bernard was glad to believe that there was an element of the unexpected in his answer.

"From California."

"You came straight from California to this place?"

"I arrived at Havre only yesterday."

"And why did you come here?"

"It would be graceful of me to be able to answer—'Because I knew you were here.' But unfortunately I did not know it.

It was a mere chance; or rather, I feel like saying it was an inspiration."

Angela looked at the geraniums again.

"It was very singular," she said. "We might have been in so many places besides this one. And you might have come to so many places besides this one."

"It is all the more singular, that one of the last persons I saw in America was your charming friend Blanche, who married Gordon Wright. She did n't tell me you were here."

"She had no reason to know it," said the girl. "She is not my friend—as you are her husband's friend."

"Ah no, I don't suppose that. But she might have heard from you."

"She does n't hear from us. My mother used to write to her for a while after she left Europe, but she has given it up." She paused a moment, and then she added—"Blanche is too silly!"

Bernard noted this, wondering how it bore upon his theory of a spiteful element in his companion. Of course Blanche was silly; but, equally of course, this young lady's perception of it was quickened by Blanche's having married a rich man whom she herself might have married.

"Gordon does n't think so," Bernard said.

Angela looked at him a moment.

"I am very glad to hear it," she rejoined, gently.

"Yes, it is very fortunate."

"Is he well?" the girl asked. "Is he happy?"

"He has all the air of it."

"I am very glad to hear it," she repeated. And then she moved the latch of the gate and passed in. At the same moment her mother appeared in the open door-way. Mrs. Vivian had apparently been summoned by the sound of her daughter's colloquy with an unrecognized voice, and when she saw Bernard she gave a sharp little cry of surprise. Then she stood gazing at him.

Since the dispersion of the little party at Baden-Baden he had not devoted much meditation to this conscientious gentlewoman who had been so tenderly anxious to establish her daughter properly in life; but there had been in his mind a tacit assumption that if Angela deemed that he had played her a trick Mrs. Vivian's view of his conduct was not more charitable. He felt that he must have seemed to her very unkind, and that in so far as a well-regulated conscience permitted the exercise of unpractical passions, she honored him with a superior detestation. The instant he beheld her on her threshold this conviction rose to the surface of his consciousness and made him feel that now, at least, his hour had come.

"It is Mr. Longueville, whom we met at Baden," said Angela to her mother, gravely.

Mrs. Vivian began to smile, and stepped down quickly toward the gate.

"Ah, Mr. Longueville," she murmured, "it 's so long—it 's so pleasant—it 's so strange—"

And suddenly she stopped, still smiling. Her smile had an odd intensity; she was trembling a little, and Bernard, who was prepared for hissing scorn, perceived with a deep, an almost violent, surprise, a touching agitation, an eager friendliness.

"Yes, it 's very long," he said; "it 's very pleasant. I have only just arrived; I met Miss Vivian."

"And you are not coming in?" asked Angela's mother, very graciously.

"Your daughter has not asked me!" said Bernard.

"Ah, my dearest," murmured Mrs. Vivian, looking at the girl.

Her daughter returned her glance, and then the elder lady paused again, and simply began to smile at Bernard, who recognized in her glance that queer little intimation—shy and cautious, yet perfectly discernible—of a desire to have a private understanding with what he felt that she mentally termed his better nature, which he had more than once perceived at Baden-Baden.

"Ah no, she has not asked me," Bernard repeated, laughing gently.

Then Angela turned her eyes upon him, and the expression of those fine organs was strikingly agreeable. It had, moreover, the merit of being easily interpreted; it said very plainly, "Please don't insist, but leave me alone." And it said it not at all sharply—very gently and pleadingly. Bernard found himself understanding it so well that he literally blushed with intelligence.

"Don't you come to the Casino in the evening, as you used to come to the Kursaal?" he asked.

Mrs. Vivian looked again at her daughter, who had passed into the door-way of the cottage; then she said—

"We will go this evening."

"I shall look for you eagerly," Bernard rejoined. "*Auf wiedersehen*, as we used to say at Baden!"

Mrs. Vivian waved him a response over the gate, her daughter gave him a glance from the threshold, and he took his way back to his inn.

He awaited the evening with great impatience; he fancied he had made a discovery, and he wished to confirm it. The discovery was that his idea that she bore him a grudge, that she was conscious of an injury, that he was associated in her mind with a wrong, had all been a morbid illusion. She had forgiven, she had forgotten, she did n't care, she had possibly never cared! This, at least, was his theory now, and he longed for a little more light upon it. His old sense of her being a complex and intricate girl had, in that quarter of an hour of talk with her, again become lively, so that he was not absolutely sure his apprehensions had been vain. But, with his quick vision of things, he had got the impression, at any rate, that she had no vulgar resentment of any slight he might have put upon her, or any disadvantage he might have caused her. Her feeling about such a matter would be large and original. Bernard desired to see more of that, and in the evening, in fact, it seemed to him that he did so.

The terrace of the Casino was far from offering the brilliant spectacle of the promenade in front of the gaming-rooms at Baden. It had neither the liberal illumination, the distinguished frequenters, nor the superior music which formed the attraction of that celebrated spot; but it had a modest animation of its own, in which the starlight on the open sea took the place of clustered lamps, and the mighty resonance of the waves performed the function of an orchestra. Mrs. Vivian made her appearance with her daughter, and Bernard, as he used to do at Baden, chose a corner to place some chairs for them. The crowd was small, for most of the visitors had com-

pressed themselves into one of the rooms, where a shrill operetta was being performed by a strolling troupe. Mrs.
Vivian's visit was a short one; she remained at the Casino less
than half an hour. But Bernard had some talk with Angela.
He sat beside her—her mother was on the other side, talking
with an old French lady whose acquaintance she had made on
the beach. Between Bernard and Angela several things were
said. When his friends went away Bernard walked home with
them. He bade them good-night at the door of their chalet,
and then slowly strolled back to the Casino. The terrace was
nearly empty; every one had gone to listen to the operetta,
the sound of whose contemporary gayety came through the
open, hot-looking windows in little thin quavers and catches.
The ocean was rumbling just beneath; it made a ruder but
richer music. Bernard stood looking at it a moment; then he
went down the steps to the beach. The tide was rather low;
he walked slowly down to the line of the breaking waves. The
sea looked huge and black and simple; everything was vague
in the unassisted darkness. Bernard stood there some time;
there was nothing but the sound and the sharp, fresh smell.
Suddenly he put his hand to his heart; it was beating very
fast. An immense conviction had come over him—abruptly,
then and there—and for a moment he held his breath. It was
like a word spoken in the darkness—he held his breath to
listen. He was in love with Angela Vivian, and his love was a
throbbing passion! He sat down on the stones where he
stood—it filled him with a kind of awe.

XXI

IT FILLED HIM with a kind of awe, and the feeling was by no means agreeable. It was not a feeling to which even a man of Bernard Longueville's easy power of extracting the savour from a sensation could rapidly habituate himself, and for the rest of that night it was far from making of our hero the happy man that a lover just coming to self-consciousness is supposed to be. It was wrong—it was dishonorable—it was impossible—and yet it *was*; it was, as nothing in his own personal experience had ever been. He seemed hitherto to have been living by proxy, in a vision, in reflection—to have been an echo, a shadow, a futile attempt; but this at last was life itself, this was a fact, this was reality. For these things one lived; these were the things that people had died for. Love had been a fable before this—doubtless a very pretty one; and passion had been a literary phrase—employed obviously with considerable effect. But now he stood in a personal relation to these familiar ideas, which gave them a very much keener import; they had laid their hand upon him in the darkness, he felt it upon his shoulder, and he knew by its pressure that it was the hand of destiny. What made this sensation a shock was the element that was mixed with it; the fact that it came not simply and singly, but with an attendant shadow in which it immediately merged and lost itself. It was forbidden fruit—he knew it the instant he had touched it. He felt that he had pledged himself *not* to do just this thing which was gleaming before him so divinely—not to widen the crevice, not to open the door that would flood him with light. Friendship and honor were at stake; they stood at his left hand, as his new-born passion stood already at his right; they claimed him as well, and their grasp had a pressure which might become acutely painful. The soul is a still more tender organism than the body, and it shrinks from the prospect of being subjected to violence. Violence—spiritual violence—was what our luxurious hero feared; and it is not too much to say that as he lingered there by the sea, late into the night, while the gurgitation of the waves grew deeper to his ear, the prospect came to have an element of positive terror. The two

faces of his situation stood confronting each other; it was a rigid, brutal opposition, and Bernard held his breath for a while
with the wonder of what would come of it. He sat a long
time upon the beach; the night grew very cold, but he had
no sense of it. Then he went away and passed before the
Casino again, and wandered through the village. The Casino
was shrouded in darkness and silence, and there was nothing
in the streets of the little town but the salt smell of the sea, a
vague aroma of fish and the distant sound of the breakers.
Little by little, Bernard lost the feeling of having been startled, and began to perceive that he could reason about his
trouble. Trouble it was, though this seems an odd name for
the consciousness of a bright enchantment; and the first thing
that reason, definitely consulted, told him about the matter
was that he had been in love with Angela Vivian any time
these three years. This sapient faculty supplied him with further information; only two or three of the items of which,
however, it is necessary to reproduce. He had been a great
fool—an incredible fool—not to have discovered before this
what was the matter with him! Bernard's sense of his own
shrewdness—always tolerably acute—had never received
such a bruise as this present perception that a great many
things had been taking place in his clever mind without his
clever mind suspecting them. But it little mattered, his reason
went on to declare, what he had suspected or what he might
now feel about it; his present business was to leave Blanquais-
les-Galets at sunrise the next morning and never rest his eyes
upon Angela Vivian again. This was his duty; it had the merit
of being perfectly plain and definite, easily apprehended, and
unattended, as far as he could discover, with the smallest material difficulties. Not only this, reason continued to remark;
but the moral difficulties were equally inconsiderable. He had
never breathed a word of his passion to Miss Vivian—quite
the contrary; he had never committed himself nor given her
the smallest reason to suspect his hidden flame; and he was
therefore perfectly free to turn his back upon her—he could
never incur the reproach of trifling with her affections. Bernard was in that state of mind when it is the greatest of blessings to be saved the distress of choice—to see a straight path
before you and to feel that you have only to follow it. Upon

the straight path I have indicated, he fixed his eyes very hard; of course he would take his departure at the earliest possible hour on the morrow. There was a streak of morning in the eastern sky by the time he knocked for re-admittance at the door of the inn, which was opened to him by a mysterious old woman in a nightcap and meagre accessories, whose identity he failed to ascertain; and he laid himself down to rest— he was very tired—with his attention fastened, as I say, on the idea—on the very image—of departure.

On waking up the next morning, rather late, he found, however, that it had attached itself to a very different object. His vision was filled with the brightness of the delightful fact itself, which seemed to impregnate the sweet morning air and to flutter in the light, fresh breeze that came through his open window from the sea. He saw a great patch of the sea between a couple of red-tiled roofs; it was bluer than any sea had ever been before. He had not slept long—only three or four hours; but he had quite slept off his dread. The shadow had dropped away and nothing was left but the beauty of his love, which seemed to shine in the freshness of the early day. He felt absurdly happy—as if he had discovered El Dorado; quite apart from consequences—he was not thinking of consequences, which of course were another affair—the feeling was intrinsically the finest one he had ever had, and—as a mere feeling—he had not done with it yet. The consideration of consequences could easily be deferred, and there would, meanwhile, be no injury to any one in his extracting, very quietly, a little subjective joy from the state of his heart. He would let the flower bloom for a day before plucking it up by the roots. Upon this latter course he was perfectly resolved, and in view of such an heroic resolution the subjective interlude appeared no more than his just privilege. The project of leaving Blanquais-les-Galets at nine o'clock in the morning dropped lightly from his mind, making no noise as it fell; but another took its place, which had an air of being still more excellent and which consisted of starting off on a long walk and absenting himself for the day. Bernard grasped his stick and wandered away; he climbed the great shoulder of the further cliff and found himself on the level downs. Here there was apparently no obstacle whatever to his walking as far as his fancy should carry him. The summer was still in a splendid mood, and the hot and quiet day—it was a Sunday—seemed to constitute a deep, silent smile on the face of nature. The sea glistened on one side, and the crops ripened on the other; the larks, losing themselves in the dense sunshine, made it ring here and there in undiscoverable spots; this was the only sound save when Bernard, pausing now and then in his walk, found himself hearing far below him, at the base of the cliff, the drawling murmur of a wave. He walked a great many miles and passed through half a dozen of those rude fishing-hamlets, lodged in some sloping hollow of the cliffs, so many of which, of late years, all along the Norman coast, have adorned themselves with a couple of hotels and a row of bathing-machines. He walked so far that the shadows had begun to lengthen before he bethought himself of stopping; the afternoon had come on and had already begun to wane. The grassy downs still stretched before him, shaded here and there with shallow but windless dells. He looked for the softest place and then flung himself down on the grass; he lay there for a long time, thinking of many things. He had determined to give himself up to a day's happiness; it was happiness of a very harmless kind—the satisfaction of thought, the bliss of mere consciousness; but such as it was it did not elude him nor turn bitter in his heart, and the long summer day closed upon him before his spirit, hovering in perpetual circles round the idea of what *might* be, had begun to rest its wing. When he rose to his feet again it was too late to return to Blanquais in the same way that he had come; the evening was at hand, the light was already fading, and the walk he had taken was one which even if he had not felt very tired, he would have thought it imprudent to attempt to repeat in the darkness. He made his way to the nearest village, where he was able to hire a rustic *carriole*, in which primitive conveyance, gaining the high-road, he jogged and jostled through the hours of the evening slowly back to his starting-point. It wanted an hour of midnight by the time he reached his inn, and there was nothing left for him but to go to bed.

He went in the unshaken faith that he should leave Blanquais early on the morrow. But early on the morrow it occurred to him that it would be simply grotesque to go off without taking leave of Mrs. Vivian and her daughter, and offering them some explanation of his intention. He had given them to understand that, so delighted was he to find them there, he would remain at Blanquais at least as long as they. He must have seemed to them wanting in civility, to spend a whole bright Sunday without apparently troubling his head about them, and if the unlucky fact of his being in love with the girl were a reason for doing his duty, it was at least not a reason for being rude. He had not yet come to that—to accepting rudeness as an incident of virtue; it had always been his theory that virtue had the best manners in the world, and he flattered himself at any rate that he could guard his integrity without making himself ridiculous. So, at what he thought a proper hour, in the course of the morning, he retraced his steps along the little lane through which, two days ago, Angela Vivian had shown him the way to her mother's door. At this humble portal he knocked; the windows of the little chalet were open, and the white curtains, behind the flower-pots, were fluttering as he had seen them before. The door was opened by a neat young woman, who informed him very promptly that Madame and Mademoiselle had left Blanquais a couple of hours earlier. They had gone to Paris—yes, very suddenly, taking with them but little luggage, and they had left her—she had the honor of being the *femme de chambre* of *ces dames*—to put up their remaining possessions and follow as soon as possible. On Bernard's expressing surprise and saying that he had supposed them to be fixed at the sea-side for the rest of the season, the femme de chambre, who seemed a very intelligent person, begged to remind him that the season was drawing to a close, that Madame had taken the chalet but for five weeks, only ten days of which period were yet to expire, that *ces dames*, as Monsieur perhaps knew, were great travellers, who had been half over the world and thought nothing of breaking camp at an hour's notice, and that, in fine, Madame might very well have received a telegram summoning her to another part of the country.

"And where have the ladies gone?" asked Bernard.

"For the moment, to Paris."

"And in Paris where have they gone?"

"*Dame, chez elles*—to their house," said the femme de chambre, who appeared to think that Bernard asked too many questions.

But Bernard persisted.

"Where is their house?"

The waiting-maid looked at him from head to foot.

"If Monsieur wishes to write, many of Madame's letters come to her banker," she said, inscrutably.

"And who is her banker?"

"He lives in the Rue de Provence."

"Very good—I will find him out," said our hero, turning away.

The discriminating reader who has been so good as to interest himself in this little narrative will perhaps at this point exclaim with a pardonable consciousness of shrewdness: "Of course he went the next day to the Rue de Provence!" Of course, yes; only as it happens Bernard did nothing of the kind. He did one of the most singular things he ever did in his life—a thing that puzzled him even at the time, and with regard to which he often afterward wondered whence he had drawn the ability for so remarkable a feat—he simply spent a fortnight at Blanquais-les-Galets. It was a very quiet fortnight; he spoke to no one, he formed no relations, he was company to himself. It may be added that he had never found his own company half so good. He struck himself as a reasonable, delicate fellow, who looked at things in such a way as to make him refrain—refrain successfully, that was the point—from concerning himself practically about Angela Vivian. His saying that he would find out the banker in the Rue de Provence had been for the benefit of the femme de chambre, whom he thought rather impertinent; he had really no intention whatever of entering that classic thoroughfare. He took long walks, rambled on the beach, along the base of the cliffs and among the brown sea-caves, and he thought a good deal of certain incidents which have figured at an earlier stage of this narrative. He had forbidden himself the future, as an object of contemplation, and it was therefore a matter of necessity that his imagination should take refuge among the warm and familiar episodes of the past. He wondered why Mrs. Vivian should have left the place so suddenly, and was of course struck with the analogy between this incident and her abrupt departure from Baden. It annoyed him, it troubled him, but it by no means rekindled the alarm he had felt on first perceiving the injured Angela on the beach. That alarm had been quenched by Angela's manner during the hour that followed and during their short talk in the evening. This evening was to be forever memorable, for it had brought with it the revelation which still, at moments, suddenly made Bernard tremble; but it had also brought him the assurance that Angela cared as little as possible for anything that a chance acquaintance might have said about her. It is all the more singular, therefore, that one evening, after he had been at Blanquais a fortnight, a train of thought should suddenly have been set in motion in his mind. It was kindled by no outward occurrence, but by some wandering spark of fancy or of memory, and the immediate effect of it was to startle our hero very much as he had been startled on the evening I have described. The circumstances were the same; he had wandered down to the beach alone, very late, and he stood looking at the duskily-tumbling sea. Suddenly the same voice that had spoken before murmured another phrase in the darkness, and it rang upon his ear for the rest of the night. It startled him, as I have said, at first; then, the next morning, it led him to take his departure for Paris. During the journey it lingered in his ear; he sat in the corner of the railway-carriage with his eyes closed, abstracted, on purpose to prolong the reverberation. If it were not true it was at least, as the Italians have it, *ben trovato*, and it was wonderful how well it bore thinking of. It bears telling less well; but I can at least give a hint of it. The theory that Angela hated him had evaporated in her presence, and another of a very different sort had sprung into being. It fitted a great many of the facts, it explained a great many contradictions, anomalies, mysteries, and it accounted for Miss Vivian's insisting upon her mother's leaving Blanquais at a few hours' notice, even better than the theory of her resentment could have done. At any rate, it obliterated Bernard's scruples very effectually, and led him on his arrival in Paris to repair instantly to the Rue de Provence. This street contains more than one banker, but there is one with whom Bernard deemed Mrs. Vivian most likely to have dealings. He found he had reckoned rightly, and he had no difficulty in procuring her address. Having done so, however, he by no means went immediately to see her; he waited a couple of days—perhaps to give those obliterated scruples I have spoken of a chance to revive. They kept very quiet, and it must be confessed that Bernard took no great pains to recall them to life. After he had been in Paris three days, he knocked at Mrs. Vivian's door.

XXII

I T WAS OPENED by the little waiting-maid whom he had
seen at Blanquais, and who looked at him very hard before
she answered his inquiry.

"You see I have found Mrs. Vivian's dwelling, though you
would n't give me the address," Bernard said to her, smiling.

"Monsieur has put some time to it!" the young woman answered dryly. And she informed him that Madame was at
home, though Mademoiselle, for whom he had not asked,
was not.

Mrs. Vivian occupied a diminutive apartment at the summit of one of the tall white houses which ornament the neighborhood of the Arc de Triomphe. The early days of
September had arrived, but Paris was still a city of absentees.
The weather was warm and charming, and a certain savour of
early autumn in the air was in accord with the somewhat melancholy aspect of the empty streets and closed shutters of this
honorable quarter, where the end of the monumental vistas
seemed to be curtained with a hazy emanation from the
Seine. It was late in the afternoon when Bernard was ushered
into Mrs. Vivian's little high-nestling drawing-room, and a
patch of sunset tints, faintly red, rested softly upon the
gilded wall. Bernard had seen these ladies only in borrowed
and provisional abodes; but here was a place where they
were really living and which was stamped with their tastes,
their habits, their charm. The little *salon* was very elegant;
it contained a multitude of pretty things, and it appeared
to Bernard to be arranged in perfection. The long windows—the ceiling being low, they were really very short—
opened upon one of those solid balconies, occupying the
width of the apartment, which are often in Paris a compensation for living up five flights of stairs, and this balcony
was filled with flowers and cushions. Bernard stepped out
upon it to await the coming of Mrs. Vivian, and, as she
was not quick to appear, he had time to see that his friends
enjoyed a magnificent view. They looked up at the trium-
phal Arch, which presented itself at a picturesque angle,
and near the green tree-tops of the Champs Elysées, be-

yond which they caught a broad gleam of the Seine and a glimpse, blue in the distance, of the great towers of Notre Dame. The whole vast city lay before them and beneath them, with its ordered brilliancy and its mingled aspect of compression and expansion; and yet the huge Parisian murmur died away before it reached Mrs. Vivian's sky-parlor, which seemed to Bernard the brightest and quietest little habitation he had ever known.

His hostess came rustling in at last; she seemed agitated; she knocked over with the skirt of her dress a little gilded chair which was reflected in the polished *parquet* as in a sheet of looking-glass. Mrs. Vivian had a fixed smile—she hardly knew what to say.

"I found your address at the banker's," said Bernard. "Your maid, at Blanquais, refused to give it to me."

Mrs. Vivian gave him a little look—there was always more or less of it in her face—which seemed equivalent to an entreaty that her interlocutor should spare her.

"Maids are so strange," she murmured; "especially the French!"

It pleased Bernard for the moment not to spare her, though he felt a sort of delight of kindness for her.

"Your going off from Blanquais so suddenly, without leaving me any explanation, any clue, any message of any sort— made me feel at first as if you did n't wish that I should look you up. It reminded me of the way you left Baden—do you remember?—three years ago."

"Baden was so charming—but one could n't stay forever," said Mrs. Vivian.

"I had a sort of theory one could. Our life was so pleasant that it seemed a shame to break the spell, and if no one had moved I am sure we might be sitting there now."

Mrs. Vivian stared, still with her little fixed smile.

"I think we should have had bad weather."

"Very likely," said Bernard, laughing. "Nature would have grown jealous of our good-humor—of our tranquil happiness. And after all, here we are together again—that is, some of us. But I have only my own audacity to thank for it. I was quite free to believe that you were not at all pleased to see me re-appear—and it is only because I am not easy to discourage—am indeed probably a rather impudent fellow—that I have ventured to come here to-day."

"I am very glad to see you re-appear, Mr. Longueville," Mrs. Vivian declared with the accent of veracity.

"It was your daughter's idea, then, running away from Blanquais?"

Mrs. Vivian lowered her eyes.

"We were obliged to go to Fontainebleau. We have but just come back. I thought of writing to you," she softly added.

"Ah, what pleasure that would have given me!"

"I mean, to tell you where we were, and that we should have been so happy to see you."

"I thank you for the intention. I suppose your daughter would n't let you carry it out."

"Angela is so peculiar," Mrs. Vivian said, simply.

"You told me that the first time I saw you."

"Yes, at Siena," said Mrs. Vivian.

"I am glad to hear you speak frankly of that place!"

"Perhaps it 's better," Mrs. Vivian murmured. She got up and went to the window; then stepping upon the balcony, she looked down a moment into the street. "She will come back in a moment," she said, coming into the room again. "She has gone to see a friend who lives just beside us. We don't mind about Siena now," she added, softly.

Bernard understood her—understood this to be a retraction of the request she had made of him at Baden.

"Dear little woman," he said to himself, "she wants to marry her daughter still—only now she wants to marry her to me!"

He wished to show her that he understood her, and he was on the point of seizing her hand, to do he did n't know what—to hold it, to press it, to kiss it—when he heard the sharp twang of the bell at the door of the little apartment.

Mrs. Vivian fluttered away.

"It 's Angela," she cried, and she stood there waiting and listening, smiling at Bernard, with her handkerchief pressed to her lips.

In a moment the girl came into the drawing-room, but on

seeing Bernard she stopped, with her hand on the door-knob. Her mother went to her and kissed her.

"It's Mr. Longueville, dearest—he has found us out."

"Found us out?" repeated Angela, with a little laugh. "What a singular expression!"

She was blushing as she had blushed when she first saw him at Blanquais. She seemed to Bernard now to have a great and peculiar brightness—something she had never had before.

"I certainly have been looking for you," he said. "I was greatly disappointed when I found you had taken flight from Blanquais."

"Taken flight?" She repeated his words as she had repeated her mother's. "That is also a strange way of speaking!"

"I don't care what I say," said Bernard, "so long as I make you understand that I have wanted very much to see you again, and that I have wondered every day whether I might venture—"

"I don't know why you should n't venture!" she interrupted, giving her little laugh again. "We are not so terrible, are we, mamma?—that is, when once you have climbed our five flights of stairs."

"I came up very fast," said Bernard, "and I find your apartment magnificent."

"Mr. Longueville must come again, must he not, dear?" asked mamma.

"I shall come very often, with your leave," Bernard declared.

"It will be immensely kind," said Angela, looking away.

"I am not sure that you will think it that."

"I don't know what you are trying to prove," said Angela; "first that we ran away from you, and then that we are not nice to our visitors."

"Oh no, not that!" Bernard exclaimed; "for I assure you I shall not care how cold you are with me."

She walked away toward another door, which was masked with a curtain that she lifted.

"I am glad to hear that, for it gives me courage to say that I am very tired, and that I beg you will excuse me."

She glanced at him a moment over her shoulder; then she passed out, dropping the curtain.

Bernard stood there face to face with Mrs. Vivian, whose eyes seemed to plead with him more than ever. In his own there was an excited smile.

"Please don't mind that," she murmured. "I know it 's true that she is tired."

"Mind it, dear lady?" cried the young man. "I delight in it. It 's just what I like."

"Ah, she 's very peculiar!" sighed Mrs. Vivian.

"She is strange—yes. But I think I understand her a little."

"You must come back to-morrow, then."

"I hope to have many to-morrows!" cried Bernard as he took his departure.

XXIII

A ND HE HAD THEM in fact. He called the next day at the
same hour, and he found the mother and the daughter
together in their pretty *salon*. Angela was very gentle and gracious; he suspected Mrs. Vivian had given her a tender little
lecture upon the manner in which she had received him the
day before. After he had been there five minutes, Mrs. Vivian
took a decanter of water that was standing upon a table and
went out on the balcony to irrigate her flowers. Bernard
watched her a while from his place in the room; then she
moved along the balcony and out of sight. Some ten minutes
elapsed without her re-appearing, and then Bernard stepped
to the threshold of the window and looked for her. She was
not there, and as he came and took his seat near Angela again,
he announced, rather formally, that Mrs. Vivian had passed
back into one of the other windows.

Angela was silent a moment—then she said—

"Should you like me to call her?"

She *was* very peculiar—that was very true; yet Bernard
held to his declaration of the day before that he now understood her a little.

"No, I don't desire it," he said. "I wish to see you alone; I
have something particular to say to you."

She turned her face toward him, and there was something
in its expression that showed him that he looked to her more
serious than he had ever looked. He sat down again; for some
moments he hesitated to go on.

"You frighten me," she said laughing; and in spite of her
laugh this was obviously true.

"I assure you my state of mind is anything but formidable. I
am afraid of *you*, on the contrary; I am humble and apologetic."

"I am sorry for that," said Angela. "I particularly dislike
receiving apologies, even when I know what they are for.
What yours are for, I can't imagine."

"You don't dislike me—you don't hate me?" Bernard suddenly broke out.

"You don't ask me that humbly. Excuse me therefore if I
say I have other, and more practical, things to do."

"You despise me," said Bernard.

"That is not humble either, for you seem to insist upon it."

"It would be after all a way of thinking of me, and I have a reason for wishing you to do that."

"I remember very well that you used to have a reason for everything. It was not always a good one."

"This one is excellent," said Bernard, gravely. "I have been in love with you for three years."

She got up slowly, turning away.

"Is that what you wished to say to me?"

She went toward the open window, and he followed her.

"I hope it does n't offend you. I don't say it lightly—it 's not a piece of gallantry. It 's the very truth of my being. I did n't know it till lately—strange as that may seem. I loved you long before I knew it—before I ventured or presumed to know it. I was thinking of you when I seemed to myself to be thinking of other things. It is very strange—there are things in it I don't understand. I travelled over the world, I tried to interest, to divert myself; but at bottom it was a perfect failure. To see you again—that was what I wanted. When I saw you last month at Blanquais I knew it; then everything became clear. It was the answer to the riddle. I wished to read it very clearly—I wished to be sure; therefore I did n't follow you immediately. I questioned my heart—I cross-questioned it. It has borne the examination, and now I am sure. I am very sure. I love you as my life—I beg you to listen to me!"

She had listened—she had listened intently, looking straight out of the window and without moving.

"You have seen very little of me," she said, presently, turning her illuminated eye on him.

"I have seen enough," Bernard added, smiling. "You must remember that at Baden I saw a good deal of you."

"Yes, but that did n't make you like me. I don't understand."

Bernard stood there a moment, frowning, with his eyes lowered.

"I can imagine that. But I think I can explain."

"Don't explain now," said Angela. "You have said enough; explain some other time." And she went out on the balcony.

Bernard, of course, in a moment was beside her, and, disregarding her injunction, he began to explain.

"I thought I disliked you—but I have come to the conclusion it was just the contrary. In reality I was in love with you. I had been so from the first time I saw you—when I made that sketch of you at Siena."

"That in itself needs an explanation. I was not at all nice then—I was very rude, very perverse. I was horrid!"

"Ah, you admit it!" cried Bernard, with a sort of quick elation.

She had been pale, but she suddenly blushed.

"Your own conduct was singular, as I remember it. It was not exactly agreeable."

"Perhaps not; but at least it was meant to be. I did n't know how to please you then, and I am far from supposing that I have learned now. But I entreat you to give me a chance."

She was silent a while; her eyes wandered over the great prospect of Paris.

"Do you know how you can please me now?" she said, at last. "By leaving me alone."

Bernard looked at her a moment, then came straight back into the drawing-room and took his hat.

"You see I avail myself of the first chance. But I shall come back to-morrow."

"I am greatly obliged to you for what you have said. Such a speech as that deserves to be listened to with consideration. You may come back to-morrow," Angela added.

On the morrow, when he came back, she received him alone.

"How did you know, at Baden, that I did n't like you?" he asked, as soon as she would allow him.

She smiled, very gently.

"You assured me yesterday that you did like me."

"I mean that I supposed I did n't. How did you know that?"

"I can only say that I observed."

"You must have observed very closely, for, superficially, I rather had the air of admiring you," said Bernard.

"It was very superficial."

"You don't mean that; for, after all, that is just what my admiration, my interest in you, were not. They were deep, they were latent. They were not superficial—they were subterranean."

"You are contradicting yourself, and I am perfectly consistent," said Angela. "Your sentiments were so well hidden that I supposed I displeased you."

"I remember that at Baden, you used to contradict yourself," Bernard answered.

"You have a terrible memory!"

"Don't call it terrible, for it sees everything now in a charming light—in the light of this understanding that we have at last arrived at, which seems to shine backward—to shine full on those Baden days."

"Have we at last arrived at an understanding?" she asked, with a grave directness which Bernard thought the most beautiful thing he had ever seen.

"It only depends upon you," he declared; and then he broke out again into a protestation of passionate tenderness. "Don't put me off this time," he cried. "You have had time to think about it; you have had time to get over the surprise, the shock. I love you, and I offer you everything that belongs to me in this world." As she looked at him with her dark, clear eyes, weighing this precious vow and yet not committing herself—"Ah, you don't forgive me!" he murmured.

She gazed at him with the same solemn brightness.

"What have I to forgive you?"

This question seemed to him enchanting. He reached forward and took her hands, and if Mrs. Vivian had come in she would have seen him kneeling at her daughter's feet.

But Mrs. Vivian remained in seclusion, and Bernard saw her only the next time he came.

"I am very happy, because I think my daughter is happy," she said.

"And what do you think of me?"

"I think you are very clever. You must promise me to be very good to her."

"I am clever enough to promise that."

"I think you are good enough to keep it," said Mrs. Vivian. She looked as happy as she said, and her happiness gave her a communicative, confidential tendency. "It is very strange how things come about—how the wheel turns round," she went on. "I suppose there is no harm in my telling you that I believe she always cared for you."

"Why did n't you tell me before?" said Bernard, with almost filial reproachfulness.

"How could I? I don't go about the world offering my daughter to people—especially to indifferent people."

"At Baden you did n't think I was indifferent. You were afraid of my not being indifferent enough."

Mrs. Vivian colored.

"Ah, at Baden I was a little too anxious!"

"Too anxious I should n't speak to your daughter!" said Bernard, laughing.

"At Baden," Mrs. Vivian went on, "I had views. But I have n't any now—I have given them up."

"That makes your acceptance of me very flattering!" Bernard exclaimed, laughing still more gaily.

"I have something better," said Mrs. Vivian, laying her finger-tips on his arm. "I have confidence."

Bernard did his best to encourage this gracious sentiment, and it seemed to him that there was something yet to be done to implant it more firmly in Angela's breast.

"I have a confession to make to you," he said to her one day. "I wish you would listen to it."

"Is it something very horrible?" Angela asked.

"Something very horrible indeed. I once did you an injury."

"An injury?" she repeated, in a tone which seemed to reduce the offence to contemptible proportions by simple vagueness of mind about it.

"I don't know what to call it," said Bernard. "A poor service—an ill-turn."

Angela gave a shrug, or rather an imitation of a shrug; for she was not a shrugging person.

"I never knew it."

"I misrepresented you to Gordon Wright," Bernard went on.

"Why do you speak to me of him?" she asked rather sadly.

"Does it displease you?"

She hesitated a little.

"Yes, it displeases me. If your confession has anything to do with him, I would rather not hear it."

Bernard returned to the subject another time—he had plenty of opportunities. He spent a portion of every day in the company of these dear women; and these days were the happiest of his life. The autumn weather was warm and soothing, the *quartier* was still deserted, and the uproar of the great city, which seemed a hundred miles away, reached them through the dense October air with a softened and muffled sound. The evenings, however, were growing cool, and before long they lighted the first fire of the season in Mrs. Vivian's heavily draped little chimney-piece. On this occasion Bernard sat there with Angela, watching the bright crackle of the wood and feeling that the charm of winter nights had begun. These two young persons were alone together in the gathering dusk; it was the hour before dinner, before the lamp had been lighted.

"I insist upon making you my confession," said Bernard. "I shall be very unhappy until you let me do it."

"Unhappy? You are the happiest of men."

"I lie upon roses, if you will; but this memory, this remorse, is a folded rose-leaf. I was completely mistaken about you at Baden; I thought all manner of evil of you—or at least I said it."

"Men are dull creatures," said Angela.

"I think they are. So much so that, as I look back upon that time, there are some things I don't understand even now."

"I don't see why you should look back. People in our position are supposed to look forward."

"You don't like those Baden days yourself," said Bernard. "You don't like to think of them."

"What a wonderful discovery!"

Bernard looked at her a moment in the brightening firelight.

"What part was it you tried to play there?"

Angela shook her head.

"Men are dull creatures."

"I have already granted that, and I am eating humble pie in asking for an explanation."

"What did you say of me?" Angela asked, after a silence.

"I said you were a coquette. Remember that I am simply historical."

She got up and stood in front of the fire, having her hand on the chimney-piece and looking down at the blaze. For some moments she remained there. Bernard could not see her face.

"I said you were a dangerous woman to marry," he went on deliberately. "I said it because I thought it. I gave Gordon an opinion about you—it was a very unfavorable one. I could n't make you out—I thought you were playing a double part. I believed that you were ready to marry him, and yet I saw—I thought I saw—" and Bernard paused again.

"What did you see?" and Angela turned toward him.

"That you were encouraging me—playing with me."

"And you did n't like that?"

"I liked it immensely—for myself! But did n't like it for Gordon; and I must do myself the justice to say that I thought more of him than of myself."

"You were an excellent friend," said Angela, simply.

"I believe I was. And I am so still," Bernard added.

She shook her head sadly.

"Poor Mr. Wright!"

"He is a dear good fellow," said Bernard.

"Thoroughly good, and dear, doubtless to his wife, the affectionate Blanche."

"You don't like him—you don't like her," said Bernard.

"Those are two very different matters. I am very sorry for Mr. Wright."

"You need n't be that. He is doing very well."

"So you have already informed me. But I am sorry for him, all the same."

"That does n't answer my question," Bernard exclaimed, with a certain irritation. "What part were you playing?"

"What part do you think?"

"Have n't I told you I gave it up, long ago?"

Angela stood with her back to the fire, looking at him; her hands were locked behind her.

"Did it ever strike you that my position at Baden was a charming one?—knowing that I had been handed over to you to be put under the microscope—like an insect with a pin stuck through it!"

"How in the world did you know it? I thought we were particularly careful."

"How can a woman help knowing such a thing? She guesses it—she discovers it by instinct; especially if she be a proud woman."

"Ah," said Bernard, "if pride is a source of information, you must be a prodigy of knowledge!"

"I don't know that you are particularly humble!" the girl retorted. "The meekest and most submissive of her sex would not have consented to have such a bargain as that made about her—such a trick played upon her!"

"My dearest Angela, it was no bargain—no trick!" Bernard interposed.

"It was a clumsy trick—it was a bad bargain!" she declared. "At any rate I hated it—I hated the idea of your pretending to pass judgment upon me; of your having come to Baden for the purpose. It was as if Mr. Wright had been buying a horse and you had undertaken to put me through my paces!"

"I undertook nothing—I declined to undertake."

"You certainly made a study of me—and I was determined you should get your lesson wrong. I determined to embarrass, to mislead, to defeat you. Or rather, I did n't determine; I simply obeyed a natural impulse of self-defence—the impulse to evade the fierce light of criticism. I wished to put you in the wrong."

"You did it all very well. You put me admirably in the wrong."

"The only justification for my doing it at all was my doing it well," said Angela.

"You were justified then! You must have hated me fiercely."

She turned her back to him and stood looking at the fire again.

"Yes, there are some things that I did that can be accounted for only by an intense aversion."

She said this so naturally that in spite of a certain theory that was touched upon a few pages back, Bernard was a good deal bewildered. He rose from the sofa where he had been lounging and went and stood beside her a moment. Then he passed his arm round her waist and murmured an almost timorous—

"Really?"

"I don't know what you are trying to make me say!" she answered.

He looked down at her for a moment as he held her close to him.

"I don't see, after all, why I should wish to make you say it. It would only make my remorse more acute."

She was musing, with her eyes on the fire, and for a moment she made no answer; then, as if her attention were returning—

"Are you still talking about your remorse?" she asked.

"You see I put it very strongly."

"That I was a horrid creature?"

"That you were not a woman to marry."

"Ah, my poor Bernard," said Angela, "I can't attempt to prove to you that you are not inconsistent!"

The month of September drew to a close, and she consented to fix a day for their wedding. The last of October was the moment selected, and the selection was almost all that was wanting to Bernard's happiness. I say "almost," for there was a solitary spot in his consciousness which felt numb and dead—unpervaded by the joy with which the rest of his spirit seemed to thrill and tingle. The removal of this hard grain in the sweet savour of life was needed to complete his felicity. Bernard felt that he had made the necessary excision when, at the end of the month, he wrote to Gordon Wright of his engagement. He had been putting off the performance of this duty from day to day—it seemed so hard to accomplish it gracefully. He did it at the end very briefly; it struck him that this was the best way. Three days after he had sent his letter there arrived one from Gordon himself, informing Bernard that he had suddenly determined to bring Blanche to

Europe. She was not well, and they would lose no time. They were to sail within a week after his writing. The letter contained a postscript—"Captain Lovelock comes with us."

XXIV

Bernard prepared for Gordon's arrival in Paris, which, according to his letter, would take place in a few days. He was not intending to stop in England; Blanche desired to proceed immediately to the French capital, to confer with her man-milliner, after which it was probable that they would go to Italy or to the East for the winter. "I have given her a choice of Rome or the Nile," said Gordon, "but she tells me she does n't care a fig where we go."

I say that Bernard prepared to receive his friends, and I mean that he prepared morally—or even intellectually. Materially speaking, he could simply hold himself in readiness to engage an apartment at a hotel and to go to meet them at the station. He expected to hear from Gordon as soon as this interesting trio should reach England, but the first notification he received came from a Parisian hotel. It came to him in the shape of a very short note, in the morning, shortly before lunch, and was to the effect that his friends had alighted in the Rue de la Paix the night before.

"We were tired, and I have slept late," said Gordon; "otherwise you should have heard from me earlier. Come to lunch, if possible. I want extremely to see you."

Bernard, of course, made a point of going to lunch. In as short a time as possible he found himself in Gordon's sitting-room at the Hôtel Middlesex. The table was laid for the mid-day repast, and a gentleman stood with his back to the door, looking out of the window. As Bernard came in, this gentleman turned and exhibited the ambrosial beard, the symmetrical shape, the monocular appendage, of Captain Lovelock.

The Captain screwed his glass into his eye, and greeted Bernard in his usual fashion—that is, as if he had parted with him overnight.

"Oh, good morning! Beastly morning, is n't it? I suppose you are come to luncheon—I have come to luncheon. It ought to be on table, you know—it 's nearly two o'clock. But I dare say you have noticed foreigners are never punctual—it 's only English servants that are punctual. And they don't understand luncheon, you know—they can't make out our eating at this sort of hour. You know they always dine so beastly early. Do you remember the sort of time they used to dine at Baden?—half-past five, half-past six; some unearthly hour of that kind. That 's the sort of time you dine in America. I found they 'd invite a man at half-past six. That 's what I call being in a hurry for your food. You know they always accuse the Americans of making a rush for their victuals. I am bound to say that in New York, and that sort of place, the victuals were very good when you got them. I hope you don't mind my saying anything about America? You know the Americans are so deucedly thin-skinned—they always bristle up if you say anything against their institutions. The English don't care a rap what you say—they 've got a different sort of temper, you know. With the Americans I 'm deuced careful—I never breathe a word about anything. While I was over there I went in for being complimentary. I laid it on thick, and I found they would take all I could give them. I did n't see much of their institutions, after all; I went in for seeing the people. Some of the people were charming—upon my soul, I was surprised at some of the people. I dare say you know some of the people I saw; they were as nice people as you would see anywhere. There were always a lot of people about Mrs. Wright, you know; they told me they were all the best people. You know she is always late for everything. She always comes in after every one is there—looking so devilish pretty, pulling on her gloves. She wears the longest gloves I ever saw in my life. Upon my word, if they don't come, I think I will ring the bell and ask the waiter what 's the matter. Would n't you ring the bell? It 's a great mistake, their trying to carry out their ideas of lunching. That 's Wright's character, you know; he 's always trying to carry out some idea. When I am abroad, I go in for the foreign breakfast myself. You may depend upon it they had better give up trying to do this sort of thing at this hour."

Captain Lovelock was more disposed to conversation than Bernard had known him before. His discourse of old had been languid and fragmentary, and our hero had never heard him pursue a train of ideas through so many involutions. To Bernard's observant eye, indeed, the Captain was an altered man. His manner betrayed a certain restless desire to be agreeable, to anticipate judgment—a disposition to smile, and be civil, and entertain his auditor, a tendency to move about and look out of the window and at the clock. He struck Bernard as a trifle nervous—as less solidly planted on his feet than when he lounged along the Baden gravel-walks by the side of his usual companion—a lady for whom, apparently, his admiration was still considerable. Bernard was curious to see whether he would ring the bell to inquire into the delay attending the service of lunch; but before this sentiment, rather idle under the circumstances, was gratified, Blanche passed into the room from a neighboring apartment. To Bernard's perception Blanche, at least, was always Blanche; she was a person in whom it would not have occurred to him to expect any puzzling variation, and the tone of her little, soft, thin voice instantly rang in his ear like an echo of yesterday's talk. He had already remarked to himself that after however long an interval one might see Blanche, she re-appeared with an air of familiarity. This was in some sense, indeed, a proof of the agreeable impression she made, and she looked exceed-ingly pretty as she now suddenly stopped on seeing our two gentlemen, and gave a little cry of surprise.

"Ah! I did n't know you were here. They never told me. Have you been waiting a long time? How d' ye do? You must think we are polite." She held out her hand to Bernard, smil-ing very graciously. At Captain Lovelock she barely glanced. "I hope you are very well," she went on to Longueville; "but I need n't ask that. You 're as blooming as a rose. What in the world has happened to you? You look so brilliant—so fresh. Can you say that to a man—that he looks fresh? Or can you only say that about butter and eggs?"

"It depends upon the man," said Captain Lovelock. "You can't say that a man 's fresh who spends his time in running about after *you*!"

"Ah, are you here?" cried Blanche with another little cry of surprise. "I did n't notice you—I thought you were the waiter. This is what he calls running about after me," she added, to Bernard; "coming to breakfast without being asked. How queerly they have arranged the table!" she went on, gaz-ing with her little elevated eyebrows at this piece of furniture. "I always thought that in Paris, if they could n't do anything else, they could arrange a table. I don't like that at all—those horrid little dishes on each side! Don't you think those things ought to be off the table, Mr. Longueville? I don't like to see a lot of things I 'm not eating. And I told them to have some flowers—pray, where are the flowers? Do they call those things flowers? They look as if they had come out of the land-lady's bonnet! Mr. Longueville, do look at those objects."

"They are not like me—they are not very fresh," laughed Bernard.

"It 's no great matter—we have not got to eat them," growled Captain Lovelock.

"I should think you would expect to—with the luncheon you usually make!" rejoined Blanche. "Since you are here, though I did n't ask you, you might as well make yourself useful. Will you be so good as to ring the bell? If Gordon expects that we are going to wait another quarter of an hour for him he exaggerates the patience of a long-suffering wife. If you are very curious to know what he is about, he is writ-ing letters, by way of a change. He writes about eighty a day; his correspondents must be strong people! It 's a lucky thing for me that I am married to Gordon; if I were not he might write to me—to me, to whom it 's a misery to have to answer even an invitation to dinner! To begin with, I don't know how to spell. If Captain Lovelock ever boasts that he has had letters from me, you may know it 's an invention. He has never had anything but telegrams—three telegrams—that I sent him in America about a pair of slippers that he had left at our house and that I did n't know what to do with. Cap-tain Lovelock's slippers are no trifle to have on one's hands—on one's feet, I suppose I ought to say. For telegrams the spelling does n't matter; the people at the office correct it—or if they don't you can put it off on them. I never see any-thing nowadays but Gordon's back," she went on, as they took their places at table—"his noble broad back, as he sits writing his letters. That 's my principal view of my husband. I think that now we are in Paris I ought to have a portrait of it by one of the great artists. It would be such a characteristic pose. I have quite forgotten his face and I don't think I should know it."

Gordon's face, however, presented itself just at this moment; he came in quickly, with his countenance flushed with the pleasure of meeting his old friend again. He had the sun-scorched look of a traveller who has just crossed the Atlantic, and he smiled at Bernard with his honest eyes.

"Don't think me a great brute for not being here to receive you," he said, as he clasped his hand. "I was writing an important letter and I put it to myself in this way: 'If I interrupt my letter I shall have to come back and finish it; whereas if I finish it now, I can have all the rest of the day to spend with him.' So I stuck to it to the end, and now we can be inseparable."

"You may be sure Gordon reasoned it out," said Blanche, while her husband offered his hand in silence to Captain Lovelock.

"Gordon's reasoning is as fine as other people's feeling!" declared Bernard, who was conscious of a desire to say something very pleasant to Gordon, and who did not at all approve of Blanche's little ironical tone about her husband.

"And Bernard's compliments are better than either," said Gordon, laughing and taking his seat at table.

"I have been paying him compliments," Blanche went on. "I have been telling him he looks so brilliant, so blooming—as if something had happened to him, as if he had inherited a fortune. He must have been doing something very wicked, and he ought to tell us all about it, to amuse us. I am sure you are a dreadful Parisian, Mr. Longueville. Remember that we are three dull, virtuous people, exceedingly bored with each other's society, and wanting to hear something strange and exciting. If it 's a little improper, that won't spoil it."

"You certainly are looking uncommonly well," said Gordon, still smiling, across the table, at his friend. "I see what Blanche means—"

"My dear Gordon, that 's a great event," his wife interposed.

"It 's a good deal to pretend, certainly," he went on, smiling always, with his red face and his blue eyes. "But this is no great credit to me, because Bernard's superb condition would strike any one. You look as if you were going to marry the Lord Mayor's daughter!"

If Bernard was blooming, his bloom at this juncture must

have deepened, and in so doing indeed have contributed an even brighter tint to his expression of salubrious happiness. It was one of the rare occasions of his life when he was at a loss for a verbal expedient.

"It 's a great match," he nevertheless murmured, jestingly. "You must excuse my inflated appearance."

"It has absorbed you so much that you have had no time to write to me," said Gordon. "I expected to hear from you after you arrived."

"I wrote to you a fortnight ago—just before receiving your own letter. You left New York before my letter reached it."

"Ah, it will have crossed us," said Gordon. "But now that we have your society I don't care. Your letters, of course, are delightful, but that is still better."

In spite of this sympathetic statement Bernard cannot be said to have enjoyed his lunch; he was thinking of something else that lay before him and that was not agreeable. He was like a man who has an acrobatic feat to perform—a wide ditch to leap, a high pole to climb—and who has a presentiment of fractures and bruises. Fortunately he was not obliged to talk much, as Mrs. Gordon displayed even more than her usual vivacity, rendering her companions the graceful service of lifting the burden of conversation from their shoulders.

"I suppose you were surprised to see us rushing out here so suddenly," she observed in the course of the repast. "We had said nothing about it when you last saw us, and I believe we are supposed to tell you everything, ain't we? I certainly have told you a great many things, and there are some of them I hope you have n't repeated. I have no doubt you have told them all over Paris, but I don't care what you tell in Paris—Paris is n't so easily shocked. Captain Lovelock does n't repeat what I tell him; I set him up as a model of discretion. I have told him some pretty bad things, and he has liked them so much he has kept them all to himself. I say my bad things to Captain Lovelock, and my good things to other people; he does n't know the difference and he is perfectly content."

"Other people as well often don't know the difference," said Gordon, gravely. "You ought always to tell us which are which."

Blanche gave her husband a little impertinent stare.

"When I am not appreciated," she said, with an attempt at superior dryness, "I am too proud to point it out. I don't know whether you know that I 'm proud," she went on, turning to Gordon and glancing at Captain Lovelock; "it 's a good thing to know. I suppose Gordon will say that I ought to be too proud to point *that* out; but what are you to do when no one has any imagination? You have a grain or two, Mr. Longueville; but Captain Lovelock has n't a speck. As for Gordon, *je n'en parle pas!* But even you, Mr. Longueville, would never imagine that I am an interesting invalid—that we are travelling for my delicate health. The doctors have n't given me up, but I have given them up. I know I don't look as if I were out of health; but that 's because I always try to look my best. My appearance proves nothing—absolutely nothing. Do you think my appearance proves anything, Captain Lovelock?"

Captain Lovelock scrutinized Blanche's appearance with a fixed and solemn eye; and then he replied—

"It proves you are very lovely."

Blanche kissed her finger-tips to him in return for this compliment.

"You only need to give Captain Lovelock a chance," she rattled on, "and he is as clever as any one. That 's what I like to do to my friends—I like to make chances for them. Captain Lovelock is like my dear little blue terrier that I left at home. If I hold out a stick he will jump over it. He won't jump without the stick; but as soon as I produce it he knows what he has to do. He looks at it a moment and then he gives his little hop. He knows he will have a lump of sugar, and Captain Lovelock expects one as well. Dear Captain Lovelock, shall I ring for a lump? Would n't it be touching? *Garçon, un morceau de sucre pour Monsieur le Capitaine!* But what I give Monsieur le Capitaine is *moral* sugar! I usually administer it in private, and he shall have a good big morsel when you go away."

Gordon got up, turning to Bernard and looking at his watch.

"Let us go away, in that case," he said, smiling, "and leave Captain Lovelock to receive his reward. We will go and take a walk; we will go up the Champs Elysées. Good morning, Monsieur le Capitaine."

Neither Blanche nor the Captain offered any opposition to this proposal, and Bernard took leave of his hostess and joined Gordon, who had already passed into the ante-chamber.

XXV

GORDON took his arm and they gained the street; they strolled in the direction of the Champs Elysées.

"For a little exercise and a good deal of talk, it 's the pleasantest place," said Gordon. "I have a good deal to say; I have a good deal to ask you."

Bernard felt the familiar pressure of his friend's hand, as it rested on his arm, and it seemed to him never to have lain there with so heavy a weight. It held him fast—it held him to account; it seemed a physical symbol of responsibility. Bernard was not re-assured by hearing that Gordon had a great deal to say, and he expected a sudden explosion of bitterness on the subject of Blanche's irremediable triviality. The afternoon was a lovely one—the day was a perfect example of the mellowest mood of autumn. The air was warm and filled with a golden haze, which seemed to hang about the bare Parisian trees, as if with a tender impulse to drape their nakedness. A fine day in Paris brings out a wonderfully bright and appreciative multitude of strollers and loungers, and the liberal spaces of the Champs Elysées were on this occasion filled with those placid votaries of inexpensive entertainment who abound in the French capital. The benches and chairs on the edge of the great avenue exhibited a dense fraternity of gazers, and up and down the broad walk passed the slow-moving and easily pleased pedestrians. Gordon, in spite of his announcement that he had a good deal to say, confined himself at first to superficial allusions, and Bernard after a while had the satisfaction of perceiving that he was not likely, for the moment, to strike the note of conjugal discord. He appeared, indeed, to feel no desire to speak of Blanche in any manner whatever. He fell into the humor of the hour and the scene, looked at the crowd, talked about trifles. He remarked that Paris was a wonderful place after all, and that a little glimpse of the Parisian picture was a capital thing as a change; said he was very glad they had come, and that for his part he was willing to stay three months.

"And what have you been doing with yourself?" he asked.

"How have you been occupied, and what are you meaning to do?"

Bernard said nothing for a moment, and Gordon presently glanced at his face to see why he was silent. Bernard, looking askance, met his companion's eyes, and then, resting his own upon them, he stopped short. His heart was beating; it was a question of saying to Gordon outright, "I have been occupied in becoming engaged to Angela Vivian." But he could n't say it, and yet he must say something. He tried to invent something; but he could think of nothing, and still Gordon was looking at him.

"I am so glad to see you!" he exclaimed, for want of something better; and he blushed—he felt foolish, he felt false—as he said it.

"My dear Bernard!" Gordon murmured gratefully, as they walked on. "It 's very good of you to say that; I am very glad we are together again. I want to say something," he added, in a moment; "I hope you won't mind it—" Bernard gave a little laugh at his companion's scruples, and Gordon continued. "To tell the truth, it has sometimes seemed to me that we were not so good friends as we used to be—that something had come between us—I don't know what, I don't know why. I don't know what to call it but a sort of lowering of the temperature. I don't know whether you have felt it, or whether it has been simply a fancy of mine. Whatever it may have been, it 's all over, is n't it? We are too old friends—too good friends—not to stick together. Of course, the rubs of life may occasionally loosen the cohesion; but it is very good to feel that, with a little direct contact, it may easily be re-established. Is n't that so? But we should n't reason about these things; one feels them, and that 's enough."

Gordon spoke in his clear, cheerful voice, and Bernard listened intently. It seemed to him there was an undertone of pain and effort in his companion's speech; it was that of an unhappy man trying to be wise and make the best of things.

"Ah, the rubs of life—the rubs of life!" Bernard repeated vaguely.

"We must n't mind them," said Gordon, with a conscientious laugh. "We must toughen our hides; or, at the worst, we must plaster up our bruises. But why should we choose this particular place and hour for talking of the pains of life?" he went on. "Are we not in the midst of its pleasures? I mean, henceforth, to cultivate its pleasures. What are yours, just now, Bernard? Is n't it supposed that in Paris one must amuse one's self? How have you been amusing yourself?"

"I have been leading a very quiet life," said Bernard.

"I notice that 's what people always say when they have been particularly dissipated. What have you done? Whom have you seen that one knows?"

Bernard was silent a moment.

"I have seen some old friends of yours," he said at last. "I have seen Mrs. Vivian and her daughter."

"Ah!" Gordon made this exclamation, and then stopped short. Bernard looked at him, but Gordon was looking away; his eyes had caught some one in the crowd. Bernard followed the direction they had taken, and then Gordon went on: "Talk of the devil—excuse the adage! Are not those the ladies in question?"

Mrs. Vivian and her daughter were, in fact, seated among a great many other quiet people, in a couple of hired chairs, at the edge of the great avenue. They were turned toward our two friends, and when Bernard distinguished them, in the well-dressed multitude, they were looking straight at Gordon Wright.

"They see you!" said Bernard.

"You say that as if I wished to run away," Gordon answered. "I don't want to run away; on the contrary, I want to speak to them."

"That 's easily done," said Bernard, and they advanced to the two ladies.

Mrs. Vivian and her daughter rose from their chairs as they came; they had evidently rapidly exchanged observations, and had decided that it would facilitate their interview with Gordon Wright to receive him standing. He made his way to them through the crowd, blushing deeply, as he always did when excited; then he stood there bare-headed, shaking hands with each of them, with a fixed smile, and with nothing, apparently, to say. Bernard watched Angela's face; she was giving his companion a beautiful smile. Mrs. Vivian was delicately cordial.

"I was sure it was you," said Gordon at last. "We were just talking of you."

"Did Mr. Longueville deny it was we?" asked Mrs. Vivian, archly; "after we had supposed that we had made an impression on him!"

"I knew you were in Paris—we were in the act of talking of you," Gordon went on. "I am very glad to see you."

Bernard had shaken hands with Angela, looking at her intently; and in her eyes, as his own met them, it seemed to him that there was a gleam of mockery. At whom was she mocking—at Gordon, or at himself? Bernard was uncomfortable enough not to care to be mocked; but he felt even more sorry that Gordon should be.

"We also knew you were coming—Mr. Longueville had told us," said Mrs. Vivian; "and we have been expecting the pleasure of seeing Blanche. Dear little Blanche!"

"Dear little Blanche will immediately come and see you," Gordon replied.

"Immediately, we hope," said Mrs. Vivian. "We shall be so very glad." Bernard perceived that she wished to say something soothing and sympathetic to poor Gordon; having it, as he supposed, on her conscience that, after having once encouraged him to regard himself as indispensable (in the capacity of son-in-law) to her happiness, she should now present to him the spectacle of a felicity which had established itself without his aid. "We were so very much interested in your marriage," she went on. "We thought it so—so delightful."

Gordon fixed his eyes on the ground for a moment.

"I owe it partly to you," he answered. "You had done so much for Blanche. You had so cultivated her mind and polished her manners that her attractions were doubled, and I fell an easy victim to them."

He uttered these words with an exaggerated solemnity, the result of which was to produce, for a moment, an almost embarrassing silence. Bernard was rapidly becoming more and more impatient of his own embarrassment, and now he exclaimed, in a loud and jovial voice—

"Blanche makes victims by the dozen! I was a victim last winter; we are all victims!"

"Dear little Blanche!" Mrs. Vivian murmured again.

Angela had said nothing; she had simply stood there, making no attempt to address herself to Gordon, and yet with no affectation of reserve or of indifference. Now she seemed to feel the impulse to speak to him.

"When Blanche comes to see us, you must be sure to come with her," she said, with a friendly smile.

Gordon looked at her, but he said nothing.

"We were so sorry to hear she is out of health," Angela went on.

Still Gordon was silent, with his eyes fixed on her expressive and charming face.

"It is not serious," he murmured at last.

"She used to be so well—so bright," said Angela, who also appeared to have the desire to say something kind and comfortable.

Gordon made no response to this; he only looked at her.

"I hope you are well, Miss Vivian," he broke out at last.

"Very well, thank you."

"Do you live in Paris?"

"We have pitched our tent here for the present."

"Do you like it?"

"I find it no worse than other places."

Gordon appeared to desire to talk with her; but he could think of nothing to say. Talking with her was a pretext for looking at her; and Bernard, who thought she had never been so handsome as at that particular moment, smiling at her troubled ex-lover, could easily conceive that his friend should desire to prolong this privilege.

"Have you been sitting here long?" Gordon asked, thinking of something at last.

"Half an hour. We came out to walk, and my mother felt tired. It is time we should turn homeward," Angela added.

"Yes, I am tired, my daughter. We must take a *voiture*, if Mr. Longueville will be so good as to find us one," said Mrs. Vivian.

Bernard, professing great alacrity, looked about him; but he still lingered near his companions. Gordon had thought of something else. "Have you been to Baden again?" Bernard heard him ask. But at this moment Bernard espied at a distance an empty hackney-carriage crawling up the avenue, and he was obliged to go and signal to it. When he came back, followed by the vehicle, the two ladies, accompanied by Gordon, had come to the edge of the pavement. They shook hands with Gordon before getting into the cab, and Mrs. Vivian exclaimed—

"Be sure you give our love to your dear wife!"

Then the two ladies settled themselves and smiled their adieux, and the little victoria rumbled away at an easy pace, while Bernard stood with Gordon, looking after it. They watched it a moment, and then Gordon turned to his companion. He looked at Bernard for some moments intently, with a singular expression.

"It is strange for me to see her!" he said, presently.

"I hope it is not altogether disagreeable," Bernard answered smiling.

"She is delightfully handsome," Gordon went on.

"She is a beautiful woman."

"And the strange thing is that she strikes me now so differently," Gordon continued. "I used to think her so mysterious—so ambiguous. She seems to be now so simple."

"Ah," said Bernard, laughing, "that 's an improvement!"

"So simple and so good!" Gordon exclaimed.

Bernard laid his hand on his companion's shoulder, shaking his head slowly.

"You must not think too much about that," he said.

"So simple—so good—so charming!" Gordon repeated.

"Ah, my dear Gordon!" Bernard murmured.

But still Gordon continued.

"So intelligent, so reasonable, so sensible."

"Have you discovered all that in two minutes' talk?"

"Yes, in two minutes' talk. I should n't hesitate about her now!"

"It 's better you should n't say that," said Bernard.

"Why should n't I say it? It seems to me it 's my duty to say it."

"No—your duty lies elsewhere," said Bernard. "There are two reasons. One is that you have married another woman."

"What difference does that make?" cried Gordon.

Bernard made no attempt to answer this inquiry; he simply went on—

"The other is—the other is—"

But here he paused.

"What is the other?" Gordon asked.

"That I am engaged to marry Miss Vivian."

And with this Bernard took his hand off Gordon's shoulder.

Gordon stood staring.

"To marry Miss Vivian?"

Now that Bernard had heard himself say it, audibly, distinctly, loudly, the spell of his apprehension seemed broken, and he went on bravely.

"We are to be married very shortly. It has all come about within a few weeks. It will seem to you very strange—perhaps you won't like it. That 's why I have hesitated to tell you."

Gordon turned pale; it was the first time Bernard had ever seen him do so; evidently he did not like it. He stood staring and frowning.

"Why, I thought—I thought," he began at last—"I thought that you disliked her!"

"I supposed so, too," said Bernard. "But I have got over that."

Gordon turned away, looking up the great avenue into the crowd. Then turning back, he said—

"I am very much surprised."

"And you are not pleased!"

Gordon fixed his eyes on the ground a moment.

"I congratulate you on your engagement," he said at last, looking up with a face that seemed to Bernard hard and unnatural.

"It is very good of you to say that, but of course you can't like it! I was sure you would n't like it. But what could I do? I fell in love with her, and I could n't run away simply to spare you a surprise. My dear Gordon," Bernard added, "you will get used to it."

"Very likely," said Gordon, dryly. "But you must give me time."

"As long as you like!"

Gordon stood for a moment again staring down at the ground.

"Very well, then, I will take my time," he said. "Good-bye!"

And he turned away, as if to walk off alone.

"Where are you going?" asked Bernard, stopping him.

"I don't know—to the hotel, anywhere. To try to get used to what you have told me."

"Don't try too hard; it will come of itself," said Bernard.

"We shall see!"

And Gordon turned away again.

"Do you prefer to go alone?"

"Very much—if you will excuse me!"

"I have asked you to excuse a greater want of ceremony!" said Bernard, smiling.

"I have not done so yet!" Gordon rejoined; and marching off, he mingled with the crowd.

Bernard watched him till he lost sight of him, and then, dropping into the first empty chair that he saw, he sat and reflected that his friend liked it quite as little as he had feared.

XXVI

B ERNARD sat thinking for a long time; at first with a good
deal of mortification—at last with a good deal of bitterness. He felt angry at last; but he was not angry with himself.
He was displeased with poor Gordon, and with Gordon's displeasure. He was uncomfortable, and he was vexed at his discomfort. It formed, it seemed to him, no natural part of his
situation; he had had no glimpse of it in the book of fate
where he registered on a fair blank page his betrothal to a
charming girl. That Gordon should be surprised, and even a
little shocked and annoyed—this was his right and his privilege; Bernard had been prepared for that, and had determined
to make the best of it. But it must not go too far; there were
limits to the morsel of humble pie that he was disposed to
swallow. Something in Gordon's air and figure, as he went
off in a huff, looking vicious and dangerous—yes, that was
positively his look—left a sinister impression on Bernard's
mind, and, after a while, made him glad to take refuge in
being angry. One would like to know what Gordon expected,
par exemple! Did he expect Bernard to give up Angela simply
to save him a shock; or to back out of his engagement by way
of an ideal reparation? No, it was too absurd, and, if Gordon
had a wife of his own, why in the name of justice should not
Bernard have one?

Being angry was a relief, but it was not exactly a solution,
and Bernard, at last, leaving his place, where for an hour or
two he had been absolutely unconscious of everything that
went on around him, wandered about for some time in deep
restlessness and irritation. At one moment he thought of
going back to Gordon's hotel, to see him, to explain. But
then he became aware that he was too angry for that—to say
nothing of Gordon's being too angry also; and, moreover,
that there was nothing to explain. He was to marry Angela
Vivian; that was a very simple fact—it needed no explanation. Was it so wonderful, so inconceivable, an incident so
unlikely to happen? He went, as he always did on Sunday, to
dine with Mrs. Vivian, and it seemed to him that he perceived
in the two ladies some symptoms of a discomposure which

had the same origin as his own. Bernard, on this occasion, at dinner, failed to make himself particularly agreeable; he ate fast—as if he had no idea what he was eating, and talked little; every now and then his eyes rested for some time upon Angela, with a strange, eagerly excited expression, as if he were looking her over and trying to make up his mind about her afresh. This young lady bore his inscrutable scrutiny with a deal of superficial composure; but she was also silent, and she returned his gaze, from time to time, with an air of unusual anxiety. She was thinking, of course, of Gordon, Bernard said to himself; and a woman's first meeting, in after years, with an ex-lover must always make a certain impression upon her. Gordon, however, had never been a lover, and if Bernard noted Angela's gravity it was not because he felt jealous. "She is simply sorry for him," he said to himself; and by the time he had finished his dinner it began to come back to him that he was sorry, too. Mrs. Vivian was probably sorry as well, for she had a slightly confused and preoccupied look—a look from which, even in the midst of his chagrin, Bernard extracted some entertainment. It was Mrs. Vivian's intermittent conscience that had been reminded of one of its lapses; her meeting with Gordon Wright had recalled the least exemplary episode of her life—the time when she whispered mercenary counsel in the ear of a daughter who sat, grave and pale, looking at her with eyes that wondered. Mrs. Vivian blushed a little now, when she met Bernard's eyes; and to remind herself that she was after all a virtuous woman, talked as much as possible about superior and harmless things—the beauty of the autumn weather, the pleasure of seeing French papas walking about on Sunday with their progeny in their hands, the peculiarities of the pulpit-oratory of the country as exemplified in the discourse of a Protestant *pasteur* whom she had been to hear in the morning.

When they rose from table and went back into her little drawing-room, she left her daughter alone for awhile with Bernard. The two were standing together before the fire; Bernard watched Mrs. Vivian close the door softly behind her. Then, looking for a moment at his companion—

"He is furious!" he announced at last.

"Furious?" said Angela. "Do you mean Mr. Wright?"

"The amiable, reasonable Gordon. He takes it very hard."

"Do you mean about me?" asked Angela.

"It 's not with you he 's furious, of course; it is with me. He won't let me off easily."

Angela looked for a moment at the fire.

"I am very sorry for him," she said, at last.

"It seems to me I am the one to be pitied," said Bernard; "and I don't see what compassion you, of all people in the world, owe him."

Angela again rested her eyes on the fire; then presently, looking up—

"He liked me very much," she remarked.

"All the more shame to him!" cried Bernard.

"What do you mean?" asked the girl, with her beautiful stare.

"If he liked you, why did he give you up?"

"He did n't give me up."

"What do *you* mean, please?" asked Bernard, staring back at her.

"I sent him away—I refused him," said Angela.

"Yes; but you thought better of it, and your mother had persuaded you that if he should ask you again, you had better accept him. Then it was that he backed out—in consequence of what I said to him on his return from England."

She shook her head slowly, with a strange smile.

"My poor Bernard, you are talking very wildly. *He did* ask me again."

"That night?" cried Bernard.

"The night he came back from England—the last time I saw him, until to-day."

"After I had denounced you?" our puzzled hero exclaimed, frowning portentously.

"I am sorry to let you know the small effect of your words!"

Bernard folded his hands together—almost devoutly—and stood gazing at her with a long, inarticulate murmur of satisfaction.

"Ah! then, I did n't injure you—I did n't deprive you of a chance?"

"Oh, sir, the intention on your part was the same!" Angela exclaimed.

"Then all my uneasiness, all my remorse, were wasted?" he went on.

But she kept the same tone, and its tender archness only gave a greater sweetness to his sense of relief.

"It was a very small penance for you to pay."

"You dismissed him definitely, and that was why he vanished?" asked Bernard, wondering still.

"He gave me another 'chance,' as you elegantly express it, and I declined to take advantage of it."

"Ah, well, now," cried Bernard, "I *am* sorry for him!"

"I was very kind—very respectful," said Angela. "I thanked him from the bottom of my heart; I begged his pardon very humbly for the wrong—if wrong it was—that I was doing him. I did n't in the least require of him that he should leave Baden at seven o'clock the next morning. I had no idea that he would do so, and that was the reason that I insisted to my mother that we ourselves should go away. When we went I knew nothing about his having gone, and I supposed he was still there. I did n't wish to meet him again."

Angela gave this information slowly, softly, with pauses between the sentences, as if she were recalling the circumstances with a certain effort; and meanwhile Bernard, with his transfigured face and his eyes fixed upon her lips, was moving excitedly about the room.

"Well, he can't accuse me, then!" he broke out again. "If what I said had no more effect upon him than that, I certainly did him no wrong."

"I think you are rather vexed he did n't believe you," said Angela.

"I confess I don't understand it. He had all the air of it. He certainly had not the air of a man who was going to rush off and give you the last proof of his confidence."

"It was not a proof of confidence," said Angela. "It had nothing to do with me. It was as between himself and you; it was a proof of independence. He did believe you, more or less, and what you said fell in with his own impressions—strange impressions that they were, poor man! At the same time, as I say, he liked me, too; it was out of his liking me that all his trouble came! He caught himself in the act of listening to you too credulously—and that seemed to him unmanly and dishonorable. The sensation brought with it a reaction, and to prove to himself that in such a matter he could be influenced by nobody, he marched away, an hour after he had talked with you, and, in the teeth of his perfect mistrust, confirmed by your account of my irregularities— heaven forgive you both!—again asked me to be his wife. But he hoped I would refuse!"

"Ah," cried Bernard, "the recreant! He deserved—he deserved—"

"That I should accept him?" Angela asked, smiling still.

Bernard was so much affected by this revelation, it seemed to him to make such a difference in his own responsibility and to lift such a weight off his conscience, that he broke out again into the liveliest ejaculations of relief.

"Oh, I don't care for anything, now, and I can do what I please! Gordon may hate me, and I shall be sorry for him; but it 's not my fault, and I owe him no reparation. No, no; I am free!"

"It 's only I who am not, I suppose," said Angela, "and the reparation must come from me! If he is unhappy, I must take the responsibility."

"Ah yes, of course," said Bernard, kissing her.

"But why should he be unhappy?" asked Angela. "If I refused him, it was what he wanted."

"He is hard to please," Bernard rejoined. "He has got a wife of his own."

"If Blanche does n't please him, he is certainly difficult;" and Angela mused a little. "But you told me the other day that they were getting on so well."

"Yes, I believe I told you," Bernard answered, musing a little too.

"You are not attending to what I say."

"No, I am thinking of something else—I am thinking of what it was that made you refuse him that way, at the last, after you had let your mother hope." And Bernard stood there, smiling at her.

"Don't think any more; you will not find out," the girl declared, turning away.

"Ah, it was cruel of you to let me think I was wrong all these years," he went on; "and, at the time, since you meant to refuse him, you might have been more frank with me."

"I thought my fault had been that I was too frank."

"I was densely stupid, and you might have made me understand better."

"Ah," said Angela, "you ask a great deal of a girl!"

"Why have you let me go on so long thinking that my deluded words had had an effect upon Gordon—feeling that I had done you a brutal wrong? It was real to me, the wrong—and I have told you of the pangs and the shame which, for so many months, it has cost me! Why have you never undeceived me until to-day, and then only by accident?"

At this question Angela blushed a little; then she answered, smiling—

"It was my vengeance."

Bernard shook his head.

"That won't do—you don't mean it. You never cared—you were too proud to care; and when I spoke to you about my fault, you did n't even know what I meant. You might have told me, therefore, that my remorse was idle, that what I said to Gordon had not been of the smallest consequence, and that the rupture had come from yourself."

For some time Angela said nothing, then at last she gave him one of the deeply serious looks with which her face was occasionally ornamented.

"If you want really to know, then—can't you see that your remorse seemed to me connected in a certain way with your affection; a sort of guarantee of it? You thought you had injured some one or other, and that seemed to be mixed up with your loving me, and therefore I let it alone."

"Ah," said Bernard, "my remorse is all gone, and yet I think I love you about as much as ever! So you see how wrong you were not to tell me."

"The wrong to you I don't care about. It is very true I might have told you for Mr. Wright's sake. It would perhaps have made him look better. But as you never attacked him for deserting me, it seemed needless for me to defend him."

"I confess," said Bernard, "I am quite at sea about Gordon's look in the matter. Is he looking better now—or is he looking worse? You put it very well just now; I was attending to you, though you said I was not. If he hoped you would refuse him, with whom is his quarrel at present? And why was he so cool to me for months after we parted at Baden? If that was his state of mind, why should he accuse me of inconsistency?"

"There is something in it, after all, that a woman can understand. I don't know whether a man can. He hoped I would refuse him, and yet when I had done so he was vexed. After a while his vexation subsided, and he married poor Blanche; but, on learning to-day that I had accepted you, it flickered up again. I suppose that was natural enough; but it won't be serious."

"What will not be serious, my dear?" asked Mrs. Vivian, who had come back to the drawing-room, and who, apparently, could not hear that the attribute in question was wanting in any direction, without some alarm.

"Shall I tell mamma, Bernard?" said Angela.

"Ah, my dear child, I hope it 's nothing that threatens your mutual happiness," mamma murmured, with gentle earnestness.

"Does it threaten our mutual happiness, Bernard?" the girl went on, smiling.

"Let Mrs. Vivian decide whether we ought to let it make us miserable," said Bernard. "Dear Mrs. Vivian, you are a casuist, and this is a nice case."

"Is it anything about poor Mr. Wright?" the elder lady inquired.

"Why do you say 'poor' Mr. Wright?" asked Bernard.

"Because I am sadly afraid he is not happy with Blanche."

"How did you discover that—without seeing them together?"

"Well, perhaps you will think me very fanciful," said Mrs. Vivian; "but it was by the way he looked at Angela. He has such an expressive face."

"He looked at me very kindly, mamma," Angela observed.

"He regularly stared, my daughter. In any one else I should

have said it was rude. But his situation is so peculiar; and one could see that he admired you still." And Mrs. Vivian gave a little soft sigh.

"Ah! she is thinking of the thirty thousand a year," Bernard said to himself.

"I am sure I hope he admires me still," the girl cried, laughing. "There is no great harm in that."

"He was comparing you with Blanche—and he was struck with the contrast."

"It could n't have been in my favor. If it 's a question of being looked at, Blanche bears it better than I."

"Poor little Blanche!" murmured Mrs. Vivian, sweetly.

"Why did you tell me he was so happy with her?" Angela asked, turning to Bernard, abruptly.

Bernard gazed at her a moment, with his eyebrows raised.

"I never saw any one ask such sudden questions!" he exclaimed.

"You can answer me at your leisure," she rejoined, turning away.

"It was because I adored you."

"You would n't say that at your leisure," said the girl.

Mrs. Vivian stood watching them.

"You, who are so happy together, you ought to think kindly of others who are less fortunate."

"That is very true, Mrs. Vivian; and I have never thought of any one so kindly as I have of Gordon for the last year."

Angela turned round again.

"Is Blanche so very bad, then?"

"You will see for yourself!"

"Ah, no," said Mrs. Vivian, "she is not bad; she is only very light. I am so glad she is to be near us again. I think a great deal can be done by association. We must help her, Angela. I think we helped her before."

"It is also very true that she is light, Mrs. Vivian," Bernard observed, "and if you could make her a little heavier, I should be tremendously grateful."

Bernard's prospective mother-in-law looked at him a little.

"I don't know whether you are laughing at me—I always think you are. But I shall not give up Blanche for that. I never give up any one that I have once tried to help. Blanche will come back to me."

Mrs. Vivian had hardly spoken when the sharp little vibration of her door-bell was heard in the hall. Bernard stood for a moment looking at the door of the drawing-room.

"It is poor Gordon come to make a scene!" he announced.

"Is that what you mean—that he opposed your marriage?" asked Mrs. Vivian, with a frightened air.

"I don't know what he proposes to do with Blanche," said Bernard, laughing.

There were voices in the hall. Angela had been listening.

"You say she will come back to you, mamma," she exclaimed. "Here she is arrived!"

XXVII

A T THE SAME MOMENT the door was thrown open, and
Mrs. Gordon appeared on the threshold with a gentleman behind her. Blanche stood an instant looking into the
lighted room and hesitating—flushed a little, smiling, extremely pretty.

"May I come in?" she said, "and may I bring in Captain
Lovelock?"

The two ladies, of course, fluttering toward her with every
demonstration of hospitality, drew her into the room, while
Bernard proceeded to greet the Captain, who advanced with
a certain awkward and bashful majesty, almost sweeping with
his great stature Mrs. Vivian's humble ceiling. There was a
tender exchange of embraces between Blanche and her
friends, and the charming visitor, losing no time, began to
chatter with her usual volubility. Mrs. Vivian and Angela
made her companion graciously welcome; but Blanche
begged they would n't mind him—she had only brought him
as a watch-dog.

"His place is on the rug," she said. "Captain Lovelock, go
and lie down on the rug."

"Upon my soul, there is nothing else but rugs in these
French places!" the Captain rejoined, looking round Mrs.
Vivian's *salon*. "Which rug do you mean?"

Mrs. Vivian had remarked to Blanche that it was very kind
of her to come first, and Blanche declared that she could not
have laid her head on her pillow before she had seen her dear
Mrs. Vivian.

"Do you suppose I would wait because I am married?" she
inquired, with a keen little smile in her charming eyes. "I am
not so much married as that, I can tell you! Do you think I
look much as if I were married, with no one to bring me here
to-night but Captain Lovelock?"

"I am sure Captain Lovelock is a very gallant escort," said
Mrs. Vivian.

"Oh, he was not afraid—that is, he was not afraid of the
journey, though it lay all through those dreadful wild
Champs Elysées. But when we arrived, he was afraid to come

in—to come up here. Captain Lovelock is so modest, you know—in spite of all the success he had in America. He will tell you about the success he had in America; it quite makes up for the defeat of the British army in the Revolution. They *were* defeated in the Revolution, the British, were n't they? I always told him so, but he insists they were not. 'How do we come to be free, then?' I always ask him; 'I suppose you admit that we are free.' Then he becomes personal and says that I am free enough, certainly. But it 's the general fact I mean; I wish you would tell him about the general fact. I think he would believe you, because he knows you know a great deal about history and all that. I don't mean this evening, but some time when it is convenient. He did n't want to come in—he wanted to stay in the carriage and smoke a cigar; he thought you would n't like it, his coming with me the first time. But I told him he need n't mind that, for I would certainly explain. I would be very careful to let you know that I brought him only as a substitute. A substitute for whom? A substitute for my husband, of course. My dear Mrs. Vivian, of course I ought to bring you some pretty message from Gordon—that he is dying to come and see you, only that he had nineteen letters to write and that he could n't possibly stir from his fireside. I suppose a good wife ought to invent excuses for her husband—ought to throw herself into the breach; is n't that what they call it? But I am afraid I am not a good wife. Do you think I am a good wife, Mr. Longueville? You once stayed three months with us, and you had a chance to see. I don't ask you that seriously, because you never tell the truth. I always do; so I will say I am not a good wife. And then the breach is too big, and I am too little. Oh, I am too little, Mrs. Vivian; I know I am too little. I am the smallest woman living; Gordon can scarcely see me with a microscope, and I believe he has the most powerful one in America. He is going to get another here; that is one of the things he came abroad for; perhaps it will do better. I *do* tell the truth, don't I, Mrs. Vivian? I have that merit, if I have n't any other. You once told me so at Baden; you said you could say one thing for me, at any rate—that I did n't tell fibs. You were very nice to me at Baden," Blanche went on, with her little intent smile, laying her hand in that of her hostess. "You see, I have never forgotten it. So, to keep up my reputation, I must tell the truth about Gordon. He simply said he would n't come— *voilà!* He gave no reason and he did n't send you any pretty message. He simply declined, and he went out somewhere else. So you see he is n't writing letters. I don't know where he can have gone; perhaps he has gone to the theatre. I know it is n't proper to go to the theatre on Sunday evening; but they say charity begins at home, and as Gordon's does n't begin at home, perhaps it does n't begin anywhere. I told him that if he would n't come with me I would come alone, and he said I might do as I chose—that he was not in a humor for making visits. I wanted to come to you very much; I had been thinking about it all day; and I am so fond of a visit like this in the evening, without being invited. Then I thought perhaps you had a *salon*—does n't every one in Paris have a *salon*? I tried to have a *salon* in New York, only Gordon said it would n't do. He said it was n't in our manners. Is this a *salon* to-night, Mrs. Vivian? Oh, do say it is; I should like so much to see Captain Lovelock in a *salon*! By good fortune he happened to have been dining with us; so I told him he must bring me here. I told you I would explain, Captain Lovelock," she added, "and I hope you think I have made it clear."

The Captain had turned very red during this wandering discourse. He sat pulling his beard and shifting the position which, with his stalwart person, he had taken up on a little gilded chair—a piece of furniture which every now and then gave a delicate creak.

"I always understand you well enough till you begin to explain," he rejoined, with a candid, even if embarrassed, laugh. "Then, by Jove, I 'm quite in the woods. You see such a lot more in things than most people. Does n't she, Miss Vivian?"

"Blanche has a fine imagination," said Angela, smiling frankly at the charming visitor.

When Blanche was fairly adrift upon the current of her articulate reflections, it was the habit of her companions—indeed, it was a sort of tacit agreement among them—simply to make a circle and admire. They sat about and looked at her—yawning, perhaps, a little at times, but on the whole very well entertained, and often exchanging a smiling commentary with each other. She looked at them, smiled at them each, in succession. Every one had his turn, and this always helped to give Blanche an audience. Incoherent and aimless as much of her talk was, she never looked prettier than in the attitude of improvisation—or rather, I should say, than in the hundred attitudes which she assumed at such a time. Perpetually moving, she was yet constantly graceful, and while she twisted her body and turned her head, with charming hands that never ceased to gesticulate, and little, conscious, brilliant eyes that looked everywhere at once—eyes that seemed to chatter even faster than her lips—she made you forget the nonsense she poured forth, or think of it only as a part of her personal picturesqueness. The thing was a regular performance; the practice of unlimited chatter had made her perfect. She rested upon her audience and held it together, and the sight of half a dozen pairs of amused and fascinated faces led her from one piece of folly to another. On this occasion, her audience was far from failing her, for they were all greatly interested. Captain Lovelock's interest, as we know, was chronic, and our three other friends were much occupied with a matter with which Blanche was intimately connected. Bernard, as he listened to her, smiling mechanically, was not encouraged. He remembered what Mrs. Vivian had said shortly before she came in, and it was not pleasant to him to think that Gordon had been occupied half the day in contrasting the finest girl in the world with this magnified butterfly. The contrast was sufficiently striking as Angela sat there near her, very still, bending her handsome head a little, with her hands crossed in her lap, and on her lips a kind but inscrutable smile. Mrs. Vivian was on the sofa next to Blanche, one of whose hands, when it was not otherwise occupied, she occasionally took into her own.

"Dear little Blanche!" she softly murmured, at intervals.

These few remarks represent a longer pause than Mrs. Gordon often suffered to occur. She continued to deliver herself upon a hundred topics, and it hardly matters where we take her up.

"I have n't the least idea what we are going to do. I have nothing to say about it whatever. Gordon tells me every day I must decide, and then I ask Captain Lovelock what he thinks; because, you see, he always thinks a great deal. Captain Lovelock says he does n't care a fig—that he will go wherever I go. So you see that does n't carry us very far. I want to settle on some place where Captain Lovelock won't go, but he won't help me at all. I think it will look better for him not to follow us; don't you think it will look better, Mrs. Vivian? Not that I care in the least where we go—or whether Captain Lovelock follows us, either. I don't take any interest in anything, Mrs. Vivian; don't you think that is very sad? Gordon may go anywhere he likes—to St. Petersburg, or to Bombay."

"You might go to a worse place than Bombay," said Captain Lovelock, speaking with the authority of an Anglo-Indian rich in reminiscences.

Blanche gave him a little stare.

"Ah well, that 's knocked on the head! From the way you speak of it, I think you would come after us; and the more I think of that, the more I see it would n't do. But we have got to go to some southern place, because I am very unwell. I have n't the least idea what 's the matter with me, and neither has any one else; but that does n't make any difference. It 's settled that I am out of health. One might as well be out of it as in it, for all the advantage it is. If you are out of health, at any rate you can come abroad. It was Gordon's discovery —he 's always making discoveries. You see it 's because I 'm so silly; he can always put it down to my being an invalid. What I should like to do, Mrs. Vivian, would be to spend the winter with you—just sitting on the sofa beside you and holding your hand. It would be rather tiresome for you; but I really think it would be better for me than anything else. I have never forgotten how kind you were to me before my marriage—that summer at Baden. You were everything to me—you and Captain Lovelock. I am sure I should be happy if I never went out of this lovely room. You have got it so beautifully arranged—I mean to do my own room just like it when I go home. And you have got such lovely clothes. You never used to say anything about it, but you and Angela always had better clothes than I. Are you always so quiet and serious—never talking about *chiffons*—always reading some wonderful book? I wish you would let me come and stay with you. If you only ask me, Gordon would be too delighted. He would n't have to trouble about me any more. He could go and live over in the Latin Quarter—that 's the desire of his heart—and think of nothing but old bottles. I know it is n't very good manners to beg for an invitation," Blanche went on, smiling with a gentler radiance; "but when it 's a question of one's health. One wants to keep one's self alive—does n't one? One wants to keep one's self going. It would be so good for me, Mrs. Vivian; it would really be very good for me!"

She had turned round more and more to her hostess as she talked; and at last she had given both her hands to Mrs. Vivian, and sat looking at her with a singular mixture of earnestness and jocosity. It was hard to know whether Blanche were expressing a real desire or a momentary caprice, and whether this abrupt little petition were to be taken seriously, or treated merely as a dramatic *pose* in a series of more or less effective attitudes. Her smile had become almost a grimace, she was flushed, she showed her pretty teeth; but there was a little passionate quiver in her voice.

"My dear child," said Mrs. Vivian, "we should be delighted to have you pay us a visit, and we should be so happy if we could do you any good. But I am afraid you would very soon get tired of us, and I ought to tell you, frankly, that our little home is to be—a—broken up. You know there is to be a—a change," the good lady continued, with a hesitation which apparently came from a sense of walking on uncertain ground, while she glanced with a smile at Bernard and Angela.

Blanche sat there with her little excited, yet innocent—too innocent—stare; her eyes followed Mrs. Vivian's. They met Bernard's for an instant, and for some reason, at this moment, Bernard flushed.

He rose quickly and walked away to the window where he stood looking out into the darkness. "The devil—the devil!" he murmured to himself; "she does n't even know we are to be married—Gordon has n't been able to trust himself to tell her!" And this fact seemed pregnant with evidence as to Gordon's state of mind; it did not appear to simplify the situation. After a moment, while Bernard stood there with his back turned—he felt rather awkward and foolish—he heard Blanche begin with her little surprised voice.

"Ah, you are going away? You are going to travel? But that 's charming; we can travel together. You are not going to travel? What then are you going to do? You are going back to America? Ah, but you must n't do that, as soon as I come abroad; that 's not nice or friendly, Mrs. Vivian, to your poor little old Blanche. You are not going back to America? Ah, then, I give it up! What 's the great mystery? Is it something about Angela? There was always a mystery about Angela. I hope you won't mind my saying it, my dear; but I was always afraid of you. My husband—he admires you so much, you know—has often tried to explain you to me; but I have never understood. What are you going to do now? Are you going into a convent? Are you going to be—A-a-h!"

And, suddenly, quickly, interrupting herself, Mrs. Gordon gave a long, wondering cry. Bernard heard her spring to her feet, and the two other ladies rise from their seats. Captain Lovelock got up as well; Bernard heard him knock over his little gilded chair. There was a pause, during which Blanche went through a little mute exhibition of amazement and pleasure. Bernard turned round, to receive half a dozen quick questions.

"What are you hiding away for? What are you blushing for? I never saw you do anything like that before! Why do you look so strange, and what are you making me say? Angela, is it true—is there something like that?" Without waiting for the answer to this last question, Blanche threw herself upon Mrs. Vivian. "My own Mrs. Vivian," she cried, "*is* she married?"

"My dear Blanche," said Bernard, coming forward, "has not Gordon told you? Angela and I are not married, but we hope to be before long. Gordon only knew it this morning; we ourselves have only known it a short time. There is no mystery about it, and we only want your congratulations."

"Well, I must say you have been very quiet about it!" cried Blanche. "When I was engaged, I wrote you all a letter."

"By Jove, she wrote to me!" observed Captain Lovelock.

Angela went to her and kissed her.

"Your husband does n't seem to have explained me very successfully!"

Mrs. Gordon held Bernard's intended for a moment at arm's length, with both her hands, looking at her with eyes of real excitement and wonder. Then she folded her in a prolonged, an exaggerated, embrace.

"Why did n't he tell me—why did n't he tell me?" she presently began. "He has had all day to tell me, and it was very cruel of him to let me come here without knowing it. Could anything be more absurd—more awkward? You don't think it 's awkward—you don't mind it? Ah well, you are very good! But I like it, Angela—I like it extremely, immensely. I think it 's delightful, and I wonder it never occurred to me. Has it been going on long? Ah, of course, it has been going on! Did n't it begin at Baden, and did n't I see it there? Do you mind my alluding to that? At Baden we were all so mixed up that one could n't tell who was attentive to whom! But Bernard has been very faithful, my dear; I can assure you of that. When he was in America he would n't look at another woman. I know something about that! He stayed three months in my house and he never spoke to me. Now I know why, Mr. Bernard; but you might have told me at the time. The reason was certainly good enough. I always want to know why, you know. Why Gordon never told me, for instance; that 's what I want to know!"

Blanche refused to sit down again; she declared that she was so agitated by this charming news that she could not be quiet, and that she must presently take her departure. Meanwhile she congratulated each of her friends half a dozen times; she kissed Mrs. Vivian again, she almost kissed Bernard; she inquired about details; she longed to hear all about Angela's "things." Of course they would stop for the wedding; but meantime she must be very discreet; she must not intrude too much. Captain Lovelock addressed to Angela a few fragmentary, but well-intentioned sentences, pulling his beard and fixing his eyes on the door-knob—an implement which presently turned in his manly fist, as he opened the door for his companion to withdraw. Blanche went away in a flutter of ejaculations and protestations which left our three friends in Mrs. Vivian's little drawing-room standing looking at each other as the door closed behind her.

"It certainly would have been better taste in him to tell her," said Bernard, frowning, "and not let other people see how little communication there is between them. It has mortified her."

"Poor Mr. Wright had his reasons," Mrs. Vivian suggested, and then she ventured to explain: "He still cares for Angela, and it was painful to him to talk about her marrying some one else."

This had been Bernard's own reflection, and it was no more agreeable as Mrs. Vivian presented it; though Angela herself seemed indifferent to it—seemed, indeed, not to hear it, as if she were thinking of something else.

"We must simply marry as soon as possible; to-morrow, if necessary," said Bernard, with some causticity. "That 's the best thing we can do for every one. When once Angela is married, Gordon will stop thinking of her. He will never permit his imagination to hover about a married woman; I am very sure of that. He does n't approve of that sort of thing, and he has the same law for himself as for other people."

"It does n't matter," said Angela, simply.

"How do you mean, my daughter, it does n't matter?"

"I don't feel obliged to feel so sorry for him now."

"Now? Pray, what has happened? I am more sorry than ever, since I have heard poor Blanche's dreadful tone about him."

The girl was silent a moment; then she shook her head, lightly.

"Her tone—her tone? Dearest mother, don't you see? She is intensely in love with him!"

XXVIII

T HIS OBSERVATION struck Bernard as extremely ingenious and worthy of his mistress's fine intelligence; he greeted it with enthusiasm, and thought of it for the next twelve hours. The more he thought of it the more felicitous it seemed to him, and he went to Mrs. Vivian's the next day almost for the express purpose of saying to Angela that, decidedly, she was right. He was admitted by his old friend, the little *femme de chambre*, who had long since bestowed upon him, definitively, her confidence; and as in the ante-chamber he heard the voice of a gentleman raised and talking with some emphasis, come to him from the *salon*, he paused a moment, looking at her with an interrogative eye.

"Yes," said Mrs. Vivian's attendant, "I must tell Monsieur frankly that another gentleman is there. Moreover, what does it matter? Monsieur would perceive it for himself!"

"Has he been here long?" asked Bernard.

"A quarter of an hour. It probably does n't seem long to the gentleman!"

"Is he alone with Mademoiselle?"

"He asked for Mademoiselle only. I introduced him into the *salon*, and Mademoiselle, after conversing a little while with Madame, consented to receive him. They have been alone together, as I have told Monsieur, since about three o'clock. Madame is in her own apartment. The position of Monsieur," added this discriminating woman, "certainly justifies him in entering the *salon*."

Bernard was quite of this opinion, and in a moment more he had crossed the threshold of the little drawing-room and closed the door behind him.

Angela sat there on a sofa, leaning back with her hands clasped in her lap and her eyes fixed upon Gordon Wright, who stood squarely before her, as if he had been making her a resolute speech. Her face wore a look of distress, almost of alarm; she kept her place, but her eyes gave Bernard a mute welcome. Gordon turned and looked at him slowly from head to foot. Bernard remembered, with a good deal of vividness, the last look his friend had given him in the Champs Elysées the day before; and he saw with some satisfaction that this was not exactly a repetition of that expression of cold horror. It was a question, however, whether the horror were changed for the better. Poor Gordon looked intensely sad and grievously wronged. The keen resentment had faded from his face, but an immense reproach was there—a heavy, helpless, appealing reproach. Bernard saw that he had not a scene of violence to dread—and yet, when he perceived what was coming, he would almost have preferred violence. Gordon did not offer him his hand, and before Bernard had had time to say anything, began to speak again, as if he were going on with what he had been saying to Angela.

"You have done me a great wrong—you have done me a cruel wrong! I have been telling it to Miss Vivian; I came on purpose to tell her. I can't really tell her; I can't tell her the details; it 's too painful! But you know what I mean! I could n't stand it any longer. I thought of going away—but I could n't do that. I must come and say what I feel. I can't bear it now."

This outbreak of a passionate sense of injury in a man habitually so undemonstrative, so little disposed to call attention to himself, had in it something at once of the touching and the terrible. Bernard, for an instant, felt almost bewildered; he asked himself whether he had not, after all, been a monster of duplicity. He was guilty of the weakness of taking refuge in what is called, I believe, in legal phrase, a side-issue.

"Don't say all this before Angela!" he exclaimed, with a kind of artificial energy. "You know she is not in the least at fault, and that it can only give her pain. The thing is between ourselves."

Angela was sitting there, looking up at both the men. "I like to hear it," she said.

"You have a singular taste!" Bernard declared.

"I know it 's between ourselves," cried Gordon, "and that Miss Vivian is not at fault. She is only too lovely, too wise, too good! It is you and I that are at fault—horribly at fault! You see I admit it, and you don't. I never dreamed that I should live to say such things as this to you; but I never dreamed you would do what you have done! It 's horrible, most horrible, that such a difference as this should come between two men who believed themselves—or whom I believed, at least—the best friends in the world. For it is a difference—it 's a great gulf, and nothing will ever fill it up. I must say so; I can't help it. You know I don't express myself easily; so, if I break out this way, you may know what I feel. I know it is a pain to Miss Vivian, and I beg her to forgive me. She has so much to forgive that she can forgive that, too. I can't pretend to accept it; I can't sit down and let it pass. And then, it is n't only my feelings; it 's the right; it 's the justice. I must say to her that you have no right to marry her; and beg of her to listen to me and let you go."

"My dear Gordon, are you crazy?" Bernard demanded, with an energy which, this time at least, was sufficiently real.

"Very likely I am crazy. I am crazy with disappointment and the bitterness of what I have lost. Add to that the wretchedness of what I have found!"

"Ah, don't say that, Mr. Wright," Angela begged.

He stood for an instant looking at her, but not heeding her words. "Will you listen to me again? Will you forget the wrong I did you?—my stupidity and folly and unworthiness? Will you blot out the past and let me begin again. I see you as clearly now as the light of that window. Will you give me another chance?"

Angela turned away her eyes and covered her face with her hands. "You *do* pain me!" she murmured.

"You go too far," said Bernard. "To what position does your extraordinary proposal relegate your wife?"

Gordon turned his pleading eyes on his old friend without a ray of concession; but for a moment he hesitated. "Don't speak to me of my wife. I have no wife."

"Ah, poor girl!" said Angela, springing up from the sofa.

"I am perfectly serious," Gordon went on, addressing himself again to her. "No, after all, I am not crazy; I see only too clearly—I see what *should* be; when people see that, you call them crazy. Bernard has no right—he must give you up. If you really care for him, you should help him. He is in a very false position; you should n't wish to see him in such a position. I can't explain to you—if it were even for my own sake. But Bernard must have told you; it is not possible that he has not told you?"

"I have told Angela everything, Gordon," said Bernard.

"I don't know what you mean by your having done me a wrong!" the girl exclaimed.

"If he has told you, then—I may say it! In listening to him, in believing him."

"But you did n't believe me," Bernard exclaimed, "since you immediately went and offered yourself to Miss Vivian!"

"I believed you all the same! When did I ever not believe you?"

"The last words I ever heard from Mr. Wright were words of the deepest kindness," said Angela.

She spoke with such a serious, tender grace, that Gordon seemed stirred to his depths again.

"Ah, give me another chance!" he moaned.

The poor girl could not help her tone, and it was in the same tone that she continued—

"If you think so well of me, try and be reasonable."

Gordon looked at her, slowly shaking his head.

"Reasonable—reasonable? Yes, you have a right to say that, for you are full of reason. But so am I. What I ask is within reasonable limits."

"Granting your happiness were lost," said Bernard—"I say that only for the argument—is that a ground for your wishing to deprive me of mine?"

"It is not yours—it is mine, that you have taken! You put me off my guard, and then you took it! Yours is elsewhere, and you are welcome to it!"

"Ah," murmured Bernard, giving him a long look and turning away, "it is well for you that I am willing still to regard you as my best friend!"

Gordon went on, more passionately, to Angela.

"He put me off my guard—I can't call it anything else. I know I gave him a great chance—I encouraged him, urged him, tempted him. But when once he had spoken, he should have stood to it. He should n't have had two opinions—one for me, and one for himself! He put me off my guard. It was because I still resisted him that I went to you again, that last time. But I was still afraid of you, and in my heart I believed him. As I say, I always believed him; it was his great influence upon me. He is the cleverest, the most intelligent, the most brilliant of men. I don't think that a grain less than I ever thought it," he continued, turning again to Bernard. "I think it only the more, and I don't wonder that you find a woman to believe it. But what have you done but deceive me? It was just my belief in your intelligence that reassured me. When Miss Vivian refused me a second time, and I left Baden, it was at first with a sort of relief. But there came back a better feeling—a feeling faint compared to this feeling of to-day, but strong enough to make me uneasy and to fill me with regret. To quench my regret, I kept thinking of what you had said, and it kept me quiet. Your word had such weight with me!"

"How many times more would you have wished to be refused, and how many refusals would have been required to give me my liberty?" asked Bernard.

"That question means nothing, because you never knew that I had again offered myself to Miss Vivian."

"No; you told me very little, considering all that you made me tell you."

"I told you beforehand that I should do exactly as I chose."

"You should have allowed me the same liberty!"

"Liberty!" cried Gordon. "Had n't you liberty to range the whole world over? Could n't he have found a thousand other women?"

"It is not for me to think so," said Angela, smiling a little. Gordon looked at her a moment.

"Ah, you cared for him from the first!" he cried.

"I had seen him before I ever saw you," said the girl.

Bernard suppressed an exclamation. There seemed to flash through these words a sort of retrospective confession which told him something that she had not directly told him. She blushed as soon as she had spoken, and Bernard found a beauty in this of which the brightness blinded him to the awkward aspect of the fact she had just presented to Gordon. At this fact Gordon stood staring; then at last he apprehended it—largely.

"Ah, then, it had been a plot between you!" he cried out.

Bernard and Angela exchanged a glance of pity.

"We had met for five minutes, and had exchanged a few words before I came to Baden. It was in Italy—at Siena. It was a simple accident that I never told you," Bernard explained.

"I wished that nothing should be said about it," said Angela.

"Ah, you loved him!" Gordon exclaimed.

Angela turned away—she went to the window. Bernard followed her for three seconds with his eyes; then he went on—

"If it were so, I had no reason to suppose it. You have accused me of deceiving you, but I deceived only myself. You say I put you off your guard, but you should rather say you put me on mine. It was, thanks to that, that I fell into the most senseless, the most brutal of delusions. The delusion passed away—it had contained the germ of better things. I saw my error, and I bitterly repented of it; and on the day you were married I felt free."

"Ah, yes, I have no doubt you waited for that!" cried Gordon. "It may interest you to know that my marriage is a miserable failure."

"I am sorry to hear it—but I can't help it."

"You have seen it with your own eyes. You know all about it, and I need n't tell you."

"My dear Mr. Wright," said Angela, pleadingly, turning round, "in Heaven's name, don't say that!"

"Why should n't I say it? I came here on purpose to say it. I came here with an intention—with a plan. You know what Blanche is—you need n't pretend, for kindness to me, that you don't. You know what a precious, what an inestimable wife she must make me—how devoted, how sympathetic she must be, and what a household blessing at every hour of the day. Bernard can tell you all about us—he has seen us in the sanctity of our home." Gordon gave a bitter laugh and went on, with the same strange, serious air of explaining his plan. "She despises me, she hates me, she cares no more for me than for the button on her glove—by which I mean that she does n't care a hundredth part as much. You may say that it serves me right, and that I have got what I deserve. I married her because she was silly. I wanted a silly wife; I had an idea you were too wise. Oh, yes, that 's what I thought of you! Blanche knew why I picked her out, and undertook to supply the article required. Heaven forgive her! She has certainly kept her engagement. But you can imagine how it must have made her like me—knowing why I picked her out! She has disappointed me all the same. I thought she had a heart; but that was a mistake. It does n't matter, though, because everything is over between us."

"What do you mean, everything is over?" Bernard demanded.

"Everything will be over in a few weeks. Then I can speak to Miss Vivian seriously."

"Ah! I am glad to hear this is not serious," said Bernard.

"Miss Vivian, wait a few weeks," Gordon went on. "Give me another chance then. Then it will be perfectly right; I shall be free."

"You speak as if you were going to put an end to your wife!"

"She is rapidly putting an end to herself. She means to leave me."

"Poor, unhappy man, do you know what you are saying?" Angela murmured.

"Perfectly. I came here to say it. She means to leave me, and I mean to offer her every facility. She is dying to take a lover, and she has got an excellent one waiting for her. Bernard knows whom I mean; I don't know whether you do. She was ready to take one three months after our marriage. It is really very good of her to have waited all this time; but I don't think she can go more than a week or two longer. She is recommended a southern climate, and I am pretty sure that in the course of another ten days I may count upon their starting together for the shores of the Mediterranean. The shores of the Mediterranean, you know, are lovely, and I hope they will do her a world of good. As soon as they have left Paris I will let you know; and then you will of course admit that, virtually, I am free."

"I don't understand you."

"I suppose you are aware," said Gordon, "that we have the advantage of being natives of a country in which marriages may be legally dissolved."

Angela stared; then, softly—

"Are you speaking of a divorce?"

"I believe that is what they call it," Gordon answered, gazing back at her with his densely clouded blue eyes. "The lawyers do it for you; and if she goes away with Lovelock, nothing will be more simple than for me to have it arranged."

Angela stared, I say; and Bernard was staring, too. Then the latter, turning away, broke out into a tremendous, irrepressible laugh.

Gordon looked at him a moment; then he said to Angela, with a deeper tremor in his voice—

"He was my dearest friend."

"I never felt more devoted to you than at this moment!" Bernard declared, smiling still.

Gordon had fixed his sombre eyes upon the girl again.

"Do you understand me now?"

Angela looked back at him for some instants.

"Yes," she murmured at last.

"And will you wait, and give me another chance?"

"Yes," she said, in the same tone.

Bernard uttered a quick exclamation, but Angela checked him with a glance, and Gordon looked from one of them to the other.

"Can I trust you?" Gordon asked.

"I will make you happy," said Angela.

Bernard wondered what under the sun she meant; but he thought he might safely add—

"I will abide by her choice."

Gordon actually began to smile.

"It won't be long, I think; two or three weeks."

Angela made no answer to this; she fixed her eyes on the floor.

"I shall see Blanche as often as possible," she presently said.

"By all means! The more you see her the better you will understand me."

"I understand you very well now. But you have shaken me very much, and you must leave me. I shall see you also— often."

Gordon took up his hat and stick; he saw that Bernard did not do the same.

"And Bernard?" he exclaimed.

"I shall ask him to leave Paris," said Angela.

"Will you go?"

"I will do what Angela requests," said Bernard.

"You have heard what she requests; it 's for you to come now."

"Ah, you must at least allow me to take leave!" cried Bernard.

Gordon went to the door, and when he had opened it he stood for a while, holding it and looking at his companions. Then—

"I assure you she won't be long!" he said to Angela, and rapidly passed out.

The others stood silent till they heard the outer door of the apartment close behind him.

"And now please to elucidate!" said Bernard, folding his arms.

Angela gave no answer for some moments; then she turned upon him a smile which appeared incongruous, but which her words presently helped to explain.

"He is intensely in love with his wife!"

XXIX

THIS STATEMENT was very effective, but it might well have seemed at first to do more credit to her satiric powers than to her faculty of observation. This was the light in which it presented itself to Bernard; but, little by little, as she amplified the text, he grew to think well of it, and at last he was quite ready to place it, as a triumph of sagacity, on a level with that other discovery which she had made the evening before and with regard to which his especial errand to-day had been to congratulate her afresh. It brought him, however, less satisfaction than it appeared to bring to his clever companion; for, as he observed plausibly enough, Gordon was quite out of his head, and, this being the case, of what importance was the secret of his heart?

"The secret of his heart and the condition of his head are one and the same thing," said Angela. "He is turned upside down by the wretchedly false position that he has got into with his wife. She has treated him badly, but he has treated her wrongly. They are in love with each other, and yet they both do nothing but hide it. He is not in the least in love with poor me—not to-day any more than he was three years ago. He thinks he is, because he is full of sorrow and bitterness, and because the news of our engagement has given him a shock. But that 's only a pretext—a chance to pour out the grief and pain which have been accumulating in his heart under a sense of his estrangement from Blanche. He is too proud to attribute his feelings to that cause, even to himself; but he wanted to cry out and say he was hurt, to demand justice for a wrong; and the revelation of the state of things between you and me—which of course strikes him as incongruous; we must allow largely for that—came to him as a sudden opportunity. No, no," the girl went on, with a generous ardor in her face, following further the train of her argument, which she appeared to find extremely attractive, "I know what you are going to say and I deny it. I am not fanciful, or sophistical, or irrational, and I know perfectly what I am about. Men are so stupid; it 's only women that have real discernment. Leave me alone, and I shall do something. Blanche is silly, yes, very silly; but she is not so bad as her husband accused her of being, in those dreadful words which he will live to repent of. She is wise enough to care for him, greatly, at bottom, and to feel her little heart filled with rage and shame that he does n't appear to care for her. If he would take her a little more seriously—it 's an immense pity he married her *because* she was silly!—she would be flattered by it, and she would try and deserve it. No, no, no! she does n't, in reality, care a straw for Captain Lovelock, I assure you, I promise you she does n't. A woman can tell. She is in danger, possibly, and if her present situation, as regards her husband, lasts, she might do something as horrid as he said. But she would do it out of spite—not out of affection for the Captain, who must be got immediately out of the way. She only keeps him to torment her husband and make Gordon come back to her. She would drop him forever to-morrow." Angela paused a moment, reflecting, with a kindled eye. "And she shall!"

Bernard looked incredulous.

"How will that be, Miss Solomon?"

"You shall see when you come back."

"When I come back? Pray, where am I going?"

"You will leave Paris for a fortnight—as I promised our poor friend."

Bernard gave an irate laugh.

"My dear girl, you are ridiculous! Your promising it was almost as childish as his asking it."

"To play with a child you must be childish. Just see the effect of this abominable passion of love, which you have been crying up to me so! By its operation Gordon Wright, the most sensible man of our acquaintance, is reduced to the level of infancy! If you will only go away, I will manage him."

"You certainly manage me! Pray, where shall I go?"

"Wherever you choose. I will write to you every day."

"That will be an inducement," said Bernard. "You know I have never received a letter from you."

"I write the most delightful ones!" Angela exclaimed; and she succeeded in making him promise to start that night for London.

She had just done so when Mrs. Vivian presented herself,

and the good lady was not a little astonished at being informed of his intention.

"You surely are not going to give up my daughter to oblige Mr. Wright?" she observed.

"Upon my word, I feel as if I were!" said Bernard.

"I will explain it, dear mamma," said Angela. "It is very interesting. Mr. Wright has made a most fearful scene; the state of things between him and Blanche is dreadful."

Mrs. Vivian opened her clear eyes.

"You really speak as if you liked it!"

"She does like it—she told Gordon so," said Bernard. "I don't know what she is up to! Gordon has taken leave of his wits; he wishes to put away his wife."

"To put her away?"

"To repudiate her, as the historians say!"

"To repudiate little Blanche!" murmured Mrs. Vivian, as if she were struck with the incongruity of the operation.

"I mean to keep them together," said Angela, with a firm decision.

Her mother looked at her with admiration.

"My dear daughter, I will assist you."

The two ladies had such an air of mysterious competence to the task they had undertaken that it seemed to Bernard that nothing was left to him but to retire into temporary exile. He accordingly betook himself to London, where he had social resources which would, perhaps, make exile endurable. He found himself, however, little disposed to avail himself of these resources, and he treated himself to no pleasures but those of memory and expectation. He ached with a sense of his absence from Mrs. Vivian's deeply familiar sky-parlor, which seemed to him for the time the most sacred spot on earth—if on earth it could be called—and he consigned to those generous postal receptacles which ornament with their brilliant hue the London street-corners, an inordinate number of the most voluminous epistles that had ever been dropped into them. He took long walks, alone, and thought all the way of Angela, to whom, it seemed to him, that the character of ministering angel was extremely becoming. She was faithful to her promise of writing to him every day, and she was an angel who wielded—so at least Bernard thought, and he was particular about letters—a very ingenious pen. Of course she had only one topic—the success of her operations with regard to Gordon. "Mamma has undertaken Blanche," she wrote, "and I am devoting myself to Mr. W. It is really very interesting." She told Bernard all about it in detail, and he also found it interesting; doubly so, indeed, for it must be confessed that the charming figure of the mistress of his affections attempting to heal a great social breach with her light and delicate hands, divided his attention pretty equally with the distracted, the distorted, the almost ludicrous, image of his old friend.

Angela wrote that Gordon had come back to see her the day after his first visit, and had seemed greatly troubled on learning that Bernard had taken himself off. "It was because you insisted on it, of course," he said; "it was not from feeling the justice of it himself." "I told him," said Angela, in her letter, "that I had made a point of it, but that we certainly ought to give you a little credit for it. But I could n't insist upon this, for fear of sounding a wrong note and exciting afresh what I suppose he would be pleased to term his jealousy. He asked me where you had gone, and when I told him—'Ah, how he must hate me!' he exclaimed. 'There you are quite wrong,' I answered. 'He feels as kindly to you as—as I do.' He looked as if he by no means believed this; but, indeed, he looks as if he believed nothing at all. He is quite upset and demoralized. He stayed half an hour and paid me his visit—trying hard to 'please' me again! Poor man, he is in a charming state to please the fair sex! But if he does n't please me, he interests me more and more; I make bold to say that to you. You would have said it would be very awkward; but, strangely enough, I found it very easy. I suppose it is because I am so interested. Very likely it was awkward for him, poor fellow, for I can certify that he was not a whit happier at the end of his half-hour, in spite of the privilege he had enjoyed. He said nothing more about you, and we talked of Paris and New York, of Baden and Rome. Imagine the situation! I shall make no resistance whatever to it; I shall simply let him perceive that conversing with me on these topics does not make him feel a bit more comfortable, and that he must look elsewhere for a remedy. I said not a word about Blanche."

She spoke of Blanche, however, the next time. "He came again this afternoon," she said in her second letter, "and he wore exactly the same face as yesterday—namely, a very unhappy one. If I were not entirely too wise to believe his account of himself, I might suppose that he was unhappy because Blanche shows symptoms of not taking flight. She has been with us a great deal—she has no idea what is going on—and I can't honestly say that she chatters any less than usual. But she is greatly interested in certain shops that she is buying out, and especially in her visits to her tailor. Mamma has proposed to her—in view of your absence—to come and stay with us, and she does n't seem afraid of the idea. I told her husband to-day that we had asked her, and that we hoped he had no objection. 'None whatever; but she won't come.' 'On the contrary, she says she will.' 'She will pretend to, up to the last minute; and then she will find a pretext for backing out.' 'Decidedly, you think very ill of her,' I said. 'She hates me,' he answered, looking at me strangely. 'You say that of every one,' I said. 'Yesterday you said it of Bernard.' 'Ah, for him there would be more reason!' he exclaimed. 'I won't attempt to answer for Bernard,' I went on, 'but I will answer for Blanche. Your idea of her hating you is a miserable delusion. She cares for you more than for any one in the world. You only misunderstand each other, and with a little good will on both sides you can easily get out of your tangle.' But he would n't listen to me; he stopped me short. I saw I should excite him if I insisted; so I dropped the subject. But it is not for long; he *shall* listen to me."

Later she wrote that Blanche had in fact "backed out," and would not come to stay with them, having given as an excuse that she was perpetually trying on dresses, and that at Mrs. Vivian's she should be at an inconvenient distance from the temple of these sacred rites, and the high priest who conducted the worship. "But we see her every day," said Angela, "and mamma is constantly with her. She likes mamma better than me. Mamma listens to her a great deal and talks to her a little—I can't do either when we are alone. I don't know what she says—I mean what mamma says; what Blanche says I know as well as if I heard it. We see nothing of Captain Lovelock, and mamma tells me she has not spoken of him for two days. She thinks this is a better symptom, but I am not so sure. Poor Mr. Wright treats it as a great triumph that Blanche should behave as he foretold. He is welcome to the comfort he can get out of this, for he certainly gets none from anything else. The society of your correspondent is not that balm to his spirit which he appeared to expect, and this in spite of the fact that I have been as gentle and kind with him as I know how to be. He is very silent—he sometimes sits for ten minutes without speaking; I assure you it is n't amusing. Sometimes he looks at me as if he were going to break out with that crazy idea to which he treated me the other day. But he says nothing, and then I see that he is not thinking of me—he is simply thinking of Blanche. The more he thinks of her the better."

"My dear Bernard," she began on another occasion, "I hope you are not dying of *ennui*, etc. Over here things are going so-so. He asked me yesterday to go with him to the Louvre, and we walked about among the pictures for half an hour. Mamma thinks it a very strange sort of thing for me to be doing, and though she delights, of all things, in a good cause, she is not sure that this cause is good enough to justify the means. I admit that the means are very singular, and, as far as the Louvre is concerned, they were not successful. We sat and looked for a quarter of an hour at the great Venus who has lost her arms, and he said never a word. I think he does n't know what to say. Before we separated he asked me if I heard from you. 'Oh, yes,' I said, 'every day.' 'And does he speak of me?' 'Never!' I answered; and I think he looked disappointed." Bernard had, in fact, in writing to Angela, scarcely mentioned his name. "He had not been here for two days," she continued, at the end of a week; "but last evening, very late—too late for a visitor—he came in. Mamma had left the drawing-room, and I was sitting alone; I immediately saw that we had reached a crisis. I thought at first he was going to tell me that Blanche had carried out his prediction; but I presently saw that this was not where the shoe pinched; and, besides, I knew that mamma was watching her too closely. 'How can I have ever been such a dull-souled idiot?' he broke out, as soon as he had got into the room. 'I like to hear you say that,' I said, 'because it does n't seem to me that you have been at all wise.' 'You are cleverness, kindness, tact, in the most perfect form!' he went on. As a veracious historian I am bound to tell you that he paid me a bushel of compliments, and thanked me in the most flattering terms for my having let him bore me so for a week. 'You have not bored me,' I said; 'you have interested me.' 'Yes,' he cried, 'as a curious case of monomania. It 's a part of your kindness to say that; but I know I have bored you to death; and the end of it all is that you despise me. You can't help despising me; I despise myself. I used to think that I was a man, but I have given that up; I am a poor creature! I used to think I could take things quietly and bear them bravely. But I can't! If it were not for very shame I could sit here and cry to you.' 'Don't mind me,' I said; 'you know it is a part of our agreement that I was not to be critical.' 'Our agreement?' he repeated, vaguely. 'I see you have forgotten it,' I answered; 'but it does n't in the least matter; it is not of that I wish to talk to you. All the more that it has n't done you a particle of good. I have been extremely nice with you for a week; but you are just as unhappy now as you were at the beginning. Indeed, I think you are rather worse.' 'Heaven forgive me, Miss Vivian, I believe I am!' he cried. 'Heaven will easily forgive you; you are on the wrong road. To catch up with your happiness, which has been running away from you, you must take another; you must travel in the same direction as Blanche; you must not separate yourself from your wife.' At the sound of Blanche's name he jumped up and took his usual tone; he knew all about his wife, and needed no information. But I made him sit down again, and I made him listen to me. I made him listen for half an hour, and at the end of the time he was interested. He had all the appearance of it; he sat gazing at me, and at last the tears came into his eyes. I believe I had a moment of eloquence. I don't know what I said, nor how I said it, to what point it would bear examination, nor how, if you had been there, it would seem to you, as a disinterested critic, to hang together; but I know that after a while there were tears in my own eyes. I begged him not to give up Blanche; I assured him that she is not so foolish as she seems; that she is a very delicate little creature to handle, and that, in reality, whatever she does, she is thinking only of him. He had been all goodness and kindness to her, I knew that; but he had not, from the first, been able to conceal from her that he regarded her chiefly as a pretty kitten. She wished to be more than that, and she took refuge in flirting, simply to excite his jealousy and make him feel strongly about her. He has felt strongly, and he was feeling strongly now; he was feeling passionately—that was my whole contention. But he had perhaps never made it plain to those rather near-sighted little mental eyes of hers, and he had let her suppose something that could n't fail to rankle in her mind and torment it. 'You have let her suppose,' I said, 'that you were thinking of me, and the poor girl has been jealous of me. I know it, but from nothing she herself has said. She has said nothing; she has been too proud and too considerate. If you don't think that 's to her honor, I do. She has had a chance every day for a week, but she has treated me without a grain of spite. I have appreciated it, I have understood it, and it has touched me very much. It ought to touch you, Mr. Wright. When she heard I was engaged to Mr. Longueville, it gave her an immense relief. And yet, at the same moment you were protesting, and denouncing, and saying those horrible things about her! I know how she appears—she likes admiration. But the admiration in the world which she would most delight in just now would be yours. She plays with Captain Lovelock as a child does with a wooden harlequin, she pulls a string and he throws up his arms and legs. She has about as much intention of eloping with him as a little girl might have of eloping with a pasteboard Jim Crow. If you were to have a frank explanation with her, Blanche would very soon throw Jim Crow out of the window. I very humbly entreat you to cease thinking of me. I don't know what wrong you have ever done me, or what kindness I have ever done you, that you should feel obliged to trouble your head about me. You see all I am—I tell you now. I am nothing in the least remarkable. As for your thinking ill of me at Baden, I never knew it nor cared about it. If it had been so, you see how I should have got over it. Dear Mr. Wright, we might be such good friends, if you would only believe me. She 's so pretty, so charming, so universally admired. You said just now you had bored me, but it 's nothing—in spite of all the compliments you have paid me—to the way I have bored you. If *she* could only know it—that I have bored you! Let her see for half an hour that I am out of your mind—the rest will take care of itself. She might so easily have made a quarrel with me. The way she has behaved to me is one of the prettiest things I have ever seen, and you shall see the way I shall always behave to her! Don't think it necessary to say out of politeness that I have not bored you; it is not in the least necessary. You know perfectly well that you are disappointed in the charm of my society. And I have done my best, too. I can honestly affirm that!' For some time he said nothing, and then he remarked that I was very clever, but he did n't see a word of sense in what I said. 'It only proves,' I said, 'that the merit of my conversation is smaller than you had taken it into your head to fancy. But I have done you good, all the same. Don't contradict me; you don't know yet; and it 's too late for us to argue about it. You will tell me to-morrow.' "

XXX

S OME THREE EVENINGS after he received this last report of
the progress of affairs in Paris, Bernard, upon whom the
burden of exile sat none the more lightly as the days went on,
turned out of the Strand into one of the theatres. He had
been gloomily pushing his way through the various London
densities—the November fog, the nocturnal darkness, the
jostling crowd. He was too restless to do anything but walk,
and he had been saying to himself, for the thousandth time,
that if he had been guilty of a misdemeanor in succumbing to
the attractions of the admirable girl who showed to such advantage in letters of twelve pages, his fault was richly expiated
by these days of impatience and bereavement. He gave little
heed to the play; his thoughts were elsewhere, and, while
they rambled, his eyes wandered round the house. Suddenly,
on the other side of it, he beheld Captain Lovelock, seated
squarely in his orchestra-stall, but, if Bernard was not mistaken, paying as little attention to the stage as he himself had
done. The Captain's eyes, it is true, were fixed upon the
scene; his head was bent a little, his magnificent beard rippled
over the expanse of his shirt-front. But Bernard was not slow
to see that his gaze was heavy and opaque, and that, though
he was staring at the actresses, their charms were lost upon
him. He saw that, like himself, poor Lovelock had matter for
reflection in his manly breast, and he concluded that Blanche's
ponderous swain was also suffering from a sense of disjunc-
tion. Lovelock sat in the same posture all the evening, and
that his imagination had not projected itself into the play was
proved by the fact that during the entractes he gazed with the
same dull fixedness at the curtain. Bernard forebore to interrupt him; we know that he was not at this moment socially
inclined, and he judged that the Captain was as little so, inasmuch as causes even more imperious than those which had
operated in his own case must have been at the bottom of his
sudden appearance in London. On leaving the theatre, however, Bernard found himself detained with the crowd in the
vestibule near the door, which, wide open to the street, was
a scene of agitation and confusion. It had come on to rain,

and the raw dampness mingled itself with the dusky uproar of the Strand. At last, among the press of people, as he was passing out, our hero became aware that he had been brought into contact with Lovelock, who was walking just beside him. At the same moment Lovelock noticed him—looked at him for an instant, and then looked away. But he looked back again the next instant, and the two men then uttered that inarticulate and inexpressive exclamation which passes for a sign of greeting among gentlemen of the Anglo-Saxon race, in their moments of more acute self-consciousness.

"Oh, are you here?" said Bernard. "I thought you were in Paris."

"No; I ain't in Paris," Lovelock answered with some dryness. "Tired of the beastly hole!"

"Oh, I see," said Bernard. "Excuse me while I put up my umbrella."

He put up his umbrella, and from under it, the next moment, he saw the Captain waving two fingers at him out of the front of a hansom. When he returned to his hotel he found on his table a letter superscribed in Gordon Wright's hand. This communication ran as follows:

"I believe you are making a fool of me. In Heaven's name, come back to Paris! G. W."

Bernard hardly knew whether to regard these few words as a further declaration of war, or as an overture to peace; but he lost no time in complying with the summons they conveyed. He started for Paris the next morning, and in the evening, after he had removed the dust of his journey and swallowed a hasty dinner, he rang at Mrs. Vivian's door. This lady and her daughter gave him a welcome which—I will not say satisfied him, but which, at least, did something toward soothing the still unhealed wounds of separation.

"And what is the news of Gordon?" he presently asked.

"We have not seen him in three days," said Angela.

"He is cured, dear Bernard; he must be. Angela has been wonderful," Mrs. Vivian declared.

"You should have seen mamma with Blanche," her daughter said, smiling. "It was most remarkable."

Mrs. Vivian smiled, too, very gently.

"Dear little Blanche! Captain Lovelock has gone to London."

"Yes, he thinks it a beastly hole. Ah, no," Bernard added, "I have got it wrong."

But it little mattered. Late that night, on his return to his own rooms, Bernard sat gazing at his fire. He had not begun to undress; he was thinking of a good many things. He was in the midst of his reflections when there came a rap at his door, which the next moment was flung open. Gordon Wright stood there, looking at him—with a gaze which Bernard returned for a moment before bidding him to come in. Gordon came in and came up to him; then he held out his hand. Bernard took it with great satisfaction; his last feeling had been that he was very weary of this ridiculous quarrel, and it was an extreme relief to find it was over.

"It was very good of you to go to London," said Gordon, looking at him with all the old serious honesty of his eyes.

"I have always tried to do what I could to oblige you," Bernard answered, smiling.

"You must have cursed me over there," Gordon went on.

"I did, a little. As you were cursing me here, it was permissible."

"That's over now," said Gordon. "I came to welcome you back. It seemed to me I could n't lay my head on my pillow without speaking to you."

"I am glad to get back," Bernard admitted, smiling still. "I can't deny that. And I find you as I believed I should." Then he added, seriously—"I knew Angela would keep us good friends."

For a moment Gordon said nothing. Then, at last—

"Yes, for that purpose it did n't matter which of us should marry her. If it had been I," he added, "she would have made you accept it."

"Ah, I don't know!" Bernard exclaimed.

"I am sure of it," said Gordon earnestly—almost argumentatively. "She's an extraordinary woman."

"Keeping you good friends with me—that's a great thing. But it's nothing to her keeping you good friends with your wife."

Gordon looked at Bernard for an instant; then he fixed his eyes for some time on the fire.

"Yes, that is the greatest of all things. A man should value his wife. He should believe in her. He has taken her, and he should keep her—especially when there is a great deal of good in her. I was a great fool the other day," he went on. "I don't remember what I said. It was very weak."

"It seemed to me feeble," said Bernard. "But it is quite within a man's rights to be a fool once in a while, and you had never abused of the license."

"Well, I have done it for a lifetime—for a lifetime." And Gordon took up his hat. He looked into the crown of it for a moment, and then he fixed his eyes on Bernard's again. "But there is one thing I hope you won't mind my saying. I have come back to my old impression of Miss Vivian."

"Your old impression?"

And Miss Vivian's accepted lover frowned a little.

"I mean that she 's not simple. She 's very strange."

Bernard's frown cleared away in a sudden, almost eager smile.

"Say at once that you dislike her! That will do capitally."

Gordon shook his head, and he, too, almost smiled a little.

"It 's not true. She 's very wonderful. And if I did dislike her, I should struggle with it. It would never do for me to dislike your wife!"

After he had gone, when the night was half over, Bernard, lying awake a while, gave a laugh in the still darkness, as this last sentence came back to him.

On the morrow he saw Blanche, for he went to see Gordon. The latter, at first, was not at home; but he had a quarter of an hour's talk with his wife, whose powers of conversation were apparently not in the smallest degree affected by anything that had occurred.

"I hope you enjoyed your visit to London," she said. "Did you go to buy Angela a set of diamonds in Bond Street? You did n't buy anything—you did n't go into a shop? Then pray what did you go for? Excuse my curiosity—it seems to me it 's rather flattering. I never know anything unless I am told. I have n't any powers of observation. I noticed you went— oh, yes, I observed that very much; and I thought it very strange, under the circumstances. Your most intimate friend arrived in Paris, and you choose the next day to make a little tour! I don't like to see you treat my husband so; he would never have done it to you. And if you did n't stay for Gordon, you might have staid for Angela. I never heard of anything so monstrous as a gentleman rushing away from the object of his affection, for no particular purpose that any one could discover, the day after she has accepted him. It was not the day after? Well, it was too soon, at any rate. Angela could n't in the least tell me what you had gone for; she said it was for a 'change.' That was a charming reason! But she was very much ashamed of you—and so was I; and at last we all sent Captain Lovelock after you to bring you back. You came back without him? Ah, so much the better; I suppose he is still looking for you, and, as he is n't very clever, that will occupy him for some time. We want to occupy him; we don't approve of his being so idle. However, for my own part, I am very glad you were away. I was a great deal at Mrs. Vivian's, and I should n't have felt nearly so much at liberty to go if I had known I should always find you there making love to Mademoiselle. It would n't have seemed to me discreet,—I know what you are going to say—that it 's the first time you ever heard of my wishing to avoid an indiscretion. It 's a taste I have taken up lately,—for the same reason you went to London, for a 'change.' " Here Blanche paused for an appreciable moment; and then she added—"Well, I must say, I have never seen anything so lovely as Mrs. Vivian's influence. I hope mamma won't be disappointed in it this time."

When Bernard next saw the other two ladies, he said to them that he was surprised at the way in which clever women incurred moral responsibilities.

"We like them," said Mrs. Vivian. "We delight in them!"

"Well," said Bernard, "I would n't for the world have it on my conscience to have reconciled poor Gordon to Mrs. Blanche."

"You are not to say a word against Blanche," Angela declared. "She 's a little miracle."

"It will be all right, dear Bernard," Mrs. Vivian added, with soft authority.

"I have taken a great fancy to her," the younger lady went on.

Bernard gave a little laugh.

"Gordon is right in his ultimate opinion. You are very strange!"

"You may abuse me as much as you please; but I will never hear a word against Mrs. Gordon."

And she never would in future; though it is not recorded that Bernard availed himself in any special degree of the license offered him in conjunction with this warning.

Blanche's health within a few days had, according to her own account, taken a marvellous turn for the better; but her husband appeared still to think it proper that they should spend the winter beneath a brilliant sun, and he presently informed his friends that they had at last settled it between them that a voyage up the Nile must be, for a thoroughly united couple, a very agreeable pastime. To perform this expedition advantageously they must repair to Cairo without delay, and for this reason he was sure that Bernard and Angela would easily understand their not making a point of waiting for the wedding. These happy people quite understood it. Their nuptials were to be celebrated with extreme simplicity. If, however, Gordon was not able to be present, he, in conjunction with his wife, bought for Angela, as a bridal gift, a necklace of the most beautiful pearls the Rue de la Paix could furnish; and on his arrival at Cairo, while he waited for his dragoman to give the signal for starting, he found time, in spite of the exactions of that large correspondence which has been more than once mentioned in the course of our narrative, to write Bernard the longest letter he had ever addressed to him. The letter reached Bernard in the middle of his honeymoon.

Chronology

1843   Born April 15 at 21 Washington Place, New York City, the
            second child (after William, born January 11, 1842, N.Y.)
            of Henry James of Albany and Mary Robertson Walsh of
            New York. Father lives on inheritance of $10,000 a year,
            his share of litigated $3,000,000 fortune of his Albany fa-
            ther William James, an Irish immigrant who came to the
            U.S. immediately after the Revolution.

1843–45   Accompanied by mother's sister, Catharine Walsh, and
            servants, the James parents take infant children to England
            and later to France. Reside at Windsor, where father has
            nervous collapse ("vastation") and experiences spiritual il-
            lumination. He becomes a Swedenborgian (May 1844),
            devoting his time to lecturing and religious-philosophical
            writings. James later claimed his earliest memory was a
            glimpse, during his second year, of the Place Vendôme in
            Paris with its Napoleonic column.

1845–47   Family returns to New York. Garth Wilkinson James
            (Wilky) born July 21, 1845. Family moves to Albany at 50
            N. Pearl St., a few doors from grandmother Catharine
            Barber James. Robertson James (Bob or Rob) born Au-
            gust 29, 1846.

1847–55   Family moves to a large house at 58 W. 14th St., New
            York. Alice James born August 7, 1848. Relatives and fa-
            ther's friends and acquaintances—Horace Greeley, George
            Ripley, Charles Anderson Dana, William Cullen Bryant,
            Bronson Alcott, and Ralph Waldo Emerson ("I knew he
            was great, greater than any of our friends")—are frequent
            visitors. Thackeray calls during his lecture tour on the En-
            glish humorists. Summers at New Brighton on Staten Is-
            land and Fort Hamilton on Long Island's south shore. On
            steamboat to Fort Hamilton August 1850, hears Washing-
            ton Irving tell his father of Margaret Fuller's drowning in
            shipwreck off Fire Island. Frequently visits Barnum's
            American Museum on free days. Taken to art shows and
            theaters; writes and draws stage scenes. Described by fa-
            ther as "a devourer of libraries." Taught in assorted private

schools and by tutors in lower Broadway and Greenwich Village. But father claims in 1848 that American schooling fails to provide "sensuous education" for his children and plans to take them to Europe.

1855–58 Family (with Aunt Kate) sails for Liverpool, June 27. James is intermittently sick with malarial fever as they travel to Paris, Lyon, and Geneva. After Swiss summer, leaves for London where Robert Thomson (later Robert Louis Stevenson's tutor) is engaged. Early summer 1856, family moves to Paris. Another tutor engaged and children attend experimental Fourierist school. Acquires fluency in French. Family goes to Boulogne-sur-mer in summer, where James contracts typhoid. Spends late October in Paris, but American crash of 1857 returns family to Boulogne where they can live more cheaply. Attends public school (fellow classmate is Coquelin, the future French actor).

1858–59 Family returns to America and settles in Newport, Rhode Island. Goes boating, fishing, and riding. Attends Reverend W. C. Leverett's Berkeley Institute, and forms friendship with classmate Thomas Sergeant Perry. Takes long walks and sketches with the painter John La Farge.

1859–60 Father, still dissatisfied with American education, returns family to Geneva in October. James attends a pre-engineering school, Institution Rochette, because parents, with "a flattering misconception of my aptitudes," feel he might benefit from less reading and more mathematics. After a few months withdraws from all classes except French, German, and Latin, and joins William as a special student at the Academy (later the University of Geneva) where he attends lectures on literary subjects. Studies German in Bonn during summer 1860.

1860–62 Family returns to Newport in September where William studies with William Morris Hunt, and James sits in on his classes. La Farge introduces him to works of Balzac, Merimée, Musset, and Browning. Wilky and Bob attend Frank Sanborn's experimental school in Concord with children of Hawthorne and Emerson and John Brown's daughter. Early in 1861, orphaned Temple cousins come to live in Newport. Develops close friendship with cousin

Mary (Minnie) Temple. Goes on a week's walking tour in July in New Hampshire with Perry. William abandons art in autumn 1861 and enters Lawrence Scientific School at Harvard. James suffers back injury in a stable fire while serving as a volunteer fireman. Reads Hawthorne ("an American could be an artist, one of the finest").

1862–63   Enters Harvard Law School (Dane Hall). Wilky enlists in the Massachusetts 44th Regiment, and later in Colonel Robert Gould Shaw's 54th, one of the first black regiments. Summer 1863, Bob joins the Massachusetts 55th, another black regiment, under Colonel Hollowell. James withdraws from law studies to try writing. Sends unsigned stories to magazines. Wilky is badly wounded and brought home to Newport in August.

1864   Family moves from Newport to 13 Ashburton Place, Boston. First tale, "A Tragedy of Error" (unsigned), published in *Continental Monthly* (Feb. 1864). Stays in Northampton, Massachusetts, early August–November. Begins writing book reviews for *North American Review* and forms friendship with its editor, Charles Eliot Norton, and his family, including his sister Grace (with whom he maintains a long-lasting correspondence). Wilky returns to his regiment.

1865   First signed tale, "The Story of a Year," published in *Atlantic Monthly* (March 1865). Begins to write reviews for the newly founded *Nation* and publishes anonymously in it during next fifteen years. William sails on a scientific expedition with Louis Agassiz to the Amazon. During summer James vacations in the White Mountains with Minnie Temple and her family; joined by Oliver Wendell Holmes Jr. and John Chipman Gray, both recently demobilized. Father subsidizes plantation for Wilky and Bob in Florida with black hired workers. The idealistic but impractical venture fails in 1870.

1866–68   Continues to publish reviews and tales in Boston and New York journals. William returns from Brazil and resumes medical education. James has recurrence of back ailment and spends summer in Swampscott, Massachusetts. Begins friendship with William Dean Howells. Family moves to 20 Quincy St., Cambridge. William, suffering from nervous ailments, goes to Germany in spring 1867. "Poor Richard," James's longest story to date, published in *Atlantic Monthly* (June–Aug. 1867). William begins intermittent criticism of Henry's story-telling and style (which will continue throughout their careers). Momentary meeting with Charles Dickens at Norton's house. Vacations in Jefferson, New Hampshire, summer 1868. William returns from Europe.

1869–70   Sails in February for European tour. Visits English towns and cathedrals. Through Nortons meets Leslie Stephen, William Morris, Dante Gabriel Rossetti, Edward Burne-Jones, John Ruskin, Charles Darwin, and George Eliot (the "one marvel" of his stay in London). Goes to Paris in May, then travels in Switzerland in summer and hikes into Italy in autumn, where he stays in Milan, Venice (Sept.), Florence, and Rome (Oct. 30–Dec. 28). Returns to England to drink the waters at Malvern health spa in Worcestershire because of digestive troubles. Stays in Paris en route and has first experience of Comédie Française. Learns that his beloved cousin, Minnie Temple, has died of tuberculosis.

1870–72   Returns to Cambridge in May. Travels to Rhode Island, Vermont, and New York to write travel sketches for *The Nation*. Spends a few days with Emerson in Concord. Meets Bret Harte at Howells' home April 1871. *Watch and Ward*, his first novel, published in *Atlantic Monthly* (Aug.–Dec. 1871). Serves as occasional art reviewer for the *Atlantic* January–March 1872.

1872–74   Accompanies Aunt Kate and sister Alice on tour of England, France, Switzerland, Italy, Austria, and Germany from May through October. Writes travel sketches for *The Nation*. Spends autumn in Paris, becoming friends with James Russell Lowell. Escorts Emerson through the Louvre. (Later, on Emerson's return from Egypt, will show him the Vatican.) Goes to Florence in December and from there to Rome, where he becomes friends with actress Fanny Kemble, her daughter Sarah Butler Wister, and William Wetmore Story and his family. In Italy sees old family friend Francis Boott and his daughter Elizabeth (Lizzie), expatriates who have lived for many years in Florentine villa on Bellosguardo. Takes up horseback riding on the Campagna. Encounters Matthew Arnold in April 1873 at Story's. Moves from Rome hotel to rooms of his own. Continues writing and now earns enough to support himself. Leaves Rome in June, spends summer in Bad Homburg. In October goes to Florence, where William joins him. They also visit Rome, William returning to America in March. In Baden-Baden June–August and returns to America September 4, with *Roderick Hudson* all but finished.

1875   *Roderick Hudson* serialized in *Atlantic Monthly* from January (published by Osgood at the end of the year). First book, *A Passionate Pilgrim and Other Tales*, published January 31. Tries living and writing in New York, in rooms at 111 E. 25th Street. Earns $200 a month from novel installments and continued reviewing, but finds New York too expensive. *Transatlantic Sketches*, published in April, sells almost 1,000 copies in three months. In Cambridge in July decides to return to Europe; arranges with John Hay, assistant to the publisher, to write Paris letters for the New York *Tribune*.

1875–76   Arriving in Paris in November, he takes rooms at 29 Rue de Luxembourg (since renamed Cambon). Becomes friend of Ivan Turgenev and is introduced by him to Gustave Flaubert's Sunday parties. Meets Edmond de Goncourt, Émile Zola, G. Charpentier (the publisher), Catulle Mendès, Alphonse Daudet, Guy de Maupassant, Ernest Renan, Gustave Doré. Makes friends with Charles Sanders Peirce, who is in Paris. Reviews (unfavorably) the early Impressionists at the Durand-Ruel gallery. By midsummer has received $400 for *Tribune* pieces, but editor asks for more Parisian gossip and James resigns. Travels in France during July, visiting Normandy and the Midi, and in September crosses to San Sebastian, Spain, to see a bullfight ("I thought the bull, in any case, a finer fellow than any of his tormentors"). Moves to London in December, taking rooms at 3 Bolton Street, Piccadilly, where he will live for the next decade.

1877   *The American* published. Meets Robert Browning and George du Maurier. Leaves London in midsummer for visit to Paris and then goes to Italy. In Rome rides again in Campagna and hears of an episode that inspires "Daisy

Miller." Back in England, spends Christmas at Stratford with Fanny Kemble.

1878 Publishes first book in England, *French Poets and Novelists* (by Macmillan). Appearance of "Daisy Miller" in *Cornhill Magazine*, edited by Leslie Stephen, is international success, but by publishing it abroad loses American copyright and story is pirated in U.S. *Cornhill* also prints "An International Episode." *The Europeans* is serialized in *Atlantic*. Now a celebrity, he dines out often, visits country houses, gains weight, takes long walks, fences, and does weight-lifting to reduce. Elected to Reform Club. Meets Tennyson, George Meredith, and James McNeill Whistler. William marries Alice Howe Gibbens.

1879 Immersed in London society (". . . dined out during the past winter 107 times!"). Meets Edmund Gosse and Robert Louis Stevenson, who will later become his close friends. Sees much of Henry Adams and his wife, Marian (Clover), in London and later in Paris. Takes rooms in Paris, September–December. *Confidence* is serialized in *Scribner's* and published by Chatto & Windus. *Hawthorne* appears in Macmillan's "English Men of Letters" series.

1880–81 Stays in Florence March–May to work on *The Portrait of a Lady*. Meets Constance Fenimore Woolson, American novelist and grandniece of James Fenimore Cooper. Returns to Bolton Street in June, where William visits him. *Washington Square* serialized in *Cornhill Magazine* and published in U.S. by Harper & Brothers (Dec. 1880). *The Portrait of a Lady* serialized in *Macmillan's Magazine* (Oct. 1880–Nov. 1881) and *Atlantic Monthly*; published by Macmillan and Houghton, Mifflin (Nov. 1881). Publication both in United States and in England yields him the then-large income of $500 a month, though book sales are disappointing. Leaves London in February for Paris, the south of France, the Italian Riviera, and Venice, and returns home in July. Sister Alice comes to London with her friend Katharine Loring. James goes to Scotland in September.

1881–83 In November revisits America after absence of six years. Lionized in New York. Returns to Quincy Street for Christmas and sees ailing brother Wilky for the first time in ten years. In January visits Washington and the Henry Adamses and meets President Chester A. Arthur. Summoned to Cambridge by mother's death January 29 ("the sweetest, gentlest, most beneficent human being I have ever known"). All four brothers are together for the first time in fifteen years at her funeral. Alice and father move from Cambridge to Boston. Prepares a stage version of "Daisy Miller" and returns to England in May. William, now a Harvard professor, comes to Europe in September. Proposed by Leslie Stephen, James becomes member, without the usual red tape, of the Atheneum Club. Travels in France in October to write *A Little Tour in France* (published 1884) and has last visit with Turgenev, who is dying. Returns to England in December and learns of father's illness. Sails for America but Henry James Sr. dies December 18, 1882, before his arrival. Made executor of father's will. Visits brothers Wilky and Bob in Milwaukee in January. Quarrels with William over division of property—James wants to restore Wilky's share. Macmillan publishes a collected pocket edition of James's novels and tales in fourteen volumes. *Siege of London* and *Portraits of Places* published. Returns to Bolton Street in September. Wilky dies in November. Constance Fenimore Woolson comes to London for the winter.

1884–86   Goes to Paris in February and visits Daudet, Zola, and Goncourt. Again impressed with their intense concern with "art, form, manner" but calls them "mandarins." Misses Turgenev, who had died a few months before. Meets John Singer Sargent and persuades him to settle in London. Returns to Bolton Street. Sargent introduces him to young Paul Bourget. During country visits encounters many British political and social figures, including W. E. Gladstone, John Bright, and Charles Dilke. Alice, suffering from nervous ailment, arrives in England for visit in November but is too ill to travel and settles near her brother. *Tales of Three Cities* ("The Impressions of a Cousin," "Lady Barbarina," "A New England Winter") and "The Art of Fiction" published 1884. Alice goes to Bournemouth in late January. James joins her in May and becomes an intimate of Robert Louis Stevenson, who resides nearby. Spends August at Dover and is visited by Paul Bourget. Stays in Paris for the next two months. Moves into a flat at 34 De Vere Gardens in Kensington early in March 1886. Alice takes rooms in London. *The Bostonians* serialized in *Century* (Feb. 1885–Feb. 1886; published 1886), *Princess Casamassima* serialized in *Atlantic Monthly* (Sept. 1885–Oct. 1886; published 1886).

1886–87   Leaves for Italy in December for extended stay, mainly in Florence and Venice. Sees much of Constance Fenimore Woolson and stays in her villa. Writes "The Aspern Papers" and other tales. Returns to De Vere Gardens in July and begins work on *The Tragic Muse*. Pays several country visits. Dines out less often ("I know it all—all that one sees by 'going out'—today, as if I had made it. But if I had, I would have made it better!").

1888   *The Reverberator*, *The Aspern Papers*, *Louisa Pallant*, *The Modern Warning*, and *Partial Portraits* published. Elizabeth Boott Duveneck dies. Robert Louis Stevenson leaves for the South Seas. Engages fencing teacher to combat "symptoms of a portentous corpulence." Goes abroad in October to Geneva (where he visits Miss Woolson), Genoa, Monte Carlo, and Paris.

1889–90   Catharine Walsh (Aunt Kate) dies March 1889. William comes to England to visit Alice in August. James goes to Dover in September and then to Paris for five weeks. Writes account of Robert Browning's funeral in Westminster Abbey. Dramatizes *The American* for the Compton Comedy Company. Meets and becomes close friends with American journalist William Morton Fullerton and young American publisher Wolcott Balestier. Goes to Italy for the summer, staying in Venice and Florence, and takes a brief walking tour in Tuscany with W. W. Baldwin, an American physician practicing in Florence. Miss Woolson moves to Cheltenham, England, to be near James. *Atlantic Monthly* rejects his story "The Pupil," but it appears in England. Writes series of drawing-room comedies for theater. Meets Rudyard Kipling. *The Tragic Muse* serialized in *Atlantic Monthly* (Jan. 1889–May 1890; published 1890). *A London Life* (including "The Patagonia," "The Liar," "Mrs. Temperly") published 1889.

1891   *The American* produced at Southport has a success during road tour. After residence in Leamington, Alice returns to London, cared for by Katharine Loring. Doctors discover she has breast cancer. James circulates comedies (*Mrs. Vibert*, later called *Tenants*, and *Mrs. Jasper*, later named *Disengaged*) among theater managers who are cool to his work. Unimpressed at first by Ibsen, writes an appreciative review after seeing a performance of *Hedda Gabler* with Elizabeth Robins, a young Kentucky actress; persuades her to take the part of Mme. de Cintré in the London production of *The American*. Recuperates from flu in Ireland. James Russell Lowell dies. *The American* opens in London, September 26, and runs for seventy nights. Wolcott Balestier dies, and James attends his funeral in Dresden in December.

1892　　Alice James dies March 6. James travels to Siena to be near the Paul Bourgets, and Venice, June–July, to visit the Daniel Curtises, then to Lausanne to meet William and his family, who have come abroad for sabbatical. Attends funeral of Tennyson at Westminster Abbey. Augustin Daly agrees to produce *Mrs. Jasper*. *The American* continues to be performed on the road by the Compton Company. *The Lesson of the Master* (with a collection of stories including "The Marriages," "The Pupil," "Brooksmith," "The Solution," and "Sir Edmund Orme") published.

1893　　Fanny Kemble dies in January. Continues to write unproduced plays. In March goes to Paris for two months. Sends Edward Compton first act and scenario for *Guy Domville*. Meets William and family in Lucerne and stays a month, returning to London in June. Spends July completing *Guy Domville* in Ramsgate. George Alexander, actor-manager, agrees to produce the play. Daly stages first reading of *Mrs. Jasper*, and James withdraws it, calling the rehearsal a mockery. *The Real Thing and Other Tales* (including "The Wheel of Time," "Lord Beaupré," "The Visit") published.

1894　　Constance Fenimore Woolson dies in Venice, January. Shocked and upset, James prepares to attend funeral in Rome but changes his mind on learning she is a suicide. Goes to Venice in April to help her family settle her affairs. Receives one of four copies, privately printed by Miss Loring, of Alice's diary. Finds it impressive but is concerned that so much gossip he told Alice in private has been included (later burns his copy). Robert Louis Stevenson dies in the South Pacific. *Guy Domville* goes into rehearsal. *Theatricals: Two Comedies* and *Theatricals: Second Series* published.

1895   *Guy Domville* opens January 5 at St. James's Theatre. At play's end James is greeted by a fifteen-minute roar of boos, catcalls, and applause. Horrified and depressed, abandons the theater. Play earns him $1,300 after five-week run. Feels he can salvage something useful from playwriting for his fiction ("a key that, working in the same *general* way fits the complicated chambers of *both* the dramatic and the narrative lock"). Writes scenario for *The Spoils of Poynton*. Visits Lord Wolseley and Lord Houghton in Ireland. In the summer goes to Torquay in Devonshire and stays until November while electricity is being installed in De Vere Gardens flat. Friendship with W. E. Norris, who resides at Torquay. Writes a one-act play ("Mrs. Gracedew") at request of Ellen Terry. *Terminations* (containing "The Death of the Lion," "The Coxon Fund," "The Middle Years," "The Altar of the Dead") published.

1896–97   Finishes *The Spoils of Poynton* (serialized in *Atlantic Monthly* April–Oct. 1896 as *The Old Things;* published 1897). *Embarrassments* ("The Figure in the Carpet," "Glasses," "The Next Time," "The Way It Came") published. Takes a house on Point Hill, Playden, opposite the old town of Rye, Sussex, August–September. Ford Madox Hueffer (later Ford Madox Ford) visits him. Converts play *The Other House* into novel and works on *What Maisie Knew* (published Sept. 1897). George du Maurier dies early in October. Because of increasing pain in wrist, hires stenographer William MacAlpine in February and then purchases a typewriter; soon begins direct dictation to MacAlpine at the machine. Invites Joseph Conrad to lunch at De Vere Gardens and begins their friendship. Goes to Bournemouth in July. Serves on jury in London before going to Dunwich, Suffolk, to spend time with Temple-Emmet cousins. In late September 1897 signs a twenty-one-year lease for Lamb House in Rye for £70 a year ($350). Takes on extra work to pay for setting up his house—the life of William Wetmore Story ($1,250 advance) and will furnish an "American Letter" for new magazine *Literature* (precursor of *Times Literary Supplement*) for $200 a month. Howells visits.

1898   "The Turn of the Screw" (serialized in *Collier's* Jan.–April; published with "Covering End" under the title *The Two Magics*) proves his most popular work since "Daisy Miller." Sleeps in Lamb House for first time June 28. Soon after is visited by William's son, Henry James Jr. (Harry), followed by a stream of visitors: future Justice Oliver Wendell Holmes, Mrs. J. T. Fields, Sarah Orne Jewett, the Paul Bourgets, the Edward Warrens, the Daniel Curtises, the Edmund Gosses, and Howard Sturgis. His witty friend Jonathan Sturges, a young crippled New Yorker, stays for two months during autumn. *In the Cage* published. Meets neighbors Stephen Crane and H. G. Wells.

1899   Finishes *The Awkward Age* and plans trip to the Continent. Fire in Lamb House delays departure. To Paris in March and then visits the Paul Bourgets at Hyères. Stays with the Curtises in their Venice palazzo, where he meets and becomes friends with Jessie Allen. In Rome meets young American-Norwegian sculptor Hendrik C. Andersen; buys one of his busts. Returns to England in July and Andersen comes for three days in August. William, his wife, Alice, and daughter, Peggy, arrive at Lamb House in October. First meeting of brothers in six years. William now has confirmed heart condition. James B. Pinker becomes literary agent and for first time James's professional relations are systematically organized; he reviews copyrights, finds new publishers, and obtains better prices for work ("the germ of a new career"). Purchases Lamb House for $10,000 with an easy mortgage.

1900   Unhappy at whiteness of beard which he has worn since the Civil War, he shaves it off. Alternates between Rye and London. Works on *The Sacred Fount* and begins *The Ambassadors*. *The Soft Side*, a collection of twelve tales, published. Niece Peggy comes to Lamb House for Christmas.

1901   Obtains permanent room at the Reform Club for London visits and spends eight weeks in town. Sees funeral of Queen Victoria. Decides to employ a woman typist, Mary Weld, to replace the more expensive shorthand stenographer, MacAlpine. Completes *The Ambassadors* and begins *The Wings of the Dove*. *The Sacred Fount* published. Has meeting with George Gissing. William James, much improved, returns home after two years in Europe. Young Cambridge admirer, Percy Lubbock visits. Discharges his alcoholic servants of sixteen years (the Smiths). Mrs. Paddington is new housekeeper.

1902   In London for the winter but gout and stomach disorder force him home earlier. Finishes *The Wings of the Dove* (published in August). William James Jr. (Billy) visits in October and becomes a favorite nephew. Writes "The Beast in the Jungle" and "The Birthplace."

1903   *The Ambassadors, The Better Sort* (a collection of twelve tales), and *William Wetmore Story and His Friends* published. After another spell in town, returns to Lamb House in May and begins work on *The Golden Bowl*. Meets and establishes close friendship with Dudley Jocelyn Persse, a nephew of Lady Gregory. First meeting with Edith Wharton in December.

1904–05 Completes *The Golden Bowl* (published Nov. 1904). Rents Lamb House for six months, and sails in August for America after twenty years absence. Sees new Manhattan skyline from New Jersey on arrival and stays with Colonel George Harvey, president of Harper's, in Jersey shore house with Mark Twain as fellow guest. Goes to William's country house at Chocorua in the White Mountains, New Hampshire. Re-explores Cambridge, Boston, Salem, Newport, and Concord, where he visits brother Bob. In October stays with Edith Wharton in the Berkshires and motors with her through Massachusetts and New York. Later visits New York, Philadelphia (where he delivers lecture "The Lesson of Balzac"), and then Washington, D.C., as a guest in Henry Adams' house. Meets (and is critical of) President Theodore Roosevelt. Returns to Philadelphia to lecture at Bryn Mawr. Travels to Richmond, Charleston, Jacksonville, Palm Beach, and St. Augustine. Then lectures in St. Louis, Chicago, South Bend, Indianapolis, Los Angeles (with a short vacation at Coronado Beach near San Diego), San Francisco, Portland, and Seattle. Returns to explore New York City ("the terrible town"), May–June. Lectures on "The Question of Our Speech" at Bryn Mawr commencement. Elected to newly founded American Academy of Arts and Letters (William declines). Returns to England in July; lectures had more than covered expenses of his trip. Begins revision of novels for the New York Edition.

1906–08   Writes "The Jolly Corner" and *The American Scene* (published 1907). Writes 18 prefaces for the New York Edition (twenty-four volumes published 1907–09). Visits Paris and Edith Wharton in spring 1907 and motors with her in Midi. Travels to Italy for the last time, visiting Hendrik Andersen in Rome, and goes on to Florence and Venice. Engages Theodora Bosanquet as his typist in autumn. Again visits Mrs. Wharton in Paris, spring 1908. William comes to England to give a series of lectures at Oxford and receives an honorary Doctor of Science degree. James goes to Edinburgh in March to see a tryout by the Forbes-Robertsons of his play, *The High Bid*, a rewrite in three acts of the one-act play originally written for Ellen Terry (revised earlier as the story "Covering End"). Play gets only five special matinees in London. Shocked by slim royalties from sales of the New York Edition.

1909   Growing acquaintance with young writers and artists of Bloomsbury, including Virginia and Vanessa Stephen and others. Meets and befriends young Hugh Walpole in February. Goes to Cambridge in June as guest of admiring dons and undergraduates and meets John Maynard Keynes. Feels unwell and sees doctors about what he believes may be heart trouble. They reassure him. Late in year burns forty years of his letters and papers at Rye. Suffers severe attacks of gout. *Italian Hours* published.

1910   Very ill in January ("food-loathing") and spends much time in bed. Nephew Harry comes to be with him in February. In March is examined by Sir William Osler, who finds nothing physically wrong. James begins to realize that he has had "a sort of nervous breakdown." William, in spite of now severe heart trouble, and his wife, Alice, come to England to give him support. Brothers and Alice go to Bad Nauheim for cure, then travel to Zurich, Lucerne, and Geneva, where they learn Robertson (Bob) James has died in America of heart attack. James's health begins to improve but William is failing. Sails with William and Alice for America in August. William dies at Chocorua soon after arrival, and James remains with the family for the winter. *The Finer Grain* and *The Outcry* published.

1911   Honorary degree from Harvard in spring. Visits with Howells and Grace Norton. Sails for England July 30. On return to Lamb House, decides he will be too lonely there and starts search for a London flat. Theodora Bosanquet obtains two work rooms adjoining her flat in Chelsea and he begins autobiography, *A Small Boy and Others*. Continues to reside at the Reform Club.

1912   Delivers "The Novel in *The Ring and the Book*," on the 100th anniversary of Browning's birth, to the Royal Society of Literature. Honorary Doctor of Letters from Oxford University June 26. Spends summer at Lamb House. Sees much of Edith Wharton ("the Firebird"), who spends summer in England. (She secretly arranges to have Scribner's put $8,000 into James's account.) Takes 21 Carlyle Mansions, in Cheyne Walk, Chelsea, as London quarters. Writes a long admiring letter for William Dean Howells' seventy-fifth birthday. Meets André Gide. Contracts bad case of shingles and is ill four months, much of the time not able to leave bed.

1913   Moves into Cheyne Walk flat. Two hundred and seventy friends and admirers subscribe for seventieth birthday portrait by Sargent and present also a silver-gilt Charles II porringer and dish ("Golden Bowl"). Sargent turns over his payment to young sculptor Derwent Wood, who does a bust of James. Autobiography *A Small Boy and Others* published. Goes with niece Peggy to Lamb House for the summer.

1914   *Notes of a Son and Brother* published. Works on "The Ivory Tower." Returns to Lamb House in July. Niece Peggy joins him. Horrified by the war ("this crash of our civilisation," "a nightmare from which there is no waking"). In London in September participates in Belgian Relief, visits wounded in St. Bartholomew's and other hospitals; feels less "finished and useless and doddering" and recalls Walt Whitman and his Civil War hospital visits. Accepts chairmanship of American Volunteer Motor Ambulance Corps in France. *Notes on Novelists* (essays on Balzac, Flaubert, Zola) published.

1915–16   Continues work with the wounded and war relief. Has occasional lunches with Prime Minister Asquith and family, and meets Winston Churchill and other war leaders. Discovers that he is considered an alien and has to report to police before going to coastal Rye. Decides to become a British national and asks Asquith to be one of his sponsors. Is granted citizenship on July 28. H. G. Wells satirizes him in *Boon* ("leviathan retrieving pebbles") and James, in the correspondence that follows, writes: "Art *makes* life, makes interest, makes importance." Burns more papers and photographs at Lamb House in autumn. Has a stroke December 2 in his flat, followed by another two days later. Develops pneumonia and during delirium gives his last confused dictation (dealing with the Napoleonic legend) to Theodora Bosanquet, who types it on the familiar typewriter. Mrs. William James arrives December 13 to care for him. On New Year's Day, George V confers the Order of Merit. Dies February 28. Funeral services held at the Chelsea Old Church. The body is cremated and the ashes are buried in Cambridge Cemetery family plot.

Note on the Texts

Presented in this volume of Henry James's works are early texts of his first five novels—*Watch and Ward* (1871), *Roderick Hudson* (1875), *The American* (1877), *The Europeans* (1878), and *Confidence* (1880). The first four were published in serial form in the *Atlantic Monthly,* where James's good friend William Dean Howells was editor; the last was published in *Scribner's Monthly.* With the exception of *Watch and Ward,* the texts printed here are those of the first American book editions, all published by the Boston firm of J. R. Osgood (later Houghton, Osgood and Company), and issued within a month or two of the final installments of the serial versions. Though James later made revisions in some of these novels, those revisions were made by a more experienced and sophisticated writer. This volume reprints the works of a young Henry James just beginning his long and productive career. The earlier versions offer the best opportunity to recapture that beginning.

James began to write his first novel, *Watch and Ward,* in 1870, after his return to America from travel abroad. It appeared in the *Atlantic Monthly* in five installments from August through December of 1871 (XXVIII, 232–246, 320–339, 415–431, 577–586, 689–710). Seven years later, in May 1878, Houghton, Osgood and Company of Boston published the book version in a first printing of 1000 copies with a note added by Henry James explaining that it "has been minutely revised, and has received many verbal alterations." More than 800 revisions were made in the text at this time by an older James who had since published two major novels and numerous short stories. The edition went through at least six reprintings. No other edition was published in Henry James's lifetime. This volume reprints the serial version in order to present the work in its original form.

Roderick Hudson, James's second novel, exists in four different versions, all prepared by James at different times in his life. The first is the *Atlantic Monthly* serial edition, published in twelve installments, January through December 1875, each of which makes up a chapter with separate title. According to James, in his Preface to the New York Edition, the novel was not yet complete when the first serial installment appeared. In November 1875, before the final installment, J. R. Osgood ("Late Ticknor & Fields, Fields, Osgood & Co.") brought out the first American book edition. The differences between the serial and book editions are relatively minor. The last and longest serial chapter was made into two chapters in the book. The new chapter title, "The Princess Casamassima," was given to chapter XII, and chapter XIII retained the former title, "Switzerland"; all other chapter titles remained the same. James never again used chapter titles in any of his fiction. A few changes in wording and punctuation were also made, a sampling of which is given in the Notes to this volume. Four years later, in June 1879, Macmillan and Company published the three-volume, first English edition, to which James appended the following note: " 'Roderick Hudson' was originally published in Boston, in 1875. It has now been minutely revised, and has received a large number of verbal alterations. Several passages have been rewritten." The revisions were extensive. Chapter titles were eliminated; the thirteen chapters in the American edition were each divided in two, giving the book twenty-six chapters; several long passages were deleted or radically revised (see sampling in the Notes); and wording and punctuation were changed throughout, though sometimes only to bring the text into agreement with current British usage. James preferred this version of the text, and Houghton, Mifflin imported sheets from Macmillan and Company in 1882 to bind under their own imprint. James made even more extensive revisions in the text in 1907 for the New York Edition, making this final version a very different book from the one which first appeared in 1875. This volume reprints the first American book edition of 1875 because its revisions were made soon after composition and best represent Henry James at that time.

Henry James wrote most of *The American*, his third novel, during his stay in Paris in 1875–76. The twelve serial installments appeared in the *Atlantic Monthly* from June 1876 through May 1877; the first book edition was issued by J. R. Osgood in May 1877. Copies of the Osgood edition were exported for the English market soon after. In December 1877, Ward, Lock and Co. published a pirated edition, carelessly printed, which omitted large portions of the text. James authorized Bernard Tauchnitz to issue a two-volume edition (using the American Osgood edition as copy) in his continental series, "Collection of British Authors," in 1878. An authorized English edition was brought out by Macmillan and Company in March 1879 (this edition later served as copy for the collected novels and tales published by Macmillan in 1883). *The American* was completely revised for the New York Edition published by Scribner's in 1907. Henry James did not read proofs for the serial version since there was not enough time to send them back and forth across the ocean. In a letter dated December 18 (1876) to William Dean Howells, then editor of *Atlantic Monthly,* he wrote: "I received a few days since a letter from my brother William, in which he speaks of some phrases (on Newman's part) as being so shocking as to make the 'reader's flesh creep.' Two or three that he quotes are indeed infelicitous, as I perceive as soon as my attention is called to them. He mentioned having persuaded you to omit one or two of the same sort. I am very glad you have done so, and would give you *carte blanche.* It is all along of my not seeing a proof. . . ." A week later, in a letter to his mother, James wrote: "The story, as it stands, is full of things I should have altered; but I think none of them are so inalterable but that I shall be easily able in preparing the volume, to remove effectually, by a few verbal corrections, that Newmanesque taint on which William dwells."

It is impossible to know what alterations were made in the serial version of the novel since no manuscript or printer's copy exists, but a collation of the serial version with the first book edition reveals that James was able to make revisions in the text published by Osgood. Hundreds of verbal changes occur throughout the text, some of them perhaps influenced by William's objections—for example, a passage in the serial version of chapter XVI, in which Newman refers to Madame de Cintré as "a high class of goods" and calls her "the best thing in the market," was cut from the book version. Other changes reflect James's desire to improve the style or add more precision. Sentences were tightened, unnecessary words were eliminated, words were exchanged for other words (for example, "heavy" was changed to "gloomy," "excesses" to "extravagance," "perfectly" to "quite," "could not come to pass in a moment" to "was an operation that was necessarily gradual," "greeting" to "aspect," "noble" to "fine" or "grand"), and street and place names were changed. It is not known what copy James used to make these changes. He could have used tear-sheets from the *Atlantic Monthly* for some of them, and, because he had sent the final installment to the *Atlantic Monthly* by late January or early February of 1877, Osgood or Howells might have been able to send him proof sheets for the final chapters. At any rate, James made extensive revisions throughout the text, including the last two chapters, between the serial appearance of the novel and its publication in book form. When the American and English editions are compared, however, the case is very different. Few verbal changes occur (examples are given in the Notes), and the differences in punctuation seem to be more a matter of house-styling than authorial revision. In fact, except for the few changes mentioned above, James does not seem to have done much to the English edition. Therefore, this volume reprints the first American book edition of 1877 because it seems most clearly representative of Henry James at the time of its composition.

The Europeans is the first novel by James for which most of the original manuscript is known to survive. (A facsimile of all but the last three chapters of the manuscript was published by Howard Fertig, New York, in 1979, with an introduction by Leon Edel.) The novel was serialized in the *Atlantic Monthly* in four installments between July and October 1878. It was first published in book form on September 18 of the same year, in a two-volume edition by Macmillan and Co. of London. Less than four weeks later, on October 12, 1878, an American edition (in one volume) was issued by Houghton, Osgood and Company in Boston. *The Europeans* was included as Volume IX of the 1883

Macmillan collected edition, but it was not included in Scribner's later New York Edition.

Many minor revisions were made in *The Europeans* between its serial publication and its English and American book editions, but the American edition is in fact closer to the manuscript in punctuation, spelling, and wording, and is unmarred, as it were, by English conventions of typography and usage. A collation of chapters I and VII of the two book editions with the facsimile of the manuscript reveals that, in fifteen cases of differing punctuation between the two editions, the Osgood text accurately reflects the manuscript eleven times, reproduces James's spelling seven of eight times, and, in eleven cases of different wording, is faithful to James's manuscript eight times. While the Osgood edition contained some errors (for example, printing "horse-thief" for the manuscript's "house-thief"), the Macmillan edition made changes more freely, such as altering the description of the sky after a winter storm from "violent blue" to "violet blue," apparently because an incredulous English compositor was unfamiliar with New England weather. The Osgood edition supplies the text reprinted here, and a sampling of the variants between this and the Macmillan edition is given in the Notes.

James's fifth novel, *Confidence,* poses the most complicated—and provocative—textual problem of any of the novels presented in this volume. It is the only novel for which the complete manuscript is known to survive. (The manuscripts of *The Princess Casamassima* and *The Europeans* are incomplete.) The germ of the tale and original plans for its development constitute the first entry in James's surviving *Notebooks. Confidence* first appeared serially in *Scribner's Monthly* (from August 1879 through January 1880), a magazine James thoroughly disliked but which paid high rates. He consequently urged family and friends to await its revised version in book form. To protect his copyright, James published it first in England in December 1879 (in two volumes) under the imprint of Chatto & Windus, who had offered better terms for the work than Macmillan. The American edition, again published by Houghton, Osgood and Company, appeared two months later, in February

1880. The English text was republished by Chatto & Windus in one volume in October 1880 and republished again in September 1882. *Confidence,* like *The Europeans,* was collected in Macmillan's uniform edition, as Volume x, but was not included in the New York Edition. In 1891, with James's permission, Houghton, Mifflin of Boston republished the original American text.

Both the English and American texts differ substantially from the serial, and each also differs widely from the other in punctuation and wording. The English edition, for example, contains thirty-one chapters, the American only thirty. The number and range of variants make it unlikely that they are compositorial; in fact, a collation of the two editions suggests that James deliberately directed one version to an English audience and the other to an American one. He specifically "authorized" both editions, which complicates the decision of which edition to present in this volume.

Unpublished letters in the files of Chatto & Windus show that James corrected tear-sheets from the *Scribner's* serial version for the English edition and that he participated in the redivision of the chapters in order to spread the novel into two volumes. It appears likely that he did the same for the American edition, probably at a slightly earlier date. The additional chapter in the English edition, for example, is simply a redivision of chapter x in the American edition, suggesting that its chapters had already been redivided from the serial chapters sometime earlier. Examination of the manuscript in the James collection of the Harvard Library does not supply proof of when or how James revised the manuscript for serial publication. He may, however, have revised proofs for at least some of the serial installments and returned them to *Scribner's* if, as published letters to his mother and to Howells indicate, he had indeed sent half of his manuscript to the journal by May 14 and the other half by June 14 or 15.

The nature of the variants themselves, however, constitutes the most persuasive evidence of James' deliberate slanting of the two editions. For example, the word *couturière* in the manuscript, referring to the person with whom Blanche Evers will confer soon after her arrival in Paris, is replaced by "man-milliner" in both the serial and the Osgood editions. In the English edition, however, it appears as "tailor." The words "insipid drivel" in both the serial and Osgood editions become, in the English edition, "stupid stuff." On the other hand, the manuscript phrase "those vague dissatisfactions" is retained in the English edition but changed to "that chronic chagrin" in the American edition. And in still another kind of variant, the word "outrageous" in the serial and Osgood editions appears as "exorbitant" in the English version.

This sampling of variants is perhaps sufficient to suggest the complexity of the differences between manuscript, serial, American, and English editions. But the crucial differences are those between the two book editions that reveal word choices slanted toward a British audience in one edition and toward an American one in the other. A brief sampling of such examples—"awfully" in the American edition is "fearfully" in the English one; "a couple of" is "a brace of"; "had no vulgar resentment" is "cared in no small way"; "whence he had drawn the ability for so remarkable a feat" is "how the deuce he had managed it"; "bosky darkness" is "fragrant dusk" (clearly wrong in context); "El Dorado" is "a hidden treasure"; "I stuck it to the end" is "I saw it through"; "a man of oddities" is "an eccentric man"; "simply hit upon" is "simply conceived"—shows the American edition to be the more appropriate choice for this edition of the early novels of Henry James. The Houghton, Osgood edition was authorized by James to be reprinted in America, it is the edition closest to the serial and manuscript versions, and it may well be the most self-consciously "American" edition of any of these early novels—a not inappropriate criterion for a Henry James who was himself, at that time, facing the personal problem of national identity. This volume reprints the text of *Confidence* from the Osgood (American) edition, and a sampling of variants, from manuscript, serial, and British editions, is given in the Notes.

The standards for American English continue to fluctuate and in some ways were different in earlier periods from what they are now. In nineteenth-century writings, for example, a word might be spelled in more than one way, even in the same work. Commas could be used expressively to suggest the movements of voice, and capitals were sometimes meant to give significances to a word beyond those it might have in its uncapitalized form. Since modernization would remove such effects, this volume has preserved the spelling, punctuation, capitalization, and wording of the editions reprinted here. The present edition is concerned only with representing the *texts* of these editions; it does not attempt to reproduce features of their typographic design—such as the display capitalization of chapter openings. Open contractions are retained when they appear in the original editions. Some changes, however, have been made. James's recurrent complaints of printer's errors were certainly justified, and obvious typographical errors have been corrected for this edition. The following is a list of those errors by page and line number: 24.40, his; 36.33, for past; 57.21, needfu; 60.4, graciously,; 61.7, clapsed; 80.35, cause; 129.19, increasd; 157.14, personally,; 174.36, illustratd; 177.26, to to; 197.30, officious.; 218.12, "We; 242.18, "You; 245.23, Schafgans; 257.18, The Newcomes; 266.15, understandings; 268.8, dres,s; 278.23, monoply; 284.9, beggar,; 289.25, raphsodizing; 351.28, hen; 354.34, I; 364.24, a a; 380.22, alter; 399.8, It 's; 400.27, "Roderick; 402.4, you,; 423.39, "He; 435.38, "Rowland; 436.3–4, is be; 447.4, suggest.; 474.24, Appenines; 475.10, looked as; 487.30, And; 488.21, on.; 489.13, Paris,; 493.2, What; 502.13, Roland; 504.24, cried; 506.2, sometimes; 529.9, should 'nt; 548.16, women; 550.38, up.; 563.11, But; 563.31, Noemie; 590.26, at if; 615.16, think,; 627.7, sitting-soom; 631.34, that."; 641.31, rather,; 658.40–659.1, matter. For; 659.2–3, her. If; 664.7, my; 670.20, law; 680.25, Pray; 692.11, me,; 706.3, Madémoiselle; 707.14, Madamoiselle; 713.39, that?"; 714.3, don't; 721.38, But; 727.29, You; 737.29, "Never,; 752.10, Is; 757.33, A; 801.29, Did n't; 806.9, if; 820.2, Fleuriéres; 820.12, long,; 860.13, I; 876.16, satchel; 917.16, influences; 918.38, usual; 945.5, monoply; 956.7, Felix; 974.35, me?"; 979.33, Don't; 985.3, "Mr.; 985.21, that?"; 987.29, hard,; 1020.19, *voilá;* 1025.17, slowly,; 1036.23, to morrow; 1063.29, Lovelock,; 1068.33, forgotten; 1069.29, But; 1070.34, Lovelock!"; 1099.10, It 's; 1149.18, but;; 1192.21, At;

1215.25, If; 1227.15, Did 'nt; 1238.7, place, as; 1239.32, infamy; 1251.11, 'chance'. Errors corrected second printing: 92.23, nt (*LOA*); 393.34, you.

Notes

In the notes below, the reference numbers denote page and line of the present volume (the line count includes chapter headings). No note is made for material included in a standard desk-reference book.

WATCH AND WARD

23.14–15   Hubert . . . ministry;]   This clause was changed in the Osgood edition to read "Hubert had just commenced parson."

24.37   "Child's Own Book"]   A London edition by this title, consisting of stories illustrated with 250 engravings "by Eminent artists," was reprinted in Boston by Munroe and Frances in 1843.

25.15   *Prince Avenant.*]   Probably a character or tale in the "Child's Own Book." See note 24.37.

29.12–13   Of . . . experience.]   This sentence was revised as follows in the Osgood edition: "Of the utmost that women can be and do he wished to have personal experience."

31.26   one]   This word was inexplicably deleted in the Osgood edition.

38.13–14   him about him]   The first and obtrusive "him" in this phrase was deleted in the Osgood edition.

39.18   "The Initials."]   A popular "three-decker" English novel, subtitled "A Story of Modern Life," set in Germany. Its anonymous author, later identified as Jemima (Montgomery) Tautphoeus, was the daughter of an English lord and wife of a German nobleman. In the Osgood edition, this title was changed to "The Heir of Redcliffe," a popular English novel by Charlotte Mary Yonge (1823–1901), published by D. Appleton in New York in 1853. "The Heir of Redcliffe" is referred to later in this serial version of the novel.

39.30   Mr. Hamilton.]   This character, from "The Initials," was changed in the Osgood edition to "Phillip" (from "The Heir of Redcliffe").

44.40   Mahomet's Paradise]   Probably a reference to the houris, the dark-eyed virgins of perfect beauty, who are said to live with the blessed in Mahomet's "Paradise."

52.21   a tongs]   Although "tongs" can be singular, James removed the "s" in the Osgood edition.

52.33   infinite]   The adjective was changed to "natural" in the Osgood edition.

62.27 "Heir of Redcliffe,"] See note 39.18.

65.35 "Is . . . vicious?"] The question was changed in the Osgood edition to "Has she—a—low tastes?"

74.9 surely,] Although this error could have been corrected by transposing the comma, James instead deleted the word from the Osgood edition.

78.3 Miss Sandys?] Changed to "Miss Sands" in the Osgood edition.

82.39 curtesied] An archaic spelling of "curtsied," which, with its variant "curtesy" (that is, "curtsey"), appears several times in the American editions of James's early novels.

101.1–4 if . . . man.] This sentence was changed in the Osgood edition to read: "If, financially, Roger should be found wanting, she could easily prevail upon him to make way for a millionaire."

144.18 the Fifth Avenue] Although unidiomatic to modern readers, "the . . . Avenue" was current usage in James's time and appears throughout these early novels.

161.20–28 Another . . . lady.] James deleted these last sentences of the novel in the Osgood edition.

RODERICK HUDSON

167.2 Rowland] Chapter titles were eliminated in the 1879 English edition, and James never again used them in any of his fiction. The 1879 English edition also divided each chapter into two, making twenty-six in all, by breaking the text at the following additional points: 179.26, 212.2, 236.11, 263.36, 290.33, 317.12, 344.26, 366.10, 389.6, 416.31, 455.13, 480.23, and 503.2.

171.11–12 Mignon . . . egg-dance.] An allusion to Ambroise Thomas's opera Mignon, first presented in 1866.

182.12 vivid blue cravat,] In the English edition, this was revised to "bright red cravat."

182.25–26 He . . . them.] Emended to "In conversation he was a colourist," in the English edition.

211.33–34 "The . . . story!"] From Tennyson's "The Princess," part 4, stanza 1.

226.29–30 their . . . towns.] Revised in the English edition to "the wanderings and contemplations that beguiled their pilgrimage to Rome."

229.2 a young . . . twenty.] James's first reference to Christina Light who later in the novel becomes the Princess Casamassima. She reappears later, a rare occurrence in James's fiction, as a central character of his novel by that title, published in 1886. Her husband, Prince Gennaro Casamassima, also reappears in that later novel.

229.37–40   black dog . . . Mephistopheles.] Mephistopheles appears in the form of a black poodle in Part I of Goethe's *Faust*.

236.14   Gloriani.] He reappears with Mme. Gloriani in James's late novel *The Ambassadors* (1903) and in the short story "The Velvet Glove" (1909).

256.33–34   in . . . toilets,] An alternative spelling of "toilettes." The phrase was deleted in the English edition.

259.26   A Reminiscence.] In the English edition this was changed to: "A Lady Listening."

279.21–23   He . . . success.] In the English edition this long sentence was compressed to: "He had not undertaken to make him over."

290.8   Herodias] Mother of Salome and second wife of Herod Antipas, she had John the Baptist executed; see Matthew 14:6–11.

291.1–2   "And . . . rose?"] From the "Moral" of Tennyson's poem "Day-Dream."

296.21   courtesy] Changed to "salutation" in the English edition; see note 82.39.

308.26   outer barbarian] Emended to "amiable simpleton" in the English edition.

330.13–16   "since . . . world,] A reference to Garibaldi's revolution of 1860, which ended Bourbon control of the kingdom of Naples and led to its incorporation by Italy under Victor Emmanuel.

333.33–34   chance anfractuosities] Simplified to "accidents of ruggedness" in the English edition.

340.1–2   I . . . infatuated."] In the serial version this read "I'm completely enslaved."

346.22   Imitation . . . Catherine.] A reference to *De imitatione Christi* by Thomas à Kempis (1379–1471) and probably to a Life of Saint Catherine of Siena. The serial version had referred to the Life of Saint Theresa, probably Saint Theresa of Avila. One possible reason for the change is James's discovery that a reader of the *Imitatione* would be more likely to read a Life of Saint Catherine of Siena than one of Saint Theresa of Avila. Saint Catherine and Saint Theresa, both mystics, are referred to later in the text (367.31–32).

348.14–349.7   "Beware . . . first."] This long passage (which is also in the serial version) was deleted from the English edition and from the New York Edition.

355.29 definitely] The word was "definitively" in the serial version.

371.39 English . . . Florence.] The poet is Robert Browning; the phrase—"How the March sun feels like May!"—is from his "A Lover's Quarrel."

380.36 "Corinne"] The popular novel by Mme. de Staël (Ann Louise Germaine Necker de Staël-Holstein, 1766–1817), which exalted woman's right to love.

380.40 Sismondi's Italian Republics] The monumental *History of the Italian Republics* by Jean Charles Léonard Simonde de Sismondi (1773–1842).

381.3–4 Roscoe's . . . Tenth] English historian William Roscoe (1753–1831), whose *Life of Leo X*, although severely criticized, was widely read.

391.32–33 confronted . . . sublimity,] Revised to "a mere sentient point in the brilliant immensity" in the English edition.

394.11 Murray] Author of the well-known nineteenth-century travel guides to Europe.

401.11–12 Listen . . . me!] These repeated imperatives were deleted from the English edition.

407.39 courtesy] See note 82.39.

468.2 *The Princess Casamassima*] James added this title when he divided chapter XII of the serial version ("Switzerland") into two chapters for the Osgood edition.

475.36 Burd Helen] Varied title of the Scottish ballads "Fair Annie" and "Child Waters," and alternate title to "Browghty Wa's."

511.31–34 Cecilia . . . mortals.] Apparently to correct the syntactical problem, James revised this penultimate sentence to read: "Cecilia, who having her shrewd impression that he comes to see the young lady at the other house as much as to see herself, does not feel obliged to seem unduly flattered, calls him whenever he reappears the most restless of mortals." James revised the sentence again for the New York Edition to read: "Cecilia, who, having her shrewd impression that he comes for the young person, the still young person, of interest at the other house as much as for any one else, fails to show as unduly flattered, and in fact pronounced him, at each reappearance, the most restless of mortals."

511.35 patient!"] In the New York Edition James added the following sentence: "And then he talks to her of Roderick, of whose history she never wearies and whom he never elsewhere names."

THE AMERICAN

551.34–35 quarterings] "Quartering" was the practice of dividing the coat of arms or escutcheon to denote the alliances of families. Fifty quarterings would indicate a particularly elaborate and prestigious lineage.

584.26   tolerably]   Revised to "extremely," probably by James, in the 1879 English edition.

591.7   the . . . Avenue!]   See note 144.18.

596.40   courtesy]   See note 82.39.

659.1–3   "For . . . her."]   These two sentences are clearly meant to have been uttered by Valentin rather than Newman, although they are included in Newman's dialogue in the original American and English editions. They are punctuated and paragraphed in this printing to indicate that the words are Valentin's. The corresponding passage in the New York Edition was so extensively revised that it yields no clue of James's recognition of the problem. In a facsimile edition of the 1883 Macmillan text as revised by James in autograph and typescript (London: Scolar Press, 1976), the passage is replaced by an inserted typescript similar to the text of the New York Edition.

668.30   a famous taper]   Urbain's wife translates the French idiom *devoir une fière chandelle à* literally—"to owe a proud candle"; that is, to owe a debt of gratitude.

669.17   *talon rouge*]   Literally "red heel," a fashion of boots frequently affected by courtiers and dandies.

677.29   any.]   The English edition has no paragraph break here.

690.7   La Pomme de Paris]   Offenbach wrote no work by this title, and some have speculated that the passage was intended to characterize the obtuseness of Lord Deepmere. It was retained in the New York Edition.

704.17–18   read . . . "Figaro,"]   The missing "of" or "about" here may have been intentional. The passage is identical in the serial and the English edition.

720.38   silver dagger]   James changed this to "dagger of diamonds" in the English edition.

769.35   "Faublas."]   Short title of Jean Baptiste Louvet de Couvrai's *Les Amours du Chevalier de Faublas* (1821). In the English edition, James substituted the more suggestive *Les Liaisons Dangereuses* (1782), by Choderlos de Laclos.

782.18   tranquil river]   Emended to "quiet water" by James in the English edition.

833.26–27   convent . . . street]   In the English edition the word "and" was removed.

843.18   meditated]   Altered to "hesitated" in the 1883 Macmillan edition, the only substantive change (from the earlier English edition) in that text.

872.3–4   Newman . . . it.]   James's deletion of this final sentence from the New York Edition of 1907 was one of the more controversial changes in that edition.

THE EUROPEANS

876.21   jingling]   Changed to "jangling" in the English edition.

880.15–16   Mid-May's Eldest Child]   Keats's poem is "Ode to a Nightingale."

883.31   violent]   Erroneously altered to "violet" in the English edition.

CONFIDENCE

1051.1   II]   There was no chapter break at this point in the serial version; nor at 1056, 1064, 1072, 1077, 1089, 1094, 1110, 1118, 1130, 1147, 1155, 1166, 1180, 1185, 1203, 1220, 1229, or 1247.

1052.21–23   each . . . wit.]   This passage in the serial version reads: "who had for mutual exercise a collection of acknowledged peculiarities."

1053.17   revolutions]   The serial version had read "resolutions."

1059.3–4   daughter, though, indeed]   The English edition reads "daughter; though indeed she."

1061.3   Marienbad]   The serial version had read "Franzensbad"; "Marienbad" is retained in the English edition.

1064.20–21   a man of oddities]   The English edition reads "an eccentric man."

1065.4   concession]   The serial version reads "confession."

1080.37–38   louis d'or]   James had written "napoleons" in the serial version, but retained "louis d'or" in the English edition.

1090.33   "I 'guess' so!"]   "*Je crois bien!*" is the phrase in the serial version, but the English edition reads as here.

1093.20   intellectual fencing]   In the serial version it is "delicate play of wit"; the English edition reads as here.

1098.31   cases.]   The English edition begins chapter XI at this point, making each subsequent chapter in that edition one number higher than in the American edition.

1103.36   beyond . . . out]   The serial version had read "too knotty a point."

1107.31   pleading]   The word in the English edition is "pleasing."

1110.29   bosky darkness]   The English edition reads "fragrant dusk."

1112.37   'outrageous']   The English edition reads "exorbitant."

1114.35   unconscious]   The English edition reads "involuntary."

1119.20   sentimental fatuity]   This phrase is also in the English edition, although it had been "masculine coquetry" in the serial.

1123.18   test]   The English edition reads "testify."

1127.1   ten thousand]   In the serial version Bernard's winnings were only "five thousand."

1136.22   strikingly inane]   The English edition has this same phrase, but it appears as "a rather senseless piece of play" in the serial.

1141.2–3   detect . . . friend]   The English edition reads "suggest amendments to his friend's behavior."

1147.7–8   as . . . lady]   Rephrased in the English edition to read "should have declined, as the ghost of Hamlet says, upon a young lady." The phrase in *Hamlet* is "decline upon a wretch" (I, v).

1147.28   particle]   Changed to "fraction" in the English edition.

1152.34   loathesome gossip]   The English edition reads "idiotic fiction."

1152.40   half suspicion]   The English edition reads "vague suspicion."

1153.8–9   of . . . monopoly]   The English edition reads " which includes the husband and excludes everyone else."

1154.5   insipid drivel]   The English edition reads "stupid stuff."

1155.6   that chronic chagrin]   The manuscript, serial version, and English edition read "those vague dissatisfactions."

1155.23   hit upon]   The serial version had read "devised"; the English edition has "conceived."

1158.2   France.]   The English edition does not break the paragraph at this point.

1161.14   accident]   The English edition reads "admonition."

1166.4   aware]   The English edition reads "conscious."

1166.21–22   salt-looking]   The English edition reads "soft-looking."

1167.35, 36   California]   In the serial and English editions, Bernard arrives from "New York."

1169.37   strikingly agreeable]   In the serial and English editions the phrase is "agreeably striking."

1172.5   habituate]   The English edition reads "accommodate."

1174.16   a couple] The English edition reads "a brace."

1174.21   El Dorado] The English edition reads "a hidden treasure."

1174.30   roots] The English edition reads "root."

1175.11   cliffs] The English edition reads "cliff."

1178.28   *ben trovato*] Literally "well found," that is, a happy coincidence.

1195.6   man-milliner] The manuscript reads *"couturière"*; the serial version "man-milliner"; and the English edition "tailor."

1211.35–36   incident . . . happen] The English edition has the same wording, but the serial reads simply "accident."

1220.3   Mrs. Gordon] Here and at subsequent points (1223.34–35, 1226.16, 1227.3, and 1252.5) Gordon Wright's wife is called "Mrs. Gordon." In the serial version she is called "Mrs. Wright." The British practice of referring to the wife of a younger son of nobility by her husband's first name, to distinguish her from the wife of an older brother, would not apply in this case. Curiously enough, she is called "Mrs. Gordon" in her last appearance in the serial version.

1235.15–16   an end . . . wife!"] James had originally planned the story to end with Gordon Wright's murder of his wife; see his published *Notebooks* (New York: Oxford University Press, 1961), pp. 3–6. In this early plan, the name "Bernard Longueville" was assigned to the character later called "Gordon Wright," and the name "Harold Stanmer" was used for the character who would become "Bernard Longueville" in the published version.

1245.28, 29   Jim Crow] Thomas B. Rice's minstrel song and dance "Jim Crow" became popular in both England and America in the late 1820s. The act inspired numerous toys, puppets, dolls, and cookies in the shape of a dancing Negro minstrel.

1250.10   abused of the license] The English edition reads simply "abused the license."

This book is set in 10 point Linotron Galliard,
a face designed for photocomposition by Matthew Carter
and based on the sixteenth-century face Granjon. The paper
is acid-free lightweight opaque and meets the requirements
for permanence of the American National Standards Institute.
The binding material is Brillianta, a woven rayon cloth made
by Van Heek-Scholco Textielfabrieken, Holland. Com-
position by The Clarinda Company. Printing by
Malloy Incorporated. Binding by Dekker Book-
binding. Designed by Bruce Campbell.

THE LIBRARY OF AMERICA SERIES

The Library of America fosters appreciation and pride in America's literary heritage by publishing, and keeping permanently in print, authoritative editions of America's best and most significant writing. An independent nonprofit organization, it was founded in 1979 with seed money from the National Endowment for the Humanities and the Ford Foundation.

To subscribe to the series or to order individual copies,
please visit www.loa.org or call (800) 964.5778.

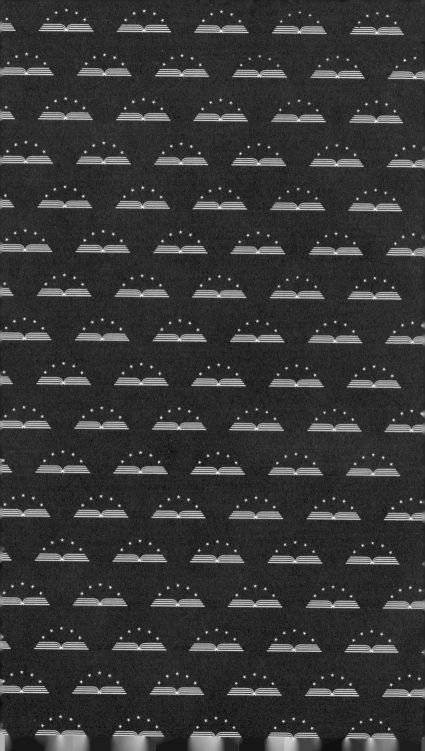